William Wilkie Collins (8 January 1824 – 23 September 1889) was an English novelist, playwright, and short story writer, best known for The Woman in White (1859), No Name (1862), Armadale (1866) and The Moonstone (1868). The last has been called the first modern English detective novel. Born to the family of painter William Collins in London, he grew up in Italy and France, learning French and Italian. He began work as a clerk for a tea merchant. After his first novel, Antonina, appeared in 1850, he met Charles Dickens, who became a close friend and mentor. Some of Collins's works appeared first in Dickens's journals All the Year Round and Household Words and they collaborated on drama and fiction. Collins published his best known works in the 1860s, achieving financial stability and an international following. However, he began suffering from gout. Taking opium for the pain developed into an addiction. In the 1870s and 1880s the quality of his writing declined along with his health. Collins was critical of the institution of marriage: he split his time between Caroline Graves, except for a two-year separation, and his common-law wife Martha Rudd, with whom he had three children. (Source: Wikipedia)

Literary works:
Basil (1852)
Hide and Seek (1854)
The Dead Secret (1856)
The Frozen Deep (1857)
"A House to Let" (1858)
"The Haunted House"
The Woman in White (1860)
No Name (1862)
Armadale (1866)
No Thoroughfare (1867)
The Moonstone (1868)
Man and Wife (1870)
Poor Miss Finch (1872)
The Law and the Lady (1875)
The Fallen Leaves (1879)

THRONE CLASSICS

I Say No
&
Little Novels
wilkie collins

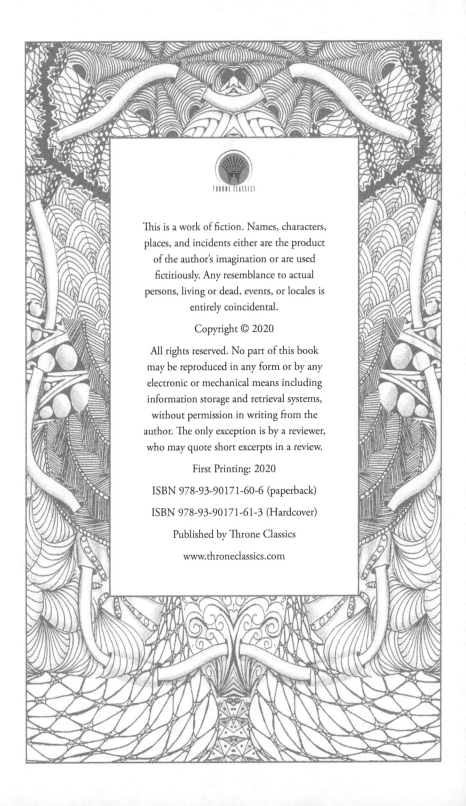

First Printing: 2020

ISBN 978-93-90171-60-6 (paperback)

ISBN 978-93-90171-61-3 (Hardcover)

Published by Throne Classics

www.throneclassics.com

Contents

I Say No
&
Little Novels

I SAY NO

BOOK THE FIRST—AT SCHOOL.

CHAPTER I. THE SMUGGLED SUPPER.

Outside the bedroom the night was black and still. The small rain fell too softly to be heard in the garden; not a leaf stirred in the airless calm; the watch-dog was asleep, the cats were indoors; far or near, under the murky heaven, not a sound was stirring.

Inside the bedroom the night was black and still.

Miss Ladd knew her business as a schoolmistress too well to allow night-lights; and Miss Ladd's young ladies were supposed to be fast asleep, in accordance with the rules of the house. Only at intervals the silence was faintly disturbed, when the restless turning of one of the girls in her bed betrayed itself by a gentle rustling between the sheets. In the long intervals of stillness, not even the softly audible breathing of young creatures asleep was to be heard.

The first sound that told of life and movement revealed the mechanical movement of the clock. Speaking from the lower regions, the tongue of Father Time told the hour before midnight.

A soft voice rose wearily near the door of the room. It counted the strokes of the clock—and reminded one of the girls of the lapse of time.

"Emily! eleven o'clock."

There was no reply. After an interval the weary voice tried again, in louder tones:

"Emily!"

A girl, whose bed was at the inner end of the room, sighed under the heavy heat of the night—and said, in peremptory tones, "Is that Cecilia?"

"Yes."

"What do you want?"

"I'm getting hungry, Emily. Is the new girl asleep?"

The new girl answered promptly and spitefully, "No, she isn't."

Having a private object of their own in view, the five wise virgins of Miss Ladd's first class had waited an hour, in wakeful anticipation of the falling asleep of the stranger—and it had ended in this way! A ripple of laughter ran round the room. The new girl, mortified and offended, entered her protest in plain words.

"You are treating me shamefully! You all distrust me, because I am a stranger."

"Say we don't understand you," Emily answered, speaking for her schoolfellows; "and you will be nearer the truth."

"Who expected you to understand me, when I only came here to-day? I have told you already my name is Francine de Sor. If want to know more, I'm nineteen years old, and I come from the West Indies."

Emily still took the lead. "Why do you come here?" she asked. "Who ever heard of a girl joining a new school just before the holidays? You are nineteen years old, are you? I'm a year younger than you—and I have finished my education. The next big girl in the room is a year younger than me—and she has finished her education. What can you possibly have left to learn at your age?"

"Everything!" cried the stranger from the West Indies, with an outburst of tears. "I'm a poor ignorant creature. Your education ought to have taught you to pity me instead of making fun of me. I hate you all. For shame, for shame!"

14

Some of the girls laughed. One of them—the hungry girl who had counted the strokes of the clock—took Francine's part.

"Never mind their laughing, Miss de Sor. You are quite right, you have good reason to complain of us."

Miss de Sor dried her eyes. "Thank you—whoever you are," she answered briskly.

"My name is Cecilia Wyvil," the other proceeded. "It was not, perhaps, quite nice of you to say you hated us all. At the same time we have forgotten our good breeding—and the least we can do is to beg your pardon."

This expression of generous sentiment appeared to have an irritating effect on the peremptory young person who took the lead in the room. Perhaps she disapproved of free trade in generous sentiment.

"I can tell you one thing, Cecilia," she said; "you shan't beat ME in generosity. Strike a light, one of you, and lay the blame on me if Miss Ladd finds us out. I mean to shake hands with the new girl—and how can I do it in the dark? Miss de Sor, my name's Brown, and I'm queen of the bedroom. I—not Cecilia—offer our apologies if we have offended you. Cecilia is my dearest friend, but I don't allow her to take the lead in the room. Oh, what a lovely nightgown!"

The sudden flow of candle-light had revealed Francine, sitting up in her bed, and displaying such treasures of real lace over her bosom that the queen lost all sense of royal dignity in irrepressible admiration. "Seven and sixpence," Emily remarked, looking at her own night-gown and despising it. One after another, the girls yielded to the attraction of the wonderful lace. Slim and plump, fair and dark, they circled round the new pupil in their flowing white robes, and arrived by common consent at one and the same conclusion: "How rich her father must be!"

Favored by fortune in the matter of money, was this enviable person possessed of beauty as well?

In the disposition of the beds, Miss de Sor was placed between Cecilia on the right hand, and Emily on the left. If, by some fantastic turn of events, a man—say in the interests of propriety, a married doctor, with Miss Ladd to look after him—had been permitted to enter the room, and had been asked what he thought of the girls when he came out, he would not even have mentioned Francine. Blind to the beauties of the expensive night-gown, he would have noticed her long upper lip, her obstinate chin, her sallow complexion, her eyes placed too close together—and would have turned his attention to her nearest neighbors. On one side his languid interest would have been instantly roused by Cecilia's glowing auburn hair, her exquisitely pure skin, and her tender blue eyes. On the other, he would have discovered a bright little creature, who would have fascinated and perplexed him at one and the same time. If he had been questioned about her by a stranger, he would have been at a loss to say positively whether she was dark or light: he would have remembered how her eyes had held him, but he would not have known of what color they were. And yet, she would have remained a vivid picture in his memory when other impressions, derived at the same time, had vanished. "There was one little witch among them, who was worth all the rest put together; and I can't tell you why. They called her Emily. If I wasn't a married man—" There he would have thought of his wife, and would have sighed and said no more.

While the girls were still admiring Francine, the clock struck the half-hour past eleven.

Cecilia stole on tiptoe to the door—looked out, and listened—closed the door again—and addressed the meeting with the irresistible charm of her sweet voice and her persuasive smile.

"Are none of you hungry yet?" she inquired. "The teachers are safe in their rooms; we have set ourselves right with Francine. Why keep the supper waiting under Emily's bed?"

Such reasoning as this, with such personal attractions to recommend it, admitted of but one reply. The queen waved her hand graciously, and said, "Pull it out."

Is a lovely girl—whose face possesses the crowning charm of expression, whose slightest movement reveals the supple symmetry of her figure—less lovely because she is blessed with a good appetite, and is not ashamed to acknowledge it? With a grace all her own, Cecilia dived under the bed, and produced a basket of jam tarts, a basket of fruit and sweetmeats, a basket of sparkling lemonade, and a superb cake—all paid for by general subscriptions, and smuggled into the room by kind connivance of the servants. On this occasion, the feast was especially plentiful and expensive, in commemoration not only of the arrival of the Midsummer holidays, but of the coming freedom of Miss Ladd's two leading young ladies. With widely different destinies before them, Emily and Cecilia had completed their school life, and were now to go out into the world.

The contrast in the characters of the two girls showed itself, even in such a trifle as the preparations for supper.

Gentle Cecilia, sitting on the floor surrounded by good things, left it to the ingenuity of others to decide whether the baskets should be all emptied at once, or handed round from bed to bed, one at a time. In the meanwhile, her lovely blue eyes rested tenderly on the tarts.

Emily's commanding spirit seized on the reins of government, and employed each of her schoolfellows in the occupation which she was fittest to undertake. "Miss de Sor, let me look at your hand. Ah! I thought so. You have got the thickest wrist among us; you shall draw the corks. If you let the lemonade pop, not a drop of it goes down your throat. Effie, Annis, Priscilla, you are three notoriously lazy girls; it's doing you a true kindness to set you to work. Effie, clear the toilet-table for supper; away with the combs, the brushes, and the looking-glass. Annis, tear the leaves out of your book of exercises, and set them out for plates. No! I'll unpack; nobody touches the baskets but me. Priscilla, you have the prettiest ears in the room. You shall act as sentinel, my dear, and listen at the door. Cecilia, when you have done devouring those tarts with your eyes, take that pair of scissors (Miss de Sor, allow me to apologize for the mean manner in which this school is carried on; the knives and forks are counted and locked up every night)—I say take that pair of scissors, Cecilia, and carve the cake, and don't keep the largest bit for yourself. Are we all ready? Very well. Now take example by me. Talk as much as you like, so long as you don't talk too loud. There is one other thing before we begin. The men always propose toasts on these occasions; let's be like the men. Can any of you make a speech? Ah, it falls on me as usual. I propose the first toast. Down with all schools and teachers—especially the

17

new teacher, who came this half year. Oh, mercy, how it stings!" The fixed gas in the lemonade took the orator, at that moment, by the throat, and effectually checked the flow of her eloquence. It made no difference to the girls. Excepting the ease of feeble stomachs, who cares for eloquence in the presence of a supper-table? There were no feeble stomachs in that bedroom. With what inexhaustible energy Miss Ladd's young ladies ate and drank! How merrily they enjoyed the delightful privilege of talking nonsense! And—alas! alas!—how vainly they tried, in after life, to renew the once unalloyed enjoyment of tarts and lemonade!

In the unintelligible scheme of creation, there appears to be no human happiness—not even the happiness of schoolgirls—which is ever complete. Just as it was drawing to a close, the enjoyment of the feast was interrupted by an alarm from the sentinel at the door.

"Put out the candle!" Priscilla whispered "Somebody on the stairs."

CHAPTER II. BIOGRAPHY IN THE BEDROOM.

The candle was instantly extinguished. In discreet silence the girls stole back to their beds, and listened.

As an aid to the vigilance of the sentinel, the door had been left ajar. Through the narrow opening, a creaking of the broad wooden stairs of the old house became audible. In another moment there was silence. An interval passed, and the creaking was heard again. This time, the sound was distant and diminishing. On a sudden it stopped. The midnight silence was disturbed no more.

What did this mean?

Had one among the many persons in authority under Miss Ladd's roof heard the girls talking, and ascended the stairs to surprise them in the act of violating one of the rules of the house? So far, such a proceeding was by no means uncommon. But was it within the limits of probability that a teacher should alter her opinion of her own duty half-way up the stairs, and deliberately go back to her own room again? The bare idea of such a thing was absurd on the face of it. What more rational explanation could ingenuity discover on the spur of the moment?

Francine was the first to offer a suggestion. She shook and shivered in her bed, and said, "For heaven's sake, light the candle again! It's a Ghost."

"Clear away the supper, you fools, before the ghost can report us to Miss Ladd."

With this excellent advice Emily checked the rising panic. The door was closed, the candle was lit; all traces of the supper disappeared. For five minutes more they listened again. No sound came from the stairs; no teacher, or ghost of a teacher, appeared at the door.

Having eaten her supper, Cecilia's immediate anxieties were at an end; she was at leisure to exert her intelligence for the benefit of her schoolfellows. In her gentle ingratiating way, she offered a composing suggestion. "When we heard the creaking, I don't believe there was anybody on the stairs. In these old houses there are always strange noises at night—and they say the stairs here were made more than two hundred years since."

The girls looked at each other with a sense of relief—but they waited to hear the opinion of the queen. Emily, as usual, justified the confidence placed in her. She discovered an ingenious method of putting Cecilia's suggestion to the test.

"Let's go on talking," she said. "If Cecilia is right, the teachers are all asleep, and we have nothing to fear from them. If she's wrong, we shall sooner or later see one of them at the door. Don't be alarmed, Miss de Sor. Catching us talking at night, in this school, only means a reprimand. Catching us with a light, ends in punishment. Blow out the candle."

Francine's belief in the ghost was too sincerely superstitious to be shaken: she started up in bed. "Oh, don't leave me in the dark! I'll take the punishment, if we are found out."

"On your sacred word of honor?" Emily stipulated.

"Yes—yes."

The queen's sense of humor was tickled.

"There's something funny," she remarked, addressing her subjects, "in a big girl like this coming to a new school and beginning with a punishment. May I ask if you are a foreigner, Miss de Sor?"

"My papa is a Spanish gentleman," Francine answered, with dignity.

"And your mamma?"

"My mamma is English."

"And you have always lived in the West Indies?"

"I have always lived in the Island of St. Domingo."

Emily checked off on her fingers the different points thus far discovered in the character of Mr. de Sor's daughter. "She's ignorant, and superstitious, and foreign, and rich. My dear (forgive the familiarity), you are an interesting girl—and we must really know more of you. Entertain the bedroom. What have you been about all your life? And what in the name of wonder, brings you here? Before you begin I insist on one condition, in the name of all the young ladies in the room. No useful information about the West Indies!"

Francine disappointed her audience.

She was ready enough to make herself an object of interest to her companions; but she was not possessed of the capacity to arrange events in their proper order, necessary to the recital of the simplest narrative. Emily was obliged to help her, by means of questions. In one respect, the result justified the trouble taken to obtain it. A sufficient reason was discovered for the extraordinary appearance of a new pupil, on the day before the school closed for the holidays.

Mr. de Sor's elder brother had left him an estate in St. Domingo, and a fortune in money as well; on the one easy condition that he continued to reside in the island. The question of expense being now beneath the notice of the family, Francine had been sent to England, especially recommended to Miss Ladd as a young lady with grand prospects, sorely in need of a fashionable education. The voyage had been so timed, by the advice of the schoolmistress, as to make the holidays a means of obtaining this object privately. Francine was to be taken to Brighton, where excellent masters could be obtained to assist Miss Ladd. With six weeks before her, she might in some degree make up for lost time; and, when the school opened again, she would avoid the mortification of being put down in the lowest class, along with the children.

The examination of Miss de Sor having produced these results was pursued no further. Her character now appeared in a new, and not very attractive, light. She audaciously took to herself the whole credit of telling her story:

"I think it's my turn now," she said, "to be interested and amused. May I ask you to begin, Miss Emily? All I know of you at present is, that your family name is Brown."

Emily held up her hand for silence.

Was the mysterious creaking on the stairs making itself heard once more? No. The sound that had caught Emily's quick ear came from the beds, on the opposite side of the room, occupied by the three lazy girls. With no new alarm to disturb them, Effie, Annis, and Priscilla had yielded to the composing influences of a good supper and a warm night. They were fast asleep—and the stoutest of the three (softly, as became a young lady) was snoring!

The unblemished reputation of the bedroom was dear to Emily, in her capacity of queen. She felt herself humiliated in the presence of the new pupil.

"If that fat girl ever gets a lover," she said indignantly, "I shall consider it my duty to warn the poor man before he marries her. Her ridiculous name is Euphemia. I have christened her (far more appropriately) Boiled Veal. No color in her hair, no color in her eyes, no color in her complexion. In short, no flavor in Euphemia. You naturally object to snoring. Pardon me if I turn my back on you—I am going to throw my slipper at her."

The soft voice of Cecilia—suspiciously drowsy in tone—interposed in the interests of mercy.

"She can't help it, poor thing; and she really isn't loud enough to disturb

21

us."

"She won't disturb you, at any rate! Rouse yourself, Cecilia. We are wide awake on this side of the room —and Francine says it's our turn to amuse her."

A low murmur, dying away gently in a sigh, was the only answer. Sweet Cecilia had yielded to the somnolent influences of the supper and the night. The soft infection of repose seemed to be in some danger of communicating itself to Francine. Her large mouth opened luxuriously in a long-continued yawn.

"Good-night!" said Emily.

Miss de Sor became wide awake in an instant.

"No," she said positively; "you are quite mistaken if you think I am going to sleep. Please exert yourself, Miss Emily—I am waiting to be interested."

Emily appeared to be unwilling to exert herself. She preferred talking of the weather.

"Isn't the wind rising?" she said.

There could be no doubt of it. The leaves in the garden were beginning to rustle, and the pattering of the rain sounded on the windows.

Francine (as her straight chin proclaimed to all students of physiognomy) was an obstinate girl. Determined to carry her point she tried Emily's own system on Emily herself—she put questions.

"Have you been long at this school?"

"More than three years."

"Have you got any brothers and sisters?"

"I am the only child."

"Are your father and mother alive?"

Emily suddenly raised herself in bed.

"Wait a minute," she said; "I think I hear it again."

"The creaking on the stairs?"

"Yes."

Either she was mistaken, or the change for the worse in the weather made it not easy to hear slight noises in the house. The wind was still rising. The passage of it through the great trees in the garden began to sound like the fall of waves on a distant beach. It drove the rain—a heavy downpour by this time—rattling against the windows.

"Almost a storm, isn't it?" Emily said

Francine's last question had not been answered yet. She took the earliest opportunity of repeating it:

"Never mind the weather," she said. "Tell me about your father and mother. Are they both alive?"

Emily's reply only related to one of her parents.

"My mother died before I was old enough to feel my loss."

"And your father?"

Emily referred to another relative—her father's sister. "Since I have grown up," she proceeded, "my good aunt has been a second mother to me. My story is, in one respect, the reverse of yours. You are unexpectedly rich; and I am unexpectedly poor. My aunt's fortune was to have been my fortune, if I outlived her. She has been ruined by the failure of a bank. In her old age, she must live on an income of two hundred a year—and I must get my own living when I leave school."

"Surely your father can help you?" Francine persisted.

"His property is landed property." Her voice faltered, as she referred to him, even in that indirect manner. "It is entailed; his nearest male relative inherits it."

The delicacy which is easily discouraged was not one of the weaknesses in the nature of Francine.

"Do I understand that your father is dead?" she asked.

Our thick-skinned fellow-creatures have the rest of us at their mercy: only give them time, and they carry their point in the end. In sad subdued tones—telling of deeply-rooted reserves of feeling, seldom revealed to strangers—Emily yielded at last.

"Yes," she said, "my father is dead."

"Long ago?"

"Some people might think it long ago. I was very fond of my father. It's nearly four years since he died, and my heart still aches when I think of him. I'm not easily depressed by troubles, Miss de Sor. But his death was sudden— he was in his grave when I first heard of it—and—Oh, he was so good to me; he was so good to me!"

The gay high-spirited little creature who took the lead among them all—who was the life and soul of the school—hid her face in her hands, and burst out crying.

Startled and—to do her justice—ashamed, Francine attempted to make excuses. Emily's generous nature passed over the cruel persistency that had tortured her. "No no; I have nothing to forgive. It isn't your fault. Other girls have not mothers and brothers and sisters—and get reconciled to such a loss as mine. Don't make excuses."

"Yes, but I want you to know that I feel for you," Francine insisted, without the slightest approach to sympathy in face, voice, or manner. "When my uncle died, and left us all the money, papa was much shocked. He trusted to time to help him."

"Time has been long about it with me, Francine. I am afraid there is something perverse in my nature; the hope of meeting again in a better world seems so faint and so far away. No more of it now! Let us talk of that good creature who is asleep on the other side of you. Did I tell you that I must earn my own bread when I leave school? Well, Cecilia has written home and found an employment for me. Not a situation as governess—something quite out of

24

the common way. You shall hear all about it."

In the brief interval that had passed, the weather had begun to change again. The wind was as high as ever; but to judge by the lessening patter on the windows the rain was passing away.

Emily began.

She was too grateful to her friend and school-fellow, and too deeply interested in her story, to notice the air of indifference with which Francine settled herself on her pillow to hear the praises of Cecilia. The most beautiful girl in the school was not an object of interest to a young lady with an obstinate chin and unfortunately-placed eyes. Pouring warm from the speaker's heart the story ran smoothly on, to the monotonous accompaniment of the moaning wind. By fine degrees Francine's eyes closed, opened and closed again. Toward the latter part of the narrative Emily's memory became, for the moment only, confused between two events. She stopped to consider—noticed Francine's silence, in an interval when she might have said a word of encouragement— and looked closer at her. Miss de Sor was asleep.

"She might have told me she was tired," Emily said to herself quietly. "Well! the best thing I can do is to put out the light and follow her example."

As she took up the extinguisher, the bedroom door was suddenly opened from the outer side. A tall woman, robed in a black dressing-gown, stood on the threshold, looking at Emily.

CHAPTER III. THE LATE MR. BROWN.

The woman's lean, long-fingered hand pointed to the candle.

"Don't put it out." Saying those words, she looked round the room, and satisfied herself that the other girls were asleep.

Emily laid down the extinguisher. "You mean to report us, of course," she said. "I am the only one awake, Miss Jethro; lay the blame on me."

"I have no intention of reporting you. But I have something to say."

She paused, and pushed her thick black hair (already streaked with gray) back from her temples. Her eyes, large and dark and dim, rested on Emily with a sorrowful interest. "When your young friends wake to-morrow morning," she went on, "you can tell them that the new teacher, whom nobody likes, has left the school."

For once, even quick-witted Emily was bewildered. "Going away," she said, "when you have only been here since Easter!"

Miss Jethro advanced, not noticing Emily's expression of surprise. "I am not very strong at the best of times," she continued, "may I sit down on your bed?" Remarkable on other occasions for her cold composure, her voice trembled as she made that request—a strange request surely, when there were chairs at her disposal.

Emily made room for her with the dazed look of a girl in a dream. "I beg your pardon, Miss Jethro, one of the things I can't endure is being puzzled. If you don't mean to report us, why did you come in and catch me with the light?"

Miss Jethro's explanation was far from relieving the perplexity which her conduct had caused.

"I have been mean enough," she answered, "to listen at the door, and I heard you talking of your father. I want to hear more about him. That is why I came in."

"You knew my father!" Emily exclaimed.

"I believe I knew him. But his name is so common—there are so many thousands of 'James Browns' in England—that I am in fear of making a mistake. I heard you say that he died nearly four years since. Can you mention any particulars which might help to enlighten me? If you think I am taking a liberty—"

Emily stopped her. "I would help you if I could," she said. "But I was in poor health at the time; and I was staying with friends far away in Scotland, to try change of air. The news of my father's death brought on a relapse. Weeks passed before I was strong enough to travel—weeks and weeks before

I saw his grave! I can only tell you what I know from my aunt. He died of heart-complaint."

Miss Jethro started.

Emily looked at her for the first time, with eyes that betrayed a feeling of distrust. "What have I said to startle you?" she asked.

"Nothing! I am nervous in stormy weather—don't notice me." She went on abruptly with her inquiries. "Will you tell me the date of your father's death?"

"The date was the thirtieth of September, nearly four years since."

She waited, after that reply.

Miss Jethro was silent.

"And this," Emily continued, "is the thirtieth of June, eighteen hundred and eighty-one. You can now judge for yourself. Did you know my father?"

Miss Jethro answered mechanically, using the same words.

"I did know your father."

Emily's feeling of distrust was not set at rest. "I never heard him speak of you," she said.

In her younger days the teacher must have been a handsome woman. Her grandly-formed features still suggested the idea of imperial beauty—perhaps Jewish in its origin. When Emily said, "I never heard him speak of you," the color flew into her pallid cheeks: her dim eyes became alive again with a momentary light. She left her seat on the bed, and, turning away, mastered the emotion that shook her.

"How hot the night is!" she said: and sighed, and resumed the subject with a steady countenance. "I am not surprised that your father never mentioned me—to you." She spoke quietly, but her face was paler than ever. She sat down again on the bed. "Is there anything I can do for you," she asked, "before I go away? Oh, I only mean some trifling service that would lay you under no obligation, and would not oblige you to keep up your acquaintance with me."

Her eyes—the dim black eyes that must once have been irresistibly beautiful—looked at Emily so sadly that the generous girl reproached herself for having doubted her father's friend. "Are you thinking of him," she said gently, "when you ask if you can be of service to me?"

Miss Jethro made no direct reply. "You were fond of your father?" she added, in a whisper. "You told your schoolfellow that your heart still aches when you speak of him."

"I only told her the truth," Emily answered simply.

Miss Jethro shuddered—on that hot night!—shuddered as if a chill had struck her.

Emily held out her hand; the kind feeling that had been roused in her glittered prettily in her eyes. "I am afraid I have not done you justice," she said. "Will you forgive me and shake hands?"

Miss Jethro rose, and drew back. "Look at the light!" she exclaimed.

The candle was all burned out. Emily still offered her hand—and still Miss Jethro refused to see it.

"There is just light enough left," she said, "to show me my way to the door. Good-night—and good-by."

Emily caught at her dress, and stopped her. "Why won't you shake hands with me?" she asked.

The wick of the candle fell over in the socket, and left them in the dark. Emily resolutely held the teacher's dress. With or without light, she was still bent on making Miss Jethro explain herself.

They had throughout spoken in guarded tones, fearing to disturb the sleeping girls. The sudden darkness had its inevitable effect. Their voices sank to whispers now. "My father's friend," Emily pleaded, "is surely my friend?"

"Drop the subject."

28

"Why?"

"You can never be my friend."

"Why not?"

"Let me go!"

Emily's sense of self-respect forbade her to persist any longer. "I beg your pardon for having kept you here against your will," she said—and dropped her hold on the dress.

Miss Jethro instantly yielded on her side. "I am sorry to have been obstinate," she answered. "If you do despise me, it is after all no more than I have deserved." Her hot breath beat on Emily's face: the unhappy woman must have bent over the bed as she made her confession. "I am not a fit person for you to associate with."

"I don't believe it!"

Miss Jethro sighed bitterly. "Young and warm hearted—I was once like you!" She controlled that outburst of despair. Her next words were spoken in steadier tones. "You will have it—you shall have it!" she said. "Some one (in this house or out of it; I don't know which) has betrayed me to the mistress of the school. A wretch in my situation suspects everybody, and worse still, does it without reason or excuse. I heard you girls talking when you ought to have been asleep. You all dislike me. How did I know it mightn't be one of you? Absurd, to a person with a well-balanced mind! I went halfway up the stairs, and felt ashamed of myself, and went back to my room. If I could only have got some rest! Ah, well, it was not to be done. My own vile suspicions kept me awake; I left my bed again. You know what I heard on the other side of that door, and why I was interested in hearing it. Your father never told me he had a daughter. 'Miss Brown,' at this school, was any 'Miss Brown,' to me. I had no idea of who you really were until to-night. I'm wandering. What does all this matter to you? Miss Ladd has been merciful; she lets me go without exposing me. You can guess what has happened. No? Not even yet? Is it innocence or kindness that makes you so slow to understand? My dear, I have obtained admission to this respectable house by means of false references, and I have been discovered. Now you know why you must not be the friend of such a woman as I am! Once more, good-night—and good-by."

Emily shrank from that miserable farewell.

"Bid me good-night," she said, "but don't bid me good-by. Let me see you again."

"Never!"

The sound of the softly-closed door was just audible in the darkness. She had spoken—she had gone—never to be seen by Emily again.

Miserable, interesting, unfathomable creature—the problem that night of Emily's waking thoughts: the phantom of her dreams. "Bad? or good?" she asked herself. "False; for she listened at the door. True; for she told me the tale of her own disgrace. A friend of my father; and she never knew that he had a daughter. Refined, accomplished, lady-like; and she stoops to use a false reference. Who is to reconcile such contradictions as these?"

Dawn looked in at the window—dawn of the memorable day which was, for Emily, the beginning of a new life. The years were before her; and the years in their course reveal baffling mysteries of life and death.

CHAPTER IV. MISS LADD'S DRAWING-MASTER.

Francine was awakened the next morning by one of the housemaids, bringing up her breakfast on a tray. Astonished at this concession to laziness, in an institution devoted to the practice of all virtues, she looked round. The bedroom was deserted.

"The other young ladies are as busy as bees, miss," the housemaid explained. "They were up and dressed two hours ago: and the breakfast has been cleared away long since. It's Miss Emily's fault. She wouldn't allow them to wake you; she said you could be of no possible use downstairs, and you had better be treated like a visitor. Miss Cecilia was so distressed at your missing your breakfast that she spoke to the housekeeper, and I was sent up to you. Please to excuse it if the tea's cold. This is Grand Day, and we are all topsy-turvy in consequence."

Inquiring what "Grand Day" meant, and why it produced this extraordinary result in a ladies' school, Francine discovered that the first day of the vacation was devoted to the distribution of prizes, in the presence of parents, guardians and friends. An Entertainment was added, comprising those merciless tests of human endurance called Recitations; light refreshments and musical performances being distributed at intervals, to encourage the exhausted audience. The local newspaper sent a reporter to describe the proceedings, and some of Miss Ladd's young ladies enjoyed the intoxicating luxury of seeing their names in print.

"It begins at three o'clock," the housemaid went on, "and, what with practicing and rehearsing, and ornamenting the schoolroom, there's a hubbub fit to make a person's head spin. Besides which," said the girl, lowering her voice, and approaching a little nearer to Francine, "we have all been taken by surprise. The first thing in the morning Miss Jethro left us, without saying good-by to anybody."

"Who is Miss Jethro?"

"The new teacher, miss. We none of us liked her, and we all suspect there's something wrong. Miss Ladd and the clergyman had a long talk together yesterday (in private, you know), and they sent for Miss Jethro—which looks bad, doesn't it? Is there anything more I can do for you, miss? It's a beautiful day after the rain. If I was you, I should go and enjoy myself in the garden."

Having finished her breakfast, Francine decided on profiting by this sensible suggestion.

The servant who showed her the way to the garden was not favorably impressed by the new pupil: Francine's temper asserted itself a little too plainly in her face. To a girl possessing a high opinion of her own importance it was not very agreeable to feel herself excluded, as an illiterate stranger, from the one absorbing interest of her schoolfellows. "Will the time ever come," she wondered bitterly, "when I shall win a prize, and sing and play before all the company? How I should enjoy making the girls envy me!"

A broad lawn, overshadowed at one end by fine old trees—flower beds and shrubberies, and winding paths prettily and invitingly laid out—made the garden a welcome refuge on that fine summer morning. The novelty of the scene, after her experience in the West Indies, the delicious breezes cooled by the rain of the night, exerted their cheering influence even on the sullen disposition of Francine. She smiled, in spite of herself, as she followed the pleasant paths, and heard the birds singing their summer songs over her head.

Wandering among the trees, which occupied a considerable extent of ground, she passed into an open space beyond, and discovered an old fish-pond, overgrown by aquatic plants. Driblets of water trickled from a dilapidated fountain in the middle. On the further side of the pond the ground sloped downward toward the south, and revealed, over a low paling, a pretty view of a village and its church, backed by fir woods mounting the heathy sides of a range of hills beyond. A fanciful little wooden building, imitating the form of a Swiss cottage, was placed so as to command the prospect. Near it, in the shadow of the building, stood a rustic chair and table—with a color-box on one, and a portfolio on the other. Fluttering over the grass, at the mercy of the capricious breeze, was a neglected sheet of drawing-paper. Francine ran round the pond, and picked up the paper just as it was on the point of being tilted into the water. It contained a sketch in water colors of the village and the woods, and Francine had looked at the view itself with indifference—the picture of the view interested her. Ordinary visitors to Galleries of Art, which admit students, show the same strange perversity. The work of the copyist commands their whole attention; they take no interest in the original picture.

Looking up from the sketch, Francine was startled. She discovered a man, at the window of the Swiss summer-house, watching her.

"When you have done with that drawing," he said quietly, "please let me have it back again."

He was tall and thin and dark. His finely-shaped intelligent face— hidden, as to the lower part of it, by a curly black beard—would have been absolutely handsome, even in the eyes of a schoolgirl, but for the deep furrows that marked it prematurely between the eyebrows, and at the sides of the mouth. In the same way, an underlying mockery impaired the attraction of his otherwise refined and gentle manner. Among his fellow-creatures, children and dogs were the only critics who appreciated his merits without discovering the defects which lessened the favorable appreciation of him by men and women. He dressed neatly, but his morning coat was badly made, and his picturesque felt hat was too old. In short, there seemed to be no good quality about him which was not perversely associated with a drawback of some kind. He was one of those harmless and luckless men, possessed of excellent qualities, who fail nevertheless to achieve popularity in their social sphere.

Francine handed his sketch to him, through the window; doubtful whether the words that he had addressed to her were spoken in jest or in earnest.

"I only presumed to touch your drawing," she said, "because it was in danger."

"What danger?" he inquired.

Francine pointed to the pond. "If I had not been in time to pick it up, it would have been blown into the water."

"Do you think it was worth picking up?"

Putting that question, he looked first at the sketch—then at the view which it represented—then back again at the sketch. The corners of his mouth turned upward with a humorous expression of scorn. "Madam Nature," he said, "I beg your pardon." With those words, he composedly tore his work of art into small pieces, and scattered them out of the window.

"What a pity!" said Francine.

He joined her on the ground outside the cottage. "Why is it a pity?" he asked.

"Such a nice drawing."

"It isn't a nice drawing."

"You're not very polite, sir."

He looked at her—and sighed as if he pitied so young a woman for having a temper so ready to take offense. In his flattest contradictions he always preserved the character of a politely-positive man.

"Put it in plain words, miss," he replied. "I have offended the predominant sense in your nature—your sense of self-esteem. You don't like to be told, even indirectly, that you know nothing of Art. In these days, everybody knows everything—and thinks nothing worth knowing after all. But beware how you presume on an appearance of indifference, which is nothing but conceit in disguise. The ruling passion of civilized humanity is, Conceit. You may try the regard of your dearest friend in any other way, and be forgiven. Ruffle the smooth surface of your friend's self-esteem—and there will be an acknowledged coolness between you which will last for life. Excuse me for giving you the benefit of my trumpery experience. This sort of smart talk is my form of conceit. Can I be of use to you in some better way? Are you looking for one of our young ladies?"

Francine began to feel a certain reluctant interest in him when he spoke of "our young ladies." She asked if he belonged to the school.

The corners of his mouth turned up again. "I'm one of the masters," he said. "Are you going to belong to the school, too?"

Francine bent her head, with a gravity and condescension intended to keep him at his proper distance. Far from being discouraged, he permitted his curiosity to take additional liberties. "Are you to have the misfortune of being one of my pupils?" he asked.

"I don't know who you are."

"You won't be much wiser when you do know. My name is Alban Morris."

Francine corrected herself. "I mean, I don't know what you teach."

Alban Morris pointed to the fragments of his sketch from Nature. "I am a bad artist," he said. "Some bad artists become Royal Academicians. Some take to drink. Some get a pension. And some—I am one of them—

find refuge in schools. Drawing is an 'Extra' at this school. Will you take my advice? Spare your good father's pocket; say you don't want to learn to draw."

He was so gravely in earnest that Francine burst out laughing. "You are a strange man," she said.

"Wrong again, miss. I am only an unhappy man."

The furrows in his face deepened, the latent humor died out of his eyes. He turned to the summer-house window, and took up a pipe and tobacco pouch, left on the ledge.

"I lost my only friend last year," he said. "Since the death of my dog, my pipe is the one companion I have left. Naturally I am not allowed to enjoy the honest fellow's society in the presence of ladies. They have their own taste in perfumes. Their clothes and their letters reek with the foetid secretion of the musk deer. The clean vegetable smell of tobacco is unendurable to them. Allow me to retire—and let me thank you for the trouble you took to save my drawing."

The tone of indifference in which he expressed his gratitude piqued Francine. She resented it by drawing her own conclusion from what he had said of the ladies and the musk deer. "I was wrong in admiring your drawing," she remarked; "and wrong again in thinking you a strange man. Am I wrong, for the third time, in believing that you dislike women?"

"I am sorry to say you are right," Alban Morris answered gravely.

"Is there not even one exception?"

The instant the words passed her lips, she saw that there was some secretly sensitive feeling in him which she had hurt. His black brows gathered into a frown, his piercing eyes looked at her with angry surprise. It was over in a moment. He raised his shabby hat, and made her a bow.

"There is a sore place still left in me," he said; "and you have innocently hit it. Good-morning."

Before she could speak again, he had turned the corner of the summer-house, and was lost to view in a shrubbery on the westward side of the grounds.

CHAPTER V. DISCOVERIES IN THE GARDEN.

Left by herself, Miss de Sor turned back again by way of the trees.

So far, her interview with the drawing-master had helped to pass the time. Some girls might have found it no easy task to arrive at a true view of the character of Alban Morris. Francine's essentially superficial observation set him down as "a little mad," and left him there, judged and dismissed to her own entire satisfaction.

Arriving at the lawn, she discovered Emily pacing backward and forward, with her head down and her hands behind her, deep in thought. Francine's high opinion of herself would have carried her past any of the other girls, unless they had made special advances to her. She stopped and looked at Emily.

It is the sad fate of little women in general to grow too fat and to be born with short legs. Emily's slim finely-strung figure spoke for itself as to the first of these misfortunes, and asserted its happy freedom from the second, if she only walked across a room. Nature had built her, from head to foot, on a skeleton-scaffolding in perfect proportion. Tall or short matters little to the result, in women who possess the first and foremost advantage of beginning well in their bones. When they live to old age, they often astonish thoughtless men, who walk behind them in the street. "I give you my honor, she was as easy and upright as a young girl; and when you got in front of her and looked—white hair, and seventy years of age."

Francine approached Emily, moved by a rare impulse in her nature—the impulse to be sociable. "You look out of spirits," she began. "Surely you don't regret leaving school?"

In her present mood, Emily took the opportunity (in the popular phrase) of snubbing Francine. "You have guessed wrong; I do regret," she answered. "I have found in Cecilia my dearest friend at school. And school brought with it the change in my life which has helped me to bear the loss of my father. If you must know what I was thinking of just now, I was thinking of my aunt. She has not answered my last letter—and I'm beginning to be afraid she is ill."

"I'm very sorry," said Francine.

"Why? You don't know my aunt; and you have only known me since yesterday afternoon. Why are you sorry?"

Francine remained silent. Without realizing it, she was beginning to feel the dominant influence that Emily exercised over the weaker natures that came in contact with her. To find herself irresistibly attracted by a stranger at a new school—an unfortunate little creature, whose destiny was to earn her own living—filled the narrow mind of Miss de Sor with perplexity. Having waited in vain for a reply, Emily turned away, and resumed the train of thought which her schoolfellow had interrupted.

By an association of ideas, of which she was not herself aware, she now passed from thinking of her aunt to thinking of Miss Jethro. The interview of the previous night had dwelt on her mind at intervals, in the hours of the new day.

Acting on instinct rather than on reason, she had kept that remarkable incident in her school life a secret from every one. No discoveries had been made by other persons. In speaking to her staff of teachers, Miss Ladd had alluded to the affair in the most cautious terms. "Circumstances of a private nature have obliged the lady to retire from my school. When we meet after the holidays, another teacher will be in her place." There, Miss Ladd's explanation had begun and ended. Inquiries addressed to the servants had led to no result. Miss Jethro's luggage was to be forwarded to the London terminus of the railway—and Miss Jethro herself had baffled investigation by leaving the school on foot. Emily's interest in the lost teacher was not the transitory interest of curiosity; her father's mysterious friend was a person whom she honestly desired to see again. Perplexed by the difficulty of finding a means of tracing Miss Jethro, she reached the shady limit of the trees, and turned to walk back again. Approaching the place at which she and Francine had met, an idea occurred to her. It was just possible that Miss Jethro might not be unknown to her aunt.

Still meditating on the cold reception that she had encountered, and still feeling the influence which mastered her in spite of herself, Francine interpreted Emily's return as an implied expression of regret. She advanced with a constrained smile, and spoke first.

"How are the young ladies getting on in the schoolroom?" she asked, by way of renewing the conversation.

Emily's face assumed a look of surprise which said plainly, Can't you take a hint and leave me to myself?

Francine was constitutionally impenetrable to reproof of this sort; her thick skin was not even tickled. "Why are you not helping them," she went on; "you who have the clearest head among us and take the lead in everything?"

It may be a humiliating confession to make, yet it is surely true that we are all accessible to flattery. Different tastes appreciate different methods of burning incense—but the perfume is more or less agreeable to all varieties of noses. Francine's method had its tranquilizing effect on Emily. She answered indulgently, "Miss de Sor, I have nothing to do with it."

"Nothing to do with it? No prizes to win before you leave school?"

"I won all the prizes years ago."

"But there are recitations. Surely you recite?"

Harmless words in themselves, pursuing the same smooth course of flattery as before—but with what a different result! Emily's face reddened with anger the moment they were spoken. Having already irritated Alban Morris, unlucky Francine, by a second mischievous interposition of accident, had succeeded in making Emily smart next. "Who has told you," she burst out; "I insist on knowing!"

"Nobody has told me anything!" Francine declared piteously.

"Nobody has told you how I have been insulted?"

"No, indeed! Oh, Miss Brown, who could insult you?"

In a man, the sense of injury does sometimes submit to the discipline of silence. In a woman—never. Suddenly reminded of her past wrongs (by the pardonable error of a polite schoolfellow), Emily committed the startling inconsistency of appealing to the sympathies of Francine!

"Would you believe it? I have been forbidden to recite—I, the head girl of the school. Oh, not to-day! It happened a month ago—when we were all in consultation, making our arrangements. Miss Ladd asked me if I had decided on a piece to recite. I said, 'I have not only decided, I have learned the piece.' 'And what may it be?' 'The dagger-scene in Macbeth.' There was a howl—I can call it by no other name—a howl of indignation. A man's soliloquy, and, worse still, a murdering man's soliloquy, recited by one of Miss Ladd's young ladies, before an audience of parents and guardians! That was the tone they took with me. I was as firm as a rock. The dagger-scene or nothing. The result is—nothing! An insult to Shakespeare, and an insult to Me. I felt it—I feel it still. I was prepared for any sacrifice in the cause of the drama. If Miss Ladd had met me in a proper spirit, do you know what I would have done? I would have played Macbeth in costume. Just hear me, and judge for yourself. I begin with a dreadful vacancy in my eyes, and a hollow moaning in my voice: 'Is this a dagger that I see before me—?'"

Reciting with her face toward the trees, Emily started, dropped the character of Macbeth, and instantly became herself again: herself, with a rising color and an angry brightening of the eyes. "Excuse me, I can't trust my memory: I must get the play." With that abrupt apology, she walked away rapidly in the direction of the house.

In some surprise, Francine turned, and looked at the trees. She discovered—in full retreat, on his side—the eccentric drawing-master, Alban Morris.

Did he, too, admire the dagger-scene? And was he modestly desirous of hearing it recited, without showing himself? In that case, why should Emily (whose besetting weakness was certainly not want of confidence in her own resources) leave the garden the moment she caught sight of him? Francine consulted her instincts. She had just arrived at a conclusion which expressed itself outwardly by a malicious smile, when gentle Cecilia appeared on the lawn—a lovable object in a broad straw hat and a white dress, with a nosegay in her bosom—smiling, and fanning herself.

"It's so hot in the schoolroom," she said, "and some of the girls, poor things, are so ill-tempered at rehearsal—I have made my escape. I hope you got your breakfast, Miss de Sor. What have you been doing here, all by yourself?"

"I have been making an interesting discovery," Francine replied.

"An interesting discovery in our garden? What can it be?"

"The drawing-master, my dear, is in love with Emily. Perhaps she doesn't care about him. Or, perhaps, I have been an innocent obstacle in the way of an appointment between them."

Cecilia had breakfasted to her heart's content on her favorite dish—buttered eggs. She was in such good spirits that she was inclined to be coquettish, even when there was no man present to fascinate. "We are not allowed to talk about love in this school," she said—and hid her face behind her fan. "Besides, if it came to Miss Ladd's ears, poor Mr. Morris might lose his situation."

"But isn't it true?" asked Francine.

"It may be true, my dear; but nobody knows. Emily hasn't breathed a word about it to any of us. And Mr. Morris keeps his own secret. Now and then we catch him looking at her—and we draw our own conclusions."

"Did you meet Emily on your way here?"

"Yes, and she passed without speaking to me."

"Thinking perhaps of Mr. Morris."

Cecilia shook her head. "Thinking, Francine, of the new life before her—and regretting, I am afraid, that she ever confided her hopes and wishes to me. Did she tell you last night what her prospects are when she leaves school?"

"She told me you had been very kind in helping her. I daresay I should have heard more, if I had not fallen asleep. What is she going to do?"

"To live in a dull house, far away in the north," Cecilia answered; "with only old people in it. She will have to write and translate for a great scholar, who is studying mysterious inscriptions—hieroglyphics, I think they are called—found among the ruins of Central America. It's really no laughing matter, Francine! Emily made a joke of it, too. 'I'll take anything but a situation as a governess,' she said; 'the children who have Me to teach them would be to be pitied indeed!' She begged and prayed me to help her to get an honest living. What could I do? I could only write home to papa. He is a member of Parliament: and everybody who wants a place seems to think he is bound to find it for them. As it happened, he had heard from an old friend of his (a certain Sir Jervis Redwood), who was in search of a secretary. Being in favor of letting the women compete for employment with the men, Sir Jervis was willing to try, what he calls, 'a female.' Isn't that a horrid way of speaking of us? and Miss Ladd says it's ungrammatical, besides. Papa had written back to say he knew of no lady whom he could recommend. When he got my letter speaking of Emily, he kindly wrote again. In the interval, Sir Jervis had received two applications for the vacant place. They were both from old ladies—and he declined to employ them."

"Because they were old," Francine suggested maliciously.

"You shall hear him give his own reasons, my dear. Papa sent me an extract from his letter. It made me rather angry; and (perhaps for that reason) I think I can repeat it word for word:—'We are four old people in this house, and we don't want a fifth. Let us have a young one to cheer us. If your daughter's friend likes the terms, and is not encumbered with a sweetheart, I will send for her when the school breaks up at midsummer.' Coarse and selfish—isn't it? However, Emily didn't agree with me, when I showed her the extract. She accepted the place, very much to her aunt's surprise and regret, when that excellent person heard of it. Now that the time has come (though Emily won't acknowledge it), I believe she secretly shrinks, poor dear, from the prospect."

"Very likely," Francine agreed—without even a pretense of sympathy.

"But tell me, who are the four old people?"

"First, Sir Jervis himself—seventy, last birthday. Next, his unmarried sister—nearly eighty. Next, his man-servant, Mr. Rook—well past sixty. And last, his man-servant's wife, who considers herself young, being only a little over forty. That is the household. Mrs. Rook is coming to-day to attend Emily on the journey to the North; and I am not at all sure that Emily will like her."

"A disagreeable woman, I suppose?"

"No—not exactly that. Rather odd and flighty. The fact is, Mrs. Rook has had her troubles; and perhaps they have a little unsettled her. She and her husband used to keep the village inn, close to our park: we know all about them at home. I am sure I pity these poor people. What are you looking at, Francine?"

Feeling no sort of interest in Mr. and Mrs. Rook, Francine was studying her schoolfellow's lovely face in search of defects. She had already discovered that Cecilia's eyes were placed too widely apart, and that her chin wanted size and character.

"I was admiring your complexion, dear," she answered coolly. "Well, and why do you pity the Rooks?"

Simple Cecilia smiled, and went on with her story.

"They are obliged to go out to service in their old age, through a misfortune for which they are in no way to blame. Their customers deserted the inn, and Mr. Rook became bankrupt. The inn got what they call a bad name—in a very dreadful way. There was a murder committed in the house."

"A murder?" cried Francine. "Oh, this is exciting! You provoking girl, why didn't you tell me about it before?"

"I didn't think of it," said Cecilia placidly.

"Do go on! Were you at home when it happened?"

"I was here, at school."

"You saw the newspapers, I suppose?"

"Miss Ladd doesn't allow us to read newspapers. I did hear of it, however, in letters from home. Not that there was much in the letters. They said it was too horrible to be described. The poor murdered gentleman—"

Francine was unaffectedly shocked. "A gentleman!" she exclaimed. "How dreadful!"

"The poor man was a stranger in our part of the country," Cecilia resumed; "and the police were puzzled about the motive for a murder. His pocketbook was missing; but his watch and his rings were found on the body. I remember the initials on his linen because they were the same as my mother's initial before she was married—'J. B.' Really, Francine, that's all I know about it."

"Surely you know whether the murderer was discovered?"

"Oh, yes—of course I know that! The government offered a reward; and clever people were sent from London to help the county police. Nothing came of it. The murderer has never been discovered, from that time to this."

"When did it happen?"

"It happened in the autumn."

"The autumn of last year?"

"No! no! Nearly four years since."

CHAPTER VI. ON THE WAY TO THE VILLAGE.

Alban Morris—discovered by Emily in concealment among the trees—was not content with retiring to another part of the grounds. He pursued his retreat, careless in what direction it might take him, to a footpath across the fields, which led to the highroad and the railway station.

Miss Ladd's drawing-master was in that state of nervous irritability which seeks relief in rapidity of motion. Public opinion in the neighborhood (especially public opinion among the women) had long since decided that his manners were offensive, and his temper incurably bad. The men who happened to pass him on the footpath said "Good-morning" grudgingly.

The women took no notice of him—with one exception. She was young and saucy, and seeing him walking at the top of his speed on the way to the railway station, she called after him, "Don't be in a hurry, sir! You're in plenty of time for the London train."

To her astonishment he suddenly stopped. His reputation for rudeness was so well established that she moved away to a safe distance, before she ventured to look at him again. He took no notice of her—he seemed to be considering with himself. The frolicsome young woman had done him a service: she had suggested an idea.

"Suppose I go to London?" he thought. "Why not?—the school is breaking up for the holidays—and she is going away like the rest of them." He looked round in the direction of the schoolhouse. "If I go back to wish her good-by, she will keep out of my way, and part with me at the last moment like a stranger. After my experience of women, to be in love again—in love with a girl who is young enough to be my daughter—what a fool, what a driveling, degraded fool I must be!"

Hot tears rose in his eyes. He dashed them away savagely, and went on again faster than ever—resolved to pack up at once at his lodgings in the village, and to take his departure by the next train.

At the point where the footpath led into the road, he came to a standstill for the second time.

The cause was once more a person of the sex associated in his mind with a bitter sense of injury. On this occasion the person was only a miserable little child, crying over the fragments of a broken jug.

Alban Morris looked at her with his grimly humorous smile. "So you've broken a jug?" he remarked.

"And spilt father's beer," the child answered. Her frail little body shook with terror. "Mother'll beat me when I go home," she said.

"What does mother do when you bring the jug back safe and sound?" Alban asked.

"Gives me bren-butter."

"Very well. Now listen to me. Mother shall give you bread and butter again this time."

The child stared at him with the tears suspended in her eyes. He went on talking to her as seriously as ever.

"You understand what I have just said to you?"

"Yes, sir."

"Have you got a pocket-handkerchief?"

"No, sir."

"Then dry your eyes with mine."

He tossed his handkerchief to her with one hand, and picked up a fragment of the broken jug with the other. "This will do for a pattern," he said to himself. The child stared at the handkerchief—stared at Alban—took courage—and rubbed vigorously at her eyes. The instinct, which is worth all the reason that ever pretended to enlighten mankind—the instinct that never deceives—told this little ignorant creature that she had found a friend. She returned the handkerchief in grave silence. Alban took her up in his arms.

"Your eyes are dry, and your face is fit to be seen," he said. "Will you give me a kiss?" The child gave him a resolute kiss, with a smack in it. "Now come and get another jug," he said, as he put her down. Her red round eyes opened wide in alarm. "Have you got money enough?" she asked. Alban slapped his pocket. "Yes, I have," he answered. "That's a good thing," said the child; "come along."

They went together hand in hand to the village, and bought the new jug, and had it filled at the beer-shop. The thirsty father was at the upper end of the fields, where they were making a drain. Alban carried the jug until they were within sight of the laborer. "You haven't far to go," he said. "Mind you don't drop it again—What's the matter now?"

"I'm frightened."

"Why?"

"Oh, give me the jug."

She almost snatched it out of his hand. If she let the precious minutes slip away, there might be another beating in store for her at the drain: her father was not of an indulgent disposition when his children were late in bringing his beer. On the point of hurrying away, without a word of farewell, she remembered the laws of politeness as taught at the infant school—and dropped her little curtsey—and said, "Thank you, sir." That bitter sense of injury was still in Alban's mind as he looked after her. "What a pity she should grow up to be a woman!" he said to himself.

The adventure of the broken jug had delayed his return to his lodgings by more than half an hour. When he reached the road once more, the cheap up-train from the North had stopped at the station. He heard the ringing of the bell as it resumed the journey to London.

One of the passengers (judging by the handbag that she carried) had not stopped at the village.

As she advanced toward him along the road, he remarked that she was a small wiry active woman—dressed in bright colors, combined with a deplorable want of taste. Her aquiline nose seemed to be her most striking feature as she came nearer. It might have been fairly proportioned to the rest of her face, in her younger days, before her cheeks had lost flesh and roundness. Being probably near-sighted, she kept her eyes half-closed; there were cunning little wrinkles at the corners of them. In spite of appearances, she was unwilling to present any outward acknowledgment of the march of time. Her hair was palpably dyed—her hat was jauntily set on her head, and ornamented with a gay feather. She walked with a light tripping step, swinging her bag, and holding her head up smartly. Her manner, like her dress, said as plainly as words could speak, "No matter how long I may have lived, I mean to be young and charming to the end of my days." To Alban's surprise she stopped and addressed him.

"Oh, I beg your pardon. Could you tell me if I am in the right road to

Miss Ladd's school?"

She spoke with nervous rapidity of articulation, and with a singularly unpleasant smile. It parted her thin lips just widely enough to show her suspiciously beautiful teeth; and it opened her keen gray eyes in the strangest manner. The higher lid rose so as to disclose, for a moment, the upper part of the eyeball, and to give her the appearance—not of a woman bent on making herself agreeable, but of a woman staring in a panic of terror. Careless to conceal the unfavorable impression that she had produced on him, Alban answered roughly, "Straight on," and tried to pass her.

She stopped him with a peremptory gesture. "I have treated you politely," she said, "and how do you treat me in return? Well! I am not surprised. Men are all brutes by nature—and you are a man. 'Straight on'?" she repeated contemptuously; "I should like to know how far that helps a person in a strange place. Perhaps you know no more where Miss Ladd's school is than I do? or, perhaps, you don't care to take the trouble of addressing me? Just what I should have expected from a person of your sex! Good-morning."

Alban felt the reproof; she had appealed to his most readily-impressible sense—his sense of humor. He rather enjoyed seeing his own prejudice against women grotesquely reflected in this flighty stranger's prejudice against men. As the best excuse for himself that he could make, he gave her all the information that she could possibly want—then tried again to pass on—and again in vain. He had recovered his place in her estimation: she had not done with him yet.

"You know all about the way there," she said "I wonder whether you know anything about the school?"

No change in her voice, no change in her manner, betrayed any special motive for putting this question. Alban was on the point of suggesting that she should go on to the school, and make her inquiries there—when he happened to notice her eyes. She had hitherto looked him straight in the face. She now looked down on the road. It was a trifling change; in all probability it meant nothing—and yet, merely because it was a change, it roused his curiosity. "I ought to know something about the school," he answered. "I am one of the masters."

"Then you're just the man I want. May I ask your name?"

"Alban Morris."

"Thank you. I am Mrs. Rook. I presume you have heard of Sir Jervis Redwood?"

"No."

"Bless my soul! You are a scholar, of course—and you have never heard of one of your own trade. Very extraordinary. You see, I am Sir Jervis's housekeeper; and I am sent here to take one of your young ladies back with me to our place. Don't interrupt me! Don't be a brute again! Sir Jervis is not of a communicative disposition. At least, not to me. A man—that explains it—a man! He is always poring over his books and writings; and Miss Redwood, at her great age, is in bed half the day. Not a thing do I know about this new inmate of ours, except that I am to take her back with me. You would feel some curiosity yourself in my place, wouldn't you? Now do tell me. What sort of girl is Miss Emily Brown?"

The name that he was perpetually thinking of—on this woman's lips! Alban looked at her.

"Well," said Mrs. Rook, "am I to have no answer? Ah, you want leading. So like a man again! Is she pretty?"

Still examining the housekeeper with mingled feelings of interest and distrust, Alban answered ungraciously:

"Yes."

"Good-tempered?"

Alban again said "Yes."

"So much about herself," Mrs. Rook remarked. "About her family now?" She shifted her bag restlessly from one hand to another. "Perhaps you can tell me if Miss Emily's father—" she suddenly corrected herself—"if Miss Emily's parents are living?"

"I don't know."

"You mean you won't tell me."

"I mean exactly what I have said."

"Oh, it doesn't matter," Mrs. Rook rejoined; "I shall find out at the school. The first turning to the left, I think you said—across the fields?"

He was too deeply interested in Emily to let the housekeeper go without putting a question on his side:

"Is Sir Jervis Redwood one of Miss Emily's old friends?" he asked.

"He? What put that into your head? He has never even seen Miss Emily. She's going to our house—ah, the women are getting the upper hand now, and serve the men right, I say!—she's going to our house to be Sir Jervis's secretary. You would like to have the place yourself, wouldn't you? You would like to keep a poor girl from getting her own living? Oh, you may look as fierce as you please—the time's gone by when a man could frighten me. I like her Christian name. I call Emily a nice name enough. But 'Brown'! Good-morning, Mr. Morris; you and I are not cursed with such a contemptibly common name as that! 'Brown'? Oh, Lord!"

She tossed her head scornfully, and walked away, humming a tune.

Alban stood rooted to the spot. The effort of his later life had been to conceal the hopeless passion which had mastered him in spite of himself. Knowing nothing from Emily—who at once pitied and avoided him—of her family circumstances or of her future plans, he had shrunk from making inquiries of others, in the fear that they, too, might find out his secret, and that their contempt might be added to the contempt which he felt for himself. In this position, and with these obstacles in his way, the announcement of Emily's proposed journey—under the care of a stranger, to fill an employment in the house of a stranger—not only took him by surprise, but inspired him with a strong feeling of distrust. He looked after Sir Jervis Redwood's flighty housekeeper, completely forgetting the purpose which had brought him thus far on the way to his lodgings. Before Mrs. Rook was out of sight, Alban Morris was following her back to the school.

CHAPTER VII. "COMING EVENTS CAST THEIR SHADOWS BEFORE."

Miss De Sor and Miss Wyvil were still sitting together under the trees, talking of the murder at the inn.

"And is that really all you can tell me?" said Francine.

"That is all," Cecilia answered.

"Is there no love in it?"

"None that I know of."

"It's the most uninteresting murder that ever was committed. What shall we do with ourselves? I'm tired of being here in the garden. When do the performances in the schoolroom begin?"

"Not for two hours yet."

Francine yawned. "And what part do you take in it?" she asked.

"No part, my dear. I tried once—only to sing a simple little song. When I found myself standing before all the company and saw rows of ladies and gentlemen waiting for me to begin, I was so frightened that Miss Ladd had to make an apology for me. I didn't get over it for the rest of the day. For the first time in my life, I had no appetite for my dinner. Horrible!" said Cecilia, shuddering over the remembrance of it. "I do assure you, I thought I was going to die."

Perfectly unimpressed by this harrowing narrative, Francine turned her head lazily toward the house. The door was thrown open at the same moment. A lithe little person rapidly descended the steps that led to the lawn.

"It's Emily come back again," said Francine.

"And she seems to be rather in a hurry," Cecilia remarked.

Francine's satirical smile showed itself for a moment. Did this appearance of hurry in Emily's movements denote impatience to resume the recital of "the dagger-scene"? She had no book in her hand; she never even looked toward Francine. Sorrow became plainly visible in her face as she approached the two girls.

Cecilia rose in alarm. She had been the first person to whom Emily had confided her domestic anxieties. "Bad news from your aunt?" she asked.

"No, my dear; no news at all." Emily put her arms tenderly round her friend's neck. "The time has come, Cecilia," she said. "We must wish each other good-by."

"Is Mrs. Rook here already?"

"It's you, dear, who are going," Emily answered sadly. "They have sent the governess to fetch you. Miss Ladd is too busy in the schoolroom to see her—and she has told me all about it. Don't be alarmed. There is no bad news from home. Your plans are altered; that's all."

"Altered?" Cecilia repeated. "In what way?"

"In a very agreeable way—you are going to travel. Your father wishes you to be in London, in time for the evening mail to France."

Cecilia guessed what had happened. "My sister is not getting well," she said, "and the doctors are sending her to the Continent."

"To the baths at St. Moritz," Emily added. "There is only one difficulty in the way; and you can remove it. Your sister has the good old governess to take care of her, and the courier to relieve her of all trouble on the journey. They were to have started yesterday. You know how fond Julia is of you. At the last moment, she won't hear of going away, unless you go too. The rooms are waiting at St. Moritz; and your father is annoyed (the governess says) by the delay that has taken place already."

She paused. Cecilia was silent. "Surely you don't hesitate?" Emily said.

"I am too happy to go wherever Julia goes," Cecilia answered warmly; "I was thinking of you, dear." Her tender nature, shrinking from the hard necessities of life, shrank from the cruelly-close prospect of parting. "I thought we were to have had some hours together yet," she said. "Why are we hurried in this way? There is no second train to London, from our station, till late in the afternoon."

"There is the express," Emily reminded her; "and there is time to catch it, if you drive at once to the town." She took Cecilia's hand and pressed it to her bosom. "Thank you again and again, dear, for all you have done for me. Whether we meet again or not, as long as I live I shall love you. Don't cry!" She made a faint attempt to resume her customary gayety, for Cecilia's sake. "Try to be as hard-hearted as I am. Think of your sister—don't think of me. Only kiss me."

Cecilia's tears fell fast. "Oh, my love, I am so anxious about you! I am so afraid that you will not be happy with that selfish old man—in that dreary house. Give it up, Emily! I have got plenty of money for both of us; come abroad with me. Why not? You always got on well with Julia, when you came to see us in the holidays. Oh, my darling! my darling! What shall I do without you?"

All that longed for love in Emily's nature had clung round her school-friend since her father's death. Turning deadly pale under the struggle to control herself, she made the effort—and bore the pain of it without letting a cry or a tear escape her. "Our ways in life lie far apart," she said gently. "There is the hope of meeting again, dear—if there is nothing more."

The clasp of Cecilia's arm tightened round her. She tried to release herself; but her resolution had reached its limits. Her hands dropped, trembling. She could still try to speak cheerfully, and that was all.

"There is not the least reason, Cecilia, to be anxious about my prospects. I mean to be Sir Jervis Redwood's favorite before I have been a week in his service."

She stopped, and pointed to the house. The governess was approaching them. "One more kiss, darling. We shall not forget the happy hours we have spent together; we shall constantly write to each other." She broke down at last. "Oh, Cecilia! Cecilia! leave me for God's sake—I can't bear it any longer!"

The governess parted them. Emily dropped into the chair that her friend had left. Even her hopeful nature sank under the burden of life at that moment.

A hard voice, speaking close at her side, startled her.

"Would you rather be Me," the voice asked, "without a creature to care for you?"

Emily raised her head. Francine, the unnoticed witness of the parting interview, was standing by her, idly picking the leaves from a rose which had dropped out of Cecilia's nosegay.

Had she felt her own isolated position? She had felt it resentfully.

Emily looked at her, with a heart softened by sorrow. There was no answering kindness in the eyes of Miss de Sor—there was only a dogged endurance, sad to see in a creature so young.

"You and Cecilia are going to write to each other," she said. "I suppose there is some comfort in that. When I left the island they were glad to get rid of me. They said, 'Telegraph when you are safe at Miss Ladd's school.' You see, we are so rich, the expense of telegraphing to the West Indies is nothing to us. Besides, a telegram has an advantage over a letter—it doesn't take long to read. I daresay I shall write home. But they are in no hurry; and I am in no hurry. The school's breaking up; you are going your way, and I am going mine—and who cares what becomes of me? Only an ugly old schoolmistress, who is paid for caring. I wonder why I am saying all this? Because I like you? I don't know that I like you any better than you like me. When I wanted to be friends with you, you treated me coolly; I don't want to force myself on you. I don't particularly care about you. May I write to you from Brighton?"

Under all this bitterness—the first exhibition of Francine's temper, at its worst, which had taken place since she joined the school—Emily saw, or thought she saw, distress that was too proud, or too shy, to show itself. "How can you ask the question?" she answered cordially.

Francine was incapable of meeting the sympathy offered to her, even half way. "Never mind how," she said. "Yes or no is all I want from you."

"Oh, Francine! Francine! what are you made of! Flesh and blood? or stone and iron? Write to me of course—and I will write back again."

"Thank you. Are you going to stay here under the trees?"

"Yes."

"All by yourself?"

"All by myself."

"With nothing to do?"

"I can think of Cecilia."

Francine eyed her with steady attention for a moment.

"Didn't you tell me last night that you were very poor?" she asked.

"I did."

"So poor that you are obliged to earn your own living?"

"Yes."

Francine looked at her again.

"I daresay you won't believe me," she said. "I wish I was you."

She turned away irritably, and walked back to the house.

Were there really longings for kindness and love under the surface of this girl's perverse nature? Or was there nothing to be hoped from a better knowledge of her?—In place of tender remembrances of Cecilia, these were the perplexing and unwelcome thoughts which the more potent personality of Francine forced upon Emily's mind.

She rose impatiently, and looked at her watch. When would it be her turn to leave the school, and begin the new life?

Still undecided what to do next, her interest was excited by the appearance of one of the servants on the lawn. The woman approached her, and presented a visiting-card; bearing on it the name of Sir Jervis Redwood. Beneath the name, there was a line written in pencil: "Mrs. Rook, to wait on Miss Emily Brown." The way to the new life was open before her at last!

Looking again at the commonplace announcement contained in the line of writing, she was not quite satisfied. Was it claiming a deference toward herself, to which she was not entitled, to expect a letter either from Sir Jervis, or from Miss Redwood; giving her some information as to the journey which she was about to undertake, and expressing with some little politeness the wish to make her comfortable in her future home? At any rate, her employer had done her one service: he had reminded her that her station in life was not what it had been in the days when her father was living, and when her aunt was in affluent circumstances.

She looked up from the card. The servant had gone. Alban Morris was waiting at a little distance—waiting silently until she noticed him.

CHAPTER VIII. MASTER AND PUPIL.

Emily's impulse was to avoid the drawing-master for the second time. The moment afterward, a kinder feeling prevailed. The farewell interview with Cecilia had left influences which pleaded for Alban Morris. It was the day of parting good wishes and general separations: he had only perhaps come to say good-by. She advanced to offer her hand, when he stopped her by pointing to Sir Jervis Redwood's card.

"May I say a word, Miss Emily, about that woman?" he asked

"Do you mean Mrs. Rook?"

"Yes. You know, of course, why she comes here?"

"She comes here by appointment, to take me to Sir Jervis Redwood's house. Are you acquainted with her?"

"She is a perfect stranger to me. I met her by accident on her way here. If Mrs. Rook had been content with asking me to direct her to the school, I should not be troubling you at this moment. But she forced her conversation on me. And she said something which I think you ought to know. Have you heard of Sir Jervis Redwood's housekeeper before to-day?"

"I have only heard what my friend—Miss Cecilia Wyvil—has told me."

"Did Miss Cecilia tell you that Mrs. Rook was acquainted with your father or with any members of your family?"

"Certainly not!"

Alban reflected. "It was natural enough," he resumed, "that Mrs. Rook should feel some curiosity about You. What reason had she for putting a question to me about your father—and putting it in a very strange manner?"

Emily's interest was instantly excited. She led the way back to the seats in the shade. "Tell me, Mr. Morris, exactly what the woman said." As she spoke, she signed to him to be seated.

Alban observed the natural grace of her action when she set him the example of taking a chair, and the little heightening of her color caused by anxiety to hear what he had still to tell her. Forgetting the restraint that he had hitherto imposed on himself, he enjoyed the luxury of silently admiring her. Her manner betrayed none of the conscious confusion which would have shown itself, if her heart had been secretly inclined toward him. She saw the man looking at her. In simple perplexity she looked at the man.

"Are you hesitating on my account?" she asked. "Did Mrs. Rook say something of my father which I mustn't hear?"

"No, no! nothing of the sort!"

"You seem to be confused."

Her innocent indifference tried his patience sorely. His memory went back to the past time—recalled the ill-placed passion of his youth, and the cruel injury inflicted on him—his pride was roused. Was he making himself ridiculous? The vehement throbbing of his heart almost suffocated him. And there she sat, wondering at his odd behavior. "Even this girl is as cold-blooded as the rest of her sex!" That angry thought gave him back his self-control. He made his excuses with the easy politeness of a man of the world.

"I beg your pardon, Miss Emily; I was considering how to put what I have to say in the fewest and plainest words. Let me try if I can do it. If Mrs. Rook had merely asked me whether your father and mother were living, I should have attributed the question to the commonplace curiosity of a gossiping woman, and have thought no more of it. What she actually did say was this: 'Perhaps you can tell me if Miss Emily's father—' There she checked herself, and suddenly altered the question in this way: 'If Miss Emily's parents are living?' I may be making mountains out of molehills; but I thought at the time (and think still) that she had some special interest in inquiring after your father, and, not wishing me to notice it for reasons of her own, changed the form of the question so as to include your mother. Does this strike you as a far-fetched conclusion?"

"Whatever it may be," Emily said, "it is my conclusion, too. How did you answer her?"

"Quite easily. I could give her no information—and I said so."

"Let me offer you the information, Mr. Morris, before we say anything more. I have lost both my parents."

Alban's momentary outbreak of irritability was at an end. He was earnest and yet gentle, again; he forgave her for not understanding how dear and how delightful to him she was. "Will it distress you," he said, "if I ask how long it is since your father died?"

"Nearly four years," she replied. "He was the most generous of men; Mrs. Rook's interest in him may surely have been a grateful interest. He may have been kind to her in past years—and she may remember him thankfully. Don't you think so?"

Alban was unable to agree with her. "If Mrs. Rook's interest in your father was the harmless interest that you have suggested," he said, "why should she have checked herself in that unaccountable manner, when she first asked me if he was living? The more I think of it now, the less sure I feel that she knows anything at all of your family history. It may help me to decide, if you will tell me at what time the death of your mother took place."

"So long ago," Emily replied, "that I can't even remember her death. I was an infant at the time."

"And yet Mrs. Rook asked me if your 'parents' were living! One of two things," Alban concluded. "Either there is some mystery in this matter, which we cannot hope to penetrate at present—or Mrs. Rook may have been speaking at random; on the chance of discovering whether you are related to some 'Mr. Brown' whom she once knew."

"Besides," Emily added, "it's only fair to remember what a common family name mine is, and how easily people may make mistakes. I should like to know if my dear lost father was really in her mind when she spoke to you. Do you think I could find it out?"

"If Mrs. Rook has any reasons for concealment, I believe you would have no chance of finding it out—unless, indeed, you could take her by surprise."

"In what way, Mr. Morris?"

"Only one way occurs to me just now," he said. "Do you happen to have a miniature or a photograph of your father?"

Emily held out a handsome locket, with a monogram in diamonds, attached to her watch chain. "I have his photograph here," she rejoined; "given to me by my dear old aunt, in the days of her prosperity. Shall I show it to Mrs. Rook?"

"Yes—if she happens, by good luck, to offer you an opportunity."

Impatient to try the experiment, Emily rose as he spoke. "I mustn't keep Mrs. Rook waiting," she said.

Alban stopped her, on the point of leaving him. The confusion and hesitation which she had already noticed began to show themselves in his manner once more.

"Miss Emily, may I ask you a favor before you go? I am only one of the masters employed in the school; but I don't think—let me say, I hope I am

58

not guilty of presumption—if I offer to be of some small service to one of my pupils—"

There his embarrassment mastered him. He despised himself not only for yielding to his own weakness, but for faltering like a fool in the expression of a simple request. The next words died away on his lips.

This time, Emily understood him.

The subtle penetration which had long since led her to the discovery of his secret—overpowered, thus far, by the absorbing interest of the moment—now recovered its activity. In an instant, she remembered that Alban's motive for cautioning her, in her coming intercourse with Mrs. Rook, was not the merely friendly motive which might have actuated him, in the case of one of the other girls. At the same time, her quickness of apprehension warned her not to risk encouraging this persistent lover, by betraying any embarrassment on her side. He was evidently anxious to be present (in her interests) at the interview with Mrs. Rook. Why not? Could he reproach her with raising false hope, if she accepted his services, under circumstances of doubt and difficulty which he had himself been the first to point out? He could do nothing of the sort. Without waiting until he had recovered himself, she answered him (to all appearances) as composedly as if he had spoken to her in the plainest terms.

"After all that you have told me," she said, "I shall indeed feel obliged if you will be present when I see Mrs. Rook."

The eager brightening of his eyes, the flush of happiness that made him look young on a sudden, were signs not to be mistaken. The sooner they were in the presence of a third person (Emily privately concluded) the better it might be for both of them. She led the way rapidly to the house.

CHAPTER IX. MRS. ROOK AND THE LOCKET.

As mistress of a prosperous school, bearing a widely-extended reputation, Miss Ladd prided herself on the liberality of her household arrangements. At breakfast and dinner, not only the solid comforts but the elegant luxuries of the table, were set before the young ladies "Other schools may, and no doubt do, offer to pupils the affectionate care to which they have been accustomed under the parents' roof," Miss Ladd used to say. "At my school, that care extends to their meals, and provides them with a cuisine which, I flatter myself, equals the most successful efforts of the cooks at home." Fathers, mothers, and friends, when they paid visits to this excellent lady, brought away with them the most gratifying recollections of her hospitality. The men, in particular, seldom failed to recognize in their hostess the rarest virtue that a single lady can possess—the virtue of putting wine on the table which may be gratefully remembered by her guests the next morning.

An agreeable surprise awaited Mrs. Rook when she entered the house of bountiful Miss Ladd.

Luncheon was ready for Sir Jervis Redwood's confidential emissary in the waiting-room. Detained at the final rehearsals of music and recitation, Miss Ladd was worthily represented by cold chicken and ham, a fruit tart, and a pint decanter of generous sherry. "Your mistress is a perfect lady!" Mrs. Rook said to the servant, with a burst of enthusiasm. "I can carve for myself, thank you; and I don't care how long Miss Emily keeps me waiting."

As they ascended the steps leading into the house, Alban asked Emily if he might look again at her locket.

"Shall I open it for you?" she suggested.

"No: I only want to look at the outside of it."

He examined the side on which the monogram appeared, inlaid with diamonds. An inscription was engraved beneath.

"May I read it?" he said.

"Certainly!"

The inscription ran thus: "In loving memory of my father. Died 30th September, 1877."

"Can you arrange the locket," Alban asked, "so that the side on which the diamonds appear hangs outward?"

She understood him. The diamonds might attract Mrs. Rook's notice; and in that case, she might ask to see the locket of her own accord. "You are beginning to be of use to me, already," Emily said, as they turned into the corridor which led to the waiting-room.

They found Sir Jervis's housekeeper luxuriously recumbent in the easiest chair in the room.

Of the eatable part of the lunch some relics were yet left. In the pint decanter of sherry, not a drop remained. The genial influence of the wine (hastened by the hot weather) was visible in Mrs. Rook's flushed face, and in a special development of her ugly smile. Her widening lips stretched to new lengths; and the white upper line of her eyeballs were more freely and horribly visible than ever.

"And this is the dear young lady?" she said, lifting her hands in over-acted admiration. At the first greetings, Alban perceived that the impression produced was, in Emily's case as in his case, instantly unfavorable.

The servant came in to clear the table. Emily stepped aside for a minute to give some directions about her luggage. In that interval Mrs. Rook's cunning little eyes turned on Alban with an expression of malicious scrutiny.

"You were walking the other way," she whispered, "when I met you." She stopped, and glanced over her shoulder at Emily. "I see what attraction has brought you back to the school. Steal your way into that poor little fool's heart; and then make her miserable for the rest of her life!—No need, miss, to hurry," she said, shifting the polite side of her toward Emily, who returned at the moment. "The visits of the trains to your station here are like the visits of the angels described by the poet, 'few and far between.' Please excuse the quotation. You wouldn't think it to look at me—I'm a great reader."

"Is it a long journey to Sir Jervis Redwood's house?" Emily asked, at a loss what else to say to a woman who was already becoming unendurable to her.

Mrs. Rook looked at the journey from an oppressively cheerful point of view.

"Oh, Miss Emily, you shan't feel the time hang heavy in my company. I can converse on a variety of topics, and if there is one thing more than another that I like, it's amusing a pretty young lady. You think me a strange creature, don't you? It's only my high spirits. Nothing strange about me— unless it's my queer Christian name. You look a little dull, my dear. Shall I begin amusing you before we are on the railway? Shall I tell you how I came by my queer name?"

Thus far, Alban had controlled himself. This last specimen of the housekeeper's audacious familiarity reached the limits of his endurance.

"We don't care to know how you came by your name," he said.

"Rude," Mrs. Rook remarked, composedly. "But nothing surprises me, coming from a man."

She turned to Emily. "My father and mother were a wicked married couple," she continued, "before I was born. They 'got religion,' as the saying is, at a Methodist meeting in a field. When I came into the world—I don't know how you feel, miss; I protest against being brought into the world without asking my leave first—my mother was determined to dedicate me to piety, before I was out of my long clothes. What name do you suppose she had me christened by? She chose it, or made it, herself—the name of 'Righteous'! Righteous Rook! Was there ever a poor baby degraded by such a ridiculous name before? It's needless to say, when I write letters, I sign R. Rook—and leave people to think it's Rosamond, or Rosabelle, or something sweetly pretty of that kind. You should have seen my husband's face when he first heard that his sweetheart's name was 'Righteous'! He was on the point of kissing me, and he stopped. I daresay he felt sick. Perfectly natural under the circumstances."

Alban tried to stop her again. "What time does the train go?" he asked.

Emily entreated him to restrain himself, by a look. Mrs. Rook was still too inveterately amiable to take offense. She opened her traveling-bag briskly, and placed a railway guide in Alban's hands.

"I've heard that the women do the men's work in foreign parts," she said.

"But this is England; and I am an Englishwoman. Find out when the train goes, my dear sir, for yourself."

Alban at once consulted the guide. If there proved to be no immediate need of starting for the station, he was determined that Emily should not be condemned to pass the interval in the housekeeper's company. In the meantime, Mrs. Rook was as eager as ever to show her dear young lady what an amusing companion she could be.

"Talking of husbands," she resumed, "don't make the mistake, my dear, that I committed. Beware of letting anybody persuade you to marry an old man. Mr. Rook is old enough to be my father. I bear with him. Of course, I bear with him. At the same time, I have not (as the poet says) 'passed through the ordeal unscathed.' My spirit—I have long since ceased to believe in anything of the sort: I only use the word for want of a better—my spirit, I say, has become embittered. I was once a pious young woman; I do assure you I was nearly as good as my name. Don't let me shock you; I have lost faith and hope; I have become—what's the last new name for a free-thinker? Oh, I keep up with the times, thanks to old Miss Redwood! She takes in the newspapers, and makes me read them to her. What is the new name? Something ending in ic. Bombastic? No, Agnostic?—that's it! I have become an Agnostic. The inevitable result of marrying an old man; if there's any blame it rests on my husband."

"There's more than an hour yet before the train starts," Alban interposed. "I am sure, Miss Emily, you would find it pleasanter to wait in the garden."

"Not at all a bad notion," Mrs. Rook declared. "Here's a man who can make himself useful, for once. Let's go into the garden."

She rose, and led the way to the door. Alban seized the opportunity of whispering to Emily.

"Did you notice the empty decanter, when we first came in? That horrid woman is drunk."

Emily pointed significantly to the locket. "Don't let her go. The garden will distract her attention: keep her near me here."

Mrs. Rook gayly opened the door. "Take me to the flower-beds," she said. "I believe in nothing—but I adore flowers."

Mrs. Rook waited at the door, with her eye on Emily. "What do you say, miss?"

"I think we shall be more comfortable if we stay where we are."

"Whatever pleases you, my dear, pleases me." With this reply, the compliant housekeeper—as amiable as ever on the surface—returned to her chair.

Would she notice the locket as she sat down? Emily turned toward the window, so as to let the light fall on the diamonds.

No: Mrs. Rook was absorbed, at the moment, in her own reflections. Miss Emily, having prevented her from seeing the garden, she was maliciously bent on disappointing Miss Emily in return. Sir Jervis's secretary (being young) took a hopeful view no doubt of her future prospects. Mrs. Rook decided on darkening that view in a mischievously-suggestive manner, peculiar to herself.

"You will naturally feel some curiosity about your new home," she began, "and I haven't said a word about it yet. How very thoughtless of me! Inside and out, dear Miss Emily, our house is just a little dull. I say our house, and why not—when the management of it is all thrown on me. We are built of stone; and we are much too long, and are not half high enough. Our situation is on the coldest side of the county, away in the west. We are close to the Cheviot hills; and if you fancy there is anything to see when you look out of window, except sheep, you will find yourself woefully mistaken. As for walks, if you go out on one side of the house you may, or may not, be gored by cattle. On the other side, if the darkness overtakes you, you may, or may not, tumble down a deserted lead mine. But the company, inside the house, makes amends for it all," Mrs. Rook proceeded, enjoying the expression of dismay which was beginning to show itself on Emily's face. "Plenty of excitement for you, my dear, in our small family. Sir Jervis will introduce you to plaster casts of hideous Indian idols; he will keep you writing for him, without mercy, from morning to night; and when he does let you go, old Miss Redwood will find she can't sleep, and will send for the pretty young lady-secretary to read to her. My husband I am sure you will like. He is a respectable man, and bears the highest character. Next to the idols, he's the most hideous object in the house. If you are good enough to encourage him, I don't say that he won't amuse you; he will tell you, for instance, he never in his life hated any human being as he hates his wife. By the way, I must not forget—in the interests of truth, you know—to mention one drawback that does exist in our domestic circle. One of these days we shall have our brains blown out or our throats cut. Sir Jervis's mother left him ten thousand pounds' worth of precious stones all contained in a little cabinet with drawers. He won't let the banker take care of his jewels; he won't sell them; he won't even wear one of the rings on his finger, or one of the pins at his breast. He keeps his cabinet on his dressing-room table; and he says, 'I like to gloat over my jewels, every night, before I go to bed.' Ten thousand pounds' worth of diamonds, rubies, emeralds, sapphires, and what not—at the mercy of the first robber who happens to hear of them. Oh, my dear, he would have no choice, I do assure you, but to use his pistols. We shouldn't quietly submit to be robbed. Sir Jervis inherits the spirit of his ancestors. My husband has the temper of a game cock. I myself, in defense of the property of my employers, am capable of becoming a perfect fiend. And we none of us understand the use of firearms!"

While she was in full enjoyment of this last aggravation of the horrors of the prospect, Emily tried another change of position—and, this time, with success. Greedy admiration suddenly opened Mrs. Rook's little eyes to their utmost width. "My heart alive, miss, what do I see at your watch-chain? How they sparkle! Might I ask for a closer view?"

Emily's fingers trembled; but she succeeded in detaching the locket from the chain. Alban handed it to Mrs. Rook.

She began by admiring the diamonds—with a certain reserve. "Nothing like so large as Sir Jervis's diamonds; but choice specimens no doubt. Might I ask what the value—?"

She stopped. The inscription had attracted her notice: she began to read it aloud: "In loving memory of my father. Died—"

Her face instantly became rigid. The next words were suspended on her lips.

Alban seized the chance of making her betray herself—under pretense of helping her. "Perhaps you find the figures not easy to read," he said. "The date is 'thirtieth September, eighteen hundred and seventy-seven'—nearly four years since."

Not a word, not a movement, escaped Mrs. Rook. She held the locket before her as she had held it from the first. Alban looked at Emily. Her eyes were riveted on the housekeeper: she was barely capable of preserving the appearance of composure. Seeing the necessity of acting for her, he at once said the words which she was unable to say for herself.

"Perhaps, Mrs. Rook, you would like to look at the portrait?" he suggested. "Shall I open the locket for you?"

Without speaking, without looking up, she handed the locket to Alban.

He opened it, and offered it to her. She neither accepted nor refused it: her hands remained hanging over the arms of the chair. He put the locket on her lap.

The portrait produced no marked effect on Mrs. Rook. Had the date prepared her to see it? She sat looking at it—still without moving: still without saying a word. Alban had no mercy on her. "That is the portrait of Miss Emily's father," he said. "Does it represent the same Mr. Brown whom you had in your mind when you asked me if Miss Emily's father was still living?"

That question roused her. She looked up, on the instant; she answered loudly and insolently: "No!"

"And yet," Alban persisted, "you broke down in reading the inscription: and considering what talkative woman you are, the portrait has had a strange effect on you—to say the least of it."

She eyed him steadily while he was speaking—and turned to Emily when he had done. "You mentioned the heat just now, miss. The heat has overcome me; I shall soon get right again."

The insolent futility of that excuse irritated Emily into answering her. "You will get right again perhaps all the sooner," she said, "if we trouble you with no more questions, and leave you to recover by yourself."

The first change of expression which relaxed the iron tensity of the housekeeper's face showed itself when she heard that reply. At last there was a feeling in Mrs. Rook which openly declared itself—a feeling of impatience to see Alban and Emily leave the room.

They left her, without a word more.

CHAPTER X. GUESSES AT THE TRUTH.

"What are we to do next? Oh, Mr. Morris, you must have seen all sorts of people in your time—you know human nature, and I don't. Help me with a word of advice!"

Emily forgot that he was in love with her—forgot everything, but the effect produced by the locket on Mrs. Rook, and the vaguely alarming conclusion to which it pointed. In the fervor of her anxiety she took Alban's arm as familiarly as if he had been her brother. He was gentle, he was considerate; he tried earnestly to compose her. "We can do nothing to any good purpose," he said, "unless we begin by thinking quietly. Pardon me for saying so—you are needlessly exciting yourself."

There was a reason for her excitement, of which he was necessarily ignorant. Her memory of the night interview with Miss Jethro had inevitably intensified the suspicion inspired by the conduct of Mrs. Rook. In less than twenty-four hours, Emily had seen two women shrinking from secret remembrances of her father—which might well be guilty remembrances—innocently excited by herself! How had they injured him? Of what infamy, on their parts, did his beloved and stainless memory remind them? Who could fathom the mystery of it? "What does it mean?" she cried, looking wildly in Alban's compassionate face. "You must have formed some idea of your own. What does it mean?"

"Come, and sit down, Miss Emily. We will try if we can find out what it means, together."

They returned to the shady solitude under the trees. Away, in front of the house, the distant grating of carriage wheels told of the arrival of Miss Ladd's guests, and of the speedy beginning of the ceremonies of the day.

"We must help each other," Alban resumed.

"When we first spoke of Mrs. Rook, you mentioned Miss Cecilia Wyvil as a person who knew something about her. Have you any objection to tell me what you may have heard in that way?"

In complying with his request Emily necessarily repeated what Cecilia had told Francine, when the two girls had met that morning in the garden.

Alban now knew how Emily had obtained employment as Sir Jervis's secretary; how Mr. and Mrs. Rook had been previously known to Cecilia's father as respectable people keeping an inn in his own neighborhood; and, finally, how they had been obliged to begin life again in domestic service, because the terrible event of a murder had given the inn a bad name, and had driven away the customers on whose encouragement their business depended.

Listening in silence, Alban remained silent when Emily's narrative had come to an end.

"Have you nothing to say to me?" she asked.

"I am thinking over what I have just heard," he answered.

Emily noticed a certain formality in his tone and manner, which disagreeably surprised her. He seemed to have made his reply as a mere concession to politeness, while he was thinking of something else which really interested him.

"Have I disappointed you in any way?" she asked.

"On the contrary, you have interested me. I want to be quite sure that I remember exactly what you have said. You mentioned, I think, that your friendship with Miss Cecilia Wyvil began here, at the school?"

"Yes."

"And in speaking of the murder at the village inn, you told me that the crime was committed—I have forgotten how long ago?"

His manner still suggested that he was idly talking about what she had told him, while some more important subject for reflection was in possession of his mind.

"I don't know that I said anything about the time that had passed since the crime was committed," she answered, sharply. "What does the murder matter to us? I think Cecilia told me it happened about four years since. Excuse me for noticing it, Mr. Morris—you seem to have some interests of your own to occupy your attention. Why couldn't you say so plainly when we came out here? I should not have asked you to help me, in that case. Since my poor father's death, I have been used to fight through my troubles by myself."

She rose, and looked at him proudly. The next moment her eyes filled with tears.

In spite of her resistance, Alban took her hand. "Dear Miss Emily," he said, "you distress me: you have not done me justice. Your interests only are in my mind."

Answering her in those terms, he had not spoken as frankly as usual. He had only told her a part of the truth.

Hearing that the woman whom they had just left had been landlady of an inn, and that a murder had been committed under her roof, he was led to ask himself if any explanation might be found, in these circumstances, of the otherwise incomprehensible effect produced on Mrs. Rook by the inscription on the locket.

In the pursuit of this inquiry there had arisen in his mind a monstrous suspicion, which pointed to Mrs. Rook. It impelled him to ascertain the date at which the murder had been committed, and (if the discovery encouraged further investigation) to find out next the manner in which Mr. Brown had died.

Thus far, what progress had he made? He had discovered that the date of Mr. Brown's death, inscribed on the locket, and the date of the crime committed at the inn, approached each other nearly enough to justify further investigation.

In the meantime, had he succeeded in keeping his object concealed from Emily? He had perfectly succeeded. Hearing him declare that her interests only had occupied his mind, the poor girl innocently entreated him to forgive her little outbreak of temper. "If you have any more questions to ask me, Mr. Morris, pray go on. I promise never to think unjustly of you again."

He went on with an uneasy conscience—for it seemed cruel to deceive her, even in the interests of truth—but still he went on.

"Suppose we assume that this woman had injured your father in some way," he said. "Am I right in believing that it was in his character to forgive injuries?"

"Entirely right."

"In that case, his death may have left Mrs. Rook in a position to be called to account, by those who owe a duty to his memory—I mean the surviving members of his family."

"There are but two of us, Mr. Morris. My aunt and myself."

"There are his executors."

"My aunt is his only executor."

"Your father's sister—I presume?"

"Yes."

"He may have left instructions with her, which might be of the greatest use to us."

"I will write to-day, and find out," Emily replied. "I had already planned to consult my aunt," she added, thinking again of Miss Jethro.

"If your aunt has not received any positive instructions," Alban continued, "she may remember some allusion to Mrs. Rook, on your father's part, at the time of his last illness—"

Emily stopped him. "You don't know how my dear father died," she said. "He was struck down—apparently in perfect health—by disease of the heart."

"Struck down in his own house?"

"Yes—in his own house."

Those words closed Alban's lips. The investigation so carefully and so delicately conducted had failed to serve any useful purpose. He had now ascertained the manner of Mr. Brown's death and the place of Mr. Brown's death—and he was as far from confirming his suspicions of Mrs. Rook as ever.

CHAPTER XI. THE DRAWING-MASTER'S CONFESSION.

"Is there nothing else you can suggest?" Emily asked.

"Nothing—at present."

"If my aunt fails us, have we no other hope?"

"I have hope in Mrs. Rook," Alban answered. "I see I surprise you; but I really mean what I say. Sir Jervis's housekeeper is an excitable woman, and she is fond of wine. There is always a weak side in the character of such a person as that. If we wait for our chance, and turn it to the right use when it comes, we may yet succeed in making her betray herself."

Emily listened to him in bewilderment.

"You talk as if I was sure of your help in the future," she said. "Have you forgotten that I leave school to-day, never to return? In half an hour more, I shall be condemned to a long journey in the company of that horrible creature—with a life to look forward to, in the same house with her, among strangers! A miserable prospect, and a hard trial of a girl's courage—is it not, Mr. Morris?"

"You will at least have one person, Miss Emily, who will try with all his heart and soul to encourage you."

"What do you mean?"

"I mean," said Alban, quietly, "that the Midsummer vacation begins today; and that the drawing-master is going to spend his holidays in the North."

Emily jumped up from her chair. "You!" she exclaimed. "You are going to Northumberland? With me?"

"Why not?" Alban asked. "The railway is open to all travelers alike, if they have money enough to buy a ticket."

"Mr. Morris! what can you be thinking of? Indeed, indeed, I am not ungrateful. I know you mean kindly—you are a good, generous man. But do remember how completely a girl, in my position, is at the mercy of appearances. You, traveling in the same carriage with me! and that woman putting her own vile interpretation on it, and degrading me in Sir Jervis Redwood's estimation, on the day when I enter his house! Oh, it's worse than thoughtless—it's madness, downright madness."

"You are quite right," Alban gravely agreed, "it is madness. I lost whatever little reason I once possessed, Miss Emily, on the day when I first met you out walking with the young ladies of the school."

Emily turned away in significant silence. Alban followed her.

"You promised just now," he said, "never to think unjustly of me again. I respect and admire you far too sincerely to take a base advantage of this occasion—the only occasion on which I have been permitted to speak with you alone. Wait a little before you condemn a man whom you don't understand. I will say nothing to annoy you—I only ask leave to explain myself. Will you take your chair again?"

She returned unwillingly to her seat. "It can only end," she thought, sadly, "in my disappointing him!"

"I have had the worst possible opinion of women for years past," Alban resumed; "and the only reason I can give for it condemns me out of my own mouth. I have been infamously treated by one woman; and my wounded self-esteem has meanly revenged itself by reviling the whole sex. Wait a little, Miss Emily. My fault has received its fit punishment. I have been thoroughly humiliated—and you have done it."

"Mr. Morris!"

"Take no offense, pray, where no offense is meant. Some few years since it was the great misfortune of my life to meet with a Jilt. You know what I mean?"

"Yes."

"She was my equal by birth (I am a younger son of a country squire), and my superior in rank. I can honestly tell you that I was fool enough to love her with all my heart and soul. She never allowed me to doubt—I may say this without conceit, remembering the miserable end of it—that my feeling for her was returned. Her father and mother (excellent people) approved of the contemplated marriage. She accepted my presents; she allowed all the customary preparations for a wedding to proceed to completion; she had not even mercy enough, or shame enough, to prevent me from publicly degrading myself by waiting for her at the altar, in the presence of a large congregation. The minutes passed—and no bride appeared. The clergyman, waiting like me, was requested to return to the vestry. I was invited to follow him. You foresee the end of the story, of course? She had run away with another man. But can you guess who the man was? Her groom!"

Emily's face reddened with indignation. "She suffered for it? Oh, Mr. Morris, surely she suffered for it?"

"Not at all. She had money enough to reward the groom for marrying her; and she let herself down easily to her husband's level. It was a suitable marriage in every respect. When I last heard of them, they were regularly in the habit of getting drunk together. I am afraid I have disgusted you? We will drop the subject, and resume my precious autobiography at a later date. One showery day in the autumn of last year, you young ladies went out with Miss Ladd for a walk. When you were all trotting back again, under your umbrellas, did you (in particular) notice an ill-tempered fellow standing in the road, and getting a good look at you, on the high footpath above him?"

Emily smiled, in spite of herself. "I don't remember it," she said.

"You wore a brown jacket which fitted you as if you had been born in it—and you had the smartest little straw hat I ever saw on a woman's head. It was the first time I ever noticed such things. I think I could paint a portrait of the boots you wore (mud included), from memory alone. That was the impression you produced on me. After believing, honestly believing, that love was one of the lost illusions of my life—after feeling, honestly feeling, that I would as soon look at the devil as look at a woman—there was the state of mind to which retribution had reduced me; using for his instrument Miss Emily Brown. Oh, don't be afraid of what I may say next! In your presence, and out of your presence, I am man enough to be ashamed of my own folly. I am resisting your influence over me at this moment, with the strongest of all resolutions—the resolution of despair. Let's look at the humorous side of the story again. What do you think I did when the regiment of young ladies had passed by me?"

Emily declined to guess.

"I followed you back to the school; and, on pretense of having a daughter to educate, I got one of Miss Ladd's prospectuses from the porter at the lodge gate. I was in your neighborhood, you must know, on a sketching tour. I went back to my inn, and seriously considered what had happened to me. The result of my cogitations was that I went abroad. Only for a change—not at all because I was trying to weaken the impression you had produced on me! After a while I returned to England. Only because I was tired of traveling—not at all because your influence drew me back! Another interval passed; and luck turned my way, for a wonder. The drawing-master's place became vacant here. Miss Ladd advertised; I produced my testimonials; and took the situation. Only because the salary was a welcome certainty to a poor man—not at all because the new position brought me into personal association with Miss Emily Brown! Do you begin to see why I have troubled you with all this talk about myself? Apply the contemptible system of self-delusion which my confession has revealed, to that holiday arrangement for a tour in the north which has astonished and annoyed you. I am going to travel this afternoon by your train. Only because I feel an intelligent longing to see the northernmost county of England—not at all because I won't let you trust yourself alone with

Mrs. Rook! Not at all because I won't leave you to enter Sir Jervis Redwood's service without a friend within reach in case you want him! Mad? Oh, yes—perfectly mad. But, tell me this: What do all sensible people do when they find themselves in the company of a lunatic? They humor him. Let me take your ticket and see your luggage labeled: I only ask leave to be your traveling servant. If you are proud—I shall like you all the better, if you are—pay me wages, and keep me in my proper place in that way."

Some girls, addressed with this reckless intermingling of jest and earnest, would have felt confused, and some would have felt flattered. With a good-tempered resolution, which never passed the limits of modesty and refinement, Emily met Alban Morris on his own ground.

"You have said you respect me," she began; "I am going to prove that I believe you. The least I can do is not to misinterpret you, on my side. Am I to understand, Mr. Morris—you won't think the worse of me, I hope, if I speak plainly—am I to understand that you are in love with me?"

"Yes, Miss Emily—if you please."

He had answered with the quaint gravity which was peculiar to him; but he was already conscious of a sense of discouragement. Her composure was a bad sign—from his point of view.

"My time will come, I daresay," she proceeded. "At present I know nothing of love, by experience; I only know what some of my schoolfellows talk about in secret. Judging by what they tell me, a girl blushes when her lover pleads with her to favor his addresses. Am I blushing?"

"Must I speak plainly, too?" Alban asked.

"If you have no objection," she answered, as composedly as if she had been addressing her grandfather.

"Then, Miss Emily, I must say—you are not blushing."

She went on. "Another token of love—as I am informed—is to tremble. Am I trembling?"

"No."

"Am I too confused to look at you?"

"No."

"Do I walk away with dignity—and then stop, and steal a timid glance at my lover, over my shoulder?"

"I wish you did!"

"A plain answer, Mr. Morris! Yes or No."

"No—of course."

"In one last word, do I give you any sort of encouragement to try again?"

"In one last word, I have made a fool of myself—and you have taken the kindest possible way of telling me so."

This time, she made no attempt to reply in his own tone. The good-humored gayety of her manner disappeared. She was in earnest—truly, sadly in earnest—when she said her next words.

"Is it not best, in your own interests, that we should bid each other good-by?" she asked. "In the time to come—when you only remember how kind you once were to me—we may look forward to meeting again. After all that you have suffered, so bitterly and so undeservedly, don't, pray don't, make me feel that another woman has behaved cruelly to you, and that I—so grieved to distress you—am that heartless creature!"

Never in her life had she been so irresistibly charming as she was at that moment. Her sweet nature showed all its innocent pity for him in her face.

He saw it—he felt it—he was not unworthy of it. In silence, he lifted her hand to his lips. He turned pale as he kissed it.

"Say that you agree with me?" she pleaded.

"I obey you."

As he answered, he pointed to the lawn at their feet. "Look," he said, "at that dead leaf which the air is wafting over the grass. Is it possible that such sympathy as you feel for Me, such love as I feel for You, can waste, wither, and fall to the ground like that leaf? I leave you, Emily—with the firm conviction that there is a time of fulfillment to come in our two lives. Happen what may in the interval—I trust the future."

The words had barely passed his lips when the voice of one of the servants reached them from the house. "Miss Emily, are you in the garden?"

Emily stepped out into the sunshine. The servant hurried to meet her, and placed a telegram in her hand. She looked at it with a sudden misgiving. In her small experience, a telegram was associated with the communication of bad news. She conquered her hesitation—opened it—read it. The color left her face: she shuddered. The telegram dropped on the grass.

"Read it," she said, faintly, as Alban picked it up.

He read these words: "Come to London directly. Miss Letitia is dangerously ill."

"Your aunt?" he asked.

"Yes—my aunt."

BOOK THE SECOND—IN LONDON.

CHAPTER XII. MRS. ELLMOTHER.

The metropolis of Great Britain is, in certain respects, like no other metropolis on the face of the earth. In the population that throngs the streets, the extremes of Wealth and the extremes of Poverty meet, as they meet nowhere else. In the streets themselves, the glory and the shame of architecture—the mansion and the hovel—are neighbors in situation, as they are neighbors nowhere else. London, in its social aspect, is the city of contrasts.

Toward the close of evening Emily left the railway terminus for the place of residence in which loss of fortune had compelled her aunt to take refuge. As she approached her destination, the cab passed—by merely crossing a road—from a spacious and beautiful Park, with its surrounding houses topped by statues and cupolas, to a row of cottages, hard by a stinking ditch miscalled a canal. The city of contrasts: north and south, east and west, the city of social contrasts.

Emily stopped the cab before the garden gate of a cottage, at the further end of the row. The bell was answered by the one servant now in her aunt's employ—Miss Letitia's maid.

Personally, this good creature was one of the ill-fated women whose appearance suggests that Nature intended to make men of them and altered her mind at the last moment. Miss Letitia's maid was tall and gaunt and awkward. The first impression produced by her face was an impression of bones. They rose high on her forehead; they projected on her cheeks; and they reached their boldest development in her jaws. In the cavernous eyes of this unfortunate person rigid obstinacy and rigid goodness looked out together, with equal severity, on all her fellow-creatures alike. Her mistress (whom she had served for a quarter of a century and more) called her "Bony." She accepted this cruelly appropriate nick-name as a mark of affectionate familiarity which honored a servant. No other person was allowed to take liberties with her: to every one but her mistress she was known as Mrs. Ellmother.

"How is my aunt?" Emily asked.

"Bad."

"Why have I not heard of her illness before?"

"Because she's too fond of you to let you be distressed about her. 'Don't tell Emily'; those were her orders, as long as she kept her senses."

"Kept her senses? Good heavens! what do you mean?"

"Fever—that's what I mean."

"I must see her directly; I am not afraid of infection."

"There's no infection to be afraid of. But you mustn't see her, for all that."

"I insist on seeing her."

"Miss Emily, I am disappointing you for your own good. Don't you know me well enough to trust me by this time?"

"I do trust you."

"Then leave my mistress to me—and go and make yourself comfortable in your own room."

Emily's answer was a positive refusal. Mrs. Ellmother, driven to her last resources, raised a new obstacle.

"It's not to be done, I tell you! How can you see Miss Letitia when she can't bear the light in her room? Do you know what color her eyes are? Red, poor soul—red as a boiled lobster."

With every word the woman uttered, Emily's perplexity and distress increased.

"You told me my aunt's illness was fever," she said—"and now you speak of some complaint in her eyes. Stand out of the way, if you please, and let me go to her."

Mrs. Ellmother, still keeping her place, looked through the open door.

"Here's the doctor," she announced. "It seems I can't satisfy you; ask him what's the matter. Come in, doctor." She threw open the door of the parlor, and introduced Emily. "This is the mistress's niece, sir. Please try if you can keep her quiet. I can't." She placed chairs with the hospitable politeness of the old school—and returned to her post at Miss Letitia's bedside.

Doctor Allday was an elderly man, with a cool manner and a ruddy complexion—thoroughly acclimatized to the atmosphere of pain and grief in which it was his destiny to live. He spoke to Emily (without any undue familiarity) as if he had been accustomed to see her for the greater part of her life.

"That's a curious woman," he said, when Mrs. Ellmother closed the door; "the most headstrong person, I think, I ever met with. But devoted to her mistress, and, making allowance for her awkwardness, not a bad nurse. I am afraid I can't give you an encouraging report of your aunt. The rheumatic fever (aggravated by the situation of this house—built on clay, you know, and close to stagnant water) has been latterly complicated by delirium."

"Is that a bad sign, sir?"

"The worst possible sign; it shows that the disease has affected the heart. Yes: she is suffering from inflammation of the eyes, but that is an unimportant symptom. We can keep the pain under by means of cooling lotions and a dark room. I've often heard her speak of you—especially since the illness assumed a serious character. What did you say? Will she know you, when you go into her room? This is about the time when the delirium usually sets in. I'll see if there's a quiet interval."

He opened the door—and came back again.

"By the way," he resumed, "I ought perhaps to explain how it was that I took the liberty of sending you that telegram. Mrs. Ellmother refused to inform you of her mistress's serious illness. That circumstance, according to my view of it, laid the responsibility on the doctor's shoulders. The form taken by your aunt's delirium—I mean the apparent tendency of the words that escape her in that state—seems to excite some incomprehensible feeling in the mind of her crabbed servant. She wouldn't even let me go into the bedroom, if she could possibly help it. Did Mrs. Ellmother give you a warm welcome when you came here?"

"Far from it. My arrival seemed to annoy her."

"Ah—just what I expected. These faithful old servants always end by presuming on their fidelity. Did you ever hear what a witty poet—I forget his name: he lived to be ninety—said of the man who had been his valet for more than half a century? 'For thirty years he was the best of servants; and for thirty years he has been the hardest of masters.' Quite true—I might say the same of my housekeeper. Rather a good story, isn't it?"

The story was completely thrown away on Emily; but one subject interested her now. "My poor aunt has always been fond of me," she said. "Perhaps she might know me, when she recognizes nobody else."

"Not very likely," the doctor answered. "But there's no laying down any rule in cases of this kind. I have sometimes observed that circumstances which have produced a strong impression on patients, when they are in a state of health, give a certain direction to the wandering of their minds, when they are in a state of fever. You will say, 'I am not a circumstance; I don't see how this encourages me to hope'—and you will be quite right. Instead of talking of my medical experience, I shall do better to look at Miss Letitia, and let you know the result. You have got other relations, I suppose? No? Very distressing—very distressing."

Who has not suffered as Emily suffered, when she was left alone? Are there not moments—if we dare to confess the truth—when poor humanity loses its hold on the consolations of religion and the hope of immortality, and feels the cruelty of creation that bids us live, on the condition that we die, and leads the first warm beginnings of love, with merciless certainty, to the cold conclusion of the grave?

"She's quiet, for the time being," Dr. Allday announced, on his return. "Remember, please, that she can't see you in the inflamed state of her eyes, and don't disturb the bed-curtains. The sooner you go to her the better, perhaps—if you have anything to say which depends on her recognizing your voice. I'll call to-morrow morning. Very distressing," he repeated, taking his hat and making his bow—"Very distressing."

Emily crossed the narrow little passage which separated the two rooms, and opened the bed-chamber door. Mrs. Ellmother met her on the threshold. "No," said the obstinate old servant, "you can't come in."

The faint voice of Miss Letitia made itself heard, calling Mrs. Ellmother by her familiar nick-name.

"Bony, who is it?"

"Never mind."

"Who is it?"

"Miss Emily, if you must know."

"Oh! poor dear, why does she come here? Who told her I was ill?"

"The doctor told her."

"Don't come in, Emily. It will only distress you—and it will do me no good. God bless you, my love. Don't come in."

"There!" said Mrs. Ellmother. "Do you hear that? Go back to the sitting-room."

Thus far, the hard necessity of controlling herself had kept Emily silent. She was now able to speak without tears. "Remember the old times, aunt," she pleaded, gently. "Don't keep me out of your room, when I have come here to nurse you!"

"I'm her nurse. Go back to the sitting-room," Mrs. Ellmother repeated.

True love lasts while life lasts. The dying woman relented.

"Bony! Bony! I can't be unkind to Emily. Let her in."

Mrs. Ellmother still insisted on having her way.

"You're contradicting your own orders," she said to her mistress. "You don't know how soon you may begin wandering in your mind again. Think, Miss Letitia—think."

This remonstrance was received in silence. Mrs. Ellmother's great gaunt figure still blocked up the doorway.

"If you force me to it," Emily said, quietly, "I must go to the doctor, and ask him to interfere."

"Do you mean that?" Mrs. Ellmother said, quietly, on her side.

"I do mean it," was the answer.

The old servant suddenly submitted—with a look which took Emily by surprise. She had expected to see anger; the face that now confronted her was a face subdued by sorrow and fear.

"I wash my hands of it," Mrs. Ellmother said. "Go in—and take the consequences."

CHAPTER XIII. MISS LETITIA.

Emily entered the room. The door was immediately closed on her from the outer side. Mrs. Ellmother's heavy steps were heard retreating along the passage. Then the banging of the door that led into the kitchen shook the flimsily-built cottage. Then, there was silence.

The dim light of a lamp hidden away in a corner and screened by a dingy green shade, just revealed the closely-curtained bed, and the table near it bearing medicine-bottles and glasses. The only objects on the chimney-piece were a clock that had been stopped in mercy to the sufferer's irritable nerves, and an open case containing a machine for pouring drops into the eyes. The smell of fumigating pastilles hung heavily on the air. To Emily's excited imagination, the silence was like the silence of death. She approached the bed trembling. "Won't you speak to me, aunt?"

"Is that you, Emily? Who let you come in?"

"You said I might come in, dear. Are you thirsty? I see some lemonade on the table. Shall I give it to you?"

"No! If you open the bed-curtains, you let in the light. My poor eyes! Why are you here, my dear? Why are you not at the school?"

"It's holiday-time, aunt. Besides, I have left school for good."

"Left school?" Miss Letitia's memory made an effort, as she repeated those words. "You were going somewhere when you left school," she said, "and Cecilia Wyvil had something to do with it. Oh, my love, how cruel of you to go away to a stranger, when you might live here with me!" She paused—her sense of what she had herself just said began to grow confused. "What stranger?" she asked abruptly. "Was it a man? What name? Oh, my mind! Has death got hold of my mind before my body?"

"Hush! hush! I'll tell you the name. Sir Jervis Redwood."

"I don't know him. I don't want to know him. Do you think he means to send for you. Perhaps he has sent for you. I won't allow it! You shan't go!"

"Don't excite yourself, dear! I have refused to go; I mean to stay here with you."

The fevered brain held to its last idea. "Has he sent for you?" she said again, louder than before.

Emily replied once more, in terms carefully chosen with the one purpose of pacifying her. The attempt proved to be useless, and worse—it seemed to make her suspicious. "I won't be deceived!" she said; "I mean to know all about it. He did send for you. Whom did he send?"

"His housekeeper."

"What name?" The tone in which she put the question told of excitement that was rising to its climax. "Don't you know that I'm curious about names?" she burst out. "Why do you provoke me? Who is it?"

"Nobody you know, or need care about, dear aunt. Mrs. Rook."

Instantly on the utterance of that name, there followed an unexpected result. Silence ensued.

Emily waited—hesitated—advanced, to part the curtains, and look in at her aunt. She was stopped by a dreadful sound of laughter—the cheerless laughter that is heard among the mad. It suddenly ended in a dreary sigh.

Afraid to look in, she spoke, hardly knowing what she said. "Is there anything you wish for? Shall I call—?"

Miss Letitia's voice interrupted her. Dull, low, rapidly muttering, it was unlike, shockingly unlike, the familiar voice of her aunt. It said strange words.

"Mrs. Rook? What does Mrs. Rook matter? Or her husband either? Bony, Bony, you're frightened about nothing. Where's the danger of those two people turning up? Do you know how many miles away the village is? Oh, you fool—a hundred miles and more. Never mind the coroner, the coroner must keep in his own district—and the jury too. A risky deception? I call it a pious fraud. And I have a tender conscience, and a cultivated mind. The newspaper? How is our newspaper to find its way to her, I should like to know? You poor old Bony! Upon my word you do me good—you make me laugh."

The cheerless laughter broke out again—and died away again drearily in a sigh.

Accustomed to decide rapidly in the ordinary emergencies of her life, Emily felt herself painfully embarrassed by the position in which she was now placed.

After what she had already heard, could she reconcile it to her sense of duty to her aunt to remain any longer in the room?

In the hopeless self-betrayal of delirium, Miss Letitia had revealed some act of concealment, committed in her past life, and confided to her faithful old servant. Under these circumstances, had Emily made any discoveries which convicted her of taking a base advantage of her position at the bedside? Most assuredly not! The nature of the act of concealment; the causes that had led to it; the person (or persons) affected by it—these were mysteries which left her entirely in the dark. She had found out that her aunt was acquainted with Mrs. Rook, and that was literally all she knew.

Blameless, so far, in the line of conduct that she had pursued, might she still remain in the bed-chamber—on this distinct understanding with herself: that she would instantly return to the sitting-room if she heard anything which could suggest a doubt of Miss Letitia's claim to her affection and respect? After some hesitation, she decided on leaving it to her conscience to answer that question. Does conscience ever say, No—when inclination says, Yes? Emily's conscience sided with her reluctance to leave her aunt.

Throughout the time occupied by these reflections, the silence had remained unbroken. Emily began to feel uneasy. She timidly put her hand through the curtains, and took Miss Letitia's hand. The contact with the burning skin startled her. She turned away to the door, to call the servant—when the sound of her aunt's voice hurried her back to the bed.

"Are you there, Bony?" the voice asked.

Was her mind getting clear again? Emily tried the experiment of making a plain reply. "Your niece is with you," she said. "Shall I call the servant?"

Miss Letitia's mind was still far away from Emily, and from the present time.

"The servant?" she repeated. "All the servants but you, Bony, have been sent away. London's the place for us. No gossiping servants and no curious neighbors in London. Bury the horrid truth in London. Ah, you may well say I look anxious and wretched. I hate deception—and yet, it must be done. Why do you waste time in talking? Why don't you find out where the vile woman lives? Only let me get at her—and I'll make Sara ashamed of herself."

Emily's heart beat fast when she heard the woman's name. "Sara" (as she and her school-fellows knew) was the baptismal name of Miss Jethro. Had her aunt alluded to the disgraced teacher, or to some other woman?

She waited eagerly to hear more. There was nothing to be heard. At this most interesting moment, the silence remained undisturbed.

In the fervor of her anxiety to set her doubts at rest, Emily's faith in her own good resolutions began to waver. The temptation to say something which might set her aunt talking again was too strong to be resisted—if she remained at the bedside. Despairing of herself she rose and turned to the door. In the moment that passed while she crossed the room the very words occurred to her that would suit her purpose. Her cheeks were hot with shame—she hesitated—she looked back at the bed—the words passed her lips.

"Sara is only one of the woman's names," she said. "Do you like her other name?"

The rapidly-muttering tones broke out again instantly—but not in answer to Emily. The sound of a voice had encouraged Miss Letitia to pursue her own confused train of thought, and had stimulated the fast-failing capacity of speech to exert itself once more.

"No! no! He's too cunning for you, and too cunning for me. He doesn't leave letters about; he destroys them all. Did I say he was too cunning for us? It's false. We are too cunning for him. Who found the morsels of his letter in the basket? Who stuck them together? Ah, we know! Don't read it, Bony. 'Dear Miss Jethro'—don't read it again. 'Miss Jethro' in his letter; and 'Sara,' when he talks to himself in the garden. Oh, who would have believed it of him, if we hadn't seen and heard it ourselves!"

There was no more doubt now.

But who was the man, so bitterly and so regretfully alluded to?

No: this time Emily held firmly by the resolution which bound her to respect the helpless position of her aunt. The speediest way of summoning Mrs. Ellmother would be to ring the bell. As she touched the handle a faint cry of suffering from the bed called her back.

"Oh, so thirsty!" murmured the failing voice—"so thirsty!"

She parted the curtains. The shrouded lamplight just showed her the green shade over Miss Letitia's eyes—the hollow cheeks below it—the arms laid helplessly on the bed-clothes. "Oh, aunt, don't you know my voice? Don't you know Emily? Let me kiss you, dear!" Useless to plead with her; useless to kiss her; she only reiterated the words, "So thirsty! so thirsty!" Emily raised the poor tortured body with a patient caution which spared it pain, and put the glass to her aunt's lips. She drank the lemonade to the last drop. Refreshed for the moment, she spoke again—spoke to the visionary servant of her delirious fancy, while she rested in Emily's arms.

"For God's sake, take care how you answer if she questions you. If she knew what we know! Are men ever ashamed? Ha! the vile woman! the vile woman!"

Her voice, sinking gradually, dropped to a whisper. The next few words that escaped her were muttered inarticulately. Little by little, the false energy of fever was wearing itself out. She lay silent and still. To look at her now was to look at the image of death. Once more, Emily kissed her—closed the curtains—and rang the bell. Mrs. Ellmother failed to appear. Emily left the room to call her.

Arrived at the top of the kitchen stairs, she noted a slight change. The door below, which she had heard banged on first entering her aunt's room, now stood open. She called to Mrs. Ellmother. A strange voice answered her. Its accent was soft and courteous; presenting the strongest imaginable contrast to the harsh tones of Miss Letitia's crabbed old maid.

"Is there anything I can do for you, miss?"

The person making this polite inquiry appeared at the foot of the stairs—a plump and comely woman of middle age. She looked up at the young lady with a pleasant smile.

"I beg your pardon," Emily said; "I had no intention of disturbing you. I called to Mrs. Ellmother."

The stranger advanced a little way up the stairs, and answered, "Mrs. Ellmother is not here."

"Do you expect her back soon?"

"Excuse me, miss—I don't expect her back at all."

"Do you mean to say that she has left the house?"

"Yes, miss. She has left the house."

CHAPTER XIV. MRS. MOSEY.

Emily's first act—after the discovery of Mrs. Ellmother's incomprehensible disappearance—was to invite the new servant to follow her into the sitting-room.

"Can you explain this?" she began.

"No, miss."

"May I ask if you have come here by Mrs. Ellmother's invitation?"

"By Mrs. Ellmother's request, miss."

"Can you tell me how she came to make the request?"

"With pleasure, miss. Perhaps—as you find me here, a stranger to yourself, in place of the customary servant—I ought to begin by giving you a reference."

"And, perhaps (if you will be so kind), by mentioning your name," Emily added.

"Thank you for reminding me, miss. My name is Elizabeth Mosey. I am well known to the gentleman who attends Miss Letitia. Dr. Allday will speak to my character and also to my experience as a nurse. If it would be in any way satisfactory to give you a second reference—"

"Quite needless, Mrs. Mosey."

"Permit me to thank you again, miss. I was at home this evening, when Mrs. Ellmother called at my lodgings. Says she, 'I have come here, Elizabeth, to ask a favor of you for old friendship's sake.' Says I, 'My dear, pray command me, whatever it may be.' If this seems rather a hasty answer to make, before I knew what the favor was, might I ask you to bear in mind that Mrs. Ellmother put it to me 'for old friendship's sake'—alluding to my late husband, and to the business which we carried on at that time? Through no fault of ours, we got into difficulties. Persons whom we had trusted proved unworthy. Not to trouble you further, I may say at once, we should have been ruined, if our old friend Mrs. Ellmother had not come forward, and trusted us with the savings of her lifetime. The money was all paid back again, before my husband's death. But I don't consider—and, I think you won't consider—that the obligation was paid back too. Prudent or not prudent, there is nothing Mrs. Ellmother can ask of me that I am not willing to do. If I have put myself in an awkward situation (and I don't deny that it looks so) this is the only excuse, miss, that I can make for my conduct."

Mrs. Mosey was too fluent, and too fond of hearing the sound of her own eminently persuasive voice. Making allowance for these little drawbacks, the impression that she produced was decidedly favorable; and, however rashly she might have acted, her motive was beyond reproach. Having said some kind words to this effect, Emily led her back to the main interest of her narrative.

"Did Mrs. Ellmother give no reason for leaving my aunt, at such a time as this?" she asked.

"The very words I said to her, miss."

"And what did she say, by way of reply?"

"She burst out crying—a thing I have never known her to do before, in an experience of twenty years."

"And she really asked you to take her place here, at a moment's notice?"

"That was just what she did," Mrs. Mosey answered. "I had no need to tell her I was astonished; my lips spoke for me, no doubt. She's a hard woman in speech and manner, I admit. But there's more feeling in her than you would suppose. 'If you are the good friend I take you for,' she says, 'don't ask me for reasons; I am doing what is forced on me, and doing it with a heavy heart.' In my place, miss, would you have insisted on her explaining herself, after that? The one thing I naturally wanted to know was, if I could speak to some lady, in the position of mistress here, before I ventured to intrude. Mrs.

90

Ellmother understood that it was her duty to help me in this particular. Your poor aunt being out of the question she mentioned you."

"How did she speak of me? In an angry way?"

"No, indeed—quite the contrary. She says, 'You will find Miss Emily at the cottage. She is Miss Letitia's niece. Everybody likes her—and everybody is right.'"

"She really said that?"

"Those were her words. And, what is more, she gave me a message for you at parting. 'If Miss Emily is surprised' (that was how she put it) 'give her my duty and good wishes; and tell her to remember what I said, when she took my place at her aunt's bedside.' I don't presume to inquire what this means," said Mrs. Mosey respectfully, ready to hear what it meant, if Emily would only be so good as to tell her. "I deliver the message, miss, as it was delivered to me. After which, Mrs. Ellmother went her way, and I went mine."

"Do you know where she went?"

"No, miss."

"Have you nothing more to tell me?"

"Nothing more; except that she gave me my directions, of course, about the nursing. I took them down in writing—and you will find them in their proper place, with the prescriptions and the medicines."

Acting at once on this hint, Emily led the way to her aunt's room.

Miss Letitia was silent, when the new nurse softly parted the curtains—looked in—and drew them together again. Consulting her watch, Mrs. Mosey compared her written directions with the medicine-bottles on the table, and set one apart to be used at the appointed time. "Nothing, so far, to alarm us," she whispered. "You look sadly pale and tired, miss. Might I advise you to rest a little?"

"If there is any change, Mrs. Mosey—either for the better or the worse—

of course you will let me know?"

"Certainly, miss."

Emily returned to the sitting-room: not to rest (after all that she had heard), but to think.

Amid much that was unintelligible, certain plain conclusions presented themselves to her mind.

After what the doctor had already said to Emily, on the subject of delirium generally, Mrs. Ellmother's proceedings became intelligible: they proved that she knew by experience the perilous course taken by her mistress's wandering thoughts, when they expressed themselves in words. This explained the concealment of Miss Letitia's illness from her niece, as well as the reiterated efforts of the old servant to prevent Emily from entering the bedroom.

But the event which had just happened—that is to say, Mrs. Ellmother's sudden departure from the cottage—was not only of serious importance in itself, but pointed to a startling conclusion.

The faithful maid had left the mistress, whom she had loved and served, sinking under a fatal illness—and had put another woman in her place, careless of what that woman might discover by listening at the bedside—rather than confront Emily after she had been within hearing of her aunt while the brain of the suffering woman was deranged by fever. There was the state of the case, in plain words.

In what frame of mind had Mrs. Ellmother adopted this desperate course of action?

To use her own expression, she had deserted Miss Letitia "with a heavy heart." To judge by her own language addressed to Mrs. Mosey, she had left Emily to the mercy of a stranger—animated, nevertheless, by sincere feelings of attachment and respect. That her fears had taken for granted suspicion which Emily had not felt, and discoveries which Emily had (as yet) not made, in no way modified the serious nature of the inference which her conduct justified. The disclosure which this woman dreaded—who could doubt it now?—directly threatened Emily's peace of mind. There was no disguising it: the innocent niece was associated with an act of deception, which had been, until that day, the undetected secret of the aunt and the aunt's maid.

In this conclusion, and in this only, was to be found the rational explanation of Mrs. Ellmother's choice—placed between the alternatives of submitting to discovery by Emily, or of leaving the house.

Poor Miss Letitia's writing-table stood near the window of the sitting-room. Shrinking from the further pursuit of thoughts which might end in disposing her mind to distrust of her dying aunt, Emily looked round in search of some employment sufficiently interesting to absorb her attention. The writing-table reminded her that she owed a letter to Cecilia. That helpful friend had surely the first claim to know why she had failed to keep her engagement with Sir Jervis Redwood.

After mentioning the telegram which had followed Mrs. Rook's arrival at the school, Emily's letter proceeded in these terms:

"As soon as I had in some degree recovered myself, I informed Mrs. Rook of my aunt's serious illness.

"Although she carefully confined herself to commonplace expressions of sympathy, I could see that it was equally a relief to both of us to feel that we were prevented from being traveling companions. Don't suppose that I have taken a capricious dislike to Mrs. Rook—or that you are in any way to blame for the unfavorable impression which she has produced on me. I will make this plain when we meet. In the meanwhile, I need only tell you that I gave her a letter of explanation to present to Sir Jervis Redwood. I also informed him of my address in London: adding a request that he would forward your letter, in case you have written to me before you receive these lines.

"Kind Mr. Alban Morris accompanied me to the railway-station, and arranged with the guard to take special care of me on the journey to London. We used to think him rather a heartless man. We were quite wrong. I don't know what his plans are for spending the summer holidays. Go where he may, I remember his kindness; my best wishes go with him.

"My dear, I must not sadden your enjoyment of your pleasant visit to the Engadine, by writing at any length of the sorrow that I am suffering. You know how I love my aunt, and how gratefully I have always felt her motherly goodness to me. The doctor does not conceal the truth. At her age, there is no hope: my father's last-left relation, my one dearest friend, is dying.

"No! I must not forget that I have another friend—I must find some comfort in thinking of you.

"I do so long in my solitude for a letter from my dear Cecilia. Nobody comes to see me, when I most want sympathy; I am a stranger in this vast city. The members of my mother's family are settled in Australia: they have not even written to me, in all the long years that have passed since her death. You remember how cheerfully I used to look forward to my new life, on leaving school? Good-by, my darling. While I can see your sweet face, in my thoughts, I don't despair—dark as it looks now—of the future that is before me."

Emily had closed and addressed her letter, and was just rising from her chair, when she heard the voice of the new nurse at the door.

CHAPTER XV. EMILY.

"May I say a word?" Mrs. Mosey inquired. She entered the room—pale and trembling. Seeing that ominous change, Emily dropped back into her chair.

"Dead?" she said faintly.

Mrs. Mosey looked at her in vacant surprise.

"I wish to say, miss, that your aunt has frightened me."

Even that vague allusion was enough for Emily.

"You need say no more," she replied. "I know but too well how my aunt's mind is affected by the fever."

Confused and frightened as she was, Mrs. Mosey still found relief in her customary flow of words.

"Many and many a person have I nursed in fever," she announced. "Many and many a person have I heard say strange things. Never yet, miss, in all my experience—!"

"Don't tell me of it!" Emily interposed.

"Oh, but I must tell you! In your own interests, Miss Emily—in your own interests. I won't be inhuman enough to leave you alone in the house to-night; but if this delirium goes on, I must ask you to get another nurse. Shocking suspicions are lying in wait for me in that bedroom, as it were. I can't resist them as I ought, if I go back again, and hear your aunt saying what she has been saying for the last half hour and more. Mrs. Ellmother has expected impossibilities of me; and Mrs. Ellmother must take the consequences. I don't say she didn't warn me—speaking, you will please to understand, in the strictest confidence. 'Elizabeth,' she says, 'you know how wildly people talk in Miss Letitia's present condition. Pay no heed to it,' she says. 'Let it go in at one ear and out at the other,' she says. 'If Miss Emily asks questions—you know nothing about it. If she's frightened—you know nothing about it. If she bursts into fits of crying that are dreadful to see, pity her, poor thing, but take no notice.' All very well, and sounds like speaking out, doesn't it? Nothing of the sort! Mrs. Ellmother warns me to expect this, that, and the other. But there is one horrid thing (which I heard, mind, over and over again at your aunt's bedside) that she does not prepare me for; and that horrid thing is—Murder!"

At that last word, Mrs. Mosey dropped her voice to a whisper—and waited to see what effect she had produced.

Sorely tried already by the cruel perplexities of her position, Emily's courage failed to resist the first sensation of horror, aroused in her by the climax of the nurse's hysterical narrative. Encouraged by her silence, Mrs. Mosey went on. She lifted one hand with theatrical solemnity—and luxuriously terrified herself with her own horrors.

"An inn, Miss Emily; a lonely inn, somewhere in the country; and a comfortless room at the inn, with a makeshift bed at one end of it, and a makeshift bed at the other—I give you my word of honor, that was how your aunt put it. She spoke of two men next; two men asleep (you understand) in the two beds. I think she called them 'gentlemen'; but I can't be sure, and I wouldn't deceive you—you know I wouldn't deceive you, for the world. Miss Letitia muttered and mumbled, poor soul. I own I was getting tired of listening—when she burst out plain again, in that one horrid word—Oh, miss, don't be impatient! don't interrupt me!"

Emily did interrupt, nevertheless. In some degree at least she had recovered herself. "No more of it!" she said—"I won't hear a word more."

But Mrs. Mosey was too resolutely bent on asserting her own importance, by making the most of the alarm that she had suffered, to be repressed by any ordinary method of remonstrance. Without paying the slightest attention to what Emily had said, she went on again more loudly and more excitably than ever.

"Listen, miss—listen! The dreadful part of it is to come; you haven't heard about the two gentlemen yet. One of them was murdered—what do you think of that!—and the other (I heard your aunt say it, in so many words) committed the crime. Did Miss Letitia fancy she was addressing a lot of people when you were nursing her? She called out, like a person making public proclamation, when I was in her room. 'Whoever you are, good people' (she says), 'a hundred pounds reward, if you find the runaway murderer. Search everywhere for a poor weak womanish creature, with rings on his little white hands. There's nothing about him like a man, except his voice—a fine round voice. You'll know him, my friends—the wretch, the monster—you'll know him by his voice.' That was how she put it; I tell you again, that was how she put it. Did you hear her scream? Ah, my dear young lady, so much the better for you! 'O the horrid murder' (she says)—'hush it up!' I'll take my Bible oath before the magistrate," cried Mrs. Mosey, starting out of her chair, "your aunt said, 'Hush it up!'"

Emily crossed the room. The energy of her character was roused at last. She seized the foolish woman by the shoulders, forced her back in the chair, and looked her straight in the face without uttering a word.

For the moment, Mrs. Mosey was petrified. She had fully expected—

having reached the end of her terrible story—to find Emily at her feet, entreating her not to carry out her intention of leaving the cottage the next morning; and she had determined, after her sense of her own importance had been sufficiently flattered, to grant the prayer of the helpless young lady. Those were her anticipations—and how had they been fulfilled? She had been treated like a mad woman in a state of revolt!

"How dare you assault me?" she asked piteously. "You ought to be ashamed of yourself. God knows I meant well."

"You are not the first person," Emily answered, quietly releasing her, "who has done wrong with the best intentions."

"I did my duty, miss, when I told you what your aunt said."

"You forgot your duty when you listened to what my aunt said."

"Allow me to explain myself."

"No: not a word more on that subject shall pass between us. Remain here, if you please; I have something to suggest in your own interests. Wait, and compose yourself."

The purpose which had taken a foremost place in Emily's mind rested on the firm foundation of her love and pity for her aunt.

Now that she had regained the power to think, she felt a hateful doubt pressed on her by Mrs. Mosey's disclosures. Having taken for granted that there was a foundation in truth for what she herself had heard in her aunt's room, could she reasonably resist the conclusion that there must be a foundation in truth for what Mrs. Mosey had heard, under similar circumstances?

There was but one way of escaping from this dilemma—and Emily deliberately took it. She turned her back on her own convictions; and persuaded herself that she had been in the wrong, when she had attached importance to anything that her aunt had said, under the influence of delirium. Having adopted this conclusion, she resolved to face the prospect of a night's solitude by the death-bed—rather than permit Mrs. Mosey to have a second opportunity of drawing her own inferences from what she might hear in Miss Letitia's room.

"Do you mean to keep me waiting much longer, miss?"

"Not a moment longer, now you are composed again," Emily answered. "I have been thinking of what has happened; and I fail to see any necessity for putting off your departure until the doctor comes to-morrow morning. There is really no objection to your leaving me to-night."

"I beg your pardon, miss; there is an objection. I have already told you I can't reconcile it to my conscience to leave you here by yourself. I am not an inhuman woman," said Mrs. Mosey, putting her handkerchief to her eyes—smitten with pity for herself.

Emily tried the effect of a conciliatory reply. "I am grateful for your kindness in offering to stay with me," she said.

"Very good of you, I'm sure," Mrs. Mosey answered ironically. "But for all that, you persist in sending me away."

"I persist in thinking that there is no necessity for my keeping you here until to-morrow."

"Oh, have it your own way! I am not reduced to forcing my company on anybody."

Mrs. Mosey put her handkerchief in her pocket, and asserted her dignity. With head erect and slowly-marching steps she walked out of the room. Emily was left in the cottage, alone with her dying aunt.

CHAPTER XVI. MISS JETHRO.

A fortnight after the disappearance of Mrs. Ellmother, and the dismissal of Mrs. Mosey, Doctor Allday entered his consulting-room, punctual to the hour at which he was accustomed to receive patients.

An occasional wrinkling of his eyebrows, accompanied by an intermittent restlessness in his movements, appeared to indicate some disturbance of this worthy man's professional composure. His mind was indeed not at ease. Even the inexcitable old doctor had felt the attraction which had already conquered three such dissimilar people as Alban Morris, Cecilia Wyvil, and Francine de Sor. He was thinking of Emily.

A ring at the door-bell announced the arrival of the first patient.

The servant introduced a tall lady, dressed simply and elegantly in dark apparel. Noticeable features, of a Jewish cast—worn and haggard, but still preserving their grandeur of form—were visible through her veil. She moved with grace and dignity; and she stated her object in consulting Doctor Allday with the ease of a well-bred woman.

"I come to ask your opinion, sir, on the state of my heart," she said; "and I am recommended by a patient, who has consulted you with advantage to herself." She placed a card on the doctor's writing-desk, and added: "I have become acquainted with the lady, by being one of the lodgers in her house."

The doctor recognized the name—and the usual proceedings ensued. After careful examination, he arrived at a favorable conclusion. "I may tell you at once," he said—"there is no reason to be alarmed about the state of your heart."

"I have never felt any alarm about myself," she answered quietly. "A sudden death is an easy death. If one's affairs are settled, it seems, on that account, to be the death to prefer. My object was to settle my affairs—such as they are—if you had considered my life to be in danger. Is there nothing the matter with me?"

"I don't say that," the doctor replied. "The action of your heart is very feeble. Take the medicine that I shall prescribe; pay a little more attention to eating and drinking than ladies usually do; don't run upstairs, and don't fatigue yourself by violent exercise—and I see no reason why you shouldn't live to be an old woman."

"God forbid!" the lady said to herself. She turned away, and looked out of the window with a bitter smile.

Doctor Allday wrote his prescription. "Are you likely to make a long stay in London?" he asked.

"I am here for a little while only. Do you wish to see me again?"

"I should like to see you once more, before you go away—if you can make it convenient. What name shall I put on the prescription?"

"Miss Jethro."

"A remarkable name," the doctor said, in his matter-of-fact way.

Miss Jethro's bitter smile showed itself again.

Without otherwise noticing what Doctor Allday had said, she laid the consultation fee on the table. At the same moment, the footman appeared with a letter. "From Miss Emily Brown," he said. "No answer required."

He held the door open as he delivered the message, seeing that Miss Jethro was about to leave the room. She dismissed him by a gesture; and, returning to the table, pointed to the letter.

"Was your correspondent lately a pupil at Miss Ladd's school?" she inquired.

"My correspondent has just left Miss Ladd," the doctor answered. "Are you a friend of hers?"

"I am acquainted with her."

"You would be doing the poor child a kindness, if you would go and see her. She has no friends in London."

"Pardon me—she has an aunt."

"Her aunt died a week since."

"Are there no other relations?"

"None. A melancholy state of things, isn't it? She would have been absolutely alone in the house, if I had not sent one of my women servants to stay with her for the present. Did you know her father?"

Miss Jethro passed over the question, as if she had not heard it. "Has the young lady dismissed her aunt's servants?" she asked.

"Her aunt kept but one servant, ma'am. The woman has spared Miss Emily the trouble of dismissing her." He briefly alluded to Mrs. Ellmother's desertion of her mistress. "I can't explain it," he said when he had done. "Can you?"

"What makes you think, sir, that I can help you? I have never even heard of the servant—and the mistress was a stranger to me."

At Doctor Allday's age a man is not easily discouraged by reproof, even when it is administered by a handsome woman. "I thought you might have known Miss Emily's father," he persisted.

Miss Jethro rose, and wished him good-morning. "I must not occupy any more of your valuable time," she said.

"Suppose you wait a minute?" the doctor suggested.

Impenetrable as ever, he rang the bell. "Any patients in the waiting-room?" he inquired. "You see I have time to spare," he resumed, when the man had replied in the negative. "I take an interest in this poor girl; and I thought—"

"If you think that I take an interest in her, too," Miss Jethro interposed, "you are perfectly right—I knew her father," she added abruptly; the allusion to Emily having apparently reminded her of the question which she had hitherto declined to notice.

"In that case," Doctor Allday proceeded, "I want a word of advice. Won't you sit down?"

She took a chair in silence. An irregular movement in the lower part of her veil seemed to indicate that she was breathing with difficulty. The doctor observed her with close attention. "Let me see my prescription again," he said. Having added an ingredient, he handed it back with a word of explanation. "Your nerves are more out of order than I supposed. The hardest disease to cure that I know of is—worry."

The hint could hardly have been plainer; but it was lost on Miss Jethro. Whatever her troubles might be, her medical adviser was not made acquainted with them. Quietly folding up the prescription, she reminded him that he had proposed to ask her advice.

"In what way can I be of service to you?" she inquired.

"I am afraid I must try your patience," the doctor acknowledged, "if I am to answer that question plainly."

With these prefatory words, he described the events that had followed Mrs. Mosey's appearance at the cottage. "I am only doing justice to this foolish woman," he continued, "when I tell you that she came here, after she had left Miss Emily, and did her best to set matters right. I went to the poor girl directly—and I felt it my duty, after looking at her aunt, not to leave her alone for that night. When I got home the next morning, whom do you think I found waiting for me? Mrs. Ellmother!"

He stopped—in the expectation that Miss Jethro would express some surprise. Not a word passed her lips.

"Mrs. Ellmother's object was to ask how her mistress was going on," the doctor proceeded. "Every day while Miss Letitia still lived, she came here to make the same inquiry—without a word of explanation. On the day of the funeral, there she was at the church, dressed in deep mourning; and, as I can personally testify, crying bitterly. When the ceremony was over—can you believe it?—she slipped away before Miss Emily or I could speak to her. We have seen nothing more of her, and heard nothing more, from that time to this."

He stopped again, the silent lady still listening without making any remark.

"Have you no opinion to express?" the doctor asked bluntly.

"I am waiting," Miss Jethro answered.

"Waiting—for what?"

"I haven't heard yet, why you want my advice."

Doctor Allday's observation of humanity had hitherto reckoned want of caution among the deficient moral qualities in the natures of women. He set down Miss Jethro as a remarkable exception to a general rule.

"I want you to advise me as to the right course to take with Miss Emily," he said. "She has assured me she attaches no serious importance to her aunt's wanderings, when the poor old lady's fever was at its worst. I don't doubt that she speaks the truth—but I have my own reasons for being afraid that she is deceiving herself. Will you bear this in mind?"

"Yes—if it's necessary."

"In plain words, Miss Jethro, you think I am still wandering from the point. I have got to the point. Yesterday, Miss Emily told me that she hoped to be soon composed enough to examine the papers left by her aunt."

Miss Jethro suddenly turned in her chair, and looked at Doctor Allday.

"Are you beginning to feel interested?" the doctor asked mischievously.

She neither acknowledged nor denied it. "Go on"—was all she said.

"I don't know how you feel," he proceeded; "I am afraid of the discoveries which she may make; and I am strongly tempted to advise her to leave the proposed examination to her aunt's lawyer. Is there anything in your knowledge of Miss Emily's late father, which tells you that I am right?"

"Before I reply," said Miss Jethro, "it may not be amiss to let the young lady speak for herself."

"How is she to do that?" the doctor asked.

Miss Jethro pointed to the writing table. "Look there," she said. "You have not yet opened Miss Emily's letter."

CHAPTER XVII. DOCTOR ALLDAY.

Absorbed in the effort to overcome his patient's reserve, the doctor had forgotten Emily's letter. He opened it immediately.

After reading the first sentence, he looked up with an expression of annoyance. "She has begun the examination of the papers already," he said.

"Then I can be of no further use to you," Miss Jethro rejoined. She made a second attempt to leave the room.

Doctor Allday turned to the next page of the letter. "Stop!" he cried. "She has found something—and here it is."

He held up a small printed Handbill, which had been placed between the first and second pages. "Suppose you look at it?" he said.

"Whether I am interested in it or not?" Miss Jethro asked.

"You may be interested in what Miss Emily says about it in her letter."

"Do you propose to show me her letter?"

"I propose to read it to you."

Miss Jethro took the Handbill without further objection. It was expressed in these words:

"MURDER. 100 POUNDS REWARD.—Whereas a murder was committed on the thirtieth September, 1877, at the Hand-in-Hand Inn, in the village of Zeeland, Hampshire, the above reward will be paid to any person or persons whose exertions shall lead to the arrest and conviction of the suspected murderer. Name not known. Supposed age, between twenty and thirty years. A well-made man, of small stature. Fair complexion, delicate features, clear blue eyes. Hair light, and cut rather short. Clean shaven, with the exception of narrow half-whiskers. Small, white, well-shaped hands. Wore valuable rings on the two last fingers of the left hand. Dressed neatly in a dark-gray tourist-suit. Carried a knapsack, as if on a pedestrian excursion. Remarkably good voice, smooth, full, and persuasive. Ingratiating manners. Apply to the Chief Inspector, Metropolitan Police Office, London."

Miss Jethro laid aside the Handbill without any visible appearance of agitation. The doctor took up Emily's letter, and read as follows:

"You will be as much relieved as I was, my kind friend, when you look at the paper inclosed. I found it loose in a blank book, with cuttings from newspapers, and odd announcements of lost property and other curious things (all huddled together between the leaves), which my aunt no doubt intended to set in order and fix in their proper places. She must have been thinking of her book, poor soul, in her last illness. Here is the origin of those 'terrible words' which frightened stupid Mrs. Mosey! Is it not encouraging to have discovered such a confirmation of my opinion as this? I feel a new interest in looking over the papers that still remain to be examined—"

Before he could get to the end of the sentence Miss Jethro's agitation broke through her reserve.

"Do what you proposed to do!" she burst out vehemently. "Stop her at once from carrying her examination any further! If she hesitates, insist on it!"

At last Doctor Allday had triumphed! "It has been a long time coming," he remarked, in his cool way; "and it's all the more welcome on that account. You dread the discoveries she may make, Miss Jethro, as I do. And you know what those discoveries may be."

"What I do know, or don't know, is of no importance," she answered sharply.

"Excuse me, it is of very serious importance. I have no authority over this poor girl—I am not even an old friend. You tell me to insist. Help me to declare honestly that I know of circumstances which justify me; and I may insist to some purpose."

Miss Jethro lifted her veil for the first time, and eyed him searchingly.

"I believe I can trust you," she said. "Now listen! The one consideration on which I consent to open my lips, is consideration for Miss Emily's tranquillity. Promise me absolute secrecy, on your word of honor."

He gave the promise.

"I want to know one thing, first," Miss Jethro proceeded. "Did she tell you—as she once told me—that her father had died of heart-complaint?"

"Yes."

"Did you put any questions to her?"

"I asked how long ago it was."

"And she told you?"

"She told me."

"You wish to know, Doctor Allday, what discoveries Miss Emily may yet make, among her aunt's papers. Judge for yourself, when I tell you that she has been deceived about her father's death."

"Do you mean that he is still living?"

"I mean that she has been deceived—purposely deceived—about the manner of his death."

"Who was the wretch who did it?"

"You are wronging the dead, sir! The truth can only have been concealed out of the purest motives of love and pity. I don't desire to disguise the conclusion at which I have arrived after what I have heard from yourself. The person responsible must be Miss Emily's aunt—and the old servant must have been in her confidence. Remember! You are bound in honor not to repeat to any living creature what I have just said."

The doctor followed Miss Jethro to the door. "You have not yet told me," he said, "how her father died."

"I have no more to tell you."

With those words she left him.

He rang for his servant. To wait until the hour at which he was accustomed to go out, might be to leave Emily's peace of mind at the mercy of an accident. "I am going to the cottage," he said. "If anybody wants me, I shall be back in a quarter of an hour."

On the point of leaving the house, he remembered that Emily would probably expect him to return the Handbill. As he took it up, the first lines caught his eye: he read the date at which the murder had been committed, for the second time. On a sudden the ruddy color left his face.

"Good God!" he cried, "her father was murdered—and that woman was concerned in it."

Following the impulse that urged him, he secured the Handbill in his pocketbook—snatched up the card which his patient had presented as her introduction—and instantly left the house. He called the first cab that passed him, and drove to Miss Jethro's lodgings.

"Gone"—was the servant's answer when he inquired for her. He insisted on speaking to the landlady. "Hardly ten minutes have passed," he said, "since she left my house."

"Hardly ten minutes have passed," the landlady replied, "since that message was brought here by a boy."

The message had been evidently written in great haste: "I am unexpectedly obliged to leave London. A bank note is inclosed in payment of my debt to you. I will send for my luggage."

The doctor withdrew.

"Unexpectedly obliged to leave London," he repeated, as he got into the cab again. "Her flight condemns her: not a doubt of it now. As fast as you can!" he shouted to the man; directing him to drive to Emily's cottage.

CHAPTER XVIII. MISS LADD.

Arriving at the cottage, Doctor Allday discovered a gentleman, who was just closing the garden gate behind him.

"Has Miss Emily had a visitor?" he inquired, when the servant admitted him.

"The gentleman left a letter for Miss Emily, sir."

"Did he ask to see her?"

"He asked after Miss Letitia's health. When he heard that she was dead, he seemed to be startled, and went away immediately."

"Did he give his name?"

"No, sir."

The doctor found Emily absorbed over her letter. His anxiety to forestall any possible discovery of the deception which had concealed the terrible story of her father's death, kept Doctor Allday's vigilance on the watch. He doubted the gentleman who had abstained from giving his name; he even distrusted the other unknown person who had written to Emily.

She looked up. Her face relieved him of his misgivings, before she could speak.

"At last, I have heard from my dearest friend," she said. "You remember what I told you about Cecilia? Here is a letter—a long delightful letter—from the Engadine, left at the door by some gentleman unknown. I was questioning the servant when you rang the bell."

"You may question me, if you prefer it. I arrived just as the gentleman was shutting your garden gate."

"Oh, tell me! what was he like?"

"Tall, and thin, and dark. Wore a vile republican-looking felt hat. Had nasty ill-tempered wrinkles between his eyebrows. The sort of man I distrust by instinct."

"Why?"

"Because he doesn't shave."

"Do you mean that he wore a beard?"

"Yes; a curly black beard."

Emily clasped her hands in amazement. "Can it be Alban Morris?" she exclaimed.

The doctor looked at her with a sardonic smile; he thought it likely that he had discovered her sweetheart.

"Who is Mr. Alban Morris?" he asked.

"The drawing-master at Miss Ladd's school."

Doctor Allday dropped the subject: masters at ladies' schools were not persons who interested him. He returned to the purpose which had brought him to the cottage—and produced the Handbill that had been sent to him in Emily's letter.

"I suppose you want to have it back again?" he said.

She took it from him, and looked at it with interest.

"Isn't it strange," she suggested, "that the murderer should have escaped, with such a careful description of him as this circulated all over England?"

She read the description to the doctor.

"'Name not known. Supposed age, between twenty-five and thirty years. A well-made man, of small stature. Fair complexion, delicate features, clear blue eyes. Hair light, and cut rather short. Clean shaven, with the exception of narrow half-whiskers. Small, white, well-shaped hands. Wore valuable rings on the two last fingers of the left hand. Dressed neatly—'"

"That part of the description is useless," the doctor remarked; "he would change his clothes."

"But could he change his voice?" Emily objected. "Listen to this: 'Remarkably good voice, smooth, full, and persuasive.' And here again! 'Ingratiating manners.' Perhaps you will say he could put on an appearance of rudeness?"

"I will say this, my dear. He would be able to disguise himself so effectually that ninety-nine people out of a hundred would fail to identify him, either by his voice or his manner."

"How?"

"Look back at the description: 'Hair cut rather short, clean shaven, with the exception of narrow half-whiskers.' The wretch was safe from pursuit; he had ample time at his disposal—don't you see how he could completely alter the appearance of his head and face? No more, my dear, of this disagreeable subject! Let us get to something interesting. Have you found anything else among your aunt's papers?"

"I have met with a great disappointment," Emily replied. "Did I tell you how I discovered the Handbill?"

"No."

"I found it, with the scrap-book and the newspaper cuttings, under a collection of empty boxes and bottles, in a drawer of the washhand-stand. And I naturally expected to make far more interesting discoveries in this room. My search was over in five minutes. Nothing in the cabinet there, in the corner, but a few books and some china. Nothing in the writing-desk, on that side-table, but a packet of note-paper and some sealing-wax. Nothing here, in the drawers, but tradesmen's receipts, materials for knitting, and old photographs. She must have destroyed all her papers, poor dear, before her last illness; and the Handbill and the other things can only have escaped, because they were left in a place which she never thought of examining. Isn't it provoking?"

With a mind inexpressibly relieved, good Doctor Allday asked permission to return to his patients: leaving Emily to devote herself to her friend's letter.

On his way out, he noticed that the door of the bed-chamber on the opposite side of the passage stood open. Since Miss Letitia's death the room had not been used. Well within view stood the washhand-stand to which Emily had alluded. The doctor advanced to the house door—reflected—hesitated—and looked toward the empty room.

It had struck him that there might be a second drawer which Emily had overlooked. Would he be justified in setting this doubt at rest? If he passed over ordinary scruples it would not be without excuse. Miss Letitia had spoken to him of her affairs, and had asked him to act (in Emily's interest) as co-executor with her lawyer. The rapid progress of the illness had made it impossible for her to execute the necessary codicil. But the doctor had been morally (if not legally) taken into her confidence—and, for that reason, he decided that he had a right in this serious matter to satisfy his own mind.

A glance was enough to show him that no second drawer had been overlooked.

There was no other discovery to detain the doctor. The wardrobe only contained the poor old lady's clothes; the one cupboard was open and empty. On the point of leaving the room, he went back to the washhand-stand. While he had the opportunity, it might not be amiss to make sure that Emily had thoroughly examined those old boxes and bottles, which she had alluded to with some little contempt.

The drawer was of considerable length. When he tried to pull it completely out from the grooves in which it ran, it resisted him. In his present frame of mind, this was a suspicious circumstance in itself. He cleared away the litter so as to make room for the introduction of his hand and arm into the drawer. In another moment his fingers touched a piece of paper, jammed between the inner end of the drawer and the bottom of the flat surface of the washhand-stand. With a little care, he succeeded in extricating the paper. Only pausing to satisfy himself that there was nothing else to be found, and to close the drawer after replacing its contents, he left the cottage.

The cab was waiting for him. On the drive back to his own house, he opened the crumpled paper. It proved to be a letter addressed to Miss Letitia; and it was signed by no less a person than Emily's schoolmistress. Looking back from the end to the beginning, Doctor Allday discovered, in the first sentence, the name of—Miss Jethro.

But for the interview of that morning with his patient he might have doubted the propriety of making himself further acquainted with the letter. As things were, he read it without hesitation.

"DEAR MADAM—I cannot but regard it as providential circumstance that your niece, in writing to you from my house, should have mentioned, among other events of her school life, the arrival of my new teacher, Miss Jethro.

"To say that I was surprised is to express very inadequately what I felt when I read your letter, informing me confidentially that I had employed a woman who was unworthy to associate with the young persons placed under my care. It is impossible for me to suppose that a lady in your position, and possessed of your high principles, would make such a serious accusation as this, without unanswerable reasons for doing so. At the same time I cannot, consistently with my duty as a Christian, suffer my opinion of Miss Jethro to be in any way modified, until proofs are laid before me which it is impossible to dispute.

"Placing the same confidence in your discretion, which you have placed in mine, I now inclose the references and testimonials which Miss Jethro submitted to me, when she presented herself to fill the vacant situation in my school.

"I earnestly request you to lose no time in instituting the confidential inquiries which you have volunteered to make. Whatever the result may be, pray return to me the inclosures which I have trusted to your care, and believe me, dear madam, in much suspense and anxiety, sincerely yours,

"AMELIA LADD."

It is needless to describe, at any length, the impression which these lines produced on the doctor.

If he had heard what Emily had heard at the time of her aunt's last illness, he would have called to mind Miss Letitia's betrayal of her interest in some man unknown, whom she believed to have been beguiled by Miss Jethro— and he would have perceived that the vindictive hatred, thus produced, must have inspired the letter of denunciation which the schoolmistress had acknowledged. He would also have inferred that Miss Letitia's inquiries had proved her accusation to be well founded—if he had known of the new teacher's sudden dismissal from the school. As things were, he was merely confirmed in his bad opinion of Miss Jethro; and he was induced, on reflection, to keep his discovery to himself.

"If poor Miss Emily saw the old lady exhibited in the character of an informer," he thought, "what a blow would be struck at her innocent respect for the memory of her aunt!"

CHAPTER XIX. SIR JERVIS REDWOOD.

In the meantime, Emily, left by herself, had her own correspondence to occupy her attention. Besides the letter from Cecilia (directed to the care of Sir Jervis Redwood), she had received some lines addressed to her by Sir Jervis himself. The two inclosures had been secured in a sealed envelope, directed to the cottage.

If Alban Morris had been indeed the person trusted as messenger by Sir Jervis, the conclusion that followed filled Emily with overpowering emotions of curiosity and surprise.

Having no longer the motive of serving and protecting her, Alban must, nevertheless, have taken the journey to Northumberland. He must have gained Sir Jervis Redwood's favor and confidence—and he might even have been a guest at the baronet's country seat—when Cecilia's letter arrived. What did it mean?

Emily looked back at her experience of her last day at school, and recalled her consultation with Alban on the subject of Mrs. Rook. Was he still bent on clearing up his suspicions of Sir Jervis's housekeeper? And, with that end in view, had he followed the woman, on her return to her master's place of abode?

Suddenly, almost irritably, Emily snatched up Sir Jervis's letter. Before the doctor had come in, she had glanced at it, and had thrown it aside in her impatience to read what Cecilia had written. In her present altered frame of mind, she was inclined to think that Sir Jervis might be the more interesting correspondent of the two.

On returning to his letter, she was disappointed at the outset.

In the first place, his handwriting was so abominably bad that she was obliged to guess at his meaning. In the second place, he never hinted at the circumstances under which Cecilia's letter had been confided to the gentleman who had left it at her door.

She would once more have treated the baronet's communication with

113

contempt—but for the discovery that it contained an offer of employment in London, addressed to herself.

Sir Jervis had necessarily been obliged to engage another secretary in Emily's absence. But he was still in want of a person to serve his literary interests in London. He had reason to believe that discoveries made by modern travelers in Central America had been reported from time to time by the English press; and he wished copies to be taken of any notices of this sort which might be found, on referring to the files of newspapers kept in the reading-room of the British Museum. If Emily considered herself capable of contributing in this way to the completeness of his great work on "the ruined cities," she had only to apply to his bookseller in London, who would pay her the customary remuneration and give her every assistance of which she might stand in need. The bookseller's name and address followed (with nothing legible but the two words "Bond Street"), and there was an end of Sir Jervis's proposal.

Emily laid it aside, deferring her answer until she had read Cecilia's letter.

CHAPTER XX. THE REVEREND MILES MIRABEL.

"I am making a little excursion from the Engadine, my dearest of all dear friends. Two charming fellow-travelers take care of me; and we may perhaps get as far as the Lake of Como.

"My sister (already much improved in health) remains at St. Moritz with the old governess. The moment I know what exact course we are going to take, I shall write to Julia to forward any letters which arrive in my absence. My life, in this earthly paradise, will be only complete when I hear from my darling Emily.

"In the meantime, we are staying for the night at some interesting place, the name of which I have unaccountably forgotten; and here I am in my room, writing to you at last—dying to know if Sir Jervis has yet thrown himself at your feet, and offered to make you Lady Redwood with magnificent settlements.

"But you are waiting to hear who my new friends are. My dear, one of

114

them is, next to yourself, the most delightful creature in existence. Society knows her as Lady Janeaway. I love her already, by her Christian name; she is my friend Doris. And she reciprocates my sentiments.

"You will now understand that union of sympathies made us acquainted with each other.

"If there is anything in me to be proud of, I think it must be my admirable appetite. And, if I have a passion, the name of it is Pastry. Here again, Lady Doris reciprocates my sentiments. We sit next to each other at the table d'hote.

"Good heavens, I have forgotten her husband! They have been married rather more than a month. Did I tell you that she is just two years older than I am?

"I declare I am forgetting him again! He is Lord Janeaway. Such a quiet modest man, and so easily amused. He carries with him everywhere a dirty little tin case, with air holes in the cover. He goes softly poking about among bushes and brambles, and under rocks, and behind old wooden houses. When he has caught some hideous insect that makes one shudder, he blushes with pleasure, and looks at his wife and me, and says, with the prettiest lisp: 'This is what I call enjoying the day.' To see the manner in which he obeys Her is, between ourselves, to feel proud of being a woman.

"Where was I? Oh, at the table d'hote.

"Never, Emily—I say it with a solemn sense of the claims of truth— never have I eaten such an infamous, abominable, maddeningly bad dinner, as the dinner they gave us on our first day at the hotel. I ask you if I am not patient; I appeal to your own recollection of occasions when I have exhibited extraordinary self-control. My dear, I held out until they brought the pastry round. I took one bite, and committed the most shocking offense against good manners at table that you can imagine. My handkerchief, my poor innocent handkerchief, received the horrid—please suppose the rest. My hair stands on end, when I think of it. Our neighbors at the table saw me. The coarse men laughed. The sweet young bride, sincerely feeling for me, said,

'Will you allow me to shake hands? I did exactly what you have done the day before yesterday.' Such was the beginning of my friendship with Lady Doris Janeaway.

"We are two resolute women— I mean that she is resolute, and that I follow her—and we have asserted our right of dining to our own satisfaction, by means of an interview with the chief cook.

"This interesting person is an ex-Zouave in the French army. Instead of making excuses, he confessed that the barbarous tastes of the English and American visitors had so discouraged him, that he had lost all pride and pleasure in the exercise of his art. As an example of what he meant, he mentioned his experience of two young Englishmen who could speak no foreign language. The waiters reported that they objected to their breakfasts, and especially to the eggs. Thereupon (to translate the Frenchman's own way of putting it) he exhausted himself in exquisite preparations of eggs. Eggs a la tripe, au gratin, a l'Aurore, a la Dauphine, a la Poulette, a la Tartare, a la Venitienne, a la Bordelaise, and so on, and so on. Still the two young gentlemen were not satisfied. The ex-Zouave, infuriated; wounded in his honor, disgraced as a professor, insisted on an explanation. What, in heaven's name, did they want for breakfast? They wanted boiled eggs; and a fish which they called a Bloaterre. It was impossible, he said, to express his contempt for the English idea of a breakfast, in the presence of ladies. You know how a cat expresses herself in the presence of a dog—and you will understand the allusion. Oh, Emily, what dinners we have had, in our own room, since we spoke to that noble cook!

"Have I any more news to send you? Are you interested, my dear, in eloquent young clergymen?

"On our first appearance at the public table we noticed a remarkable air of depression among the ladies. Had some adventurous gentleman tried to climb a mountain, and failed? Had disastrous political news arrived from England; a defeat of the Conservatives, for instance? Had a revolution in the fashions broken out in Paris, and had all our best dresses become of no earthly value to us? I applied for information to the only lady present who shone on the company with a cheerful face—my friend Doris, of course. "'What day was yesterday?' she asked.

"'Sunday,' I answered.

"'Of all melancholy Sundays,' she continued, the most melancholy in the calendar. Mr. Miles Mirabel preached his farewell sermon, in our temporary chapel upstairs.'

"'And you have not recovered it yet?'

"'We are all heart-broken, Miss Wyvil.'

"This naturally interested me. I asked what sort of sermons Mr. Mirabel preached. Lady Janeaway said: 'Come up to our room after dinner. The subject is too distressing to be discussed in public.'

"She began by making me personally acquainted with the reverend gentleman—that is to say, she showed me the photographic portraits of him. They were two in number. One only presented his face. The other exhibited him at full length, adorned in his surplice. Every lady in the congregation had received the two photographs as a farewell present. 'My portraits,' Lady Doris remarked, 'are the only complete specimens. The others have been irretrievably ruined by tears.'

"You will now expect a personal description of this fascinating man. What the photographs failed to tell me, my friend was so kind as to complete from the resources of her own experience. Here is the result presented to the best of my ability.

"He is young—not yet thirty years of age. His complexion is fair; his features are delicate, his eyes are clear blue. He has pretty hands, and rings prettier still. And such a voice, and such manners! You will say there are plenty of pet parsons who answer to this description. Wait a little—I have kept his chief distinction till the last. His beautiful light hair flows in profusion over his shoulders; and his glossy beard waves, at apostolic length, down to the lower buttons of his waistcoat.

"What do you think of the Reverend Miles Mirabel now?

"The life and adventures of our charming young clergyman, bear eloquent testimony to the saintly patience of his disposition, under trials which would have overwhelmed an ordinary man. (Lady Doris, please notice, quotes in this place the language of his admirers; and I report Lady Doris.)

"He has been clerk in a lawyer's office—unjustly dismissed. He has given readings from Shakespeare—infamously neglected. He has been secretary to a promenade concert company—deceived by a penniless manager. He has been employed in negotiations for making foreign railways—repudiated by an unprincipled Government. He has been translator to a publishing house—declared incapable by envious newspapers and reviews. He has taken refuge in dramatic criticism—dismissed by a corrupt editor. Through all these means of purification for the priestly career, he passed at last into the one sphere that was worthy of him: he entered the Church, under the protection of influential friends. Oh, happy change! From that moment his labors have been blessed. Twice already he has been presented with silver tea-pots filled with sovereigns. Go where he may, precious sympathies environ him; and domestic affection places his knife and fork at innumerable family tables. After a continental career, which will leave undying recollections, he is now recalled to England—at the suggestion of a person of distinction in the Church, who prefers a mild climate. It will now be his valued privilege to represent an absent rector in a country living; remote from cities, secluded in pastoral solitude, among simple breeders of sheep. May the shepherd prove worthy of the flock!

"Here again, my dear, I must give the merit where the merit is due. This memoir of Mr. Mirabel is not of my writing. It formed part of his farewell sermon, preserved in the memory of Lady Doris—and it shows (once more in the language of his admirers) that the truest humility may be found in the character of the most gifted man.

"Let me only add, that you will have opportunities of seeing and hearing this popular preacher, when circumstances permit him to address congregations in the large towns. I am at the end of my news; and I begin to feel—after this long, long letter—that it is time to go to bed. Need I say that I have often spoken of you to Doris, and that she entreats you to be her friend as well as mine, when we meet again in England?

"Good-by, darling, for the present. With fondest love,

"Your CECILIA."

"P.S.—I have formed a new habit. In case of feeling hungry in the night, I keep a box of chocolate under the pillow. You have no idea what a comfort it is. If I ever meet with the man who fulfills my ideal, I shall make it a condition of the marriage settlement, that I am to have chocolate under the pillow."

CHAPTER XXI. POLLY AND SALLY.

Without a care to trouble her; abroad or at home, finding inexhaustible varieties of amusement; seeing new places, making new acquaintances—what a disheartening contrast did Cecilia's happy life present to the life of her friend! Who, in Emily's position, could have read that joyously-written letter from Switzerland, and not have lost heart and faith, for the moment at least, as the inevitable result?

A buoyant temperament is of all moral qualities the most precious, in this respect; it is the one force in us—when virtuous resolution proves insufficient—which resists by instinct the stealthy approaches of despair. "I shall only cry," Emily thought, "if I stay at home; better go out."

Observant persons, accustomed to frequent the London parks, can hardly have failed to notice the number of solitary strangers sadly endeavoring to vary their lives by taking a walk. They linger about the flower-beds; they sit for hours on the benches; they look with patient curiosity at other people who have companions; they notice ladies on horseback and children at play, with submissive interest; some of the men find company in a pipe, without appearing to enjoy it; some of the women find a substitute for dinner, in little dry biscuits wrapped in crumpled scraps of paper; they are not sociable; they are hardly ever seen to make acquaintance with each other; perhaps they are shame-faced, or proud, or sullen; perhaps they despair of others, being accustomed to despair of themselves; perhaps they have their reasons for never venturing to encounter curiosity, or their vices which dread detection, or their virtues which suffer hardship with the resignation that is sufficient for itself. The one thing certain is, that these unfortunate people resist discovery. We know that they are strangers in London—and we know no more.

And Emily was one of them.

Among the other forlorn wanderers in the Parks, there appeared latterly a trim little figure in black (with the face protected from notice behind a crape veil), which was beginning to be familiar, day after day, to nursemaids and children, and to rouse curiosity among harmless solitaries meditating on benches, and idle vagabonds strolling over the grass. The woman-servant, whom the considerate doctor had provided, was the one person in Emily's absence left to take care of the house. There was no other creature who could be a companion to the friendless girl. Mrs. Ellmother had never shown herself again since the funeral. Mrs. Mosey could not forget that she had been (no matter how politely) requested to withdraw. To whom could Emily say, "Let us go out for a walk?" She had communicated the news of her aunt's death to Miss Ladd, at Brighton; and had heard from Francine. The worthy schoolmistress had written to her with the truest kindness. "Choose your own time, my poor child, and come and stay with me at Brighton; the sooner the better." Emily shrank—not from accepting the invitation—but from encountering Francine. The hard West Indian heiress looked harder than ever with a pen in her hand. Her letter announced that she was "getting on wretchedly with her studies (which she hated); she found the masters appointed to instruct her ugly and disagreeable (and loathed the sight of them); she had taken a dislike to Miss Ladd (and time only confirmed that unfavorable impression); Brighton was always the same; the sea was always the same; the drives were always the same. Francine felt a presentiment that she should do something desperate, unless Emily joined her, and made Brighton endurable behind the horrid schoolmistress's back." Solitude in London was a privilege and a pleasure, viewed as the alternative to such companionship as this.

Emily wrote gratefully to Miss Ladd, and asked to be excused.

Other days had passed drearily since that time; but the one day that had brought with it Cecilia's letter set past happiness and present sorrow together so vividly and so cruelly that Emily's courage sank. She had forced back the tears, in her lonely home; she had gone out to seek consolation and encouragement under the sunny sky—to find comfort for her sore heart in the radiant summer beauty of flowers and grass, in the sweet breathing of the air, in the happy heavenward soaring of the birds. No! Mother Nature is stepmother to the sick at heart. Soon, too soon, she could hardly see where she went. Again and again she resolutely cleared her eyes, under the shelter of her veil, when passing strangers noticed her; and again and again the tears found their way back. Oh, if the girls at the school were to see her now—the girls who used to say in their moments of sadness, "Let us go to Emily and be cheered"—would they know her again? She sat down to rest and recover herself on the nearest bench. It was unoccupied. No passing footsteps were audible on the remote path to which she had strayed. Solitude at home! Solitude in the Park! Where was Cecilia at that moment? In Italy, among the lakes and mountains, happy in the company of her light-hearted friend.

The lonely interval passed, and persons came near. Two sisters, girls like herself, stopped to rest on the bench.

They were full of their own interests; they hardly looked at the stranger in mourning garments. The younger sister was to be married, and the elder was to be bridesmaid. They talked of their dresses and their presents; they compared the dashing bridegroom of one with the timid lover of the other; they laughed over their own small sallies of wit, over their joyous dreams of the future, over their opinions of the guests invited to the wedding. Too joyfully restless to remain inactive any longer, they jumped up again from the seat. One of them said, "Polly, I'm too happy!" and danced as she walked away. The other cried, "Sally, for shame!" and laughed, as if she had hit on the most irresistible joke that ever was made.

Emily rose and went home.

By some mysterious influence which she was unable to trace, the boisterous merriment of the two girls had roused in her a sense of revolt against the life that she was leading. Change, speedy change, to some occupation that would force her to exert herself, presented the one promise of brighter days that she could see. To feel this was to be inevitably reminded of Sir Jervis Redwood. Here was a man, who had never seen her, transformed by the incomprehensible operation of Chance into the friend of whom she stood in need—the friend who pointed the way to a new world of action, the busy world of readers in the library of the Museum.

Early in the new week, Emily had accepted Sir Jervis's proposal, and had so interested the bookseller to whom she had been directed to apply, that he took it on himself to modify the arbitrary instructions of his employer.

"The old gentleman has no mercy on himself, and no mercy on others," he explained, "where his literary labors are concerned. You must spare yourself, Miss Emily. It is not only absurd, it's cruel, to expect you to ransack old newspapers for discoveries in Yucatan, from the time when Stephens published his 'Travels in Central America'—nearly forty years since! Begin with back numbers published within a few years—say five years from the present date—and let us see what your search over that interval will bring forth."

Accepting this friendly advice, Emily began with the newspaper-volume dating from New Year's Day, 1876.

The first hour of her search strengthened the sincere sense of gratitude with which she remembered the bookseller's kindness. To keep her attention steadily fixed on the one subject that interested her employer, and to resist the temptation to read those miscellaneous items of news which especially interest women, put her patience and resolution to a merciless test. Happily for herself, her neighbors on either side were no idlers. To see them so absorbed over their work that they never once looked at her, after the first moment when she took her place between them, was to find exactly the example of which she stood most in need. As the hours wore on, she pursued her weary way, down one column and up another, resigned at least (if not quite reconciled yet) to her task. Her labors ended, for the day, with such encouragement as she might derive from the conviction of having, thus far, honestly pursued a useless search.

News was waiting for her when she reached home, which raised her sinking spirits.

On leaving the cottage that morning she had given certain instructions, relating to the modest stranger who had taken charge of her correspondence—in case of his paying a second visit, during her absence at the Museum. The first words spoken by the servant, on opening the door, informed her that the unknown gentleman had called again. This time he had boldly left his card. There was the welcome name that she had expected to see—Alban Morris.

CHAPTER XXII. ALBAN MORRIS.

Having looked at the card, Emily put her first question to the servant.

"Did you tell Mr. Morris what your orders were?" she asked.

"Yes, miss; I said I was to have shown him in, if you had been at home. Perhaps I did wrong; I told him what you told me when you went out this morning—I said you had gone to read at the Museum."

"What makes you think you did wrong?"

"Well, miss, he didn't say anything, but he looked upset."

"Do you mean that he looked angry?"

The servant shook her head. "Not exactly angry—puzzled and put out."

"Did he leave any message?"

"He said he would call later, if you would be so good as to receive him."

In half an hour more, Alban and Emily were together again. The light fell full on her face as she rose to receive him.

"Oh, how you have suffered!"

The words escaped him before he could restrain himself. He looked at her with the tender sympathy, so precious to women, which she had not seen in the face of any human creature since the loss of her aunt. Even the good doctor's efforts to console her had been efforts of professional routine—the inevitable result of his life-long familiarity with sorrow and death. While Alban's eyes rested on her, Emily felt her tears rising. In the fear that he might misinterpret her reception of him, she made an effort to speak with some appearance of composure.

"I lead a lonely life," she said; "and I can well understand that my face shows it. You are one of my very few friends, Mr. Morris"—the tears rose again; it discouraged her to see him standing irresolute, with his hat in his hand, fearful of intruding on her. "Indeed, indeed, you are welcome," she said, very earnestly.

In those sad days her heart was easily touched. She gave him her hand for the second time. He held it gently for a moment. Every day since they had parted she had been in his thoughts; she had become dearer to him than ever. He was too deeply affected to trust himself to answer. That silence pleaded for him as nothing had pleaded for him yet. In her secret self she remembered with wonder how she had received his confession in the school garden. It was a little hard on him, surely, to have forbidden him even to hope.

Conscious of her own weakness—even while giving way to it—she felt the necessity of turning his attention from herself. In some confusion, she pointed to a chair at her side, and spoke of his first visit, when he had left her letters at the door. Having confided to him all that she had discovered, and all that she had guessed, on that occasion, it was by an easy transition that she alluded next to the motive for his journey to the North.

"I thought it might be suspicion of Mrs. Rook," she said. "Was I mistaken?"

"No; you were right."

"They were serious suspicions, I suppose?"

"Certainly! I should not otherwise have devoted my holiday-time to clearing them up."

"May I know what they were?"

"I am sorry to disappoint you," he began.

"But you would rather not answer my question," she interposed.

"I would rather hear you tell me if you have made any other guess."

"One more, Mr. Morris. I guessed that you had become acquainted with Sir Jervis Redwood."

"For the second time, Miss Emily, you have arrived at a sound conclusion. My one hope of finding opportunities for observing Sir Jervis's housekeeper depended on my chance of gaining admission to Sir Jervis's house."

"How did you succeed? Perhaps you provided yourself with a letter of introduction?"

"I knew nobody who could introduce me," Alban replied. "As the event proved, a letter would have been needless. Sir Jervis introduced himself—and, more wonderful still, he invited me to his house at our first interview."

"Sir Jervis introduced himself?" Emily repeated, in amazement. "From Cecilia's description of him, I should have thought he was the last person in the world to do that!"

Alban smiled. "And you would like to know how it happened?" he suggested.

"The very favor I was going to ask of you," she replied.

Instead of at once complying with her wishes, he paused—hesitated—and made a strange request. "Will you forgive my rudeness, if I ask leave to walk up and down the room while I talk? I am a restless man. Walking up and down helps me to express myself freely."

Her face brightened for the first time. "How like You that is!" she exclaimed.

Alban looked at her with surprise and delight. She had betrayed an interest in studying his character, which he appreciated at its full value. "I should never have dared to hope," he said, "that you knew me so well already."

"You are forgetting your story," she reminded him.

He moved to the opposite side of the room, where there were fewer impediments in the shape of furniture. With his head down, and his hands crossed behind him, he paced to and fro. Habit made him express himself in his usual quaint way—but he became embarrassed as he went on. Was he disturbed by his recollections? or by the fear of taking Emily into his confidence too freely?

"Different people have different ways of telling a story," he said. "Mine is the methodical way—I begin at the beginning. We will start, if you please, in the railway—we will proceed in a one-horse chaise—and we will stop at a village, situated in a hole. It was the nearest place to Sir Jervis's house, and it was therefore my destination. I picked out the biggest of the cottages—I mean the huts—and asked the woman at the door if she had a bed to let. She evidently thought me either mad or drunk. I wasted no time in persuasion; the right person to plead my cause was asleep in her arms. I began by admiring the baby; and I ended by taking the baby's portrait. From that moment I became a member of the family—the member who had his own way. Besides the room occupied by the husband and wife, there was a sort of kennel in which the husband's brother slept. He was dismissed (with five shillings of mine to comfort him) to find shelter somewhere else; and I was promoted to the vacant place. It is my misfortune to be tall. When I went to bed, I slept with my head on the pillow, and my feet out of the window. Very cool and pleasant in summer weather. The next morning, I set my trap for Sir Jervis."

"Your trap?" Emily repeated, wondering what he meant.

"I went out to sketch from Nature," Alban continued. "Can anybody (with or without a title, I don't care), living in a lonely country house, see a stranger hard at work with a color-box and brushes, and not stop to look at what he is doing? Three days passed, and nothing happened. I was quite patient; the grand open country all round me offered lessons of inestimable value in what we call aerial perspective. On the fourth day, I was absorbed over the hardest of all hard tasks in landscape art, studying the clouds straight from Nature. The magnificent moorland silence was suddenly profaned by a man's voice, speaking (or rather croaking) behind me. 'The worst curse of human life,' the voice said, 'is the detestable necessity of taking exercise. I hate losing my time; I hate fine scenery; I hate fresh air; I hate a pony. Go on, you brute!' Being too deeply engaged with the clouds to look round, I had supposed this pretty speech to be addressed to some second person. Nothing of the sort; the croaking voice had a habit of speaking to itself. In a minute more, there came within my range of view a solitary old man, mounted on a rough pony."

"Was it Sir Jervis?"

Alban hesitated.

"It looked more like the popular notion of the devil," he said.

"Oh, Mr. Morris!"

"I give you my first impression, Miss Emily, for what it is worth. He had his high-peaked hat in his hand, to keep his head cool. His wiry iron-gray hair looked like hair standing on end; his bushy eyebrows curled upward toward his narrow temples; his horrid old globular eyes stared with a wicked brightness; his pointed beard hid his chin; he was covered from his throat to his ankles in a loose black garment, something between a coat and a cloak; and, to complete him, he had a club foot. I don't doubt that Sir Jervis Redwood is the earthly alias which he finds convenient—but I stick to that first impression which appeared to surprise you. 'Ha! an artist; you seem to be the sort of man I want!' In those terms he introduced himself. Observe, if you please, that my trap caught him the moment he came my way. Who wouldn't be an artist?"

"Did he take a liking to you?" Emily inquired.

"Not he! I don't believe he ever took a liking to anybody in his life."

"Then how did you get your invitation to his house?"

"That's the amusing part of it, Miss Emily. Give me a little breathing time, and you shall hear."

CHAPTER XXIII. MISS REDWOOD.

"I got invited to Sir Jervis's house," Alban resumed, "by treating the old savage as unceremoniously as he had treated me. 'That's an idle trade of yours,' he said, looking at my sketch. 'Other ignorant people have made the same remark,' I answered. He rode away, as if he was not used to be spoken to in that manner, and then thought better of it, and came back. 'Do you understand wood engraving?' he asked. 'Yes.' 'And etching?' 'I have practiced etching myself.' 'Are you a Royal Academician?' 'I'm a drawing-master at a ladies' school.' 'Whose school?' 'Miss Ladd's.' 'Damn it, you know the girl who ought to have been my secretary.' I am not quite sure whether you will take it as a compliment—Sir Jervis appeared to view you in the light of a reference to my respectability. At any rate, he went on with his questions. 'How long do you stop in these parts?' 'I haven't made up my mind.' 'Look here; I want to consult you—are you listening?' 'No; I'm sketching.' He burst into a horrid scream. I asked if he felt himself taken ill. 'Ill?' he said—'I'm laughing.' It was a diabolical laugh, in one syllable—not 'ha! ha! ha!' only 'ha!'—and it made him look wonderfully like that eminent person, whom I persist in thinking he resembles. 'You're an impudent dog,' he said; 'where are you living?' He was so delighted when he heard of my uncomfortable position in the kennel-bedroom, that he offered his hospitality on the spot. 'I can't go to you in such a pigstye as that,' he said; 'you must come to me. What's your name?' 'Alban Morris; what's yours?' 'Jervis Redwood. Pack up your traps when you've done your job, and come and try my kennel. There it is, in a corner of your drawing, and devilish like, too.' I packed up my traps, and I tried his kennel. And now you have had enough of Sir Jervis Redwood."

"Not half enough!" Emily answered. "Your story leaves off just at the interesting moment. I want you to take me to Sir Jervis's house."

"And I want you, Miss Emily, to take me to the British Museum. Don't let me startle you! When I called here earlier in the day, I was told that you had gone to the reading-room. Is your reading a secret?"

His manner, when he made that reply, suggested to Emily that there was some foregone conclusion in his mind, which he was putting to the test. She answered without alluding to the impression which he had produced on her.

"My reading is no secret. I am only consulting old newspapers."

He repeated the last words to himself. "Old newspapers?" he said—as if he was not quite sure of having rightly understood her.

She tried to help him by a more definite reply.

"I am looking through old newspapers," she resumed, "beginning with the year eighteen hundred and seventy-six."

"And going back from that time," he asked eagerly; "to earlier dates still?"

"No—just the contrary—advancing from 'seventy-six' to the present time."

He suddenly turned pale—and tried to hide his face from her by looking out of the window. For a moment, his agitation deprived him of his presence of mind. In that moment, she saw that she had alarmed him.

"What have I said to frighten you?" she asked.

He tried to assume a tone of commonplace gallantry. "There are limits even to your power over me," he replied. "Whatever else you may do, you can never frighten me. Are you searching those old newspapers with any particular object in view?"

"Yes."

"May I know what it is?"

"May I know why I frightened you?"

He began to walk up and down the room again—then checked himself abruptly, and appealed to her mercy.

"Don't be hard on me," he pleaded. "I am so fond of you—oh, forgive me! I only mean that it distresses me to have any concealments from you. If I could open my whole heart at this moment, I should be a happier man."

She understood him and believed him. "My curiosity shall never embarrass you again," she answered warmly. "I won't even remember that I wanted to hear how you got on in Sir Jervis's house."

His gratitude seized the opportunity of taking her harmlessly into his confidence. "As Sir Jervis's guest," he said, "my experience is at your service. Only tell me how I can interest you."

She replied, with some hesitation, "I should like to know what happened when you first saw Mrs. Rook." To her surprise and relief, he at once complied with her wishes.

"We met," he said, "on the evening when I first entered the house. Sir Jervis took me into the dining-room—and there sat Miss Redwood, with a large black cat on her lap. Older than her brother, taller than her brother, leaner than her brother—with strange stony eyes, and a skin like parchment—she looked (if I may speak in contradictions) like a living corpse. I was presented, and the corpse revived. The last lingering relics of former good breeding showed themselves faintly in her brow and in her smile. You will hear more of Miss Redwood presently. In the meanwhile, Sir Jervis made me reward his hospitality by professional advice. He wished me to decide whether the artists whom he had employed to illustrate his wonderful book had cheated him by overcharges and bad work—and Mrs. Rook was sent to fetch the engravings from his study upstairs. You remember her petrified appearance, when she first read the inscription on your locket? The same result followed when she found herself face to face with me. I saluted her civilly—she was deaf and blind to my politeness. Her master snatched the illustrations out of her hand, and told her to leave the room. She stood stockstill, staring helplessly. Sir Jervis looked round at his sister; and I followed his example. Miss Redwood was observing the housekeeper too attentively to notice anything else; her brother was obliged to speak to her. 'Try Rook with the bell,' he said. Miss Redwood took a fine old bronze hand-bell from the table at her side, and rang it. At the shrill silvery sound of the bell, Mrs. Rook put her hand to her head as if the ringing had hurt her—turned instantly, and left us. 'Nobody can manage Rook but my sister,' Sir Jervis explained; 'Rook is crazy.' Miss Redwood differed with him. 'No!' she said. Only one word, but there were volumes of contradiction in it. Sir Jervis looked at me slyly; meaning, perhaps, that he thought his sister crazy too. The dinner was brought in at the same moment, and my attention was diverted to Mrs. Rook's husband."

"What was he like?" Emily asked.

"I really can't tell you; he was one of those essentially commonplace persons, whom one never looks at a second time. His dress was shabby, his head was bald, and his hands shook when he waited on us at table—and that is all I remember. Sir Jervis and I feasted on salt fish, mutton, and beer. Miss Redwood had cold broth, with a wine-glass full of rum poured into it by Mr. Rook. 'She's got no stomach,' her brother informed me; 'hot things come up again ten minutes after they have gone down her throat; she lives on that beastly mixture, and calls it broth-grog!' Miss Redwood sipped her elixir of life, and occasionally looked at me with an appearance of interest which I was at a loss to understand. Dinner being over, she rang her antique bell. The shabby old man-servant answered her call. 'Where's your wife?' she inquired. 'Ill, miss.' She took Mr. Rook's arm to go out, and stopped as she passed me. 'Come to my room, if you please, sir, to-morrow at two o'clock,' she said. Sir Jervis explained again: 'She's all to pieces in the morning' (he invariably called his sister 'She'); 'and gets patched up toward the middle of the day. Death has forgotten her, that's about the truth of it.' He lighted his pipe and pondered over the hieroglyphics found among the ruined cities of Yucatan; I lighted my pipe, and read the only book I could find in the dining-room—a dreadful record of shipwrecks and disasters at sea. When the room was full of tobacco-smoke we fell asleep in our chairs—and when we awoke again we got up and went to bed. There is the true story of my first evening at Redwood Hall."

Emily begged him to go on. "You have interested me in Miss Redwood," she said. "You kept your appointment, of course?"

"I kept my appointment in no very pleasant humor. Encouraged by my favorable report of the illustrations which he had submitted to my judgment, Sir Jervis proposed to make me useful to him in a new capacity. 'You have nothing particular to do,' he said, 'suppose you clean my pictures?' I gave him one of my black looks, and made no other reply. My interview with his sister tried my powers of self-command in another way. Miss Redwood declared her purpose in sending for me the moment I entered the room. Without any preliminary remarks—speaking slowly and emphatically, in a wonderfully strong voice for a woman of her age—she said, 'I have a favor to ask of you, sir. I want you to tell me what Mrs. Rook has done.' I was so staggered that I stared at her like a fool. She went on: 'I suspected Mrs. Rook, sir, of having guilty remembrances on her conscience before she had been a week in our service.' Can you imagine my astonishment when I heard that Miss Redwood's view of Mrs. Rook was my view? Finding that I still said nothing, the old lady entered into details: 'We arranged, sir,' (she persisted in calling me 'sir,' with the formal politeness of the old school)—'we arranged, sir, that Mrs. Rook and her husband should occupy the bedroom next to mine, so that I might have her near me in case of my being taken ill in the night. She looked at the door between the two rooms—suspicious! She asked if there was any objection to her changing to another room—suspicious! suspicious! Pray take a seat, sir, and tell me which Mrs. Rook is guilty of— theft or murder?'"

"What a dreadful old woman!" Emily exclaimed. "How did you answer her?"

"I told her, with perfect truth, that I knew nothing of Mrs. Rook's secrets. Miss Redwood's humor took a satirical turn. 'Allow me to ask, sir, whether your eyes were shut, when our housekeeper found herself unexpectedly in your presence?' I referred the old lady to her brother's opinion. 'Sir Jervis believes Mrs. Rook to be crazy,' I reminded her. 'Do you refuse to trust me, sir?' 'I have no information to give you, madam.' She waved her skinny old hand in the direction of the door. I made my bow, and retired. She called me back. 'Old women used to be prophets, sir, in the bygone time,' she said. 'I will venture on a prediction. You will be the means of depriving us of the services of Mr. and Mrs. Rook. If you will be so good as to stay here a day or two longer you will hear that those two people have given us notice to quit. It will be her doing, mind—he is a mere cypher. I wish you good-morning.' Will you believe me, when I tell you that the prophecy was fulfilled?"

"Do you mean that they actually left the house?"

"They would certainly have left the house," Alban answered, "if Sir Jervis had not insisted on receiving the customary month's warning. He asserted his resolution by locking up the old husband in the pantry. His sister's suspicions never entered his head; the housekeeper's conduct (he said) simply proved that she was, what he had always considered her to be, crazy. 'A capital servant, in spite of that drawback,' he remarked; 'and you will see, I shall bring her to her senses.' The impression produced on me was naturally of a very different kind. While I was still uncertain how to entrap Mrs. Rook into confirming my suspicions, she herself had saved me the trouble. She had placed her own guilty interpretation on my appearance in the house—I had driven her away!"

Emily remained true to her resolution not to let her curiosity embarrass Alban again. But the unexpressed question was in her thoughts—"Of what guilt does he suspect Mrs. Rook? And, when he first felt his suspicions, was my father in his mind?"

Alban proceeded.

"I had only to consider next, whether I could hope to make any further discoveries, if I continued to be Sir Jervis's guest. The object of my journey had been gained; and I had no desire to be employed as picture-cleaner. Miss Redwood assisted me in arriving at a decision. I was sent for to speak to her again. The success of her prophecy had raised her spirits. She asked, with ironical humility, if I proposed to honor them by still remaining their guest, after the disturbance that I had provoked. I answered that I proposed to leave by the first train the next morning. 'Will it be convenient for you to travel to some place at a good distance from this part of the world?' she asked. I had my own reasons for going to London, and said so. 'Will you mention that to my brother this evening, just before we sit down to dinner?' she continued. 'And will you tell him plainly that you have no intention of returning to the North? I shall make use of Mrs. Rook's arm, as usual, to help me downstairs—and I will take care that she hears what you say. Without venturing on another prophecy, I will only hint to you that I have my own idea of what will happen; and I should like you to see for yourself, sir, whether my anticipations are realized.' Need I tell you that this strange old woman proved to be right once more? Mr. Rook was released; Mrs. Rook made humble apologies, and laid the whole blame on her husband's temper: and Sir Jervis bade me remark that his method had succeeded in bringing the housekeeper to her senses. Such were the results produced by the announcement of my departure for London—purposely made in Mrs. Rook's hearing. Do you agree with me, that my journey to Northumberland has not been taken in vain?"

Once more, Emily felt the necessity of controlling herself.

133

Alban had said that he had "reasons of his own for going to London." Could she venture to ask him what those reasons were? She could only persist in restraining her curiosity, and conclude that he would have mentioned his motive, if it had been (as she had at one time supposed) connected with herself. It was a wise decision. No earthly consideration would have induced Alban to answer her, if she had put the question to him.

All doubt of the correctness of his own first impression was now at an end; he was convinced that Mrs. Rook had been an accomplice in the crime committed, in 1877, at the village inn. His object in traveling to London was to consult the newspaper narrative of the murder. He, too, had been one of the readers at the Museum—had examined the back numbers of the newspaper—and had arrived at the conclusion that Emily's father had been the victim of the crime. Unless he found means to prevent it, her course of reading would take her from the year 1876 to the year 1877, and under that date, she would see the fatal report, heading the top of a column, and printed in conspicuous type.

In the meanwhile Emily had broken the silence, before it could lead to embarrassing results, by asking if Alban had seen Mrs. Rook again, on the morning when he left Sir Jervis's house.

"There was nothing to be gained by seeing her," Alban replied. "Now that she and her husband had decided to remain at Redwood Hall, I knew where to find her in case of necessity. As it happened I saw nobody, on the morning of my departure, but Sir Jervis himself. He still held to his idea of having his pictures cleaned for nothing. 'If you can't do it yourself,' he said, 'couldn't you teach my secretary?' He described the lady whom he had engaged in your place as a 'nasty middle-aged woman with a perpetual cold in her head.' At the same time (he remarked) he was a friend to the women, 'because he got them cheap.' I declined to teach the unfortunate secretary the art of picture-cleaning. Finding me determined, Sir Jervis was quite ready to say good-by. But he made use of me to the last. He employed me as postman and saved a stamp. The letter addressed to you arrived at breakfast-time. Sir Jervis said, 'You are going to London; suppose you take it with you?'"

"Did he tell you that there was a letter of his own inclosed in the envelope?"

"No. When he gave me the envelope it was already sealed."

Emily at once handed to him Sir Jervis's letter. "That will tell you who employs me at the Museum, and what my work is," she said.

He looked through the letter, and at once offered—eagerly offered—to help her.

"I have been a student in the reading-room at intervals, for years past," he said. "Let me assist you, and I shall have something to do in my holiday time." He was so anxious to be of use that he interrupted her before she could thank him. "Let us take alternate years," he suggested. "Did you not tell me you were searching the newspapers published in eighteen hundred and seventy-six?"

"Yes."

"Very well. I will take the next year. You will take the year after. And so on."

"You are very kind," she answered—"but I should like to propose an improvement on your plan."

"What improvement?" he asked, rather sharply.

"If you will leave the five years, from 'seventy-six to 'eighty-one, entirely to me," she resumed, "and take the next five years, reckoning backward from 'seventy-six, you will help me to better purpose. Sir Jervis expects me to look for reports of Central American Explorations, through the newspapers of the last forty years; and I have taken the liberty of limiting the heavy task imposed on me. When I report my progress to my employer, I should like to say that I have got through ten years of the examination, instead of five. Do you see any objection to the arrangement I propose?"

He proved to be obstinate—incomprehensibly obstinate.

"Let us try my plan to begin with," he insisted. "While you are looking through 'seventy-six, let me be at work on 'seventy-seven. If you still prefer your own arrangement, after that, I will follow your suggestion with pleasure. Is it agreed?"

Her acute perception—enlightened by his tone as wall as by his words—detected something under the surface already.

"It isn't agreed until I understand you a little better," she quietly replied. "I fancy you have some object of your own in view."

She spoke with her usual directness of look and manner. He was evidently disconcerted. "What makes you think so?" he asked.

"My own experience of myself makes me think so," she answered. "If I had some object to gain, I should persist in carrying it out—like you."

"Does that mean, Miss Emily, that you refuse to give way?"

"No, Mr. Morris. I have made myself disagreeable, but I know when to stop. I trust you—and submit."

If he had been less deeply interested in the accomplishment of his merciful design, he might have viewed Emily's sudden submission with some distrust. As it was, his eagerness to prevent her from discovering the narrative of the murder hurried him into an act of indiscretion. He made an excuse to leave her immediately, in the fear that she might change her mind.

"I have inexcusably prolonged my visit," he said. "If I presume on your kindness in this way, how can I hope that you will receive me again? We meet to-morrow in the reading-room."

He hastened away, as if he was afraid to let her say a word in reply.

Emily reflected.

"Is there something he doesn't want me to see, in the news of the year 'seventy-seven?" The one explanation which suggested itself to her mind assumed that form of expression—and the one method of satisfying her curiosity that seemed likely to succeed, was to search the volume which Alban had reserved for his own reading.

For two days they pursued their task together, seated at opposite desks.

On the third day Emily was absent.

Was she ill?

She was at the library in the City, consulting the file of The Times for the year 1877.

CHAPTER XXIV. MR. ROOK.

Emily's first day in the City library proved to be a day wasted.

She began reading the back numbers of the newspaper at haphazard, without any definite idea of what she was looking for. Conscious of the error into which her own impatience had led her, she was at a loss how to retrace the false step that she had taken. But two alternatives presented themselves: either to abandon the hope of making any discovery—or to attempt to penetrate Alban 's motives by means of pure guesswork, pursued in the dark.

How was the problem to be solved? This serious question troubled her all through the evening, and kept her awake when she went to bed. In despair of her capacity to remove the obstacle that stood in her way, she decided on resuming her regular work at the Museum—turned her pillow to get at the cool side of it—and made up her mind to go asleep.

In the case of the wiser animals, the Person submits to Sleep. It is only the superior human being who tries the hopeless experiment of making Sleep submit to the Person. Wakeful on the warm side of the pillow, Emily remained wakeful on the cool side—thinking again and again of the interview with Alban which had ended so strangely.

Little by little, her mind passed the limits which had restrained it thus far. Alban's conduct in keeping his secret, in the matter of the newspapers, now began to associate itself with Alban's conduct in keeping that other secret, which concealed from her his suspicions of Mrs. Rook.

She started up in bed as the next possibility occurred to her.

In speaking of the disaster which had compelled Mr. and Mrs. Rook to close the inn, Cecilia had alluded to an inquest held on the body of the murdered man. Had the inquest been mentioned in the newspapers, at the time? And had Alban seen something in the report, which concerned Mrs. Rook?

Led by the new light that had fallen on her, Emily returned to the library the next morning with a definite idea of what she had to look for. Incapable of giving exact dates, Cecilia had informed her that the crime was committed "in the autumn." The month to choose, in beginning her examination, was therefore the month of August.

No discovery rewarded her. She tried September, next—with the same unsatisfactory results. On Monday the first of October she met with some encouragement at last. At the top of a column appeared a telegraphic summary of all that was then known of the crime. In the number for the Wednesday following, she found a full report of the proceedings at the inquest.

Passing over the preliminary remarks, Emily read the evidence with the closest attention.

The jury having viewed the body, and having visited an outhouse in which the murder had been committed, the first witness called was Mr. Benjamin Rook, landlord of the Hand-in-Hand inn.

On the evening of Sunday, September 30th, 1877, two gentlemen presented themselves at Mr. Rook's house, under circumstances which especially excited his attention.

The youngest of the two was short, and of fair complexion. He carried a knapsack, like a gentleman on a pedestrian excursion; his manners were pleasant; and he was decidedly good-looking. His companion, older, taller, and darker—and a finer man altogether—leaned on his arm and seemed to be exhausted. In every respect they were singularly unlike each other. The younger stranger (excepting little half-whiskers) was clean shaved. The elder wore his whole beard. Not knowing their names, the landlord distinguished them, at the coroner's suggestion, as the fair gentleman, and the dark gentleman.

It was raining when the two arrived at the inn. There were signs in the heavens of a stormy night.

On accosting the landlord, the fair gentleman volunteered the following statement:

Approaching the village, he had been startled by seeing the dark gentleman (a total stranger to him) stretched prostrate on the grass at the roadside—so far as he could judge, in a swoon. Having a flask with brandy in it, he revived the fainting man, and led him to the inn.

This statement was confirmed by a laborer, who was on his way to the village at the time.

The dark gentleman endeavored to explain what had happened to him. He had, as he supposed, allowed too long a time to pass (after an early breakfast that morning), without taking food: he could only attribute the fainting fit to that cause. He was not liable to fainting fits. What purpose (if any) had brought him into the neighborhood of Zeeland, he did not state. He had no intention of remaining at the inn, except for refreshment; and he asked for a carriage to take him to the railway station.

The fair gentleman, seeing the signs of bad weather, desired to remain in Mr. Rook's house for the night, and proposed to resume his walking tour the next day.

Excepting the case of supper, which could be easily provided, the landlord had no choice but to disappoint both his guests. In his small way of business, none of his customers wanted to hire a carriage—even if he could have afforded to keep one. As for beds, the few rooms which the inn contained were all engaged; including even the room occupied by himself and his wife. An exhibition of agricultural implements had been opened in the neighborhood, only two days since; and a public competition between rival machines was to be decided on the coming Monday. Not only was the Hand-in-Hand inn crowded, but even the accommodation offered by the nearest town had proved barely sufficient to meet the public demand.

The gentlemen looked at each other and agreed that there was no help for it but to hurry the supper, and walk to the railway station—a distance of between five and six miles—in time to catch the last train.

While the meal was being prepared, the rain held off for a while. The dark man asked his way to the post-office and went out by himself.

He came back in about ten minutes, and sat down afterward to supper with his companion. Neither the landlord, nor any other person in the public room, noticed any change in him on his return. He was a grave, quiet sort of person, and (unlike the other one) not much of a talker.

As the darkness came on, the rain fell again heavily; and the heavens were black.

A flash of lightning startled the gentlemen when they went to the window to look out: the thunderstorm began. It was simply impossible that two strangers to the neighborhood could find their way to the station, through storm and darkness, in time to catch the train. With or without bedrooms, they must remain at the inn for the night. Having already given up their own room to their lodgers, the landlord and landlady had no other place to sleep in than the kitchen. Next to the kitchen, and communicating with it by a door, was an outhouse; used, partly as a scullery, partly as a lumber-room. There was an old truckle-bed among the lumber, on which one of the gentlemen might rest. A mattress on the floor could be provided for the other. After adding a table and a basin, for the purposes of the toilet, the accommodation which Mr. Rook was able to offer came to an end.

The travelers agreed to occupy this makeshift bed-chamber.

The thunderstorm passed away; but the rain continued to fall heavily. Soon after eleven the guests at the inn retired for the night. There was some little discussion between the two travelers, as to which of them should take possession of the truckle-bed. It was put an end to by the fair gentleman, in his own pleasant way. He proposed to "toss up for it"—and he lost. The dark gentleman went to bed first; the fair gentleman followed, after waiting a while. Mr. Rook took his knapsack into the outhouse; and arranged on the table his appliances for the toilet—contained in a leather roll, and including a razor—ready for use in the morning.

Having previously barred the second door of the outhouse, which led into the yard, Mr. Rook fastened the other door, the lock and bolts of which were on the side of the kitchen. He then secured the house door, and the shutters over the lower windows. Returning to the kitchen, he noticed that the time was ten minutes short of midnight. Soon afterward, he and his wife went to bed.

Nothing happened to disturb Mr. and Mrs. Rook during the night.

At a quarter to seven the next morning, he got up; his wife being still asleep. He had been instructed to wake the gentlemen early; and he knocked at their door. Receiving no answer, after repeatedly knocking, he opened the door and stepped into the outhouse.

At this point in his evidence, the witness's recollections appeared to overpower him. "Give me a moment, gentlemen," he said to the jury. "I have had a dreadful fright; and I don't believe I shall get over it for the rest of my life."

The coroner helped him by a question: "What did you see when you opened the door?"

Mr. Rook answered: "I saw the dark man stretched out on his bed—dead, with a frightful wound in his throat. I saw an open razor, stained with smears of blood, at his side."

"Did you notice the door, leading into the yard?"

"It was wide open, sir. When I was able to look round me, the other traveler—I mean the man with the fair complexion, who carried the knapsack—was nowhere to be seen."

"What did you do, after making these discoveries?"

"I closed the yard door. Then I locked the other door, and put the key in my pocket. After that I roused the servant, and sent him to the constable—who lived near to us—while I ran for the doctor, whose house was at the other end of our village. The doctor sent his groom, on horseback, to the police-office in the town. When I returned to the inn, the constable was there—and he and the police took the matter into their own hands."

"You have nothing more to tell us?"

"Nothing more."

CHAPTER XXV. "J. B."

Mr. Rook having completed his evidence, the police authorities were the next witnesses examined.

They had not found the slightest trace of any attempt to break into the house in the night. The murdered man's gold watch and chain were discovered under his pillow. On examining his clothes the money was found in his purse, and the gold studs and sleeve buttons were left in his shirt. But his pocketbook (seen by witnesses who had not yet been examined) was missing. The search for visiting cards and letters had proved to be fruitless. Only the initials, "J. B.," were marked on his linen. He had brought no luggage with him to the inn. Nothing could be found which led to the discovery of his name or of the purpose which had taken him into that part of the country.

The police examined the outhouse next, in search of circumstantial evidence against the missing man.

He must have carried away his knapsack, when he took to flight, but he had been (probably) in too great a hurry to look for his razor—or perhaps too terrified to touch it, if it had attracted his notice. The leather roll, and the other articles used for his toilet, had been taken away. Mr. Rook identified the blood-stained razor. He had noticed overnight the name of the Belgian city, "Liege," engraved on it.

The yard was the next place inspected. Foot-steps were found on the muddy earth up to the wall. But the road on the other side had been recently mended with stones, and the trace of the fugitive was lost. Casts had been taken of the footsteps; and no other means of discovery had been left untried. The authorities in London had also been communicated with by telegraph.

The doctor being called, described a personal peculiarity, which he had noticed at the post-mortem examination, and which might lead to the identification of the murdered man.

As to the cause of death, the witness said it could be stated in two words. The internal jugular vein had been cut through, with such violence, judging by the appearances, that the wound could not have been inflicted, in the act of suicide, by the hand of the deceased person. No other injuries, and no sign of disease, was found on the body. The one cause of death had been Hemorrhage; and the one peculiarity which called for notice had been discovered in the mouth. Two of the front teeth, in the upper jaw, were false. They had been so admirably made to resemble the natural teeth on either side of them, in form and color, that the witness had only hit on the discovery by accidentally touching the inner side of the gum with one of his fingers.

The landlady was examined, when the doctor had retired. Mrs. Rook was able, in answering questions put to her, to give important information, in reference to the missing pocketbook.

Before retiring to rest, the two gentlemen had paid the bill—intending to leave the inn the first thing in the morning. The traveler with the knapsack paid his share in money. The other unfortunate gentleman looked into his purse, and found only a shilling and a sixpence in it. He asked Mrs. Rook if she could change a bank-note. She told him it could be done, provided the note was for no considerable sum of money. Upon that he opened his pocketbook (which the witness described minutely) and turned out the contents on the table. After searching among many Bank of England notes, some in one pocket of the book and some in another, he found a note of the value of five pounds. He thereupon settled his bill, and received the change from Mrs. Rook—her husband being in another part of the room, attending to the guests. She noticed a letter in an envelope, and a few cards which looked (to her judgment) like visiting cards, among the bank-notes which he had turned out on the table. When she returned to him with the change, he had just put them back, and was closing the pocketbook. She saw him place it in one of the breast pockets of his coat.

The fellow-traveler who had accompanied him to the inn was present all the time, sitting on the opposite side of the table. He made a remark when he saw the notes produced. He said, "Put all that money back—don't tempt a poor man like me!" It was said laughing, as if by way of a joke.

Mrs. Rook had observed nothing more that night; had slept as soundly as usual; and had been awakened when her husband knocked at the outhouse door, according to instructions received from the gentlemen, overnight.

Three of the guests in the public room corroborated Mrs. Rook's evidence. They were respectable persons, well and widely known in that part of Hampshire. Besides these, there were two strangers staying in the house. They referred the coroner to their employers—eminent manufacturers at Sheffield and Wolverhampton—whose testimony spoke for itself.

The last witness called was a grocer in the village, who kept the post-office.

On the evening of the 30th, a dark gentleman, wearing his beard, knocked at the door, and asked for a letter addressed to "J. B., Post-office, Zeeland." The letter had arrived by that morning's post; but, being Sunday evening, the grocer requested that application might be made for it the next morning. The stranger said the letter contained news, which it was of importance to him to receive without delay. Upon this, the grocer made an exception to customary rules and gave him the letter. He read it by the light of the lamp in the passage. It must have been short, for the reading was done in a moment. He seemed to think over it for a while; and then he turned round to go out. There was nothing to notice in his look or in his manner. The witness offered a remark on the weather; and the gentleman said, "Yes, it looks like a bad night"—and so went away.

The postmaster's evidence was of importance in one respect: it suggested the motive which had brought the deceased to Zeeland. The letter addressed to "J. B." was, in all probability, the letter seen by Mrs. Rook among the contents of the pocketbook, spread out on the table.

The inquiry being, so far, at an end, the inquest was adjourned—on the chance of obtaining additional evidence, when the reported proceedings were read by the public.

....

Consulting a later number of the newspaper Emily discovered that the deceased person had been identified by a witness from London.

Henry Forth, gentleman's valet, being examined, made the following statement:

He had read the medical evidence contained in the report of the inquest; and, believing that he could identify the deceased, had been sent by his present master to assist the object of the inquiry. Ten days since, being then out of place, he had answered an advertisement. The next day, he was instructed to call at Tracey's Hotel, London, at six o'clock in the evening, and to ask for Mr. James Brown. Arriving at the hotel he saw the gentleman for a few minutes only. Mr. Brown had a friend with him. After glancing over the valet's references, he said, "I haven't time enough to speak to you this evening. Call here to-morrow morning at nine o'clock." The gentleman who was present laughed, and said, "You won't be up!" Mr. Brown answered, "That won't matter; the man can come to my bedroom, and let me see how he understands his duties, on trial." At nine the next morning, Mr. Brown was reported to be still in bed; and the witness was informed of the number of the room. He knocked at the door. A drowsy voice inside said something, which he interpreted as meaning "Come in." He went in. The toilet-table was on his left hand, and the bed (with the lower curtain drawn) was on his right. He saw on the table a tumbler with a little water in it, and with two false teeth in the water. Mr. Brown started up in bed—looked at him furiously—abused him for daring to enter the room—and shouted to him to "get out." The witness, not accustomed to be treated in that way, felt naturally indignant, and at once withdrew—but not before he had plainly seen the vacant place which the false teeth had been made to fill. Perhaps Mr. Brown had forgotten that he had left his teeth on the table. Or perhaps he (the valet) had misunderstood what had been said to him when he knocked at the door. Either way, it seemed to be plain enough that the gentleman resented the discovery of his false teeth by a stranger.

Having concluded his statement the witness proceeded to identify the remains of the deceased.

He at once recognized the gentleman named James Brown, whom he had twice seen—once in the evening, and again the next morning—at Tracey's Hotel. In answer to further inquiries, he declared that he knew nothing of the family, or of the place of residence, of the deceased. He complained to the proprietor of the hotel of the rude treatment that he had received, and asked if Mr. Tracey knew anything of Mr. James Brown. Mr. Tracey knew nothing of him. On consulting the hotel book it was found that he had given notice to leave, that afternoon.

Before returning to London, the witness produced references which gave him an excellent character. He also left the address of the master who had engaged him three days since.

The last precaution adopted was to have the face of the corpse photographed, before the coffin was closed. On the same day the jury agreed on their verdict: "Willful murder against some person unknown."

....

Two days later, Emily found a last allusion to the crime—extracted from the columns of the South Hampshire Gazette.

A relative of the deceased, seeing the report of the adjourned inquest, had appeared (accompanied by a medical gentleman); had seen the photograph; and had declared the identification by Henry Forth to be correct.

Among other particulars, now communicated for the first time, it was stated that the late Mr. James Brown had been unreasonably sensitive on the subject of his false teeth, and that the one member of his family who knew of his wearing them was the relative who now claimed his remains.

The claim having been established to the satisfaction of the authorities, the corpse was removed by railroad the same day. No further light had been thrown on the murder. The Handbill offering the reward, and describing the suspected man, had failed to prove of any assistance to the investigations of the police.

146

From that date, no further notice of the crime committed at the Hand-in-Hand inn appeared in the public journals.

....

Emily closed the volume which she had been consulting, and thankfully acknowledged the services of the librarian.

The new reader had excited this gentleman's interest. Noticing how carefully she examined the numbers of the old newspaper, he looked at her, from time to time, wondering whether it was good news or bad of which she was in search. She read steadily and continuously; but she never rewarded his curiosity by any outward sign of the impression that had been produced on her. When she left the room there was nothing to remark in her manner; she looked quietly thoughtful—and that was all.

The librarian smiled—amused by his own folly. Because a stranger's appearance had attracted him, he had taken it for granted that circumstances of romantic interest must be connected with her visit to the library. Far from misleading him, as he supposed, his fancy might have been employed to better purpose, if it had taken a higher flight still—and had associated Emily with the fateful gloom of tragedy, in place of the brighter interest of romance.

There, among the ordinary readers of the day, was a dutiful and affectionate daughter following the dreadful story of the death of her father by murder, and believing it to be the story of a stranger—because she loved and trusted the person whose short-sighted mercy had deceived her. That very discovery, the dread of which had shaken the good doctor's firm nerves, had forced Alban to exclude from his confidence the woman whom he loved, and had driven the faithful old servant from the bedside of her dying mistress—that very discovery Emily had now made, with a face which never changed color, and a heart which beat at ease. Was the deception that had won this cruel victory over truth destined still to triumph in the days which were to come? Yes—if the life of earth is a foretaste of the life of hell. No—if a lie is a lie, be the merciful motive for the falsehood what it may. No—if all deceit contains in it the seed of retribution, to be ripened inexorably in the lapse of time.

CHAPTER XXVI. MOTHER EVE.

The servant received Emily, on her return from the library, with a sly smile. "Here he is again, miss, waiting to see you."

She opened the parlor door, and revealed Alban Morris, as restless as ever, walking up and down the room.

"When I missed you at the Museum, I was afraid you might be ill," he said. "Ought I to have gone away, when my anxiety was relieved? Shall I go away now?"

"You must take a chair, Mr. Morris, and hear what I have to say for myself. When you left me after your last visit, I suppose I felt the force of example. At any rate I, like you, had my suspicions. I have been trying to confirm them—and I have failed."

He paused, with the chair in his hand. "Suspicions of Me?" he asked.

"Certainly! Can you guess how I have been employed for the last two days? No—not even your ingenuity can do that. I have been hard at work, in another reading-room, consulting the same back numbers of the same newspaper, which you have been examining at the British Museum. There is my confession—and now we will have some tea."

She moved to the fireplace, to ring the bell, and failed to see the effect produced on Alban by those lightly-uttered words. The common phrase is the only phrase that can describe it. He was thunderstruck.

"Yes," she resumed, "I have read the report of the inquest. If I know nothing else, I know that the murder at Zeeland can't be the discovery which you are bent on keeping from me. Don't be alarmed for the preservation of your secret! I am too much discouraged to try again."

The servant interrupted them by answering the bell; Alban once more escaped detection. Emily gave her orders with an approach to the old gayety of her school days. "Tea, as soon as possible—and let us have the new cake. Are you too much of a man, Mr. Morris, to like cake?"

In this state of agitation, he was unreasonably irritated by that playful question. "There is one thing I like better than cake," he said; "and that one thing is a plain explanation."

His tone puzzled her. "Have I said anything to offend you?" she asked. "Surely you can make allowance for a girl's curiosity? Oh, you shall have your explanation—and, what is more, you shall have it without reserve!"

She was as good as her word. What she had thought, and what she had planned, when he left her after his last visit, was frankly and fully told. "If you wonder how I discovered the library," she went on, "I must refer you to my aunt's lawyer. He lives in the City—and I wrote to him to help me. I don't consider that my time has been wasted. Mr. Morris, we owe an apology to Mrs. Rook."

Alban's astonishment, when he heard this, forced its way to expression in words. "What can you possibly mean?" he asked.

The tea was brought in before Emily could reply. She filled the cups, and sighed as she looked at the cake. "If Cecilia was here, how she would enjoy it!" With that complimentary tribute to her friend, she handed a slice to Alban. He never even noticed it.

"We have both of us behaved most unkindly to Mrs. Rook," she resumed. "I can excuse your not seeing it; for I should not have seen it either, but for the newspaper. While I was reading, I had an opportunity of thinking over what we said and did, when the poor woman's behavior so needlessly offended us. I was too excited to think, at the time—and, besides, I had been upset, only the night before, by what Miss Jethro said to me."

Alban started. "What has Miss Jethro to do with it?" he asked.

"Nothing at all," Emily answered. "She spoke to me of her own private affairs. A long story—and you wouldn't be interested in it. Let me finish what I had to say. Mrs. Rook was naturally reminded of the murder, when she heard that my name was Brown; and she must certainly have been struck— as I was—by the coincidence of my father's death taking place at the same time when his unfortunate namesake was killed. Doesn't this sufficiently account for her agitation when she looked at the locket? We first took her by

149

surprise: and then we suspected her of Heaven knows what, because the poor creature didn't happen to have her wits about her, and to remember at the right moment what a very common name 'James Brown' is. Don't you see it as I do?"

"I see that you have arrived at a remarkable change of opinion, since we spoke of the subject in the garden at school."

"In my place, you would have changed your opinion too. I shall write to Mrs. Rook by tomorrow's post."

Alban heard her with dismay. "Pray be guided by my advice!" he said earnestly. "Pray don't write that letter!"

"Why not?"

It was too late to recall the words which he had rashly allowed to escape him. How could he reply?

To own that he had not only read what Emily had read, but had carefully copied the whole narrative and considered it at his leisure, appeared to be simply impossible after what he had now heard. Her peace of mind depended absolutely on his discretion. In this serious emergency, silence was a mercy, and silence was a lie. If he remained silent, might the mercy be trusted to atone for the lie? He was too fond of Emily to decide that question fairly, on its own merits. In other words, he shrank from the terrible responsibility of telling her the truth.

"Isn't the imprudence of writing to such a person as Mrs. Rook plain enough to speak for itself?" he suggested cautiously.

"Not to me."

She made that reply rather obstinately. Alban seemed (in her view) to be trying to prevent her from atoning for an act of injustice. Besides, he despised her cake. "I want to know why you object," she said; taking back the neglected slice, and eating it herself.

"I object," Alban answered, "because Mrs. Rook is a coarse presuming woman. She may pervert your letter to some use of her own, which you may have reason to regret."

"Is that all?"

"Isn't it enough?"

"It may be enough for you. When I have done a person an injury, and wish to make an apology, I don't think it necessary to inquire whether the person's manners happen to be vulgar or not."

Alban's patience was still equal to any demands that she could make on it. "I can only offer you advice which is honestly intended for your own good," he gently replied.

"You would have more influence over me, Mr. Morris, if you were a little readier to take me into your confidence. I daresay I am wrong—but I don't like following advice which is given to me in the dark."

It was impossible to offend him. "Very naturally," he said; "I don't blame you."

Her color deepened, and her voice rose. Alban's patient adherence to his own view—so courteously and considerately urged—was beginning to try her temper. "In plain words," she rejoined, "I am to believe that you can't be mistaken in your judgment of another person."

There was a ring at the door of the cottage while she was speaking. But she was too warmly interested in confuting Alban to notice it.

He was quite willing to be confuted. Even when she lost her temper, she was still interesting to him. "I don't expect you to think me infallible," he said. "Perhaps you will remember that I have had some experience. I am unfortunately older than you are."

"Oh if wisdom comes with age," she smartly reminded him, "your friend Miss Redwood is old enough to be your mother—and she suspected Mrs. Rook of murder, because the poor woman looked at a door, and disliked being in the next room to a fidgety old maid."

Alban's manner changed: he shrank from that chance allusion to doubts and fears which he dare not acknowledge. "Let us talk of something else," he said.

She looked at him with a saucy smile. "Have I driven you into a corner at last? And is that your way of getting out of it?"

Even his endurance failed. "Are you trying to provoke me?" he asked. "Are you no better than other women? I wouldn't have believed it of you, Emily."

"Emily?" She repeated the name in a tone of surprise, which reminded him that he had addressed her with familiarity at a most inappropriate time—the time when they were on the point of a quarrel. He felt the implied reproach too keenly to be able to answer her with composure.

"I think of Emily—I love Emily—my one hope is that Emily may love me. Oh, my dear, is there no excuse if I forget to call you 'Miss' when you distress me?"

All that was tender and true in her nature secretly took his part. She would have followed that better impulse, if he had only been calm enough to understand her momentary silence, and to give her time. But the temper of a gentle and generous man, once roused, is slow to subside. Alban abruptly left his chair. "I had better go!" he said.

"As you please," she answered. "Whether you go, Mr. Morris, or whether you stay, I shall write to Mrs. Rook."

The ring at the bell was followed by the appearance of a visitor. Doctor Allday opened the door, just in time to hear Emily's last words. Her vehemence seemed to amuse him.

"Who is Mrs. Rook?" he asked.

"A most respectable person," Emily answered indignantly; "housekeeper to Sir Jervis Redwood. You needn't sneer at her, Doctor Allday! She has not always been in service—she was landlady of the inn at Zeeland."

The doctor, about to put his hat on a chair, paused. The inn at Zeeland

152

reminded him of the Handbill, and of the visit of Miss Jethro.

"Why are you so hot over it?" he inquired

"Because I detest prejudice!" With this assertion of liberal feeling she pointed to Alban, standing quietly apart at the further end of the room. "There is the most prejudiced man living—he hates Mrs. Rook. Would you like to be introduced to him? You're a philosopher; you may do him some good. Doctor Allday—Mr. Alban Morris."

The doctor recognized the man, with the felt hat and the objectionable beard, whose personal appearance had not impressed him favorably.

Although they may hesitate to acknowledge it, there are respectable Englishmen still left, who regard a felt hat and a beard as symbols of republican disaffection to the altar and the throne. Doctor Allday's manner might have expressed this curious form of patriotic feeling, but for the associations which Emily had revived. In his present frame of mind, he was outwardly courteous, because he was inwardly suspicious. Mrs. Rook had been described to him as formerly landlady of the inn at Zeeland. Were there reasons for Mr. Morris's hostile feeling toward this woman which might be referable to the crime committed in her house that might threaten Emily's tranquillity if they were made known? It would not be amiss to see a little more of Mr. Morris, on the first convenient occasion.

"I am glad to make your acquaintance, sir."

"You are very kind, Doctor Allday."

The exchange of polite conventionalities having been accomplished, Alban approached Emily to take his leave, with mingled feelings of regret and anxiety—regret for having allowed himself to speak harshly; anxiety to part with her in kindness.

"Will you forgive me for differing from you?" It was all he could venture to say, in the presence of a stranger.

"Oh, yes!" she said quietly.

"Will you think again, before you decide?"

"Certainly, Mr. Morris. But it won't alter my opinion, if I do."

The doctor, hearing what passed between them, frowned. On what subject had they been differing? And what opinion did Emily decline to alter?

Alban gave it up. He took her hand gently. "Shall I see you at the Museum, to-morrow?" he asked.

She was politely indifferent to the last. "Yes—unless something happens to keep me at home."

The doctor's eyebrows still expressed disapproval. For what object was the meeting proposed? And why at a museum?

"Good-afternoon, Doctor Allday."

"Good-afternoon, sir."

For a moment after Alban's departure, the doctor stood irresolute. Arriving suddenly at a decision, he snatched up his hat, and turned to Emily in a hurry.

"I bring you news, my dear, which will surprise you. Who do you think has just left my house? Mrs. Ellmother! Don't interrupt me. She has made up her mind to go out to service again. Tired of leading an idle life—that's her own account of it—and asks me to act as her reference."

"Did you consent?"

"Consent! If I act as her reference, I shall be asked how she came to leave her last place. A nice dilemma! Either I must own that she deserted her mistress on her deathbed—or tell a lie. When I put it to her in that way, she walked out of the house in dead silence. If she applies to you next, receive her as I did—or decline to see her, which would be better still."

"Why am I to decline to see her?"

"In consequence of her behavior to your aunt, to be sure! No: I have said all I wanted to say—and I have no time to spare for answering idle questions. Good-by."

Socially-speaking, doctors try the patience of their nearest and dearest friends, in this respect—they are almost always in a hurry. Doctor Allday's precipitate departure did not tend to soothe Emily's irritated nerves. She began to find excuses for Mrs. Ellmother in a spirit of pure contradiction. The old servant's behavior might admit of justification: a friendly welcome might persuade her to explain herself. "If she applies to me," Emily determined, "I shall certainly receive her."

Having arrived at this resolution, her mind reverted to Alban.

Some of the sharp things she had said to him, subjected to after-reflection in solitude, failed to justify themselves. Her better sense began to reproach her. She tried to silence that unwelcome monitor by laying the blame on Alban. Why had he been so patient and so good? What harm was there in his calling her "Emily"? If he had told her to call him by his Christian name, she might have done it. How noble he looked, when he got up to go away; he was actually handsome! Women may say what they please and write what they please: their natural instinct is to find their master in a man—especially when they like him. Sinking lower and lower in her own estimation, Emily tried to turn the current of her thoughts in another direction. She took up a book—opened it, looked into it, threw it across the room.

If Alban had returned at that moment, resolved on a reconciliation—if he had said, "My dear, I want to see you like yourself again; will you give me a kiss, and make it up"—would he have left her crying, when he went away? She was crying now.

CHAPTER XXVII. MENTOR AND TELEMACHUS.

If Emily's eyes could have followed Alban as her thoughts were following him, she would have seen him stop before he reached the end of the road in which the cottage stood. His heart was full of tenderness and sorrow: the longing to return to her was more than he could resist. It would be easy to wait, within view of the gate, until the doctor's visit came to an end. He had just decided to go back and keep watch—when he heard rapid footsteps approaching. There (devil take him!) was the doctor himself.

"I have something to say to you, Mr. Morris. Which way are you walking?"

"Any way," Alban answered—not very graciously.

"Then let us take the turning that leads to my house. It's not customary for strangers, especially when they happen to be Englishmen, to place confidence in each other. Let me set the example of violating that rule. I want to speak to you about Miss Emily. May I take your arm? Thank you. At my age, girls in general—unless they are my patients—are not objects of interest to me. But that girl at the cottage—I daresay I am in my dotage—I tell you, sir, she has bewitched me! Upon my soul, I could hardly be more anxious about her, if I was her father. And, mind, I am not an affectionate man by nature. Are you anxious about her too?"

"Yes."

"In what way?"

"In what way are you anxious, Doctor Allday?"

The doctor smiled grimly.

"You don't trust me? Well, I have promised to set the example. Keep your mask on, sir—mine is off, come what may of it. But, observe: if you repeat what I am going to say—"

Alban would hear no more. "Whatever you may say, Doctor Allday, is trusted to my honor. If you doubt my honor, be so good as to let go my arm—I am not walking your way."

The doctor's hand tightened its grasp. "That little flourish of temper, my dear sir, is all I want to set me at my ease. I feel I have got hold of the right man. Now answer me this. Have you ever heard of a person named Miss Jethro?"

Alban suddenly came to a standstill.

"All right!" said the doctor. "I couldn't have wished for a more satisfactory reply."

"Wait a minute," Alban interposed. "I know Miss Jethro as a teacher at

Miss Ladd's school, who left her situation suddenly—and I know no more."

The doctor's peculiar smile made its appearance again.

"Speaking in the vulgar tone," he said, "you seem to be in a hurry to wash your hands of Miss Jethro."

"I have no reason to feel any interest in her," Alban replied.

"Don't be too sure of that, my friend. I have something to tell you which may alter your opinion. That ex-teacher at the school, sir, knows how the late Mr. Brown met his death, and how his daughter has been deceived about it."

Alban listened with surprise—and with some little doubt, which he thought it wise not to acknowledge.

"The report of the inquest alludes to a 'relative' who claimed the body," he said. "Was that 'relative' the person who deceived Miss Emily? And was the person her aunt?"

"I must leave you to take your own view," Doctor Allday replied. "A promise binds me not to repeat the information that I have received. Setting that aside, we have the same object in view—and we must take care not to get in each other's way. Here is my house. Let us go in, and make a clean breast of it on both sides."

Established in the safe seclusion of his study, the doctor set the example of confession in these plain terms:

"We only differ in opinion on one point," he said. "We both think it likely (from our experience of the women) that the suspected murderer had an accomplice. I say the guilty person is Miss Jethro. You say—Mrs. Rook."

"When you have read my copy of the report," Alban answered, "I think you will arrive at my conclusion. Mrs. Rook might have entered the outhouse in which the two men slept, at any time during the night, while her husband was asleep. The jury believed her when she declared that she never woke till the morning. I don't."

"I am open to conviction, Mr. Morris. Now about the future. Do you

157

mean to go on with your inquiries?"

"Even if I had no other motive than mere curiosity," Alban answered, "I think I should go on. But I have a more urgent purpose in view. All that I have done thus far, has been done in Emily's interests. My object, from the first, has been to preserve her from any association—in the past or in the future—with the woman whom I believe to have been concerned in her father's death. As I have already told you, she is innocently doing all she can, poor thing, to put obstacles in my way."

"Yes, yes," said the doctor; "she means to write to Mrs. Rook—and you have nearly quarreled about it. Trust me to take that matter in hand. I don't regard it as serious. But I am mortally afraid of what you are doing in Emily's interests. I wish you would give it up."

"Why?"

"Because I see a danger. I don't deny that Emily is as innocent of suspicion as ever. But the chances, next time, may be against us. How do you know to what lengths your curiosity may lead you? Or on what shocking discoveries you may not blunder with the best intentions? Some unforeseen accident may open her eyes to the truth, before you can prevent it. I seem to surprise you?"

"You do, indeed, surprise me."

"In the old story, my dear sir, Mentor sometimes surprised Telemachus. I am Mentor—without being, I hope, quite so long-winded as that respectable philosopher. Let me put it in two words. Emily's happiness is precious to you. Take care you are not made the means of wrecking it! Will you consent to a sacrifice, for her sake?"

"I will do anything for her sake."

"Will you give up your inquiries?"

"From this moment I have done with them!"

"Mr. Morris, you are the best friend she has."

158

"The next best friend to you, doctor."

In that fond persuasion they now parted—too eagerly devoted to Emily to look at the prospect before them in its least hopeful aspect. Both clever men, neither one nor the other asked himself if any human resistance has ever yet obstructed the progress of truth—when truth has once begun to force its way to the light.

For the second time Alban stopped, on his way home. The longing to be reconciled with Emily was not to be resisted. He returned to the cottage, only to find disappointment waiting for him. The servant reported that her young mistress had gone to bed with a bad headache.

Alban waited a day, in the hope that Emily might write to him. No letter arrived. He repeated his visit the next morning. Fortune was still against him. On this occasion, Emily was engaged.

"Engaged with a visitor?" he asked.

"Yes, sir. A young lady named Miss de Sor."

Where had he heard that name before? He remembered immediately that he had heard it at the school. Miss de Sor was the unattractive new pupil, whom the girls called Francine. Alban looked at the parlor window as he left the cottage. It was of serious importance that he should set himself right with Emily. "And mere gossip," he thought contemptuously, "stands in my way!"

If he had been less absorbed in his own interests, he might have remembered that mere gossip is not always to be despised. It has worked fatal mischief in its time.

CHAPTER XXVIII. FRANCINE.

"You're surprised to see me, of course?" Saluting Emily in those terms, Francine looked round the parlor with an air of satirical curiosity. "Dear me, what a little place to live in!"

"What brings you to London?" Emily inquired.

"You ought to know, my dear, without asking. Why did I try to make friends with you at school? And why have I been trying ever since? Because I hate you—I mean because I can't resist you—no! I mean because I hate myself for liking you. Oh, never mind my reasons. I insisted on going to London with Miss Ladd—when that horrid woman announced that she had an appointment with her lawyer. I said, 'I want to see Emily.' 'Emily doesn't like you.' 'I don't care whether she likes me or not; I want to see her.' That's the way we snap at each other, and that's how I always carry my point. Here I am, till my duenna finishes her business and fetches me. What a prospect for You! Have you got any cold meat in the house? I'm not a glutton, like Cecilia—but I'm afraid I shall want some lunch."

"Don't talk in that way, Francine!"

"Do you mean to say you're glad to see me?"

"If you were only a little less hard and bitter, I should always be glad to see you."

"You darling! (excuse my impetuosity). What are you looking at? My new dress? Do you envy me?"

"No; I admire the color—that's all."

Francine rose, and shook out her dress, and showed it from every point of view. "See how it's made: Paris, of course! Money, my dear; money will do anything—except making one learn one's lessons."

"Are you not getting on any better, Francine?"

"Worse, my sweet friend—worse. One of the masters, I am happy to say, has flatly refused to teach me any longer. 'Pupils without brains I am accustomed to,' he said in his broken English; 'but a pupil with no heart is beyond my endurance.' Ha! ha! the mouldy old refugee has an eye for character, though. No heart—there I am, described in two words."

"And proud of it," Emily remarked.

"Yes—proud of it. Stop! let me do myself justice. You consider tears a sign that one has some heart, don't you? I was very near crying last Sunday.

A popular preacher did it; no less a person that Mr. Mirabel—you look as if you had heard of him."

"I have heard of him from Cecilia."

"Is she at Brighton? Then there's one fool more in a fashionable watering place. Oh, she's in Switzerland, is she? I don't care where she is; I only care about Mr. Mirabel. We all heard he was at Brighton for his health, and was going to preach. Didn't we cram the church! As to describing him, I give it up. He is the only little man I ever admired—hair as long as mine, and the sort of beard you see in pictures. I wish I had his fair complexion and his white hands. We were all in love with him—or with his voice, which was it?—when he began to read the commandments. I wish I could imitate him when he came to the fifth commandment. He began in his deepest bass voice: 'Honor thy father—' He stopped and looked up to heaven as if he saw the rest of it there. He went on with a tremendous emphasis on the next word. 'And thy mother,' he said (as if that was quite a different thing) in a tearful, fluty, quivering voice which was a compliment to mothers in itself. We all felt it, mothers or not. But the great sensation was when he got into the pulpit. The manner in which he dropped on his knees, and hid his face in his hands, and showed his beautiful rings was, as a young lady said behind me, simply seraphic. We understood his celebrity, from that moment—I wonder whether I can remember the sermon."

"You needn't attempt it on my account," Emily said.

"My dear, don't be obstinate. Wait till you hear him."

"I am quite content to wait."

"Ah, you're just in the right state of mind to be converted; you're in a fair way to become one of his greatest admirers. They say he is so agreeable in private life; I am dying to know him.—Do I hear a ring at the bell? Is somebody else coming to see you?"

The servant brought in a card and a message.

"The person will call again, miss."

Emily looked at the name written on the card.

"Mrs. Ellmother!" she exclaimed.

"What an extraordinary name!" cried Francine. "Who is she?"

"My aunt's old servant."

"Does she want a situation?"

Emily looked at some lines of writing at the back of the card. Doctor Allday had rightly foreseen events. Rejected by the doctor, Mrs. Ellmother had no alternative but to ask Emily to help her.

"If she is out of place," Francine went on, "she may be just the sort of person I am looking for."

"You?" Emily asked, in astonishment.

Francine refused to explain until she got an answer to her question. "Tell me first," she said, "is Mrs. Ellmother engaged?"

"No; she wants an engagement, and she asks me to be her reference."

"Is she sober, honest, middle-aged, clean, steady, good-tempered, industrious?" Francine rattled on. "Has she all the virtues, and none of the vices? Is she not too good-looking, and has she no male followers? In one terrible word—will she satisfy Miss Ladd?"

"What has Miss Ladd to do with it?"

"How stupid you are, Emily! Do put the woman's card down on the table, and listen to me. Haven't I told you that one of my masters has declined to have anything more to do with me? Doesn't that help you to understand how I get on with the rest of them? I am no longer Miss Ladd's pupil, my dear. Thanks to my laziness and my temper, I am to be raised to the dignity of 'a parlor boarder.' In other words, I am to be a young lady who patronizes the school; with a room of my own, and a servant of my own. All provided for by a private arrangement between my father and Miss Ladd, before I left the West Indies. My mother was at the bottom of it, I have not the least doubt.

You don't appear to understand me."

"I don't, indeed!"

Francine considered a little. "Perhaps they were fond of you at home," she suggested.

"Say they loved me, Francine—and I loved them."

"Ah, my position is just the reverse of yours. Now they have got rid of me, they don't want me back again at home. I know as well what my mother said to my father, as if I had heard her. 'Francine will never get on at school, at her age. Try her, by all means; but make some other arrangement with Miss Ladd in case of a failure—or she will be returned on our hands like a bad shilling.' There is my mother, my anxious, affectionate mother, hit off to a T."

"She is your mother, Francine; don't forget that."

"Oh, no; I won't forget it. My cat is my kitten's mother—there! there! I won't shock your sensibilities. Let us get back to matter of fact. When I begin my new life, Miss Ladd makes one condition. My maid is to be a model of discretion—an elderly woman, not a skittish young person who will only encourage me. I must submit to the elderly woman, or I shall be sent back to the West Indies after all. How long did Mrs. Ellmother live with your aunt?"

"Twenty-five years, and more.'

"Good heavens, it's a lifetime! Why isn't this amazing creature living with you, now your aunt is dead? Did you send her away?"

"Certainly not."

"Then why did she go?"

"I don't know."

"Do you mean that she went away without a word of explanation?"

"Yes; that is exactly what I mean."

"When did she go? As soon as your aunt was dead?"

"That doesn't matter, Francine."

"In plain English, you won't tell me? I am all on fire with curiosity—and that's how you put me out! My dear, if you have the slightest regard for me, let us have the woman in here when she comes back for her answer. Somebody must satisfy me. I mean to make Mrs. Ellmother explain herself."

"I don't think you will succeed, Francine."

"Wait a little, and you will see. By-the-by, it is understood that my new position at the school gives me the privilege of accepting invitations. Do you know any nice people to whom you can introduce me?"

"I am the last person in the world who has a chance of helping you," Emily answered. "Excepting good Doctor Allday—" On the point of adding the name of Alban Morris, she checked herself without knowing why, and substituted the name of her school-friend. "And not forgetting Cecilia," she resumed, "I know nobody."

"Cecilia's a fool," Francine remarked gravely; "but now I think of it, she may be worth cultivating. Her father is a member of Parliament—and didn't I hear that he has a fine place in the country? You see, Emily, I may expect to be married (with my money), if I can only get into good society. (Don't suppose I am dependent on my father; my marriage portion is provided for in my uncle's will.) Cecilia may really be of some use to me. Why shouldn't I make a friend of her, and get introduced to her father—in the autumn, you know, when the house is full of company? Have you any idea when she is coming back?"

"No."

"Do you think of writing to her?"

"Of course!"

"Give her my kind love; and say I hope she enjoys Switzerland."

"Francine, you are positively shameless! After calling my dearest friend a fool and a glutton, you send her your love for your own selfish ends; and you expect me to help you in deceiving her! I won't do it."

"Keep your temper, my child. We are all selfish, you little goose. The only difference is—some of us own it, and some of us don't. I shall find my own way to Cecilia's good graces quite easily: the way is through her mouth. You mentioned a certain Doctor Allday. Does he give parties? And do the right sort of men go to them? Hush! I think I hear the bell again. Go to the door, and see who it is."

Emily waited, without taking any notice of this suggestion. The servant announced that "the person had called again, to know if there was any answer."

"Show her in here," Emily said.

The servant withdrew, and came back again.

"The person doesn't wish to intrude, miss; it will be quite sufficient if you will send a message by me."

Emily crossed the room to the door.

"Come in, Mrs. Ellmother," she said. "You have been too long away already. Pray come in."

CHAPTER XXIX. "BONY."

Mrs. Ellmother reluctantly entered the room.

Since Emily had seen her last, her personal appearance doubly justified the nickname by which her late mistress had distinguished her. The old servant was worn and wasted; her gown hung loose on her angular body; the big bones of her face stood out, more prominently than ever. She took Emily's offered hand doubtingly. "I hope I see you well, miss," she said—with hardly a vestige left of her former firmness of voice and manner.

"I am afraid you have been suffering from illness," Emily answered gently.

"It's the life I'm leading that wears me down; I want work and change."

Making that reply, she looked round, and discovered Francine observing her with undisguised curiosity. "You have got company with you," she said to Emily. "I had better go away, and come back another time."

Francine stopped her before she could open the door. "You mustn't go away; I wish to speak to you."

"About what, miss?"

The eyes of the two women met—one, near the end of her life, concealing under a rugged surface a nature sensitively affectionate and incorruptibly true: the other, young in years, without the virtues of youth, hard in manner and hard at heart. In silence on either side, they stood face to face; strangers brought together by the force of circumstances, working inexorably toward their hidden end.

Emily introduced Mrs. Ellmother to Francine. "It may be worth your while," she hinted, "to hear what this young lady has to say."

Mrs. Ellmother listened, with little appearance of interest in anything that a stranger might have to say: her eyes rested on the card which contained her written request to Emily. Francine, watching her closely, understood what was passing in her mind. It might be worth while to conciliate the old woman by a little act of attention. Turning to Emily, Francine pointed to the card lying on the table. "You have not attended yet to Mr. Ellmother's request," she said.

Emily at once assured Mrs. Ellmother that the request was granted. "But is it wise," she asked, "to go out to service again, at your age?"

"I have been used to service all my life, Miss Emily—that's one reason. And service may help me to get rid of my own thoughts—that's another. If you can find me a situation somewhere, you will be doing me a good turn."

"Is it useless to suggest that you might come back, and live with me?" Emily ventured to say.

Mrs. Ellmother's head sank on her breast. "Thank you kindly, miss; it is useless."

"Why is it useless?" Francine asked.

Mrs. Ellmother was silent.

"Miss de Sor is speaking to you," Emily reminded her.

"Am I to answer Miss de Sor?"

Attentively observing what passed, and placing her own construction on looks and tones, it suddenly struck Francine that Emily herself might be in Mrs. Ellmother's confidence, and that she might have reasons of her own for assuming ignorance when awkward questions were asked. For the moment at least, Francine decided on keeping her suspicions to herself.

"I may perhaps offer you the employment you want," she said to Mrs. Ellmother. "I am staying at Brighton, for the present, with the lady who was Miss Emily's schoolmistress, and I am in need of a maid. Would you be willing to consider it, if I proposed to engage you?"

"Yes, miss."

"In that case, you can hardly object to the customary inquiry. Why did you leave your last place?"

Mrs. Ellmother appealed to Emily. "Did you tell this young lady how long I remained in my last place?"

Melancholy remembrances had been revived in Emily by the turn which the talk had now taken. Francine's cat-like patience, stealthily feeling its way to its end, jarred on her nerves. "Yes," she said; "in justice to you, I have mentioned your long term of service."

Mrs. Ellmother addressed Francine. "You know, miss, that I served my late mistress for over twenty-five years. Will you please remember that—and let it be a reason for not asking me why I left my place."

Francine smiled compassionately. "My good creature, you have mentioned the very reason why I should ask. You live five-and-twenty years with your mistress—and then suddenly leave her—and you expect me to pass over this extraordinary proceeding without inquiry. Take a little time to think."

"I want no time to think. What I had in my mind, when I left Miss Letitia, is something which I refuse to explain, miss, to you, or to anybody."

She recovered some of her old firmness, when she made that reply. Francine saw the necessity of yielding—for the time at least, Emily remained silent, oppressed by remembrance of the doubts and fears which had darkened the last miserable days of her aunt's illness. She began already to regret having made Francine and Mrs. Ellmother known to each other.

"I won't dwell on what appears to be a painful subject," Francine graciously resumed. "I meant no offense. You are not angry, I hope?"

"Sorry, miss. I might have been angry, at one time. That time is over."

It was said sadly and resignedly: Emily heard the answer. Her heart ached as she looked at the old servant, and thought of the contrast between past and present. With what a hearty welcome this broken woman had been used to receive her in the bygone holiday-time! Her eyes moistened. She felt the merciless persistency of Francine, as if it had been an insult offered to herself. "Give it up!" she said sharply.

"Leave me, my dear, to manage my own business," Francine replied. "About your qualifications?" she continued, turning coolly to Mrs. Ellmother. "Can you dress hair?"

"Yes."

"I ought to tell you," Francine insisted, "that I am very particular about my hair."

"My mistress was very particular about her hair," Mrs. Ellmother answered.

"Are you a good needlewoman?"

"As good as ever I was—with the help of my spectacles."

Francine turned to Emily. "See how well we get on together. We are beginning to understand each other already. I am an odd creature, Mrs. Ellmother. Sometimes, I take sudden likings to persons—I have taken a liking to you. Do you begin to think a little better of me than you did? I hope you will produce the right impression on Miss Ladd; you shall have every assistance that I can give. I will beg Miss Ladd, as a favor to me, not to ask you that one forbidden question."

Poor Mrs. Ellmother, puzzled by the sudden appearance of Francine in the character of an eccentric young lady, the creature of genial impulse, thought it right to express her gratitude for the promised interference in her favor. "That's kind of you, miss," she said.

"No, no, only just. I ought to tell you there's one thing Miss Ladd is strict about—sweethearts. Are you quite sure," Francine inquired jocosely, "that you can answer for yourself, in that particular?"

This effort of humor produced its intended effect. Mrs. Ellmother, thrown off her guard, actually smiled. "Lord, miss, what will you say next!"

"My good soul, I will say something next that is more to the purpose. If Miss Ladd asks me why you have so unaccountably refused to be a servant again in this house, I shall take care to say that it is certainly not out of dislike to Miss Emily."

"You need say nothing of the sort," Emily quietly remarked.

"And still less," Francine proceeded, without noticing the interruption— "still less through any disagreeable remembrances of Miss Emily's aunt."

Mrs. Ellmother saw the trap that had been set for her. "It won't do, miss," she said.

"What won't do?"

"Trying to pump me."

Francine burst out laughing. Emily noticed an artificial ring in her gayety which suggested that she was exasperated, rather than amused, by the repulse which had baffled her curiosity once more.

Mrs. Ellmother reminded the merry young lady that the proposed arrangement between them had not been concluded yet. "Am I to understand, miss, that you will keep a place open for me in your service?"

"You are to understand," Francine replied sharply, "that I must have Miss Ladd's approval before I can engage you. Suppose you come to Brighton? I will pay your fare, of course."

"Never mind my fare, miss. Will you give up pumping?"

"Make your mind easy. It's quite useless to attempt pumping you. When will you come?"

Mrs. Ellmother pleaded for a little delay. "I'm altering my gowns," she said. "I get thinner and thinner—don't I, Miss Emily? My work won't be done before Thursday."

"Let us say Friday, then," Francine proposed.

"Friday!" Mrs. Ellmother exclaimed. "You forget that Friday is an unlucky day."

"I forgot that, certainly! How can you be so absurdly superstitious."

"You may call it what you like, miss. I have good reason to think as I do. I was married on a Friday—and a bitter bad marriage it turned out to be. Superstitious, indeed! You don't know what my experience has been. My only sister was one of a party of thirteen at dinner; and she died within the year. If we are to get on together nicely, I'll take that journey on Saturday, if you please."

"Anything to satisfy you," Francine agreed; "there is the address. Come in the middle of the day, and we will give you your dinner. No fear of our being thirteen in number. What will you do, if you have the misfortune to spill the salt?"

"Take a pinch between my finger and thumb, and throw it over my left shoulder," Mrs. Ellmother answered gravely. "Good-day, miss."

"Good-day."

Emily followed the departing visitor out to the hall. She had seen and heard enough to decide her on trying to break off the proposed negotiation—with the one kind purpose of protecting Mrs. Ellmother against the pitiless curiosity of Francine.

"Do you think you and that young lady are likely to get on well together?" she asked.

"I have told you already, Miss Emily, I want to get away from my own home and my own thoughts; I don't care where I go, so long as I do that." Having answered in those words, Mrs. Ellmother opened the door, and waited a while, thinking. "I wonder whether the dead know what is going on in the world they have left?" she said, looking at Emily. "If they do, there's one among them knows my thoughts, and feels for me. Good-by, miss—and don't think worse of me than I deserve."

Emily went back to the parlor. The only resource left was to plead with Francine for mercy to Mrs. Ellmother.

"Do you really mean to give it up?" she asked.

"To give up—what? 'Pumping,' as that obstinate old creature calls it?"

Emily persisted. "Don't worry the poor old soul! However strangely she may have left my aunt and me her motives are kind and good—I am sure of that. Will you let her keep her harmless little secret?"

"Oh, of course!"

"I don't believe you, Francine!"

"Don't you? I am like Cecilia—I am getting hungry. Shall we have some lunch?"

"You hard-hearted creature!"

"Does that mean—no luncheon until I have owned the truth? Suppose you own the truth? I won't tell Mrs. Ellmother that you have betrayed her."

"For the last time, Francine—I know no more of it than you do. If you persist in taking your own view, you as good as tell me I lie; and you will oblige me to leave the room."

Even Francine's obstinacy was compelled to give way, so far as appearances went. Still possessed by the delusion that Emily was deceiving her, she was now animated by a stronger motive than mere curiosity. Her sense of her own importance imperatively urged her to prove that she was not a person who could be deceived with impunity.

"I beg your pardon," she said with humility. "But I must positively have it out with Mrs. Ellmother. She has been more than a match for me—my turn next. I mean to get the better of her; and I shall succeed."

"I have already told you, Francine—you will fail."

"My dear, I am a dunce, and I don't deny it. But let me tell you one thing. I haven't lived all my life in the West Indies, among black servants, without learning something."

"What do you mean?"

"More, my clever friend, than you are likely to guess. In the meantime, don't forget the duties of hospitality. Ring the bell for luncheon."

CHAPTER XXX. LADY DORIS.

The arrival of Miss Ladd, some time before she had been expected, interrupted the two girls at a critical moment. She had hurried over her business in London, eager to pass the rest of the day with her favorite pupil. Emily's affectionate welcome was, in some degree at least, inspired by a sensation of relief. To feel herself in the embrace of the warm-hearted schoolmistress was like finding a refuge from Francine.

When the hour of departure arrived, Miss Ladd invited Emily to Brighton for the second time. "On the last occasion, my dear, you wrote me an excuse; I won't be treated in that way again. If you can't return with us now, come to-morrow." She added in a whisper, "Otherwise, I shall think you include me in your dislike of Francine."

There was no resisting this. It was arranged that Emily should go to Brighton on the next day.

Left by herself, her thoughts might have reverted to Mrs. Ellmother's doubtful prospects, and to Francine's strange allusion to her life in the West Indies, but for the arrival of two letters by the afternoon post. The handwriting on one of them was unknown to her. She opened that one first. It was an answer to the letter of apology which she had persisted in writing to Mrs. Rook. Happily for herself, Alban's influence had not been without its effect, after his departure. She had written kindly—but she had written briefly at the same time.

Mrs. Rook's reply presented a nicely compounded mixture of gratitude and grief. The gratitude was addressed to Emily as a matter of course. The grief related to her "excellent master." Sir Jervis's strength had suddenly failed. His medical attendant, being summoned, had expressed no surprise. "My patient is over seventy years of age," the doctor remarked. "He will sit up late at night, writing his book; and he refuses to take exercise, till headache and giddiness force him to try the fresh air. As the necessary result, he has broken down at last. It may end in paralysis, or it may end in death." Reporting this expression of medical opinion, Mrs. Rook's letter glided imperceptibly from respectful sympathy to modest regard for her own interests in the future. It might be the sad fate of her husband and herself to be thrown on the world again. If necessity brought them to London, would "kind Miss Emily grant her the honor of an interview, and favor a poor unlucky woman with a word of advice?"

"She may pervert your letter to some use of her own, which you may have reason to regret." Did Emily remember Alban's warning words? No: she accepted Mrs. Rook's reply as a gratifying tribute to the justice of her own opinions.

Having proposed to write to Alban, feeling penitently that she had been in the wrong, she was now readier than ever to send him a letter, feeling compassionately that she had been in the right. Besides, it was due to the faithful friend, who was still working for her in the reading room, that he should be informed of Sir Jervis's illness. Whether the old man lived or whether he died, his literary labors were fatally interrupted in either case; and one of the consequences would be the termination of her employment at the Museum. Although the second of the two letters which she had received was addressed to her in Cecilia's handwriting, Emily waited to read it until she had first written to Alban. "He will come to-morrow," she thought; "and we shall both make apologies. I shall regret that I was angry with him and he will regret that he was mistaken in his judgment of Mrs. Rook. We shall be as good friends again as ever."

In this happy frame of mind she opened Cecilia's letter. It was full of good news from first to last.

The invalid sister had made such rapid progress toward recovery that the travelers had arranged to set forth on their journey back to England in a fortnight. "My one regret," Cecilia added, "is the parting with Lady Doris. She and her husband are going to Genoa, where they will embark in Lord Janeaway's yacht for a cruise in the Mediterranean. When we have said that miserable word good-by—oh, Emily, what a hurry I shall be in to get back to you! Those allusions to your lonely life are so dreadful, my dear, that I have destroyed your letter; it is enough to break one's heart only to look at it. When once I get to London, there shall be no more solitude for my poor afflicted friend. Papa will be free from his parliamentary duties in August—and he has promised to have the house full of delightful people to meet you. Who do you think will be one of our guests? He is illustrious; he is fascinating; he deserves a line all to himself, thus:

"The Reverend Miles Mirabel!

"Lady Doris has discovered that the country parsonage, in which this brilliant clergyman submits to exile, is only twelve miles away from our house. She has written to Mr. Mirabel to introduce me, and to mention the date of my return. We will have some fun with the popular preacher—we will both fall in love with him together.

"Is there anybody to whom you would like me to send an invitation? Shall we have Mr. Alban Morris? Now I know how kindly he took care of you at the railway station, your good opinion of him is my opinion. Your letter also mentions a doctor. Is he nice? and do you think he will let me eat pastry, if we have him too? I am so overflowing with hospitality (all for your sake) that I am ready to invite anybody, and everybody, to cheer you and make you happy. Would you like to meet Miss Ladd and the whole school?

"As to our amusements, make your mind easy.

"I have come to a distinct understanding with Papa that we are to have dances every evening—except when we try a little concert as a change. Private theatricals are to follow, when we want another change after the dancing and the music. No early rising; no fixed hour for breakfast; everything that is most exquisitely delicious at dinner—and, to crown all, your room next to mine, for delightful midnight gossipings, when we ought to be in bed. What do you say, darling, to the programme?

"A last piece of news—and I have done.

"I have actually had a proposal of marriage, from a young gentleman who sits opposite me at the table d'hote! When I tell you that he has white eyelashes, and red hands, and such enormous front teeth that he can't shut his mouth, you will not need to be told that I refused him. This vindictive person has abused me ever since, in the most shameful manner. I heard him last night, under my window, trying to set one of his friends against me. 'Keep clear of her, my dear fellow; she's the most heartless creature living.' The friend took my part; he said, 'I don't agree with you; the young lady is a person of great sensibility.' 'Nonsense!' says my amiable lover; 'she eats too much—her sensibility is all stomach.' There's a wretch for you. What a shameful advantage to take of sitting opposite to me at dinner! Good-by, my love, till we meet soon, and are as happy together as the day is long."

Emily kissed the signature. At that moment of all others, Cecilia was such a refreshing contrast to Francine!

Before putting the letter away, she looked again at that part of it which mentioned Lady Doris's introduction of Cecilia to Mr. Mirabel. "I don't feel the slightest interest in Mr. Mirabel," she thought, smiling as the idea occurred to her; "and I need never have known him, but for Lady Doris—who is a perfect stranger to me."

She had just placed the letter in her desk, when a visitor was announced.

Doctor Allday presented himself (in a hurry as usual).

"Another patient waiting?" Emily asked mischievously. "No time to spare, again?"

"Not a moment," the old gentleman answered. "Have you heard from Mrs. Ellmother?"

"Yes."

"You don't mean to say you have answered her?"

"I have done better than that, doctor—I have seen her this morning."

"And consented to be her reference, of course?"

"How well you know me!"

Doctor Allday was a philosopher: he kept his temper. "Just what I might have expected," he said. "Eve and the apple! Only forbid a woman to do anything, and she does it directly—because you have forbidden her. I'll try the other way with you now, Miss Emily. There was something else that I meant to have forbidden."

"What was it?"

"May I make a special request?"

"Certainly."

"Oh, my dear, write to Mrs. Rook! I beg and entreat of you, write to Mrs. Rook!"

Emily's playful manner suddenly disappeared.

Ignoring the doctor's little outbreak of humor, she waited in grave surprise, until it was his pleasure to explain himself.

Doctor Allday, on his side, ignored the ominous change in Emily; he went on as pleasantly as ever. "Mr. Morris and I have had a long talk about you, my dear. Mr. Morris is a capital fellow; I recommend him as a sweetheart. I also back him in the matter of Mrs. Rook.—What's the matter now? You're as red as a rose. Temper again, eh?"

"Hatred of meanness!" Emily answered indignantly. "I despise a man who plots, behind my back, to get another man to help him. Oh, how I have been mistaken in Alban Morris!"

"Oh, how little you know of the best friend you have!" cried the doctor, imitating her. "Girls are all alike; the only man they can understand, is the man who flatters them. Will you oblige me by writing to Mrs. Rook?"

Emily made an attempt to match the doctor, with his own weapons. "Your little joke comes too late," she said satirically. "There is Mrs. Rook's answer. Read it, and—" she checked herself, even in her anger she was incapable of speaking ungenerously to the old man who had so warmly befriended her. "I won't say to you," she resumed, "what I might have said to another person."

"Shall I say it for you?" asked the incorrigible doctor. "'Read it, and be ashamed of yourself'—That was what you had in your mind, isn't it? Anything to please you, my dear." He put on his spectacles, read the letter, and handed it back to Emily with an impenetrable countenance. "What do you think of my new spectacles?" he asked, as he took the glasses off his nose. "In the experience of thirty years, I have had three grateful patients." He put the spectacles back in the case. "This comes from the third. Very gratifying—very gratifying."

Emily's sense of humor was not the uppermost sense in her at that moment. She pointed with a peremptory forefinger to Mrs. Rook's letter. "Have you nothing to say about this?"

The doctor had so little to say about it that he was able to express himself in one word:

"Humbug!"

He took his hat—nodded kindly to Emily—and hurried away to feverish pulses waiting to be felt, and to furred tongues that were ashamed to show themselves.

CHAPTER XXXI. MOIRA.

When Alban presented himself the next morning, the hours of the night had exercised their tranquilizing influence over Emily. She remembered sorrowfully how Doctor Allday had disturbed her belief in the man who loved her; no feeling of irritation remained. Alban noticed that her manner was unusually subdued; she received him with her customary grace, but not with her customary smile.

"Are you not well?" he asked.

"I am a little out of spirits," she replied. "A disappointment—that is all."

He waited a moment, apparently in the expectation that she might tell him what the disappointment was. She remained silent, and she looked away from him. Was he in any way answerable for the depression of spirits to which she alluded? The doubt occurred to him—but he said nothing.

"I suppose you have received my letter?" she resumed.

"I have come here to thank you for your letter."

"It was my duty to tell you of Sir Jervis's illness; I deserve no thanks."

"You have written to me so kindly," Alban reminded her; "you have referred to our difference of opinion, the last time I was here, so gently and so forgivingly—"

"If I had written a little later," she interposed, "the tone of my letter might have been less agreeable to you. I happened to send it to the post, before I received a visit from a friend of yours—a friend who had something to say to me after consulting with you."

"Do you mean Doctor Allday?"

"Yes."

"What did he say?"

"What you wished him to say. He did his best; he was as obstinate and unfeeling as you could possibly wish him to be; but he was too late. I have written to Mrs. Rook, and I have received a reply." She spoke sadly, not angrily—and pointed to the letter lying on her desk.

Alban understood: he looked at her in despair. "Is that wretched woman doomed to set us at variance every time we meet!" he exclaimed.

Emily silently held out the letter.

He refused to take it. "The wrong you have done me is not to be set right in that way," he said. "You believe the doctor's visit was arranged between us. I never knew that he intended to call on you; I had no interest in sending him here—and I must not interfere again between you and Mrs. Rook."

"I don't understand you."

"You will understand me when I tell you how my conversation with Doctor Allday ended. I have done with interference; I have done with advice. Whatever my doubts may be, all further effort on my part to justify them—all further inquiries, no matter in what direction—are at an end: I made the sacrifice, for your sake. No! I must repeat what you said to me just now; I deserve no thanks. What I have done, has been done in deference to Doctor Allday—against my own convictions; in spite of my own fears. Ridiculous convictions! ridiculous fears! Men with morbid minds are their own tormentors. It doesn't matter how I suffer, so long as you are at ease. I shall never thwart you or vex you again. Have you a better opinion of me now?"

She made the best of all answers—she gave him her hand.

"May I kiss it?" he asked, as timidly as if he had been a boy addressing his first sweetheart.

She was half inclined to laugh, and half inclined to cry. "Yes, if you like," she said softly.

"Will you let me come and see you again?"

"Gladly—when I return to London."

"You are going away?"

"I am going to Brighton this afternoon, to stay with Miss Ladd."

It was hard to lose her, on the happy day when they understood each other at last. An expression of disappointment passed over his face. He rose, and walked restlessly to the window. "Miss Ladd?" he repeated, turning to Emily as if an idea had struck him. "Did I hear, at the school, that Miss de Sor was to spend the holidays under the care of Miss Ladd?"

"Yes."

"The same young lady," he went on, "who paid you a visit yesterday morning?"

"The same."

That haunting distrust of the future, which he had first betrayed and then affected to ridicule, exercised its depressing influence over his better sense. He was unreasonable enough to feel doubtful of Francine, simply because she was a stranger.

"Miss de Sor is a new friend of yours," he said. "Do you like her?"

It was not an easy question to answer—without entering into particulars which Emily's delicacy of feeling warned her to avoid. "I must know a little more of Miss de Sor," she said, "before I can decide."

Alban's misgivings were naturally encouraged by this evasive reply. He began to regret having left the cottage, on the previous day, when he had heard that Emily was engaged. He might have sent in his card, and might have been admitted. It was an opportunity lost of observing Francine. On the morning of her first day at school, when they had accidentally met at the summer house, she had left a disagreeable impression on his mind. Ought he to allow his opinion to be influenced by this circumstance? or ought he to follow Emily's prudent example, and suspend judgment until he knew a little more of Francine?

"Is any day fixed for your return to London?" he asked.

"Not yet," she said; "I hardly know how long my visit will be."

"In little more than a fortnight," he continued, "I shall return to my classes—they will be dreary classes, without you. Miss de Sor goes back to the school with Miss Ladd, I suppose?"

Emily was at a loss to account for the depression in his looks and tones, while he was making these unimportant inquiries. She tried to rouse him by speaking lightly in reply.

"Miss de Sor returns in quite a new character; she is to be a guest instead of a pupil. Do you wish to be better acquainted with her?"

"Yes," he said gravely, "now I know that she is a friend of yours." He returned to his place near her. "A pleasant visit makes the days pass quickly," he resumed. "You may remain at Brighton longer than you anticipate; and we may not meet again for some time to come. If anything happens—"

"Do you mean anything serious?" she asked.

"No, no! I only mean—if I can be of any service. In that case, will you write to me?"

"You know I will!"

She looked at him anxiously. He had completely failed to hide from her the uneasy state of his mind: a man less capable of concealment of feeling never lived. "You are anxious, and out of spirits," she said gently. "Is it my fault?"

"Your fault? oh, don't think that! I have my dull days and my bright days—and just now my barometer is down at dull." His voice faltered, in spite of his efforts to control it; he gave up the struggle, and took his hat to go. "Do you remember, Emily, what I once said to you in the garden at the school? I still believe there is a time of fulfillment to come in our lives." He suddenly checked himself, as if there had been something more in his mind to which he hesitated to give expression—and held out his hand to bid her good-by.

"My memory of what you said in the garden is better than yours," she reminded him. "You said 'Happen what may in the interval, I trust the future.' Do you feel the same trust still?"

He sighed—drew her to him gently—and kissed her on the forehead. Was that his own reply? She was not calm enough to ask him the question: it remained in her thoughts for some time after he had gone.

....

On the same day Emily was at Brighton.

Francine happened to be alone in the drawing-room. Her first proceeding, when Emily was shown in, was to stop the servant.

"Have you taken my letter to the post?"

"Yes, miss."

"It doesn't matter." She dismissed the servant by a gesture, and burst into such effusive hospitality that she actually insisted on kissing Emily. "Do you know what I have been doing?" she said. "I have been writing to Cecilia— directing to the care of her father, at the House of Commons. I stupidly forgot that you would be able to give me the right address in Switzerland. You don't object, I hope, to my making myself agreeable to our dear, beautiful, greedy girl? It is of such importance to me to surround myself with influential friends—and, of course, I have given her your love. Don't look disgusted! Come, and see your room.—Oh, never mind Miss Ladd. You will see her when she wakes. Ill? Is that sort of old woman ever ill? She's only taking her nap after bathing. Bathing in the sea, at her age! How she must frighten the fishes!"

Having seen her own bed-chamber, Emily was next introduced to the room occupied by Francine.

One object that she noticed in it caused her some little surprise— not unmingled with disgust. She discovered on the toilet-table a coarsely caricatured portrait of Mrs. Ellmother. It was a sketch in pencil—wretchedly drawn; but spitefully successful as a likeness. "I didn't know you were an artist," Emily remarked, with an ironical emphasis on the last word. Francine laughed scornfully—crumpled the drawing up in her hand—and threw it into the waste-paper basket.

"You satirical creature!" she burst out gayly. "If you had lived a dull life at St. Domingo, you would have taken to spoiling paper too. I might really have turned out an artist, if I had been clever and industrious like you. As it was, I learned a little drawing—and got tired of it. I tried modeling in wax—and got tired of it. Who do you think was my teacher? One of our slaves."

"A slave!" Emily exclaimed.

"Yes—a mulatto, if you wish me to be particular; the daughter of an English father and a negro mother. In her young time (at least she said so herself) she was quite a beauty, in her particular style. Her master's favorite; he educated her himself. Besides drawing and painting, and modeling in wax, she could sing and play—all the accomplishments thrown away on a slave! When her owner died, my uncle bought her at the sale of the property."

A word of natural compassion escaped Emily—to Francine's surprise.

"Oh, my dear, you needn't pity her! Sappho (that was her name) fetched a high price, even when she was no longer young. She came to us, by inheritance, with the estates and the rest of it; and took a fancy to me, when she found out I didn't get on well with my father and mother. 'I owe it to my father and mother,' she used to say, 'that I am a slave. When I see affectionate daughters, it wrings my heart.' Sappho was a strange compound. A woman with a white side to her character, and a black side. For weeks together, she would be a civilized being. Then she used to relapse, and become as complete a negress as her mother. At the risk of her life she stole away, on those occasions, into the interior of the island, and looked on, in hiding, at the horrid witchcrafts and idolatries of the blacks; they would have murdered a half-blood, prying into their ceremonies, if they had discovered her. I followed her once, so far as I dared. The frightful yellings and drummings in the darkness of the forests frightened me. The blacks suspected her, and it came to my ears. I gave her the warning that saved her life (I don't know what I should have done without Sappho to amuse me!); and, from that time, I do believe the curious creature loved me. You see I can speak generously even of a slave!"

"I wonder you didn't bring her with you to England," Emily said.

"In the first place," Francine answered, "she was my father's property, not mine. In the second place, she's dead. Poisoned, as the other half-bloods supposed, by some enemy among the blacks. She said herself, she was under a spell!"

"What did she mean?"

Francine was not interested enough in the subject to explain. "Stupid superstition, my dear. The negro side of Sappho was uppermost when she was dying—there is the explanation. Be off with you! I hear the old woman on the stairs. Meet her before she can come in here. My bedroom is my only refuge from Miss Ladd."

On the morning of the last day in the week, Emily had a little talk in private with her old schoolmistress. Miss Ladd listened to what she had to say of Mrs. Ellmother, and did her best to relieve Emily's anxieties. "I think you are mistaken, my child, in supposing that Francine is in earnest. It is her great fault that she is hardly ever in earnest. You can trust to my discretion; leave the rest to your aunt's old servant and to me."

Mrs. Ellmother arrived, punctual to the appointed time. She was shown into Miss Ladd's own room. Francine—ostentatiously resolved to take no personal part in the affair—went for a walk. Emily waited to hear the result.

After a long interval, Miss Ladd returned to the drawing-room, and announced that she had sanctioned the engagement of Mrs. Ellmother.

"I have considered your wishes, in this respect," she said. "It is arranged that a week's notice, on either side, shall end the term of service, after the first month. I cannot feel justified in doing more than that. Mrs. Ellmother is such a respectable woman; she is so well known to you, and she was so long in your aunt's service, that I am bound to consider the importance of securing a person who is exactly fitted to attend on such a girl as Francine. In one word, I can trust Mrs. Ellmother."

"When does she enter on her service?" Emily inquired.

"On the day after we return to the school," Miss Ladd replied. "You will be glad to see her, I am sure. I will send her here."

"One word more before you go," Emily said.

"Did you ask her why she left my aunt?"

"My dear child, a woman who has been five-and-twenty years in one place is entitled to keep her own secrets. I understand that she had her reasons, and that she doesn't think it necessary to mention them to anybody. Never trust people by halves—especially when they are people like Mrs. Ellmother."

It was too late now to raise any objections. Emily felt relieved, rather than disappointed, on discovering that Mrs. Ellmother was in a hurry to get back to London by the next train. She had found an opportunity of letting her lodgings; and she was eager to conclude the bargain. "You see I couldn't say Yes," she explained, "till I knew whether I was to get this new place or not—and the person wants to go in tonight."

Emily stopped her at the door. "Promise to write and tell me how you get on with Miss de Sor."

"You say that, miss, as if you didn't feel hopeful about me."

"I say it, because I feel interested about you. Promise to write."

Mrs. Ellmother promised, and hastened away. Emily looked after her from the window, as long as she was in view. "I wish I could feel sure of Francine!" she said to herself.

"In what way?" asked the hard voice of Francine, speaking at the door.

It was not in Emily's nature to shrink from a plain reply. She completed her half-formed thought without a moment's hesitation.

"I wish I could feel sure," she answered, "that you will be kind to Mrs. Ellmother."

"Are you afraid I shall make her life one scene of torment?" Francine inquired. "How can I answer for myself? I can't look into the future."

"For once in your life, can you be in earnest?" Emily said.

"For once in your life, can you take a joke?" Francine replied.

Emily said no more. She privately resolved to shorten her visit to Brighton.

BOOK THE THIRD—NETHERWOODS.

CHAPTER XXXII. IN THE GRAY ROOM.

The house inhabited by Miss Ladd and her pupils had been built, in the early part of the present century, by a wealthy merchant—proud of his money, and eager to distinguish himself as the owner of the largest country seat in the neighborhood.

After his death, Miss Ladd had taken Netherwoods (as the place was called), finding her own house insufficient for the accommodation of the increasing number of her pupils. A lease was granted to her on moderate terms. Netherwoods failed to attract persons of distinction in search of a country residence. The grounds were beautiful; but no landed property—not even a park—was attached to the house. Excepting the few acres on which the building stood, the surrounding land belonged to a retired naval officer of old family, who resented the attempt of a merchant of low birth to assume the position of a gentleman. No matter what proposals might be made to the admiral, he refused them all. The privilege of shooting was not one of the attractions offered to tenants; the country presented no facilities for hunting; and the only stream in the neighborhood was not preserved. In consequence of these drawbacks, the merchant's representatives had to choose between a proposal to use Netherwoods as a lunatic asylum, or to accept as tenant the respectable mistress of a fashionable and prosperous school. They decided in favor of Miss Ladd.

The contemplated change in Francine's position was accomplished, in that vast house, without inconvenience. There were rooms unoccupied, even when the limit assigned to the number of pupils had been reached. On the re-opening of the school, Francine was offered her choice between two rooms on one of the upper stories, and two rooms on the ground floor. She chose these last.

Her sitting-room and bedroom, situated at the back of the house, communicated with each other. The sitting-room, ornamented with a pretty paper of delicate gray, and furnished with curtains of the same color, had been accordingly named, "The Gray Room." It had a French window, which opened on the terrace overlooking the garden and the grounds. Some fine old engravings from the grand landscapes of Claude (part of a collection of prints possessed by Miss Ladd's father) hung on the walls. The carpet was in harmony with the curtains; and the furniture was of light-colored wood, which helped the general effect of subdued brightness that made the charm of the room. "If you are not happy here," Miss Ladd said, "I despair of you." And Francine answered, "Yes, it's very pretty, but I wish it was not so small."

On the twelfth of August the regular routine of the school was resumed. Alban Morris found two strangers in his class, to fill the vacancies left by Emily and Cecilia. Mrs. Ellmother was duly established in her new place. She produced an unfavorable impression in the servants' hall—not (as the handsome chief housemaid explained) because she was ugly and old, but because she was "a person who didn't talk." The prejudice against habitual silence, among the lower order of the people, is almost as inveterate as the prejudice against red hair.

In the evening, on that first day of renewed studies—while the girls were in the grounds, after tea—Francine had at last completed the arrangement of her rooms, and had dismissed Mrs. Ellmother (kept hard at work since the morning) to take a little rest. Standing alone at her window, the West Indian heiress wondered what she had better do next. She glanced at the girls on the lawn, and decided that they were unworthy of serious notice, on the part of a person so specially favored as herself. She turned sidewise, and looked along the length of the terrace. At the far end a tall man was slowly pacing to and fro, with his head down and his hands in his pockets. Francine recognized the rude drawing-master, who had torn up his view of the village, after she had saved it from being blown into the pond.

She stepped out on the terrace, and called to him. He stopped, and looked up.

"Do you want me?" he called back.

"Of course I do!"

She advanced a little to meet him, and offered encouragement under the form of a hard smile. Although his manners might be unpleasant, he had claims on the indulgence of a young lady, who was at a loss how to employ her idle time. In the first place, he was a man. In the second place, he was not as old as the music-master, or as ugly as the dancing-master. In the third place, he was an admirer of Emily; and the opportunity of trying to shake his allegiance by means of a flirtation, in Emily's absence, was too good an opportunity to be lost.

"Do you remember how rude you were to me, on the day when you were sketching in the summer-house?" Francine asked with snappish playfulness. "I expect you to make yourself agreeable this time—I am going to pay you a compliment."

He waited, with exasperating composure, to hear what the proposed compliment might be. The furrow between his eyebrows looked deeper than ever. There were signs of secret trouble in that dark face, so grimly and so resolutely composed. The school, without Emily, presented the severest trial of endurance that he had encountered, since the day when he had been deserted and disgraced by his affianced wife.

"You are an artist," Francine proceeded, "and therefore a person of taste. I want to have your opinion of my sitting-room. Criticism is invited; pray come in."

He seemed to be unwilling to accept the invitation—then altered his mind, and followed Francine. She had visited Emily; she was perhaps in a fair way to become Emily's friend. He remembered that he had already lost an opportunity of studying her character, and—if he saw the necessity—of warning Emily not to encourage the advances of Miss de Sor.

"Very pretty," he remarked, looking round the room—without appearing to care for anything in it, except the prints.

Francine was bent on fascinating him. She raised her eyebrows and lifted her hands, in playful remonstrance. "Do remember it's my room," she said, "and take some little interest in it, for my sake!"

"What do you want me to say?" he asked.

"Come and sit down by me." She made room for him on the sofa. Her one favorite aspiration—the longing to excite envy in others—expressed itself in her next words. "Say something pretty," she answered; "say you would like to have such a room as this."

"I should like to have your prints," he remarked. "Will that do?"

"It wouldn't do—from anybody else. Ah, Mr. Morris, I know why you are not as nice as you might be! You are not happy. The school has lost its one attraction, in losing our dear Emily. You feel it—I know you feel it." She assisted this expression of sympathy to produce the right effect by a sigh. "What would I not give to inspire such devotion as yours! I don't envy Emily; I only wish—" She paused in confusion, and opened her fan. "Isn't it pretty?" she said, with an ostentatious appearance of changing the subject. Alban behaved like a monster; he began to talk of the weather.

"I think this is the hottest day we have had," he said; "no wonder you want your fan. Netherwoods is an airless place at this season of the year."

She controlled her temper. "I do indeed feel the heat," she admitted, with a resignation which gently reproved him; "it is so heavy and oppressive here after Brighton. Perhaps my sad life, far away from home and friends, makes me sensitive to trifles. Do you think so, Mr. Morris?"

The merciless man said he thought it was the situation of the house.

"Miss Ladd took the place in the spring," he continued; "and only discovered the one objection to it some months afterward. We are in the highest part of the valley here—but, you see, it's a valley surrounded by hills; and on three sides the hills are near us. All very well in winter; but in summer I have heard of girls in this school so out of health in the relaxing atmosphere that they have been sent home again."

Francine suddenly showed an interest in what he was saying. If he had cared to observe her closely, he might have noticed it.

"Do you mean that the girls were really ill?" she asked.

"No. They slept badly—lost appetite—started at trifling noises. In short, their nerves were out of order."

"Did they get well again at home, in another air?"

"Not a doubt of it," he answered, beginning to get weary of the subject. "May I look at your books?"

Francine's interest in the influence of different atmospheres on health was not exhausted yet. "Do you know where the girls lived when they were at home?" she inquired.

"I know where one of them lived. She was the best pupil I ever had—and I remember she lived in Yorkshire." He was so weary of the idle curiosity—as it appeared to him—which persisted in asking trifling questions, that he left his seat, and crossed the room. "May I look at your books?" he repeated.

"Oh, yes!"

The conversation was suspended for a while. The lady thought, "I should like to box his ears!" The gentleman thought, "She's only an inquisitive fool after all!" His examination of her books confirmed him in the delusion that there was really nothing in Francine's character which rendered it necessary to caution Emily against the advances of her new friend. Turning away from the book-case, he made the first excuse that occurred to him for putting an end to the interview.

"I must beg you to let me return to my duties, Miss de Sor. I have to correct the young ladies' drawings, before they begin again to-morrow."

Francine's wounded vanity made a last expiring attempt to steal the heart of Emily's lover.

"You remind me that I have a favor to ask," she said. "I don't attend the other classes—but I should so like to join your class! May I?" She looked up at him with a languishing appearance of entreaty which sorely tried Alban's capacity to keep his face in serious order. He acknowledged the compliment paid to him in studiously commonplace terms, and got a little nearer to the open window. Francine's obstinacy was not conquered yet.

"My education has been sadly neglected," she continued; "but I have had some little instruction in drawing. You will not find me so ignorant as some of the other girls." She waited a little, anticipating a few complimentary words. Alban waited also—in silence. "I shall look forward with pleasure to my lessons under such an artist as yourself," she went on, and waited again, and was disappointed again. "Perhaps," she resumed, "I may become your favorite pupil—Who knows?"

"Who indeed!"

It was not much to say, when he spoke at last—but it was enough to encourage Francine. She called him "dear Mr. Morris"; she pleaded for permission to take her first lesson immediately; she clasped her hands— "Please say Yes!"

"I can't say Yes, till you have complied with the rules."

"Are they your rules?"

Her eyes expressed the readiest submission—in that case. He entirely failed to see it: he said they were Miss Ladd's rules—and wished her good-evening.

She watched him, walking away down the terrace. How was he paid? Did he receive a yearly salary, or did he get a little extra money for each new pupil who took drawing lessons? In this last case, Francine saw her opportunity of being even with him "You brute! Catch me attending your class!"

CHAPTER XXXIII. RECOLLECTIONS OF ST. DOMINGO.

The night was oppressively hot. Finding it impossible to sleep, Francine lay quietly in her bed, thinking. The subject of her reflections was a person who occupied the humble position of her new servant.

Mrs. Ellmother looked wretchedly ill. Mrs. Ellmother had told Emily that her object, in returning to domestic service, was to try if change would relieve her from the oppression of her own thoughts. Mrs. Ellmother believed in vulgar superstitions which declared Friday to be an unlucky day; and which recommended throwing a pinch over your left shoulder, if you happened to spill the salt.

In themselves, these were trifling recollections. But they assumed a certain importance, derived from the associations which they called forth.

They reminded Francine, by some mental process which she was at a loss to trace, of Sappho the slave, and of her life at St. Domingo.

She struck a light, and unlocked her writing desk. From one of the drawers she took out an old household account-book.

The first page contained some entries, relating to domestic expenses, in her own handwriting. They recalled one of her efforts to occupy her idle time, by relieving her mother of the cares of housekeeping. For a day or two, she had persevered—and then she had ceased to feel any interest in her new employment. The remainder of the book was completely filled up, in a beautifully clear handwriting, beginning on the second page. A title had been found for the manuscript by Francine. She had written at the top of the page: Sappho's Nonsense.

After reading the first few sentences she rapidly turned over the leaves, and stopped at a blank space near the end of the book. Here again she had added a title. This time it implied a compliment to the writer: the page was headed: Sappho's Sense.

She read this latter part of the manuscript with the closest attention.

"I entreat my kind and dear young mistress not to suppose that I believe in witchcraft—after such an education as I have received. When I wrote down, at your biding, all that I had told you by word of mouth, I cannot imagine what delusion possessed me. You say I have a negro side to my character, which I inherit from my mother. Did you mean this, dear mistress, as a joke? I am almost afraid it is sometimes not far off from the truth.

"Let me be careful, however, to avoid leading you into a mistake. It is really true that the man-slave I spoke of did pine and die, after the spell had been cast on him by my witch-mother's image of wax. But I ought also to have told you that circumstances favored the working of the spell: the fatal end was not brought about by supernatural means.

"The poor wretch was not in good health at the time; and our owner had occasion to employ him in the valley of the island far inland. I have been told, and can well believe, that the climate there is different from the climate on the coast—in which the unfortunate slave had been accustomed to live. The overseer wouldn't believe him when he said the valley air would be his death—and the negroes, who might otherwise have helped him, all avoided a man whom they knew to be under a spell.

"This, you see, accounts for what might appear incredible to civilized persons. If you will do me a favor, you will burn this little book, as soon as you have read what I have written here. If my request is not granted, I can only implore you to let no eyes but your own see these pages. My life might be in danger if the blacks knew what I have now told you, in the interests of truth."

Francine closed the book, and locked it up again in her desk. "Now I know," she said to herself, "what reminded me of St. Domingo."

When Francine rang her bell the next morning, so long a time elapsed without producing an answer that she began to think of sending one of the house-servants to make inquiries. Before she could decide, Mrs. Ellmother presented herself, and offered her apologies.

"It's the first time I have overslept myself, miss, since I was a girl. Please to excuse me, it shan't happen again."

"Do you find that the air here makes you drowsy?" Francine asked.

Mrs. Ellmother shook her head. "I didn't get to sleep," she said, "till morning, and so I was too heavy to be up in time. But air has got nothing to do with it. Gentlefolks may have their whims and fancies. All air is the same to people like me."

"You enjoy good health, Mrs. Ellmother?"

"Why not, miss? I have never had a doctor."

"Oh! That's your opinion of doctors, is it?"

"I won't have anything to do with them—if that's what you mean by my opinion," Mrs. Ellmother answered doggedly. "How will you have your hair done?"

"The same as yesterday. Have you seen anything of Miss Emily? She went back to London the day after you left us."

"I haven't been in London. I'm thankful to say my lodgings are let to a good tenant."

"Then where have you lived, while you were waiting to come here?"

"I had only one place to go to, miss; I went to the village where I was born. A friend found a corner for me. Ah, dear heart, it's a pleasant place, there!"

"A place like this?"

"Lord help you! As little like this as chalk is to cheese. A fine big moor, miss, in Cumberland, without a tree in sight—look where you may. Something like a wind, I can tell you, when it takes to blowing there."

"Have you never been in this part of the country?"

"Not I! When I left the North, my new mistress took me to Canada. Talk about air! If there was anything in it, the people in that air ought to live to be a hundred. I liked Canada."

"And who was your next mistress?"

Thus far, Mrs. Ellmother had been ready enough to talk. Had she failed to hear what Francine had just said to her? or had she some reason for feeling reluctant to answer? In any case, a spirit of taciturnity took sudden possession of her—she was silent.

Francine (as usual) persisted. "Was your next place in service with Miss Emily's aunt?"

"Yes."

"Did the old lady always live in London?"

"No."

"What part of the country did she live in?"

"Kent."

"Among the hop gardens?"

"No."

"In what other part, then?"

"Isle of Thanet."

"Near the sea coast?"

"Yes."

Even Francine could insist no longer: Mrs. Ellmother's reserve had beaten her—for that day at least. "Go into the hall," she said, "and see if there are any letters for me in the rack."

There was a letter bearing the Swiss postmark. Simple Cecilia was flattered and delighted by the charming manner in which Francine had written to her. She looked forward with impatience to the time when their present acquaintance might ripen into friendship. Would "Dear Miss de Sor" waive all ceremony, and consent to be a guest (later in the autumn) at her father's house? Circumstances connected with her sister's health would delay their return to England for a little while. By the end of the month she hoped to be at home again, and to hear if Francine was disengaged. Her address, in England, was Monksmoor Park, Hants.

Having read the letter, Francine drew a moral from it: "There is great use in a fool, when one knows how to manage her."

Having little appetite for her breakfast, she tried the experiment of a walk on the terrace. Alban Morris was right; the air at Netherwoods, in the summer time, was relaxing. The morning mist still hung over the lowest part of the valley, between the village and the hills beyond. A little exercise produced a feeling of fatigue. Francine returned to her room, and trifled with her tea and toast.

Her next proceeding was to open her writing-desk, and look into the old account-book once more. While it lay open on her lap, she recalled what had passed that morning, between Mrs. Ellmother and herself.

The old woman had been born and bred in the North, on an open moor. She had been removed to the keen air of Canada when she left her birthplace. She had been in service after that, on the breezy eastward coast of Kent. Would the change to the climate of Netherwoods produce any effect on Mrs. Ellmother? At her age, and with her seasoned constitution, would she feel it as those school-girls had felt it—especially that one among them, who lived in the bracing air of the North, the air of Yorkshire?

Weary of solitary thinking on one subject, Francine returned to the terrace with a vague idea of finding something to amuse her—that is to say, something she could turn into ridicule—if she joined the girls.

The next morning, Mrs. Ellmother answered her mistress's bell without delay. "You have slept better, this time?" Francine said.

"No, miss. When I did get to sleep I was troubled by dreams. Another bad night—and no mistake!"

"I suspect your mind is not quite at ease," Francine suggested.

"Why do you suspect that, if you please?"

"You talked, when I met you at Miss Emily's, of wanting to get away from your own thoughts. Has the change to this place helped you?"

"It hasn't helped me as I expected. Some people's thoughts stick fast."

"Remorseful thoughts?" Francine inquired.

Mrs. Ellmother held up her forefinger, and shook it with a gesture of reproof. "I thought we agreed, miss, that there was to be no pumping."

196

The business of the toilet proceeded in silence.

A week passed. During an interval in the labors of the school, Miss Ladd knocked at the door of Francine's room.

"I want to speak to you, my dear, about Mrs. Ellmother. Have you noticed that she doesn't seem to be in good health?"

"She looks rather pale, Miss Ladd."

"It's more serious than that, Francine. The servants tell me that she has hardly any appetite. She herself acknowledges that she sleeps badly. I noticed her yesterday evening in the garden, under the schoolroom window. One of the girls dropped a dictionary. She started at that slight noise, as if it terrified her. Her nerves are seriously out of order. Can you prevail upon her to see the doctor?"

Francine hesitated—and made an excuse. "I think she would be much more likely, Miss Ladd, to listen to you. Do you mind speaking to her?"

"Certainly not!"

Mrs. Ellmother was immediately sent for. "What is your pleasure, miss?" she said to Francine.

Miss Ladd interposed. "It is I who wish to speak to you, Mrs. Ellmother. For some days past, I have been sorry to see you looking ill."

"I never was ill in my life, ma'am."

Miss Ladd gently persisted. "I hear that you have lost your appetite."

"I never was a great eater, ma'am."

It was evidently useless to risk any further allusion to Mrs. Ellmother's symptoms. Miss Ladd tried another method of persuasion. "I daresay I may be mistaken," she said; "but I do really feel anxious about you. To set my mind at rest, will you see the doctor?"

"The doctor! Do you think I'm going to begin taking physic, at my time of life? Lord, ma'am! you amuse me—you do indeed!" She burst into a

197

sudden fit of laughter; the hysterical laughter which is on the verge of tears. With a desperate effort, she controlled herself. "Please, don't make a fool of me again," she said—and left the room.

"What do you think now?" Miss Ladd asked.

Francine appeared to be still on her guard.

"I don't know what to think," she said evasively.

Miss Ladd looked at her in silent surprise, and withdrew.

Left by herself, Francine sat with her elbows on the table and her face in her hands, absorbed in thought. After a long interval, she opened her desk—and hesitated. She took a sheet of note-paper—and paused, as if still in doubt. She snatched up her pen, with a sudden recovery of resolution—and addressed these lines to the wife of her father's agent in London:

"When I was placed under your care, on the night of my arrival from the West Indies, you kindly said I might ask you for any little service which might be within your power. I shall be greatly obliged if you can obtain for me, and send to this place, a supply of artists' modeling wax—sufficient for the production of a small image."

CHAPTER XXXIV. IN THE DARK.

A week later, Alban Morris happened to be in Miss Ladd's study, with a report to make on the subject of his drawing-class. Mrs. Ellmother interrupted them for a moment. She entered the room to return a book which Francine had borrowed that morning.

"Has Miss de Sor done with it already?" Miss Ladd asked.

"She won't read it, ma'am. She says the leaves smell of tobacco-smoke."

Miss Ladd turned to Alban, and shook her head with an air of good-humored reproof. "I know who has been reading that book last!" she said.

Alban pleaded guilty, by a look. He was the only master in the school who smoked. As Mrs. Ellmother passed him, on her way out, he noticed the signs of suffering in her wasted face.

"That woman is surely in a bad state of health," he said. "Has she seen the doctor?"

"She flatly refuses to consult the doctor," Miss Ladd replied. "If she was a stranger, I should meet the difficulty by telling Miss de Sor (whose servant she is) that Mrs. Ellmother must be sent home. But I cannot act in that peremptory manner toward a person in whom Emily is interested."

From that moment Mrs. Ellmother became a person in whom Alban was interested. Later in the day, he met her in one of the lower corridors of the house, and spoke to her. "I am afraid the air of this place doesn't agree with you," he said.

Mrs. Ellmother's irritable objection to being told (even indirectly) that she looked ill, expressed itself roughly in reply. "I daresay you mean well, sir—but I don't see how it matters to you whether the place agrees with me or not."

"Wait a minute," Alban answered good-humoredly. "I am not quite a stranger to you."

"How do you make that out, if you please?"

"I know a young lady who has a sincere regard for you."

"You don't mean Miss Emily?"

"Yes, I do. I respect and admire Miss Emily; and I have tried, in my poor way, to be of some little service to her."

Mrs. Ellmother's haggard face instantly softened. "Please to forgive me, sir, for forgetting my manners," she said simply. "I have had my health since the day I was born—and I don't like to be told, in my old age, that a new place doesn't agree with me."

Alban accepted this apology in a manner which at once won the heart of the North-countrywoman. He shook hands with her. "You're one of the right sort," she said; "there are not many of them in this house."

Was she alluding to Francine? Alban tried to make the discovery. Polite circumlocution would be evidently thrown away on Mrs. Ellmother. "Is your new mistress one of the right sort?" he asked bluntly.

The old servant's answer was expressed by a frowning look, followed by a plain question.

"Do you say that, sir, because you like my new mistress?"

"No."

"Please to shake hands again!" She said it—took his hand with a sudden grip that spoke for itself—and walked away.

Here was an exhibition of character which Alban was just the man to appreciate. "If I had been an old woman," he thought in his dryly humorous way, "I believe I should have been like Mrs. Ellmother. We might have talked of Emily, if she had not left me in such a hurry. When shall I see her again?"

He was destined to see her again, that night—under circumstances which he remembered to the end of his life.

The rules of Netherwoods, in summer time, recalled the young ladies from their evening's recreation in the grounds at nine o'clock. After that hour, Alban was free to smoke his pipe, and to linger among trees and flower-beds before he returned to his hot little rooms in the village. As a relief to the drudgery of teaching the young ladies, he had been using his pencil, when the day's lessons were over, for his own amusement. It was past ten o'clock before he lighted his pipe, and began walking slowly to and fro on the path which led to the summer-house, at the southern limit of the grounds.

In the perfect stillness of the night, the clock of the village church was distinctly audible, striking the hours and the quarters. The moon had not risen; but the mysterious glimmer of starlight trembled on the large open space between the trees and the house.

Alban paused, admiring with an artist's eye the effect of light, so faintly and delicately beautiful, on the broad expanse of the lawn. "Does the man live who could paint that?" he asked himself. His memory recalled the works of the greatest of all landscape painters—the English artists of fifty years since. While recollections of many a noble picture were still passing through his mind, he was startled by the sudden appearance of a bareheaded woman on the terrace steps.

She hurried down to the lawn, staggering as she ran—stopped, and looked back at the house—hastened onward toward the trees—stopped again, looking backward and forward, uncertain which way to turn next—and then advanced once more. He could now hear her heavily gasping for breath. As she came nearer, the starlight showed a panic-stricken face—the face of Mrs. Ellmother.

Alban ran to meet her. She dropped on the grass before he could cross the short distance which separated them. As he raised her in his arms she looked at him wildly, and murmured and muttered in the vain attempt to speak. "Look at me again," he said. "Don't you remember the man who had some talk with you to-day?" She still stared at him vacantly: he tried again. "Don't you remember Miss Emily's friend?"

As the name passed his lips, her mind in some degree recovered its balance. "Yes," she said; "Emily's friend; I'm glad I have met with Emily's friend." She caught at Alban's arm—starting as if her own words had alarmed her. "What am I talking about? Did I say 'Emily'? A servant ought to say 'Miss Emily.' My head swims. Am I going mad?"

Alban led her to one of the garden chairs. "You're only a little frightened," he said. "Rest, and compose yourself."

She looked over her shoulder toward the house. "Not here! I've run away from a she-devil; I want to be out of sight. Further away, Mister—I don't know your name. Tell me your name; I won't trust you, unless you tell me your name!"

"Hush! hush! Call me Alban."

"I never heard of such a name; I won't trust you."

"You won't trust your friend, and Emily's friend? You don't mean that, I'm sure. Call me by my other name—call me 'Morris.'"

"Morris?" she repeated. "Ah, I've heard of people called 'Morris.' Look back! Your eyes are young—do you see her on the terrace?"

"There isn't a living soul to be seen anywhere."

With one hand he raised her as he spoke—and with the other he took up the chair. In a minute more, they were out of sight of the house. He seated her so that she could rest her head against the trunk of a tree.

"What a good fellow!" the poor old creature said, admiring him; "he knows how my head pains me. Don't stand up! You're a tall man. She might see you."

"She can see nothing. Look at the trees behind us. Even the starlight doesn't get through them."

Mrs. Ellmother was not satisfied yet. "You take it coolly," she said. "Do you know who saw us together in the passage to-day? You good Morris, she saw us—she did. Wretch! Cruel, cunning, shameless wretch."

In the shadows that were round them, Alban could just see that she was shaking her clinched fists in the air. He made another attempt to control her. "Don't excite yourself! If she comes into the garden, she might hear you."

The appeal to her fears had its effect.

"That's true," she said, in lowered tones. A sudden distrust of him seized her the next moment. "Who told me I was excited?" she burst out. "It's you who are excited. Deny it if you dare; I begin to suspect you, Mr. Morris; I don't like your conduct. What has become of your pipe? I saw you put your pipe in your coat pocket. You did it when you set me down among the trees where she could see me! You are in league with her—she is coming to meet you here—you know she does not like tobacco-smoke. Are you two going to put me in the madhouse?"

She started to her feet. It occurred to Alban that the speediest way of pacifying her might be by means of the pipe. Mere words would exercise no persuasive influence over that bewildered mind. Instant action, of some kind, would be far more likely to have the right effect. He put his pipe and his tobacco pouch into her hands, and so mastered her attention before he spoke.

"Do you know how to fill a man's pipe for him?" he asked.

"Haven't I filled my husband's pipe hundreds of times?" she answered sharply.

"Very well. Now do it for me."

She took her chair again instantly, and filled the pipe. He lighted it, and seated himself on the grass, quietly smoking. "Do you think I'm in league with her now?" he asked, purposely adopting the rough tone of a man in her own rank of life.

She answered him as she might have answered her husband, in the days of her unhappy marriage.

"Oh, don't gird at me, there's a good man! If I've been off my head for a minute or two, please not to notice me. It's cool and quiet here," the poor woman said gratefully. "Bless God for the darkness; there's something comforting in the darkness—along with a good man like you. Give me a word of advice. You are my friend in need. What am I to do? I daren't go back to the house!"

She was quiet enough now, to suggest the hope that she might be able to give Alban some information "Were you with Miss de Sor," he asked, "before you came out here? What did she do to frighten you?"

There was no answer; Mrs. Ellmother had abruptly risen once more. "Hush!" she whispered. "Don't I hear somebody near us?"

Alban at once went back, along the winding path which they had followed. No creature was visible in the gardens or on the terrace. On returning, he found it impossible to use his eyes to any good purpose in the obscurity among the trees. He waited a while, listening intently. No sound was audible: there was not even air enough to stir the leaves.

As he returned to the place that he had left, the silence was broken by the chimes of the distant church clock, striking the three-quarters past ten.

Even that familiar sound jarred on Mrs. Ellmother's shattered nerves. In her state of mind and body, she was evidently at the mercy of any false alarm which might be raised by her own fears. Relieved of the feeling of distrust which had thus far troubled him, Alban sat down by her again—opened his match-box to relight his pipe—and changed his mind. Mrs. Ellmother had unconsciously warned him to be cautious.

For the first time, he thought it likely that the heat in the house might induce some of the inmates to try the cooler atmosphere in the grounds. If this happened, and if he continued to smoke, curiosity might tempt them to follow the scent of tobacco hanging on the stagnant air.

"Is there nobody near us?" Mrs. Ellmother asked. "Are you sure?"

"Quite sure. Now tell me, did you really mean it, when you said just now that you wanted my advice?"

"Need you ask that, sir? Who else have I got to help me?"

"I am ready and willing to help you—but I can't do it unless I know first what has passed between you and Miss de Sor. Will you trust me?"

"I will!"

"May I depend on you?"

"Try me!"

CHAPTER XXXV. THE TREACHERY OF THE PIPE.

Alban took Mrs. Ellmother at her word. "I am going to venture on a guess," he said. "You have been with Miss de Sor to-night."

"Quite true, Mr. Morris."

"I am going to guess again. Did Miss de Sor ask you to stay with her, when you went into her room?"

"That's it! She rang for me, to see how I was getting on with my needlework—and she was what I call hearty, for the first time since I have been in her service. I didn't think badly of her when she first talked of engaging me; and I've had reason to repent of my opinion ever since. Oh, she showed the cloven foot to-night! 'Sit down,' she says; 'I've nothing to read, and I hate work; let's have a little chat.' She's got a glib tongue of her own. All I could do was to say a word now and then to keep her going. She talked and talked till it was time to light the lamp. She was particular in telling me to put the shade over it. We were half in the dark, and half in the light. She trapped me (Lord knows how!) into talking about foreign parts; I mean the place she lived in before they sent her to England. Have you heard that she comes from the West Indies?"

"Yes; I have heard that. Go on."

"Wait a bit, sir. There's something, by your leave, that I want to know. Do you believe in Witchcraft?"

"I know nothing about it. Did Miss de Sor put that question to you?"

"She did."

"And how did you answer?"

"Neither in one way nor the other. I'm in two minds about that matter of Witchcraft. When I was a girl, there was an old woman in our village, who was a sort of show. People came to see her from all the country round— gentlefolks among them. It was her great age that made her famous. More than a hundred years old, sir! One of our neighbors didn't believe in her age, and she heard of it. She cast a spell on his flock. I tell you, she sent a plague on his sheep, the plague of the Bots. The whole flock died; I remember it well. Some said the sheep would have had the Bots anyhow. Some said it was the spell. Which of them was right? How am I to settle it?"

"Did you mention this to Miss de Sor?"

"I was obliged to mention it. Didn't I tell you, just now, that I can't make up my mind about Witchcraft? 'You don't seem to know whether you believe or disbelieve,' she says. It made me look like a fool. I told her I had my reasons, and then I was obliged to give them."

"And what did she do then?"

"She said, 'I've got a better story of Witchcraft than yours.' And she opened a little book, with a lot of writing in it, and began to read. Her story made my flesh creep. It turns me cold, sir, when I think of it now."

He heard her moaning and shuddering. Strongly as his interest was excited, there was a compassionate reluctance in him to ask her to go on. His merciful scruples proved to be needless. The fascination of beauty it is possible to resist. The fascination of horror fastens its fearful hold on us, struggle against it as we may. Mrs. Ellmother repeated what she had heard, in spite of herself.

"It happened in the West Indies," she said; "and the writing of a woman slave was the writing in the little book. The slave wrote about her mother. Her mother was a black—a Witch in her own country. There was a forest in her own country. The devil taught her Witchcraft in the forest. The serpents and the wild beasts were afraid to touch her. She lived without eating. She was sold for a slave, and sent to the island—an island in the West Indies. An old man lived there; the wickedest man of them all. He filled the black Witch with devilish knowledge. She learned to make the image of wax. The image of wax casts spells. You put pins in the image of wax. At every pin you put, the person under the spell gets nearer and nearer to death. There was a poor black in the island. He offended the Witch. She made his image in wax; she cast spells on him. He couldn't sleep; he couldn't eat; he was such a coward that common noises frightened him. Like Me! Oh, God, like me!"

"Wait a little," Alban interposed. "You are exciting yourself again—wait."

"You're wrong, sir! You think it ended when she finished her story, and shut up her book; there's worse to come than anything you've heard yet. I don't know what I did to offend her. She looked at me and spoke to me, as if I was the dirt under her feet. 'If you're too stupid to understand what I have been reading,' she says, 'get up and go to the glass. Look at yourself, and remember what happened to the slave who was under the spell. You're getting paler and paler, and thinner and thinner; you're pining away just as he did. Shall I tell you why?' She snatched off the shade from the lamp, and put her hand under the table, and brought out an image of wax. My image! She pointed to three pins in it. 'One,' she says, 'for no sleep. One for no appetite. One for broken nerves.' I asked her what I had done to make such a bitter enemy of her. She says, 'Remember what I asked of you when we talked of your being my servant. Choose which you will do? Die by inches' (I swear she said it as I hope to be saved); 'die by inches, or tell me—'"

There—in the full frenzy of the agitation that possessed her—there, Mrs. Ellmother suddenly stopped.

Alban's first impression was that she might have fainted. He looked closer, and could just see her shadowy figure still seated in the chair. He asked if she was ill. No.

"Then why don't you go on?"

"I have done," she answered.

"Do you think you can put me off," he rejoined sternly, "with such an excuse as that? What did Miss de Sor ask you to tell her? You promised to trust me. Be as good as your word."

In the days of her health and strength, she would have set him at defiance. All she could do now was to appeal to his mercy.

"Make some allowance for me," she said. "I have been terribly upset. What has become of my courage? What has broken me down in this way? Spare me, sir."

He refused to listen. "This vile attempt to practice on your fears may be repeated," he reminded her. "More cruel advantage may be taken of the nervous derangement from which you are suffering in the climate of this place. You little know me, if you think I will allow that to go on."

She made a last effort to plead with him. "Oh sir, is this behaving like the good kind man I thought you were? You say you are Miss Emily's friend? Don't press me—for Miss Emily's sake!"

"Emily!" Alban exclaimed. "Is she concerned in this?"

There was a change to tenderness in his voice, which persuaded Mrs. Ellmother that she had found her way to the weak side of him. Her one effort now was to strengthen the impression which she believed herself to have produced. "Miss Emily is concerned in it," she confessed.

"In what way?"

"Never mind in what way."

"But I do mind."

"I tell you, sir, Miss Emily must never know it to her dying day!"

The first suspicion of the truth crossed Alban's mind.

"I understand you at last," he said. "What Miss Emily must never know—is what Miss de Sor wanted you to tell her. Oh, it's useless to contradict me! Her motive in trying to frighten you is as plain to me now as if she had confessed it. Are you sure you didn't betray yourself, when she showed the image of wax?"

"I should have died first!" The reply had hardly escaped her before she regretted it. "What makes you want to be so sure about it?" she said. "It looks as if you knew—"

"I do know."

"What!"

The kindest thing that he could do now was to speak out. "Your secret is no secret to me," he said.

Rage and fear shook her together. For the moment she was like the Mrs. Ellmother of former days. "You lie!" she cried.

"I speak the truth."

"I won't believe you! I daren't believe you!"

"Listen to me. In Emily's interests, listen to me. I have read of the murder at Zeeland—"

208

"That's nothing! The man was a namesake of her father."

"The man was her father himself. Keep your seat! There is nothing to be alarmed about. I know that Emily is ignorant of the horrid death that her father died. I know that you and your late mistress have kept the discovery from her to this day. I know the love and pity which plead your excuse for deceiving her, and the circumstances that favored the deception. My good creature, Emily's peace of mind is as sacred to me as it is to you! I love her as I love my own life—and better. Are you calmer, now?"

He heard her crying: it was the best relief that could come to her. After waiting a while to let the tears have their way, he helped her to rise. There was no more to be said now. The one thing to do was to take her back to the house.

"I can give you a word of advice," he said, "before we part for the night. You must leave Miss de Sor's service at once. Your health will be a sufficient excuse. Give her warning immediately."

Mrs. Ellmother hung back, when he offered her his arm. The bare prospect of seeing Francine again was revolting to her. On Alban's assurance that the notice to leave could be given in writing, she made no further resistance. The village clock struck eleven as they ascended the terrace steps.

A minute later, another person left the grounds by the path which led to the house. Alban's precaution had been taken too late. The smell of tobacco-smoke had guided Francine, when she was at a loss which way to turn next in search of Mrs. Ellmother. For the last quarter of an hour she had been listening, hidden among the trees.

CHAPTER XXXVI. CHANGE OF AIR.

The inmates of Netherwoods rose early, and went to bed early. When Alban and Mrs. Ellmother arrived at the back door of the house, they found it locked.

The only light visible, along the whole length of the building, glimmered through the Venetian blind of the window-entrance to Francine's sitting-room. Alban proposed to get admission to the house by that way. In her horror of again encountering Francine, Mrs. Ellmother positively refused to follow him when he turned away from the door. "They can't be all asleep yet," she said—and rang the bell.

One person was still out of bed—and that person was the mistress of the house. They recognized her voice in the customary question: "Who's there?" The door having been opened, good Miss Ladd looked backward and forward between Alban and Mrs. Ellmother, with the bewildered air of a lady who doubted the evidence of her own eyes. The next moment, her sense of humor overpowered her. She burst out laughing.

"Close the door, Mr. Morris," she said, "and be so good as to tell me what this means. Have you been giving a lesson in drawing by starlight?"

Mrs. Ellmother moved, so that the light of the lamp in Miss Ladd's hand fell on her face. "I am faint and giddy," she said; "let me go to my bed."

Miss Ladd instantly followed her. "Pray forgive me! I didn't see you were ill, when I spoke," she gently explained. "What can I do for you?"

"Thank you kindly, ma'am. I want nothing but peace and quiet. I wish you good-night."

Alban followed Miss Ladd to her study, on the front side of the house. He had just mentioned the circumstances under which he and Mrs. Ellmother had met, when they were interrupted by a tap at the door. Francine had got back to her room unperceived, by way of the French window. She now presented herself, with an elaborate apology, and with the nearest approach to a penitent expression of which her face was capable.

"I am ashamed, Miss Ladd, to intrude on you at this time of night. My only excuse is, that I am anxious about Mrs. Ellmother. I heard you just now in the hall. If she is really ill, I am the unfortunate cause of it."

"In what way, Miss de Sor?"

"I am sorry to say I frightened her—while we were talking in my room—quite unintentionally. She rushed to the door and ran out. I supposed she had gone to her bedroom; I had no idea she was in the grounds."

210

In this false statement there was mingled a grain of truth. It was true that Francine believed Mrs. Ellmother to have taken refuge in her room—for she had examined the room. Finding it empty, and failing to discover the fugitive in other parts of the house, she had become alarmed, and had tried the grounds next—with the formidable result which has been already related. Concealing this circumstance, she had lied in such a skillfully artless manner that Alban (having no suspicion of what had really happened to sharpen his wits) was as completely deceived as Miss Ladd. Proceeding to further explanation—and remembering that she was in Alban's presence—Francine was careful to keep herself within the strict limit of truth. Confessing that she had frightened her servant by a description of sorcery, as it was practiced among the slaves on her father's estate, she only lied again, in declaring that Mrs. Ellmother had supposed she was in earnest, when she was guilty of no more serious offense than playing a practical joke.

In this case, Alban was necessarily in a position to detect the falsehood. But it was so evidently in Francine's interests to present her conduct in the most favorable light, that the discovery failed to excite his suspicion. He waited in silence, while Miss Ladd administered a severe reproof. Francine having left the room, as penitently as she had entered it (with her handkerchief over her tearless eyes), he was at liberty, with certain reserves, to return to what had passed between Mrs. Ellmother and himself.

"The fright which the poor old woman has suffered," he said, "has led to one good result. I have found her ready at last to acknowledge that she is ill, and inclined to believe that the change to Netherwoods has had something to do with it. I have advised her to take the course which you suggested, by leaving this house. Is it possible to dispense with the usual delay, when she gives notice to leave Miss de Sor's service?"

"She need feel no anxiety, poor soul, on that account," Miss Ladd replied. "In any case, I had arranged that a week's notice on either side should be enough. As it is, I will speak to Francine myself. The least she can do, to express her regret, is to place no difficulties in Mrs. Ellmother's way."

The next day was Sunday.

Miss Ladd broke through her rule of attending to secular affairs on week days only; and, after consulting with Mrs. Ellmother, arranged with Francine that her servant should be at liberty to leave Netherwoods (health permitting) on the next day. But one difficulty remained. Mrs. Ellmother was in no condition to take the long journey to her birthplace in Cumberland; and her own lodgings in London had been let.

Under these circumstances, what was the best arrangement that could be made for her? Miss Ladd wisely and kindly wrote to Emily on the subject, and asked for a speedy reply.

Later in the day, Alban was sent for to see Mrs. Ellmother. He found her anxiously waiting to hear what had passed, on the previous night, between Miss Ladd and himself. "Were you careful, sir, to say nothing about Miss Emily?"

"I was especially careful; I never alluded to her in any way."

"Has Miss de Sor spoken to you?"

"I have not given her the opportunity."

"She's an obstinate one—she might try."

"If she does, she shall hear my opinion of her in plain words." The talk between them turned next on Alban's discovery of the secret, of which Mrs. Ellmother had believed herself to be the sole depositary since Miss Letitia's death. Without alarming her by any needless allusion to Doctor Allday or to Miss Jethro, he answered her inquiries (so far as he was himself concerned) without reserve. Her curiosity once satisfied, she showed no disposition to pursue the topic. She pointed to Miss Ladd's cat, fast asleep by the side of an empty saucer.

"Is it a sin, Mr. Morris, to wish I was Tom? He doesn't trouble himself about his life that is past or his life that is to come. If I could only empty my saucer and go to sleep, I shouldn't be thinking of the number of people in this world, like myself, who would be better out of it than in it. Miss Ladd has got me my liberty tomorrow; and I don't even know where to go, when I leave this place."

"Suppose you follow Tom's example?" Alban suggested. "Enjoy to-day (in that comfortable chair) and let to-morrow take care of itself."

To-morrow arrived, and justified Alban's system of philosophy. Emily answered Miss Ladd's letter, to excellent purpose, by telegraph.

"I leave London to-day with Cecilia" (the message announced) "for Monksmoor Park, Hants. Will Mrs. Ellmother take care of the cottage in my absence? I shall be away for a month, at least. All is prepared for her if she consents."

Mrs. Ellmother gladly accepted this proposal. In the interval of Emily's absence, she could easily arrange to return to her own lodgings. With words of sincere gratitude she took leave of Miss Ladd; but no persuasion would induce her to say good-by to Francine. "Do me one more kindness, ma'am; don't tell Miss de Sor when I go away." Ignorant of the provocation which had produced this unforgiving temper of mind, Miss Ladd gently remonstrated. "Miss de Sor received my reproof in a penitent spirit; she expresses sincere sorrow for having thoughtlessly frightened you. Both yesterday and to-day she has made kind inquiries after your health. Come! come! don't bear malice—wish her good-by." Mrs. Ellmother's answer was characteristic. "I'll say good-by by telegraph, when I get to London."

Her last words were addressed to Alban. "If you can find a way of doing it, sir, keep those two apart."

"Do you mean Emily and Miss de Sor?

"Yes."

"What are you afraid of?"

"I don't know."

"Is that quite reasonable, Mrs. Ellmother?"

"I daresay not. I only know that I am afraid."

The pony chaise took her away. Alban's class was not yet ready for him.

He waited on the terrace.

Innocent alike of all knowledge of the serious reason for fear which did really exist, Mrs. Ellmother and Alban felt, nevertheless, the same vague distrust of an intimacy between the two girls. Idle, vain, malicious, false—to know that Francine's character presented these faults, without any discoverable merits to set against them, was surely enough to justify a gloomy view of the prospect, if she succeeded in winning the position of Emily's friend. Alban reasoned it out logically in this way—without satisfying himself, and without accounting for the remembrance that haunted him of Mrs. Ellmother's farewell look. "A commonplace man would say we are both in a morbid state of mind," he thought; "and sometimes commonplace men turn out to be right."

He was too deeply preoccupied to notice that he had advanced perilously near Francine's window. She suddenly stepped out of her room, and spoke to him.

"Do you happen to know, Mr. Morris, why Mrs. Ellmother has gone away without bidding me good-by?"

"She was probably afraid, Miss de Sor, that you might make her the victim of another joke."

Francine eyed him steadily. "Have you any particular reason for speaking to me in that way?"

"I am not aware that I have answered you rudely—if that is what you mean."

"That is not what I mean. You seem to have taken a dislike to me. I should be glad to know why."

"I dislike cruelty—and you have behaved cruelly to Mrs. Ellmother."

"Meaning to be cruel?" Francine inquired.

"You know as well as I do, Miss de Sor, that I can't answer that question."

Francine looked at him again "Am I to understand that we are enemies?"

214

she asked.

"You are to understand," he replied, "that a person whom Miss Ladd employs to help her in teaching, cannot always presume to express his sentiments in speaking to the young ladies."

"If that means anything, Mr. Morris, it means that we are enemies."

"It means, Miss de Sor, that I am the drawing-master at this school, and that I am called to my class."

Francine returned to her room, relieved of the only doubt that had troubled her. Plainly no suspicion that she had overheard what passed between Mrs. Ellmother and himself existed in Alban's mind. As to the use to be made of her discovery, she felt no difficulty in deciding to wait, and be guided by events. Her curiosity and her self-esteem had been alike gratified—she had got the better of Mrs. Ellmother at last, and with that triumph she was content. While Emily remained her friend, it would be an act of useless cruelty to disclose the terrible truth. There had certainly been a coolness between them at Brighton. But Francine—still influenced by the magnetic attraction which drew her to Emily—did not conceal from herself that she had offered the provocation, and had been therefore the person to blame. "I can set all that right," she thought, "when we meet at Monksmoor Park." She opened her desk and wrote the shortest and sweetest of letters to Cecilia. "I am entirely at the disposal of my charming friend, on any convenient day— may I add, my dear, the sooner the better?"

CHAPTER XXXVII. "THE LADY WANTS YOU, SIR."

The pupils of the drawing-class put away their pencils and color-boxes in high good humor: the teacher's vigilant eye for faults had failed him for the first time in their experience. Not one of them had been reproved; they had chattered and giggled and drawn caricatures on the margin of the paper, as freely as if the master had left the room. Alban's wandering attention was indeed beyond the reach of control. His interview with Francine had doubled his sense of responsibility toward Emily—while he was further than ever from seeing how he could interfere, to any useful purpose, in his present position, and with his reasons for writing under reserve.

One of the servants addressed him as he was leaving the schoolroom. The landlady's boy was waiting in the hall, with a message from his lodgings.

"Now then! what is it?" he asked, irritably.

"The lady wants you, sir." With this mysterious answer, the boy presented a visiting card. The name inscribed on it was—"Miss Jethro."

She had arrived by the train, and she was then waiting at Alban's lodgings. "Say I will be with her directly." Having given the message, he stood for a while, with his hat in his hand—literally lost in astonishment. It was simply impossible to guess at Miss Jethro's object: and yet, with the usual perversity of human nature, he was still wondering what she could possibly want with him, up to the final moment when he opened the door of his sitting-room.

She rose and bowed with the same grace of movement, and the same well-bred composure of manner, which Doctor Allday had noticed when she entered his consulting-room. Her dark melancholy eyes rested on Alban with a look of gentle interest. A faint flush of color animated for a moment the faded beauty of her face—passed away again—and left it paler than before.

"I cannot conceal from myself," she began, "that I am intruding on you under embarrassing circumstances."

"May I ask, Miss Jethro, to what circumstances you allude?"

"You forget, Mr. Morris, that I left Miss Ladd's school, in a manner which justified doubt of me in the minds of strangers."

"Speaking as one of those strangers," Alban replied, "I cannot feel that I had any right to form an opinion, on a matter which only concerned Miss Ladd and yourself."

Miss Jethro bowed gravely. "You encourage me to hope," she said. "I think you will place a favorable construction on my visit when I mention my motive. I ask you to receive me, in the interests of Miss Emily Brown."

Stating her purpose in calling on him in those plain terms, she added to the amazement which Alban already felt, by handing to him—as if she was presenting an introduction—a letter marked, "Private," addressed to her by Doctor Allday.

"I may tell you," she premised, "that I had no idea of troubling you, until Doctor Allday suggested it. I wrote to him in the first instance; and there is his reply. Pray read it."

The letter was dated, "Penzance"; and the doctor wrote, as he spoke, without ceremony.

"MADAM—Your letter has been forwarded to me. I am spending my autumn holiday in the far West of Cornwall. However, if I had been at home, it would have made no difference. I should have begged leave to decline holding any further conversation with you, on the subject of Miss Emily Brown, for the following reasons:

"In the first place, though I cannot doubt your sincere interest in the young lady's welfare, I don't like your mysterious way of showing it. In the second place, when I called at your address in London, after you had left my house, I found that you had taken to flight. I place my own interpretation on this circumstance; but as it is not founded on any knowledge of facts, I merely allude to it, and say no more."

Arrived at that point, Alban offered to return the letter. "Do you really mean me to go on reading it?" he asked.

"Yes," she said quietly.

Alban returned to the letter.

"In the third place, I have good reason to believe that you entered Miss Ladd's school as a teacher, under false pretenses. After that discovery, I tell you plainly I hesitate to attach credit to any statement that you may wish to make. At the same time, I must not permit my prejudices (as you will probably call them) to stand in the way of Miss Emily's interests—supposing them to be really depending on any interference of yours. Miss Ladd's drawing-master, Mr. Alban Morris, is even more devoted to Miss Emily's service than I am. Whatever you might have said to me, you can say to him—with this possible advantage, that he may believe you."

There the letter ended. Alban handed it back in silence.

Miss Jethro pointed to the words, "Mr. Alban Morris is even more devoted to Miss Emily's service than I am."

"Is that true?" she asked.

"Quite true."

"I don't complain, Mr. Morris, of the hard things said of me in that letter; you are at liberty to suppose, if you like, that I deserve them. Attribute it to pride, or attribute it to reluctance to make needless demands on your time—I shall not attempt to defend myself. I leave you to decide whether the woman who has shown you that letter—having something important to say to you—is a person who is mean enough to say it under false pretenses."

"Tell me what I can do for you, Miss Jethro: and be assured, beforehand, that I don't doubt your sincerity."

"My purpose in coming here," she answered, "is to induce you to use your influence over Miss Emily Brown—"

"With what object?" Alban asked, interrupting her.

"My object is her own good. Some years since, I happened to become acquainted with a person who has attained some celebrity as a preacher. You have perhaps heard of Mr. Miles Mirabel?"

"I have heard of him."

"I have been in correspondence with him," Miss Jethro proceeded. "He tells me he has been introduced to a young lady, who was formerly one of Miss Ladd's pupils, and who is the daughter of Mr. Wyvil, of Monksmoor Park. He has called on Mr. Wyvil; and he has since received an invitation to stay at Mr. Wyvil's house. The day fixed for the visit is Monday, the fifth of next month."

Alban listened—at a loss to know what interest he was supposed to have in being made acquainted with Mr. Mirabel's engagements. Miss Jethro's next words enlightened him.

"You are perhaps aware," she resumed, "that Miss Emily Brown is Miss Wyvil's intimate friend. She will be one of the guests at Monksmoor Park. If there are any obstacles which you can place in her way—if there is any influence which you can exert, without exciting suspicion of your motive—prevent her, I entreat you, from accepting Miss Wyvil's invitation, until Mr. Mirabel's visit has come to an end."

"Is there anything against Mr. Mirabel?" he asked.

"I say nothing against him."

"Is Miss Emily acquainted with him?"

"No."

"Is he a person with whom it would be disagreeable to her to associate?"

"Quite the contrary."

"And yet you expect me to prevent them from meeting! Be reasonable, Miss Jethro."

"I can only be in earnest, Mr. Morris—more truly, more deeply in earnest than you can suppose. I declare to you that I am speaking in Miss Emily's interests. Do you still refuse to exert yourself for her sake?"

"I am spared the pain of refusal," Alban answered. "The time for interference has gone by. She is, at this moment, on her way to Monksmoor Park."

Miss Jethro attempted to rise—and dropped back into her chair. "Water!" she said faintly. After drinking from the glass to the last drop, she began to revive. Her little traveling-bag was on the floor at her side. She took out a railway guide, and tried to consult it. Her fingers trembled incessantly; she was unable to find the page to which she wished to refer. "Help me," she said, "I must leave this place—by the first train that passes."

"To see Emily?" Alban asked.

"Quite useless! You have said it yourself—the time for interference has gone by. Look at the guide."

"What place shall I look for?"

"Look for Vale Regis."

Alban found the place. The train was due in ten minutes. "Surely you are not fit to travel so soon?" he suggested.

"Fit or not, I must see Mr. Mirabel—I must make the effort to keep them apart by appealing to him."

"With any hope of success?"

"With no hope—and with no interest in the man himself. Still I must try."

"Out of anxiety for Emily's welfare?"

"Out of anxiety for more than that."

"For what?"

"If you can't guess, I daren't tell you."

That strange reply startled Alban. Before he could ask what it meant, Miss Jethro had left him.

In the emergencies of life, a person readier of resource than Alban Morris it would not have been easy to discover. The extraordinary interview that had now come to an end had found its limits. Bewildered and helpless, he stood at the window of his room, and asked himself (as if he had been the weakest man living), "What shall I do?"

BOOK THE FOURTH—THE COUNTRY HOUSE.

CHAPTER XXXVIII. DANCING.

The windows of the long drawing-room at Monksmoor are all thrown open to the conservatory. Distant masses of plants and flowers, mingled in ever-varying forms of beauty, are touched by the melancholy luster of the rising moon. Nearer to the house, the restful shadows are disturbed at intervals, where streams of light fall over them aslant from the lamps in the room. The fountain is playing. In rivalry with its lighter music, the nightingales are singing their song of ecstasy. Sometimes, the laughter of girls is heard—and, sometimes, the melody of a waltz. The younger guests at Monksmoor are dancing.

Emily and Cecilia are dressed alike in white, with flowers in their hair. Francine rivals them by means of a gorgeous contrast of color, and declares that she is rich with the bright emphasis of diamonds and the soft persuasion of pearls.

Miss Plym (from the rectory) is fat and fair and prosperous: she overflows with good spirits; she has a waist which defies tight-lacing, and she dances joyously on large flat feet. Miss Darnaway (officer's daughter with small means) is the exact opposite of Miss Plym. She is thin and tall and faded—poor soul. Destiny has made it her hard lot in life to fill the place of head-nursemaid at home. In her pensive moments, she thinks of the little brothers and sisters, whose patient servant she is, and wonders who comforts them in their tumbles and tells them stories at bedtime, while she is holiday-making at the pleasant country house.

Tender-hearted Cecilia, remembering how few pleasures this young friend has, and knowing how well she dances, never allows her to be without a partner. There are three invaluable young gentlemen present, who are excellent dancers. Members of different families, they are nevertheless fearfully and wonderfully like each other. They present the same rosy complexions and straw-colored mustachios, the same plump cheeks, vacant eyes and low forehead; and they utter, with the same stolid gravity, the same imbecile small talk. On sofas facing each other sit the two remaining guests, who have not joined the elders at the card-table in another room. They are both men. One of them is drowsy and middle-aged—happy in the possession of large landed property: happier still in a capacity for drinking Mr. Wyvil's famous port-wine without gouty results.

The other gentleman—ah, who is the other? He is the confidential adviser and bosom friend of every young lady in the house. Is it necessary to name the Reverend Miles Mirabel?

There he sits enthroned, with room for a fair admirer on either side of him—the clerical sultan of a platonic harem. His persuasive ministry is felt as well as heard: he has an innocent habit of fondling young persons. One of his arms is even long enough to embrace the circumference of Miss Plym—while the other clasps the rigid silken waist of Francine. "I do it everywhere else," he says innocently, "why not here?" Why not indeed—with that delicate complexion and those beautiful blue eyes; with the glorious golden hair that rests on his shoulders, and the glossy beard that flows over his breast? Familiarities, forbidden to mere men, become privileges and condescensions when an angel enters society—and more especially when that angel has enough of mortality in him to be amusing. Mr. Mirabel, on his social side, is an irresistible companion. He is cheerfulness itself; he takes a favorable view of everything; his sweet temper never differs with anybody. "In my humble way," he confesses, "I like to make the world about me brighter." Laughter (harmlessly produced, observe!) is the element in which he lives and breathes. Miss Darnaway's serious face puts him out; he has laid a bet with Emily—not in money, not even in gloves, only in flowers—that he will make Miss Darnaway laugh; and he has won the wager. Emily's flowers are in his button-hole, peeping through the curly interstices of his beard. "Must you leave me?" he asks tenderly, when there is a dancing man at liberty, and it is Francine's turn to claim him. She leaves her seat not very willingly. For a while, the place is vacant; Miss Plym seizes the opportunity of consulting the ladies' bosom friend.

"Dear Mr. Mirabel, do tell me what you think of Miss de Sor?"

Dear Mr. Mirabel bursts into enthusiasm and makes a charming reply. His large experience of young ladies warns him that they will tell each other what he thinks of them, when they retire for the night; and he is careful on these occasions to say something that will bear repetition.

"I see in Miss de Sor," he declares, "the resolution of a man, tempered by the sweetness of a woman. When that interesting creature marries, her husband will be—shall I use the vulgar word?—henpecked. Dear Miss Plym, he will enjoy it; and he will be quite right too; and, if I am asked to the wedding, I shall say, with heartfelt sincerity, Enviable man!"

In the height of her admiration for Mr. Mirabel's wonderful eye for character, Miss Plym is called away to the piano. Cecilia succeeds to her friend's place—and has her waist taken in charge as a matter of course.

"How do you like Miss Plym?" she asks directly.

Mr. Mirabel smiles, and shows the prettiest little pearly teeth. "I was just thinking of her," he confesses pleasantly; "Miss Plym is so nice and plump, so comforting and domestic—such a perfect clergyman's daughter. You love her, don't you? Is she engaged to be married? In that case—between ourselves, dear Miss Wyvil, a clergyman is obliged to be cautious—I may own that I love her too."

Delicious titillations of flattered self-esteem betray themselves in Cecilia's lovely complexion. She is the chosen confidante of this irresistible man; and she would like to express her sense of obligation. But Mr. Mirabel is a master in the art of putting the right words in the right places; and simple Cecilia distrusts herself and her grammar.

At that moment of embarrassment, a friend leaves the dance, and helps Cecilia out of the difficulty.

Emily approaches the sofa-throne, breathless—followed by her partner, entreating her to give him "one turn more." She is not to be tempted; she means to rest. Cecilia sees an act of mercy, suggested by the presence of the disengaged young man. She seizes his arm, and hurries him off to poor Miss Darnaway; sitting forlorn in a corner, and thinking of the nursery at home. In the meanwhile a circumstance occurs. Mr. Mirabel's all-embracing arm shows itself in a new character, when Emily sits by his side.

It becomes, for the first time, an irresolute arm. It advances a little—and hesitates. Emily at once administers an unexpected check; she insists on preserving a free waist, in her own outspoken language. "No, Mr. Mirabel, keep that for the others. You can't imagine how ridiculous you and the young ladies look, and how absurdly unaware of it you all seem to be." For the first time in his life, the reverend and ready-witted man of the world is at a loss for an answer. Why?

For this simple reason. He too has felt the magnetic attraction of the irresistible little creature whom every one likes. Miss Jethro has been doubly defeated. She has failed to keep them apart; and her unexplained misgivings have not been justified by events: Emily and Mr. Mirabel are good friends already. The brilliant clergyman is poor; his interests in life point to a marriage for money; he has fascinated the heiresses of two rich fathers, Mr. Tyvil and Mr. de Sor—and yet he is conscious of an influence (an alien influence, without a balance at its bankers), which has, in some mysterious way, got between him and his interests.

On Emily's side, the attraction felt is of another nature altogether. Among the merry young people at Monksmoor she is her old happy self again; and she finds in Mr. Mirabel the most agreeable and amusing man whom she has ever met. After those dismal night watches by the bed of her dying aunt, and the dreary weeks of solitude that followed, to live in this new world of luxury and gayety is like escaping from the darkness of night, and basking in the fall brightness of day. Cecilia declares that she looks, once more, like the joyous queen of the bedroom, in the bygone time at school; and Francine (profaning Shakespeare without knowing it), says, "Emily is herself again!"

"Now that your arm is in its right place, reverend sir," she gayly resumes,

"I may admit that there are exceptions to all rules. My waist is at your disposal, in a case of necessity—that is to say, in a case of waltzing."

"The one case of all others," Mirabel answers, with the engaging frankness that has won him so many friends, "which can never happen in my unhappy experience. Waltzing, I blush to own it, means picking me up off the floor, and putting smelling salts to my nostrils. In other words, dear Miss Emily, it is the room that waltzes—not I. I can't look at those whirling couples there, with a steady head. Even the exquisite figure of our young hostess, when it describes flying circles, turns me giddy."

Hearing this allusion to Cecilia, Emily drops to the level of the other girls. She too pays her homage to the Pope of private life. "You promised me your unbiased opinion of Cecilia," she reminds him; "and you haven't given it yet."

The ladies' friend gently remonstrates. "Miss Wyvil's beauty dazzles me. How can I give an unbiased opinion? Besides, I am not thinking of her; I can only think of you."

Emily lifts her eyes, half merrily, half tenderly, and looks at him over the top of her fan. It is her first effort at flirtation. She is tempted to engage in the most interesting of all games to a girl—the game which plays at making love. What has Cecilia told her, in those bedroom gossipings, dear to the hearts of the two friends? Cecilia has whispered, "Mr. Mirabel admires your figure; he calls you 'the Venus of Milo, in a state of perfect abridgment.'" Where is the daughter of Eve, who would not have been flattered by that pretty compliment—who would not have talked soft nonsense in return? "You can only think of Me," Emily repeats coquettishly. "Have you said that to the last young lady who occupied my place, and will you say it again to the next who follows me?"

"Not to one of them! Mere compliments are for the others—not for you."

"What is for me, Mr. Mirabel?"

"What I have just offered you—a confession of the truth."

Emily is startled by the tone in which he replies. He seems to be in earnest; not a vestige is left of the easy gayety of his manner. His face shows an expression of anxiety which she has never seen in it yet. "Do you believe me?" he asks in a whisper.

She tries to change the subject.

"When am I to hear you preach, Mr. Mirabel?"

He persists. "When you believe me," he says.

His eyes add an emphasis to that reply which is not to be mistaken. Emily turns away from him, and notices Francine. She has left the dance, and is looking with marked attention at Emily and Mirabel. "I want to speak to you," she says, and beckons impatiently to Emily.

Mirabel whispers, "Don't go!"

Emily rises nevertheless—ready to avail herself of the first excuse for leaving him. Francine meets her half way, and takes her roughly by the arm.

"What is it?" Emily asks.

"Suppose you leave off flirting with Mr. Mirabel, and make yourself of some use."

"In what way?"

"Use your ears—and look at that girl."

She points disdainfully to innocent Miss Plym. The rector's daughter possesses all the virtues, with one exception—the virtue of having an ear for music. When she sings, she is out of tune; and, when she plays, she murders time.

"Who can dance to such music as that?" says Francine. "Finish the waltz for her."

Emily naturally hesitates. "How can I take her place, unless she asks me?"

Francine laughs scornfully. "Say at once, you want to go back to Mr.

226

Mirabel."

"Do you think I should have got up, when you beckoned to me," Emily rejoins, "if I had not wanted to get away from Mr. Mirabel?"

Instead of resenting this sharp retort, Francine suddenly breaks into good humor. "Come along, you little spit-fire; I'll manage it for you."

She leads Emily to the piano, and stops Miss Plym without a word of apology: "It's your turn to dance now. Here's Miss Brown waiting to relieve you."

Cecilia has not been unobservant, in her own quiet way, of what has been going on. Waiting until Francine and Miss Plym are out of hearing, she bends over Emily, and says, "My dear, I really do think Francine is in love with Mr. Mirabel."

"After having only been a week in the same house with him!" Emily exclaims.

"At any rate," said Cecilia, more smartly than usual, "she is jealous of you."

CHAPTER XXXIX. FEIGNING.

The next morning, Mr. Mirabel took two members of the circle at Monksmoor by surprise. One of them was Emily; and one of them was the master of the house.

Seeing Emily alone in the garden before breakfast, he left his room and joined her. "Let me say one word," he pleaded, "before we go to breakfast. I am grieved to think that I was so unfortunate as to offend you, last night."

Emily's look of astonishment answered for her before she could speak. "What can I have said or done," she asked, "to make you think that?"

"Now I breathe again!" he cried, with the boyish gayety of manner which was one of the secrets of his popularity among women. "I really feared that I had spoken thoughtlessly. It is a terrible confession for a clergyman to make—but it is not the less true that I am one of the most indiscreet men living. It is my rock ahead in life that I say the first thing which comes uppermost, without stopping to think. Being well aware of my own defects, I naturally distrust myself."

"Even in the pulpit?" Emily inquired.

He laughed with the readiest appreciation of the satire—although it was directed against himself.

"I like that question," he said; "it tells me we are as good friends again as ever. The fact is, the sight of the congregation, when I get into the pulpit, has the same effect upon me that the sight of the footlights has on an actor. All oratory (though my clerical brethren are shy of confessing it) is acting—without the scenery and the costumes. Did you really mean it, last night, when you said you would like to hear me preach?"

"Indeed, I did."

"How very kind of you. I don't think myself the sermon is worth the sacrifice. (There is another specimen of my indiscreet way of talking!) What I mean is, that you will have to get up early on Sunday morning, and drive twelve miles to the damp and dismal little village, in which I officiate for a man with a rich wife who likes the climate of Italy. My congregation works in the fields all the week, and naturally enough goes to sleep in church on Sunday. I have had to counteract that. Not by preaching! I wouldn't puzzle the poor people with my eloquence for the world. No, no: I tell them little stories out of the Bible—in a nice easy gossiping way. A quarter of an hour is my limit of time; and, I am proud to say, some of them (mostly the women) do to a certain extent keep awake. If you and the other ladies decide to honor me, it is needless to say you shall have one of my grand efforts. What will be the effect on my unfortunate flock remains to be seen. I will have the church brushed up, and luncheon of course at the parsonage. Beans, bacon, and beer—I haven't got anything else in the house. Are you rich? I hope not!"

"I suspect I am quite as poor as you are, Mr. Mirabel."

"I am delighted to hear it. (More of my indiscretion!) Our poverty is another bond between us."

Before he could enlarge on this text, the breakfast bell rang.

He gave Emily his arm, quite satisfied with the result of the morning's talk. In speaking seriously to her on the previous night, he had committed the mistake of speaking too soon. To amend this false step, and to recover his position in Emily's estimation, had been his object in view—and it had been successfully accomplished. At the breakfast-table that morning, the companionable clergyman was more amusing than ever.

The meal being over, the company dispersed as usual—with the one exception of Mirabel. Without any apparent reason, he kept his place at the table. Mr. Wyvil, the most courteous and considerate of men, felt it an attention due to his guest not to leave the room first. All that he could venture to do was to give a little hint. "Have you any plans for the morning?" he asked.

"I have a plan that depends entirely on yourself," Mirabel answered; "and I am afraid of being as indiscreet as usual, if I mention it. Your charming daughter tells me you play on the violin."

Modest Mr. Wyvil looked confused. "I hope you have not been annoyed," he said; "I practice in a distant room so that nobody may hear me."

"My dear sir, I am eager to hear you! Music is my passion; and the violin is my favorite instrument."

Mr. Wyvil led the way to his room, positively blushing with pleasure. Since the death of his wife he had been sadly in want of a little encouragement. His daughters and his friends were careful—over-careful, as he thought—of intruding on him in his hours of practice. And, sad to say, his daughters and his friends were, from a musical point of view, perfectly right.

Literature has hardly paid sufficient attention to a social phenomenon of a singularly perplexing kind. We hear enough, and more than enough, of persons who successfully cultivate the Arts—of the remarkable manner in which fitness for their vocation shows itself in early life, of the obstacles which family prejudice places in their way, and of the unremitting devotion which has led to the achievement of glorious results.

But how many writers have noticed those other incomprehensible persons, members of families innocent for generations past of practicing Art or caring for Art, who have notwithstanding displayed from their earliest years the irresistible desire to cultivate poetry, painting, or music; who have surmounted obstacles, and endured disappointments, in the single-hearted resolution to devote their lives to an intellectual pursuit—being absolutely without the capacity which proves the vocation, and justifies the sacrifice. Here is Nature, "unerring Nature," presented in flat contradiction with herself. Here are men bent on performing feats of running, without having legs; and women, hopelessly barren, living in constant expectation of large families to the end of their days. The musician is not to be found more completely deprived than Mr. Wyvil of natural capacity for playing on an instrument— and, for twenty years past, it had been the pride and delight of his heart to let no day of his life go by without practicing on the violin.

"I am sure I must be tiring you," he said politely—after having played without mercy for an hour and more.

No: the insatiable amateur had his own purpose to gain, and was not exhausted yet. Mr. Wyvil got up to look for some more music. In that interval desultory conversation naturally took place. Mirabel contrived to give it the necessary direction—the direction of Emily.

"The most delightful girl I have met with for many a long year past!" Mr. Wyvil declared warmly. "I don't wonder at my daughter being so fond of her. She leads a solitary life at home, poor thing; and I am honestly glad to see her spirits reviving in my house."

"An only child?" Mirabel asked.

In the necessary explanation that followed, Emily's isolated position in the world was revealed in few words. But one more discovery—the most important of all—remained to be made. Had she used a figure of speech in saying that she was as poor as Mirabel himself? or had she told him the shocking truth? He put the question with perfect delicacy—-but with unerring directness as well.

Mr. Wyvil, quoting his daughter's authority, described Emily's income as falling short even of two hundred a year. Having made that disheartening reply, he opened another music book. "You know this sonata, of course?" he said. The next moment, the violin was under his chin and the performance began.

While Mirabel was, to all appearance, listening with the utmost attention, he was actually endeavoring to reconcile himself to a serious sacrifice of his own inclinations. If he remained much longer in the same house with Emily, the impression that she had produced on him would be certainly strengthened—and he would be guilty of the folly of making an offer of marriage to a woman who was as poor as himself. The one remedy that could be trusted to preserve him from such infatuation as this, was absence. At the end of the week, he had arranged to return to Vale Regis for his Sunday duty; engaging to join his friends again at Monksmoor on the Monday following. That rash promise, there could be no further doubt about it, must not be fulfilled.

He had arrived at this resolution, when the terrible activity of Mr. Wyvil's bow was suspended by the appearance of a third person in the room.

Cecilia's maid was charged with a neat little three-cornered note from her young lady, to be presented to her master. Wondering why his daughter should write to him, Mr. Wyvil opened the note, and was informed of Cecilia's motive in these words:

"DEAREST PAPA—I hear Mr. Mirabel is with you, and as this is a secret, I must write. Emily has received a very strange letter this morning, which puzzles her and alarms me. When you are quite at liberty, we shall be so much obliged if you will tell us how Emily ought to answer it."

Mr. Wyvil stopped Mirabel, on the point of trying to escape from the music. "A little domestic matter to attend to," he said. "But we will finish the sonata first."

CHAPTER XL. CONSULTING.

Out of the music room, and away from his violin, the sound side of Mr. Wyvil's character was free to assert itself. In his public and in his private capacity, he was an eminently sensible man.

As a member of parliament, he set an example which might have been followed with advantage by many of his colleagues. In the first place he abstained from hastening the downfall of representative institutions by asking questions and making speeches. In the second place, he was able to distinguish between the duty that he owed to his party, and the duty that he owed to his country. When the Legislature acted politically—that is to say, when it dealt with foreign complications, or electoral reforms—he followed his leader. When the Legislature acted socially—that is to say, for the good of the people—he followed his conscience. On the last occasion when the great Russian bugbear provoked a division, he voted submissively with his Conservative allies. But, when the question of opening museums and picture galleries on Sundays arrayed the two parties in hostile camps, he broke into open mutiny, and went over to the Liberals. He consented to help in preventing an extension of the franchise; but he refused to be concerned in obstructing the repeal of taxes on knowledge. "I am doubtful in the first case," he said, "but I am sure in the second." He was asked for an explanation: "Doubtful of what? and sure of what?" To the astonishment of his leader, he answered: "The benefit to the people." The same sound sense appeared in the transactions of his private life. Lazy and dishonest servants found that the gentlest of masters had a side to his character which took them by surprise. And, on certain occasions in the experience of Cecilia and her sister, the most indulgent of fathers proved to be as capable of saying No, as the sternest tyrant who ever ruled a fireside.

Called into council by his daughter and his guest, Mr. Wyvil assisted them by advice which was equally wise and kind—but which afterward proved, under the perverse influence of circumstances, to be advice that he had better not have given.

The letter to Emily which Cecilia had recommended to her father's consideration, had come from Netherwoods, and had been written by Alban Morris.

He assured Emily that he had only decided on writing to her, after some hesitation, in the hope of serving interests which he did not himself understand, but which might prove to be interests worthy of consideration, nevertheless. Having stated his motive in these terms, he proceeded to relate what had passed between Miss Jethro and himself. On the subject of Francine, Alban only ventured to add that she had not produced a favorable impression on him, and that he could not think her likely, on further experience, to prove a desirable friend.

On the last leaf were added some lines, which Emily was at no loss how to answer. She had folded back the page, so that no eyes but her own should see how the poor drawing-master finished his letter: "I wish you all possible happiness, my dear, among your new friends; but don't forget the old friend who thinks of you, and dreams of you, and longs to see you again. The little world I live in is a dreary world, Emily, in your absence. Will you write to me now and then, and encourage me to hope?"

Mr. Wyvil smiled, as he looked at the folded page, which hid the signature.

"I suppose I may take it for granted," he said slyly, "that this gentleman really has your interests at heart? May I know who he is?"

Emily answered the last question readily enough. Mr. Wyvil went on with his inquiries. "About the mysterious lady, with the strange name," he proceeded—"do you know anything of her?"

Emily related what she knew; without revealing the true reason for Miss Jethro's departure from Netherwoods. In after years, it was one of her most treasured remembrances, that she had kept secret the melancholy confession which had startled her, on the last night of her life at school.

Mr. Wyvil looked at Alban's letter again. "Do you know how Miss Jethro became acquainted with Mr. Mirabel?" he asked.

"I didn't even know that they were acquainted."

"Do you think it likely—if Mr. Morris had been talking to you instead of writing to you—that he might have said more than he has said in his letter?"

Cecilia had hitherto remained a model of discretion. Seeing Emily hesitate, temptation overcame her. "Not a doubt of it, papa!" she declared confidently.

"Is Cecilia right?" Mr. Wyvil inquired.

Reminded in this way of her influence over Alban, Emily could only make one honest reply. She admitted that Cecilia was right.

Mr. Wyvil thereupon advised her not to express any opinion, until she was in a better position to judge for herself. "When you write to Mr. Morris," he continued, "say that you will wait to tell him what you think of Miss Jethro, until you see him again."

"I have no prospect at present of seeing him again," Emily said.

"You can see Mr. Morris whenever it suits him to come here," Mr. Wyvil replied. "I will write and ask him to visit us, and you can inclose the invitation in your letter."

"Oh, Mr. Wyvil, how good of you!"

"Oh, papa, the very thing I was going to ask you to do!"

The excellent master of Monksmoor looked unaffectedly surprised. "What are you two young ladies making a fuss about?" he said. "Mr. Morris is a gentleman by profession; and—may I venture to say it, Miss Emily?—a valued friend of yours as well. Who has a better claim to be one of my guests?"

Cecilia stopped her father as he was about to leave the room. "I suppose we mustn't ask Mr. Mirabel what he knows of Miss Jethro?" she said.

"My dear, what can you be thinking of? What right have we to question Mr. Mirabel about Miss Jethro?"

"It's so very unsatisfactory, papa. There must be some reason why Emily and Mr. Mirabel ought not to meet—or why should Miss Jethro have been so very earnest about it?"

"Miss Jethro doesn't intend us to know why, Cecilia. It will perhaps come out in time. Wait for time."

Left together, the girls discussed the course which Alban would probably take, on receiving Mr. Wyvil's invitation.

"He will only be too glad," Cecilia asserted, "to have the opportunity of seeing you again."

"I doubt whether he will care about seeing me again, among strangers," Emily replied. "And you forget that there are obstacles in his way. How is he to leave his class?"

"Quite easily! His class doesn't meet on the Saturday half-holiday. He can be here, if he starts early, in time for luncheon; and he can stay till Monday or Tuesday."

"Who is to take his place at the school?"

"Miss Ladd, to be sure—if you make a point of it. Write to her, as well as to Mr. Morris."

The letters being written—and the order having been given to prepare a room for the expected guest—Emily and Cecilia returned to the drawing-room. They found the elders of the party variously engaged—the men with newspapers, and the ladies with work. Entering the conservatory next, they discovered Cecilia's sister languishing among the flowers in an easy chair. Constitutional laziness, in some young ladies, assumes an invalid character, and presents the interesting spectacle of perpetual convalescence. The doctor declared that the baths at St. Moritz had cured Miss Julia. Miss Julia declined to agree with the doctor.

"Come into the garden with Emily and me," Cecilia said.

"Emily and you don't know what it is to be ill," Julia answered.

The two girls left her, and joined the young people who were amusing themselves in the garden. Francine had taken possession of Mirabel, and had condemned him to hard labor in swinging her. He made an attempt to get away when Emily and Cecilia approached, and was peremptorily recalled to his duty. "Higher!" cried Miss de Sor, in her hardest tones of authority. "I want to swing higher than anybody else!" Mirabel submitted with gentleman-like resignation, and was rewarded by tender encouragement expressed in a look.

"Do you see that?" Cecilia whispered. "He knows how rich she is—I wonder whether he will marry her."

Emily smiled. "I doubt it, while he is in this house," she said. "You are as rich as Francine—and don't forget that you have other attractions as well."

Cecilia shook her head. "Mr. Mirabel is very nice," she admitted; "but I wouldn't marry him. Would you?"

Emily secretly compared Alban with Mirabel. "Not for the world!" she answered.

The next day was the day of Mirabel's departure. His admirers among the ladies followed him out to the door, at which Mr. Wyvil's carriage was waiting. Francine threw a nosegay after the departing guest as he got in. "Mind you come back to us on Monday!" she said. Mirabel bowed and thanked her; but his last look was for Emily, standing apart from the others at the top of the steps. Francine said nothing; her lips closed convulsively—she turned suddenly pale.

CHAPTER XLI. SPEECHIFYING.

On the Monday, a plowboy from Vale Regis arrived at Monksmoor.

In respect of himself, he was a person beneath notice. In respect of his errand, he was sufficiently important to cast a gloom over the household. The faithless Mirabel had broken his engagement, and the plowboy was the herald of misfortune who brought his apology. To his great disappointment (he wrote) he was detained by the affairs of his parish. He could only trust to Mr. Wyvil's indulgence to excuse him, and to communicate his sincere sense of regret (on scented note paper) to the ladies.

Everybody believed in the affairs of the parish—with the exception of Francine. "Mr. Mirabel has made the best excuse he could think of for shortening his visit; and I don't wonder at it," she said, looking significantly at Emily.

Emily was playing with one of the dogs; exercising him in the tricks which he had learned. She balanced a morsel of sugar on his nose—and had no attention to spare for Francine.

Cecilia, as the mistress of the house, felt it her duty to interfere. "That is a strange remark to make," she answered. "Do you mean to say that we have driven Mr. Mirabel away from us?"

"I accuse nobody," Francine began with spiteful candor.

"Now she's going to accuse everybody!" Emily interposed, addressing herself facetiously to the dog.

"But when girls are bent on fascinating men, whether they like it or not," Francine proceeded, "men have only one alternative—they must keep out of the way." She looked again at Emily, more pointedly than ever.

Even gentle Cecilia resented this. "Whom do you refer to?" she said sharply.

"My dear!" Emily remonstrated, "need you ask?" She glanced at Francine as she spoke, and then gave the dog his signal. He tossed up the sugar, and caught it in his mouth. His audience applauded him—and so, for that time, the skirmish ended.

Among the letters of the next morning's delivery, arrived Alban's reply. Emily's anticipations proved to be correct. The drawing-master's du ties would not permit him to leave Netherwoods; and he, like Mirabel, sent his apologies. His short letter to Emily contained no further allusion to Miss Jethro; it began and ended on the first page.

Had he been disappointed by the tone of reserve in which Emily had written to him, under Mr. Wyvil's advice? Or (as Cecilia suggested) had his detention at the school so bitterly disappointed him that he was too disheartened to write at any length? Emily made no attempt to arrive at a conclusion, either one way or the other. She seemed to be in depressed spirits; and she spoke superstitiously, for the first time in Cecilia's experience of her.

"I don't like this reappearance of Miss Jethro," she said. "If the mystery about that woman is ever cleared up, it will bring trouble and sorrow to me—and I believe, in his own secret heart, Alban Morris thinks so too."

"Write, and ask him," Cecilia suggested.

"He is so kind and so unwilling to distress me," Emily answered, "that he wouldn't acknowledge it, even if I am right."

In the middle of the week, the course of private life at Monksmoor suffered an interruption—due to the parliamentary position of the master of the house.

The insatiable appetite for making and hearing speeches, which represents one of the marked peculiarities of the English race (including their cousins in the United States), had seized on Mr. Wyvil's constituents. There was to be a political meeting at the market hall, in the neighboring town; and the member was expected to make an oration, passing in review contemporary events at home and abroad. "Pray don't think of accompanying me," the good man said to his guests. "The hall is badly ventilated, and the speeches, including my own, will not be worth hearing."

This humane warning was ungratefully disregarded. The gentlemen were all interested in "the objects of the meeting"; and the ladies were firm in the resolution not to be left at home by themselves. They dressed with a view to the large assembly of spectators before whom they were about to appear; and they outtalked the men on political subjects, all the way to the town.

The most delightful of surprises was in store for them, when they reached the market hall. Among the crowd of ordinary gentlemen, waiting under the portico until the proceedings began, appeared one person of distinction, whose title was "Reverend," and whose name was Mirabel.

Francine was the first to discover him. She darted up the steps and held out her hand.

"This is a pleasure!" she cried. "Have you come here to see—" she was about to say Me, but, observing the strangers round her, altered the word to Us. "Please give me your arm," she whispered, before her young friends had arrived within hearing. "I am so frightened in a crowd!"

She held fast by Mirabel, and kept a jealous watch on him. Was it only her fancy? or did she detect a new charm in his smile when he spoke to Emily?

Before it was possible to decide, the time for the meeting had arrived. Mr. Wyvil's friends were of course accommodated with seats on the platform. Francine, still insisting on her claim to Mirabel's arm, got a chair next to him. As she seated herself, she left him free for a moment. In that moment, the infatuated man took an empty chair on the other side of him, and placed it for Emily. He communicated to that hated rival the information which he ought to have reserved for Francine. "The committee insist," he said, "on my proposing one of the Resolutions. I promise not to bore you; mine shall be the shortest speech delivered at the meeting."

The proceedings began.

Among the earlier speakers not one was inspired by a feeling of mercy for the audience. The chairman reveled in words. The mover and seconder of the first Resolution (not having so much as the ghost of an idea to trouble either of them), poured out language in flowing and overflowing streams, like water from a perpetual spring. The heat exhaled by the crowded audience was already becoming insufferable. Cries of "Sit down!" assailed the orator of the moment. The chairman was obliged to interfere. A man at the back of the hall roared out, "Ventilation!" and broke a window with his stick. He was rewarded with three rounds of cheers; and was ironically invited to mount the platform and take the chair.

Under these embarrassing circumstances, Mirabel rose to speak.

He secured silence, at the outset, by a humorous allusion to the prolix speaker who had preceded him. "Look at the clock, gentlemen," he said; "and limit my speech to an interval of ten minutes." The applause which followed was heard, through the broken window, in the street. The boys among the mob outside intercepted the flow of air by climbing on each other's shoulders and looking in at the meeting, through the gaps left by the shattered glass. Having proposed his Resolution with discreet brevity of speech, Mirabel courted popularity on the plan adopted by the late Lord Palmerston in the House of Commons—he told stories, and made jokes, adapted to the intelligence of the dullest people who were listening to him. The charm of his voice and manner completed his success. Punctually at the tenth minute, he sat down amid cries of "Go on." Francine was the first to take his hand, and to express admiration mutely by pressing it. He returned the pressure—but he looked at the wrong lady—the lady on the other side.

Although she made no complaint, he instantly saw that Emily was overcome by the heat. Her lips were white, and her eyes were closing. "Let me take you out," he said, "or you will faint."

Francine started to her feet to follow them. The lower order of the audience, eager for amusement, put their own humorous construction on the young lady's action. They roared with laughter. "Let the parson and his sweetheart be," they called out; "two's company, miss, and three isn't." Mr. Wyvil interposed his authority and rebuked them. A lady seated behind Francine interfered to good purpose by giving her a chair, which placed her out of sight of the audience. Order was restored—and the proceedings were resumed.

On the conclusion of the meeting, Mirabel and Emily were found waiting for their friends at the door. Mr. Wyvil innocently added fuel to the fire that was burning in Francine. He insisted that Mirabel should return to Monksmoor, and offered him a seat in the carriage at Emily's side.

Later in the evening, when they all met at dinner, there appeared a change in Miss de Sor which surprised everybody but Mirabel. She was gay and good-humored, and especially amiable and attentive to Emily—who sat opposite to her at the table. "What did you and Mr. Mirabel talk about while you were away from us?" she asked innocently. "Politics?"

Emily readily adopted Francine's friendly tone. "Would you have talked politics, in my place?" she asked gayly.

"In your place, I should have had the most delightful of companions," Francine rejoined; "I wish I had been overcome by the heat too!"

Mirabel—attentively observing her—acknowledged the compliment by a bow, and left Emily to continue the conversation. In perfect good faith she owned to having led Mirabel to talk of himself. She had heard from Cecilia that his early life had been devoted to various occupations, and she was interested in knowing how circumstances had led him into devoting himself to the Church. Francine listened with the outward appearance of implicit belief, and with the inward conviction that Emily was deliberately deceiving her. When the little narrative was at an end, she was more agreeable than ever. She admired Emily's dress, and she rivaled Cecilia in enjoyment of the good things on the table; she entertained Mirabel with humorous anecdotes of the priests at St. Domingo, and was so interested in the manufacture of violins, ancient and modern, that Mr. Wyvil promised to show her his famous collection of instruments, after dinner. Her overflowing amiability included even poor Miss Darnaway and the absent brothers and sisters. She heard with flattering sympathy, how they had been ill and had got well again; what amusing tricks they played, what alarming accidents happened to them, and how remarkably clever they were—"including, I do assure you, dear Miss de Sor, the baby only ten months old." When the ladies rose to retire, Francine was, socially speaking, the heroine of the evening.

While the violins were in course of exhibition, Mirabel found an opportunity of speaking to Emily, unobserved.

"Have you said, or done, anything to offend Miss de Sor?" he asked.

"Nothing whatever!" Emily declared, startled by the question. "What makes you think I have offended her?"

"I have been trying to find a reason for the change in her," Mirabel answered—"especially the change toward yourself."

"Well?"

"Well—she means mischief."

"Mischief of what sort?"

"Of a sort which may expose her to discovery—unless she disarms suspicion at the outset. That is (as I believe) exactly what she has been doing this evening. I needn't warn you to be on your guard."

All the next day Emily was on the watch for events—and nothing happened. Not the slightest appearance of jealousy betrayed itself in Francine. She made no attempt to attract to herself the attentions of Mirabel; and she showed no hostility to Emily, either by word, look, or manner.

....

The day after, an event occurred at Netherwoods. Alban Morris received an anonymous letter, addressed to him in these terms:

"A certain young lady, in whom you are supposed to be interested, is forgetting you in your absence. If you are not mean enough to allow yourself to be supplanted by another man, join the party at Monksmoor before it is too late."

CHAPTER XLII. COOKING.

The day after the political meeting was a day of departures, at the pleasant country house.

Miss Darnaway was recalled to the nursery at home. The old squire who did justice to Mr. Wyvil's port-wine went away next, having guests to entertain at his own house. A far more serious loss followed. The three dancing men had engagements which drew them to new spheres of activity in other drawing-rooms. They said, with the same dreary grace of manner, "Very sorry to go"; they drove to the railway, arrayed in the same perfect traveling suits of neutral tint; and they had but one difference of opinion among them—each firmly believed that he was smoking the best cigar to be got in London.

The morning after these departures would have been a dull morning indeed, but for the presence of Mirabel.

When breakfast was over, the invalid Miss Julia established herself on the sofa with a novel. Her father retired to the other end of the house, and profaned the art of music on music's most expressive instrument. Left with

Emily, Cecilia, and Francine, Mirabel made one of his happy suggestions. "We are thrown on our own resources," he said. "Let us distinguish ourselves by inventing some entirely new amusement for the day. You young ladies shall sit in council—and I will be secretary." He turned to Cecilia. "The meeting waits to hear the mistress of the house."

Modest Cecilia appealed to her school friends for help; addressing herself in the first instance (by the secretary's advice) to Francine, as the eldest. They all noticed another change in this variable young person. She was silent and subdued; and she said wearily, "I don't care what we do—shall we go out riding?"

The unanswerable objection to riding as a form of amusement, was that it had been more than once tried already. Something clever and surprising was anticipated from Emily when it came to her turn. She, too, disappointed expectation. "Let us sit under the trees," was all that she could suggest, "and ask Mr. Mirabel to tell us a story."

Mirabel laid down his pen and took it on himself to reject this proposal. "Remember," he remonstrated, "that I have an interest in the diversions of the day. You can't expect me to be amused by my own story. I appeal to Miss Wyvil to invent a pleasure which will include the secretary."

Cecilia blushed and looked uneasy. "I think I have got an idea," she announced, after some hesitation. "May I propose that we all go to the keeper's lodge?" There her courage failed her, and she hesitated again.

Mirabel gravely registered the proposal, as far as it went. "What are we to do when we get to the keeper's lodge?" he inquired.

"We are to ask the keeper's wife," Cecilia proceeded, "to lend us her kitchen."

"To lend us her kitchen," Mirabel repeated.

"And what are we to do in the kitchen?"

Cecilia looked down at her pretty hands crossed on her lap, and answered softly, "Cook our own luncheon."

Here was an entirely new amusement, in the most attractive sense of the words! Here was charming Cecilia's interest in the pleasures of the table so happily inspired, that the grateful meeting offered its tribute of applause—even including Francine. The members of the council were young; their daring digestions contemplated without fear the prospect of eating their own amateur cookery. The one question that troubled them now was what they were to cook.

"I can make an omelet," Cecilia ventured to say.

"If there is any cold chicken to be had," Emily added, "I undertake to follow the omelet with a mayonnaise."

"There are clergymen in the Church of England who are even clever enough to fry potatoes," Mirabel announced—"and I am one of them. What shall we have next? A pudding? Miss de Sor, can you make a pudding?"

Francine exhibited another new side to her character—a diffident and humble side. "I am ashamed to say I don't know how to cook anything," she confessed; "you had better leave me out of it."

But Cecilia was now in her element. Her plan of operations was wide enough even to include Francine. "You shall wash the lettuce, my dear, and stone the olives for Emily's mayonnaise. Don't be discouraged! You shall have a companion; we will send to the rectory for Miss Plym—the very person to chop parsley and shallot for my omelet. Oh, Emily, what a morning we are going to have!" Her lovely blue eyes sparkled with joy; she gave Emily a kiss which Mirabel must have been more or less than man not to have coveted. "I declare," cried Cecilia, completely losing her head, "I'm so excited, I don't know what to do with myself!"

Emily's intimate knowledge of her friend applied the right remedy. "You don't know what to do with yourself?" she repeated. "Have you no sense of duty? Give the cook your orders."

Cecilia instantly recovered her presence of mind. She sat down at the writing-table, and made out a list of eatable productions in the animal and vegetable world, in which every other word was underlined two or three times over. Her serious face was a sight to see, when she rang for the cook, and the two held a privy council in a corner.

On the way to the keeper's lodge, the young mistress of the house headed a procession of servants carrying the raw materials. Francine followed, held in custody by Miss Plym—who took her responsibilities seriously, and clamored for instruction in the art of chopping parsley. Mirabel and Emily were together, far behind; they were the only two members of the company whose minds were not occupied in one way or another by the kitchen.

"This child's play of ours doesn't seem to interest you," Mirabel remarked.

"I am thinking," Emily answered, "of what you said to me about Francine."

"I can say something more," he rejoined. "When I noticed the change in her at dinner, I told you she meant mischief. There is another change to-day, which suggests to my mind that the mischief is done."

"And directed against me?" Emily asked.

Mirabel made no direct reply. It was impossible for him to remind her that she had, no matter how innocently, exposed herself to the jealous hatred of Francine. "Time will tell us, what we don't know now," he replied evasively.

"You seem to have faith in time, Mr. Mirabel."

"The greatest faith. Time is the inveterate enemy of deceit. Sooner or later, every hidden thing is a thing doomed to discovery."

"Without exception?"

"Yes," he answered positively, "without exception."

At that moment Francine stopped and looked back at them. Did she think that Emily and Mirabel had been talking together long enough? Miss Plym—with the parsley still on her mind—advanced to consult Emil y's experience. The two walked on together, leaving Mirabel to overtake Francine. He saw, in her first look at him, the effort that it cost her to suppress those emotions which the pride of women is most deeply interested in concealing.

Before a word had passed, he regretted that Emily had left them together.

"I wish I had your cheerful disposition," she began, abruptly. "I am out of spirits or out of temper—I don't know which; and I don't know why. Do you ever trouble yourself with thinking of the future?"

"As seldom as possible, Miss de Sor. In such a situation as mine, most people have prospects—I have none."

He spoke gravely, conscious of not feeling at ease on his side. If he had been the most modest man that ever lived, he must have seen in Francine's face that she loved him.

When they had first been presented to each other, she was still under the influence of the meanest instincts in her scheming and selfish nature. She had thought to herself, "With my money to help him, that man's celebrity would do the rest; the best society in England would be glad to receive Mirabel's wife." As the days passed, strong feeling had taken the place of those contemptible aspirations: Mirabel had unconsciously inspired the one passion which was powerful enough to master Francine—sensual passion. Wild hopes rioted in her. Measureless desires which she had never felt before, united themselves with capacities for wickedness, which had been the horrid growth of a few nights—capacities which suggested even viler attempts to rid herself of a supposed rivalry than slandering Emily by means of an anonymous letter. Without waiting for it to be offered, she took Mirabel's arm, and pressed it to her breast as they slowly walked on. The fear of discovery which had troubled her after she had sent her base letter to the post, vanished at that inspiriting moment. She bent her head near enough to him when he spoke to feel his breath on her face.

"There is a strange similarity," she said softly, "between your position and mine. Is there anything cheering in my prospects? I am far away from home—my father and mother wouldn't care if they never saw me again. People talk about my money! What is the use of money to such a lonely wretch as I am? Suppose I write to London, and ask the lawyer if I may give it all away to some deserving person? Why not to you?"

"My dear Miss de Sor—!"

"Is there anything wrong, Mr. Mirabel, in wishing that I could make you a prosperous man?"

"You must not even talk of such a thing!"

"How proud you are!" she said submissively.

"Oh, I can't bear to think of you in that miserable village—a position so unworthy of your talents and your claims! And you tell me I must not talk about it. Would you have said that to Emily, if she was as anxious as I am to see you in your right place in the world?"

"I should have answered her exactly as I have answered you."

"She will never embarrass you, Mr. Mirabel, by being as sincere as I am. Emily can keep her own secrets."

"Is she to blame for doing that?"

"It depends on your feeling for her."

"What feeling do you mean?"

"Suppose you heard she was engaged to be married?" Francine suggested.

Mirabel's manner—studiously cold and formal thus far—altered on a sudden. He looked with unconcealed anxiety at Francine. "Do you say that seriously?" he asked.

"I said 'suppose.' I don't exactly know that she is engaged."

"What do you know?"

"Oh, how interested you are in Emily! She is admired by some people. Are you one of them?"

Mirabel's experience of women warned him to try silence as a means of provoking her into speaking plainly. The experiment succeeded: Francine returned to the question that he had put to her, and abruptly answered it.

"You may believe me or not, as you like—I know of a man who is in love with her. He has had his opportunities; and he has made good use of them.

Would you like to know who he is?"

"I should like to know anything which you may wish to tell me." He did his best to make the reply in a tone of commonplace politeness—and he might have succeeded in deceiving a man. The woman's quicker ear told her that he was angry. Francine took the full advantage of that change in her favor.

"I am afraid your good opinion of Emily will be shaken," she quietly resumed, "when I tell you that she has encouraged a man who is only drawing-master at a school. At the same time, a person in her circumstances—I mean she has no money—ought not to be very hard to please. Of course she has never spoken to you of Mr. Alban Morris?"

"Not that I remember."

Only four words—but they satisfied Francine.

The one thing wanting to complete the obstacle which she had now placed in Emily's way, was that Alban Morris should enter on the scene. He might hesitate; but, if he was really fond of Emily, the anonymous letter would sooner or later bring him to Monksmoor. In the meantime, her object was gained. She dropped Mirabel's arm.

"Here is the lodge," she said gayly—"I declare Cecilia has got an apron on already! Come, and cook."

CHAPTER XLIII. SOUNDING.

Mirabel left Francine to enter the lodge by herself. His mind was disturbed: he felt the importance of gaining time for reflection before he and Emily met again.

The keeper's garden was at the back of the lodge. Passing through the wicket-gate, he found a little summer-house at a turn in the path. Nobody was there: he went in and sat down.

At intervals, he had even yet encouraged himself to underrate the true importance of the feeling which Emily had awakened in him. There was an end to all self-deception now. After what Francine had said to him, this shallow and frivolous man no longer resisted the all-absorbing influence of love. He shrank under the one terrible question that forced itself on his mind:—Had that jealous girl spoken the truth?

In what process of investigation could he trust, to set this anxiety at rest? To apply openly to Emily would be to take a liberty, which Emily was the last person in the world to permit. In his recent intercourse with her he had felt more strongly than ever the importance of speaking with reserve. He had been scrupulously careful to take no unfair advantage of his opportunity, when he had removed her from the meeting, and when they had walked together, with hardly a creature to observe them, in the lonely outskirts of the town. Emily's gaiety and good humor had not led him astray: he knew that these were bad signs, viewed in the interests of love. His one hope of touching her deeper sympathies was to wait for the help that might yet come from time and chance. With a bitter sigh, he resigned himself to the necessity of being as agreeable and amusing as ever: it was just possible that he might lure her into alluding to Alban Morris, if he began innocently by making her laugh.

As he rose to return to the lodge, the keeper's little terrier, prowling about the garden, looked into the summer-house. Seeing a stranger, the dog showed his teeth and growled.

Mirabel shrank back against the wall behind him, trembling in every limb. His eyes stared in terror as the dog came nearer: barking in high triumph over the discovery of a frightened man whom he could bully. Mirabel called out for help. A laborer at work in the garden ran to the place—and stopped with a broad grin of amusement at seeing a grown man terrified by a barking dog. "Well," he said to himself, after Mirabel had passed out under protection, "there goes a coward if ever there was one yet!"

Mirabel waited a minute behind the lodge to recover himself. He had been so completely unnerved that his hair was wet with perspiration. While he used his handkerchief, he shuddered at other recollections than the recollection of the dog. "After that night at the inn," he thought, "the least thing frightens me!"

He was received by the young ladies with cries of derisive welcome.

"Oh, for shame! for shame! here are the potatoes already cut, and nobody to fry them!"

Mirabel assumed the mask of cheerfulness—with the desperate resolution of an actor, amusing his audience at a time of domestic distress. He astonished the keeper's wife by showing that he really knew how to use her frying-pan. Cecilia's omelet was tough—but the young ladies ate it. Emily's mayonnaise sauce was almost as liquid as water—they swallowed it nevertheless by the help of spoons. The potatoes followed, crisp and dry and delicious—and Mirabel became more popular than ever. "He is the only one of us," Cecilia sadly acknowledged, "who knows how to cook."

When they all left the lodge for a stroll in the park, Francine attached herself to Cecilia and Miss Plym. She resigned Mirabel to Emily—in the happy belief that she had paved the way for a misunderstanding between them.

The merriment at the luncheon table had revived Emily's good spirits. She had a light-hearted remembrance of the failure of her sauce. Mirabel saw her smiling to herself. "May I ask what amuses you?" he said.

"I was thinking of the debt of gratitude that we owe to Mr. Wyvil," she replied. "If he had not persuaded you to return to Monksmoor, we should never have seen the famous Mr. Mirabel with a frying pan in his hand, and never have tasted the only good dish at our luncheon."

Mirabel tried vainly to adopt his companion's easy tone. Now that he was alone with her, the doubts that Francine had aroused shook the prudent resolution at which he had arrived in the garden. He ran the risk, and told Emily plainly why he had returned to Mr. Wyvil's house.

"Although I am sensible of our host's kindness," he answered, "I should have gone back to my parsonage—but for You."

She declined to understand him seriously. "Then the affairs of your parish are neglected—and I am to blame!" she said.

"Am I the first man who has neglected his duties for your sake?" he asked. "I wonder whether the masters at school had the heart to report you when you neglected your lessons?"

She thought of Alban—and betrayed herself by a heightened color. The moment after, she changed the subject. Mirabel could no longer resist the conclusion that Francine had told him the truth.

"When do you leave us," she inquired.

"To-morrow is Saturday—I must go back as usual."

"And how will your deserted parish receive you?"

He made a desperate effort to be as amusing as usual.

"I am sure of preserving my popularity," he said, "while I have a cask in the cellar, and a few spare sixpences in my pocket. The public spirit of my parishioners asks for nothing but money and beer. Before I went to that wearisome meeting, I told my housekeeper that I was going to make a speech about reform. She didn't know what I meant. I explained that reform might increase the number of British citizens who had the right of voting at elections for parliament. She brightened up directly. 'Ah,' she said, 'I've heard my husband talk about elections. The more there are of them (he says) the more money he'll get for his vote. I'm all for reform.' On my way out of the house, I tried the man who works in my garden on the same subject. He didn't look at the matter from the housekeeper's sanguine point of view. 'I don't deny that parliament once gave me a good dinner for nothing at the public-house,' he admitted. 'But that was years ago—and (you'll excuse me, sir) I hear nothing of another dinner to come. It's a matter of opinion, of course. I don't myself believe in reform.' There are specimens of the state of public spirit in our village!" He paused. Emily was listening—but he had not succeeded in choosing a subject that amused her. He tried a topic more nearly connected with his own interests; the topic of the future. "Our good friend has asked me to prolong my visit, after Sunday's duties are over," he said. "I hope I shall find you here, next week?"

"Will the affairs of your parish allow you to come back?" Emily asked mischievously.

"The affairs of my parish—if you force me to confess it—were only an excuse."

"An excuse for what?"

"An excuse for keeping away from Monksmoor—in the interests of my own tranquillity. The experiment has failed. While you are here, I can't keep away."

She still declined to understand him seriously. "Must I tell you in plain words that flattery is thrown away on me?" she said.

"Flattery is not offered to you," he answered gravely. "I beg your pardon for having led to the mistake by talking of myself." Having appealed to her indulgence by that act of submission, he ventured on another distant allusion to the man whom he hated and feared. "Shall I meet any friends of yours," he resumed, "when I return on Monday?"

"What do you mean?"

"I only meant to ask if Mr. Wyvil expects any new guests?"

As he put the question, Cecilia's voice was heard behind them, calling to Emily. They both turned round. Mr. Wyvil had joined his daughter and her two friends. He advanced to meet Emily.

"I have some news for you that you little expect," he said. "A telegram has just arrived from Netherwoods. Mr. Alban Morris has got leave of absence, and is coming here to-morrow."

CHAPTER XLIV. COMPETING.

Time at Monksmoor had advanced to the half hour before dinner, on Saturday evening.

Cecilia and Francine, Mr. Wyvil and Mirabel, were loitering in the conservatory. In the drawing-room, Emily had been considerately left alone with Alban. He had missed the early train from Netherwoods; but he had arrived in time to dress for dinner, and to offer the necessary explanations.

If it had been possible for Alban to allude to the anonymous letter, he might have owned that his first impulse had led him to destroy it, and to assert his confidence in Emily by refusing Mr. Wyvil's invitation. But try as he might to forget them, the base words that he had read remained in his memory. Irritating him at the outset, they had ended in rousing his jealousy. Under that delusive influence, he persuaded himself that he had acted, in the first instance, without due consideration. It was surely his interest—it might even be his duty—to go to Mr. Wyvil's house, and judge for himself. After some last wretched moments of hesitation, he had decided on effecting a compromise with his own better sense, by consulting Miss Ladd. That excellent lady did exactly what he had expected her to do. She made arrangements which granted him leave of absence, from the Saturday to the Tuesday following. The excuse which had served him, in telegraphing to Mr. Wyvil, must now be repeated, in accounting for his unexpected appearance to Emily. "I found a person to take charge of my class," he said; "and I gladly availed myself of the opportunity of seeing you again."

After observing him attentively, while he was speaking to her, Emily owned, with her customary frankness, that she had noticed something in his manner which left her not quite at her ease.

"I wonder," she said, "if there is any foundation for a doubt that has troubled me?" To his unutterable relief, she at once explained what the doubt was. "I am afraid I offended you, in replying to your letter about Miss Jethro."

In this case, Alban could enjoy the luxury of speaking unreservedly. He confessed that Emily's letter had disappointed him.

"I expected you to answer me with less reserve," he replied; "and I began to think I had acted rashly in writing to you at all. When there is a better opportunity, I may have a word to say—" He was apparently interrupted by something that he saw in the conservatory. Looking that way, Emily perceived that Mirabel was the object which had attracted Alban's attention. The vile anonymous letter was in his mind again. Without a preliminary word to prepare Emily, he suddenly changed the subject. "How do you like the clergyman?" he asked.

"Very much indeed," she replied, without the slightest embarrassment.

"Mr. Mirabel is clever and agreeable—and not at all spoiled by his success. I am sure," she said innocently, "you will like him too."

Alban's face answered her unmistakably in the negative sense—but Emily's attention was drawn the other way by Francine. She joined them at the moment, on the lookout for any signs of an encouraging result which her treachery might already have produced. Alban had been inclined to suspect her when he had received the letter. He rose and bowed as she approached. Something—he was unable to realize what it was—told him, in the moment when they looked at each other, that his suspicion had hit the mark.

In the conservatory the ever-amiable Mirabel had left his friends for a while in search of flowers for Cecilia. She turned to her father when they were alone, and asked him which of the gentlemen was to take her in to dinner—Mr. Mirabel or Mr. Morris?

"Mr. Morris, of course," he answered. "He is the new guest—and he turns out to be more than the equal, socially-speaking, of our other friend. When I showed him his room, I asked if he was related to a man who bore the same name—a fellow student of mine, years and years ago, at college. He is my friend's younger son; one of a ruined family—but persons of high distinction in their day."

Mirabel returned with the flowers, just as dinner was announced.

"You are to take Emily to-day," Cecilia said to him, leading the way out of the conservatory. As they entered the drawing-room, Alban was just offering his arm to Emily. "Papa gives you to me, Mr. Morris," Cecilia explained pleasantly. Alban hesitated, apparently not understanding the allusion. Mirabel interfered with his best grace: "Mr. Wyvil offers you the honor of taking his daughter to the dining-room." Alban's face darkened ominously, as the elegant little clergyman gave his arm to Emily, and followed Mr. Wyvil and Francine out of the room. Cecilia looked at her silent and surly companion, and almost envied her lazy sister, dining—under cover of a convenient headache—in her own room.

Having already made up his mind that Alban Morris required careful handling, Mirabel waited a little before he led the conversation as usual. Between the soup and the fish, he made an interesting confession, addressed to Emily in the strictest confidence.

"I have taken a fancy to your friend Mr. Morris," he said. "First impressions, in my case, decide everything; I like people or dislike them on impulse. That man appeals to my sympathies. Is he a good talker?"

"I should say Yes," Emily answered prettily, "if you were not present."

Mirabel was not to be beaten, even by a woman, in the art of paying compliments. He looked admiringly at Alban (sitting opposite to him), and said: "Let us listen."

This flattering suggestion not only pleased Emily—it artfully served Mirabel's purpose. That is to say, it secured him an opportunity for observation of what was going on at the other side of the table.

Alban's instincts as a gentleman had led him to control his irritation and to regret that he had suffered it to appear. Anxious to please, he presented himself at his best. Gentle Cecilia forgave and forgot the angry look which had startled her. Mr. Wyvil was delighted with the son of his old friend. Emily felt secretly proud of the good opinions which her admirer was gathering; and Francine saw with pleasure that he was asserting his claim to Emily's preference, in the way of all others which would be most likely to discourage his rival. These various impressions—produced while Alban's enemy was ominously silent—began to suffer an imperceptible change, from the moment when Mirabel decided that his time had come to take the lead. A remark made by Alban offered him the chance for which he had been on the watch. He agreed with the remark; he enlarged on the remark; he was brilliant and familiar, and instructive and amusing—and still it was all due to the remark. Alban's temper was once more severely tried. Mirabel's mischievous object had not escaped his penetration. He did his best to put obstacles in the adversary's way—and was baffled, time after time, with the readiest ingenuity. If he interrupted—the sweet-tempered clergyman submitted, and went on. If he differed—modest Mr. Mirabel said, in the most amiable manner, "I daresay I am wrong," and handled the topic from his opponent's point of view. Never

255

had such a perfect Christian sat before at Mr. Wyvil's table: not a hard word, not an impatient look, escaped him. The longer Alban resisted, the more surely he lost ground in the general estimation. Cecilia was disappointed; Emily was grieved; Mr. Wyvil's favorable opinion began to waver; Francine was disgusted. When dinner was over, and the carriage was waiting to take the shepherd back to his flock by moonlight, Mirabel's triumph was complete. He had made Alban the innocent means of publicly exhibiting his perfect temper and perfect politeness, under their best and brightest aspect.

So that day ended. Sunday promised to pass quietly, in the absence of Mirabel. The morning came—and it seemed doubtful whether the promise would be fulfilled.

Francine had passed an uneasy night. No such encouraging result as she had anticipated had hitherto followed the appearance of Alban Morris at Monksmoor. He had clumsily allowed Mirabel to improve his position—while he had himself lost ground—in Emily's estimation. If this first disastrous consequence of the meeting between the two men was permitted to repeat itself on future occasions, Emily and Mirabel would be brought more closely together, and Alban himself would be the unhappy cause of it. Francine rose, on the Sunday morning, before the table was laid for breakfast—resolved to try the effect of a timely word of advice.

Her bedroom was situated in the front of the house. The man she was looking for presently passed within her range of view from the window, on his way to take a morning walk in the park. She followed him immediately.

"Good-morning, Mr. Morris."

He raised his hat and bowed—without speaking, and without looking at her.

"We resemble each other in one particular," she proceeded, graciously; "we both like to breathe the fresh air before breakfast."

He said exactly what common politeness obliged him to say, and no more—he said, "Yes."

Some girls might have been discouraged. Francine went on.

"It is no fault of mine, Mr. Morris, that we have not been better friends. For some reason, into which I don't presume to inquire, you seem to distrust me. I really don't know what I have done to deserve it."

"Are you sure of that?" he asked—eying her suddenly and searchingly as he spoke.

Her hard face settled into a rigid look; her eyes met his eyes with a stony defiant stare. Now, for the first time, she knew that he suspected her of having written the anonymous letter. Every evil quality in her nature steadily defied him. A hardened old woman could not have sustained the shock of discovery with a more devilish composure than this girl displayed. "Perhaps you will explain yourself," she said.

"I have explained myself," he answered.

"Then I must be content," she rejoined, "to remain in the dark. I had intended, out of my regard for Emily, to suggest that you might—with advantage to yourself, and to interests that are very dear to you—be more careful in your behavior to Mr. Mirabel. Are you disposed to listen to me?"

"Do you wish me to answer that question plainly, Miss de Sor?"

"I insist on your answering it plainly."

"Then I am not disposed to listen to you."

"May I know why? or am I to be left in the dark again?"

"You are to be left, if you please, to your own ingenuity."

Francine looked at him, with a malignant smile. "One of these days, Mr. Morris—I will deserve your confidence in my ingenuity." She said it, and went back to the house.

This was the only element of disturbance that troubled the perfect tranquillity of the day. What Francine had proposed to do, with the one idea of making Alban serve her purpose, was accomplished a few hours later by Emily's influence for good over the man who loved her.

They passed the afternoon together uninterruptedly in the distant solitudes of the park. In the course of conversation Emily found an opportunity of discreetly alluding to Mirabel. "You mustn't be jealous of our clever little friend," she said; "I like him, and admire him; but—"

"But you don't love him?"

She smiled at the eager way in which Alban put the question.

"There is no fear of that," she answered brightly.

"Not even if you discovered that he loves you?"

"Not even then. Are you content at last? Promise me not to be rude to Mr. Mirabel again."

"For his sake?"

"No—for my sake. I don't like to see you place yourself at a disadvantage toward another man; I don't like you to disappoint me."

The happiness of hearing her say those words transfigured him—the manly beauty of his earlier and happier years seemed to have returned to Alban. He took her hand—he was too agitated to speak.

"You are forgetting Mr. Mirabel," she reminded him gently.

"I will be all that is civil and kind to Mr. Mirabel; I will like him and admire him as you do. Oh, Emily, are you a little, only a very little, fond of me?"

"I don't quite know."

"May I try to find out?"

"How?" she asked.

Her fair cheek was very near to him. The softly-rising color on it said, Answer me here—and he answered.

CHAPTER XLV. MISCHIEF—MAKING.

On Monday, Mirabel made his appearance—and the demon of discord returned with him.

Alban had employed the earlier part of the day in making a sketch in the park—intended as a little present for Emily. Presenting himself in the drawing-room, when his work was completed, he found Cecilia and Francine alone. He asked where Emily was.

The question had been addressed to Cecilia. Francine answered it.

"Emily mustn't be disturbed," she said.

"Why not?"

"She is with Mr. Mirabel in the rose garden. I saw them talking together—evidently feeling the deepest interest in what they were saying to each other. Don't interrupt them—you will only be in the way."

Cecilia at once protested against this last assertion. "She is trying to make mischief, Mr. Morris—don't believe her. I am sure they will be glad to see you, if you join them in the garden."

Francine rose, and left the room. She turned, and looked at Alban as she opened the door. "Try it," she said—"and you will find I am right."

"Francine sometimes talks in a very ill-natured way," Cecilia gently remarked. "Do you think she means it, Mr. Morris?'

"I had better not offer an opinion," Alban replied.

"Why?"

"I can't speak impartially; I dislike Miss de Sor."

There was a pause. Alban's sense of self-respect forbade him to try the experiment which Francine had maliciously suggested. His thoughts—less easy to restrain—wandered in the direction of the garden. The attempt to make him jealous had failed; but he was conscious, at the same time, that Emily had disappointed him. After what they had said to each other in the park, she ought to have remembered that women are at the mercy of appearances. If Mirabel had something of importance to say to her, she might have avoided exposing herself to Francine's spiteful misconstruction: it would have been easy to arrange with Cecilia that a third person should be present at the interview.

While he was absorbed in these reflections, Cecilia—embarrassed by the silence—was trying to find a topic of conversation. Alban roughly pushed his sketch-book away from him, on the table. Was he displeased with Emily? The same question had occurred to Cecilia at the time of the correspondence, on the subject of Miss Jethro. To recall those letters led her, by natural sequence, to another effort of memory. She was reminded of the person who had been the cause of the correspondence: her interest was revived in the mystery of Miss Jethro.

"Has Emily told you that I have seen your letter?" she asked.

He roused himself with a start. "I beg your pardon. What letter are you thinking of?"

"I was thinking of the letter which mentions Miss Jethro's strange visit. Emily was so puzzled and so surprised that she showed it to me—and we both consulted my father. Have you spoken to Emily about Miss Jethro?"

"I have tried—but she seemed to be unwilling to pursue the subject."

"Have you made any discoveries since you wrote to Emily?"

"No. The mystery is as impenetrable as ever."

As he replied in those terms, Mirabel entered the conservatory from the garden, evidently on his way to the drawing-room.

To see the man, whose introduction to Emily it had been Miss Jethro's mysterious object to prevent—at the very moment when he had been speaking of Miss Jethro herself—was, not only a temptation of curiosity, but a direct incentive (in Emily's own interests) to make an effort at discovery. Alban pursued the conversation with Cecilia, in a tone which was loud enough to be heard in the conservatory.

"The one chance of getting any information that I can see," he proceeded, "is to speak to Mr. Mirabel."

"I shall be only too glad, if I can be of any service to Miss Wyvil and

Mr. Morris."

With those obliging words, Mirabel made a dramatic entry, and looked at Cecilia with his irresistible smile. Startled by his sudden appearance, she unconsciously assisted Alban's design. Her silence gave him the opportunity of speaking in her place.

"We were talking," he said quietly to Mirabel, "of a lady with whom you are acquainted."

"Indeed! May I ask the lady's name?"

"Miss Jethro."

Mirabel sustained the shock with extraordinary self-possession—so far as any betrayal by sudden movement was concerned. But his color told the truth: it faded to paleness—it revealed, even to Cecilia's eyes, a man overpowered by fright.

Alban offered him a chair. He refused to take it by a gesture. Alban tried an apology next. "I am afraid I have ignorantly revived some painful associations. Pray excuse me."

The apology roused Mirabel: he felt the necessity of offering some explanation. In timid animals, the one defensive capacity which is always ready for action is cunning. Mirabel was too wily to dispute the inference— the inevitable inference—which any one must have drawn, after seeing the effect on him that the name of Miss Jethro had produced. He admitted that "painful associations" had been revived, and deplored the "nervous sensibility" which had permitted it to be seen.

"No blame can possibly attach to you, my dear sir," he continued, in his most amiable manner. "Will it be indiscreet, on my part, if I ask how you first became acquainted with Miss Jethro?"

"I first became acquainted with her at Miss Ladd's school," Alban answered. "She was, for a short time only, one of the teachers; and she left her situation rather suddenly." He paused—but Mirabel made no remark. "After an interval of a few months," he resumed, "I saw Miss Jethro again. She called on me at my lodgings, near Netherwoods."

"Merely to renew your former acquaintance?"

Mirabel made that inquiry with an eager anxiety for the reply which he was quite unable to conceal. Had he any reason to dread what Miss Jethro might have it in her power to say of him to another person? Alban was in no way pledged to secrecy, and he was determined to leave no means untried of throwing light on Miss Jethro's mysterious warning. He repeated the plain narrative of the interview, which he had communicated by letter to Emily. Mirabel listened without making any remark.

"After what I have told you, can you give me no explanation?" Alban asked.

"I am quite unable, Mr. Morris, to help you."

Was he lying? or speaking, the truth? The impression produced on Alban was that he had spoken the truth.

Women are never so ready as men to resign themselves to the disappointment of their hopes. Cecilia, silently listening up to this time, now ventured to speak—animated by her sisterly interest in Emily.

"Can you not tell us," she said to Mirabel, "why Miss Jethro tried to prevent Emily Brown from meeting you here?"

"I know no more of her motive than you do," Mirabel replied.

Alban interposed. "Miss Jethro left me," he said, "with the intention— quite openly expressed—of trying to prevent you from accepting Mr. Wyvil's invitation. Did she make the attempt?"

Mirabel admitted that she had made the attempt. "But," he added, "without mentioning Miss Emily's name. I was asked to postpone my visit, as a favor to herself, because she had her own reasons for wishing it. I had my reasons" (he bowed with gallantry to Cecilia) "for being eager to have the honor of knowing Mr. Wyvil and his daughter; and I refused."

Once more, the doubt arose: was he lying? or speaking the truth? And, once more, Alban could not resist the conclusion that he was speaking the truth.

"There is one thing I should like to know," Mirabel continued, after some hesitation. "Has Miss Emily been informed of this strange affair?"

"Certainly!"

Mirabel seemed to be disposed to continue his inquiries—and suddenly changed his mind. Was he beginning to doubt if Alban had spoken without concealment, in describing Miss Jethro's visit? Was he still afraid of what Miss Jethro might have said of him? In any case, he changed the subject, and made an excuse for leaving the room.

"I am forgetting my errand," he said to Alban. "Miss Emily was anxious to know if you had finished your sketch. I must tell her that you have returned."

He bowed and withdrew.

Alban rose to follow him—and checked himself.

"No," he thought, "I trust Emily!" He sat down again by Cecilia's side.

Mirabel had indeed returned to the rose garden. He found Emily employed as he had left her, in making a crown of roses, to be worn by Cecilia in the evening. But, in one other respect, there was a change. Francine was present.

"Excuse me for sending you on a needless errand," Emily said to Mirabel; "Miss de Sor tells me Mr. Morris has finished his sketch. She left him in the drawing-room—why didn't you bring him here?"

"He was talking with Miss Wyvil."

Mirabel answered absently—with his eyes on Francine. He gave her one of those significant looks, which says to a third person, "Why are you here?" Francine's jealousy declined to understand him. He tried a broader hint, in words.

"Are you going to walk in the garden?" he said.

Francine was impenetrable. "No," she answered, "I am going to stay here with Emily."

Mirabel had no choice but to yield. Imperative anxieties forced him to say, in Francine's presence, what he had hoped to say to Emily privately.

"When I joined Miss Wyvil and Mr. Morris," he began, "what do you think they were doing? They were talking of—Miss Jethro."

Emily dropped the rose-crown on her lap. It was easy to see that she had been disagreeably surprised.

"Mr. Morris has told me the curious story of Miss Jethro's visit," Mirabel continued; "but I am in some doubt whether he has spoken to me without reserve. Perhaps he expressed himself more freely when he spoke to you. Miss Jethro may have said something to him which tended to lower me in your estimation?"

"Certainly not, Mr. Mirabel—so far as I know. If I had heard anything of the kind, I should have thought it my duty to tell you. Will it relieve your anxiety, if I go at once to Mr. Morris, and ask him plainly whether he has concealed anything from you or from me?"

Mirabel gratefully kissed her hand. "Your kindness overpowers me," he said—speaking, for once, with true emotion.

Emily immediately returned to the house. As soon as she was out of sight, Francine approached Mirabel, trembling with suppressed rage.

CHAPTER XLVI. PRETENDING.

Miss de Sor began cautiously with an apology. "Excuse me, Mr. Mirabel, for reminding you of my presence."

Mr. Mirabel made no reply.

"I beg to say," Francine proceeded, "that I didn't intentionally see you kiss Emily's hand."

Mirabel stood, looking at the roses which Emily had left on her chair, as completely absorbed in his own thoughts as if he had been alone in the garden.

"Am I not even worth notice?" Francine asked. "Ah, I know to whom I am indebted for your neglect!" She took him familiarly by the arm, and burst into a harsh laugh. "Tell me now, in confidence—do you think Emily is fond of you?"

The impression left by Emily's kindness was still fresh in Mirabel's memory: he was in no humor to submit to the jealous resentment of a woman whom he regarded with perfect indifference. Through the varnish of politeness which overlaid his manner, there rose to the surface the underlying insolence, hidden, on all ordinary occasions, from all human eyes. He answered Francine—mercilessly answered her—at last.

"It is the dearest hope of my life that she may be fond of me," he said.

Francine dropped his arm "And fortune favors your hopes," she added, with an ironical assumption of interest in Mirabel's prospects. "When Mr. Morris leaves us to-morrow, he removes the only obstacle you have to fear. Am I right?"

"No; you are wrong."

"In what way, if you please?"

"In this way. I don't regard Mr. Morris as an obstacle. Emily is too delicate and too kind to hurt his feelings—she is not in love with him. There is no absorbing interest in her mind to divert her thoughts from me. She is idle and happy; she thoroughly enjoys her visit to this house, and I am associated with her enjoyment. There is my chance—!"

He suddenly stopped. Listening to him thus far, unnaturally calm and cold, Francine now showed that she felt the lash of his contempt. A hideous smile passed slowly over her white face. It threatened the vengeance which knows no fear, no pity, no remorse—the vengeance of a jealous woman. Hysterical anger, furious language, Mirabel was prepared for. The smile frightened him.

"Well?" she said scornfully, "why don't you go on?"

A bolder man might still have maintained the audacious position which he had assumed. Mirabel's faint heart shrank from it. He was eager to shelter himself under the first excuse that he could find. His ingenuity, paralyzed by his fears, was unable to invent anything new. He feebly availed himself of the commonplace trick of evasion which he had read of in novels, and seen in action on the stage.

"Is it possible," he asked, with an overacted assumption of surprise, "that you think I am in earnest?"

In the case of any other person, Francine would have instantly seen through that flimsy pretense. But the love which accepts the meanest crumbs of comfort that can be thrown to it—which fawns and grovels and deliberately deceives itself, in its own intensely selfish interests—was the love that burned in Francine's breast. The wretched girl believed Mirabel with such an ecstatic sense of belief that she trembled in every limb, and dropped into the nearest chair.

"I was in earnest," she said faintly. "Didn't you see it?"

He was perfectly shameless; he denied that he had seen it, in the most positive manner. "Upon my honor, I thought you were mystifying me, and I humored the joke."

She sighed, and looking at him with an expression of tender reproach. "I wonder whether I can believe you," she said softly.

"Indeed you may believe me!" he assured her.

She hesitated—for the pleasure of hesitating. "I don't know. Emily is very much admired by some men. Why not by you?"

"For the best of reasons," he answered "She is poor, and I am poor. Those are facts which speak for themselves."

"Yes—but Emily is bent on attracting you. She would marry you to-morrow, if you asked her. Don't attempt to deny it! Besides, you kissed her hand."

"Oh, Miss de Sor!"

"Don't call me 'Miss de Sor'! Call me Francine. I want to know why you kissed her hand."

He humored her with inexhaustible servility. "Allow me to kiss your hand, Francine!—and let me explain that kissing a lady's hand is only a form of thanking her for her kindness. You must own that Emily—"

She interrupted him for the third time. "Emily?" she repeated. "Are you as familiar as that already? Does she call you 'Miles,' when you are by yourselves? Is there any effort at fascination which this charming creature has left untried? She told you no doubt what a lonely life she leads in her poor little home?"

Even Mirabel felt that he must not permit this to pass.

"She has said nothing to me about herself," he answered. "What I know of her, I know from Mr. Wyvil."

"Oh, indeed! You asked Mr. Wyvil about her family, of course? What did he say?"

"He said she lost her mother when she was a child—and he told me her father had died suddenly, a few years since, of heart complaint."

"Well, and what else?—Never mind now! Here is somebody coming."

The person was only one of the servants. Mirabel felt grateful to the man for interrupting them. Animated by sentiments of a precisely opposite nature, Francine spoke to him sharply.

"What do you want here?"

"A message, miss."

"From whom?"

"From Miss Brown."

"For me?"

"No, miss." He turned to Mirabel. "Miss Brown wishes to speak to you, sir, if you are not engaged."

Francine controlled herself until the man was out of hearing.

"Upon my word, this is too shameless!" she declared indignantly. "Emily can't leave you with me for five minutes, without wanting to see you again. If you go to her after all that you have said to me," she cried, threatening Mirabel with her outstretched hand, "you are the meanest of men!"

He was the meanest of men—he carried out his cowardly submission to the last extremity.

"Only say what you wish me to do," he replied.

Even Francine expected some little resistance from a creature bearing the outward appearance of a man. "Oh, do you really mean it?" she asked "I want you to disappoint Emily. Will you stay here, and let me make your excuses?"

"I will do anything to please you."

Francine gave him a farewell look. Her admiration made a desperate effort to express itself appropriately in words. "You are not a man," she said, "you are an angel!"

Left by himself, Mirabel sat down to rest. He reviewed his own conduct with perfect complacency. "Not one man in a hundred could have managed that she-devil as I have done," he thought. "How shall I explain matters to Emily?"

Considering this question, he looked by chance at the unfinished crown of roses. "The very thing to help me!" he said—and took out his pocketbook, and wrote these lines on a blank page: "I have had a scene of jealousy with Miss de Sor, which is beyond all description. To spare you a similar infliction, I have done violence to my own feelings. Instead of instantly obeying the message which you have so kindly sent to me, I remain here for a little while—entirely for your sake."

Having torn out the page, and twisted it up among the roses, so that only a corner of the paper appeared in view, Mirabel called to a lad who was at work in the garden, and gave him his directions, accompanied by a shilling. "Take those flowers to the servants' hall, and tell one of the maids to put them in Miss Brown's room. Stop! Which is the way to the fruit garden?"

The lad gave the necessary directions. Mirabel walked away slowly, with his hands in his pockets. His nerves had been shaken; he thought a little fruit might refresh him.

CHAPTER XLVII. DEBATING.

In the meanwhile Emily had been true to her promise to relieve Mirabel's anxieties, on the subject of Miss Jethro. Entering the drawing-room in search of Alban, she found him talking with Cecilia, and heard her own name mentioned as she opened the door.

"Here she is at last!" Cecilia exclaimed. "What in the world has kept you all this time in the rose garden?"

"Has Mr. Mirabel been more interesting than usual?" Alban asked gayly. Whatever sense of annoyance he might have felt in Emily's absence, was forgotten the moment she appeared; all traces of trouble in his face vanished when they looked at each other.

"You shall judge for yourself," Emily replied with a smile. "Mr. Mirabel has been speaking to me of a relative who is very dear to him—his sister."

Cecilia was surprised. "Why has he never spoken to us of his sister?" she asked.

"It's a sad subject to speak of, my dear. His sister lives a life of suffering— she has been for years a prisoner in her room. He writes to her constantly. His letters from Monksmoor have interested her, poor soul. It seems he said something about me—and she has sent a kind message, inviting me to visit her one of these days. Do you understand it now, Cecilia?"

"Of course I do! Tell me—is Mr. Mirabel's sister older or younger than he is?"

"Older."

"Is she married?"

"She is a widow."

"Does she live with her brother?" Alban asked.

"Oh, no! She has her own house—far away in Northumberland."

"Is she near Sir Jervis Redwood?"

"I fancy not. Her house is on the coast."

"Any children?" Cecilia inquired.

"No; she is quite alone. Now, Cecilia, I have told you all I know—and I have something to say to Mr. Morris. No, you needn't leave us; it's a subject in which you are interested. A subject," she repeated, turning to Alban, "which you may have noticed is not very agreeable to me."

"Miss Jethro?" Alban guessed.

"Yes; Miss Jethro."

Cecilia's curiosity instantly asserted itself.

"We have tried to get Mr. Mirabel to enlighten us, and tried in vain," she said. "You are a favorite. Have you succeeded?"

"I have made no attempt to succeed," Emily replied. "My only object is to relieve Mr. Mirabel's anxiety, if I can—with your help, Mr. Morris."

"In what way can I help you?"

"You mustn't be angry."

"Do I look angry?"

"You look serious. It is a very simple thing. Mr. Mirabel is afraid that Miss Jethro may have said something disagreeable about him, which you might hesitate to repeat. Is he making himself uneasy without any reason?"

"Without the slightest reason. I have concealed nothing from Mr. Mirabel."

"Thank you for the explanation." She turned to Cecilia. "May I send one of the servants with a message? I may as well put an end to Mr. Mirabel's suspense."

The man was summoned, and was dispatched with the message. Emily would have done well, after this, if she had abstained from speaking further of Miss Jethro. But Mirabel's doubts had, unhappily, inspired a similar feeling of uncertainty in her own mind. She was now disposed to attribute the tone of mystery in Alban's unlucky letter to some possible concealment suggested by regard for herself. "I wonder whether I have any reason to feel uneasy?" she said—half in jest, half in earnest.

"Uneasy about what?" Alban inquired.

"About Miss Jethro, of course! Has she said anything of me which your kindness has concealed?"

Alban seemed to be a little hurt by the doubt which her question implied. "Was that your motive," he asked, "for answering my letter as cautiously as if you had been writing to a stranger?"

"Indeed you are quite wrong!" Emily earnestly assured him. "I was perplexed and startled—and I took Mr. Wyvil's advice, before I wrote to you. Shall we drop the subject?"

Alban would have willingly dropped the subject—but for that unfortunate allusion to Mr. Wyvil. Emily had unconsciously touched him on a sore place. He had already heard from Cecilia of the consultation over his letter, and had disapproved of it. "I think you were wrong to trouble Mr. Wyvil," he said.

The altered tone of his voice suggested to Emily that he would have spoken more severely, if Cecilia had not been in the room. She thought him needlessly ready to complain of a harmless proceeding—and she too returned to the subject, after having proposed to drop it not a minute since!

"You didn't tell me I was to keep your letter a secret," she replied.

Cecilia made matters worse—with the best intentions. "I'm sure, Mr.

Morris, my father was only too glad to give Emily his advice."

Alban remained silent—ungraciously silent as Emily thought, after Mr. Wyvil's kindness to him.

"The thing to regret," she remarked, "is that Mr. Morris allowed Miss Jethro to leave him without explaining herself. In his place, I should have insisted on knowing why she wanted to prevent me from meeting Mr. Mirabel in this house."

Cecilia made another unlucky attempt at judicious interference. This time, she tried a gentle remonstrance.

"Remember, Emily, how Mr. Morris was situated. He could hardly be rude to a lady. And I daresay Miss Jethro had good reasons for not wishing to explain herself."

Francine opened the drawing-room door and heard Cecilia's last words.

"Miss Jethro again!" she exclaimed.

"Where is Mr. Mirabel?" Emily asked. "I sent him a message."

"He regrets to say he is otherwise engaged for the present," Francine replied with spiteful politeness. "Don't let me interrupt the conversation. Who is this Miss Jethro, whose name is on everybody's lips?"

Alban could keep silent no longer. "We have done with the subject," he said sharply.

"Because I am here?"

"Because we have said more than enough about Miss Jethro already."

"Speak for yourself, Mr. Morris," Emily answered, resenting the masterful tone which Alban's interference had assumed. "I have not done with Miss Jethro yet, I can assure you."

"My dear, you don't know where she lives," Cecilia reminded her.

"Leave me to discover it!" Emily answered hotly. "Perhaps Mr. Mirabel knows. I shall ask Mr. Mirabel."

272

"I thought you would find a reason for returning to Mr. Mirabel," Francine remarked.

Before Emily could reply, one of the maids entered the room with a wreath of roses in her hand.

"Mr. Mirabel sends you these flowers, miss," the woman said, addressing Emily. "The boy told me they were to be taken to your room. I thought it was a mistake, and I have brought them to you here."

Francine, who happened to be nearest to the door, took the roses from the girl on pretense of handing them to Emily. Her jealous vigilance detected the one visible morsel of Mirabel's letter, twisted up with the flowers. Had Emily entrapped him into a secret correspondence with her? "A scrap of waste paper among your roses," she said, crumpling it up in her hand as if she meant to throw it away.

But Emily was too quick for her. She caught Francine by the wrist. "Waste paper or not," she said; "it was among my flowers and it belongs to me."

Francine gave up the letter, with a look which might have startled Emily if she had noticed it. She handed the roses to Cecilia. "I was making a wreath for you to wear this evening, my dear—and I left it in the garden. It's not quite finished yet."

Cecilia was delighted. "How lovely it is!" she exclaimed. "And how very kind of you! I'll finish it myself." She turned away to the conservatory.

"I had no idea I was interfering with a letter," said Francine; watching Emily with fiercely-attentive eyes, while she smoothed out the crumpled paper.

Having read what Mirabel had written to her, Emily looked up, and saw that Alban was on the point of following Cecilia into the conservatory. He had noticed something in Francine's face which he was at a loss to understand, but which made her presence in the room absolutely hateful to him. Emily followed and spoke to him.

273

"I am going back to the rose garden," she said.

"For any particular purpose?" Alban inquired

"For a purpose which, I am afraid, you won't approve of. I mean to ask Mr. Mirabel if he knows Miss Jethro's address."

"I hope he is as ignorant of it as I am," Alban answered gravely.

"Are we going to quarrel over Miss Jethro, as we once quarreled over Mrs. Rook?" Emily asked—with the readiest recovery of her good humor. "Come! come! I am sure you are as anxious, in your own private mind, to have this matter cleared up as I am."

"With one difference—that I think of consequences, and you don't." He said it, in his gentlest and kindest manner, and stepped into the conservatory.

"Never mind the consequences," she called after him, "if we can only get at the truth. I hate being deceived!"

"There is no person living who has better reason than you have to say that."

Emily looked round with a start. Alban was out of hearing. It was Francine who had answered her.

"What do you mean?" she said.

Francine hesitated. A ghastly paleness overspread her face.

"Are you ill?" Emily asked.

"No—I am thinking."

After waiting for a moment in silence, Emily moved away toward the door of the drawing-room. Francine suddenly held up her hand.

"Stop!" she cried.

Emily stood still.

"My mind is made up," Francine said.

"Made up—to what?"

"You asked what I meant, just now."

"I did."

"Well, my mind is made up to answer you. Miss Emily Brown, you are leading a sadly frivolous life in this house. I am going to give you something more serious to think about than your flirtation with Mr. Mirabel. Oh, don't be impatient! I am coming to the point. Without knowing it yourself, you have been the victim of deception for years past—cruel deception—wicked deception that puts on the mask of mercy."

"Are you alluding to Miss Jethro?" Emily asked, in astonishment. "I thought you were strangers to each other. Just now, you wanted to know who she was."

"I know nothing about her. I care nothing about her. I am not thinking of Miss Jethro."

"Who are you thinking of?"

"I am thinking," Francine answered, "of your dead father."

CHAPTER XLVIII. INVESTIGATING.

Having revived his sinking energies in the fruit garden, Mirabel seated himself under the shade of a tree, and reflected on the critical position in which he was placed by Francine's jealousy.

If Miss de Sor continued to be Mr. Wyvil's guest, there seemed to be no other choice before Mirabel than to leave Monksmoor—and to trust to a favorable reply to his sister's invitation for the free enjoyment of Emily's society under another roof. Try as he might, he could arrive at no more satisfactory conclusion than this. In his preoccupied state, time passed quickly. Nearly an hour had elapsed before he rose to return to the house.

Entering the hall, he was startled by a cry of terror in a woman's voice, coming from the upper regions. At the same time Mr. Wyvil, passing along the bedroom corridor after leaving the music-room, was confronted by his daughter, hurrying out of Emily's bedchamber in such a state of alarm that she could hardly speak.

"Gone!" she cried, the moment she saw her father.

Mr. Wyvil took her in his arms and tried to compose her. "Who has gone?" he asked.

"Emily! Oh, papa, Emily has left us! She has heard dreadful news—she told me so herself."

"What news? How did she hear it?"

"I don't know how she heard it. I went back to the drawing-room to show her my roses—"

"Was she alone?"

"Yes! She frightened me—she seemed quite wild. She said, 'Let me be by myself; I shall have to go home.' She kissed me—and ran up to her room. Oh, I am such a fool! Anybody else would have taken care not to lose sight of her."

"How long did you leave her by herself?"

"I can't say. I thought I would go and tell you. And then I got anxious about her, and knocked at her door, and looked into the room. Gone! Gone!"

Mr. Wyvil rang the bell and confided Cecilia to the care of her maid. Mirabel had already joined him in the corridor. They went downstairs together and consulted with Alban. He volunteered to make immediate inquiries at the railway station. Mr. Wyvil followed him, as far as the lodge gate which opened on the highroad—while Mirabel went to a second gate, at the opposite extremity of the park.

Mr. Wyvil obtained the first news of Emily. The lodge keeper had seen her pass him, on her way out of the park, in the greatest haste. He had called after her, "Anything wrong, miss?" and had received no reply. Asked what time had elapsed since this had happened, he was too confused to be able to answer with any certainty. He knew that she had taken the road which led to the station—and he knew no more.

Mr. Wyvil and Mirabel met again at the house, and instituted an examination of the servants. No further discoveries were made.

The question which occurred to everybody was suggested by the words which Cecilia had repeated to her father. Emily had said she had "heard dreadful news"—how had that news reached her? The one postal delivery at Monksmoor was in the morning. Had any special messenger arrived, with a letter for Emily? The servants were absolutely certain that no such person had entered the house. The one remaining conclusion suggested that somebody must have communicated the evil tidings by word of mouth. But here again no evidence was to be obtained. No visitor had called during the day, and no new guests had arrived. Investigation was completely baffled.

Alban returned from the railway, with news of the fugitive.

He had reached the station, some time after the departure of the London train. The clerk at the office recognized his description of Emily, and stated that she had taken her ticket for London. The station-master had opened the carriage door for her, and had noticed that the young lady appeared to be very much agitated. This information obtained, Alban had dispatched a telegram to Emily—in Cecilia's name: "Pray send us a few words to relieve our anxiety, and let us know if we can be of any service to you."

This was plainly all that could be done—but Cecilia was not satisfied. If her father had permitted it, she would have followed Emily. Alban comforted her. He apologized to Mr. Wyvil for shortening his visit, and announced his intention of traveling to London by the next train. "We may renew our inquiries to some advantage," he added, after hearing what had happened in his absence, "if we can find out who was the last person who saw her, and spoke to her, before your daughter found her alone in the drawing-room. When I went out of the room, I left her with Miss de Sor."

The maid who waited on Miss de Sor was sent for. Francine had been out, by herself, walking in the park. She was then in her room, changing her dress. On hearing of Emily's sudden departure, she had been (as the maid reported) "much shocked and quite at a loss to understand what it meant."

Joining her friends a few minutes later, Francine presented, so far as personal appearance went, a strong contrast to the pale and anxious faces round her. She looked wonderfully well, after her walk. In other respects, she was in perfect harmony with the prevalent feeling. She expressed herself with the utmost propriety; her sympathy moved poor Cecilia to tears.

"I am sure, Miss de Sor, you will try to help us?" Mr. Wyvil began

"With the greatest pleasure," Francine answered.

"How long were you and Miss Emily Brown together, after Mr. Morris left you?"

"Not more than a quarter of an hour, I should think."

"Did anything remarkable occur in the course of conversation?"

"Nothing whatever."

Alban interfered for the first time. "Did you say anything," he asked, "which agitated or offended Miss Brown?"

"That's rather an extraordinary question," Francine remarked.

"Have you no other answer to give?" Alban inquired.

"I answer—No!" she said, with a sudden outburst of anger.

There, the matter dropped. While she spoke in reply to Mr. Wyvil, Francine had confronted him without embarrassment. When Alban interposed, she never looked at him—except when he provoked her to anger. Did she remember that the man who was questioning her, was also the man who had suspected her of writing the anonymous letter? Alban was on his guard against himself, knowing how he disliked her. But the conviction in his own mind was not to be resisted. In some unimaginable way, Francine was associated with Emily's flight from the house.

The answer to the telegram sent from the railway station had not arrived, when Alban took his departure for London. Cecilia's suspense began to grow unendurable: she looked to Mirabel for comfort, and found none. His office was to console, and his capacity for performing that office was notorious among his admirers; but he failed to present himself to advantage, when Mr. Wyvil's lovely daughter had need of his services. He was, in truth, too sincerely anxious and distressed to be capable of commanding his customary resources of ready-made sentiment and fluently-pious philosophy. Emily's influence had awakened the only earnest and true feeling which had ever ennobled the popular preacher's life.

Toward evening, the long-expected telegram was received at last. What could be said, under the circumstances, it said in these words:

"Safe at home—don't be uneasy about me—will write soon."

With that promise they were, for the time, forced to be content.

BOOK THE FIFTH—THE COTTAGE.

CHAPTER XLIX. EMILY SUFFERS.

Mrs. Ellmother—left in charge of Emily's place of abode, and feeling sensible of her lonely position from time to time—had just thought of trying the cheering influence of a cup of tea, when she heard a cab draw up at the cottage gate. A violent ring at the bell followed. She opened the door—and found Emily on the steps. One look at that dear and familiar face was enough for the old servant.

"God help us," she cried, "what's wrong now?"

Without a word of reply, Emily led the way into the bedchamber which had been the scene of Miss Letitia's death. Mrs. Ellmother hesitated on the threshold.

"Why do you bring me in here?" she asked.

"Why did you try to keep me out?" Emily answered.

"When did I try to keep you out, miss?"

"When I came home from school, to nurse my aunt. Ah, you remember now! Is it true—I ask you here, where your old mistress died—is it true that my aunt deceived me about my father's death? And that you knew it?"

There was dead silence. Mrs. Ellmother trembled horribly—her lips dropped apart—her eyes wandered round the room with a stare of idiotic terror. "Is it her ghost tells you that?" she whispered. "Where is her ghost? The room whirls round and round, miss—and the air sings in my ears."

Emily sprang forward to support her. She staggered to a chair, and lifted her great bony hands in wild entreaty. "Don't frighten me," she said. "Stand back."

Emily obeyed her. She dashed the cold sweat off her forehead. "You were talking about your father's death just now," she burst out, in desperate defiant tones. "Well! we know it and we are sorry for it—your father died suddenly."

"My father died murdered in the inn at Zeeland! All the long way to London, I have tried to doubt it. Oh, me, I know it now!"

Answering in those words, she looked toward the bed. Harrowing remembrances of her aunt's delirious self-betrayal made the room unendurable to her. She ran out. The parlor door was open. Entering the room, she passed by a portrait of her father, which her aunt had hung on the wall over the fireplace. She threw herself on the sofa and burst into a passionate fit of crying. "Oh, my father—my dear, gentle, loving father; my first, best, truest friend—murdered! murdered! Oh, God, where was your justice, where was your mercy, when he died that dreadful death?"

A hand was laid on her shoulder; a voice said to her, "Hush, my child! God knows best."

Emily looked up, and saw that Mrs. Ellmother had followed her. "You poor old soul," she said, suddenly remembering; "I frightened you in the other room."

"I have got over it, my dear. I am old; and I have lived a hard life. A hard life schools a person. I make no complaints." She stopped, and began to shudder again. "Will you believe me if I tell you something?" she asked. "I warned my self-willed mistress. Standing by your father's coffin, I warned her. Hide the truth as you may (I said), a time will come when our child will know what you are keeping from her now. One or both of us may live to see it. I am the one who has lived; no refuge in the grave for me. I want to hear about it—there's no fear of frightening or hurting me now. I want to hear how you found it out. Was it by accident, my dear? or did a person tell you?"

Emily's mind was far away from Mrs. Ellmother. She rose from the sofa, with her hands held fast over her aching heart.

"The one duty of my life," she said—"I am thinking of the one duty of my life. Look! I am calm now; I am resigned to my hard lot. Never, never

281

again, can the dear memory of my father be what it was! From this time, it is the horrid memory of a crime. The crime has gone unpunished; the man has escaped others. He shall not escape Me." She paused, and looked at Mrs. Ellmother absently. "What did you say just now? You want to hear how I know what I know? Naturally! naturally! Sit down here—sit down, my old friend, on the sofa with me—and take your mind back to Netherwoods. Alban Morris—"

Mrs. Ellmother recoiled from Emily in dismay. "Don't tell me he had anything to do with it! The kindest of men; the best of men!"

"The man of all men living who least deserves your good opinion or mine," Emily answered sternly.

"You!" Mrs. Ellmother exclaimed, "you say that!"

"I say it. He—who won on me to like him—he was in the conspiracy to deceive me; and you know it! He heard me talk of the newspaper story of the murder of my father—I say, he heard me talk of it composedly, talk of it carelessly, in the innocent belief that it was the murder of a stranger—and he never opened his lips to prevent that horrid profanation! He never even said, speak of something else; I won't hear you! No more of him! God forbid I should ever see him again. No! Do what I told you. Carry your mind back to Netherwoods. One night you let Francine de Sor frighten you. You ran away from her into the garden. Keep quiet! At your age, must I set you an example of self-control?

"I want to know, Miss Emily, where Francine de Sor is now?"

"She is at the house in the country, which I have left."

"Where does she go next, if you please? Back to Miss Ladd?"

"I suppose so. What interest have you in knowing where she goes next?"

"I won't interrupt you, miss. It's true that I ran away into the garden. I can guess who followed me. How did she find her way to me and Mr. Morris, in the dark?"

"The smell of tobacco guided her—she knew who smoked—she had seen him talking to you, on that very day—she followed the scent—she heard what you two said to each other—and she has repeated it to me. Oh, my old friend, the malice of a revengeful girl has enlightened me, when you, my nurse—and he, my lover—left me in the dark: it has told me how my father died!"

"That's said bitterly, miss!"

"Is it said truly?"

"No. It isn't said truly of myself. God knows you would never have been kept in the dark, if your aunt had listened to me. I begged and prayed—I went down on my knees to her—I warned her, as I told you just now. Must I tell you what a headstrong woman Miss Letitia was? She insisted. She put the choice before me of leaving her at once and forever—or giving in. I wouldn't have given in to any other creature on the face of this earth. I am obstinate, as you have often told me. Well, your aunt's obstinacy beat mine; I was too fond of her to say No. Besides, if you ask me who was to blame in the first place, I tell you it wasn't your aunt; she was frightened into it."

"Who frightened her?"

"Your godfather—the great London surgeon—he who was visiting in our house at the time."

"Sir Richard?"

"Yes—Sir Richard. He said he wouldn't answer for the consequences, in the delicate state of your health, if we told you the truth. Ah, he had it all his own way after that. He went with Miss Letitia to the inquest; he won over the coroner and the newspaper men to his will; he kept your aunt's name out of the papers; he took charge of the coffin; he hired the undertaker and his men, strangers from London; he wrote the certificate—who but he! Everybody was cap in hand to the famous man!"

"Surely, the servants and the neighbors asked questions?"

"Hundreds of questions! What did that matter to Sir Richard? They were like so many children, in his hands. And, mind you, the luck helped him. To begin with, there was the common name. Who was to pick out your poor father among the thousands of James Browns? Then, again, the house and lands went to the male heir, as they called him—the man your father quarrelled with in the bygone time. He brought his own establishment with him. Long before you got back from the friends you were staying with—don't you remember it?—we had cleared out of the house; we were miles and miles away; and the old servants were scattered abroad, finding new situations wherever they could. How could you suspect us? We had nothing to fear in that way; but my conscience pricked me. I made another attempt to prevail on Miss Letitia, when you had recovered your health. I said, 'There's no fear of a relapse now; break it to her gently, but tell her the truth.' No! Your aunt was too fond of you. She daunted me with dreadful fits of crying, when I tried to persuade her. And that wasn't the worst of it. She bade me remember what an excitable man your father was—she reminded me that the misery of your mother's death laid him low with brain fever—she said, 'Emily takes after her father; I have heard you say it yourself; she has his constitution, and his sensitive nerves. Don't you know how she loved him—how she talks of him to this day? Who can tell (if we are not careful) what dreadful mischief we may do?' That was how my mistress worked on me. I got infected with her fears; it was as if I had caught an infection of disease. Oh, my dear, blame me if it must be; but don't forget how I have suffered for it since! I was driven away from my dying mistress, in terror of what she might say, while you were watching at her bedside. I have lived in fear of what you might ask me—and have longed to go back to you—and have not had the courage to do it. Look at me now!"

The poor woman tried to take out her handkerchief; her quivering hand helplessly entangled itself in her dress. "I can't even dry my eyes," she said faintly. "Try to forgive me, miss!"

Emily put her arms round the old nurse's neck. "It is you," she said sadly, "who must forgive me."

For a while they were silent. Through the window that was open to the little garden, came the one sound that could be heard—the gentle trembling of leaves in the evening wind.

284

The silence was harshly broken by the bell at the cottage door. They both started.

Emily's heart beat fast. "Who can it be?" she said.

Mrs. Ellmother rose. "Shall I say you can't see anybody?" she asked, before leaving the room.

"Yes! yes!"

Emily heard the door opened—heard low voices in the passage. There was a momentary interval. Then, Mrs. Ellmother returned. She said nothing. Emily spoke to her.

"Is it a visitor?"

"Yes."

"Have you said I can't see anybody?"

"I couldn't say it."

"Why not?"

"Don't be hard on him, my dear. It's Mr. Alban Morris."

CHAPTER L. MISS LADD ADVISES.

Mrs. Ellmother sat by the dying embers of the kitchen fire; thinking over the events of the day in perplexity and distress.

She had waited at the cottage door for a friendly word with Alban, after he had left Emily. The stern despair in his face warned her to let him go in silence. She had looked into the parlor next. Pale and cold, Emily lay on the sofa—sunk in helpless depression of body and mind. "Don't speak to me," she whispered; "I am quite worn out." It was but too plain that the view of Alban's conduct which she had already expressed, was the view to which she had adhered at the interview between them. They had parted in grief—-perhaps in anger—perhaps forever. Mrs. Ellmother lifted Emily in compassionate silence, and carried her upstairs, and waited by her until she slept.

In the still hours of the night, the thoughts of the faithful old servant—dwelling for a while on past and present—advanced, by slow degrees, to consideration of the doubtful future. Measuring, to the best of her ability, the responsibility which had fallen on her, she felt that it was more than she could bear, or ought to bear, alone. To whom could she look for help?

The gentlefolks at Monksmoor were strangers to her. Doctor Allday was near at hand—but Emily had said, "Don't send for him; he will torment me with questions—and I want to keep my mind quiet, if I can." But one person was left, to whose ever-ready kindness Mrs. Ellmother could appeal—and that person was Miss Ladd.

It would have been easy to ask the help of the good schoolmistress in comforting and advising the favorite pupil whom she loved. But Mrs. Ellmother had another object in view: she was determined that the cold-blooded cruelty of Emily's treacherous friend should not be allowed to triumph with impunity. If an ignorant old woman could do nothing else, she could tell the plain truth, and could leave Miss Ladd to decide whether such a person as Francine deserved to remain under her care.

To feel justified in taking this step was one thing: to put it all clearly in writing was another. After vainly making the attempt overnight, Mrs. Ellmother tore up her letter, and communicated with Miss Ladd by means of a telegraphic message, in the morning. "Miss Emily is in great distress. I must not leave her. I have something besides to say to you which cannot be put into a letter. Will you please come to us?"

Later in the forenoon, Mrs. Ellmother was called to the door by the arrival of a visitor. The personal appearance of the stranger impressed her favorably. He was a handsome little gentleman; his manners were winning, and his voice was singularly pleasant to hear.

"I have come from Mr. Wyvil's house in the country," he said; "and I bring a letter from his daughter. May I take the opportunity of asking if Miss Emily is well?"

"Far from it, sir, I am sorry to say. She is so poorly that she keeps her bed."

At this reply, the visitor's face revealed such sincere sympathy and regret, that Mrs. Ellmother was interested in him: she added a word more. "My mistress has had a hard trial to bear, sir. I hope there is no bad news for her in the young lady's letter?"

"On the contrary, there is news that she will be glad to hear—Miss Wyvil is coming here this evening. Will you excuse my asking if Miss Emily has had medical advice?"

"She won't hear of seeing the doctor, sir. He's a good friend of hers—and he lives close by. I am unfortunately alone in the house. If I could leave her, I would go at once and ask his advice."

"Let me go!" Mirabel eagerly proposed.

Mrs. Ellmother's face brightened. "That's kindly thought of, sir—if you don't mind the trouble."

"My good lady, nothing is a trouble in your young mistress's service. Give me the doctor's name and address—and tell me what to say to him."

"There's one thing you must be careful of," Mrs. Ellmother answered. "He mustn't come here, as if he had been sent for—she would refuse to see him."

Mirabel understood her. "I will not forget to caution him. Kindly tell Miss Emily I called—my name is Mirabel. I will return to-morrow."

He hastened away on his errand—only to find that he had arrived too late. Doctor Allday had left London; called away to a serious case of illness. He was not expected to get back until late in the afternoon. Mirabel left a message, saying that he would return in the evening.

The next visitor who arrived at the cottage was the trusty friend, in whose generous nature Mrs. Ellmother had wisely placed confidence. Miss Ladd had resolved to answer the telegram in person, the moment she read it.

"If there is bad news," she said, "let me hear it at once. I am not well enough to bear suspense; my busy life at the school is beginning to tell on me."

"There is nothing that need alarm you, ma'am—but there is a great deal to say, before you see Miss Emily. My stupid head turns giddy with thinking of it. I hardly know where to begin."

"Begin with Emily," Miss Ladd suggested.

Mrs. Ellmother took the advice. She described Emily's unexpected arrival on the previous day; and she repeated what had passed between them afterward. Miss Ladd's first impulse, when she had recovered her composure, was to go to Emily without waiting to hear more. Not presuming to stop her, Mrs. Ellmother ventured to put a question "Do you happen to have my telegram about you, ma'am?" Miss Ladd produced it. "Will you please look at the last part of it again?"

Miss Ladd read the words: "I have something besides to say to you which cannot be put into a letter." She at once returned to her chair.

"Does what you have still to tell me refer to any person whom I know?" she said.

"It refers, ma'am, to Miss de Sor. I am afraid I shall distress you."

"What did I say, when I came in?" Miss Ladd asked. "Speak out plainly; and try—it's not easy, I know—but try to begin at the beginning."

Mrs. Ellmother looked back through her memory of past events, and began by alluding to the feeling of curiosity which she had excited in Francine, on the day when Emily had made them known to one another. From this she advanced to the narrative of what had taken place at Netherwoods—to the atrocious attempt to frighten her by means of the image of wax—to the discovery made by Francine in the garden at night—and to the circumstances under which that discovery had been communicated to Emily.

Miss Ladd's face reddened with indignation. "Are you sure of all that you have said?" she asked.

"I am quite sure, ma'am. I hope I have not done wrong," Mrs. Ellmother added simply, "in telling you all this?"

"Wrong?" Miss Ladd repeated warmly. "If that wretched girl has no defense to offer, she is a disgrace to my school—and I owe you a debt of gratitude for showing her to me in her true character. She shall return at once to Netherwoods; and she shall answer me to my entire satisfaction—or leave my house. What cruelty! what duplicity! In all my experience of girls, I have never met with the like of it. Let me go to my dear little Emily—and try to forget what I have heard."

Mrs. Ellmother led the good lady to Emily's room—and, returning to the lower part of the house, went out into the garden. The mental effort that she had made had left its result in an aching head, and in an overpowering sense of depression. "A mouthful of fresh air will revive me," she thought.

The front garden and back garden at the cottage communicated with each other. Walking slowly round and round, Mrs. Ellmother heard footsteps on the road outside, which stopped at the gate. She looked through the grating, and discovered Alban Morris.

"Come in, sir!" she said, rejoiced to see him. He obeyed in silence. The full view of his face shocked Mrs. Ellmother. Never in her experience of the friend who had been so kind to her at Netherwoods, had he looked so old and so haggard as he looked now. "Oh, Mr. Alban, I see how she has distressed you! Don't take her at her word. Keep a good heart, sir—young girls are never long together of the same mind."

Alban gave her his hand. "I mustn't speak about it," he said. "Silence helps me to bear my misfortune as becomes a man. I have had some hard blows in my time: they don't seem to have blunted my sense of feeling as I thought they had. Thank God, she doesn't know how she has made me suffer! I want to ask her pardon for having forgotten myself yesterday. I spoke roughly to her, at one time. No: I won't intrude on her; I have said I am sorry, in writing. Do you mind giving it to her? Good-by—and thank you. I mustn't stay longer; Miss Ladd expects me at Netherwoods."

"Miss Ladd is in the house, sir, at this moment."

"Here, in London!"

"Upstairs, with Miss Emily."

"Upstairs? Is Emily ill?"

"She is getting better, sir. Would you like to see Miss Ladd?"

"I should indeed! I have something to say to her—and time is of importance to me. May I wait in the garden?"

"Why not in the parlor, sir?"

"The parlor reminds me of happier days. In time, I may have courage enough to look at the room again. Not now."

"If she doesn't make it up with that good man," Mrs. Ellmother thought, on her way back to the house, "my nurse-child is what I have never believed her to be yet—she's a fool."

In half an hour more, Miss Ladd joined Alban on the little plot of grass behind the cottage. "I bring Emily's reply to your letter," she said. "Read it, before you speak to me."

Alban read it: "Don't suppose you have offended me—and be assured that I feel gratefully the tone in which your note is written. I try to write forbearingly on my side; I wish I could write acceptably as well. It is not to be done. I am as unable as ever to enter into your motives. You are not my relation; you were under no obligation of secrecy: you heard me speak ignorantly of the murder of my father, as if it had been the murder of a stranger; and yet you kept me—deliberately, cruelly kept me—deceived! The remembrance of it burns me like fire. I cannot—oh, Alban, I cannot restore you to the place in my estimation which you have lost! If you wish to help me to bear my trouble, I entreat you not to write to me again."

Alban offered the letter silently to Miss Ladd. She signed to him to keep it.

"I know what Emily has written," she said; "and I have told her, what I now tell you—she is wrong; in every way, wrong. It is the misfortune of her impetuous nature that she rushes to conclusions—and those conclusions once formed, she holds to them with all the strength of her character. In this matter, she has looked at her side of the question exclusively; she is blind to your side."

"Not willfully!" Alban interposed.

Miss Ladd looked at him with admiration. "You defend Emily?" she said.

"I love her," Alban answered.

Miss Ladd felt for him, as Mrs. Ellmother had felt for him. "Trust to time, Mr. Morris," she resumed. "The danger to be afraid of is—the danger of some headlong action, on her part, in the interval. Who can say what the end may be, if she persists in her present way of thinking? There is something monstrous, in a young girl declaring that it is her duty to pursue a murderer, and to bring him to justice! Don't you see it yourself?"

Alban still defended Emily. "It seems to me to be a natural impulse," he said—"natural, and noble."

"Noble!" Miss Ladd exclaimed.

"Yes—for it grows out of the love which has not died with her father's death."

"Then you encourage her?"

"With my whole heart—if she would give me the opportunity!"

"We won't pursue the subject, Mr. Morris. I am told by Mrs. Ellmother that you have something to say to me. What is it?"

"I have to ask you," Alban replied, "to let me resign my situation at Netherwoods."

Miss Ladd was not only surprised; she was also—a very rare thing with her—inclined to be suspicious. After what he had said to Emily, it occurred to her that Alban might be meditating some desperate project, with the hope of recovering his lost place in her favor.

"Have you heard of some better employment?" she asked.

"I have heard of no employment. My mind is not in a state to give the necessary attention to my pupils."

"Is that your only reason for wishing to leave me?"

"It is one of my reasons."

"The only one which you think it necessary to mention?"

"Yes."

"I shall be sorry to lose you, Mr. Morris."

"Believe me, Miss Ladd, I am not ungrateful for your kindness."

"Will you let me, in all kindness, say something more?" Miss Ladd answered. "I don't intrude on your secrets—I only hope that you have no rash project in view."

"I don't understand you, Miss Ladd."

"Yes, Mr. Morris—you do."

She shook hands with him—and went back to Emily.

CHAPTER LI. THE DOCTOR SEES.

Alban returned to Netherwoods—to continue his services, until another master could be found to take his place.

By a later train Miss Ladd followed him. Emily was too well aware of the importance of the mistress's presence to the well-being of the school, to permit her to remain at the cottage. It was understood that they were to correspond, and that Emily's room was waiting for her at Netherwoods, whenever she felt inclined to occupy it.

Mrs. Ellmother made the tea, that evening, earlier than usual. Being alone again with Emily, it struck her that she might take advantage of her position to say a word in Alban's favor. She had chosen her time unfortunately.

The moment she pronounced the name, Emily checked her by a look, and spoke of another person—that person being Miss Jethro.

Mrs. Ellmother at once entered her protest, in her own downright way. "Whatever you do," she said, "don't go back to that! What does Miss Jethro matter to you?"

"I am more interested in her than you suppose—I happen to know why she left the school."

"Begging your pardon, miss, that's quite impossible!"

"She left the school," Emily persisted, "for a serious reason. Miss Ladd discovered that she had used false references."

"Good Lord! who told you that?"

"You see I know it. I asked Miss Ladd how she got her information. She was bound by a promise never to mention the person's name. I didn't say it to her—but I may say it to you. I am afraid I have an idea of who the person was."

"No," Mrs. Ellmother obstinately asserted, "you can't possibly know who it was! How should you know?"

"Do you wish me to repeat what I heard in that room opposite, when my aunt was dying?"

"Drop it, Miss Emily! For God's sake, drop it!"

"I can't drop it. It's dreadful to me to have suspicions of my aunt—and no better reason for them than what she said in a state of delirium. Tell me, if you love me, was it her wandering fancy? or was it the truth?"

"As I hope to be saved, Miss Emily, I can only guess as you do—I don't rightly know. My mistress trusted me half way, as it were. I'm afraid I have a rough tongue of my own sometimes. I offended her—and from that time she kept her own counsel. What she did, she did in the dark, so far as I was concerned."

"How did you offend her?"

293

"I shall be obliged to speak of your father if I tell you how?"

"Speak of him."

"He was not to blame—mind that!" Mrs. Ellmother said earnestly. "If I wasn't certain of what I say now you wouldn't get a word out of me. Good harmless man—there's no denying it—he was in love with Miss Jethro! What's the matter?"

Emily was thinking of her memorable conversation with the disgraced teacher on her last night at school. "Nothing" she answered. "Go on."

"If he had not tried to keep it secret from us," Mrs. Ellmother resumed, "your aunt might never have taken it into her head that he was entangled in a love affair of the shameful sort. I don't deny that I helped her in her inquiries; but it was only because I felt sure from the first that the more she discovered the more certainly my master's innocence would show itself. He used to go away and visit Miss Jethro privately. In the time when your aunt trusted me, we never could find out where. She made that discovery afterward for herself (I can't tell you how long afterward); and she spent money in employing mean wretches to pry into Miss Jethro's past life. She had (if you will excuse me for saying it) an old maid's hatred of the handsome young woman, who lured your father away from home, and set up a secret (in a manner of speaking) between her brother and herself. I won't tell you how we looked at letters and other things which he forgot to leave under lock and key. I will only say there was one bit, in a journal he kept, which made me ashamed of myself. I read it out to Miss Letitia; and I told her in so many words, not to count any more on me. No; I haven't got a copy of the words—I can remember them without a copy. 'Even if my religion did not forbid me to peril my soul by leading a life of sin with this woman whom I love'—that was how it began—'the thought of my daughter would keep me pure. No conduct of mine shall ever make me unworthy of my child's affection and respect.' There! I'm making you cry; I won't stay here any longer. All that I had to say has been said. Nobody but Miss Ladd knows for certain whether your aunt was innocent or guilty in the matter of Miss Jethro's disgrace. Please to excuse me; my work's waiting downstairs."

From time to time, as she pursued her domestic labors, Mrs. Ellmother thought of Mirabel. Hours on hours had passed—and the doctor had not appeared. Was he too busy to spare even a few minutes of his time? Or had the handsome little gentleman, after promising so fairly, failed to perform his errand? This last doubt wronged Mirabel. He had engaged to return to the doctor's house; and he kept his word.

Doctor Allday was at home again, and was seeing patients. Introduced in his turn, Mirabel had no reason to complain of his reception. At the same time, after he had stated the object of his visit, something odd began to show itself in the doctor's manner.

He looked at Mirabel with an appearance of uneasy curiosity; and he contrived an excuse for altering the visitor's position in the room, so that the light fell full on Mirabel's face.

"I fancy I must have seen you," the doctor said, "at some former time."

"I am ashamed to say I don't remember it," Mirabel answered.

"Ah, very likely I'm wrong! I'll call on Miss Emily, sir, you may depend on it."

Left in his consulting-room, Doctor Allday failed to ring the bell which summoned the next patient who was waiting for him. He took his diary from the table drawer, and turned to the daily entries for the past month of July.

Arriving at the fifteenth day of the month, he glanced at the first lines of writing: "A visit from a mysterious lady, calling herself Miss Jethro. Our conference led to some very unexpected results."

No: that was not what he was in search of. He looked a little lower down: and read on regularly, from that point, as follows:

"Called on Miss Emily, in great anxiety about the discoveries which she might make among her aunt's papers. Papers all destroyed, thank God—except the Handbill, offering a reward for discovery of the murderer, which she found in the scrap-book. Gave her back the Handbill. Emily much surprised that the wretch should have escaped, with such a careful description of him circulated everywhere. She read the description aloud to me, in her nice clear voice: 'Supposed age between twenty-five and thirty years. A well-made man of small stature. Fair complexion, delicate features, clear blue eyes. Hair light, and cut rather short. Clean shaven, with the exception of narrow half-whiskers'—and so on. Emily at a loss to understand how the fugitive could disguise himself. Reminded her that he could effectually disguise his head and face (with time to help him) by letting his hair grow long, and cultivating his beard. Emily not convinced, even by this self-evident view of the case. Changed the subject."

The doctor put away his diary, and rang the bell.

"Curious," he thought. "That dandified little clergyman has certainly reminded me of my discussion with Emily, more than two months since. Was it his flowing hair, I wonder? or his splendid beard? Good God! suppose it should turn out—?"

He was interrupted by the appearance of his patient. Other ailing people followed. Doctor Allday's mind was professionally occupied for the rest of the evening.

CHAPTER LII. "IF I COULD FIND A FRIEND!"

Shortly after Miss Ladd had taken her departure, a parcel arrived for Emily, bearing the name of a bookseller printed on the label. It was large, and it was heavy. "Reading enough, I should think, to last for a lifetime," Mrs. Ellmother remarked, after carrying the parcel upstairs.

Emily called her back as she was leaving the room. "I want to caution you," she said, "before Miss Wyvil comes. Don't tell her—don't tell anybody—how my father met his death. If other persons are taken into our confidence, they will talk of it. We don't know how near to us the murderer may be. The slightest hint may put him on his guard."

"Oh, miss, are you still thinking of that!"

"I think of nothing else."

"Bad for your mind, Miss Emily—and bad for your body, as your looks show. I wish you would take counsel with some discreet person, before you move in this matter by yourself."

Emily sighed wearily. "In my situation, where is the person whom I can trust?"

"You can trust the good doctor."

"Can I? Perhaps I was wrong when I told you I wouldn't see him. He might be of some use to me."

Mrs. Ellmother made the most of this concession, in the fear that Emily might change her mind. "Doctor Allday may call on you tomorrow," she said.

"Do you mean that you have sent for him?"

"Don't be angry! I did it for the best—and Mr. Mirabel agreed with me."

"Mr. Mirabel! What have you told Mr. Mirabel?"

"Nothing, except that you are ill. When he heard that, he proposed to go for the doctor. He will be here again to-morrow, to ask for news of your health. Will you see him?"

"I don't know yet—I have other things to think of. Bring Miss Wyvil up here when she comes."

"Am I to get the spare room ready for her?"

"No. She is staying with her father at the London house."

Emily made that reply almost with an air of relief. When Cecilia arrived, it was only by an effort that she could show grateful appreciation of the sympathy of her dearest friend. When the visit came to an end, she felt an ungrateful sense of freedom: the restraint was off her mind; she could think again of the one terrible subject that had any interest for her now. Over love, over friendship, over the natural enjoyment of her young life, predominated the blighting resolution which bound her to avenge her father's death. Her dearest remembrances of him—tender remembrances once—now burned in her (to use her own words) like fire. It was no ordinary love that had bound parent and child together in the bygone time. Emily had grown from infancy to girlhood, owing all the brightness of her life—a life without a mother, without brothers, without sisters—to her father alone. To submit to lose this beloved, this only companion, by the cruel stroke of disease was of all trials of resignation the hardest to bear. But to be severed from him by the murderous hand of a man, was more than Emily's fervent nature could passively endure. Before the garden gate had closed on her friend she had returned to her one thought, she was breathing again her one aspiration. The books that she had ordered, with her own purpose in view—books that might supply her want of experience, and might reveal the perils which beset the course that lay before her—were unpacked and spread out on the table. Hour after hour, when the old servant believed that her mistress was in bed, she was absorbed over biographies in English and French, which related the stratagems by means of which famous policemen had captured the worst criminals of their time. From these, she turned to works of fiction, which found their chief topic of interest in dwelling on the discovery of hidden crime. The night passed, and dawn glimmered through the window—and still she opened book after book with sinking courage—and still she gained nothing but the disheartening conviction of her inability to carry out her own plans. Almost every page that she turned over revealed the immovable obstacles set in her way by her sex and her age. Could she mix with the people, or visit the scenes, familiar to the experience of men (in fact and in fiction), who had traced the homicide to his hiding-place, and had marked him among his harmless fellow-creatures with the brand of Cain? No! A young girl following, or attempting to follow, that career, must reckon with insult and outrage—paying their abominable tribute to her youth and her beauty, at every turn. What proportion would the men who might respect her bear to the men who might make her the object of advances, which it was hardly possible to imagine without shuddering. She crept exhausted to her bed, the most helpless, hopeless creature on the wide surface of the earth—a girl self-devoted to the task of a man.

Careful to perform his promise to Mirabel, without delay, the doctor called on Emily early in the morning—before the hour at which he usually entered his consulting-room.

"Well? What's the matter with the pretty young mistress?" he asked, in his most abrupt manner, when Mrs. Ellmother opened the door. "Is it love? or jealousy? or a new dress with a wrinkle in it?"

"You will hear about it, sir, from Miss Emily herself. I am forbidden to say anything."

"But you mean to say something—for all that?"

"Don't joke, Doctor Allday! The state of things here is a great deal too serious for joking. Make up your mind to be surprised—I say no more."

Before the doctor could ask what this meant, Emily opened the parlor door. "Come in!" she said, impatiently.

Doctor Allday's first greeting was strictly professional. "My dear child, I never expected this," he began. "You are looking wretchedly ill." He attempted to feel her pulse. She drew her hand away from him.

"It's my mind that's ill," she answered. "Feeling my pulse won't cure me of anxiety and distress. I want advice; I want help. Dear old doctor, you have always been a good friend to me—be a better friend than ever now."

"What can I do?"

"Promise you will keep secret what I am going to say to you—and listen, pray listen patiently, till I have done."

Doctor Allday promised, and listened. He had been, in some degree at least, prepared for a surprise—but the disclosure which now burst on him was more than his equanimity could sustain. He looked at Emily in silent dismay. She had surprised and shocked him, not only by what she said, but by what she unconsciously suggested. Was it possible that Mirabel's personal appearance had produced on her the same impression which was present in his own mind? His first impulse, when he was composed enough to speak, urged him to put the question cautiously.

"If you happened to meet with the suspected man," he said, "have you any means of identifying him?"

"None whatever, doctor. If you would only think it over—"

He stopped her there; convinced of the danger of encouraging her, and resolved to act on his conviction.

"I have enough to occupy me in my profession," he said. "Ask your other friend to think it over."

"What other friend?"

"Mr. Alban Morris."

The moment he pronounced the name, he saw that he had touched on some painful association. "Has Mr. Morris refused to help you?" he inquired.

"I have not asked him to help me."

"Why?"

There was no choice (with such a man as Doctor Allday) between offending him or answering him. Emily adopted the last alternative. On this occasion she had no reason to complain of his silence.

"Your view of Mr. Morris's conduct surprises me," he replied—"surprises me more than I can say," he added; remembering that he too was guilty of having kept her in ignorance of the truth, out of regard—mistaken regard, as it now seemed to be—for her peace of mind.

"Be good to me, and pass it over if I am wrong," Emily said: "I can't dispute with you; I can only tell you what I feel. You have always been so kind to me—may I count on your kindness still?"

Doctor Allday relapsed into silence.

"May I at least ask," she went on, "if you know anything of persons—" She paused, discouraged by the cold expression of inquiry in the old man's eyes as he looked at her.

"What persons?" he said.

"Persons whom I suspect."

"Name them."

Emily named the landlady of the inn at Zeeland: she could now place the right interpretation on Mrs. Rook's conduct, when the locket had been put into her hand at Netherwoods. Doctor Allday answered shortly and stiffly: he had never even seen Mrs. Rook. Emily mentioned Miss Jethro next—and saw at once that she had interested him.

"What do you suspect Miss Jethro of doing?" he asked.

"I suspect her of knowing more of my father's death than she is willing to acknowledge," Emily replied.

The doctor's manner altered for the better. "I agree with you," he said frankly. "But I have some knowledge of that lady. I warn you not to waste time and trouble in trying to discover the weak side of Miss Jethro."

"That was not my experience of her at school," Emily rejoined. "At the same time I don't know what may have happened since those days. I may perhaps have lost the place I once held in her regard."

"How?"

"Through my aunt."

"Through your aunt?"

"I hope and trust I am wrong," Emily continued; "but I fear my aunt had something to do with Miss Jethro's dismissal from the school—and in that case Miss Jethro may have found it out." Her eyes, resting on the doctor, suddenly brightened. "You know something about it!" she exclaimed.

He considered a little—whether he should or should not tell her of the letter addressed by Miss Ladd to Miss Letitia, which he had found at the cottage.

"If I could satisfy you that your fears are well founded," he asked, "would the discovery keep you away from Miss Jethro?"

"I should be ashamed to speak to her—even if we met."

"Very well. I can tell you positively, that your aunt was the person who turned Miss Jethro out of the school. When I get home, I will send you a letter that proves it."

Emily's head sank on her breast. "Why do I only hear of this now?" she said.

"Because I had no reason for letting you know of it, before to-day. If I have done nothing else, I have at least succeeded in keeping you and Miss Jethro apart."

Emily looked at him in alarm. He went on without appearing to notice that he had startled her. "I wish to God I could as easily put a stop to the mad project which you are contemplating."

"The mad project?" Emily repeated. "Oh, Doctor Allday. Do you cruelly leave me to myself, at the time of all others, when I am most in need of your sympathy?"

That appeal moved him. He spoke more gently; he pitied, while he condemned her.

"My poor dear child, I should be cruel indeed, if I encouraged you. You are giving yourself up to an enterprise, so shockingly unsuited to a young girl like you, that I declare I contemplate it with horror. Think, I entreat you, think; and let me hear that you have yielded—not to my poor entreaties— but to your own better sense!" His voice faltered; his eyes moistened. "I shall make a fool of myself," he burst out furiously, "if I stay here any longer. Good-by."

He left her.

She walked to the window, and looked out at the fair morning. No one to feel for her—no one to understand her—nothing nearer that could speak to poor mortality of hope and encouragement than the bright heaven, so far away! She turned from the window. "The sun shines on the murderer," she thought, "as it shines on me."

She sat down at the table, and tried to quiet her mind; to think steadily to some good purpose. Of the few friends that she possessed, every one had declared that she was in the wrong. Had they lost the one loved being of all beings on earth, and lost him by the hand of a homicide—and that homicide free? All that was faithful, all that was devoted in the girl's nature, held her to her desperate resolution as with a hand of iron. If she shrank at that miserable moment, it was not from her design—it was from the sense of her own helplessness. "Oh, if I had been a man!" she said to herself. "Oh, if I could find a friend!"

CHAPTER LIII. THE FRIEND IS FOUND.

Mrs. Ellmother looked into the parlor. "I told you Mr. Mirabel would call again," she announced. "Here he is."

"Has he asked to see me?"

"He leaves it entirely to you."

For a moment, and a moment only, Emily was undecided. "Show him in," she said.

Mirabel's embarrassment was visible the moment he entered the room. For the first time in his life—in the presence of a woman—the popular preacher was shy. He who had taken hundreds of fair hands with sympathetic pressure—he who had offered fluent consolation, abroad and at home, to beauty in distress—was conscious of a rising color, and was absolutely at a loss for words when Emily received him. And yet, though he appeared at disadvantage—and, worse still, though he was aware of it himself—there was nothing contemptible in his look and manner. His silence and confusion revealed a change in him which inspired respect. Love had developed this spoiled darling of foolish congregations, this effeminate pet of drawing-rooms and boudoirs, into the likeness of a Man—and no woman, in Emily's position, could have failed to see that it was love which she herself had inspired.

Equally ill at ease, they both took refuge in the commonplace phrases suggested by the occasion. These exhausted there was a pause. Mirabel alluded to Cecilia, as a means of continuing the conversation.

"Have you seen Miss Wyvil?" he inquired.

"She was here last night; and I expect to see her again to-day before she returns to Monksmoor with her father. Do you go back with them?"

"Yes—if you do."

"I remain in London."

"Then I remain in London, too."

The strong feeling that was in him had forced its way to expression at last. In happier days—when she had persistently refused to let him speak to her seriously—she would have been ready with a light-hearted reply. She was silent now. Mirabel pleaded with her not to misunderstand him, by an honest confession of his motives which presented him under a new aspect. The easy plausible man, who had hardly ever seemed to be in earnest before—meant, seriously meant, what he said now.

"May I try to explain myself?" he asked.

"Certainly, if you wish it."

"Pray, don't suppose me capable," Mirabel said earnestly, "of presuming to pay you an idle compliment. I cannot think of you, alone and in trouble, without feeling anxiety which can only be relieved in one way—I must be near enough to hear of you, day by day. Not by repeating this visit! Unless you wish it, I will not again cross the threshold of your door. Mrs. Ellmother will tell me if your mind is more at ease; Mrs. Ellmother will tell me if there is any new trial of your fortitude. She needn't even mention that I have been speaking to her at the door; and she may be sure, and you may be sure, that I shall ask no inquisitive questions. I can feel for you in your misfortune, without wishing to know what that misfortune is. If I can ever be of the smallest use, think of me as your other servant. Say to Mrs. Ellmother, 'I want him'—and say no more."

Where is the woman who could have resisted such devotion as this— inspired, truly inspired, by herself? Emily's eyes softened as she answered him.

"You little know how your kindness touches me," she said.

"Don't speak of my kindness until you have put me to the proof," he interposed. "Can a friend (such a friend as I am, I mean) be of any use?"

"Of the greatest use if I could feel justified in trying you."

"I entreat you to try me!"

"But, Mr. Mirabel, you don't know what I am thinking of."

"I don't want to know."

"I may be wrong. My friends all say I am wrong."

"I don't care what your friends say; I don't care about any earthly thing but your tranquillity. Does your dog ask whether you are right or wrong? I am your dog. I think of You, and I think of nothing else."

She looked back through the experience of the last few days. Miss Ladd—Mrs. Ellmother—Doctor Allday: not one of them had felt for her, not one of them had spoken to her, as this man had felt and had spoken. She remembered the dreadful sense of solitude and helplessness which had wrung her heart, in the interval before Mirabel came in. Her father himself could hardly have been kinder to her than this friend of a few weeks only. She looked at him through her tears; she could say nothing that was eloquent, nothing even that was adequate. "You are very good to me," was her only acknowledgment of all that he had offered. How poor it seemed to be! and yet how much it meant!

He rose—saying considerately that he would leave her to recover herself, and would wait to hear if he was wanted.

"No," she said; "I must not let you go. In common gratitude I ought to decide before you leave me, and I do decide to take you into my confidence." She hesitated; her color rose a little. "I know how unselfishly you offer me your help," she resumed; "I know you speak to me as a brother might speak to a sister—"

He gently interrupted her. "No," he said; "I can't honestly claim to do that. And—may I venture to remind you?—you know why."

She started. Her eyes rested on him with a momentary expression of reproach.

"Is it quite fair," she asked, "in my situation, to say that?"

"Would it have been quite fair," he rejoined, "to allow you to deceive yourself? Should I deserve to be taken into your confidence, if I encouraged you to trust me, under false pretenses? Not a word more of those hopes on which the happiness of my life depends shall pass my lips, unless you permit it. In my devotion to your interests, I promise to forget myself. My motives may be misinterpreted; my position may be misunderstood. Ignorant people may take me for that other happier man, who is an object of interest to you—"

"Stop, Mr. Mirabel! The person to whom you refer has no such claim on me as you suppose."

"Dare I say how happy I am to hear it? Will you forgive me?"

"I will forgive you if you say no more."

Their eyes met. Completely overcome by the new hope that she had inspired, Mirabel was unable to answer her. His sensitive nerves trembled under emotion, like the nerves of a woman; his delicate complexion faded away slowly into whiteness. Emily was alarmed—he seemed to be on the point of fainting. She ran to the window to open it more widely.

"Pray don't trouble yourself," he said, "I am easily agitated by any sudden sensation—and I am a little overcome at this moment by my own happiness."

"Let me give you a glass of wine."

"Thank you—I don't need it indeed."

"You really feel better?"

"I feel quite well again—and eager to hear how I can serve you."

"It's a long story, Mr. Mirabel—and a dreadful story."

"Dreadful?"

"Yes! Let me tell you first how you can serve me. I am in search of a man who has done me the cruelest wrong that one human creature can inflict on another. But the chances are all against me—I am only a woman; and I don't know how to take even the first step toward discovery."

"You will know, when I guide you."

He reminded her tenderly of what she might expect from him, and was rewarded by a grateful look. Seeing nothing, suspecting nothing, they advanced together nearer and nearer to the end.

"Once or twice," Emily continued, "I spoke to you of my poor father, when we were at Monksmoor—and I must speak of him again. You could have no interest in inquiring about a stranger—and you cannot have heard how he died."

"Pardon me, I heard from Mr. Wyvil how he died."

"You heard what I had told Mr. Wyvil," Emily said: "I was wrong."

"Wrong!" Mirabel exclaimed, in a tone of courteous surprise. "Was it not a sudden death?"

"It was a sudden death."

"Caused by disease of the heart?"

"Caused by no disease. I have been deceived about my father's death—and I have only discovered it a few days since."

At the impending moment of the frightful shock which she was innocently about to inflict on him, she stopped—doubtful whether it would be best to relate how the discovery had been made, or to pass at once to the result. Mirabel supposed that she had paused to control her agitation. He was so immeasurably far away from the faintest suspicion of what was coming that he exerted his ingenuity, in the hope of sparing her.

"I can anticipate the rest," he said. "Your sad loss has been caused by some fatal accident. Let us change the subject; tell me more of that man whom I must help you to find. It will only distress you to dwell on your father's death."

"Distress me?" she repeated. "His death maddens me!"

"Oh, don't say that!"

"Hear me! hear me! My father died murdered, at Zeeland—and the man you must help me to find is the wretch who killed him."

She started to her feet with a cry of terror. Mirabel dropped from his chair senseless to the floor.

CHAPTER LIV. THE END OF THE FAINTING FIT.

Emily recovered her presence of mind. She opened the door, so as to make a draught of air in the room, and called for water. Returning to Mirabel, she loosened his cravat. Mrs. Ellmother came in, just in time to prevent her from committing a common error in the treatment of fainting persons, by raising Mirabel's head. The current of air, and the sprinkling of water over his face, soon produced their customary effect. "He'll come round, directly," Mrs. Ellmother remarked. "Your aunt was sometimes taken with these swoons, miss; and I know something about them. He looks a poor weak creature, in spite of his big beard. Has anything frightened him?"

Emily little knew how correctly that chance guess had hit on the truth!

"Nothing can possibly have frightened him," she replied; "I am afraid he is in bad health. He turned suddenly pale while we were talking; and I thought he was going to be taken ill; he made light of it, and seemed to recover. Unfortunately, I was right; it was the threatening of a fainting fit—he dropped on the floor a minute afterward."

A sigh fluttered over Mirabel's lips. His eyes opened, looked at Mrs. Ellmother in vacant terror, and closed again. Emily whispered to her to leave the room. The old woman smiled satirically as she opened the door—then looked back, with a sudden change of humor. To see the kind young mistress bending over the feeble little clergyman set her—by some strange association of ideas—thinking of Alban Morris. "Ah," she muttered to herself, on her way out, "I call him a Man!"

There was wine in the sideboard—the wine which Emily had once already offered in vain. Mirabel drank it eagerly, this time. He looked round the room, as if he wished to be sure that they were alone. "Have I fallen to a low place in your estimation?" he asked, smiling faintly. "I am afraid you will think poorly enough of your new ally, after this?"

"I only think you should take more care of your health," Emily replied, with sincere interest in his recovery. "Let me leave you to rest on the sofa."

He refused to remain at the cottage—he asked, with a sudden change to fretfulness, if she would let her servant get him a cab. She ventured to doubt whether he was quite strong enough yet to go away by himself. He reiterated, piteously reiterated, his request. A passing cab was stopped directly. Emily accompanied him to the gate. "I know what to do," he said, in a hurried absent way. "Rest and a little tonic medicine will soon set me right." The clammy coldness of his skin made Emily shudder, as they shook hands. "You won't think the worse of me for this?" he asked.

"How can you imagine such a thing!" she answered warmly.

"Will you see me, if I come to-morrow?"

"I shall be anxious to see you."

So they parted. Emily returned to the house, pitying him with all her heart.

BOOK THE SIXTH—HERE AND THERE.

CHAPTER LV. MIRABEL SEES HIS WAY.

Reaching the hotel at which he was accustomed to stay when he was in London, Mirabel locked the door of his room. He looked at the houses on the opposite side of the street. His mind was in such a state of morbid distrust that he lowered the blind over the window. In solitude and obscurity, the miserable wretch sat down in a corner, and covered his face with his hands, and tried to realize what had happened to him.

Nothing had been said at the fatal interview with Emily, which could have given him the slightest warning of what was to come. Her father's name—absolutely unknown to him when he fled from the inn—had only been communicated to the public by the newspaper reports of the adjourned inquest. At the time when those reports appeared, he was in hiding, under circumstances which prevented him from seeing a newspaper. While the murder was still a subject of conversation, he was in France—far out of the track of English travelers—and he remained on the continent until the summer of eighteen hundred and eighty-one. No exercise of discretion, on his part, could have extricated him from the terrible position in which he was now placed. He stood pledged to Emily to discover the man suspected of the murder of her father; and that man was—himself!

What refuge was left open to him?

If he took to flight, his sudden disappearance would be a suspicious circumstance in itself, and would therefore provoke inquiries which might lead to serious results. Supposing that he overlooked the risk thus presented, would he be capable of enduring a separation from Emily, which might be a separation for life? Even in the first horror of discovering his situation, her influence remained unshaken—the animating spirit of the one manly capacity for resistance which raised him above the reach of his own fears. The only prospect before him which he felt himself to be incapable of contemplating, was the prospect of leaving Emily.

Having arrived at this conclusion, his fears urged him to think of providing for his own safety.

The first precaution to adopt was to separate Emily from friends whose advice might be hostile to his interests—perhaps even subversive of his security. To effect this design, he had need of an ally whom he could trust. That ally was at his disposal, far away in the north.

At the time when Francine's jealousy began to interfere with all freedom of intercourse between Emily and himself at Monksmoor, he had contemplated making arrangements which might enable them to meet at the house of his invalid sister, Mrs. Delvin. He had spoken of her, and of the bodily affliction which confined her to her room, in terms which had already interested Emily. In the present emergency, he decided on returning to the subject, and on hastening the meeting between the two women which he had first suggested at Mr. Wyvil's country seat.

No time was to be lost in carrying out this intention. He wrote to Mrs. Delvin by that day's post; confiding to her, in the first place, the critical position in which he now found himself. This done, he proceeded as follows:

"To your sound judgment, dearest Agatha, it may appear that I am making myself needlessly uneasy about the future. Two persons only know that I am the man who escaped from the inn at Zeeland. You are one of them, and Miss Jethro is the other. On you I can absolutely rely; and, after my experience of her, I ought to feel sure of Miss Jethro. I admit this; but I cannot get over my distrust of Emily's friends. I fear the cunning old doctor; I doubt Mr. Wyvil; I hate Alban Morris.

"Do me a favor, my dear. Invite Emily to be your guest, and so separate her from these friends. The old servant who attends on her will be included in the invitation, of course. Mrs. Ellmother is, as I believe, devoted to the interests of Mr. Alban Morris: she will be well out of the way of doing mischief, while we have her safe in your northern solitude.

"There is no fear that Emily will refuse your invitation.

"In the first place, she is already interested in you. In the second place, I shall consider the small proprieties of social life; and, instead of traveling with her to your house, I shall follow by a later train. In the third place, I am now the chosen adviser in whom she trusts; and what I tell her to do, she will do. It pains me, really and truly pains me, to be compelled to deceive her—but the other alternative is to reveal myself as the wretch of whom she is in search. Was there ever such a situation? And, oh, Agatha, I am so fond of her! If I fail to persuade her to be my wife, I don't care what becomes of me. I used to think disgrace, and death on the scaffold, the most frightful prospect that a man can contemplate. In my present frame of mind, a life without Emily may just as well end in that way as in any other. When we are together in your old sea-beaten tower, do your best, my dear, to incline the heart of this sweet girl toward me. If she remains in London, how do I know that Mr. Morris may not recover the place he has lost in her good opinion? The bare idea of it turns me cold.

"There is one more point on which I must touch, before I can finish my letter.

"When you last wrote, you told me that Sir Jervis Redwood was not expected to live much longer, and that the establishment would be broken up after his death. Can you find out for me what will become, under the circumstances, of Mr. and Mrs. Rook? So far as I am concerned, I don't doubt that the alteration in my personal appearance, which has protected me for years past, may be trusted to preserve me from recognition by these two people. But it is of the utmost importance, remembering the project to which Emily has devoted herself, that she should not meet with Mrs. Rook. They have been already in correspondence; and Mrs. Rook has expressed an intention (if the opportunity offers itself) of calling at the cottage. Another reason, and a pressing reason, for removing Emily from London! We can easily keep the Rooks out of your house; but I own I should feel more at my ease, if I heard that they had left Northumberland."

With that confession, Mrs. Delvin's brother closed his letter.

CHAPTER LVI. ALBAN SEES HIS WAY.

During the first days of Mirabel's sojourn at his hotel in London, events were in progress at Netherwoods, affecting the interests of the man who was the especial object of his distrust. Not long after Miss Ladd had returned to her school, she heard of an artist who was capable of filling the place to be vacated by Alban Morris. It was then the twenty-third of the month. In four days more the new master would be ready to enter on his duties; and Alban would be at liberty.

On the twenty-fourth, Alban received a telegram which startled him. The person sending the message was Mrs. Ellmother; and the words were: "Meet me at your railway station to-day, at two o'clock."

He found the old woman in the waiting-room; and he met with a rough reception.

"Minutes are precious, Mr. Morris," she said; "you are two minutes late. The next train to London stops here in half an hour—and I must go back by it."

"Good heavens, what brings you here? Is Emily—?"

"Emily is well enough in health—if that's what you mean? As to why I come here, the reason is that it's a deal easier for me (worse luck!) to take this journey than to write a letter. One good turn deserves another. I don't forget how kind you were to me, away there at the school—and I can't, and won't, see what's going on at the cottage, behind your back, without letting you know of it. Oh, you needn't be alarmed about her! I've made an excuse to get away for a few hours—but I haven't left her by herself. Miss Wyvil has come to London again; and Mr. Mirabel spends the best part of his time with her. Excuse me for a moment, will you? I'm so thirsty after the journey, I can hardly speak."

She presented herself at the counter in the waiting-room. "I'll trouble you, young woman, for a glass of ale." She returned to Alban in a better humor. "It's not bad stuff, that! When I have said my say, I'll have a drop more—just to wash the taste of Mr. Mirabel out of my mouth. Wait a bit; I have something to ask you. How much longer are you obliged to stop here, teaching the girls to draw?"

"I leave Netherwoods in three days more," Alban replied.

"That's all right! You may be in time to bring Miss Emily to her senses, yet."

"What do you mean?"

"I mean—if you don't stop it—she will marry the parson."

"I can't believe it, Mrs. Ellmother! I won't believe it!"

"Ah, it's a comfort to him, poor fellow, to say that! Look here, Mr. Morris; this is how it stands. You're in disgrace with Miss Emily—and he profits by it. I was fool enough to take a liking to Mr. Mirabel when I first opened the door to him; I know better now. He got on the blind side of me; and now he has got on the blind side of her. Shall I tell you how? By doing what you would have done if you had had the chance. He's helping her—or pretending to help her, I don't know which—to find the man who murdered poor Mr. Brown. After four years! And when all the police in England (with a reward to encourage them) did their best, and it came to nothing!"

"Never mind that!" Alban said impatiently. "I want to know how Mr. Mirabel is helping her?"

"That's more than I can tell you. You don't suppose they take me into their confidence? All I can do is to pick up a word, here and there, when fine weather tempts them out into the garden. She tells him to suspect Mrs. Rook, and to make inquiries after Miss Jethro. And he has his plans; and he writes them down, which is dead against his doing anything useful, in my opinion. I don't hold with your scribblers. At the same time I wouldn't count too positively, in your place, on his being likely to fail. That little Mirabel—if it wasn't for his beard, I should believe he was a woman, and a sickly woman too; he fainted in our house the other day—that little Mirabel is in earnest. Rather than leave Miss Emily from Saturday to Monday, he has got a parson out of employment to do his Sunday work for him. And, what's more, he has persuaded her (for some reasons of his own) to leave London next week."

"Is she going back to Monksmoor?"

"Not she! Mr. Mirabel has got a sister, a widow lady; she's a cripple, or something of the sort. Her name is Mrs. Delvin. She lives far away in the north country, by the sea; and Miss Emily is going to stay with her."

"Are you sure of that?"

"Sure? I've seen the letter."

"Do you mean the letter of invitation?"

"Yes—I do. Miss Emily herself showed it to me. I'm to go with her—'in attendance on my mistress,' as the lady puts it. This I will say for Mrs. Delvin: her handwriting is a credit to the school that taught her; and the poor bedridden creature words her invitation so nicely, that I myself couldn't have resisted it—and I'm a hard one, as you know. You don't seem to heed me, Mr. Morris."

"I beg your pardon, I was thinking."

"Thinking of what—if I may make so bold?"

"Of going back to London with you, instead of waiting till the new master comes to take my place."

"Don't do that, sir! You would do harm instead of good, if you showed yourself at the cottage now. Besides, it would not be fair to Miss Ladd, to leave her before the other man takes your girls off your hands. Trust me to look after your interests; and don't go near Miss Emily—don't even write to her—unless you have got something to say about the murder, which she will be eager to hear. Make some discovery in that direction, Mr. Morris, while the parson is only trying to do it or pretending to do it—and I'll answer for the result. Look at the clock! In ten minutes more the train will be here. My memory isn't as good as it was; but I do think I have told you all I had to tell."

"You are the best of good friends!" Alban said warmly.

"Never mind about that, sir. If you want to do a friendly thing in return, tell me if you know what has become of Miss de Sor."

"She has returned to Netherwoods."

"Aha! Miss Ladd is as good as her word. Would you mind writing to tell me of it, if Miss de Sor leaves the school again? Good Lord! there she is on the platform with bag and baggage. Don't let her see me, Mr. Morris! If she comes in here, I shall set the marks of my ten finger-nails on that false face of hers, as sure as I am a Christian woman."

Alban placed himself at the door, so as to hide Mrs. Ellmother. There indeed was Francine, accompanied by one of the teachers at the school. She took a seat on the bench outside the booking-office, in a state of sullen indifference—absorbed in herself—noticing nothing. Urged by ungovernable curiosity, Mrs. Ellmother stole on tiptoe to Alban's side to look at her. To a person acquainted with the circumstances there could be no possible doubt of what had happened. Francine had failed to excuse herself, and had been dismissed from Miss Ladd's house.

"I would have traveled to the world's end," Mrs. Ellmother said, "to see that!"

She returned to her place in the waiting-room, perfectly satisfied.

The teacher noticed Alban, on leaving the booking-office after taking the tickets. "I shall be glad," she said, looking toward Francine, "when I have resigned the charge of that young lady to the person who is to receive her in London."

"Is she to be sent back to her parents?" Alban asked.

"We don't know yet. Miss Ladd will write to St. Domingo by the next mail. In the meantime, her father's agent in London—the same person who pays her allowance—takes care of her until he hears from the West Indies."

"Does she consent to this?"

"She doesn't seem to care what becomes of her. Miss Ladd has given her every opportunity of explaining and excusing herself, and has produced

316

no impression. You can see the state she is in. Our good mistress—always hopeful even in the worst cases, as you know—thinks she is feeling ashamed of herself, and is too proud and self-willed to own it. My own idea is, that some secret disappointment is weighing on her mind. Perhaps I am wrong."

No. Miss Ladd was wrong; and the teacher was right.

The passion of revenge, being essentially selfish in its nature, is of all passions the narrowest in its range of view. In gratifying her jealous hatred of Emily, Francine had correctly foreseen consequences, as they might affect the other object of her enmity—Alban Morris. But she had failed to perceive the imminent danger of another result, which in a calmer frame of mind might not have escaped discovery. In triumphing over Emily and Alban, she had been the indirect means of inflicting on herself the bitterest of all disappointments—she had brought Emily and Mirabel together. The first forewarning of this catastrophe had reached her, on hearing that Mirabel would not return to Monksmoor. Her worst fears had been thereafter confirmed by a letter from Cecilia, which had followed her to Netherwoods. From that moment, she, who had made others wretched, paid the penalty in suffering as keen as any that she had inflicted. Completely prostrated; powerless, through ignorance of his address in London, to make a last appeal to Mirabel; she was literally, as had just been said, careless what became of her. When the train approached, she sprang to her feet—advanced to the edge of the platform—and suddenly drew back, shuddering. The teacher looked in terror at Alban. Had the desperate girl meditated throwing herself under the wheels of the engine? The thought had been in both their minds; but neither of them acknowledged it. Francine stepped quietly into the carriage, when the train drew up, and laid her head back in a corner, and closed her eyes. Mrs. Ellmother took her place in another compartment, and beckoned to Alban to speak to her at the window.

"Where can I see you, when you go to London?" she asked.

"At Doctor Allday's house."

"On what day?"

"On Tuesday next."

CHAPTER LVII. APPROACHING THE END.

Alban reached London early enough in the afternoon to find the doctor at his luncheon. "Too late to see Mrs. Ellmother," he announced. "Sit down and have something to eat."

"Has she left any message for me?"

"A message, my good friend, that you won't like to hear. She is off with her mistress, this morning, on a visit to Mr. Mirabel's sister."

"Does he go with them?"

"No; he follows by a later train."

"Has Mrs. Ellmother mentioned the address?"

"There it is, in her own handwriting."

Alban read the address:—"Mrs. Delvin, The Clink, Belford, Northumberland."

"Turn to the back of that bit of paper," the doctor said. "Mrs. Ellmother has written something on it."

She had written these words: "No discoveries made by Mr. Mirabel, up to this time. Sir Jervis Redwood is dead. The Rooks are believed to be in Scotland; and Miss Emily, if need be, is to help the parson to find them. No news of Miss Jethro."

"Now you have got your information," Doctor Allday resumed, "let me have a look at you. You're not in a rage: that's a good sign to begin with."

"I am not the less determined," Alban answered.

"To bring Emily to her senses?" the doctor asked.

"To do what Mirabel has not done—and then to let her choose between us."

"Ay? ay? Your good opinion of her hasn't altered, though she has treated you so badly?"

"My good opinion makes allowance for the state of my poor darling's mind, after the shock that has fallen on her," Alban answered quietly. "She is not my Emily now. She will be my Emily yet. I told her I was convinced of it, in the old days at school—and my conviction is as strong as ever. Have you seen her, since I have been away at Netherwoods?"

"Yes; and she is as angry with me as she is with you."

"For the same reason?"

"No, no. I heard enough to warn me to hold my tongue. I refused to help her—that's all. You are a man, and you may run risks which no young girl ought to encounter. Do you remember when I asked you to drop all further inquiries into the murder, for Emily's sake? The circumstances have altered since that time. Can I be of any use?"

"Of the greatest use, if you can give me Miss Jethro's address."

"Oh! You mean to begin in that way, do you?"

"Yes. You know that Miss Jethro visited me at Netherwoods?"

"Go on."

"She showed me your answer to a letter which she had written to you. Have you got that letter?"

Doctor Allday produced it. The address was at a post-office, in a town on the south coast. Looking up when he had copied it, Alban saw the doctor's eyes fixed on him with an oddly-mingled expression: partly of sympathy, partly of hesitation.

"Have you anything to suggest?" he asked.

"You will get nothing out of Miss Jethro," the doctor answered, "unless—" there he stopped.

"Unless, what?"

"Unless you can frighten her."

"How am I to do that?"

After a little reflection, Doctor Allday returned, without any apparent reason, to the subject of his last visit to Emily.

"There was one thing she said, in the course of our talk," he continued, "which struck me as being sensible: possibly (for we are all more or less conceited), because I agreed with her myself. She suspects Miss Jethro of knowing more about that damnable murder than Miss Jethro is willing to acknowledge. If you want to produce the right effect on her—" he looked hard at Alban and checked himself once more.

"Well? what am I to do?"

"Tell her you have an idea of who the murderer is."

"But I have no idea."

"But I have."

"Good God! what do you mean?"

"Don't mistake me! An impression has been produced on my mind— that's all. Call it a freak or fancy; worth trying perhaps as a bold experiment, and worth nothing more. Come a little nearer. My housekeeper is an excellent woman, but I have once or twice caught her rather too near to that door. I think I'll whisper it."

He did whisper it. In breathless wonder, Alban heard of the doubt which had crossed Doctor Allday's mind, on the evening when Mirabel had called at his house.

"You look as if you didn't believe it," the doctor remarked.

"I'm thinking of Emily. For her sake I hope and trust you are wrong. Ought I to go to her at once? I don't know what to do!"

"Find out first, my good fellow, whether I am right or wrong. You can do it, if you will run the risk with Miss Jethro."

Alban recovered himself. His old friend's advice was clearly the right advice to follow. He examined his railway guide, and then looked at his watch.

"If I can find Miss Jethro," he answered, "I'll risk it before the day is out."

The doctor accompanied him to the door. "You will write to me, won't you?"

"Without fail. Thank you—and good-by."

BOOK THE SEVENTH—THE CLINK.

CHAPTER LVIII. A COUNCIL OF TWO.

Early in the last century one of the picturesque race of robbers and murderers, practicing the vices of humanity on the borderlands watered by the river Tweed, built a tower of stone on the coast of Northumberland. He lived joyously in the perpetration of atrocities; and he died penitent, under the direction of his priest. Since that event, he has figured in poems and pictures; and has been greatly admired by modern ladies and gentlemen, whom he would have outraged and robbed if he had been lucky enough to meet with them in the good old times.

His son succeeded him, and failed to profit by the paternal example: that is to say, he made the fatal mistake of fighting for other people instead of fighting for himself.

In the rebellion of Forty-Five, this northern squire sided to serious purpose with Prince Charles and the Highlanders. He lost his head; and his children lost their inheritance. In the lapse of years, the confiscated property fell into the hands of strangers; the last of whom (having a taste for the turf) discovered, in course of time, that he was in want of money. A retired merchant, named Delvin (originally of French extraction), took a liking to the wild situation, and purchased the tower. His wife—already in failing health—had been ordered by the doctors to live a quiet life by the sea. Her husband's death left her a rich and lonely widow; by day and night alike, a prisoner in her room; wasted by disease, and having but two interests which reconciled her to life—writing poetry in the intervals of pain, and paying the debts of a reverend brother who succeeded in the pulpit, and prospered nowhere else.

In the later days of its life, the tower had been greatly improved as a place of residence. The contrast was remarkable between the dreary gray outer walls, and the luxuriously furnished rooms inside, rising by two at a time to the lofty eighth story of the building. Among the scattered populace of the country round, the tower was still known by the odd name given to it in the bygone time—"The Clink." It had been so called (as was supposed) in allusion to the noise made by loose stones, washed backward and forward at certain times of the tide, in hollows of the rock on which the building stood.

On the evening of her arrival at Mrs. Delvin's retreat, Emily retired at an early hour, fatigued by her long journey. Mirabel had an opportunity of speaking with his sister privately in her own room.

"Send me away, Agatha, if I disturb you," he said, "and let me know when I can see you in the morning."

"My dear Miles, have you forgotten that I am never able to sleep in calm weather? My lullaby, for years past, has been the moaning of the great North Sea, under my window. Listen! There is not a sound outside on this peaceful night. It is the right time of the tide, just now—and yet, 'the clink' is not to be heard. Is the moon up?"

Mirabel opened the curtains. "The whole sky is one great abyss of black," he answered. "If I was superstitious, I should think that horrid darkness a bad omen for the future. Are you suffering, Agatha?"

"Not just now. I suppose I look sadly changed for the worse since you saw me last?"

But for the feverish brightness of her eyes, she would have looked like a corpse. Her wrinkled forehead, her hollow cheeks, her white lips told their terrible tale of the suffering of years. The ghastly appearance of her face was heightened by the furnishing of the room. This doomed woman, dying slowly day by day, delighted in bright colors and sumptuous materials. The paper on the walls, the curtains, the carpet presented the hues of the rainbow. She lay on a couch covered with purple silk, under draperies of green velvet to keep her warm. Rich lace hid her scanty hair, turning prematurely gray; brilliant rings glittered on her bony fingers. The room was in a blaze of light from lamps and candles. Even the wine at her side that kept her alive had been decanted into a bottle of lustrous Venetian glass. "My grave is open," she used to say; "and I want all these beautiful things to keep me from looking at it. I should die at once, if I was left in the dark."

Her brother sat by the couch, thinking "Shall I tell you what is in your mind?" she asked.

Mirabel humored the caprice of the moment. "Tell me!" he said.

"You want to know what I think of Emily," she answered. "Your letter told me you were in love; but I didn't believe your letter. I have always doubted whether you were capable of feeling true love—until I saw Emily. The moment she entered the room, I knew that I had never properly appreciated my brother. You are in love with her, Miles; and you are a better man than I thought you. Does that express my opinion?"

Mirabel took her wasted hand, and kissed it gratefully.

"What a position I am in!" he said. "To love her as I love her; and, if she knew the truth, to be the object of her horror—to be the man whom she would hunt to the scaffold, as an act of duty to the memory of her father!"

"You have left out the worst part of it," Mrs. Delvin reminded him. "You have bound yourself to help her to find the man. Your one hope of persuading her to become your wife rests on your success in finding him. And you are the man. There is your situation! You can't submit to it. How can you escape from it?"

"You are trying to frighten me, Agatha."

"I am trying to encourage you to face your position boldly."

"I am doing my best," Mirabel said, with sullen resignation. "Fortune has favored me so far. I have, really and truly, been unable to satisfy Emily by discovering Miss Jethro. She has left the place at which I saw her last—there is no trace to be found of her—and Emily knows it."

"Don't forget," Mrs. Delvin replied, "that there is a trace to be found of

Mrs. Rook, and that Emily expects you to follow it."

Mirabel shuddered. "I am surrounded by dangers, whichever way I look," he said. "Do what I may, it turns out to be wrong. I was wrong, perhaps, when I brought Emily here."

"No!"

"I could easily make an excuse," Mirabel persisted "and take her back to London."

"And for all you know to the contrary," his wiser sister replied, "Mrs. Rook may go to London; and you may take Emily back in time to receive her at the cottage. In every way you are safer in my old tower. And—don't forget—you have got my money to help you, if you want it. In my belief, Miles, you will want it."

"You are the dearest and best of sisters! What do you recommend me to do?"

"What you would have been obliged to do," Mrs. Delvin answered, "if you had remained in London. You must go to Redwood Hall tomorrow, as Emily has arranged it. If Mrs. Rook is not there, you must ask for her address in Scotland. If nobody knows the address, you must still bestir yourself in trying to find it. And, when you do fall in with Mrs. Rook—"

"Well?"

"Take care, wherever it may be, that you see her privately."

Mirabel was alarmed. "Don't keep me in suspense," he burst out. "Tell me what you propose."

"Never mind what I propose, to-night. Before I can tell you what I have in my mind, I must know whether Mrs. Rook is in England or Scotland. Bring me that information to-morrow, and I shall have something to say to you. Hark! The wind is rising, the rain is falling. There is a chance of sleep for me—I shall soon hear the sea. Good-night."

"Good-night, dearest—and thank you again, and again!"

CHAPTER LIX. THE ACCIDENT AT BELFORD.

Early in the morning Mirabel set forth for Redwood Hall, in one of the vehicles which Mrs. Delvin still kept at "The Clink" for the convenience of visitors. He returned soon after noon; having obtained information of the whereabout of Mrs. Rook and her husband. When they had last been heard of, they were at Lasswade, near Edinburgh. Whether they had, or had not, obtained the situation of which they were in search, neither Miss Redwood nor any one else at the Hall could tell.

In half an hour more, another horse was harnessed, and Mirabel was on his way to the railway station at Belford, to follow Mrs. Rook at Emily's urgent request. Before his departure, he had an interview with his sister.

Mrs. Delvin was rich enough to believe implicitly in the power of money. Her method of extricating her brother from the serious difficulties that beset him, was to make it worth the while of Mr. and Mrs. Rook to leave England. Their passage to America would be secretly paid; and they would take with them a letter of credit addressed to a banker in New York. If Mirabel failed to discover them, after they had sailed, Emily could not blame his want of devotion to her interests. He understood this; but he remained desponding and irresolute, even with the money in his hands. The one person who could rouse his courage and animate his hope, was also the one person who must know nothing of what had passed between his sister and himself. He had no choice but to leave Emily, without being cheered by her bright looks, invigorated by her inspiriting words. Mirabel went away on his doubtful errand with a heavy heart.

"The Clink" was so far from the nearest post town, that the few letters, usually addressed to the tower, were delivered by private arrangement with a messenger. The man's punctuality depended on the convenience of his superiors employed at the office. Sometimes he arrived early, and sometimes he arrived late. On this particular morning he presented himself, at half past one o'clock, with a letter for Emily; and when Mrs. Ellmother smartly reproved him for the delay, he coolly attributed it to the hospitality of friends whom he had met on the road.

The letter, directed to Emily at the cottage, had been forwarded from London by the person left in charge. It addressed her as "Honored Miss." She turned at once to the end—and discovered the signature of Mrs. Rook!

"And Mr. Mirabel has gone," Emily exclaimed, "just when his presence is of the greatest importance to us!"

Shrewd Mrs. Ellmother suggested that it might be as well to read the letter first—and then to form an opinion.

Emily read it.

"Lasswade, near Edinburgh, Sept. 26th.

"HONORED MISS—I take up my pen to bespeak your kind sympathy for my husband and myself; two old people thrown on the world again by the death of our excellent master. We are under a month's notice to leave Redwood Hall.

"Hearing of a situation at this place (also that our expenses would be paid if we applied personally), we got leave of absence, and made our application. The lady and her son are either the stingiest people that ever lived—or they have taken a dislike to me and my husband, and they make money a means of getting rid of us easily. Suffice it to say that we have refused to accept starvation wages, and that we are still out of place. It is just possible that you may have heard of something to suit us. So I write at once, knowing that good chances are often lost through needless delay.

"We stop at Belford on our way back, to see some friends of my husband, and we hope to get to Redwood Hall in good time on the 28th. Would you please address me to care of Miss Redwood, in case you know of any good situation for which we could apply. Perhaps we may be driven to try our luck in London. In this case, will you permit me to have the honor of presenting my respects, as I ventured to propose when I wrote to you a little time since.

"I beg to remain, Honored Miss,

"Your humble servant,

"R. ROOK."

Emily handed the letter to Mrs. Ellmother. "Read it," she said, "and tell me what you think."

"I think you had better be careful."

"Careful of Mrs. Rook?"

"Yes—and careful of Mrs. Delvin too."

Emily was astonished. "Are you really speaking seriously?" she said. "Mrs. Delvin is a most interesting person; so patient under her sufferings; so kind, so clever; so interested in all that interests me. I shall take the letter to her at once, and ask her advice."

"Have your own way, miss. I can't tell you why—but I don't like her!"

Mrs. Delvin's devotion to the interests of her guest took even Emily by surprise. After reading Mrs. Rook's letter, she rang the bell on her table in a frenzy of impatience. "My brother must be instantly recalled," she said. "Telegraph to him in your own name, telling him what has happened. He will find the message waiting for him, at the end of his journey."

The groom, summoned by the bell, was ordered to saddle the third and last horse left in the stables; to take the telegram to Belford, and to wait there until the answer arrived.

"How far is it to Redwood Hall?" Emily asked, when the man had received his orders.

"Ten miles," Mrs. Delvin answered.

"How can I get there to-day?"

"My dear, you can't get there."

"Pardon me, Mrs. Delvin, I must get there."

"Pardon me. My brother represents you in this matter. Leave it to my brother."

The tone taken by Mirabel's sister was positive, to say the least of it.

Emily thought of what her faithful old servant had said, and began to doubt her own discretion in so readily showing the letter. The mistake—if a mistake it was—had however been committed; and, wrong or right, she was not disposed to occupy the subordinate position which Mrs. Delvin had assigned to her.

"If you will look at Mrs. Rook's letter again," Emily replied, "you will see that I ought to answer it. She supposes I am in London."

"Do you propose to tell Mrs. Rook that you are in this house?" Mrs. Delvin asked.

"Certainly."

"You had better consult my brother, before you take any responsibility on yourself."

Emily kept her temper. "Allow me to remind you," she said, "that Mr. Mirabel is not acquainted with Mrs. Rook—and that I am. If I speak to her personally, I can do much to assist the object of our inquiries, before he returns. She is not an easy woman to deal with—"

"And therefore," Mrs. Delvin interposed, "the sort of person who requires careful handling by a man like my brother—a man of the world."

"The sort of person, as I venture to think," Emily persisted, "whom I ought to see with as little loss of time as possible."

Mrs. Delvin waited a while before she replied. In her condition of health, anxiety was not easy to bear. Mrs. Rook's letter and Emily's obstinacy had seriously irritated her. But, like all persons of ability, she was capable, when there was serious occasion for it, of exerting self-control. She really liked and admired Emily; and, as the elder woman and the hostess, she set an example of forbearance and good humor.

"It is out of my power to send you to Redwood Hall at once," she resumed. "The only one of my three horses now at your disposal is the horse which took my brother to the Hall this morning. A distance, there and back, of twenty miles. You are not in too great a hurry, I am sure, to allow the horse

329

time to rest?"

Emily made her excuses with perfect grace and sincerity. "I had no idea the distance was so great," she confessed. "I will wait, dear Mrs. Delvin, as long as you like."

They parted as good friends as ever—with a certain reserve, nevertheless, on either side. Emily's eager nature was depressed and irritated by the prospect of delay. Mrs. Delvin, on the other hand (devoted to her brother's interests), thought hopefully of obstacles which might present themselves with the lapse of time. The horse might prove to be incapable of further exertion for that day. Or the threatening aspect of the weather might end in a storm.

But the hours passed—and the sky cleared—and the horse was reported to be fit for work again. Fortune was against the lady of the tower; she had no choice but to submit.

Mrs. Delvin had just sent word to Emily that the carriage would be ready for her in ten minutes, when the coachman who had driven Mirabel to Belford returned. He brought news which agreeably surprised both the ladies. Mirabel had reached the station five minutes too late; the coachman had left him waiting the arrival of the next train to the North. He would now receive the telegraphic message at Belford, and might return immediately by taking the groom's horse. Mrs. Delvin left it to Emily to decide whether she would proceed by herself to Redwood Hall, or wait for Mirabel's return.

Under the changed circumstances, Emily would have acted ungraciously if she had persisted in holding to her first intention. She consented to wait.

The sea still remained calm. In the stillness of the moorland solitude on the western side of "The Clink," the rapid steps of a horse were heard at some little distance on the highroad.

Emily ran out, followed by careful Mrs. Ellmother, expecting to meet Mirabel.

She was disappointed: it was the groom who had returned. As he pulled up at the house, and dismounted, Emily noticed that the man looked excited.

"Is there anything wrong?" she asked.

"There has been an accident, miss."

"Not to Mr. Mirabel!"

"No, no, miss. An accident to a poor foolish woman, traveling from Lasswade."

Emily looked at Mrs. Ellmother. "It can't be Mrs. Rook!" she said.

"That's the name, miss! She got out before the train had quite stopped, and fell on the platform."

"Was she hurt?"

"Seriously hurt, as I heard. They carried her into a house hard by—and sent for the doctor."

"Was Mr. Mirabel one of the people who helped her?"

"He was on the other side of the platform, miss; waiting for the train from London. I got to the station and gave him the telegram, just as the accident took place. We crossed over to hear more about it. Mr. Mirabel was telling me that he would return to 'The Clink' on my horse—when he heard the woman's name mentioned. Upon that, he changed his mind and went to the house."

"Was he let in?"

"The doctor wouldn't hear of it. He was making his examination; and he said nobody was to be in the room but her husband and the woman of the house."

"Is Mr. Mirabel waiting to see her?"

"Yes, miss. He said he would wait all day, if necessary; and he gave me this bit of a note to take to the mistress."

Emily turned to Mrs. Ellmother. "It's impossible to stay here, not knowing whether Mrs. Rook is going to live or die," she said. "I shall go to

331

Belford—and you will go with me."

The groom interfered. "I beg your pardon, miss. It was Mr. Mirabel's most particular wish that you were not, on any account, to go to Belford."

"Why not?"

"He didn't say."

Emily eyed the note in the man's hand with well-grounded distrust. In all probability, Mirabel's object in writing was to instruct his sister to prevent her guest from going to Belford. The carriage was waiting at the door. With her usual promptness of resolution, Emily decided on taking it for granted that she was free to use as she pleased a carriage which had been already placed at her disposal.

"Tell your mistress," she said to the groom, "that I am going to Belford instead of to Redwood Hall."

In a minute more, she and Mrs. Ellmother were on their way to join Mirabel at the station.

CHAPTER LX. OUTSIDE THE ROOM.

Emily found Mirabel in the waiting room at Belford. Her sudden appearance might well have amazed him; but his face expressed a more serious emotion than surprise—he looked at her as if she had alarmed him.

"Didn't you get my message?" he asked. "I told the groom I wished you to wait for my return. I sent a note to my sister, in case he made any mistake."

"The man made no mistake," Emily answered. "I was in too great a hurry to be able to speak with Mrs. Delvin. Did you really suppose I could endure the suspense of waiting till you came back? Do you think I can be of no use—I who know Mrs. Rook?"

"They won't let you see her."

"Why not? You seem to be waiting to see her."

"I am waiting for the return of the rector of Belford. He is at Berwick;

and he has been sent for at Mrs. Rook's urgent request."

"Is she dying?"

"She is in fear of death—whether rightly or wrongly, I don't know. There is some internal injury from the fall. I hope to see her when the rector returns. As a brother clergyman, I may with perfect propriety ask him to use his influence in my favor."

"I am glad to find you so eager about it."

"I am always eager in your interests."

"Don't think me ungrateful," Emily replied gently. "I am no stranger to Mrs. Rook; and, if I send in my name, I may be able to see her before the clergyman returns."

She stopped. Mirabel suddenly moved so as to place himself between her and the door. "I must really beg of you to give up that idea," he said; "you don't know what horrid sight you may see—what dreadful agonies of pain this unhappy woman may be suffering."

His manner suggested to Emily that he might be acting under some motive which he was unwilling to acknowledge. "If you have a reason for wishing that I should keep away from Mrs. Rook," she said, "let me hear what it is. Surely we trust each other? I have done my best to set the example, at any rate."

Mirabel seemed to be at a loss for a reply.

While he was hesitating, the station-master passed the door. Emily asked him to direct her to the house in which Mrs. Rook had been received. He led the way to the end of the platform, and pointed to the house. Emily and Mrs. Ellmother immediately left the station. Mirabel accompanied them, still remonstrating, still raising obstacles.

The house door was opened by an old man. He looked reproachfully at Mirabel. "You have been told already," he said, "that no strangers are to see my wife?"

Encouraged by discovering that the man was Mr. Rook, Emily mentioned her name. "Perhaps you may have heard Mrs. Rook speak of me," she added.

"I've heard her speak of you oftentimes."

"What does the doctor say?"

"He thinks she may get over it. She doesn't believe him."

"Will you say that I am anxious to see her, if she feels well enough to receive me?"

Mr. Rook looked at Mrs. Ellmother. "Are there two of you wanting to go upstairs?" he inquired.

"This is my old friend and servant," Emily answered. "She will wait for me down here."

"She can wait in the parlor; the good people of this house are well known to me." He pointed to the parlor door—and then led the way to the first floor. Emily followed him. Mirabel, as obstinate as ever, followed Emily.

Mr. Rook opened a door at the end of the landing; and, turning round to speak to Emily, noticed Mirabel standing behind her. Without making any remarks, the old man pointed significantly down the stairs. His resolution was evidently immovable. Mirabel appealed to Emily to help him.

"She will see me, if you ask her," he said, "Let me wait here?"

The sound of his voice was instantly followed by a cry from the bed-chamber—a cry of terror.

Mr. Rook hurried into the room, and closed the door. In less than a minute, he opened it again, with doubt and horror plainly visible in his face. He stepped up to Mirabel—eyed him with the closest scrutiny—and drew back again with a look of relief.

"She's wrong," he said; "you are not the man."

This strange proceeding startled Emily.

"What man do you mean?" she asked.

Mr. Rook took no notice of the question. Still looking at Mirabel, he pointed down the stairs once more. With vacant eyes—moving mechanically, like a sleep-walker in his dream—Mirabel silently obeyed. Mr. Rook turned to Emily.

"Are you easily frightened?" he said

"I don't understand you," Emily replied. "Who is going to frighten me? Why did you speak to Mr. Mirabel in that strange way?"

Mr. Rook looked toward the bedroom door. "Maybe you'll hear why, inside there. If I could have my way, you shouldn't see her—but she's not to be reasoned with. A caution, miss. Don't be too ready to believe what my wife may say to you. She's had a fright." He opened the door. "In my belief," he whispered, "she's off her head."

Emily crossed the threshold. Mr. Rook softly closed the door behind her.

CHAPTER LXI. INSIDE THE ROOM.

A decent elderly woman was seated at the bedside. She rose, and spoke to Emily with a mingling of sorrow and confusion strikingly expressed on her face. "It isn't my fault," she said, "that Mrs. Rook receives you in this manner; I am obliged to humor her."

She drew aside, and showed Mrs. Rook with her head supported by many pillows, and her face strangely hidden from view under a veil. Emily started back in horror. "Is her face injured?" she asked.

Mrs. Rook answered the question herself. Her voice was low and weak; but she still spoke with the same nervous hurry of articulation which had been remarked by Alban Morris, on the day when she asked him to direct her to Netherwoods.

"Not exactly injured," she explained; "but one's appearance is a matter of some anxiety even on one's death-bed. I am disfigured by a thoughtless use of water, to bring me to when I had my fall—and I can't get at my toilet-things to put myself right again. I don't wish to shock you. Please excuse the veil."

Emily remembered the rouge on her cheeks, and the dye on her hair, when they had first seen each other at the school. Vanity—of all human frailties the longest-lived—still held its firmly-rooted place in this woman's nature; superior to torment of conscience, unassailable by terror of death!

The good woman of the house waited a moment before she left the room. "What shall I say," she asked, "if the clergyman comes?"

Mrs. Rook lifted her hand solemnly "Say," she answered, "that a dying sinner is making atonement for sin. Say this young lady is present, by the decree of an all-wise Providence. No mortal creature must disturb us." Her hand dropped back heavily on the bed. "Are we alone?" she asked.

"We are alone," Emily answered. "What made you scream just before I came in?"

"No! I can't allow you to remind me of that," Mrs. Rook protested. "I must compose myself. Be quiet. Let me think."

Recovering her composure, she also recovered that sense of enjoyment in talking of herself, which was one of the marked peculiarities in her character.

"You will excuse me if I exhibit religion," she resumed. "My dear parents were exemplary people; I was most carefully brought up. Are you pious? Let us hope so."

Emily was once more reminded of the past.

The bygone time returned to her memory—the time when she had accepted Sir Jervis Redwood's offer of employment, and when Mrs. Rook had arrived at the school to be her traveling companion to the North. The wretched creature had entirely forgotten her own loose talk, after she had drunk Miss Ladd's good wine to the last drop in the bottle. As she was boasting now of her piety, so she had boasted then of her lost faith and hope, and had mockingly declared her free-thinking opinions to be the result of her ill-assorted marriage. Forgotten—all forgotten, in this later time of pain and fear. Prostrate under the dread of death, her innermost nature—stripped of

336

the concealments of her later life—was revealed to view. The early religious training, at which she had scoffed in the insolence of health and strength, revealed its latent influence—intermitted, but a living influence always from first to last. Mrs. Rook was tenderly mindful of her exemplary parents, and proud of exhibiting religion, on the bed from which she was never to rise again.

"Did I tell you that I am a miserable sinner?" she asked, after an interval of silence.

Emily could endure it no longer. "Say that to the clergyman," she answered—"not to me."

"Oh, but I must say it," Mrs. Rook insisted. "I am a miserable sinner. Let me give you an instance of it," she continued, with a shameless relish of the memory of her own frailties. "I have been a drinker, in my time. Anything was welcome, when the fit was on me, as long as it got into my head. Like other persons in liquor, I sometimes talked of things that had better have been kept secret. We bore that in mind—my old man and I—-when we were engaged by Sir Jervis. Miss Redwood wanted to put us in the next bedroom to hers—a risk not to be run. I might have talked of the murder at the inn; and she might have heard me. Please to remark a curious thing. Whatever else I might let out, when I was in my cups, not a word about the pocketbook ever dropped from me. You will ask how I know it. My dear, I should have heard of it from my husband, if I had let that out—and he is as much in the dark as you are. Wonderful are the workings of the human mind, as the poet says; and drink drowns care, as the proverb says. But can drink deliver a person from fear by day, and fear by night? I believe, if I had dropped a word about the pocketbook, it would have sobered me in an instant. Have you any remark to make on this curious circumstance?"

Thus far, Emily had allowed the woman to ramble on, in the hope of getting information which direct inquiry might fail to produce. It was impossible, however, to pass over the allusion to the pocketbook. After giving her time to recover from the exhaustion which her heavy breathing sufficiently revealed, Emily put the question:

"Who did the pocketbook belong to?"

"Wait a little," said Mrs. Rook. "Everything in its right place, is my motto. I mustn't begin with the pocketbook. Why did I begin with it? Do you think this veil on my face confuses me? Suppose I take it off. But you must promise first—solemnly promise you won't look at my face. How can I tell you about the murder (the murder is part of my confession, you know), with this lace tickling my skin? Go away—and stand there with your back to me. Thank you. Now I'll take it off. Ha! the air feels refreshing; I know what I am about. Good heavens, I have forgotten something! I have forgotten him. And after such a fright as he gave me! Did you see him on the landing?"

"Who are you talking of?" Emily asked.

Mrs. Rook's failing voice sank lower still.

"Come closer," she said, "this must be whispered. Who am I talking of?" she repeated. "I am talking of the man who slept in the other bed at the inn; the man who did the deed with his own razor. He was gone when I looked into the outhouse in the gray of the morning. Oh, I have done my duty! I have told Mr. Rook to keep an eye on him downstairs. You haven't an idea how obstinate and stupid my husband is. He says I couldn't know the man, because I didn't see him. Ha! there's such a thing as hearing, when you don't see. I heard—and I knew it again."

Emily turned cold from head to foot.

"What did you know again?" she said.

"His voice," Mrs. Rook answered. "I'll swear to his voice before all the judges in England."

Emily rushed to the bed. She looked at the woman who had said those dreadful words, speechless with horror.

"You're breaking your promise!" cried Mrs. Rook. "You false girl, you're breaking your promise!"

She snatched at the veil, and put it on again. The sight of her face, momentary as it had been, reassured Emily. Her wild eyes, made wilder still by the blurred stains of rouge below them, half washed away—her disheveled hair, with streaks of gray showing through the dye—presented a spectacle which would have been grotesque under other circumstances, but which now reminded Emily of Mr. Rook's last words; warning her not to believe what his wife said, and even declaring his conviction that her intellect was deranged. Emily drew back from the bed, conscious of an overpowering sense of self-reproach. Although it was only for a moment, she had allowed her faith in Mirabel to be shaken by a woman who was out of her mind.

"Try to forgive me," she said. "I didn't willfully break my promise; you frightened me."

Mrs. Rook began to cry. "I was a handsome woman in my time," she murmured. "You would say I was handsome still, if the clumsy fools about me had not spoiled my appearance. Oh, I do feel so weak! Where's my medicine?"

The bottle was on the table. Emily gave her the prescribed dose, and revived her failing strength.

"I am an extraordinary person," she resumed. "My resolution has always been the admiration of every one who knew me. But my mind feels—how shall I express it?—a little vacant. Have mercy on my poor wicked soul! Help me."

"How can I help you?"

"I want to recollect. Something happened in the summer time, when we were talking at Netherwoods. I mean when that impudent master at the school showed his suspicions of me. (Lord! how he frightened me, when he turned up afterward at Sir Jervis's house.) You must have seen yourself he suspected me. How did he show it?"

"He showed you my locket," Emily answered.

"Oh, the horrid reminder of the murder!" Mrs. Rook exclaimed. "I didn't mention it: don't blame Me. You poor innocent, I have something dreadful to tell you."

Emily's horror of the woman forced her to speak. "Don't tell me!" she cried. "I know more than you suppose; I know what I was ignorant of when you saw the locket."

Mrs. Rook took offense at the interruption.

"Clever as you are, there's one thing you don't know," she said. "You asked me, just now, who the pocketbook belonged to. It belonged to your father. What's the matter? Are you crying?"

Emily was thinking of her father. The pocketbook was the last present she had given to him—a present on his birthday. "Is it lost?" she asked sadly.

"No; it's not lost. You will hear more of it directly. Dry your eyes, and expect something interesting—I'm going to talk about love. Love, my dear, means myself. Why shouldn't it? I'm not the only nice-looking woman, married to an old man, who has had a lover."

"Wretch! what has that got to do with it?"

"Everything, you rude girl! My lover was like the rest of them; he would bet on race-horses, and he lost. He owned it to me, on the day when your father came to our inn. He said, 'I must find the money—or be off to America, and say good-by forever.' I was fool enough to be fond of him. It broke my heart to hear him talk in that way. I said, 'If I find the money, and more than the money, will you take me with you wherever you go?' Of course, he said Yes. I suppose you have heard of the inquest held at our old place by the coroner and jury? Oh, what idiots! They believed I was asleep on the night of the murder. I never closed my eyes—I was so miserable, I was so tempted."

"Tempted? What tempted you?"

"Do you think I had any money to spare? Your father's pocketbook tempted me. I had seen him open it, to pay his bill over-night. It was full of bank-notes. Oh, what an overpowering thing love is! Perhaps you have known it yourself."

Emily's indignation once more got the better of her prudence. "Have you no feeling of decency on your death-bed!" she said.

Mrs. Rook forgot her piety; she was ready with an impudent rejoinder. "You hot-headed little woman, your time will come," she answered. "But you're right—I am wandering from the point; I am not sufficiently sensible of this solemn occasion. By-the-by, do you notice my language? I inherit correct English from my mother—a cultivated person, who married beneath her. My paternal grandfather was a gentleman. Did I tell you that there came a time, on that dreadful night, when I could stay in bed no longer? The pocketbook—I did nothing but think of that devilish pocketbook, full of bank-notes. My husband was fast asleep all the time. I got a chair and stood on it. I looked into the place where the two men were sleeping, through the glass in the top of the door. Your father was awake; he was walking up and down the room. What do you say? Was he agitated? I didn't notice. I don't know whether the other man was asleep or awake. I saw nothing but the pocketbook stuck under the pillow, half in and half out. Your father kept on walking up and down. I thought to myself, 'I'll wait till he gets tired, and then I'll have another look at the pocketbook.' Where's the wine? The doctor said I might have a glass of wine when I wanted it."

Emily found the wine and gave it to her. She shuddered as she accidentally touched Mrs. Rook's hand.

The wine helped the sinking woman.

"I must have got up more than once," she resumed. "And more than once my heart must have failed me. I don't clearly remember what I did, till the gray of the morning came. I think that must have been the last time I looked through the glass in the door."

She began to tremble. She tore the veil off her face. She cried out piteously, "Lord, be merciful to me a sinner! Come here," she said to Emily. "Where are you? No! I daren't tell you what I saw; I daren't tell you what I did. When you're possessed by the devil, there's nothing, nothing, nothing you can't do! Where did I find the courage to unlock the door? Where did I find the courage to go in? Any other woman would have lost her senses, when she found blood on her fingers after taking the pocketbook—"

Emily's head swam; her heart beat furiously—she staggered to the door, and opened it to escape from the room.

"I'm guilty of robbing him; but I'm innocent of his blood!" Mrs. Rook called after her wildly. "The deed was done—the yard door was wide open, and the man was gone—when I looked in for the last time. Come back, come back!"

Emily looked round.

"I can't go near you," she said, faintly.

"Come near enough to see this."

She opened her bed-gown at the throat, and drew up a loop of ribbon over her head. The pocketbook was attached to the ribbon. She held it out.

"Your father's book," she said. "Won't you take your father's book?"

For a moment, and only for a moment, Emily was repelled by the profanation associated with her birthday gift. Then, the loving remembrance of the dear hands that had so often touched that relic, drew the faithful daughter back to the woman whom she abhorred. Her eyes rested tenderly on the book. Before it had lain in that guilty bosom, it had been his book. The beloved memory was all that was left to her now; the beloved memory consecrated it to her hand. She took the book.

"Open it," said Mrs. Rook.

There were two five-pound bank-notes in it.

"His?" Emily asked.

"No; mine—the little I have been able to save toward restoring what I stole."

"Oh!" Emily cried, "is there some good in this woman, after all?"

"There's no good in the woman!" Mrs. Rook answered desperately. "There's nothing but fear—fear of hell now; fear of the pocketbook in the past time. Twice I tried to destroy it—and twice it came back, to remind me of the duty that I owed to my miserable soul. I tried to throw it into the fire. It struck the bar, and fell back into the fender at my feet. I went out, and cast it into the well. It came back again in the first bucket of water that was drawn up. From that moment, I began to save what I could. Restitution! Atonement! I tell you the book found a tongue—and those were the grand words it dinned in my ears, morning and night." She stooped to fetch her breath—stopped, and struck her bosom. "I hid it here, so that no person should see it, and no person take it from me. Superstition? Oh, yes, superstition! Shall tell you something? You may find yourself superstitious, if you are ever cut to the heart as I was. He left me! The man I had disgraced myself for, deserted me on the day when I gave him the stolen money. He suspected it was stolen; he took care of his own cowardly self—and left me to the hard mercy of the law, if the theft was found out. What do you call that, in the way of punishment? Haven't I suffered? Haven't I made atonement? Be a Christian—say you forgive me."

"I do forgive you."

"Say you will pray for me."

"I will."

"Ah! that comforts me! Now you can go."

Emily looked at her imploringly. "Don't send me away, knowing no more of the murder than I knew when I came here! Is there nothing, really nothing, you can tell me?"

Mrs. Rook pointed to the door.

"Haven't I told you already? Go downstairs, and see the wretch who escaped in the dawn of the morning!"

"Gently, ma'am, gently! You're talking too loud," cried a mocking voice from outside.

"It's only the doctor," said Mrs. Rook. She crossed her hands over her bosom with a deep-drawn sigh. "I want no doctor, now. My peace is made with my Maker. I'm ready for death; I'm fit for Heaven. Go away! go away!"

343

CHAPTER LXII. DOWNSTAIRS.

In a moment more, the doctor came in—a brisk, smiling, self-sufficient man—smartly dressed, with a flower in his button-hole. A stifling odor of musk filled the room, as he drew out his handkerchief with a flourish, and wiped his forehead.

"Plenty of hard work in my line, just now," he said. "Hullo, Mrs. Rook! somebody has been allowing you to excite yourself. I heard you, before I opened the door. Have you been encouraging her to talk?" he asked, turning to Emily, and shaking his finger at her with an air of facetious remonstrance.

Incapable of answering him; forgetful of the ordinary restraints of social intercourse—with the one doubt that preserved her belief in Mirabel, eager for confirmation—Emily signed to this stranger to follow her into a corner of the room, out of hearing. She made no excuses: she took no notice of his look of surprise. One hope was all she could feel, one word was all she could say, after that second assertion of Mirabel's guilt. Indicating Mrs. Rook by a glance at the bed, she whispered the word:

"Mad?"

Flippant and familiar, the doctor imitated her; he too looked at the bed.

"No more mad than you are, miss. As I said just now, my patient has been exciting herself; I daresay she has talked a little wildly in consequence. Hers isn't a brain to give way, I can tell you. But there's somebody else—"

Emily had fled from the room. He had destroyed her last fragment of belief in Mirabel's innocence. She was on the landing trying to console herself, when the doctor joined her.

"Are you acquainted with the gentleman downstairs?" he asked.

"What gentleman?"

"I haven't heard his name; he looks like a clergyman. If you know him—"

"I do know him. I can't answer questions! My mind—"

344

"Steady your mind, miss! and take your friend home as soon as you can. He hasn't got Mrs. Rook's hard brain; he's in a state of nervous prostration, which may end badly. Do you know where he lives?"

"He is staying with his sister—Mrs. Delvin."

"Mrs. Delvin! she's a friend and patient of mine. Say I'll look in to-morrow morning, and see what I can do for her brother. In the meantime, get him to bed, and to rest; and don't be afraid of giving him brandy."

The doctor returned to the bedroom. Emily heard Mrs. Ellmother's voice below.

"Are you up there, miss?"

"Yes."

Mrs. Ellmother ascended the stairs. "It was an evil hour," she said, "that you insisted on going to this place. Mr. Mirabel—" The sight of Emily's face suspended the next words on her lips. She took the poor young mistress in her motherly arms. "Oh, my child! what has happened to you?"

"Don't ask me now. Give me your arm—let us go downstairs."

"You won't be startled when you see Mr. Mirabel—will you, my dear? I wouldn't let them disturb you; I said nobody should speak to you but myself. The truth is, Mr. Mirabel has had a dreadful fright. What are you looking for?"

"Is there a garden here? Any place where we can breathe the fresh air?"

There was a courtyard at the back of the house. They found their way to it. A bench was placed against one of the walls. They sat down.

"Shall I wait till you're better before I say any more?" Mrs. Ellmother asked. "No? You want to hear about Mr. Mirabel? My dear, he came into the parlor where I was; and Mr. Rook came in too—-and waited, looking at him. Mr. Mirabel sat down in a corner, in a dazed state as I thought. It wasn't for long. He jumped up, and clapped his hand on his heart as if his heart hurt him. 'I must and will know what's going on upstairs,' he says. Mr.

Rook pulled him back, and told him to wait till the young lady came down. Mr. Mirabel wouldn't hear of it. 'Your wife's frightening her,' he says; 'your wife's telling her horrible things about me.' He was taken on a sudden with a shivering fit; his eyes rolled, and his teeth chattered. Mr. Rook made matters worse; he lost his temper. 'I'm damned,' he says, 'if I don't begin to think you are the man, after all; I've half a mind to send for the police.' Mr. Mirabel dropped into his chair. His eyes stared, his mouth fell open. I took hold of his hand. Cold—cold as ice. What it all meant I can't say. Oh, miss, you know! Let me tell you the rest of it some other time."

Emily insisted on hearing more. "The end!" she cried. "How did it end?"

"I don't know how it might have ended, if the doctor hadn't come in—to pay his visit, you know, upstairs. He said some learned words. When he came to plain English, he asked if anybody had frightened the gentleman. I said Mr. Rook had frightened him. The doctor says to Mr. Rook, 'Mind what you are about. If you frighten him again, you may have his death to answer for.' That cowed Mr. Rook. He asked what he had better do. 'Give me some brandy for him first,' says the doctor; 'and then get him home at once.' I found the brandy, and went away to the inn to order the carriage. Your ears are quicker than mine, miss—do I hear it now?"

They rose, and went to the house door. The carriage was there.

Still cowed by what the doctor had said, Mr. Rook appeared, carefully leading Mirabel out. He had revived under the action of the stimulant. Passing Emily he raised his eyes to her—trembled—and looked down again. When Mr. Rook opened the door of the carriage he paused, with one of his feet on the step. A momentary impulse inspired him with a false courage, and brought a flush into his ghastly face. He turned to Emily.

"May I speak to you?" he asked.

She started back from him. He looked at Mrs. Ellmother. "Tell her I am innocent," he said. The trembling seized on him again. Mr. Rook was obliged to lift him into the carriage.

Emily caught at Mrs. Ellmother's arm. "You go with him," she said. "I can't."

"How are you to get back, miss?"

She turned away and spoke to the coachman. "I am not very well. I want the fresh air—I'll sit by you."

Mrs. Ellmother remonstrated and protested, in vain. As Emily had determined it should be, so it was.

"Has he said anything?" she asked, when they had arrived at their journey's end.

"He has been like a man frozen up; he hasn't said a word; he hasn't even moved."

"Take him to his sister; and tell her all that you know. Be careful to repeat what the doctor said. I can't face Mrs. Delvin. Be patient, my good old friend; I have no secrets from you. Only wait till to-morrow; and leave me by myself to-night."

Alone in her room, Emily opened her writing-case. Searching among the letters in it, she drew out a printed paper. It was the Handbill describing the man who had escaped from the inn, and offering a reward for the discovery of him.

At the first line of the personal description of the fugitive, the paper dropped from her hand. Burning tears forced their way into her eyes. Feeling for her handkerchief, she touched the pocketbook which she had received from Mrs. Rook. After a little hesitation she took it out. She looked at it. She opened it.

The sight of the bank-notes repelled her; she hid them in one of the pockets of the book. There was a second pocket which she had not yet examined. She pat her hand into it, and, touching something, drew out a letter.

The envelope (already open) was addressed to "James Brown, Esq., Post Office, Zeeland." Would it be inconsistent with her respect for her father's memory to examine the letter? No; a glance would decide whether she ought to read it or not.

It was without date or address; a startling letter to look at—for it only contained three words:

"I say No."

The words were signed in initials:

"S. J."

In the instant when she read the initials, the name occurred to her.

Sara Jethro.

CHAPTER LXIII. THE DEFENSE OF MIRABEL.

The discovery of the letter gave a new direction to Emily's thoughts—and so, for the time at least, relieved her mind from the burden that weighed on it. To what question, on her father's part, had "I say No" been Miss Jethro's brief and stern reply? Neither letter nor envelope offered the slightest hint that might assist inquiry; even the postmark had been so carelessly impressed that it was illegible.

Emily was still pondering over the three mysterious words, when she was interrupted by Mrs. Ellmother's voice at the door.

"I must ask you to let me come in, miss; though I know you wished to be left by yourself till to-morrow. Mrs. Delvin says she must positively see you to-night. It's my belief that she will send for the servants, and have herself carried in here, if you refuse to do what she asks. You needn't be afraid of seeing Mr. Mirabel."

"Where is he?"

"His sister has given up her bedroom to him," Mrs. Ellmother answered. "She thought of your feelings before she sent me here—and had the curtains closed between the sitting-room and the bedroom. I suspect my nasty temper misled me, when I took a dislike to Mrs. Delvin. She's a good creature; I'm sorry you didn't go to her as soon as we got back."

"Did she seem to be angry, when she sent you here?"

"Angry! She was crying when I left her."

Emily hesitated no longer.

She noticed a remarkable change in the invalid's sitting-room—so brilliantly lighted on other occasions—the moment she entered it. The lamps were shaded, and the candles were all extinguished. "My eyes don't bear the light so well as usual," Mrs. Delvin said. "Come and sit near me, Emily; I hope to quiet your mind. I should be grieved if you left my house with a wrong impression of me."

Knowing what she knew, suffering as she must have suffered, the quiet kindness of her tone implied an exercise of self-restraint which appealed irresistibly to Emily's sympathies. "Forgive me," she said, "for having done you an injustice. I am ashamed to think that I shrank from seeing you when I returned from Belford."

"I will endeavor to be worthy of your better opinion of me," Mrs. Delvin replied. "In one respect at least, I may claim to have had your best interests at heart—while we were still personally strangers. I tried to prevail on my poor brother to own the truth, when he discovered the terrible position in which he was placed toward you. He was too conscious of the absence of any proof which might induce you to believe him, if he attempted to defend himself—in one word, he was too timid—to take my advice. He has paid the penalty, and I have paid the penalty, of deceiving you."

Emily started. "In what way have you deceived me?" she asked.

"In the way that was forced on us by our own conduct," Mrs. Delvin said. "We have appeared to help you, without really doing so; we calculated on inducing you to marry my brother, and then (when he could speak with the authority of a husband) on prevailing on you to give up all further inquiries. When you insisted on seeing Mrs. Rook, Miles had the money in his hand to bribe her and her husband to leave England."

"Oh, Mrs. Delvin!"

"I don't attempt to excuse myself. I don't expect you to consider how sorely I was tempted to secure the happiness of my brother's life, by marriage with such a woman as yourself. I don't remind you that I knew—when I put obstacles in your way—that you were blindly devoting yourself to the discovery of an innocent man."

Emily heard her with angry surprise. "Innocent?" she repeated. "Mrs. Rook recognized his voice the instant she heard him speak."

Impenetrable to interruption, Mrs. Delvin went on. "But what I do ask," she persisted, "even after our short acquaintance, is this. Do you suspect me of deliberately scheming to make you the wife of a murderer?"

Emily had never viewed the serious question between them in this light. Warmly, generously, she answered the appeal that had been made to her. "Oh, don't think that of me! I know I spoke thoughtlessly and cruelly to you, just now—"

"You spoke impulsively," Mrs. Delvin interposed; "that was all. My one desire before we part—how can I expect you to remain here, after what has happened?—is to tell you the truth. I have no interested object in view; for all hope of your marriage with my brother is now at an end. May I ask if you have heard that he and your father were strangers, when they met at the inn?"

"Yes; I know that."

"If there had been any conversation between them, when they retired to rest, they might have mentioned their names. But your father was preoccupied; and my brother, after a long day's walk, was so tired that he fell asleep as soon as his head was on the pillow. He only woke when the morning dawned. What he saw when he looked toward the opposite bed might have struck with terror the boldest man that ever lived. His first impulse was naturally to alarm the house. When he got on his feet, he saw his own razor—a blood-stained razor on the bed by the side of the corpse. At that discovery, he lost all control over himself. In a panic of terror, he snatched up his knapsack, unfastened the yard door, and fled from the house. Knowing him, as you and I know him, can we wonder at it? Many a man has been hanged for murder, on circumstantial

350

evidence less direct than the evidence against poor Miles. His horror of his own recollections was so overpowering that he forbade me even to mention the inn at Zeeland in my letters, while he was abroad. 'Never tell me (he wrote) who that wretched murdered stranger was, if I only heard of his name, I believe it would haunt me to my dying day. I ought not to trouble you with these details—and yet, I am surely not without excuse. In the absence of any proof, I cannot expect you to believe as I do in my brother's innocence. But I may at least hope to show you that there is some reason for doubt. Will you give him the benefit of that doubt?"

"Willingly!" Emily replied. "Am I right in supposing that you don't despair of proving his innocence, even yet'?"

"I don't quite despair. But my hopes have grown fainter and fainter, as the years have gone on. There is a person associated with his escape from Zeeland; a person named Jethro—"

"You mean Miss Jethro!"

"Yes. Do you know her?"

"I know her—and my father knew her. I have found a letter, addressed to him, which I have no doubt was written by Miss Jethro. It is barely possible that you may understand what it means. Pray look at it."

"I am quite unable to help you," Mrs. Delvin answered, after reading the letter. "All I know of Miss Jethro is that, but for her interposition, my brother might have fallen into the hands of the police. She saved him."

"Knowing him, of course?"

"That is the remarkable part of it: they were perfect strangers to each other."

"But she must have had some motive."

"There is the foundation of my hope for Miles. Miss Jethro declared, when I wrote and put the question to her, that the one motive by which she was actuated was the motive of mercy. I don't believe her. To my mind, it is

351

in the last degree improbable that she would consent to protect a stranger from discovery, who owned to her (as my brother did) that he was a fugitive suspected of murder. She knows something, I am firmly convinced, of that dreadful event at Zeeland—and she has some reason for keeping it secret. Have you any influence over her?"

"Tell me where I can find her."

"I can't tell you. She has removed from the address at which my brother saw her last. He has made every possible inquiry—without result."

As she replied in those discouraging terms, the curtains which divided Mrs. Delvin's bedroom from her sitting-room were drawn aside. An elderly woman-servant approached her mistress's couch.

"Mr. Mirabel is awake, ma'am. He is very low; I can hardly feel his pulse. Shall I give him some more brandy?"

Mrs. Delvin held out her hand to Emily. "Come to me to-morrow morning," she said—and signed to the servant to wheel her couch into the next room. As the curtain closed over them, Emily heard Mirabel's voice. "Where am I?" he said faintly. "Is it all a dream?"

The prospect of his recovery the next morning was gloomy indeed. He had sunk into a state of deplorable weakness, in mind as well as in body. The little memory of events that he still preserved was regarded by him as the memory of a dream. He alluded to Emily, and to his meeting with her unexpectedly. But from that point his recollection failed him. They had talked of something interesting, he said—but he was unable to remember what it was. And they had waited together at a railway station—but for what purpose he could not tell. He sighed and wondered when Emily would marry him—and so fell asleep again, weaker than ever.

Not having any confidence in the doctor at Belford, Mrs. Delvin had sent an urgent message to a physician at Edinburgh, famous for his skill in treating diseases of the nervous system. "I cannot expect him to reach this remote place, without some delay," she said; "I must bear my suspense as well as I can."

352

"You shall not bear it alone," Emily answered. "I will wait with you till the doctor comes."

Mrs. Delvin lifted her frail wasted hands to Emily's face, drew it a little nearer—and kissed her.

CHAPTER LXIV. ON THE WAY TO LONDON.

The parting words had been spoken. Emily and her companion were on their way to London.

For some little time, they traveled in silence—alone in the railway carriage. After submitting as long as she could to lay an embargo on the use of her tongue, Mrs. Ellmother started the conversation by means of a question: "Do you think Mr. Mirabel will get over it, miss?"

"It's useless to ask me," Emily said. "Even the great man from Edinburgh is not able to decide yet, whether he will recover or not."

"You have taken me into your confidence, Miss Emily, as you promised—and I have got something in my mind in consequence. May I mention it without giving offense?"

"What is it?"

"I wish you had never taken up with Mr. Mirabel."

Emily was silent. Mrs. Ellmother, having a design of her own to accomplish, ventured to speak more plainly. "I often think of Mr. Alban Morris," she proceeded. "I always did like him, and I always shall."

Emily suddenly pulled down her veil. "Don't speak of him!" she said.

"I didn't mean to offend you."

"You don't offend me. You distress me. Oh, how often I have wished—!" She threw herself back in a corner of the carriage and said no more.

Although not remarkable for the possession of delicate tact, Mrs. Ellmother discovered that the best course she could now follow was a course of silence.

Even at the time when she had most implicitly trusted Mirabel, the fear that she might have acted hastily and harshly toward Alban had occasionally troubled Emily's mind. The impression produced by later events had not only intensified this feeling, but had presented the motives of that true friend under an entirely new point of view. If she had been left in ignorance of the manner of her father's death—as Alban had designed to leave her; as she would have been left, but for the treachery of Francine—how happily free she would have been from thoughts which it was now a terror to her to recall. She would have parted from Mirabel, when the visit to the pleasant country house had come to an end, remembering him as an amusing acquaintance and nothing more. He would have been spared, and she would have been spared, the shock that had so cruelly assailed them both. What had she gained by Mrs. Rook's detestable confession? The result had been perpetual disturbance of mind provoked by self-torturing speculations on the subject of the murder. If Mirabel was innocent, who was guilty? The false wife, without pity and without shame—or the brutal husband, who looked capable of any enormity? What was her future to be? How was it all to end? In the despair of that bitter moment—seeing her devoted old servant looking at her with kind compassionate eyes—Emily's troubled spirit sought refuge in impetuous self-betrayal; the very betrayal which she had resolved should not escape her, hardly a minute since!

She bent forward out of her corner, and suddenly drew up her veil. "Do you expect to see Mr. Alban Morris, when we get back?" she asked.

"I should like to see him, miss—if you have no objection."

"Tell him I am ashamed of myself! and say I ask his pardon with all my heart!"

"The Lord be praised!" Mrs. Ellmother burst out—and then, when it was too late, remembered the conventional restraints appropriate to the occasion. "Gracious, what a fool I am!" she said to herself. "Beautiful weather, Miss Emily, isn't it?" she continued, in a desperate hurry to change the subject.

Emily reclined again in her corner of the carriage. She smiled, for the first time since she had become Mrs. Delvin's guest at the tower.

BOOK THE LAST—AT HOME AGAIN.

CHAPTER LXV. CECILIA IN A NEW CHARACTER.

Reaching the cottage at night, Emily found the card of a visitor who had called during the day. It bore the name of "Miss Wyvil," and had a message written on it which strongly excited Emily's curiosity.

"I have seen the telegram which tells your servant that you return to-night. Expect me early to-morrow morning—with news that will deeply interest you."

To what news did Cecilia allude? Emily questioned the woman who had been left in charge of the cottage, and found that she had next to nothing to tell. Miss Wyvil had flushed up, and had looked excited, when she read the telegraphic message—that was all. Emily's impatience was, as usual, not to be concealed. Expert Mrs. Ellmother treated the case in the right way—first with supper, and then with an adjournment to bed. The clock struck twelve, when she put out the young mistress's candle. "Ten hours to pass before Cecilia comes here!" Emily exclaimed. "Not ten minutes," Mrs. Ellmother reminded her, "if you will only go to sleep."

Cecilia arrived before the breakfast-table was cleared; as lovely, as gentle, as affectionate as ever—but looking unusually serious and subdued.

"Out with it at once!" Emily cried. "What have you got to tell me?'

"Perhaps, I had better tell you first," Cecilia said, "that I know what you kept from me when I came here, after you left us at Monksmoor. Don't think, my dear, that I say this by way of complaint. Mr. Alban Morris says you had good reasons for keeping your secret."

"Mr. Alban Morris! Did you get your information from him?"

"Yes. Do I surprise you?"

"More than words can tell!"

"Can you bear another surprise? Mr. Morris has seen Miss Jethro, and has discovered that Mr. Mirabel has been wrongly suspected of a dreadful crime. Our amiable little clergyman is guilty of being a coward—and guilty of nothing else. Are you really quiet enough to read about it?"

She produced some leaves of paper filled with writing. "There," she explained, "is Mr. Morris's own account of all that passed between Miss Jethro and himself."

"But how do you come by it?"

"Mr. Morris gave it to me. He said, 'Show it to Emily as soon as possible; and take care to be with her while she reads it.' There is a reason for this—" Cecilia's voice faltered. On the brink of some explanation, she seemed to recoil from it. "I will tell you by-and-by what the reason is," she said.

Emily looked nervously at the manuscript. "Why doesn't he tell me himself what he has discovered? Is he—" The leaves began to flutter in her trembling fingers—"is he angry with me?"

"Oh, Emily, angry with You! Read what he has written and you shall know why he keeps away."

Emily opened the manuscript.

CHAPTER LXVI. ALBAN'S NARRATIVE.

"The information which I have obtained from Miss Jethro has been communicated to me, on the condition that I shall not disclose the place of her residence. 'Let me pass out of notice (she said) as completely as if I had passed out of life; I wish to be forgotten by some, and to be unknown by others.'" With this one stipulation, she left me free to write the present narrative of what passed at the interview between us. I feel that the discoveries which I have made are too important to the persons interested to be trusted to memory.

1. She Receives Me.

"Finding Miss Jethro's place of abode, with far less difficulty than I had anticipated (thanks to favoring circumstances), I stated plainly the object of my visit. She declined to enter into conversation with me on the subject of the murder at Zeeland.

"I was prepared to meet with this rebuke, and to take the necessary measures for obtaining a more satisfactory reception. 'A person is suspected of having committed the murder,' I said; 'and there is reason to believe that you are in a position to say whether the suspicion is justified or not. Do you refuse to answer me, if I put the question?'

"Miss Jethro asked who the person was.

"I mentioned the name—Mr. Miles Mirabel.

"It is not necessary, and it would certainly be not agreeable to me, to describe the effect which this reply produced on Miss Jethro. After giving her time to compose herself, I entered into certain explanations, in order to convince her at the outset of my good faith. The result justified my anticipations. I was at once admitted to her confidence.

"She said, 'I must not hesitate to do an act of justice to an innocent man. But, in such a serious matter as this, you have a right to judge for yourself whether the person who is now speaking to you is a person whom you can trust. You may believe that I tell the truth about others, if I begin—whatever it may cost me—by telling the truth about myself.'"

2. She Speaks of Herself.

"I shall not attempt to place on record the confession of a most unhappy woman. It was the common story of sin bitterly repented, and of vain effort to recover the lost place in social esteem. Too well known a story, surely, to be told again.

"But I may with perfect propriety repeat what Miss Jethro said to me, in allusion to later events in her life which are connected with my own personal experience. She recalled to my memory a visit which she had paid to me at Netherwoods, and a letter addressed to her by Doctor Allday, which I had read at her express request.

"She said, 'You may remember that the letter contained some severe reflections on my conduct. Among other things, the doctor mentions that he called at the lodging I occupied during my visit to London, and found I had taken to flight: also that he had reason to believe I had entered Miss Ladd's service, under false pretenses.'

"I asked if the doctor had wronged her.

"She answered 'No: in one case, he is ignorant; in the other, he is right. On leaving his house, I found myself followed in the street by the man to whom I owe the shame and misery of my past life. My horror of him is not to be described in words. The one way of escaping was offered by an empty cab that passed me. I reached the railway station safely, and went back to my home in the country. Do you blame me?'

"It was impossible to blame her—and I said so.

"She then confessed the deception which she had practiced on Miss Ladd. 'I have a cousin,' she said, 'who was a Miss Jethro like me. Before her marriage she had been employed as a governess. She pitied me; she sympathized with my longing to recover the character that I had lost. With her permission, I made use of the testimonials which she had earned as a teacher—I was betrayed (to this day I don't know by whom)—and I was dismissed from Netherwoods. Now you know that I deceived Miss Ladd, you may reasonably conclude that I am likely to deceive You.'

"I assured her, with perfect sincerity, that I had drawn no such conclusion. Encouraged by my reply, Miss Jethro proceeded as follows."

3. She Speaks of Mirabel.

"'Four years ago, I was living near Cowes, in the Isle of Wight—in a cottage which had been taken for me by a gentleman who was the owner of a yacht. We had just returned from a short cruise, and the vessel was under orders to sail for Cherbourg with the next tide.

"'While I was walking in my garden, I was startled by the sudden appearance Of a man (evidently a gentleman) who was a perfect stranger to me. He was in a pitiable state of terror, and he implored my protection. In reply to my first inquiries, he mentioned the inn at Zeeland, and the dreadful death of a person unknown to him; whom I recognized (partly by the description given, and partly by comparison of dates) as Mr. James Brown. I shall say nothing of the shock inflicted on me: you don't want to know what I felt. What I did (having literally only a minute left for decision) was to hide the fugitive from discovery, and to exert my influence in his favor with the owner of the yacht. I saw nothing more of him. He was put on board, as soon as the police were out of sight, and was safely landed at Cherbourg.'

"I asked what induced her to run the risk of protecting a stranger, who was under suspicion of having committed a murder.

"She said, 'You shall hear my explanation directly. Let us have done with Mr. Mirabel first. We occasionally corresponded, during the long absence on the continent; never alluding, at his express request, to the horrible event at the inn. His last letter reached me, after he had established himself at Vale Regis. Writing of the society in the neighborhood, he informed me of his introduction to Miss Wyvil, and of the invitation that he had received to meet her friend and schoolfellow at Monksmoor. I knew that Miss Emily possessed a Handbill describing personal peculiarities in Mr. Mirabel, not hidden under the changed appearance of his head and face. If she remembered or happened to refer to that description, while she was living in the same house with him, there was a possibility at least of her suspicion being excited. The fear of this took me to you. It was a morbid fear, and, as events turned out, an unfounded fear: but I was unable to control it. Failing to produce any effect on you, I went to Vale Regis, and tried (vainly again) to induce Mr. Mirabel to send an excuse to Monksmoor. He, like you, wanted to know what my motive was. When I tell you that I acted solely in Miss Emily's interests, and that I knew how she had been deceived about her father's death, need I say why I was afraid to acknowledge my motive?'

"I understood that Miss Jethro might well be afraid of the consequences, if she risked any allusion to Mr. Brown's horrible death, and if it afterward chanced to reach his daughter's ears. But this state of feeling implied an extraordinary interest in the preservation of Emily's peace of mind. I asked

Miss Jethro how that interest had been excited?

"She answered, 'I can only satisfy you in one way. I must speak of her father now.'"

Emily looked up from the manuscript. She felt Cecilia's arm tenderly caressing her. She heard Cecilia say, "My poor dear, there is one last trial of your courage still to come. I am afraid of what you are going to read, when you turn to the next page. And yet—"

"And yet," Emily replied gently, "it must be done. I have learned my hard lesson of endurance, Cecilia, don't be afraid."

Emily turned to the next page.

4. She Speaks of the Dead.

"For the first time, Miss Jethro appeared to be at a loss how to proceed. I could see that she was suffering. She rose, and opening a drawer in her writing table, took a letter from it.

"She said, 'Will you read this? It was written by Miss Emily's father. Perhaps it may say more for me than I can say for myself?'

"I copy the letter. It was thus expressed:

"'You have declared that our farewell to-day is our farewell forever. For the second time, you have refused to be my wife; and you have done this, to use your own words, in mercy to Me.

"'In mercy to Me, I implore you to reconsider your decision.

"'If you condemn me to live without you—I feel it, I know it—you condemn me to despair which I have not fortitude enough to endure. Look at the passages which I have marked for you in the New Testament. Again and again, I say it; your true repentance has made you worthy of the pardon of God. Are you not worthy of the love, admiration, and respect of man? Think! oh, Sara, think of what our lives might be, and let them be united for time and for eternity.

"'I can write no more. A deadly faintness oppresses me. My mind is in a state unknown to me in past years. I am in such confusion that I sometimes think I hate you. And then I recover from my delusion, and know that man never loved woman as I love you.

"'You will have time to write to me by this evening's post. I shall stop at Zeeland to-morrow, on my way back, and ask for a letter at the post office. I forbid explanations and excuses. I forbid heartless allusions to your duty. Let me have an answer which does not keep me for a moment in suspense.

"'For the last time, I ask you: Do you consent to be my wife? Say, Yes— or say, No.'

"I gave her back the letter—with the one comment on it, which the circumstances permitted me to make:

"'You said No?'

"She bent her head in silence.

"I went on—not willingly, for I would have spared her if it had been possible. I said, 'He died, despairing, by his own hand—and you knew it?'

"She looked up. 'No! To say that I knew it is too much. To say that I feared it is the truth.'

"'Did you love him?'

"She eyed me in stern surprise. 'Have I any right to love? Could I disgrace an honorable man by allowing him to marry me? You look as if you held me responsible for his death.'

"'Innocently responsible,' I said.

"She still followed her own train of thought. 'Do you suppose I could for a moment anticipate that he would destroy himself, when I wrote my reply? He was a truly religious man. If he had been in his right mind, he would have shrunk from the idea of suicide as from the idea of a crime.'

"On reflection, I was inclined to agree with her. In his terrible position, it was at least possible that the sight of the razor (placed ready, with the other appliances of the toilet, for his fellow-traveler's use) might have fatally tempted a man whose last hope was crushed, whose mind was tortured by despair. I should have been merciless indeed, if I had held Miss Jethro accountable thus far. But I found it hard to sympathize with the course which she had pursued, in permitting Mr. Brown's death to be attributed to murder without a word of protest. 'Why were you silent?' I said.

"She smiled bitterly.

"'A woman would have known why, without asking,' she replied. 'A woman would have understood that I shrank from a public confession of my shameful past life. A woman would have remembered what reasons I had for pitying the man who loved me, and for accepting any responsibility rather than associate his memory, before the world, with an unworthy passion for a degraded creature, ending in an act of suicide. Even if I had made that cruel sacrifice, would public opinion have believed such a person as I am—against the evidence of a medical man, and the verdict of a jury? No, Mr. Morris! I said nothing, and I was resolved to say nothing, so long as the choice of alternatives was left to me. On the day when Mr. Mirabel implored me to save him, that choice was no longer mine—and you know what I did. And now again when suspicion (after all the long interval that had passed) has followed and found that innocent man, you know what I have done. What more do you ask of me?'

"'Your pardon,' I said, 'for not having understood you—and a last favor. May I repeat what I have heard to the one person of all others who ought to know, and who must know, what you have told me?'

"It was needless to hint more plainly that I was speaking of Emily. Miss Jethro granted my request.

"'It shall be as you please,' she answered. 'Say for me to his daughter, that the grateful remembrance of her is my one refuge from the thoughts that tortured me, when we spoke together on her last night at school. She has made this dead heart of mine feel a reviving breath of life, when I think of her. Never, in our earthly pilgrimage, shall we meet again—I implore her to pity and forget me. Farewell, Mr. Morris; farewell forever.'

"I confess that the tears came into my eyes. When I could see clearly again, I was alone in the room."

CHAPTER LXVII. THE TRUE CONSOLATION.

Emily closed the pages which told her that her father had died by his own hand.

Cecilia still held her tenderly embraced. By slow degrees, her head dropped until it rested on her friend's bosom. Silently she suffered. Silently Cecilia bent forward, and kissed her forehead. The sounds that penetrated to the room were not out of harmony with the time. From a distant house the voices of children were just audible, singing the plaintive melody of a hymn; and, now and then, the breeze blew the first faded leaves of autumn against the window. Neither of the girls knew how long the minutes followed each other uneventfully, before there was a change. Emily raised her head, and looked at Cecilia.

"I have one friend left," she said.

"Not only me, love—oh, I hope not only me!"

"Yes. Only you."

"I want to say something, Emily; but I am afraid of hurting you."

"My dear, do you remember what we once read in a book of history at school? It told of the death of a tortured man, in the old time, who was broken on the wheel. He lived through it long enough to say that the agony, after the first stroke of the club, dulled his capacity for feeling pain when the next blows fell. I fancy pain of the mind must follow the same rule. Nothing you can say will hurt me now."

"I only wanted to ask, Emily, if you were engaged—at one time—to marry Mr. Mirabel. Is it true?"

"False! He pressed me to consent to an engagement—and I said he must not hurry me."

"What made you say that?"

"I thought of Alban Morris."

Vainly Cecilia tried to restrain herself. A cry of joy escaped her.

"Are you glad?" Emily asked. "Why?"

Cecilia made no direct reply. "May I tell you what you wanted to know, a little while since?" she said. "You asked why Mr. Morris left it all to me, instead of speaking to you himself. When I put the same question to him, he told me to read what he had written. 'Not a shadow of suspicion rests on Mr. Mirabel,' he said. 'Emily is free to marry him—and free through Me. Can I tell her that? For her sake, and for mine, it must not be. All that I can do is to leave old remembrances to plead for me. If they fail, I shall know that she will be happier with Mr. Mirabel than with me.' 'And you will submit?' I asked. 'Because I love her,' he answered, 'I must submit.' Oh, how pale you are! Have I distressed you?"

"You have done me good."

"Will you see him?"

Emily pointed to the manuscript. "At such a time as this?" she said.

Cecilia still held to her resolution. "Such a time as this is the right time," she answered. "It is now, when you most want to be comforted, that you ought to see him. Who can quiet your poor aching heart as he can quiet it?" She impulsively snatched at the manuscript and threw it out of sight. "I can't bear to look at it," she said. "Emily! if I have done wrong, will you forgive me? I saw him this morning before I came here. I was afraid of what might happen—I refused to break the dreadful news to you, unless he was somewhere near us. Your good old servant knows where to go. Let me send her—"

Mrs. Ellmother herself opened the door, and stood doubtful on the threshold, hysterically sobbing and laughing at the same time. "I'm everything that's bad!" the good old creature burst out. "I've been listening—I've been lying—I said you wanted him. Turn me out of my situation, if you like. I've got him! Here he is!"

In another moment, Emily was in his arms—and they were alone. On his faithful breast the blessed relief of tears came to her at last: she burst out crying.

"Oh, Alban, can you forgive me?"

He gently raised her head, so that he could see her face.

"My love, let me look at you," he said. "I want to think again of the day when we parted in the garden at school. Do you remember the one conviction that sustained me? I told you, Emily, there was a time of fulfillment to come in our two lives; and I have never wholly lost the dear belief. My own darling, the time has come!"

POSTSCRIPT. GOSSIP IN THE STUDIO.

The winter time had arrived. Alban was clearing his palette, after a hard day's work at the cottage. The servant announced that tea was ready, and that Miss Ladd was waiting to see him in the next room.

Alban ran in, and received the visitor cordially with both hands. "Welcome back to England! I needn't ask if the sea-voyage has done you good. You are looking ten years younger than when you went away."

Miss Ladd smiled. "I shall soon be ten years older again, if I go back to Netherwoods," she replied. "I didn't believe it at the time; but I know better now. Our friend Doctor Allday was right, when he said that my working days were over. I must give up the school to a younger and stronger successor, and make the best I can in retirement of what is left of my life. You and Emily may expect to have me as a near neighbor. Where is Emily?"

"Far away in the North."

"In the North! You don't mean that she has gone back to Mrs. Delvin?"

"She has gone back—with Mrs. Ellmother to take care of her—at my express request. You know what Emily is, when there is an act of mercy to be done. That unhappy man has been sinking (with intervals of partial recovery) for months past. Mrs. Delvin sent word to us that the end was near, and that the one last wish her brother was able to express was the wish to see Emily. He had been for some hours unable to speak when my wife arrived. But he knew her, and smiled faintly. He was just able to lift his hand. She took it, and waited by him, and spoke words of consolation and kindness from time to time. As the night advanced, he sank into sleep, still holding her hand. They only knew that he had passed from sleep to death—passed without a movement or a sigh—when his hand turned cold. Emily remained for a day at the tower to comfort poor Mrs. Delvin—and she comes home, thank God, this evening!"

"I needn't ask if you are happy?" Miss Ladd said.

"Happy? I sing, when I have my bath in the morning. If that isn't happiness (in a man of my age) I don't know what is!"

"And how are you getting on?"

"Famously! I have turned portrait painter, since you were sent away for your health. A portrait of Mr. Wyvil is to decorate the town hall in the place that he represents; and our dear kind-hearted Cecilia has induced a fascinated mayor and corporation to confide the work to my hands."

"Is there no hope yet of that sweet girl being married?" Miss Ladd asked. "We old maids all believe in marriage, Mr. Morris—though some of us don't own it."

"There seems to be a chance," Alban answered. "A young lord has turned up at Monksmoor; a handsome pleasant fellow, and a rising man in politics. He happened to be in the house a few days before Cecilia's birthday; and he asked my advice about the right present to give her. I said, 'Try something new in Tarts.' When he found I was in earnest, what do you think he did? Sent his steam yacht to Rouen for some of the famous pastry! You should have seen Cecilia, when the young lord offered his delicious gift. If I could paint that smile and those eyes, I should be the greatest artist living. I believe she will marry him. Need I say how rich they will be? We shall not envy them—we are rich too. Everything is comparative. The portrait of Mr. Wyvil will put three hundred pounds in my pocket. I have earned a hundred and twenty more by illustrations, since we have been married. And my wife's income (I like to be particular) is only five shillings and tenpence short of two hundred a year. Moral! we are rich as well as happy."

"Without a thought of the future?" Miss Ladd asked slyly.

"Oh, Doctor Allday has taken the future in hand! He revels in the old-fashioned jokes, which used to be addressed to newly-married people, in his time. 'My dear fellow,' he said the other day, 'you may possibly be under a joyful necessity of sending for the doctor, before we are all a year older. In that case, let it be understood that I am Honorary Physician to the family.' The warm-hearted old man talks of getting me another portrait to do. 'The greatest ass in the medical profession (he informed me) has just been made a baronet; and his admiring friends have decided that he is to be painted at full length, with his bandy legs hidden under a gown, and his great globular eyes staring at the spectator—I'll get you the job.' Shall I tell you what he says of Mrs. Rook's recovery?"

Miss Ladd held up her hands in amazement. "Recovery!" she exclaimed.

"And a most remarkable recovery too," Alban informed her. "It is the first case on record of any person getting over such an injury as she has received. Doctor Allday looked grave when he heard of it. 'I begin to believe in the devil,' he said; 'nobody else could have saved Mrs. Rook.' Other people don't take that view. She has been celebrated in all the medical newspapers—and she has been admitted to come excellent almshouse, to live in comfortable idleness to a green old age. The best of it is that she shakes her head, when her wonderful recovery is mentioned. 'It seems such a pity,' she says; 'I was so fit for heaven.' Mr. Rook having got rid of his wife, is in excellent spirits. He is occupied in looking after an imbecile old gentleman; and, when he is asked if he likes the employment, he winks mysteriously and slaps his pocket. Now, Miss Ladd, I think it's my turn to hear some news. What have you got to tell me?"

"I believe I can match your account of Mrs. Rook," Miss Ladd said. "Do you care to hear what has become of Francine?"

Alban, rattling on hitherto in boyish high spirits, suddenly became serious. "I have no doubt Miss de Sor is doing well," he said sternly. "She is too heartless and wicked not to prosper."

"You are getting like your old cynical self again, Mr. Morris—and you are wrong. I called this morning on the agent who had the care of Francine, when I left England. When I mentioned her name, he showed me a telegram, sent to him by her father. 'There's my authority,' he said, 'for letting her leave my house.' The message was short enough to be easily remembered: 'Anything my daughter likes as long as she doesn't come back to us.' In those cruel terms Mr. de Sor wrote of his own child. The agent was just as unfeeling, in his way. He called her the victim of slighted love and clever proselytizing. 'In plain words,' he said, 'the priest of the Catholic chapel close by has converted her; and she is now a novice in a convent of Carmelite nuns in the West of England. Who could have expected it? Who knows how it may end?"

As Miss Ladd spoke, the bell rang at the cottage gate. "Here she is!" Alban cried, leading the way into the hall. "Emily has come home."

LITTLE NOVELS

MRS. ZANT AND THE GHOST.

I.

THE course of this narrative describes the return of a disembodied spirit to earth, and leads the reader on new and strange ground.

Not in the obscurity of midnight, but in the searching light of day, did the supernatural influence assert itself. Neither revealed by a vision, nor announced by a voice, it reached mortal knowledge through the sense which is least easily self-deceived: the sense that feels.

The record of this event will of necessity produce conflicting impressions. It will raise, in some minds, the doubt which reason asserts; it will invigorate, in other minds, the hope which faith justifies; and it will leave the terrible question of the destinies of man, where centuries of vain investigation have left it—in the dark.

Having only undertaken in the present narrative to lead the way along a succession of events, the writer declines to follow modern examples by thrusting himself and his opinions on the public view. He returns to the shadow from which he has emerged, and leaves the opposing forces of incredulity and belief to fight the old battle over again, on the old ground.

II.

THE events happened soon after the first thirty years of the present century had come to an end.

On a fine morning, early in the month of April, a gentleman of middle age (named Rayburn) took his little daughter Lucy out for a walk in the woodland pleasure-ground of Western London, called Kensington Gardens.

The few friends whom he possessed reported of Mr. Rayburn (not unkindly) that he was a reserved and solitary man. He might have been more accurately described as a widower devoted to his only surviving child. Although he was not more than forty years of age, the one pleasure which made life enjoyable to Lucy's father was offered by Lucy herself.

Playing with her ball, the child ran on to the southern limit of the Gardens, at that part of it which still remains nearest to the old Palace of Kensington. Observing close at hand one of those spacious covered seats, called in England "alcoves," Mr. Rayburn was reminded that he had the morning's newspaper in his pocket, and that he might do well to rest and read. At that early hour the place was a solitude.

"Go on playing, my dear," he said; "but take care to keep where I can see you."

Lucy tossed up her ball; and Lucy's father opened his newspaper. He had not been reading for more than ten minutes, when he felt a familiar little hand laid on his knee.

"Tired of playing?" he inquired—with his eyes still on the newspaper.

"I'm frightened, papa."

He looked up directly. The child's pale face startled him. He took her on his knee and kissed her.

"You oughtn't to be frightened, Lucy, when I am with you," he said, gently. "What is it?" He looked out of the alcove as he spoke, and saw a little dog among the trees. "Is it the dog?" he asked.

Lucy answered:

"It's not the dog—it's the lady."

The lady was not visible from the alcove.

"Has she said anything to you?" Mr. Rayburn inquired.

"No."

"What has she done to frighten you?"

372

The child put her arms round her father's neck.

"Whisper, papa," she said; "I'm afraid of her hearing us. I think she's mad."

"Why do you think so, Lucy?"

"She came near to me. I thought she was going to say something. She seemed to be ill."

"Well? And what then?"

"She looked at me."

There, Lucy found herself at a loss how to express what she had to say next—and took refuge in silence.

"Nothing very wonderful, so far," her father suggested.

"Yes, papa—but she didn't seem to see me when she looked."

"Well, and what happened then?"

"The lady was frightened—and that frightened me. I think," the child repeated positively, "she's mad."

It occurred to Mr. Rayburn that the lady might be blind. He rose at once to set the doubt at rest.

"Wait here," he said, "and I'll come back to you."

But Lucy clung to him with both hands; Lucy declared that she was afraid to be by herself. They left the alcove together.

The new point of view at once revealed the stranger, leaning against the trunk of a tree. She was dressed in the deep mourning of a widow. The pallor of her face, the glassy stare in her eyes, more than accounted for the child's terror—it excused the alarming conclusion at which she had arrived.

"Go nearer to her," Lucy whispered.

They advanced a few steps. It was now easy to see that the lady was young, and wasted by illness—but (arriving at a doubtful conclusion perhaps under the present circumstances) apparently possessed of rare personal attractions in happier days. As the father and daughter advanced a little, she discovered them. After some hesitation, she left the tree; approached with an evident intention of speaking; and suddenly paused. A change to astonishment and fear animated her vacant eyes. If it had not been plain before, it was now beyond all doubt that she was not a poor blind creature, deserted and helpless. At the same time, the expression of her face was not easy to understand. She could hardly have looked more amazed and bewildered, if the two strangers who were observing her had suddenly vanished from the place in which they stood.

Mr. Rayburn spoke to her with the utmost kindness of voice and manner.

"I am afraid you are not well," he said. "Is there anything that I can do—"

The next words were suspended on his lips. It was impossible to realize such a state of things; but the strange impression that she had already produced on him was now confirmed. If he could believe his senses, her face did certainly tell him that he was invisible and inaudible to the woman whom he had just addressed! She moved slowly away with a heavy sigh, like a person disappointed and distressed. Following her with his eyes, he saw the dog once more—a little smooth-coated terrier of the ordinary English breed. The dog showed none of the restless activity of his race. With his head down and his tail depressed, he crouched like a creature paralyzed by fear. His mistress roused him by a call. He followed her listlessly as she turned away.

After walking a few paces only, she suddenly stood still.

Mr. Rayburn heard her talking to herself.

"Did I feel it again?" she said, as if perplexed by some doubt that awed or grieved her. After a while her arms rose slowly, and opened with a gentle caressing action—an embrace strangely offered to the empty air! "No," she said to herself, sadly, after waiting a moment. "More perhaps when to-morrow comes—no more to-day." She looked up at the clear blue sky. "The beautiful sunlight! the merciful sunlight!" she murmured. "I should have died if it had happened in the dark."

374

Once more she called to the dog; and once more she walked slowly away.

"Is she going home, papa?' the child asked.

"We will try and find out," the father answered.

He was by this time convinced that the poor creature was in no condition to be permitted to go out without some one to take care of her. From motives of humanity, he was resolved on making the attempt to communicate with her friends.

III.

THE lady left the Gardens by the nearest gate; stopping to lower her veil before she turned into the busy thoroughfare which leads to Kensington. Advancing a little way along the High Street, she entered a house of respectable appearance, with a card in one of the windows which announced that apartments were to let.

Mr. Rayburn waited a minute—then knocked at the door, and asked if he could see the mistress of the house. The servant showed him into a room on the ground floor, neatly but scantily furnished. One little white object varied the grim brown monotony of the empty table. It was a visiting-card.

With a child's unceremonious curiosity Lucy pounced on the card, and spelled the name, letter by letter: "Z, A, N, T," she repeated. "What does that mean?"

Her father looked at the card, as he took it away from her, and put it back on the table. The name was printed, and the address was added in pencil: "Mr. John Zant, Purley's Hotel."

The mistress made her appearance. Mr. Rayburn heartily wished himself out of the house again, the moment he saw her. The ways in which it is possible to cultivate the social virtues are more numerous and more varied than is generally supposed. This lady's way had apparently accustomed her to meet her fellow-creatures on the hard ground of justice without mercy. Something in her eyes, when she looked at Lucy, said: "I wonder whether that child gets punished when she deserves it?"

"Do you wish to see the rooms which I have to let?" she began.

Mr. Rayburn at once stated the object of his visit—as clearly, as civilly, and as concisely as a man could do it. He was conscious (he added) that he had been guilty perhaps of an act of intrusion.

The manner of the mistress of the house showed that she entirely agreed with him. He suggested, however, that his motive might excuse him. The mistress's manner changed, and asserted a difference of opinion.

"I only know the lady whom you mention," she said, "as a person of the highest respectability, in delicate health. She has taken my first-floor apartments, with excellent references; and she gives remarkably little trouble. I have no claim to interfere with her proceedings, and no reason to doubt that she is capable of taking care of herself."

Mr. Rayburn unwisely attempted to say a word in his own defense.

"Allow me to remind you—" he began.

"Of what, sir?"

"Of what I observed, when I happened to see the lady in Kensington Gardens."

"I am not responsible for what you observed in Kensington Gardens. If your time is of any value, pray don't let me detain you."

Dismissed in those terms, Mr. Rayburn took Lucy's hand and withdrew. He had just reached the door, when it was opened from the outer side. The Lady of Kensington Gardens stood before him. In the position which he and his daughter now occupied, their backs were toward the window. Would she remember having seen them for a moment in the Gardens?

"Excuse me for intruding on you," she said to the landlady. "Your servant tells me my brother-in-law called while I was out. He sometimes leaves a message on his card."

She looked for the message, and appeared to be disappointed: there was no writing on the card.

Mr. Rayburn lingered a little in the doorway on the chance of hearing something more. The landlady's vigilant eyes discovered him.

"Do you know this gentleman?" she said maliciously to her lodger.

"Not that I remember."

Replying in those words, the lady looked at Mr. Rayburn for the first time; and suddenly drew back from him.

"Yes," she said, correcting herself; "I think we met—"

Her embarrassment overpowered her; she could say no more.

Mr. Rayburn compassionately finished the sentence for her.

"We met accidentally in Kensington Gardens," he said.

She seemed to be incapable of appreciating the kindness of his motive. After hesitating a little she addressed a proposal to him, which seemed to show distrust of the landlady.

"Will you let me speak to you upstairs in my own rooms?" she asked.

Without waiting for a reply, she led the way to the stairs. Mr. Rayburn and Lucy followed. They were just beginning the ascent to the first floor, when the spiteful landlady left the lower room, and called to her lodger over their heads: "Take care what you say to this man, Mrs. Zant! He thinks you're mad."

Mrs. Zant turned round on the landing, and looked at him. Not a word fell from her lips. She suffered, she feared, in silence. Something in the sad submission of her face touched the springs of innocent pity in Lucy's heart. The child burst out crying.

That artless expression of sympathy drew Mrs. Zant down the few stairs which separated her from Lucy.

"May I kiss your dear little girl?" she said to Mr. Rayburn. The landlady, standing on the mat below, expressed her opinion of the value of caresses, as compared with a sounder method of treating young persons in tears: "If that

377

child was mine," she remarked, "I would give her something to cry for."

In the meantime, Mrs. Zant led the way to her rooms.

The first words she spoke showed that the landlady had succeeded but too well in prejudicing her against Mr. Rayburn.

"Will you let me ask your child," she said to him, "why you think me mad?"

He met this strange request with a firm answer.

"You don't know yet what I really do think. Will you give me a minute's attention?"

"No," she said positively. "The child pities me, I want to speak to the child. What did you see me do in the Gardens, my dear, that surprised you?" Lucy turned uneasily to her father; Mrs. Zant persisted. "I first saw you by yourself, and then I saw you with your father," she went on. "When I came nearer to you, did I look very oddly—as if I didn't see you at all?"

Lucy hesitated again; and Mr. Rayburn interfered.

"You are confusing my little girl," he said. "Allow me to answer your questions—or excuse me if I leave you."

There was something in his look, or in his tone, that mastered her. She put her hand to her head.

"I don't think I'm fit for it," she answered vacantly. "My courage has been sorely tried already. If I can get a little rest and sleep, you may find me a different person. I am left a great deal by myself; and I have reasons for trying to compose my mind. Can I see you tomorrow? Or write to you? Where do you live?"

Mr. Rayburn laid his card on the table in silence. She had strongly excited his interest. He honestly desired to be of some service to this forlorn creature—abandoned so cruelly, as it seemed, to her own guidance. But he had no authority to exercise, no sort of claim to direct her actions, even if she consented to accept his advice. As a last resource he ventured on an allusion to the relative of whom she had spoken downstairs.

"When do you expect to see your brother-in-law again?" he said.

"I don't know," she answered. "I should like to see him—he is so kind to me."

She turned aside to take leave of Lucy.

"Good-by, my little friend. If you live to grow up, I hope you will never be such a miserable woman as I am." She suddenly looked round at Mr. Rayburn. "Have you got a wife at home?" she asked.

"My wife is dead."

"And you have a child to comfort you! Please leave me; you harden my heart. Oh, sir, don't you understand? You make me envy you!"

Mr. Rayburn was silent when he and his daughter were out in the street again. Lucy, as became a dutiful child, was silent, too. But there are limits to human endurance—and Lucy's capacity for self-control gave way at last.

"Are you thinking of the lady, papa?" she said.

He only answered by nodding his head. His daughter had interrupted him at that critical moment in a man's reflections, when he is on the point of making up his mind. Before they were at home again Mr. Rayburn had arrived at a decision. Mrs. Zant's brother-in-law was evidently ignorant of any serious necessity for his interference—or he would have made arrangements for immediately repeating his visit. In this state of things, if any evil happened to Mrs. Zant, silence on Mr. Rayburn's part might be indirectly to blame for a serious misfortune. Arriving at that conclusion, he decided upon running the risk of being rudely received, for the second time, by another stranger.

Leaving Lucy under the care of her governess, he went at once to the address that had been written on the visiting-card left at the lodging-house, and sent in his name. A courteous message was returned. Mr. John Zant was at home, and would be happy to see him.

IV.

MR. RAYBURN was shown into one of the private sitting-rooms of the hotel.

He observed that the customary position of the furniture in a room had been, in some respects, altered. An armchair, a side-table, and a footstool had all been removed to one of the windows, and had been placed as close as possible to the light. On the table lay a large open roll of morocco leather, containing rows of elegant little instruments in steel and ivory. Waiting by the table, stood Mr. John Zant. He said "Good-morning" in a bass voice, so profound and so melodious that those two commonplace words assumed a new importance, coming from his lips. His personal appearance was in harmony with his magnificent voice—he was a tall, finely-made man of dark complexion; with big brilliant black eyes, and a noble curling beard, which hid the whole lower part of his face. Having bowed with a happy mingling of dignity and politeness, the conventional side of this gentleman's character suddenly vanished; and a crazy side, to all appearance, took its place. He dropped on his knees in front of the footstool. Had he forgotten to say his prayers that morning, and was he in such a hurry to remedy the fault that he had no time to spare for consulting appearances? The doubt had hardly suggested itself, before it was set at rest in a most unexpected manner. Mr. Zant looked at his visitor with a bland smile, and said:

"Please let me see your feet."

For the moment, Mr. Rayburn lost his presence of mind. He looked at the instruments on the side-table.

"Are you a corn-cutter?" was all he could say.

"Excuse me, sir," returned the polite operator, "the term you use is quite obsolete in our profession." He rose from his knees, and added modestly: "I am a Chiropodist."

"I beg your pardon."

"Don't mention it! You are not, I imagine, in want of my professional services. To what motive may I attribute the honor of your visit?"

By this time Mr. Rayburn had recovered himself.

"I have come here," he answered, "under circumstances which require apology as well as explanation."

Mr. Zant's highly polished manner betrayed signs of alarm; his suspicions pointed to a formidable conclusion—a conclusion that shook him to the innermost recesses of the pocket in which he kept his money.

"The numerous demands on me—" he began.

Mr. Rayburn smiled.

"Make your mind easy," he replied. "I don't want money. My object is to speak with you on the subject of a lady who is a relation of yours."

"My sister-in-law!" Mr. Zant exclaimed. "Pray take a seat."

Doubting if he had chosen a convenient time for his visit, Mr. Rayburn hesitated.

"Am I likely to be in the way of persons who wish to consult you?" he asked.

"Certainly not. My morning hours of attendance on my clients are from eleven to one." The clock on the mantelpiece struck the quarter-past one as he spoke. "I hope you don't bring me bad news?" he said, very earnestly. "When I called on Mrs. Zant this morning, I heard that she had gone out for a walk. Is it indiscreet to ask how you became acquainted with her?"

Mr. Rayburn at once mentioned what he had seen and heard in Kensington Gardens; not forgetting to add a few words, which described his interview afterward with Mrs. Zant.

The lady's brother-in-law listened with an interest and sympathy, which offered the strongest possible contrast to the unprovoked rudeness of the mistress of the lodging-house. He declared that he could only do justice to his sense of obligation by following Mr. Rayburn's example, and expressing

381

himself as frankly as if he had been speaking to an old friend.

"The sad story of my sister-in-law's life," he said, "will, I think, explain certain things which must have naturally perplexed you. My brother was introduced to her at the house of an Australian gentleman, on a visit to England. She was then employed as governess to his daughters. So sincere was the regard felt for her by the family that the parents had, at the entreaty of their children, asked her to accompany them when they returned to the Colony. The governess thankfully accepted the proposal."

"Had she no relations in England?" Mr. Rayburn asked.

"She was literally alone in the world, sir. When I tell you that she had been brought up in the Foundling Hospital, you will understand what I mean. Oh, there is no romance in my sister-in-law's story! She never has known, or will know, who her parents were or why they deserted her. The happiest moment in her life was the moment when she and my brother first met. It was an instance, on both sides, of love at first sight. Though not a rich man, my brother had earned a sufficient income in mercantile pursuits. His character spoke for itself. In a word, he altered all the poor girl's prospects, as we then hoped and believed, for the better. Her employers deferred their return to Australia, so that she might be married from their house. After a happy life of a few weeks only—"

His voice failed him; he paused, and turned his face from the light.

"Pardon me," he said; "I am not able, even yet, to speak composedly of my brother's death. Let me only say that the poor young wife was a widow, before the happy days of the honeymoon were over. That dreadful calamity struck her down. Before my brother had been committed to the grave, her life was in danger from brain-fever."

Those words placed in a new light Mr. Rayburn's first fear that her intellect might be deranged. Looking at him attentively, Mr. Zant seemed to understand what was passing in the mind of his guest.

"No!" he said. "If the opinions of the medical men are to be trusted, the result of the illness is injury to her physical strength—not injury to her mind. I have observed in her, no doubt, a certain waywardness of temper since her illness; but that is a trifle. As an example of what I mean, I may tell you that I invited her, on her recovery, to pay me a visit. My house is not in London—the air doesn't agree with me—my place of residence is at St. Sallins-on-Sea. I am not myself a married man; but my excellent housekeeper would have received Mrs. Zant with the utmost kindness. She was resolved—obstinately resolved, poor thing—to remain in London. It is needless to say that, in her melancholy position, I am attentive to her slightest wishes. I took a lodging for her; and, at her special request, I chose a house which was near Kensington Gardens.

"Is there any association with the Gardens which led Mrs. Zant to make that request?"

"Some association, I believe, with the memory of her husband. By the way, I wish to be sure of finding her at home, when I call to-morrow. Did you say (in the course of your interesting statement) that she intended—as you supposed—to return to Kensington Gardens to-morrow? Or has my memory deceived me?"

"Your memory is perfectly accurate."

"Thank you. I confess I am not only distressed by what you have told me of Mrs. Zant—I am at a loss to know how to act for the best. My only idea, at present, is to try change of air and scene. What do you think yourself?"

"I think you are right."

Mr. Zant still hesitated.

"It would not be easy for me, just now," he said, "to leave my patients and take her abroad."

The obvious reply to this occurred to Mr. Rayburn. A man of larger worldly experience might have felt certain suspicions, and might have remained silent. Mr. Rayburn spoke.

"Why not renew your invitation and take her to your house at the seaside?" he said.

In the perplexed state of Mr. Zant's mind, this plain course of action had apparently failed to present itself. His gloomy face brightened directly.

"The very thing!" he said. "I will certainly take your advice. If the air of St. Sallins does nothing else, it will improve her health and help her to recover her good looks. Did she strike you as having been (in happier days) a pretty woman?"

This was a strangely familiar question to ask—almost an indelicate question, under the circumstances A certain furtive expression in Mr. Zant's fine dark eyes seemed to imply that it had been put with a purpose. Was it possible that he suspected Mr. Rayburn's interest in his sister-in-law to be inspired by any motive which was not perfectly unselfish and perfectly pure? To arrive at such a conclusion as this might be to judge hastily and cruelly of a man who was perhaps only guilty of a want of delicacy of feeling. Mr. Rayburn honestly did his best to assume the charitable point of view. At the same time, it is not to be denied that his words, when he answered, were carefully guarded, and that he rose to take his leave.

Mr. John Zant hospitably protested.

"Why are you in such a hurry? Must you really go? I shall have the honor of returning your visit to-morrow, when I have made arrangements to profit by that excellent suggestion of yours. Good-by. God bless you."

He held out his hand: a hand with a smooth surface and a tawny color, that fervently squeezed the fingers of a departing friend. "Is that man a scoundrel?" was Mr. Rayburn's first thought, after he had left the hotel. His moral sense set all hesitation at rest—and answered: "You're a fool if you doubt it."

V.

DISTURBED by presentiments, Mr. Rayburn returned to his house on foot, by way of trying what exercise would do toward composing his mind.

The experiment failed. He went upstairs and played with Lucy; he drank an extra glass of wine at dinner; he took the child and her governess to a circus in the evening; he ate a little supper, fortified by another glass of wine, before he went to bed—and still those vague forebodings of evil persisted in torturing him. Looking back through his past life, he asked himself if any woman (his late wife of course excepted!) had ever taken the predominant place in his thoughts which Mrs. Zant had assumed—without any discernible reason to account for it? If he had ventured to answer his own question, the reply would have been: Never!

All the next day he waited at home, in expectation of Mr. John Zant's promised visit, and waited in vain.

Toward evening the parlor-maid appeared at the family tea-table, and presented to her master an unusually large envelope sealed with black wax, and addressed in a strange handwriting. The absence of stamp and postmark showed that it had been left at the house by a messenger.

"Who brought this?" Mr. Rayburn asked.

"A lady, sir—in deep mourning."

"Did she leave any message?"

"No, sir."

Having drawn the inevitable conclusion, Mr. Rayburn shut himself up in his library. He was afraid of Lucy's curiosity and Lucy's questions, if he read Mrs. Zant's letter in his daughter's presence.

Looking at the open envelope after he had taken out the leaves of writing which it contained, he noticed these lines traced inside the cover:

"My one excuse for troubling you, when I might have consulted my brother-in-law, will be found in the pages which I inclose. To speak plainly, you have been led to fear that I am not in my right senses. For this very reason, I now appeal to you. Your dreadful doubt of me, sir, is my doubt too. Read what I have written about myself—and then tell me, I entreat you, which I am: A person who has been the object of a supernatural revelation? or an unfortunate creature who is only fit for imprisonment in a mad-house?"

Mr. Rayburn opened the manuscript. With steady attention, which soon quickened to breathless interest, he read what follows:

VI. THE LADY'S MANUSCRIPT.

YESTERDAY morning the sun shone in a clear blue sky—after a succession of cloudy days, counting from the first of the month.

The radiant light had its animating effect on my poor spirits. I had passed the night more peacefully than usual; undisturbed by the dream, so cruelly familiar to me, that my lost husband is still living—the dream from which I always wake in tears. Never, since the dark days of my sorrow, have I been so little troubled by the self-tormenting fancies and fears which beset miserable women, as when I left the house, and turned my steps toward Kensington Gardens—for the first time since my husband's death.

Attended by my only companion, the little dog who had been his favorite as well as mine, I went to the quiet corner of the Gardens which is nearest to Kensington.

On that soft grass, under the shade of those grand trees, we had loitered together in the days of our betrothal. It was his favorite walk; and he had taken me to see it in the early days of our acquaintance. There, he had first asked me to be his wife. There, we had felt the rapture of our first kiss. It was surely natural that I should wish to see once more a place sacred to such memories as these? I am only twenty-three years old; I have no child to comfort me, no companion of my own age, nothing to love but the dumb creature who is so faithfully fond of me.

I went to the tree under which we stood, when my dear one's eyes told his love before he could utter it in words. The sun of that vanished day shone on me again; it was the same noontide hour; the same solitude was around me. I had feared the first effect of the dreadful contrast between past and present. No! I was quiet and resigned. My thoughts, rising higher than earth, dwelt on the better life beyond the grave. Some tears came into my eyes. But I was not unhappy. My memory of all that happened may be trusted, even in trifles which relate only to myself—I was not unhappy.

The first object that I saw, when my eyes were clear again, was the dog. He crouched a few paces away from me, trembling pitiably, but uttering no cry. What had caused the fear that overpowered him?

I was soon to know.

I called to the dog; he remained immovable—conscious of some mysterious coming thing that held him spellbound. I tried to go to the poor creature, and fondle and comfort him.

At the first step forward that I took, something stopped me.

It was not to be seen, and not to be heard. It stopped me.

The still figure of the dog disappeared from my view: the lonely scene round me disappeared—excepting the light from heaven, the tree that sheltered me, and the grass in front of me. A sense of unutterable expectation kept my eyes riveted on the grass. Suddenly, I saw its myriad blades rise erect and shivering. The fear came to me of something passing over them with the invisible swiftness of the wind. The shivering advanced. It was all round me. It crept into the leaves of the tree over my head; they shuddered, without a sound to tell of their agitation; their pleasant natural rustling was struck dumb. The song of the birds had ceased. The cries of the water-fowl on the pond were heard no more. There was a dreadful silence.

But the lovely sunshine poured down on me, as brightly as ever.

In that dazzling light, in that fearful silence, I felt an Invisible Presence near me. It touched me gently.

At the touch, my heart throbbed with an overwhelming joy. Exquisite pleasure thrilled through every nerve in my body. I knew him! From the unseen world—himself unseen—he had returned to me. Oh, I knew him!

And yet, my helpless mortality longed for a sign that might give me assurance of the truth. The yearning in me shaped itself into words. I tried to utter the words. I would have said, if I could have spoken: "Oh, my angel, give me a token that it is You!" But I was like a person struck dumb—I could only think it.

The Invisible Presence read my thought. I felt my lips touched, as my husband's lips used to touch them when he kissed me. And that was my answer. A thought came to me again. I would have said, if I could have spoken: "Are you here to take me to the better world?"

I waited. Nothing that I could feel touched me.

I was conscious of thinking once more. I would have said, if I could have spoken: "Are you here to protect me?"

I felt myself held in a gentle embrace, as my husband's arms used to hold me when he pressed me to his breast. And that was my answer.

The touch that was like the touch of his lips, lingered and was lost; the clasp that was like the clasp of his arms, pressed me and fell away. The garden-scene resumed its natural aspect. I saw a human creature near, a lovely little girl looking at me.

At that moment, when I was my own lonely self again, the sight of the child soothed and attracted me. I advanced, intending to speak to her. To my horror I suddenly ceased to see her. She disappeared as if I had been stricken blind.

And yet I could see the landscape round me; I could see the heaven above me. A time passed—only a few minutes, as I thought—and the child became visible to me again; walking hand-in-hand with her father. I approached them; I was close enough to see that they were looking at me with pity and surprise. My impulse was to ask if they saw anything strange in my face or my manner. Before I could speak, the horrible wonder happened again. They vanished from my view.

Was the Invisible Presence still near? Was it passing between me and my fellow-mortals; forbidding communication, in that place and at that time?

It must have been so. When I turned away in my ignorance, with a heavy heart, the dreadful blankness which had twice shut out from me the beings of my own race, was not between me and my dog. The poor little creature filled me with pity; I called him to me. He moved at the sound of my voice, and followed me languidly; not quite awakened yet from the trance of terror that had possessed him.

Before I had retired by more than a few steps, I thought I was conscious of the Presence again. I held out my longing arms to it. I waited in the hope of a touch to tell me that I might return. Perhaps I was answered by indirect means? I only know that a resolution to return to the same place, at the same hour, came to me, and quieted my mind.

The morning of the next day was dull and cloudy; but the rain held off. I set forth again to the Gardens.

My dog ran on before me into the street—and stopped: waiting to see in which direction I might lead the way. When I turned toward the Gardens, he dropped behind me. In a little while I looked back. He was following me no longer; he stood irresolute. I called to him. He advanced a few steps—hesitated—and ran back to the house.

I went on by myself. Shall I confess my superstition? I thought the dog's desertion of me a bad omen.

Arrived at the tree, I placed myself under it. The minutes followed each other uneventfully. The cloudy sky darkened. The dull surface of the grass showed no shuddering consciousness of an unearthly creature passing over it.

I still waited, with an obstinacy which was fast becoming the obstinacy of despair. How long an interval elapsed, while I kept watch on the ground before me, I am not able to say. I only know that a change came.

Under the dull gray light I saw the grass move—but not as it had moved, on the day before. It shriveled as if a flame had scorched it. No flame appeared. The brown underlying earth showed itself winding onward in a thin strip—which might have been a footpath traced in fire. It frightened me. I longed for the protection of the Invisible Presence. I prayed for a warning of it, if danger was near.

A touch answered me. It was as if a hand unseen had taken my hand—had raised it, little by little—had left it, pointing to the thin brown path that wound toward me under the shriveled blades of grass.

I looked to the far end of the path.

The unseen hand closed on my hand with a warning pressure: the revelation of the coming danger was near me—I waited for it. I saw it.

The figure of a man appeared, advancing toward me along the thin brown path. I looked in his face as he came nearer. It showed me dimly the face of my husband's brother—John Zant.

The consciousness of myself as a living creature left me. I knew nothing; I felt nothing. I was dead.

When the torture of revival made me open my eyes, I found myself on the grass. Gentle hands raised my head, at the moment when I recovered my senses. Who had brought me to life again? Who was taking care of me?

I looked upward, and saw—bending over me—John Zant.

VII.

THERE, the manuscript ended.

Some lines had been added on the last page; but they had been so carefully erased as to be illegible. These words of explanation appeared below the canceled sentences:

"I had begun to write the little that remains to be told, when it struck me that I might, unintentionally, be exercising an unfair influence on your opinion. Let me only remind you that I believe absolutely in the supernatural revelation which I have endeavored to describe. Remember this—and decide for me what I dare not decide for myself."

There was no serious obstacle in the way of compliance with this request.

Judged from the point of view of the materialist, Mrs. Zant might no doubt be the victim of illusions (produced by a diseased state of the nervous system), which have been known to exist—as in the celebrated case of the book-seller, Nicolai, of Berlin—without being accompanied by derangement of the intellectual powers. But Mr. Rayburn was not asked to solve any such intricate problem as this. He had been merely instructed to read the manuscript, and to say what impression it had left on him of the mental condition of the writer; whose doubt of herself had been, in all probability, first suggested by remembrance of the illness from which she had suffered—brain-fever.

Under these circumstances, there could be little difficulty in forming an opinion. The memory which had recalled, and the judgment which had arranged, the succession of events related in the narrative, revealed a mind in full possession of its resources.

Having satisfied himself so far, Mr. Rayburn abstained from considering the more serious question suggested by what he had read.

At any time his habits of life and his ways of thinking would have rendered him unfit to weigh the arguments, which assert or deny supernatural revelation among the creatures of earth. But his mind was now so disturbed by the startling record of experience which he had just read, that he was only conscious of feeling certain impressions—without possessing the capacity to reflect on them. That his anxiety on Mrs. Zant's account had been increased, and that his doubts of Mr. John Zant had been encouraged, were the only practical results of the confidence placed in him of which he was thus far aware. In the ordinary exigencies of life a man of hesitating disposition, his interest in Mrs. Zant's welfare, and his desire to discover what had passed between her brother-in-law and herself, after their meeting in the Gardens, urged him into instant action. In half an hour more, he had arrived at her lodgings. He was at once admitted.

VIII.

MRS. ZANT was alone, in an imperfectly lighted room.

"I hope you will excuse the bad light," she said; "my head has been burning as if the fever had come back again. Oh, don't go away! After what I have suffered, you don't know how dreadful it is to be alone."

The tone of her voice told him that she had been crying. He at once tried the best means of setting the poor lady at ease, by telling her of the conclusion at which he had arrived, after reading her manuscript. The happy result showed itself instantly: her face brightened, her manner changed; she was eager to hear more.

"Have I produced any other impression on you?" she asked.

He understood the allusion. Expressing sincere respect for her own convictions, he told her honestly that he was not prepared to enter on the obscure and terrible question of supernatural interposition. Grateful for the tone in which he had answered her, she wisely and delicately changed the subject.

"I must speak to you of my brother-in-law," she said. "He has told me of your visit; and I am anxious to know what you think of him. Do you like Mr. John Zant?"

Mr. Rayburn hesitated.

The careworn look appeared again in her face. "If you had felt as kindly toward him as he feels toward you," she said, "I might have gone to St. Sallins with a lighter heart."

Mr. Rayburn thought of the supernatural appearances, described at the close of her narrative. "You believe in that terrible warning," he remonstrated; "and yet, you go to your brother-in-law's house!"

"I believe," she answered, "in the spirit of the man who loved me in the days of his earthly bondage. I am under his protection. What have I to do but to cast away my fears, and to wait in faith and hope? It might have helped my resolution if a friend had been near to encourage me." She paused and smiled sadly. "I must remember," she resumed, "that your way of understanding my position is not my way. I ought to have told you that Mr. John Zant feels needless anxiety about my health. He declares that he will not lose sight of me until his mind is at ease. It is useless to attempt to alter his opinion. He says my nerves are shattered—and who that sees me can doubt it? He tells me that my only chance of getting better is to try change of air and perfect repose— how can I contradict him? He reminds me that I have no relation but himself, and no house open to me but his own—and God knows he is right!"

She said those last words in accents of melancholy resignation, which grieved the good man whose one merciful purpose was to serve and console her. He spoke impulsively with the freedom of an old friend,

"I want to know more of you and Mr. John Zant than I know now," he said. "My motive is a better one than mere curiosity. Do you believe that I feel a sincere interest in you?"

"With my whole heart."

That reply encouraged him to proceed with what he had to say. "When you recovered from your fainting-fit," he began, "Mr. John Zant asked questions, of course?"

"He asked what could possibly have happened, in such a quiet place as Kensington Gardens, to make me faint."

"And how did you answer?"

"Answer? I couldn't even look at him!"

"You said nothing?"

"Nothing. I don't know what he thought of me; he might have been surprised, or he might have been offended."

"Is he easily offended?" Mr. Rayburn asked.

"Not in my experience of him."

"Do you mean your experience of him before your illness?"

"Yes. Since my recovery, his engagements with country patients have kept him away from London. I have not seen him since he took these lodgings for me. But he is always considerate. He has written more than once to beg that I will not think him neglectful, and to tell me (what I knew already through my poor husband) that he has no money of his own, and must live by his profession."

"In your husband's lifetime, were the two brothers on good terms?"

"Always. The one complaint I ever heard my husband make of John Zant was that he didn't come to see us often enough, after our marriage. Is there some wickedness in him which we have never suspected? It may be—but how can it be? I have every reason to be grateful to the man against whom I have been supernaturally warned! His conduct to me has been always perfect. I can't tell you what I owe to his influence in quieting my mind, when a dreadful doubt arose about my husband's death."

"Do you mean doubt if he died a natural death?"

"Oh, no! no! He was dying of rapid consumption—but his sudden death took the doctors by surprise. One of them thought that he might have taken an overdose of his sleeping drops, by mistake. The other disputed this conclusion, or there might have been an inquest in the house. Oh, don't speak of it any more! Let us talk of something else. Tell me when I shall see you again."

"I hardly know. When do you and your brother-in-law leave London?"

"To-morrow." She looked at Mr. Rayburn with a piteous entreaty in her eyes; she said, timidly: "Do you ever go to the seaside, and take your dear little girl with you?"

The request, at which she had only dared to hint, touched on the idea which was at that moment in Mr. Rayburn's mind.

Interpreted by his strong prejudice against John Zant, what she had said of her brother-in-law filled him with forebodings of peril to herself; all the more powerful in their influence, for this reason—that he shrank from distinctly realizing them. If another person had been present at the interview, and had said to him afterward: "That man's reluctance to visit his sister-in-law, while her husband was living, is associated with a secret sense of guilt which her innocence cannot even imagine: he, and he alone, knows the cause of her husband's sudden death: his feigned anxiety about her health is adopted as the safest means of enticing her into his house,"—if those formidable conclusions had been urged on Mr. Rayburn, he would have felt it his duty to reject them, as unjustifiable aspersions on an absent man. And yet, when he took leave that evening of Mrs. Zant, he had pledged himself to give Lucy a holiday at the seaside: and he had said, without blushing, that the child really deserved it, as a reward for general good conduct and attention to her lessons!

IX.

THREE days later, the father and daughter arrived toward evening at St. Sallins-on-Sea. They found Mrs. Zant at the station.

The poor woman's joy, on seeing them, expressed itself like the joy of a child. "Oh, I am so glad! so glad!" was all she could say when they met. Lucy was half-smothered with kisses, and was made supremely happy by a present of the finest doll she had ever possessed. Mrs. Zant accompanied her friends to the rooms which had been secured at the hotel. She was able to speak confidentially to Mr. Rayburn, while Lucy was in the balcony hugging her doll, and looking at the sea.

The one event that had happened during Mrs. Zant's short residence at St. Sallins was the departure of her brother-in-law that morning, for London. He had been called away to operate on the feet of a wealthy patient who knew the value of his time: his housekeeper expected that he would return to dinner.

As to his conduct toward Mrs. Zant, he was not only as attentive as ever—he was almost oppressively affectionate in his language and manner. There was no service that a man could render which he had not eagerly offered to her. He declared that he already perceived an improvement in her health; he congratulated her on having decided to stay in his house; and (as a proof, perhaps, of his sincerity) he had repeatedly pressed her hand. "Have you any idea what all this means?" she said, simply.

Mr. Rayburn kept his idea to himself. He professed ignorance; and asked next what sort of person the housekeeper was.

Mrs. Zant shook her head ominously.

"Such a strange creature," she said, "and in the habit of taking such liberties that I begin to be afraid she is a little crazy."

"Is she an old woman?"

"No—only middle-aged." This morning, after her master had left the house, she actually asked me what I thought of my brother-in-law! I told her, as coldly as possible, that I thought he was very kind. She was quite insensible to the tone in which I had spoken; she went on from bad to worse. "Do you call him the sort of man who would take the fancy of a young woman?" was her next question. She actually looked at me (I might have been wrong; and I hope I was) as if the "young woman" she had in her mind was myself! I said: "I don't think of such things, and I don't talk about them." Still, she was not in the least discouraged; she made a personal remark next: "Excuse me—but you do look wretchedly pale." I thought she seemed to enjoy the defect in my complexion; I really believe it raised me in her estimation. "We shall get on better in time," she said; "I am beginning to like you." She walked out humming a tune. Don't you agree with me? Don't you think she's crazy?"

"I can hardly give an opinion until I have seen her. Does she look as if she might have been a pretty woman at one time of her life?"

"Not the sort of pretty woman whom I admire!"

Mr. Rayburn smiled. "I was thinking," he resumed, "that this person's odd conduct may perhaps be accounted for. She is probably jealous of any young lady who is invited to her master's house—and (till she noticed your complexion) she began by being jealous of you."

Innocently at a loss to understand how she could become an object of the housekeeper's jealousy, Mrs. Zant looked at Mr. Rayburn in astonishment. Before she could give expression to her feeling of surprise, there was an interruption—a welcome interruption. A waiter entered the room, and announced a visitor; described as "a gentleman."

Mrs. Zant at once rose to retire.

"Who is the gentleman?" Mr. Rayburn asked—detaining Mrs. Zant as he spoke.

A voice which they both recognized answered gayly, from the outer side of the door:

"A friend from London."

X.

"WELCOME to St. Sallins!" cried Mr. John Zant. "I knew that you were expected, my dear sir, and I took my chance at finding you at the hotel." He turned to his sister-in-law, and kissed her hand with an elaborate gallantry worthy of Sir Charles Grandison himself. "When I reached home, my dear, and heard that you had gone out, I guessed that your object was to receive our excellent friend. You have not felt lonely while I have been away? That's right! that's right!" he looked toward the balcony, and discovered Lucy at the open window, staring at the magnificent stranger. "Your little daughter, Mr. Rayburn? Dear child! Come and kiss me."

Lucy answered in one positive word: "No."

Mr. John Zant was not easily discouraged.

"Show me your doll, darling," he said. "Sit on my knee."

Lucy answered in two positive words—"I won't."

Her father approached the window to administer the necessary reproof. Mr. John Zant interfered in the cause of mercy with his best grace. He held up his hands in cordial entreaty. "Dear Mr. Rayburn! The fairies are sometimes shy; and this little fairy doesn't take to strangers at first sight. Dear child! All in good time. And what stay do you make at St. Sallins? May we hope that our poor attractions will tempt you to prolong your visit?"

He put his flattering little question with an ease of manner which was rather too plainly assumed; and he looked at Mr. Rayburn with a watchfulness which appeared to attach undue importance to the reply. When he said: "What stay do you make at St. Sallins?" did he really mean: "How soon do you leave us?" Inclining to adopt this conclusion, Mr. Rayburn answered cautiously that his stay at the seaside would depend on circumstances. Mr. John Zant looked at his sister-in-law, sitting silent in a corner with Lucy on her lap. "Exert your attractions," he said; "make the circumstances agreeable to our good friend. Will you dine with us to-day, my dear sir, and bring your little fairy with you?"

Lucy was far from receiving this complimentary allusion in the spirit in which it had been offered. "I'm not a fairy," she declared. "I'm a child."

"And a naughty child," her father added, with all the severity that he could assume.

"I can't help it, papa; the man with the big beard puts me out."

The man with the big beard was amused—amiably, paternally amused— by Lucy's plain speaking. He repeated his invitation to dinner; and he did his best to look disappointed when Mr. Rayburn made the necessary excuses.

"Another day," he said (without, however, fixing the day). "I think you will find my house comfortable. My housekeeper may perhaps be eccentric— but in all essentials a woman in a thousand. Do you feel the change from London already? Our air at St. Sallins is really worthy of its reputation. Invalids who come here are cured as if by magic. What do you think of Mrs. Zant? How does she look?"

Mr. Rayburn was evidently expected to say that she looked better. He said it. Mr. John Zant seemed to have anticipated a stronger expression of opinion.

"Surprisingly better!" he pronounced. "Infinitely better! We ought both to be grateful. Pray believe that we are grateful."

"If you mean grateful to me," Mr. Rayburn remarked, "I don't quite understand—"

"You don't quite understand? Is it possible that you have forgotten our conversation when I first had the honor of receiving you? Look at Mrs. Zant again."

Mr. Rayburn looked; and Mrs. Zant's brother-in-law explained himself.

"You notice the return of her color, the healthy brightness of her eyes. (No, my dear, I am not paying you idle compliments; I am stating plain facts.) For that happy result, Mr. Rayburn, we are indebted to you."

"Surely not?"

"Surely yes! It was at your valuable suggestion that I thought of inviting my sister-in-law to visit me at St. Sallins. Ah, you remember it now. Forgive me if I look at my watch; the dinner hour is on my mind. Not, as your dear little daughter there seems to think, because I am greedy, but because I am always punctual, in justice to the cook. Shall we see you to-morrow? Call early, and you will find us at home."

He gave Mrs. Zant his arm, and bowed and smiled, and kissed his hand to Lucy, and left the room. Recalling their interview at the hotel in London, Mr. Rayburn now understood John Zant's object (on that occasion) in assuming the character of a helpless man in need of a sensible suggestion. If Mrs. Zant's residence under his roof became associated with evil consequences, he could declare that she would never have entered the house but for Mr. Rayburn's advice.

With the next day came the hateful necessity of returning this man's visit.

Mr. Rayburn was placed between two alternatives. In Mrs. Zant's interests he must remain, no matter at what sacrifice of his own inclinations, on good terms with her brother-in-law—or he must return to London, and leave the poor woman to her fate. His choice, it is needless to say, was never a matter of doubt. He called at the house, and did his innocent best—without in the least deceiving Mr. John Zant—to make himself agreeable during the short duration of his visit. Descending the stairs on his way out, accompanied by Mrs. Zant, he was surprised to see a middle-aged woman in the hall, who looked as if she was waiting there expressly to attract notice.

"The housekeeper," Mrs. Zant whispered. "She is impudent enough to try to make acquaintance with you."

This was exactly what the housekeeper was waiting in the hall to do.

"I hope you like our watering-place, sir," she began. "If I can be of service to you, pray command me. Any friend of this lady's has a claim on me—and you are an old friend, no doubt. I am only the housekeeper; but I presume to take a sincere interest in Mrs. Zant; and I am indeed glad to see you here. We none of us know—do we?—how soon we may want a friend. No offense, I hope? Thank you, sir. Good-morning."

There was nothing in the woman's eyes which indicated an unsettled mind; nothing in the appearance of her lips which suggested habits of intoxication. That her strange outburst of familiarity proceeded from some strong motive seemed to be more than probable. Putting together what Mrs. Zant had already told him, and what he had himself observed, Mr. Rayburn suspected that the motive might be found in the housekeeper's jealousy of her master.

XI.

REFLECTING in the solitude of his own room, Mr. Rayburn felt that the one prudent course to take would be to persuade Mrs. Zant to leave St. Sallins. He tried to prepare her for this strong proceeding, when she came the next day to take Lucy out for a walk.

"If you still regret having forced yourself to accept your brother-in-law's invitation," was all he ventured to say, "don't forget that you are perfect mistress of your own actions. You have only to come to me at the hotel, and I will take you back to London by the next train."

She positively refused to entertain the idea.

"I should be a thankless creature, indeed," she said, "if I accepted your proposal. Do you think I am ungrateful enough to involve you in a personal quarrel with John Zant? No! If I find myself forced to leave the house, I will go away alone."

There was no moving her from this resolution. When she and Lucy had gone out together, Mr. Rayburn remained at the hotel, with a mind ill at ease. A man of readier mental resources might have felt at a loss how to act for the best, in the emergency that now confronted him. While he was still as far as ever from arriving at a decision, some person knocked at the door.

Had Mrs. Zant returned? He looked up as the door was opened, and saw to his astonishment—Mr. John Zant's housekeeper.

"Don't let me alarm you, sir," the woman said. "Mrs. Zant has been taken a little faint, at the door of our house. My master is attending to her."

"Where is the child?" Mr. Rayburn asked.

"I was bringing her back to you, sir, when we met a lady and her little girl at the door of the hotel. They were on their way to the beach—and Miss Lucy begged hard to be allowed to go with them. The lady said the two children were playfellows, and she was sure you would not object."

"The lady is quite right. Mrs. Zant's illness is not serious, I hope?"

"I think not, sir. But I should like to say something in her interests. May I? Thank you." She advanced a step nearer to him, and spoke her next words in a whisper. "Take Mrs. Zant away from this place, and lose no time in doing it."

Mr. Rayburn was on his guard. He merely asked: "Why?"

The housekeeper answered in a curiously indirect manner—partly in jest, as it seemed, and partly in earnest.

"When a man has lost his wife," she said, "there's some difference of opinion in Parliament, as I hear, whether he does right or wrong, if he marries his wife's sister. Wait a bit! I'm coming to the point. My master is one who has a long head on his shoulders; he sees consequences which escape the notice of people like me. In his way of thinking, if one man may marry his wife's sister, and no harm done, where's the objection if another man pays a compliment to the family, and marries his brother's widow? My master, if you please, is that other man. Take the widow away before she marries him."

This was beyond endurance.

"You insult Mrs. Zant," Mr. Rayburn answered, "if you suppose that such a thing is possible!"

"Oh! I insult her, do I? Listen to me. One of three things will happen. She will be entrapped into consenting to it—or frightened into consenting to it—or drugged into consenting to it—"

Mr. Rayburn was too indignant to let her go on.

401

"You are talking nonsense," he said. "There can be no marriage; the law forbids it."

"Are you one of the people who see no further than their noses?" she asked insolently. "Won't the law take his money? Is he obliged to mention that he is related to her by marriage, when he buys the license?" She paused; her humor changed; she stamped furiously on the floor. The true motive that animated her showed itself in her next words, and warned Mr. Rayburn to grant a more favorable hearing than he had accorded to her yet. "If you won't stop it," she burst out, "I will! If he marries anybody, he is bound to marry ME. Will you take her away? I ask you, for the last time—will you take her away?"

The tone in which she made that final appeal to him had its effect.

"I will go back with you to John Zant's house," he said, "and judge for myself."

She laid her hand on his arm:

"I must go first—or you may not be let in. Follow me in five minutes; and don't knock at the street door."

On the point of leaving him, she abruptly returned.

"We have forgotten something," she said. "Suppose my master refuses to see you. His temper might get the better of him; he might make it so unpleasant for you that you would be obliged to go."

"My temper might get the better of me," Mr. Rayburn replied; "and—if I thought it was in Mrs. Zant's interests—I might refuse to leave the house unless she accompanied me."

"That will never do, sir."

"Why not?"

"Because I should be the person to suffer."

"In what way?"

"In this way. If you picked a quarrel with my master, I should be blamed for it because I showed you upstairs. Besides, think of the lady. You might frighten her out of her senses, if it came to a struggle between you two men."

The language was exaggerated; but there was a force in this last objection which Mr. Rayburn was obliged to acknowledge.

"And, after all," the housekeeper continued, "he has more right over her than you have. He is related to her, and you are only her friend."

Mr. Rayburn declined to let himself be influenced by this consideration, "Mr. John Zant is only related to her by marriage," he said. "If she prefers trusting in me—come what may of it, I will be worthy of her confidence."

The housekeeper shook her head.

"That only means another quarrel," she answered. "The wise way, with a man like my master, is the peaceable way. We must manage to deceive him."

"I don't like deceit."

"In that case, sir, I'll wish you good-by. We will leave Mrs. Zant to do the best she can for herself."

Mr. Rayburn was unreasonable. He positively refused to adopt this alternative.

"Will you hear what I have got to say?" the housekeeper asked.

"There can be no harm in that," he admitted. "Go on."

She took him at his word.

"When you called at our house," she began, "did you notice the doors in the passage, on the first floor? Very well. One of them is the door of the drawing-room, and the other is the door of the library. Do you remember the drawing-room, sir?"

"I thought it a large well-lighted room," Mr. Rayburn answered. "And I noticed a doorway in the wall, with a handsome curtain hanging over it."

"That's enough for our purpose," the housekeeper resumed. "On the other side of the curtain, if you had looked in, you would have found the library. Suppose my master is as polite as usual, and begs to be excused for not receiving you, because it is an inconvenient time. And suppose you are polite on your side and take yourself off by the drawing-room door. You will find me waiting downstairs, on the first landing. Do you see it now?"

"I can't say I do."

"You surprise me, sir. What is to prevent us from getting back softly into the library, by the door in the passage? And why shouldn't we use that second way into the library as a means of discovering what may be going on in the drawing-room? Safe behind the curtain, you will see him if he behaves uncivilly to Mrs. Zant, or you will hear her if she calls for help. In either case, you may be as rough and ready with my master as you find needful; it will be he who has frightened her, and not you. And who can blame the poor housekeeper because Mr. Rayburn did his duty, and protected a helpless woman? There is my plan, sir. Is it worth trying?"

He answered, sharply enough: "I don't like it."

The housekeeper opened the door again, and wished him good-by.

If Mr. Rayburn had felt no more than an ordinary interest in Mrs. Zant, he would have let the woman go. As it was, he stopped her; and, after some further protest (which proved to be useless), he ended in giving way.

"You promise to follow my directions?" she stipulated.

He gave the promise. She smiled, nodded, and left him. True to his instructions, Mr. Rayburn reckoned five minutes by his watch, before he followed her.

XII.

THE housekeeper was waiting for him, with the street-door ajar.

"They are both in the drawing-room," she whispered, leading the way upstairs. "Step softly, and take him by surprise."

A table of oblong shape stood midway between the drawing-room walls.

At the end of it which was nearest to the window, Mrs. Zant was pacing to and fro across the breadth of the room. At the opposite end of the table, John Zant was seated. Taken completely by surprise, he showed himself in his true character. He started to his feet, and protested with an oath against the intrusion which had been committed on him.

Heedless of his action and his language, Mr. Rayburn could look at nothing, could think of nothing, but Mrs. Zant. She was still walking slowly to and fro, unconscious of the words of sympathy which he addressed to her, insensible even as it seemed to the presence of other persons in the room.

John Zant's voice broke the silence. His temper was under control again: he had his reasons for still remaining on friendly terms with Mr. Rayburn.

"I am sorry I forgot myself just now," he said.

Mr. Rayburn's interest was concentrated on Mrs. Zant; he took no notice of the apology.

"When did this happen?" he asked.

"About a quarter of an hour ago. I was fortunately at home. Without speaking to me, without noticing me, she walked upstairs like a person in a dream."

Mr. Rayburn suddenly pointed to Mrs. Zant.

"Look at her!" he said. "There's a change!"

All restlessness in her movements had come to an end. She was standing at the further end of the table, which was nearest to the window, in the full flow of sunlight pouring at that moment over her face. Her eyes looked out straight before her—void of all expression. Her lips were a little parted: her head drooped slightly toward her shoulder, in an attitude which suggested listening for something or waiting for something. In the warm brilliant light, she stood before the two men, a living creature self-isolated in a stillness like the stillness of death.

John Zant was ready with the expression of his opinion.

"A nervous seizure," he said. "Something resembling catalepsy, as you see."

"Have you sent for a doctor?"

"A doctor is not wanted."

"I beg your pardon. It seems to me that medical help is absolutely necessary."

"Be so good as to remember," Mr. John Zant answered, "that the decision rests with me, as the lady's relative. I am sensible of the honor which your visit confers on me. But the time has been unhappily chosen. Forgive me if I suggest that you will do well to retire."

Mr. Rayburn had not forgotten the housekeeper's advice, or the promise which she had exacted from him. But the expression in John Zant's face was a serious trial to his self-control. He hesitated, and looked back at Mrs. Zant.

If he provoked a quarrel by remaining in the room, the one alternative would be the removal of her by force. Fear of the consequences to herself, if she was suddenly and roughly roused from her trance, was the one consideration which reconciled him to submission. He withdrew.

The housekeeper was waiting for him below, on the first landing. When the door of the drawing-room had been closed again, she signed to him to follow her, and returned up the stairs. After another struggle with himself, he obeyed. They entered the library from the corridor—and placed themselves behind the closed curtain which hung over the doorway. It was easy so to arrange the edge of the drapery as to observe, without exciting suspicion, whatever was going on in the next room.

Mrs. Zant's brother-in-law was approaching her at the time when Mr. Rayburn saw him again.

In the instant afterward, she moved—before he had completely passed over the space between them. Her still figure began to tremble. She lifted her drooping head. For a moment there was a shrinking in her—as if she had been touched by something. She seemed to recognize the touch: she was still again.

John Zant watched the change. It suggested to him that she was beginning to recover her senses. He tried the experiment of speaking to her.

"My love, my sweet angel, come to the heart that adores you!"

He advanced again; he passed into the flood of sunlight pouring over her.

"Rouse yourself!" he said.

She still remained in the same position; apparently at his mercy, neither hearing him nor seeing him.

"Rouse yourself!" he repeated. "My darling, come to me!"

At the instant when he attempted to embrace her—at the instant when Mr. Rayburn rushed into the room—John Zant's arms, suddenly turning rigid, remained outstretched. With a shriek of horror, he struggled to draw them back—struggled, in the empty brightness of the sunshine, as if some invisible grip had seized him.

"What has got me?" the wretch screamed. "Who is holding my hands? Oh, the cold of it! the cold of it!"

His features became convulsed; his eyes turned upward until only the white eyeballs were visible. He fell prostrate with a crash that shook the room.

The housekeeper ran in. She knelt by her master's body. With one hand she loosened his cravat. With the other she pointed to the end of the table.

Mrs. Zant still kept her place; but there was another change. Little by little, her eyes recovered their natural living expression—then slowly closed. She tottered backward from the table, and lifted her hands wildly, as if to grasp at something which might support her. Mr. Rayburn hurried to her before she fell—lifted her in his arms—and carried her out of the room.

One of the servants met them in the hall. He sent her for a carriage. In a quarter of an hour more, Mrs. Zant was safe under his care at the hotel.

XIII.

THAT night a note, written by the housekeeper, was delivered to Mrs. Zant.

"The doctors give little hope. The paralytic stroke is spreading upward to his face. If death spares him, he will live a helpless man. I shall take care of him to the last. As for you—forget him."

Mrs. Zant gave the note to Mr. Rayburn.

"Read it, and destroy it," she said. "It is written in ignorance of the terrible truth."

He obeyed—and looked at her in silence, waiting to hear more. She hid her face. The few words she had addressed to him, after a struggle with herself, fell slowly and reluctantly from her lips.

She said: "No mortal hand held the hands of John Zant. The guardian spirit was with me. The promised protection was with me. I know it. I wish to know no more."

Having spoken, she rose to retire. He opened the door for her, seeing that she needed rest in her own room.

Left by himself, he began to consider the prospect that was before him in the future. How was he to regard the woman who had just left him? As a poor creature weakened by disease, the victim of her own nervous delusion? or as the chosen object of a supernatural revelation—unparalleled by any similar revelation that he had heard of, or had found recorded in books? His first discovery of the place that she really held in his estimation dawned on his mind, when he felt himself recoiling from the conclusion which presented her to his pity, and yielding to the nobler conviction which felt with her faith, and raised her to a place apart among other women.

XIV.

THEY left St. Sallins the next day.

Arrived at the end of the journey, Lucy held fast by Mrs. Zant's hand. Tears were rising in the child's eyes.

"Are we to bid her good-by?" she said sadly to her father.

He seemed to be unwilling to trust himself to speak; he only said:

"My dear, ask her yourself."

But the result justified him. Lucy was happy again.

MISS MORRIS AND THE STRANGER.

I.

WHEN I first saw him, he was lost in one of the Dead Cities of England—situated on the South Coast, and called Sandwich.

Shall I describe Sandwich? I think not. Let us own the truth; descriptions of places, however nicely they may be written, are always more or less dull. Being a woman, I naturally hate dullness. Perhaps some description of Sandwich may drop out, as it were, from my report of our conversation when we first met as strangers in the street.

He began irritably. "I've lost myself," he said.

"People who don't know the town often do that," I remarked.

He went on: "Which is my way to the Fleur de Lys Inn?"

His way was, in the first place, to retrace his steps. Then to turn to the left. Then to go on until he found two streets meeting. Then to take the street on the right. Then to look out for the second turning on the left. Then to follow the turning until he smelled stables—and there was the inn. I put it in the clearest manner, and never stumbled over a word.

"How the devil am I to remember all that?" he said.

This was rude. We are naturally and properly indignant with any man who is rude to us. But whether we turn our backs on him in contempt, or whether we are merciful and give him a lesson in politeness, depends entirely on the man. He may be a bear, but he may also have his redeeming qualities. This man had redeeming qualities. I cannot positively say that he was either handsome or ugly, young or old, well or ill dressed. But I can speak with certainty to the personal attractions which recommended him to notice. For instance, the tone of his voice was persuasive. (Did you ever read a story, written by one of us, in which we failed to dwell on our hero's voice?) Then, again, his hair was reasonably long. (Are you acquainted with any woman who can endure a man with a cropped head?) Moreover, he was of a good height. (It must be a very tall woman who can feel favorably inclined toward a short man.) Lastly, although his eyes were not more than fairly presentable in form and color, the wretch had in some unaccountable manner become possessed of beautiful eyelashes. They were even better eyelashes than mine. I write quite seriously. There is one woman who is above the common weakness of vanity—and she holds the present pen.

So I gave my lost stranger a lesson in politeness. The lesson took the form of a trap. I asked him if he would like me to show him the way to the inn. He was still annoyed at losing himself. As I had anticipated, he bluntly answered: "Yes."

"When you were a boy, and you wanted something," I said, "did your mother teach you to say 'Please'?"

He positively blushed. "She did," he admitted; "and she taught me to say 'Beg your pardon' when I was rude. I'll say it now: 'Beg your pardon.'"

This curious apology increased my belief in his redeeming qualities. I led the way to the inn. He followed me in silence. No woman who respects herself can endure silence when she is in the company of a man. I made him talk.

"Do you come to us from Ramsgate?" I began. He only nodded his head. "We don't think much of Ramsgate here," I went on. "There is not an old building in the place. And their first Mayor was only elected the other day!"

This point of view seemed to be new to him. He made no attempt to dispute it; he only looked around him, and said: "Sandwich is a melancholy place, miss." He was so rapidly improving in politeness, that I encouraged him by a smile. As a citizen of Sandwich, I may say that we take it as a compliment when we are told that our town is a melancholy place. And why not? Melancholy is connected with dignity. And dignity is associated with age. And we are old. I teach my pupils logic, among other things—there is a specimen. Whatever may be said to the contrary, women can reason. They

411

can also wander; and I must admit that I am wandering. Did I mention, at starting, that I was a governess? If not, that allusion to "pupils" must have come in rather abruptly. Let me make my excuses, and return to my lost stranger.

"Is there any such thing as a straight street in all Sandwich?" he asked.

"Not one straight street in the whole town."

"Any trade, miss?"

"As little as possible—and that is expiring."

"A decayed place, in short?"

"Thoroughly decayed."

My tone seemed to astonish him. "You speak as if you were proud of its being a decayed place," he said.

I quite respected him; this was such an intelligent remark to make. We do enjoy our decay: it is our chief distinction. Progress and prosperity everywhere else; decay and dissolution here. As a necessary consequence, we produce our own impression, and we like to be original. The sea deserted us long ago: it once washed our walls, it is now two miles away from us— we don't regret the sea. We had sometimes ninety-five ships in our harbor, Heaven only knows how many centuries ago; we now have one or two small coasting vessels, half their time aground in a muddy little river—we don't regret our harbor. But one house in the town is daring enough to anticipate the arrival of resident visitors, and announces furnished apartments to let. What a becoming contrast to our modern neighbor, Ramsgate! Our noble market-place exhibits the laws made by the corporation; and every week there are fewer and fewer people to obey the laws. How convenient! Look at our one warehouse by the river side—with the crane generally idle, and the windows mostly boarded up; and perhaps one man at the door, looking out for the job which his better sense tells him cannot possibly come. What a wholesome protest against the devastating hurry and over-work elsewhere, which has shattered the nerves of the nation! "Far from me and from my friends" (to borrow the eloquent language of Doctor Johnson) "be such frigid enthusiasm as shall conduct us indifferent and unmoved" over the bridge by which you enter Sandwich, and pay a toll if you do it in a carriage. "That man is little to be envied (Doctor Johnson again) who can lose himself in our labyrinthine streets, and not feel that he has reached the welcome limits of progress, and found a haven of rest in an age of hurry."

I am wandering again. Bear with the unpremeditated enthusiasm of a citizen who only attained years of discretion at her last birthday. We shall soon have done with Sandwich; we are close to the door of the inn.

"You can't mistake it now, sir," I said. "Good-morning."

He looked down at me from under his beautiful eyelashes (have I mentioned that I am a little woman?), and he asked in his persuasive tones: "Must we say good-by?"

I made him a bow.

"Would you allow me to see you safe home?" he suggested.

Any other man would have offended me. This man blushed like a boy, and looked at the pavement instead of looking at me. By this time I had made up my mind about him. He was not only a gentleman beyond all doubt, but a shy gentleman as well. His bluntness and his odd remarks were, as I thought, partly efforts to disguise his shyness, and partly refuges in which he tried to forget his own sense of it. I answered his audacious proposal amiably and pleasantly. "You would only lose your way again," I said, "and I should have to take you back to the inn for the second time."

Wasted words! My obstinate stranger only made another proposal.

"I have ordered lunch here," he said, "and I am quite alone." He stopped in confusion, and looked as if he rather expected me to box his ears. "I shall be forty next birthday," he went on; "I am old enough to be your father." I all but burst out laughing, and stepped across the street, on my way home. He followed me. "We might invite the landlady to join us," he said, looking the picture of a headlong man, dismayed by the consciousness of his own imprudence. "Couldn't you honor me by lunching with me if we had the landlady?" he asked.

This was a little too much. "Quite out of the question, sir—and you ought to know it," I said with severity. He half put out his hand. "Won't you even shake hands with me?" he inquired piteously. When we have most properly administered a reproof to a man, what is the perversity which makes us weakly pity him the minute afterward? I was fool enough to shake hands with this perfect stranger. And, having done it, I completed the total loss of my dignity by running away. Our dear crooked little streets hid me from him directly.

As I rang at the door-bell of my employer's house, a thought occurred to me which might have been alarming to a better regulated mind than mine.

"Suppose he should come back to Sandwich?"

II.

BEFORE many more days passed I had troubles of my own to contend with, which put the eccentric stranger out of my head for the time.

Unfortunately, my troubles are part of my story; and my early life mixes itself up with them. In consideration of what is to follow, may I say two words relating to the period before I was a governess?

I am the orphan daughter of a shopkeeper of Sandwich. My father died, leaving to his widow and child an honest name and a little income of L80 a year. We kept on the shop—neither gaining nor losing by it. The truth is nobody would buy our poor little business. I was thirteen years old at the time; and I was able to help my mother, whose health was then beginning to fail. Never shall I forget a certain bright summer's day, when I saw a new customer enter our shop. He was an elderly gentleman; and he seemed surprised to find so young a girl as myself in charge of the business, and, what is more, competent to support the charge. I answered his questions in a manner which seemed to please him. He soon discovered that my education (excepting my knowledge of the business) had been sadly neglected; and he inquired if he could see my mother. She was resting on the sofa in the back parlor—and she received him there. When he came out, he patted me on the cheek. "I have taken a fancy to you," he said, "and perhaps I shall come back again." He did come back again. My mother had referred him to the rector for our characters in the town, and he had heard what our clergyman could say for us. Our only relations had emigrated to Australia, and were not doing well there. My mother's death would leave me, so far as relatives were concerned, literally alone in the world. "Give this girl a first-rate education," said our elderly customer, sitting at our tea-table in the back parlor, "and she will do. If you will send her to school, ma'am, I'll pay for her education." My poor mother began to cry at the prospect of parting with me. The old gentleman said: "Think of it," and got up to go. He gave me his card as I opened the shop-door for him. "If you find yourself in trouble," he whispered, so that my mother could not hear him, "be a wise child, and write and tell me of it." I looked at the card. Our kind-hearted customer was no less a person than Sir Gervase Damian, of Garrum Park, Sussex—with landed property in our county as well! He had made himself (through the rector, no doubt) far better acquainted than I was with the true state of my mother's health. In four months from the memorable day when the great man had taken tea with us, my time had come to be alone in the world. I have no courage to dwell on it; my spirits sink, even at this distance of time, when I think of myself in those days. The good rector helped me with his advice—I wrote to Sir Gervase Damian.

A change had come over his life as well as mine in the interval since we had met.

Sir Gervase had married for the second time—and, what was more foolish still, perhaps, at his age, had married a young woman. She was said to be consumptive, and of a jealous temper as well. Her husband's only child by his first wife, a son and heir, was so angry at his father's second marriage that he left the house. The landed property being entailed, Sir Gervase could only express his sense of his son's conduct by making a new will, which left all his property in money to his young wife.

These particulars I gathered from the steward, who was expressly sent to visit me at Sandwich.

"Sir Gervase never makes a promise without keeping it," this gentleman informed me. "I am directed to take you to a first-rate ladies' school in the neighborhood of London, and to make all the necessary arrangements for your remaining there until you are eighteen years of age. Any written communications in the future are to pass, if you please, through the hands of the rector of Sandwich. The delicate health of the new Lady Damian makes it only too likely that the lives of her husband and herself will be passed, for the most part, in a milder climate than the climate of England. I am instructed to say this, and to convey to you Sir Gervase's best wishes."

By the rector's advice, I accepted the position offered to me in this unpleasantly formal manner—concluding (quite correctly, as I afterward discovered) that I was indebted to Lady Damian for the arrangement which personally separated me from my benefactor. Her husband's kindness and my gratitude, meeting on the neutral ground of Garrum Park, were objects of conjugal distrust to this lady. Shocking! shocking! I left a sincerely grateful letter to be forwarded to Sir Gervase; and, escorted by the steward, I went to school—being then just fourteen years old.

I know I am a fool. Never mind. There is some pride in me, though I am only a small shopkeeper's daughter. My new life had its trials—my pride held me up.

For the four years during which I remained at the school, my poor welfare might be a subject of inquiry to the rector, and sometimes even the steward—never to Sir Gervase himself. His winters were no doubt passed abroad; but in the summer time he and Lady Damian were at home again. Not even for a day or two in the holiday time was there pity enough felt for my lonely position to ask me to be the guest of the housekeeper (I expected nothing more) at Garrum Park. But for my pride, I might have felt it bitterly. My pride said to me, "Do justice to yourself." I worked so hard, I behaved so well, that the mistress of the school wrote to Sir Gervase to tell him how thoroughly I had deserved the kindness that he had shown to me. No answer was received. (Oh, Lady Damian!) No change varied the monotony of my life—except when one of my schoolgirl friends sometimes took me home with her for a few days at vacation time. Never mind. My pride held me up.

As the last half-year of my time at school approached, I began to consider the serious question of my future life.

Of course, I could have lived on my eighty pounds a year; but what a lonely, barren existence it promised to be!—unless somebody married me; and where, if you please, was I to find him? My education had thoroughly fitted me to be a governess. Why not try my fortune, and see a little of the world in that way? Even if I fell among ill-conditioned people, I could be independent of them, and retire on my income.

The rector, visiting London, came to see me. He not only approved of my idea—he offered me a means of carrying it out. A worthy family, recently settled at Sandwich, were in want of a governess. The head of the household was partner in a business (the exact nature of which it is needless to mention) having "branches" out of London. He had become superintendent of a new "branch"—tried as a commercial experiment, under special circumstances, at Sandwich. The idea of returning to my native place pleased me—dull as the place was to others. I accepted the situation.

When the steward's usual half-yearly letter arrived soon afterward, inquiring what plans I had formed on leaving school, and what he could do to help them, acting on behalf of Sir Gervase, a delicious tingling filled me from head to foot when I thought of my own independence. It was not ingratitude toward my benefactor; it was only my little private triumph over Lady Damian. Oh, my sisters of the sex, can you not understand and forgive me?

So to Sandwich I returned; and there, for three years, I remained with the kindest people who ever breathed the breath of life. Under their roof I was still living when I met with my lost gentleman in the street.

Ah, me! the end of that quiet, pleasant life was near. When I lightly spoke to the odd stranger of the expiring trade of the town, I never expected that my employer's trade was expiring too. The speculation had turned out to be a losing one; and all his savings had been embarked in it. He could no longer remain at Sandwich, or afford to keep a governess. His wife broke the sad news to me. I was so fond of the children, I proposed to her to give up my salary. Her husband refused even to consider the proposal. It was the old story of poor humanity over again. We cried, we kissed, we parted.

What was I to do next?—Write to Sir Gervase?

I had already written, soon after my return to Sandwich; breaking through the regulations by directly addressing Sir Gervase. I expressed my grateful sense of his generosity to a poor girl who had no family claim on him; and I promised to make the one return in my power by trying to be worthy of the interest he had taken in me. The letter was written without any alloy of mental reserve. My new life as a governess was such a happy one that I had forgotten my paltry bitterness of feeling against Lady Damian.

It was a relief to think of this change for the better, when the secretary at Garrum Park informed me that he had forwarded my letter to Sir Gervase, then at Madeira with his sick wife. She was slowly and steadily wasting away in a decline. Before another year had passed, Sir Gervase was left a widower for the second time, with no child to console him under his loss. No answer came to my grateful letter. I should have been unreasonable indeed if I had expected the bereaved husband to remember me in his grief and loneliness. Could I write to him again, in my own trumpery little interests, under these circumstances? I thought (and still think) that the commonest feeling of delicacy forbade it. The only other alternative was to appeal to the ever-ready friends of the obscure and helpless public. I advertised in the newspapers.

The tone of one of the answers which I received impressed me so favorably, that I forwarded my references. The next post brought my written engagement, and the offer of a salary which doubled my income.

The story of the past is told; and now we may travel on again, with no more stoppages by the way.

III.

THE residence of my present employer was in the north of England. Having to pass through London, I arranged to stay in town for a few days to make some necessary additions to my wardrobe. An old servant of the rector, who kept a lodging-house in the suburbs, received me kindly, and guided my choice in the serious matter of a dressmaker. On the second morning after my arrival an event happened. The post brought me a letter forwarded from the rectory. Imagine my astonishment when my correspondent proved to be Sir Gervase Damian himself!

The letter was dated from his house in London. It briefly invited me to call and see him, for a reason which I should hear from his own lips. He naturally supposed that I was still at Sandwich, and requested me, in a postscript, to consider my journey as made at his expense.

I went to the house the same day. While I was giving my name, a gentleman came out into the hall. He spoke to me without ceremony.

"Sir Gervase," he said, "believes he is going to die. Don't encourage him in that idea. He may live for another year or more, if his friends will only persuade him to be hopeful about himself."

With that, the gentleman left me; the servant said it was the doctor.

The change in my benefactor, since I had seen him last, startled and distressed me. He lay back in a large arm-chair, wearing a grim black dressing-gown, and looking pitiably thin and pinched and worn. I do not think I should have known him again, if we had met by accident. He signed to me to be seated on a little chair by his side.

"I wanted to see you," he said quietly, "before I die. You must have thought me neglectful and unkind, with good reason. My child, you have not been forgotten. If years have passed without a meeting between us, it has not been altogether my fault—"

He stopped. A pained expression passed over his poor worn face; he was evidently thinking of the young wife whom he had lost. I repeated—fervently and sincerely repeated—what I had already said to him in writing. "I owe everything, sir, to your fatherly kindness." Saying this, I ventured a little further. I took his wan white hand, hanging over the arm of the chair, and respectfully put it to my lips.

He gently drew his hand away from me, and sighed as he did it. Perhaps she had sometimes kissed his hand.

"Now tell me about yourself," he said.

I told him of my new situation, and how I had got it. He listened with evident interest.

"I was not self-deceived," he said, "when I first took a fancy to you in the shop. I admire your independent feeling; it's the right kind of courage in a girl like you. But you must let me do something more for you—some little service to remember me by when the end has come. What shall it be?"

"Try to get better, sir; and let me write to you now and then," I answered. "Indeed, indeed, I want nothing more."

"You will accept a little present, at least?" With those words he took from the breast-pocket of his dressing-gown an enameled cross attached to a gold chain. "Think of me sometimes," he said, as he put the chain round my neck. He drew me to him gently, and kissed my forehead. It was too much for me. "Don't cry, my dear," he said; "don't remind me of another sad young face—"

Once more he stopped; once more he was thinking of the lost wife. I pulled down my veil, and ran out of the room.

IV.

THE next day I was on my way to the north. My narrative brightens again—but let us not forget Sir Gervase Damian.

I ask permission to introduce some persons of distinction:—Mrs. Fosdyke, of Carsham Hall, widow of General Fosdyke; also Master Frederick, Miss Ellen, and Miss Eva, the pupils of the new governess; also two ladies and three gentlemen, guests staying in the house.

Discreet and dignified; handsome and well-bred—such was my impression of Mrs. Fosdyke, while she harangued me on the subject of her children, and communicated her views on education. Having heard the views before from others, I assumed a listening position, and privately formed my opinion of the schoolroom. It was large, lofty, perfectly furnished for the purpose; it had a big window and a balcony looking out over the garden terrace and the park beyond—a wonderful schoolroom, in my limited experience. One of the two doors which it possessed was left open, and showed me a sweet little bedroom, with amber draperies and maplewood furniture, devoted to myself. Here were wealth and liberality, in the harmonious combination so seldom discovered by the spectator of small means. I controlled my first feeling of bewilderment just in time to answer Mrs. Fosdyke on the subject of reading and recitation—viewed as minor accomplishments which a good governess might be expected to teach.

"While the organs are young and pliable," the lady remarked, "I regard it as of great importance to practice children in the art of reading aloud, with an agreeable variety of tone and correctness of emphasis. Trained in this way, they will produce a favorable impression on others, even in ordinary conversation, when they grow up. Poetry, committed to memory and recited, is a valuable means toward this end. May I hope that your studies have enabled you to carry out my views?"

Formal enough in language, but courteous and kind in manner. I relieved Mrs. Fosdyke from anxiety by informing her that we had a professor of elocution at school. And then I was left to improve my acquaintance with my three pupils.

They were fairly intelligent children; the boy, as usual, being slower than the girls. I did my best—with many a sad remembrance of the far dearer pupils whom I had left—to make them like me and trust me; and I succeeded in winning their confidence. In a week from the time of my arrival at Carsham Hall, we began to understand each other.

The first day in the week was one of our days for reciting poetry, in obedience to the instructions with which I had been favored by Mrs. Fosdyke. I had done with the girls, and had just opened (perhaps I ought to say profaned) Shakespeare's "Julius Caesar," in the elocutionary interests of Master Freddy. Half of Mark Antony's first glorious speech over Caesar's dead body he had learned by heart; and it was now my duty to teach him, to the best of my small ability, how to speak it. The morning was warm. We had our big window open; the delicious perfume of flowers in the garden beneath filled the room.

I recited the first eight lines, and stopped there feeling that I must not exact too much from the boy at first. "Now, Freddy," I said, "try if you can speak the poetry as I have spoken it."

"Don't do anything of the kind, Freddy," said a voice from the garden; "it's all spoken wrong."

Who was this insolent person? A man unquestionably—and, strange to say, there was something not entirely unfamiliar to me in his voice. The girls began to giggle. Their brother was more explicit. "Oh," says Freddy, "it's only Mr. Sax."

The one becoming course to pursue was to take no notice of the interruption. "Go on," I said. Freddy recited the lines, like a dear good boy, with as near an imitation of my style of elocution as could be expected from him.

"Poor devil!" cried the voice from the garden, insolently pitying my attentive pupil.

I imposed silence on the girls by a look—and then, without stirring from my chair, expressed my sense of the insolence of Mr. Sax in clear and commanding tones. "I shall be obliged to close the window if this is repeated." Having spoken to that effect, I waited in expectation of an apology. Silence was the only apology. It was enough for me that I had produced the right impression. I went on with my recitation.

> *"Here, under leave of Brutus, and the rest*
>
> *(For Brutus is an honorable man;*
>
> *So are they all, all honorable men),*
>
> *Come I to speak in Caesar's funeral.*
>
> *He was my friend, faithful and just to me—"*

"Oh, good heavens, I can't stand that! Why don't you speak the last line properly? Listen to me."

Dignity is a valuable quality, especially in a governess. But there are limits to the most highly trained endurance. I bounced out into the balcony—and there, on the terrace, smoking a cigar, was my lost stranger in the streets of Sandwich!

He recognized me, on his side, the instant I appeared. "Oh, Lord!" he cried in tones of horror, and ran round the corner of the terrace as if my eyes had been mad bulls in close pursuit of him. By this time it is, I fear, useless for me to set myself up as a discreet person in emergencies. Another woman might have controlled herself. I burst into fits of laughter. Freddy and the girls joined me. For the time, it was plainly useless to pursue the business of education. I shut up Shakespeare, and allowed—no, let me tell the truth, encouraged—the children to talk about Mr. Sax.

They only seemed to know what Mr. Sax himself had told them. His father and mother and brothers and sisters had all died in course of time. He was the sixth and last of the children, and he had been christened "Sextus" in consequence, which is Latin (here Freddy interposed) for sixth. Also christened "Cyril" (here the girls recovered the lead) by his mother's request; "Sextus" being such a hideous name. And which of his Christian names does he use? You wouldn't ask if you knew him! "Sextus," of course, because it is the ugliest. Sextus Sax? Not the romantic sort of name that one likes, when one is a woman. But I have no right to be particular. My own name (is it possible that I have not mentioned it in these pages yet?) is only Nancy Morris. Do not despise me—and let us return to Mr. Sax.

Is he married? The eldest girl thought not. She had heard mamma say to a lady, "An old German family, my dear, and, in spite of his oddities, an excellent man; but so poor—barely enough to live on—and blurts out the truth, if people ask his opinion, as if he had twenty thousand a year!" "Your mamma knows him well, of course?" "I should think so, and so do we. He often comes here. They say he's not good company among grown-up people. We think him jolly. He understands dolls, and he's the best back at leap-frog in the whole of England." Thus far we had advanced in the praise of

Sextus Sax, when one of the maids came in with a note for me. She smiled mysteriously, and said, "I'm to wait for an answer, miss."

I opened the note, and read these lines:—

"I am so ashamed of myself, I daren't attempt to make my apologies personally. Will you accept my written excuses? Upon my honor, nobody told me when I got here yesterday that you were in the house. I heard the recitation, and—can you excuse my stupidity?—I thought it was a stage-struck housemaid amusing herself with the children. May I accompany you when you go out with the young ones for your daily walk? One word will do. Yes or no. Penitently yours—S. S."

In my position, there was but one possible answer to this. Governesses must not make appointments with strange gentlemen—even when the children are present in the capacity of witnesses. I said, No. Am I claiming too much for my readiness to forgive injuries, when I add that I should have preferred saying Yes?

We had our early dinner, and then got ready to go out walking as usual. These pages contain a true confession. Let me own that I hoped Mr. Sax would understand my refusal, and ask Mrs. Fosdyke's leave to accompany us. Lingering a little as we went downstairs, I heard him in the hall—actually speaking to Mrs. Fosdyke! What was he saying? That darling boy, Freddy, got into a difficulty with one of his boot-laces exactly at the right moment. I could help him, and listen—and be sadly disappointed by the result. Mr. Sax was offended with me.

"You needn't introduce me to the new governess," I heard him say. "We have met on a former occasion, and I produced a disagreeable impression on her. I beg you will not speak of me to Miss Morris."

Before Mrs. Fosdyke could say a word in reply, Master Freddy changed suddenly from a darling boy to a detestable imp. "I say, Mr. Sax!" he called out, "Miss Morris doesn't mind you a bit—she only laughs at you."

The answer to this was the sudden closing of a door. Mr. Sax had taken refuge from me in one of the ground-floor rooms. I was so mortified, I could almost have cried.

Getting down into the hall, we found Mrs. Fosdyke with her garden hat on, and one of the two ladies who were staying in the house (the unmarried one) whispering to her at the door of the morning-room. The lady—Miss Melbury—looked at me with a certain appearance of curiosity which I was quite at a loss to understand, and suddenly turned away toward the further end of the hall.

"I will walk with you and the children," Mrs. Fosdyke said to me. "Freddy, you can ride your tricycle if you like." She turned to the girls. "My dears, it's cool under the trees. You may take your skipping-ropes."

She had evidently something special to say to me; and she had adopted the necessary measures for keeping the children in front of us, well out of hearing. Freddy led the way on his horse on three wheels; the girls followed, skipping merrily. Mrs. Fosdyke opened the business by the most embarrassing remark that she could possibly have made under the circumstances.

"I find that you are acquainted with Mr. Sax," she began; "and I am surprised to hear that you dislike him."

She smiled pleasantly, as if my supposed dislike of Mr. Sax rather amused her. What "the ruling passion" may be among men, I cannot presume to consider. My own sex, however, I may claim to understand. The ruling passion among women is Conceit. My ridiculous notion of my own consequence was wounded in some way. I assumed a position of the loftiest indifference.

"Really, ma'am," I said, "I can't undertake to answer for any impression that Mr. Sax may have formed. We met by the merest accident. I know nothing about him."

Mrs. Fosdyke eyed me slyly, and appeared to be more amused than ever.

"He is a very odd man," she admitted, "but I can tell you there is a fine nature under that strange surface of his. However," she went on, "I am forgetting that he forbids me to talk about him in your presence. When the opportunity offers, I shall take my own way of teaching you two to understand each other: you will both be grateful to me when I have succeeded. In the meantime, there is a third person who will be sadly disappointed to hear that you know nothing about Mr. Sax."

"May I ask, ma'am, who the person is?"

"Can you keep a secret, Miss Morris? Of course you can! The person is Miss Melbury."

(Miss Melbury was a dark woman. It cannot be because I am a fair woman myself—I hope I am above such narrow prejudices as that—but it is certainly true that I don't admire dark women.)

"She heard Mr. Sax telling me that you particularly disliked him," Mrs. Fosdyke proceeded. "And just as you appeared in the hall, she was asking me to find out what your reason was. My own opinion of Mr. Sax, I ought to tell you, doesn't satisfy her; I am his old friend, and I present him of course from my own favorable point of view. Miss Melbury is anxious to be made acquainted with his faults—and she expected you to be a valuable witness against him."

Thus far we had been walking on. We now stopped, as if by common consent, and looked at one another.

In my previous experience of Mrs. Fosdyke, I had only seen the more constrained and formal side of her character. Without being aware of my own success, I had won the mother's heart in winning the goodwill of her children. Constraint now seized its first opportunity of melting away; the latent sense of humor in the great lady showed itself, while I was inwardly wondering what the nature of Miss Melbury's extraordinary interest in Mr. Sax might be. Easily penetrating my thoughts, she satisfied my curiosity without committing herself to a reply in words. Her large gray eyes sparkled as they rested on my face, and she hummed the tune of the old French song, "C'est l'amour, l'amour, l'amour!" There is no disguising it—something in this disclosure made me excessively angry. Was I angry with Miss Melbury? or with Mr. Sax? or with myself? I think it must have been with myself.

Finding that I had nothing to say on my side, Mrs. Fosdyke looked at her watch, and remembered her domestic duties. To my relief, our interview came to an end.

"I have a dinner-party to-day," she said, "and I have not seen the housekeeper yet. Make yourself beautiful, Miss Morris, and join us in the drawing-room after dinner."

V.

I WORE my best dress; and, in all my life before, I never took such pains with my hair. Nobody will be foolish enough, I hope, to suppose that I did this on Mr. Sax's account. How could I possibly care about a man who was little better than a stranger to me? No! the person I dressed at was Miss Melbury.

She gave me a look, as I modestly placed myself in a corner, which amply rewarded me for the time spent on my toilet. The gentlemen came in. I looked at Mr. Sax (mere curiosity) under shelter of my fan. His appearance was greatly improved by evening dress. He discovered me in my corner, and seemed doubtful whether to approach me or not. I was reminded of our first odd meeting; and I could not help smiling as I called it to mind. Did he presume to think that I was encouraging him? Before I could decide that question, he took the vacant place on the sofa. In any other man—after what had passed in the morning—this would have been an audacious proceeding. He looked so painfully embarrassed, that it became a species of Christian duty to pity him.

"Won't you shake hands?" he said, just as he had said it at Sandwich.

I peeped round the corner of my fan at Miss Melbury. She was looking at us. I shook hands with Mr. Sax.

"What sort of sensation is it," he asked, "when you shake hands with a man whom you hate?"

"I really can't tell you," I answered innocently; "I have never done such a thing."

"You would not lunch with me at Sandwich," he protested; "and, after the humblest apology on my part, you won't forgive me for what I did this morning. Do you expect me to believe that I am not the special object of your antipathy? I wish I had never met with you! At my age, a man gets angry when he is treated cruelly and doesn't deserve it. You don't understand that, I dare say."

"Oh, yes, I do. I heard what you said about me to Mrs. Fosdyke, and I heard you bang the door when you got out of my way."

He received this reply with every appearance of satisfaction. "So you listened, did you? I'm glad to hear that."

"Why?"

"It shows you take some interest in me, after all."

Throughout this frivolous talk (I only venture to report it because it shows that I bore no malice on my side) Miss Melbury was looking at us like the basilisk of the ancients. She owned to being on the wrong side of thirty; and she had a little money—but these were surely no reasons why she should glare at a poor governess. Had some secret understanding of the tender sort been already established between Mr. Sax and herself? She provoked me into trying to find out—especially as the last words he had said offered me the opportunity.

"I can prove that I feel a sincere interest in you," I resumed. "I can resign you to a lady who has a far better claim to your attention than mine. You are neglecting her shamefully."

He stared at me with an appearance of bewilderment, which seemed to imply that the attachment was on the lady's side, so far. It was of course impossible to mention names; I merely turned my eyes in the right direction. He looked where I looked—and his shyness revealed itself, in spite of his resolution to conceal it. His face flushed; he looked mortified and surprised. Miss Melbury could endure it no longer. She rose, took a song from the music-stand, and approached us.

"I am going to sing," she said, handing the music to him. "Please turn over for me, Mr. Sax."

I think he hesitated—but I cannot feel sure that I observed him correctly. It matters little. With or without hesitation, he followed her to the piano.

Miss Melbury sang—with perfect self-possession, and an immense compass of voice. A gentleman near me said she ought to be on the stage. I thought so too. Big as it was, our drawing-room was not large enough for her. The gentleman sang next. No voice at all—but so sweet, such true feeling! I turned over the leaves for him. A dear old lady, sitting near the piano, entered into conversation with me. She spoke of the great singers at the beginning of the present century. Mr. Sax hovered about, with Miss Melbury's eye on him. I was so entranced by the anecdotes of my venerable friend, that I could take no notice of Mr. Sax. Later, when the dinner-party was over, and we were retiring for the night, he still hovered about, and ended in offering me a bedroom candle. I immediately handed it to Miss Melbury. Really a most enjoyable evening!

VI.

THE next morning we were startled by an extraordinary proceeding on the part of one of the guests. Mr. Sax had left Carsham Hall by the first train—nobody knew why.

Nature has laid—so, at least, philosophers say—some heavy burdens upon women. Do those learned persons include in their list the burden of hysterics? If so, I cordially agree with them. It is hardly worth speaking of in my case—a constitutional outbreak in the solitude of my own room, treated with eau-de-cologne and water, and quite forgotten afterward in the absorbing employment of education. My favorite pupil, Freddy, had been up earlier than the rest of us—breathing the morning air in the fruit-garden. He had seen Mr. Sax and had asked him when he was coming back again. And Mr. Sax had said, "I shall be back again next month." (Dear little Freddy!)

In the meanwhile we, in the schoolroom, had the prospect before us of a dull time in an empty house. The remaining guests were to go away at the end of the week, their hostess being engaged to pay a visit to some old friends in Scotland.

During the next three or four days, though I was often alone with Mrs. Fosdyke, she never said one word on the subject of Mr. Sax. Once or twice I caught her looking at me with that unendurably significant smile of hers. Miss Melbury was equally unpleasant in another way. When we accidentally met on the stairs, her black eyes shot at me passing glances of hatred and scorn. Did these two ladies presume to think—?

No; I abstained from completing that inquiry at the time, and I abstain from completing it here.

The end of the week came, and I and the children were left alone at Carsham Hall.

I took advantage of the leisure hours at my disposal to write to Sir Gervase; respectfully inquiring after his health, and informing him that I had been again most fortunate in my engagement as a governess. By return of post an answer arrived. I eagerly opened it. The first lines informed me of Sir Gervase Damian's death.

The letter dropped from my hand. I looked at my little enameled cross. It is not for me to say what I felt. Think of all that I owed to him; and remember how lonely my lot was in the world. I gave the children a holiday; it was only the truth to tell them that I was not well.

How long an interval passed before I could call to mind that I had only read the first lines of the letter, I am not able to say. When I did take it up I was surprised to see that the writing covered two pages. Beginning again where I had left off, my head, in a moment more, began to swim. A horrid fear overpowered me that I might not be in my right mind, after I had read the first three sentences. Here they are, to answer for me that I exaggerate nothing:—

"The will of our deceased client is not yet proved. But, with the sanction of the executors, I inform you confidentially that you are the person chiefly interested in it. Sir Gervase Damian bequeaths to you, absolutely, the whole of his personal property, amounting to the sum of seventy thousand pounds."

If the letter had ended there, I really cannot imagine what extravagances

430

I might not have committed. But the writer (head partner in the firm of Sir Gervase's lawyers) had something more to say on his own behalf. The manner in which he said it strung up my nerves in an instant. I can not, and will not, copy the words here. It is quite revolting enough to give the substance of them.

The man's object was evidently to let me perceive that he disapproved of the will. So far I do not complain of him—he had, no doubt, good reason for the view he took. But, in expressing his surprise "at this extraordinary proof of the testator's interest in a perfect stranger to the family," he hinted his suspicion of an influence, on my part, exercised over Sir Gervase, so utterly shameful, that I cannot dwell on the subject. The language, I should add, was cunningly guarded. Even I could see that it would bear more than one interpretation, and would thus put me in the wrong if I openly resented it. But the meaning was plain; and part at least of the motive came out in the following sentences:

"The present Sir Gervase, as you are doubtless aware, is not seriously affected by his father's will. He is already more liberally provided for, as heir under the entail to the whole of the landed property. But, to say nothing of old friends who are forgotten, there is a surviving relative of the late Sir Gervase passed over, who is nearly akin to him by blood. In the event of this person disputing the will, you will of course hear from us again, and refer us to your legal adviser."

The letter ended with an apology for delay in writing to me, caused by difficulty in discovering my address.

And what did I do?—Write to the rector, or to Mrs. Fosdyke, for advice? Not I!

At first I was too indignant to be able to think of what I ought to do. Our post-time was late, and my head ached as if it would burst into pieces. I had plenty of leisure to rest and compose myself. When I got cool again, I felt able to take my own part, without asking any one to help me.

Even if I had been treated kindly, I should certainly not have taken the money when there was a relative living with a claim to it. What did I want with a large fortune! To buy a husband with it, perhaps? No, no! from all that I have heard, the great Lord Chancellor was quite right when he said that a woman with money at her own disposal was "either kissed out of it or kicked out of it, six weeks after her marriage." The one difficulty before me was not to give up my legacy, but to express my reply with sufficient severity, and at the same time with due regard to my own self-respect. Here is what I wrote:

"SIR—I will not trouble you by attempting to express my sorrow on hearing of Sir Gervase Damian's death. You would probably form your own opinion on that subject also; and I have no wish to be judged by your unenviable experience of humanity for the second time.

"With regard to the legacy, feeling the sincerest gratitude to my generous benefactor, I nevertheless refuse to receive the money.

"Be pleased to send me the necessary document to sign, for transferring my fortune to that relative of Sir Gervase mentioned in your letter. The one condition on which I insist is, that no expression of thanks shall be addressed to me by the person in whose favor I resign the money. I do not desire (even supposing that justice is done to my motives on this occasion) to be made the object of expressions of gratitude for only doing my duty."

So it ended. I may be wrong, but I call that strong writing.

In due course of post a formal acknowledgment arrived. I was requested to wait for the document until the will had been proved, and was informed that my name should be kept strictly secret in the interval. On this occasion the executors were almost as insolent as the lawyer. They felt it their duty to give me time to reconsider a decision which had been evidently formed on impulse. Ah, how hard men are—at least, some of them! I locked up the acknowledgment in disgust, resolved to think no more of it until the time came for getting rid of my legacy. I kissed poor Sir Gervase's little keepsake. While I was still looking at it, the good children came in, of their own accord, to ask how I was. I was obliged to draw down the blind in my room, or they would have seen the tears in my eyes. For the first time since my mother's death, I felt the heartache. Perhaps the children made me think of the happier time when I was a child myself.

VII.

THE will had been proved, and I was informed that the document was in course of preparation when Mrs. Fosdyke returned from her visit to Scotland.

She thought me looking pale and worn.

"The time seems to me to have come," she said, "when I had better make you and Mr. Sax understand each other. Have you been thinking penitently of your own bad behavior?"

I felt myself blushing. I had been thinking of my conduct to Mr. Sax—and I was heartily ashamed of it, too.

Mrs. Fosdyke went on, half in jest, half in earnest. "Consult your own sense of propriety!" she said. "Was the poor man to blame for not being rude enough to say No, when a lady asked him to turn over her music? Could he help it, if the same lady persisted in flirting with him? He ran away from her the next morning. Did you deserve to be told why he left us? Certainly not—after the vixenish manner in which you handed the bedroom candle to Miss Melbury. You foolish girl! Do you think I couldn't see that you were in love with him? Thank Heaven, he's too poor to marry you, and take you away from my children, for some time to come. There will be a long marriage engagement, even if he is magnanimous enough to forgive you. Shall I ask Miss Melbury to come back with him?"

She took pity on me at last, and sat down to write to Mr. Sax. His reply, dated from a country house some twenty miles distant, announced that he would be at Carsham Hall in three days' time.

On that third day the legal paper that I was to sign arrived by post. It was Sunday morning; I was alone in the schoolroom.

In writing to me, the lawyer had only alluded to "a surviving relative of Sir Gervase, nearly akin to him by blood." The document was more explicit. It described the relative as being a nephew of Sir Gervase, the son of his sister. The name followed.

It was Sextus Cyril Sax.

I have tried on three different sheets of paper to describe the effect which this discovery produced on me—and I have torn them up one after another. When I only think of it, my mind seems to fall back into the helpless surprise and confusion of that time. After all that had passed between us—the man himself being then on his way to the house! what would he think of me when he saw my name at the bottom of the document? what, in Heaven's name, was I to do?

How long I sat petrified, with the document on my lap, I never knew. Somebody knocked at the schoolroom door, and looked in and said something, and went out again. Then there was an interval. Then the door was opened again. A hand was laid kindly on my shoulder. I looked up—and there was Mrs. Fosdyke, asking, in the greatest alarm, what was the matter with me.

The tone of her voice roused me into speaking. I could think of nothing but Mr. Sax; I could only say, "Has he come?"

"Yes—and waiting to see you."

Answering in those terms, she glanced at the paper in my lap. In the extremity of my helplessness, I acted like a sensible creature at last. I told Mrs. Fosdyke all that I have told here.

She neither moved nor spoke until I had done. Her first proceeding, after that, was to take me in her arms and give me a kiss. Having so far encouraged me, she next spoke of poor Sir Gervase.

"We all acted like fools," she announced, "in needlessly offending him by protesting against his second marriage. I don't mean you—I mean his son, his nephew, and myself. If his second marriage made him happy, what business had we with the disparity of years between husband and wife? I can tell you this, Sextus was the first of us to regret what he had done. But for his stupid fear of being suspected of an interested motive, Sir Gervase might have known there was that much good in his sister's son."

She snatched up a copy of the will, which I had not even noticed thus far.

"See what the kind old man says of you," she went on, pointing to the words. I could not see them; she was obliged to read them for me. "I leave my money to the one person living who has been more than worthy of the little I have done for her, and whose simple unselfish nature I know that I can trust."

I pressed Mrs. Fosdyke's hand; I was not able to speak. She took up the legal paper next.

"Do justice to yourself, and be above contemptible scruples," she said. "Sextus is fond enough of you to be almost worthy of the sacrifice that you are making. Sign—and I will sign next as the witness."

I hesitated.

"What will he think of me?" I said.

"Sign!" she repeated, "and we will see to that."

I obeyed. She asked for the lawyer's letter. I gave it to her, with the lines which contained the man's vile insinuation folded down, so that only the words above were visible, which proved that I had renounced my legacy, not even knowing whether the person to be benefited was a man or a woman. She took this, with the rough draft of my own letter, and the signed renunciation—and opened the door.

"Pray come back, and tell me about it!" I pleaded.

She smiled, nodded, and went out.

Oh, what a long time passed before I heard the long-expected knock at the door! "Come in," I cried impatiently.

Mrs. Fosdyke had deceived me. Mr. Sax had returned in her place. He closed the door. We two were alone.

He was deadly pale; his eyes, as they rested on me, had a wild startled look. With icy cold fingers he took my hand, and lifted it in silence to his lips. The sight of his agitation encouraged me—I don't to this day know why, unless it appealed in some way to my compassion. I was bold enough to look at him. Still silent, he placed the letters on the table—and then he laid the signed paper beside them. When I saw that, I was bolder still. I spoke first.

"Surely you don't refuse me?" I said.

He answered, "I thank you with my whole heart; I admire you more than words can say. But I can't take it."

"Why not?"

"The fortune is yours," he said gently. "Remember how poor I am, and feel for me if I say no more."

His head sank on his breast. He stretched out one hand, silently imploring me to understand him. I could endure it no longer. I forgot every consideration which a woman, in my position, ought to have remembered. Out came the desperate words, before I could stop them.

"You won't take my gift by itself?" I said.

"No."

"Will you take Me with it?"

That evening, Mrs. Fosdyke indulged her sly sense of humor in a new way. She handed me an almanac.

"After all, my dear," she remarked, "you needn't be ashamed of having spoken first. You have only used the ancient privilege of the sex. This is Leap Year."

436

MR. COSWAY AND THE LANDLADY.

I.

THE guests would have enjoyed their visit to Sir Peter's country house—but for Mr. Cosway. And to make matters worse, it was not Mr. Cosway but the guests who were to blame. They repeated the old story of Adam and Eve, on a larger scale. The women were the first sinners; and the men were demoralized by the women.

Mr. Cosway's bitterest enemy could not have denied that he was a handsome, well-bred, unassuming man. No mystery of any sort attached to him. He had adopted the Navy as a profession—had grown weary of it after a few years' service—and now lived on the moderate income left to him, after the death of his parents. Out of this unpromising material the lively imaginations of the women built up a romance. The men only noticed that Mr. Cosway was rather silent and thoughtful; that he was not ready with his laugh; and that he had a fancy for taking long walks by himself. Harmless peculiarities, surely? And yet, they excited the curiosity of the women as signs of a mystery in Mr. Cosway's past life, in which some beloved object unknown must have played a chief part.

As a matter of course, the influence of the sex was tried, under every indirect and delicate form of approach, to induce Mr. Cosway to open his heart, and tell the tale of his sorrows. With perfect courtesy, he baffled curiosity, and kept his supposed secret to himself. The most beautiful girl in the house was ready to offer herself and her fortune as consolations, if this impenetrable bachelor would only have taken her into his confidence. He smiled sadly, and changed the subject.

Defeated so far, the women accepted the next alternative.

One of the guests staying in the house was Mr. Cosway's intimate friend—formerly his brother-officer on board ship. This gentleman was now subjected to the delicately directed system of investigation which had failed with his friend. With unruffled composure he referred the ladies, one after another, to Mr. Cosway. His name was Stone. The ladies decided that his nature was worthy of his name.

The last resource left to our fair friends was to rouse the dormant interest of the men, and to trust to the confidential intercourse of the smoking-room for the enlightenment which they had failed to obtain by other means.

In the accomplishment of this purpose, the degree of success which rewarded their efforts was due to a favoring state of affairs in the house. The shooting was not good for much; the billiard-table was under repair; and there were but two really skilled whist-players among the guests. In the atmosphere of dullness thus engendered, the men not only caught the infection of the women's curiosity, but were even ready to listen to the gossip of the servants' hall, repeated to their mistresses by the ladies' maids. The result of such an essentially debased state of feeling as this was not slow in declaring itself. But for a lucky accident, Mr. Cosway would have discovered to what extremities of ill-bred curiosity idleness and folly can lead persons holding the position of ladies and gentlemen, when he joined the company at breakfast on the next morning.

The newspapers came in before the guests had risen from the table. Sir Peter handed one of them to the lady who sat on his right hand.

She first looked, it is needless to say, at the list of births, deaths, and marriages; and then she turned to the general news—the fires, accidents, fashionable departures, and so on. In a few minutes, she indignantly dropped the newspaper in her lap.

"Here is another unfortunate man," she exclaimed, "sacrificed to the stupidity of women! If I had been in his place, I would have used my knowledge of swimming to save myself, and would have left the women to go to the bottom of the river as they deserved!"

"A boat accident, I suppose?" said Sir Peter.

"Oh yes—the old story. A gentleman takes two ladies out in a boat. After a while they get fidgety, and feel an idiotic impulse to change places. The boat upsets as usual; the poor dear man tries to save them—and is drowned along with them for his pains. Shameful! shameful!"

"Are the names mentioned?"

"Yes. They are all strangers to me; I speak on principle." Asserting herself in those words, the indignant lady handed the newspaper to Mr. Cosway, who happened to sit next to her. "When you were in the navy," she continued, "I dare say your life was put in jeopardy by taking women in boats. Read it yourself, and let it be a warning to you for the future."

Mr. Cosway looked at the narrative of the accident—and revealed the romantic mystery of his life by a burst of devout exclamation, expressed in the words:

"Thank God, my wife's drowned!"

II.

To declare that Sir Peter and his guests were all struck speechless, by discovering in this way that Mr. Cosway was a married man, is to say very little. The general impression appeared to be that he was mad. His neighbors at the table all drew back from him, with the one exception of his friend. Mr. Stone looked at the newspaper: pressed Mr. Cosway's hand in silent sympathy—and addressed himself to his host.

"Permit me to make my friend's apologies," he said, "until he is composed enough to act for himself. The circumstances are so extraordinary that I venture to think they excuse him. Will you allow us to speak to you privately?"

Sir Peter, with more apologies addressed to his visitors, opened the door which communicated with his study. Mr. Stone took Mr. Cosway's arm, and led him out of the room. He noticed no one, spoke to no one—he moved mechanically, like a man walking in his sleep.

After an unendurable interval of nearly an hour's duration, Sir Peter returned alone to the breakfast-room. Mr. Cosway and Mr. Stone had already taken their departure for London, with their host's entire approval.

"It is left to my discretion," Sir Peter proceeded, "to repeat to you what I have heard in my study. I will do so, on one condition—that you all consider yourselves bound in honor not to mention the true names and the real places, when you tell the story to others."

Subject to this wise reservation, the narrative is here repeated by one of the company. Considering how he may perform his task to the best advantage, he finds that the events which preceded and followed Mr. Cosway's disastrous marriage resolve themselves into certain well-marked divisions. Adopting this arrangement, he proceeds to relate:

The First Epoch in Mr. Cosway's Life.

The sailing of her Majesty's ship Albicore was deferred by the severe illness of the captain. A gentleman not possessed of political influence might, after the doctor's unpromising report of him, have been superseded by another commanding officer. In the present case, the Lords of the Admiralty showed themselves to be models of patience and sympathy. They kept the vessel in port, waiting the captain's recovery.

Among the unimportant junior officers, not wanted on board under these circumstances, and favored accordingly by obtaining leave to wait for orders on shore, were two young men, aged respectively twenty-two and twenty-three years, and known by the names of Cosway and Stone. The scene which now introduces them opens at a famous seaport on the south coast of England, and discloses the two young gentlemen at dinner in a private room at their inn.

"I think that last bottle of champagne was corked," Cosway remarked. "Let's try another. You're nearest the bell, Stone. Ring."

Stone rang, under protest. He was the elder of the two by a year, and he set an example of discretion.

"I am afraid we are running up a terrible bill," he said. "We have been here more than three weeks—"

"And we have denied ourselves nothing," Cosway added. "We have lived like princes. Another bottle of champagne, waiter. We have our riding-horses, and our carriage, and the best box at the theater, and such cigars as London itself could not produce. I call that making the most of life. Try the new bottle. Glorious drink, isn't it? Why doesn't my father have champagne at the family dinner-table?"

"Is your father a rich man, Cosway?"

"I should say not. He didn't give me anything like the money I expected, when I said good-by—and I rather think he warned me solemnly, at parting, to take the greatest care of it.' There's not a farthing more for you,' he said, 'till your ship returns from her South American station.' Your father is a clergyman, Stone."

"Well, and what of that?"

"And some clergymen are rich."

"My father is not one of them, Cosway."

"Then let us say no more about him. Help yourself, and pass the bottle."

Instead of adopting this suggestion, Stone rose with a very grave face, and once more rang the bell. "Ask the landlady to step up," he said, when the waiter appeared.

"What do you want with the landlady?" Cosway inquired.

"I want the bill."

The landlady—otherwise Mrs. Pounce—entered the room. She was short, and old, and fat, and painted, and a widow. Students of character, as revealed in the face, would have discovered malice and cunning in her bright black eyes, and a bitter vindictive temper in the lines about her thin red lips. Incapable of such subtleties of analysis as these, the two young officers differed widely, nevertheless, in their opinions of Mrs. Pounce. Cosway's reckless sense of humor delighted in pretending to be in love with her. Stone took a dislike to her from the first. When his friend asked for the reason, he made a strangely obscure answer. "Do you remember that morning in the wood when you killed the snake?" he said. "I took a dislike to the snake." Cosway made no further inquiries.

"Well, my young heroes," said Mrs. Pounce (always loud, always cheerful, and always familiar with her guests), "what do you want with me now?"

"Take a glass of champagne, my darling," said Cosway; "and let me try if I can get my arm round your waist. That's all I want with you."

The landlady passed this over without notice. Though she had spoken to both of them, her cunning little eyes rested on Stone from the moment when she appeared in the room. She knew by instinct the man who disliked her—and she waited deliberately for Stone to reply.

"We have been here some time," he said, "and we shall be obliged, ma'am, if you will let us have our bill."

Mrs. Pounce lifted her eyebrows with an expression of innocent surprise.

"Has the captain got well, and must you go on board to-night?" she asked.

"Nothing of the sort!" Cosway interposed. "We have no news of the captain, and we are going to the theater to-night."

"But," persisted Stone, "we want, if you please, to have the bill."

"Certainly, sir," said Mrs. Pounce, with a sudden assumption of respect. "But we are very busy downstairs, and we hope you will not press us for it to-night?"

"Of course not!" cried Cosway.

Mrs. Pounce instantly left the room, without waiting for any further remark from Cosway's friend.

"I wish we had gone to some other house," said Stone. "You mark my words—that woman means to cheat us."

Cosway expressed his dissent from this opinion in the most amiable

442

manner. He filled his friend's glass, and begged him not to say ill-natured things of Mrs. Pounce.

But Stone's usually smooth temper seemed to be ruffled; he insisted on his own view. "She's impudent and inquisitive, if she is not downright dishonest," he said. "What right had she to ask you where we lived when we were at home; and what our Christian names were; and which of us was oldest, you or I? Oh, yes—it's all very well to say she only showed a flattering interest in us! I suppose she showed a flattering interest in my affairs, when I awoke a little earlier than usual, and caught her in my bedroom with my pocketbook in her hand. Do you believe she was going to lock it up for safety's sake? She knows how much money we have got as well as we know it ourselves. Every half-penny we have will be in her pocket tomorrow. And a good thing, too—we shall be obliged to leave the house."

Even this cogent reasoning failed in provoking Cosway to reply. He took Stone's hat, and handed it with the utmost politeness to his foreboding friend. "There's only one remedy for such a state of mind as yours," he said. "Come to the theater."

At ten o'clock the next morning Cosway found himself alone at the breakfast-table. He was informed that Mr. Stone had gone out for a little walk, and would be back directly. Seating himself at the table, he perceived an envelope on his plate, which evidently inclosed the bill. He took up the envelope, considered a little, and put it back again unopened. At the same moment Stone burst into the room in a high state of excitement.

"News that will astonish you!" he cried. "The captain arrived yesterday evening. His doctors say that the sea-voyage will complete his recovery. The ship sails to-day—and we are ordered to report ourselves on board in an hour's time. Where's the bill?"

Cosway pointed to it. Stone took it out of the envelope.

It covered two sides of a prodigiously long sheet of paper. The sum total was brightly decorated with lines in red ink. Stone looked at the total, and passed it in silence to Cosway. For once, even Cosway was prostrated.

In dreadful stillness the two young men produced their pocketbooks; added up their joint stores of money, and compared the result with the bill. Their united resources amounted to a little more than one-third of their debt to the landlady of the inn.

The only alternative that presented itself was to send for Mrs. Pounce; to state the circumstances plainly; and to propose a compromise on the grand commercial basis of credit.

Mrs. Pounce presented herself superbly dressed in walking costume. Was she going out; or had she just returned to the inn? Not a word escaped her; she waited gravely to hear what the gentlemen wanted. Cosway, presuming on his position as favorite, produced the contents of the two pocketbooks and revealed the melancholy truth.

"There is all the money we have," he concluded. "We hope you will not object to receive the balance in a bill at three months."

Mrs. Pounce answered with a stern composure of voice and manner entirely new in the experience of Cosway and Stone.

"I have paid ready money, gentlemen, for the hire of your horses and carriages," she said; "here are the receipts from the livery stables to vouch for me; I never accept bills unless I am quite sure beforehand that they will be honored. I defy you to find an overcharge in the account now rendered; and I expect you to pay it before you leave my house."

Stone looked at his watch.

"In three-quarters of an hour," he said, "we must be on board."

Mrs. Pounce entirely agreed with him. "And if you are not on board," she remarked, "you will be tried by court-martial, and dismissed the service with your characters ruined for life."

"My dear creature, we haven't time to send home, and we know nobody in the town," pleaded Cosway. "For God's sake take our watches and jewelry, and our luggage—and let us go."

"I am not a pawnbroker," said the inflexible lady. "You must either pay your lawful debt to me in honest money, or—"

She paused and looked at Cosway. Her fat face brightened—she smiled graciously for the first time.

Cosway stared at her in unconcealed perplexity. He helplessly repeated her last words. "We must either pay the bill," he said, "or what?"

"Or," answered Mrs. Pounce, "one of you must marry ME."

Was she joking? Was she intoxicated? Was she out of her senses? Neither of the three; she was in perfect possession of herself; her explanation was a model of lucid and convincing arrangement of facts.

"My position here has its drawbacks," she began. "I am a lone widow; I am known to have an excellent business, and to have saved money. The result is that I am pestered to death by a set of needy vagabonds who want to marry me. In this position, I am exposed to slanders and insults. Even if I didn't know that the men were after my money, there is not one of them whom I would venture to marry. He might turn out a tyrant and beat me; or a drunkard, and disgrace me; or a betting man, and ruin me. What I want, you see, for my own peace and protection, is to be able to declare myself married, and to produce the proof in the shape of a certificate. A born gentleman, with a character to lose, and so much younger in years than myself that he wouldn't think of living with me—there is the sort of husband who suits my book! I'm a reasonable woman, gentlemen. I would undertake to part with my husband at the church door—never to attempt to see him or write to him afterward—and only to show my certificate when necessary, without giving any explanations. Your secret would be quite safe in my keeping. I don't care a straw for either of you, so long as you answer my purpose. What do you say to paying my bill (one or the other of you) in this way? I am ready dressed for the altar; and the clergyman has notice at the church. My preference is for Mr. Cosway," proceeded this terrible woman with the cruelest irony, "because he has been so particular in his attentions toward me. The license (which I provided on the chance a fortnight since) is made out in his name. Such is my weakness for Mr. Cosway. But that don't matter if Mr. Stone would like to take his place. He can hail by his friend's name. Oh, yes, he can! I have consulted my lawyer. So long as the bride and bridegroom agree to it, they may be married in any name they like, and it stands good. Look at your watch again, Mr. Stone. The church is in the next street. By my calculation, you have just got five minutes to decide. I'm a punctual woman, my little dears; and I will be back to the moment."

She opened the door, paused, and returned to the room.

"I ought to have mentioned," she resumed, "that I shall make you a present of the bill, receipted, on the conclusion of the ceremony. You will be taken to the ship in my own boat, with all your money in your pockets, and a hamper of good things for the mess. After that I wash my hands of you. You may go to the devil your own way."

With this parting benediction, she left them.

Caught in the landlady's trap, the two victims looked at each other in expressive silence. Without time enough to take legal advice; without friends on shore; without any claim on officers of their own standing in the ship, the prospect before them was literally limited to Marriage or Ruin. Stone made a proposal worthy of a hero.

"One of us must marry her," he said; "I'm ready to toss up for it."

Cosway matched him in generosity. "No," he answered. "It was I who brought you here; and I who led you into these infernal expenses. I ought to pay the penalty—and I will."

Before Stone could remonstrate, the five minutes expired. Punctual Mrs. Pounce appeared again in the doorway.

"Well?" she inquired, "which is it to be—Cosway, or Stone?"

Cosway advanced as reckless as ever, and offered his arm.

"Now then, Fatsides," he said, "come and be married!"

In five-and-twenty minutes more, Mrs. Pounce had become Mrs. Cosway; and the two officers were on their way to the ship.

The Second Epoch in Mr. Cosway's Life.

Four years elapsed before the Albicore returned to the port from which she had sailed.

In that interval, the death of Cosway's parents had taken place. The lawyer who had managed his affairs, during his absence from England, wrote to inform him that his inheritance from his late father's "estate" was eight hundred a year. His mother only possessed a life interest in her fortune; she had left her jewels to her son, and that was all.

Cosway's experience of the life of a naval officer on foreign stations (without political influence to hasten his promotion) had thoroughly disappointed him. He decided on retiring from the service when the ship was "paid off." In the meantime, to the astonishment of his comrades, he seemed to be in no hurry to make use of the leave granted him to go on shore. The faithful Stone was the only man on board who knew that he was afraid of meeting his "wife." This good friend volunteered to go to the inn, and make the necessary investigation with all needful prudence. "Four years is a long time, at her age," he said. "Many things may happen in four years."

An hour later, Stone returned to the ship, and sent a written message on board, addressed to his brother-officer, in these words: "Pack up your things at once, and join me on shore."

"What news?" asked the anxious husband.

Stone looked significantly at the idlers on the landing-place. "Wait," he said, "till we are by ourselves."

"Where are we going?"

"To the railway station."

They got into an empty carriage; and Stone at once relieved his friend of all further suspense.

"Nobody is acquainted with the secret of your marriage, but our two selves," he began quietly. "I don't think, Cosway, you need go into mourning."

"You don't mean to say she's dead!"

"I have seen a letter (written by her own lawyer) which announces her death," Stone replied. "It was so short that I believe I can repeat it word for word: 'Dear Sir—I have received information of the death of my client. Please address your next and last payment, on account of the lease and goodwill of the inn, to the executors of the late Mrs. Cosway.' There, that is the letter. 'Dear Sir' means the present proprietor of the inn. He told me your wife's previous history in two words. After carrying on the business with her customary intelligence for more than three years, her health failed, and she went to London to consult a physician. There she remained under the doctor's care. The next event was the appearance of an agent, instructed to sell the business in consequence of the landlady's declining health. Add the death at a later time—and there is the beginning and the end of the story. Fortune owed you a good turn, Cosway—and Fortune has paid the debt. Accept my best congratulations."

Arrived in London, Stone went on at once to his relations in the North. Cosway proceeded to the office of the family lawyer (Mr. Atherton), who had taken care of his interests in his absence. His father and Mr. Atherton had been schoolfellows and old friends. He was affectionately received, and was invited to pay a visit the next day to the lawyer's villa at Richmond.

"You will be near enough to London to attend to your business at the Admiralty," said Mr. Atherton, "and you will meet a visitor at my house, who is one of the most charming girls in England—the only daughter of the great Mr. Restall. Good heavens! have you never heard of him? My dear sir, he's one of the partners in the famous firm of Benshaw, Restall, and Benshaw."

Cosway was wise enough to accept this last piece of information as quite conclusive. The next day, Mrs. Atherton presented him to the charming Miss Restall; and Mrs. Atherton's young married daughter (who had been his playfellow when they were children) whispered to him, half in jest, half in earnest: "Make the best use of your time; she isn't engaged yet."

Cosway shuddered inwardly at the bare idea of a second marriage. Was Miss Restall the sort of woman to restore his confidence?

She was small and slim and dark—a graceful, well-bred, brightly

448

intelligent person, with a voice exquisitely sweet and winning in tone. Her ears, hands, and feet were objects to worship; and she had an attraction, irresistibly rare among the women of the present time—the attraction of a perfectly natural smile. Before Cosway had been an hour in the house, she discovered that his long term of service on foreign stations had furnished him with subjects of conversation which favorably contrasted with the commonplace gossip addressed to her by other men. Cosway at once became a favorite, as Othello became a favorite in his day.

The ladies of the household all rejoiced in the young officer's success, with the exception of Miss Restall's companion (supposed to hold the place of her lost mother, at a large salary), one Mrs. Margery.

Too cautious to commit herself in words, this lady expressed doubt and disapprobation by her looks. She had white hair, iron-gray eyebrows, and protuberant eyes; her looks were unusually expressive. One evening, she caught poor Mr. Atherton alone, and consulted him confidentially on the subject of Mr. Cosway's income. This was the first warning which opened the eyes of the good lawyer to the nature of the "friendship" already established between his two guests. He knew Miss Restall's illustrious father well, and he feared that it might soon be his disagreeable duty to bring Cosway's visit to an end.

On a certain Saturday afternoon, while Mr. Atherton was still considering how he could most kindly and delicately suggest to Cosway that it was time to say good-by, an empty carriage arrived at the villa. A note from Mr. Restall was delivered to Mrs. Atherton, thanking her with perfect politeness for her kindness to his daughter. "Circumstances," he added, "rendered it necessary that Miss Restall should return home that afternoon."

The "circumstances" were supposed to refer to a garden-party to be given by Mr. Restall in the ensuing week. But why was his daughter wanted at home before the day of the party?

The ladies of the family, still devoted to Cosway's interests, entertained no doubt that Mrs. Margery had privately communicated with Mr. Restall, and that the appearance of the carriage was the natural result. Mrs. Atherton's married daughter did all that could be done: she got rid of Mrs. Margery for one minute, and so arranged it that Cosway and Miss Restall took leave of each other in her own sitting-room.

When the young lady appeared in the hall she had drawn her veil down. Cosway escaped to the road and saw the last of the carriage as it drove away. In a little more than a fortnight his horror of a second marriage had become one of the dead and buried emotions of his nature. He stayed at the villa until Monday morning, as an act of gratitude to his good friends, and then accompanied Mr. Atherton to London. Business at the Admiralty was the excuse. It imposed on nobody. He was evidently on his way to Miss Restall.

"Leave your business in my hands," said the lawyer, on the journey to town, "and go and amuse yourself on the Continent. I can't blame you for falling in love with Miss Restall; I ought to have foreseen the danger, and waited till she had left us before I invited you to my house. But I may at least warn you to carry the matter no further. If you had eight thousand instead of eight hundred a year, Mr. Restall would think it an act of presumption on your part to aspire to his daughter's hand, unless you had a title to throw into the bargain. Look at it in the true light, my dear boy; and one of these days you will thank me for speaking plainly."

Cosway promised to "look at it in the true light."

The result, from his point of view, led him into a change of residence. He left his hotel and took a lodging in the nearest bystreet to Mr. Restall's palace at Kensington.

On the same evening he applied (with the confidence due to a previous arrangement) for a letter at the neighboring post-office, addressed to E. C.—the initials of Edwin Cosway. "Pray be careful," Miss Restall wrote; "I have tried to get you a card for our garden party. But that hateful creature, Margery, has evidently spoken to my father; I am not trusted with any invitation cards. Bear it patiently, dear, as I do, and let me hear if you have succeeded in finding a lodging near us."

Not submitting to this first disappointment very patiently, Cosway sent his reply to the post-office, addressed to A. R.—the initials of Adela Restall. The next day the impatient lover applied for another letter. It was waiting for him, but it was not directed in Adela's handwriting. Had their correspondence been discovered? He opened the letter in the street; and read, with amazement, these lines:

"Dear Mr. Cosway, my heart sympathizes with two faithful lovers, in spite of my age and my duty. I inclose an invitation to the party tomorrow. Pray don't betray me, and don't pay too marked attention to Adela. Discretion is easy. There will be twelve hundred guests. Your friend, in spite of appearances, Louisa Margery."

How infamously they had all misjudged this excellent woman! Cosway went to the party a grateful, as well as a happy man. The first persons known to him, whom he discovered among the crowd of strangers, were the Athertons. They looked, as well they might, astonished to see him. Fidelity to Mrs. Margery forbade him to enter into any explanations. Where was that best and truest friend? With some difficulty he succeeded in finding her. Was there any impropriety in seizing her hand and cordially pressing it? The result of this expression of gratitude was, to say the least of it, perplexing.

Mrs. Margery behaved like the Athertons! She looked astonished to see him and she put precisely the same question: "How did you get here?" Cosway could only conclude that she was joking. "Who should know that, dear lady, better than yourself?" he rejoined. "I don't understand you," Mrs. Margery answered, sharply. After a moment's reflection, Cosway hit on another solution of the mystery. Visitors were near them; and Mrs. Margery had made her own private use of one of Mr. Restall's invitation cards. She might have serious reasons for pushing caution to its last extreme. Cosway looked at her significantly. "The least I can do is not to be indiscreet," he whispered—and left her.

He turned into a side walk; and there he met Adela at last!

It seemed like a fatality. She looked astonished; and she said: "How did you get here?" No intrusive visitors were within hearing, this time. "My dear!" Cosway remonstrated, "Mrs. Margery must have told you, when she sent me my invitation." Adela turned pale. "Mrs. Margery?" she repeated. "Mrs. Margery has said nothing to me; Mrs. Margery detests you. We must have this cleared up. No; not now—I must attend to our guests. Expect a letter; and, for heaven's sake, Edwin, keep out of my father's way. One of our visitors whom he particularly wished to see has sent an excuse—and he is dreadfully angry about it."

She left him before Cosway could explain that he and Mr. Restall had thus far never seen each other.

He wandered away toward the extremity of the grounds, troubled by vague suspicions; hurt at Adela's cold reception of him. Entering a shrubbery, which seemed intended to screen the grounds, at this point, from a lane outside, he suddenly discovered a pretty little summer-house among the trees. A stout gentleman, of mature years, was seated alone in this retreat. He looked up with a frown. Cosway apologized for disturbing him, and entered into conversation as an act of politeness.

"A brilliant assembly to-day, sir."

The stout gentleman replied by an inarticulate sound—something between a grunt and a cough.

"And a splendid house and grounds," Cosway continued.

The stout gentleman repeated the inarticulate sound.

Cosway began to feel amused. Was this curious old man deaf and dumb?

"Excuse my entering into conversation," he persisted. "I feel like a stranger here. There are so many people whom I don't know."

The stout gentleman suddenly burst into speech. Cosway had touched a sympathetic fiber at last.

"There are a good many people here whom I don't know," he said, gruffly. "You are one of them. What's your name?"

"My name is Cosway, sir. What's yours?"

The stout gentleman rose with fury in his looks. He burst out with an oath; and added the in tolerable question, already three times repeated by others: "How did you get here?" The tone was even more offensive than the oath. "Your age protects you, sir," said Cosway, with the loftiest composure. "I'm sorry I gave my name to so rude a person."

"Rude?" shouted the old gentleman. "You want my name in return, I suppose? You young puppy, you shall have it! My name is Restall."

He turned his back and walked off. Cosway took the only course now open to him. He returned to his lodgings.

The next day no letter reached him from Adela. He went to the postoffice. No letter was there. The day wore on to evening—and, with the evening, there appeared a woman who was a stranger to him. She looked like a servant; and she was the bearer of a mysterious message.

"Please be at the garden-door that opens on the lane, at ten o'clock to-morrow morning. Knock three times at the door—and then say 'Adela.' Some one who wishes you well will be alone in the shrubbery, and will let you in. No, sir! I am not to take anything; and I am not to say a word more." She spoke—and vanished.

Cosway was punctual to his appointment. He knocked three times; he pronounced Miss Restall's Christian name. Nothing happened. He waited a while, and tried again. This time Adela's voice answered strangely from the shrubbery in tones of surprise: "Edwin, is it really you?"

"Did you expect any one else?" Cosway asked. "My darling, your message said ten o'clock—and here I am."

The door was suddenly unlocked.

"I sent no message," said Adela, as they confronted each other on the threshold.

In the silence of utter bewilderment they went together into the summer-house. At Adela's request, Cosway repeated the message that he had received, and described the woman who had delivered it. The description applied to no person known to Miss Restall. "Mrs. Margery never sent you the invitation;

and I repeat, I never sent you the message. This meeting has been arranged by some one who knows that I always walk in the shrubbery after breakfast. There is some underhand work going on—"

Still mentally in search of the enemy who had betrayed them, she checked herself, and considered a little. "Is it possible—?" she began, and paused again. Her eyes filled with tears. "My mind is so completely upset," she said, "that I can't think clearly of anything. Oh, Edwin, we have had a happy dream, and it has come to an end. My father knows more than we think for. Some friends of ours are going abroad tomorrow—and I am to go with them. Nothing I can say has the least effect upon my father. He means to part us forever—and this is his cruel way of doing it!"

She put her arm round Cosway's neck and lovingly laid her head on his shoulder. With tenderest kisses they reiterated their vows of eternal fidelity until their voices faltered and failed them. Cosway filled up the pause by the only useful suggestion which it was now in his power to make—he proposed an elopement.

Adela received this bold solution of the difficulty in which they were placed exactly as thousands of other young ladies have received similar proposals before her time, and after.

She first said positively No. Cosway persisted. She began to cry, and asked if he had no respect for her. Cosway declared that his respect was equal to any sacrifice except the sacrifice of parting with her forever. He could, and would, if she preferred it, die for her, but while he was alive he must refuse to give her up. Upon this she shifted her ground. Did he expect her to go away with him alone? Certainly not. Her maid could go with her, or, if her maid was not to be trusted, he would apply to his landlady, and engage "a respectable elderly person" to attend on her until the day of their marriage. Would she have some mercy on him, and just consider it? No: she was afraid to consider it. Did she prefer misery for the rest of her life? Never mind his happiness: it was her happiness only that he had in his mind. Traveling with unsympathetic people; absent from England, no one could say for how long; married, when she did return, to some rich man whom she hated—would she, could she, contemplate that prospect? She contemplated it through tears; she contemplated it to an accompaniment of sighs, kisses, and protestations—she trembled, hesitated, gave way. At an appointed hour of the coming night, when her father would be in the smoking-room, and Mrs. Margery would be in bed, Cosway was to knock at the door in the lane once more; leaving time to make all the necessary arrangements in the interval.

The one pressing necessity, under these circumstances, was to guard against the possibility of betrayal and surprise. Cosway discreetly alluded to the unsolved mysteries of the invitation and the message. "Have you taken anybody into our confidence?" he asked.

Adela answered with some embarrassment. "Only one person," She said—"dear Miss Benshaw."

"Who is Miss Benshaw?"

"Don't you really know, Edwin? She is richer even than papa—she has inherited from her late brother one half-share in the great business in the City. Miss Benshaw is the lady who disappointed papa by not coming to the garden-party. You remember, dear, how happy we were when we were together at Mr. Atherton's? I was very miserable when they took me away. Miss Benshaw happened to call the next day and she noticed it. 'My dear,' she said (Miss Benshaw is quite an elderly lady now), 'I am an old maid, who has missed the happiness of her life, through not having had a friend to guide and advise her when she was young. Are you suffering as I once suffered?' She spoke so nicely—and I was so wretched—that I really couldn't help it. I opened my heart to her."

Cosway looked grave. "Are you sure she is to be trusted?" he asked.

"Perfectly sure."

"Perhaps, my love, she has spoken about us (not meaning any harm) to some friend of hers? Old ladies are so fond of gossip. It's just possible—don't you think so?"

Adela hung her head.

"I have thought it just possible myself," she admitted. "There is plenty of time to call on her to-day. I will set our doubts at rest before Miss Benshaw goes out for her afternoon drive."

On that understanding they parted.

Toward evening Cosway's arrangements for the elopement were completed. He was eating his solitary dinner when a note was brought to him. It had been left at the door by a messenger. The man had gone away without waiting for an answer. The note ran thus:

"Miss Benshaw presents her compliments to Mr. Cosway, and will be obliged if he can call on her at nine o'clock this evening, on business which concerns himself."

This invitation was evidently the result of Adela's visit earlier in the day. Cosway presented himself at the house, troubled by natural emotions of anxiety and suspense. His reception was not of a nature to compose him. He was shown into a darkened room. The one lamp on the table was turned down low, and the little light thus given was still further obscured by a shade. The corners of the room were in almost absolute darkness.

A voice out of one of the corners addressed him in a whisper:

"I must beg you to excuse the darkened room. I am suffering from a severe cold. My eyes are inflamed, and my throat is so bad that I can only speak in a whisper. Sit down, sir. I have got news for you."

"Not bad news, I hope, ma'am?" Cosway ventured to inquire.

"The worst possible news," said the whispering voice. "You have an enemy striking at you in the dark."

Cosway asked who it was, and received no answer. He varied the form of inquiry, and asked why the unnamed person struck at him in the dark. The experiment succeeded; he obtained a reply.

"It is reported to me," said Miss Benshaw, "that the person thinks it necessary to give you a lesson, and takes a spiteful pleasure in doing it as mischievously as possible. The person, as I happen to know, sent you your invitation to the party, and made the appointment which took you to the door in the lane. Wait a little, sir; I have not done yet. The person has put it into Mr. Restall's head to send his daughter abroad tomorrow."

Cosway attempted to make her speak more plainly.

"Is this wretch a man or a woman?" he said.

Miss Benshaw proceeded without noticing the interruption.

"You needn't be afraid, Mr. Cosway; Miss Restall will not leave England. Your enemy is all-powerful. Your enemy's object could only be to provoke you into planning an elopement—and, your arrangements once completed, to inform Mr. Restall, and to part you and Miss Adela quite as effectually as if you were at opposite ends of the world. Oh, you will undoubtedly be parted! Spiteful, isn't it? And, what is worse, the mischief is as good as done already."

Cosway rose from his chair.

"Do you wish for any further explanation?" asked Miss Benshaw.

"One thing more," he replied. "Does Adela know of this?"

"No," said Miss Benshaw; "it is left to you to tell her."

There was a moment of silence. Cosway looked at the lamp. Once roused, as usual with men of his character, his temper was not to be trifled with.

"Miss Benshaw," he said, "I dare say you think me a fool; but I can draw my own conclusion, for all that. You are my enemy."

The only reply was a chuckling laugh. All voices can be more or less effectually disguised by a whisper but a laugh carries the revelation of its own identity with it. Cosway suddenly threw off the shade over the lamp and turned up the wick.

The light flooded the room, and showed him—His Wife.

The Third Epoch in Mr. Cosway's Life.

Three days had passed. Cosway sat alone in his lodging—pale and worn: the shadow already of his former self.

He had not seen Adela since the discovery. There was but one way in which he could venture to make the inevitable disclosure—he wrote to her; and Mr. Atherton's daughter took care that the letter should be received. Inquiries made afterward, by help of the same good friend, informed him that Miss Restall was suffering from illness.

The mistress of the house came in.

"Cheer up, sir," said the good woman. "There is better news of Miss Restall to-day."

He raised his head.

"Don't trifle with me!" he answered fretfully; "tell me exactly what the servant said."

The mistress repeated the words. Miss Restall had passed a quieter night, and had been able for a few hours to leave her room. He asked next if any reply to his letter had arrived. No reply had been received.

If Adela definitely abstained from writing to him, the conclusion would be too plain to be mistaken. She had given him up—and who could blame her?

There was a knock at the street-door. The mistress looked out.

"Here's Mr. Stone come back, sir!" she exclaimed joyfully—and hurried away to let him in.

Cosway never looked up when his friend appeared.

"I knew I should succeed," said Stone. "I have seen your wife."

"Don't speak of her," cried Cosway. "I should have murdered her when I saw her face, if I had not instantly left the house. I may be the death of the wretch yet, if you presist in speaking of her!"

Stone put his hand kindly on his friend's shoulder.

458

"Must I remind you that you owe something to your old comrade?" he asked. "I left my father and mother, the morning I got your letter—and my one thought has been to serve you. Reward me. Be a man, and hear what is your right and duty to know. After that, if you like, we will never refer to the woman again."

Cosway took his hand, in silent acknowledgment that he was right. They sat down together. Stone began.

"She is so entirely shameless," he said, "that I had no difficulty in getting her to speak. And she so cordially hates you that she glories in her own falsehood and treachery."

"Of course, she lies," Cosway said bitterly, "when she calls herself Miss Benshaw?"

"No; she is really the daughter of the man who founded the great house in the City. With every advantage that wealth and position could give her the perverse creature married one of her father's clerks, who had been deservedly dismissed from his situation. From that moment her family discarded her. With the money procured by the sale of her jewels, her husband took the inn which we have such bitter cause to remember—and she managed the house after his death. So much for the past. Carry your mind on now to the time when our ship brought us back to England. At that date, the last surviving member of your wife's family—her elder brother—lay at the point of death. He had taken his father's place in the business, besides inheriting his father's fortune. After a happy married life he was left a widower, without children; and it became necessary that he should alter his will. He deferred performing his duty. It was only at the time of his last illness that he had dictated instructions for a new will, leaving his wealth (excepting certain legacies to old friends) to the hospitals of Great Britain and Ireland. His lawyer lost no time in carrying out the instructions. The new will was ready for signature (the old will having been destroyed by his own hand), when the doctors sent a message to say that their patient was insensible, and might die in that condition."

"Did the doctors prove to be right?"

"Perfectly right. Our wretched landlady, as next of kin, succeeded, not

459

only to the fortune, but (under the deed of partnership) to her late brother's place in the firm: on the one easy condition of resuming the family name. She calls herself "Miss Benshaw." But as a matter of legal necessity she is set down in the deed as "Mrs. Cosway Benshaw." Her partners only now know that her husband is living, and that you are the Cosway whom she privately married. Will you take a little breathing time? or shall I go on, and get done with it?"

Cosway signed to him to go on.

"She doesn't in the least care," Stone proceeded, "for the exposure. 'I am the head partner,' she says 'and the rich one of the firm; they daren't turn their backs on Me.' You remember the information I received—in perfect good faith on his part—from the man who keeps the inn? The visit to the London doctor, and the assertion of failing health, were adopted as the best means of plausibly severing the lady's connection (the great lady now!) with a calling so unworthy of her as the keeping of an inn. Her neighbors at the seaport were all deceived by the stratagem, with two exceptions. They were both men— vagabonds who had pertinaciously tried to delude her into marrying them in the days when she was a widow. They refused to believe in the doctor and the declining health; they had their own suspicion of the motives which had led to the sale of the inn, under very unfavorable circumstances; and they decided on going to London, inspired by the same base hope of making discoveries which might be turned into a means of extorting money."

"She escaped them, of course," said Cosway. "How?"

"By the help of her lawyer, who was not above accepting a handsome private fee. He wrote to the new landlord of the inn, falsely announcing his client's death, in the letter which I repeated to you in the railway carriage on our journey to London. Other precautions were taken to keep up the deception, on which it is needless to dwell. Your natural conclusion that you were free to pay your addresses to Miss Restall, and the poor young lady's innocent confidence in 'Miss Benshaw's' sympathy, gave this unscrupulous woman the means of playing the heartless trick on you which is now exposed. Malice and jealousy—I have it, mind, from herself!—were not her only motives. 'But for that Cosway,' she said (I spare you the epithet which she put before your name), 'with my money and position, I might have married a needy lord, and sunned myself in my old age in the full blaze of the peerage.' Do you understand how she hated you, now? Enough of the subject! The moral of it, my dear Cosway, is to leave this place, and try what change of scene will do for you. I have time to spare; and I will go abroad with you. When shall it be?"

"Let me wait a day or two more," Cosway pleaded.

Stone shook his head. "Still hoping, my poor friend, for a line from Miss Restall? You distress me."

"I am sorry to distress you, Stone. If I can get one pitying word from her, I can submit to the miserable life that lies before me."

"Are you not expecting too much?"

"You wouldn't say so, if you were as fond of her as I am."

They were silent. The evening slowly darkened; and the mistress came in as usual with the candles. She brought with her a letter for Cosway.

He tore it open; read it in an instant; and devoured it with kisses. His highly wrought feelings found their vent in a little allowable exaggeration. "She has saved my life!" he said, as he handed the letter to Stone.

It only contained these lines:

"My love is yours, my promise is yours. Through all trouble, through all profanation, through the hopeless separation that may be before us in this world, I live yours—and die yours. My Edwin, God bless and comfort you."

The Fourth Epoch in Mr. Cosway's Life.

The separation had lasted for nearly two years, when Cosway and Stone paid that visit to the country house which is recorded at the outset of the present narrative. In the interval nothing had been heard of Miss Restall, except through Mr. Atherton. He reported that Adela was leading a very quiet life. The one remarkable event had been an interview between "Miss Benshaw" and herself. No other person had been present; but the little that

461

was reported placed Miss Restall's character above all praise. She had forgiven the woman who had so cruelly injured her!

The two friends, it may be remembered, had traveled to London, immediately after completing the fullest explanation of Cosway's startling behavior at the breakfast-table. Stone was not by nature a sanguine man. "I don't believe in our luck," he said. "Let us be quite sure that we are not the victims of another deception."

The accident had happened on the Thames; and the newspaper narrative proved to be accurate in every respect. Stone personally attended the inquest. From a natural feeling of delicacy toward Adela, Cosway hesitated to write to her on the subject. The ever-helpful Stone wrote in his place.

After some delay, the answer was received. It inclosed a brief statement (communicated officially by legal authority) of the last act of malice on the part of the late head-partner in the house of Benshaw and Company. She had not died intestate, like her brother. The first clause of her will contained the testator's grateful recognition of Adela Restall's Christian act of forgiveness. The second clause (after stating that there were neither relatives nor children to be benefited by the will) left Adela Restall mistress of Mrs. Cosway Benshaw's fortune—on the one merciless condition that she did not marry Edwin Cosway. The third clause—if Adela Restall violated the condition—handed over the whole of the money to the firm in the City, "for the extension of the business, and the benefit of the surviving partners."

Some months later, Adela came of age. To the indignation of Mr. Restall, and the astonishment of the "Company," the money actually went to the firm. The fourth epoch in Mr. Cosway's life witnessed his marriage to a woman who cheerfully paid half a million of money for the happiness of passing her life, on eight hundred a year, with the man whom she loved.

But Cosway felt bound in gratitude to make a rich woman of his wife, if work and resolution could do it. When Stone last heard of him, he was reading for the bar; and Mr. Atherton was ready to give him his first brief.

NOTE.—That "most improbable" part of the present narrative,

which is contained in the division called The First Epoch, is founded on an adventure which actually occurred to no less a person than a cousin of Sir Walter Scott. In Lockhart's delightful "Life," the anecdote will be found as told by Sir Walter to Captain Basil Hall. The remainder of the present story is entirely imaginary. The writer wondered what such a woman as the landlady would do under certain given circumstances, after her marriage to the young midshipman—and here is the result.

MR. MEDHURST AND THE PRINCESS.

I.

THE day before I left London, to occupy the post of second secretary of legation at a small German Court, I took leave of my excellent French singing-master, Monsieur Bonnefoy, and of his young and pretty daughter named Jeanne.

Our farewell interview was saddened by Monsieur Bonnefoy's family anxieties. His elder brother, known in the household as Uncle David, had been secretly summoned to Paris by order of a republican society. Anxious relations in London (whether reasonably or not, I am unable to say) were in some fear of the political consequences that might follow.

At parting, I made Mademoiselle Jeanne a present, in the shape of a plain gold brooch. For some time past, I had taken my lessons at Monsieur Bonnefoy's house; his daughter and I often sang together under his direction. Seeing much of Jeanne, under these circumstances, the little gift that I had offered to her was only the natural expression of a true interest in her welfare. Idle rumor asserted—quite falsely—that I was in love with her. I was sincerely the young lady's friend: no more, no less.

Having alluded to my lessons in singing, it may not be out of place to mention the circumstances under which I became Monsieur Bonnefoy's pupil, and to allude to the change in my life that followed in due course of time.

Our family property—excepting the sum of five thousand pounds left to me by my mother—is landed property strictly entailed. The estates were inherited by my only brother, Lord Medhurst; the kindest, the best, and, I grieve to say it, the unhappiest of men. He lived separated from a bad wife; he had no children to console him; and he only enjoyed at rare intervals the blessing of good health. Having myself nothing to live on but the interest of my mother's little fortune, I had to make my own way in the world. Poor younger sons, not possessed of the commanding ability which achieves distinction, find the roads that lead to prosperity closed to them, with one exception. They can always apply themselves to the social arts which make a man agreeable in society. I had naturally a good voice, and I cultivated it. I was ready to sing, without being subject to the wretched vanity which makes objections and excuses—I pleased the ladies—the ladies spoke favorably of me to their husbands—and some of their husbands were persons of rank and influence. After no very long lapse of time, the result of this combination of circumstances declared itself. Monsieur Bonnefoy's lessons became the indirect means of starting me on a diplomatic career—and the diplomatic career made poor Ernest Medhurst, to his own unutterable astonishment, the hero of a love story!

The story being true, I must beg to be excused, if I abstain from mentioning names, places, and dates, when I enter on German ground. Let it be enough to say that I am writing of a bygone year in the present century, when no such thing as a German Empire existed, and when the revolutionary spirit of France was still an object of well-founded suspicion to tyrants by right divine on the continent of Europe.

II.

ON joining the legation, I was not particularly attracted by my chief, the Minister. His manners were oppressively polite; and his sense of his own importance was not sufficiently influenced by diplomatic reserve. I venture to describe him (mentally speaking) as an empty man, carefully trained to look full on public occasions.

My colleague, the first secretary, was a far more interesting person. Bright, unaffected, and agreeable, he at once interested me when we were introduced to each other. I pay myself a compliment, as I consider, when I add that he became my firm and true friend.

We took a walk together in the palace gardens on the evening of my arrival. Reaching a remote part of the grounds, we were passed by a lean, sallow, sour-looking old man, drawn by a servant in a chair on wheels. My companion stopped, whispered to me, "Here is the Prince," and bowed bareheaded. I followed his example as a matter of course. The Prince feebly returned our salutation. "Is he ill?" I asked, when we had put our hats on again.

"Shakespeare," the secretary replied, "tells us that 'one man in his time plays many parts.' Under what various aspects the Prince's character may have presented itself, in his younger days, I am not able to tell you. Since I have been here, he has played the part of a martyr to illness, misunderstood by his doctors."

"And his daughter, the Princess—what do you say of her?"

"Ah, she is not so easily described! I can only appeal to your memory of other women like her, whom you must often have seen—women who are tall and fair, and fragile and elegant; who have delicate aquiline noses and melting blue eyes—women who have often charmed you by their tender smiles and their supple graces of movement. As for the character of this popular young lady, I must not influence you either way; study it for yourself."

"Without a hint to guide me?"

"With a suggestion," he replied, "which may be worth considering. If you wish to please the Princess, begin by endeavoring to win the good graces of the Baroness."

"Who is the Baroness?"

"One of the ladies in waiting—bosom friend of her Highness, and chosen repository of all her secrets. Personally, not likely to attract you; short and fat, and ill-tempered and ugly. Just at this time, I happen myself to get on with her better than usual. We have discovered that we possess one sympathy in common—we are the only people at Court who don't believe in the Prince's new doctor."

"Is the new doctor a quack?"

The secretary looked round, before he answered, to see that nobody was near us.

"It strikes me," he said, "that the Doctor is a spy. Mind! I have no right

466

to speak of him in that way; it is only my impression—and I ought to add that appearances are all in his favor. He is in the service of our nearest royal neighbor, the Grand Duke; and he has been sent here expressly to relieve the sufferings of the Duke's good friend and brother, our invalid Prince. This is an honorable mission no doubt. And the man himself is handsome, well-bred, and (I don't quite know whether this is an additional recommendation) a countryman of ours. Nevertheless I doubt him, and the Baroness doubts him. You are an independent witness; I shall be anxious to hear if your opinion agrees with ours."

I was presented at Court, toward the end of the week; and, in the course of the next two or three days, I more than once saw the Doctor. The impression that he produced on me surprised my colleague. It was my opinion that he and the Baroness had mistaken the character of a worthy and capable man.

The secretary obstinately adhered to his own view.

"Wait a little," he answered, "and we shall see."

He was quite right. We did see.

III.

BUT the Princess—the gentle, gracious, beautiful Princess—what can I say of her Highness?

I can only say that she enchanted me.

I had been a little discouraged by the reception that I met with from her father. Strictly confining himself within the limits of politeness, he bade me welcome to his Court in the fewest possible words, and then passed me by without further notice. He afterward informed the English Minister that I had been so unfortunate as to try his temper: "Your new secretary irritates me, sir—he is a person in an offensively perfect state of health." The Prince's charming daughter was not of her father's way of thinking; it is impossible to say how graciously, how sweetly I was received. She honored me by speaking to me in my own language, of which she showed herself to be a perfect mistress. I was not only permitted, but encouraged, to talk of my family, and to dwell on my own tastes, amusements, and pursuits. Even when her Highness's attention was claimed by other persons waiting to be presented, I was not forgotten. The Baroness was instructed to invite me for the next evening to the Princess's tea-table; and it was hinted that I should be especially welcome if I brought my music with me, and sang.

My friend the secretary, standing near us at the time, looked at me with a mysterious smile. He had suggested that I should make advances to the Baroness—and here was the Baroness (under royal instructions) making advances to Me!

"We know what that means," he whispered.

In justice to myself, I must declare that I entirely failed to understand him.

On the occasion of my second reception by the Princess, at her little evening party, I detected the Baroness, more than once, in the act of watching her Highness and myself, with an appearance of disapproval in her manner, which puzzled me. When I had taken my leave, she followed me out of the room.

"I have a word of advice to give you," she said. "The best thing you can do, sir, is to make an excuse to your Minister, and go back to England."

I declare again, that I entirely failed to understand the Baroness.

IV.

BEFORE the season came to an end, the Court removed to the Prince's country-seat, in the interests of his Highness's health. Entertainments were given (at the Doctor's suggestion), with a view of raising the patient's depressed spirits. The members of the English legation were among the guests invited. To me it was a delightful visit. I had again every reason to feel gratefully sensible of the Princess's condescending kindness. Meeting the secretary one day in the library, I said that I thought her a perfect creature. Was this an absurd remark to make? I could see nothing absurd in it—and yet my friend burst out laughing.

"My good fellow, nobody is a perfect creature," he said. "The Princess has her faults and failings, like the rest of us."

I denied it positively.

"Use your eyes," he went on; "and you will see, for example, that she is shallow and frivolous. Yesterday was a day of rain. We were all obliged to employ ourselves somehow indoors. Didn't you notice that she had no resources in herself? She can't even read."

"There you are wrong at any rate," I declared. "I saw her reading the newspaper."

"You saw her with the newspaper in her hand. If you had not been deaf and blind to her defects, you would have noticed that she couldn't fix her attention on it. She was always ready to join in the chatter of the ladies about her. When even their stores of gossip were exhausted, she let the newspaper drop on her lap, and sat in vacant idleness smiling at nothing."

I reminded him that she might have met with a dull number of the newspaper. He took no notice of this unanswerable reply.

"You were talking the other day of her warmth of feeling," he proceeded. "She has plenty of sentiment (German sentiment), I grant you, but no true feeling. What happened only this morning, when the Prince was in the breakfast-room, and when the Princess and her ladies were dressed to go out riding? Even she noticed the wretchedly depressed state of her father's spirits. A man of that hypochondriacal temperament suffers acutely, though he may only fancy himself to be ill. The Princess overflowed with sympathy, but she never proposed to stay at home, and try to cheer the old man. Her filial duty was performed to her own entire satisfaction when she had kissed her hand to the Prince. The moment after, she was out of the room—eager to enjoy her ride. We all heard her laughing gayly among the ladies in the hall."

I could have answered this also, if our discussion had not been interrupted at the moment. The Doctor came into the library in search of a book. When he had left us, my colleague's strong prejudice against him instantly declared itself.

"Be on your guard with that man," he said.

"Why?" I asked.

"Haven't you noticed," he replied, "that when the Princess is talking to you, the Doctor always happens to be in that part of the room?"

"What does it matter where the Doctor is?"

My friend looked at me with an oddly mingled expression of doubt and surprise. "Do you really not understand me?" he said.

"I don't indeed."

"My dear Ernest, you are a rare and admirable example to the rest of us—you are a truly modest man."

What did he mean?

V.

EVENTS followed, on the next day, which (as will presently be seen) I have a personal interest in relating.

The Baroness left us suddenly, on leave of absence. The Prince wearied of his residence in the country; and the Court returned to the capital. The charming Princess was reported to be "indisposed," and retired to the seclusion of her own apartments.

A week later, I received a note from the Baroness, marked "private and confidential." It informed me that she had resumed her duties as lady-in-waiting, and that she wished to see me at my earliest convenience. I obeyed at once; and naturally asked if there were better accounts of her Highness's health.

The Baroness's reply a little surprised me. She said, "The Princess is perfectly well."

"Recovered already!" I exclaimed.

"She has never been ill," the Baroness answered. "Her indisposition was a sham; forced on her by me, in her own interests. Her reputation is in peril; and you—you hateful Englishman—are the cause of it."

470

Not feeling disposed to put up with such language as this, even when it was used by a lady, I requested that she would explain herself. She complied without hesitation. In another minute my eyes were opened to the truth. I knew—no; that is too positive—let me say I had reason to believe that the Princess loved me!

It is simply impossible to convey to the minds of others any idea of the emotions that overwhelmed me at that critical moment of my life. I was in a state of confusion at the time; and, when my memory tries to realize it, I am in a state of confusion now. The one thing I can do is to repeat what the Baroness said to me when I had in some degree recovered my composure.

"I suppose you are aware," she began, "of the disgrace to which the Princess's infatuation exposes her, if it is discovered? On my own responsibility I repeat what I said to you a short time since. Do you refuse to leave this place immediately?"

Does the man live, honored as I was, who would have hesitated to refuse? Find him if you can!

"Very well," she resumed. "As the friend of the Princess, I have no choice now but to take things as they are, and to make the best of them. Let us realize your position to begin with. If you were (like your elder brother) a nobleman possessed of vast estates, my royal mistress might be excused. As it is, whatever you may be in the future, you are nothing now but an obscure young man, without fortune or title. Do you see your duty to the Princess? or must I explain it to you?"

I saw my duty as plainly as she did. "Her Highness's secret is a sacred secret," I said. "I am bound to shrink from no sacrifice which may preserve it."

The Baroness smiled maliciously. "I may have occasion," she answered, "to remind you of what you have just said. In the meanwhile the Princess's secret is in danger of discovery."

"By her father?"

"No. By the Doctor."

At first, I doubted whether she was in jest or in earnest. The next instant, I remembered that the secretary had expressly cautioned me against that man.

"It is evidently one of your virtues," the Baroness proceeded, "to be slow to suspect. Prepare yourself for a disagreeable surprise. The Doctor has been watching the Princess, on every occasion when she speaks to you, with some object of his own in view. During my absence, young sir, I have been engaged in discovering what that object is. My excellent mother lives at the Court of the Grand Duke, and enjoys the confidence of his Ministers. He is still a bachelor; and, in the interests of the succession to the throne, the time has arrived when he must marry. With my mother's assistance, I have found out that the Doctor's medical errand here is a pretense. Influenced by the Princess's beauty the Grand Duke has thought of her first as his future duchess. Whether he has heard slanderous stories, or whether he is only a cautious man, I can't tell you. But this I know: he has instructed his physician—if he had employed a professed diplomatist his motive might have been suspected—to observe her Highness privately, and to communicate the result. The object of the report is to satisfy the Duke that the Princess's reputation is above the reach of scandal; that she is free from entanglements of a certain kind; and that she is in every respect a person to whom he can with propriety offer his hand in marriage. The Doctor, Mr. Ernest, is not disposed to allow you to prevent him from sending in a favorable report. He has drawn his conclusions from the Princess's extraordinary kindness to the second secretary of the English legation; and he is only waiting for a little plainer evidence to communicate his suspicions to the Prince. It rests with you to save the Princess."

"Only tell me how I am to do it!" I said.

"There is but one way of doing it," she answered; "and that way has (comically enough) been suggested to me by the Doctor himself."

Her tone and manner tried my patience.

"Come to the point!" I said.

She seemed to enjoy provoking me.

"No hurry, Mr. Ernest—no hurry! You shall be fully enlightened, if you

472

will only wait a little. The Prince, I must tell you, believes in his daughter's indisposition. When he visited her this morning, he was attended by his medical adviser. I was present at the interview. To do him justice, the Doctor is worthy of the trust reposed in him—he boldly attempted to verify his suspicions of the daughter in the father's presence."

"How?"

"Oh, in the well-known way that has been tried over and over again, under similar circumstances! He merely invented a report that you were engaged in a love-affair with some charming person in the town. Don't be angry; there's no harm done."

"But there is harm done," I insisted. "What must the Princess think of me?"

"Do you suppose she is weak enough to believe the Doctor? Her Highness beat him at his own weapons; not the slightest sign of agitation on her part rewarded his ingenuity. All that you have to do is to help her to mislead this medical spy. It's as easy as lying: and easier. The Doctor's slander declares that you have a love-affair in the town. Take the hint—and astonish the Doctor by proving that he has hit on the truth."

It was a hot day; the Baroness was beginning to get excited. She paused and fanned herself.

"Do I startle you?" she asked.

"You disgust me."

She laughed.

"What a thick-headed man this is!" she said, pleasantly. "Must I put it more plainly still? Engage in what your English prudery calls a 'flirtation,' with some woman here—the lower in degree the better, or the Princess might be jealous—and let the affair be seen and known by everybody about the Court. Sly as he is, the Doctor is not prepared for that! At your age, and with your personal advantages, he will take appearances for granted; he will conclude that he has wronged you, and misinterpreted the motives of the

Princess. The secret of her Highness's weakness will be preserved—thanks to that sacrifice, Mr. Ernest, which you are so willing and so eager to make."

It was useless to remonstrate with such a woman as this. I simply stated my own objection to her artfully devised scheme.

"I don't wish to appear vain," I said; "but the woman to whom I am to pay these attentions may believe that I really admire her—and it is just possible that she may honestly return the feeling which I am only assuming."

"Well—and what then?"

"It's hard on the woman, surely?"

The Baroness was shocked, unaffectedly shocked.

"Good heavens!" she exclaimed, "how can anything that you do for the Princess be hard on a woman of the lower orders? There must be an end of this nonsense, sir! You have heard what I propose, and you know what the circumstances are. My mistress is waiting for your answer. What am I to say?"

"Let me see her Highness, and speak for myself," I said.

"Quite impossible to-day, without running too great a risk. Your reply must be made through me."

There was to be a Court concert at the end of the week. On that occasion I should be able to make my own reply. In the meanwhile I only told the Baroness I wanted time to consider.

"What time?" she asked.

"Until to-morrow. Do you object?"

"On the contrary, I cordially agree. Your base hesitation may lead to results which I have not hitherto dared to anticipate."

"What do you mean?"

"Between this and to-morrow," the horrid woman replied, "the Princess may end in seeing you with my eyes. In that hope I wish you good-morning."

VI.

MY enemies say that I am a weak man, unduly influenced by persons of rank—because of their rank. If this we re true, I should have found little difficulty in consenting to adopt the Baroness's suggestion. As it was, the longer I reflected on the scheme the less I liked it. I tried to think of some alternative that might be acceptably proposed. The time passed, and nothing occurred to me. In this embarrassing position my mind became seriously disturbed; I felt the necessity of obtaining some relief, which might turn my thoughts for a while into a new channel. The secretary called on me, while I was still in doubt what to do. He reminded me that a new prima donna was advertised to appear on that night; and he suggested that we should go to the opera. Feeling as I did at the time, I readily agreed.

We found the theater already filled, before the performance began. Two French gentlemen were seated in the row of stalls behind us. They were talking of the new singer.

"She is advertised as 'Mademoiselle Fontenay,'" one of them said. "That sounds like an assumed name."

"It is an assumed name," the other replied. "She is the daughter of a French singing-master, named Bonnefoy."

To my friend's astonishment I started to my feet, and left him without a word of apology. In another minute I was at the stage-door, and had sent in my card to "Mademoiselle Fontenay." While I was waiting, I had time to think. Was it possible that Jeanne had gone on the stage? Or were there two singing-masters in existence named Bonnefoy? My doubts were soon decided. The French woman-servant whom I remembered when I was Monsieur Bonnefoy's pupil, made her appearance, and conducted me to her young mistress's dressing-room. Dear good Jeanne, how glad she was to see me!

I found her standing before the glass, having just completed her preparations for appearing on the stage. Dressed in her picturesque costume, she was so charming that I expressed my admiration heartily, as became her old friend. "Do you really like me?" she said, with the innocent familiarity which I recollected so well. "See how I look in the glass—that is the great test." It was not easy to apply the test. Instead of looking at her image in the glass, it was far more agreeable to look at herself. We were interrupted—too soon interrupted—by the call-boy. He knocked at the door, and announced that the overture had begun.

"I have a thousand things to ask you," I told her. "What has made this wonderful change in your life? How is it that I don't see your father—"

Her face instantly saddened; her hand trembled as she laid it on my arm to silence me.

"Don't speak of him now," she said, "or you will unnerve me. Come to me to-morrow when the stage will not be waiting; Annette will give you my address." She opened the door to go out, and returned. "Will you think me very unreasonable if I ask you not to make one of my audience to-night? You have reminded me of the dear old days that can never come again. If I feel that I am singing to you—" She left me to understand the rest, and turned away again to the door. As I followed her out, to say good-by, she drew from her bosom the little brooch which had been my parting gift, and held it out to me. "On the stage, or off," she said, "I always wear it. Good-night, Ernest."

I was prepared to hear sad news when we met the next morning.

My good old friend and master had died suddenly. To add to the bitterness of that affliction, he had died in debt to a dear and intimate friend. For his daughter's sake he had endeavored to add to his little savings by speculating with borrowed money on the Stock Exchange. He had failed, and the loan advanced had not been repaid, when a fit of apoplexy struck him down. Offered the opportunity of trying her fortune on the operatic stage, Jeanne made the attempt, and was now nobly employed in earning the money to pay her father's debt.

"It was the only way in which I could do justice to his memory," she said, simply. "I hope you don't object to my going on the stage?"

I took her hand, poor child—and let that simple action answer for me. I was too deeply affected to be able to speak.

476

"It is not in me to be a great actress," she resumed; "but you know what an admirable musician my father was. He has taught me to sing, so that I can satisfy the critics, as well as please the public. There was what they call a great success last night. It has earned me an engagement for another year to come, and an increase of salary. I have already sent some money to our good old friend at home, and I shall soon send more. It is my one consolation—I feel almost happy again when I am paying my poor father's debt. No more now of my sad story! I want to hear all that you can tell me of yourself." She moved to the window, and looked out. "Oh, the beautiful blue sky! We used sometimes to take a walk, when we were in London, on fine days like this. Is there a park here?"

I took her to the palace gardens, famous for their beauty in that part of Germany.

Arm in arm we loitered along the pleasant walks. The lovely flowers, the bright sun, the fresh fragrant breeze, all helped her to recover her spirits. She began to be like the happy Jeanne of my past experience, as easily pleased as a child. When we sat down to rest, the lap of her dress was full of daisies. "Do you remember," she said, "when you first taught me to make a daisy-chain? Are you too great a man to help me again now?"

We were still engaged with our chain, seated close together, when the smell of tobacco-smoke was wafted to us on the air.

I looked up and saw the Doctor passing us, enjoying his cigar. He bowed; eyed my pretty companion with a malicious smile; and passed on.

"Who is that man?" she asked.

"The Prince's physician," I replied.

"I don't like him," she said; "why did he smile when he looked at me?"

"Perhaps," I suggested, "he thought we were lovers."

She blushed. "Don't let him think that! tell him we are only old friends."

We were not destined to finish our flower chain on that day.

Another person interrupted us, whom I recognized as the elder brother of Monsieur Bonnefoy—already mentioned in these pages, under the name of Uncle David. Having left France for political reasons, the old republican had taken care of his niece after her father's death, and had accepted the position of Jeanne's business manager in her relations with the stage. Uncle David's object, when he joined us in the garden, was to remind her that she was wanted at rehearsal, and must at once return with him to the theater. We parted, having arranged that I was to see the performance on that night.

Later in the day, the Baroness sent for me again.

"Let me apologize for having misunderstood you yesterday," she said: "and let me offer you my best congratulations. You have done wonders already in the way of misleading the Doctor. There is only one objection to that girl at the theater—I hear she is so pretty that she may possibly displease the Princess. In other respects, she is just in the public position which will make your attentions to her look like the beginning of a serious intrigue. Bravo, Mr. Ernest—bravo!"

I was too indignant to place any restraint on the language in which I answered her.

"Understand, if you please," I said, "that I am renewing an old friendship with Mademoiselle Jeanne—begun under the sanction of her father. Respect that young lady, madam, as I respect her."

The detestable Baroness clapped her hands, as if she had been at the theater.

"If you only say that to the Princess," she remarked, "as well as you have said it to me, there will be no danger of arousing her Highness's jealousy. I have a message for you. At the concert, on Saturday, you are to retire to the conservatory, and you may hope for an interview when the singers begin the second part of the programme. Don't let me detain you any longer. Go back to your young lady, Mr. Ernest—pray go back!"

VII.

ON the second night of the opera the applications for places were too numerous to be received. Among the crowded audience, I recognized many of my friends. They persisted in believing an absurd report (first circulated, as I imagine, by the Doctor), which asserted that my interest in the new singer was something more than the interest of an old friend. When I went behind the scenes to congratulate Jeanne on her success, I was annoyed in another way—and by the Doctor again. He followed me to Jeanne's room, to offer his congratulations; and he begged that I would introduce him to the charming prima donna. Having expressed his admiration, he looked at me with his insolently suggestive smile, and said he could not think of prolonging his intrusion. On leaving the room, he noticed Uncle David, waiting as usual to take care of Jeanne on her return from the theater—looked at him attentively—bowed, and went out.

The next morning, I received a note from the Baroness, expressed in these terms:

"More news! My rooms look out on the wing of the palace in which the Doctor is lodged. Half an hour since, I discovered him at his window, giving a letter to a person who is a stranger to me. The man left the palace immediately afterward. My maid followed him, by my directions. Instead of putting the letter in the post, he took a ticket at the railway-station—for what place the servant was unable to discover. Here, you will observe, is a letter important enough to be dispatched by special messenger, and written at a time when we have succeeded in freeing ourselves from the Doctor's suspicions. It is at least possible that he has decided on sending a favorable report of the Princess to the Grand Duke. If this is the case, please consider whether you will not act wisely (in her Highness's interests) by keeping away from the concert."

Viewing this suggestion as another act of impertinence on the part of the Baroness, I persisted in my intention of going to the concert. It was for the Princess to decide what course of conduct I was bound to follow. What did I care for the Doctor's report to the Duke! Shall I own my folly? I do really believe I was jealous of the Duke.

VIII.

ENTERING the Concert Room, I found the Princess alone on the dais, receiving the company. "Nervous prostration" had made it impossible for the

Prince to be present. He was confined to his bed-chamber; and the Doctor was in attendance on him.

I bowed to the Baroness, but she was too seriously offended with me for declining to take her advice to notice my salutation. Passing into the conservatory, it occurred to me that I might be seen, and possibly suspected, in the interval between the first and second parts of the programme, when the music no longer absorbed the attention of the audience. I went on, and waited outside on the steps that led to the garden; keeping the glass door open, so as to hear when the music of the second part of the concert began.

After an interval which seemed to be endless, I saw the Princess approaching me.

She had made the heat in the Concert Room an excuse for retiring for a while; and she had the Baroness in attendance on her to save appearances. Instead of leaving us to ourselves, the malicious creature persisted in paying the most respectful attentions to her mistress. It was impossible to make her understand that she was not wanted any longer until the Princess said sharply, "Go back to the music!" Even then, the detestable woman made a low curtsey, and answered: "I will return, Madam, in five minutes."

I ventured to present myself in the conservatory.

The Princess was dressed with exquisite simplicity, entirely in white. Her only ornaments were white roses in her hair and in her bosom. To say that she looked lovely is to say nothing. She seemed to be the ethereal creature of some higher sphere; too exquisitely delicate and pure to be approached by a mere mortal man like myself. I was awed; I was silent. Her Highness's sweet smile encouraged me to venture a little nearer. She pointed to a footstool which the Baroness had placed for her. "Are you afraid of me, Ernest?" she asked softly.

Her divinely beautiful eyes rested on me with a look of encouragement. I dropped on my knees at her feet. She had asked if I was afraid of her. This, if I may use such an expression, roused my manhood. My own boldness astonished me. I answered: "Madam, I adore you."

She laid her fair hand on my head, and looked at me thoughtfully.

"Forget my rank," she whispered—"have I not set you the example? Suppose that I am nothing but an English Miss. What would you say to Miss?"

"I should say, I love you."

"Say it to Me."

My lips said it on her hand. She bent forward. My heart beats fast at the bare remembrance of it. Oh, heavens, her Highness kissed me!

"There is your reward," she murmured, "for all you have sacrificed for my sake. What an effort it must have been to offer the pretense of love to an obscure stranger! The Baroness tells me this actress—this singer—what is she?—is pretty. Is it true?"

The Baroness was quite mischievous enough to have also mentioned the false impression, prevalent about the Court, that I was in love with Jeanne. I attempted to explain. The gracious Princess refused to hear me.

"Do you think I doubt you?" she said. "Distinguished by me, could you waste a look on a person in that rank of life?" She laughed softly, as if the mere idea of such a thing amused her. It was only for a moment: her thoughts took a new direction—they contemplated the uncertain future. "How is this to end?" she asked. "Dear Ernest, we are not in Paradise; we are in a hard cruel world which insists on distinctions in rank. To what unhappy destiny does the fascination which you exercise over me condemn us both?"

She paused—took one of the white roses out of her bosom—touched it with her lips—and gave it to me.

"I wonder whether you feel the burden of life as I feel it?" she resumed. "It is immaterial to me, whether we are united in this world or in the next. Accept my rose, Ernest, as an assurance that I speak with perfect sincerity. I see but two alternatives before us. One of them (beset with dangers) is elopement. And the other," she added, with truly majestic composure, "is suicide."

Would Englishmen in general have rightly understood such fearless confidence in them as this language implied? I am afraid they might have attributed it to what my friend the secretary called "German sentiment." Perhaps they might even have suspected the Princess of quoting from some old-fashioned German play. Under the irresistible influence of that glorious creature, I contemplated with such equal serenity the perils of elopement and the martyrdom of love, that I was for the moment at a loss how to reply. In that moment, the evil genius of my life appeared in the conservatory. With haste in her steps, with alarm in her face, the Baroness rushed up to her royal mistress, and said, "For God's sake, Madam, come away! The Prince desires to speak with you instantly."

Her Highness rose, calmly superior to the vulgar excitement of her lady in waiting. "Think of it to-night," she said to me, "and let me hear from you to-morrow."

She pressed my hand; she gave me a farewell look. I sank into the chair that she had just left. Did I think of elopement? Did I think of suicide? The elevating influence of the Princess no longer sustained me; my nature became degraded. Horrid doubts rose in my mind. Did her father suspect us?

IX.

NEED I say that I passed a sleepless night?

The morning found me with my pen in my hand, confronting the serious responsibility of writing to the Princess, and not knowing what to say. I had already torn up two letters, when Uncle David presented himself with a message from his niece. Jeanne was in trouble, and wanted to ask my advice.

My state of mind, on hearing this, became simply inexplicable. Here was an interruption which ought to have annoyed me. It did nothing of the kind—it inspired me with a feeling of relief!

I naturally expected that the old Frenchman would return with me to his niece, and tell me what had happened. To my surprise, he begged that I would excuse him, and left me without a word of explanation. I found Jeanne walking up and down her little sitting-room, flushed and angry. Fragments of torn paper and heaps of flowers littered the floor; and three unopen jewel-cases appeared to have been thrown into the empty fireplace. She caught me excitedly by the hand the moment I entered the room.

"You are my true friend," she said; "you were present the other night when I sang. Was there anything in my behavior on the stage which could justify men who call themselves gentlemen in insulting me?"

"My dear, how can you ask the question?"

"I must ask it. Some of them send flowers, and some of them send jewels; and every one of them writes letters—infamous, abominable letters— saying they are in love with me, and asking for appointments as if I was—"

She could say no more. Poor dear Jeanne—her head dropped on my shoulder; she burst out crying. Who could see her so cruelly humiliated— the faithful loving daughter, whose one motive for appearing on the stage had been to preserve her father's good name—and not feel for her as I did? I forgot all considerations of prudence; I thought of nothing but consoling her; I took her in my arms; I dried her tears; I kissed her; I said, "Tell me the name of any one of the wretches who has written to you, and I will make him an example to the rest!" She shook her head, and pointed to the morsels of paper on the floor. "Oh, Ernest, do you think I asked you to come here for any such purpose as that? Those jewels, those hateful jewels, tell me how I can send them back! spare me the sight of them!"

So far it was easy to console her. I sent the jewels at once to the manager of the theater—with a written notice to be posted at the stage door, stating that they were waiting to be returned to the persons who could describe them.

"Try, my dear, to forget what has happened," I said. "Try to find consolation and encouragement in your art."

"I have lost all interest in my success on the stage," she answered, "now I know the penalty I must pay for it. When my father's memory is clear of reproach, I shall leave the theater never to return to it again."

"Take time to consider, Jeanne."

"I will do anything you ask of me."

For a while we were silent. Without any influence to lead to it that

I could trace, I found myself recalling the language that the Princess had used in alluding to Jeanne. When I thought of them now, the words and the tone in which they had been spoken jarred on me. There is surely something mean in an assertion of superiority which depends on nothing better than the accident of birth. I don't know why I took Jeanne's hand; I don't know why I said, "What a good girl you are! how glad I am to have been of some little use to you!" Is my friend the secretary right, when he reproaches me with acting on impulse, like a woman? I don't like to think so; and yet, this I must own— it was well for me that I was obliged to leave her, before I had perhaps said other words which might have been alike unworthy of Jeanne, of the Princess, and of myself. I was called away to speak to my servant. He brought with him the secretary's card, having a line written on it: "I am waiting at your rooms, on business which permits of no delay."

As we shook hands, Jeanne asked me if I knew where her uncle was. I could only tell her that he had left me at my own door. She made no remark; but she seemed to be uneasy on receiving that reply.

X.

WHEN I arrived at my rooms, my colleague hurried to meet me the moment I opened the door.

"I am going to surprise you," he said; "and there is no time to prepare you for it. Our chief, the Minister, has seen the Prince this morning, and has been officially informed of an event of importance in the life of the Princess. She is engaged to be married to the Grand Duke."

Engaged to the Duke—and not a word from her to warn me of it! Engaged—after what she had said to me no longer ago than the past night! Had I been made a plaything to amuse a great lady? Oh, what degradation! I was furious; I snatched up my hat to go to the palace—to force my way to her—to overwhelm her with reproaches. My friend stopped me. He put an official document into my hand.

"There is your leave of absence from the legation," he said; "beginning from to-day. I have informed the Minister, in strict confidence, of the critical position in which you are placed. He agrees with me that the Princess's inexcusable folly is alone to blame. Leave us, Ernest, by the next train. There is some intrigue going on, and I fear you may be involved in it. You know that the rulers of these little German States can exercise despotic authority when they choose?"

"Yes! yes!"

"Whether the Prince has acted of his own free will—or whether he has been influenced by some person about him—I am not able to tell you. He has issued an order to arrest an old Frenchman, known to be a republican, and suspected of associating with one of the secret societies in this part of Germany. The conspirator has taken to flight; having friends, as we suppose, who warned him in time. But this, Ernest, is not the worst of it. That charming singer, that modest, pretty girl—"

"You don't mean Jeanne?"

"I am sorry to say I do. Advantage has been taken of her relationship to the old man, to include that innocent creature in political suspicions which it is simply absurd to suppose that she has deserved. She is ordered to leave the Prince's domains immediately.—Are you going to her?"

"Instantly!" I replied.

Could I feel a moment's hesitation, after the infamous manner in which the Princess had sacrificed me to the Grand Duke? Could I think of the poor girl, friendless, helpless—with nobody near her but a stupid woman-servant, unable to speak the language of the country—and fail to devote myself to the protection of Jeanne? Thank God, I reached her lodgings in time to tell her what had happened, and to take it on myself to receive the police.

XI.

IN three days more, Jeanne was safe in London; having traveled under my escort. I was fortunate enough to find a home for her, in the house of a lady who had been my mother's oldest and dearest friend.

We were separated, a few days afterward, by the distressing news which reached me of the state of my brother's health. I went at once to his house in the country. His medical attendants had lost all hope of saving him: they told me plainly that his release from a life of suffering was near at hand.

While I was still in attendance at his bedside, I heard from the secretary. He inclosed a letter, directed to me in a strange handwriting. I opened the envelope and looked for the signature. My friend had been entrapped into sending me an anonymous letter.

Besides addressing me in French (a language seldom used in my experience at the legation), the writer disguised the identity of the persons mentioned by the use of classical names. In spite of these precautions, I felt no difficulty in arriving at a conclusion. My correspondent's special knowledge of Court secrets, and her malicious way of communicating them, betrayed the Baroness.

I translate the letter; restoring to the persons who figure in it the names under which they are already known. The writer began in these satirically familiar terms:

"When you left the Prince's dominions, my dear sir, you no doubt believed yourself to be a free agent. Quite a mistake! You were a mere puppet; and the strings that moved you were pulled by the Doctor.

"Let me tell you how.

"On a certain night, which you well remember, the Princess was unexpectedly summoned to the presence of her father. His physician's skill had succeeded in relieving the illustrious Prince, prostrate under nervous miseries. He was able to attend to a state affair of importance, revealed to him by the Doctor—who then for the first time acknowledged that he had presented himself at Court in a diplomatic, as well as in a medical capacity.

"This state affair related to a proposal for the hand of the Princess, received from the Grand Duke through the authorized medium of the Doctor. Her Highness, being consulted, refused to consider the proposal. The Prince asked for her reason. She answered: 'I have no wish to be married.' Naturally irritated by such a ridiculous excuse, her father declared positively that the marriage should take place.

"The impression produced on the Grand Duke's favorite and emissary was of a different kind.

"Certain suspicions of the Princess and yourself, which you had successfully contrived to dissipate, revived in the Doctor's mind when he heard the lady's reason for refusing to marry his royal master. It was now too late to regret that he had suffered himself to be misled by cleverly managed appearances. He could not recall the favorable report which he had addressed to the Duke—or withdraw the proposal of marriage which he had been commanded to make.

"In this emergency, the one safe course open to him was to get rid of You—and, at the same time, so to handle circumstances as to excite against you the pride and anger of the Princess. In the pursuit of this latter object he was assisted by one of the ladies in waiting, sincerely interested in the welfare of her gracious mistress, and therefore ardently desirous of seeing her Highness married to the Duke.

"A wretched old French conspirator was made the convenient pivot on which the intrigue turned.

"An order for the arrest of this foreign republican having been first obtained, the Prince was prevailed on to extend his distrust of the Frenchman to the Frenchman's niece. You know this already; but you don't know why it was done. Having believed from the first that you were really in love with the young lady, the Doctor reckoned confidently on your devoting yourself to the protection of a friendless girl, cruelly exiled at an hour's notice.

"The one chance against us was that tender considerations, associated with her Highness, might induce you to hesitate. The lady in waiting easily moved this obstacle out of the way. She abstained from delivering a letter addressed to you, intrusted to her by the Princess. When the great lady asked why she had not received your reply, she was informed (quite truly) that you and the charming opera singer had taken your departure together. You may imagine what her Highness thought of you, and said of you, when I mention in conclusion that she consented, the same day, to marry the Duke.

"So, Mr. Ernest, these clever people tricked you into serving their interests, blindfold. In relating how it was done, I hope I may have assisted you in forming a correct estimate of the state of your own intelligence. You have made a serious mistake in adopting your present profession. Give up diplomacy—and get a farmer to employ you in keeping his sheep."

Do I sometimes think regretfully of the Princess?

Permit me to mention a circumstance, and to leave my answer to be inferred. Jeanne is Lady Medhurst.

MR. LISMORE AND THE WIDOW.

I.

LATE in the autumn, not many years since, a public meeting was held at the Mansion House, London, under the direction of the Lord Mayor.

The list of gentlemen invited to address the audience had been chosen with two objects in view. Speakers of celebrity, who would rouse public enthusiasm, were supported by speakers connected with commerce, who would be practically useful in explaining the purpose for which the meeting was convened. Money wisely spent in advertising had produced the customary result—every seat was occupied before the proceedings began.

Among the late arrivals, who had no choice but to stand or to leave the hall, were two ladies. One of them at once decided on leaving the hall. "I shall go back to the carriage," she said, "and wait for you at the door." Her friend answered, "I shan't keep you long. He is advertised to support the second Resolution; I want to see him—and that is all."

An elderly gentleman, seated at the end of a bench, rose and offered his place to the lady who remained. She hesitated to take advantage of his kindness, until he reminded her that he had heard what she said to her friend. Before the third Resolution was proposed, his seat would be at his own disposal again. She thanked him, and without further ceremony took his place He was provided with an opera-glass, which he more than once offered to her, when famous orators appeared on the platform; she made no use of it until a speaker—known in the City as a ship-owner—stepped forward to support the second Resolution.

His name (announced in the advertisements) was Ernest Lismore.

The moment he rose, the lady asked for the opera-glass. She kept it to her eyes for such a length of time, and with such evident interest in Mr. Lismore, that the curiosity of her neighbors was aroused. Had he anything to say in which a lady (evidently a stranger to him) was personally interested? There was nothing in the address that he delivered which appealed to the enthusiasm of women. He was undoubtedly a handsome man, whose appearance proclaimed him to be in the prime of life—midway perhaps between thirty and forty years of age. But why a lady should persist in keeping an opera-glass fixed on him all through his speech, was a question which found the general ingenuity at a loss for a reply.

Having returned the glass with an apology, the lady ventured on putting a question next. "Did it strike you, sir, that Mr. Lismore seemed to be out of spirits?" she asked.

"I can't say it did, ma'am."

"Perhaps you noticed that he left the platform the moment he had done?"

This betrayal of interest in the speaker did not escape the notice of a lady, seated on the bench in front. Before the old gentleman could answer, she volunteered an explanation.

"I am afraid Mr. Lismore is troubled by anxieties connected with his business," she said. "My husband heard it reported in the City yesterday that he was seriously embarrassed by the failure—"

A loud burst of applause made the end of the sentence inaudible. A famous member of Parliament had risen to propose the third Resolution. The polite old man took his seat, and the lady left the hall to join her friend.

"Well, Mrs. Callender, has Mr. Lismore disappointed you?"

"Far from it! But I have heard a report about him which has alarmed me: he is said to be seriously troubled about money matters. How can I find out his address in the City?"

"We can stop at the first stationer's shop we pass, and ask to look at the Directory. Are you going to pay Mr. Lismore a visit?"

"I am going to think about it."

II.

THE next day a clerk entered Mr. Lismore's private room at the office, and presented a visiting-card. Mrs. Callender had reflected, and had arrived at a decision. Underneath her name she had written these explanatory words: "On important business."

"Does she look as if she wanted money?" Mr. Lismore inquired.

"Oh dear, no! She comes in her carriage."

"Is she young or old?"

"Old, sir."

To Mr. Lismore—conscious of the disastrous influence occasionally exercised over busy men by youth and beauty—this was a recommendation in itself. He said: "Show her in."

Observing the lady, as she approached him, with the momentary curiosity of a stranger, he noticed that she still preserved the remains of beauty. She had also escaped the misfortune, common to persons at her time of life, of becoming too fat. Even to a man's eye, her dressmaker appeared to have made the most of that favorable circumstance. Her figure had its defects concealed, and its remaining merits set off to advantage. At the same time she evidently held herself above the common deceptions by which some women seek to conceal their age. She wore her own gray hair; and her complexion bore the test of daylight. On entering the room, she made her apologies with some embarrassment. Being the embarrassment of a stranger (and not of a youthful stranger), it failed to impress Mr. Lismore favorably.

"I am afraid I have chosen an inconvenient time for my visit," she began.

"I am at your service," he answered a little stiffly; "especially if you will be so kind as to mention your business with me in few words."

She was a woman of some spirit, and that reply roused her.

"I will mention it in one word," she said smartly. "My business is—gratitude."

He was completely at a loss to understand what she meant, and he said so plainly. Instead of explaining herself, she put a question.

"Do you remember the night of the eleventh of March, between five and six years since?"

He considered for a moment.

"No," he said, "I don't remember it. Excuse me, Mrs. Callender, I have affairs of my own to attend to which cause me some anxiety—"

"Let me assist your memory, Mr. Lismore; and I will leave you to your affairs. On the date that I have referred to, you were on your way to the railway-station at Bexmore, to catch the night express from the North to London."

As a hint that his time was valuable the ship-owner had hitherto remained standing. He now took his customary seat, and began to listen with some interest. Mrs. Callender had produced her effect on him already.

"It was absolutely necessary," she proceeded, "that you should be on board your ship in the London Docks at nine o'clock the next morning. If you had lost the express, the vessel would have sailed without you."

The expression of his face began to change to surprise. "Who told you that?" he asked.

"You shall hear directly. On your way into the town, your carriage was stopped by an obstruction on the highroad. The people of Bexmore were looking at a house on fire."

He started to his feet.

"Good heavens! are you the lady?"

She held up her hand in satirical protest.

"Gently, sir! You suspected me just now of wasting your valuable time. Don't rashly conclude that I am the lady, until you find that I am acquainted with the circumstances."

"Is there no excuse for my failing to recognize you?" Mr. Lismore asked. "We were on the dark side of the burning house; you were fainting, and I—"

"And you," she interposed, "after saving me at the risk of your own life, turned a deaf ear to my poor husband's entreaties, when he asked you to wait till I had recovered my senses."

"Your poor husband? Surely, Mrs. Callender, he received no serious injury from the fire?"

"The firemen rescued him under circumstances of peril," she answered, "and at his great age he sank under the shock. I have lost the kindest and best of men. Do you remember how you parted from him—burned and bruised in saving me? He liked to talk of it in his last illness. 'At least' (he said to you), 'tell me the name of the man who has preserved my wife from a dreadful death.' You threw your card to him out of the carriage window, and away you went at a gallop to catch your train! In all the years that have passed I have kept that card, and have vainly inquired for my brave sea-captain. Yesterday I saw your name on the list of speakers at the Mansion House. Need I say that I attended the meeting? Need I tell you now why I come here and interrupt you in business hours?"

She held out her hand. Mr. Lismore took it in silence, and pressed it warmly.

"You have not done with me yet," she resumed with a smile. "Do you remember what I said of my errand, when I first came in?"

"You said it was an errand of gratitude."

"Something more than the gratitude which only says 'Thank you,'" she added. "Before I explain myself, however, I want to know what you have been doing, and how it was that my inquiries failed to trace you after that terrible night."

The appearance of depression which Mrs. Callender had noticed at the public meeting showed itself again in Mr. Lismore's face. He sighed as he answered her.

"My story has one merit," he said; "it is soon told. I cannot wonder that you failed to discover me. In the first place, I was not captain of my ship at that time; I was only mate. In the second place, I inherited some money, and ceased to lead a sailor's life, in less than a year from the night of the fire. You will now understand what obstacles were in the way of your tracing me. With my little capital I started successfully in business as a ship-owner. At the time, I naturally congratulated myself on my own good fortune. We little know, Mrs. Callender, what the future has in store for us."

He stopped. His handsome features hardened—as if he was suffering (and concealing) pain. Before it was possible to speak to him, there was a knock at the door. Another visitor, without an appointment, had called; the clerk appeared again, with a card and a message.

"The gentleman begs you will see him, sir. He has something to tell you which is too important to be delayed."

Hearing the message, Mrs. Callender rose immediately.

"It is enough for to-day that we understand each other," she said. "Have you any engagement to-morrow, after the hours of business?"

"None."

She pointed to her card on the writing-table. "Will you come to me to-morrow evening at that address? I am like the gentleman who has just called; I, too, have my reason for wishing to see you."

He gladly accepted the invitation. Mrs. Callender stopped him as he opened the door for her.

"Shall I offend you," she said, "if I ask a strange question before I go? I have a better motive, mind, than mere curiosity. Are you married?"

"No."

"Forgive me again," she resumed. "At my age, you cannot possibly misunderstand me; and yet—"

She hesitated. Mr. Lismore tried to give her confidence. "Pray don't

494

stand on ceremony, Mrs. Callender. Nothing that you can ask me need be prefaced by an apology."

Thus encouraged, she ventured to proceed.

"You may be engaged to be married?" she suggested. "Or you may be in love?"

He found it impossible to conceal his surprise. But he answered without hesitation.

"There is no such bright prospect in my life," he said. "I am not even in love."

She left him with a little sigh. It sounded like a sigh of relief.

Ernest Lismore was thoroughly puzzled. What could be the old lady's object in ascertaining that he was still free from a matrimonial engagement? If the idea had occurred to him in time, he might have alluded to her domestic life, and might have asked if she had children? With a little tact he might have discovered more than this. She had described her feeling toward him as passing the ordinary limits of gratitude; and she was evidently rich enough to be above the imputation of a mercenary motive. Did she propose to brighten those dreary prospects to which he had alluded in speaking of his own life? When he presented himself at her house the next evening, would she introduce him to a charming daughter?

He smiled as the idea occurred to him. "An appropriate time to be thinking of my chances of marriage!" he said to himself. "In another month I may be a ruined man."

III.

THE gentleman who had so urgently requested an interview was a devoted friend—who had obtained a means of helping Ernest at a serious crisis in his affairs.

It had been truly reported that he was in a position of pecuniary embarrassment, owing to the failure of a mercantile house with which he had been intimately connected. Whispers affecting his own solvency had followed on the bankruptcy of the firm. He had already endeavored to obtain advances of money on the usual conditions, and had been met by excuses for delay. His friend had now arrived with a letter of introduction to a capitalist, well known in commercial circles for his daring speculations and for his great wealth.

Looking at the letter, Ernest observed that the envelope was sealed. In spite of that ominous innovation on established usage, in cases of personal introduction, he presented the letter. On this occasion, he was not put off with excuses. The capitalist flatly declined to discount Mr. Lismore's bills, unless they were backed by responsible names.

Ernest made a last effort.

He applied for help to two mercantile men whom he had assisted in their difficulties, and whose names would have satisfied the money-lender. They were most sincerely sorry—but they, too, refused.

The one security that he could offer was open, it must be owned, to serious objections on the score of risk. He wanted an advance of twenty thousand pounds, secured on a homeward-bound ship and cargo. But the vessel was not insured; and, at that stormy season, she was already more than a month overdue. Could grateful colleagues be blamed if they forgot their obligations when they were asked to offer pecuniary help to a merchant in this situation? Ernest returned to his office, without money and without credit.

A man threatened by ruin is in no state of mind to keep an engagement at a lady's tea-table. Ernest sent a letter of apology to Mrs. Call ender, alleging extreme pressure of business as the excuse for breaking his engagement.

"Am I to wait for an answer, sir?" the messenger asked.

"No; you are merely to leave the letter."

IV.

IN an hour's time—to Ernest's astonishment—the messenger returned with a reply.

"The lady was just going out, sir, when I rang at the door," he explained,

496

"and she took the letter from me herself. She didn't appear to know your handwriting, and she asked me who I came from. When I mentioned your name, I was ordered to wait."

Ernest opened the letter.

"DEAR MR. LISMORE—One of us must speak out, and your letter of apology forces me to be that one. If you are really so proud and so distrustfull as you seem to be, I shall offend you. If not, I shall prove myself to be your friend.

"Your excuse is 'pressure of business.' The truth (as I have good reason to believe) is 'want of money.' I heard a stranger, at that public meeting, say that you were seriously embarrassed by some failure in the City.

"Let me tell you what my own pecuniary position is in two words. I am the childless widow of a rich man—"

Ernest paused. His anticipated discovery of Mrs. Callender's "charming daughter" was in his mind for the moment. "That little romance must return to the world of dreams," he thought—and went on with the letter.

"After what I owe to you, I don't regard it as repaying an obligation—I consider myself as merely performing a duty when I offer to assist you by a loan of money.

"Wait a little before you throw my letter into the wastepaper basket.

"Circumstances (which it is impossible for me to mention before we meet) put it out of my power to help you—unless I attach to my most sincere offer of service a very unusual and very embarrassing condition. If you are on the brink of ruin, that misfortune will plead my excuse—and your excuse, too, if you accept the loan on my terms. In any case, I rely on the sympathy and forbearance of the man to whom I owe my life.

"After what I have now written, there is only one thing to add. I beg to decline accepting your excuses; and I shall expect to see you tomorrow evening, as we arranged. I am an obstinate old woman—but I am also your faithful friend and servant,

"MARY CALLENDER."

Ernest looked up from the letter. "What can this possibly mean?" he wondered.

But he was too sensible a man to be content with wondering—he decided on keeping his engagement.

V.

WHAT Doctor Johnson called "the insolence of wealth" appears far more frequently in the houses of the rich than in the manners of the rich. The reason is plain enough. Personal ostentation is, in the very nature of it, ridiculous. But the ostentation which exhibits magnificent pictures, priceless china, and splendid furniture, can purchase good taste to guide it, and can assert itself without affording the smallest opening for a word of depreciation, or a look of contempt. If I am worth a million of money, and if I am dying to show it, I don't ask you to look at me—I ask you to look at my house.

Keeping his engagement with Mrs. Callender, Ernest discovered that riches might be lavishly and yet modestly used.

In crossing the hall and ascending the stairs, look where he might, his notice was insensibly won by proofs of the taste which is not to be purchased, and the wealth which uses but never exhibits its purse. Conducted by a man-servant to the landing on the first floor, he found a maid at the door of the boudoir waiting to announce him. Mrs. Callender advanced to welcome her guest, in a simple evening dress perfectly suited to her age. All that had looked worn and faded in her fine face, by daylight, was now softly obscured by shaded lamps. Objects of beauty surrounded her, which glowed with subdued radiance from their background of sober color. The influence of appearances is the strongest of all outward influences, while it lasts. For the moment, the scene produced its impression on Ernest, in spite of the terrible anxieties which consumed him. Mrs. Callender, in his office, was a woman who had stepped out of her appropriate sphere. Mrs. Callender, in her own house, was a woman who had risen to a new place in his estimation.

"I am afraid you don't thank me for forcing you to keep your engagement," she said, with her friendly tones and her pleasant smile.

"Indeed I do thank you," he replied. "Your beautiful house and your gracious welcome have persuaded me into forgetting my troubles—for a while."

The smile passed away from her face. "Then it is true," she said gravely.

"Only too true."

She led him to a seat beside her, and waited to speak again until her maid had brought in the tea.

"Have you read my letter in the same friendly spirit in which I wrote it?" she asked, when they were alone again.

"I have read your letter gratefully, but—"

"But you don't know yet what I have to say. Let us understand each other before we make any objections on either side. Will you tell me what your present position is—at its worst? I can and will speak plainly when my turn comes, if you will honor me with your confidence. Not if it distresses you," she added, observing him attentively.

He was ashamed of his hesitation—and he made amends for it.

"Do you thoroughly understand me?" he asked, when the whole truth had been laid before her without reserve.

She summed up the result in her own words.

"If your overdue ship returns safely, within a month from this time, you can borrow the money you want, without difficulty. If the ship is lost, you have no alternative (when the end of the month comes) but to accept a loan from me or to suspend payment. Is that the hard truth?"

"It is."

"And the sum you require is—twenty thousand pounds?"

"Yes."

"I have twenty times as much money as that, Mr. Lismore, at my sole disposal—on one condition."

"The condition alluded to in your letter?"

"Yes."

"Does the fulfillment of the condition depend in some way on any decision of mine?"

"It depends entirely on you."

That answer closed his lips.

With a composed manner and a steady hand she poured herself out a cup of tea.

"I conceal it from you," she said; "but I want confidence. Here" (she pointed to the cup) "is the friend of women, rich or poor, when they are in trouble. What I have now to say obliges me to speak in praise of myself. I don't like it—let me get it over as soon as I can. My husband was very fond of me: he had the most absolute confidence in my discretion, and in my sense of duty to him and to myself. His last words, before he died, were words that thanked me for making the happiness of his life. As soon as I had in some degree recovered, after the affliction that had fallen on me, his lawyer and executor produced a copy of his will, and said there were two clauses in it which my husband had expressed a wish that I should read. It is needless to say that I obeyed."

She still controlled her agitation—but she was now unable to conceal it. Ernest made an attempt to spare her.

"Am I concerned in this?" he asked.

"Yes. Before I tell you why, I want to know what you would do—in a certain case which I am unwilling even to suppose. I have heard of men, unable to pay the demands made on them, who began business again, and succeeded, and in course of time paid their creditors."

"And you want to know if there is any likelihood of my following their example?" he said. "Have you also heard of men who have made that second effort—who have failed again—and who have doubled the debts they owed to their brethren in business who trusted them? I knew one of those men myself. He committed suicide."

She laid her hand for a moment on his.

"I understand you," she said. "If ruin comes—"

"If ruin comes," he interposed, "a man without money and without credit can make but one last atonement. Don't speak of it now."

She looked at him with horror.

"I didn't mean that!" she said.

"Shall we go back to what you read in the will?" he suggested.

"Yes—if you will give me a minute to compose myself."

VI.

IN less than the minute she had asked for, Mrs. Callender was calm enough to go on.

"I now possess what is called a life-interest in my husband's fortune," she said. "The money is to be divided, at my death, among charitable institutions; excepting a certain event—"

"Which is provided for in the will?" Ernest added, helping her to go on.

"Yes. I am to be absolute mistress of the whole of the four hundred thousand pounds—" her voice dropped, and her eyes looked away from him as she spoke the next words—"on this one condition, that I marry again."

He looked at her in amazement.

"Surely I have mistaken you," he said. "You mean on this one condition, that you do not marry again?"

"No, Mr. Lismore; I mean exactly what I have said. You now know that the recovery of your credit and your peace of mind rests entirely with yourself."

After a moment of reflection he took her hand and raised it respectfully to his lips. "You are a noble woman!" he said.

She made no reply. With drooping head and downcast eyes she waited for his decision. He accepted his responsibility.

"I must not, and dare not, think of the hardship of my own position," he said; "I owe it to you to speak without reference to the future that may be in store for me. No man can be worthy of the sacrifice which your generous forgetfulness of yourself is willing to make. I respect you; I admire you; I thank you with my whole heart. Leave me to my fate, Mrs. Callender—and let me go."

He rose. She stopped him by a gesture.

"A young woman," she answered, "would shrink from saying—what I, as an old woman, mean to say now. I refuse to leave you to your fate. I ask you to prove that you respect me, admire me, and thank me with your whole heart. Take one day to think—and let me hear the result. You promise me this?"

He promised. "Now go," she said.

VII.

NEXT morning Ernest received a letter from Mrs. Callender. She wrote to him as follows:

"There are some considerations which I ought to have mentioned yesterday evening, before you left my house.

"I ought to have reminded you—if you consent to reconsider your decision—that the circumstances do not require you to pledge yourself to me absolutely.

"At my age, I can with perfect propriety assure you that I regard our marriage simply and solely as a formality which we must fulfill, if I am to carry out my intention of standing between you and ruin.

"Therefore—if the missing ship appears in time, the only reason for the marriage is at an end. We shall be as good friends as ever; without the encumbrance of a formal tie to bind us.

"In the other event, I should ask you to submit to certain restrictions which, remembering my position, you will understand and excuse.

"We are to live together, it is unnecessary to say, as mother and son. The marriage ceremony is to be strictly private; and you are so to arrange your affairs that, immediately afterward, we leave England for any foreign place which you prefer. Some of my friends, and (perhaps) some of your friends, will certainly misinterpret our motives—if we stay in our own country—in a manner which would be unendurable to a woman like me.

"As to our future lives, I have the most perfect confidence in you, and I should leave you in the same position of independence which you occupy now. When you wish for my company you will always be welcome. At other times, you are your own master. I live on my side of the house, and you live on yours—and I am to be allowed my hours of solitude every day, in the pursuit of musical occupations, which have been happily associated with all my past life and which I trust confidently to your indulgence.

"A last word, to remind you of what you may be too kind to think of yourself.

"At my age, you cannot, in the course of Nature, be troubled by the society of a grateful old woman for many years. You are young enough to look forward to another marriage, which shall be something more than a mere form. Even if you meet with the happy woman in my lifetime, honestly tell me of it—and I promise to tell her that she has only to wait.

"In the meantime, don't think, because I write composedly, that I write heartlessly. You pleased and interested me, when I first saw you, at the public meeting. I don't think I could have proposed, what you call this sacrifice of myself, to a man who had personally repelled me—though I might have felt my debt of gratitude as sincerely as ever. Whether your ship is saved, or whether your ship is lost, old Mary Callender likes you—and owns it without false shame.

"Let me have your answer this evening, either personally or by letter—whichever you like best."

VIII.

MRS. CALLENDER received a written answer long before the evening. It said much in few words:

"A man impenetrable to kindness might be able to resist your letter. I am not that man. Your great heart has conquered me."

The few formalities which precede marriage by special license were observed by Ernest. While the destiny of their future lives was still in suspense, an unacknowledged feeling of embarrassment, on either side, kept Ernest and Mrs. Callender apart. Every day brought the lady her report of the state of affairs in the City, written always in the same words: "No news of the ship."

IX.

ON the day before the ship-owner's liabilities became due, the terms of the report from the City remained unchanged—and the special license was put to its contemplated use. Mrs. Callender's lawyer and Mrs. Callender's maid were the only persons trusted with the secret. Leaving the chief clerk in charge of the business, with every pecuniary demand on his employer satisfied in full, the strangely married pair quitted England.

They arranged to wait for a few days in Paris, to receive any letters of importance which might have been addressed to Ernest in the interval. On the evening of their arrival, a telegram from London was waiting at their hotel. It announced that the missing ship had passed up Channel—undiscovered in a fog, until she reached the Downs—on the day before Ernest's liabilities fell due.

"Do you regret it?" Mrs. Lismore said to her husband.

"Not for a moment!" he answered.

They decided on pursuing their journey as far as Munich.

Mrs. Lismore's taste for music was matched by Ernest's taste for painting. In his leisure hours he cultivated the art, and delighted in it. The picture-galleries of Munich were almost the only galleries in Europe which he had not seen. True to the engagements to which she had pledged herself, his wife was willing to go wherever it might please him to take her. The one suggestion she made was, that they should hire furnished apartments. If they lived at an hotel, friends of the husband or the wife (visitors like themselves to the famous city) might see their names in the book, or might meet them at the door.

They were soon established in a house large enough to provide them with every accommodation which they required.

Ernest's days were passed in the galleries; Mrs. Lismore remaining at home, devoted to her music, until it was time to go out with her husband for a drive. Living together in perfect amity and concord, they were nevertheless not living happily. Without any visible reason for the change, Mrs. Lismore's spirits were depressed. On the one occasion when Ernest noticed it she made an effort to be cheerful, which it distressed him to see. He allowed her to think that she had relieved him of any further anxiety. Whatever doubts he might feel were doubts delicately concealed from that time forth.

But when two people are living together in a state of artificial tranquillity, it seems to be a law of Nature that the element of disturbance gathers unseen, and that the outburst comes inevitably with the lapse of time.

In ten days from the date of their arrival at Munich, the crisis came. Ernest returned later than usual from the picture-gallery, and—for the first time in his wife's experience—shut himself up in his own room.

He appeared at the dinner-hour with a futile excuse. Mrs. Lismore waited until the servant had withdrawn. "Now, Ernest," she said, "it's time to tell me the truth."

Her manner, when she said those few words, took him by surprise. She was unquestionably confused; and, instead of looking at him, she trifled with the fruit on her plate. Embarrassed on his side, he could only answer:

"I have nothing to tell."

"Were there many visitors at the gallery?" she asked.

"About the same as usual."

"Any that you particularly noticed?" she went on. "I mean, among the ladies."

He laughed uneasily. "You forget how interested I am in the pictures," he said.

There was a pause. She looked up at him—and suddenly looked away again. But he saw it plainly: there were tears in her eyes.

"Do you mind turning down the gas?" she said. "My eyes have been weak all day."

He complied with her request—the more readily, having his own reasons for being glad to escape the glaring scrutiny of the light.

"I think I will rest a little on the sofa," she resumed. In the position which he occupied, his back would have been now turned on her. She stopped him when he tried to move his chair. "I would rather not look at you, Ernest," she said, "when you have lost confidence in me."

Not the words, but the tone, touched all that was generous and noble in his nature. He left his place, and knelt beside her—and opened to her his whole heart.

"Am I not unworthy of you?" he asked, when it was over.

She pressed his hand in silence.

"I should be the most ungrateful wretch living," he said, "if I did not think of you, and you only, now that my confession is made. We will leave Munich to-morrow—and, if resolution can help me, I will only remember the sweetest woman my eyes ever looked on as the creature of a dream."

She hid her face on his breast, and reminded him of that letter of her writing, which had decided the course of their lives.

"When I thought you might meet the happy woman in my life-time, I said to you, 'Tell me of it—and I promise to tell her that she has only to wait.' Time must pass, Ernest, before it can be needful to perform my promise. But you might let me see her. If you find her in the gallery to-morrow, you might bring her here."

Mrs. Lismore's request met with no refusal. Ernest was only at a loss to know how to grant it.

"You tell me she is a copyist of pictures," his wife reminded him. "She will be interested in hearing of the portfolio of drawings by the great French artists which I bought for you in Paris. Ask her to come and see them, and to tell you if she can make some copies. And say, if you like, that I shall be glad to become acquainted with her."

He felt her breath beating fast on his bosom. In the fear that she might lose all control over herself, he tried to relieve her by speaking lightly. "What an invention yours is!" he said. "If my wife ever tries to deceive me, I shall be a mere child in her hands."

She rose abruptly from the sofa—kissed him on the forehead—and said wildly, "I shall be better in bed!" Before he could move or speak, she had left him.

X.

THE next morning he knocked at the door of his wife's room and asked how she had passed the night.

"I have slept badly," she answered, "and I must beg you to excuse my absence at breakfast-time." She called him back as he was about to withdraw. "Remember," she said, "when you return from the gallery to-day, I expect that you will not return alone."

Three hours later he was at home again. The young lady's services as a copyist were at his disposal; she had returned with him to look at the drawings.

The sitting-room was empty when they entered it. He rang for his wife's maid—and was informed that Mrs. Lismore had gone out. Refusing to believe the woman, he went to his wife's apartments. She was not to be found.

When he returned to the sitting-room, the young lady was not unnaturally offended. He could make allowances for her being a little out of temper at the slight that had been put on her; but he was inexpressibly disconcerted by the manner—almost the coarse manner—in which she expressed herself.

"I have been talking to your wife's maid, while you have been away," she said. "I find you have married an old lady for her money. She is jealous of me, of course?"

"Let me beg you to alter your opinion," he answered. "You are wronging my wife; she is incapable of any such feeling as you attribute to her."

The young lady laughed. "At any rate you are a good husband," she said satirically. "Suppose you own the truth? Wouldn't you like her better if she was young and pretty like me?"

He was not merely surprised—he was disgusted. Her beauty had so completely fascinated him, when he first saw her, that the idea of associating any want of refinement and good breeding with such a charming creature never entered his mind. The disenchantment to him was already so complete that he was even disagreeably affected by the tone of her voice: it was almost as repellent to him as the exhibition of unrestrained bad temper which she seemed perfectly careless to conceal.

"I confess you surprise me," he said, coldly.

The reply produced no effect on her. On the contrary, she became more insolent than ever.

"I have a fertile fancy," she went on, "and your absurd way of taking a joke only encourages me! Suppose you could transform this sour old wife of yours, who has insulted me, into the sweetest young creature that ever lived, by only holding up your finger—wouldn't you do it?"

This passed the limits of his endurance. "I have no wish," he said, "to forget the consideration which is due to a woman. You leave me but one alternative." He rose to go out of the room.

She ran to the door as he spoke, and placed herself in the way of his going out.

He signed to her to let him pass.

She suddenly threw her arms round his neck, kissed him passionately, and whispered, with her lips at his ear: "Oh, Ernest, forgive me! Could I have asked you to marry me for my money if I had not taken refuge in a disguise?"

XI.

WHEN he had sufficiently recovered to think, he put her back from him. "Is there an end of the deception now?" he asked, sternly. "Am I to trust you in your new character?"

"You are not to be harder on me than I deserve," she answered, gently. "Did you ever hear of an actress named Miss Max?"

He began to understand her. "Forgive me if I spoke harshly," he said. "You have put me to a severe trial."

She burst into tears. "Love," she murmured, "is my only excuse."

From that moment she had won her pardon. He took her hand, and made her sit by him.

"Yes," he said, "I have heard of Miss Max and of her wonderful powers of personation—and I have always regretted not having seen her while she was on the stage."

"Did you hear anything more of her, Ernest?"

"Yes, I heard that she was a pattern of modesty and good conduct, and that she gave up her profession, at the height of her success, to marry an old man."

"Will you come with me to my room?" she asked. "I have something there which I wish to show you."

It was the copy of her husband's will.

"Read the lines, Ernest, which begin at the top of the page. Let my dead husband speak for me."

The lines ran thus:

"My motive in marrying Miss Max must be stated in this place, in justice to her—and, I will venture to add, in justice to myself. I felt the sincerest sympathy for her position. She was without father, mother, or friends; one of the poor forsaken children, whom the mercy of the Foundling Hospital provides with a home. Her after life on the stage was the life of a virtuous woman: persecuted by profligates; insulted by some of the baser creatures associated with her, to whom she was an object of envy. I offered her a home, and the protection of a father—on the only terms which the world would recognize as worthy of us. My experience of her since our marriage has been the experience of unvarying goodness, sweetness, and sound sense. She has behaved so nobly, in a trying position, that I wish her (even in this life) to have her reward. I entreat her to make a second choice in marriage, which shall not be a mere form. I firmly believe that she will choose well and wisely—that she will make the happiness of a man who is worthy of her—and that, as wife and mother, she will set an example of inestimable value in the social sphere that she occupies. In proof of the heartfelt sincerity with which I pay my tribute to her virtues, I add to this my will the clause that follows."

With the clause that followed, Ernest was already acquainted.

"Will you now believe that I never loved till I saw your face for the first time?" said his wife. "I had no experience to place me on my guard against the fascination—the madness some people might call it—which possesses a woman when all her heart is given to a man. Don't despise me, my dear! Remember that I had to save you from disgrace and ruin. Besides, my old stage remembrances tempted me. I had acted in a play in which the heroine did—what I have done! It didn't end with me, as it did with her in the story. She was represented as rejoicing in the success of her disguise. I have known some miserable hours of doubt and shame since our marriage. When I went to meet you in my own person at the picture-gallery—oh, what relief, what joy I felt, when I saw how you admired me—it was not because I could no longer carry on the disguise. I was able to get hours of rest from the effort; not only at night, but in the daytime, when I was shut up in my retirement in the music-room; and when my maid kept watch against discovery. No, my love! I hurried on the disclosure, because I could no longer endure the hateful triumph of my own deception. Ah, look at that witness against me! I can't bear even to see it!"

She abruptly left him. The drawer that she had opened to take out the copy of the will also contained the false gray hair which she had discarded. It had only that moment attracted her notice. She snatched it up, and turned to the fireplace.

Ernest took it from her, before she could destroy it. "Give it to me," he said.

"Why?"

He drew her gently to his bosom, and answered: "I must not forget my old wife."

MISS JEROMETTE AND THE CLERGYMAN.

I.

MY brother, the clergyman, looked over my shoulder before I was aware of him, and discovered that the volume which completely absorbed my attention was a collection of famous Trials, published in a new edition and in a popular form.

He laid his finger on the Trial which I happened to be reading at the moment. I looked up at him; his face startled me. He had turned pale. His eyes were fixed on the open page of the book with an expression which puzzled and alarmed me.

"My dear fellow," I said, "what in the world is the matter with you?"

He answered in an odd absent manner, still keeping his finger on the open page.

"I had almost forgotten," he said. "And this reminds me."

"Reminds you of what?" I asked. "You don't mean to say you know anything about the Trial?"

"I know this," he said. "The prisoner was guilty."

"Guilty?" I repeated. "Why, the man was acquitted by the jury, with the full approval of the judge! What call you possibly mean?"

"There are circumstances connected with that Trial," my brother answered, "which were never communicated to the judge or the jury—which were never so much as hinted or whispered in court. I know them—of my own knowledge, by my own personal experience. They are very sad, very strange, very terrible. I have mentioned them to no mortal creature. I have done my best to forget them. You—quite innocently—have brought them back to my mind. They oppress, they distress me. I wish I had found you reading any book in your library, except that book!"

My curiosity was now strongly excited. I spoke out plainly.

"Surely," I suggested, "you might tell your brother what you are unwilling to mention to persons less nearly related to you. We have followed different professions, and have lived in different countries, since we were boys at school. But you know you can trust me."

He considered a little with himself.

"Yes," he said. "I know I can trust you." He waited a moment, and then he surprised me by a strange question.

"Do you believe," he asked, "that the spirits of the dead can return to earth, and show themselves to the living?"

I answered cautiously—adopting as my own the words of a great English writer, touching the subject of ghosts.

"You ask me a question," I said, "which, after five thousand years, is yet undecided. On that account alone, it is a question not to be trifled with."

My reply seemed to satisfy him.

"Promise me," he resumed, "that you will keep what I tell you a secret as long as I live. After my death I care little what happens. Let the story of my strange experience be added to the published experience of those other men who have seen what I have seen, and who believe what I believe. The world will not be the worse, and may be the better, for knowing one day what I am now about to trust to your ear alone."

My brother never again alluded to the narrative which he had confided to me, until the later time when I was sitting by his deathbed. He asked if I still remembered the story of Jeromette. "Tell it to others," he said, "as I have told it to you."

I repeat it after his death—as nearly as I can in his own words.

II.

ON a fine summer evening, many years since, I left my chambers in the Temple, to meet a fellow-student, who had proposed to me a night's amusement in the public gardens at Cremorne.

You were then on your way to India; and I had taken my degree at Oxford. I had sadly disappointed my father by choosing the Law as my profession, in preference to the Church. At that time, to own the truth, I had no serious intention of following any special vocation. I simply wanted an excuse for enjoying the pleasures of a London life. The study of the Law supplied me with that excuse. And I chose the Law as my profession accordingly.

On reaching the place at which we had arranged to meet, I found that my friend had not kept his appointment. After waiting vainly for ten minutes, my patience gave way and I went into the Gardens by myself.

I took two or three turns round the platform devoted to the dancers without discovering my fellow-student, and without seeing any other person with whom I happened to be acquainted at that time.

For some reason which I cannot now remember, I was not in my usual good spirits that evening. The noisy music jarred on my nerves, the sight of the gaping crowd round the platform irritated me, the blandishments of the painted ladies of the profession of pleasure saddened and disgusted me. I opened my cigar-case, and turned aside into one of the quiet by-walks of the Gardens.

A man who is habitually careful in choosing his cigar has this advantage over a man who is habitually careless. He can always count on smoking the best cigar in his case, down to the last. I was still absorbed in choosing my cigar, when I heard these words behind me—spoken in a foreign accent and in a woman's voice:

"Leave me directly, sir! I wish to have nothing to say to you."

I turned round and discovered a little lady very simply and tastefully dressed, who looked both angry and alarmed as she rapidly passed me on her way to the more frequented part of the Gardens. A man (evidently the worse for the wine he had drunk in the course of the evening) was following her, and was pressing his tipsy attentions on her with the coarsest insolence of speech and manner. She was young and pretty, and she cast one entreating

514

look at me as she went by, which it was not in manhood—perhaps I ought to say, in young-manhood—to resist.

I instantly stepped forward to protect her, careless whether I involved myself in a discreditable quarrel with a blackguard or not. As a matter of course, the fellow resented my interference, and my temper gave way. Fortunately for me, just as I lifted my hand to knock him down, at policeman appeared who had noticed that he was drunk, and who settled the dispute officially by turning him out of the Gardens.

I led her away from the crowd that had collected. She was evidently frightened—I felt her hand trembling on my arm—but she had one great merit; she made no fuss about it.

"If I can sit down for a few minutes," she said in her pretty foreign accent, "I shall soon be myself again, and I shall not trespass any further on your kindness. I thank you very much, sir, for taking care of me."

We sat down on a bench in a retired par t of the Gardens, near a little fountain. A row of lighted lamps ran round the outer rim of the basin. I could see her plainly.

I have said that she was "a little lady." I could not have described her more correctly in three words.

Her figure was slight and small: she was a well-made miniature of a woman from head to foot. Her hair and her eyes were both dark. The hair curled naturally; the expression of the eyes was quiet, and rather sad; the complexion, as I then saw it, very pale; the little mouth perfectly charming. I was especially attracted, I remembered, by the carriage of her head; it was strikingly graceful and spirited; it distinguished her, little as she was and quiet as she was, among the thousands of other women in the Gardens, as a creature apart. Even the one marked defect in her—a slight "cast" in the left eye—seemed to add, in some strange way, to the quaint attractiveness of her face. I have already spoken of the tasteful simplicity of her dress. I ought now to add that it was not made of any costly material, and that she wore no jewels or ornaments of any sort. My little lady was not rich; even a man's eye could see that.

She was perfectly unembarrassed and unaffected. We fell as easily into talk as if we had been friends instead of strangers.

I asked how it was that she had no companion to take care of her. "You are too young and too pretty," I said in my blunt English way, "to trust yourself alone in such a place as this."

She took no notice of the compliment. She calmly put it away from her as if it had not reached her ears.

"I have no friend to take care of me," she said simply. "I was sad and sorry this evening, all by myself, and I thought I would go to the Gardens and hear the music, just to amuse me. It is not much to pay at the gate; only a shilling."

"No friend to take care of you?" I repeated. "Surely there must be one happy man who might have been here with you to-night?"

"What man do you mean?" she asked.

"The man," I answered thoughtlessly, "whom we call, in England, a Sweetheart."

I would have given worlds to have recalled those foolish words the moment they passed my lips. I felt that I had taken a vulgar liberty with her. Her face saddened; her eyes dropped to the ground. I begged her pardon.

"There is no need to beg my pardon," she said. "If you wish to know, sir—yes, I had once a sweetheart, as you call it in England. He has gone away and left me. No more of him, if you please. I am rested now. I will thank you again, and go home."

She rose to leave me.

I was determined not to part with her in that way. I begged to be allowed to see her safely back to her own door. She hesitated. I took a man's unfair advantage of her, by appealing to her fears. I said, "Suppose the blackguard who annoyed you should be waiting outside the gates?" That decided her.

She took my arm. We went away together by the bank of the Thames, in the balmy summer night.

A walk of half an hour brought us to the house in which she lodged—a shabby little house in a by-street, inhabited evidently by very poor people.

She held out her hand at the door, and wished me good-night. I was too much interested in her to consent to leave my little foreign lady without the hope of seeing her again. I asked permission to call on her the next day. We were standing under the light of the street-lamp. She studied my face with a grave and steady attention before she made any reply.

"Yes," she said at last. "I think I do know a gentleman when I see him. You may come, sir, if you please, and call upon me to-morrow."

So we parted. So I entered—doubting nothing, foreboding nothing—on a scene in my life which I now look back on with unfeigned repentance and regret.

III.

I AM speaking at this later time in the position of a clergyman, and in the character of a man of mature age. Remember that; and you will understand why I pass as rapidly as possible over the events of the next year of my life—why I say as little as I can of the errors and the delusions of my youth.

I called on her the next day. I repeated my visits during the days and weeks that followed, until the shabby little house in the by-street had become a second and (I say it with shame and self-reproach) a dearer home to me.

All of herself and her story which she thought fit to confide to me under these circumstances may be repeated to you in few words.

The name by which letters were addressed to her was "Mademoiselle Jeromette." Among the ignorant people of the house and the small tradesmen of the neighborhood—who found her name not easy of pronunciation by the average English tongue—she was known by the friendly nickname of "The French Miss." When I knew her, she was resigned to her lonely life among strangers. Some years had elapsed since she had lost her parents, and had

517

left France. Possessing a small, very small, income of her own, she added to it by coloring miniatures for the photographers. She had relatives still living in France; but she had long since ceased to correspond with them. "Ask me nothing more about my family," she used to say. "I am as good as dead in my own country and among my own people."

This was all—literally all—that she told me of herself. I have never discovered more of her sad story from that day to this.

She never mentioned her family name—never even told me what part of France she came from or how long she had lived in England. That she was by birth and breeding a lady, I could entertain no doubt; her manners, her accomplishments, her ways of thinking and speaking, all proved it. Looking below the surface, her character showed itself in aspects not common among young women in these days. In her quiet way she was an incurable fatalist, and a firm believer in the ghostly reality of apparitions from the dead. Then again in the matter of money, she had strange views of her own. Whenever my purse was in my hand, she held me resolutely at a distance from first to last. She refused to move into better apartments; the shabby little house was clean inside, and the poor people who lived in it were kind to her—and that was enough. The most expensive present that she ever permitted me to offer her was a little enameled ring, the plainest and cheapest thing of the kind in the jeweler's shop. In all relations with me she was sincerity itself. On all occasions, and under all circumstances, she spoke her mind (as the phrase is) with the same uncompromising plainness.

"I like you," she said to me; "I respect you; I shall always be faithful to you while you are faithful to me. But my love has gone from me. There is another man who has taken it away with him, I know not where."

Who was the other man?

She refused to tell me. She kept his rank and his name strict secrets from me. I never discovered how he had met with her, or why he had left her, or whether the guilt was his of making of her an exile from her country and her friends. She despised herself for still loving him; but the passion was too strong for her—she owned it and lamented it with the frankness which was so

518

preeminently a part of her character. More than this, she plainly told me, in the early days of our acquaintance, that she believed he would return to her. It might be to-morrow, or it might be years hence. Even if he failed to repent of his own cruel conduct, the man would still miss her, as something lost out of his life; and, sooner or later, he would come back.

"And will you receive him if he does come back?" I asked.

"I shall receive him," she replied, "against my own better judgment—in spite of my own firm persuasion that the day of his return to me will bring with it the darkest days of my life."

I tried to remonstrate with her.

"You have a will of your own," I said. "Exert it if he attempts to return to you."

"I have no will of my own," she answered quietly, "where he is concerned. It is my misfortune to love him." Her eyes rested for a moment on mine, with the utter self-abandonment of despair. "We have said enough about this," she added abruptly. "Let us say no more."

From that time we never spoke again of the unknown man. During the year that followed our first meeting, she heard nothing of him directly or indirectly. He might be living, or he might be dead. There came no word of him, or from him. I was fond enough of her to be satisfied with this—he never disturbed us.

IV.

THE year passed—and the end came. Not the end as you may have anticipated it, or as I might have foreboded it.

You remember the time when your letters from home informed you of the fatal termination of our mother's illness? It is the time of which I am now speaking. A few hours only before she breathed her last, she called me to her bedside, and desired that we might be left together alone. Reminding me that her death was near, she spoke of my prospects in life; she noticed my want of interest in the studies which were then supposed to be engaging my attention, and she ended by entreating me to reconsider my refusal to enter the Church.

"Your father's heart is set upon it," she said. "Do what I ask of you, my dear, and you will help to comfort him when I am gone."

Her strength failed her: she could say no more. Could I refuse the last request she would ever make to me? I knelt at the bedside, and took her wasted hand in mine, and solemnly promised her the respect which a son owes to his mother's last wishes.

Having bound myself by this sacred engagement, I had no choice but to accept the sacrifice which it imperatively exacted from me. The time had come when I must tear myself free from all unworthy associations. No matter what the effort cost me, I must separate myself at once and forever from the unhappy woman who was not, who never could be, my wife.

At the close of a dull foggy day I set forth with a heavy heart to say the words which were to part us forever.

Her lodging was not far from the banks of the Thames. As I drew near the place the darkness was gathering, and the broad surface of the river was hidden from me in a chill white mist. I stood for a while, with my eyes fixed on the vaporous shroud that brooded over the flowing water—I stood and asked myself in despair the one dreary question: "What am I to say to her?"

The mist chilled me to the bones. I turned from the river-bank, and made my way to her lodgings hard by. "It must be done!" I said to myself, as I took out my key and opened the house door.

She was not at her work, as usual, when I entered her little sitting-room. She was standing by the fire, with her head down and with an open letter in her hand.

The instant she turned to meet me, I saw in her face that something was wrong. Her ordinary manner was the manner of an unusually placid and self-restrained person. Her temperament had little of the liveliness which we associate in England with the French nature. She was not ready with her laugh; and in all my previous experience, I had never yet known her to cry.

Now, for the first time, I saw the quiet face disturbed; I saw tears in the pretty brown eyes. She ran to meet me, and laid her head on my breast, and burst into a passionate fit of weeping that shook her from head to foot.

Could she by any human possibility have heard of the coming change in my life? Was she aware, before I had opened my lips, of the hard necessity which had brought me to the house?

It was simply impossible; the thing could not be.

I waited until her first burst of emotion had worn itself out. Then I asked—with an uneasy conscience, with a sinking heart—what had happened to distress her.

She drew herself away from me, sighing heavily, and gave me the open letter which I had seen in her hand.

"Read that," she said. "And remember I told you what might happen when we first met."

I read the letter.

It was signed in initials only; but the writer plainly revealed himself as the man who had deserted her. He had repented; he had returned to her. In proof of his penitence he was willing to do her the justice which he had hitherto refused—he was willing to marry her, on the condition that she would engage to keep the marriage a secret, so long as his parents lived. Submitting this proposal, he waited to know whether she would consent, on her side, to forgive and forget.

I gave her back the letter in silence. This unknown rival had done me the service of paving the way for our separation. In offering her the atonement of marriage, he had made it, on my part, a matter of duty to her, as well as to myself, to say the parting words. I felt this instantly. And yet, I hated him for helping me.

She took my hand, and led me to the sofa. We sat down, side by side. Her face was composed to a sad tranquillity. She was quiet; she was herself again.

"I have refused to see him," she said, "until I had first spoken to you. You have read his letter. What do you say?"

I could make but one answer. It was my duty to tell her what my own position was in the plainest terms. I did my duty—leaving her free to decide on the future for herself. Those sad words said, it was useless to prolong the wretchedness of our separation. I rose, and took her hand for the last time.

I see her again now, at that final moment, as plainly as if it had happened yesterday. She had been suffering from an affection of the throat; and she had a white silk handkerchief tied loosely round her neck. She wore a simple dress of purple merino, with a black-silk apron over it. Her face was deadly pale; her fingers felt icily cold as they closed round my hand.

"Promise me one thing," I said, "before I go. While I live, I am your friend—if I am nothing more. If you are ever in trouble, promise that you will let me know it."

She started, and drew back from me as if I had struck her with a sudden terror.

"Strange!" she said, speaking to herself. "He feels as I feel. He is afraid of what may happen to me, in my life to come."

I attempted to reassure her. I tried to tell her what was indeed the truth—that I had only been thinking of the ordinary chances and changes of life, when I spoke.

She paid no heed to me; she came back and put her hands on my shoulders and thoughtfully and sadly looked up in my face.

"My mind is not your mind in this matter," she said. "I once owned to you that I had my forebodings, when we first spoke of this man's return. I may tell you now, more than I told you then. I believe I shall die young, and die miserably. If I am right, have you interest enough still left in me to wish to hear of it?"

She paused, shuddering—and added these startling words:

"You shall hear of it."

The tone of steady conviction in which she spoke alarmed and distressed me. My face showed her how deeply and how painfully I was affected.

"There, there!" she said, returning to her natural manner; "don't take what I say too seriously. A poor girl who has led a lonely life like mine thinks strangely and talks strangely—sometimes. Yes; I give you my promise. If I am ever in trouble, I will let you know it. God bless you—you have been very kind to me—good-by!"

A tear dropped on my face as she kissed me. The door closed between us. The dark street received me.

It was raining heavily. I looked up at her window, through the drifting shower. The curtains were parted: she was standing in the gap, dimly lit by the lamp on the table behind her, waiting for our last look at each other. Slowly lifting her hand, she waved her farewell at the window, with the unsought native grace which had charmed me on the night when we first met. The curtain fell again—she disappeared—nothing was before me, nothing was round me, but the darkness and the night.

V.

IN two years from that time, I had redeemed the promise given to my mother on her deathbed. I had entered the Church.

My father's interest made my first step in my new profession an easy one. After serving my preliminary apprenticeship as a curate, I was appointed, before I was thirty years of age, to a living in the West of England.

My new benefice offered me every advantage that I could possibly desire—with the one exception of a sufficient income. Although my wants were few, and although I was still an unmarried man, I found it desirable, on many accounts, to add to my resources. Following the example of other young clergymen in my position, I determined to receive pupils who might stand in need of preparation for a career at the Universities. My relatives exerted themselves; and my good fortune still befriended me. I obtained two pupils to start with. A third would complete the number which I was at present prepared to receive. In course of time, this third pupil made his appearance, under circumstances sufficiently remarkable to merit being mentioned in detail.

It was the summer vacation; and my two pupils had gone home. Thanks to a neighboring clergyman, who kindly undertook to perform my duties for me, I too obtained a fortnight's holiday, which I spent at my father's house in London.

During my sojourn in the metropolis, I was offered an opportunity of preaching in a church, made famous by the eloquence of one of the popular pulpit-orators of our time. In accepting the proposal, I felt naturally anxious to do my best, before the unusually large and unusually intelligent congregation which would be assembled to hear me.

At the period of which I am now speaking, all England had been startled by the discovery of a terrible crime, perpetrated under circumstances of extreme provocation. I chose this crime as the main subject of my sermon. Admitting that the best among us were frail mortal creatures, subject to evil promptings and provocations like the worst among us, my object was to show how a Christian man may find his certain refuge from temptation in the safeguards of his religion. I dwelt minutely on the hardship of the Christian's first struggle to resist the evil influence—on the help which his Christianity inexhaustibly held out to him in the worst relapses of the weaker and viler part of his nature—on the steady and certain gain which was the ultimate reward of his faith and his firmness—and on the blessed sense of peace and happiness which accompanied the final triumph. Preaching to this effect, with the fervent conviction which I really felt, I may say for myself, at least, that I did no discredit to the choice which had placed me in the pulpit. I held the attention of my congregation, from the first word to the last.

While I was resting in the vestry on the conclusion of the service, a note was brought to me written in pencil. A member of my congregation—a gentleman—wished to see me, on a matter of considerable importance to himself. He would call on me at any place, and at any hour, which I might choose to appoint. If I wished to be satisfied of his respectability, he would beg leave to refer me to his father, with whose name I might possibly be acquainted.

The name given in the reference was undoubtedly familiar to me, as the name of a man of some celebrity and influence in the world of London. I sent back my card, appointing an hour for the visit of my correspondent on the afternoon of the next day.

VI.

THE stranger made his appearance punctually. I guessed him to be some two or three years younger than myself. He was undeniably handsome; his manners were the manners of a gentleman—and yet, without knowing why, I felt a strong dislike to him the moment he entered the room.

After the first preliminary words of politeness had been exchanged between us, my visitor informed me as follows of the object which he had in view.

"I believe you live in the country, sir?" he began.

"I live in the West of England," I answered.

"Do you make a long stay in London?"

"No. I go back to my rectory to-morrow."

"May I ask if you take pupils?"

"Yes."

"Have you any vacancy?"

"I have one vacancy."

"Would you object to let me go back with you to-morrow, as your pupil?"

The abruptness of the proposal took me by surprise. I hesitated.

In the first place (as I have already said), I disliked him. In the second place, he was too old to be a fit companion for my other two pupils—both lads in their teens. In the third place, he had asked me to receive him at least three weeks before the vacation came to an end. I had my own pursuits and amusements in prospect during that interval, and saw no reason why I should inconvenience myself by setting them aside.

He noticed my hesitation, and did not conceal from me that I had disappointed him.

"I have it very much at heart," he said, "to repair without delay the time that I have lost. My age is against me, I know. The truth is—I have wasted my opportunities since I left school, and I am anxious, honestly anxious, to mend my ways, before it is too late. I wish to prepare myself for one of the Universities—I wish to show, if I can, that I am not quite unworthy to inherit my father's famous name. You are the man to help me, if I can only persuade you to do it. I was struck by your sermon yesterday; and, if I may venture to make the confession in your presence, I took a strong liking to you. Will you see my father, before you decide to say No? He will be able to explain whatever may seem strange in my present application; and he will be happy to see you this afternoon, if you can spare the time. As to the question of terms, I am quite sure it can be settled to your entire satisfaction."

He was evidently in earnest—gravely, vehemently in earnest. I unwillingly consented to see his father.

Our interview was a long one. All my questions were answered fully and frankly.

The young man had led an idle and desultory life. He was weary of it, and ashamed of it. His disposition was a peculiar one. He stood sorely in need of a guide, a teacher, and a friend, in whom he was disposed to confide. If I disappointed the hopes which he had centered in me, he would be discouraged, and he would relapse into the aimless and indolent existence of which he was now ashamed. Any terms for which I might stipulate were at my disposal if I would consent to receive him, for three months to begin with, on trial.

Still hesitating, I consulted my father and my friends.

They were all of opinion (and justly of opinion so far) that the new connection would be an excellent one for me. They all reproached me for taking a purely capricious dislike to a well-born and well-bred young man, and for permitting it to influence me, at the outset of my career, against my own interests. Pressed by these considerations, I allowed myself to be persuaded to give the new pupil a fair trial. He accompanied me, the next day, on my way back to the rectory.

VII.

LET me be careful to do justice to a man whom I personally disliked. My senior pupil began well: he produced a decidedly favorable impression on the persons attached to my little household.

The women, especially, admired his beautiful light hair, his crisply-curling beard, his delicate complexion, his clear blue eyes, and his finely shaped hands and feet. Even the inveterate reserve in his manner, and the downcast, almost sullen, look which had prejudiced me against him, aroused a common feeling of romantic enthusiasm in my servants' hall. It was decided, on the high authority of the housekeeper herself, that "the new gentleman" was in love—and, more interesting still, that he was the victim of an unhappy attachment which had driven him away from his friends and his home.

For myself, I tried hard, and tried vainly, to get over my first dislike to the senior pupil.

I could find no fault with him. All his habits were quiet and regular; and he devoted himself conscientiously to his reading. But, little by little, I became satisfied that his heart was not in his studies. More than this, I had my reasons for suspecting that he was concealing something from me, and that he felt painfully the reserve on his own part which he could not, or dared not, break through. There were moments when I almost doubted whether he had not chosen my remote country rectory as a safe place of refuge from some person or persons of whom he stood in dread.

For example, his ordinary course of proceeding, in the matter of his correspondence, was, to say the least of it, strange.

He received no letters at my house. They waited for him at the village post office. He invariably called for them himself, and invariably forbore to trust any of my servants with his own letters for the post. Again, when we were out walking together, I more than once caught him looking furtively over his shoulder, as if he suspected some person of following him, for some evil purpose. Being constitutionally a hater of mysteries, I determined, at an early stage of our intercourse, on making an effort to clear matters up. There might be just a chance of my winning the senior pupil's confidence, if I spoke to him while the last days of the summer vacation still left us alone together in the house.

"Excuse me for noticing it," I said to him one morning, while we were engaged over our books—"I cannot help observing that you appear to have some trouble on your mind. Is it indiscreet, on my part, to ask if I can be of any use to you?"

He changed color—looked up at me quickly—looked down again at his book—struggled hard with some secret fear or secret reluctance that was in him—and suddenly burst out with this extraordinary question: "I suppose you were in earnest when you preached that sermon in London?"

"I am astonished that you should doubt it," I replied.

He paused again; struggled with himself again; and startled me by a second outbreak, even stranger than the first.

"I am one of the people you preached at in your sermon," he said. "That's the true reason why I asked you to take me for your pupil. Don't turn me out! When you talked to your congregation of tortured and tempted people, you talked of Me."

I was so astonished by the confession, that I lost my presence of mind. For the moment, I was unable to answer him.

"Don't turn me out!" he repeated. "Help me against myself. I am telling you the truth. As God is my witness, I am telling you the truth!"

"Tell me the whole truth," I said; "and rely on my consoling and helping you—rely on my being your friend."

In the fervor of the moment, I took his hand. It lay cold and still in mine; it mutely warned me that I had a sullen and a secret nature to deal with.

"There must be no concealment between us," I resumed. "You have entered my house, by your own confession, under false pretenses. It is your duty to me, and your duty to yourself, to speak out."

The man's inveterate reserve—cast off for the moment only—renewed its hold on him. He considered, carefully considered, his next words before he permitted them to pass his lips.

"A person is in the way of my prospects in life," he began slowly, with his eyes cast down on his book. "A person provokes me horribly. I feel dreadful temptations (like the man you spoke of in your sermon) when I am in the person's company. Teach me to resist temptation. I am afraid of myself, if I see the person again. You are the only man who can help me. Do it while you can."

He stopped, and passed his handkerchief over his forehead.

"Will that do?" he asked—still with his eyes on his book.

"It will not do," I answered. "You are so far from really opening your heart to me, that you won't even let me know whether it is a man or a woman who stands in the way of your prospects in life. You used the word 'person,' over and over again—rather than say 'he' or 'she' when you speak of the provocation which is trying you. How can I help a man who has so little confidence in me as that?"

My reply evidently found him at the end of his resources. He tried, tried desperately, to say more than he had said yet. No! The words seemed to stick in his throat. Not one of them would pass his lips.

"Give me time," he pleaded piteously. "I can't bring myself to it, all at once. I mean well. Upon my soul, I mean well. But I am slow at this sort of thing. Wait till to-morrow."

To-morrow came—and again he put it off.

"One more day!" he said. "You don't know how hard it is to speak plainly. I am half afraid; I am half ashamed. Give me one more day."

I had hitherto only disliked him. Try as I might (and did) to make merciful allowance for his reserve, I began to despise him now.

VIII.

THE day of the deferred confession came, and brought an event with it, for which both he and I were alike unprepared. Would he really have confided in me but for that event? He must either have done it, or have abandoned the purpose which had led him into my house.

We met as usual at the breakfast-table. My housekeeper brought in my letters of the morning. To my surprise, instead of leaving the room again as usual, she walked round to the other side of the table, and laid a letter before my senior pupil—the first letter, since his residence with me, which had been delivered to him under my roof.

He started, and took up the letter. He looked at the address. A spasm of suppressed fury passed across his face; his breath came quickly; his hand trembled as it held the letter. So far, I said nothing. I waited to see whether he would open the envelope in my presence or not.

He was afraid to open it in my presence. He got on his feet; he said, in tones so low that I could barely hear him: "Please excuse me for a minute"— and left the room.

I waited for half an hour—for a quarter of an hour after that—and then I sent to ask if he had forgotten his breakfast.

In a minute more, I heard his footstep in the hall. He opened the breakfast-room door, and stood on the threshold, with a small traveling-bag in his hand.

"I beg your pardon," he said, still standing at the door. "I must ask for leave of absence for a day or two. Business in London."

"Can I be of any use?" I asked. "I am afraid your letter has brought you bad news?"

"Yes," he said shortly. "Bad news. I have no time for breakfast."

"Wait a few minutes," I urged. "Wait long enough to treat me like your friend—to tell me what your trouble is before you go."

He made no reply. He stepped into the hall and closed the door—then opened it again a little way, without showing himself.

"Business in London," he repeated—as if he thought it highly important to inform me of the nature of his errand. The door closed for the second time. He was gone.

I went into my study, and carefully considered what had happened.

The result of my reflections is easily described. I determined on discontinuing my relations with my senior pupil. In writing to his father (which I did, with all due courtesy and respect, by that day's post), I mentioned as my reason for arriving at this decision:—First, that I had found it impossible to win the confidence of his son. Secondly, that his son had that morning suddenly and mysteriously left my house for London, and that I must decline accepting any further responsibility toward him, as the necessary consequence.

I had put my letter in the post-bag, and was beginning to feel a little easier after having written it, when my housekeeper appeared in the study, with a very grave face, and with something hidden apparently in her closed hand.

"Would you please look, sir, at what we have found in the gentleman's bedroom, since he went away this morning?"

I knew the housekeeper to possess a woman's full share of that amicable weakness of the sex which goes by the name of "Curiosity." I had also, in various indirect ways, become aware that my senior pupil's strange departure had largely increased the disposition among the women of my household to regard him as the victim of an unhappy attachment. The time was ripe, as it seemed to me, for checking any further gossip about him, and any renewed attempts at prying into his affairs in his absence.

"Your only business in my pupil's bedroom," I said to the housekeeper, "is to see that it is kept clean, and that it is properly aired. There must be no interference, if you please, with his letters, or his papers, or with anything else that he has left behind him. Put back directly whatever you may have found in his room."

The housekeeper had her full share of a woman's temper as well as of a woman's curiosity. She listened to me with a rising color, and a just perceptible toss of the head.

"Must I put it back, sir, on the floor, between the bed and the wall?" she inquired, with an ironical assumption of the humblest deference to my wishes. "That's where the girl found it when she was sweeping the room. Anybody can see for themselves," pursued the housekeeper indignantly, "that the poor gentleman has gone away broken-hearted. And there, in my opinion, is the hussy who is the cause of it!"

With those words, she made me a low curtsey, and laid a small photographic portrait on the desk at which I was sitting.

I looked at the photograph.

In an instant, my heart was beating wildly—my head turned giddy—the housekeeper, the furniture, the walls of the room, all swayed and whirled round me.

The portrait that had been found in my senior pupil's bedroom was the portrait of Jeromette!

IX.

I HAD sent the housekeeper out of my study. I was alone, with the photograph of the Frenchwoman on my desk.

There could surely be little doubt about the discovery that had burst upon me. The man who had stolen his way into my house, driven by the terror of a temptation that he dared not reveal, and the man who had been my unknown rival in the by-gone time, were one and the same!

Recovering self-possession enough to realize this plain truth, the inferences that followed forced their way into my mind as a matter of course.

The unnamed person who was the obstacle to my pupil's prospects in life, the unnamed person in whose company he was assailed by temptations which made him tremble for himself, stood revealed to me now as being, in all human probability, no other than Jeromette. Had she bound him in the fetters of the marriage which he had himself proposed? Had she discovered his place of refuge in my house? And was the letter that had been delivered to him of her writing? Assuming these questions to be answered in the affirmative, what, in that case, was his "business in London"? I remembered how he had spoken to me of his temptations, I recalled the expression that had crossed his face when he recognized the handwriting on the letter—and the conclusion that followed literally shook me to the soul. Ordering my horse to be saddled, I rode instantly to the railway-station.

The train by which he had traveled to London had reached the terminus nearly an hour since. The one useful course that I could take, by way of quieting the dreadful misgivings crowding one after another on my mind, was to telegraph to Jeromette at the address at which I had last seen her. I sent the subjoined message—prepaying the reply:

"If you are in any trouble, telegraph to me. I will be with you by the first train. Answer, in any case."

There was nothing in the way of the immediate dispatch of my message. And yet the hours passed, and no answer was received. By the advice of the clerk, I sent a second telegram to the London office, requesting an explanation. The reply came back in these terms:

"Improvements in street. Houses pulled down. No trace of person named in telegram."

I mounted my horse, and rode back slowly to the rectory.

"The day of his return to me will bring with it the darkest days of my life."..... "I shall die young, and die miserably. Have you interest enough still left in me to wish to hear of it?" .... "You shall hear of it." Those words were in my memory while I rode home in the cloudless moonlight night. They were so vividly present to me that I could hear again her pretty foreign accent, her quiet clear tones, as she spoke them. For the rest, the emotions of that memorable day had worn me out. The answer from the telegraph office had struck me with a strange and stony despair. My mind was a blank. I had no thoughts. I had no tears.

I was about half-way on my road home, and I had just heard the clock of a village church strike ten, when I became conscious, little by little, of a chilly sensation slowly creeping through and through me to the bones. The warm, balmy air of a summer night was abroad. It was the month of July. In the month of July, was it possible that any living creature (in good health) could feel cold? It was not possible—and yet, the chilly sensation still crept through and through me to the bones.

I looked up. I looked all round me.

My horse was walking along an open highroad. Neither trees nor waters were near me. On either side, the flat fields stretched away bright and broad in the moonlight.

I stopped my horse, and looked round me again.

Yes: I saw it. With my own eyes I saw it. A pillar of white mist—between five and six feet high, as well as I could judge—was moving beside me at the edge of the road, on my left hand. When I stopped, the white mist stopped. When I went on, the white mist went on. I pushed my horse to a trot—the pillar of mist was with me. I urged him to a gallop—-the pillar of mist was with me. I stopped him again—the pillar of mist stood still.

The white color of it was the white color of the fog which I had seen over the river—on the night when I had gone to bid her farewell. And the chill which had then crept through me to the bones was the chill that was creeping through me now.

I went on again slowly. The white mist went on again slowly—with the clear bright night all round it.

I was awed rather than frightened. There was one moment, and one only, when the fear came to me that my reason might be shaken. I caught myself keeping time to the slow tramp of the horse's feet with the slow utterances of these words, repeated over and over again: "Jeromette is dead. Jeromette is dead." But my will was still my own: I was able to control myself, to impose silence on my own muttering lips. And I rode on quietly. And the pillar of mist went quietly with me.

My groom was waiting for my return at the rectory gate. I pointed to the mist, passing through the gate with me.

"Do you see anything there?" I said.

The man looked at me in astonishment.

I entered the rectory. The housekeeper met me in the hall. I pointed to the mist, entering with me.

"Do you see anything at my side?" I asked.

The housekeeper looked at me as the groom had looked at me.

"I am afraid you are not well, sir," she said. "Your color is all gone—you are shivering. Let me get you a glass of wine."

I went into my study, on the ground-floor, and took the chair at my desk. The photograph still lay where I had left it. The pillar of mist floated round the table, and stopped opposite to me, behind the photograph.

The housekeeper brought in the wine. I put the glass to my lips, and set it down again. The chill of the mist was in the wine. There was no taste, no reviving spirit in it. The presence of the housekeeper oppressed me. My dog had followed her into the room. The presence of the animal oppressed me. I said to the woman: "Leave me by myself, and take the dog with you."

They went out, and left me alone in the room.

I sat looking at the pillar of mist, hovering opposite to me.

It lengthened slowly, until it reached to the ceiling. As it lengthened, it grew bright and luminous. A time passed, and a shadowy appearance showed itself in the center of the light. Little by little, the shadowy appearance took the outline of a human form. Soft brown eyes, tender and melancholy, looked at me through the unearthly light in the mist. The head and the rest of the face broke next slowly on my view. Then the figure gradually revealed itself, moment by moment, downward and downward to the feet. She stood before me as I had last seen her, in her purple-merino dress, with the black-silk apron, with the white handkerchief tied loosely round her neck. She stood before me, in the gentle beauty that I remembered so well; and looked at me as she had looked when she gave me her last kiss—when her tears had dropped on my cheek.

I fell on my knees at the table. I stretched out my hands to her imploringly. I said: "Speak to me—O, once again speak to me, Jeromette."

Her eyes rested on me with a divine compassion in them. She lifted her hand, and pointed to the photograph on my desk, with a gesture which bade me turn the card. I turned it. The name of the man who had left my house that morning was inscribed on it, in her own handwriting.

I looked up at her again, when I had read it. She lifted her hand once more, and pointed to the handkerchief round her neck. As I looked at it, the fair white silk changed horribly in color—the fair white silk became darkened and drenched in blood.

A moment more—and the vision of her began to grow dim. By slow degrees, the figure, then the face, faded back into the shadowy appearance that I had first seen. The luminous inner light died out in the white mist. The mist itself dropped slowly downward—floated a moment in airy circles on the floor—vanished. Nothing was before me but the familiar wall of the room, and the photograph lying face downward on my desk.

X.

THE next day, the newspapers reported the discovery of a murder in London. A Frenchwoman was the victim. She had been killed by a wound in the throat. The crime had been discovered between ten and eleven o'clock on the previous night.

I leave you to draw your conclusion from what I have related. My own faith in the reality of the apparition is immovable. I say, and believe, that Jeromette kept her word with me. She died young, and died miserably. And I heard of it from herself.

Take up the Trial again, and look at the circumstances that were revealed during the investigation in court. His motive for murdering her is there.

You will see that she did indeed marry him privately; that they lived together contentedly, until the fatal day when she discovered that his fancy had been caught by another woman; that violent quarrels took place between them, from that time to the time when my sermon showed him his own deadly hatred toward her, reflected in the case of another man; that she discovered his place of retreat in my house, and threatened him by letter with the public assertion of her conjugal rights; lastly, that a man, variously described by different witnesses, was seen leaving the door of her lodgings on the night of the murder. The Law—advancing no further than this—may have discovered circumstances of suspicion, but no certainty. The Law, in default of direct evidence to convict the prisoner, may have rightly decided in letting him go free.

But I persisted in believing that the man was guilty. I declare that he, and he alone, was the murderer of Jeromette. And now, you know why.

MISS MINA AND THE GROOM

I.

I HEAR that the "shocking story of my conduct" was widely circulated at the ball, and that public opinion (among the ladies), in every part of the room, declared I had disgraced myself. But there was one dissentient voice in this chorus of general condemnation. You spoke, Madam, with all the authority of your wide celebrity and your high rank. You said: "I am personally a stranger to the young lady who is the subject of remark. If I venture to interfere, it is only to remind you that there are two sides to every question. May I ask if you have waited to pass sentence, until you have heard what the person accused has to say in her own defense?"

These just and generous words produced, if I am correctly informed, a dead silence. Not one of the women who had condemned me had heard me in my own defense. Not one of them ventured to answer you.

How I may stand in the opinions of such persons as these, is a matter of perfect indifference to me. My one anxiety is to show that I am not quite unworthy of your considerate interference in my favor. Will you honor me by reading what I have to say for myself in these pages?

I will pass as rapidly as I can over the subject of my family; and I will abstain (in deference to motives of gratitude and honor) from mentioning surnames in my narrative.

My father was the second son of an English nobleman. A German lady was his first wife, and my mother. Left a widower, he married for the second time; the new wife being of American birth. She took a stepmother's dislike to me—which, in some degree at least, I must own that I deserved.

When the newly married pair went to the United States they left me in England, by my own desire, to live under the protection of my uncle—a General in the army. This good man's marriage had been childless, and his wife (Lady Claudia) was, perhaps on that account, as kindly ready as her husband to receive me in the character of an adopted daughter. I may add here, that I bear my German mother's Christian name, Wilhelmina. All my friends, in the days when I had friends, used to shorten this to Mina. Be my friend so far, and call me Mina, too.

After these few words of introduction, will your patience bear with me, if I try to make you better acquainted with my uncle and aunt, and if I allude to circumstances connected with my new life which had, as I fear, some influence in altering my character for the worse?

II.

WHEN I think of the good General's fatherly kindness to me, I really despair of writing about him in terms that do justice to his nature. To own the truth, the tears get into my eyes, and the lines mingle in such confusion that I cannot read them myself. As for my relations with my aunt, I only tell the truth when I say that she performed her duties toward me without the slightest pretension, and in the most charming manner.

At nearly fifty years old, Lady Claudia was still admired, though she had lost the one attraction which distinguished her before my time—the attraction of a perfectly beautiful figure. With fine hair and expressive eyes, she was otherwise a plain woman. Her unassuming cleverness and her fascinating manners were the qualities no doubt which made her popular everywhere. We never quarreled. Not because I was always amiable, but because my aunt would not allow it. She managed me, as she managed her husband, with perfect tact. With certain occasional checks, she absolutely governed the General. There were eccentricities in his character which made him a man easily ruled by a clever woman. Deferring to his opinion, so far as appearances went, Lady Claudia generally contrived to get her own way in the end. Except when he was at his Club, happy in his gossip, his good dinners, and his whist, my excellent uncle lived under a despotism, in the happy delusion that he was master in his own house.

Prosperous and pleasant as it appeared on the surface, my life had its sad side for a young woman.

In the commonplace routine of our existence, as wealthy people in the upper rank, there was nothing to ripen the growth of any better capacities which may have been in my nature. Heartily as I loved and admired my uncle, he was neither of an age nor of a character to be the chosen depositary of my most secret thoughts, the friend of my inmost heart who could show me how to make the best and the most of my life. With friends and admirers in plenty, I had found no one who could hold this position toward me. In the midst of society I was, unconsciously, a lonely woman.

As I remember them, my hours of happiness were the hours when I took refuge in my music and my books. Out of the house, my one diversion, always welcome and always fresh, was riding. Without, any false modesty, I may mention that I had lovers as well as admirers; but not one of them produced an impression on my heart. In all that related to the tender passion, as it is called, I was an undeveloped being. The influence that men have on women, because they are men, was really and truly a mystery to me. I was ashamed of my own coldness—I tried, honestly tried, to copy other girls; to feel my heart beating in the presence of the one chosen man. It was not to be done. When a man pressed my hand, I felt it in my rings, instead of my heart.

These confessions made, I have done with the past, and may now relate the events which my enemies, among the ladies, have described as presenting a shocking story.

III.

WE were in London for the season. One morning, I went out riding with my uncle, as usual, in Hyde Park.

The General's service in the army had been in a cavalry regiment—service distinguished by merits which justified his rapid rise to the high places in his profession. In the hunting-field, he was noted as one of the most daring and most accomplished riders in our county. He had always delighted in riding young and high-spirited horses; and the habit remained with him after he had quitted the active duties of his profession in later life. From first to last he had met with no accident worth remembering, until the unlucky morning when he went out with me.

His horse, a fiery chestnut, ran away with him, in that part of the Park-ride called Rotten Row. With the purpose of keeping clear of other riders, he spurred his runaway horse at the rail which divides the Row from the grassy inclosure at its side. The terrified animal swerved in taking the leap, and dashed him against a tree. He was dreadfully shaken and injured; but his strong constitution carried him through to recovery—with the serious drawback of an incurable lameness in one leg.

The doctors, on taking leave of their patient, united in warning him (at his age, and bearing in mind his weakened leg) to ride no more restive horses. "A quiet cob, General," they all suggested. My uncle was sorely mortified and offended. "If I am fit for nothing but a quiet cob," he said, bitterly, "I will ride no more." He kept his word. No one ever saw the General on horseback again.

Under these sad circumstances (and my aunt being no horsewoman), I had apparently no other choice than to give up riding also. But my kind-hearted uncle was not the man to let me be sacrificed to his own disappointment. His riding-groom had been one of his soldier-servants in the cavalry regiment—a quaint sour tempered old man, not at all the sort of person to attend on a young lady taking her riding-exercise alone. "We must find a smart fellow who can be trusted," said the General. "I shall inquire at the club."

For a week afterward, a succession of grooms, recommended by friends, applied for the vacant place.

The General found insurmountable objections to all of them. "I'll tell you what I have done," he announced one day, with the air of a man who had hit on a grand discovery; "I have advertised in the papers."

Lady Claudia looked up from her embroidery with the placid smile that was peculiar to her. "I don't quite like advertising for a servant," she said. "You are at the mercy of a stranger; you don't know that you are not engaging a drunkard or a thief."

"Or you may be deceived by a false character," I added on my side. I seldom ventured, at domestic consultations, on giving my opinion unasked—but the new groom represented a subject in which I felt a strong personal interest. In a certain sense, he was to be my groom.

"I'm much obliged to you both for warning me that I am so easy to deceive," the General remarked satirically. "Unfortunately, the mischief is done. Three men have answered my advertisement already. I expect them here tomorrow to be examined for the place."

Lady Claudia looked up from her embroidery again. "Are you going to see them yourself?" she asked softly. "I thought the steward—"

"I have hitherto considered myself a better judge of a groom than my steward," the General interposed. "However, don't be alarmed; I won't act on my own sole responsibility, after the hint you have given me. You and Mina shall lend me your valuable assistance, and discover whether they are thieves, drunkards, and what not, before I feel the smallest suspicion of it, myself."

IV.

WE naturally supposed that the General was joking. No. This was one of those rare occasions on which Lady Claudia's tact—infallible in matters of importance—proved to be at fault in a trifle. My uncle's self-esteem had been touched in a tender place; and he had resolved to make us feel it. The next morning a polite message came, requesting our presence in the library, to see the grooms. My aunt (always ready with her smile, but rarely tempted into laughing outright) did for once laugh heartily. "It is really too ridiculous!" she said. However, she pursued her policy of always yielding, in the first instance. We went together to the library.

The three grooms were received in the order in which they presented themselves for approval. Two of them bore the ineffaceable mark of the public-house so plainly written on their villainous faces, that even I could see it. My uncle ironically asked us to favor him with our opinions. Lady Claudia answered with her sweetest smile: "Pardon me, General—we are here to learn." The words were nothing; but the manner in which they were spoken was perfect. Few men could have resisted that gentle influence—and the General was not one of the few. He stroked his mustache, and returned to his petticoat government. The two grooms were dismissed.

The entry of the third and last man took me completely by surprise.

If the stranger's short coat and light trousers had not proclaimed his vocation in life, I should have taken it for granted that there had been some mistake, and that we were favored with a visit from a gentleman unknown. He was between dark and light in complexion, with frank clear blue eyes; quiet and intelligent, if appearances were to be trusted; easy in his movements; respectful in his manner, but perfectly free from servility. "I say!" the General blurted out, addressing my aunt confidentially, "he looks as if he would do, doesn't he?"

The appearance of the new man seemed to have had the same effect on Lady Claudia which it had produced on me. But she got over her first feeling of surprise sooner than I did. "You know best," she answered, with the air of a woman who declined to trouble herself by giving an opinion.

"Step forward, my man," said the General. The groom advanced from the door, bowed, and stopped at the foot of the table—my uncle sitting at the head, with my aunt and myself on either side of him. The inevitable questions began.

"What is your name?"

"Michael Bloomfield."

"Your age?"

"Twenty-six."

My aunt's want of interest in the proceedings expressed itself by a little weary sigh. She leaned back resignedly in her chair.

The General went on with his questions: "What experience have you had as a groom?"

"I began learning my work, sir, before I was twelve years old."

"Yes! yes! I mean what private families have you served in?"

"Two, sir."

"How long have you been in your two situations?"

"Four years in the first; and three in the second."

The General looked agreeably surprised. "Seven years in only two situations is a good character in itself," he remarked. "Who are your references?"

The groom laid two papers on the table.

"I don't take written references," said the General.

"Be pleased to read my papers, sir," answered the groom.

My uncle looked sharply across the table. The groom sustained the look with respectful but unshaken composure. The General took up the papers, and seemed to be once more favorably impressed as he read them. "Personal references in each case if required in support of strong written recommendations from both his employers," he informed my aunt. "Copy the addresses, Mina. Very satisfactory, I must say. Don't you think so yourself?" he resumed, turning again to my aunt.

Lady Claudia replied by a courteous bend of her head. The General went on with his questions. They related to the management of horses; and they were answered to his complete satisfaction.

"Michael Bloomfield, you know your business," he said, "and you have a good character. Leave your address. When I have consulted your references, you shall hear from me."

The groom took out a blank card, and wrote his name and address on it. I looked over my uncle's shoulder when he received the card. Another surprise! The handwriting was simply irreproachable—the lines running perfectly straight, and every letter completely formed. As this perplexing person made his modest bow, and withdrew, the General, struck by an after-thought, called him back from the door.

"One thing more," said my uncle. "About friends and followers? I consider it my duty to my servants to allow them to see their relations; but I expect them to submit to certain conditions in return—"

"I beg your pardon, sir," the groom interposed. "I shall not give you any trouble on that score. I have no relations."

"No brothers or sisters?" asked the General.

"None, sir."

"Father and mother both dead?"

"I don't know, sir."

"You don't know! What does that mean?"

"I am telling you the plain truth, sir. I never heard who my father and mother were—and I don't expect to hear now."

He said those words with a bitter composure which impressed me painfully. Lady Claudia was far from feeling it as I did. Her languid interest in the engagement of the groom seemed to be completely exhausted—and that was all. She rose, in her easy graceful way, and looked out of the window at the courtyard and fountain, the house-dog in his kennel, and the box of flowers in the coachman's window.

In the meanwhile, the groom remained near the table, respectfully waiting for his dismissal. The General spoke to him sharply, for the first time. I could see that my good uncle had noticed the cruel tone of that passing reference to the parents, and thought of it as I did.

"One word more, before you go," he said. "If I don't find you more mercifully inclined toward my horses than you seem to be toward your father and mother, you won't remain long in my service. You might have told me you had never heard who your parents were, without speaking as if you didn't care to hear."

"May I say a bold word, sir, in my own defense?"

He put the question very quietly, but, at the same time, so firmly that he even surprised my aunt. She looked round from the window—then turned back again, and stretched out her hand toward the curtain, intending, as I supposed, to alter the arrangement of it. The groom went on.

"May I ask, sir, why I should care about a father and mother who deserted me? Mind what you are about, my lady!" he cried—suddenly addressing my aunt. "There's a cat in the folds of that curtain; she might frighten you."

He had barely said the words before the housekeeper's large tabby cat, taking its noonday siesta in the looped-up fold of the curtain, leaped out and made for the door.

Lady Claudia was, naturally enough, a little perplexed by the man's discovery of an animal completely hidden in the curtain. She appeared to think that a person who was only a groom had taken a liberty in presuming to puzzle her. Like her husband, she spoke to Michael sharply.

"Did you see the cat?" she asked.

"No, my lady."

"Then how did you know the creature was in the curtain?"

For the first time since he had entered the room the groom looked a little confused.

"It's a sort of presumption for a man in my position to be subject to a nervous infirmity," he answered. "I am one of those persons (the weakness is not uncommon, as your ladyship is aware) who know by their own unpleasant sensations when a cat is in the room. It goes a little further than that with me. The 'antipathy,' as the gentlefolks call it, tells me in what part of the room the cat is."

My aunt turned to her husband, without attempting to conceal that she took no sort of interest in the groom's antipathies.

"Haven't you done with the man yet?" she asked.

The General gave the groom his dismissal.

"You shall hear from me in three days' time. Good-morning."

Michael Bloomfield seemed to have noticed my aunt's ungracious manner. He looked at her for a moment with steady attention before he left the room.

V.

"You don't mean to engage that man?" said Lady Claudia as the door closed.

"Why not?" asked my uncle.

"I have taken a dislike to him."

This short answer was so entirely out of the character of my aunt that the General took her kindly by the hand, and said:

"I am afraid you are not well."

She irritably withdrew her hand.

"I don't feel well. It doesn't matter."

"It does matter, Claudia. What can I do for you?"

"Write to the man—" She paused and smiled contemptuously. "Imagine a groom with an antipathy to cats!" she said, turning to me. "I don't know what you think, Mina. I have a strong objection, myself, to servants who hold themselves above their position in life. Write," she resumed, addressing her husband, "and tell him to look for another place."

"What objection can I make to him?" the General asked, helplessly.

"Good heavens! can't you make an excuse? Say he is too young."

My uncle looked at me in expressive silence—walked slowly to the writing-table—and glanced at his wife, in the faint hope that she might change her mind. Their eyes met—and she seemed to recover the command of her temper. She put her hand caressingly on the General's shoulder.

"I remember the time," she said, softly, "when any caprice of mine was a command to you. Ah, I was younger then!"

The General's reception of this little advance was thoroughly characteristic of him. He first kissed Lady Claudia's hand, and then he wrote the letter. My aunt rewarded him by a look, and left the library.

"What the deuce is the matter with her?" my uncle said to me when we were alone. "Do you dislike the man, too?"

"Certainly not. As far as I can judge, he appears to be just the sort of person we want."

"And knows thoroughly well how to manage horses, my dear. What can be your aunt's objection to him?"

As the words passed his lips Lady Claudia opened the library door.

"I am so ashamed of myself," she said, sweetly. "At my age, I have been behaving like a spoiled child. How good you are to me, General! Let me try to make amends for my misconduct. Will you permit me?"

She took up the General's letter, without waiting for permission; tore it to pieces, smiling pleasantly all the while; and threw the fragments into the waste-paper basket. "As if you didn't know better than I do!" she said, kissing him on the forehead. "Engage the man by all means."

She left the room for the second time. For the second time my uncle looked at me in blank perplexity—and I looked back at him in the same condition of mind. The sound of the luncheon bell was equally a relief to both of us. Not a word more was spoken on the subject of the new groom. His references were verified; and he entered the General's service in three days' time.

VI.

ALWAYS careful in anything that concerned my welfare, no matter how trifling it might be, my uncle did not trust me alone with the new groom when he first entered our service. Two old friends of the General accompanied me at his special request, and reported the man to be perfectly competent and trustworthy. After that, Michael rode out with me alone; my friends among young ladies seldom caring to accompany me, when I abandoned the park for the quiet country roads on the north and west of London. Was it wrong in me to talk to him on these expeditions? It would surely have been treating a man like a brute never to take the smallest notice of him—especially as his conduct was uniformly respectful toward me. Not once, by word or look, did he presume on the position which my favor permitted him to occupy.

Ought I to blush when I confess (though he was only a groom) that he interested me?

In the first place, there was something romantic in the very blankness of the story of his life.

He had been left, in his infancy, in the stables of a gentleman living in Kent, near the highroad between Gravesend and Rochester. The same day, the stable-boy had met a woman running out of the yard, pursued by the dog. She was a stranger, and was not well-dressed. While the boy was protecting her by chaining the dog to his kennel, she was quick enough to place herself beyond the reach of pursuit.

The infant's clothing proved, on examination, to be of the finest linen. He was warmly wrapped in a beautiful shawl of some foreign manufacture, entirely unknown to all the persons present, including the master and mistress of the house. Among the folds of the shawl there was discovered an open letter, without date, signature, or address, which it was presumed the woman must have forgotten.

Like the shawl, the paper was of foreign manufacture. The handwriting presented a strongly marked character; and the composition plainly revealed the mistakes of a person imperfectly acquainted with the English language. The contents of the letter, after alluding to the means supplied for the support of the child, announced that the writer had committed the folly of inclosing a sum of a hundred pounds in a banknote, "to pay expenses." In a postscript, an appointment was made for a meeting in six months' time, on the eastward side of London Bridge. The stable-boy's description of the woman who had passed him showed that she belonged to the lower class. To such a person a hundred pounds would be a fortune. She had, no doubt, abandoned the child, and made off with the money.

No trace of her was ever discovered. On the day of the appointment the police watched the eastward side of London Bridge without obtaining any result. Through the kindness of the gentleman in whose stable he had been found, the first ten years of the boy's life were passed under the protection of a charitable asylum. They gave him the name of one of the little inmates who had died; and they sent him out to service before he was eleven years old. He was harshly treated and ran away; wandered to some training-stables near Newmarket; attracted the favorable notice of the head-groom, was employed among the other boys, and liked the occupation. Growing up to manhood, he had taken service in private families as a groom. This was the story of twenty-six years of Michael's life.

But there was something in the man himself which attracted attention, and made one think of him in his absence.

I mean by this, that there was a spirit of resistance to his destiny in him, which is very rarely found in serving-men of his order. I remember accompanying the General "on one of his periodical visits of inspection to the stable." He was so well satisfied that he proposed extending his investigations to the groom's own room.

"If you don object, Michael?" he added, with his customary consideration for the self-respect of all persons in his employment. Michael's color rose a little; he looked at me. "I am afraid the young lady will not find my room quite so tidy as it ought to be," he said as he opened the door for us.

The only disorder in the groom's room was produced, to our surprise, by the groom's books and papers.

Cheap editions of the English poets, translations of Latin and Greek classics, handbooks for teaching French and German "without a master," carefully written "exercises" in both languages, manuals of shorthand, with more "exercises" in that art, were scattered over the table, round the central object of a reading-lamp, which spoke plainly of studies by night. "Why, what is all this?" cried the General. "Are you going to leave me, Michael, and set up a school?" Michael answered in sad, submissive tones. "I try to improve myself, sir—though I sometimes lose heart and hope." "Hope of what?" asked my uncle. "Are you not content to be a servant? Must you rise in the world, as the saying is?" The groom shrank a little at that abrupt question. "If I had relations to care for me and help me along the hard ways of life," he said, "I might be satisfied, sir, to remain as I am. As it is, I have no one to think about but myself—and I am foolish enough sometimes to look beyond myself."

So far, I had kept silence; but I could no longer resist giving him a word of encouragement—his confession was so sadly and so patiently made. "You speak too harshly of yourself," I said; "the best and greatest men have begun like you by looking beyond themselves." For a moment our eyes met. I admired the poor lonely fellow trying so modestly and so bravely to teach himself—and I did not care to conceal it. He was the first to look away; some suppressed emotion turned him deadly pale. Was I the cause of it? I felt myself tremble as that bold question came into my mind. The General, with one sharp glance at me, diverted the talk (not very delicately, as I thought) to the misfortune of Michael's birth.

"I have heard of your being deserted in your infancy by some woman unknown," he said. "What has become of the things you were wrapped in, and the letter that was found on you? They might lead to a discovery, one of these days." The groom smiled. "The last master I served thought of it as you do, Sir. He was so good as to write to the gentleman who was first burdened with the care of me—and the things were sent to me in return."

He took up an unlocked leather bag, which opened by touching a brass knob, and showed us the shawl, the linen (sadly faded by time) and the letter. We were puzzled by the shawl. My uncle, who had served in the East, thought it looked like a very rare kind of Persian work. We examined with interest the letter, and the fine linen. When Michael quietly remarked, as we handed them back to him, "They keep the secret, you see," we could only look at each other, and own there was nothing more to be said.

VII.

THAT night, lying awake thinking, I made my first discovery of a great change that had come over me. I felt like a new woman.

Never yet had my life been so enjoyable to me as it was now. I was conscious of a delicious lightness of heart. The simplest things pleased me; I was ready to be kind to everybody, and to admire everything. Even the familiar scenery of my rides in the park developed beauties which I had never noticed before. The enchantments of music affected me to tears. I was absolutely in love with my dogs and my birds—and, as for my maid, I bewildered the girl with presents, and gave her holidays almost before she could ask for them. In a bodily sense, I felt an extraordinary accession of strength and activity. I romped with the dear old General, and actually kissed Lady Claudia, one morning, instead of letting her kiss me as usual. My friends noticed my new outburst of gayety and spirit—and wondered what had produced it. I can honestly say that I wondered too! Only on that wakeful night which followed our visit to Michael's room did I arrive at something like a clear understanding of myself. The next morning completed the process of enlightenment. I went out riding as usual. The instant when Michael put his hand under my foot as I sprang into the saddle, his touch flew all over me like a flame. I knew who had made a new woman of me from that moment.

As to describing the first sense of confusion that overwhelmed me, even if I were a practiced writer I should be incapable of doing it. I pulled down my veil, and rode on in a sort of trance. Fortunately for me, our house looked on the park, and I had only to cross the road. Otherwise I should have met with some accident if I had ridden through the streets. To this day, I don't know where I rode. The horse went his own way quietly—and the groom followed me.

The groom! Is there any human creature so free from the hateful and anti-Christian pride of rank as a woman who loves with all her heart and soul, for the first time in her life? I only tell the truth (in however unfavorable a light it may place me) when I declare that my confusion was entirely due to the discovery that I was in love. I was not ashamed of myself for being in love with the groom. I had given my heart to the man. What did the accident of his position matter? Put money into his pocket and a title before his name—by another accident: in speech, manners, and attainments, he would be a gentleman worthy of his wealth and worthy of his rank.

Even the natural dread of what my relations and friends might say, if they discovered my secret, seemed to be a sensation so unworthy of me and of him, that I looked round, and called to him to speak to me, and asked him questions about himself which kept him riding nearly side by side with me. Ah, how I enjoyed the gentle deference and respect of his manner as he answered me! He was hardly bold enough to raise his eyes to mine, when I looked at him. Absorbed in the Paradise of my own making, I rode on slowly, and was only aware that friends had passed and had recognized me, by seeing him touch his hat. I looked round and discovered the women smiling ironically as they rode by. That one circumstance roused me rudely from my dream. I let Michael fall back again to his proper place, and quickened my horse's pace; angry with myself, angry with the world in general, then suddenly changing, and being fool enough and child enough to feel ready to cry. How long these varying moods lasted, I don't know. On returning, I slipped off my horse without waiting for Michael to help me, and ran into the house without even wishing him "Good-day."

VIII.

AFTER taking off my riding-habit, and cooling my hot face with eau-de-cologne and water, I went down to the room which we called the morning-room. The piano there was my favorite instrument and I had the idea of trying what music would do toward helping me to compose myself.

As I sat down before the piano, I heard the opening of the door of the breakfast-room (separated from me by a curtained archway), and the voice of Lady Claudia asking if Michael had returned to the stable. On the servant's reply in the affirmative, she desired that he might be sent to her immediately.

No doubt, I ought either to have left the morning-room, or to have let my aunt know of my presence there. I did neither the one nor the other. Her first dislike of Michael had, to all appearance, subsided. She had once or twice actually taken opportunities of speaking to him kindly. I believed this was due to the caprice of the moment. The tone of her voice too suggested, on this occasion, that she had some spiteful object in view, in sending for him. I knew it was unworthy of me—and yet, I deliberately waited to hear what passed between them.

Lady Claudia began.

553

"You were out riding to-day with Miss Mina?"

"Yes, my lady."

"Turn to the light. I wish to see people when I speak to them. You were observed by some friends of mine; your conduct excited remark. Do you know your business as a lady's groom?"

"I have had seven years' experience, my lady."

"Your business is to ride at a certain distance behind your mistress. Has your experience taught you that?"

"Yes, my lady."

"You were not riding behind Miss Mina—your horse was almost side by side with hers. Do you deny it?"

"No, my lady."

"You behaved with the greatest impropriety—you were seen talking to Miss Mina. Do you deny that?"

"No, my lady."

"Leave the room. No! come back. Have you any excuse to make?"

"None, my lady."

"Your insolence is intolerable! I shall speak to the General."

The sound of the closing door followed.

I knew now what the smiles meant on the false faces of those women-friends of mine who had met me in the park. An ordinary man, in Michael's place, would have mentioned my own encouragement of him as a sufficient excuse. He, with the inbred delicacy and reticence of a gentleman, had taken all the blame on himself. Indignant and ashamed, I advanced to the breakfast-room, bent on instantly justifying him. Drawing aside the curtain, I was startled by a sound as of a person sobbing. I cautiously looked in. Lady Claudia was prostrate on the sofa, hiding her face in her hands, in a passion of tears.

I withdrew, completely bewildered. The extraordinary contradictions in my aunt's conduct were not at an end yet. Later in the day, I went to my uncle, resolved to set Michael right in his estimation, and to leave him to speak to Lady Claudia. The General was in the lowest spirits; he shook his head ominously the moment. I mentioned the groom's name. "I dare say the man meant no harm—but the thing has been observed. I can't have you made the subject of scandal, Mina. My wife makes a point of it—Michael must go.

"You don't mean to say that she has insisted on your sending Michael away?"

Before he could answer me, a footman appeared with a message. "My lady wishes to see you, sir."

The General rose directly. My curiosity had got, by this time, beyond all restraint. I was actually indelicate enough to ask if I might go with him! He stared at me, as well he might. I persisted; I said I particularly wished to see Lady Claudia. My uncle's punctilious good breeding still resisted me. "Your aunt may wish to speak to me in private," he said. "Wait a moment, and I will send for you."

I was incapable of waiting: my obstinacy was something superhuman. The bare idea that Michael might lose his place, through my fault, made me desperate, I suppose. "I won't trouble you to send for me," I persisted; "I will go with you at once as far as the door, and wait to hear if I may come in." The footman was still present, holding the door open; the General gave way. I kept so close behind him that my aunt saw me as her husband entered the room. "Come in, Mina," she said, speaking and looking like the charming Lady Claudia of everyday life. Was this the woman whom I had seen crying her heart out on the sofa hardly an hour ago?

"On second thoughts," she continued, turning to the General, "I fear I may have been a little hasty. Pardon me for troubling you about it again— have you spoken to Michael yet? No? Then let us err on the side of kindness; let us look over his misconduct this time."

My uncle was evidently relieved. I seized the opportunity of making my confession, and taking the whole blame on myself. Lady Claudia stopped me with the perfect grace of which she was mistress.

"My good child, don't distress yourself! don't make mountains out of molehills!" She patted me on the cheek with two plump white fingers which felt deadly cold. "I was not always prudent, Mina, when I was your age. Besides, your curiosity is naturally excited about a servant who is—what shall I call him?—a foundling."

She paused and fixed her eyes on me attentively. "What did he tell you?" she asked. "Is it a very romantic story?"

The General began to fidget in his chair. If I had kept my attention on him, I should have seen in his face a warning to me to be silent. But my interest at the moment was absorbed in my aunt. Encouraged by her amiable reception, I was not merely unsuspicious of the trap that she had set for me—I was actually foolish enough to think that I could improve Michael's position in her estimation (remember that I was in love with him!) by telling his story exactly as I have already told it in these pages. I spoke with fervor. Will you believe it?—her humor positively changed again! She flew into a passion with me for the first time in her life.

"Lies!" she cried. "Impudent lies on the face of them—invented to appeal to your interest. How dare you repeat them? General! if Mina had not brought it on herself, this man's audacity would justify you in instantly dismissing him. Don't you agree with me?"

The General's sense of fair play roused him for once into openly opposing his wife.

"You are completely mistaken," he said. "Mina and I have both had the shawl and the letter in our hands—and (what was there besides?)—ah, yes, the very linen the child was wrapped in."

What there was in those words to check Lady Claudia's anger in its full flow I was quite unable to understand. If her husband had put a pistol to her head, he could hardly have silenced her more effectually. She did not appear to be frightened, or ashamed of her outbreak of rage—she sat vacant and speechless, with her eyes on the General and her hands crossed on her lap. After waiting a moment (wondering as I did what it meant) my uncle rose with his customary resignation and left her. I followed him. He was unusually silent and thoughtful; not a word passed between us. I afterward discovered that he was beginning to fear, poor man, that his wife's mind must be affected in some way, and was meditating a consultation with the physician who helped us in cases of need.

As for myself, I was either too stupid or too innocent to feel any positive forewarning of the truth, so far. After luncheon, while I was alone in the conservatory, my maid came to me from Michael, asking if I had any commands for him in the afternoon. I thought this rather odd; but it occurred to me that he might want some hours to himself. I made the inquiry.

To my astonishment, the maid announced that Lady Claudia had employed Michael to go on an errand for her. The nature of the errand was to take a letter to her bookseller, and to bring back the books which she had ordered. With three idle footmen in the house, whose business it was to perform such service as this, why had she taken the groom away from his work? The question obtained such complete possession of my mind that I actually summoned courage enough to go to my aunt. I said I had thought of driving out in my pony-carriage that afternoon, and I asked if she objected to sending one of the three indoor servants for her books in Michael's place.

She received me with a strange hard stare, and answered with obstinate self-possession: "I wish Michael to go!" No explanation followed. With reason or without it, agreeable to me or not agreeable to me, she wished Michael to go.

I begged her pardon for interfering, and replied that I would give up the idea of driving on that day. She made no further remark. I left the room, determining to watch her. There is no defense for my conduct; it was mean and unbecoming, no doubt. I was drawn on, by some force in me which I could not even attempt to resist. Indeed, indeed I am not a mean person by nature!

At first, I thought of speaking to Michael; not with any special motive, but simply because I felt drawn toward him as the guide and helper in whom my heart trusted at this crisis in my life. A little consideration, however, suggested to me that I might be seen speaking to him, and might so do him an injury. While I was still hesitating, the thought came to me that my aunt's motive for sending him to her bookseller might be to get him out of her way.

Out of her way in the house? No: his place was not in the house. Out of her way in the stable? The next instant, the idea flashed across my mind of watching the stable door.

The best bedrooms, my room included, were all in front of the house. I went up to my maid's room, which looked on the courtyard; ready with my excuse, if she happened to be there. She was not there. I placed myself at the window, in full view of the stable opposite.

An interval elapsed—long or short, I cannot say which; I was too much excited to look at my watch. All I know is that I discovered her! She crossed the yard, after waiting to make sure that no one was there to see her; and she entered the stable by the door which led to that part of the building occupied by Michael. This time I looked at my watch.

Forty minutes passed before I saw her again. And then, instead of appearing at the door, she showed herself at the window of Michael's room; throwing it wide open. I concealed myself behind the window curtain, just in time to escape discovery, as she looked up at the house. She next appeared in the yard, hurrying back. I waited a while, trying to compose myself in case I met any one on the stairs. There was little danger of a meeting at that hour. The General was at his club; the servants were at their tea. I reached my own room without being seen by any one, and locked myself in.

What had my aunt been doing for forty minutes in Michael's room? And why had she opened the window?

I spare you my reflections on these perplexing questions. A convenient headache saved me from the ordeal of meeting Lady Claudia at the dinner-table. I passed a restless and miserable night; conscious that I had found my way blindly, as it were, to some terrible secret which might have its influence on my whole future life, and not knowing what to think, or what to do next. Even then, I shrank instinctively from speaking to my uncle. This was not wonderful. But I felt afraid to speak to Michael—and that perplexed and alarmed me. Consideration for Lady Claudia was certainly not the motive that kept me silent, after what I had seen.

The next morning my pale face abundantly justified the assertion that I was still ill.

My aunt, always doing her maternal duty toward me, came herself to inquire after my health before I was out of my room. So certain was she of not having been observed on the previous day—or so prodigious was her power of controlling herself—that she actually advised me to go out riding before lunch, and try what the fresh air and the exercise would do to relieve me! Feeling that I must end in speaking to Michael, it struck me that this would be the one safe way of consulting him in private. I accepted her advice, and had another approving pat on the cheek from her plump white fingers. They no longer struck cold on my skin; the customary vital warmth had returned to them. Her ladyship's mind had recovered its tranquillity.

IX.

I LEFT the house for my morning ride.

Michael was not in his customary spirits. With some difficulty, I induced him to tell me the reason. He had decided on giving notice to leave his situation in the General's employment. As soon as I could command myself, I asked what had happened to justify this incomprehensible proceeding on his part. He silently offered me a letter. It was written by the master whom he had served before he came to us; and it announced that an employment as secretary was offered to him, in the house of a gentleman who was "interested in his creditable efforts to improve his position in the world."

What it cost me to preserve the outward appearance of composure as I handed back the letter, I am ashamed to tell. I spoke to him with some bitterness. "Your wishes are gratified," I said; "I don't wonder that you are eager to leave your place." He reined back his horse and repeated my words.

"Eager to leave my place? I am heart-broken at leaving it." I was reckless enough to ask why. His head sank. "I daren't tell you," he said. I went on from one imprudence to another. "What are you afraid of?" I asked. He suddenly looked up at me. His eyes answered: "You."

Is it possible to fathom the folly of a woman in love? Can any sensible person imagine the enormous importance which the veriest trifles assume in her poor little mind? I was perfectly satisfied—even perfectly happy, after that one look. I rode on briskly for a minute or two—then the forgotten scene at the stable recurred to my memory. I resumed a foot-pace and beckoned to him to speak to me.

"Lady Claudia's bookseller lives in the City, doesn't he?" I began.

"Yes, miss."

"Did you walk both ways?"

"Yes."

"You must have felt tired when you got back?"

"I hardly remember what I felt when I got back—I was met by a surprise."

"May I ask what it was?"

"Certainly, miss. Do you remember a black bag of mine?"

"Perfectly."

"When I returned from the City I found the bag open; and the things I kept in it—the shawl, the linen, and the letter—"

"Gone?"

"Gone."

My heart gave one great leap in me, and broke into vehement throbbings, which made it impossible for me to say a word more. I reined up my horse, and fixed my eyes on Michael. He was startled; he asked if I felt faint. I could only sign to him that I was waiting to hear more.

"My own belief," he proceeded, "is that some person burned the things in my absence, and opened the window to prevent any suspicion being excited by the smell. I am certain I shut the window before I left my room. When I closed it on my return, the fresh air had not entirely removed the smell of burning; and, what is more, I found a heap of ashes in the grate. As to the person who has done me this injury, and why it has been done, those are mysteries beyond my fathoming—I beg your pardon, miss—I am sure you are not well. Might I advise you to return to the house?"

I accepted his advice and turned back.

In the tumult of horror and amazement that filled my mind, I could still feel a faint triumph stirring in me through it all, when I saw how alarmed and how anxious he was about me. Nothing more passed between us on the way back. Confronted by the dreadful discovery that I had now made, I was silent and helpless. Of the guilty persons concerned in the concealment of the birth, and in the desertion of the infant, my nobly-born, highly-bred, irreproachable aunt now stood revealed before me as one! An older woman than I might have been hard put to it to preserve her presence of mind, in such a position as mine. Instinct, not reason, served me in my sore need. Instinct, not reason, kept me passively and stupidly silent when I got back to the house. "We will talk about it to-morrow," was all I could say to Michael, when he gently lifted me from my horse.

I excused myself from appearing at the luncheon-table; and I drew down the blinds in my sitting-room, so that my face might not betray me when Lady Claudia's maternal duty brought her upstairs to make inquiries. The same excuse served in both cases—my ride had failed to relieve me of my headache. My aunt's brief visit led to one result which is worth mentioning. The indescribable horror of her that I felt forced the conviction on my mind that we two could live no longer under the same roof. While I was still trying to face this alternative with the needful composure, my uncle presented himself, in some anxiety about my continued illness. I should certainly have burst out crying, when the kind and dear old man condoled with me, if he had not brought news with him which turned back all my thoughts on myself and my aunt. Michael had shown the General his letter and had given notice to leave. Lady Claudia was present at the time. To her husband's amazement, she abruptly interfered with a personal request to Michael to think better of it, and to remain in his place!

"I should not have troubled you, my dear, on this unpleasant subject," said my uncle, "if Michael had not told me that you were aware of the circumstances under which he feels it his duty to leave us. After your aunt's interference (quite incomprehensible to me), the man hardly knows what to do. Being your groom, he begs me to ask if there is any impropriety in his leaving the difficulty to your decision. I tell you of his request, Mina; but I strongly advise you to decline taking any responsibility on yourself."

I answered mechanically, accepting my uncle's suggestion, while my thoughts were wholly absorbed in this last of the many extraordinary proceedings on Lady Claudia's part since Michael had entered the house. There are limits—out of books and plays—to the innocence of a young unmarried woman. After what I had just heard the doubts which had thus far perplexed me were suddenly and completely cleared up. I said to my secret self: "She has some human feeling left. If her son goes away, she knows that they may never meet again!"

From the moment when my mind emerged from the darkness, I recovered the use of such intelligence and courage as I naturally possessed. From this point, you will find that, right or wrong, I saw my way before me, and took it.

To say that I felt for the General with my whole heart, is merely to own that I could be commonly grateful. I sat on his knee, and laid my cheek against his cheek, and thanked him for his long, long years of kindness to me. He stopped me in his simple generous way. "Why, Mina, you talk as if you were going to leave us!" I started up, and went to the window, opening it and complaining of the heat, and so concealing from him that he had unconsciously anticipated the event that was indeed to come. When I returned to my chair, he helped me to recover myself by alluding once more to his wife. He feared that her health was in some way impaired. In the time when they had first met, she was subject to nervous maladies, having their origin in a "calamity" which was never mentioned by either of them in later days. She might possibly be suffering again, from some other form of nervous derangement, and he seriously thought of persuading her to send for medical advice.

Under ordinary circumstances, this vague reference to a "calamity" would not have excited any special interest in me. But my mind was now in a state of morbid suspicion. I had not heard how long my uncle and aunt had been married; but I remembered that Michael had described himself as being twenty-six years old. Bearing these circumstances in mind, it struck me that I might be acting wisely (in Michael's interest) if I persuaded the General to speak further of what had happened, at the time when he met the woman whom an evil destiny had bestowed on him for a wife. Nothing but the consideration of serving the man I loved would have reconciled me to making my own secret use of the recollections which my uncle might innocently confide to me. As it was, I thought the means would, in this case, he for once justified by the end. Before we part, I have little doubt that you will think so too.

I found it an easier task than I had anticipated to turn the talk back again to the days when the General had seen Lady Claudia for the first time. He was proud of the circumstances under which he had won his wife. Ah, how my heart ached for him as I saw his eyes sparkle, and the color mount in his fine rugged face!

This is the substance of what I heard from him. I tell it briefly, because it is still painful to me to tell it at all.

My uncle had met Lady Claudia at her father's country house. She had then reappeared in society, after a period of seclusion, passed partly in England, partly on the Continent. Before the date of her retirement, she had been engaged to marry a French nobleman, equally illustrious by his birth and by his diplomatic services in the East. Within a few weeks of the wedding-day, he was drowned by the wreck of his yacht. This was the calamity to which my uncle had referred.

Lady Claudia's mind was so seriously affected by the dreadful event, that the doctors refused to answer for the consequences, unless she was at once placed in the strictest retirement. Her mother, and a French maid devotedly attached to her, were the only persons whom it was considered safe for the young lady to see, until time and care had in some degree composed her. Her return to her friends and admirers, after the necessary interval of seclusion, was naturally a subject of sincere rejoicing among the guests assembled in her father's house. My uncle's interest in Lady Claudia soon developed into love. They were equals in rank, and well suited to each other in age. The parents raised no obstacles; but they did not conceal from their guest that the disaster which had befallen their daughter was but too likely to disincline her to receive his addresses, or any man's addresses, favorably. To their surprise, they proved to be wrong. The young lady was touched by the simplicity and the delicacy with which her lover urged his suit. She had lived among worldly people. This was a man whose devotion she could believe to be sincere. They were married.

Had no unusual circumstances occurred? Had nothing happened which the General had forgotten? Nothing.

X.

IT is surely needless that I should stop here, to draw the plain inferences from the events just related.

Any person who remembers that the shawl in which the infant was wrapped came from those Eastern regions which were associated with the French nobleman's diplomatic services—also, that the faults of composition in the letter found on the child were exactly the faults likely to have been committed by the French maid—any person who follows these traces can find his way to the truth as I found mine.

Returning for a moment to the hopes which I had formed of being of some service to Michael, I have only to say that they were at once destroyed, when I heard of the death by drowning of the man to whom the evidence pointed as his father. The prospect looked equally barren when I thought of the miserable mother. That she should openly acknowledge her son in her position was perhaps not to be expected of any woman. Had she courage enough, or, in plainer words, heart enough to acknowledge him privately?

I called to mind again some of the apparent caprices and contradictions in Lady Claudia's conduct, on the memorable day when Michael had presented himself to fill the vacant place. Look back with me to the record of what she said and did on that occasion, by the light of your present knowledge, and you will see that his likeness to his father must have struck her when he entered the room, and that his statement of his age must have correctly described the age of her son. Recall the actions that followed, after she had been exhausted by her first successful efforts at self-control—the withdrawal to the window to conceal her face; the clutch at the curtain when she felt herself sinking; the harshness of manner under which she concealed her emotions when she ventured to speak to him; the reiterated inconsistencies and vacillations of conduct that followed, all alike due to the protest of Nature, desperately resisted to the last—and say if I did her injustice when I believed her to be incapable of running the smallest risk of discovery at the prompting of maternal love.

There remained, then, only Michael to think of. I remember how he had spoken of the unknown parents whom he neither expected nor cared to discover. Still, I could not reconcile it to my conscience to accept a chance outbreak of temper as my sufficient justification for keeping him in ignorance of a discovery which so nearly concerned him. It seemed at least to be my duty to make myself acquainted with the true state of his feelings, before I decided to bear the burden of silence with me to my grave.

What I felt it my duty to do in this serious matter, I determined to do at once. Besides, let me honestly own that I felt lonely and desolate, oppressed by the critical situation in which I was placed, and eager for the relief that it would be to me only to hear the sound of Michael's voice. I sent my maid to say that I wished to speak to him immediately. The crisis was already hanging over my head. That one act brought it down.

XI.

He came in, and stood modestly waiting at the door.

After making him take a chair, I began by saying that I had received his message, and that, acting on my uncle's advice, I must abstain from interfering in the question of his leaving, or not leaving, his place. Having in this way established a reason for sending for him, I alluded next to the loss that he had sustained, and asked if he had any prospect of finding out the person who had entered his room in his absence. On his reply in the negative, I spoke of the serious results to him of the act of destruction that had been committed. "Your last chance of discovering your parents," I said, "has been cruelly destroyed."

He smiled sadly. "You know already, miss, that I never expected to discover them."

I ventured a little nearer to the object I had in view.

"Do you never think of your mother?" I asked. "At your age, she might be still living. Can you give up all hope of finding her, without feeling your heart ache?"

"If I have done her wrong, in believing that she deserted me," he answered, "the heart-ache is but a poor way of expressing the remorse that I should feel."

I ventured nearer still.

"Even if you were right," I began—"even if she did desert you—"

He interrupted me sternly. "I would not cross the street to see her," he said. "A woman who deserts her child is a monster. Forgive me for speaking so, miss! When I see good mothers and their children it maddens me when I think of what my childhood was."

Hearing these words, and watching him attentively while he spoke, I could see that my silence would be a mercy, not a crime. I hastened to speak of other things.

566

"If you decide to leave us," I said, "when shall you go?"

His eyes softened instantly. Little by little the color faded out of his face as he answered me.

"The General kindly said, when I spoke of leaving my place—" His voice faltered, and he paused to steady it. "My master," he resumed, "said that I need not keep my new employer waiting by staying for the customary month, provided—provided you were willing to dispense with my services."

So far, I had succeeded in controlling myself. At that reply I felt my resolution failing me. I saw how he suffered; I saw how manfully he struggled to conceal it.

"I am not willing," I said. "I am sorry—very, very sorry to lose you. But I will do anything that is for your good. I can say no more."

He rose suddenly, as if to leave the room; mastered himself; stood for a moment silently looking at me—then looked away again, and said his parting words.

"If I succeed, Miss Mina, in my new employment—if I get on to higher things—is it—is it presuming too much, to ask if I might, some day—perhaps when you are out riding alone—if I might speak to you—only to ask if you are well and happy—"

He could say no more. I saw the tears in his eyes; saw him shaken by the convulsive breathings which break from men in the rare moments when they cry. He forced it back even then. He bowed to me—oh, God, he bowed to me, as if he were only my servant! as if he were too far below me to take my hand, even at that moment! I could have endured anything else; I believe I could still have restrained myself under any other circumstances. It matters little now; my confession must be made, whatever you may think of me. I flew to him like a frenzied creature—I threw my arms round his neck—I said to him, "Oh, Michael, don't you know that I love you?" And then I laid my head on his breast, and held him to me, and said no more.

In that moment of silence, the door of the room was opened. I started, and looked up. Lady Claudia was standing on the threshold.

I saw in her face that she had been listening—she must have followed him when he was on his way to my room. That conviction steadied me. I took his hand in mine, and stood side by side with him, waiting for her to speak first. She looked at Michael, not at me. She advanced a step or two, and addressed him in these words:

"It is just possible that you have some sense of decency left. Leave the room."

That deliberate insult was all that I wanted to make me completely mistress of myself. I told Michael to wait a moment, and opened my writing desk. I wrote on an envelope the address in London of a faithful old servant, who had attended my mother in her last moments. I gave it to Michael. "Call there to-morrow morning," I said. "You will find me waiting for you."

He looked at Lady Claudia, evidently unwilling to leave me alone with her. "Fear nothing," I said; "I am old enough to take care of myself. I have only a word to say to this lady before I leave the house." With that, I took his arm, and walked with him to the door, and said good-by almost as composedly as if we had been husband and wife already.

Lady Claudia's eyes followed me as I shut the door again and crossed the room to a second door which led into my bed-chamber. She suddenly stepped up to me, just as I was entering the room, and laid her hand on my arm.

"What do I see in your face?" she asked as much of herself as of me—with her eyes fixed in keen inquiry on mine.

"You shall know directly," I answered. "Let me get my bonnet and cloak first."

"Do you mean to leave the house?"

"I do."

She rang the bell. I quietly dressed myself, to go out.

568

The servant answered the bell, as I returned to the sitting-room.

"Tell your master I wish to see him instantly," said Lady Claudia.

"My master has gone out, my lady."

"To his club?"

"I believe so, my lady."

"I will send you with a letter to him. Come back when I ring again." She turned to me as the man withdrew. "Do you refuse to stay here until the General returns?"

"I shall be happy to see the General, if you will inclose my address in your letter to him."

Replying in those terms, I wrote the address for the second time. Lady Claudia knew perfectly well, when I gave it to her, that I was going to a respectable house kept by a woman who had nursed me when I was a child.

"One last question," she said. "Am I to tell the General that it is your intention to marry your groom?"

Her tone stung me into making an answer which I regretted the moment it had passed my lips.

"You can put it more plainly, if you like," I said. "You can tell the General that it is my intention to marry your son."

She was near the door, on the point of leaving me. As I spoke, she turned with a ghastly stare of horror—felt about her with her hands as if she was groping in darkness—and dropped on the floor.

I instantly summoned help. The women-servants carried her to my bed. While they were restoring her to herself, I wrote a few lines telling the miserable woman how I had discovered her secret.

"Your husband's tranquillity," I added, "is as precious to me as my own. As for your son, you know what he thinks of the mother who deserted him. Your secret is safe in my keeping—safe from your husband, safe from your son, to the end of my life."

I sealed up those words, and gave them to her when she had come to herself again. I never heard from her in reply. I have never seen her from that time to this. She knows she can trust me.

And what did my good uncle say, when we next met? I would rather report what he did, when he had got the better of his first feelings of anger and surprise on hearing of my contemplated marriage. He consented to receive us on our wedding-day; and he gave my husband the appointment which places us both in an independent position for life.

But he had his misgivings. He checked me when I tried to thank him.

"Come back in a year's time," he said. "I will wait to be thanked till the experience of your married life tells me that I have deserved it."

The year passed; and the General received the honest expression of my gratitude. He smiled and kissed me; but there was something in his face which suggested that he was not quite satisfied yet.

"Do you believe that I have spoken sincerely?" I asked.

"I firmly believe it," he answered—and there he stopped.

A wiser woman would have taken the hint and dropped the subject. My folly persisted in putting another question:

"Tell me, uncle. Haven't I proved that I was right when I married my groom?"

"No, my dear. You have only proved that you are a lucky woman!"

MR. LEPEL AND THE HOUSEKEEPER

FIRST EPOCH.

THE Italians are born actors.

At this conclusion I arrived, sitting in a Roman theater—now many years since. My friend and traveling companion, Rothsay, cordially agreed with me. Experience had given us some claim to form an opinion. We had visited, at that time, nearly every city in Italy. Where-ever a theater was open, we had attended the performances of the companies which travel from place to place; and we had never seen bad acting from first to last. Men and women, whose names are absolutely unknown in England, played (in modern comedy and drama for the most part) with a general level of dramatic ability which I have never seen equaled in the theaters of other nations. Incapable Italian actors there must be, no doubt. For my own part I have only discovered them, by ones and twos, in England; appearing among the persons engaged to support Salvini and Ristori before the audiences of London.

On the occasion of which I am now writing, the night's performances consisted of two plays. An accident, to be presently related, prevented us from seeing more than the introductory part of the second piece. That one act—in respect of the influence which the remembrance of it afterward exercised over Rothsay and myself—claims a place of its own in the opening pages of the present narrative.

The scene of the story was laid in one of the principalities of Italy, in the bygone days of the Carbonaro conspiracies. The chief persons were two young noblemen, friends affectionately attached to each other, and a beautiful girl born in the lower ranks of life.

On the rising of the curtain, the scene before us was the courtyard of a prison. We found the beautiful girl (called Celia as well as I can recollect) in great distress; confiding her sorrows to the jailer's daughter. Her father was pining in the prison, charged with an offense of which he was innocent;

and she herself was suffering the tortures of hopeless love. She was on the point of confiding her secret to her friend, when the appearance of the young nobleman closed her lips. The girls at once withdrew; and the two friends— whom I now only remember as the Marquis and the Count—began the dialogue which prepared us for the story of the play.

The Marquis had been tried for conspiracy against the reigning Prince and his government; had been found guilty, and is condemned to be shot that evening. He accepts his sentence with the resignation of a man who is weary of his life. Young as he is, he has tried the round of pleasures without enjoyment; he has no interests, no aspirations, no hopes; he looks on death as a welcome release. His friend the Count, admitted to a farewell interview, has invented a stratagem by which the prisoner may escape and take to flight. The Marquis expresses a grateful sense of obligation, and prefers being shot. "I don't value my life," he says; "I am not a happy man like you." Upon this the Count mentions circumstances which he has hitherto kept secret. He loves the charming Celia, and loves in vain. Her reputation is unsullied; she possesses every good quality that a man can desire in a wife—but the Count's social position forbids him to marry a woman of low birth. He is heart-broken; and he too finds life without hope a burden that is not to be borne. The Marquis at once sees a way of devoting himself to his friend's interests. He is rich; his money is at his own disposal; he will bequeath a marriage portion to Celia which will make her one of the richest women in Italy. The Count receives this proposal with a sigh. "No money," he says, "will remove the obstacle that still remains. My father's fatal objection to Celia is her rank in life." The Marquis walks apart—considers a little—consults his watch—and returns with a new idea. "I have nearly two hours of life still left," he says. "Send for Celia: she was here just now, and she is probably in her father's cell." The Count is at a loss to understand what this proposal means. The Marquis explains himself. "I ask your permission," he resumes, "to offer marriage to Celia—for your sake. The chaplain of the prison will perform the ceremony. Before dark, the girl you love will be my widow. My widow is a lady of title—a fit wife for the greatest nobleman in the land." The Count protests and refuses in vain. The jailer is sent to find Celia. She appears. Unable to endure the scene, the Count rushes out in horror. The Marquis takes the girl into his confidence, and makes his excuses. If she becomes a widow of rank, she may not only marry the Count, but will be in a position to procure the liberty of the innocent old man, whose strength is failing him under the rigors of imprisonment. Celia hesitates. After a struggle with herself, filial love prevails, and she consents. The jailer announces that the chaplain is waiting; the bride and bridegroom withdraw to the prison chapel. Left on the stage, the jailer hears a distant sound in the city, which he is at a loss to understand. It sinks, increases again, travels nearer to the prison, and now betrays itself as the sound of multitudinous voices in a state of furious uproar. Has the conspiracy broken out again? Yes! The whole population has risen; the soldiers have refused to fire on the people; the terrified Prince has dismissed his ministers, and promises a constitution. The Marquis, returning from the ceremony which has just made Celia his wife, is presented with a free pardon, and with the offer of a high place in the re-formed ministry. A new life is opening before him—and he has innocently ruined his friend's prospects! On this striking situation the drop-curtain falls.

While we were still applauding the first act, Rothsay alarmed me: he dropped from his seat at my side, like a man struck dead. The stifling heat in the theater had proved too much for him. We carried him out at once into the fresh air. When he came to his senses, my friend entreated me to leave him, and see the end of the play. To my mind, he looked as if he might faint again. I insisted on going back with him to our hotel.

On the next day I went to the theater, to ascertain if the play would be repeated. The box-office was closed. The dramatic company had left Rome.

My interest in discovering how the story ended led me next to the booksellers' shops—in the hope of buying the play. Nobody knew anything about it. Nobody could tell me whether it was the original work of an Italian writer, or whether it had been stolen (and probably disfigured) from the French. As a fragment I had seen it. As a fragment it has remained from that time to this.

SECOND EPOCH.

ONE of my objects in writing these lines is to vindicate the character of an innocent woman (formerly in my service as housekeeper) who has been cruelly slandered. Absorbed in the pursuit of my purpose, it has only now occurred to me that strangers may desire to know something more than they know now of myself and my friend. "Give us some idea," they may say, "of what sort of persons you are, if you wish to interest us at the outset of your story."

A most reasonable suggestion, I admit. Unfortunately, I am not the right man to comply with it.

In the first place, I cannot pretend to pronounce judgment on my own character. In the second place, I am incapable of writing impartially of my friend. At the imminent risk of his own life, Rothsay rescued me from a dreadful death by accident, when we were at college together. Who can expect me to speak of his faults? I am not even capable of seeing them.

Under these embarrassing circumstances—and not forgetting, at the same time, that a servant's opinion of his master and his master's friends may generally be trusted not to err on the favorable side—I am tempted to call my valet as a witness to character.

I slept badly on our first night at Rome; and I happened to be awake while the man was talking of us confidentially in the courtyard of the hotel—just under my bedroom window. Here, to the best of my recollection, is a faithful report of what he said to some friend among the servants who understood English:

"My master's well connected, you must know—though he's only plain Mr. Lepel. His uncle's the great lawyer, Lord Lepel; and his late father was a banker. Rich, did you say? I should think he was rich—and be hanged to him! No, not married, and not likely to be. Owns he was forty last birthday; a regular old bachelor. Not a bad sort, taking him altogether. The worst of him is, he is one of the most indiscreet persons I ever met with. Does the queerest things, when the whim takes him, and doesn't care what other people think of it. They say the Lepels have all got a slate loose in the upper story. Oh, no; not a very old family—I mean, nothing compared to the family of his friend, young Rothsay. They count back, as I have heard, to the ancient kings of Scotland. Between ourselves, the ancient kings haven't left the Rothsays much money. They would be glad, I'll be bound, to get my rich master for one of their daughters. Poor as Job, I tell you. This young fellow, traveling with us, has never had a spare five-pound note since he was born. Plenty of brains in his head, I grant you; and a little too apt sometimes to be suspicious of other people. But liberal—oh, give him his due—liberal in a small way. Tips me with a sovereign now and then. I take it—Lord bless you, I take it. What do you say? Has he got any employment? Not he! Dabbles in chemistry (experiments, and that sort of thing) by way of amusing himself; and tells the most infernal lies about it. The other day he showed me a bottle about as big as a thimble, with what looked like water in it, and said it was enough to poison everybody in the hotel. What rot! Isn't that the clock striking again? Near about bedtime, I should say. Wish you good night."

There are our characters—drawn on the principle of justice without mercy, by an impudent rascal who is the best valet in England. Now you know what sort of persons we are; and now we may go on again.

Rothsay and I parted, soon after our night at the theater. He went to Civita Vecchia to join a friend's yacht, waiting for him in the harbor. I turned homeward, traveling at a leisurely rate through the Tyrol and Germany.

After my arrival in England, certain events in my life occurred which did not appear to have any connection at the time. They led, nevertheless, to consequences which seriously altered the relations of happy past years between Rothsay and myself.

The first event took place on my return to my house in London. I found among the letters waiting for me an invitation from Lord Lepel to spend a few weeks with him at his country seat in Sussex.

I had made so many excuses, in past years, when I received invitations from my uncle, that I was really ashamed to plead engagements in London again. There was no unfriendly feeling between us. My only motive for keeping away from him took its rise in dislike of the ordinary modes of life in an English country-house. A man who feels no interest in politics, who cares nothing for field sports, who is impatient of amateur music and incapable of small talk, is a man out of his element in country society. This was my unlucky case. I went to Lord Lepel's house sorely against my will; longing already for the day when it would be time to say good-by.

The routine of my uncle's establishment had remained unaltered since my last experience of it.

I found my lord expressing the same pride in his collection of old masters, and telling the same story of the wonderful escape of his picture-gallery from fire—I renewed my acquaintance with the same members of Parliament among the guests, all on the same side in politics—I joined in the same dreary amusements—I saluted the same resident priest (the Lepels are all born and bred Roman Catholics)—I submitted to the same rigidly early breakfast hour; and inwardly cursed the same peremptory bell, ringing as a means of reminding us of our meals. The one change that presented itself was a change out of the house. Death had removed the lodgekeeper at the park-gate. His widow and daughter (Mrs. Rymer and little Susan) remained in their pretty cottage. They had been allowed by my lord's kindness to take charge of the gate.

Out walking, on the morning after my arrival, I was caught in a shower on my way back to the park, and took shelter in the lodge.

In the bygone days I had respected Mrs. Rymer's husband as a thoroughly worthy man—but Mrs. Rymer herself was no great favorite of mine. She had married beneath her, as the phrase is, and she was a little too conscious of it. A woman with a sharp eye to her own interests; selfishly discontented with her position in life, and not very scrupulous in her choice of means when she had an end in view: that is how I describe Mrs. Rymer. Her daughter, whom I only remembered as a weakly child, astonished me when I saw her again after the interval that had elapsed. The backward flower had bloomed into perfect health. Susan was now a lovely little modest girl of seventeen—with a natural delicacy and refinement of manner, which marked her to my mind as one of Nature's gentlewomen. When I entered the lodge she was writing at a table in a corner, having some books on it, and rose to withdraw. I begged that she would proceed with her employment, and asked if I might know what it was. She answered me with a blush, and a pretty brightening of her clear blue eyes. "I am trying, sir, to teach myself French," she said. The weather showed no signs of improving—I volunteered to help her, and found her such an attentive and intelligent pupil that I looked in at the lodge from time to time afterward, and continued my instructions. The younger men among my uncle's guests set their own stupid construction on my attentions "to the girl at the gate," as they called her—rather too familiarly, according to my notions of propriety. I contrived to remind them that I was old enough to be Susan's father, in a manner which put an end to their jokes; and I was pleased to hear, when I next went to the lodge, that Mrs. Rymer had been wise enough to keep these facetious gentlemen at their proper distance.

The day of my departure arrived. Lord Leper took leave of me kindly, and asked for news of Rothsay. "Let me know when your friend returns," my uncle said; "he belongs to a good old stock. Put me in mind of him when I next invite you to come to my house."

On my way to the train I stopped of course at the lodge to say good-by. Mrs. Rymer came out alone I asked for Susan.

"My daughter is not very well to-day."

"Is she confined to her room?"

"She is in the parlor."

I might have been mistaken, but I thought Mrs. Rymer answered me in no very friendly way. Resolved to judge for myself, I entered the lodge, and found my poor little pupil sitting in a corner, crying. When I asked her what was the matter, the excuse of a "bad headache" was the only reply that I received. The natures of young girls are a hopeless puzzle to me. Susan seemed, for some reason which it was impossible to understand, to be afraid to look at me.

"Have you and your mother been quarreling?" I asked.

"Oh, no!"

She denied it with such evident sincerity that I could not for a moment suspect her of deceiving me. Whatever the cause of her distress might be, it was plain that she had her own reasons for keeping it a secret.

Her French books were on the table. I tried a little allusion to her lessons.

"I hope you will go on regularly with your studies," I said.

"I will do my best, sir—without you to help me."

She said it so sadly that I proposed—purely from the wish to encourage her—a continuation of our lessons through the post.

"Send your exercises to me once a week," I suggested; "and I will return them corrected."

She thanked me in low tones, with a shyness of manner which I had never noticed in her before. I had done my best to cheer her—and I was conscious, as we shook hands at parting, that I had failed. A feeling of disappointment overcomes me when I see young people out of spirits. I was sorry for Susan.

THIRD EPOCH.

ONE of my faults (which has not been included in the list set forth by my valet) is a disinclination to occupy myself with my own domestic affairs. The proceedings of my footman, while I had been away from home, left me no alternative but to dismiss him on my return. With this exertion of authority my interference as chief of the household came to an end. I left it to my excellent housekeeper, Mrs. Mozeen, to find a sober successor to the drunken vagabond who had been sent away. She discovered a respectable young man—tall, plump, and rosy—whose name was Joseph, and whose character was beyond reproach. I have but one excuse for noticing such a trifling event as this. It took its place, at a later period, in the chain which was slowly winding itself round me.

My uncle had asked me to prolong my visit and I should probably have consented, but for anxiety on the subject of a near and dear relative—my sister. Her health had been failing since the death of her husband, to whom she was tenderly attached. I heard news of her while I was in Sussex, which hurried me back to town. In a month more, her death deprived me of my last living relation. She left no children; and my two brothers had both died unmarried while they were still young men.

This affliction placed me in a position of serious embarrassment, in regard to the disposal of my property after my death.

I had hitherto made no will; being well aware that my fortune (which was entirely in money) would go in due course of law to the person of all others who would employ it to the best purpose—that is to say, to my sister as my nearest of kin. As I was now situated, my property would revert to my uncle if I died intestate. He was a richer man than I was. Of his two children, both sons, the eldest would inherit his estates: the youngest had already succeeded to his mother's ample fortune. Having literally no family claims on me, I felt bound to recognize the wider demands of poverty and misfortune, and to devote my superfluous wealth to increasing the revenues of charitable institutions. As to minor legacies, I owed it to my good housekeeper, Mrs. Mozeen, not to forget the faithful services of past years. Need I add—if I had been free to act as I pleased—that I should have gladly made Rothsay the object of a handsome bequest? But this was not to be. My friend was a man morbidly sensitive on the subject of money. In the early days of our intercourse we had been for the first and only time on the verge of a quarrel, when I had asked (as a favor to myself) to be allowed to provide for him in my will.

"It is because I am poor," he explained, "that I refuse to profit by your kindness—though I feel it gratefully."

I failed to understand him—and said so plainly.

"You will understand this," he resumed; "I should never recover my sense of degradation, if a mercenary motive on my side was associated with our friendship. Don't say it's impossible! You know as well as I do that appearances would be against me, in the eyes of the world. Besides, I don't want money; my own small income is enough for me. Make me your executor if you like, and leave me the customary present of five hundred pounds. If you exceed that sum I declare on my word of honor that I will not touch one farthing of it." He took my hand, and pressed it fervently. "Do me a favor," he said. "Never let us speak of this again!"

I understood that I must yield—or lose my friend.

In now making my will, I accordingly appointed Rothsay one of my executors, on the terms that he had prescribed. The minor legacies having been next duly reduced to writing, I left the bulk of my fortune to public charities.

My lawyer laid the fair copy of the will on my table.

"A dreary disposition of property for a man of your age," he said, "I hope to receive a new set of instructions before you are a year older."

"What instructions?" I asked.

"To provide for your wife and children," he answered.

My wife and children! The idea seemed to be so absurd that I burst out laughing. It never occurred to me that there could be any absurdity from my own point of view.

I was sitting alone, after my legal adviser had taken his leave, looking absently at the newly-engrossed will, when I heard a sharp knock at the house-door which I thought I recognized. In another minute Rothsay's bright face enlivened my dull room. He had returned from the Mediterranean that morning.

"Am I interrupting you?" he asked, pointing to the leaves of manuscript before me. "Are you writing a book?"

"I am making my will."

His manner changed; he looked at me seriously.

"Do you remember what I said, when we once talked of your will?" he asked. I set his doubts at rest immediately—but he was not quite satisfied yet. "Can't you put your will away?" he suggested. "I hate the sight of anything that reminds me of death."

"Give me a minute to sign it," I said—and rang to summon the witnesses.

Mrs. Mozeen answered the bell. Rothsay looked at her, as if he wished to have my housekeeper put away as well as my will. From the first moment when he had seen her, he conceived a great dislike to that good creature.

There was nothing, I am sure, personally repellent about her. She was a little slim quiet woman, with a pale complexion and bright brown eyes. Her movements were gentle; her voice was low; her decent gray dress was adapted to her age. Why Rothsay should dislike her was more than he could explain himself. He turned his unreasonable prejudice into a joke—and said he hated a woman who wore slate colored cap-ribbons!

I explained to Mrs. Mozeen that I wanted witnesses to the signature of my will. Naturally enough—being in the room at the time—she asked if she could be one of them.

I was obliged to say No; and not to mortify her, I gave the reason.

"My will recognizes what I owe to your good services," I said. "If you are one of the witnesses, you will lose your legacy. Send up the men-servants."

With her customary tact, Mrs. Mozeen expressed her gratitude silently, by a look—and left the room.

"Why couldn't you tell that woman to send the servants, without mentioning her legacy?" Rothsay asked. "My friend Lepel, you have done a very foolish thing."

"In what way?"

"You have given Mrs. Mozeen an interest in your death."

It was impossible to make a serious reply to this ridiculous exhibition of Rothsay's prejudice against poor Mrs. Mozeen.

"When am I to be murdered?" I asked. "And how is it to be done? Poison?"

"I'm not joking," Rothsay answered. "You are infatuated about your housekeeper. When you spoke of her legacy, did you notice her eyes."

"Yes."

"Did nothing strike you?"

"It struck me that they were unusually well preserved eyes for a woman of her age."

The appearance of the valet and the footman put an end to this idle talk. The will was executed, and locked up. Our conversation turned on Rothsay's travels by sea. The cruise had been in every way successful. The matchless shores of the Mediterranean defied description; the sailing of the famous yacht had proved to be worthy of her reputation; and, to crown all, Rothsay had come back to England, in a fair way, for the first time in his life, of making money.

"I have discovered a treasure," he announced.

"It was a dirty little modern picture, picked up in a by-street at Palermo. It is a Virgin and Child, by Guido."

On further explanation it appeared that the picture exposed for sale was painted on copper. Noticing the contrast between the rare material and the wretchedly bad painting that covered it, Rothsay had called to mind some of the well-known stories of valuable works of art that had been painted over for purposes of disguise. The price asked for the picture amounted to little more than the value of the metal. Rothsay bought it. His knowledge of chemistry enabled him to put his suspicion successfully to the test; and one of the guests on board the yacht—a famous French artist—had declared his conviction that the picture now revealed to view was a genuine work by Guido. Such an opinion as this convinced me that it would be worth while to submit my friend's discovery to the judgment of other experts. Consulted independently, these critics confirmed the view taken by the celebrated personage who had first seen the work. This result having been obtained, Rothsay asked my advice next on the question of selling his picture. I at once thought of my uncle. An undoubted work by Guido would surely be an acquisition to his gallery. I had only (in accordance with his own request) to let him know that my friend had returned to England. We might take the picture with us, when we received our invitation to Lord Lepel's house.

FOURTH EPOCH.

My uncle's answer arrived by return of post. Other engagements obliged him to defer receiving us for a month. At the end of that time, we were cordially invited to visit him, and to stay as long as we liked.

In the interval that now passed, other events occurred—still of the trifling kind.

One afternoon, just as I was thinking of taking my customary ride in the park, the servant appeared charged with a basket of flowers, and with a message from Mrs. Rymer, requesting me to honor her by accepting a little offering from her daughter. Hearing that she was then waiting in the hall, I told the man to show her in. Susan (as I ought to have already mentioned) had sent her exercises to me regularly every week. In returning them corrected, I had once or twice added a word of well-deserved approval. The offering of flowers was evidently intended to express my pupil's grateful sense of the interest taken in her by her teacher.

I had no reason, this time, to suppose that Mrs. Rymer entertained an unfriendly feeling toward me. At the first words of greeting that passed between us I perceived a change in her manner, which ran in the opposite extreme. She overwhelmed me with the most elaborate demonstrations of politeness and respect; dwelling on her gratitude for my kindness in receiving her, and on her pride at seeing her daughter's flowers on my table, until I made a resolute effort to stop her by asking (as if it was actually a matter of importance to me!) whether she was in London on business or on pleasure.

"Oh, on business, sir! My poor husband invested his little savings in bank stock, and I have just been drawing my dividend. I do hope you don't think my girl over-bold in venturing to send you a few flowers. She wouldn't allow me to interfere. I do assure you she would gather and arrange them with her own hands. In themselves I know they are hardly worth accepting; but if you will allow the motive to plead—"

I made another effort to stop Mrs. Rymer; I said her daughter could not have sent me a prettier present.

The inexhaustible woman only went on more fluently than ever.

"She is so grateful, sir, and so proud of your goodness in looking at her exercises. The difficulty of the French language seem as nothing to her, now her motive is to please you. She is so devoted to her studies that I find it difficult to induce her to take the exercise necessary to her health; and, as you may perhaps remember, Susan was always rather weakly as a child. She inherits her father's constitution, Mr. Lepel—not mine."

Here, to my infinite relief, the servant appeared, announcing that my horse was at the door.

Mrs. Rymer opened her mouth. I saw a coming flood of apologies on the point of pouring out—and seized my hat on the spot. I declared I had an appointment; I sent kind remembrances to Susan (pitying her for having such a mother with my whole heart); I said I hoped to return to my uncle's house soon, and to continue the French lessons. The one thing more that I remember was finding myself safe in the saddle, and out of the reach of Mrs. Rymer's tongue.

Reflecting on what had passed, it was plain to me that this woman had some private end in view, and that my abrupt departure had prevented her from finding the way to it. What motive could she possibly have for that obstinate persistence in presenting poor Susan under a favorable aspect, to a man who had already shown that he was honestly interested in her pretty modest daughter? I tried hard to penetrate the mystery—and gave it up in despair.

Three days before the date at which Rothsay and I were to pay our visit to Lord Lepel, I found myself compelled to undergo one of the minor miseries of human life. In other words I became one of the guests at a large dinner-party. It was a rainy day in October. My position at the table placed me between a window that was open and a door that was hardly ever shut. I went to bed shivering; and woke the next morning with a headache and a difficulty in breathing. On consulting the doctor, I found that I was suffering from an attack of bronchitis. There was no reason to be alarmed. If I remained indoors, and submitted to the necessary treatment, I might hope to keep my engagement with my uncle in ten days or a fortnight.

There was no alternative but to submit. I accordingly arranged with Rothsay that he should present himself at Lord Lepel's house (taking the picture with him), on the date appointed for our visit, and that I should follow as soon as I was well enough to travel.

On the day when he was to leave London, my friend kindly came to keep me company for a while. He was followed into my room by Mrs. Mozeen, with a bottle of medicine in her hand. This worthy creature, finding that the doctor's directions occasionally escaped my memory, devoted herself to the duty of administering the remedies at the prescribed intervals of time. When she left the room, having performed her duties as usual, I saw Rothsay's eyes follow her to the door with an expression of sardonic curiosity. He put a strange question to me as soon as we were alone.

"Who engaged that new servant of yours?" he asked. "I mean the fat fellow, with the curly flaxen hair."

"Hiring servants," I replied, "is not much in my way. I left the engagement of the new man to Mrs. Mozeen."

Rothsay walked gravely up to my bedside.

"Lepel," he said, "your respectable housekeeper is in love with the fat young footman."

It is not easy to amuse a man suffering from bronchitis. But this new outbreak of absurdity was more than I could resist, even with a mustard-plaster on my chest.

"I thought I should raise your spirits," Rothsay proceeded. "When I came to your house this morning, the valet opened the door to me. I expressed my surprise at his condescending to take that trouble. He informed me that Joseph was otherwise engaged. 'With anybody in particular?' I asked, humoring the joke. 'Yes, sir, with the housekeeper. She's teaching him how to brush his hair, so as to show off his good looks to the best advantage.' Make up your mind, my friend, to lose Mrs. Mozeen—especially if she happens to have any money."

"Nonsense, Rothsay! The poor woman is old enough to be Joseph's mother."

"My good fellow, that won't make any difference to Joseph. In the days when we were rich enough to keep a man-servant, our footman—as handsome a fellow as ever you saw, and no older than I am—married a witch with a lame leg. When I asked him why he had made such a fool of himself he looked quite indignant, and said: 'Sir! she has got six hundred pounds.' He and the witch keep a public house. What will you bet me that we don't see your housekeeper drawing beer at the bar, and Joseph getting drunk in the parlor, before we are a year older?"

I was not well enough to prolong my enjoyment of Rothsay's boyish humor. Besides, exaggeration to be really amusing must have some relation, no matter how slender it may be, to the truth. My housekeeper belonged to a respectable family, and was essentially a person accustomed to respect herself. Her brother occupied a position of responsibility in the establishment of a firm of chemists whom I had employed for years past. Her late husband had farmed his own land, and had owed his ruin to calamities for which he was in no way responsible. Kind-hearted Mrs. Mozeen was just the woman to take a motherly interest in a well-disposed lad like Joseph; and it was equally characteristic of my valet—especially when Rothsay was thoughtless enough to encourage him—to pervert an innocent action for the sake of indulging in a stupid jest. I took advantage of my privilege as an invalid, and changed the subject.

A week passed. I had expected to hear from Rothsay. To my surprise and disappointment no letter arrived.

Susan was more considerate. She wrote, very modestly and prettily, to say that she and her mother had heard of my illness from Mr. Rothsay, and to express the hope that I should soon be restored to health. A few days later, Mrs. Rymer's politeness carried her to the length of taking the journey to London to make inquiries at my door. I did not see her, of course. She left word that she would have the honor of calling again.

The second week followed. I had by that time perfectly recovered from my attack of bronchitis—and yet I was too ill to leave the house.

The doctor himself seemed to be at a loss to understand the symptoms that now presented themselves. A vile sensation of nausea tried my endurance, and an incomprehensible prostration of strength depressed my spirits. I felt such a strange reluctance to exert myself that I actually left it to Mrs. Mozeen to write to my uncle in my name, and say that I was not yet well enough to visit him. My medical adviser tried various methods of treatment; my housekeeper administered the prescribed medicines with unremitting care; but nothing came of it. A physician of great authority was called into consultation. Being completely puzzled, he retreated to the last refuge of bewildered doctors. I asked him what was the matter with me. And he answered: "Suppressed gout."

FIFTH EPOCH.

MIDWAY in the third week, my uncle wrote to me as follows:

"I have been obliged to request your friend Rothsay to bring his visit to a conclusion. Although he refuses to confess it, I have reason to believe that he has committed the folly of falling seriously in love with the young girl at my lodge gate. I have tried remonstrance in vain; and I write to his father at the same time that I write to you. There is much more that I might say. I reserve it for the time when I hope to have the pleasure of seeing you, restored to health."

Two days after the receipt of this alarming letter Rothsay returned to me.

Ill as I was, I forgot my sufferings the moment I looked at him. Wild and haggard, he stared at me with bloodshot eyes like a man demented.

"Do you think I am mad? I dare say I am. I can't live without her." Those were the first words he said when we shook hands.

But I had more influence over him than any other person; and, weak as I was, I exerted it. Little by little, he became more reasonable; he began to speak like his old self again.

To have expressed any surprise, on my part, at what had happened, would have been not only imprudent, but unworthy of him and of me. My first inquiry was suggested by the fear that he might have been hurried into openly confessing his passion to Susan—although his position forbade him to offer marriage. I had done him an injustice. His honorable nature had shrunk from the cruelty of raising hopes, which, for all he knew to the contrary, might never be realized. At the same time, he had his reasons for believing that he was at least personally acceptable to her.

"She was always glad to see me," said poor Rothsay. "We constantly talked of you. She spoke of your kindness so prettily and so gratefully. Oh, Lepel, it is not her beauty only that has won my heart! Her nature is the nature of an angel."

His voice failed him. For the first time in my remembrance of our long companionship, he burst into tears.

I was so shocked and distressed that I had the greatest difficulty in preserving my own self-control. In the effort to comfort him, I asked if he had ventured to confide in his father.

"You are the favorite son," I reminded him. "Is there no gleam of hope in the future?"

He had written to his father. In silence he gave me the letter in reply.

It was expressed with a moderation which I had hardly dared to expect. Mr. Rothsay the elder admitted that he had himself married for love, and that his wife's rank in the social scale (although higher than Susan's) had not been equal to his own.

"In such a family as ours," he wrote—perhaps with pardonable pride—"we raise our wives to our own degree. But this young person labors under a double disadvantage. She is obscure, and she is poor. What have you to offer her? Nothing. And what have I to give you? Nothing."

This meant, as I interpreted it, that the main obstacle in the way was Susan's poverty. And I was rich! In the excitement that possessed me, I followed the impulse of the moment headlong, like a child.

"While you were away from me," I said to Rothsay, "did you never once think of your old friend? Must I remind you that I can make Susan your wife with one stroke of my pen?" He looked at me in silent surprise. I took my check-book from the drawer of the table, and placed the inkstand within reach. "Susan's marriage portion," I said, "is a matter of a line of writing, with my name at the end of it."

He burst out with an exclamation that stopped me, just as my pen touched the paper.

"Good heavens!" he cried, "you are thinking of that play we saw at Rome! Are we on the stage? Are you performing the part of the Marquis—and am I the Count?"

I was so startled by this wild allusion to the past—I recognized with such astonishment the reproduction of one of the dramatic situations in the play, at a crisis in his life and mine—that the use of the pen remained suspended in my hand. For the first time in my life I was conscious of a sensation which resembled superstitious dread.

Rothsay recovered himself first. He misinterpreted what was passing in my mind.

"Don't think me ungrateful," he said. "You dear, kind, good fellow, consider for a moment, and you will see that it can't be. What would be said of her and of me, if you made Susan rich with your money, and if I married her? The poor innocent would be called your cast-off mistress. People would say: 'He has behaved liberally to her, and his needy friend has taken advantage of it.'"

The point of view which I had failed to see was put with terrible directness of expression: the conviction that I was wrong was literally forced on me. What reply could I make? Rothsay evidently felt for me.

"You are ill," he said, gently; "let me leave you to rest."

He held out his hand to say good-by. I insisted on his taking up his abode with me, for the present at least. Ordinary persuasion failed to induce him to yield. I put it on selfish grounds next.

"You have noticed that I am ill," I said, "I want you to keep me company."

He gave way directly.

Through the wakeful night, I tried to consider what moral remedies might be within our reach. The one useful conclusion at which I could arrive was to induce Rothsay to try what absence and change might do to compose his mind. To advise him to travel alone was out of the question. I wrote to his one other old friend besides myself—the friend who had taken him on a cruise in the Mediterranean.

The owner of the yacht had that very day given directions to have his vessel laid up for the winter season. He at once countermanded the order by telegraph. "I am an idle man," he said, "and I am as fond of Rothsay as you are. I will take him wherever he likes to go." It was not easy to persuade the object of these kind intentions to profit by them. Nothing that I could say roused him. I spoke to him of his picture. He had left it at my uncle's house, and neither knew nor cared to know whether it had been sold or not. The one consideration which ultimately influenced Rothsay was presented by the doctor; speaking as follows (to quote his own explanation) in the interests of my health:

"I warned your friend," he said, "that his conduct was causing anxiety which you were not strong enough to bear. On hearing this he at once promised to follow the advice which you had given to him, and to join the yacht. As you know, he has kept his word. May I ask if he has ever followed the medical profession?"

Replying in the negative, I begged the doctor to tell me why he had put his question.

He answered, "Mr. Rothsay requested me to tell him all that I knew about your illness. I complied, of course; mentioning that I had lately adopted a new method of treatment, and that I had every reason to feel confident of the results. He was so interested in the symptoms of your illness, and in the remedies being tried, that he took notes in his pocketbook of what I had said. When he paid me that compliment, I thought it possible that I might be speaking to a colleague."

I was pleased to hear of my friend's anxiety for my recovery. If I had been in better health, I might have asked myself what reason he could have had for making those entries in his pocketbook.

Three days later, another proof reached me of Rothsay's anxiety for my welfare.

The owner of the yacht wrote to beg that I would send him a report of my health, addressed to a port on the south coast of England, to which they were then bound. "If we don't hear good news," he added, "I have reason to fear that Rothsay will overthrow our plans for the recovery of his peace of mind by leaving the vessel, and making his own inquiries at your bedside."

With no small difficulty I roused myself sufficiently to write a few words with my own hand. They were words that lied—for my poor friend's sake. In a postscript, I begged my correspondent to let me hear if the effect produced on Rothsay had answered to our hopes and expectations.

SIXTH EPOCH.

THE weary days followed each other—and time failed to justify the doctor's confidence in his new remedies. I grew weaker and weaker.

My uncle came to see me. He was so alarmed that he insisted on a consultation being held with his own physician. Another great authority was called in, at the same time, by the urgent request of my own medical man. These distinguished persons held more than one privy council, before they would consent to give a positive opinion. It was an evasive opinion (encumbered with hard words of Greek and Roman origin) when it was at last pronounced. I waited until they had taken their leave, and then appealed to my own doctor. "What do these men really think?" I asked. "Shall I live, or die?"

The doctor answered for himself as well as for his illustrious colleagues. "We have great faith in the new prescriptions," he said.

I understood what that meant. They were afraid to tell me the truth. I insisted on the truth.

"How long shall I live?" I said. "Till the end of the year?"

The reply followed in one terrible word:

"Perhaps."

It was then the first week in December. I understood that I might reckon—at the utmost—on three weeks of life. What I felt, on arriving at this conclusion, I shall not say. It is the one secret I keep from the readers of these lines.

The next day, Mrs. Rymer called once more to make inquiries. Not satisfied with the servant's report, she entreated that I would consent to see her. My housekeeper, with her customary kindness, undertook to convey the message. If she had been a wicked woman, would she have acted in this way? "Mrs. Rymer seems to be sadly distressed," she pleaded. "As I understand, sir, she is suffering under some domestic anxiety which can only be mentioned to yourself."

Did this anxiety relate to Susan? The bare doubt of it decided me. I consented to see Mrs. Rymer. Feeling it necessary to control her in the use of her tongue, I spoke the moment the door was opened.

"I am suffering from illness; and I must ask you to spare me as much as possible. What do you wish to say to me?"

The tone in which I addressed Mrs. Rymer would have offended a more sensitive woman. The truth is, she had chosen an unfortunate time for her visit. There were fluctuations in the progress of my malady; there were days when I felt better, and days when I felt worse—and this was a bad day. Moreover, my uncle had tried my temper that morning. He had called to see me, on his way to winter in the south of France by his physician's advice; and he recommended a trial of change of air in my case also. His country house (only thirty miles from London) was entirely at my disposal; and the railway supplied beds for invalids. It was useless to answer that I was not equal to the effort. He reminded me that I had exerted myself to leave my bedchamber for my arm-chair in the next room, and that a little additional resolution would enable me to follow his advice. We parted in a state of irritation on either side which, so far as I was concerned, had not subsided yet.

"I wish to speak to you, sir, about my daughter," Mrs. Rymer answered.

The mere allusion to Susan had its composing effect on me. I said kindly that I hoped she was well.

"Well in body," Mrs. Rymer announced. "Far from it, sir, in mind."

Before I could ask what this meant, we were interrupted by the appearance of the servant, bringing the letters which had arrived for me by the afternoon post. I told the man, impatiently, to put them on the table at my side.

"What is distressing Susan?" I inquired, without stopping to look at the letters.

"She is fretting, sir, about your illness. Oh, Mr. Lepel, if you would only try the sweet country air! If you only had my good little Susan to nurse you!"

She, too, taking my uncle's view! And talking of Susan as my nurse!

"What are you thinking of?" I asked her. "A young girl like your daughter nursing Me! You ought to have more regard for Susan's good name!"

"I know what you ought to do!" She made that strange reply with a furtive look at me, half in anger, half in alarm.

"Go on," I said.

"Will you turn me out of your house for my impudence?" she asked.

"I will hear what you have to say to me. What ought I to do?"

"Marry Susan."

I heard the woman plainly—and yet, I declare, I doubted the evidence of my senses.

"She's breaking her heart for you," Mrs. Rymer burst out. "She's been in love with you since you first darkened our doors—and it will end in the neighbors finding it out. I did my duty to her; I tried to stop it; I tried to prevent you from seeing her, when you went away. Too late; the mischief was done. When I see my girl fading day by day—crying about you in secret, talking about you in her dreams—I can't stand it; I must speak out. Oh, yes,

I know how far beneath you she is—the daughter of your uncle's servant. But she's your equal, sir, in the sight of Heaven. My lord's priest converted her only last year—and my Susan is as good a Papist as yourself."

How could I let this go on? I felt that I ought to have stopped it before.

"It's possible," I said, "that you may not be deliberately deceiving me. If you are yourself deceived, I am bound to tell you the truth. Mr. Rothsay loves your daughter, and, what is more, Mr. Rothsay has reason to know that Susan—"

"That Susan loves him?" she interposed, with a mocking laugh. "Oh, Mr. Lepel, is it possible that a clever man like you can't see clearer than that? My girl in love with Mr. Rothsay! She wouldn't have looked at him a second time if he hadn't talked to her about you. When I complained privately to my lord of Mr. Rothsay hanging about the lodge, do you think she turned as pale as ashes, and cried when he passed through the gate, and said good-by?"

She had complained of Rothsay to Lord Lepel—I understood her at last! She knew that my friend and all his family were poor. She had put her own construction on the innocent interest that I had taken in her daughter. Careless of the difference in rank, blind to the malady that was killing me, she was now bent on separating Rothsay and Susan, by throwing the girl into the arms of a rich husband like myself!

"You are wasting your breath," I told her; "I don't believe one word you say to me."

"Believe Susan, then!" cried the reckless woman. "Let me bring her here. If she's too shamefaced to own the truth, look at her—that's all I ask—look at her, and judge for yourself!"

This was intolerable. In justice to Susan, in justice to Rothsay, I insisted on silence. "No more of it!" I said. "Take care how you provoke me. Don't you see that I am ill? don't you see that you are irritating me to no purpose?"

She altered her tone. "I'll wait," she said, quietly, "while you compose yourself."

With those words, she walked to the window, and stood there with her back toward me. Was the wretch taking advantage of my helpless condition? I stretched out my hand to ring the bell, and have her sent away—and hesitated to degrade Susan's mother, for Susan's sake. In my state of prostration, how could I arrive at a decision? My mind was dreadfully disturbed; I felt the imperative necessity of turning my thoughts to some other subject. Looking about me, the letters on the table attracted my attention. Mechanically, I took them up; mechanically I put them down again. Two of them slipped from my trembling fingers; my eyes fell on the uppermost of the two. The address was in the handwriting of the good friend with whom Rothsay was sailing.

Just as I had been speaking of Rothsay, here was the news of him for which I had been waiting.

I opened the letter and read these words:

"There is, I fear, but little hope for our friend—unless this girl on whom he has set his heart can (by some lucky change of circumstances) become his wife. He has tried to master his weakness; but his own infatuation is too much for him. He is really and truly in a state of despair. Two evenings since—to give you a melancholy example of what I mean—I was in my cabin, when I heard the alarm of a man overboard. The man was Rothsay. My sailing-master, seeing that he was unable to swim, jumped into the sea and rescued him, as I got on deck. Rothsay declares it to have been an accident; and everybody believes him but myself. I know the state of his mind. Don't be alarmed; I will have him well looked after; and I won't give him up just yet. We are still bound southward, with a fair wind. If the new scenes which I hope to show him prove to be of no avail, I must reluctantly take him back to England. In that case, which I don't like to contemplate, you may see him again—perhaps in a month's time."

He might return in a month's time—return to hear of the death of the one friend, on whose power and will to help him he might have relied. If I failed to employ in his interests the short interval of life still left to me, could I doubt (after what I had just read) what the end would be? How could I help him? Oh, God! how could I help him?

Mrs. Rymer left the window, and returned to the chair which she had occupied when I first received her.

"Are you quieter in your mind now?" she asked.

I neither answered her nor looked at her.

Still determined to reach her end, she tried again to force her unhappy daughter on me. "Will you consent," she persisted, "to see Susan?"

If she had been a little nearer to me, I am afraid I should have struck her. "You wretch!" I said, "do you know that I am a dying man?"

"While there's life there's hope," Mrs. Rymer remarked.

I ought to have controlled myself; but it was not to be done.

"Hope of your daughter being my rich widow?" I asked.

Her bitter answer followed instantly.

"Even then," she said, "Susan wouldn't marry Rothsay."

A lie! If circumstances favored her, I knew, on Rothsay's authority, what Susan would do.

The thought burst on my mind, like light bursting on the eyes of a man restored to sight. If Susan agreed to go through the form of marriage with a dying bridegroom, my rich widow could (and would) become Rothsay's wife. Once more, the remembrance of the play at Rome returned, and set the last embers of resolution, which sickness and suffering had left to me, in a flame. The devoted friend of that imaginary story had counted on death to complete his generous purpose in vain: he had been condemned by the tribunal of man, and had been reprieved. I—in his place, and with his self-sacrifice in my mind—might found a firmer trust in the future; for I had been condemned by the tribunal of God.

Encouraged by my silence, the obstinate woman persisted. "Won't you even send a message to Susan?" she asked.

Rashly, madly, without an instant's hesitation, I answered:

"Go back to Susan, and say I leave it to her."

Mrs. Rymer started to her feet. "You leave it to Susan to be your wife, if she likes?"

"I do."

"And if she consents?"

"I consent."

In two weeks and a day from that time, the deed was done. When Rothsay returned to England, he would ask for Susan—and he would find my virgin-widow rich and free.

SEVENTH EPOCH.

WHATEVER may be thought of my conduct, let me say this in justice to myself—I was resolved that Susan should not be deceived.

Half an hour after Mrs. Rymer had left my house, I wrote to her daughter, plainly revealing the motive which led me to offer marriage, solely in the future interest of Rothsay and herself. "If you refuse," I said in conclusion, "you may depend on my understanding you and feeling for you. But, if you consent—then I have a favor to ask Never let us speak to one another of the profanation that we have agreed to commit, for your faithful lover's sake."

I had formed a high opinion of Susan—too high an opinion as it seemed. Her reply surprised and disappointed me. In other words, she gave her consent.

I stipulated that the marriage should be kept strictly secret, for a certain period. In my own mind I decided that the interval should be held to expire, either on the day of my death, or on the day when Rothsay returned.

My next proceeding was to write in confidence to the priest whom I have already mentioned, in an earlier part of these pages. He has reasons of his own for not permitting me to disclose the motive which induced him to celebrate my marriage privately in the chapel at Lord Lepel's house. My uncle's desire that I should try change of air, as offering a last chance of recovery, was known to my medical attendant, and served as a sufficient reason (although he protested against the risk) for my removal to the country. I was carried to the station, and placed on a bed—slung by ropes to the ceiling of a saloon carriage, so as to prevent me from feeling the vibration when the train was in motion. Faithful Mrs. Mozeen entreated to be allowed to accompany me. I was reluctantly compelled to refuse compliance with this request, in justice to the claims of my lord's housekeeper; who had been accustomed to exercise undivided authority in the household, and who had made every preparation for my comfort. With her own hands, Mrs. Mozeen packed everything that I required, including the medicines prescribed for the occasion. She was deeply affected, poor soul, when we parted.

I bore the journey—happily for me, it was a short one—better than had been anticipated. For the first few days that followed, the purer air of the country seemed, in some degree, to revive me. But the deadly sense of weakness, the slow sinking of the vital power in me, returned as the time drew near for the marriage. The ceremony was performed at night. Only Susan and her mother were present. No persons in the house but ourselves had the faintest suspicion of what had happened.

I signed my new will (the priest and Mrs. Rymer being the witnesses) in my bed that night. It left everything that I possessed, excepting a legacy to Mrs. Mozeen, to my wife.

Obliged, it is needless to say, to preserve appearances, Susan remained at the lodge as usual. But it was impossible to resist her entreaty to be allowed to attend on me, for a few hours daily, as assistant to the regular nurse. When she was alone with me, and had no inquisitive eyes to dread, the poor girl showed a depth of feeling, which I was unable to reconcile with the motives that could alone have induced her (as I then supposed) to consent to the mockery of our marriage. On occasions when I was so far able to resist the languor that oppressed me as to observe what was passing at my bedside—I saw Susan look at me as if there were thoughts in her pressing for utterance which she hesitated to express. Once, she herself acknowledged this. "I have so much to say to you," she owned, "when you are stronger and fitter to hear me." At other times, her nerves seemed to be shaken by the spectacle of my sufferings. Her kind hands trembled and made mistakes, when they had any nursing duties to perform near me. The servants, noticing her, used to say, "That pretty girl seems to be the most awkward person in the house." On the day that followed the ceremony in the chapel, this want of self-control brought about an accident which led to serious results.

In removing the small chest which held my medicines from the shelf on which it was placed, Susan let it drop on the floor. The two full bottles still left were so completely shattered that not even a teaspoonful of the contents was saved.

Shocked at what she had done, the poor girl volunteered to go herself to my chemist in London by the first train. I refused to allow it. What did it matter to me now, if my death from exhaustion was hastened by a day or two? Why need my life be prolonged artificially by drugs, when I had nothing left to live for? An excuse for me which would satisfy others was easily found. I said that I had been long weary of physic, and that the accident had decided me on refusing to take more.

That night I did not wake quite so often as usual. When she came to me the next day, Susan noticed that I looked better. The day after, the other nurse made the same observation. At the end of the week, I was able to leave my bed, and sit by the fireside, while Susan read to me. Some mysterious change in my health had completely falsified the prediction of the medical men. I sent to London for my doctor—and told him that the improvement in me had begun on the day when I left off taking his remedies. "Can you explain it?" I asked.

He answered that no such "resurrection from the dead" (as he called it) had ever happened in his long experience. On leaving me, he asked for the latest prescriptions that had been written. I inquired what he was going to do with them. "I mean to go to the chemist," he replied, "and to satisfy myself that your medicines have been properly made up."

I owed it to Mrs. Mozeen's true interest in me to tell her what had happened. The same day I wrote to her. I also mentioned what the doctor had said, and asked her to call on him, and ascertain if the prescriptions had been shown to the chemist, and if any mistake had been made.

A more innocently intended letter than this never was written. And yet there are people who have declared that it was inspired by suspicion of Mrs. Mozeen!

EIGHTH EPOCH.

WHETHER I was so weakened by illness as to be incapable of giving my mind to more than one subject for reflection at a time (that subject being now the extraordinary recovery of my health)—or whether I was preoccupied by the effort, which I was in honor bound to make, to resist the growing attraction to me of Susan's society—I cannot presume to say. This only I know: when the discovery of the terrible position toward Rothsay in which I now stood suddenly overwhelmed me, an interval of some days had passed. I cannot account for it. I can only say—so it was.

Susan was in the room. I was wholly unable to hide from her the sudden change of color which betrayed the horror that had overpowered me. She said, anxiously: "What has frightened you?"

I don't think I heard her. The play was in my memory again—the fatal play, which had wound itself into the texture of Rothsay's life and mine. In vivid remembrance, I saw once more the dramatic situation of the first act, and shrank from the reflection of it in the disaster which had fallen on my friend and myself.

"What has frightened you?" Susan repeated.

I answered in one word—I whispered his name: "Rothsay!"

She looked at me in innocent surprise. "Has he met with some misfortune?" she asked, quietly.

"Misfortune"—did she call it? Had I not said enough to disturb her tranquillity in mentioning Rothsay's name? "I am living!" I said. "Living— and likely to live!"

Her answer expressed fervent gratitude. "Thank God for it!"

I looked at her, astonished as she had been astonished when she looked

600

at me.

"Susan, Susan," I cried—"must I own it? I love you!"

She came nearer to me with timid pleasure in her eyes—with the first faint light of a smile playing round her lips.

"You say it very strangely," she murmured. "Surely, my dear one, you ought to love me? Since the first day when you gave me my French lesson—haven't I loved You?"

"You love me?" I repeated. "Have you read—?" My voice failed me; I could say no more.

She turned pale. "Read what?" she asked.

"My letter."

"What letter?"

"The letter I wrote to you before we were married."

Am I a coward? The bare recollection of what followed that reply makes me tremble. Time has passed. I am a new man now; my health is restored; my happiness is assured: I ought to be able to write on. No: it is not to be done. How can I think coolly? how force myself to record the suffering that I innocently, most innocently, inflicted on the sweetest and truest of women? Nothing saved us from a parting as absolute as the parting that follows death but the confession that had been wrung from me at a time when my motive spoke for itself. The artless avowal of her affection had been justified, had been honored, by the words which laid my heart at her feet when I said "I love you."

She had risen to leave me. In a last look, we had silently resigned ourselves to wait, apart from each other, for the day of reckoning that must follow Rothsay's return, when we heard the sound of carriage-wheels on the drive that led to the house. In a minute more the man himself entered the room.

He looked first at Susan—then at me. In both of us he saw the traces that told of agitation endured, but not yet composed. Worn and weary he waited, hesitating, near the door.

"Am I intruding?" he asked.

"We were thinking of you, and speaking of you," I replied, "just before you came in."

"We?" he repeated, turning toward Susan once more. After a pause, he offered me his hand—and drew it back.

"You don't shake hands with me," he said.

"I am waiting, Rothsay, until I know that we are the same firm friends as ever."

For the third time he looked at Susan.

"Will you shake hands?" he asked.

She gave him her hand cordially. "May I stay here?" she said, addressing herself to me.

In my situation at that moment, I understood the generous purpose that animated her. But she had suffered enough already—I led her gently to the door. "It will be better," I whispered, "if you will wait downstairs in the library." She hesitated. "What will they say in the house?" she objected, thinking of the servants and of the humble position which she was still supposed to occupy. "It matters nothing what they say, now," I told her. She left us.

"There seems to be some private understanding between you," Rothsay said, when we were alone.

"You shall hear what it is," I answered. "But I must beg you to excuse me if I speak first of myself."

"Are you alluding to your health?"

"Yes."

"Quite needless, Lepel. I met your doctor this morning. I know that a council of physicians decided you would die before the year was out."

He paused there.

"And they proved to be wrong," I added.

"They might have proved to be right," Rothsay rejoined, "but for the accident which spilled your medicine and the despair of yourself which decided you on taking no more."

I could hardly believe that I understood him. "Do you assert," I said, "that my medicine would have killed me, if I had taken the rest of it?"

"I have no doubt that it would."

"Will you explain what you mean?"

"Let me have your explanation first. I was not prepared to find Susan in your room. I was surprised to see traces of tears in her face. Something has happened in my absence. Am I concerned in it?"

"You are."

I said it quietly—in full possession of myself. The trial of fortitude through which I had already passed seemed to have blunted my customary sense of feeling. I approached the disclosure which I was now bound to make with steady resolution, resigned to the worst that could happen when the truth was known.

"Do you remember the time," I resumed, "when I was so eager to serve you that I proposed to make Susan your wife by making her rich?"

"Yes."

"Do you remember asking me if I was thinking of the play we saw together at Rome? Is the story as present to your mind now, as it was then?"

"Quite as present."

"You asked if I was performing the part of the Marquis—and if you were the Count. Rothsay! the devotion of that ideal character to his friend has been my devotion; his conviction that his death would justify what he had done for his friend's sake, has been my conviction; and as it ended with him, so it has ended with me—his terrible position is my terrible position toward you, at this moment."

"Are you mad?" Rothsay asked, sternly.

I passed over that first outbreak of his anger in silence.

"Do you mean to tell me you have married Susan?" he went on.

"Bear this in mind," I said. "When I married her, I was doomed to death. Nay, more. In your interests—as God is my witness—I welcomed death."

He stepped up to me, in silence, and raised his hand with a threatening gesture.

That action at once deprived me of my self-possession. I spoke with the ungovernable rashness of a boy.

"Carry out your intention," I said. "Insult me."

His hand dropped.

"Insult me," I repeated; "it is one way out of the unendurable situation in which we are placed. You may trust me to challenge you. Duels are still fought on the Continent; I will follow you abroad; I will choose pistols; I will take care that we fight on the fatal foreign system; and I will purposely miss you. Make her what I intended her to be—my rich widow."

He looked at me attentively.

"Is that your refuge?" he asked, scornfully. "No! I won't help you to commit suicide."

God forgive me! I was possessed by a spirit of reckless despair; I did my best to provoke him.

"Reconsider your decision," I said; "and remember—you tried to commit suicide yourself."

He turned quickly to the door, as if he distrusted his own powers of self-control.

"I wish to speak to Susan," he said, keeping his back turned on me.

"You will find her in the library."

He left me.

I went to the window. I opened it and let the cold wintry air blow over my burning head. I don't know how long I sat at the window. There came a time when I saw Rothsay on the house steps. He walked rapidly toward the park gate. His head was down; he never once looked back at the room in which he had left me.

As he passed out of my sight, I felt a hand laid gently on my shoulder. Susan had returned to me.

"He will not come back," she said. "Try still to remember him as your old friend. He asks you to forgive and forget."

She had made the peace between us. I was deeply touched; my eyes filled with tears as I looked at her. She kissed me on the forehead and went out. I afterward asked what had passed between them when Rothsay spoke with her in the library. She never has told me what they said to each other; and she never will. She is right.

Later in the day I was told that Mrs. Rymer had called, and wished to "pay her respects."

I refused to see her. Whatever claim she might have otherwise had on my consideration had been forfeited by the infamy of her conduct, when she intercepted my letter to Susan. Her sense of injury on receiving my message was expressed in writing, and was sent to me the same evening. The last sentence in her letter was characteristic of the woman.

"However your pride may despise me," she wrote, "I am indebted to you for the rise in life that I have always desired. You may refuse to see me—but you can't prevent my being the mother-in-law of a gentleman."

Soon afterward, I received a visit which I had hardly ventured to expect.

Busy as he was in London, my doctor came to see me. He was not in his usual good spirits.

"I hope you don't bring me any bad news?" I said.

"You shall judge for yourself," he replied. "I come from Mr. Rothsay, to say for him what he is not able to say for himself."

"Where is he?"

"He has left England."

"For any purpose that you know of?"

"Yes. He has sailed to join the expedition of rescue—I ought rather to call it the forlorn hope—which is to search for the lost explorers in Central Australia."

In other words, he had gone to seek death in the fatal footsteps of Burke and Wills. I could not trust myself to speak.

The doctor saw that there was a reason for my silence, and that he would do well not to notice it. He changed the subject.

"May I ask," he said, "if you have heard from the servants left in charge at your house in London?"

"Has anything happened?"

"Something has happened which they are evidently afraid to tell you, knowing the high opinion which you have of Mrs. Mozeen. She has suddenly quitted your service, and has gone, nobody knows where. I have taken charge of a letter which she left for you."

He handed me the letter. As soon as I had recovered myself, I looked at it.

There was this inscription on the address: "For my good master, to wait until he returns home." The few lines in the letter itself ran thus:

"Distressing circumstances oblige me to leave you, sir, and do not permit me to enter into particulars. In asking your pardon, I offer my sincere thanks for your kindness, and my fervent prayers for your welfare."

That was all. The date had a special interest for me. Mrs. Mozeen had written on the day when she must have received my letter—the letter which has already appeared in these pages.

"Is there really nothing known of the poor woman's motives?" I asked.

"There are two explanations suggested," the doctor informed me. "One of them, which is offered by your female servants, seems to me absurd. They declare that Mrs. Mozeen, at her mature age, was in love with the young man who is your footman! It is even asserted that she tried to recommend herself to him, by speaking of the money which she expected to bring to the man who would make her his wife. The footman's reply, informing her that he was already engaged to be married, is alleged to be the cause which has driven her from your house."

I begged that the doctor would not trouble himself to repeat more of what my women servants had said.

"If the other explanation," I added, "is equally unworthy of notice—"

"The other explanation," the doctor interposed, "comes from Mr. Rothsay, and is of a very serious kind."

Rothsay's opinion demanded my respect.

"What view does he take?" I inquired.

"A view that startles me," the doctor said. "You remember my telling you of the interest he took in your symptoms, and in the remedies I had employed? Well! Mr. Rothsay accounts for the incomprehensible recovery of your health by asserting that poison—probably administered in small quantities, and intermitted at intervals in fear of discovery—has been mixed with your medicine; and he asserts that the guilty person is Mrs. Mozeen."

It was impossible that I could openly express the indignation that I felt on hearing this. My position toward Rothsay forced me to restrain myself.

"May I ask," the doctor continued, "if Mrs. Mozeen was aware that she had a legacy to expect at your death?"

"Certainly."

"Has she a brother who is one of the dispensers employed by your chemists?"

"Yes."

"Did she know that I doubted if my prescriptions had been properly prepared, and that I intended to make inquiries?"

"I wrote to her myself on the subject."

"Do you think her brother told her that I was referred to him, when I went to the chemists?"

"I have no means of knowing what her brother did."

"Can you at least tell me when she received your letter?"

"She must have received it on the day when she left my house."

The doctor rose with a grave face.

"These are rather extraordinary coincidences," he remarked.

I merely replied, "Mrs. Mozeen is as incapable of poisoning as I am."

The doctor wished me good-morning.

I repeat here my conviction of my housekeeper's innocence. I protest against the cruelty which accuses her. And, whatever may have been her motive in suddenly leaving my service, I declare that she still possesses my sympathy and esteem, and I invite her to return to me if she ever sees these lines.

I have only to add, by way of postscript, that we have heard of the safe return of the expedition of rescue. Time, as my wife and I both hope, may yet convince Rothsay that he will not be wrong in counting on Susan's love—the love of a sister.

In the meanwhile we possess a memorial of our absent friend. We have bought his picture.

608

MR. CAPTAIN AND THE NYMPH.

I.

"THE Captain is still in the prime of life," the widow remarked. "He has given up his ship; he possesses a sufficient income, and he has nobody to live with him. I should like to know why he doesn't marry."

"The Captain was excessively rude to Me," the widow's younger sister added, on her side. "When we took leave of him in London, I asked if there was any chance of his joining us at Brighton this season. He turned his back on me as if I had mortally offended him; and he made me this extraordinary answer: 'Miss! I hate the sight of the sea.' The man has been a sailor all his life. What does he mean by saying that he hates the sight of the sea?"

These questions were addressed to a third person present—and the person was a man. He was entirely at the mercy of the widow and the widow's sister. The other ladies of the family—who might have taken him under their protection—had gone to an evening concert. He was known to be the Captain's friend, and to be well acquainted with events in the Captain's life. As it happened, he had reasons for hesitating to revive associations connected with those events. But what polite alternative was left to him? He must either inflict disappointment, and, worse still, aggravate curiosity—or he must resign himself to circumstances, and tell the ladies why the Captain would never marry, and why (sailor as he was) he hated the sight of the sea. They were both young women and handsome women—and the person to whom they had appealed (being a man) followed the example of submission to the sex, first set in the garden of Eden. He enlightened the ladies, in the terms that follow:

THE British merchantman, Fortuna, sailed from the port of Liverpool (at a date which it is not necessary to specify) with the morning tide. She was bound for certain islands in the Pacific Ocean, in search of a cargo of sandal-wood—a commodity which, in those days, found a ready and profitable market in the Chinese Empire.

A large discretion was reposed in the Captain by the owners, who knew him to be not only trustworthy, but a man of rare ability, carefully cultivated during the leisure hours of a seafaring life. Devoted heart and soul to his professional duties, he was a hard reader and an excellent linguist as well. Having had considerable experience among the inhabitants of the Pacific Islands, he had attentively studied their characters, and had mastered their language in more than one of its many dialects. Thanks to the valuable information thus obtained, the Captain was never at a loss to conciliate the islanders. He had more than once succeeded in finding a cargo under circumstances in which other captains had failed.

Possessing these merits, he had also his fair share of human defects. For instance, he was a little too conscious of his own good looks—of his bright chestnut hair and whiskers, of his beautiful blue eyes, of his fair white skin, which many a woman had looked at with the admiration that is akin to envy. His shapely hands were protected by gloves; a broad-brimmed hat sheltered his complexion in fine weather from the sun. He was nice in the choice of his perfumes; he never drank spirits, and the smell of tobacco was abhorrent to him. New men among his officers and his crew, seeing him in his cabin, perfectly dressed, washed, and brushed until he was an object speckless to look upon—a merchant-captain soft of voice, careful in his choice of words, devoted to study in his leisure hours—were apt to conclude that they had trusted themselves at sea under a commander who was an anomalous mixture of a schoolmaster and a dandy. But if the slightest infraction of discipline took place, or if the storm rose and the vessel proved to be in peril, it was soon discovered that the gloved hands held a rod of iron; that the soft voice could make itself heard through wind and sea from one end of the deck to the other; and that it issued orders which the greatest fool on board discovered to be orders that had saved the ship. Throughout his professional life, the general impression that this variously gifted man produced on the little world about him was always the same. Some few liked him; everybody respected him; nobody understood him. The Captain accepted these results. He persisted in reading his books and protecting his complexion, with this result: his owners shook hands with him, and put up with his gloves.

The Fortuna touched at Rio for water, and for supplies of food which might prove useful in case of scurvy. In due time the ship rounded Cape Horn, favored by the finest weather ever known in those latitudes by the oldest hand on board. The mate—one Mr. Duncalf—a boozing, wheezing, self-confident old sea-dog, with a flaming face and a vast vocabulary of oaths, swore that he didn't like it. "The foul weather's coming, my lads," said Mr. Duncalf. "Mark my words, there'll be wind enough to take the curl out of the Captain's whiskers before we are many days older!"

For one uneventful week, the ship cruised in search of the islands to which the owners had directed her. At the end of that time the wind took the predicted liberties with the Captain's whiskers; and Mr. Duncalf stood revealed to an admiring crew in the character of a true prophet.

For three days and three nights the Fortuna ran before the storm, at the mercy of wind and sea. On the fourth morning the gale blew itself out, the sun appeared again toward noon, and the Captain was able to take an observation. The result informed him that he was in a part of the Pacific Ocean with which he was entirely unacquainted. Thereupon, the officers were called to a council in the cabin.

Mr. Duncalf, as became his rank, was consulted first. His opinion possessed the merit of brevity. "My lads, this ship's bewitched. Take my word for it, we shall wish ourselves back in our own latitudes before we are many days older." Which, being interpreted, meant that Mr. Duncalf was lost, like his superior officer, in a part of the ocean of which he knew nothing.

The remaining members of the council having no suggestions to offer, left the Captain to take his own way. He decided (the weather being fine again) to stand on under an easy press of sail for four-and-twenty hours more, and to see if anything came of it.

Soon after nightfall, something did come of it. The lookout forward hailed the quarter-deck with the dread cry, "Breakers ahead!" In less than a minute more, everybody heard the crash of the broken water. The Fortuna was put about, and came round slowly in the light wind. Thanks to the timely alarm and the fine weather, the safety of the vessel was easily provided for. They kept her under a short sail; and they waited for the morning.

The dawn showed them in the distance a glorious green island, not marked in the ship's charts—an island girt about by a coral-reef, and having in its midst a high-peaked mountain which looked, through the telescope, like a mountain of volcanic origin. Mr. Duncalf, taking his morning draught of rum and water, shook his groggy old head and said (and swore): "My lads, I don't like the look of that island." The Captain was of a different opinion. He had one of the ship's boats put into the water; he armed himself and four of his crew who accompanied him; and away he went in the morning sunlight to visit the island.

Skirting round the coral reef, they found a natural breach, which proved to be broad enough and deep enough not only for the passage of the boat, but of the ship herself if needful. Crossing the broad inner belt of smooth water, they approached the golden sands of the island, strew ed with magnificent shells, and crowded by the dusky islanders—men, women, and children, all waiting in breathless astonishment to see the strangers land.

The Captain kept the boat off, and examined the islanders carefully. The innocent, simple people danced, and sang, and ran into the water, imploring their wonderful white visitors by gestures to come on shore. Not a creature among them carried arms of any sort; a hospitable curiosity animated the entire population. The men cried out, in their smooth musical language, "Come and eat!" and the plump black-eyed women, all laughing together, added their own invitation, "Come and be kissed!" Was it in mortals to resist such temptations as these? The Captain led the way on shore, and the women surrounded him in an instant, and screamed for joy at the glorious spectacle of his whiskers, his complexion, and his gloves. So the mariners from the far north were welcomed to the newly-discovered island.

III.

THE morning wore on. Mr. Duncalf, in charge of the ship, cursing the island over his rum and water, as a "beastly green strip of a place, not laid down in any Christian chart," was kept waiting four mortal hours before the Captain returned to his command, and reported himself to his officers as follows:

He had found his knowledge of the Polynesian dialects sufficient to make himself in some degree understood by the natives of the new island. Under the guidance of the chief he had made a first journey of exploration, and had seen for himself that the place was a marvel of natural beauty and fertility. The one barren spot in it was the peak of the volcanic mountain, composed of crumbling rock; originally no doubt lava and ashes, which had cooled and consolidated with the lapse of time. So far as he could see, the crater at the top was now an extinct crater. But, if he had understood rightly, the chief had spoken of earthquakes and eruptions at certain bygone periods, some of which lay within his own earliest recollections of the place.

Adverting next to considerations of practical utility, the Captain announced that he had seen sandal-wood enough on the island to load a dozen ships, and that the natives were willing to part with it for a few toys and trinkets generally distributed among them. To the mate's disgust, the Fortuna was taken inside the reef that day, and was anchored before sunset in a natural harbor. Twelve hours of recreation, beginning with the next morning, were granted to the men, under the wise restrictions in such cases established by the Captain. That interval over, the work of cutting the precious wood and loading the ship was to be unremittingly pursued.

Mr. Duncalf had the first watch after the Fortuna had been made snug. He took the boatswain aside (an ancient sea-dog like himself), and he said in a gruff whisper: "My lad, this here ain't the island laid down in our sailing orders. See if mischief don't come of disobeying orders before we are many days older."

Nothing in the shape of mischief happened that night. But at sunrise the next morning a suspicious circumstance occurred; and Mr. Duncalf whispered to the boatswain: "What did I tell you?" The Captain and the chief of the islanders held a private conference in the cabin, and the Captain, after first forbidding any communication with the shore until his return, suddenly left the ship, alone with the chief, in the chief's own canoe.

What did this strange disappearance mean? The Captain himself, when he took his seat in the canoe, would have been puzzled to answer that question. He asked, in the nearest approach that his knowledge could make to the language used in the island, whether he would be a long time or a short time absent from his ship.

The chief answered mysteriously (as the Captain understood him) in these words: "Long time or short time, your life depends on it, and the lives of your men."

Paddling his light little boat in silence over the smooth water inside the reef, the chief took his visitor ashore at a part of the island which was quite new to the Captain. The two crossed a ravine, and ascended an eminence beyond. There the chief stopped, and silently pointed out to sea.

The Captain looked in the direction indicated to him, and discovered a second and a smaller island, lying away to the southwest. Taking out his telescope from the case by which it was slung at his back, he narrowly examined the place. Two of the native canoes were lying off the shore of the new island; and the men in them appeared to be all kneeling or crouching in curiously chosen attitudes. Shifting the range of his glass, he next beheld a white-robed figure, tall and solitary—the one inhabitant of the island whom he could discover. The man was standing on the highest point of a rocky cape. A fire was burning at his feet. Now he lifted his arms solemnly to the sky; now he dropped some invisible fuel into the fire, which made a blue smoke; and now he cast other invisible objects into the canoes floating beneath him, which the islanders reverently received with bodies that crouched in abject submission. Lowering his telescope, the Captain looked round at the chief for an explanation. The chief gave the explanation readily. His language was interpreted by the English stranger in these terms:

"Wonderful white man! the island you see yonder is a Holy Island. As such it is Taboo—an island sanctified and set apart. The honorable person whom you notice on the rock is an all-powerful favorite of the gods. He is by vocation a Sorcerer, and by rank a Priest. You now see him casting charms and blessings into the canoes of our fishermen, who kneel to him for fine weather and great plenty of fish. If any profane person, native or stranger, presumes to set foot on that island, my otherwise peaceful subjects will (in the performance of a religious duty) put that person to death. Mention this to your men. They will be fed by my male people, and fondled by my female people, so long as they keep clear of the Holy Isle. As they value their lives, let them respect this prohibition. Is it understood between us? Wonderful white man! my canoe is waiting for you. Let us go back."

Understanding enough of the chief's language (illustrated by his gestures) to receive in the right spirit the communication thus addressed to him, the Captain repeated the warning to the ship's company in the plainest possible English. The officers and men then took their holiday on shore, with the exception of Mr. Duncalf, who positively refused to leave the ship. For twelve delightful hours they were fed by the male people, and fondled by the female people, and then they were mercilessly torn from the flesh-pots and the arms of their new friends, and set to work on the sandal-wood in good earnest. Mr. Duncalf superintended the loading, and waited for the mischief that was to come of disobeying the owners' orders with a confidence worthy of a better cause.

IV.

STRANGELY enough, chance once more declared itself in favor of the mate's point of view. The mischief did actually come; and the chosen instrument of it was a handsome young islander, who was one of the sons of the chief.

The Captain had taken a fancy to the sweet-tempered, intelligent lad. Pursuing his studies in the dialect of the island, at leisure hours, he had made the chief's son his tutor, and had instructed the youth in English by way of return. More than a month had passed in this intercourse, and the ship's lading was being rapidly completed—when, in an evil hour, the talk between the two turned on the subject of the Holy Island.

"Does nobody live on the island but the Priest?" the Captain asked.

The chief's son looked round him suspiciously. "Promise me you won't tell anybody!" he began very earnestly.

The Captain gave his promise.

"There is one other person on the island," the lad whispered; "a person to feast your eyes upon, if you could only see her! She is the Priest's daughter. Removed to the island in her infancy, she has never left it since. In that sacred solitude she has only looked on two human beings—her father and her mother. I once saw her from my canoe, taking care not to attract her notice, or to approach too near the holy soil. Oh, so young, dear master, and, oh, so beautiful!" The chief's son completed the description by kissing his own hands as an expression of rapture.

The Captain's fine blue eyes sparkled. He asked no more questions; but, later on that day, he took his telescope with him, and paid a secret visit to the eminence which overlooked the Holy Island. The next day, and the next, he privately returned to the same place. On the fourth day, fatal Destiny favored him. He discovered the nymph of the island.

Standing alone upon the cape on which he had already seen her father, she was feeding some tame birds which looked like turtle-doves. The glass showed the Captain her white robe, fluttering in the sea-breeze; her long black hair falling to her feet; her slim and supple young figure; her simple grace of attitude, as she turned this way and that, attending to the wants of her birds. Before her was the blue ocean; behind her rose the lustrous green of the island forest. He looked and looked until his eyes and arms ached. When she disappeared among the trees, followed by her favorite birds, the Captain shut up his telescope with a sigh, and said to himself: "I have seen an angel!"

From that hour he became an altered man; he was languid, silent, interested in nothing. General opinion, on board his ship, decided that he was going to be taken ill.

A week more elapsed, and the officers and crew began to talk of the voyage to their market in China. The Captain refused to fix a day for sailing. He even took offense at being asked to decide. Instead of sleeping in his cabin, he went ashore for the night.

Not many hours afterward (just before daybreak), Mr. Duncalf, snoring in his cabin on deck, was aroused by a hand laid on his shoulder. The swinging lamp, still alight, showed him the dusky face of the chief's son, convulsed with terror. By wild signs, by disconnected words in the little English which he had learned, the lad tried to make the mate understand him. Dense Mr. Duncalf, understanding nothing, hailed the second officer, on the opposite side of the deck. The second officer was young and intelligent; he rightly interpreted the terrible news that had come to the ship.

The Captain had broken his own rules. Watching his opportunity, under cover of the night, he had taken a canoe, and had secretly crossed the channel to the Holy Island. No one had been near him at the time but the chief's son. The lad had vainly tried to induce him to abandon his desperate enterprise, and had vainly waited on the shore in the hope of hearing the sound of the paddle announcing his return. Beyond all reasonable doubt, the infatuated man had set foot on the shores of the tabooed island.

The one chance for his life was to conceal what he had done, until the ship could be got out of the harbor, and then (if no harm had come to him in the interval) to rescue him after nightfall. It was decided to spread the report that he had really been taken ill, and that he was confined to his cabin. The chief's son, whose heart the Captain's kindness had won, could be trusted to do this, and to keep the secret faithfully for his good friend's sake.

Toward noon, the next day, they attempted to take the ship to sea, and failed for want of wind. Hour by hour, the heat grew more oppressive. As the day declined, there were ominous appearances in the western heaven. The natives, who had given some trouble during the day by their anxiety to see the Captain, and by their curiosity to know the cause of the sudden preparations for the ship's departure, all went ashore together, looking suspiciously at the sky, and reappeared no more. Just at midnight, the ship (still in her snug berth inside the reef) suddenly trembled from her keel to her uppermost masts. Mr. Duncalf, surrounded by the startled crew, shook his knotty fist at the island as if he could see it in the dark. "My lads, what did I tell you? That was a shock of earthquake."

With the morning the threatening aspect of the weather unexpectedly disappeared. A faint hot breeze from the land, just enough to give the ship steerage-way, offered Mr. Duncalf a chance of getting to sea. Slowly the

Fortuna, with the mate himself at the wheel, half sailed, half drifted into the open ocean. At a distance of barely two miles from the island the breeze was felt no more, and the vessel lay becalmed for the rest of the day.

At night the men waited their orders, expecting to be sent after their Captain in one of the boats. The intense darkness, the airless heat, and a second shock of earthquake (faintly felt in the ship at her present distance from the land) warned the mate to be cautious. "I smell mischief in the air," said Mr. Duncalf. "The Captain must wait till I am surer of the weather."

Still no change came with the new day. The dead calm continued, and the airless heat. As the day declined, another ominous appearance became visible. A thin line of smoke was discovered through the telescope, ascending from the topmost peak of the mountain on the main island. Was the volcano threatening an eruption? The mate, for one, entertained no doubt of it. "By the Lord, the place is going to burst up!" said Mr. Duncalf. "Come what may of it, we must find the Captain to-night!"

V.

WHAT was the Captain doing? and what chance had the crew of finding him that night?

He had committed himself to his desperate adventure, without forming any plan for the preservation of his own safety; without giving even a momentary consideration to the consequences which might follow the risk that he had run. The charming figure that he had seen haunted him night and day. The image of the innocent creature, secluded from humanity in her island solitude, was the one image that filled his mind. A man, passing a woman in the street, acts on the impulse to turn and follow her, and in that one thoughtless moment shapes the destiny of his future life. The Captain had acted on a similar impulse, when he took the first canoe he had found on the beach, and shaped his reckless course for the tabooed island.

Reaching the shore while it was still dark, he did one sensible thing—he hid the canoe so that it might not betray him when the daylight came. That done, he waited for the morning on the outskirts of the forest.

The trembling light of dawn revealed the mysterious solitude around him. Following the outer limits of the trees, first in one direction, then in another, and finding no trace of any living creature, he decided on penetrating to the interior of the island. He entered the forest.

An hour of walking brought him to rising ground. Continuing the ascent, he got clear of the trees, and stood on the grassy top of a broad cliff which overlooked the sea. An open hut was on the cliff. He cautiously looked in, and discovered that it was empty. The few household utensils left about, and the simple bed of leaves in a corner, were covered with fine sandy dust. Night-birds flew blundering out of the inner cavities of the roof, and took refuge in the shadows of the forest below. It was plain that the hut had not been inhabited for some time past.

Standing at the open doorway and considering what he should do next, the Captain saw a bird flying toward him out of the forest. It was a turtle-dove, so tame that it fluttered close up to him. At the same moment the sound of sweet laughter became audible among the trees. His heart beat fast; he advanced a few steps and stopped. In a moment more the nymph of the island appeared, in her white robe, ascending the cliff in pursuit of her truant bird. She saw the strange man, and suddenly stood still; struck motionless by the amazing discovery that had burst upon her. The Captain approached, smiling and holding out his hand. She never moved; she stood before him in helpless wonderment—her lovely black eyes fixed spellbound on his face; her dusky bosom palpitating above the fallen folds of her robe; her rich red lips parted in mute astonishment. Feasting his eyes on her beauty in silence, the Captain after a while ventured to speak to her in the language of the main island. The sound of his voice, addressing her in the words that she understood, roused the lovely creature to action. She started, stepped close up to him, and dropped on her knees at his feet.

"My father worships invisible deities," she said, softly. "Are you a visible deity? Has my mother sent you?" She pointed as she spoke to the deserted hut behind them. "You appear," she went on, "in the place where my mother died. Is it for her sake that you show yourself to her child? Beautiful deity, come to the Temple—come to my father!"

The Captain gently raised her from the ground. If her father saw him, he was a doomed man.

Infatuated as he was, he had sense enough left to announce himself plainly in his own character, as a mortal creature arriving from a distant land. The girl instantly drew back from him with a look of terror.

"He is not like my father," she said to herself; "he is not like me. Is he the lying demon of the prophecy? Is he the predestined destroyer of our island?"

The Captain's experience of the sex showed him the only sure way out of the awkward position in which he was now placed. He appealed to his personal appearance.

"Do I look like a demon?" he asked.

Her eyes met his eyes; a faint smile trembled on her lips. He ventured on asking what she meant by the predestined destruction of the island. She held up her hand solemnly, and repeated the prophecy.

The Holy Island was threatened with destruction by an evil being, who would one day appear on its shores. To avert the fatality the place had been sanctified and set apart, under the protection of the gods and their priest. Here was the reason for the taboo, and for the extraordinary rigor with which it was enforced. Listening to her with the deepest interest, the Captain took her hand and pressed it gently.

"Do I feel like a demon?" he whispered.

Her slim brown fingers closed frankly on his hand. "You feel soft and friendly," she said with the fearless candor of a child. "Squeeze me again. I like it!"

The next moment she snatched her hand away from him; the sense of his danger had suddenly forced itself on her mind. "If my father sees you," she said, "he will light the signal fire at the Temple, and the people from the other island will come here and put you to death. Where is your canoe? No! It is daylight. My father may see you on the water." She considered a little, and, approaching him, laid her hands on his shoulders. "Stay here till nightfall," she resumed. "My father never comes this way. The sight of the place where my mother died is horrible to him. You are safe here. Promise to stay where you are till night-time."

The Captain gave his promise.

Freed from anxiety so far, the girl's mobile temperament recovered its native cheerfulness, its sweet gayety and spirit. She admired the beautiful stranger as she might have admired a new bird that had flown to her to be fondled with the rest. She patted his fair white skin, and wished she had a skin like it. She lifted the great glossy folds of her long black hair, and compared it with the Captain's bright curly locks, and longed to change colors with him from the bottom of her heart. His dress was a wonder to her; his watch was a new revelation. She rested her head on his shoulder to listen delightedly to the ticking, as he held the watch to her ear. Her fragrant breath played on his face, her warm, supple figure rested against him softly. The Captain's arm stole round her waist, and the Captain's lips gently touched her cheek. She lifted her head with a look of pleased surprise. "Thank you," said the child of Nature, simply. "Kiss me again; I like it. May I kiss you?" The tame turtle-dove perched on her shoulder as she gave the Captain her first kiss, and diverted her thoughts to the pets that she had left, in pursuit of the truant dove. "Come," she said, "and see my birds. I keep them on this side of the forest. There is no danger, so long as you don't show yourself on the other side. My name is Aimata. Aimata will take care of you. Oh, what a beautiful white neck you have!" She put her arm admiringly round his neck. The Captain's arm held her tenderly to him. Slowly the two descended the cliff, and were lost in the leafy solitudes of the forest. And the tame dove fluttered before them, a winged messenger of love, cooing to his mate.

VI.

THE night had come, and the Captain had not left the island.

Aimata's resolution to send him away in the darkness was a forgotten resolution already. She had let him persuade her that he was in no danger, so long as he remained in the hut on the cliff; and she had promised, at parting, to return to him while the Priest was still sleeping, at the dawn of day.

He was alone in the hut. The thought of the innocent creature whom he loved was sorrowfully as well as tenderly present to his mind. He almost regretted his rash visit to the island. "I will take her with me to England," he said to himself. "What does a sailor care for the opinion of the world? Aimata shall be my wife."

The intense heat oppressed him. He stepped out on the cliff, toward midnight, in search of a breath of air.

At that moment, the first shock of earthquake (felt in the ship while she was inside the reef) shook the ground he stood on. He instantly thought of the volcano on the main island. Had he been mistaken in supposing the crater to be extinct? Was the shock that he had just felt a warning from the volcano, communicated through a submarine connection between the two islands? He waited and watched through the hours of darkness, with a vague sense of apprehension, which was not to be reasoned away. With the first light of daybreak he descended into the forest, and saw the lovely being whose safety was already precious to him as his own, hurrying to meet him through the trees.

She waved her hand distractedly as she approached him. "Go!" she cried; "go away in your canoe before our island is destroyed!"

He did his best to quiet her alarm. Was it the shock of earthquake that had frightened her? No: it was more than the shock of earthquake—it was something terrible which had followed the shock. There was a lake near the Temple, the waters of which were supposed to be heated by subterranean fires. The lake had risen with the earthquake, had bubbled furiously, and had then melted away into the earth and been lost. Her father, viewing the portent with horror, had gone to the cape to watch the volcano on the main island, and to implore by prayers and sacrifices the protection of the gods. Hearing this, the Captain entreated Aimata to let him see the emptied lake, in the absence of the Priest. She hesitated; but his influence was all-powerful. He prevailed on her to turn back with him through the forest.

Reaching the furthest limit of the trees, they came out upon open rocky ground which sloped gently downward toward the center of the island.

Having crossed this space, they arrived at a natural amphitheater of rock. On one side of it the Temple appeared, partly excavated, partly formed by a natural cavern. In one of the lateral branches of the cavern was the dwelling of the Priest and his daughter. The mouth of it looked out on the rocky basin of the lake. Stooping over the edge, the Captain discovered, far down in the empty depths, a light cloud of steam. Not a drop of water was visible, look where he might.

Aimata pointed to the abyss, and hid her face on his bosom. "My father says," she whispered, "that it is your doing."

The Captain started. "Does your father know that I am on the island?"

She looked up at him with a quick glance of reproach. "Do you think I would tell him, and put your life in peril?" she asked. "My father felt the destroyer of the island in the earthquake; my father saw the coming destruction in the disappearance of the lake." Her eyes rested on him with a loving languor. "Are you indeed the demon of the prophecy?" she said, winding his hair round her finger. "I am not afraid of you, if you are. I am a creature bewitched; I love the demon." She kissed him passionately. "I don't care if I die," she whispered between the kisses, "if I only die with you!"

The Captain made no attempt to reason with her. He took the wiser way—he appealed to her feelings.

"You will come and live with me happily in my own country," he said. "My ship is waiting for us. I will take you home with me, and you shall be my wife."

She clapped her hands for joy. Then she thought of her father, and drew back from him in tears.

The Captain understood her. "Let us leave this dreary place," he suggested. "We will talk about it in the cool glades of the forest, where you first said you loved me."

She gave him her hand. "Where I first said I loved you!" she repeated, smiling tenderly as she looked at him. They left the lake together.

VII.

THE darkness had fallen again; and the ship was still becalmed at sea.

Mr. Duncalf came on deck after his supper. The thin line of smoke, seen rising from the peak of the mountain that evening, was now succeeded by ominous flashes of fire from the same quarter, intermittently visible. The faint hot breeze from the land was felt once more. "There's just an air of wind," Mr. Duncalf remarked. "I'll try for the Captain while I have the chance."

One of the boats was lowered into the water—under command of the second mate, who had already taken the bearings of the tabooed island by daylight. Four of the men were to go with him, and they were all to be well armed. Mr. Duncalf addressed his final instructions to the officer in the boat.

"You will keep a lookout, sir, with a lantern in the bows. If the natives annoy you, you know what to do. Always shoot natives. When you get anigh the island, you will fire a gun and sing out for the Captain."

"Quite needless," interposed a voice from the sea. "The Captain is here!"

Without taking the slightest notice of the astonishment that he had caused, the commander of the Fortuna paddled his canoe to the side of the ship. Instead of ascending to the deck, he stepped into the boat, waiting alongside. "Lend me your pistols," he said quietly to the second officer, "and oblige me by taking your men back to their duties on board." He looked up at Mr. Duncalf and gave some further directions. "If there is any change in the weather, keep the ship standing off and on, at a safe distance from the land, and throw up a rocket from time to time to show your position. Expect me on board again by sunrise."

"What!" cried the mate. "Do you mean to say you are going back to the island—in that boat—all by yourself?"

"I am going back to the island," answered the Captain, as quietly as ever; "in this boat—all by myself." He pushed off from the ship, and hoisted the sail as he spoke.

"You're deserting your duty!" the old sea-dog shouted, with one of his loudest oaths.

"Attend to my directions," the Captain shouted back, as he drifted away into the darkness.

Mr. Duncalf—violently agitated for the first time in his life—took leave of his superior officer, with a singular mixture of solemnity and politeness, in these words:

"The Lord have mercy on your soul! I wish you good-evening."

VIII.

ALONE in the boat, the Captain looked with a misgiving mind at the flashing of the volcano on the main island.

If events had favored him, he would have removed Aimata to the shelter of the ship on the day when he saw the emptied basin on the lake. But the smoke of the Priest's sacrifice had been discovered by the chief; and he had dispatched two canoes with instructions to make inquiries. One of the canoes had returned; the other was kept in waiting off the cape, to place a means of communicating with the main island at the disposal of the Priest. The second shock of earthquake had naturally increased the alarm of the chief. He had sent messages to the Priest, entreating him to leave the island, and other messages to Aimata suggesting that she should exert her influence over her father, if he hesitated. The Priest refused to leave the Temple. He trusted in his gods and his sacrifices—he believed they might avert the fatality that threatened his sanctuary.

Yielding to the holy man, the chief sent re-enforcements of canoes to take their turn at keeping watch off the headland. Assisted by torches, the islanders were on the alert (in superstitious terror of the demon of the prophecy) by night as well as by day. The Captain had no alternative but to keep in hiding, and to watch his opportunity of approaching the place in which he had concealed his canoe. It was only after Aimata had left him as usual, to return to her father at the close of evening, that the chances declared themselves in his favor. The fire-flashes from the mountain, visible when the night came, had struck terror into the hearts of the men on the watch. They thought of their wives, their children, and their possessions on the main island, and they one and all deserted their Priest. The Captain seized the opportunity of communicating with the ship, and of exchanging a frail canoe which he was ill able to manage, for a swift-sailing boat capable of keeping the sea in the event of stormy weather.

As he now neared the land, certain small sparks of red, moving on the distant water, informed him that the canoes of the sentinels had been ordered back to their duty.

Carefully avoiding the lights, he reached his own side of the island without accident, and, guided by the boat's lantern, anchored under the cliff. He climbed the rocks, advanced to the door of the hut, and was met, to his delight and astonishment, by Aimata on the threshold.

"I dreamed that some dreadful misfortune had parted us forever," she said; "and I came here to see if my dream was true. You have taught me what it is to be miserable; I never felt my heart ache till I looked into the hut and found that you had gone. Now I have seen you, I am satisfied. No! you must not go back with me. My father may be out looking for me. It is you that are in danger, not I. I know the forest as well by dark as by daylight."

The Captain detained her when she tried to leave him.

"Now you are here," he said, "why should I not place you at once in safety? I have been to the ship; I have brought back one of the boats. The darkness will befriend us—let us embark while we can."

She shrank away as he took her hand. "You forget my father!" she said.

"Your father is in no danger, my love. The canoes are waiting for him at the cape; I saw the lights as I passed."

With that reply he drew her out of the hut and led her toward the sea. Not a breath of the breeze was now to be felt. The dead calm had returned—and the boat was too large to be easily managed by one man alone at the oars.

"The breeze may come again," he said. "Wait here, my angel, for the chance."

As he spoke, the deep silence of the forest below them was broken by a sound. A harsh wailing voice was heard, calling:

"Aimata! Aimata!"

"My father!" she whispered; "he has missed me. If he comes here you are lost."

She kissed him with passionate fervor; she held him to her for a moment with all her strength.

"Expect me at daybreak," she said, and disappeared down the landward slope of the cliff.

He listened, anxious for her safety. The voices of the father and daughter just reached him from among the trees. The Priest spoke in no angry tones; she had apparently found an acceptable excuse for her absence. Little by little, the failing sound of their voices told him that they were on their way back together to the Temple. The silence fell again. Not a ripple broke on the beach. Not a leaf rustled in the forest. Nothing moved but the reflected flashes of the volcano on the main island over the black sky. It was an airless and an awful calm.

He went into the hut, and laid down on his bed of leaves—not to sleep, but to rest. All his energies might be required to meet the coming events of the morning. After the voyage to and from the ship, and the long watching that had preceded it, strong as he was he stood in need of repose.

For some little time he kept awake, thinking. Insensibly the oppression of the intense heat, aided in its influence by his own fatigue, treacherously closed his eyes. In spite of himself, the weary man fell into a deep sleep.

He was awakened by a roar like the explosion of a park of artillery. The volcano on the main island had burst into a state of eruption. Smoky flame-light overspread the sky, and flashed through the open doorway of the hut. He sprang from his bed—and found himself up to his knees in water.

Had the sea overflowed the land?

He waded out of the hut, and the water rose to his middle. He looked round him by the lurid light of the eruption. The one visible object within the range of view was the sea, stained by reflections from the blood-red sky, swirling and rippling strangely in the dead calm. In a moment more, he became conscious that the earth on which he stood was sinking under his feet. The water rose to his neck; the last vestige of the roof of the hut disappeared.

He looked round again, and the truth burst on him. The island was sinking—slowly, slowly sinking into volcanic depths, below even the depth of the sea! The highest object was the hut, and that had dropped inch by inch under water before his own eyes. Thrown up to the surface by occult volcanic influences, the island had sunk back, under the same influences, to the obscurity from which it had emerged!

A black shadowy object, turning in a wide circle, came slowly near him as the all-destroying ocean washed its bitter waters into his mouth. The buoyant boat, rising as the sea rose, had dragged its anchor, and was floating round in the vortex made by the slowly sinking island. With a last desperate hope that Aimata might have been saved as he had been saved, he swam to the boat, seized the heavy oars with the strength of a giant, and made for the place (so far as he could guess at it now) where the lake and the Temple had once been.

He looked round and round him; he strained his eyes in the vain attempt to penetrate below the surface of the seething dimpling sea. Had the panic-stricken watchers in the canoes saved themselves, without an effort to preserve the father and daughter? Or had they both been suffocated before they could make an attempt to escape? He called to her in his misery, as if she could hear him out of the fathomless depths: "Aimata! Aimata!" The roar of the distant eruption answered him. The mounting fires lit the solitary sea far and near over the sinking island. The boat turned slowly and more slowly in the lessening vortex. Never again would those gentle eyes look at him with unutterable love! Never again would those fresh lips touch his lips with their fervent kiss! Alone, amid the savage forces of Nature in conflict, the miserable mortal lifted his hands in frantic supplication—and the burning sky glared down on him in its pitiless grandeur, and struck him to his knees in the boat. His reason sank with his sinking limbs. In the merciful frenzy that succeeded the shock, he saw afar off, in her white robe, an angel poised on the waters, beckoning him to follow her to the brighter and the better world. He loosened the sail, he seized the oars; and the faster he pursued it, the faster the mocking vision fled from him over the empty and endless sea.

IX.

THE boat was discovered, on the next morning, from the ship.

All that the devotion of the officers of the Fortuna could do for their unhappy commander was done on the homeward voyage. Restored to his own country, and to skilled medical help, the Captain's mind by slow degrees recovered its balance. He has taken his place in society again—he lives and moves and manages his affairs like the rest of us. But his heart is dead to all new emotions; nothing remains in it but the sacred remembrance of his lost love. He neither courts nor avoids the society of women. Their sympathy finds him grateful, but their attractions seem to be lost on him; they pass from his mind as they pass from his eyes—they stir nothing in him but the memory of Aimata.

"Now you know, ladies, why the Captain will never marry, and why (sailor as he is) he hates the sight of the sea."

MR. MARMADUKE AND THE MINISTER.

I.

September 13th.—Winter seems to be upon us, on the Highland Border, already.

I looked out of window, as the evening closed in, before I barred the shutters and drew the curtains for the night. The clouds hid the hilltops on either side of our valley. Fantastic mists parted and met again on the lower slopes, as the varying breeze blew them. The blackening waters of the lake before our window seemed to anticipate the coming darkness. On the more distant hills the torrents were just visible, in the breaks of the mist, stealing their way over the brown ground like threads of silver. It was a dreary scene. The stillness of all things was only interrupted by the splashing of our little waterfall at the back of the house. I was not sorry to close the shutters, and confine the view to the four walls of our sitting-room.

The day happened to be my birthday. I sat by the peat-fire, waiting for the lamp and the tea-tray, and contemplating my past life from the vantage-ground, so to speak, of my fifty-fifth year.

There was wonderfully little to look back on. Nearly thirty years since, it pleased an all-wise Providence to cast my lot in this remote Scottish hamlet, and to make me Minister of Cauldkirk, on a stipend of seventy-four pounds sterling per annum. I and my surroundings have grown quietly older and older together. I have outlived my wife; I have buried one generation among my parishioners, and married another; I have borne the wear and tear of years better than the kirk in which I minister and the manse (or parsonage-house) in which I live—both sadly out of repair, and both still trusting for the means of reparation to the pious benefactions of people richer than myself. Not that I complain, be it understood, of the humble position which I occupy. I possess many blessings; and I thank the Lord for them. I have my little bit of land and my cow. I have also my good daughter, Felicia; named after her deceased mother, but inheriting her comely looks, it is thought, rather from myself.

Neither let me forget my elder sister, Judith; a friendless single person, sheltered under my roof, whose temperament I could wish somewhat less prone to look at persons and things on the gloomy side, but whose compensating virtues Heaven forbid that I should deny. No; I am grateful for what has been given me (from on high), and resigned to what has been taken away. With what fair prospects did I start in life! Springing from a good old Scottish stock, blessed with every advantage of education that the institutions of Scotland and England in turn could offer; with a career at the Bar and in Parliament before me—and all cast to the winds, as it were, by the measureless prodigality of my unhappy father, God forgive him! I doubt if I had five pounds left in my purse, when the compassion of my relatives on the mother's side opened a refuge to me at Cauldkirk, and hid me from the notice of the world for the rest of my life.

September 14th.—Thus far I had posted up my Diary on the evening of the 13th, when an event occurred so completely unexpected by my household and myself, that the pen, I may say, dropped incontinently from my hand.

It was the time when we had finished our tea, or supper—I hardly know which to call it. In the silence, we could hear the rain pouring against the window, and the wind that had risen with the darkness howling round the house. My sister Judith, taking the gloomy view according to custom— copious draughts of good Bohea and two helpings of such a mutton ham as only Scotland can produce no effect in raising her spirits—my sister, I say, remarked that there would be ships lost at sea and men drowned this night. My daughter Felicia, the brightest-tempered creature of the female sex that I have ever met with, tried to give a cheerful turn to her aunt's depressing prognostication. "If the ships must be lost," she said, "we may surely hope that the men will be saved." "God willing," I put in—thereby giving to my daughter's humane expression of feeling the fit religious tone that was all it wanted—and then went on with my written record of the events and reflections of the day. No more was said. Felicia took up a book. Judith took up her knitting.

On a sudden, the silence was broken by a blow on the house-door.

My two companions, as is the way of women, set up a scream. I was startled myself, wondering who could be out in the rain and the darkness and striking at the door of the house. A stranger it must be. Light or dark, any person in or near Cauldkirk, wanting admission, would know where to find the bell-handle at the side of the door. I waited a while to hear what might happen next. The stroke was repeated, but more softly. It became me as a man and a minister to set an example. I went out into the passage, and I called through the door, "Who's there?"

A man's voice answered—so faintly that I could barely hear him—"A lost traveler."

Immediately upon this my cheerful sister expressed her view of the matter through the open parlor door. "Brother Noah, it's a robber. Don't let him in!"

What would the Good Samaritan have done in my place? Assuredly he would have run the risk and opened the door. I imitated the Good Samaritan.

A man, dripping wet, with a knapsack on his back and a thick stick in his hand, staggered in, and would, I think, have fallen in the passage if I had not caught him by the arm. Judith peeped out at the parlor door, and said, "He's drunk." Felicia was behind her, holding up a lighted candle, the better to see what was going on. "Look at his face, aunt," says she. "Worn out with fatigue, poor man. Bring him in, father—bring him in."

Good Felicia! I was proud of my girl. "He'll spoil the carpet," says sister Judith. I said, "Silence, for shame!" and brought him in, and dropped him dripping into my own armchair. Would the Good Samaritan have thought of his carpet or his chair? I did think of them, but I overcame it. Ah, we are a decadent generation in these latter days!

"Be quick, father" says Felicia; "he'll faint if you don't give him something!"

I took out one of our little drinking cups (called among us a "Quaigh"), while Felicia, instructed by me, ran to the kitchen for the cream-jug. Filling the cup with whisky and cream in equal proportions, I offered it to him. He drank it off as if it had been so much water. "Stimulant and nourishment, you'll observe, sir, in equal portions," I remarked to him. "How do you feel now?"

"Ready for another," says he.

Felicia burst out laughing. I gave him another. As I turned to hand it to him, sister Judith came behind me, and snatched away the cream-jug. Never a generous person, sister Judith, at the best of times—more especially in the matter of cream.

He handed me back the empty cup. "I believe, sir, you have saved my life," he said. "Under Providence," I put in—adding, "But I would remark, looking to the state of your clothes, that I have yet another service to offer you, before you tell us how you came into this pitiable state." With that reply, I led him upstairs, and set before him the poor resources of my wardrobe, and left him to do the best he could with them. He was rather a small man, and I am in stature nigh on six feet. When he came down to us in my clothes, we had the merriest evening that I can remember for years past. I thought Felicia would have had a hysteric fit; and even sister Judith laughed—he did look such a comical figure in the minister's garments.

As for the misfortune that had befallen him, it offered one more example of the preternatural rashness of the English traveler in countries unknown to him. He was on a walking tour through Scotland; and he had set forth to go twenty miles a-foot, from a town on one side of the Highland Border, to a town on the other, without a guide. The only wonder is that he found his way to Cauldkirk, instead of perishing of exposure among the lonesome hills.

"Will you offer thanks for your preservation to the Throne of Grace, in your prayers to-night?" I asked him. And he answered, "Indeed I will!"

We have a spare room at the manse; but it had not been inhabited for more than a year past. Therefore we made his bed, for that night, on the sofa in the parlor; and so left him, with the fire on one side of his couch, and the whisky and the mutton ham on the other in case of need. He mentioned his name when we bade him good-night. Marmaduke Falmer of London, son of a minister of the English Church Establishment, now deceased. It was plain, I may add, before he spoke, that we had offered the hospitality of the manse to a man of gentle breeding.

September 15th.—I have to record a singularly pleasant day; due partly to a return of the fine weather, partly to the good social gifts of our guest.

Attired again in his own clothing, he was, albeit wanting in height, a finely proportioned man, with remarkably small hands and feet; having also a bright mobile face, and large dark eyes of an extraordinary diversity of expression. Also, he was of a sweet and cheerful humor; easily pleased with little things, and amiably ready to make his gifts agreeable to all of us. At the same time, a person of my experience and penetration could not fail to perceive that he was most content when in company with Felicia. I have already mentioned my daughter's comely looks and good womanly qualities. It was in the order of nature that a young man (to use his own phrase) getting near to his thirty-first birthday should feel drawn by sympathy toward a well-favored young woman in her four-and-twentieth year. In matters of this sort I have always cultivated a liberal turn of mind, not forgetting my own youth.

As the evening closed in, I was sorry to notice a certain change in our guest for the worse. He showed signs of fatigue—falling asleep at intervals in his chair, and waking up and shivering. The spare room was now well aired, having had a roaring fire in it all day.

I begged him not to stand on ceremony, and to betake himself at once to his bed. Felicia (having learned the accomplishment from her excellent mother) made him a warm sleeping-draught of eggs, sugar, nutmeg, and spirits, delicious alike to the senses of smell and taste. Sister Judith waited until he had closed the door behind him, and then favored me with one of her dismal predictions. "You'll rue the day, brother, when you let him into the house. He is going to fall ill on our hands."

II.

November 28th.—God be praised for all His mercies! This day, our guest, Marmaduke Falmer, joined us downstairs in the sitting-room for the first time since his illness.

He is sadly deteriorated, in a bodily sense, by the wasting rheumatic fever that brought him nigh to death; but he is still young, and the doctor (humanly speaking) has no doubt of his speedy and complete recovery. My sister takes the opposite view. She remarked, in his hearing, that nobody ever thoroughly got over a rheumatic fever. Oh, Judith! Judith! it's well for humanity that you're a single person! If haply, there had been any man desperate enough to tackle such a woman in the bonds of marriage, what a pessimist progeny must have proceeded from you!

Looking back over my Diary for the last two months and more, I see one monotonous record of the poor fellow's sufferings; cheered and varied, I am pleased to add, by the devoted services of my daughter at the sick man's bedside. With some help from her aunt (most readily given when he was nearest to the point of death), and with needful services performed in turn by two of our aged women in Cauldkirk, Felicia could not have nursed him more assiduously if he had been her own brother. Half the credit of bringing him through it belonged (as the doctor himself confessed) to the discreet young nurse, always ready through the worst of the illness, and always cheerful through the long convalescence that followed. I must also record to the credit of Marmaduke that he was indeed duly grateful. When I led him into the parlor, and he saw Felicia waiting by the armchair, smiling and patting the pillows for him, he took her by the hand, and burst out crying. Weakness, in part, no doubt—but sincere gratitude at the bottom of it, I am equally sure.

November 29th.—However, there are limits even to sincere gratitude. Of this truth Mr. Marmaduke seems to be insufficiently aware. Entering the sitting-room soon after noon today, I found our convalescent guest and his nurse alone. His head was resting on her shoulder; his arm was round her waist—and (the truth before everything) Felicia was kissing him.

A man may be of a liberal turn of mind, and may yet consistently object to freedom when it takes the form of unlicensed embracing and kissing; the person being his own daughter, and the place his own house. I signed to my girl to leave us; and I advanced to Mr. Marmaduke, with my opinion of his conduct just rising in words to my lips—when he staggered me with amazement by asking for Felicia's hand in marriage.

"You need feel no doubt of my being able to offer to your daughter a position of comfort and respectability," he said. "I have a settled income of eight hundred pounds a year."

His raptures over Felicia; his protestations that she was the first woman he had ever really loved; his profane declaration that he preferred to die, if I refused to let him be her husband—all these flourishes, as I may call them, passed in at one of my ears and out at the other. But eight hundred pounds sterling per annum, descending as it were in a golden avalanche on the mind of a Scottish minister (accustomed to thirty years' annual contemplation of seventy-four pounds)—eight hundred a year, in one young man's pocket, I say, completely overpowered me. I just managed to answer, "Wait till tomorrow"—and hurried out of doors to recover my self-respect, if the thing was to be anywise done. I took my way through the valley. The sun was shining, for a wonder. When I saw my shadow on the hillside, I saw the Golden Calf as an integral part of me, bearing this inscription in letters of flame—"Here's another of them!"

November 30th.—I have made amends for yesterday's backsliding; I have acted as becomes my parental dignity and my sacred calling.

The temptation to do otherwise, has not been wanting. Here is sister Judith's advice: "Make sure that he has got the money first; and, for Heaven's sake, nail him!" Here is Mr. Marmaduke's proposal: "Make any conditions you please, so long as you give me your daughter." And, lastly, here is Felicia's confession: "Father, my heart is set on him. Oh, don't be unkind to me for the first time in your life!"

But I have stood firm. I have refused to hear any more words on the subject from any one of them, for the next six months to come.

"So serious a venture as the venture of marriage," I said, "is not to be undertaken on impulse. As soon as Mr. Marmaduke can travel, I request him to leave us, and not to return again for six months. If, after that interval, he is still of the same mind, and my daughter is still of the same mind, let him return to Cauldkirk, and (premising that I am in all other respects satisfied) let him ask me for his wife."

There were tears, there were protestations; I remained immovable. A week later, Mr. Marmaduke left us, on his way by easy stages to the south. I am not a hard man. I rewarded the lovers for their obedience by keeping sister Judith out of the way, and letting them say their farewell words (accompaniments included) in private.

III.

May 28th.—A letter from Mr. Marmaduke, informing me that I may expect him at Cauldkirk, exactly at the expiration of the six months' interval—viz., on June the seventh.

Writing to this effect, he added a timely word on the subject of his family. Both his parents were dead; his only brother held a civil appointment in India, the place being named. His uncle (his father's brother) was a merchant resident in London; and to this near relative he referred me, if I wished to make inquiries about him. The names of his bankers, authorized to give me every information in respect to his pecuniary affairs, followed. Nothing could be more plain and straightforward. I wrote to his uncle, and I wrote to his bankers. In both cases the replies were perfectly satisfactory—nothing in the slightest degree doubtful, no prevarications, no mysteries. In a word, Mr. Marmaduke himself was thoroughly well vouched for, and Mr. Marmaduke's income was invested in securities beyond fear and beyond reproach. Even sister Judith, bent on picking a hole in the record somewhere, tried hard, and could make nothing of it.

The last sentence in Mr. Marmaduke's letter was the only part of it which I failed to read with pleasure.

He left it to me to fix the day for the marriage, and he entreated that I would make it as early a day as possible. I had a touch of the heartache when I thought of parting with Felicia, and being left at home with nobody but Judith. However, I got over it for that time, and, after consulting my daughter, we decided on naming a fortnight after Mr. Marmaduke's arrival—that is to say, the twenty-first of June. This gave Felicia time for her preparations, besides offering to me the opportunity of becoming better acquainted with my son-in-law's disposition. The happiest marriage does indubitably make its demands on human forbearance; and I was anxious, among other things, to assure myself of Mr. Marmaduke's good temper.

IV.

June 22d.—The happy change in my daughter's life (let me say nothing of the change in my life) has come: they were married yesterday. The manse is a desert; and sister Judith was never so uncongenial a companion to me as I feel her to be now. Her last words to the married pair, when they drove away, were: "Lord help you both; you have all your troubles before you!"

I had no heart to write yesterday's record, yesterday evening, as usual. The absence of Felicia at the supper-table completely overcame me. I, who have so often comforted others in their afflictions, could find no comfort for myself. Even now that the day has passed, the tears come into my eyes, only with writing about it. Sad, sad weakness! Let me close my Diary, and open the Bible—and be myself again.

June 23d.—More resigned since yesterday; a more becoming and more pious frame of mind—obedient to God's holy will, and content in the belief that my dear daughter's married life will be a happy one.

They have gone abroad for their holiday—to Switzerland, by way of France. I was anything rather than pleased when I heard that my son-in-law proposed to take Felicia to that sink of iniquity, Paris. He knows already what I think of balls and playhouses, and similar devils' diversions, and how I have brought up my daughter to think of them—the subject having occurred in conversation among us more than a week since. That he could meditate taking a child of mine to the headquarters of indecent jiggings and abominable stage-plays, of spouting rogues and painted Jezebels, was indeed a heavy blow.

However, Felicia reconciled me to it in the end. She declared that her only desire in going to Paris was to see the picture-galleries, the public buildings, and the fair outward aspect of the city generally. "Your opinions, father, are my opinions," she said; "and Marmaduke, I am sure, will so shape our arrangements as to prevent our passing a Sabbath in Paris." Marmaduke not only consented to this (with the perfect good temper of which I have observed more than one gratifying example in him), but likewise assured me that, speaking for himself personally, it would be a relief to him when they got to the mountains and the lakes. So that matter was happily settled. Go where they may, God bless and prosper them!

Speaking of relief, I must record that Judith has gone away to Aberdeen on a visit to some friends. "You'll be wretched enough here," she said at parting, "all by yourself." Pure vanity and self-complacence! It may be resignation to her absence, or it may be natural force of mind, I began to be more easy and composed the moment I was alone, and this blessed state of feeling has continued uninterruptedly ever since.

V.

September 5th.—A sudden change in my life, which it absolutely startles me to record. I am going to London!

My purpose in taking this most serious step is of a twofold nature. I have a greater and a lesser object in view.

The greater object is to see my daughter, and to judge for myself whether certain doubts on the vital question of her happiness, which now torment me night and day, are unhappily founded on truth. She and her husband returned in August from their wedding-tour, and took up their abode in Marmaduke's new residence in London. Up to this time, Felicia's letters to me were, in very truth, the delight of my life—she was so entirely happy, so amazed and delighted with all the wonderful things she saw, so full of love and admiration for the best husband that ever lived. Since her return to London, I perceive a complete change.

She makes no positive complaint, but she writes in a tone of weariness and discontent; she says next to nothing of Marmaduke, and she dwells perpetually on the one idea of my going to London to see her. I hope with my whole heart that I am wrong; but the rare allusions to her husband, and the constantly repeated desire to see her father (while she has not been yet three months married), seem to me to be bad signs. In brief, my anxiety is too great to be endured. I have so arranged matters with one of my brethren as to be free to travel to London cheaply by steamer; and I begin the journey tomorrow.

My lesser object may be dismissed in two words. Having already decided on going to London, I propose to call on the wealthy nobleman who owns all the land hereabouts, and represent to him the discreditable, and indeed dangerous, condition of the parish kirk for want of means to institute the necessary repairs. If I find myself well received, I shall put in a word for the manse, which is almost in as deplorable a condition as the church. My lord is a wealthy man—may his heart and his purse be opened unto me!

Sister Judith is packing my portmanteau. According to custom, she forbodes the worst. "Never forget," she says, "that I warned you against Marmaduke, on the first night when he entered the house."

VI.

September 10th.—After more delays than one, on land and sea, I was at last set ashore near the Tower, on the afternoon of yesterday. God help us, my worst anticipations have been realized! My beloved Felicia has urgent and serious need of me.

It is not to be denied that I made my entry into my son-in-law's house in a disturbed and irritated frame of mind. First, my temper was tried by the almost interminable journey, in the noisy and comfortless vehicle which they call a cab, from the river-wharf to the west-end of London, where Marmaduke lives. In the second place, I was scandalized and alarmed by an incident which took place—still on the endless journey from east to west—in a street hard by the market of Covent Garden.

We had just approached a large building, most profusely illuminated with gas, and exhibiting prodigious colored placards having inscribed on them nothing but the name of Barrymore. The cab came suddenly to a standstill; and looking out to see what the obstacle might be, I discovered a huge concourse of men and women, drawn across the pavement and road alike, so that it seemed impossible to pass by them. I inquired of my driver what this assembling of the people meant. "Oh," says he, "Barrymore has made another hit." This answer being perfectly unintelligible to me, I requested some further explanation, and discovered that "Barrymore" was the name of a stage-player favored by the populace; that the building was a theater, and that all these creatures with immortal souls were waiting, before the doors opened, to get places at the show!

The emotions of sorrow and indignation caused by this discovery so absorbed me that I failed to notice an attempt the driver made to pass through, where the crowd seemed to be thinner, until the offended people resented the proceeding. Some of them seized the horse's head; others were on the point of pulling the driver off his box, when providentially the police interfered. Under their protection, we drew back, and reached our destination in safety, by another way. I record this otherwise unimportant affair, because it grieved and revolted me (when I thought of the people's souls), and so indisposed my mind to take cheerful views of anything. Under these circumstances, I would fain hope that I have exaggerated the true state of the case, in respect to my daughter's married life.

My good girl almost smothered me with kisses. When I at last got a fair opportunity of observing her, I thought her looking pale and worn and anxious. Query: Should I have arrived at this conclusion if I had met with no example of the wicked dissipations of London, and if I had ridden at my ease in a comfortable vehicle?

They had a succulent meal ready for me, and, what I call, fair enough whisky out of Scotland. Here again I remarked that Felicia ate very little, and Marmaduke nothing at all. He drank wine, too—and, good heavens, champagne wine!—a needless waste of money surely when there was whisky on the table. My appetite being satisfied, my son-in-law went out of the room, and returned with his hat in his hand. "You and Felicia have many things to talk about on your first evening together. I'll leave you for a while—I shall only be in the way." So he spoke. It was in vain that his wife and I assured him he was not in the way at all. He kissed his hand, and smiled pleasantly, and left us.

"There, father!" says Felicia. "For the last ten days he has gone out like that, and left me alone for the whole evening. When we first returned from Switzerland, he left me in the same mysterious way, only it was after breakfast then. Now he stays at home in the daytime, and goes out at night."

I inquired if she had not summoned him to give her some explanation.

"I don't know what to make of his explanation," says Felicia. "When he went away in the daytime, he told me he had business in the City. Since he took to going out at night, he says he goes to his club."

"Have you asked where his club is, my dear?"

"He says it's in Pall Mall. There are dozens of clubs in that street—and he has never told me the name of his club. I am completely shut out of his confidence. Would you believe it, father? he has not introduced one of his friends to me since we came home. I doubt if they know where he lives, since he took this house."

What could I say?

I said nothing, and looked round the room. It was fitted up with perfectly palatial magnificence. I am an ignorant man in matters of this sort, and partly to satisfy my curiosity, partly to change the subject, I asked to see the house. Mercy preserve us, the same grandeur everywhere! I wondered if even such an income as eight hundred a year could suffice for it all. In a moment when I was considering this, a truly frightful suspicion crossed my mind. Did these mysterious absences, taken in connection with the unbridled luxury that surrounded us, mean that my son-in-law was a gamester? a shameless shuffler of cards, or a debauched bettor on horses? While I was still completely overcome by my own previsions of evil, my daughter put her arm in mine to take me to the top of the house.

For the first time I observed a bracelet of dazzling gems on her wrist. "Not diamonds?" I said. She answered, with as much composure as if she had been the wife of a nobleman, "Yes, diamonds—a present from Marmaduke." This was too much for me; my previsions, so to speak, forced their way into words. "Oh, my poor child!" I burst out, "I'm in mortal fear that your husband's a gamester!"

She showed none of the horror I had anticipated; she only shook her head and began to cry.

"Worse than that, I'm afraid," she said.

I was petrified; my tongue refused its office, when I would fain have asked her what she meant. Her besetting sin, poor soul, is a proud spirit. She dried her eyes on a sudden, and spoke out freely, in these words: "I am not going to cry about it. The other day, father, we were out walking in the park. A horrid, bold, yellow-haired woman passed us in an open carriage. She kissed her hand to Marmaduke, and called out to him, 'How are you, Marmy?' I was so indignant that I pushed him away from me, and told him to go and take a drive with his lady. He burst out laughing. 'Nonsense!' he said; 'she has known me for years—you don't understand our easy London manners.' We have made it up since then; but I have my own opinion of the creature in the open carriage."

Morally speaking, this was worse than all. But, logically viewed, it completely failed as a means of accounting for the diamond bracelet and the splendor of the furniture.

We went on to the uppermost story. It was cut off from the rest of the house by a stout partition of wood, and a door covered with green baize.

When I tried the door it was locked. "Ha!" says Felicia, "I wanted you to see it for yourself!" More suspicious proceedings on the part of my son-in-law! He kept the door constantly locked, and the key in his pocket. When his wife asked him what it meant, he answered: "My study is up there—and I like to keep it entirely to myself." After such a reply as that, the preservation of my daughter's dignity permitted but one answer: "Oh, keep it to yourself, by all means!"

My previsions, upon this, assumed another form.

I now asked myself—still in connection with my son-in-law's extravagant expenditure—whether the clew to the mystery might not haply be the forging of bank-notes on the other side of the baize door. My mind was prepared for anything by this time. We descended again into the dining-room. Felicia saw how my spirits were dashed, and came and perched upon my knee. "Enough of my troubles for to-night, father," she said. "I am going to be your little girl again, and we will talk of nothing but Cauldkirk, until Marmaduke comes back." I am one of the firmest men living, but I could not keep the hot tears out of my eyes when she put her arm round my neck and said those words. By good fortune I was sitting with my back to the lamp; she didn't notice me.

A little after eleven o'clock Marmaduke returned. He looked pale and weary. But more champagne, and this time something to eat with it, seemed to set him to rights again—no doubt by relieving him from the reproaches of a guilty conscience.

I had been warned by Felicia to keep what had passed between us a secret from her husband for the present; so we had (superficially speaking) a merry end to the evening. My son-in-law was nearly as good company as ever, and wonderfully fertile in suggestions and expedients when he saw they were wanted. Hearing from his wife, to whom I had mentioned it, that I purposed representing the decayed condition of the kirk and manse to the owner of Cauldkirk and the country round about, he strongly urged me to draw up a list of repairs that were most needful, before I waited on my lord. This advice, vicious and degraded as the man who offered it may be, is sound advice nevertheless. I shall assuredly take it.

So far I had written in my Diary, in the forenoon. Returning to my daily record, after a lapse of some hours, I have a new mystery of iniquity to chronicle. My abominable son-in-law now appears (I blush to write it) to be nothing less than an associate of thieves!

After the meal they call luncheon, I thought it well before recreating myself with the sights of London, to attend first to the crying necessities of the kirk and the manse. Furnished with my written list, I presented myself at his lordship's residence. I was immediately informed that he was otherwise engaged, and could not possibly receive me. If I wished to see my lord's secretary, Mr. Helmsley, I could do so. Consenting to this, rather than fail entirely in my errand, I was shown into the secretary's room.

Mr. Helmsley heard what I had to say civilly enough; expressing, however, grave doubts whether his lordship would do anything for me, the demands on his purse being insupportably numerous already. However, he undertook to place my list before his employer, and to let me know the result. "Where are you staying in London?" he asked. I answered: "With my son-in-law, Mr. Marmaduke Falmer." Before I could add the address, the secretary started to his feet and tossed my list back to me across the table in the most uncivil manner.

"Upon my word," says he, "your assurance exceeds anything I ever heard of. Your son-in-law is concerned in the robbery of her ladyship's diamond bracelet—the discovery was made not an hour ago. Leave the house, sir, and consider yourself lucky that I have no instructions to give you in charge to the police." I protested against this unprovoked outrage, with a violence of language which I would rather not recall. As a minister, I ought, under every provocation, to have preserved my self-control.

The one thing to do next was to drive back to my unhappy daughter.

Her guilty husband was with her. I was too angry to wait for a fit opportunity of speaking. The Christian humility which I have all my life cultivated as the first of virtues sank, as it were, from under me. In terms of burning indignation I told them what had happened. The result was too distressing to be described. It ended in Felicia giving her husband back the bracelet. The hardened reprobate laughed at us. "Wait till I have seen his lordship and Mr. Helmsley," he said, and left the house.

Does he mean to escape to foreign parts? Felicia, womanlike, believes in him still; she is quite convinced that there must be some mistake. I am myself in hourly expectation of the arrival of the police.

With gratitude to Providence, I note before going to bed the harmless termination of the affair of the bracelet—so far as Marmaduke is concerned. The agent who sold him the jewel has been forced to come forward and state the truth. His lordship's wife is the guilty person; the bracelet was hers—a present from her husband. Harassed by debts that she dare not acknowledge, she sold it; my lord discovered that it was gone; and in terror of his anger the wretched woman took refuge in a lie.

She declared that the bracelet had been stolen from her. Asked for the name of the thief, the reckless woman (having no other name in her mind at the moment) mentioned the man who had innocently bought the jewel of her agent, otherwise my unfortunate son-in-law. Oh, the profligacy of the modern Babylon! It was well I went to the secretary when I did or we should really have had the police in the house. Marmaduke found them in consultation over the supposed robbery, asking for his address. There was a dreadful exhibition of violence and recrimination at his lordship's residence: in the end he re-purchased the bracelet. My son-in-law's money has been returned to him; and Mr. Helmsley has sent me a written apology.

In a worldly sense, this would, I suppose, be called a satisfactory ending.

It is not so to my mind. I freely admit that I too hastily distrusted Marmaduke; but am I, on that account, to give him back immediately the place which he once occupied in my esteem? Again this evening he mysteriously quitted the house, leaving me alone with Felicia, and giving no better excuse for his conduct than that he had an engagement. And this when I have a double claim on his consideration, as his father-in-law and his guest.

September 11th.—The day began well enough. At breakfast, Marmaduke spoke feelingly of the unhappy result of my visit to his lordship, and asked me to let him look at the list of repairs. "It is just useless to expect anything from my lord, after what has happened," I said. "Besides, Mr. Helmsley gave me no hope when I stated my case to him." Marmaduke still held out his hand for the list. "Let me try if I can get some subscribers," he replied. This was kindly meant, at any rate. I gave him the list; and I began to recover some of my old friendly feeling for him. Alas! the little gleam of tranquillity proved to be of short duration.

We made out our plans for the day pleasantly enough. The check came when Felicia spoke next of our plans for the evening. "My father has only four days more to pass with us," she said to her husband. "Surely you won't go out again to-night, and leave him?" Marmaduke's face clouded over directly; he looked embarrassed and annoyed. I sat perfectly silent, leaving them to settle it by themselves.

"You will stay with us this evening, won't you?" says Felicia. No: he was not free for the evening. "What! another engagement? Surely you can put it off?" No; impossible to put it off. "Is it a ball, or a party of some kind?" No answer; he changed the subject—he offered Felicia the money repaid to him for the bracelet. "Buy one for yourself, my dear, this time." Felicia handed him back the money, rather too haughtily, perhaps. "I don't want a bracelet," she said; "I want your company in the evening."

He jumped up, good-tempered as he was, in something very like a rage—then looked at me, and checked himself on the point (as I believe) of using profane language. "This is downright persecution!" he burst out, with an angry turn of his head toward his wife. Felicia got up, in her turn. "Your language is an insult to my father and to me!" He looked thoroughly staggered at this: it was evidently their first serious quarrel.

Felicia took no notice of him. "I will get ready directly, father; and we will go out together." He stopped her as she was leaving the room—recovering his good temper with a readiness which it pleased me to see. "Come, come, Felicia! We have not quarreled yet, and we won't quarrel now. Let me off this one time more, and I will devote the next three evenings of your father's visit to him and to you. Give me a kiss, and make it up." My daughter doesn't do things by halves. She gave him a dozen kisses, I should think—and there was a happy end of it.

"But what shall we do to-morrow evening?" says Marmaduke, sitting down by his wife, and patting her hand as it lay in his.

"Take us somewhere," says she. Marmaduke laughed. "Your father objects to public amusements. Where does he want to go to?" Felicia took up the newspaper. "There is an oratorio at Exeter Hall," she said; "my father likes music." He turned to me. "You don't object to oratorios, sir?" "I don't object to music," I answered, "so long as I am not required to enter a theater." Felicia handed the newspaper to me. "Speaking of theaters, father, have you read what they say about the new play? What a pity it can't be given out of a theater!" I looked at her in speechless amazement. She tried to explain herself. "The paper says that the new play is a service rendered to the cause of virtue; and that the great actor, Barrymore, has set an example in producing it which

647

deserves the encouragement of all truly religious people. Do read it, father!" I held up my hands in dismay. My own daughter perverted! pinning her faith on a newspaper! speaking, with a perverse expression of interest, of a stage-play and an actor! Even Marmaduke witnessed this lamentable exhibition of backsliding with some appearance of alarm. "It's not her fault, sir," he said, interceding with me. "It's the fault of the newspaper. Don't blame her!" I held my peace; determining inwardly to pray for her. Shortly afterward my daughter and I went out. Marmaduke accompanied us part of the way, and left us at a telegraph office. "Who are you going to telegraph to?" Felicia asked. Another mystery! He answered, "Business of my own, my dear"—and went into the office.

September 12th.—Is my miserable son-in-law's house under a curse? The yellow-haired woman in the open carriage drove up to the door at half-past ten this morning, in a state of distraction. Felicia and I saw her from the drawing-room balcony—a tall woman in gorgeous garments. She knocked with her own hand at the door—she cried out distractedly, "Where is he? I must see him!" At the sound of her voice, Marmaduke (playing with his little dog in the drawing-room) rushed downstairs and out into the street. "Hold your tongue!" we heard him say to her. "What are you here for?"

What she answered we failed to hear; she was certainly crying. Marmaduke stamped on the pavement like a man beside himself—took her roughly by the arm, and led her into the house.

Before I could utter a word, Felicia left me and flew headlong down the stairs.

She was in time to hear the dining-room locked. Following her, I prevented the poor jealous creature from making a disturbance at the door. God forgive me—not knowing how else to quiet her—I degraded myself by advising her to listen to what they said. She instantly opened the door of the back dining-room, and beckoned to me to follow. I naturally hesitated. "I shall go mad," she whispered, "if you leave me by myself!" What could I do? I degraded myself the second time. For my own child—in pity for my own child!

We heard them, through the flimsy modern folding-doors, at those times when he was most angry, and she most distracted. That is to say, we heard them when they spoke in their loudest tones.

"How did you find out where I live?" says he. "Oh, you're ashamed of me?" says she. "Mr. Helmsley was with us yesterday evening. That's how I found out!" "What do you mean?" "I mean that Mr. Helmsley had your card and address in his pocket. Ah, you were obliged to give your address when you had to clear up that matter of the bracelet! You cruel, cruel man, what have I done to deserve such a note as you sent me this morning?" "Do what the note tells you!" "Do what the note tells me? Did anybody ever hear a man talk so, out of a lunatic asylum? Why, you haven't even the grace to carry out your own wicked deception—you haven't even gone to bed!" There the voices grew less angry, and we missed what followed. Soon the lady burst out again, piteously entreating him this time. "Oh, Marmy, don't ruin me! Has anybody offended you? Is there anything you wish to have altered? Do you want more money? It is too cruel to treat me in this way—it is indeed!" He made some answer, which we were not able to hear; we could only suppose that he had upset her temper again. She went on louder than ever "I've begged and prayed of you—and you're as hard as iron. I've told you about the Prince—and that has had no effect on you. I have done now. We'll see what the doctor says." He got angry, in his turn; we heard him again. "I won't see the doctor!" "Oh, you refuse to see the doctor?—I shall make your refusal known—and if there's law in England, you shall feel it!" Their voices dropped again; some new turn seemed to be taken by the conversation. We heard the lady once more, shrill and joyful this time. "There's a dear! You see it, don't you, in the right light? And you haven't forgotten the old times, have you? You're the same dear, honorable, kind-hearted fellow that you always were!"

I caught hold of Felicia, and put my hand over her mouth.

There was a sound in the next room which might have been—I cannot be certain—the sound of a kiss. The next moment, we heard the door of the room unlocked. Then the door of the house was opened, and the noise of retreating carriage-wheels followed. We met him in the hall, as he entered the house again.

My daughter walked up to him, pale and determined.

"I insist on knowing who that woman is, and what she wants here." Those were her first words. He looked at her like a man in utter confusion. "Wait till this evening; I am in no state to speak to you now!" With that, he snatched his hat off the hall table and rushed out of the house.

It is little more than three weeks since they returned to London from their happy wedding-tour—and it has come to this!

The clock has just struck seven; a letter has been left by a messenger, addressed to my daughter. I had persuaded her, poor soul, to lie down in her own room. God grant that the letter may bring her some tidings of her husband! I please myself in the hope of hearing good news.

My mind has not been kept long in suspense. Felicia's waiting-woman has brought me a morsel of writing paper, with these lines penciled on it in my daughter's handwriting: "Dearest father, make your mind easy. Everything is explained. I cannot trust myself to speak to you about it to-night—and he doesn't wish me to do so. Only wait till tomorrow, and you shall know all. He will be back about eleven o'clock. Please don't wait up for him—he will come straight to me."

September 13th.—The scales have fallen from my eyes; the light is let in on me at last. My bewilderment is not to be uttered in words—I am like a man in a dream.

Before I was out of my room in the morning, my mind was upset by the arrival of a telegram addressed to myself. It was the first thing of the kind I ever received; I trembled under the prevision of some new misfortune as I opened the envelope.

Of all the people in the world, the person sending the telegram was sister Judith! Never before did this distracting relative confound me as she confounded me now. Here is her message: "You can't come back. An architect from Edinburgh asserts his resolution to repair the kirk and the manse. The man only waits for his lawful authority to begin. The money is ready—but who has found it? Mr. Architect is forbidden to tell. We live in awful times. How is Felicia?"

Naturally concluding that Judith's mind must be deranged, I went downstairs to meet my son-in-law (for the first time since the events of yesterday) at the late breakfast which is customary in this house. He was waiting for me—but Felicia was not present. "She breakfasts in her room this morning," says Marmaduke; "and I am to give you the explanation which has already satisfied your daughter. Will you take it at great length, sir? or will you have it in one word?" There was something in his manner that I did not at all like—he seemed to be setting me at defiance. I said, stiffly, "Brevity is best; I will have it in one word."

"Here it is then," he answered. "I am Barrymore."

POSTSCRIPT ADDED BY FELICIA.

If the last line extracted from my dear father's Diary does not contain explanation enough in itself, I add some sentences from Marmaduke's letter to me, sent from the theater last night. (N. B.—I leave out the expressions of endearment: they are my own private property.)

... "Just remember how your father talked about theaters and actors, when I was at Cauldkirk, and how you listened in dutiful agreement with him. Would he have consented to your marriage if he had known that I was one of the 'spouting rogues,' associated with the 'painted Jezebels' of the playhouse? He would never have consented—and you yourself, my darling, would have trembled at the bare idea of marrying an actor.

"Have I been guilty of any serious deception? and have my friends been guilty in helping to keep my secret? My birth, my name, my surviving relatives, my fortune inherited from my father—all these important particulars have been truly stated. The name of Barrymore is nothing but the name that I assumed when I went on the stage.

"As to what has happened, since our return from Switzerland, I own that I ought to have made my confession to you. Forgive me if I weakly hesitated. I was so fond of you; and I so distrusted the Puritanical convictions which your education had rooted in your mind, that I put it off from day to day. Oh, my angel....!

"Yes, I kept the address of my new house a secret from all my friends, knowing they would betray me if they paid us visits. As for my mysteriously-closed study, it was the place in which I privately rehearsed my new part. When I left you in the mornings, it was to go to the theater rehearsals. My evening absences began of course with the first performance.

"Your father's arrival seriously embarrassed me. When you (most properly) insisted on my giving up some of my evenings to him, you necessarily made it impossible for me to appear on the stage. The one excuse I could make to the theater was, that I was too ill to act. It did certainly occur to me to cut the Gordian knot by owning the truth. But your father's horror, when you spoke of the newspaper review of the play, and the shame and fear you showed at your own boldness, daunted me once more.

"The arrival at the theater of my written excuse brought the manageress down upon me, in a state of distraction. Nobody could supply my place; all the seats were taken; and the Prince was expected. There was what we call a scene between the poor lady and myself. I felt I was in the wrong; I saw that the position in which I had impulsively placed myself was unworthy of me—and it ended in my doing my duty to the theater and the public. But for the affair of the bracelet, which obliged me as an honorable man to give my name and address, the manageress would not have discovered me. She, like every one else, only knew of my address at my bachelor chambers. How could you be jealous of the old theatrical comrade of my first days on the stage? Don't you know yet that you are the one woman in the world....?

"A last word relating to your father, and I have done.

"Do you remember my leaving you at the telegraph office? It was to send a message to a friend of mine, an architect in Edinburgh, instructing him to go immediately to Cauldkirk, and provide for the repairs at my expense. The theater, my dear, more than trebles my paternal income, and I can well afford it. Will your father refuse to accept a tribute of respect to a Scottish minister, because it is paid out of an actor's pocket? You shall ask him the question.

"And, I say, Felicia—will you come and see me act? I don't expect your father to enter a theater; but, by way of further reconciling him to his son-in-law, suppose you ask him to hear me read the play?"

MR. PERCY AND THE PROPHET.

PART 1.—THE PREDICTION.

CHAPTER I. THE QUACK.

THE disasters that follow the hateful offense against Christianity, which men call war, were severely felt in England during the peace that ensued on the overthrow of Napoleon at Waterloo. With rare exceptions, distress prevailed among all classes of the community. The starving nation was ripe and ready for a revolutionary rising against its rulers, who had shed the people's blood and wasted the people's substance in a war which had yielded to the popular interests absolutely nothing in return.

Among the unfortunate persons who were driven, during the disastrous early years of this century, to strange shifts and devices to obtain the means of living, was a certain obscure medical man, of French extraction, named Lagarde. The Doctor (duly qualified to bear the title) was an inhabitant of London; living in one of the narrow streets which connect the great thoroughfare of the Strand with the bank of the Thames.

The method of obtaining employment chosen by poor Lagarde, as the one alternative left in the face of starvation, was, and is still considered by the medical profession to be, the method of a quack. He advertised in the public journals.

Addressing himself especially to two classes of the community, the Doctor proceeded in these words:

"I have the honor of inviting to my house, in the first place: Persons afflicted with maladies which ordinary medical practice has failed to cure—

and, in the second place: Persons interested in investigations, the object of which is to penetrate the secrets of the future. Of the means by which I endeavor to alleviate suffering and to enlighten doubt, it is impossible to speak intelligibly within the limits of an advertisement. I can only offer to submit my system to public inquiry, without exacting any preliminary fee from ladies and gentlemen who may honor me with a visit. Those who see sufficient reason to trust me, after personal experience, will find a money-box fixed on the waiting-room table, into which they can drop their offerings according to their means. Those whom I am not fortunate enough to satisfy will be pleased to accept the expression of my regret, and will not be expected to give anything. I shall be found at home every evening between the hours of six and ten."

Toward the close of the year 1816 this strange advertisement became a general topic of conversation among educated people in London. For some weeks the Doctor's invitations were generally accepted—and, all things considered, were not badly remunerated. A faithful few believed in him, and told wonderful stories of what he had pronounced and prophesied in the sanctuary of his consulting-room. The majority of his visitors simply viewed him in the light of a public amusement, and wondered why such a gentlemanlike man should have chosen to gain his living by exhibiting himself as a quack.

CHAPTER II. THE NUMBERS.

ON a raw and snowy evening toward the latter part of January, 1817, a gentleman, walking along the Strand, turned into the street in which Doctor Lagarde lived, and knocked at the physician's door.

He was admitted by an elderly male servant to a waiting-room on the first floor. The light of one little lamp, placed on a bracket fixed to the wall, was so obscured by a dark green shade as to make it difficult, if not impossible, for visitors meeting by accident to recognize each other. The metal money-box fixed to the table was just visible. In the flickering light of a small fire, the stranger perceived the figures of three men seated, apart and silent, who were the only occupants of the room beside himself.

So far as objects were to be seen, there was nothing to attract attention in the waiting-room. The furniture was plain and neat, and nothing more. The elderly servant handed a card, with a number inscribed on it, to the new visitor, said in a whisper, "Your number will be called, sir, in your turn," and disappeared. For some minutes nothing disturbed the deep silence but the faint ticking of a clock. After a while a bell rang from an inner room, a door opened, and a gentleman appeared, whose interview with Doctor Lagarde had terminated. His opinion of the sitting was openly expressed in one emphatic word—"Humbug!" No contribution dropped from his hand as he passed the money-box on his way out.

The next number (being Number Fifteen) was called by the elderly servant, and the first incident occurred in the strange series of events destined to happen in the Doctor's house that night.

One after another the three men who had been waiting rose, examined their cards under the light of the lamp, and sat down again surprised and disappointed.

The servant advanced to investigate the matter. The numbers possessed by the three visitors, instead of being Fifteen, Sixteen and Seventeen, proved to be Sixteen, Seventeen and Eighteen. Turning to the stranger who had arrived the last, the servant said:

"Have I made a mistake, sir? Have I given you Number Fifteen instead of Number Eighteen?"

The gentleman produced his numbered card.

A mistake had certainly been made, but not the mistake that the servant supposed. The card held by the latest visitor turned out to be the card previously held by the dissatisfied stranger who had just left the room— Number Fourteen! As to the card numbered Fifteen, it was only discovered the next morning lying in a corner, dropped on the floor!

Acting on his first impulse, the servant hurried out, calling to the original holder of Fourteen to come back and bear his testimony to that fact. The street-door had been opened for him by the landlady of the house. She was a pretty woman—and the gentleman had fortunately lingered to talk to her.

He was induced, at the intercession of the landlady, to ascend the stairs again.

On returning to the waiting-room, he addressed a characteristic question to the assembled visitors. "More humbug?" asked the gentleman who liked to talk to a pretty woman.

The servant—completely puzzled by his own stupidity—attempted to make his apologies.

"Pray forgive me, gentlemen," he said. "I am afraid I have confused the cards I distribute with the cards returned to me. I think I had better consult my master."

Left by themselves, the visitors began to speak jestingly of the strange situation in which they were placed. The original holder of Number Fourteen described his experience of the Doctor in his own pithy way. "I applied to the fellow to tell my fortune. He first went to sleep over it, and then he said he could tell me nothing. I asked why. 'I don't know,' says he. ' I do,' says I—'humbug!' I'll bet you the long odds, gentlemen, that you find it humbug, too."

Before the wager could be accepted or declined, the door of the inner room was opened again. The tall, spare, black figure of a new personage appeared on the threshold, relieved darkly against the light in the room behind him. He addressed the visitors in these words:

"Gentlemen, I must beg your indulgence. The accident—as we now suppose it to be—which has given to the last comer the number already held by a gentleman who has unsuccessfully consulted me, may have a meaning which we can none of us at present see. If the three visitors who have been so good as to wait will allow the present holder of Number Fourteen to consult me out of his turn—and if the earlier visitor who left me dissatisfied with his consultation will consent to stay here a little longer—something may happen which will justify a trifling sacrifice of your own convenience. Is ten minutes' patience too much to ask of you?"

The three visitors who had waited longest consulted among themselves, and (having nothing better to do with their time) decided on accepting the

Doctor's proposal. The visitor who believed it all to be "humbug" coolly took a gold coin out of his pocket, tossed it into the air, caught it in his closed hand, and walked up to the shaded lamp on the bracket.

"Heads, stay," he said, "Tails, go." He opened his hand, and looked at the coin. "Heads! Very good. Go on with your hocus-pocus, Doctor—I'll wait."

"You believe in chance," said the Doctor, quietly observing him. "That is not my experience of life."

He paused to let the stranger who now held Number Fourteen pass him into the inner room—then followed, closing the door behind him.

CHAPTER III. THE CONSULTATION.

THE consulting-room was better lighted than the waiting-room, and that was the only difference between the two. In the one, as in the other, no attempt was made to impress the imagination. Everywhere, the commonplace furniture of a London lodging-house was left without the slightest effort to alter or improve it by changes of any kind.

Seen under the clearer light, Doctor Lagarde appeared to be the last person living who would consent to degrade himself by an attempt at imposture of any kind. His eyes were the dreamy eyes of a visionary; his look was the prematurely-aged look of a student, accustomed to give the hours to his book which ought to have been given to his bed. To state it briefly, he was a man who might easily be deceived by others, but who was incapable of consciously practicing deception himself.

Signing to his visitor to be seated, he took a chair on the opposite side of the small table that stood between them—waited a moment with his face hidden in his hands, as if to collect himself—and then spoke.

"Do you come to consult me on a case of illness?" he inquired, "or do you ask me to look to the darkness which hides your future life?"

The answer to these questions was frankly and briefly expressed. "I have no need to consult you about my health. I come to hear what you can tell me of my future life."

"I can try," pursued the Doctor; "but I cannot promise to succeed."

"I accept your conditions," the stranger rejoined. "I never believe nor disbelieve. If you will excuse my speaking frankly, I mean to observe you closely, and to decide for myself."

Doctor Lagarde smiled sadly.

"You have heard of me as a charlatan who contrives to amuse a few idle people," he said. "I don't complain of that; my present position leads necessarily to misinterpretation of myself and my motives. Still, I may at least say that I am the victim of a sincere avowal of my belief in a great science. Yes! I repeat it, a great science! New, I dare say, to the generation we live in, though it was known and practiced in the days when pyramids were built. The age is advancing; and the truths which it is my misfortune to advocate, before the time is ripe for them, are steadily forcing their way to recognition. I am resigned to wait. My sincerity in this matter has cost me the income that I derived from my medical practice. Patients distrust me; doctors refuse to consult with me. I could starve if I had no one to think of but myself. But I have another person to consider, who is very dear to me; and I am driven, literally driven, either to turn beggar in the streets, or do what I am doing now."

He paused, and looked round toward the corner of the room behind him. "Mother," he said gently, "are you ready?"

An elderly lady, dressed in deep mourning, rose from her seat in the corner. She had been, thus far, hidden from notice by the high back of the easy-chair in which her son sat. Excepting some folds of fine black lace, laid over her white hair so as to form a head-dress at once simple and picturesque, there was nothing remarkable in her attire. The visitor rose and bowed. She gravely returned his salute, and moved so as to place herself opposite to her son.

"May I ask what this lady is going to do?" said the stranger.

"To be of any use to you," answered Doctor Lagarde, "I must be thrown into the magnetic trance. The person who has the strongest influence over me is the person who will do it to-night."

He turned to his mother. "When you like," he said.

Bending over him, she took both the Doctor's hands, and looked steadily into his eyes. No words passed between them; nothing more took place. In a minute or two, his head was resting against the back of the chair, and his eyelids had closed.

"Are you sleeping?" asked Madame Lagarde.

"I am sleeping," he answered.

She laid his hands gently on the arms of the chair, and turned to address the visitor.

"Let the sleep gain on him for a minute or two more," she said. "Then take one of his hands, and put to him what questions you please."

"Does he hear us now, madam?"

"You might fire off a pistol, sir, close to his ear, and he would not hear it. The vibration might disturb him; that is all. Until you or I touch him, and so establish the nervous sympathy, he is as lost to all sense of our presence here, as if he were dead."

"Are you speaking of the thing called Animal Magnetism, madam?"

"Yes, sir."

"And you believe in it, of course?"

"My son's belief, sir, is my belief in this thing as in other things. I have heard what he has been saying to you. It is for me that he sacrifices himself by holding these exhibitions; it is in my poor interests that his hardly-earned money is made. I am in infirm health; and, remonstrate as I may, my son persists in providing for me, not the bare comforts only, but even the luxuries of life. Whatever I may suffer, I have my compensation; I can still thank God for giving me the greatest happiness that a woman can enjoy, the possession of a good son."

She smiled fondly as she looked at the sleeping man. "Draw your chair nearer to him," she resumed, "and take his hand. You may speak freely in making your inquiries. Nothing that happens in this room goes out of it."

With those words she returned to her place, in the corner behind her son's chair.

The visitor took Doctor Lagarde's hand. As they touched each other, he was conscious of a faintly-titillating sensation in his own hand—a sensation which oddly reminded him of bygone experiments with an electrical machine, in the days when he was a boy at school!

"I wish to question you about my future life," he began. "How ought I to begin?"

The Doctor spoke his first words in the monotonous tones of a man talking in his sleep.

"Own your true motive before you begin," he said. "Your interest in your future life is centered in a woman. You wish to know if her heart will be yours in the time that is to come—and there your interest in your future life ends."

This startling proof of the sleeper's capacity to look, by sympathy, into his mind, and to see there his most secret thoughts, instead of convincing the stranger, excited his suspicions. "You have means of getting information," he said, "that I don't understand."

The Doctor smiled, as if the idea amused him.

Madame Lagarde rose from her seat and interposed.

"Hundreds of strangers come here to consult my son," she said quietly. "If you believe that we know who those strangers are, and that we have the means of inquiring into their private lives before they enter this room, you believe in something much more incredible than the magnetic sleep!"

This was too manifestly true to be disputed. The visitor made his apologies.

"I should like to have some explanation," he added. "The thing is so very extraordinary. How can I prevail upon Doctor Lagarde to enlighten me?"

"He can only tell you what he sees," Madame Lagarde answered; "ask him that, and you will get a direct reply. Say to him: 'Do you see the lady?'"

The stranger repeated the question. The reply followed at once, in these words:

"I see two figures standing side by side. One of them is your figure. The other is the figure of a lady. She only appears dimly. I can discover nothing but that she is taller than women generally are, and that she is dressed in pale blue."

The man to whom he was speaking started at those last words. "Her favorite color!" he thought to himself—forgetting that, while he held the Doctor's hand, the Doctor could think with his mind.

"Yes," added the sleeper quietly, "her favorite color, as you know. She fades and fades as I look at her," he went on. "She is gone. I only see you, under a new aspect. You have a pistol in your hand. Opposite to you, there stands the figure of another man. He, too, has a pistol in his hand. Are you enemies? Are you meeting to fight a duel? Is the lady the cause? I try, but I fail to see her."

"Can you describe the man?"

"Not yet. So far, he is only a shadow in the form of a man."

There was another interval. An appearance of disturbance showed itself on the sleeper's face. Suddenly, he waved his free hand in the direction of the waiting-room.

"Send for the visitors who are there," he said. "They are all to come in. Each one of them is to take one of my hands in turn—while you remain where you are, holding the other hand. Don't let go of me, even for a moment. My mother will ring."

Madame Lagarde touched a bell on the table. The servant received his orders from her and retired. After a short absence, he appeared again in the consulting-room, with one visitor only waiting on the threshold behind him.

CHAPTER IV. THE MAN.

"The other three gentlemen have gone away, madam," the servant explained, addressing Madame Lagarde. "They were tired of waiting. I found this gentleman fast asleep; and I am afraid he is angry with me for taking the liberty of waking him."

"Sleep of the common sort is evidently not allowed in this house." With that remark the gentleman entered the room, and stood revealed as the original owner of the card numbered Fourteen.

Viewed by the clear lamplight, he was a tall, finely-made man, in the prime of life, with a florid complexion, golden-brown hair, and sparkling blue eyes. Noticing Madame Lagarde, he instantly checked the flow of his satire, with the instinctive good-breeding of a gentleman. "I beg your pardon," he said; "I have a great many faults, and a habit of making bad jokes is one of them. Is the servant right, madam, in telling me that I have the honor of presenting myself here at your request?"

Madame Lagarde briefly explained what had passed.

The florid gentleman (still privately believing it to be all "humbug") was delighted to make himself of any use. "I congratulate you, sir," he said, with his easy humor, as he passed the visitor who had become possessed of his card. "Number Fourteen seems to be a luckier number in your keeping than it was in mine."

As he spoke, he took Doctor Lagarde's disengaged hand. The instant they touched each other the sleeper started. His voice rose; his face flushed. "You are the man!" he exclaimed. "I see you plainly now!"

"What am I doing?"

"You are standing opposite to the gentleman here who is holding my other hand; and (as I have said already) you have met to fight a duel."

The unbeliever cast a shrewd look at his companion in the consultation.

"Considering that you and I are total strangers, sir," he said, "don't you think the Doctor had better introduce us, before he goes any further? We have got to fighting a duel already, and we may as well know who we are, before the pistols go off." He turned to Doctor Lagarde. "Dramatic situations don't amuse me out of the theater," he resumed. "Let me put you to a very commonplace test. I want to be introduced to this gentleman. Has he told you his name?"

"No."

"Of course, you know it, without being told?"

"Certainly. I have only to look into your own knowledge of yourselves, while I am in this trance, and while you have got my hands, to know both your names as well as you do."

"Introduce us, then!" retorted the jesting gentleman. "And take my name first."

"Mr. Percy Linwood," replied the Doctor; "I have the honor of presenting you to Captain Bervie, of the Artillery."

With one accord, the gentlemen both dropped Doctor Lagarde's hands, and looked at each other in blank amazement.

"Of course he has discovered our names somehow!" said Mr. Percy Linwood, explaining the mystery to his own perfect satisfaction in that way.

Captain Bervie had not forgotten what Madame Lagarde had said to him, when he too had suspected a trick. He now repeated it (quite ineffectually) for Mr. Linwood's benefit. "If you don't feel the force of that argument as I feel it," he added, "perhaps, as a favor to me, sir, you will not object to our each taking the Doctor's hand again, and hearing what more he can tell us while he remains in the state of trance?"

"With the greatest pleasure!" answered good-humored Mr. Linwood. "Our friend is beginning to amuse me; I am as anxious as you are to know what he is going to see next."

Captain Bervie put the next question.

"You have seen us ready to fight a duel—can you tell us the result?"

"I can tell you nothing more than I have told you already. The figures of the duelists have faded away, like the other figures I saw before them. What I see now looks like the winding gravel-path of a garden. A man and a woman are walking toward me. The man stops, and places a ring on the woman's finger, and kisses her."

Captain Bervie opened his lips to continue his inquiries—turned pale—and checked himself. Mr. Linwood put the next question.

"Who is the happy man?" he asked.

"You are the happy man," was the instantaneous reply.

"Who is the woman?" cried Captain Bervie, before Mr. Linwood could speak again.

"The same woman whom I saw before; dressed in the same color, in pale blue."

Captain Bervie positively insisted on receiving clearer information than this. "Surely you can see something of her personal appearance?" he said.

"I can see that she has long dark-brown hair, falling below her waist. I can see that she has lovely dark-brown eyes. She has the look of a sensitive nervous person. She is quite young. I can see no more."

"Look again at the man who is putting the ring on her finger," said the Captain. "Are you sure that the face you see is the face of Mr. Percy Linwood?"

"I am absolutely sure."

Captain Bervie rose from his chair.

"Thank you, madam," he said to the Doctor's mother. "I have heard enough."

664

He walked to the door. Mr. Percy Linwood dropped Doctor Lagarde's hand, and appealed to the retiring Captain with a broad stare of astonishment.

"You don't really believe this?" he said.

"I only say I have heard enough," Captain Bervie answered.

Mr. Linwood could hardly fail to see that any further attempt to treat the matter lightly might lead to undesirable results.

"It is difficult to speak seriously of this kind of exhibition," he resumed quietly. "But I suppose I may mention a mere matter of fact, without meaning or giving offense. The description of the lady, I can positively declare, does not apply in any single particular to any one whom I know."

Captain Bervie turned round at the door. His patience was in some danger of failing him. Mr. Linwood's unruffled composure, assisted in its influence by the presence of Madame Lagarde, reminded him of the claims of politeness. He restrained the rash words as they rose to his lips. "You may make new acquaintances, sir," was all that he said. "You have the future before you."

Upon that, he went out. Percy Linwood waited a little, reflecting on the Captain's conduct.

Had Doctor Lagarde's description of the lady accidentally answered the description of a living lady whom Captain Bervie knew? Was he by any chance in love with her? and had the Doctor innocently reminded him that his love was not returned? Assuming this to be likely, was it really possible that he believed in prophetic revelations offered to him under the fantastic influence of a trance? Could any man in the possession of his senses go to those lengths? The Captain's conduct was simply incomprehensible.

Pondering these questions, Percy decided on returning to his place by the Doctor's chair. "Of one thing I am certain, at any rate," he thought to himself. "I'll see the whole imposture out before I leave the house!"

He took Doctor Lagarde's hand. "Now, then! what is the next discovery?" he asked.

The sleeper seemed to find some difficulty in answering the question.

"I indistinctly see the man and the woman again," he said.

"Am I the man still?" Percy inquired.

"No. The man, this time, is the Captain. The woman is agitated by something that he is saying to her. He seems to be trying to persuade her to go away with him. She hesitates. He whispers something in her ear. She yields. He leads her away. The darkness gathers behind them. I look and look, and I can see no more."

"Shall we wait awhile?" Percy suggested, "and then try again?"

Doctor Lagarde sighed, and reclined in his chair. "My head is heavy," he said; "my spirits are dull. The darkness baffles me. I have toiled long enough for you. Drop my hand and leave me to rest."

Hearing those words, Madame Lagarde approached her son's chair.

"It will be useless, sir, to ask him any more questions to-night," she said. "He has been weak and nervous all day, and he is worn out by the effort he has made. Pardon me, if I ask you to step aside for a moment, while I give him the repose that he needs."

She laid her right hand gently on the Doctor's head, and kept it there for a minute or so. "Are you at rest now?" she asked.

"I am at rest," he answered, in faint, drowsy tones.

Madame Lagarde returned to Percy. "If you are not yet satisfied," she said, "my son will be at your service to-morrow evening, sir."

"Thank you, madam, I have only one more question to ask, and you can no doubt answer it. When your son wakes, will he remember what he has said to Captain Bervie and to myself?"

"My son will be as absolutely ignorant of everything that he has seen, and of everything that he has said in the trance, as if he had been at the other end of the world."

Percy Linwood swallowed this last outrageous assertion with an effort which he was quite unable to conceal. "Many thanks, madam," he said; "I wish you good-night."

Returning to the waiting-room, he noticed the money-box fixed to the table. "These people look poor," he thought to himself, "and I feel really indebted to them for an amusing evening. Besides, I can afford to be liberal, for I shall certainly never go back." He dropped a five-pound note into the money-box, and left the house.

Walking toward his club, Percy's natural serenity of mind was a little troubled by the remembrance of Captain Bervie's language and conduct. The Captain had interested the young man in spite of himself. His first idea was to write to Bervie, and mention what had happened at the renewed consultation with Doctor Lagarde. On second thoughts, he saw reason to doubt how the Captain might receive such an advance as this, on the part of a stranger. "After all," Percy decided, "the whole thing is too absurd to be worth thinking about seriously. Neither he nor I are likely to meet again, or to see the Doctor again—and there's an end of it."

He never was more mistaken in his life. The end of it was not to come for many a long day yet.

PART II.—THE FULFILLMENT.

CHAPTER V. THE BALLROOM.

WHILE the consultation at Doctor Lagarde's was still fresh in the memory of the persons present at it, Chance or Destiny, occupied in sowing the seeds for the harvest of the future, discovered as one of its fit instruments a retired military officer named Major Mulvany.

The Major was a smart little man, who persisted in setting up the appearance of youth as a means of hiding the reality of fifty. Being still a bachelor, and being always ready to make himself agreeable, he was generally popular in the society of women. In the ballroom he was a really welcome addition to the company. The German waltz had then been imported into England little more than three years since. The outcry raised against the dance, by persons skilled in the discovery of latent impropriety, had not yet lost its influence in certain quarters. Men who could waltz were scarce. The Major had successfully grappled with the difficulties of learning the dance in mature life; and the young ladies rewarded him nobly for the effort. That is to say, they took the assumption of youth for granted in the palpable presence of fifty.

Knowing everybody and being welcome everywhere, playing a good hand at whist, and having an inexhaustible fancy in the invention of a dinner, Major Mulvany naturally belonged to all the best clubs of his time. Percy Linwood and he constantly met in the billiard-room or at the dinner-table. The Major approved of the easy, handsome, pleasant-tempered young man. "I have lost the first freshness of youth," he used to say, with pathetic resignation, "and I see myself revived, as it were, in Percy. Naturally I like Percy."

About three weeks after the memorable evening at Doctor Lagarde's, the two friends encountered each other on the steps of a club.

"Have you got anything to do to-night?" asked the Major.

"Nothing that I know of," said Percy, "unless I go to the theater."

"Let the theater wait, my boy. My old regiment gives a ball at Woolwich to-night. I have got a ticket to spare; and I know several sweet girls who are going. Some of them waltz, Percy! Gather your rosebuds while you may. Come with me."

The invitation was accepted as readily as it was given. The Major found the carriage, and Percy paid for the post-horses. They entered the ballroom among the earlier guests; and the first person whom they met, waiting near the door, was—Captain Bervie.

Percy bowed a little uneasily. "I feel some doubt," he said, laughing, "whether we have been properly introduced to one another or not."

"Not properly introduced!" cried Major Mulvany. "I'll soon set that right. My dear friend, Percy Linwood; my dear friend, Arthur Bervie—be known to each other! esteem each other!"

Captain Bervie acknowledged the introduction by a cold salute. Percy, yielding to the good-natured impulse of the moment, alluded to what had happened in Doctor Lagarde's consulting-room.

"You missed something worth hearing when you left the Doctor the other night," he said. "We continued the sitting; and you turned up again among the persons of the drama, in a new character—"

"Excuse me for interrupting you," said Captain Bervie. "I am a member of the committee, charged with the arrangements of the ball, and I must really attend to my duties."

He withdrew without waiting for a reply. Percy looked round wonderingly at Major Mulvany. "Strange!" he said, "I feel rather attracted toward Captain Bervie; and he seems to have taken such a dislike to me that he can hardly behave with common civility. What does it mean?"

"I'll tell you," answered the Major, confidentially. "Arthur Bervie is madly in love—madly is really the word—with a Miss Bowmore. And (this is between ourselves) the young lady doesn't feel it quite in the same way. A sweet girl; I've often had her on my knee when she was a child. Her father and mother are old friends of mine. She is coming to the ball to-night. That's the true reason why Arthur left you just now. Look at him—waiting to be the first to speak to her. If he could have his way, he wouldn't let another man come near the poor girl all through the evening; he really persecutes her. I'll introduce you to Miss Bowmore; and you will see how he looks at us for presuming to approach her. It's a great pity; she will never marry him. Arthur Bervie is a man in a thousand; but he's fast becoming a perfect bear under the strain on his temper. What's the matter? You don't seem to be listening to me."

This last remark was perfectly justified. In telling the Captain's love-story, Major Mulvany had revived his young friend's memory of the lady in the blue dress, who had haunted the visions of Doctor Lagarde.

"Tell me," said Percy, "what is Miss Bowmore like? Is there anything remarkable in her personal appearance? I have a reason for asking."

As he spoke, there arose among the guests in the rapidly-filling ballroom a low murmur of surprise and admiration. The Major laid one hand on Percy's shoulder, and, lifting the other, pointed to the door.

"What is Miss Bowmore like?" he repeated. "There she is! Let her answer for herself."

Percy turned toward the lower end of the room.

A young lady was entering, dressed in plain silk, and the color of it was a pale blue! Excepting a white rose at her breast, she wore no ornament of any sort. Doubly distinguished by the perfect simplicity of her apparel, and by her tall, supple, commanding figure, she took rank at once as the most remarkable woman in the room. Moving nearer to her through the crowd, under the guidance of the complaisant Major, young Linwood gained a clearer view of her hair, her complexion, and the color of her eyes. In every one of these particulars she was the living image of the woman described by

Doctor Lagarde!

While Percy was absorbed over this strange discovery, Major Mulvany had got within speaking distance of the young lady and of her mother, as they stood together in conversation with Captain Bervie. "My dear Mrs. Bowmore, how well you are looking! My dear Miss Charlotte, what a sensation you have made already! The glorious simplicity (if I may so express myself) of your dress is—is—what was I going to say?—the ideas come thronging on me; I merely want words."

Miss Bowmore's magnificent brown eyes, wandering from the Major to Percy, rested on the young man with a modest and momentary interest, which Captain Bervie's jealous attention instantly detected.

"They are forming a dance," he said, pressing forward impatiently to claim his partner. "If we don't take our places we shall be too late."

"Stop! stop!" cried the Major. "There is a time for everything, and this is the time for presenting my dear friend here, Mr. Percy Linwood. He is like me, Miss Charlotte—he has been struck by your glorious simplicity, and he wants words." At this part of the presentation, he happened to look toward the irate Captain, and instantly gave him a hint on the subject of his temper. "I say, Arthur Bervie! we are all good-humored people here. What have you got on your eyebrows? It looks like a frown; and it doesn't become you. Send for a skilled waiter, and have it brushed off and taken away directly!"

"May I ask, Miss Bowmore, if you are disengaged for the next dance?" said Percy, the moment the Major gave him an opportunity of speaking.

"Miss Bowmore is engaged to me for the next dance," said the angry Captain, before the young lady could answer.

"The third dance, then?" Percy persisted, with his brightest smile.

"With pleasure, Mr. Linwood," said Miss Bowmore. She would have been no true woman if she had not resented the open exhibition of Arthur's jealousy; it was like asserting a right over her to which he had not the shadow of a claim. She threw a look at Percy as her partner led her away, which was the severest punishment she could inflict on the man who ardently loved her.

The third dance stood in the programme as a waltz.

In jealous distrust of Percy, the Captain took the conductor of the band aside, and used his authority as committeeman to substitute another dance. He had no sooner turned his back on the orchestra than the wife of the Colonel of the regiment, who had heard him, spoke to the conductor in her turn, and insisted on the original programme being retained. "Quote the Colonel's authority," said the lady, "if Captain Bervie ventures to object." In the meantime, the Captain, on his way to rejoin Charlotte, was met by one of his brother officers, who summoned him officially to an impending debate of the committee charged with the administrative arrangements of the supper-table. Bervie had no choice but to follow his brother officer to the committee-room.

Barely a minute later the conductor appeared at his desk, and the first notes of the music rose low and plaintive, introducing the third dance.

"Percy, my boy!" cried the Major, recognizing the melody, "you're in luck's way—it's going to be a waltz!"

Almost as he spoke, the notes of the symphony glided by subtle modulations into the inspiriting air of the waltz. Percy claimed his partner's hand. Miss Charlotte hesitated, and looked at her mother.

"Surely you waltz?" said Percy.

"I have learned to waltz," she answered, modestly; "but this is such a large room, and there are so many people!"

"Once round," Percy pleaded; "only once round!"

Miss Bowmore looked again at her mother. Her foot was keeping time with the music, under her dress; her heart was beating with a delicious excitement; kind-hearted Mrs. Bowmore smiled and said: "Once round, my dear, as Mr. Linwood suggests."

In another moment Percy's arm took possession of her waist, and they were away on the wings of the waltz!

Could words describe, could thought realize, the exquisite enjoyment of the dance? Enjoyment? It was more—it was an epoch in Charlotte's life—it was the first time she had waltzed with a man. What a difference between the fervent clasp of Percy's arm and the cold, formal contact of the mistress who had taught her! How brightly his eyes looked down into hers; admiring her with such a tender restraint, that there could surely be no harm in looking up at him now and then in return. Round and round they glided, absorbed in the music and in themselves. Occasionally her bosom just touched him, at those critical moments when she was most in need of support. At other intervals, she almost let her head sink on his shoulder in trying to hide from him the smile which acknowledged his admiration too boldly. "Once round," Percy had suggested; "once round," her mother had said. They had been ten, twenty, thirty times round; they had never stopped to rest like other dancers; they had centered the eyes of the whole room on them—including the eyes of Captain Bervie—without knowing it; her delicately pale complexion had changed to rosy-red; the neat arrangement of her hair had become disturbed; her bosom was rising and falling faster and faster in the effort to breathe— before fatigue and heat overpowered her at last, and forced her to say to him faintly, "I'm very sorry—I can't dance any more!"

Percy led her into the cooler atmosphere of the refreshment-room, and revived her with a glass of lemonade. Her arm still rested on his—she was just about to thank him for the care he had taken of her—when Captain Bervie entered the room.

"Mrs. Bowmore wishes me to take you back to her," he said to Charlotte. Then, turning to Percy, he added: "Will you kindly wait here while I take Miss Bowmore to the ballroom? I have a word to say to you—I will return directly."

The Captain spoke with perfect politeness—but his face betrayed him. It was pale with the sinister whiteness of suppressed rage.

Percy sat down to cool and rest himself. With his experience of the ways of men, he felt no surprise at the marked contrast between Captain

Bervie's face and Captain Bervie's manner. "He has seen us waltzing, and he is coming back to pick a quarrel with me." Such was the interpretation which Mr. Linwood's knowledge of the world placed on Captain Bervie's politeness. In a minute or two more the Captain returned to the refreshment-room, and satisfied Percy that his anticipations had not deceived him.

CHAPTER VI. LOVE.

FOUR days had passed since the night of the ball.

Although it was no later in the year than the month of February, the sun was shining brightly, and the air was as soft as the air of a day in spring. Percy and Charlotte were walking together in the little garden at the back of Mr. Bowmore's cottage, near the town of Dartford, in Kent.

"Mr. Linwood," said the young lady, "you were to have paid us your first visit the day after the ball. Why have you kept us waiting? Have you been too busy to remember your new friends?"

"I have counted the hours since we parted, Miss Charlotte. If I had not been detained by business—"

"I understand! For three days business has controlled you. On the fourth day, you have controlled business—and here you are? I don't believe one word of it, Mr. Linwood!"

There was no answering such a declaration as this. Guiltily conscious that Charlotte was right in refusing to accept his well-worn excuse, Percy made an awkward attempt to change the topic of conversation.

They happened, at the moment, to be standing near a small conservatory at the end of the garden. The glass door was closed, and the few plants and shrubs inside had a lonely, neglected look. "Does nobody ever visit this secluded place?" Percy asked, jocosely, "or does it hide discoveries in the rearing of plants which are forbidden mysteries to a stranger?"

"Satisfy your curiosity, Mr. Linwood, by all means," Charlotte answered in the same tone. "Open the door, and I will follow you."

Percy obeyed. In passing through the doorway, he encountered the bare

674

hanging branches of some creeping plant, long since dead, and detached from its fastenings on the woodwork of the roof. He pushed aside the branches so that Charlotte could easily follow him in, without being aware that his own forced passage through them had a little deranged the folds of spotless white cambric which a well-dressed gentleman wore round his neck in those days. Charlotte seated herself, and directed Percy's attention to the desolate conservatory with a saucy smile.

"The mystery which your lively imagination has associated with this place," she said, "means, being interpreted, that we are too poor to keep a gardener. Make the best of your disappointment, Mr. Linwood, and sit here by me. We are out of hearing and out of sight of mamma's other visitors. You have no excuse now for not telling me what has really kept you away from us."

She fixed her eyes on him as she said those words. Before Percy could think of another excuse, her quick observation detected the disordered condition of his cravat, and discovered the upper edge of a black plaster attached to one side of his neck.

"You have been hurt in the neck!" she said. "That is why you have kept away from us for the last three days!"

"A mere trifle," he answered, in great confusion; "please don't notice it."

Her eyes, still resting on his face, assumed an expression of suspicious inquiry, which Percy was entirely at a loss to understand. Suddenly, she started to her feet, as if a new idea had occurred to her. "Wait here," she said, flushing with excitement, "till I come back: I insist on it!"

Before Percy could ask for an explanation she had left the conservatory.

In a minute or two, Miss Bowmore returned, with a newspaper in her hand. "Read that," she said, pointing to a paragraph distinguished by a line drawn round it in ink.

The passage that she indicated contained an account of a duel which had recently taken place in the neighborhood of London. The names of the duelists were not mentioned. One was described as an officer, and the other as a civilian. They had quarreled at cards, and had fought with pistols. The civilian had had a narrow escape of his life. His antagonist's bullet had passed near enough to the side of his neck to tear the flesh, and had missed the vital parts, literally, by a hair's-breadth.

Charlotte's eyes, riveted on Percy, detected a sudden change of color in his face the moment he looked at the newspaper. That was enough for her. "You are the man!" she cried. "Oh, for shame, for shame! To risk your life for a paltry dispute about cards!"

"I would risk it again," said Percy, "to hear you speak as if you set some value on it."

She looked away from him without a word of reply. Her mind seemed to be busy again with its own thoughts. Did she meditate returning to the subject of the duel? Was she not satisfied with the discovery which she had just made?

No such doubts as these troubled the mind of Percy Linwood. Intoxicated by the charm of her presence, emboldened by her innocent betrayal of the interest that she felt in him, he opened his whole heart to her as unreservedly as if they had known each other from the days of their childhood. There was but one excuse for him. Charlotte was his first love.

"You don't know how completely you have become a part of my life, since we met at the ball," he went on. "That one delightful dance seemed, by some magic which I can't explain, to draw us together in a few minutes as if we had known each other for years. Oh, dear! I could make such a confession of what I felt—only I am afraid of offending you by speaking too soon. Women are so dreadfully difficult to understand. How is a man to know at what time it is considerate toward them to conceal his true feelings; and at what time it is equally considerate to express his true feelings? One doesn't know whether it is a matter of days or weeks or months—there ought to be a law to settle it. Dear Miss Charlotte, when a poor fellow loves you at first sight, as he has never loved any other woman, and when he is tormented by the fear that some other man may be preferred to him, can't you forgive him if he lets out the truth a little too soon?" He ventured, as he put that very downright question, to take her hand. "It really isn't my fault," he said, simply. "My heart is so full of you I can talk of nothing else."

To Percy's delight, the first experimental pressure of his hand, far from being resented, was softly returned. Charlotte looked at him again, with a new resolution in her face.

"I'll forgive you for talking nonsense, Mr. Linwood," she said; "and I will even permit you to come and see me again, on one condition—that you tell the whole truth about the duel. If you conceal the smallest circumstance, our acquaintance is at an end."

"Haven't I owned everything already?" Percy inquired, in great perplexity. "Did I say No, when you told me I was the man?"

"Could you say No, with that plaster on your neck?" was the ready rejoinder. "I am determined to know more than the newspaper tells me. Will you declare, on your word of honor, that Captain Bervie had nothing to do with the duel? Can you look me in the face, and say that the real cause of the quarrel was a disagreement at cards? When you were talking with me just before I left the ball, how did you answer a gentleman who asked you to make one at the whist-table? You said, 'I don't play at cards.' Ah! You thought I had forgotten that? Don't kiss my hand! Trust me with the whole truth, or say good-by forever."

"Only tell me what you wish to know, Miss Charlotte," said Percy humbly. "If you will put the questions, I will give the answers—as well as I can."

On this understanding, Percy's evidence was extracted from him as follows:

"Was it Captain Bervie who quarreled with you?"

"Yes."

"Was it about me?"

"Yes."

"What did he say?"

"He said I had committed an impropriety in waltzing with you."

"Why?"

"Because your parents disapproved of your waltzing in a public ballroom."

"That's not true! What did he say next?"

"He said I had added tenfold to my offense, by waltzing with you in such a manner as to make you the subject of remark to the whole room."

"Oh! did you let him say that?"

"No; I contradicted him instantly. And I said, besides, 'It's an insult to Miss Bowmore, to suppose that she would permit any impropriety.'"

"Quite right! And what did he say?"

"Well, he lost his temper; I would rather not repeat what he said when he was mad with jealousy. There was nothing to be done with him but to give him his way."

"Give him his way? Does that mean fight a duel with him?"

"Don't be angry—it does."

"And you kept my name out of it, by pretending to quarrel at the card-table?"

"Yes. We managed it when the cardroom was emptying at supper-time, and nobody was present but Major Mulvany and another friend as witnesses."

"And when did you fight the duel?"

"The next morning."

"You never thought of me, I suppose?"

"Indeed, I did; I was very glad that you had no suspicion of what we were at."

"Was that all?"

"No; I had your flower with me, the flower you gave me out of your nosegay, at the ball."

"Well?"

"Oh, never mind, it doesn't matter."

"It does matter. What did you do with my flower?"

"I gave it a sly kiss while they were measuring the ground; and (don't tell anybody!) I put it next to my heart to bring me luck."

"Was that just before he shot at you?"

"Yes."

"How did he shoot?"

"He walked (as the seconds had arranged it) ten paces forward; and then he stopped, and lifted his pistol—"

"Don't tell me any more! Oh, to think of my being the miserable cause of such horrors! I'll never dance again as long as I live. Did you think he had killed you, when the bullet wounded your poor neck?"

"No; I hardly felt it at first."

"Hardly felt it? How he talks! And when the wretch had done his best to kill you, and when it came to your turn, what did you do?"

"Nothing."

"What! You didn't walk your ten paces forward?"

"No."

"And you never shot at him in return?"

"No; I had no quarrel with him, poor fellow; I just stood where I was, and fired in the air—"

Before he could stop her, Charlotte seized his hand, and kissed it with an hysterical fervor of admiration, which completely deprived him of his presence of mind.

"Why shouldn't I kiss the hand of a hero?" she cried, with tears of enthusiasm sparkling in her eyes. "Nobody but a hero would have given that man his life; nobody but a hero would have pardoned him, while the blood was streaming from the wound that he had inflicted. I respect you, I admire you. Oh, don't think me bold! I can't control myself when I hear of anything noble and good. You will understand me better when we get to be old friends—won't you?"

She spoke in low sweet tones of entreaty. Percy's arm stole softly round her.

"Are we never to be nearer and dearer to each other than old friends?" he asked in a whisper. "I am not a hero—your goodness overrates me, dear Miss Charlotte. My one ambition is to be the happy man who is worthy enough to win you. At your own time! I wouldn't distress you, I wouldn't confuse you, I wouldn't for the whole world take advantage of the compliment which your sympathy has paid to me. If it offends you, I won't even ask if I may hope."

She sighed as he said the last words; trembled a little, and silently looked at him.

Percy read his answer in her eyes. Without meaning it on either side their heads drew nearer together; their cheeks, then their lips, touched. She started back from him, and rose to leave the conservatory. At the same moment, the sound of slowly-approaching footsteps became audible on the gravel walk of the garden. Charlotte hurried to the door.

"My father!" she exclaimed, turning to Percy. "Come, and be introduced to him."

Percy followed her into the garden.

CHAPTER VII. POLITICS.

JUDGING by appearances, Mr. Bowmore looked like a man prematurely wasted and worn by the cares of a troubled life. His eyes presented the one feature in which his daughter resembled him. In shape and color they were exactly reproduced in Charlotte; the difference was in the expression. The father's look was habitually restless, eager, and suspicious. Not a trace was to be seen in it of the truthfulness and gentleness which made the charm of the daughter's expression. A man whose bitter experience of the world had soured his temper and shaken his faith in his fellow-creatures—such was Mr. Bowmore as he presented himself on the surface. He received Percy politely—but with a preoccupied air. Every now and then, his restless eyes wandered from the visitor to an open letter in his hand. Charlotte, observing him, pointed to the letter.

"Have you any bad news there, papa?" she asked.

"Dreadful news!" Mr. Bowmore answered. "Dreadful news, my child, to every Englishman who respects the liberties which his ancestors won. My correspondent is a man who is in the confidence of the Ministers," he continued, addressing Percy. "What do you think is the remedy that the Government proposes for the universal distress among the population, caused by an infamous and needless war? Despotism, Mr. Linwood; despotism in this free country is the remedy! In one week more, sir, Ministers will bring in a Bill for suspending the Habeas Corpus Act!"

Before Percy could do justice in words to the impression produced on him, Charlotte innocently asked a question which shocked her father.

"What is the Habeas Corpus Act, papa?"

"Good God!" cried Mr. Bowmore, "is it possible that a child of mine has grown up to womanhood, in ignorance of the palladium of English liberty? Oh, Charlotte! Charlotte!"

"I am very sorry, papa. If you will only tell me, I will never forget it."

Mr. Bowmore reverently uncovered his head, saluting an invisible Habeas Corpus Act. He took his daughter by the hand, with a certain parental sternness: his voice trembled with emotion as he spoke his next words:

"The Habeas Corpus Act, my child, forbids the imprisonment of an English subject, unless that imprisonment can be first justified by law.

Not even the will of the reigning monarch can prevent us from appearing before the judges of the land, and summoning them to declare whether our committal to prison is legally just."

He put on his hat again. "Never forget what I have told you, Charlotte!" he said solemnly. "I would not remove my hat, sir," he continuing, turning to Percy, "in the presence of the proudest autocrat that ever sat on a throne. I uncover, in homage to the grand law which asserts the sacredness of human liberty. When Parliament has sanctioned the infamous Bill now before it, English patriots may be imprisoned, may even be hanged, on warrants privately obtained by the paid spies and informers of the men who rule us. Perhaps I weary you, sir. You are a young man; the conduct of the Ministry may not interest you."

"On the contrary," said Percy, "I have the strongest personal interest in the conduct of the Ministry."

"How? in what way?" cried Mr. Bowmore eagerly.

"My late father had a claim on government," Percy answered, "for money expended in foreign service. As his heir, I inherit the claim, which has been formally recognized by the present Ministers. My petition for a settlement will be presented by friends of mine who can advocate my interests in the House of Commons."

Mr. Bowmore took Percy's hand, and shook it warmly.

"In such a matter as this you cannot have too many friends to help you," he said. "I myself have some influence, as representing opinion outside the House; and I am entirely at your service. Come tomorrow, and let us talk over the details of your claim at my humble dinner-table. To-day I must attend a meeting of the Branch-Hampden-Club, of which I am vice-president, and to which I am now about to communicate the alarming news which my letter contains. Excuse me for leaving you—and count on a hearty welcome when we see you to-morrow."

The amiable patriot saluted his daughter with a smile, and disappeared.

"I hope you like my father?" said Charlotte. "All our friends say he ought to be in Parliament. He has tried twice. The expenses were dreadful; and each time the other man defeated him. The agent says he would be certainly elected, if he tried again; but there is no money, and we mustn't think of it."

A man of a suspicious turn of mind might have discovered, in those artless words, the secret of Mr. Bowmore's interest in the success of his young friend's claim on the Government. One British subject, with a sum of ready money at his command, may be an inestimably useful person to another British subject (without ready money) who cannot sit comfortably unless he sits in Parliament. But honest Percy Linwood was not a man of a suspicious turn of mind. He had just opened his lips to echo Charlotte's filial glorification of her father, when a shabbily-dressed man-servant met them with a message, for which they were both alike unprepared:

"Captain Bervie has called, Miss, to say good-by, and my mistress requests your company in the parlor."

CHAPTER VIII. THE WARNING.

HAVING delivered his little formula of words, the shabby servant cast a look of furtive curiosity at Percy and withdrew. Charlotte turned to her lover, with indignation sparkling in her eyes and flushing on her cheeks at the bare idea of seeing Captain Bervie again. "Does he think I will breathe the same air," she exclaimed, "with the man who attempted to take your life!"

Percy gently remonstrated with her.

"You are sadly mistaken," he said. "Captain Bervie stood to receive my fire as fairly as I stood to receive his. When I discharged my pistol in the air, he was the first man who ran up to me, and asked if I was seriously hurt. They told him my wound was a trifle; and he fell on his knees and thanked God for preserving my life from his guilty hand. 'I am no longer the rival who hates you,' he said. 'Give me time to try if change of scene will quiet my mind; and I will be your brother, and her brother.' Whatever his faults may be, Charlotte, Arthur Bervie has a great heart. Go in, I entreat you, and be friends with him as I am."

Charlotte listened with downcast eyes and changing color. "You believe him?" she asked in low and trembling tones.

"I believe him as I believe You," Percy answered.

She secretly resented the comparison, and detested the Captain more heartily than ever. "I will go in and see him, if you wish it," she said. "But not by myself. I want you to come with me."

"Why?" Percy asked.

"I want to see what his face says, when you and he meet."

"Do you still doubt him, Charlotte?"

She made no reply. Percy had done his best to convince her, and had evidently failed.

They went together into the cottage. Fixing her eyes steadily on the Captain's face, Charlotte saw it turn pale when Percy followed her into the parlor. The two men greeted one another cordially. Charlotte sat down by her mother, preserving her composure so far as appearances went. "I hear you have called to bid us good-by," she said to Bervie. "Is it to be a long absence?"

"I have got two months' leave," the Captain answered, without looking at her while he spoke.

"Are you going abroad?"

"Yes. I think so."

She turned away to her mother. Bervie seized the opportunity of speaking to Percy. "I have a word of advice for your private ear." At the same moment, Charlotte whispered to her mother: "Don't encourage him to prolong his visit."

The Captain showed no intention to prolong his visit. To Charlotte's surprise, when he took leave of the ladies, Percy also rose to go. "His carriage," he said, "was waiting at the door; and he had offered to take Captain Bervie back to London."

Charlotte instantly suspected an arrangement between the two men for a confidential interview. Her obstinate distrust of Bervie strengthened tenfold. She reluctantly gave him her hand, as he parted from her at the parlor-door. The effort of concealing her true feeling toward him gave a color and a vivacity to her face which made her irresistibly beautiful. Bervie looked at the woman whom he had lost with an immeasurable sadness in his eyes. "When we meet again," he said, "you will see me in a new character." He hurried out of the gate, as if he feared to trust himself for a moment longer in her presence.

Charlotte followed Percy into the passage. "I shall be here to-morrow, dearest!" he said, and tried to raise her hand to his lips. She abruptly drew it away. "Not that hand!" she answered. "Captain Bervie has just touched it. Kiss the other!"

"Do you still doubt the Captain?" said Percy, amused by her petulance.

She put her arm over his shoulder, and touched the plaster on his neck gently with her finger. "There's one thing I don't doubt," she said: "the Captain did that!"

Percy left her, laughing. At the front gate of the cottage he found Arthur Bervie in conversation with the same shabbily-dressed man-servant who had announced the Captain's visit to Charlotte.

"What has become of the other servant?" Bervie asked. "I mean the old man who has been with Mr. Bowmore for so many years."

"He has left his situation, sir."

"Why?"

"As I understand, sir, he spoke disrespectfully to the master."

"Oh! And how came the master to hear of you?"

"I advertised; and Mr. Bowmore answered my advertisement."

Bervie looked hard at the man for a moment, and then joined Percy at the carriage door. The two gentlemen started for London.

"What do you think of Mr. Bowmore's new servant?" asked the Captain as they drove away from the cottage. "I don't like the look of the fellow."

"I didn't particularly notice him," Percy answered.

There was a pause. When the conversation was resumed, it turned on common-place subjects. The Captain looked uneasily out of the carriage window. Percy looked uneasily at the Captain.

They had left Dartford about two miles behind them, when Percy noticed an old gabled house, sheltered by magnificent trees, and standing on an eminence well removed from the high-road. Carriages and saddle-horses were visible on the drive in front, and a flag was hoisted on a staff placed in the middle of the lawn.

"Something seems to be going on there," Percy remarked. "A fine old house! Who does it belong to?"

Bervie smiled. "It belongs to my father," he said. "He is chairman of the bench of local magistrates, and he receives his brother justices to-day, to celebrate the opening of the sessions."

He stopped and looked at Percy with some embarrassment. "I am afraid I have surprised and disappointed you," he resumed, abruptly changing the subject. "I told you when we met just now at Mr. Bowmore's cottage that I had something to say to you; and I have not yet said it. The truth is, I don't feel sure whether I have been long enough your friend to take the liberty of advising you."

"Whatever your advice is," Percy answered, "trust me to take it kindly on my side."

Thus encouraged, the Captain spoke out.

"You will probably pass much of your time at the cottage," he began, "and you will be thrown a great deal into Mr. Bowmore's society. I have known him for many years. Speaking from that knowledge, I most seriously warn you against him as a thoroughly unprincipled and thoroughly dangerous man."

This was strong language—and, naturally enough, Percy said so. The

686

Captain justified his language.

"Without alluding to Mr. Bowmore's politics," he went on, "I can tell you that the motive of everything he says and does is vanity. To the gratification of that one passion he would sacrifice you or me, his wife or his daughter, without hesitation and without remorse. His one desire is to get into Parliament. You are wealthy, and you can help him. He will leave no effort untried to reach that end; and, if he gets you into political difficulties, he will desert you without scruple."

Percy made a last effort to take Mr. Bowmore's part—for the one irresistible reason that he was Charlotte's father.

"Pray don't think I am unworthy of your kind interest in my welfare," he pleaded. "Can you tell me of any facts which justify what you have just said?"

"I can tell you of three facts," Bervie said. "Mr. Bowmore belongs to one of the most revolutionary clubs in England; he has spoken in the ranks of sedition at public meetings; and his name is already in the black book at the Home Office. So much for the past. As to the future, if the rumor be true that Ministers mean to stop the insurrectionary risings among the population by suspending the Habeas Corpus Act, Mr. Bowmore will certainly be in danger; and it may be my father's duty to grant the warrant that apprehends him. Write to my father to verify what I have said, and I will forward your letter by way of satisfying him that he can trust you. In the meantime, refuse to accept Mr. Bowmore's assistance in the matter of your claim on Parliament; and, above all things, stop him at the outset, when he tries to steal his way into your intimacy. I need not caution you to say nothing against him to his wife and daughter. His wily tongue has long since deluded them. Don't let him delude you! Have you thought any more of our evening at Doctor Lagarde's?" he asked, abruptly changing the subject.

"I hardly know," said Percy, still under the impression of the formidable warning which he had just received.

"Let me jog your memory," the other continued. "You went on with the consultation by yourself, after I had left the Doctor's house. It will be really doing me a favor if you can call to mind what Lagarde saw in the trance—in my absence?"

Thus entreated Percy roused himself. His memory of events were still fresh enough to answer the call that his friend had made on it. In describing what had happened, he accurately repeated all that the Doctor had said.

Bervie dwelt on the words with alarm in his face as well as surprise.

"A man like me, trying to persuade a woman like—" he checked himself, as if he was afraid to let Charlotte's name pass his lips. "Trying to induce a woman to go away with me," he resumed, "and persuading her at last? Pray, go on! What did the Doctor see next?"

"He was too much exhausted, he said, to see any more."

"Surely you returned to consult him again?"

"No; I had had enough of it."

"When we get to London," said the Captain, "we shall pass along the Strand, on the way to your chambers. Will you kindly drop me at the turning that leads to the Doctor's lodgings?"

Percy looked at him in amazement. "You still take it seriously?" he said.

"Is it not serious?" Bervie asked. "Have you and I, so far, not done exactly what this man saw us doing? Did we not meet, in the days when we were rivals (as he saw us meet), with the pistols in our hands? Did you not recognize his description of the lady when you met her at the ball, as I recognized it before you?"

"Mere coincidences!" Percy answered, quoting Charlotte's opinion when they had spoken together of Doctor Lagarde, but taking care not to cite his authority. "How many thousand men have been crossed in love? How many thousand men have fought duels for love? How many thousand women choose blue for their favorite color, and answer to the vague description of the lady whom the Doctor pretended to see?"

"Say that it is so," Bervie rejoined. "The thing is remarkable, even from your point of view. And if more coincidences follow, the result will be more remarkable still."

Arrived at the Strand, Percy set the Captain down at the turning which led to the Doctor's lodgings. "You will call on me or write me word, if anything remarkable happens?" he said.

"You shall hear from me without fail," Bervie replied.

That night, the Captain's pen performed the Captain's promise, in few and startling words.

"Melancholy news! Madame Lagarde is dead. Nothing is known of her son but that he has left England. I have found out that he is a political exile. If he has ventured back to France, it is barely possible that I may hear something of him. I have friends at the English embassy in Paris who will help me to make inquiries; and I start for the Continent in a day or two. Write to me while I am away, to the care of my father, at 'The Manor House, near Dartford.' He will always know my address abroad, and will forward your letters. For your own sake, remember the warning I gave you this afternoon! Your faithful friend, A. B."

CHAPTER IX. OFFICIAL SECRETS

THERE WAS a more serious reason than Bervie was aware of, at the time, for the warning which he had thought it his duty to address to Percy Linwood. The new footman who had entered Mr. Bowmore's service was a Spy.

Well practiced in the infamous vocation that he followed, the wretch had been chosen by the Department of Secret Service at the Home Office, to watch the proceedings of Mr. Bowmore and his friends, and to report the result to his superiors. It may not be amiss to add that the employment of paid spies and informers, by the English Government of that time, was openly acknowledged in the House of Lords, and was defended as a necessary measure in the speeches of Lord Redesdale and Lord Liverpool.*

The reports furnished by the Home Office Spy, under these circumstances, begin with the month of March, and take the form of a series of notes introduced as follows:

"MR. SECRETARY—Since I entered Mr. Bowmore's service, I have the honor to inform you that my eyes and ears have been kept in a state of active observation; and I can further certify that my means of making myself useful in the future to my honorable employers are in no respect diminished. Not the slightest suspicion of my true character is felt by any person in the house.

FIRST NOTE.

"The young gentleman now on a visit to Mr. Bowmore is, as you have been correctly informed, Mr. Percy Linwood. Although he is engaged to be married to Miss Bowmore, he is not discreet enough to conceal a certain want of friendly feeling, on his part, toward her father. The young lady has noticed this, and has resented it. She accuses her lover of having allowed himself to be prejudiced against Mr. Bowmore by some slanderous person unknown.

"Mr. Percy's clumsy defense of himself led (in my hearing) to a quarrel! Nothing but his prompt submission prevented the marriage engagement from being broken off.

"'If you showed a want of confidence in Me' (I heard Miss Charlotte say), 'I might forgive it. But when you show a want of confidence in a man so noble as my father, I have no mercy on you.' After such an expression of filial sentiment as this, Mr. Percy wisely took the readiest way of appealing to the lady's indulgence. The young man has a demand on Parliament for moneys due to his father's estate; and he pleased and flattered Miss Charlotte by asking Mr. Bowmore to advise him as to the best means of asserting his claim. By way of advancing his political interests, Mr. Bowmore introduced him to the local Hampden Club; and Miss Charlotte rewarded him with a generosity which must not be passed over in silence. Her lover was permitted to put an engagement ring on her finger, and to kiss her afterward to his heart's content."

SECOND NOTE.

"Mr. Percy has paid more visits to the Republican Club; and Justice Bervie (father of the Captain) has heard of it, and has written to his son. The result that might have been expected has followed. Captain Bervie announces his return to England, to exert his influence for political good against the influence of Mr. Bowmore for political evil.

"In the meanwhile, Mr. Percy's claim has been brought before the House of Commons, and has been adjourned for further consideration in six months' time. Both the gentlemen are indignant—especially Mr. Bowmore. He has called a meeting of the Club to consider his young friend's wrongs, and has proposed the election of Mr. Percy as a member of that revolutionary society."

THIRD NOTE.

"Mr. Percy has been elected. Captain Bervie has tried to awaken his mind to a sense of the danger that threatens him, if he persists in associating with his republican friends—and has utterly failed. Mr. Bowmore and Mr. Percy have made speeches at the Club, intended to force the latter gentleman's claim on the immediate attention of Government. Mr. Bowmore's flow of frothy eloquence has its influence (as you know from our shorthand writers' previous reports) on thousands of ignorant people. As it seems to me, the reasons for at once putting this man in prison are beyond dispute. Whether it is desirable to include Mr. Percy in the order of arrest, I must not venture to decide. Let me only hint that his seditious speech rivals the more elaborate efforts of Mr. Bowmore himself.

"So much for the present. I may now respectfully direct your attention to the future.

"On the second of April next the Club assembles a public meeting, 'in aid of British liberty,' in a field near Dartford. Mr. Bowmore is to preside, and is to be escorted afterward to Westminster Hall on his way to plead Mr. Percy's cause, in his own person, before the House of Commons. He is quite serious in declaring that 'the minions of Government dare not touch a hair of his head.' Miss Charlotte agrees with her father And Mr. Percy agrees with Miss Charlotte. Such is the state of affairs at the house in which I am acting the part of domestic servant.

"I inclose shorthand reports of the speeches recently delivered at the

Hampden Club, and have the honor of waiting for further orders."

FOURTH NOTE.

"Your commands have reached me by this morning's post.

"I immediately waited on Justice Bervie (in plain clothes, of course), and gave him your official letter, instructing me to arrest Mr. Bowmore and Mr. Percy Linwood.

"The venerable magistrate hesitated.

"He quite understood the necessity for keeping the arrest a strict secret, in the interests of Government. The only reluctance he felt in granting the warrant related to his son's intimate friend. But for the peremptory tone of your letter, I really believe he would have asked you to give Mr. Percy time for consideration. Not being rash enough to proceed to such an extreme as this, he slyly consulted the young man's interests by declining, on formal grounds, to date the warrant earlier than the second of April. Please note that my visit to him was paid at noon, on the thirty-first of March.

"If the object of this delay (to which I was obliged to submit) is to offer a chance of escape to Mr. Percy, the same chance necessarily includes Mr. Bowmore, whose name is also in the warrant. Trust me to keep a watchful eye on both these gentlemen; especially on Mr. Bowmore. He is the most dangerous man of the two, and the most likely, if he feels any suspicions, to slip through the fingers of the law.

"I have also to report that I discovered three persons in the hall of Justice Bervie's house, as I went out.

"One of them was his son, the Captain; one was his daughter, Miss Bervie; and the third was that smooth-tongued old soldier, Major Mulvany. If the escape of Mr. Bowmore and Mr. Linwood is in contemplation, mark my words: the persons whom I have just mentioned will be concerned in it—and perhaps Miss Charlotte herself as well. At present, she is entirely unsuspicious of any misfortune hanging over her head; her attention being absorbed in the preparation of her bridal finery. As an admirer myself of the fair sex, I must own that it seems hard on the girl to have her lover clapped into prison, before the wedding-day.

"I will bring you word of the arrest myself. There will be plenty of time to catch the afternoon coach to London.

"Here—unless something happens which it is impossible to foresee—my report may come to an end."

Readers who may desire to test the author's authority for

this statement, are referred to "The Annual Register" for

1817, Chapters I. and III.; and, further on, to page 66 in

the same volume.

CHAPTER X. THE ELOPEMENT.

ON the evening of the first of April, Mrs. Bowmore was left alone with the servants. Mr. Bowmore and Percy had gone out together to attend a special meeting of the Club. Shortly afterward Miss Charlotte had left the cottage, under very extraordinary circumstances.

A few minutes only after the departure of her father and Percy, she received a letter, which appeared to cause her the most violent agitation. She said to Mrs. Bowmore:

"Mamma, I must see Captain Bervie for a few minutes in private, on a matter of serious importance to all of us. He is waiting at the front gate, and he will come in if I show myself at the hall door."

Upon this, Mrs. Bowmore had asked for an explanation.

"There is no time for explanation," was the only answer she received; "I ask you to leave me for five minutes alone with the Captain."

Mrs. Bowmore still hesitated. Charlotte snatched up her garden hat, and declared, wildly, that she would go out to Captain Bervie, if she was not permitted to receive him at home. In the face of this declaration, Mrs. Bowmore yielded, and left the room.

In a minute more the Captain made his appearance.

Although she had given way, Mrs. Bowmore was not disposed to trust her daughter, without supervision, in the society of a man whom Charlotte herself had reviled as a slanderer and a false friend. She took up her position in the veranda outside the parlor, at a safe distance from one of the two windows of the room which had been left partially open to admit the fresh air. Here she waited and listened.

The conversation was for some time carried on in whispers.

As they became more and more excited, both Charlotte and Bervie ended in unconsciously raising their voices.

"I swear it to you on my faith as a Christian!" Mrs. Bowmore heard the Captain say. "I declare before God who hears me that I am speaking the truth!"

And Charlotte had answered, with a burst of tears:

"I can't believe you! I daren't believe you! Oh, how can you ask me to do such a thing? Let me go! let me go!"

Alarmed at those words, Mrs. Bowmore advanced to the window and looked in.

Bervie had put her daughter's arm on his arm, and was trying to induce her to leave the parlor with him. She resisted, and implored him to release her. He dropped her arm, and whispered in her ear. She looked at him—and instantly made up her mind.

"Let me tell my mother where I am going," she said; "and I will consent."

"Be it so!" he answered. "And remember one thing: every minute is precious; the fewest words are the best."

Mrs. Bowmore re-entered the cottage by the adjoining room, and met them in the passage. In few words, Charlotte spoke.

"I must go at once to Justice Bervie's house. Don't be afraid, mamma! I

694

know what I am about, and I know I am right."

"Going to Justice Bervie's!" cried Mrs. Bowmore, in the utmost extremity of astonishment. "What will your father say, what will Percy think, when they come back from the Club?"

"My sister's carriage is waiting for me close by," Bervie answered. "It is entirely at Miss Bowmore's disposal. She can easily get back, if she wishes to keep her visit a secret, before Mr. Bowmore and Mr. Linwood return."

He led her to the door as he spoke. She ran back and kissed her mother tenderly. Mrs. Bowmore called to them to wait.

"I daren't let you go," she said to her daughter, "without your father's leave!"

Charlotte seemed not to hear, the Captain seemed not to hear. They ran across the front garden, and through the gate—and were out of sight in less than a minute.

More than two hours passed; the sun sank below the horizon, and still there were no signs of Charlotte's return.

Feeling seriously uneasy, Mrs. Bowmore crossed the room to ring the bell, and send the man-servant to Justice Bervie's house to hasten her daughter's return.

As she approached the fireplace, she was startled by a sound of stealthy footsteps in the hall, followed by a loud noise as of some heavy object that had dropped on the floor. She rang the bell violently, and opened the door of the parlor. At the same moment, the spy-footman passed her, running out, apparently in pursuit of somebody, at the top of his speed. She followed him, as rapidly as she could, across the little front garden, to the gate. Arrived in the road, she was in time to see him vault upon the luggage-board at the back of a post-chaise before the cottage, just as the postilion started the horses on their way to London. The spy saw Mrs. Bowmore looking at him, and pointed, with an insolent nod of his head, first to the inside of the vehicle, and then over it to the high-road; signing to her that he designed to accompany the person in the post-chaise to the end of the journey.

Turning to go back, Mrs. Bowmore saw her own bewilderment reflected in the faces of the two female servants, who had followed her out.

"Who can the footman be after, ma'am?" asked the cook. "Do you think it's a thief?"

The housemaid pointed to the post-chaise, barely visible in the distance.

"Simpleton!" she said. "Do thieves travel in that way? I wish my master had come back," she proceeded, speaking to herself: "I'm afraid there's something wrong."

Mrs. Bowmore, returning through the garden-gate, instantly stopped and looked at the woman.

"What makes you mention your master's name, Amelia, when you fear that something is wrong?" she asked.

Amelia changed color, and looked confused.

"I am loth to alarm you, ma'am," she said; "and I can't rightly see what it is my duty to do."

Mrs. Bowmore's heart sank within her under the cruelest of all terrors, the terror of something unknown. "Don't keep me in suspense," she said faintly. "Whatever it is, let me know it."

She led the way back to the parlor. The housemaid followed her. The cook (declining to be left alone) followed the housemaid.

"It was something I heard early this afternoon, ma'am," Amelia began. "Cook happened to be busy—"

The cook interposed: she had not forgiven the housemaid for calling her a simpleton. "No, Amelia, if you must bring me into it—not busy. Uneasy in my mind on the subject of the soup."

"I don't know that your mind makes much difference," Amelia resumed. "What it comes to is this—it was I, and not you, who went into the kitchen-garden for the vegetables."

"Not by my wish, Heaven knows!" persisted the cook.

"Leave the room!" said Mrs. Bowmore. Even her patience had given way at last.

The cook looked as if she declined to believe her own ears. Mrs. Bowmore pointed to the door. The cook said "Oh?"—accenting it as a question. Mrs. Bowmore's finger still pointed. The cook, in solemn silence, yielded to circumstances, and banged the door.

"I was getting the vegetables, ma'am," Amelia proceeded, "when I heard voices on the other side of the paling. The wood is so old that one can see through the cracks easy enough. I saw my master, and Mr. Linwood, and Captain Bervie. The Captain seemed to have stopped the other two on the pathway that leads to the field; he stood, as it might be, between them and the back way to the house—and he spoke severely, that he did!"

"What did Captain Bervie say?"

"He said these words, ma'am: 'For the last time, Mr. Bowmore,' says he, 'will you understand that you are in danger, and that Mr. Linwood is in danger, unless you both leave this neighborhood to-night?' My master made light of it. 'For the last time,' says he, 'will you refer us to a proof of what you say, and allow us to judge for ourselves?' 'I have told you already,' says the Captain, 'I am bound by my duty toward another person to keep what I know a secret.' 'Very well,' says my master, 'I am bound by my duty to my country. And I tell you this,' says he, in his high and mighty way, 'neither Government, nor the spies of Government, dare touch a hair of my head: they know it, sir, for the head of the people's friend!'"

"That's quite true," said Mrs. Bowmore, still believing in her husband as firmly as ever.

Amelia went on:

"Captain Bervie didn't seem to think so," she said. "He lost his temper. 'What stuff!' says he; 'there's a Government spy in your house at this moment, disguised as your footman.' My master looked at Mr. Linwood, and burst out laughing. 'You won't beat that, Captain,' says he, 'if you talk till doomsday.' He turned about without a word more, and went home. The Captain caught Mr. Linwood by the arm, as soon as they were alone. 'For God's sake,' says he, 'don't follow that madman's example!'"

Mrs. Bowmore was shocked. "Did he really call my husband a madman?" she asked.

"He did, indeed, ma'am—and he was in earnest about it, too. 'If you value your liberty,' he says to Mr. Linwood; 'if you hope to become Charlotte's husband, consult your own safety. I can give you a passport. Escape to France and wait till this trouble is over.' Mr. Linwood was not in the best of tempers—Mr. Linwood shook him off. 'Charlotte's father will soon be my father,' says he, 'do you think I will desert him? My friends at the Club have taken up my claim; do you think I will forsake them at the meeting to-morrow? You ask me to be unworthy of Charlotte, and unworthy of my friends—you insult me, if you say more.' He whipped round on his heel, and followed my master."

"And what did the Captain do?"

"Lifted up his hands, ma'am, to the heavens, and looked—I declare it turned my blood to see him. If there's truth in mortal man, it's my firm belief—"

What the housemaid's belief was, remained unexpressed. Before she could get to her next word, a shriek of horror from the hall announced that the cook's powers of interruption were not exhausted yet.

Mistress and servant both hurried out in terror of they knew not what. There stood the cook, alone in the hall, confronting the stand on which the overcoats and hats of the men of the family were placed.

"Where's the master's traveling coat?" cried the cook, staring wildly at an unoccupied peg. "And where's his cap to match! Oh Lord, he's off in the post-chaise! and the footman's after him!"

Simpleton as she was, the woman had blundered on a very serious discovery.

Coat and cap—both made after a foreign pattern, and both strikingly remarkable in form and color to English eyes—had unquestionably disappeared. It was equally certain that they were well known to the foot man, whom the Captain had declared to be a spy, as the coat and cap which his master used in traveling. Had Mr. Bowmore discovered (since the afternoon) that he was really in danger? Had the necessities of instant flight only allowed him time enough to snatch his coat and cap out of the hall? And had the treacherous manservant seen him as he was making his escape to the post-chaise? The cook's conclusions answered all these questions in the affirmative—and, if Captain Bervie's words of warning had been correctly reported, the cook's conclusion for once was not to be despised.

Under this last trial of her fortitude, Mrs. Bowmore's feeble reserves of endurance completely gave way. The poor lady turned faint and giddy. Amelia placed her on a chair in the hall, and told the cook to open the front door, and let in the fresh air.

The cook obeyed; and instantly broke out with a second terrific scream; announcing nothing less, this time, than the appearance of Mr. Bowmore himself, alive and hearty, returning with Percy from the meeting at the Club!

The inevitable inquiries and explanations followed.

Fully assured, as he had declared himself to be, of the sanctity of his person (politically speaking), Mr. Bowmore turned pale, nevertheless, when he looked at the unoccupied peg on his clothes stand. Had some man unknown personated him? And had a post-chaise been hired to lead an impending pursuit of him in the wrong direction? What did it mean? Who was the friend to whose services he was indebted? As for the proceedings of the man-servant, but one interpretation could now be placed on them. They distinctly justified what Captain Bervie had said of him. Mr. Bowmore thought of the Captain's other assertion, relating to the urgent necessity for making his escape; and looked at Percy in silent dismay; and turned paler than ever.

Percy's thoughts, diverted for the moment only from the lady of his love, returned to her with renewed fidelity. "Let us hear what Charlotte thinks of it," he said. "Where is she?"

It was impossible to answer this question plainly and in few words.

Terrified at the effect which her attempt at explanation produced on Percy, helplessly ignorant when she was called upon to account for her daughter's absence, Mrs. Bowmore could only shed tears and express a devout trust in Providence. Her husband looked at the new misfortune from a political point of view. He sat down and slapped his forehead theatrically with the palm of his hand. "Thus far," said the patriot, "my political assailants have only struck at me through the newspapers. Now they strike at me through my child!"

Percy made no speeches. There was a look in his eyes which boded ill for Captain Bervie if the two met. "I am going to fetch her," was all he said, "as fast as a horse can carry me."

He hired his horse at an inn in the town, and set forth for Justice Bervie's house at a gallop.

During Percy's absence, Mr. Bowmore secured the front and back entrances to the cottage with his own hands.

These first precautions taken, he ascended to his room and packed his traveling-bag. "Necessaries for my use in prison," he remarked. "The bloodhounds of Government are after me." "Are they after Percy, too?" his wife ventured to ask. Mr. Bowmore looked up impatiently, and cried "Pooh!"—as if Percy was of no consequence. Mrs. Bowmore thought otherwise: the good woman privately packed a bag for Percy, in the sanctuary of her own room.

For an hour, and more than an hour, no event of any sort occurred.

Mr. Bowmore stalked up and down the parlor, meditating. At intervals, ideas of flight presented themselves attractively to his mind. At intervals, ideas of the speech that he had prepared for the public meeting on the next day took their place. "If I fly to-night," he wisely observed, "what will become of my speech? I will not fly to-night! The people shall hear me."

He sat down and crossed his arms fiercely. As he looked at his wife to see what effect he had produced on her, the sound of heavy carriage-wheels and the trampling of horses penetrated to the parlor from the garden-gate.

Mr. Bowmore started to his feet, with every appearance of having suddenly altered his mind on the question of flight. Just as he reached the hall, Percy's voice was heard at the front door. "Let me in. Instantly! Instantly!"

Mrs. Bowmore drew back the bolts before the servants could help her. "Where is Charlotte?" she cried; seeing Percy alone on the doorstep.

"Gone!" Percy answered furiously. "Eloped to Paris with Captain Bervie! Read her own confession. They were just sending the messenger with it, when I reached the house."

He handed a note to Mrs. Bowmore, and turned aside to speak to her husband while she read it. Charlotte wrote to her mother very briefly; promising to explain everything on her return. In the meantime, she had left home under careful protection—she had a lady for her companion on the journey—and she would write again from Paris. So the letter, evidently written in great haste, began and ended.

Percy took Mr. Bowmore to the window, and pointed to a carriage and four horses waiting at the garden-gate.

"Do you come with me, and back me with your authority as her father?" he asked, sternly. "Or do you leave me to go alone?"

Mr. Bowmore was famous among his admirers for his "happy replies." He made one now.

"I am not Brutus," he said. "I am only Bowmore. My daughter before everything. Fetch my traveling-bag."

While the travelers' bags were being placed in the chaise, Mr. Bowmore was struck by an idea.

He produced from his coat-pocket a roll of many papers thickly covered with writing. On the blank leaf in which they were tied up, he wrote in the largest letters: "Frightful domestic calamity! Vice-President Bowmore obliged to leave England! Welfare of a beloved daughter! His speech will be read at the meeting by Secretary Joskin, of the Club. (Private to Joskin. Have these lines printed and posted everywhere. And, when you read my speech, for God's sake don't drop your voice at the ends of the sentences.)"

He threw down the pen, and embraced Mrs. Bowmore in the most summary manner. The poor woman was ordered to send the roll of paper to the Club, without a word to comfort and sustain her from her husband's lips. Percy spoke to her hopefully and kindly, as he kissed her cheek at parting.

On the next morning, a letter, addressed to Mrs. Bowmore, was delivered at the cottage by private messenger.

Opening the letter, she recognized the handwriting of her husband's old friend, and her old friend—Major Mulvany. In breathless amazement, she read these lines:

"DEAR MRS. BOWMORE—In matters of importance, the golden rule is never to waste words. I have performed one of the great actions of my life—I have saved your husband.

"How I discovered that my friend was in danger, I must not tell you at present. Let it be enough if I say that I have been a guest under Justice Bervie's hospitable roof, and that I know of a Home Office spy who has taken you unawares, under pretense of being your footman. If I had not circumvented him, the scoundrel would have imprisoned your husband, and another dear friend of mine. This is how I did it.

"I must begin by appealing to your memory.

"Do you happen to remember that your husband and I are as near as may be of about the same height? Very good, so far. Did you, in the next place, miss Bowmore's traveling coat and cap from their customary peg? I am the thief, dearest lady; I put them on my own humble self. Did you hear a sudden noise in the hall? Oh, forgive me—I made the noise! And it did just what I wanted of it. It brought the spy up from the kitchen, suspecting that something might be wrong.

"What did the wretch see when he got into the hall? His master, in traveling costume, running out. What did he find when he reached the garden? His master escaping, in a post-chaise, on the road to London. What did he do, the born blackguard that he was? Jumped up behind the chaise to make sure of his prisoner. It was dark when we got to London. In a hop, skip, and jump, I was out of the carriage, and in at my own door, before he could look me in the face.

"The date of the warrant, you must know, obliged him to wait till the morning. All that night, he and the Bow Street runners kept watch They came in with the sunrise—and who did they find? Major Mulvany snug in his bed, and as innocent as the babe unborn. Oh, they did their duty! Searched the place from the kitchen to the garrets—and gave it up. There's but one thing I regret—I let the spy off without a good thrashing. No matter. I'll do it yet, one of these days.

"Let me know the first good news of our darling fugitives, and I shall be more than rewarded for what little I have done.

"Your always devoted,

"TERENCE MULVANY."

CHAPTER XI. PURSUIT AND DISCOVERY.

FEELING himself hurried away on the road to Dover, as fast as four horses could carry him, Mr. Bowmore had leisure to criticise Percy's conduct, from his own purely selfish point of view.

"If you had listened to my advice," he said, "you would have treated that man Bervie like the hypocrite and villain that he is. But no! you trusted to your own crude impressions. Having given him your hand after the duel (I would have given him the contents of my pistol!) you hesitated to withdraw it again, when that slanderer appealed to your friendship not to cast him off. Now you see the consequence!"

"Wait till we get to Paris!" All the ingenuity of Percy's traveling companion failed to extract from him any other answer than that.

Foiled so far, Mr. Bowmore began to start difficulties next. Had they money enough for the journey? Percy touched his pocket, and answered shortly, "Plenty." Had they passports? Percy sullenly showed a letter. "There is the necessary voucher from a magistrate," he said. "The consul at Dover will give us our passports. Mind this!" he added, in warning tones, "I have pledged my word of honor to Justice Bervie that we have no political object in view in traveling to France. Keep your politics to yourself, on the other side of the Channel."

Mr. Bowmore listened in blank amazement. Charlotte's lover was appearing in a new character—the character of a man who had lost his respect for Charlotte's father!

It was useless to talk to him. He deliberately checked any further attempts at conversation by leaning back in the carriage, and closing his eyes. The truth is, Mr. Bowmore's own language and conduct were insensibly producing the salutary impression on Percy's mind which Bervie had vainly tried to convey, under the disadvantage of having Charlotte's influence against him. Throughout the journey, Percy did exactly what Bervie had once entreated him to do—he kept Mr. Bowmore at a distance.

At every stage, they inquired after the fugitives. At every stage, they were answered by a more or less intelligible description of Bervie and Charlotte, and of the lady who accompanied them. No disguise had been attempted; no person had in any case been bribed to conceal the truth.

When the first tumult of his emotions had in some degree subsided, this strange circumstance associated itself in Percy's mind with the equally unaccountable conduct of Justice Bervie, on his arrival at the manor house.

The old gentleman met his visitor in the hall, without expressing, and apparently without feeling, any indignation at his son's conduct. It was even useless to appeal to him for information. He only said, "I am not in Arthur's confidence; he is of age, and my daughter (who has volunteered to accompany him) is of age. I have no claim to control them. I believe they have taken Miss Bowmore to Paris; and that is all I know about it."

He had shown the same dense insensibility in giving his official voucher for the passports. Percy had only to satisfy him on the question of politics; and the document was drawn out as a matter of course. Such had been the father's behavior; and the conduct of the son now exhibited the same shameless composure. To what conclusion did this discovery point? Percy abandoned the attempt to answer that question in despair.

They reached Dover toward two o'clock in the morning.

At the pier-head they found a coast-guardsman on duty, and received more information.

In 1817 the communication with France was still by sailing-vessels. Arriving long after the departure of the regular packet, Bervie had hired a lugger, and had sailed with the two ladies for Calais, having a fresh breeze in his favor. Percy's first angry impulse was to follow him instantly. The next moment he remembered the insurmountable obstacle of the passports. The Consul would certainly not grant those essentially necessary documents at two in the morning!

The only alternative was to wait for the regular packet, which sailed some hours later—between eight and nine o'clock in the forenoon. In this case, they might apply for their passports before the regular office hours, if they explained the circumstances, backed by the authority of the magistrate's letter.

Mr. Bowmore followed Percy to the nearest inn that was open, sublimely indifferent to the delays and difficulties of the journey. He ordered refreshments with the air of a man who was performing a melancholy duty to himself, in the name of humanity.

"When I think of my speech," he said, at supper, "my heart bleeds for the people. In a few hours more, they will assemble in their thousands, eager to hear me. And what will they see? Joskin in my place! Joskin with a manuscript in his hand! Joskin, who drops his voice at the ends of his sentences! I will never forgive Charlotte. Waiter, another glass of brandy and water."

After an unusually quick passage across the Channel, the travelers landed on the French coast, before the defeated spy had returned from London to

Dartford by stage-coach. Continuing their journey by post as far as Amiens, they reached that city in time to take their places by the diligence to Paris.

Arrived in Paris, they encountered another incomprehensible proceeding on the part of Captain Bervie.

Among the persons assembled in the yard to see the arrival of the diligence was a man with a morsel of paper in his hand, evidently on the lookout for some person whom he expected to discover among the travelers. After consulting his bit of paper, he looked with steady attention at Percy and Mr. Bowmore, and suddenly approached them. "If you wish to see the Captain," he said, in broken English, "you will find him at that hotel." He handed a printed card to Percy, and disappeared among the crowd before it was possible to question him.

Even Mr. Bowmore gave way to human weakness, and condescended to feel astonished in the face of such an event as this. "What next?" he exclaimed.

"Wait till we get to the hotel," said Percy.

In half an hour more the landlord had received them, and the waiter had led them to the right door. Percy pushed the man aside, and burst into the room.

Captain Bervie was alone, reading a newspaper. Before the first furious words had escaped Percy's lips, Bervie silenced him by pointing to a closed door on the right of the fireplace.

"She is in that room," he said; "speak quietly, or you may frighten her. I know what you are going to say," he added, as Percy stepped nearer to him. "Will you hear me in my own defense, and then decide whether I am the greatest scoundrel living, or the best friend you ever had?"

He put the question kindly, with something that was at once grave and tender in his look and manner. The extraordinary composure with which he acted and spoke had its tranquilizing influence over Percy. He felt himself surprised into giving Bervie a hearing.

"I will tell you first what I have done," the Captain proceeded, "and next why I did it. I have taken it on myself, Mr. Linwood, to make an alteration in your wedding arrangements. Instead of being married at Dartford church, you will be married (if you see no objection) at the chapel of the embassy in Paris, by my old college friend the chaplain."

This was too much for Percy's self-control. "Your audacity is beyond belief," he broke out.

"And beyond endurance," Mr. Bowmore added. "Understand this, sir! Whatever your defense may be, I object, under any circumstances, to be made the victim of a trick."

"You are the victim of your own obstinate refusal to profit by a plain warning," Bervie rejoined. "At the eleventh hour, I entreated you, and I entreated Mr. Linwood, to provide for your own safety; and I spoke in vain."

Percy's patience gave way once more.

"To use your own language," he said, "I have still to decide whether you have behaved toward me like a scoundrel or a friend. You have said nothing to justify yourself yet."

"Very well put!" Mr. Bowmore chimed in. "Come to the point, sir! My daughter's reputation is in question."

"Miss Bowmore's reputation is not in question for a single instant," Bervie answered. "My sister has been the companion of her journey from first to last."

"Journey?" Mr. Bowmore repeated, indignantly. "I want to know, sir, what the journey means. As an outraged father, I ask one plain question. Why did you run away with my daughter?"

Bervie took a slip of paper from his pocket, and handed it to Percy with a smile.

It was a copy of the warrant which Justice Bervie's duty had compelled him to issue for the "arrest of Orlando Bowmore and Percy Linwood." There was no danger in divulging the secret now. British warrants were waste-paper in France, in those days.

"I ran away with the bride," Bervie said coolly, "in the certain knowledge that you and Mr. Bowmore would run after me. If I had not forced you both to follow me out of England on the first of April, you would have been made State prisoners on the second. What do you say to my conduct now?"

"Wait, Percy, before you answer him," Mr. Bowmore interposed. "He is ready enough at excusing himself. But, observe—he hasn't a word to say in justification of my daughter's readiness to run away with him."

"Have you quite done?" Bervie asked, as quietly as ever.

Mr. Bowmore reserved the right of all others which he most prized, the right of using his tongue. "For the present," he answered in his loftiest manner, "I have done."

Bervie proceeded: "Your daughter consented to run away with me, because I took her to my father's house, and prevailed upon him to trust her with the secret of the coming arrests. She had no choice left but to let her obstinate father and her misguided lover go to prison—or to take her place with my sister and me in the traveling-carriage." He appealed once more to Percy. "My friend, you remember the day when you spared my life. Have I remembered it, too?"

For once, there was an Englishman who was not contented to express the noblest emotions that humanity can feel by the commonplace ceremony of shaking hands. Percy's heart overflowed. In an outburst of unutterable gratitude he threw himself on Bervie's breast. As brothers the two men embraced. As brothers they loved and trusted one another, from that day forth.

The door on the right was softly opened from within. A charming face—the dark eyes bright with happy tears, the rosy lips just opening into a smile—peeped into the room. A low sweet voice, with an under-note of trembling in it, made this modest protest, in the form of an inquiry:

"When you have quite done, Percy, with our good friend, perhaps you will have something to say to ME?"

LAST WORDS.

THE persons immediately interested in the marriage of Percy and Charlotte were the only persons present at the ceremony.

At the little breakfast afterward, in the French hotel, Mr. Bowmore insisted on making a speech to a select audience of six; namely, the bride and bridegroom, the bridesmaid, the Chaplain, the Captain, and Mrs. Bowmore. But what does a small audience matter? The English frenzy for making speeches is not to be cooled by such a trifle as that. At the end of the world, the expiring forces of Nature will hear a dreadful voice—the voice of the last Englishman delivering the last speech.

Percy wisely made his honeymoon a long one; he determined to be quite sure of his superior influence over his wife before he trusted her within reach of her father again.

Mr. and Mrs. Bowmore accompanied Captain Bervie and Miss Bervie on their way back to England, as far as Boulogne. In that pleasant town the banished patriot set up his tent. It was a cheaper place to live in than Paris, and it was conveniently close to England, when he had quite made up his mind whether to be an exile on the Continent, or to go back to his own country and be a martyr in prison. In the end, the course of events settled that question for him. Mr. Bowmore returned to England, with the return of the Habeas Corpus Act.

The years passed. Percy and Charlotte (judged from the romantic point of view) became two uninteresting married people. Bervie (always remaining a bachelor) rose steadily in his profession, through the higher grades of military rank. Mr. Bowmore, wisely overlooked by a new Government, sank back again into the obscurity from which shrewd Ministers would never have assisted him to emerge. The one subject of interest left, among the persons of this little drama, was now represented by Doctor Lagarde. Thus far, not a trace had been discovered of the French physician, who had so strangely associated the visions of his magnetic sleep with the destinies of the two men who had consulted him.

Steadfastly maintaining his own opinion of the prediction and the fulfillment, Bervie persisted in believing that he and Lagarde (or Percy and Lagarde) were yet destined to meet, and resume the unfinished consultation at the point where it had been broken off. Persons, happy in the possession of "sound common sense," who declared the prediction to be skilled guesswork, and the fulfillment manifest coincidence, ridiculed the idea of finding Doctor Lagarde as closely akin to that other celebrated idea of finding the needle in the bottle of hay. But Bervie's obstinacy was proverbial. Nothing shook his confidence in his own convictions.

More than thirteen years had elapsed since the consultation at the Doctor's lodgings, when Bervie went to Paris to spend a summer holiday with his friend, the chaplain at the English embassy. His last words to Percy and Charlotte when he took his leave were: "Suppose I meet with Doctor Lagarde?"

It was then the year 1830. Bervie arrived at his friend's rooms on the 24th of July. On the 27th of the month the famous revolution broke out which dethroned Charles the Tenth in three days.

On the second day, Bervie and his host ventured into the streets, watching the revolution (like other reckless Englishmen) at the risk of their lives. In the confusion around them they were separated. Bervie, searching for his companion, found his progress stopped by a barricade, which had been desperately attacked, and desperately defended. Men in blouses and men in uniform lay dead and dying together: the tricolored flag waved over them, in token of the victory of the people.

Bervie had just revived a poor wretch with a drink from an overthrown bowl of water, which still had a few drops left in it, when he felt a hand laid on his shoulder from behind. He turned and discovered a National Guard, who had been watching his charitable action. "Give a helping hand to that poor fellow," said the citizen-soldier, pointing to a workman standing near, grimed with blood and gunpowder. The tears were rolling down the man's cheeks. "I can't see my way, sir, for crying," he said. "Help me to carry that sad burden into the next street." He pointed to a rude wooden litter, on which lay a dead or wounded man, his face and breast covered with an old cloak. "There is the best friend the people ever had," the workman said. "He cured us, comforted us, respected us, loved us. And there he lies, shot dead while he was binding up the wounds of friends and enemies alike!"

"Whoever he is, he has died nobly," Bervie answered, "May I look at him?"

The workman signed that he might look.

Bervie lifted the cloak—and met with Doctor Lagarde once more.

MISS BERTHA AND THE YANKEE.

[PRELIMINARY STATEMENTS OF WITNESSES FOR THE DEFENSE, COLLECTED AT THE OFFICE OF THE SOLICITOR.]

No. 1.—Miss Bertha Laroche, of Nettlegrove Hall, testifies and says:—

I.

TOWARD the middle of June, in the year 1817, I went to take the waters at Maplesworth, in Derbyshire, accompanied by my nearest relative—my aunt.

I am an only child; and I was twenty-one years old at my last birthday. On coming of age I inherited a house and lands in Derbyshire, together with a fortune in money of one hundred thousand pounds. The only education which I have received has been obtained within the last two or three years of my life; and I have thus far seen nothing of Society, in England or in any other civilized part of the world. I can be a competent witness, it seems, in spite of these disadvantages. Anyhow, I mean to tell the truth.

My father was a French colonist in the island of Saint Domingo. He died while I was very young; leaving to my mother and to me just enough to live on, in the remote part of the island in which our little property was situated. My mother was an Englishwoman. Her delicate health made it necessary for her to leave me, for many hours of the day, under the care of our household slaves. I can never forget their kindness to me; but, unfortunately, their ignorance equaled their kindness. If we had been rich enough to send to France or England for a competent governess we might have done very well. But we were not rich enough. I am ashamed to say that I was nearly thirteen years old before I had learned to read and write correctly.

Four more years passed—and then there came a wonderful event in our lives, which was nothing less than the change from Saint Domingo to England.

My mother was distantly related to an ancient and wealthy English family. She seriously offended those proud people by marrying an obscure foreigner, who had nothing to live on but his morsel of land in the West Indies. Having no expectations from her relatives, my mother preferred happiness with the man she loved to every other consideration; and I, for one, think she was right. From that moment she was cast off by the head of the family. For eighteen years of her life, as wife, mother, and widow, no letters came to her from her English home. We had just celebrated my seventeenth birthday when the first letter came. It informed my mother that no less than three lives, which stood between her and the inheritance of certain portions of the family property, had been swept away by death. The estate and the fortune which I have already mentioned had fallen to her in due course of law, and her surviving relatives were magnanimously ready to forgive her at last!

We wound up our affairs at Saint Domingo, and we went to England to take possession of our new wealth.

At first, the return to her native air seemed to have a beneficial effect on my mother's health. But it was a temporary improvement only. Her constitution had been fatally injured by the West Indian climate, and just as we had engaged a competent person to look after my neglected education, my constant attendance was needed at my mother's bedside. We loved each other dearly, and we wanted no strange nurses to come between us. My aunt (my mother's sister) relieved me of my cares in the intervals when I wanted rest.

For seven sad months our dear sufferer lingered. I have only one remembrance to comfort me; my mother's last kiss was mine—she died peacefully with her head on my bosom.

I was nearly nineteen years old before I had sufficiently rallied my courage to be able to think seriously of myself and my prospects.

At that age one does not willingly submit one's self for the first time to the authority of a governess. Having my aunt for a companion and protectress, I proposed to engage my own masters and to superintend my own education.

My plans failed to meet with the approval of the head of the family. He

713

declared (most unjustly, as the event proved) that my aunt was not a fit person to take care of me. She had passed all the later years of her life in retirement. A good creature, he admitted, in her own way, but she had no knowledge of the world, and no firmness of character. The right person to act as my chaperon, and to superintend my education, was the high-minded and accomplished woman who had taught his own daughters.

I declined, with all needful gratitude and respect, to take his advice. The bare idea of living with a stranger so soon after my mother's death revolted me. Besides, I liked my aunt, and my aunt liked me. Being made acquainted with my decision, the head of the family cast me off, exactly as he had cast off my mother before me.

So I lived in retirement with my good aunt, and studied industriously to improve my mind until my twenty-first birthday came. I was now an heiress, privileged to think and act for myself. My aunt kissed me tenderly. We talked of my poor mother, and we cried in each other's arms on the memorable day that made a wealthy woman of me. In a little time more, other troubles than vain regrets for the dead were to try me, and other tears were to fill my eyes than the tears which I had given to the memory of my mother.

II.

I MAY now return to my visit, in June, 1817, to the healing springs at Maplesworth.

This famous inland watering-place was only between nine and ten miles from my new home called Nettlegrove Hall. I had been feeling weak and out of spirits for some months, and our medical adviser recommended change of scene and a trial of the waters at Maplesworth. My aunt and I established ourselves in comfortable apartments, with a letter of introduction to the chief doctor in the place. This otherwise harmless and worthy man proved, strangely enough, to be the innocent cause of the trials and troubles which beset me at the outset of my new life.

The day after we had presented our letter of introduction, we met the doctor on the public walk. He was accompanied by two strangers, both young men, and both (so far as my ignorant opinion went) persons of some distinction, judging by their dress and manners. The doctor said a few kind words to us, and rejoined his two companions. Both the gentlemen looked at me, and both took off their hats as my aunt and I proceeded on our walk.

I own I thought occasionally of the well-bred strangers during the rest of the day, especially of the shortest of the two, who was also the handsomest of the two to my thinking. If this confession seems rather a bold one, remember, if you please, that I had never been taught to conceal my feelings at Saint Domingo, and that the events which followed our arrival in England had kept me completely secluded from the society of other young ladies of my age.

The next day, while I was drinking my glass of healing water (extremely nasty water, by the way) the doctor joined us.

While he was asking me about my health, the two strangers made their appearance again, and took off their hats again. They both looked expectantly at the doctor, and the doctor (in performance of a promise which he had already made, as I privately suspected) formally introduced them to my aunt and to me. First (I put the handsomest man first) Captain Arthur Stanwick, of the army, home from India on leave, and staying at Maplesworth to take the waters; secondly, Mr. Lionel Varleigh, of Boston, in America, visiting England, after traveling all over Europe, and stopping at Maplesworth to keep company with his friend the Captain.

On their introduction, the two gentlemen, observing, no doubt, that I was a little shy, forbore delicately from pressing their society on us.

Captain Stanwick, with a beautiful smile, and with teeth worthy of the smile, stroked his whiskers, and asked me if I had found any benefit from taking the waters. He afterward spoke in great praise of the charming scenery in the neighborhood of Maplesworth, and then, turning away, addressed his next words to my aunt. Mr. Varleigh took his place. Speaking with perfect gravity, and with no whiskers to stroke, he said:

"I have once tried the waters here out of curiosity. I can sympathize, miss, with the expression which I observed on your face when you emptied your glass just now. Permit me to offer you something nice to take the taste of the waters out of your mouth." He produced from his pocket a beautiful little box filled with sugar-plums. "I bought it in Paris," h e explained. "Having lived a good deal in France, I have got into a habit of making little presents of this sort to ladies and children. I wouldn't let the doctor see it, miss, if I were you. He has the usual medical prejudice against sugar-plums." With that quaint warning, he, too, made his bow and discreetly withdrew.

Thinking it over afterward, I acknowledged to myself that the English Captain—although he was the handsomest man of the two, and possessed the smoothest manners—had failed, nevertheless, to overcome my shyness. The American traveler's unaffected sincerity and good-humor, on the other hand, set me quite at my ease. I could look at him and thank him, and feel amused at his sympathy with the grimace I had made, after swallowing the ill-flavored waters. And yet, while I lay awake at night, wondering whether we should meet our new acquaintances on the next day, it was the English Captain that I most wanted to see again, and not the American traveler! At the time, I set this down to nothing more important than my own perversity. Ah, dear! dear! I know better than that now.

The next morning brought the doctor to our hotel on a special visit to my aunt. He invented a pretext for sending me into the next room, which was so plainly a clumsy excuse that my curiosity was aroused. I gratified my curiosity. Must I make my confession plainer still? Must I acknowledge that I was mean enough to listen on the other side of the door?

I heard my dear innocent old aunt say: "Doctor! I hope you don't see anything alarming in the state of Bertha's health."

The doctor burst out laughing. "My dear madam! there is nothing in the state of the young lady's health which need cause the smallest anxiety to you or to me. The object of my visit is to justify myself for presenting those two gentlemen to you yesterday. They are both greatly struck by Miss Bertha's beauty, and they both urgently entreated me to introduce them. Such introductions, I need hardly say, are marked exceptions to my general rule. In ninety-nine cases out of a hundred I should have said No. In the cases of

Captain Stanwick and Mr. Varleigh, however, I saw no reason to hesitate. Permit me to assure you that I am not intruding on your notice two fortune-hunting adventurers. They are both men of position and men of property. The family of the Stanwicks has been well known to me for years; and Mr. Varleigh brought me a letter from my oldest living friend, answering for him as a gentleman in the highest sense of the word. He is the wealthiest man of the two; and it speaks volumes for him, in my opinion, that he has preserved his simplicity of character after a long residence in such places as Paris and Vienna. Captain Stanwick has more polish and ease of manner, but, looking under the surface, I rather fancy there may be something a little impetuous and domineering in his temper. However, we all have our faults. I can only say, for both these young friends of mine, that you need feel no scruple about admitting them to your intimacy, if they happen to please you—and your niece. Having now, I hope, removed any doubts which may have troubled you, pray recall Miss Bertha. I am afraid I have interrupted you in discussing your plans for the day."

The smoothly eloquent doctor paused for the moment; and I darted away from the door.

Our plans for the day included a drive through the famous scenery near the town. My two admirers met us on horseback. Here, again, the Captain had the advantage over his friend. His seat in the saddle and his riding-dress were both perfect things in their way. The Englishman rode on one side of the carriage and the American on the other. They both talked well, but Mr. Varleigh had seen more of the world in general than Captain Stanwick, and he made himself certainly the more interesting and more amusing companion of the two.

On our way back my admiration was excited by a thick wood, beautifully situated on rising ground at a little distance from the high-road: "Oh, dear," I said, "how I should like to take a walk in that wood!" Idle, thoughtless words; but, oh, what remembrances crowd on me as I think of them now!

Captain Stanwick and Mr. Varleigh at once dismounted and offered themselves as my escort. The coachman warned them to be careful; people had often lost themselves, he said, in that wood. I asked the name of it. The name was Herne Wood. My aunt was not very willing to leave her comfortable seat in the carriage, but it ended in her going with us.

Before we entered the wood, Mr. Varleigh noted the position of the high-road by his pocket-compass. Captain Stanwick laughed at him, and offered me his arm. Ignorant as I was of the ways of the world and the rules of coquetry, my instinct (I suppose) warned me not to distinguish one of the gentlemen too readily at the expense of the other. I took my aunt's arm and settled it in that way.

A winding path led us into the wood.

On a nearer view, the place disappointed me; the further we advanced, the more horribly gloomy it grew. The thickly-growing trees shut out the light; the damp stole over me little by little until I shivered; the undergrowth of bushes and thickets rustled at intervals mysteriously, as some invisible creeping creature passed through it. At a turn in the path we reached a sort of clearing, and saw the sky and the sunshine once more. But, even here, a disagreeable incident occurred. A snake wound his undulating way across the open space, passing close by me, and I was fool enough to scream. The Captain killed the creature with his riding-cane, taking a pleasure in doing it which I did not like to see.

We left the clearing and tried another path, and then another. And still the horrid wood preyed on my spirits. I agreed with my aunt that we should do well to return to the carriage. On our way back we missed the right path, and lost ourselves for the moment. Mr. Varleigh consulted his compass, and pointed in one direction. Captain Stanwick, consulting nothing but his own jealous humor, pointed in the other. We followed Mr. Varleigh's guidance, and got back to the clearing. He turned to the Captain, and said, good-humoredly: "You see the compass was right." Captain Stanwick, answered, sharply: "There are more ways than one out of an English wood; you talk as if we were in one of your American forests."

Mr. Varleigh seemed to be at a loss to understand his rudeness; there was a pause. The two men looked at each other, standing face to face on the brown earth of the clearing—the Englishman's ruddy countenance, light auburn hair and whiskers, and well-opened bold blue eyes, contrasting with the pale complexion, the keenly-observant look, the dark closely-cut hair, and the delicately-lined face of the American. It was only for a moment: I had barely time to feel uneasy before they controlled themselves and led us back to the carriage, talking as pleasantly as if nothing had happened. For days afterward, nevertheless, that scene in the clearing—the faces and figures of the two men, the dark line of trees hemming them in on all sides, the brown circular patch of ground on which they stood—haunted my memory, and got in the way of my brighter and happier thoughts. When my aunt inquired if I had enjoyed the day, I surprised her by saying No. And when she asked why, I could only answer: "It was all spoiled by Herne Wood."

III.

THREE weeks passed.

The terror of those dreadful days creeps over me again when I think of them. I mean to tell the truth without shrinking; but I may at least consult my own feelings by dwelling on certain particulars as briefly as I can. I shall describe my conduct toward the two men who courted me in the plainest terms, if I say that I distinguished neither of them. Innocently and stupidly I encouraged them both.

In books, women are generally represented as knowing their own minds in matters which relate to love and marriage. This is not my experience of myself. Day followed day; and, ridiculous as it may appear, I could not decide which of my two admirers I liked best!

Captain Stanwick was, at first, the man of my choice. While he kept his temper under control, h e charmed me. But when he let it escape him, he sometimes disappointed, sometimes irritated me. In that frame of mind I turned for relief to Lionel Varleigh, feeling that he was the more gentle and the more worthy man of the two, and honestly believing, at such times, that I preferred him to his rival. For the first few days after our visit to Herne Wood I had excellent opportunities of comparing them. They paid their visits to us together, and they divided their attentions carefully between me and my aunt. At the end of the week, however, they began to present themselves separately. If I had possessed any experience of the natures of men, I might have known what this meant, and might have seen the future possibility of some more serious estrangement between the two friends, of which I might be the unfortunate cause. As it was; I never once troubled my head about what might be passing out of my presence. Whether they came together, or whether they came separately, their visits were always agreeable to me. and I thought of nothing and cared for nothing more.

But the time that was to enlighten me was not far off.

One day Captain Stanwick called much earlier than usual. My aunt had not yet returned from her morning walk. The Captain made some excuse for presenting himself under these circumstances which I have now forgotten.

Without actually committing himself to a proposal of marriage he spoke with such tender feeling, he managed his hold on my inexperience so delicately, that he entrapped me into saying some words, on my side, which I remembered with a certain dismay as soon as I was left alone again. In half an hour more, Mr. Lionel Varleigh was announced as my next visitor. I at once noticed a certain disturbance in his look and manner which was quite new in my experience of him. I offered him a chair. To my surprise he declined to take it.

"I must trust to your indulgence to permit me to put an embarrassing question to you," he began. "It rests with you, Miss Laroche, to decide whether I shall remain here, or whether I shall relieve you of my presence by leaving the room."

"What can you possibly mean?" I asked.

"Is it your wish," he went on, "that I should pay you no more visits except in Captain Stanwick's company, or by Captain Stanwick's express permission?"

My astonishment deprived me for the moment of the power of answering him. "Do you really mean that Captain Stanwick has forbidden you to call on me?" I asked as soon as I could speak.

"I have exactly repeated what Captain Stanwick said to me half an hour since," Lionel Varleigh answered.

In my indignation at hearing this, I entirely forgot the rash words of encouragement which the Captain had entrapped me into speaking to him. When I think of it now, I am ashamed to repeat the language in which I resented this man's presumptuous assertion of authority over me. Having committed one act of indiscretion already, my anxiety to assert my freedom of action hurried me into committing another. I bade Mr. Varleigh welcome whenever he chose to visit me, in terms which made his face flush under the emotions of pleasure and surprise which I had aroused in him. My wounded vanity acknowledged no restraints. I signed to him to take a seat on the sofa at my side; I engaged to go to his lodgings the next day, with my aunt, and see the collection of curiosities which he had amassed in the course of his travels. I almost believe, if he had tried to kiss me, that I was angry enough with the Captain to have let him do it!

Remember what my life had been—remember how ignorantly I had passed the precious days of my youth, how insidiously a sudden accession of wealth and importance had encouraged my folly and my pride—and try, like good Christians, to make some allowance for me!

My aunt came in from her walk, before Mr. Varleigh's visit had ended. She received him rather coldly, and he perceived it. After reminding me of our appointment for the next day, he took his leave.

"What appointment does Mr. Varleigh mean?" my aunt asked, as soon as we were alone. "Is it wise, under the circumstances, to make appointments with Mr. Varleigh?" she said, when I had answered her question. I naturally inquired what she meant. My aunt replied, "I have met Captain Stanwick while I was out walking. He has told me something which I am quite at a loss to understand. Is it possible, Bertha, that you have received a proposal of marriage from him favorably, without saying one word about your intentions to me?"

I instantly denied it. However rashly I might have spoken, I had certainly said nothing to justify Captain Stanwick in claiming me as his promised wife. In his mean fear of a fair rivalry with Mr. Varleigh, he had deliberately misinterpreted me. "If I marry either of the two," I said, "it will be Mr. Varleigh!"

My aunt shook her head. "These two gentlemen seem to be both in love with you, Bertha. It is a trying position for you between them, and I am afraid you have acted with some indiscretion. Captain Stanwick tells me that he and his friend have come to a separation already. I fear you are the cause of it. Mr. Varleigh has left the hotel at which he was staying with the Captain, in consequence of a disagreement between them this morning. You were not aware of that when you accepted his invitation. Shall I write an excuse for you? We must, at least, put off the visit, my dear, until you have set yourself right with Captain Stanwick."

I began to feel a little alarmed, but I was too obstinate to yield without a struggle. "Give me time to think over it," I said. "To write an excuse seems like acknowledging the Captain's authority. Let us wait till to-morrow morning."

IV.

THE morning brought with it another visit from Captain Stanwick. This time my aunt was present. He looked at her without speaking, and turned to me, with his fiery temper showing itself already in his eyes.

"I have a word to say to you in private," he began.

"I have no secrets from my aunt," I answered. "Whatever you have to say, Captain Stanwick, may be said here."

He opened his lips to reply, and suddenly checked himself. He was controlling his anger by so violent an effort that it turned his ruddy face pale. For the moment he conquered his temper—he addressed himself to me with the outward appearance of respect at least.

"Has that man Varleigh lied?" he asked; "or have you given him hopes, too—after what you said to me yesterday?"

"I said nothing to you yesterday which gives you any right to put that question to me," I rejoined. "You have entirely misunderstood me, if you

722

think so."

My aunt attempted to say a few temperate words, in the hope of soothing him. He waved his hand, refusing to listen to her, and advanced closer to me.

"You have misunderstood me," he said, "if you think I am a man to be made a plaything of in the hands of a coquette!"

My aunt interposed once more, with a resolution which I had not expected from her.

"Captain Stanwick," she said, "you are forgetting yourself."

He paid no heed to her; he persisted in speaking to me. "It is my misfortune to love you," he burst out. "My whole heart is set on you. I mean to be your husband, and no other man living shall stand in my way. After what you said to me yesterday, I have a right to consider that you have favored my addresses. This is not a mere flirtation. Don't think it! I say it's the passion of a life! Do you hear? It's the passion of a man's whole life! I am not to be trifled with. I have had a night of sleepless misery about you—I have suffered enough for you—and you're not worth it. Don't laugh! This is no laughing matter. Take care, Bertha! Take care!"

My aunt rose from her chair. She astonished me. On all ordinary occasions the most retiring, the most feminine of women, she now walked up to Captain Stanwick and looked him full in the face, without flinching for an instant.

"You appear to have forgotten that you are speaking in the presence of two ladies," she said. "Alter your tone, sir, or I shall be obliged to take my niece out of the room."

Half angry, half frightened, I tried to speak in my turn. My aunt signed to me to be silent. The Captain drew back a step as if he felt her reproof. But his eyes, still fixed on me, were as fiercely bright as ever. There the gentleman's superficial good-breeding failed to hide the natural man beneath.

"I will leave you in undisturbed possession of the room," he said to my aunt with bitter politeness. "Before I go, permit me to give your niece an opportunity of reconsidering her conduct before it is too late." My aunt drew back, leaving him free to speak to me. After considering for a moment, he laid his hand firmly, but not roughly, on my arm. "You have accepted Lionel Varleigh's invitation to visit him," he said, "under pretense of seeing his curiosities. Think again before you decide on keeping that engagement. If you go to Varleigh tomorrow, you will repent it to the last day of your life." Saying those words, in a tone which made me tremble in spite of myself, he walked to the door. As he laid his hand on the lock, he turned toward me for the last time. "I forbid you to go to Varleigh's lodgings," he said, very distinctly and quietly. "Understand what I tell you. I forbid it."

With those words he left us.

My aunt sat down by me and took my hand kindly. "There is only one thing to be done," she said; "we must return at once to Nettlegrove. If Captain Stanwick attempts to annoy you in your own house, we have neighbors who will protect us, and we have Mr. Loring, our rector, to appeal to for advice. As for Mr. Varleigh, I will write our excuses myself before we go away."

She put out her hand to ring the bell and order the carriage. I stopped her. My childish pride urged me to assert myself in some way, after the passive position that I had been forced to occupy during the interview with Captain Stanwick.

"No," I said, "it is not acting fairly toward Mr. Varleigh to break our engagement with him. Let us return to Nettlegrove by all means, but let us first call on Mr. Varleigh and take our leave. Are we to behave rudely to a gentleman who has always treated us with the utmost consideration, because Captain Stanwick has tried to frighten us by cowardly threats? The commonest feeling of self-respect forbids it."

My aunt protested against this outbreak of folly with perfect temper and good sense. But my obstinacy (my firmness as I thought it!) was immovable. I left her to choose between going with me to Mr. Varleigh, or letting me go to him by myself. Finding it useless to resist, she decided, it is needless to say, on going with me.

We found Mr. Varleigh very courteous, but more than usually grave and quiet. Our visit only lasted for a few minutes; my aunt using the influence of her age and her position to shorten it. She mentioned family affairs as the motive which recalled us to Nettlegrove. I took it on myself to invite Mr. Varleigh to visit me at my own house. He bowed and thanked me, without engaging himself to accept the invitation. When I offered him my hand at parting, he raised it to his lips, and kissed it with a fervor that agitated me. His eyes looked into mine with a sorrowful admiration, with a lingering regret, as if they were taking their leave of me for a long while. "Don't forget me!" he whispered, as he stood at the door, while I followed my aunt out. "Come to Nettlegrove," I whispered back. His eyes dropped to the ground; he let me go without a word more.

This, I declare solemnly, was all that passed at our visit. By some unexpressed consent among us, no allusion whatever was made to Captain Stanwick; not even his name was mentioned. I never knew that the two men had met, just before we called on Mr. Varleigh. Nothing was said which could suggest to me the slightest suspicion of any arrangement for another meeting between them later in the day. Beyond the vague threats which had escaped Captain Stanwick's lips—threats which I own I was rash enough to despise—I had no warning whatever of the dreadful events which happened at Maplesworth on the day after our return to Nettlegrove Hall.

I can only add that I am ready to submit to any questions that may be put to me. Pray don't think me a heartless woman. My worst fault was ignorance. In those days, I knew nothing of the false pretenses under which men hide what is selfish and savage in their natures from the women whom it is their interest to deceive.

No. 2.—Julius Bender, fencing-master, testifies and says:—

I am of German nationality; established in England as teacher of the use of the sword and the pistol since the beginning of the present year.

Finding business slack in London, it unfortunately occurred to me to try what I could do in the country. I had heard of Maplesworth as a place largely frequented by visitors on account of the scenery, as well as by invalids in need of taking the waters; and I opened a gallery there at the beginning of the season of 1817, for fencing and pistol practice. About the visitors I had not been deceived; there were plenty of idle young gentlemen among them who might have been expected to patronize my establishment. They showed the most barbarous indifference to the noble art of attack and defense—came by twos and threes, looked at my gallery, and never returned. My small means began to fail me. After paying my expenses, I was really at my wits' end to find a few pounds to go on with, in the hope of better days.

One gentleman, I remember, who came to see me, and who behaved most liberally.

He described himself as an American, and said he had traveled a great deal. As my ill luck would have it, he stood in no need of my instructions. On the two or three occasions when he amused himself with my foils and my pistols, he proved to be one of the most expert swordsmen and one of the finest shots that I ever met with. It was not wonderful: he had by nature cool nerves and a quick eye; and he had been taught by the masters of the art in Vienna and Paris.

Early in July—the 9th or 10th of the month, I think—I was sitting alone in my gallery, looking ruefully enough at the last two sovereigns in my purse, when a gentleman was announced who wanted a lesson. "A private lesson," he said, with emphasis, looking at the man who cleaned and took care of my weapons.

I sent the man out of the room. The stranger (an Englishman, and, as I fancied, judging by outward appearances, a military man as well) took from his pocket-book a fifty-pound banknote, and held it up before me. "I have a heavy wager depending on a fencing match," he said, "and I have no time to improve myself. Teach me a trick which will make me a match for a man skilled in the use of the foil, and keep the secret—and there are fifty pounds for you."

I hesitated. I did indeed hesitate, poor as I was. But this devil of a man held his banknote before me whichever way I looked, and I had only two pounds left in the world!

"Are you going to fight a duel?" I asked.

"I have already told you what I am going to do," he answered.

I waited a little. The infernal bank-note still tempted me. In spite of myself, I tried him again.

"If I teach you the trick," I persisted, "will you undertake to make no bad use of your lesson?"

"Yes," he said, impatiently enough.

I was not quite satisfied yet.

"Will you promise it, on your word of honor?" I asked.

"Of course I will," he answered. "Take the money, and don't keep me waiting any longer."

I took the money, and I taught him the trick—and I regretted it almost as soon as it was done. Not that I knew, mind, of any serious consequences that followed; for I returned to London the next morning. My sentiments were those of a man of honor, who felt that he had degraded his art, and who could not be quite sure that he might not have armed the hand of an assassin as well. I have no more to say.

No. 3.—Thomas Outwater, servant to Captain Stanwick, testifies and says:—

If I did not firmly believe my master to be out of his senses, no punishment that I could receive would prevail upon me to tell of him what I am going to tell now.

But I say he is mad, and therefore not accountable for what he has done—mad for love of a young woman. If I could have my way, I should like to twist her neck, though she is a lady, and a great heiress into the bargain. Before she came between them, my master and Mr. Varleigh were more like brothers than anything else. She set them at variance, and whether she meant to do it or not is all the same to me. I own I took a dislike to her when I first saw her. She was one of the light-haired, blue-eyed sort, with an innocent look and a snaky waist—not at all to be depended on, as I have found them.

I hear I am not expected to give an account of the disagreement between the two gentlemen, of which this lady was the cause. I am to state what I did in Maplesworth, and what I saw afterward in Herne Wood. Poor as I am, I would give a five-pound note to anybody who could do it for me. Unfortunately, I must do it for myself.

On the 10th of July, in the evening, my master went, for the second time that day, to Mr. Varleigh's lodgings.

I am certain of the date, because it was the day of publication of the town newspaper, and there was a law report in it which set everybody talking. There had been a duel with pistols, a day or two before, between a resident in the town and a visitor, caused by some dispute about horses. Nothing very serious came of the meeting. One of the men only was hurt, and the wound proved to be of no great importance. The awkward part of the matter was that the constables appeared on the ground, before the wounded man had been removed. He and his two seconds were caught, and the prisoners were committed for trial. Dueling (the magistrates said) was an inhuman and unchristian practice, and they were determined to put the law in force and stop it. This sentence made a great stir in the town, and fixed the date, as I have just said, in my mind.

Having been accidentally within hearing of some of the disputes concerning Miss Laroche between my master and Mr. Varleigh, I had my misgivings about the Captain's second visit to the friend with whom he had quarreled already. A gentleman called on him, soon after he had gone out, on important business. This gave me an excuse for following him to Mr. Varleigh's rooms with the visitor's card, and I took the opportunity.

I heard them at high words on my way upstairs, and waited a little on the landing. The Captain was in one of his furious rages; Mr. Varleigh was firm and cool as usual. After listening for a minute or so, I heard enough (in my opinion) to justify me in entering the room. I caught my master in the act of lifting his cane—threatening to strike Mr. Varleigh. He instantly dropped his hand, and turned on me in a fury at my intrusion. Taking no notice of this outbreak of temper, I gave him his friend's card, and went out. A talk followed in voices too low for me to hear outside the room, and then the Captain approached the door. I got out of his way, feeling very uneasy about what was to come next. I could not presume to question Mr. Varleigh. The only thing I could think of was to tell the young lady's aunt what I had seen and heard, and to plead with Miss Laroche herself to make peace between them. When I inquired for the ladies at their lodgings, I was told that they had left Maplesworth.

I saw no more of the Captain that night.

The next morning he seemed to be quite himself again. He said to me, "Thomas, I am going sketching in Herne Wood. Take the paint-box and the rest of it, and put this into the carriage."

He handed me a packet as thick as my arm, and about three feet long, done up in many folds of canvas. I made bold to ask what it was. He answered that it was an artist's sketching umbrella, packed for traveling.

In an hour's time, the carriage stopped on the road below Herne Wood. My master said he would carry his sketching things himself, and I was to wait with the carriage. In giving him the so-called umbrella, I took the occasion of his eye being off me for the moment to pass my hand over it carefully; and I felt, through the canvas, the hilt of a sword. As an old soldier, I could not be mistaken—the hilt of a sword.

What I thought, on making this discovery, does not much matter. What I did was to watch the Captain into the wood, and then to follow him.

I tracked him along the path to where there was a clearing in the midst of the trees. There he stopped, and I got behind a tree. He undid the canvas, and produced two swords concealed in the packet. If I had felt any doubts before, I was certain of what was coming now. A duel without seconds or witnesses, by way of keeping the town magistrates in the dark—a duel between my master and Mr. Varleigh! As his name came into my mind, the man himself appeared, making his way into the clearing from the other side of the wood.

What could I do to stop it? No human creature was in sight. The nearest village was a mile away, reckoning from the further side of the wood. The coachman was a stupid old man, quite useless in a difficulty, even if I had had time enough to go back to the road and summon him to help me. While I was thinking about it, the Captain and Mr. Varleigh had stripped to their shirts and trousers. When they crossed their swords, I could stand it no longer—I burst in on them. "For God Almighty's sake, gentlemen," I cried out, "don't fight without seconds!" My master turned on me, like the madman he was, and threatened me with the point of his sword. Mr. Varleigh pulled me back out of harm's way. "Don't be afraid," he whispered, as he led me back to the verge of the clearing; "I have chosen the sword instead of the pistol expressly to spare his life."

Those noble words (spoken by as brave and true a man as ever breathed) quieted me. I knew Mr. Varleigh had earned the repute of being one of the finest swordsmen in Europe.

The duel began. I was placed behind my master, and was consequently opposite to his antagonist. The Captain stood on his defense, waiting for the other to attack. Mr. Varleigh made a pass. I was opposite the point of his sword; I saw it touch the Captain's left shoulder. In the same instant of time my master struck up his opponent's sword with his own weapon, seized Mr. Varleigh's right wrist in his left hand, and passed his sword clean through Mr. Varleigh's breast. He fell, the victim of a murderous trick—fell without a word or a cry.

The Captain turned slowly, and faced me with his bloody sword in his hand. I can't tell you how he looked; I can only say that the sight of him turned me faint with terror. I was at Waterloo—I am no coward. But I tell you the cold sweat poured down my face like water. I should have dropped if I had not held by the branch of a tree.

My master waited until I had in a measure recovered myself. "Feel if his heart beats," he said, pointing to the man on the ground.

I obeyed. He was dead—the heart was still; the beat of the pulse was gone. I said, "You have killed him!"

The Captain made no answer. He packed up the two swords again in the canvas, and put them under his arm. Then he told me to follow him with the sketching materials. I drew back from him without speaking; there was a horrid hollow sound in his voice that I did not like. "Do as I tell you," he said: "you have yourself to thank for it if I refuse to lose sight of you now." I managed to say that he might trust me to say nothing. He refused to trust me; he put out his hand to take hold of me. I could not stand that. "I'll go with you," I said; "don't touch me!" We reached the carriage and returned to Maplesworth. The same day we traveled by post to London.

In London I contrived to give the Captain the slip. By the first coach the next morning I want back to Maplesworth, eager to hear what had happened, and if the body had been found. Not a word of news reached me; nothing seemed to be known of the duel in Herne Wood.

I went to the wood—on foot, fearing that I might be traced if I hired a carriage. The country round was as solitary as usual. Not a creature was near when I entered the wood; not a creature was near when I looked into the clearing.

There was nothing on the ground. The body was gone.

No. 4.—The Reverend Alfred Loring, Rector of Nettlegrove, testifies and says:—

I.

EARLY in the month of October, 1817, I was informed that Miss Bertha Laroche had called at my house, and wished to see me in private.

I had first been presented to Miss Laroche on her arrival, with her aunt, to take possession of her property at Nettlegrove Hall. My opportunities of improving my acquaintance with her had not been so numerous as I could have desired, and I sincerely regretted it. She had produced a very favorable impression on me. Singularly inexperienced and impulsive—with an odd mixture of shyness and vivacity in her manner, and subject now and then to outbursts of vanity and petulance which she was divertingly incapable of concealing—I could detect, nevertheless, under the surface the signs which told of a true and generous nature, of a simple and pure heart. Her personal appearance, I should add, was attractive in a remarkable degree. There was something in it so peculiar, and at the same time so fascinating, that I am conscious it may have prejudiced me in her favor. For fear of this acknowledgment being misunderstood, I think it right to add that I am old enough to be her grandfather, and that I am also a married man.

I told the servant to show Miss Laroche into my study.

The moment she entered the room, her appearance alarmed me: she looked literally panic-stricken. I offered to send for my wife; she refused the proposal. I entreated her to take time at least to compose herself. It was not in her impulsive nature to do this. She said, "Give me your hand to encourage me, and let me speak while I can." I gave her my hand, poor soul. I said, "Speak to me, my dear, as if I were your father."

So far as I could understand the incoherent statement which she addressed to me, she had been the object of admiration (while visiting Maplesworth) of two gentlemen, who both desired to marry her. Hesitating between them and perfectly inexperienced in such matters, she had been the unfortunate cause of enmity between the rivals, and had returned to Nettlegrove, at her aunt's suggestion, as the best means of extricating herself from a very embarrassing position. The removal failing to alleviate her distressing recollections of what had happened, she and her aunt had tried a further change by making a tour of two months on the Continent. She had returned in a more quiet frame of mind. To her great surprise, she had heard nothing of either of her two suitors, from the day when she left Maplesworth to the day when she presented herself at my rectory.

Early that morning she was walking, after breakfast, in the park at Nettlegrove when she heard footsteps behind her. She turned, and found herself face to face with one of her suitors at Maplesworth. I am informed that there is no necessity now for my suppressing the name. The gentleman was Captain Stanwick.

He was so fearfully changed for the worse that she hardly knew him again.

After his first glance at her, he held his hand over his bloodshot eyes as if the sunlight hurt them. Without a word to prepare her for the disclosure, he confessed that he had killed Mr. Varleigh in a duel. His remorse (he declared) had unsettled his reason: only a few days had passed since he had been released from confinement in an asylum.

"You are the cause of it," he said wildly. "It is for love of you. I have but one hope left to live for—my hope in you. If you cast me off, my mind is made up. I will give my life for the life that I have taken; I will die by my own hand. Look at me, and you will see that I am in earnest. My future as a living man depends on your decision. Think of it to-day, and meet me here to-morrow. Not at this time; the horrid daylight feels like fire in my eyes, and goes like fire to my brain. Wait till sunset—you will find me here."

He left her as suddenly as he had appeared. When she had sufficiently recovered herself to be able to think, she decided on saying nothing of what had happened to her aunt. She took her way to the rectory to seek my advice.

It is needless to encumber my narrative by any statement of the questions which I felt it my duty to put to her under these circumstances. My inquiries informed me that Captain Stanwick had in the first instance produced a favorable impression on her. The less showy qualities of Mr. Varleigh had afterward grown on her liking; aided greatly by the repelling effect on her mind of the Captain's violent language and conduct when he had reason to suspect that his rival was being preferred to him. When she knew the horrible news of Mr. Varleigh's death, she "knew her own heart" (to repeat her exact words to me) by the shock that she felt. Toward Captain Stanwick the only feeling of which she was now conscious was, naturally, a feeling of the strongest aversion.

My own course in this difficult and painful matter appeared to me to be clear. "It is your duty as a Christian to see this miserable man again," I said. "And it is my duty as your friend and pastor, to sustain you under the trial. I will go with you to-morrow to the place of meeting."

II.

THE next evening we found Captain Stanwick waiting for us in the park.

He drew back on seeing me. I explained to him, temperately and firmly, what my position was. With sullen looks he resigned himself to endure my presence. By degrees I won his confidence. My first impression of him remains unshaken—the man's reason was unsettled. I suspected that the assertion of his release was a falsehood, and that he had really escaped from the asylum. It was impossible to lure him into telling me where the place was. He was too cunning to do this—too cunning to say anything about his relations, when I tried to turn the talk that way next. On the other hand, he spoke with a revolting readiness of the crime that he had committed, and of his settled resolution to destroy himself if Miss Laroche refused to be his wife. "I have nothing else to live for; I am alone in the world," he said. "Even my servant has deserted me. He knows how I killed Lionel Varleigh." He paused and spoke his next words in a whisper to me. "I killed him by a trick—he was the best swordsman of the two."

This confession was so horrible that I could only attribute it to an insane delusion. On pressing my inquiries, I found that the same idea must have occurred to the poor wretch's relations, and to the doctors who signed the certificates for placing him under medical care. This conclusion (as I afterward heard) was greatly strengthened by the fact that Mr. Varleigh's body had not been found on the reported scene of the duel. As to the servant, he had deserted his master in London, and had never reappeared. So far as my poor judgment went, the question before me was not of delivering a self-accused murderer to justice (with no corpse to testify against him), but of restoring an insane man to the care of the persons who had been appointed to restrain him.

I tried to test the strength of his delusion in an interval when he was not urging his shocking entreaties on Miss Laroche. "How do you know that you killed Mr. Varleigh?" I said.

He looked at me with a wild terror in his eyes. Suddenly he lifted his right hand, and shook it in the air, with a moaning cry, which was unmistakably a cry of pain. "Should I see his ghost," he asked, "if I had not killed him? I know it, by the pain that wrings me in the hand that stabbed him. Always in my right hand! always the same pain at the moment when I see him!" He stopped and ground his teeth in the agony and reality of his delusion. "Look!" he cried. "Look between the two trees behind you. There he is—with his dark hair, and his shaven face, and his steady look! There he is, standing before me as he stood in the wood, with his eyes on my eyes, and his sword feeling mine!" He turned to Miss Laroche. "Do you see him too?" he asked eagerly. "Tell me the truth. My whole life depends on your telling me the truth."

She controlled herself with a wonderful courage. "I don't see him," she answered.

He took out his handkerchief, and passed it over his face with a gasp of relief. "There is my last chance!" he said. "If she will be true to me—if she will be always near me, morning, noon, and night, I shall be released from the sight of him. See! he is fading away already! Gone!" h e cried, with a scream of exultation. He fell on his knees, and looked at Miss Laroche like a savage adoring his idol. "Will you cast me off now?" he asked, humbly. "Lionel was fond of you in his lifetime. His spirit is a merciful spirit. He shrinks from frightening you, he has left me for your sake; he will release me for your sake. Pity me, take me to live with you—and I shall never see him again!"

It was dreadful to hear him. I saw that the poor girl could endure no more. "Leave us," I whispered to her; "I will join you at the house."

He heard me, and instantly placed himself between us. "Let her promise, or she shan't go."

She felt, as I felt, the imperative necessity of saying anything that might soothe him. At a sign from me she gave him her promise to return.

He was satisfied—he insisted on kissing her hand, and then he let her go. I had by this time succeeded in inducing him to trust me. He proposed, of his own accord, that I should accompany him to the inn in the village at which he had been staying. The landlord (naturally enough distrusting his wretched guest) had warned him that morning to find some other place of shelter. I engaged to use my influence with the man to make him change his purpose, and I succeeded in effecting the necessary arrangements for having the poor wretch properly looked after. On my return to my own house, I wrote to a brother magistrate living near me, and to the superintendent of our county asylum, requesting them to consult with me on the best means of lawfully restraining Captain Stanwick until we could communicate with his relations. Could I have done more than this? The event of the next morning answered that question—answered it at once and forever.

III.

PRESENTING myself at Nettlegrove Hall toward sunset, to take charge of Miss Laroche, I was met by an obstacle in the shape of a protest from her aunt.

This good lady had been informed of the appearance of Captain Stanwick in the park, and she strongly disapproved of encouraging any further communication with him on the part of her niece. She also considered that I had failed in my duty in still leaving the Captain at liberty. I told her that I was only waiting to act on the advice of competent persons, who would arrive the next day to consult with me; and I did my best to persuade her of the wisdom of the course that I had taken in the meantime. Miss Laroche, on her side, was resolved to be true to the promise that she had given. Between us, we induced her aunt to yield on certain conditions.

"I know the part of the park in which the meeting is to take place," the old lady said; "it is my niece's favorite walk. If she is not brought back to me in half an hour's time, I shall send the men-servants to protect her."

The twilight was falling when we reached the appointed place. We found Captain Stanwick angry and suspicious; it was not easy to pacify him on the subject of our delay. His insanity seemed to me to be now more marked than ever. He had seen, or dreamed of seeing, the ghost during the past night. For the first time (he said) the apparition of the dead man had spoken to him. In solemn words it had condemned him to expiate his crime by giving his life for the life that he had taken. It had warned him not to insist on marriage with Bertha Laroche: "She shall share your punishment if she shares your life. And you shall know it by this sign—She shall see me as you see me."

I tried to compose him. He shook his head in immovable despair. "No," he answered; "if she sees him when I see him, there ends the one hope of

736

release that holds me to life. It will be good-by between us, and good-by forever!"

We had walked on, while we were speaking, to a part of the park through which there flowed a rivulet of clear water. On the further bank, the open ground led down into a wooded valley. On our side of the stream rose a thick plantation of fir-trees intersected by a winding path. Captain Stanwick stopped as we reached the place. His eyes rested, in the darkening twilight, on the narrow space pierced by the path among the trees. On a sudden he lifted his right hand, with the same cry of pain which we had heard before; with his left hand he took Miss Laroche by the arm. "There!" he said. "Look where I look! Do you see him there?"

As the words passed his lips, a dimly-visible figure appeared, advancing toward us along the path.

Was it the figure of a living man? or was it the creation of my own excited fancy? Before I could ask myself the question, the man advanced a step nearer to us. A last gleam of the dying light fell on his face through an opening in the trees. At the same instant Miss Laroche started back from Captain Stanwick with a scream of terror. She would have fallen if I had not been near enough to support her. The Captain was instantly at her side again. "Speak!" he cried. "Do you see it, too?"

She was just able to say "Yes" before she fainted in my arms.

He stooped over her, and touched her cold cheek with his lips. "Goodby!" he said, in tones suddenly and strangely changed to the most exquisite tenderness. "Good-by, forever!"

He leaped the rivulet; he crossed the open ground; he was lost to sight in the valley beyond.

As he disappeared, the visionary man among the fir-trees advanced; passed in silence; crossed the rivulet at a bound; and vanished as the figure of the Captain had vanished before him.

I was left alone with the swooning woman. Not a sound, far or near, broke the stillness of the coming night.

No 5.—Mr. Frederic Darnel, Member of the College of Surgeons, testifies and says:—

IN the intervals of my professional duty I am accustomed to occupy myself in studying Botany, assisted by a friend and neighbor, whose tastes in this respect resemble my own. When I can spare an hour or two from my patients, we go out together searching for specimens. Our favorite place is Herne Wood. It is rich in material for the botanist, and it is only a mile distant from the village in which I live.

Early in July, my friend and I made a discovery in the wood of a very alarming and unexpected kind. We found a man in the clearing, prostrated by a dangerous wound, and to all appearance dead.

We carried him to the gamekeeper's cottage on the outskirts of the woods, and on the side of it nearest to our village. He and his boy were out, but the light cart in which he makes his rounds, in the remoter part of his master's property, was in the outhouse. While my friend was putting the horse to, I examined the stranger's wound. It had been quite recently inflicted, and I doubted whether it had (as yet, at any rate) really killed him. I did what I could with the linen and cold water which the gamekeeper's wife offered to me, and then my friend and I removed him carefully to my house in the cart. I applied the necessary restoratives, and I had the pleasure of satisfying myself that the vital powers had revived. He was perfectly unconscious, of course, but the action of the heart became distinctly perceptible, and I had hopes.

In a few days more I felt fairly sure of him. Then the usual fever set in. I was obliged, in justice to his friends, to search his clothes in presence of a witness. We found his handkerchief, his purse, and his cigar-case, and nothing more. No letters or visiting cards; nothing marked on his clothes but initials. There was no help for it but to wait to identify him until he could speak.

When that time came, he acknowledged to me that he had divested himself purposely of any clew to his identity, in the fear (if some mischance happened to him) of the news of it reaching his father and mother abruptly, by means of the newspapers. He had sent a letter to his bankers in London, to be forwarded to his parents, if the bankers neither saw him nor heard from him in a month's time. His first act was to withdraw this letter. The other particulars which he communicated to me are, I am told, already known. I need only add that I willingly kept his secret, simply speaking of him in the neighborhood as a traveler from foreign parts who had met with an accident.

His convalescence was a long one. It was the beginning of October before he was completely restored to health. When he left us he went to London. He behaved most liberally to me; and we parted with sincere good wishes on either side.

No. 6.—Mr. Lionel Varleigh, of Boston, U. S. A., testifies and says:—

MY first proceeding, on my recovery, was to go to the relations of Captain Stanwick in London, for the purpose of making inquiries about him.

I do not wish to justify myself at the expense of that miserable man. It is true that I loved Miss Laroche too dearly to yield her to any rival except at her own wish. It is also true that Captain Stanwick more than once insulted me, and that I endured it. He had suffered from sunstroke in India, and in his angry moments he was hardly a responsible being. It was only when he threatened me with personal chastisement that my patience gave way. We met sword in hand. In my mind was the resolution to spare his life. In his mind was the resolution to kill me. I have forgiven him. I will say no more.

His relations informed me of the symptoms of insane delusion which he had shown after the duel; of his escape from the asylum in which he had been confined; and of the failure to find him again.

The moment I heard this news the dread crossed my mind that Stanwick had found his way to Miss Laroche. In an hour more I was traveling to Nettlegrove Hall.

I arrived late in the evening, and found Miss Laroche's aunt in great alarm about her niece's safety. The young lady was at that very moment speaking to Stanwick in the park, with only an old man (the rector) to protect her. I volunteered to go at once, and assist in taking care of her. A servant accompanied me to show me the place of meeting. We heard voices indistinctly, but saw no one. The servant pointed to a path through the fir-trees. I went on quickly by myself, leaving the man within call. In a few minutes I came upon them suddenly, at a little distance from me, on the bank of a stream.

The fear of seriously alarming Miss Laroche, if I showed myself too suddenly, deprived me for a moment of my presence of mind. Pausing to consider what it might be best to do, I was less completely protected from discovery by the trees than I had supposed. She had seen me; I heard her cry of alarm. The instant afterward I saw Stanwick leap over the rivulet and take to flight. That action roused me. Without stopping for a word of explanation, I pursued him.

Unhappily, I missed my footing in the obscure light, and fell on the open ground beyond the stream. When I had gained my feet once more, Stanwick had disappeared among the trees which marked the boundary of the park beyond me. I could see nothing of him, and I could hear nothing of him, when I came out on the high-road. There I met with a laboring man who showed me the way to the village. From the inn I sent a letter to Miss Laroche's aunt, explaining what had happened, and asking leave to call at the Hall on the next day.

Early in the morning the rector came to me at the inn. He brought sad news. Miss Laroche was suffering from a nervous attack, and my visit to the Hall must be deferred. Speaking next of the missing man, I heard all that Mr. Loring could tell me. My intimate knowledge of Stanwick enabled me to draw my own conclusion from the facts. The thought instantly crossed my mind that the poor wretch might have committed his expiatory suicide at the very spot on which he had attempted to kill me. Leaving the rector to institute the necessary inquiries, I took post-horses to Maplesworth on my way to Herne Wood.

Advancing from the high-road to the wood, I saw two persons at a little distance from me—a man in the dress of a gamekeeper, and a lad. I was too much agitated to take any special notice of them; I hurried along the path which led to the clearing. My presentiment had not misled me. There he lay, dead on the scene of the duel, with a blood-stained razor by his side! I fell on my knees by the corpse; I took his cold hand in mine; and I thanked God that I had forgiven him in the first days of my recovery.

I was still kneeling, when I felt myself seized from behind. I struggled to my feet, and confronted the gamekeeper. He had noticed my hurry in entering the wood; his suspicions had been aroused, and he and the lad had followed me. There was blood on my clothes; there was horror in my face. Appearances were plainly against me; I had no choice but to accompany the gamekeeper to the nearest magistrate.

My instructions to my solicitor forbade him to vindicate my innocence by taking any technical legal objections to the action of the magistrate or of the coroner. I insisted on my witnesses being summoned to the lawyer's office, and allowed to state, in their own way, what they could truly declare on my behalf; and I left my defense to be founded upon the materials thus obtained. In the meanwhile I was detained in custody, as a matter of course.

With this event the tragedy of the duel reached its culminating point. I was accused of murdering the man who had attempted to take my life!

This last incident having been related, all that is worth noticing in my contribution to the present narrative comes to an end. I was tried in due course of law. The evidence taken at my solicitor's office was necessarily altered in form, though not in substance, by the examination to which the witnesses were subjected in a court of justice. So thoroughly did our defense satisfy the jury, that they became restless toward the close of the proceedings, and returned their verdict of Not Guilty without quitting the box.

When I was a free man again, it is surely needless to dwell on the first use that I made of my honorable acquittal. Whether I deserved the enviable place that I occupied in Bertha's estimation, it is not for me to say. Let me leave the decision to the lady who has ceased to be Miss Laroche—I mean the lady who has been good enough to become my wife.

MISS DULANE AND MY LORD.

Part I. TWO REMONSTRATIONS.

I.

ONE afternoon old Miss Dulane entered her drawing-room; ready to receive visitors, dressed in splendor, and exhibiting every outward appearance of a defiant frame of mind.

Just as a saucy bronze nymph on the mantelpiece struck the quarter to three on an elegant clock under her arm, a visitor was announced—"Mrs. Newsham."

Miss Dulane wore her own undisguised gray hair, dressed in perfect harmony with her time of life. Without an attempt at concealment, she submitted to be too short and too stout. Her appearance (if it had only been made to speak) would have said, in effect: "I am an old woman, and I scorn to disguise it."

Mrs. Newsham, tall and elegant, painted and dyed, acted on the opposite principle in dressing, which confesses nothing. On exhibition before the world, this lady's disguise asserted that she had reached her thirtieth year on her last birthday. Her husband was discreetly silent, and Father Time was discreetly silent: they both knew that her last birthday had happened thirty years since.

"Shall we talk of the weather and the news, my dear? Or shall we come to the object of your visit at once?" So Miss Dulane opened the interview.

"Your tone and manner, my good friend, are no doubt provoked by the report in the newspaper of this morning. In justice to you, I refuse to believe the report." So Mrs. Newsham adopted her friend's suggestion.

"You kindness is thrown away, Elizabeth. The report is true."

"Matilda, you shock me!"

"Why?"

"At your age!"

"If he doesn't object to my age, what does it matter to you?"

"Don't speak of that man!"

"Why not?"

"He is young enough to be your son; and he is marrying you—impudently, undisguisedly marrying you—for your money!"

"And I am marrying him—impudently, undisguisedly marrying him—for his rank."

"You needn't remind me, Matilda, that you are the daughter of a tailor."

"In a week or two more, Elizabeth, I shall remind you that I am the wife of a nobleman's son."

"A younger son; don't forget that."

"A younger son, as you say. He finds the social position, and I find the money—half a million at my own sole disposal. My future husband is a good fellow in his way, and his future wife is another good fellow in her way. To look at your grim face, one would suppose there were no such things in the world as marriages of convenience."

"Not at your time of life. I tell you plainly, your marriage will be a public scandal."

"That doesn't frighten us," Miss Dulane remarked. "We are resigned to every ill-natured thing that our friends can say of us. In course of time, the next nine days' wonder will claim public attention, and we shall be forgotten. I shall be none the less on that account Lady Howel Beaucourt. And my husband will be happy in the enjoyment of every expensive taste which a poor man call gratify, for the first time in his life. Have you any more objections to make? Don't hesitate to speak plainly."

"I have a question to ask, my dear."

"Charmed, I am sure, to answer it—if I can."

"Am I right in supposing that Lord Howel Beaucourt is about half your age?"

"Yes, dear; my future husband is as nearly as possible half as old as I am."

Mrs. Newsham's uneasy virtue shuddered. "What a profanation of marriage!" she exclaimed.

"Nothing of the sort," her friend pronounced positively. "Marriage, by the law of England (as my lawyer tells me), is nothing but a contract. Who ever heard of profaning a contract?"

"Call it what you please, Matilda. Do you expect to live a happy life, at your age, with a young man for your husband?"

"A happy life," Miss Dulane repeated, "because it will be an innocent life." She laid a certain emphasis on the last word but one.

Mrs. Newsham resented the emphasis, and rose to go. Her last words were the bitterest words that she had spoken yet.

"You have secured such a truly remarkable husband, my dear, that I am emboldened to ask a great favor. Will you give me his lordship's photograph?"

"No," said Miss Dulane, "I won't give you his lordship's photograph."

"What is your objection, Matilda?"

"A very serious objection, Elizabeth. You are not pure enough in mind to be worthy of my husband's photograph."

With that reply the first of the remonstrances assumed hostile proportions, and came to an untimely end.

II.

THE second remonstrance was reserved for a happier fate. It took its rise in a conversation between two men who were old and true friends. In other words, it led to no quarreling.

The elder man was one of those admirable human beings who are cordial, gentle, and good-tempered, without any conscious exercise of their own virtues. He was generally known in the world about him by a fond and familiar use of his Christian name. To call him "Sir Richard" in these pages (except in the character of one of his servants) would be simply ridiculous. When he lent his money, his horses, his house, and (sometimes, after unlucky friends had dropped to the lowest social depths) even his clothes, this general benefactor was known, in the best society and the worst society alike, as "Dick." He filled the hundred mouths of Rumor with his nickname, in the days when there was an opera in London, as the proprietor of the "Beauty-box." The ladies who occupied the box were all invited under the same circumstances. They enjoyed operatic music; but their husbands and fathers were not rich enough to be able to gratify that expensive taste. Dick's carriage called for them, and took them home again; and the beauties all agreed (if he ever married) that Mrs. Dick would be the most enviable woman on the face of the civilized earth. Even the false reports, which declared that he was privately married already, and on bad terms with his wife, slandered him cordially under the popular name. And his intimate companions, when they alluded among each other to a romance in his life which would remain a hidden romance to the end of his days, forgot that the occasion justified a serious and severe use of his surname, and blamed him affectionately as "poor dear Dick."

The hour was midnight; and the friends, whom the most hospitable of men delighted to assemble round his dinner-table, had taken their leave with the exception of one guest specially detained by the host, who led him back to the dining-room.

"You were angry with our friends," Dick began, "when they asked you about that report of your marriage. You won't be angry with Me. Are you really going to be the old maid's husband?"

This plain question received a plain reply: "Yes, I am."

Dick took the young lord's hand. Simply and seriously, he said: "Accept my congratulations."

Howel Beaucourt started as if he had received a blow instead of a compliment.

"There isn't another man or woman in the whole circle of my acquaintance," he declared, "who would have congratulated me on marrying Miss Dulane. I believe you would make allowances for me if I had committed murder."

"I hope I should," Dick answered gravely. "When a man is my friend— murder or marriage—I take it for granted that he has a reason for what he does. Wait a minute. You mustn't give me more credit than I deserve. I don't agree with you. If I were a marrying man myself, I shouldn't pick an old maid—I should prefer a young one. That's a matter of taste. You are not like me. You always have a definite object in view. I may not know what the object is. Never mind! I wish you joy all the same."

Beaucourt was not unworthy of the friendship he had inspired. "I should be ungrateful indeed," he said, "if I didn't tell you what my object is. You know that I am poor?"

"The only poor friend of mine," Dick remarked, "who has never borrowed money of me."

Beaucourt went on without noticing this. "I have three expensive tastes," he said. "I want to get into Parliament; I want to have a yacht; I want to collect pictures. Add, if you like, the selfish luxury of helping poverty and wretchedness, and hearing my conscience tell me what an excellent man I am. I can't do all this on five hundred a year—but I can do it on forty times five hundred a year. Moral: marry Miss Dulane."

Listening attentively until the other had done, Dick showed a sardonic side to his character never yet discovered in Beaucourt's experience of him.

"I suppose you have made the necessary arrangements," he said. "When the old lady releases you, she will leave consolation behind her in her will."

"That's the first ill-natured thing I ever heard you say, Dick. When the old lady dies, my sense of honor takes fright, and turns its back on her will. It's a condition on my side, that every farthing of her money shall be left to her relations."

"Don't you call yourself one of them?"

"What a question! Am I her relation because the laws of society force a mock marriage on us? How can I make use of her money unless I am her husband? and how can she make use of my title unless she is my wife? As long as she lives I stand honestly by my side of the bargain. But when she dies the transaction is at an end, and the surviving partner returns to his five hundred a year."

Dick exhibited another surprising side to his character. The most compliant of men now became as obstinate as the proverbial mule.

"All very well," he said, "but it doesn't explain why—if you must sell yourself—you have sold yourself to an old lady. There are plenty of young ones and pretty ones with fortunes to tempt you. It seems odd that you haven't tried your luck with one of them."

"No, Dick. It would have been odd, and worse than odd, if I had tried my luck with a young woman."

"I don't see that."

"You shall see it directly. If I marry an old woman for her money, I have no occasion to be a hypocrite; we both know that our marriage is a mere matter of form. But if I make a young woman my wife because I want her money, and if that young woman happens to be worth a straw, I must deceive her and disgrace myself by shamming love. That, my boy, you may depend upon it, I will never do."

Dick's face suddenly brightened with a mingled expression of relief and triumph.

"Ha! my mercenary friend," he burst out, "there's something mixed up in this business which is worthier of you than anything I have heard yet. Stop! I'm going to be clever for the first time in my life. A man who talks of love as you do, must have felt love himself. Where is the young one and the pretty one? And what has she done, poor dear, to be deserted for an old woman? Good God! how you look at me! I have hurt your feelings—I have been a greater fool than ever—I am more ashamed of myself than words can say!"

Beaucourt stopped him there, gently and firmly.

"You have made a very natural mistake," he said. "There was a young lady. She has refused me—absolutely refused me. There is no more love in my life. It's a dark life and an empty life for the rest of my days. I must see what money can do for me next. When I have thoroughly hardened my heart I may not feel my misfortune as I feel it now. Pity me or despise me. In either case let us say goodnight."

He went out into the hall and took his hat. Dick went out into the hall and took his hat.

"Have your own way," he answered, "I mean to have mine—I'll go home with you."

The man was simply irresistible. Beaucourt sat down resignedly on the nearest of the hall chairs. Dick asked him to return to the dining-room. "No," he said; "it's not worth while. What I can tell you may be told in two minutes." Dick submitted, and took the next of the hall chairs. In that inappropriate place the young lord's unpremeditated confession was forced out of him, by no more formidable exercise of power than the kindness of his friend.

"When you hear where I met with her," he began, "you will most likely not want to hear any more. I saw her, for the first time, on the stage of a music hall."

He looked at Dick. Perfectly quiet and perfectly impenetrable, Dick only said, "Go on." Beaucourt continued in these words:

"She was singing Arne's delicious setting of Ariel's song in the 'Tempest,' with a taste and feeling completely thrown away on the greater part of the audience. That she was beautiful—in my eyes at least—I needn't say. That she had descended to a sphere unworthy of her and new to her, nobody could doubt. Her modest dress, her refinement of manner, seemed rather to puzzle than to please most of the people present; they applauded her, but not very warmly, when she retired. I obtained an introduction through her music-master, who happened to be acquainted professionally with some relatives of mine. He told me that she was a young widow; and he assured me that the calamity through which her family had lost their place in the world had brought no sort of disgrace on them. If I wanted to know more, he referred me to the lady herself. I found her very reserved. A long time passed before I could win her confidence—and a longer time still before I ventured to confess the feeling with which she had inspired me. You know the rest."

"You mean, of course, that you offered her marriage?"

"Certainly."

"And she refused you on account of your position in life."

"No. I had foreseen that obstacle, and had followed the example of the adventurous nobleman in the old story. Like him, I assumed a name, and presented myself as belonging to her own respectable middle class of life. You are too old a friend to suspect me of vanity if I tell you that she had no objection to me, and no suspicion that I had approached her (personally speaking) under a disguise."

"What motive could she possibly have had for refusing you?" Dick asked.

"A motive associated with her dead husband," Beaucourt answered. "He had married her—mind, innocently married her—while his first wife was living. The woman was an inveterate drunkard; they had been separated for years. Her death had been publicly reported in the newspapers, among the persons killed in a railway accident abroad. When she claimed her unhappy husband he was in delicate health. The shock killed him. His widow—I can't, and won't, speak of her misfortune as if it was her fault—knew of no living friends who were in a position to help her. Not a great artist with a wonderful voice, she could still trust to her musical accomplishments to provide for the necessities of life. Plead as I might with her to forget the past, I always got the same reply: 'If I was base enough to let myself be tempted by the happy future that you offer, I should deserve the unmerited disgrace which has fallen on me. Marry a woman whose reputation will bear inquiry, and forget me.' I was mad enough to press my suit once too often. When I visited her on the next day she was gone. Every effort to trace her has failed. Lost, my friend— irretrievably lost to me!"

He offered his hand and said good-night. Dick held him back on the doorstep.

"Break off your mad engagement to Miss Dulane," he said. "Be a man, Howel; wait and hope! You are throwing away your life when happiness is within your reach, if you will only be patient. That poor young creature is worthy of you. Lost? Nonsense! In this narrow little world people are never hopelessly lost till they are dead and underground. Help me to recognize her by a description, and tell me her name. I'll find her; I'll persuade her to come back to you—and, mark my words, you will live to bless the day when you followed my advice."

This well-meant remonstrance was completely thrown away. Beaucourt's despair was deaf to every entreaty that Dick had addressed to him. "Thank you with all my heart," he said. "You don't know her as I do. She is one of the very few women who mean No when they say No. Useless, Dick—useless!"

Those were the last words he said to his friend in the character of a single man.

Part II. PLATONIC MARRIAGE.

III.

"SEVEN months have passed, my dear Dick, since my 'inhuman obstinacy' (those were the words you used) made you one of the witnesses at my marriage to Miss Dulane, sorely against your will. Do you remember your parting prophecy when you were out of the bride's hearing? 'A miserable life is before that woman's husband—and, by Jupiter, he has deserved it!'

"Never, my dear boy, attempt to forecast the future again. Viewed as a prophet you are a complete failure. I have nothing to complain of in my married life.

"But you must not mistake me. I am far from saying that I am a happy man; I only declare myself to be a contented man. My old wife is a marvel of good temper and good sense. She trusts me implicitly, and I have given her no reason to regret it. We have our time for being together, and our time for keeping apart. Within our inevitable limits we understand each other and respect each other, and have a truer feeling of regard on both sides than many people far better matched than we are in point of age. But you shall judge for yourself. Come and dine with us, when I return on Wednesday next from the trial trip of my new yacht. In the meantime I have a service to ask of you.

"My wife's niece has been her companion for years. She has left us to be married to an officer, who has taken her to India; and we are utterly at a loss how to fill her place. The good old lady doesn't want much. A nice-tempered refined girl, who can sing and play to her with some little taste and feeling, and read to her now and then when her eyes are weary—there is what we require; and there, it seems, is more than we can get, after advertising for a week past. Of all the 'companions' who have presented themselves, not one has turned out to be the sort of person whom Lady Howel wants.

"Can you help us? In any case, my wife sends you her kind remembrances; and (true to the old times) I add my love."

On the day which followed the receipt of this letter, Dick paid a visit to Lady Howel Beaucourt.

"You seem to be excited," she said. "Has anything remarkable happened?"

"Pardon me if I ask a question first," Dick replied. "Do you object to a young widow?"

"That depends on the widow."

"Then I have found the very person you want. And, oddly enough, your husband has had something to do with it."

"Do you mean that my husband has recommended her?"

There was an undertone of jealousy in Lady Howel's voice—-jealousy excited not altogether without a motive. She had left it to Beaucourt's sense of honor to own the truth, if there had been any love affair in his past life which ought to make him hesitates before he married. He had justified Miss Dulane's confidence in him; acknowledging an attachment to a young widow, and adding that she had positively refused him. "We have not met since," he said, "and we shall never meet again." Under those circumstances, Miss Dulane had considerately abstained from asking for any further details. She had not thought of the young widow again, until Dick's language had innocently inspired her first doubt. Fortunately for both of them, he was an outspoken man; and he reassured her unreservedly in these words: "Your husband knows nothing about it."

"Now," she said, "you may tell me how you came to hear of the lady."

"Through my uncle's library," Dick replied. "His will has left me his collection of books—in such a wretchedly neglected condition that I asked Beaucourt (not being a reading man myself) if he knew of any competent person who could advise me how to set things right. He introduced me to Farleigh & Halford, the well-known publishers. The second partner is a book collector himself, as well as a bookseller. He kindly looks in now and then, to see how his instructions for mending and binding are being carried out. When he called yesterday I thought of you, and I found he could help us to a young lady employed in his office at correcting proof sheets."

"What is the lady's name?"

"Mrs. Evelin."

"Why does she leave her employment?"

"To save her eyes, poor soul. When the senior partner, Mr. Farleigh, met with her, she was reduced by family misfortunes to earn her own living. The publishers would have been only too glad to keep her in their office, but for the oculist's report. He declared that she would run the risk of blindness, if she fatigued her weak eyes much longer. There is the only objection to this otherwise invaluable person—she will not be able to read to you."

"Can she sing and play?"

"Exquisitely. Mr. Farleigh answers for her music."

"And her character?"

"Mr. Halford answers for her character."

"And her manners?"

"A perfect lady. I have seen her and spoken to her; I answer for her manners, and I guarantee her personal appearance. Charming—charming!"

For a moment Lady Howel hesitated. After a little reflection, she decided that it was her duty to trust her excellent husband. "I will receive the charming widow," she said, "to-morrow at twelve o'clock; and, if she produces the right impression, I promise to overlook the weakness of her eyes."

IV.

BEAUCOURT had prolonged the period appointed for the trial trip of his yacht by a whole week. His apology when he returned delighted the kind-hearted old lady who had made him a present of the vessel.

"There isn't such another yacht in the whole world," he declared. "I really hadn't the heart to leave that beautiful vessel after only three days experience of her." He burst out with a torrent of technical praises of the yacht, to which his wife listened as attentively as if she really understood what he was talking about. When his breath and his eloquence were exhausted alike, she said, "Now, my dear, it's my turn. I can match your perfect vessel with my perfect lady."

"What! you have found a companion?"

"Yes."

"Did Dick find her for you?"

"He did indeed. You shall see for yourself how grateful I ought to be to your friend."

She opened a door which led into the next room. "Mary, my dear, come and be introduced to my husband."

Beaucourt started when he heard the name, and instantly recovered himself. He had forgotten how many Marys there are in the world.

Lady Howel returned, leading her favorite by the hand, and gayly introduced her the moment they entered the room.

"Mrs. Evelin; Lord—"

She looked at her husband. The utterance of his name was instantly suspended on her lips. Mrs. Evelin's hand, turning cold at the same moment in her hand, warned her to look round. The face of the woman more than reflected the inconcealable agitation in the face of the man.

The wife's first words, when she recovered herself, were addressed to them both.

"Which of you can I trust," she asked, "to tell me the truth?"

"You can trust both of us," her husband answered.

The firmness of his tone irritated her. "I will judge of that for myself," she said. "Go back to the next room," she added, turning to Mrs. Evelin; "I will hear you separately."

The companion, whose duty it was to obey—whose modesty and

754

gentleness had won her mistress's heart—refused to retire.

"No," she said; "I have been deceived too. I have my right to hear what Lord Howel has to say for himself."

Beaucourt attempted to support the claim that she had advanced. His wife sternly signed to him to be silent. "What do you mean?" she said, addressing the question to Mrs. Evelin.

"I mean this. The person whom you speak of as a nobleman was presented to me as 'Mr. Vincent, an artist.' But for that deception I should never have set foot in your ladyship's house."

"Is this true, my lord?" Lady Howel asked, with a contemptuous emphasis on the title of nobility.

"Quite true," her husband answered. "I thought it possible that my rank might prove an obstacle in the way of my hopes. The blame rests on me, and on me alone. I ask Mrs. Evelin to pardon me for an act of deception which I deeply regret."

Lady Howel was a just woman. Under other circumstances she might have shown herself to be a generous woman. That brighter side of her character was incapable of revealing itself in the presence of Mrs. Evelin, young and beautiful, and in possession of her husband's heart. She could say, "I beg your pardon, madam; I have not treated you justly." But no self-control was strong enough to restrain the next bitter words from passing her lips. "At my age," she said, "Lord Howel will soon be free; you will not have long to wait for him."

The young widow looked at her sadly—answered her sadly.

"Oh, my lady, your better nature will surely regret having said that!"

For a moment her eyes rested on Beaucourt, dim with rising tears. She left the room—and left the house.

There was silence between the husband and wife. Beaucourt was the first to speak again.

"After what you have just heard, do you persist in your jealousy of that lady, and your jealousy of me?" he asked.

"I have behaved cruelly to her and to you. I am ashamed of myself," was all she said in reply. That expression of sorrow, so simple and so true, did not appeal in vain to the gentler side of Beaucourt's nature. He kissed his wife's hand; he tried to console her.

"You may forgive me," she answered. "I cannot forgive myself. That poor lady's last words have made my heart ache. What I said to her in anger I ought to have said generously. Why should she not wait for you? After your life with me—a life of kindness, a life of self-sacrifice—you deserve your reward. Promise me that you will marry the woman you love—after my death has released you."

"You distress me, and needlessly distress me," he said. "What you are thinking of, my dear, can never happen; no, not even if—" He left the rest unsaid.

"Not even if you were free?" she asked.

"Not even then."

She looked toward the next room. "Go in, Howel, and bring Mrs. Evelin back; I have something to say to her."

The discovery that she had left the house caused no fear that she had taken to flight with the purpose of concealing herself. There was a prospect before the poor lonely woman which might be trusted to preserve her from despair, to say the least of it.

During her brief residence in Beaucourt's house she had shown to Lady Howel a letter received from a relation, who had emigrated to New Zealand with her husband and her infant children some years since. They had steadily prospered; they were living in comfort, and they wanted for nothing but a trustworthy governess to teach their children. The mother had accordingly written, asking if her relative in England could recommend a competent person, and offering a liberal salary. In showing the letter to Lady Howel,

Mrs. Evelin had said: "If I had not been so happy as to attract your notice, I might have offered to be the governess myself."

Assuming that it had now occurred to her to act on this idea, Lady Howel felt assured that she would apply for advice either to the publishers who had recommended her, or to Lord Howel's old friend.

Beaucourt at once offered to make the inquiries which might satisfy his wife that she had not been mistaken. Readily accepting his proposal, she asked at the same time for a few minutes of delay.

"I want to say to you," she explained, "what I had in my mind to say to Mrs. Evelin. Do you object to tell me why she refused to marry you? I couldn't have done it in her place."

"You would have done it, my dear, as I think, if her misfortune had been your misfortune." With those prefatory words he told the miserable story of Mrs. Evelin's marriage.

Lady Howel's sympathies, strongly excited, appeared to have led her to a conclusion which she was not willing to communicate to her husband. She asked him, rather abruptly, if he would leave it to her to find Mrs. Evelin. "I promise," she added, "to tell you what I am thinking of, when I come back."

In two minutes more she was ready to go out, and had hurriedly left the house.

V.

AFTER a long absence Lady Howel returned, accompanied by Dick. His face and manner betrayed unusual agitation; Beaucourt noticed it.

"I may well be excited," Dick declared, "after what I have heard, and after what we have done. Lady Howel, yours is the brain that thinks to some purpose. Make our report—I wait for you."

But my lady preferred waiting for Dick. He consented to speak first, for the thoroughly characteristic reason that he could "get over it in no time."

"I shall try the old division," he said, "into First, Second, and Third.

Don't be afraid; I am not going to preach—quite the contrary; I am going to be quick about it. First, then, Mrs. Evelin has decided, under sound advice, to go to New Zealand. Second, I have telegraphed to her relations at the other end of the world to tell them that she is coming. Third, and last, Farleigh & Halford have sent to the office, and secured a berth for her in the next ship that sails—date the day after to-morrow. Done in half a minute. Now, Lady Howel!"

"I will begin and end in half a minute too," she said, "if I can. First," she continued, turning to her husband, "I found Mrs. Evelin at your friend's house. She kindly let me say all that I could say for the relief of my poor heart. Secondly—"

She hesitated, smiled uneasily, and came to a full stop.

"I can't do it, Howel," she confessed; "I speak to you as usual, or I can never get on. Saying many things in few words—if the ladies who assert our rights will forgive me for confessing it—is an accomplishment in which we are completely beaten by the men. You must have thought me rude, my dear, for leaving you very abruptly, without a word of explanation. The truth is, I had an idea in my head, and I kept it to myself (old people are proverbially cautious, you know) till I had first found out whether it was worth mentioning. When you were speaking of the wretched creature who had claimed Mrs. Evelin's husband as her own, you said she was an inveterate drunkard. A woman in that state of degradation is capable, as I persist in thinking, of any wickedness. I suppose this put it into my head to doubt her—no; I mean, to wonder whether Mr. Evelin—do you know that she keeps her husband's name by his own entreaty addressed to her on his deathbed?—oh, I am losing myself in a crowd of words of my own collecting! Say the rest of it for me, Sir Richard!"

"No, Lady Howel. Not unless you call me 'Dick.'"

"Then say it for me—Dick."

"No, not yet, on reflection. Dick is too short, say 'Dear Dick.'"

"Dear Dick—there!"

"Thank you, my lady. Now we had better remember that your husband is present." He turned to Beaucourt. "Lady Howel had the idea," he proceeded, "which ought to have presented itself to you and to me. It was a serious misfortune (as she thought) that Mr. Evelin's sufferings in his last illness, and his wife's anxiety while she was nursing him, had left them unfit to act in their own defense. They might otherwise not have submitted to the drunken wretch's claim, without first making sure that she had a right to advance it. Taking her character into due consideration, are we quite certain that she was herself free to marry, when Mr. Evelin unfortunately made her his wife? To that serious question we now mean to find an answer. With Mrs. Evelin's knowledge of the affair to help us, we have discovered the woman's address, to begin with. She keeps a small tobacconist's shop at the town of Grailey in the north of England. The rest is in the hands of my lawyer. If we make the discovery that we all hope for, we have your wife to thank for it." He paused, and looked at his watch. "I've got an appointment at the club. The committee will blackball the best fellow that ever lived if I don't go and stop them. Good-by."

The last day of Mrs. Evelin's sojourn in England was memorable in more ways than one.

On the first occasion in Beaucourt's experience of his married life, his wife wrote to him instead of speaking to him, although they were both in the house at the time. It was a little note only containing these words: "I thought you would like to say good-by to Mrs. Evelin. I have told her to expect you in the library, and I will take care that you are not disturbed."

Waiting at the window of her sitting-room, on the upper floor, Lady Howel perceived that the delicate generosity of her conduct had been gratefully felt. The interview in the library barely lasted for five minutes. She saw Mrs. Evelin leave the house with her veil down. Immediately afterward, Beaucourt ascended to his wife's room to thank her. Carefully as he had endeavored to hide them, the traces of tears in his eyes told her how cruelly the parting scene had tried him. It was a bitter moment for his admirable wife. "Do you wish me dead?" she asked with sad self-possession. "Live," he said, "and live happily, if you wish to make me happy too." He drew her to him and kissed her forehead. Lady Howel had her reward.

Part III. NEWS FROM THE COLONY.

<u>VI.</u>

FURNISHED with elaborate instructions to guide him, which included golden materials for bribery, a young Jew holding the place of third clerk in the office of Dick's lawyer was sent to the town of Grailey to make discoveries. In the matter of successfully instituting private inquiries, he was justly considered to be a match for any two Christians who might try to put obstacles in his way. His name was Moses Jackling.

Entering the cigar-shop, the Jew discovered that he had presented himself at a critical moment.

A girl and a man were standing behind the counter. The girl looked like a maid-of-all-work: she was rubbing the tears out of her eyes with a big red fist. The man, smart in manner and shabby in dress, received the stranger with a peremptory eagerness to do business. "Now, then! what for you?" Jackling bought the worst cigar he had ever smoked, in the course of an enormous experience of bad tobacco, and tried a few questions with this result. The girl had lost her place; the man was in "possession"; and the stock and furniture had been seized for debt. Jackling thereupon assumed the character of a creditor, and ask to speak with the mistress.

"She's too ill to see you, sir," the girl said.

"Tell the truth, you fool," cried the man in possession. He led the way to a door with a glass in the upper part of it, which opened into a parlor behind the shop. As soon as his back was turned, Jackling whispered to the maid, "When I go, slip out after me; I've got something for you." The man lifted the curtain over the glass. "Look through," he said, "and see what's the matter with her for yourself."

Jackling discovered the mistress flat on her back on the floor, helplessly drunk. That was enough for the clerk—so far. He took leave of the man in possession, with the one joke which never wears out in the estimation of

Englishmen; the joke that foresees the drinker's headache in the morning. In a minute or two more the girl showed herself, carrying an empty jug. She had been sent for the man's beer, and she was expected back directly. Jackling, having first overwhelmed her by a present of five shillings, proposed another appointment in the evening. The maid promised to be at the place of meeting; and in memory of the five shillings she kept her word.

"What wages do you get?" was the first question that astonished her.

"Three pounds a year, sir," the unfortunate creature replied.

"All paid?"

"Only one pound paid—and I say it's a crying shame."

"Say what you like, my dear, so long as you listen to me. I want to know everything that your mistress says and does—first when she's drunk, and then when she's sober. Wait a bit; I haven't done yet. If you tell me everything you can remember—mind everything—I'll pay the rest of your wages."

Madly excited by this golden prospect, the victim of domestic service answered inarticulately with a scream. Jackling's right hand and left hand entered his pockets, and appeared again holding two sovereigns separately between two fingers and thumbs. From that moment, he was at liberty to empty the maid-of-all-work's memory of every saying and doing that it contained.

The sober moments of the mistress yielded little or nothing to investigation. The report of her drunken moments produced something worth hearing. There were two men whom it was her habit to revile bitterly in her cups. One of them was Mr. Evelin, whom she abused—sometimes for the small allowance that he made to her; sometimes for dying before she could prosecute him for bigamy. Her drunken remembrances of the other man were associated with two names. She called him "Septimus"; she called him "Darts"; and she despised him occasionally for being a "common sailor." It was clearly demonstrated that he was one man, and not two. Whether he was "Septimus," or whether he was "Darts," he had always committed the same atrocities. He had taken her money away from her; he had called her by an atrocious name; and he had knocked her down on more than one occasion. Provided with this information, Jackling rewarded the girl, and paid a visit to her mistress the next day.

The miserable woman was exactly in the state of nervous prostration (after the excess of the previous evening) which offered to the clerk his best chance of gaining his end. He presented himself as the representative of friends, bent on helping her, whose modest benevolence had positively forbidden him to mention their names.

"What sum of money must you pay," he asked, "to get rid of the man in possession?"

Too completely bewildered to speak, her trembling hand offered to him a slip of paper on which the amount of the debt and the expenses was set forth: L51 12s. 10d.

With some difficulty the Jew preserved his gravity. "Very well," he resumed. "I will make it up to sixty pounds (to set you going again) on two conditions."

She suddenly recovered her power of speech. "Give me the money!" she cried, with greedy impatience of delay.

"First condition," he continued, without noticing the interruption: "you are not to suffer, either in purse or person, if you give us the information that we want."

She interrupted him again. "Tell me what it is, and be quick about it."

"Second condition," he went on as impenetrably as ever; "you take me to the place where I can find the certificate of your marriage to Septimus Darts."

Her eyes glared at him like the eyes of a wild animal. Furies, hysterics, faintings, denials, threats—Jackling endured them all by turns. It was enough for him that his desperate guess of the evening before, had hit the mark on the morning after. When she had completely exhausted herself he returned to the experiment which he had already tried with the maid. Well aware of the advantage of exhibiting gold instead of notes, when the object is to tempt poverty, he produced the promised bribe in sovereigns, pouring them playfully backward and forward from one big hand to the other.

The temptation was more than the woman could resist. In another half-hour the two were traveling together to a town in one of the midland counties.

The certificate was found in the church register, and duly copied.

It also appeared that one of the witnesses to the marriage was still living. His name and address were duly noted in the clerk's pocketbook. Subsequent inquiry, at the office of the Customs Comptroller, discovered the name of Septimus Darts on the captain's official list of the crew of an outward bound merchant vessel. With this information, and with a photographic portrait to complete it, the man was discovered, alive and hearty, on the return of the ship to her port.

His wife's explanation of her conduct included the customary excuse that she had every reason to believe her husband to be dead, and was followed by a bold assertion that she had married Mr. Evelin for love. In Moses Jackling's opinion she lied when she said this, and lied again when she threatened to prosecute Mr. Evelin for bigamy. "Take my word for it," said this new representative of the unbelieving Jew, "she would have extorted money from him if he had lived." Delirium tremens left this question unsettled, and closed the cigar shop soon afterward, under the authority of death.

The good news, telegraphed to New Zealand, was followed by a letter containing details.

At a later date, a telegram arrived from Mrs. Evelin. She had reached her destination, and had received the dispatch which told her that she had been lawfully married. A letter to Lady Howel was promised by the next mail.

While the necessary term of delay was still unexpired, the newspapers received the intelligence of a volcanic eruption in the northern island of the New Zealand group. Later particulars, announcing a terrible destruction of life and property, included the homestead in which Mrs. Evelin was living. The farm had been overwhelmed, and every member of the household had perished.

Part IV. THE NIGHT NURSE.

VII.

Indorsed as follows: "Reply from Sir Richard, addressed to Farleigh & Halford."

"Your courteous letter has been forwarded to my house in the country.

"I really regret that you should have thought it necessary to apologize for troubling me. Your past kindness to the unhappy Mrs. Evelin gives you a friendly claim on me which I gladly recognize—as you shall soon see.

"'The extraordinary story,' as you very naturally call it, is nevertheless true. I am the only person now at your disposal who can speak as an eye-witness of the events.

"In the first place I must tell you that the dreadful intelligence, received from New Zealand, had an effect on Lord Howel Beaucourt which shocked his friends and inexpressibly distressed his admirable wife. I can only describe him, at that time, as a man struck down in mind and body alike.

"Lady Howel was unremitting in her efforts to console him. He was thankful and gentle. It was true that no complaint could be made of him. It was equally true that no change for the better rewarded the devotion of his wife.

"The state of feeling which this implied imbittered the disappointment that Lady Howel naturally felt. As some relief to her overburdened mind, she associated herself with the work of mercy, carried on under the superintendence of the rector of the parish. I thought he was wrong in permitting a woman, at her advanced time of life, to run the risk encountered in visiting the sick and suffering poor at their own dwelling-places. Circumstances, however, failed to justify my dread of the perilous influences of infection and foul air. The one untoward event that happened, seemed to be too trifling to afford any cause for anxiety. Lady Howel caught cold.

"Unhappily, she treated that apparently trivial accident with indifference. Her husband tried in vain to persuade her to remain at home. On one of her charitable visits she was overtaken by a heavy fall of rain; and a shivering fit seized her on returning to the house. At her age the results were serious. A bronchial attack followed. In a week more, the dearest and best of women had left us nothing to love but the memory of the dead.

"Her last words were faintly whispered to me in her husband's presence: 'Take care of him,' the dying woman said, 'when I am gone.'

"No effort of mine to be worthy of that sacred trust was left untried. How could I hope to succeed where she had failed? My house in London and my house in the country were both open to Beaucourt; I entreated him to live with me, or (if he preferred it) to be my guest for a short time only, or (if he wished to be alone) to choose the place of abode which he liked best for his solitary retreat. With sincere expressions of gratitude, his inflexible despair refused my proposals.

"In one of the ancient 'Inns,' built centuries since for the legal societies of London, he secluded himself from friends and acquaintances alike. One by one, they were driven from his dreary chambers by a reception which admitted them with patient resignation and held out little encouragement to return. After an interval of no great length, I was the last of his friends who intruded on his solitude.

"Poor Lady Howel's will (excepting some special legacies) had left her fortune to me in trust, on certain conditions with which it is needless to trouble you. Beaucourt's resolution not to touch a farthing of his dead wife's money laid a heavy responsibility on my shoulders; the burden being ere long increased by forebodings which alarmed me on the subject of his health.

"He devoted himself to the reading of old books, treating (as I was told) of that branch of useless knowledge generally described as 'occult science.' These unwholesome studies so absorbed him, that he remained shut up in his badly ventilated chambers for weeks together, without once breathing the outer air even for a few minutes. Such defiance of the ordinary laws of nature as this could end but in one way; his health steadily declined and feverish symptoms showed themselves. The doctor said plainly, 'There is no chance for him if he stays in this place.'

"Once more he refused to be removed to my London house. The development of the fever, he reminded me, might lead to consequences dangerous to me and to my household. He had heard of one of the great London hospitals, which reserved certain rooms for the occupation of persons capable of paying for the medical care bestowed on them. If he were to be removed at all, to that hospital he would go. Many advantages, and no objections of importance, were presented by this course of proceeding. We conveyed him to the hospital without a moment's loss of time.

"When I think of the dreadful illness that followed, and when I recall the days of unrelieved suspense passed at the bedside, I have not courage enough to dwell on this part of my story. Besides, you know already that Beaucourt recovered—or, as I might more correctly describe it, that he was snatched back to life when the grasp of death was on him. Of this happier period of his illness I have something to say which may surprise and interest you.

"On one of the earlier days of his convalescence my visit to him was paid later than usual. A matter of importance, neglected while he was in danger, had obliged me to leave town for a few days, after there was nothing to be feared. Returning, I had missed the train which would have brought me to London in better time.

"My appearance evidently produced in Beaucourt a keen feeling of relief. He requested the day nurse, waiting in the room, to leave us by ourselves.

"'I was afraid you might not have come to me to-day,' he said. 'My last moments would have been imbittered, my friend, by your absence.'

"'Are you anticipating your death,' I asked, 'at the very time when the doctors answer for your life?'

"'The doctors have not seen her,' he said; 'I saw her last night.'

"'Of whom are you speaking?'

"'Of my lost angel, who perished miserably in New Zealand. Twice her spirit has appeared to me. I shall see her for the third time, tonight; I shall follow her to the better world.'

"Had the delirium of the worst time of the fever taken possession of him again? In unutterable dread of a relapse, I took his hand. The skin was cool. I laid my fingers on his pulse. It was beating calmly.

"'You think I am wandering in my mind,' he broke out. 'Stay here tonight—I command you, stay!—and see her as I have seen her.'

"I quieted him by promising to do what he had asked of me. He had still one more condition to insist on.

"'I won't be laughed at,' he said. 'Promise that you will not repeat to any living creature what I have just told you.'

"My promise satisfied him. He wearily closed his eyes. In a few minutes more his poor weak body was in peaceful repose.

"The day-nurse returned, and remained with us later than usual. Twilight melted into darkness. The room was obscurely lit by a shaded lamp, placed behind a screen that kept the sun out of the sick man's eyes in the daytime.

"'Are we alone?' Beaucourt asked.

"'Yes.'

"'Watch the door.'

"'Why?'

"'You will see her on the threshold.'

"As he said those words the door slowly opened. In the dim light I could only discern at first the figure of a woman. She slowly advanced toward me. I saw the familiar face in shadow; the eyes were large and faintly luminous— the eyes of Mrs. Evelin.

"The wild words spoken to me by Beaucourt, the stillness and the obscurity in the room, had their effect, I suppose, on my imagination. You will think me a poor creature when I confess it. For the moment I did assuredly feel a thrill of superstitious terror.

"My delusion was dispelled by a change in her face. Its natural expression of surprise, when she saw me, set my mind free to feel the delight inspired by the discovery that she was a living woman. I should have spoken to her if she had not stopped me by a gesture.

"Beaucourt's voice broke the silence. 'Ministering Spirit!' he said, 'free me from the life of earth. Take me with you to the life eternal.'

"She made no attempt to enlighten him. 'Wait,' she answered calmly, 'wait and rest.'

"Silently obeying her, he turned his head on the pillow; we saw his face no more.

"I have related the circumstances exactly as they happened: the ghost story which report has carried to your ears has no other foundation than this.

"Mrs. Evelin led the way to that further end of the room in which the screen stood. Placing ourselves behind it, we could converse in whispers without being heard. Her first words told me that she had been warned by one of the hospital doctors to respect my friend's delusion for the present. His mind partook in some degree of the weakness of his body, and he was not strong enough yet to bear the shock of discovering the truth.

"She had been saved almost by a miracle.

"Released (in a state of insensibility) from the ruins of the house, she had been laid with her dead relatives awaiting burial. Happily for her, an English traveler visiting the island was among the first men who volunteered to render help. He had been in practice as a medical man, and he saved her from being buried alive. Nearly a month passed before she was strong enough to bear removal to Wellington (the capital city) and to be received into the hospital.

"I asked why she had not telegraphed or written to me.

"'When I was strong enough to write,' she said, 'I was strong enough to bear the sea-voyage to England. The expenses so nearly exhausted my small savings that I had no money to spare for the telegraph.'

"On her arrival in London, only a few days since, she had called on me at the time when I had left home on the business which I have already mentioned. She had not heard of Lady Howel's death, and had written ignorantly to prepare that good friend for seeing her. The messenger sent with the letter had found the house in the occupation of strangers, and had been referred to the agent employed in letting it. She went herself to this person, and so heard that Lord Howel Beaucourt had lost his wife, and was reported to be dying in one of the London hospitals.

"'If he had been in his usual state of health,' she said, 'it would have been indelicate on my part—I mean it would have seemed like taking a selfish advantage of the poor lady's death—to have let him know that my life had been saved, in any other way than by writing to him. But when I heard he was dying, I forgot all customary considerations. His name was so well-known in London that I easily discovered at what hospital he had been received. There I heard that the report was false and that he was out of danger. I ought to have been satisfied with that—but oh, how could I be so near him and not long to see him? The old doctor with whom I had been speaking discovered, I suppose, that I was in trouble about something. He was so kind and fatherly, and he seemed to take such interest in me, that I confessed everything to him. After he had made me promise to be careful, he told the night-nurse to let me take her place for a little while, when the dim light in the room would not permit his patient to see me too plainly. He waited at the door when we tried the experiment. Neither he nor I foresaw that Lord Howel would put such a strange interpretation on my presence. The nurse doesn't approve of my coming back—even for a little while only—and taking her place again to-night. She is right. I have had my little glimpse of happiness, and with that little I must be content.'

"What I said in answer to this, and what I did as time advanced, it is surely needless to tell you. You have read the newspapers which announce their marriage, and their departure for Italy. What else is there left for me to say?

"There is, perhaps, a word more still wanting.

"Obstinate Lord Howel persisted in refusing to take the fortune that was waiting for him. In this difficulty, the conditions under which I was acting permitted me to appeal to the bride. When she too said No, I was not to be trifled with. I showed her poor Lady's Howel's will. After reading the terms in which my dear old friend alluded to her she burst out crying. I interpreted those grateful tears as an expression of repentance for the ill-considered reply which I had just received. As yet, I have not been told that I was wrong."

MR. POLICEMAN AND THE COOK.

A FIRST WORD FOR MYSELF.

BEFORE the doctor left me one evening, I asked him how much longer I was likely to live. He answered: "It's not easy to say; you may die before I can get back to you in the morning, or you may live to the end of the month."

I was alive enough on the next morning to think of the needs of my soul, and (being a member of the Roman Catholic Church) to send for the priest.

The history of my sins, related in confession, included blameworthy neglect of a duty which I owed to the laws of my country. In the priest's opinion—and I agreed with him—I was bound to make public acknowledgment of my fault, as an act of penance becoming to a Catholic Englishman. We concluded, thereupon, to try a division of labor. I related the circumstances, while his reverence took the pen and put the matter into shape.

Here follows what came of it:

I.

WHEN I was a young man of five-and-twenty, I became a member of the London police force. After nearly two years' ordinary experience of the responsible and ill-paid duties of that vocation, I found myself employed on my first serious and terrible case of official inquiry—relating to nothing less than the crime of Murder.

The circumstances were these:

I was then attached to a station in the northern district of London—which I beg permission not to mention more particularly. On a certain Monday in the week, I took my turn of night duty. Up to four in the morning, nothing occurred at the station-house out of the ordinary way. It was then springtime, and, between the gas and the fire, the room became rather hot.

I went to the door to get a breath of fresh air—much to the surprise of our Inspector on duty, who was constitutionally a chilly man. There was a fine rain falling; and a nasty damp in the air sent me back to the fireside. I don't suppose I had sat down for more than a minute when the swinging-door was violently pushed open. A frantic woman ran in with a scream, and said: "Is this the station-house?"

Our Inspector (otherwise an excellent officer) had, by some perversity of nature, a hot temper in his chilly constitution. "Why, bless the woman, can't you see it is?" he says. "What's the matter now?"

"Murder's the matter!" she burst out. "For God's sake, come back with me. It's at Mrs. Crosscapel's lodging-house, number 14 Lehigh Street. A young woman has murdered her husband in the night! With a knife, sir. She says she thinks she did it in her sleep."

I confess I was startled by this; and the third man on duty (a sergeant) seemed to feel it too. She was a nice-looking young woman, even in her terrified condition, just out of bed, with her clothes huddled on anyhow. I was partial in those days to a tall figure—and she was, as they say, my style. I put a chair for her; and the sergeant poked the fire. As for the Inspector, nothing ever upset him. He questioned her as coolly as if it had been a case of petty larceny.

"Have you seen the murdered man?" he asked.

"No, sir."

"Or the wife?"

"No, sir. I didn't dare go into the room; I only heard about it!"

"Oh? And who are You? One of the lodgers?"

"No, sir. I'm the cook."

"Isn't there a master in the house?"

"Yes, sir. He's frightened out of his wits. And the housemaid's gone for the doctor. It all falls on the poor servants, of course. Oh, why did I ever set

772

foot in that horrible house?"

The poor soul burst out crying, and shivered from head to foot. The Inspector made a note of her statement, and then asked her to read it, and sign it with her name. The object of this proceeding was to get her to come near enough to give him the opportunity of smelling her breath. "When people make extraordinary statements," he afterward said to me, "it sometimes saves trouble to satisfy yourself that they are not drunk. I've known them to be mad—but not often. You will generally find that in their eyes."

She roused herself and signed her name—"Priscilla Thurlby." The Inspector's own test proved her to be sober; and her eyes—a nice light blue color, mild and pleasant, no doubt, when they were not staring with fear, and red with crying—satisfied him (as I supposed) that she was not mad. He turned the case over to me, in the first instance. I saw that he didn't believe in it, even yet.

"Go back with her to the house," he says. "This may be a stupid hoax, or a quarrel exaggerated. See to it yourself, and hear what the doctor says. If it is serious, send word back here directly, and let nobody enter the place or leave it till we come. Stop! You know the form if any statement is volunteered?"

"Yes, sir. I am to caution the persons that whatever they say will be taken down, and may be used against them."

"Quite right. You'll be an Inspector yourself one of these days. Now, miss!" With that he dismissed her, under my care.

Lehigh Street was not very far off—about twenty minutes' walk from the station. I confess I thought the Inspector had been rather hard on Priscilla. She was herself naturally angry with him. "What does he mean," she says, "by talking of a hoax? I wish he was as frightened as I am. This is the first time I have been out at service, sir—and I did think I had found a respectable place."

I said very little to her—feeling, if the truth must be told, rather anxious about the duty committed to me. On reaching the house the door was opened from within, before I could knock. A gentleman stepped out, who proved to be the doctor. He stopped the moment he saw me.

"You must be careful, policeman," he says. "I found the man lying on his back, in bed, dead—with the knife that had killed him left sticking in the wound."

Hearing this, I felt the necessity of sending at once to the station. Where could I find a trustworthy messenger? I took the liberty of asking the doctor if he would repeat to the police what he had already said to me. The station was not much out of his way home. He kindly granted my request.

The landlady (Mrs. Crosscapel) joined us while we were talking. She was still a young woman; not easily frightened, as far as I could see, even by a murder in the house. Her husband was in the passage behind her. He looked old enough to be her father; and he so trembled with terror that some people might have taken him for the guilty person. I removed the key from the street door, after locking it; and I said to the landlady: "Nobody must leave the house, or enter the house, till the Inspector comes. I must examine the premises to see if any one has broken in."

"There is the key of the area gate," she said, in answer to me. "It's always kept locked. Come downstairs and see for yourself." Priscilla went with us. Her mistress set her to work to light the kitchen fire. "Some of us," says Mrs. Crosscapel, "may be the better for a cup of tea." I remarked that she took things easy, under the circumstances. She answered that the landlady of a London lodging-house could not afford to lose her wits, no matter what might happen.

I found the gate locked, and the shutters of the kitchen window fastened. The back kitchen and back door were secured in the same way. No person was concealed anywhere. Returning upstairs, I examined the front parlor window. There, again, the barred shutters answered for the security of that room. A cracked voice spoke through the door of the back parlor. "The policeman can come in," it said, "if he will promise not to look at me." I turned to the landlady for information. "It's my parlor lodger, Miss Mybus," she said, "a most respectable lady." Going into the room, I saw something rolled up perpendicularly in the bed curtains. Miss Mybus had made herself modestly invisible in that way. Having now satisfied my mind about the security of the lower part of the house, and having the keys safe in my pocket, I was ready to go upstairs.

On our way to the upper regions I asked if there had been any visitors on the previous day. There had been only two visitors, friends of the lodgers—and Mrs. Crosscapel herself had let them both out. My next inquiry related to the lodgers themselves. On the ground floor there was Miss Mybus. On the first floor (occupying both rooms) Mr. Barfield, an old bachelor, employed in a merchant's office. On the second floor, in the front room, Mr. John Zebedee, the murdered man, and his wife. In the back room, Mr. Deluc; described as a cigar agent, and supposed to be a Creole gentleman from Martinique. In the front garret, Mr. and Mrs. Crosscapel. In the back garret, the cook and the housemaid. These were the inhabitants, regularly accounted for. I asked about the servants. "Both excellent characters," says the landlady, "or they would not be in my service."

We reached the second floor, and found the housemaid on the watch outside the door of the front room. Not as nice a woman, personally, as the cook, and sadly frightened of course. Her mistress had posted her, to give the alarm in the case of an outbreak on the part of Mrs. Zebedee, kept locked up in the room. My arrival relieved the housemaid of further responsibility. She ran downstairs to her fellow-servant in the kitchen.

I asked Mrs. Crosscapel how and when the alarm of the murder had been given.

"Soon after three this morning," says she, "I was woke by the screams of Mrs. Zebedee. I found her out here on the landing, and Mr. Deluc, in great alarm, trying to quiet her. Sleeping in the next room he had only to open his door, when her screams woke him. 'My dear John's murdered! I am the miserable wretch—I did it in my sleep!' She repeated these frantic words over and over again, until she dropped in a swoon. Mr. Deluc and I carried her back into the bedroom. We both thought the poor creature had been driven distracted by some dreadful dream. But when we got to the bedside—don't ask me what we saw; the doctor has told you about it already. I was once a nurse in a hospital, and accustomed, as such, to horrid sights. It turned me cold and giddy, notwithstanding. As for Mr. Deluc, I thought he would have had a fainting fit next."

Hearing this, I inquired if Mrs. Zebedee had said or done any strange things since she had been Mrs. Crosscapel's lodger.

"You think she's mad?" says the landlady. "And anybody would be of your mind, when a woman accuses herself of murdering her husband in her sleep. All I can say is that, up to this morning, a more quiet, sensible, well-behaved little person than Mrs. Zebedee I never met with. Only just married, mind, and as fond of her unfortunate husband as a woman could be. I should have called them a pattern couple, in their own line of life."

There was no more to be said on the landing. We unlocked the door and went into the room.

II.

HE lay in bed on his back as the doctor had described him. On the left side of his nightgown, just over his heart, the blood on the linen told its terrible tale. As well as one could judge, looking unwillingly at a dead face, he must have been a handsome young man in his lifetime. It was a sight to sadden anybody—but I think the most painful sensation was when my eyes fell next on his miserable wife.

She was down on the floor, crouched up in a corner—a dark little woman, smartly dressed in gay colors. Her black hair and her big brown eyes made the horrid paleness of her face look even more deadly white than perhaps it really was. She stared straight at us without appearing to see us. We spoke to her, and she never answered a word. She might have been dead—like her husband—except that she perpetually picked at her fingers, and shuddered every now and then as if she was cold. I went to her and tried to lift her up. She shrank back with a cry that well-nigh frightened me—not because it was loud, but because it was more like the cry of some animal than of a human being. However quietly she might have behaved in the landlady's previous experience of her, she was beside herself now. I might have been moved by a natural pity for her, or I might have been completely upset in my mind—I only know this, I could not persuade myself that she was guilty. I even said to

Mrs. Crosscapel, "I don't believe she did it."

While I spoke there was a knock at the door. I went downstairs at once, and admitted (to my great relief) the Inspector, accompanied by one of our men.

He waited downstairs to hear my report, and he approved of what I had done. "It looks as if the murder had been committed by somebody in the house." Saying this, he left the man below, and went up with me to the second floor.

Before he had been a minute in the room, he discovered an object which had escaped my observation.

It was the knife that had done the deed.

The doctor had found it left in the body—had withdrawn it to probe the wound—and had laid it on the bedside table. It was one of those useful knives which contain a saw, a corkscrew, and other like implements. The big blade fastened back, when open, with a spring. Except where the blood was on it, it was as bright as when it had been purchased. A small metal plate was fastened to the horn handle, containing an inscription, only partly engraved, which ran thus: "To John Zebedee, from—" There it stopped, strangely enough.

Who or what had interrupted the engraver's work? It was impossible even to guess. Nevertheless, the Inspector was encouraged.

"This ought to help us," he said—and then he gave an attentive ear (looking all the while at the poor creature in the corner) to what Mrs. Crosscapel had to tell him.

The landlady having done, he said he must now see the lodger who slept in the next bed-chamber.

Mr. Deluc made his appearance, standing at the door of the room, and turning away his head with horror from the sight inside.

He was wrapped in a splendid blue dressing-gown, with a golden girdle and trimmings. His scanty brownish hair curled (whether artificially or not, I am unable to say) in little ringlets. His complexion was yellow; his greenish-brown eyes were of the sort called "goggle"—they looked as if they might drop out of his face, if you held a spoon under them. His mustache and goat's beard were beautifully oiled; and, to complete his equipment, he had a long black cigar in his mouth.

"It isn't insensibility to this terrible tragedy," he explained. "My nerves have been shattered, Mr. Policeman, and I can only repair the mischief in this way. Be pleased to excuse and feel for me."

The Inspector questioned this witness sharply and closely. He was not a man to be misled by appearances; but I could see that he was far from liking, or even trusting, Mr. Deluc. Nothing came of the examination, except what Mrs. Crosscapel had in substance already mentioned to me. Mr. Deluc returned to his room.

"How long has he been lodging with you?" the Inspector asked, as soon as his back was turned.

"Nearly a year," the landlady answered.

"Did he give you a reference?"

"As good a reference as I could wish for." Thereupon, she mentioned the names of a well-known firm of cigar merchants in the city. The Inspector noted the information in his pocketbook.

I would rather not relate in detail what happened next: it is too distressing to be dwelt on. Let me only say that the poor demented woman was taken away in a cab to the station-house. The Inspector possessed himself of the knife, and of a book found on the floor, called "The World of Sleep." The portmanteau containing the luggage was locked—and then the door of the room was secured, the keys in both cases being left in my charge. My instructions were to remain in the house, and allow nobody to leave it, until I heard again shortly from the Inspector.

III.

THE coroner's inquest was adjourned; and the examination before the magistrate ended in a remand—Mrs. Zebedee being in no condition to understand the proceedings in either case. The surgeon reported her to be completely prostrated by a terrible nervous shock. When he was asked if he considered her to have been a sane woman before the murder took place, he refused to answer positively at that time.

A week passed. The murdered man was buried; his old father attending the funeral. I occasionally saw Mrs. Crosscapel, and the two servants, for the purpose of getting such further information as was thought desirable. Both the cook and the housemaid had given their month's notice to quit; declining, in the interest of their characters, to remain in a house which had been the scene of a murder. Mr. Deluc's nerves led also to his removal; his rest was now disturbed by frightful dreams. He paid the necessary forfeit-money, and left without notice. The first-floor lodger, Mr. Barfield, kept his rooms, but obtained leave of absence from his employers, and took refuge with some friends in the country. Miss Mybus alone remained in the parlors. "When I am comfortable," the old lady said, "nothing moves me, at my age. A murder up two pairs of stairs is nearly the same thing as a murder in the next house. Distance, you see, makes all the difference."

It mattered little to the police what the lodgers did. We had men in plain clothes watching the house night and day. Everybody who went away was privately followed; and the police in the district to which they retired were warned to keep an eye on them, after that. As long as we failed to put Mrs. Zebedee's extraordinary statement to any sort of test—to say nothing of having proved unsuccessful, thus far, in tracing the knife to its purchaser—we were bound to let no person living under Mr. Crosscapel's roof, on the night of the murder, slip through our fingers.

IV.

IN a fortnight more, Mrs. Zebedee had sufficiently recovered to make the necessary statement—after the preliminary caution addressed to persons in such cases. The surgeon had no hesitation, now, in reporting her to be a sane woman.

Her station in life had been domestic service. She had lived for four years in her last place as lady's-maid, with a family residing in Dorsetshire.

The one objection to her had been the occasional infirmity of sleep-walking, which made it necessary that one of the other female servants should sleep in the same room, with the door locked and the key under her pillow. In all other respects the lady's-maid was described by her mistress as "a perfect treasure."

In the last six months of her service, a young man named John Zebedee entered the house (with a written character) as a footman. He soon fell in love with the nice little lady's-maid, and she heartily returned the feeling. They might have waited for years before they were in a pecuniary position to marry, but for the death of Zebedee's uncle, who left him a little fortune of two thousand pounds. They were now, for persons in their station, rich enough to please themselves; and they were married from the house in which they had served together, the little daughters of the family showing their affection for Mrs. Zebedee by acting as her bridesmaids.

The young husband was a careful man. He decided to employ his small capital to the best advantage, by sheep-farming in Australia. His wife made no objection; she was ready to go wherever John went.

Accordingly they spent their short honeymoon in London, so as to see for themselves the vessel in which their passage was to be taken. They went to Mrs. Crosscapel's lodging-house because Zebedee's uncle had always stayed there when in London. Ten days were to pass before the day of embarkation arrived. This gave the young couple a welcome holiday, and a prospect of amusing themselves to their heart's content among the sights and shows of the great city.

On their first evening in London they went to the theater. They were both accustomed to the fresh air of the country, and they felt half stifled by the heat and the gas. However, they were so pleased with an amusement which was new to them that they went to another theater on the next evening. On this second occasion, John Zebedee found the heat unendurable. They left the theater, and got back to their lodgings toward ten o'clock.

Let the rest be told in the words used by Mrs. Zebedee herself. She said:

"We sat talking for a little while in our room, and John's headache got worse and worse. I persuaded him to go to bed, and I put out the candle (the fire giving sufficient light to undress by), so that he might the sooner fall asleep. But he was too restless to sleep. He asked me to read him something. Books always made him drowsy at the best of times.

"I had not myself begun to undress. So I lit the candle again, and I opened the only book I had. John had noticed it at the railway bookstall by the name of 'The World of Sleep.' He used to joke with me about my being a sleepwalker; and he said, 'Here's something that's sure to interest you'—and he made me a present of the book.

"Before I had read to him for more than half an hour he was fast asleep. Not feeling that way inclined, I went on reading to myself.

"The book did indeed interest me. There was one terrible story which took a hold on my mind—the story of a man who stabbed his own wife in a sleep-walking dream. I thought of putting down my book after that, and then changed my mind again and went on. The next chapters were not so interesting; they were full of learned accounts of why we fall asleep, and what our brains do in that state, and such like. It ended in my falling asleep, too, in my armchair by the fireside.

"I don't know what o'clock it was when I went to sleep. I don't know how long I slept, or whether I dreamed or not. The candle and the fire had both burned out, and it was pitch dark when I woke. I can't even say why I woke—unless it was the coldness of the room.

"There was a spare candle on the chimney-piece. I found the matchbox, and got a light. Then for the first time, I turned round toward the bed; and I saw—"

She had seen the dead body of her husband, murdered while she was unconsciously at his side—and she fainted, poor creature, at the bare remembrance of it.

The proceedings were adjourned. She received every possible care and attention; the chaplain looking after her welfare as well as the surgeon.

I have said nothing of the evidence of the landlady and servants. It was taken as a mere formality. What little they knew proved nothing against Mrs. Zebedee. The police made no discoveries that supported her first frantic accusation of herself. Her master and mistress, where she had been last in service, spoke of her in the highest terms. We were at a complete deadlock.

It had been thought best not to surprise Mr. Deluc, as yet, by citing him as a witness. The action of the law was, however, hurried in this case by a private communication received from the chaplain.

After twice seeing, and speaking with, Mrs. Zebedee, the reverend gentleman was persuaded that she had no more to do than himself with the murder of her husband. He did not consider that he was justified in repeating a confidential communication—he would only recommend that Mr. Deluc should be summoned to appear at the next examination. This advice was followed.

The police had no evidence against Mrs. Zebedee when the inquiry was resumed. To assist the ends of justice she was now put into the witness-box. The discovery of her murdered husband, when she woke in the small hours of the morning, was passed over as rapidly as possible. Only three questions of importance were put to her.

First, the knife was produced. Had she ever seen it in her husband's possession? Never. Did she know anything about it? Nothing whatever.

Secondly: Did she, or did her husband, lock the bedroom door when they returned from the theater? No. Did she afterward lock the door herself? No.

Thirdly: Had she any sort of reason to give for supposing that she had murdered her husband in a sleep-walking dream? No reason, except that she was beside herself at the time, and the book put the thought into her head.

After this the other witnesses were sent out of court The motive for the chaplain's communication now appeared. Mrs. Zebedee was asked if anything unpleasant had occurred between Mr. Deluc and herself.

Yes. He had caught her alone on the stairs at the lodging-house; had presumed to make love to her; and had carried the insult still farther by attempting to kiss her. She had slapped his face, and had declared that her husband should know of it, if his misconduct was repeated. He was in a furious rage at having his face slapped; and he said to her: "Madam, you may live to regret this."

After consultation, and at the request of our Inspector, it was decided to keep Mr. Deluc in ignorance of Mrs. Zebedee's statement for the present. When the witnesses were recalled, he gave the same evidence which he had already given to the Inspector—and he was then asked if he knew anything of the knife. He looked at it without any guilty signs in his face, and swore that he had never seen it until that moment. The resumed inquiry ended, and still nothing had been discovered.

But we kept an eye on Mr. Deluc. Our next effort was to try if we could associate him with the purchase of the knife.

Here again (there really did seem to be a sort of fatality in this case) we reached no useful result. It was easy enough to find out the wholesale cutlers, who had manufactured the knife at Sheffield, by the mark on the blade. But they made tens of thousands of such knives, and disposed of them to retail dealers all over Great Britain—to say nothing of foreign parts. As to finding out the person who had engraved the imperfect inscription (without knowing where, or by whom, the knife had been purchased) we might as well have looked for the proverbial needle in the bundle of hay. Our last resource was to have the knife photographed, with the inscribed side uppermost, and to send copies to every police-station in the kingdom.

At the same time we reckoned up Mr. Deluc—I mean that we made investigations into his past life—on the chance that he and the murdered man might have known each other, and might have had a quarrel, or a rivalry about a woman, on some former occasion. No such discovery rewarded us.

We found Deluc to have led a dissipated life, and to have mixed with very bad company. But he had kept out of reach of the law. A man may be a profligate vagabond; may insult a lady; may say threatening things to her, in the first stinging sensation of having his face slapped—but it doesn't follow from these blots on his character that he has murdered her husband in the dead of the night.

Once more, then, when we were called upon to report ourselves, we had no evidence to produce. The photographs failed to discover the owner of the knife, and to explain its interrupted inscription. Poor Mrs. Zebedee was allowed to go back to her friends, on entering into her own recognizance to appear again if called upon. Articles in the newspapers began to inquire how many more murderers would succeed in baffling the police. The authorities at the Treasury offered a reward of a hundred pounds for the necessary information. And the weeks passed and nobody claimed the reward.

Our Inspector was not a man to be easily beaten. More inquiries and examinations followed. It is needless to say anything about them. We were defeated—and there, so far as the police and the public were concerned, was an end of it.

The assassination of the poor young husband soon passed out of notice, like other undiscovered murders. One obscure person only was foolish enough, in his leisure hours, to persist in trying to solve the problem of Who Killed Zebedee? He felt that he might rise to the highest position in the police force if he succeeded where his elders and betters had failed—and he held to his own little ambition, though everybody laughed at him. In plain English, I was the man.

V.

WITHOUT meaning it, I have told my story ungratefully.

There were two persons who saw nothing ridiculous in my resolution to continue the investigation, single-handed. One of them was Miss Mybus; and the other was the cook, Priscilla Thurlby.

Mentioning the lady first, Miss Mybus was indignant at the resigned manner in which the police accepted their defeat. She was a little bright-eyed wiry woman; and she spoke her mind freely.

"This comes home to me," she said. "Just look back for a year or two. I can call to mind two cases of persons found murdered in London—and the assassins have never been traced. I am a person, too; and I ask myself if my turn is not coming next. You're a nice-looking fellow and I like your pluck and perseverance. Come here as often as you think right; and say you are my visitor, if they make any difficulty about letting you in. One thing more! I have nothing particular to do, and I am no fool. Here, in the parlors, I see everybody who comes into the house or goes out of the house. Leave me your address—I may get some information for you yet."

With the best intentions, Miss Mybus found no opportunity of helping me. Of the two, Priscilla Thurlby seemed more likely to be of use.

In the first place, she was sharp and active, and (not having succeeded in getting another situation as yet) was mistress of her own movements.

In the second place, she was a woman I could trust. Before she left home to try domestic service in London, the parson of her native parish gave her a written testimonial, of which I append a copy. Thus it ran:

"I gladly recommend Priscilla Thurlby for any respectable employment which she may be competent to undertake. Her father and mother are infirm old people, who have lately suffered a diminution of their income; and they have a younger daughter to maintain. Rather than be a burden on her parents, Priscilla goes to London to find domestic employment, and to devote her earnings to the assistance of her father and mother. This circumstance speaks for itself. I have known the family many years; and I only regret that I have no vacant place in my own household which I can offer to this good girl,

(Signed) "HENRY DEERINGTON, Rector of Roth."

After reading those words, I could safely ask Priscilla to help me in reopening the mysterious murder case to some good purpose.

My notion was that the proceedings of the persons in Mrs. Crosscapel's house had not been closely enough inquired into yet. By way of continuing the investigation, I asked Priscilla if she could tell me anything which associated the housemaid with Mr. Deluc. She was unwilling to answer. "I may be casting suspicion on an innocent person," she said. "Besides, I was for so short a time the housemaid's fellow servant—"

"You slept in the same room with her," I remarked; "and you had opportunities of observing her conduct toward the lodgers. If they had asked you, at the examination, what I now ask, you would have answered as an honest woman."

To this argument she yielded. I heard from her certain particulars, which threw a new light on Mr. Deluc, and on the case generally. On that information I acted. It was slow work, owing to the claims on me of my regular duties; but with Priscilla's help, I steadily advanced toward the end I had in view.

Besides this, I owed another obligation to Mrs. Crosscapel's nice-looking cook. The confession must be made sooner or later—and I may as well make it now. I first knew what love was, thanks to Priscilla. I had delicious kisses, thanks to Priscilla. And, when I asked if she would marry me, she didn't say No. She looked, I must own, a little sadly, and she said: "How can two such poor people as we are ever hope to marry?" To this I answered: "It won't be long before I lay my hand on the clew which my Inspector has failed to find. I shall be in a position to marry you, my dear, when that time comes."

At our next meeting we spoke of her parents. I was now her promised husband. Judging by what I had heard of the proceedings of other people in my position, it seemed to be only right that I should be made known to her father and mother. She entirely agreed with me; and she wrote home that day to tell them to expect us at the end of the week.

I took my turn of night-duty, and so gained my liberty for the greater part of the next day. I dressed myself in plain clothes, and we took our tickets on the railway for Yateland, being the nearest station to the village in which Priscilla's parents lived.

VI.

THE train stopped, as usual, at the big town of Waterbank. Supporting herself by her needle, while she was still unprovided with a situation, Priscilla had been at work late in the night—she was tired and thirsty. I left the carriage to get her some soda-water. The stupid girl in the refreshment room failed to pull the cork out of the bottle, and refused to let me help her. She took a corkscrew, and used it crookedly. I lost all patience, and snatched the bottle out of her hand. Just as I drew the cork, the bell rang on the platform. I only waited to pour the soda-water into a glass—but the train was moving as I left the refreshment room. The porters stopped me when I tried to jump on to the step of the carriage. I was left behind.

As soon as I had recovered my temper, I looked at the time-table. We had reached Waterbank at five minutes past one. By good luck, the next train was due at forty-four minutes past one, and arrived at Yateland (the next station) ten minutes afterward. I could only hope that Priscilla would look at the time-table too, and wait for me. If I had attempted to walk the distance between the two places, I should have lost time instead of saving it. The interval before me was not very long; I occupied it in looking over the town.

Speaking with all due respect to the inhabitants, Waterbank (to other people) is a dull place. I went up one street and down another—and stopped to look at a shop which struck me; not from anything in itself, but because it was the only shop in the street with the shutters closed.

A bill was posted on the shutters, announcing that the place was to let. The outgoing tradesman's name and business, announced in the customary painted letters, ran thus: James Wycomb, Cutler, etc.

For the first time, it occurred to me that we had forgotten an obstacle in our way, when we distributed our photographs of the knife. We had none of us remembered that a certain proportion of cutlers might be placed, by circumstances, out of our reach—either by retiring from business or by becoming bankrupt. I always carried a copy of the photograph about me; and I thought to myself, "Here is the ghost of a chance of tracing the knife to Mr. Deluc!"

The shop door was opened, after I had twice rung the bell, by an old man, very dirty and very deaf. He said, "You had better go upstairs, and speak to Mr. Scorrier—top of the house."

I put my lips to the old fellow's ear-trumpet, and asked who Mr. Scorrier was.

"Brother-in-law to Mr. Wycomb. Mr. Wycomb's dead. If you want to buy the business apply to Mr. Scorrier."

Receiving that reply, I went upstairs, and found Mr. Scorrier engaged in engraving a brass door-plate. He was a middle-aged man, with a cadaverous face and dim eyes After the necessary apologies, I produced my photograph.

"May I ask, sir, if you know anything of the inscription on that knife?" I said.

He took his magnifying glass to look at it.

"This is curious," he remarked quietly. "I remember the queer name—Zebedee. Yes, sir; I did the engraving, as far as it goes. I wonder what prevented me from finishing it?"

The name of Zebedee, and the unfinished inscription on the knife, had appeared in every English newspaper. He took the matter so coolly that I was doubtful how to interpret his answer. Was it possible that he had not seen the account of the murder? Or was he an accomplice with prodigious powers of self-control?

"Excuse me," I said, "do you read the newspapers?"

"Never! My eyesight is failing me. I abstain from reading, in the interests of my occupation."

"Have you not heard the name of Zebedee mentioned—particularly by people who do read the newspapers?"

"Very likely; but I didn't attend to it. When the day's work is done, I take my walk. Then I have my supper, my drop of grog, and my pipe. Then I go to bed. A dull existence you think, I daresay! I had a miserable life, sir, when I was young. A bare subsistence, and a little rest, before the last perfect rest in the grave—that is all I want. The world has gone by me long ago. So much the better."

The poor man spoke honestly. I was ashamed of having doubted him. I returned to the subject of the knife.

"Do you know where it was purchased, and by whom?" I asked.

"My memory is not so good as it was," he said; "but I have got something by me that helps it."

He took from a cupboard a dirty old scrapbook. Strips of paper, with writing on them, were pasted on the pages, as well as I could see. He turned to an index, or table of contents, and opened a page. Something like a flash of life showed itself on his dismal face.

"Ha! now I remember," he said. "The knife was bought of my late brother-in-law, in the shop downstairs. It all comes back to me, sir. A person in a state of frenzy burst into this very room, and snatched the knife away from me, when I was only half way through the inscription!"

I felt that I was now close on discovery. "May I see what it is that has assisted your memory?" I asked.

"Oh yes. You must know, sir, I live by engraving inscriptions and addresses, and I paste in this book the manuscript instructions which I receive, with marks of my own on the margin. For one thing, they serve as a reference to new customers. And for another thing, they do certainly help my memory."

He turned the book toward me, and pointed to a slip of paper which occupied the lower half of a page.

I read the complete inscription, intended for the knife that killed Zebedee, and written as follows:

"To John Zebedee. From Priscilla Thurlby."

VII.

I DECLARE that it is impossible for me to describe what I felt when Priscilla's name confronted me like a written confession of guilt. How long it was before I recovered myself in some degree, I cannot say. The only thing I can clearly call to mind is, that I frightened the poor engraver.

My first desire was to get possession of the manuscript inscription. I told him I was a policeman, and summoned him to assist me in the discovery of a crime. I even offered him money. He drew back from my hand. "You shall have it for nothing," he said, "if you will only go away and never come here again." He tried to cut it out of the page—but his trembling hands were helpless. I cut it out myself, and attempted to thank him. He wouldn't hear me. "Go away!" he said, "I don't like the look of you."

It may be here objected that I ought not to have felt so sure as I did of the woman's guilt, until I had got more evidence against her. The knife might have been stolen from her, supposing she was the person who had snatched it out of the engraver's hands, and might have been afterward used by the thief to commit the murder. All very true. But I never had a moment's doubt in my own mind, from the time when I read the damnable line in the engraver's book.

I went back to the railway without any plan in my head. The train by which I had proposed to follow her had left Waterbank. The next train that arrived was for London. I took my place in it—still without any plan in my head.

At Charing Cross a friend met me. He said, "You're looking miserably ill. Come and have a drink."

I went with him. The liquor was what I really wanted; it strung me up, and cleared my head. He went his way, and I went mine. In a little while more, I determined what I would do.

In the first place, I decided to resign my situation in the police, from a motive which will presently appear. In the second place, I took a bed at a public-house. She would no doubt return to London, and she would go to my lodgings to find out why I had broken my appointment. To bring to justice the one woman whom I had dearly loved was too cruel a duty for a poor creature like me. I preferred leaving the police force. On the other hand, if she and I met before time had helped me to control myself, I had a horrid fear that I might turn murderer next, and kill her then and there. The wretch had not only all but misled me into marrying her, but also into charging the innocent housemaid with being concerned in the murder.

The same night I hit on a way of clearing up such doubts as still harassed my mind. I wrote to the rector of Roth, informing him that I was engaged to marry her, and asking if he would tell me (in consideration of my position) what her former relations might have been with the person named John Zebedee.

By return of post I got this reply:

"SIR—Under the circumstances, I think I am bound to tell you confidentially what the friends and well-wishers of Priscilla have kept secret, for her sake.

"Zebedee was in service in this neighborhood. I am sorry to say it, of a man who has come to such a miserable end—but his behavior to Priscilla proves him to have been a vicious and heartless wretch. They were engaged—and, I add with indignation, he tried to seduce her under a promise of marriage. Her virtue resisted him, and he pretended to be ashamed of himself. The banns were published in my church. On the next day Zebedee disappeared, and cruelly deserted her. He was a capable servant; and I believe he got another place. I leave you to imagine what the poor girl suffered under the outrage inflicted on her. Going to London, with my recommendation, she answered the first advertisement that she saw, and was unfortunate enough to begin her career in domestic service in the very lodging-house to which (as I gather from the newspaper report of the murder) the man Zebedee took the person whom he married, after deserting Priscilla. Be assured that you are about to unite yourself to an excellent girl, and accept my best wishes for your happiness."

It was plain from this that neither the rector nor the parents and friends knew anything of the purchase of the knife. The one miserable man who knew the truth was the man who had asked her to be his wife.

I owed it to myself—at least so it seemed to me—not to let it be supposed that I, too, had meanly deserted her. Dreadful as the prospect was, I felt that I must see her once more, and for the last time.

She was at work when I went into her room. As I opened the door she

791

started to her feet. Her cheeks reddened, and her eyes flashed with anger. I stepped forward—and she saw my face. My face silenced her.

I spoke in the fewest words I could find.

"I have been to the cutler's shop at Waterbank," I said. "There is the unfinished inscription on the knife, complete in your handwriting. I could hang you by a word. God forgive me—I can't say the word."

Her bright complexion turned to a dreadful clay-color. Her eyes were fixed and staring, like the eyes of a person in a fit. She stood before me, still and silent. Without saying more, I dropped the inscription into the fire. Without saying more, I left her.

I never saw her again.

VIII.

BUT I heard from her a few days later. The letter has long since been burned. I wish I could have forgotten it as well. It sticks to my memory. If I die with my senses about me, Priscilla's letter will be my last recollection on earth.

In substance it repeated what the rector had already told me. Further, it informed me that she had bought the knife as a keepsake for Zebedee, in place of a similar knife which he had lost. On the Saturday, she made the purchase, and left it to be engraved. On the Sunday, the banns were put up. On the Monday, she was deserted; and she snatched the knife from the table while the engraver was at work.

She only knew that Zebedee had added a new sting to the insult inflicted on her when he arrived at the lodgings with his wife. Her duties as cook kept her in the kitchen—and Zebedee never discovered that she was in the house. I still remember the last lines of her confession:

"The devil entered into me when I tried their door, on my way up to bed, and found it unlocked, and listened a while, and peeped in. I saw them by the dying light of the candle—one asleep on the bed, the other asleep by the fireside. I had the knife in my hand, and the thought came to me to do it, so that they might hang her for the murder. I couldn't take the knife out again, when I had done it. Mind this! I did really like you—I didn't say Yes, because you could hardly hang your own wife, if you found out who killed Zebedee."

Since the past time I have never heard again of Priscilla Thurlby; I don't know whether she is living or dead. Many people may think I deserve to be hanged myself for not having given her up to the gallows. They may, perhaps, be disappointed when they see this confession, and hear that I have died decently in my bed. I don't blame them. I am a penitent sinner. I wish all merciful Christians good-by forever.

About Author

Early life

Collins was born at 11 New Cavendish Street, Marylebone, London, the son of a well-known Royal Academician landscape painter, William Collins and his wife, Harriet Geddes. Named after his father, he swiftly became known by his middle name, which honoured his godfather, David Wilkie. The family moved to Pond Street, Hampstead, in 1826. In 1828 Collins's brother Charles Allston Collins was born. Between 1829 and 1830, the Collins family moved twice, first to Hampstead Square and then to Porchester Terrace, Bayswater. Wilkie and Charles received their early education from their mother at home. The Collins family were deeply religious, and Collins's mother enforced strict church attendance on her sons, which Wilkie disliked.

In 1835, Collins began attending school at the Maida Vale academy. From 1836 to 1838, he lived with his parents in Italy and France, which made a great impression on him. He learned Italian while the family was in Italy and began learning French, in which he would eventually become fluent. From 1838 to 1840, he attended the Reverend Cole's private boarding school in Highbury, where he was bullied by a boy who would force Collins to tell him a story before allowing him to go to sleep. "It was this brute who first awakened in me, his poor little victim, a power of which but for him I might never have been aware.... When I left school I continued story telling for my own pleasure", Collins later said.

In 1840 the family moved to 85 Oxford Terrace, Bayswater. In late 1840, he left school and was apprenticed as a clerk to the firm of tea merchants Antrobus & Co, owned by a friend of Wilkie's father. He disliked his clerical work but remained employed by the company for more than five years. Collins's first story The Last Stage Coachman, was published in the Illuminated Magazine in August 1843. In 1844 he travelled to Paris with Charles Ward. That same year he wrote his first novel, Iolani, or Tahiti as It Was; a Romance, which was submitted to Chapman and Hall but rejected in 1845. The novel remained unpublished during his lifetime. Collins said of it:

"My youthful imagination ran riot among the noble savages, in scenes which caused the respectable British publisher to declare that it was impossible to put his name on the title page of such a novel." It was during the writing of this novel that Collins's father first learned that his assumptions that Wilkie would follow him in becoming a painter were mistaken.

William Collins had intended Wilkie for a clergyman and was disappointed in his son's lack of interest. In 1846 he instead entered Lincoln's Inn to study law, on the initiative of his father, who wanted him to have a steady income. Wilkie showed only a slight interest in law and spent most of his time with friends and on working on a second novel, Antonina, or the Fall of Rome. After his father's death in 1847, Collins produced his first published book, Memoirs of the Life of William Collins, Esq., R. A., published in 1848. The family moved to 38 Blandford Square soon afterwards, where they used their drawing room for amateur theatricals. In 1849, Collins exhibited a painting, "The Smugglers' Retreat", at the Royal Academy summer exhibition. Antonina was published by Richard Bentley in February 1850. Collins went on a walking tour of Cornwall with artist Henry Brandling in July and August 1850. He managed to complete his legal studies and be called to the bar in 1851. Though he never formally practised, he used his legal knowledge in many of his novels.

Early writing career

An instrumental event in his career was an introduction in March 1851 to Charles Dickens by a mutual friend, through the painter Augustus Egg. They became lifelong friends and collaborators. In May of that year, Collins acted with Dickens in Edward Bulwer-Lytton's play Not So Bad As We Seem. Among the audience were Queen Victoria and Prince Albert. Collins's story "A Terribly Strange Bed," his first contribution to Household Words, appeared in April, 1852. In May 1852 he went on tour with Dickens's company of amateur actors, again performing Not So Bad As We Seem, but with a more substantial role. Collins's novel Basil was published by Bentley in November. During the writing of Hide and Seek, in early 1853, Collins suffered what was probably his first attack of gout, which would plague him for the rest of his life. He was ill from April to early July. After that he stayed with Dickens in Boulogne from July to September 1853, then toured Switzerland and Italy with Dickens and Egg from October to December. Collins published Hide and Seek in June 1854.

During this period Collins extended the variety of his writing, publishing articles in George Henry Lewes's paper The Leader, short stories and essays for Bentley's Miscellany, dramatic criticism and the travel book Rambles Beyond Railways. His first play, The Lighthouse, was performed by Dickens's theatrical company at Tavistock House, in 1855. His first collection of short stories, After Dark, was published by Smith, Elder in February 1856. His novel A Rogue's Life was serialised in Household Words in March 1856. Around then, Collins began using laudanum regularly to treat his gout. He became addicted and struggled with that problem later in life.

Collins joined the staff of Household Words in October 1856. In 1856–57 he collaborated closely with Dickens on a play, The Frozen Deep, first performed in Tavistock. Collins's novel The Dead Secret was serialised in Household Words from January to June 1857 and published in volume form by Bradbury and Evans. Collins's play The Lighthouse was performed at the Olympic Theatre in August. The Lazy Tour of Two Idle Apprentices, based on Dickens's and Collins's walking tour in the north of England, was serialised in Household Words in October 1857. In 1858 he collaborated with Dickens and other writers on the story "A House to Let".

1860s

According to biographer Melisa Klimaszewski, "The novels Collins published in the 1860s are the best and most enduring of his career. The Woman in White, No Name, Armadale, and The Moonstone, written in less than a decade, show Collins not just as a master of his craft, but as an innovater and provocateur. These four works, which secured him an international reputation, and sold in large numbers, ensured his financial stability, and allowed him to support many others".

The Woman in White was serialised in All the Year Round from November 1859 to August 1860 and was a great success. The novel was published in book form soon after serial publication ended, and it reached an eighth edition by November 1860. His increased stature as a writer made Collins resign his position with All the Year Round in 1862 to focus on novel writing. During the planning of his next novel, No Name, he continued to suffer from gout, and it now especially affected his eyes. Serial publication of No Name began in early 1862 and finished in 1863. By this time the laudanum he was taking for his continual gout became a serious problem.

At the beginning of 1863, he travelled to German spas and Italy for his health, with Caroline Graves. In 1864, he began work on his novel Armadale, travelling in August to do research for it. It was published serially in The Cornhill Magazine in 1864–66. His play No Thoroughfare, co-written with Dickens, was published as the 1867 Christmas number of All the Year Round and dramatised at the Adelphi Theatre on 26 December. It enjoyed a run of 200 nights before being taken on tour.

Collins's search for background information for Armadale took him to the Norfolk Broads and the small village of Winterton-on-Sea. His novel The Moonstone was serialised in All the Year Round from January to August 1868. His mother, Harriet Collins, died that year.

Later years

In 1870, his novel Man and Wife was published. This year also saw the death of Charles Dickens, which caused him great sadness. He said of their early days together, "We saw each other every day, and were as fond of each other as men could be."

The Woman in White was dramatised and produced at the Olympic Theatre in October 1871.

Collins's novel Poor Miss Finch was serialised in Cassell's Magazine from October to March 1872. His short novel Miss or Mrs? was published in the 1872 Christmas number of the Graphic. His novel The New Magdalen was serialised from October 1872 to July 1873. His younger brother, Charles Allston Collins, died later in 1873. Charles had married Dickens's younger daughter, Kate.

In 1873–74, Collins toured the United States and Canada, giving readings of his work. The American writers he met included Oliver Wendell Holmes, Sr., and Mark Twain, and he began a friendship with the photographer Napoleon Sarony, who took several portraits of him.

His novel The Law and the Lady, serialised in the Graphic from September to March 1875, was followed by a short novel, The Haunted Hotel, which was serialised from June to November 1878. His later novels include Jezebel's Daughter (1880), The Black Robe (1881), Heart and Science (1883) and The Evil Genius (1886). In 1884, Collins was elected Vice-President of the Society of Authors, which had been founded by his friend and fellow novelist Walter Besant.

The inconsistent quality of Collins's dramatic and fictional works in the last decade of his life was accompanied by a general decline in his health, including diminished eyesight. He was often unable to leave home and had difficulty writing. During these last years, he focused on mentoring younger writers, including the novelist Hall Caine, and helped to protect other writers from copyright infringement of their works. His writing became a way for him to fight his illness without allowing it to keep him bedridden. His step-daughter Harriet also served as an amanuensis for several years. His last novel, Blind Love, was finished posthumously by Walter Besant.

Death

Collins died at 82 Wimpole Street, following a paralytic stroke. He is buried in Kensal Green Cemetery, West London. His headstone describes him as the author of The Woman in White. Caroline Graves died in 1895 and was buried with Collins. Martha Rudd died in 1919.

Personal life

In 1858 Collins began living with Caroline Graves and her daughter Harriet. Caroline came from a humble family, having married young, had a child, and been widowed. Collins lived close to the small shop kept by Caroline, and the two may have met in the neighborhood in the mid–1850s. He treated Harriet, whom he called Carrie, as his own daughter, and helped to provide for her education. Excepting one short separation, they lived together for the rest of Collins's life. Collins disliked the institution of marriage, but remained dedicated to Caroline and Harriet, considering them to be his family. Caroline had wanted to marry Collins. She left him while he wrote The Moonstone and was suffering an attack of acute gout. She then married a younger man named Joseph Clow, but returned to Collins after two years.

In 1868, Collins met Martha Rudd in Winterton-on-Sea in Norfolk, and the two began a liaison. She was 19 years old and from a large, poor family. She moved to London to be closer to him a few years later. Their daughter Marian was born in 1869, their second daughter, Harriet Constance, in 1871 and their son, William Charles, in 1874. When he was with Martha he assumed the name William Dawson, and she and their children used the last name of Dawson themselves.

For the last 20 years of his life Collins divided his time between Caroline, who lived with him at his home in Gloucester Place, and Martha who was nearby.

Like his friend Charles Dickens, Collins was a professing Christian.

Works

Collins's works were classified at the time as "sensation novels", a genre seen nowadays as the precursor to detective and suspense fiction. He also wrote penetratingly on the plight of women and on the social and domestic issues of his time. For example, his 1854 Hide and Seek contained one of the first portrayals of a deaf character in English literature. As did many writers of his time, Collins published most of his novels as serials in magazines such as Dickens's All the Year Round and was known as a master of the form, creating just the right degree of suspense to keep his audience reading from week to week. Sales of All The Year Round increased when The Woman in White followed A Tale of Two Cities.

Collins enjoyed ten years of great success following publication of The Woman in White in 1859. His next novel, No Name combined social commentary – the absurdity of the law as it applied to children of unmarried parents (see Illegitimacy in fiction) – with a densely plotted revenge thriller.

Armadale, the first and only of Collins's major novels of the 1860s to be serialised in a magazine other than All the Year Round, provoked strong criticism, generally centred upon its transgressive villainess Lydia Gwilt, and provoked in part by Collins's typically confrontational preface. The novel was simultaneously a financial coup for its author and a comparative commercial failure: the sum paid by Cornhill for the serialisation rights was exceptional, eclipsing by a substantial margin the prices paid for the vast majority of similar novels, yet the novel failed to recoup its publisher's investment. The Moonstone, published in 1868, and the last novel of what is generally regarded as the most successful decade of its author's career, was, despite a somewhat cool reception from both Dickens and the critics, a significant return to form and reestablished the market value of an author whose success on the competitive Victorian literary market had been gradually waning in the wake of his first perceived masterpiece. Viewed by many to represent the advent of the detective story within the tradition of the English novel, The Moonstone remains one of Collins's most critically acclaimed productions, identified by T. S. Eliot as "the first, the longest, and the best of modern English detective novels... in a genre invented by Collins and not by Poe," and Dorothy L. Sayers referred to it as "probably the very finest detective story ever written".

After The Moonstone, Collins's novels contained fewer thriller elements and more social commentary. The subject matter continued to be sensational, but his popularity declined. The poet Algernon Charles Swinburne commented: "What brought good Wilkie's genius nigh perdition? / Some demon whispered—'Wilkie! have a mission.'"

Factors most often cited have been the death of Dickens in 1870, and with it the loss of his literary mentoring, Collins's increased dependence upon laudanum, and his penchant for using his fiction to rail against social injustices. His novels and novellas of the 1870s and 1880s are generally regarded as inferior to his previous productions and receive comparatively little critical attention today[when?].

The Woman in White and The Moonstone share an unusual narrative structure, somewhat resembling an epistolary novel, in which different portions of the book have different narrators, each with a distinct narrative voice. Armadale has this to a lesser extent through the correspondence between some characters. (Source: Wikipedia)

CPSIA information can be obtained
at www.ICGtesting.com
Printed in the USA
LVHW090346140720
660560LV00013B/614

CONQUER WE MUST

ROBIN PRIOR

CONQUER WE MUST

A MILITARY HISTORY OF BRITAIN 1914–1945

YALE UNIVERSITY PRESS
NEW HAVEN AND LONDON

Contains public sector information licensed under the Open Government Licence v3.0.

For information about this and other Yale University Press publications, please contact:
U.S. Office: sales.press@yale.edu   yalebooks.com
Europe Office: sales@yaleup.co.uk   yalebooks.co.uk

Set in Minion Pro by IDSUK (DataConnection) Ltd
Printed in Great Britain by TJ Books, Padstow, Cornwall

Library of Congress Control Number: 2022942466

ISBN 978-0-300-23340-7

A catalogue record for this book is available from the British Library.

10 9 8 7 6 5 4 3 2 1

This book is for
Abby

CONTENTS

ILLUSTRATIONS

Plates

1. Sir Edward Grey speaking to a packed House of Commons, 3 August 1914. Michel & Gabrielle Therin-Weise / Alamy Stock Photo.
2. Mr Asquith taking an interest in the war or at least in an aeroplane. BMH Photographic / Alamy Stock Photo.
3. General Sir John French, C-in-C of the BEF, with his ADCs in 1915. KGPA Ltd / Alamy Stock Photo.
4. Lloyd George with his Cabinet colleague Lord Reading and Albert Thomas (French munitions minister) visiting the front. National Archives of the Netherlands.
5. Generals Rawlinson and Haig during the Battle of the Somme. Chronicle / Alamy Stock Photo.
6. Admiral Sir John Jellicoe. Library of Congress Prints and Photographs Division Washington, D.C., LC-B2- 6462-7 [P&P].
7. Soldiers at the Battle of the Menin Road, 1917. GRANGER - Historical Picture Archive / Alamy Stock Photo.
8. Guns on the Western Front. Colin Waters / Alamy Stock Photo.
9. Trenches at Gallipoli. Chronicle / Alamy Stock Photo.
10. Troops wading into battle in Mesopotamia. Everett Collection Historical / Alamy Stock Photo.
11. Churchill with the King and the War Cabinet, 1943. Classic Image / Alamy Stock Photo.
12. Keith Park. Pictorial Press Ltd / Alamy Stock Photo.
13. Generals O'Connor and Wavell. The Print Collector / Alamy Stock Photo.

14. Changing the guard in Cairo. Trinity Mirror / Mirrorpix / Alamy Stock Photo.
15. British troops at the invasion of Sicily in July 1943. mccool / Alamy Stock Photo.
16. Cassino and its dominating monastery. Vintage_Space / Alamy Stock Photo.
17. General William Slim. Trinity Mirror / Mirrorpix / Alamy Stock Photo.
18. The Grand Alliance at Quebec, 1944. Department of Defense. Department of the Army. Fort Leavenworth, Kansas. (9/18/1947-), National Archives, 292627.
19. The D-Day commanders: Bradley, Ramsay, Tedder, Eisenhower, Montgomery, Leigh-Mallory and Bedell Smith. Pictorial Press Ltd / Alamy Stock Photo.
20. Sherman tanks from the 3 Canadian Division pass through the village of Reviers shortly after the D-Day landings. Pictorial Press Ltd / Alamy Stock Photo.
21. A Lancaster bomber, the true instrument of strategic bombing. Shawshots / Alamy Stock Photo.
22. A convoy in mid-Atlantic, finally with air cover. Antiqua Print Gallery / Alamy Stock Photo.

Table

Maps

ACKNOWLEDGEMENTS

I HAVE INCURRED A debt to many people and institutions over the years I have been writing this book. First, I would like to thank the University of Adelaide for providing me with a home and in particular to Professor Jennie Shaw, Deputy Vice-Chancellor, for her help and encouragement and belief in this project. Without her support this book might not have been written. I would also like to acknowledge Margaret Hosking, the most superb of librarians, for her efforts in securing the Churchill Archive Online, without which this book would have been immeasurably poorer.

On a personal level I would like to thank Dr Gordon Baker, Professor Gary Sheffield and Michael David, all of whom read chapters of the book. In particular I would like to thank Gordon for listening to innumerable telephone calls and acting at times as a one-man seminar for some of my ideas. His patience and good humour were tested more than once. I also wish to thank Dr Debbie Lackerstein for her help in the difficult task of accessing the Montgomery Papers at the height of the Covid pandemic.

On the typing of the manuscript, Bonny and Cassie helped me in their own inimitable way.

In the course of writing I have made many friends, some of whom I know only as an online presence. In particular for their help and encouragement I especially thank Robert Lyman, Peter Caddick-Adams, David Morgan-Owen, Jonathan Boff, Dan Todman, Alan Allport, Christopher Bell and Andrew Harris. They have lifted my spirits more than once in this five-year journey.

My research for this book was spread over a number of years and was thankfully almost complete before the virus struck. I owe a great debt to many institutions for help in research and for copyright permission to quote from collections in their possession. In particular I want to thank Jessica Collins and the staff at Churchill College, Cambridge, notably for assistance in copyright permission to quote from Crown Copyright material in the Churchill Archive Online, published by Bloomsbury Publishing. Also thanks to Cathy Williams and the staff at the Liddell Hart Centre for Military Archives and especially for helping with copyright permission to quote from the Alanbrooke Papers. The National Library of Scotland kindly gave me permission to quote from the diaries and papers of Earl Haig. At the Imperial War Museum I thank Bryn Hammond for his individual help and in particular Tony Richards, Head of Documents and Sound, for copyright permission for collections in their possession. I would also like to thank the Australian War Memorial for their wonderful collection of digitised war diaries. I thank the Australian Defence Force Academy for access to the Montgomery Papers. Finally, I wish to thank The National Archives (UK). The majority of footnotes in this book relate to their collections. The efficiency with which they work and the help I received from their staff is beyond praise. I have endeavoured to contact all copyright holders. If I have inadvertently missed anyone, I would be happy to acknowledge them in another edition of this book.

Of course, although I have attempted to use original sources as much as possible, the book stands on the shoulders of much research done by others. The bibliography is an attempt to acknowledge that work but I should state that I have read much more than I was able to list due to the exigencies of space.

As this book was nearing its end, I suffered one heavy blow. In June 2022 my old writing partner, Trevor Wilson, died. I would have liked to have shown him this book but it was not to be. His fingerprints can however be found in many of the First World War chapters. Vale Trevor.

I owe a great debt to the team at Yale University Press London, so ably led by Heather McCallum. This was a large project and it came to fruition in some style. Heather has been encouraging and patient as my many requests poured in. Her guidance, often needed, was invariably in the right direction. I must also thank Felicity Maunder for her expertise in the production phase. Special thanks go to Jessica Cuthbert-Smith, copy-editor par excellence, and Michelle Tilling for superb proofreading. Thanks too to Katie Urquhart for managing the illustrations and to Lucy Buchan for her all-round help. I must also thank Martin Brown for drawing the maps. I am only sorry that the pandemic kept me away from London and from meeting all the members of this great team.

My greatest debt, as always, is to my wife, Heather. She has participated in every phase of the production of this book. She helped with the original research and read all the chapters from start to finish. She is able to spot and correct long-winded, circuitous or just plain muddled arguments and this book would have been a poorer effort without her. Every chapter bears her improvements. None of my books could possibly have been written without her.

My daughter Megan made a major contribution by supplying an additional member of our family when I was at the very beginning of this book. Abby is a total delight and it is appropriate that this book be dedicated to her.

INTRODUCTION

IN THE TWENTIETH CENTURY it fell to Britain to confront a number of regimes which represented a threat to the civilised world. Nazi Germany and Imperial Japan were two of the blackest regimes ever to darken the pages of human history. The Nazis with their expansionism, militarism and vile racial policies could not be endured or even tolerated because their thirst for conquest was virtually unlimited. There was no chance of peaceful co-existence with them. The very presence of democratic, liberal states was sufficient provocation for Hitler to foment a war. The Germany of the Kaiser, while it had some seemingly democratic credentials in terms of the franchise and welfare system, was in fact expansionist, militaristic and anything but liberal. Its domination of Europe would not, as some commentators have suggested, have resulted in some form of premature Common Market but in the snuffing out of liberal values in Western Europe and, when Tirpitz had got around to outbuilding the British fleet, in Britain as well. Italy was once an ally of Britain and a democracy of a kind but under Mussolini gradually succumbed to fascism and illiberalism. From the moment the Pact of Steel with Hitler was announced, oppression increased and by its end the regime was an accomplice to genocide. Japan had also been an ally of Britain but from the 1930s descended into its own form of fascism as became brutally apparent with the rape of Nanking and the barbaric medical experiments inflicted on the Chinese people. And its war against China was only a stepping-stone to wider ambitions across the Pacific basin.

Taking the two world wars together, Britain was the only power on the Allied side to fight these regimes from beginning to end. And, given the nature of the powers that it was fighting, it was essential that any chance of a liberal world order (however imperfect) emerging with peace, depended on Britain being on the winning side.

What struck me in examining Britain in these wars was the implacable nature of its effort. There was never any doubt that Britain would strive with every fibre of its being to see both wars through to successful conclusions. The Defence of the Realm Act in 1914 and the Emergency Powers Act of 1939–1940 swept away many of the civil liberties that had been won at such cost over the centuries, with hardly a murmur from the general population. Politicians thought not to be up to the rigours that such wars engendered, such as Asquith and Chamberlain, were replaced with more resolute premiers in Lloyd George and Churchill. Similarly, military leaders such as Sir John French and Archibald Wavell, who were not thought up to the job, were replaced with more unswerving commanders such as Haig and Montgomery.

As for the people, it is often said of the First World War, if members of the public had known of the carnage at the front, they would have insisted that it be stopped. The problem with this theory is that the people had a good idea of what was happening on the various fronts. The publication of lists of casualties by name by the press (helpfully totalled at the top of the page by such newspapers as the *Glasgow Herald*) and the sheer extent of the casualties demonstrated the true cost of the war. Certainly by 1916 very few families did not know of a close relative or loved one who had become a casualty. Then, for those curious to understand whether the great offensives were getting any closer to Berlin, the press published maps indicating that Berlin, even in 1918, was still some way off. Yet, even with this knowledge, the extent of an anti-war movement in Britain was small, and though by 1917 war-weariness had certainly set in, there was no strong call to end it. Indeed, there were stronger calls to prosecute it with more firmness.

A similar spirit seemed to imbue those whose lot it was to prosecute this war at close range – the soldiers. Regardless of what one thinks of the sometimes futile campaigns in which they were required to participate, overwhelmingly they did so without resorting to widespread indiscipline. Day after day, whatever the hopelessness of the task set, they attacked again and again. Churchill, a stern critic of the methods used on the Western Front, could not but admire of 'the wonderful tenacity' of the British soldier. Indeed, there is some kind of epic grandeur within the great tragedy of these endeavours. It is a matter for wonder that of the Allied armies fighting on the Western Front and elsewhere, the British army was the only one that stuck to its task without mutiny or indeed reluctance to fight.

What is remarkable about Britain and the Second World War is that, having endured the ordeal of 1914–1918, it went to war again in 1939. A claim is sometimes made that the policy of appeasement fed on the disillusionment with the Great War. But when appeasement was seen to equal dishonour – which after Munich, it rapidly was – and when it was acknowledged that Hitler's aims were indeed unlimited, the mood became resolute for war, as a startled Chamberlain was late to realise.

And when the people were tested with war directly as they were in the Blitz the mood was again uncompromising. They came out to see Churchill as he visited the bombed cities, not just to be cheered but to check that his spirit remained as determined as theirs. As for the armies, they were sent out to fight in the Middle East, India, Burma and many other places as well where they spent years away from home and loved ones. That their morale was often low seems beyond dispute. That they fought on is definitely beyond dispute.

Despite the resolution shown in Britain in both world wars, it must not be concluded that victory was a certainty. There were moments in the wars where victory might have turned into defeat or at least a prolongation of the war to the depths of exhaustion.

One such moment occurred on 7 November 1917 when Haig asked for over 1 million men to prolong his already disastrous campaign at Passchendaele into 1918. If such a policy had been pursued, the reserves (few enough as it happened) which stopped the German spring offensive in 1918 would have been consumed and the British armies not just driven back but perhaps defeated. Lloyd George refused the request, perhaps earning his sobriquet of 'the man who won the war'.

A similar decisive moment came in June 1942 during the Second World War. Then, an American delegation in London, led by General Marshall, and with the full backing of President Roosevelt, insisted that an invasion of north-western Europe take place in that year – the sooner, in fact, the better. Churchill, backed by his military advisers, refused. And as the British, under the American plan, would have been required to provide the bulk of the troops and the shipping, that was the end of the debate. If such an operation had gone ahead it would almost certainly have led to a crushing defeat – the Allies not possessing the seasoned troops, nor the sophisticated landing craft, nor the practice at amphibious operations, to carry it through to a success. What this would have meant for the war in the west and the eventual composition of Europe is highly speculative – but it would certainly have led to a prolongation of the war, with Britain playing an ever-diminishing part in its conclusion.

There are many other such moments detailed in the course of the following narrative. They show that victory in a conflict the size of a world war is never a foregone conclusion. And the alternative, as far as Western Europe and indeed Britain were concerned, was that they could have finished up under the heel of the Kaiser's Germany or even worse as provinces of a Nazified Europe. Matters of world-historical importance were therefore at stake in both conflicts.

This book, then, takes its title, *Conquer We Must,* from the stern resolve exhibited by Britain in both world wars. The book concentrates on the political and military interface that decided where Britain would fight, with what resources it would fight, and how it would fight. The forums in which these decisions would be made had to be rapidly improvised in 1914 as fighting a world war was quite outside the experience of anyone in government. A kind of War Council where selected politicians and selected military advisers would gather together was implemented with great speed and the precedent followed, with some refinements, in the Second World War. Luckily for the historian, it was also decided that such bodies would keep minutes and papers that have been almost entirely preserved for posterity. These documents allow us a bird's-eye view of decision-making at the highest level. For example, we can trace the decision to embark on various enterprises, including Gallipoli, the Somme, the war in the desert and the Normandy landings; we can observe the cut and thrust of debate which the ventures engendered and the way in which the final decision was made. Other documents allow us to see at first hand debates among coalition partners about which strategy to follow. This is particularly important in the Second World War, where the Americans take an increasingly prominent role. There we can see what compromises were reached and those instances where compromise proved impossible. We can also see disputes shifting from those within a country to those between countries, as national interests clash and solidify.

But we must record not merely high-level decision-making. The decisions taken in these forums resulted in fighting on the ground, many times in campaigns that stretched over long months or even years. It would be an anaemic history that ignored the combat operations that flowed from these decisions. Detail of the fighting enables us to examine how well thought out the original decisions at the summit were, what price had to be paid, and whether the politicians had the will or the means of intervening if these military operations seemed to be going wrong.

And what we know about a liberal state (Britain in 1914) or a democracy (Britain in 1939) is that if military operations were going wrong, the politicians had sanctions that they could apply to the military and expect to be obeyed. They could replace generals or order them to cease and desist from the methods they were employing. If they did not choose this course of action, we need to know why and we need to know the consequences for the men on the ground who were required to persist with unfruitful miliary operations. If they did order changes in command or method, we need to ask the same questions – why was the change made and what consequences were there for the soldiers?

Again, some examples are in order. In 1915 a Liberal government (on the urging of Churchill but with the ready acceptance of the other members of the War Council) decided that the strategy being carried out was perhaps not the best way to win the war. Against the advice of their First Sea Lord (Jacky Fisher) they decided to attempt to bring down an empire and shorten the war by naval power alone, and when that operation failed, their Minister of War (Lord Kitchener) – without consulting either civilian or military colleagues – decided to commit troops to the area, resulting in the rather futile and quite costly Gallipoli campaign. This was civilian intervention with a vengeance.

By contrast in 1916, having decided on the Somme campaign, the civilian War Committee decided to accept the advice of the military and to persist with it despite the enormous casualty bill, the obvious fact that the battle was not progressing according to plan and despite the palpable nonsense they were being fed by their top military adviser, General Robertson. This was civilian dereliction with a vengeance.

The Second World War represents a different scenario. Both Chamberlain and Churchill were interventionists, the difference being that Chamberlain would intervene to confine military operations to a minimum (his decision to drop leaflets on Germany instead of bombs being one of the more well known), while Churchill's interventions were almost always of the opposite type where he insisted on incessant attacks whether commanders were ready for them or not.

Clashes of personality are commonplace in politicians and not unknown among soldiers. In war, especially world war, these clashes have a heightened importance because issues of survival are at stake. We are fortunate that many of the key players (though not any of the four Prime Ministers) kept diaries. For the First World War we have the diaries of Maurice Hankey, Secretary of the variously named War Councils, and for the military we have that of Sir Douglas Haig. This diary has been described as the longest suicide note in history, but it shows like nothing else in this conflict the pressures under which a high-level commander and then Commander-in-Chief worked. It shows the war from his perspective (a narrow focus, it has been called, as though between the ears of a horse) but it is wide ranging enough and candid enough to provide an unrivalled view of general headquarters (GHQ) at work. It also shows the bitter disputes between Haig and Lloyd George, though here we need Hankey's diary, and the minutes of the various forums in which Haig and Lloyd George clashed, to gain a true perspective.

For the Second World War we have Alan Brooke's diary, in many ways the equivalent of Haig's. Here clashes with Churchill are almost a daily event, though their differences in strategy are on most occasions not as far apart as Brooke asserts. We also have Harold Nicolson's unparalleled view of the Parliamentary Churchill at war and the gossipy if rather repellent diaries of a Conservative backbencher, Chips Channon, now in an expanded form.

We also have the Roosevelt–Churchill correspondence, one of the key sources for the development of Allied strategy in the Second World War.

This is particularly important because Roosevelt was not an inveterate writer like Churchill, and his correspondence with the Prime Minister provides the best source for his thinking. This relationship, even before the US became an active partner in the war, is in some ways the best introduction to the sometimes ambivalent partnership Britain had with its great ally and the benefits and costs that such an association brought about.

The fascinating interplay between politicians and the military, the force of the personalities involved and the transcending importance of the issues at stake, make the study of Britain in two world wars, worthy of attention. It also provides a fruitful opportunity for comparison. Was anything learned from one war to the next? Was Churchill the beneficiary of events from the earlier conflict where in 1915 he was unceremoniously removed from office? Did Britain fight a more efficient second world war than a first and if so, was that experience accountable for it?

The two world wars are therefore a lens through which to see Britain in its last, best role as a Great Power. The choices it made during that period and its ultimate survival live with us still.

CHAPTER 1

A LIBERAL STATE
DECLARES WAR

AT 4 P.M. ON SUNDAY 28 June, 1914 the Foreign Office received a report from Consul Jones in Sarajevo: 'According to news received here heir apparent and his consort assassinated this morning by means of an explosive nature.'[1] Later that evening the news arrived from the British Ambassador that Franz Ferdinand and the Duchess Sophie had in fact been shot by a 'young Serbian student'.[2]

Thirty-seven days later Britain and Germany were at war. What is remarkable about Britain during this period is that not a single military figure had the slightest influence on policy. The country went to war because the Cabinet and the House of Commons decided that it must.

Sir Edward Grey, the British Foreign Secretary, as was appropriate, was the first to react to the murders. He expressed his condolences to the Austrian Emperor through the Ambassador,[3] and he expressed his sympathy to the Austrian Ambassador in London, Count Mensdorff, noting that 'every feeling political and personal makes me sympathise with you'.[4]

Grey was not at this stage particularly perturbed. What happened in the Balkans, he said, 'was not our concern', a position he maintained throughout the crisis.[5]

Certainly, if the incident remained localised, Britain would have no interest. Indeed, it is difficult to think of an area of the world in which Britain was less interested. Trade with the area was minimal, defence links, except with the Greek navy, nil. British representation was minuscule. There was an embassy in Serbia and one in Romania that covered the remainder of the Balkans. That was all. Recent events, however, had demonstrated how the Great Powers could be drawn into Balkan affairs. In 1912 war broke out between the Balkan states led by Serbia and Turkey. A second war followed in 1913 between Serbia, Romania and Bulgaria as they sought to redistribute land taken from the Ottomans in the first war for themselves. Austria sought to intervene in this conflict, mainly to prevent the emergence of an enlarged Serbia, which they feared might act as a magnet to the Slav populations living within their empire. Russia, which saw itself as the guardian of Slav interests in the Balkans, warned the Austrians to back off. On this occasion the war was confined. Grey, with German encouragement, called an Ambassadors' Conference in London. Protracted negotiations punctuated by outbreaks of fighting in the Balkans followed. Eventually Grey, with the general approval of Germany, France and Russia, shouted at the assembled Balkan representatives: 'Sign or Go'. They signed. Great Power solidarity had won through. Austria would have to live with a greater Serbia. Russia was mollified.

Grey's first intimation that the assassination of the Archduke might also have implications for the Powers arrived via a cable from the British Ambassador in Vienna, Sir Maurice de Bunsen. On 2 July he warned Grey that the murders would see a period of 'great tension' between the two countries. The Austrians thought that if the assassinations were not planned in Belgrade, the plans certainly found favour there. Was this the first step towards an even greater Serbia at the expense of the Slav populations of Austria?[6]

Due to the vagaries of the diplomatic cable traffic in those far-off days, this telegram only arrived at the Foreign Office on 6 July. It was perhaps its arrival that prompted Grey to seek an interview with the German Ambassador to Britain, Prince Lichnowsky. It is interesting that Grey sought out Lichnowsky rather than Count Mensdorff, the Austrian Ambassador. Clearly the Foreign Secretary was thinking that the crisis might be managed by a re-run of the methods used in the Balkan wars. Germany would act as a restraint on Austria while Britain and France could use their influence on Russia.

On this occasion Grey was to be disappointed. Lichnowsky had just returned to London from Berlin. He reported that the anti-Serb feeling in Austria was very strong. But more alarming was the mood in the German capital. There was a feeling that Germany could not ask for restraint from its main ally again. In any case, some in Berlin were nervous about the increases in the size of the Russian army and concerned that Russia had signed some kind of naval convention with Britain. Men with close ties with the military were saying, Lichnowsky told Grey in the utmost confidence, that if Austria saw fit to punish the Serbs and Russia intervened to protect them, Germany should stand up for its ally – better a war now than later against an even stronger Russia.[7]

Grey sought to reassure Lichnowsky. He had heard nothing from Russia to indicate ill-will towards Germany; there had been no naval convention signed between Britain and Russia, merely conversations between naval authorities; all must work to pacify the Austrian–Serb situation; they would meet again for further talks.[8]

Despite his calm outward demeanour, this talk with Lichnowsky thoroughly alarmed Grey. He immediately arranged a meeting with Count Benkendorff, the Russian Ambassador to Britain (who happened to be Lichnowsky's cousin), to establish if there was any reason for German fear of Russia. Benkendorff assured him there was 'no indication whatever from St. Petersburg of ill-will towards Germany'.[9] He went on to say, however, that the increase in the Russian army in recent years was an 'undoubted fact' that might have fuelled German fears. Grey urged him to reassure Germany that no one was preparing any kind of coup against it. This the Ambassador promised to do, noting that Grey had said that 'the idea that the terrible crime might unexpectedly produce a general war with all its attendant catastrophes . . . made his hair stand on edge'.[10]

Had Grey been aware of events in Berlin and Vienna that had taken place at the time of these interviews, his hair would not have stood on edge, it would have fallen out. Count Berchtold, the Austrian Foreign Minister, and Conrad, the Austrian Chief of Staff, had pushed for war against Serbia since the time of the assassination. The Emperor was not so certain. Austria could not move without Germany's backing. Would it be given? Franz Joseph therefore insisted that a mission be despatched to Berlin to find out.

The mission would be conducted by Count Alexander Hoyos, the chief of the Foreign Minister's Private Office. He was to convey two documents to the Germans, long and rambling affairs, which in their essence made the case for war. Hoyos arrived at the Wilhelmstrasse on the very day that Grey met with Lichnowsky – 6 July. During the next two days Hoyos saw Zimmerman, the Under-Secretary of State (the Foreign Minister, Jagow, was on honeymoon in Switzerland), while the Austrian Ambassador to Germany, Count Szogyeny, presented the same documents to the Kaiser. Later both men met the German Chancellor Bethmann Hollweg.[11] What transpired at these meetings has engaged historians for decades. However the main tenor is clear. Both the Kaiser and the Chancellor left the Austrians in no doubt that 'the German Government was in favour of an **immediate** offensive on our part against Serbia'.[12] In other words the Germans were committed to back Austria at the very moment that Grey was attempting to invoke them as mediator. The blank cheque had been issued.

Grey knew nothing of these manoeuvres but his suspicions that Austria intended to take stern action against Serbia were confirmed on 16 July. On that day he learned from de Bunsen that 'a friend' (in fact Count Lutzow, a former Austrian Ambassador to Italy) was aware that 'a kind of indictment is being prepared [in Vienna] against the Serbian Government for alleged complicity in the conspiracy which led to the assassination of the Archduke'.[13] The informant went on to say that the Austrians were in no mood to parlay with the Serbians; that they would require unconditional compliance with their indictment, 'failing which force will be used' and that Germany was in 'complete agreement with this procedure'.[14]

This was escalation. Germany was now in the mix, not as a mediator but as a backer of its ally in any military action that Austria might take. Nevertheless, the nature of the Austrian indictment was not known. There was still time to urge caution on the Powers. Grey therefore began another round of diplomatic conversations. First he told the British Ambassador in St Petersburg, Sir George Buchanan, that it was important to keep the Austrians and the Russians talking. If Austria could show good justification for any demands it made on Belgrade and if the Powers concentrated on the wider issue of the peace of Europe, the situation might be contained.[15] Next he called in Benkendorff and urged him to ask the Russian Foreign Minister (Sazanov) to initiate talks between the Russians and Austria. Sazanov should emphasise that the strength of pro-Slav feeling in Russia meant that there was widespread sympathy for Serbia but that if the Austrians took the Russians into their confidence and laid before them the case they had against Serbia, any reasonable demands might be met.[16]

Grey then called in Lichnowsky and asked if he had any details of the step Austria might take against Serbia. Lichnowsky informed him that he had not, which was correct because his own government was keeping him out of the Balkan loop. Lichnowsky, however, told Grey that he was very apprehensive about the belligerence of the Austrians. Grey passed on these sentiments to the British Ambassador in Berlin and authorised him to say that the Austrians must keep their demands within reasonable limits. Then the Powers would be well placed to urge restraint on Russia.[17]

Finally Grey saw the French Ambassador to Britain, Paul Cambon. He told him of the apprehensions of the German Ambassador and that he was uncertain of the role the Germans were playing in the Balkan dispute. 'Probably', he told Cambon, 'Berlin was trying to moderate Vienna.'[18] Grey was not being entirely straightforward with Cambon here. He kept from him any hint that Germany might be playing a double game – urging Austria on in private while publicly calling for peace. Grey clearly still had hopes that Germany might in the end restrain its ally. In the meantime Grey thought that the most direct method of restraining Russia lay with its ally France, but that the French might be reluctant to act if they were suspicious of German motives.

In this period we see Grey follow a conciliatory path. He had by no means ruled out some form of reparation to Austria from Serbia for the outrage. He also communicated the same message to all the Powers – be reasonable and keep talking. And it is noteworthy that he took this line as strongly with his Entente partners as he did with the representatives of the Central Powers.[19]

Grey was certainly involved in a perilous balancing act, and this act became much more difficult on 23 July. On that day Mensdorff had seen Grey to give him advance warning of the nature of the Austrian note to Serbia, no doubt in order to cushion the blow. He led Grey to understand that the note would consist of a long list of demands with which Serbia was expected to comply. He then told Grey that there would be a time limit attached to the note. Grey interrupted and told the Austrian Ambassador that this converted the note into an ultimatum, that it would inflame opinion in Russia and that in these circumstances it would be very difficult for the Entente Powers to urge restraint.[20]

Grey concluded by saying to Mensdorff that:

the possible consequences of the present situation were terrible. If as many as four Great Powers of Europe – let us say Austria, France, Russia, and Germany – [note that Grey was prudently giving nothing away as to the position of Britain] were engaged in war, it seemed to me that it must involve the expenditure of so vast a sum of money and such an interference with trade, that a war would be accompanied or followed by a complete collapse of European credit and industry. In these days, in great industrial States, this would mean a state of things worse than that of 1848, and irrespective of who were victors in the war, many things might be completely swept away.[21]

Statesmen have been accused of marching towards war in this period without realising the consequences. If that is the case, Sir Edward Grey must be excluded from their number.

On 24 July Grey saw the ultimatum. He told the British Ambassador to Austria that he considered it 'the most formidable document I had ever seen addressed by one State to another that was independent'.[22] The merits or otherwise of the Austrian case did not interest him. It was the whole tone of the note that caused alarm. In Grey's view, it amounted to an ultimatum designed to be rejected. In particular he noted that demand No. 5 would have allowed Austrian-appointed officials to have judicial authority on Serbian territory – 'hardly consistent with maintenance of independent sovereignty of Serbia'.[23] Not that Grey was all that interested in that either – why should he be? Britain's national interests were hardly engaged. What did worry him was the threat the ultimatum posed to the peace of Europe. For, if Serbian territorial integrity was threatened, Russia might intervene. And if the Germans were standing behind the Austrians, an intervention by Russia to assist Serbia might trigger a German intervention to assist Austria. All this was made of immediate urgency because a forty-eight-hour time limit had been attached to the note. Within two days, four Great Powers might be at war. In this situation Britain might be reduced – at best – to the position of a bystander watching over the destruction of European trade – at worst dragged into a conflict the origins of which lay outside Britain's zone of interest.

Grey now repeated the tactics he had employed after the assassination. He saw the relevant ambassadors and advised that talks between Austria and Russia were essential. This time he went one step further. He suggested that he was thinking of calling a conference or a meeting of the four least interested Powers – Germany, France, Russia and Britain – to discuss the assassination crisis and to hammer out a settlement.[24] But later in the day the German Embassy issued a communication which made their participation in such a conference highly unlikely. The communiqué stated that Germany regarded the Austrian demands as 'equitable and moderate'.[25] If the terms of the ultimatum were not met then Austria would have no choice but to use 'military measures' against the Serbs.[26]

With a solid front of the Powers on the brink of dissolution, Grey suggested to Asquith that the Cabinet be immediately brought together. Some authorities have intimated that Grey should have consulted his colleagues at a much earlier date than this.[27] But the fact is that before the Austrian ultimatum Grey had no great need to speak to the Cabinet. Until then it was unclear what response the Austrians might make to the assassination. Grey certainly had intimations that their note would be stiff but it was the German communiqué that crystallised his thinking. If Germany backed Austria whatever the terms it might present to Serbia, the peace of Europe was definitely endangered. A conference of the Powers now seemed the only hope and for that he had to have Cabinet sanction.

In fact the day that Grey alerted the Cabinet to the European situation most of their time had been taken up by the Irish question – how to square the Liberal government's promise of Home Rule for Ireland with the wish of Protestant Ulster to opt out of any such agreement. Once Grey commenced talking, however, the Cabinet's attention was soon gripped; 'the muddy byways of Fermanagh and Tyrone' soon fell away.[28] He said that the Austrian note could well be the prelude to a new war in which at least four of the Great Powers might be involved. He suggested a mediating group of Italy, Germany France and Britain be set up to use their influence for moderation.[29] Asquith grasped the danger at once. He told his confidante Venetia Stanley, 'we are within measurable, or imaginable distance from a real Armageddon.'[30] 'Happily', he concluded, 'there seems to be no reason why we should be anything more than spectators.'[31]

Grey was not so sanguine. He immediately saw Lichnowsky and Cambon and pressed them to accept his idea for a four-Power conference.[32] He also urged on Lichnowsky that pressure be put on Austria to extend the deadline.[33] Grey was coming under pressure himself from various sources to take more vigorous action. The Russians strongly suggested that he openly declare for the Entente or he would have 'rendered the war more likely and should not have played a "beau role"'.[34] His own officials were also getting impatient. Sir Eyre Crowe, Assistant Under-Secretary at the Foreign Office, was urging an immediate mobilisation of the fleet.[35] Sir Arthur Nicolson, the Permanent Under-Secretary, insisted that the moment had come to support Russia.[36] Grey refused to be rushed. He thought it was premature to make any statement in support of France or Russia. As for the fleet, the First and Second Fleets were being held together at Portsmouth and Churchill, as First Lord of the Admiralty, had advised him that mobilisation could be carried out in twenty-four hours.[37] All he was prepared to do was to inform the Russians that he had given no indication to Lichnowsky that Britain would necessarily stand aside in any ensuing conflict.[38] Beyond that he was not prepared to go.

Grey then left for Itchen Abbas in Hampshire for some fishing. This action has been described as either showing 'unflappable sang-froid, or culpable disregard of duty'.[39] In fact it was neither. Grey wished to clear his head and was in any case in touch with the Foreign Office. There Nicolson had received an important communication from the Russians. They agreed to stand aside in any Austrian–Serbian dispute if a Serbian appeal for arbitration was left in the hands of Germany, England, France and Italy.[40] Nicolson considered this was the moment formally to issue his invitation for a four-Power ambassadors' meeting in London.[41] Grey agreed and telegrams were despatched to the Powers.[42]

Meanwhile the Serbian reply to the Austrian ultimatum was received in London. Modern analyses of this reply have stressed that Serbia did not agree with the majority of the Austrian demands. One account describes the Serb response as 'mendacious' on some points and 'wholly negative' or 'wilful' on others.[43] Another has the Serbs offering a 'subtle cocktail of acceptances, conditional acceptances, evasions and rejections'.[44] However, that is not the way it seemed to the Powers at the time. In London an analysis of the ultimatum and the reply noted that the Serbs had not accepted some points but that in the main it met Austrian demands.[45] The French and the Russians agreed.[46] So, in part did the Germans, telling Grey that 'there were some things in the Austrian note that Serbia could hardly be expected to accept'.[47] Even the Swiss thought that the Serbs had 'conceded practically all the Austrian demands'.[48] At the time, therefore, the Powers could see no reason for the Austrians not to take the Serbian note at least as a basis for negotiation.

And early on 27 July this seemed to be in prospect. Grey had seen Lichnowsky, who had told him that the German government accepted 'in principle' mediation between Austria and Russia by the four Powers.[49] Later in the day, however, the British Ambassador in Berlin, Sir Edwin Goschen, revealed how out of touch Lichnowsky was. He told Grey that the Foreign Minister (Jagow, now returned from his honeymoon) had said that a four-Power conference would 'practically amount to a court of arbitration and could not be called together except at the request of Austria and Russia. He could not therefore . . . fall in with your suggestion'.[50] Jagow was quite aware that Austria was already on the brink of war with Serbia and would never call for a conference. Without the backing of Germany, Grey's idea was dead. The blank cheque was still in play.

Grey now asked Asquith to summon the Cabinet, which met on the evening of the 27th. Grey, 'looking fit and in good physical trim', laid out the situation.[51] His proposal for a conference 'à quatre' looked 'more than doubtful' because of the attitude of Germany. The position was:

> Germany says to us 'if you will say at St. Petersburg that in no conditions will you come in & help, Russia will draw back & then there will be no war'. On the other hand Russia says to us 'if you won't say you are ready to side with us now, your friendship is valueless, and we shall act on that assumption in the future'.[52]

His only policy was to work for peace by keeping the Powers guessing about any actions Britain might take.[53] Two important decisions were taken at that Cabinet, however. The first was to ratify Churchill's decision to keep the First and Second Fleets concentrated at Portsmouth. The second was more revealing: 'to consider in the next Cabinet our precise obligations in regard to the neutrality of Belgium'.[54]

Events were now starting to crowd in on the British. Before another Cabinet could be called, the Austrians declared war on Serbia. In the short term this act was not as shattering as it might seem. So sclerotic was the

Austrian mobilisation mechanism that nothing happened. No Austrian troops swept into Serbia; no bombardment broke out across the Danube; no bombs fell on Belgrade. And there were some hopeful signs. France, Russia and Italy had accepted Grey's proposal for a conference. Even Germany 'no longer excluded altogether the idea of mediation'.[55] Indeed, it appeared that the main German objection was to the form of words used by Grey – Jagow thought a 'conference' implied that the Powers would dictate terms to Austria.[56] Grey quickly disabused him. He proposed to Germany any form of discussion that might produce a settlement. Further, he suggested that the Germans themselves decide on the form of the meeting, or as an alternative, intercede with the Austrians to keep them talking to the Russians.[57] The hawkish Eyre Crowe was moved to declare this 'the first ray of hope'.[58]

But although he did not know it, Grey's initiative had already been dashed. Jagow had merely passed on the mediation proposal to the Austrians. He had not urged them to accept it; rather he had left the initiative with them. As war had already been declared, Berchtold and Conrad deemed that the British offer had come too late. Jagow accepted this view without comment. Austria would have its war and the Germans would continue to back it.[59] Jagow had played a reckless and deceptive game. The last, best hope for peace – an Anglo-German agreement – had gone.

The Cabinet met on the 29th. By then Grey had heard from the British Ambassador in Berlin that Germany was not able to accept the conference proposal, and that the Austrian quarrel with Serbia was a matter for the two states to decide.[60] In other words Germany would not act to restrain Austria. This news irritated Grey and sharpened his approach. Now that he could no longer count on Germany, he determined to prepare his colleagues for the worst. As already heralded, the first item on the agenda was a consideration of Britain's treaty obligations to Belgium. This matter is of the utmost interest. In the diplomatic correspondence concerning the crisis, voluminous as it is, Belgium hardly rates a mention in any of the documents. But as Grey and several other senior Cabinet members knew, it was of vital importance to Britain. He had attended, along with Asquith, Lloyd George, McKenna and Churchill, a meeting of the Committee of Imperial Defence (CID) in 1911 where the military, in the person of General Sir Henry Wilson, who was the Director of Military Operations, laid before the meeting a detailed scenario in which Germany invaded France through

Belgium.[61] This was also a matter of public debate, one observer noting that 'every well-informed observer knew that a German attack on France would involve the invasion of Belgium'.[62]

Perhaps it would be going too far to include the entire Asquith Cabinet among the 'well-informed', but at least there were enough of them to give the lead to the others. What were Britain's obligations to Belgium should the Germans invade and the Belgians resist? The actual treaty of 1839 was produced by Grey and dusted off, as was the interpolation of the Gladstone government in 1870 when it seemed that Prussia might invade Belgium in the course of the Franco-Prussian War. A long discussion followed. The result was inconclusive. The Cabinet decided that it was uncertain how far a single state of those who had guaranteed Belgian neutrality (France, Prussia and Britain) was bound by the treaty if the other states refused to comply. The matter was therefore one of 'policy rather than of legal obligation'.[63]

As to whether Britain would in any circumstances intervene in a war, in the words of one of the more pacific members of the Cabinet ministers (John Burns) 'it was decided not to decide'.[64] Although Grey described the Austrian actions as 'brutal recklessness', he also undertook 'to continue to urge mediation by as many of the Powers as he could'.[65] As for Britain's position, he would tell both the French and German Ambassadors that 'at this stage' Britain was unable to pledge under which conditions it would join a war or stand aside.[66]

This Cabinet meeting has been regarded as one of the most indecisive of all the meetings in the lead-up to war. It was far from that. The fact was that an overwhelming proportion of the members were against war at any cost. That was not Grey's view. He was concerned that a German attack on France through Belgium might succeed and that the long-term interests of Britain would not survive a French defeat. But he also knew that of the nineteen ministers, probably only Asquith, Churchill, Crewe and Haldane supported entering a war if the Germans attacked France. That left fourteen in the 'pacific' camp. But the matter of Belgium and Britain's obligations to it had now been raised. The question of whether Britain should intervene as a matter of obligation or policy was rather disingenuous. If Belgium, on Britain's doorstep, fell to the Germans, this would raise an issue of national security of rather a different order than what might happen in the Balkans. In that case 'policy' and 'obligation' would merge into one. In introducing the matter of Belgium to the Cabinet Grey was not yet preparing them for war but he was signalling to them that in certain circumstances the crisis could lead to Britain's national interest being engaged. The 'pacific' Cabinet had received its first shock.

This was also the time to prepare Parliament for the worst. If Grey and the Cabinet eventually decided for war it would avail them little if Parliament disagreed. So, after the Cabinet meeting Grey repaired to the House of Commons. He made a short statement to the effect that the crisis was grave. Austria had declared war on Serbia and Russia had ordered a partial mobilisation of its troops. So far no other Power had reacted. The government's policy was to pursue peace.[67]

This provoked an immediate response from the leader of the Liberal Foreign Affairs Committee, Arthur Ponsonby. The group, which consisted of about thirty members of Parliament, was on the pacifist side of the Party. Ponsonby sought an immediate interview with Grey and told him that Britain should immediately declare to the Powers that it would remain neutral in any circumstances.[68] Grey played for time. He told Ponsonby that doubt about Britain's ultimate position might be a useful bargaining position with both sides. Would the group remain silent until the end of the week?[69] Ponsonby agreed but whether or not Grey could count on more than that remained to be seen.

Grey then met with the German and the French Ambassadors. He told Lichnowsky that if Germany and France were not involved in conflict, the question of British intervention would not arise, which was as close to warning Germany to stay out of Western Europe as Grey was prepared to go.[70]

The interview with Cambon was tense. Grey made it clear that he considered Britain free from any obligation to come to the aid of France and that Cambon must not be misled by the friendly nature of their conversations. Britain had no interest in Eastern Europe, but even if Germany and France became involved, Britain had not decided what to do. This was not what Cambon wanted to hear but he received the news calmly enough, noting that if the hegemony of Europe became the question, he was sure Britain would decide what it was 'necessary for us to do'.[71] Grey made no effort to contradict this statement and Cambon probably drew some comfort from that.

On 30 July affairs in Europe were delicately poised. The evening before, military action of a kind had broken out in the Balkans as Austria began shelling Belgrade from across the Danube. No troops were to be seen, however. In Russia, as Grey had been aware, a mobilisation of the military districts nearest Austria had been underway for some days. This move was very far from war, though, as it would take the Russian military machine many weeks to creak into action.[72]

At this moment the Germans acted. At 9 a.m. a telegram arrived at the Foreign Office from Goschen in Berlin. He had been summoned by Bethmann Hollweg, who told him that if Russia attacked Austria 'a European conflagration' might be inevitable. It was evident that Britain would never allow France to be crushed so the German government were willing to give an assurance that if Britain remained neutral Germany would not make territorial acquisitions at the expense of France. On questioning by Goschen, Bethmann said he could give no similar assurances in regards to French colonies. And under pressure he blurted out the following:

> As regards Belgium his Excellency could not tell to what operations Germany might be forced by the actions of France, but he could state that, provided that Belgium did not take sides against Germany, her integrity would be respected after the conclusion of the war.[73]

This was an extraordinary statement. France would not be crushed but its colonies would be stripped from it after military defeat. The Germans would definitely traverse Belgium on their way to France (thus casually did Bethmann give away the German military plan) but all would be restored after the victory. In short, Western Europe would be overrun but there was no cause for British alarm because Germany had no territorial ambitions there. France and no doubt Belgium would be quite happy with their status as German vassals.

Grey reacted furiously. Goschen was told to inform the Chancellor that British neutrality on those terms 'cannot for a moment be entertained'. Further, if France was crushed to the extent that its colonies would be forfeit it would lose its position as a Great Power – something that Britain also could not entertain. As for Belgium, Bethmann was to be told that Britain would not bargain away its obligation to uphold the neutrality of that state.[74]

He did not give up on peace, however. Bethmann was also to be told that the best way forward was for Britain and Germany to work together and that he (Grey) would work towards a policy which in the end guaranteed Germany from aggression from any of the three Entente Powers, a very conciliatory ending in the circumstances.[75]

Grey next met Cambon, who immediately reminded the Foreign Secretary of the letters they had circulated in 1912. Grey needed no reminding. The arrangements between Britain and France had been made public as a result of the furore caused by Grey's failure to disclose to the Cabinet an earlier series of Anglo-French military meetings. But he also reminded Cambon that the letters only stated that the two Powers should 'consult' in a crisis. The British and French were already doing that. Cambon left disgruntled.[76]

The Foreign Secretary had told Cambon that he would talk to him again after the next day's Cabinet. The discussion there would have given no comfort to the Frenchman. Grey laid out Bethmann's attempt to buy British neutrality and informed them that he had refused to negotiate on that basis. However, Grey went on to say that he thought if Britain and Germany worked together there was still a chance for peace.[77] It is very doubtful if Grey considered that joint British–German action was even a remote possibility but he no doubt picked up the mood of the meeting, which was still quite non-interventionist. After Grey had spoken, Harcourt (the Colonial Secretary) passed a note to Jack Pease (Board of Education) that said, 'it is clear that this Cabinet will not join the war'.[78] And Pease himself urged that 'we do nothing provocative'.[79] In the end all that was agreed was that 'public opinion' (whatever that was) would not at the moment allow Britain to support France, that a violation of Belgian neutrality might change things, but that no commitments should be given to any country.[80]

Grey then went to lunch with the Prime Minister. Asquith had had a bewildering day. In the morning he had met the Unionist leaders Andrew Bonar Law and Edward Carson who suggested that the Irish question be delayed until after the crisis.[81] What position on the crisis itself was held by the Unionists was at this point complicated. Bonar Law no doubt backed support for France, but prominent City men were in a panic over the European situation ('the greatest ninnies and funks I've ever had to tackle', Asquith told his wife[82]). The Prime Minister had also seen the King, who had received a telegram from the Kaiser lamenting the fact of Russian mobilisation and ranting about the Tsar's 'perfidy'.[83] Asquith's conclusion that 'things look almost as bad as can be & I fear much about tomorrow' summed up the day fairly well.[84]

Back at the Foreign Office, however, there was another of those brief rays of hope. Grey was informed from Berlin that talks between the Austrians and Russians had resumed.[85] He immediately revived his four-Power mediation scheme. He suggested that the Powers tell Austria that if they could obtain 'full satisfaction' of Austrian demands on Serbia, they halt all military operations around Belgrade. Then he went further:

> I said to the German Ambassador this morning that if Germany could get any reasonable proposal put forward which made it clear that Germany and Austria were striving to preserve European peace, and that Russia and France would be unreasonable if they rejected it, I would support it at St. Petersburg and Paris and go to the length of saying that if Russia and France would not accept it His Majesty's Government would have nothing more to do with the consequences.[86]

This was a remarkable offer. Austria would obtain at least most of it they wanted or Britain would leave its Entente partners to fight alone. No doubt it reflected Grey's growing alarm at the European situation and his determination not to go to war over Eastern Europe. There was a sting in the tail, however. Grey also told the Germans that 'if France became involved [in the conflict] we should be drawn in'.[87] From that point at least Germany should have had no illusions about where Britain stood.

The problem for Grey was that events in Europe were moving beyond his control. As Parliament sat that evening, Asquith told members that news that Russia had ordered general mobilisation had been received. Germany had declared martial law and mobilisation must be imminent.[88]

Grey, rather against his inner convictions, declared the situation 'not irretrievable'. But with German mobilisation looming he asked both French and German governments whether they were 'prepared to engage to respect neutrality of Belgium so long as no other Power violates it'.[89] This was now the key to Grey's policy. The Cabinet, so far, had shown no inclination to intervene, as he would have, if Germany attacked the French alone. Short of a miraculous development in Eastern Europe, all now hinged on whether Bethmann's indiscretion concerning Belgium and the German war plan in the west was accurate.

Without the Cabinet or Parliament to worry about, the officials at the Foreign Office implored Grey to take firmer action and mobilise the British Expeditionary Force (BEF) and the fleet. Eyre Crowe lamented that Germany 'is throwing dust in our eyes' and wrote Grey a lengthy memorandum which concluded by saying that 'the contention that England cannot in any circumstances go to war, is not true, and that any endorsement of it would be an act of political suicide'.[90] Arthur Nicolson observed that 'Germany has been playing with us for the past few days' and begged Grey to mobilise the army, preparatory to despatching it to France.[91]

Grey resisted these pressures. He dined with Asquith and then went home to bed announcing that he would consider the question of mobilisation on the morrow.[92]

The events of 31 July had one more twist, however. After Grey had left Downing Street, Grey's secretary, Sir William Tyrrell, arrived with the news that Russian general mobilisation had been confirmed. Asquith, Tyrrell and other Foreign Office officials set to work and drafted an appeal from the King to the Tsar to halt mobilisation and resume talks with the Austrians. Exactly how talks could resume when Belgrade was under Austrian shell fire was not spelled out. Anyway, Asquith and Tyrrell hailed a taxi, drove to Buckingham Palace, hauled the King out of bed and obtained his signature on the message.[93] All this came too late. The Tsar could not halt mobilisation without causing chaos.

Grey awoke to varying news. In a positive development the French had agreed to respect Belgian neutrality.[94] On a negative note, Germany had not replied to his telegram and was to order general mobilisation if Russia did not demobilise at once.[95]

Under these impressions the Cabinet met. Regrettably, there was no official record kept of this meeting. Nevertheless the gist can be pieced together from various members' diaries and letters. The main controversy was Belgium and its neutrality.[96] Members took varying views. Churchill, described in most accounts as 'bellicose', was no doubt convinced that Germany would attack through Belgium and wanted an immediate mobilisation of the fleet.[97] This was denied him. A large group in the Cabinet, including Lord Morley, Lord President of the Council, Louis Harcourt, Colonial Secretary, Sir John Simon, the Attorney General, Earl Beauchamp, First Commissioner of Works, and John Burns, President of the Board of Trade, and probably Walter Runciman, President of the Board of Agriculture, and T. McKinnon Wood, Secretary of State for Scotland, were for 'unconditional peace'.[98] Churchill, Grey, Asquith, Lord Crewe, Secretary of State for India, and Haldane, the Lord Chancellor, were pretty clearly for war should France be attacked. A large group of waverers remained. Herbert Samuel, President of the Local Government Board, Charles Hobhouse, Postmaster General, Augustine Birrell, Secretary of State for Ireland, and Jack Pease, President of the Board of Education, and probably Home Secretary Reginald McKenna were for war if Germany invaded Belgium but in no other circumstances.[99] That left Lloyd George, Chancellor of the Exchequer and second man in the government, and one likely to give a lead to many of the waverers. Asquith probably summed him up best by saying that although he was 'all for peace', he was 'sensible & statesmanlike for keeping the position still open'.[100] Lloyd George was no pacifist. And he was quite pro-French.[101] In all probability he was, even at this time, an interventionist. But he was also of the radical wing of the Liberal Party, the heir of Cobden and Bright, and could hardly take the lead in declaring that he would enter the war to maintain the 'foul idol of the balance of power'.[102] Yet he surely knew that, as a politician of the first order, he had leadership qualities that could flourish in war. He therefore did not want to place himself on the wrong side of history – by opposing a war that might be popular and cast him into irrelevance. What to do? For the moment he did nothing. He would wait to see what Germany did next. But his indecision on 1 August froze the Cabinet. The waverers would not move without him. The split remained unresolved.[103] In the end the only action was a unilateral one by Churchill. He told Asquith after the meeting that he was mobilising the fleet. Asquith grunted, which Churchill took for assent.[104]

The Cabinet deadlock left Grey in a difficult position. Soon after the meeting Cambon arrived at the Foreign Office. He reminded Grey that as a result of naval discussions in 1912, the French had concentrated their fleet in the Mediterranean on the understanding that Britain would protect their north-east coast. Would the British honour these obligations? Grey said that it was possible that under certain conditions Britain might help but that the Cabinet had not pronounced on these matters and he could make no further statement. Cambon stressed that the Germans could therefore come through the Channel and attack them. Grey promised to take the issue of the French coasts to the Cabinet on the 2nd but that was all.[105]

Grey also saw Lichnowsky, who caused a sensation in Berlin by suggesting that Britain had decided to remain neutral.[106] Grey disabused him of that in the afternoon, adding that the German non-response to the issue of Belgian neutrality 'was a matter of very great regret' and would affect 'feeling in this country'.[107]

The remainder of the day was largely taken up with rumours. Grey heard from the Austrian Ambassador, Count Mensdorff, that talks between Russia and Austria were still continuing.[108] They were not. Then Grey received a report 'from a reliable source' that his four-Power mediation proposal was being considered in Berlin.[109] It was not. German troops were said to be massing on the French border. French troops were also alleged to be closing on Alsace-Lorraine. Finally, an actual fact arrived. At 11.15 p.m. came the fateful news that Germany had declared war on Russia.[110]

This was in reality the end of the line for any peace proposals that Grey might make. In Germany, once mobilisation had been declared, troops would start an immediate move into Belgium via Luxembourg. And the astounding fact was that this was the only war plan the Germans had. Whatever the circumstances, even those which had so far only involved states in Eastern Europe, the first and immediate move by the German army would be to invade Belgium.[111] This was not just risking British intervention, it was virtually asking for it.

Events in London on 2 August proceeded at a hectic pace, though it was a Sunday. A Cabinet had been scheduled for 11 a.m. but before Grey could leave the Foreign Office, Cambon was once more on his doorstep. He insisted that the naval dispositions discussed the previous day meant that Britain had definite 'obligations' to France and demanded that they be met. Grey insisted there was no obligation. He had assured Parliament that Britain's hands were free, and they were. Desperately, Cambon urged Grey to raise the issue of the French coast at Cabinet. Grey said he would see if any assurances could be given. With Cambon 'white and speechless', the meeting broke up.[112]

Meanwhile the waverers were meeting at 11 Downing Street, Lloyd George's official residence. Apart from the Chancellor, present were Harcourt, Beauchamp, Simon, Runciman and Pease. All knew that Germany had declared war on Russia. Still, Simon and Harcourt strongly made the point that the 1839 treaty with Belgium was not binding. There was some dissent. The others, including apparently Lloyd George, thought that a 'wholesale' invasion of Belgium might mean Britain should enter the war. They were all agreed that they 'were not prepared to go into war now'.[113]

Then the Cabinet met. Grey told them the time had come 'for some plain speaking'. His last two meetings with the French Ambassador had left Cambon in tears. He must insist that the German fleet be prevented from entering the Channel, and he regarded the upholding of Belgian neutrality as binding. If those points were not accepted, he must go. Asquith agreed. So did Churchill. Morley and Burns then spoke from the opposite view. If Grey's points were agreed, they must go.[114] Burns then resigned anyway but was induced to keep attending Cabinets for the moment. Others were still wavering. Harcourt agreed that the Germans should be kept out of the Channel.[115] Samuel thought that they should keep out of Belgium.[116] Asquith then attempted to focus the Cabinet's attention by reading a letter of support from the Unionist leaders, Bonar Law and Lansdowne, to the effect that they would back any move to support France.[117] So if the Cabinet broke up, there was a prospect of a Unionist administration, probably supported by Asquith, Grey and Churchill. The Cabinet adjourned. What had been accomplished? Grey was to assure Cambon that the German fleet would not be allowed in the Channel. As between war or peace, there was still no decision. Cabinet would reconvene at 6.30 p.m.[118]

In the interval Grey saw Cambon and gave him the assurances about the Channel. The Frenchman was not mollified. German troops had by this time been reported in Luxembourg and he asked for the immediate despatch of the BEF. Grey refused. The whole matter of British policy was still under discussion in the Cabinet. Furthermore the 'great catastrophe' playing out in Europe was so dire that troops must be kept at home to protect the coasts. Cambon asked if that meant Britain would never send a force to France. Grey replied that his statement only applied to the present moment.[119] He then left for a quiet couple of hours communing with the birds at the zoo.

When the Cabinet reassembled in the evening, there was a definite sense that the mood was hardening towards intervention.[120] The waverers had a second meeting with Lloyd George. They were confronted with the threat of Grey's resignation and perhaps others; the possibility of a Unionist pro-war government; and the ever-closer German threat to Belgium. We know little of the trajectory of the discussion. However, Pease recorded that the meeting was 'friendly' and that they 'had agreed on a line of policy'.[121] What was agreed was that Grey's statement to Cambon about protecting the French coast reflected 'our friendships with France' and recognition that the act was required to 'preserve British interests'. As regards Belgium, 'a **substantial** violation of the neutrality of that country' would compel Britain to take action. Grey was to make a statement to Parliament on Monday afternoon and the Cabinet would meet in the morning to discuss his statement.[122]

This line of policy indicated that a definite majority of the Cabinet were now in favour of intervention, leaving Morley, Beauchamp, Burns and Simon isolated. The circumstances under which individuals would enter differed, however. Grey, Asquith, Churchill, Crewe and Haldane would have entered if France was attacked. Even a technical breach of Belgian neutrality would have brought Hobhouse in.[123] Others, including Lloyd George, Samuel, Runciman, McKenna and probably Harcourt and Birrell, were for intervention if the breach of Belgian neutrality was 'substantial'. In all, fourteen were for some form of intervention, four against and McKinnon Wood a complete mystery.[124]

In the Cabinet meetings of 2 August, Grey had achieved a victory of a kind. There was now a consensus that in some circumstances Britain could not stand aside. If those circumstances varied from person to person that was not yet a matter for concern to Grey. The circumstances that would decide British intervention were outside his control. It was the German government and their war plan that would decide whether the Liberal Cabinet would enter the conflict united. But there was another hurdle for Grey to jump and that was Parliament, because in Britain, in 1914 anyway, it was Parliament that would make the final judgement on the Cabinet's policy.[125]

The Cabinet was due to meet at 11.15 a.m. Grey was to make his final declaration on what he should include in his address to Parliament. Just twenty minutes before this crucial meeting the Foreign Office recorded this message from the British Ambassador in Belgium, Sir Francis Villiers:

> French Minister reports that Germans massed force . . . along the frontier prepared to invade Belgium.
>
> Last night at 7.30 German Minister presented ultimatum to Belgium asking whether she is prepared to assume attitude of benevolent neutrality towards German military operations in Belgium. Belgium has refused categorically. German Minister will probably leave Belgium at once.[126]

This information would have been of the greatest use to Grey. Even if a consensus in Cabinet was emerging that Britain should uphold Belgian neutrality, no one had been sure what attitude Belgium would take in the event of a German invasion. What would the position of the interventionists, and especially those in the Lloyd George camp, be if Belgium gave the Germans free passage? Could they be more Belgian that the Belgians themselves? Here was the answer – Belgium would resist. It might be thought a matter of urgency that Grey should receive this message as a soon as possible. This would not have been difficult; the Cabinet was meeting a few doors down from the Foreign Office. Perhaps the cipher clerk was slow to pass the information on to his superiors. Perhaps he never did. For whatever reason, Grey did not get the information. The Cabinet meeting remained ignorant of the German ultimatum and Belgian determination to fight.[127]

So, when the Cabinet assembled, the first news was about resignations. Burns was not present and Asquith informed them that he had received letters of resignation from Morley and Simon that morning. Beauchamp then said that he also must go.[128] 'That is 4 said the PM out of our number.'[129] Much emotion and tears followed. However, the four – Burns, Beauchamp, Morley and Simon – were hardly heavy hitters and Asquith and Grey were satisfied enough by having the support of the remaining fifteen (including the enigmatic McKinnon Wood). Interestingly Lloyd George and Harcourt both spoke in support of Grey. Neither could contemplate the wholesale invasion of Belgium by Germany, although this was based on an assumption rather than fact at that stage. Lloyd George, in a sign that he had moved into the interventionist camp, urged Morley and Simon to stay.[130] This had no effect and the Cabinet turned their attention to what Grey should say in Parliament. The general line was quickly agreed and he hurriedly returned to the Foreign Office to write it.[131]

There he was confronted by Lichnowsky, who pleaded with him not to make Belgian neutrality a *casus belli*, but Grey had no time even to record the conversation.[132] What he was not confronted by was the Villiers telegram. In an incredible display of ineptitude, no one at the Foreign Office alerted Grey to the two facts that should have been central points in his address – that Belgium was facing a full-scale invasion and that it had decided to resist. Surely if Crowe and Nicolson, the two senior clerks, and hawks for intervention, had been aware of it Grey would have been the first to know. Probably the telegram lay somewhere on a desk, unnoticed and unannounced.

Therefore when Grey rose to speak in the Commons at just after 3 p.m., four hours had passed since the decoding of Villiers telegram and he was still unaware of it. The House was packed. Chairs had been placed in the aisles to cater for the crowds, something that had not been done since Gladstone introduced the first Home Rule Bill in 1892. The Foreign Secretary spoke for over an hour. He gave a history of the Entente with France but stressed that the government had entered into no binding obligations and that Parliament was free make its own decision. The only undertaking that Britain had given was to keep the German fleet from making any incursion into the Channel. Next he turned to Belgium and noted that while France had given a pledge to uphold Belgian neutrality, Germany had not.

He then interrupted his speech. He said, 'It now appears from the news I have received today – which has come quite recently, and I am not sure how far it has reached me in an accurate form – that an ultimatum has been given to Belgium by Germany' asking for the passage of troops in return for friendly relations. Presumably, Grey had been handed a note from a Foreign Office official informing of the ultimatum but not including the vital point that Belgium had decided to resist. Consequently, especially in the rather bumbling form in which he delivered it, it hardly packed the punch it should have. Grey then resumed his speech, laying out a nightmare scenario of a beaten-down France, which would result in Belgium and eventually the Netherlands and Denmark left to the mercy of Germany. He left the House in no doubt that the government's position was that Britain had vital interest and obligations towards France and Belgium which called for intervention.[133]

Whatever 'ragged edges' the speech had (one of the most ragged being caused by the note to Grey from the Foreign Office), it won the overwhelming support of the Commons.[134] Bonar Law rose immediately to offer Unionist support. More remarkably, so did Redmond, the leader of the Irish Nationalists. Ramsay MacDonald for Labour was not persuaded and would ultimately resign but the bulk of the party were solid. Those Liberals opposed to Grey's policy were few. Just twenty-eight assembled after his speech to vote on a resolution opposing intervention. Three abstained and two opposed the motion, leaving only twenty-three dissenters.[135]

In any case any incipient opposition to intervention was finally crushed by Grey's announcement at 7 p.m. The House had risen at 4.35 p.m. and reassembled at 7 p.m. In the interval Grey had finally got the Villiers telegram and some additional information as well. He immediately read it out:

> Germany sent yesterday evening at seven o'clock a note proposing to Belgium friendly neutrality, covering free passage on Belgian territory, and promising maintenance of independence of the kingdom and possessions at the conclusion of peace, and threatening in case of refusal, to treat Belgium as an enemy. A time limit of twelve hours was fixed for the reply. The Belgians have answered that an attack on their neutrality would be a flagrant violation of the rights of nations, and to accept the German proposal would be to sacrifice the honour of the nation. Conscious of its duty, Belgium is firmly resolved to repel aggression by all possible means.[136]

That statement no doubt confirmed for the House that they had made the correct decision but, as Grey noted in his memoirs, if he had possessed that information earlier it would have eliminated the need for much of his earlier speech.[137] He had made the speech of his life without the piece of information that would have rendered it irrelevant.

During the night German troops began their assault on Belgium. In the morning the Cabinet met. Beauchamp and Simon had withdrawn their resignations. Parliament was solid. Asquith ordered an ultimatum be drawn up for Goschen to deliver to Germany stating unless it withdrew by midnight (11 p.m. Greenwich Mean Time) he was to ask for his passports.[138] He was not actually instructed to declare war but the meaning was clear enough. The hours ticked by. At 11 p.m. the lamps went out. Britain was at war with Germany.

Britain only entered this war reluctantly and at the last minute. This was an appropriate and a necessary response by a state wishing to maintain its power position. When the assassination crisis was confined to Austria and Serbia and the matter was being handled within the Foreign Office, Grey did not consider that it was a matter of British concern. It was only when other Powers, Germany and Russia, seemed to be on the brink of entering the Austro-Serb dispute that he became alarmed. Even then, there is no indication that, had a war erupted in Eastern Europe between Austria and Russia, Grey would have found any great British interest to protect. German involvement was for him the key factor because of the well-founded rumours that Germany might attack Russia's alliance partner, France, a liberal state with similar interests to Britain, through Belgium, a state with which Britain had a treaty obligation but also a state which could not be allowed to fall into the hands of a power striving for European hegemony.

This was the issue about which Grey sought to convince the Cabinet and then Parliament. Grey's own position had by then become clear. If France was beaten down, Belgium and probably the Netherlands would be at the mercy of Germany. At the very least this might mean that the industry and trade of France, Belgium and the Netherlands could fall under German direction. In this circumstance Germany, in short order, would soon have the resources to build the largest fleet in Europe as well as already being in possession of the largest efficient army. The position of liberal Britain would then be at a discount. It was this nightmare that the Cabinet was so reluctant to face. Indeed, it seems highly likely that some did not see this scenario as clearly as Grey, Churchill and Asquith. Nevertheless, they saw it clearly enough to acquiesce in war. Parliament was rather in the same position but eventually accepted the proposition put before them by Grey that it was not in the interests of the country to stand aside and watch while Germany trampled on Western Europe.

What seems so remarkable about Britain during the crisis is the rationality and relative modernity of its decision-making processes. Grey decided on a policy, took it to Cabinet, which after exhaustive and lengthy debate placed it before Parliament. If, on 3 August the House of Commons had decided on another policy, a new government would have come into being and placed its policy before the House. Compare this with the fractured and divided centres of decision-making in Austria or Germany or Russia. In those rather pre-modern states the monarchs might have one policy, the head of administration another, the Foreign Ministries yet a third and the military a different policy altogether.

What is also remarkable is what little role the military played in Britain's decision-making process. Certainly in mid-1914 the military in Britain was at a discount due to the so-called Curragh Incident, in which some soldiers had unnecessarily involved themselves in matters of politics and as a result had resigned rather than be sacked by the Liberal government. Nevertheless, the slippery Director of Military Operations, Sir Henry Wilson, kept in close touch with Arthur Nicolson at the Foreign Office. Wilson was slow to grasp that the crisis might involve Britain and then panicked when he thought the Cabinet would vote to stay out. He then tried to see Grey, failed, and raced about London seeing the Conservative leadership and a great many people of no consequence.[139] In the end the Cabinet made their own decision without the advice of Wilson, or for that matter, anyone else in the military.

Neither Grey, nor the Cabinet, nor Parliament acted as any kind of automaton during the crisis. The disaster that war would mean for Europe was widely canvassed. Indeed, Grey's final statement on the matter – that the lights then going out would not be lit again in his time – seems dire enough. It was a prediction shared by others who thought war the only option, including Asquith and Churchill. These men have often been criticised for a failure of imagination – a failure to see the appalling slaughter on the Western Front that would culminate in Verdun, the Somme and Passchendaele. Perhaps they did not envisage these horrors but they did envisage something pretty desperate: a Europe dominated by a militarised triumphant Germany. In going to war they fought to prevent such a disaster to the liberal order. Perhaps they failed. Perhaps, on the other hand, they did not.

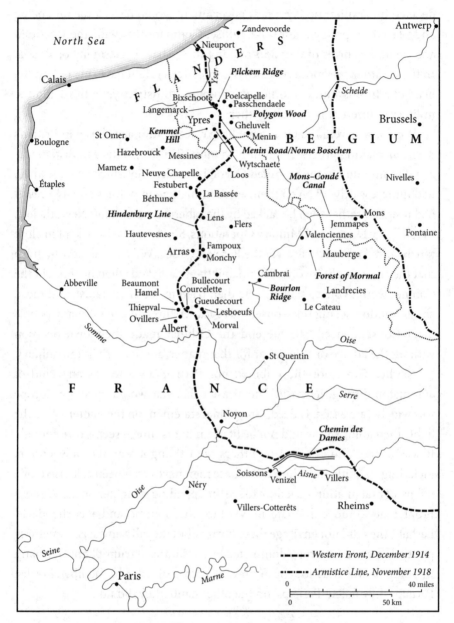

Map 1. The Western Front, 1914–1918.

CHAPTER 2

1914 – THE NEW WARFARE

Saul hath slain his thousands but David his tens of thousands
(Inscription on the Machine Gun Corps Memorial, Hyde Park)

FOR THE FIRST TIME in one hundred years Britain had entered a major European war. As noted, it was the politicians who had made this decision without intervention by the military. Yet since 1912 the military had been making plans for just such a war. Henry Wilson, as Director of Military Operations, in consultation with the French had decided that the BEF would concentrate on the left of the French armies around Mauberge in Flanders. He now found that these plans might count for nothing. As soon as war was declared, Asquith put aside this planning and determined to consult as wide a range of opinion as possible on what Britain should do to meet its commitments to France and Belgium. On 5 August at Downing Street gathered an unwieldy group of seventeen men from the great and the good of the British political and military establishment. On the political side were the Prime Minister, Grey, Churchill, Haldane and the soon-to-be-appointed Secretary of State for War, Lord Kitchener. From the military appeared Field Marshal Lord Roberts, Britain's senior soldier; Sir John French, designated commander of the BEF; General Douglas, Chief of the Imperial General Staff; General Sir Ian Hamilton, who had been Kitchener's Chief of Staff in South Africa; General Sclater, the Adjutant-General;

General Cowans, the Quarter-Master General; General von Donop, the Master-General of the Ordinance; General Archibald Murray, designated Chief of Staff to Sir John French; General Henry Wilson; and Generals Haig and Grierson, designated commanders of the I and II Corps respectively of the BEF. Finally, representing the navy was Prince Louis of Battenberg, the First Sea Lord.[1]

Asquith briefed the meeting as to the general situation (Belgium invaded but resisting, Italy neutral). Henry Wilson, whose plans had been so summarily set aside, was beside himself and noted in his diary the group set to 'discussing strategy like idiots'.[2] He was briefly mollified by Sir John French, who suggested that the Wilson plan indeed be followed. But French soon went off at a tangent by putting forward the idea that if the BEF landed at Antwerp they could act with the Dutch and the Belgians and strike the invading Germans in the flank. Grey quietly pointed out that the Dutch were neutral and Churchill added that such an expedition would violate that neutrality and that in any case the navy could not guarantee the safe passage of the army so close to waters in which the High Seas Fleet operated. The discussion then rambled to and fro, from Belgium and its needs to the employment of Indian troops in a European war (Roberts opposed this), to the offers of troops made by the Dominions and then back to how many of the BEF's six divisions could be sent out of the country with safety. In the end no decisions at all were made. Five divisions were to be readied for embarkation and the French were to be contacted about their preferred destination for the BEF.[3] It was not a good start.

The next day the same group met again. Despite arguments from the navy that Britain was safe from invasion, Kitchener declared that no more than four of the six BEF divisions were to be despatched. Asquith immediately accepted this pronouncement, indicating that two divisions should be kept at home 'to aid the civil power' in case of disturbances. The spectre of widespread rioting at home was a clearly unpalatable subject and attention soon turned to Africa and whether Indian troops could capture Dar es Salaam. Grey, probably at the end of his tether after the rigours of the July crisis, insisted that the discussion return to Western Europe. Finally, a decision was reached. Four infantry divisions and one cavalry division would be sent to France. Grey was to inform the Belgians. After that the meeting broke up.[4]

With that decision made, the machinery of mobilisation and embarkation, largely devised by Wilson, was put into motion. It ran remarkably smoothly. The experience of 6 Brigade (2 Division) was typical. On 4 August, when mobilisation was ordered, they were at their base at Aldershot. From the 5th to the 8th, officers, men, and reservists poured into the Wellington Barracks. Then there was a delay while the 2,000 horses allocated to the brigade for pulling guns, ammunition limbers and supplies of all kinds were collected. During this period the brigade was inspected by the King and Queen. Then, on 12 August it entrained at Farnborough for Southampton, where it embarked in a number of small ships for France. By the 13th the brigade disembarked at Rouen without losing a single man, horse or piece of equipment. After a night's rest they entrained for their concentration area in a number of small villages north of Cambrai. From there they marched to the front – 11 miles on the first day, 14 on the second, and 15 on the third. By 16 August they were just south-west of the mining town of Mons.[5]

The five divisions of the BEF totalled around 85,000 men. The officers came from a narrow caste, mainly of families already in the military and those described in their enlistment forms as 'gentlemen'.[6] The other ranks came largely from the unemployed.[7] It was then a small, all-volunteer force.

At the top of the hierarchy stood GHQ. This consisted of the Commander-in-Chief, General Sir John French, and a small staff of a little over twenty. Next in line were the two army corps, commanded by Haig and first Grierson (who died at Rouen on 17 August) and then General Smith-Dorrien. Each corps had a very small staff. It was their task to implement the orders received from GHQ and to issue their own orders to their constituent divisions (1 and 2 Division in I Corps and 3 and 5 Division in II Corps).

It was the division that was the key fighting unit in the BEF (and in all other European armies) in 1914. At that time, British divisions consisted of 12,000 infantrymen, organised into three brigades, each of which had four battalions of 1,000 men each. Such an organisation gave great flexibility. An attack could be made (say) with two brigades in the front line, with the third in reserve to send help forward where required. A similar organisation might apply to a brigade in a defensive position. Similarly, a brigade might deploy three of its four battalions in the front for attack or defence, with the fourth in reserve.

A division in 1914 had a formidable amount of firepower at its disposal. The artillery component of a division consisted of 4,000 men with 54 x 18-pounder guns, 18 x 4.5" howitzers and 4 x 60-pounder heavy guns. All were modern, quick-firing types with which the army had been re-equipped after the South African War.[8] Each of the lighter guns could fire seven or eight shells per minute, the 60-pounders somewhat fewer. In addition, a division had 24 Vickers machine guns, each of which could fire 600 rounds of .303 bullets per minute. Finally, each soldier was equipped with a Lee-Enfield magazine rifle and was capable of firing fifteen aimed rounds per minute.

Divisions each had a small cavalry component for scouting and liaison purposes, signal companies, field ambulances and ammunition columns.

All told, a division consisted of 18,000 men and 5,500 horses. These horses were not cavalry but draught animals used for pulling the guns, their ammunition limbers and supplies. On the march, a division took up 15 miles of road, the infantry accounting for 7 miles, the artillery 5 and the ammunition train, ambulances and miscellaneous units, 3 miles.[9]

The Cavalry Division (commanded by General Allenby) was a smaller unit. It consisted of 6,900 men and 7,500 horses. It was divided into four brigades, each of which had three regiments. The horsed soldiers had some firepower available to them. The division had 24 x 13-pounder guns and 24 machine guns. Each cavalryman also carried a Lee-Enfield magazine rifle with the idea that cavalry could move rapidly on the battlefield, dismount and act as infantrymen. Most cavalrymen still carried a sword despite the experience of the South African War where these weapons proved of limited utility. Nevertheless, in 1908 a new sword was designed and the cavalry re-equipped with it.[10] Some regiments were even equipped with lances long deemed obsolete. This weapon had been abolished in 1903 but remarkably re-installed in 1912. Along with the new-model sword, it would prove virtually useless in 1914. On the march, a cavalry division extended over 11 miles of road.[11]

On a more modern note, the BEF had an air component. The Royal Flying Corps (RFC) of twenty machines of various types, divided into four squadrons and commanded by a Brigadier-General (Sir David Henderson), left England in the second week of August. By 16 August they concentrated around Mauberge. On the 19th the first reconnaissance flight of the war over German-held territory was undertaken.[12]

The size of the BEF was dwarfed by the huge troop deployments made by the conscript armies of France and Germany. The French had just over 1 million men; the Germans 1.5 million. The offensive plans of the major belligerents had a strange symmetry. The French, under General Joffre, were to launch their main attack on their right through Alsace-Lorraine into southern Germany. From there they would wheel north and take any German forces entering Belgium in flank. The Germans would also launch their main attack on their right, advancing through Belgium in a gigantic wheeling movement. The plan was to drive the French south and then east, pinning them against their own fortifications along the Franco-German border. If both plans succeeded, the French army would be located in Germany heading north while the German army would be in France heading south.

How did the BEF fit into this scheme of things? The plan, as developed by Henry Wilson and the French, was that after the concentration around Mauberge, the BEF would move northwards to Mons in eastern Belgium where it would prolong the left of the French Fifth Army. The two armies would then advance through Belgium and forestall the German invasion.

In the first weeks of the war the balance of advantage definitely lay with the Germans. Joffre's great offensive in Alsace-Lorraine was immediately beaten back with huge loss by a markedly inferior German force using the hilly ground and the potency of defensive firepower to wipe out many of the closely packed attacking troops. On the German right the attackers had more success. After a stubborn defence of Liège, the small Belgian army was brushed aside and retreated to the ring of forts around Antwerp. The German First and Second Armies, comprising just fewer than 600,000 men then swept through Belgium towards a combined Allied force of only half that number (the French Fifth Army of 250,000 men and the BEF of 85,000). In any advance that it attempted, the BEF would be vastly outnumbered.

None of this was known by any commander at the time. When Sir John French met Joffre on 16 August he found him full of confidence. Joffre told him that his general instruction was to advance in tandem with the French Fifth Army on Nivelles, a Belgian town to the north-east of Mons. Both men formed a favourable picture of each other, and Sir John departed for his next meeting with the commander of the French Fifth Army, General Lanrezac, in good spirits.[13]

This meeting did not proceed smoothly. Partly this was because Lanrezac had a much more accurate picture of the German forces confronting him than Joffre. He feared he faced the distinct possibility of being outflanked to his west by a numerically superior force.[14] As for Sir John, the Frenchman was mainly concerned by the non-appearance of the BEF, a point he made to the British with some asperity. Worse than these petty exchanges was the impression left on Sir John by Lanrezac that the Fifth Army would soon take the offensive and advance on the right of the BEF near Mons. In fact the Frenchman had no intention of attacking and was some 9 miles in rear of the British forces.[15]

Soon, however, information began to arrive that taking the offensive might be more difficult than envisaged by the high command. The British cavalry were already scouting well in advance of Mons and by 22 August their commanders were convinced that they would soon be confronted by a great force of German infantry.[16] In addition, the RFC had been making an increasing number of reconnaissance flights. On 22 August no fewer than twelve flights were undertaken, spotting large bodies of German troops closing on the British forces and threatening to outflank them to the west.[17] But it was one thing to accumulate intelligence, it was quite another to get the high command to believe it. At GHQ (located at Le Cateau) Sir John's Deputy Chief of Staff, Henry Wilson, insouciantly remarked of the air intelligence, 'I can't believe this', and went on planning for an advance.[18] Sir John agreed with him, noting that 'there still appears to be very little on our front except cavalry supported by small bodies of infantry'.[19]

At this moment the situation was transformed by news from the French. Lieutenant Louis Spears was a British Liaison Officer with the French Fifth Army. On the evening of 22 August he met with Sir John and informed him that Lanrezac's forces had suffered a defeat by the Germans, had retreated to a point 9 miles in rear of the BEF and had no intention of attacking the next day.[20] This convinced Sir John he must halt, at least for the moment. Not even an intervention by one of Lanrezac's staff officers, begging the British to attack, could move him. He would comply with a further request from Lanrezac to stand firm for twenty-four hours and he would then consider if he was in a position to attack.[21] Orders were issued to his corps to be ready to defend or advance. The scene was set for the Battle of Mons.

As it happened, only the British II Corps would take part in the battle. It would be commanded, not by General Grierson, who had died of a heart attack on 17 August, but by General Smith-Dorrien, with whom Sir John French had not always seen eye to eye. Smith-Dorrien's corps held the Mons–Condé Canal in force, with small packets of troops and cavalry scouting to its north. On the right, almost at right angles to it and echeloned back to the south in order to keep in some contact with the left of the French Fifth Army, was I Corps. The battle was to take place in most unpromising country. Mons was the centre of a small coal-mining district. The approaches to the canal were masked by a 'cluster of hamlets' with rows of mean and crowded mining cottages. Slag heaps of waste material from the mines littered the valley and obscured observation. Many of the heaps were quite high but too hot for men to stand on and too treacherously slippery for artillery pieces to find a platform. The canal, which was only 7 feet deep and 60 feet wide, was crossed by no fewer than twenty-four bridges, any of which might give passage to the attacking troops.[22]

The II Corps held the line from just west of Condé to just east of Mons, a distance of some 24 miles, with five brigades from 5 and 3 Divisions in the front line and two in reserve. The German First Army which was about to attack them consisted of four army corps (IX, III, IV and VII) totalling eight divisions. However, the army commander, Von Kluck, had only a vague idea of the exact position of the BEF and his forces were echeloned back from left to right so that not all of his forces would engage the British at the same time.[23]

On 23 August the German infantry discovered that they were facing a type of warfare for which they were not prepared. On the British right their line arced north-eastwards along an awkward bend in the canal. It was here that the first encounter took place. Around 9 a.m. the Germans came on in close order formation in heavy masses. They were immediately shot down by the rapid rifle fire from the 8 Brigade infantry and several machine guns which had entrenched along the canal line. Attempts by the Germans to form up in the concealment of woods and rush the British line met the same fate. After two hours of futile endeavour, the Germans withdrew to regroup.[24]

It was essentially the same story as the battle spread from right to left as the echeloned German formations arrived at the canal line. At Jemmapes

33

the Germans were stopped in their tracks with heavy casualties, as they were at many points west. In some instances the Germans attempted to manoeuvre artillery in close support of their infantry assaults but the enemy gunners were also driven back by hostile machine-gun fire.[25] What the British were demonstrating even on the first day of battle was the devastating effect of defensive firepower against troops in the open. The magazine rifle and the machine gun had immediately transformed the battlefield.

What the Germans did demonstrate was that with weight of numbers and disregard for the casualty bill, attacks could be pushed home. This was especially the case with close artillery support. When the attackers brought forward some field guns and directed their fire onto the British machine-gunners and riflemen, the rudimentary British trenches provided insufficient shelter and particularly on their right the defenders were forced back.[26] Along the remainder of the canal, however, the British front held. At the end of the day II Corps had suffered 1,600 casualties, the Germans probably five times that number.[27]

Sir John French had taken no part in the events at Mons. He had left to visit a newly formed brigade at Valenciennes. He was not to return to GHQ until most of the fighting was over. Messages soon arrived from Smith-Dorrien to the effect that his troops must retreat or be overwhelmed. Sir John regarded these missives as pessimistic and ordered the army to stand fast. Then news arrived from the French that Lanrezac had issued orders for a retreat. Stunned, Sir John recast his orders. There would be a retreat, the details to be worked out by the corps commanders.[28]

In the case of I Corps and 3 Division of II Corps, the process of disengaging with the enemy proved straightforward. Haig's corps had not really been engaged and he slipped away quietly to the south. In the case of 3 Division, the shattered Germans opposing them were in no real mood to press them closely. It was different further west, where new German formations had at last arrived in the area of 5 Division. Here the Germans did press hard. They bombarded the area with newly arrived artillery and came on in solid masses. Once more they lost heavily but units in the rearguard of 5 Division were at risk of being cut off. Enter the cavalry. If it was the German infantry that learned of the new realities of war on 23 August, it was the British cavalry that was to learn a stern lesson on the 24th.[29]

So far the cavalry had performed well. Their reconnaissance work had enabled commanders to obtain a fair idea of the composition and size of the enemy forces ranged against them. But many in the cavalry did not see reconnaissance as their main function. Despite much pre-war thought that considered the day of the cavalry charge to be over, it was perfecting the shock tactics of the *arme blanche* that dominated training in these years.[30] In 1910 no less than 80 per cent of the cavalry's training time was taken up honing 'shock tactics'; a mere 10 per cent on reconnaissance duties.[31]

With this background it was only a matter of time before the cavalry tried its hand at a charge. The occasion seemed to arrive on 24 August with the impending encirclement of two battalions of the hard-pressed 5 Division. Brigadier-General de Lisle, no slouch in promoting 'the cavalry spirit', ordered a group from the 9 Lancers and the 4 Dragoons to charge the enemy in order to rescue the infantry. The result was a fiasco. Some horsemen ran into a barbed-wire fence and had to veer sharply away 'like a flock of sheep'.[32] Others were shot down by the German gun line, into which they were charging. A few advanced German scouts were speared but the main body 'never reached a point closer than 800 yards from the guns'.[33] Lieutenant Jock Marsden of the 9 Lancers remained very bitter about de Lisle's action, still reflecting on the stupidity of deploying cavalry in close proximity to enemy guns some six weeks later.[34] This futile episode cost 250 men and 300 horses. It had no effect on the German advance, 'which continued with hardly a pause'.[35] In the face of modern firepower, the 'cavalry spirit' was not enough.

Meanwhile the close attention the Germans were paying to the British left flank, coupled with the further retirement of the French Fifth Army on his right, presented problems for Sir John French. He must retreat to stay in touch with the French but in the path of I Corps lay the Forest of Mormal – through which there were no north–south roads. He had no choice therefore but to order Haig to proceed to the right of the forest and Smith-Dorrien to retreat to its left. The corps of the BEF thus became separated.

The retreat continued on the 25th, Smith-Dorrien's troops being very hard pressed by the pursuing Germans. That night the situation seemed parlous. Allenby had informed the II Corps Commander that, due to the dispersal of his cavalry division across the battlefield, it might not be able to cover a retreat on the following day.[36] The commander of 3 Division,

General Hamilton, reinforced this view. Some of his units were still coming in at nightfall and a start would be impossible before daybreak on the 26th.[37] Armed with this information, Smith-Dorrien decided to stand and fight. Sir John French reluctantly agreed.

Preparations for battle commenced immediately. At dawn, 3 Division dug a series of trenches that French workers had commenced the day before. Behind the front line a second series of trenches was completed, a sure sign that the BEF was already aware of the power of concealed troops and machine guns.[38]

The Battle of Le Cateau, like that at Mons, was fought entirely by II Corps – I Corps being some 8 miles away on the other side of the Forest of Mormal. Nor did GHQ, involved in a further backwards move to Noyon, play any role. The fighting took the form of an attempted envelopment by the Germans on both flanks. On the right they were fought off by a combination of well-placed artillery with rifle and machine-gun fire. On the left, the newly arrived 4 Division had their first taste of battle. Here the German IV Corps entered battle, also for the first time. They deployed those close-packed formations that had been so disastrous at Mons. And so they proved here. They were shot down in great numbers. The battle was in many ways a re-run of Mons, with the difference that the fighting was more intense and the German flanking movements more dangerous. Only the tenacity of the defence held them off. At the end of the day II Corps started to disengage. British casualties amounted to over 7,800 men and 38 guns.[39]

The great retreat now commenced. It was to continue for a further eleven days. In that time, in an epic of endurance, the BEF covered between 200 and 250 miles. The weather was hot, the roads crowded with refugees fleeing the oncoming Germans. Some men slept as they marched. Some fell to the ground with fatigue. Men, many of whom were reservists, found their feet so swollen that if they managed to take their boots off they could not get them back on. On an average day they got four hours' sleep.[40] By 2 September, 6 Brigade were reporting that 'the men were about done. The straggling was the worst we had seen but there was every excuse as there was little chance of getting water.'[41] Just before 2 p.m. they were forced by fatigue to stop. But at 6 p.m. they were on the march again. In all they had covered 24 miles that day.[42]

How was it in these circumstances that an army in this condition was able to escape the clutches of a numerically superior force?

Initially the explanation is straightforward. The German army had received a bloody shock at Mons and Le Cateau. It was not immediately ready to repeat the dose. Then, as the retreat went on, the Germans were often unsure of the exact position of the British. No army in these early days of the war would march or attack at night. So these hours often gave the BEF a chance to slip away in the early hours of the morning and leave their pursuers uncertain as to their exact whereabouts. For example, 8 Brigade, which had been heavily engaged in the two battles fought by II Corps, did not report a single encounter with the enemy during the entire retreat.[43]

Moreover, the pursuing armies were in a similar state of exhaustion to those they pursued. The Germans had been marching since 4 August. On the same day that 6 Brigade reported a problem with stragglers, a German officer noted:

> Our men are done up. For four days they have been marching 24 miles a day. The country is difficult, the roads are in a bad condition, and barred by trees felled across them, the fields are pitted with shell holes. The men stagger forward, their faces pitted with dust, their uniform in rags, they look like living scarecrows. They march with their eyes closed.[44]

In this condition battle was hardly a realistic proposition.

Coming to grips with an enemy in retreat was no easy matter either. All armies designated some of their units to act as rearguards. These formations would contain riflemen, machine guns and artillery which could exact a heavy price on troops rash enough to attack across the open. Even when a resting British force was surprised, as it was at Néry on 1 September, the results could be ambiguous. Here the 1 Cavalry Brigade and a battery of guns were bivouacked when they were set upon by a German cavalry force. The guns were overrun but British reinforcements rushed in and although L Battery was lost, the Germans lost more casualties than the British.[45]

There were similar incidents. At Landrecies, I Corps seemed to be endangered by a surprise night attack. In the event Haig's force escaped with few casualties. Then at Villers-Cotterêts late in the retreat the rearguard of the Guards battalion was attacked but managed to beat off the German forces. But these were minor events. In the main the retreat proceeded unmolested.[46]

Finally, it should be recalled that the whole idea of the German plan was to drive Allied forces south and then east onto their own frontier defences. Until 5 September this endeavour seemed to be working. Why risk a confrontation when the overall objective seemed within its grasp? The problem for the Germans was that this was an illusion. Joffre had been hatching a plan of his own.

Joffre's design relied on the BEF maintaining the connection between the Fifth French Army on their right and a new Sixth Army which he was forming north of Paris by transferring troops from the now aborted offensive in Alsace-Lorraine. His plan was to strike the German First Army in the flank with his Sixth Army while the remaining forces, from the BEF on the left to his armies around Verdun on the right, turned and launched a gigantic counter-attack. On 31 August Sir John French threw this whole conception into doubt. On that day he told Joffre that he wished to retire behind the Seine in order that the BEF could rest and refit.[47] Joffre had no choice but to agree. Back in London, however, Kitchener did not. He immediately asked Sir John to elaborate but he received the same message – the BEF was 'shattered' and he hoped Kitchener would approve his actions. Kitchener did not. He took the matter to the Cabinet. As Asquith told the King:

> After the Cabinet had carefully considered the matter, a further telegram to Sir J. French was drafted expressing the anxiety of the Government and dwelling on the importance of his co-operating continuously with General Joffre.[48]

This was a less than subtle reminder from his civilian masters that they required Sir John to stay in the line. But the C-in-C was in no mood for subtleties. 'I cannot do anything until I can refit', he told Kitchener.[49] In the light of this reply Asquith called a scratch Cabinet meeting consisting of Kitchener, Churchill and McKenna which resulted in the despatch of Kitchener to Paris to meet with Sir John.[50] This meeting was fraught. Kitchener rather overplayed the drama by appearing in the full dress uniform of a field marshal. This outraged Sir John and was unnecessary. A civilian suit would have sufficed for the Minister for War – it was the authority of the Cabinet, not a military rank, that Kitchener represented. In any case Sir John was told in no uncertain terms that the BEF would remain in the firing line and conform to Joffre's wishes.[51] And so it did. The importance of this episode is often thought to be that it showed the beginning of a rift between Kitchener and Sir John. It was, but that had few consequences. Its real importance lay in the assertion of authority by the civilian leadership in Britain over the military. When the Cabinet asserted itself, the command, if they wished to continue to command, listened. Here was a precedent – and another aspect of modern warfare.

There is no space here to deal with Joffre's design – the Battle of the Marne. It was largely a French affair with no fewer than five French armies in action.[52] The BEF was a small but usefully placed component on the left. The French Sixth Army north of Paris had attracted the attention of the German First Army and drew it to the west. This created a gap with the German Second Army and it was into this gap that the French Fifth Army and the BEF marched. By now the BEF consisted of three corps – the newly arrived 4 Division and 19 Brigade of Line of Communication troops had been formed into III Corps under General Pulteney. The first reinforcements had also arrived from England, so it was a force of just over 100,000 men which advanced into the gap. It made slow and uncertain progress. Initially it was not even clear to the command that there was a gap between the two enemy armies. As the Germans had found in late August, tangling with rearguards was a hazardous business. Occasionally there might be a local success. On 10 September 6 Brigade surprised the German rearguards at Hautevesnes. They pinned them down with artillery and machine-gun fire until, after several hours, they surrendered. Five hundred enemy troops were captured.[53] But such chances were rare and the BEF had had little rest – the advance was just a continuation of the long march south but in the opposite direction. On the map opportunities seemed to exist to roll up at least part of the German First Army. On the ground this was never a possibility. The Germans withdrew, not always in good order but with sufficient coherence to maintain their line until they reached the River Aisne.

It was thought by GHQ and the French that the Germans might make some kind of stand along the Aisne. It was good defensive country. The river itself meandered through a shallow valley which gave no cover to infantry attempting to cross it. Most high ground, with good artillery positions, lay on the German side of the river. Generally, the stream was unfordable. The British occupied an area between the French Sixth Army at Soissons on the left to the right wing of the French Fifth Army around Villiers. Its orders were to cross the river and proceed to a road which ran along the crest of a ridge some 5 miles beyond – this was the Chemin des Dames of later notoriety.

On the right and left of their front the BEF found passage of the Aisne surprisingly easy. On the left at Venizel, German attempts to destroy the bridge had failed and troops from 11 Brigade of 4 Division crossed and drove off the German outposts by bayonet charge. Later in the day they were reinforced by 12 Brigade. Further attempts to advance were, however, driven off with heavy casualties. On the right 2 Division found another partly intact bridge and was able to get its leading brigade across unopposed. Only in the centre were attempts thwarted by German fire. Yet even in this area, at nightfall a single plank of a bridge was found intact.[54] By the end of 13 September elements of all three British corps were across the Aisne. The German retreat seemed to bear the hallmarks of haste. An attack on the Chemin des Dames beckoned.

Such an operation began on 14 September. In the I Corps area on the right there was much excitement. Some elements of 1 Division, taking advantage of the early morning fog and the confusion actually reached the Chemin des Dames. But they were few in number (just five companies) and 1 mile apart.[55] Eventually these small groups were driven back by German counter-attacks.[56] Haig had nothing in corps reserve to support them and in any case there was no sign of 2 Division on their right.[57] The leading brigade (6) of that unit had been much held up crossing the single-plank bridge. Then both 5 and 6 Brigades ran into heavy German opposition and were well short of the ridge at nightfall. A further advance, before midnight, by some companies from both brigades was then successful. At 11.30 p.m. the Chemin des Dames was reached but, as with the morning advance, the troops were few in number and they found groups of German soldiers to their right and left. At midnight the order was given for the men to retire.[58] They would not see the Chemin des Dames again.

Elsewhere the BEF got nowhere near the ridge. In the centre II Corps were, at the end of the day, holding the same positions which they had held at dawn.[59] On the right III Corps came up against well-entrenched German troops protected by wire netting and fencing. The ground was swept by enemy artillery and machine guns. No advance was possible.[60]

Did the BEF almost capture the Chemin des Dames? Some authorities think so.[61] But, as with other ridges 'almost captured' in the First World War, this is a chimera. The men on the ridge formed no coherent front (as they knew) and there was a gap of many hours between the toe-hold gained by the men of 1 Division in the morning and that of 2 Division at 11.30 p.m. Ridges had to be occupied in numbers and for a considerable part of their length before any claims to have 'held' them had any substance. The Germans were shocked by the British incursions but ultimately in control of the situation. For most of its length the ridge was always securely in their hands.

After 14 September the initiative lay with the Germans. Sir John French seemed to realise that. On that day he issued orders to entrench. This the BEF did. At this stage there were no lines of continuous trenches but rather a succession of pits capable of holding a few men. They were just 18 inches to 2 feet wide and with small traverses. Trenches, of course, have an evil reputation but to the troops they represented at least some kind of protection against enemy shelling, machine-gun and rifle fire. They were also very small targets and difficult for enemy artillery to demolish, especially when many of the shells to hand were shrapnel rather than high explosive.

From 16 September it was the Germans that did the attacking. They repeatedly assailed sections of the British line, in part to push the BEF back over the river and in part to pin them to their positions while the Germans attempted to outflank them to the north. Neither plan worked. On 20 September the enemy broke the line of 7 Brigade and streamed towards the river, only to be beaten back by intense shelling from some British batteries.[62] During October the battle settled into artillery duels and raiding parties designed to discomfort rather than defeat the opposing trench dwellers.[63] The Germans had by far the best of these duels. They had the heavier guns and a better system of fire control. British troops often suffered from 'friendly fire' in this period as the complete lack of a decent communication system between the artillery and the infantry, obvious to many pre-war observers, made itself manifest.[64]

The BEF was not to remain on the Aisne for long. In early September Sir John French had suggested to Joffre that his force be moved north to Flanders. This made some sense. It would shorten the supply lines from Britain, allowing the BEF to receive supplies and reinforcements through the Channel ports of Dunkirk and Calais instead of the more distant Le Havre and Rouen. Also two additional divisions in England (7 and 8) being prepared for despatch to France could be sent via the shorter route. Finally, the BEF move would dovetail with Joffre's conception of turning the open flank of the German forces on the Aisne by a northward move. Gradually II Corps, III Corps and the two cavalry divisions (a second cavalry division had been established at the Marne) left the Aisne and their positions were taken over by I Corps. On 8 October this too left. The concentration in Flanders had been completed without German interference.

The British infantry moved to its concentration areas in Flanders by rail, II Corps being sent to Abbeville, III Corps to St Omer. Later, I Corps was sent to Hazebrouck. Other British forces were also in Flanders. IV Corps (7 Division, 3 Cavalry Division) commanded by General Rawlinson was astride the Menin Road, having participated in a futile attempt to save Antwerp from its German besiegers and then retreated to the vicinity of Ypres.[65] Yet more reinforcements were on the way. A corps of the Indian Army (Kitchener had ignored Lord Roberts's advice about not employing Indian troops in Europe) had landed at Marseilles on 26 September and was to be sent to Flanders in October.[66] Moreover twenty-two battalions of the Territorial Force (Britain's part-time soldiers created by the Haldane reforms in 1906) were despatched to Flanders as reinforcements for the Regular divisions during this period.[67]

Intermingled with the BEF were two French cavalry corps, while to the north of them were some French Territorial divisions and the Belgian army, which had retreated from Antwerp to Nieuport.

Joffre's grand plan for these disparate forces was to pivot on the French left flank around Béthune, get behind the German right flank and wheel forwards, driving the Germans back through Belgium to their own frontier.[68] The problem for Joffre and the BEF was that the Germans had a similar plan. Falkenhayn had now taken over from Moltke as Chief of the

General Staff. He always thought that the war would be decided on the Western Front and to that end he had formed a new Fourth Army from reservists – mainly young men aged between seventeen and twenty. Its task would be to break the Allied line between Menin and the sea. To its south the German Sixth Army would remain on the defensive until the Fourth attacked. Then it to would move forwards from Menin to La Bassée. The ultimate goal was to occupy the Channel ports, thereby cutting the British supply line. In all, ten army corps would attack the BEF, the French Territorials and the Belgians. The Germans outnumbered their opponents in infantry by at least two to one and had much more heavy artillery and unity of command – a formidable triad of advantage.[69]

The offensive plans of both the Allies and the Germans failed. On the Allied side this is hardly surprising. Their line, which due to hasty planning came into battle piecemeal, was halted at the moment it came into solid contact with the advancing Germans. In the face of overwhelming fire superiority it could go no further. Worse, the BEF was now spread out over a distance of 35 miles – it was the thin red line.[70]

The German failure needs a more thorough investigation. The Germans mounted three major attacks during the First Battle of Ypres – on 21–22 October, 29 October to 2 November and on 11 November. In the first instance, although the Germans attacked across the entire British front, their major effort was made by the Reserve Corps of their Fourth Army between Bixschoote and Langemarck. Here the columns of young soldiers advanced in massed waves. They were cut down in great numbers by the British riflemen and machine-gunners sheltered only by scrapes in the ground rather than trenches. As the day went on, machine guns boiled in their water jackets and rifle barrels grew too hot to touch, some infantrymen firing 600 rounds in a day.[71] Many German regiments lost 70 per cent of their strength.[72] The derisory amount of ground they gained was retaken by a British counter-attack on the following day.[73] It is a heavy mark against German military leadership that these untested soldiers were thrown into battle in this way. To the south the attack also failed in much the same way. But here there was one consolation for the Germans. Rawlinson's IV Corps had been given the insane order by GHQ to advance on Menin, ignoring all the evidence of massed German formations opposite them.[74] Not surprisingly, Rawlinson failed. But in selecting a defensive position, he merely drew a line on a map without regard to contours.[75] Voluntarily, therefore, he gave up the Passchendaele Ridge, a feature that would not be in British hands until the last year of the war.

The second major German effort came at the end of October. In the interval the Germans had reorganised their army. Falkenhayn's new plan was to insert a new army (Group Fabeck) of five corps between the Fourth and Sixth Armies. These were seasoned troops and their task would be to drive through from Zandevoorde to Messines and seize Kemmel Hill as a preliminary to an advance on the Channel ports. While this was proceeding, the two other German armies would mount diversionary attacks.[76] Ominously the new army group was given over 250 heavy howitzers and mortars to assist the breakthrough.[77] The overture to this attack began on 29 October with a ferocious bombardment on either side of the Menin Road and on the troops to the south holding the Messines Ridge. Furious, intense and continuous fighting followed as the German infantry came forward in waves. On the Menin Road Fabeck's troops actually broke the British line and entered the village of Gheluvelt, a key point of high ground, but they were distracted by looting the chateau. And at this very moment a counter-attack led by three companies of the 2 Worcesters fell upon the Germans and drove them back out of the village and re-established the line.[78]

Much attention has been focused on this incident but further south were more disturbing developments. Rather by accident, as the BEF advanced into Flanders in mid-October, the Cavalry Corps found itself passing over the Messines–Wytschaete Ridge. In the flatlands of Flanders this feature was of some note. Although it was only 100 metres high, it gave excellent observation over the ground around Ypres to the north that the British were endeavouring to hold. Initially the cavalry commander (Allenby) gave it little attention as the plan then was to advance right across Belgium. When that advance was halted by strong German attacks just beyond the ridge, he became concerned that his major task might now consist of holding the ridge rather than advancing beyond it. This meant that his horsed soldiers would not act as cavalry but fight on foot. As noted earlier, a division of cavalry had just 7,000 riflemen as against 12,000 in a division of infantry. But Allenby's men had been in almost continuous action for two months. Some of his brigades had just 180 men. Moreover, the artillery of the corps consisted mainly of 13-pounders – too light to inflict serious damage on German gun positions and too worn out to obtain even rudimentary accuracy.[79] Here was the moment for some dramatic intervention by the high command, who so far had played little role in the fighting around Ypres. In the week of stalemate on the ridge between 21 and 31 October there was time to relieve the cavalry on this important ground and replace them with infantry in greater numbers and with greater fire support than cavalry divisions could muster. And it might be thought that the importance of holding high ground and the difficulty of recapturing it had been impressed on GHQ by the recent struggle for the Chemin des Dames. Eventually they did send reinforcements to Allenby but they were the wrong kind. Two battalions of the Indian Corps arrived, but they were weak in numbers, quite unused to the type of warfare that confronted them and, worst of all, had not one heavy gun at their disposal.[80] The only other reinforcement was that of a Territorial battalion (the London Scottish) which suffered from the same deficiencies as the Indian force. The whole reinforcement fiasco only demonstrated how GHQ had totally failed to grasp the importance of the Messines Ridge.

For some days, however, it seemed that the situation might be saved. The cavalry fought tenaciously, holding off the greater numbers of the attackers and withstanding artillery bombardments that, for 1914, were unprecedented. The Indian and Territorial forces also fought better than their lack of experience might have predicted. But in the end they were too few in numbers and had too little firepower to withstand the Germans. First Wytschaete, at the northern end of the ridge, was lost, and then on 1 November Messines fell and the whole British line was forced to retreat.[81] The ridge was gone. It would not return to British hands until 1917, after one of the most protracted campaigns on the Western Front. The consolation was that such a heavy toll had been taken on the attackers that they could not advance further. For the second time the German army had been fought to a standstill.

The Germans tried to break the British line on a third occasion on 11 November. This time they employed the Guards Divisions – considered their best troops. The fighting was concentrated around Nonne Bosschen and Polygon Wood. The enemy made some ground but found that the Guards were no more able to withstand machine-gun, rifle, and artillery fire than any other troops. They were beaten off with heavy losses.[82]

Although fighting continued through November and December, this was the last major German effort to break through to the Channel ports. Why had they failed? The simple answer is that, as was shown at Mons and Le Cateau, the magazine rifle, the machine gun and quick-firing artillery exacted too high a price on men advancing in the open for an attack to be decisive. Ground was captured at Ypres but not much of it. Then exhaustion and high casualties brought the attempt to a halt. Nor did the German superiority in men and artillery compensate. All additional infantry amounted to in many cases was more targets for the British and a higher casualty toll for the Germans. The German heavy artillery certainly inflicted many casualties on the BEF but it was insufficiently accurate (as was all artillery at this stage of the war) to kill or neutralise the defenders in large enough numbers for the attack to get forward. In many cases it was the fire of riflemen rather than machine guns or artillery that stopped the Germans. This should not have been a matter for surprise. One hundred riflemen firing '15 rounds rapid' of aimed, accurate fire could cause havoc among the massed ranks of the enemy. That the BEF had to rely on the rifle is often celebrated in the literature as a demonstration of individual endeavour. This is misplaced. A greater number of machine guns could have inflicted an even heavier toll on the attacker for less cost. The fact was that the General Staff in the pre-war period rejected a proposal by the School of Musketry at Hythe to increase the number of machine guns per battalion.[83] This antediluvian attitude was not based on reasons of economy as is so often stated but because the staff could not see the value of machine guns. This would not be the last time that the men of the BEF would pay for the pre-industrial attitudes of its leaders.

How then are we to view the campaigns of 1914?

They are often written up as the last kick of the 'old warfare'. This is not the case. Although arms such as the cavalry played a useful role in reconnaissance in 1914, even in that capacity they were becoming obsolete. It was found, even before the clash of armies, that the RFC could range much deeper into enemy territory and provide more sweeping evaluations of enemy strength than any cavalry patrol. To some extent it was the grounding of the air arm at Ypres because of the weather that led to the often-fuzzy estimates of German numbers. In the role of shock troops the cavalry was entirely useless, and those commanders who insisted that this was not the case were regarded with suspicion by their own men. In any case, at Ypres, from the middle of October the cavalry fought dismounted – that is, as infantry.

The RFC instituted a new dimension in warfare. At an early date aeroplanes started spotting the fall of shot for the artillery. At first this was done by the clumsy method of throwing down messages tied in bags. But on the Aisne several aircraft were equipped with a wireless, by which means instant adjustments of range could be radioed to the guns.[84] This was the commencement of a long and increasingly sophisticated partnership.

At Mons, Le Cateau, the Aisne and Ypres a new paradigm was evident from the beginning. Massed infantry attacks across the open, in the face of magazine rifles, machine guns and artillery, were too costly to prosper. The volume of fire laid down by these weapons could cut down numbers far in excess of those who huddled in primitive defences. One hundred riflemen and a machine gun could fire over 2,000 bullets per minute and hit with some accuracy at ranges up to 900 yards. Even when infantry spread out into looser formations, few of their endeavours saw any great success or substantial gains of ground. Often the few exhausted survivors of such attacks were immediately pushed back to their starting line by fresh troops brought forward to counter-attack. In the face of ferocious defensive firepower, heroism and any amount of training proved futile. In the pre-war period troops had repeatedly practised fire and movement tactics. In 1914 it was soon found that where there was much fire there was little movement.

The other notable aspect of the warfare of 1914 was the appearance of trenches. They were dug at Mons on the first day of battle to provide shelter for troops obliged to fall back. They appeared again at Le Cateau and in greater numbers at the Aisne. They were again hastily dug throughout the campaign around Ypres. At this stage of the war they were often mere scrapes in the ground and rarely continuous. Nevertheless, they gave riflemen and machine-gunners sufficient protection for them to devastate the attacking infantry. And by the time that winter had ended the fighting in Flanders, some form of trenches existed from the Swiss border to the Channel coast. To prevail, an army would by some means have to force a way through these obstacles. And the appearance of rolls of barbed wire, which were occasionally placed in front of trenches at Ypres, threatened to make that task very hazardous indeed.[85]

Little need be said about the high command because it played such a small role in directing these early battles. It is doubtful if Sir John French was even aware of the Battle of Mons until after the event. Le Cateau was fought by Smith-Dorrien; the Aisne, in its crucial aspect, largely by I Corps; and the battles around Ypres mainly by the lower-order commanders. All GHQ contributed in this last instance was a series of unthinking orders to attack that were usually ignored by everyone from the corps commanders down.

Sir John French's major contribution was to Anglo-French tensions. He had a disturbing tendency to consider that he was fighting a battle quite separate from the larger movements taking place around him. It was the Cabinet who reminded him that he was a cog in a machine designed to ensure the freedom of Western Europe. There would be no Brexit from that design unless the civilians so decided.

As for the civilian direction of the war, there was little opportunity for them to intervene except to keep Sir John French in situ. They watched the progress of operations with increasing alarm but could do little to influence them. The battles were too fluid and too tied to the fortunes of the French for any opportunity to exert authority. What they were watching, however – the destruction of the original BEF – was hardly to their liking. Voices started to be heard in London about seeking other fields in which to exert what authority Britain had.

CHAPTER 3

THE NAVY GOES TO WAR
1914–1915

WHILE THE BEF PLAYED a minuscule role in events on the Western Front in 1914, at sea the British were dominant if not overwhelming. At the beginning of the war the Royal Navy represented the greatest concentration of naval power ever seen. In all it could deploy 645 warships compared to Germany's 318.[1] It could also rely on the considerable fleet of its French ally. The only other major naval powers (Japan and the United States) were neutral.

Britain also had a lead in the type of ship that ensured naval supremacy – the all big-gun dreadnought battleship. On the outbreak of war Britain had twenty-two such battleships and was building thirteen more. Germany had just fifteen and was building five more.[2] British battleships also tended to have a heavier armament than their German equivalents. This tilted the margin in Britain's favour more than mere numbers would indicate.

But while Britain entered the war with a healthy naval supremacy there were several factors that were to make the enforcement of that supremacy difficult. In the first place Britain had worldwide interests that had to be protected: trade routes to keep the home country supplied with warlike materiel and food; and convoy routes which troops from the Empire would need to traverse to add to the power of the small British army on the Western Front. The Germans had no global interests. Certainly they had colonies scattered across the world, but these were forfeit to Britain's greater naval power and of little importance to what Germany could deploy on the major war fronts.

There was in the Royal Navy, however, a certain sclerotic quality, perhaps borne of a century of unrivalled naval supremacy. Churchill noticed this when he became First Lord of the Admiralty in 1911. He set about trying to rectify what he regarded as a rather ingrained complacency by creating a Naval Staff along the same lines as the General Staff of the army, but that process only commenced in 1912 and had hardly become established on the outbreak of war.

Various negative factors flowed from this sclerosis. New technology had arrived, particularly the development of radio telephony (R/T), whereby ships could communicate with each other via radio while the Admiralty in London could communicate with ships in far distant waters. This gave the Admiralty a chance to centralise control of naval operations or interfere with the discretion of local naval commanders according to perspective.

An additional problem came from the fact that Britain, to counter the German fleet, had been forced to concentrate the overwhelming proportion of its ships in the North Sea. This left little to spare for the outer seas and also meant that admirals and captains of any promise were also concentrated in those North Sea squadrons. Elsewhere, as would become evident, the second eleven were definitely in control, a factor that added to the Admiralty's centralising tendencies.

On the outbreak of war the Home Fleet, or (as it was soon renamed) the Grand Fleet, steamed north to its war station at Scapa Flow. It says little for the Admiralty that this base, though long designated as the home of the Grand Fleet, was not entirely secure. Partly this came about over disputes within the Admiralty between the relative merits of Cromarty and Scapa as bases. In 1912 a decision had been made in favour of Cromarty, largely on the grounds of cost.[3] Then expert opinion in the navy swung in favour of Scapa. A dispute between the Treasury, the War Office and the Admiralty followed over which department would pay for the required defences at Scapa. Some, including Admiral Bridgeman, the First Sea Lord, argued once more for Cromarty.[4] Indecision reigned. The result was that, when war came, Scapa had few gun defences and no defences against submarines. Consequently the Grand Fleet had on occasion to hastily retreat to the west coast of Scotland until these defences were in place.

As it happened, this mattered little because there was no naval action on the outbreak of war. Much naval opinion in Britain considered that the

German High Seas Fleet would seek an early encounter in a major naval engagement fought somewhere in the North Sea. Why else, the reasoning went, had the Germans built such a fleet? This was a good question which had no certain answer. The German fleet might be formidable but its masters were not about to sail blithely into the North Sea and allow it to be sunk by the superior Grand Fleet. The High Seas Fleet remained in harbour, its purpose unsure. The Germans, it turns out, had built a fleet large enough to antagonise the British but not large enough to fight them. Such was the folly of pre-war German naval policy.

It was in the Mediterranean then that naval action, if it can be so described, began. In that sea the British had three battlecruisers (the battlecruiser was a lightly armoured and faster version of the dreadnought) with attendant light cruisers, four heavy cruisers and sixteen destroyers.[5] The Germans had one battlecruiser (*Goeben*) and one light cruiser (*Breslau*) in the area, commanded by Admiral Souchon. Complicating matters in those waters was the fact that Italy (in whose waters the *Goeben* and *Breslau* were lurking) was neutral and that Austria-Hungary, which had a considerable fleet at the head of the Adriatic, was not yet at war with Britain. The other major fleet in the Mediterranean was the French (with four dreadnoughts) guarding the route by which their Algerian army would cross to the Western Front via Marseilles.[6]

The action against the *Goeben* was the first in which the Admiralty could directly communicate with an admiral on the spot. It proved not to be an auspicious beginning for the new technology. The British commander in the Mediterranean was Admiral Sir Berkeley Milne, a Churchill appoint-ment in whom he and the Admiralty more generally had lost confidence. He was about to be replaced when war broke out.[7] This deficit of trust led the Admiralty to attempt to direct the campaign against the *Goeben* from London, with unfortunate results.

The two main problems were that the Admiralty were not able to articu-late the policy Milne should follow in the Mediterranean with any clarity and that the admiral himself was a man of limited initiative. In the first instance the admiral was told to bring the *Goeben* to action if possible but not to engage with superior forces (not defined), observe Italian neutrality 'rigidly' and to regard the protection of the French troops from Algeria to Marseilles as 'his first task'.[8] This was a strange priority as the French had ample ships of their own with which to protect their transports.

51

The first move made by the German ships on the outbreak of war was to sail into the neutral waters of the Strait of Messina to coal. Milne of course was unable to follow because of the instruction to observe Italian neutrality. But his subsequent actions were peculiar. He stationed all three of his battlecruisers at the northern end of the straits in what he considered a blocking position between the Germans and the French transports.[9] This left the southern end of the straits unguarded, with the added problem that the German ships could easily sail through this passage and, if they chose, double back towards the French. Thus Milne's dispositions produced the worst of all worlds

And, after coaling, Souchon promptly left by the unguarded southern exit. He did not turn west towards the French, however, but east towards Turkey, which was indeed his destination. The Admiralty were well aware that tensions between Turkey and Britain were running high over the seizure by Britain of two battleships being built for Turkey. They also knew that the Turkish army had just mobilised under German direction. None of this intelligence was passed on to Milne.[10]

But Milne now knew that the Germans were out of the straits and heading east. It might be thought that, as he had been instructed to bring the *Goeben* to action, he would follow hot-foot on Souchon's path and seek a fleet action with his stronger squadron at the first opportunity. He did nothing of the kind, merely following the German ships at some distance and at a leisurely pace. In this manner he and his three battlecruisers gradually faded from the scene. It well might have been the case that he recalled the Admiralty's instruction not to become engaged with a superior force and chose to regard the German squadron as fitting that bill. This was hardly Nelsonic, but then neither were the Admiralty's desperately vague instructions.

However, there was another British force between the *Goeben*, *Breslau* and Turkey. The First Cruiser Squadron, commanded by Admiral Troubridge, with four heavy cruisers and eight destroyers was at the entrance of the Adriatic watching lest the Austro-Hungarians declare war and make a move into the central Mediterranean. Troubridge had been alerted to the movements of the German squadron by the Admiralty. But he had also been instructed not to become engaged with a superior force, which the Admiralty had yet again not defined. He therefore moved south towards Souchon, but as he was about to come into range he signalled 'am obliged to give up the chase'.[11] His defence at his court martial was that he regarded the German ships as representing a 'superior force' and therefore he was only obeying orders.[12] In the event, the court came down on his side, reasoning that his instructions were ambiguous and that he was entitled to his interpretation of them.[13] He never served at sea again, however.

Eventually the *Goeben* and *Breslau* reached the Dardanelles and proceeded to Constantinople. There the crews donned fezzes and the ships became units of the Turkish navy. There was an outcry in London, which did some damage to Churchill's reputation. It was thought that the Admiralty had bungled the pursuit and that the arrival of the German ships had helped Turkey decide to throw in its lot with the Central Powers. The bungling was real enough but the fact was that Turkey had already decided on a German alliance. The ships were just additional glue to bind the two countries together.[14]

No one emerges with any credit from this incident. The Admiralty (and Churchill, who was in the war room for at least some of the action – or inaction) proved incapable of expressing their wishes clearly and the admirals on the spot proved incapable of demonstrating any initiative. The naval war had not got off to a good start.

* * * * *

While the not-so-great chase had been proceeding in the Mediterranean, the navy had acted with much more decision, if not precision, in the North Sea. Churchill had been chafing at the lack of naval action since the outbreak of war and the non-event in the Mediterranean made him all the more impatient. On 24 August Churchill summoned a meeting with Prince Louis, as First Sea Lord, his principal naval adviser, Vice-Admiral Sturdee, the Chief of the Naval Staff, and Commodore Tyrwhitt, in command of two destroyer flotillas which were part of the Grand Fleet but stationed on the east coast at Harwich.[15] A plan was concocted whereby Tyrwhitt's destroyer flotillas, led by its cruisers and supported by a force of submarines commanded by Commodore Roger Keyes, would sweep through the waters of the Heligoland Bight with the idea of surprising and destroying any German warships returning to port.[16]

This was at best a half-baked plan. For in the waters of the Heligoland Bight lurked not only German light forces but at least some of their dreadnought battleships. If the British cruisers and destroyers were to encounter one or two dreadnoughts, they risked annihilation. Of course British heavy forces were available in number in the form of the Grand Fleet. But not only did the Admiralty not ask the commander of this force, Admiral Jellicoe, to lend support, they failed even to inform him of the plan. Somehow, at the last minute, Jellicoe got wind of the scheme and offered his help. He was told that his ships were not required but that his battlecruiser force under Admiral Beatty 'can support if convenient'.[17] This was desperately vague but Jellicoe acted with despatch, sending Beatty with three battlecruisers and an attendant cruiser squadron (under Commodore Goodenough) south.[18] But neither Beatty nor Goodenough was given any details about the plan or what forces were involved, Beatty commenting that he hoped 'to learn more as we go along'.[19]

Nor did Admiralty incompetence stop there. They neglected to inform Tyrwhitt and Keyes that reinforcements were on the way. When someone at the Admiralty finally twigged to this omission, a message was sent but it was never delivered. Tyrwhitt and Keyes had by this time left port and were out of radio range.[20] This mistake was almost disastrous. During the morning of 28 August, Tyrwhitt saw Goodenough's cruisers looming out of the gloom. He was on the point of opening fire but prudently decided to challenge first. He received the startling reply that the cruiser squadron was British and that Beatty's battlecruisers were not far behind.[21] Keyes, however, never learned of the reinforcements. Nor were Beatty's ships aware of the presence of Keyes's submarines. At one point Keyes was on the verge of torpedoing a British cruiser and at another one of Beatty's cruisers attempted to ram a British submarine.[22]

As for the battle, it started badly for the British. Tyrwhitt's flagship, *Arethusa*, was wrecked by an early encounter with a German cruiser and a little later the British flotillas were engaged by three German cruisers, all of which outgunned them.[23] But Tyrwhitt had taken the precaution of calling urgently to Beatty and at exactly the opportune moment Beatty's battlecruisers appeared to the north. They made short work of the German cruisers, sinking three in moments.[24] In the end the Germans lost three cruisers and a destroyer – 781 officers and men killed and a further 381 picked up as prisoners by the British. The Royal Navy had a cruiser and three destroyers damaged (the *Arethusa* badly damaged) with just thirty-five killed and forty wounded.[25] The greatest deficiency on the British side was not the plan or the fighting sailors; it was the Admiralty Staff. The greatest naval instrument on earth was seemingly run by amateurs.

That the Naval Staff were not exactly at the pinnacle of their profession soon manifested itself again. Since the beginning of the war, a patrol of five ageing cruisers had been maintained off the coast of the Netherlands. Their purpose was to keep these waters clear of enemy torpedo craft and mine-layers. In mid-September Churchill became concerned about the safety of the patrol. He minuted the First Sea Lord that the risk to the old ships was too great and that they should be withdrawn.[26] The staff decided that the patrol should indeed be withdrawn, but not immediately.[27] Four days later, three of the old cruisers were torpedoed by a German submarine with the loss of 1,400 lives.[28]

What of the high seas? Here the only impressive concentration of German naval power was the Far East Asiatic Squadron under Admiral von Spee at Tsing-Tao in northern China. The squadron consisted of the modern heavy cruisers, *Scharnhorst* and *Gneisenau* and three light cruisers, *Emden*, *Nurnberg* and *Leipzig*. All ships could make over 20 knots and the 8″ guns of the heavy cruisers could outrange the rather motley collection of British ships concentrated at Singapore.[29] This force, under Admiral Jerram, had just one battleship, the *Triumph*, which was obsolete, of slow speed and weak armament. There were also two ancient armoured cruisers and three vener-able light cruisers. Any encounter between these two squadrons would have resulted in a crushing victory for the Germans, so the British kept well away.

In Pacific waters, however, lay ships that could deal with Von Spee. These were the battlecruiser *Australia* and the fast light cruisers *Sydney* and *Melbourne* under Admiral Patey. The *Australia* had 8 x 12″ guns and a speed of 24 knots and could probably have sunk Von Spee's cruisers single-handed.[30] And on the outbreak of war Patey moved his force north of New Guinea, anticipating that his main task would be to bring Von Spee to action while at the same time protecting Australian trade routes from a swoop south by the German ships.[31]

Patey's plan was soon derailed by the failure of the Naval Staff to estab-lish firm priorities for outlying squadrons. On the outbreak of war this had been clear – hunt down and destroy enemy warships. Then a cross-service committee chaired by the Admiralty decided that scooping up German colonies should be given priority. This caused no difficulty when there were no German warships present, as in Africa – where small forces landed from British ships overran Togoland and Cameroon – but in the Far East there was the matter of Von Spee's squadron and the German colonies of Samoa and New Guinea. The Admiralty decided that the colonies were of greater importance than Von Spee and ordered Patey to occupy the colonies as an 'urgent Imperial service'.[32]

Patey therefore had in the first instance to devote his force to colonial expeditions. First the *Australia* escorted the New Zealanders to Samoa, which was captured without a shot.[33] Then Patey returned and escorted the Australian contingent first to Rabaul and then to New Guinea, which was captured at a cost of six Australian casualties.[34]

Meanwhile Von Spee, who had rather been forgotten, revealed himself. On 15 September his squadron appeared off Apia in Samoa and bombarded the town. The New Zealand occupation force was alarmed but the Germans soon disappeared into the vastness of the Pacific. What was their destination? Patey thought he knew. He considered that Von Spee was proceeding to the west coast of South America where he might attack British shipping, especially the crucial nitrate trade from Chile. Patey begged to be allowed to follow, but the Admiralty had other ideas.[35] They thought the Germans might double back and return to Samoa or even Fiji and New Zealand.[36] Therefore they ordered Patey to patrol these waters, which he did fruitlessly for the next three weeks.

That policy caused tensions to run high between Britain and New Zealand. While Patey was patrolling the Pacific he could not be escorting New Zealand troops which had been raised for the war in Europe to Australia. Churchill assured New Zealand that the rusting P Class cruisers he was willing to provide were escort enough and that the risks they would run were 'fair and good'.[37] The New Zealanders, however, considered the risks neither fair nor good and the government threatened to resign unless a stronger escort was provided.[38] Negotiations followed, not to the reassurance of New Zealand. Finally, the Prime Minister (Massey) again threated resignation and to make his reasons public unless a stronger escort was provided.[39] That had a sobering effect on the Admiralty. They would not, though, provide Patey, who continued to cruise aimlessly in the South Pacific waiting for Von Spee. In some haste they prevailed upon the now-allied Japanese government to send the heavy cruiser *Ibuki* to New Zealand.[40] This calmed the New Zealanders but allowed Von Spee to escape. On 15 October the Admiralty learned that an intercepted radio message placed the German ships at the Marquesas Islands in the mid-Pacific.[41] Patey was still keen to follow him but the Admiralty, now thoroughly alarmed by the crisis with New Zealand, kept him in the South Pacific. Any action along the coast of South America would take place without the battlecruiser *Australia*.

In those waters the Admiralty had managed to assemble a similar motley collection of ships that characterised the China Squadron. The South American Squadron, under Admiral Sir Christopher Cradock, began life as a force searching for the German cruisers *Dresden* and *Karlsruhe* known to be in the Caribbean. After an unsuccessful trawl through the West Indies and off the coast of Brazil, the Admiralty, now believing that Patey might have been correct in his prediction that Von Spee might appear in South American waters, ordered Cradock south. His squadron consisted of the heavy cruisers *Good Hope* and *Monmouth* and weirdly the P&O liner *Otranto*. He was to be reinforced, however. The light cruiser *Glasgow*, then on the west coast of South America, was to be added, as was the pre-dreadnought battleship *Canopus* from African waters.[42] His instructions were clear. He was to meet and destroy Von Spee (now accompanied by the *Dresden* and *Nurnberg*).[43]

This was in fact a ludicrous order. All Cradock's ships were obsolete, too weak to stand in a line of battle against Von Spee and too slow to run away. Clearly the Admiralty were relying on *Canopus* to tilt the scales in Cradock's favour. It had the heaviest armament of any ship in South American waters with 4 x 12″ and 12 x 6″ guns. But the ship was old (built 1899), its guns were out-ranged by Von Spee's heavy cruisers and it was slow. Other indicators for the *Canopus* were even gloomier. The rifling on its guns was so worn that when it fired at the Dardanelles, just four weeks later, some of the shells left the barrel head over heels.[44] In these circumstances it is doubtful if it could have come close to hitting a fast-moving ship.

Cradock was aware of the deficiencies of his squadron. While concentrating his force at the Falklands he signalled the Admiralty that he thought his squadron inadequate, adding, 'Does *Defence* [a heavy cruiser] join my command?'.[45] This aroused Churchill's concern. He minuted that he presumed if Cradock felt he had insufficient forces to attack, he would shadow Von Spee, pending reinforcements.[46] But at this point staff work at the Admiralty broke down. Churchill's message was not sent to Cradock but a signal ordering him to concentrate his squadron against Von Spee was.[47] The message was clear – Cradock could fight Von Spee with what he had and that would not include the *Defence*.

Yet Cradock's doubts had not been stilled. Indeed, after he inspected the *Canopus* they increased. He told the Admiralty that its slow speed might prevent him from forcing an action.[48] This having elicited no reply, he informed their lordships that he was leaving for the Strait of Magellan with his faster ships and instructing the *Canopus* to follow with the squadron's colliers.[49] As he headed south, Cradock made one last attempt to convince the Admiralty of the inadequacies of his ships. He told them that it was 'impracticable' to force an action with the slow speed of the battleship and that he had ordered *Defence* to join him. Meanwhile the *Canopus* would continue to convoy his colliers.[50] This order was quickly countermanded by the Admiralty, *Defence* being ordered to remain on the east coast of South America. No comment was made about the lowly use to which Cradock had assigned the *Canopus*.[51]

Cradock was now proceeding up the west coast of South America with the *Good Hope, Monmouth, Glasgow* and *Otranto. Canopus* was 300 miles behind with the colliers. On 29 October *Glasgow* called at the Chilean port of Coronel to collect mails. While in port it picked up wireless signals from Von Spee's squadron. At the same time Von Spee learned of the presence of the *Glasgow*. On 1 November both sides began to search. Late in the afternoon the two fleets met about 50 miles east of Coronel. Cradock immediately turned towards the enemy but Von Spee used his superior speed to keep out of range until the sun had set and the British ships were sharply silhouetted against the horizon. Then he opened fire. Cradock replied but he was hopelessly outgunned and the stormy conditions made it impossible to fire many of the guns on the lower decks of the *Monmouth* and *Good Hope*. The battle was over in two hours. The *Good Hope* blew up; the *Monmouth* was sunk with all hands.[52] Dark and moonless conditions allowed the *Glasgow* and *Otranto* to escape.

Why Cradock joined battle without the *Canopus* is a riddle. Perhaps he thought the ship so obsolete that it would add nothing to his force. Yet the practically unarmed *Otranto* was present. Perhaps he was determined to show the Admiralty that his force was inadequate. Perhaps he acted upon impulse. As for the Admiralty, their staff work was deficient, their overall risk assessment disastrous and their failure to pass on Churchill's instructions woeful. Their misuse of the *Australia* at this time is also a mark against them. But whatever the explanation, British naval supremacy in the South Atlantic had been lost.

The loss at Coronel sent shock waves through the Admiralty. Two battlecruisers, previously held back as essential for Britain's naval supremacy in the North Sea, were immediately ordered by the new First Sea Lord Admiral Fisher with Churchill's full concurrence, to the South Atlantic. The *Invincible* and the *Inflexible* left Devonport on 11 November, with the dockyard workers that were still refitting them aboard.[53] Their departure was supposed to be secret in case the Germans took the opportunity to attack the Grand Fleet. But the commander, Admiral Sturdee, soon alerted the Germans by calling at a Spanish port where there were several German merchant ships. He also continually broke wireless silence as he crossed the Atlantic which was picked up by German agents in Montevideo. Luckily for the British, none of this information reached Von Spee.[54]

There was no sense of urgency in Sturdee's voyage. He frequently stopped to examine merchant ships for contraband and proceeded at an economical speed to save coal. At the Abrolhos Rocks off Brazil he was joined by the cruisers *Carnarvon, Cornwall, Kent, Bristol* and *Glasgow*. At last the Admiralty had assembled a force to take on Von Spee. After coaling, Captain Luce of the *Glasgow* convinced Sturdee to make haste to the Falklands to reinforce the lone *Canopus*.[55] Even then Sturdee did not hurry, maintaining his slow speed and conducting sweeps for enemy shipping. He finally arrived at the Falklands on 7 December, five weeks after Coronel.

As it happened, Von Spee had been just as lethargic. After Coronel he had spent an inordinate amount of time on the coast of Chile, coaling and resting. His plan was to attack and occupy the Falklands but he too stopped to capture a collier and transfer its cargo. As a result he arrived off Port Stanley one day after Sturdee.[56]

He was greeted by a shot from the beached *Canopus* which ricocheted off the water in front of the *Gneisenau* and hit the base of its after funnel.[57] Von Spee then sheered off, much to the relief of Sturdee, whose battlecruisers were coaling and quite vulnerable to attack. He soon raised steam for battle and at 10 a.m. the *Inflexible* and the *Invincible* with the four attendant cruisers set off in pursuit.[58]

Sturdee's tactics were simple. The battlecruisers would engage Von Spee's heavy ships at extreme range, while the cruisers dealt with the *Nurnberg*,

Leipzig and *Dresden*. The battle developed according to this plan. As the battlecruisers closed, Von Spee ordered his smaller ships to break away. This they did but they were pursued by their British opposite numbers. The main action began at 1.20 p.m. when Sturdee opened fire at 16,000 yards.[59] Initially his fire was bad. For the first 150 rounds fired, the British probably scored just five hits.[60] Nor did Sturdee's tactics aid his gunners. The course he steered continually fouled the range with smoke and for a time the path of one battlecruiser hampered the other. Nevertheless, British superiority soon began to tell. Hits were scored on the German heavy cruisers which slowed their speed. They were then plastered with shells. The *Scharnhorst* sank at 4.17 p.m. and the *Gneisenau* two hours later. Sturdee's battlecruisers were practically untouched, just two casualties having been suffered.

The lighter British cruisers pursued and sank the *Leipzig* and *Nurnberg*. The *Dresden* escaped and was not to be hunted down in Chilean waters until March 1915. Naval supremacy in the South Atlantic had been regained.

This period of the naval war finished early in the new year with a British victory of a kind at the Dogger Bank. In January the Germans planned a battlecruiser sweep into the North Sea. British Naval Intelligence was aware of the move and ordered Beatty's five battlecruisers with attendant light craft to a rendezvous point designed to cut Admiral Hipper's squadron off from its base.[61] The plan worked perfectly and on the morning of 24 January the four enemy battlecruisers were sighted. Hipper immediately turned for home and a chase developed. But errors began to accumulate on the British side. The *Tiger* misread the fire distribution signal, with the result that one German ship (*Moltke*) was left unattended to score damaging hits on the *Lion*, Beatty's flagship.[62] Nevertheless, British fire quickly reduced the German heavy cruiser *Blücher* to a smouldering wreck. Eventually, though, the *Lion* began to lose speed. Desperate for his remaining ships to concentrate on the enemy rather than following the stricken *Lion*, Beatty made two signals: 'Course N.E.' and then 'Attack the rear of the enemy'.[63] However, Seymour, his signalling officer, passed these to the other ships as one signal: 'Attack the rear of the enemy bearing North East'.[64] At the time the signal was read, the crippled *Blücher* lay exactly north-east of Beatty's battlecruisers and it was by this time the rearward German ship. So instead of attacking Hipper's squadron, the four battlecruisers concentrated on the already-sinking *Blücher*. Beatty, seeing his plan going awry, sent another signal: 'Keep nearer the enemy' but by that time the *Lion* was too far astern for it to be read.[65] He then transferred to a destroyer, caught up with the remainder of the squadron and ordered the chase resumed. It was too late. Hipper had escaped.

Publicly much was made by Beatty over the destruction of the *Blücher*. Privately he was furious at the lack of initiative shown by the battlecruiser captains. The lesson he did not learn was that he needed a signal officer capable of translating his wishes into action. Seymour was not that man but remained in place. On the German side a more valuable lesson was learned. British hits on the *Seydlitz* had almost resulted in a disaster. Flash penetrated down the shell shaft to the magazine where the doors were open to assist the rapid handling of shells. On this occasion the magazine was flooded and the doors closed just in time to prevent a ship-destroying explosion. From then on magazine doors in German warships were securely closed during an action. This was not the case on British ships, where that flaw would prove most costly.[66]

Overall, neither the Admiralty, nor to a lesser extent Churchill, emerges well from these early naval skirmishes. Churchill was partly responsible for the vague orders sent to Milne and for concocting the Heligoland Bight scheme and not informing the Commander-in-Chief that he had done so. However, it has to be said that he did not have much to work with. With the *Goeben* incident neither Milne nor Troubridge showed any dash or initiative. Neither man queried or asked for clarification of their vague orders. As for the Heligoland Bight operation, Jellicoe saved both the Admiralty and Tyrwhitt and Keyes, who had concocted the scheme without reference to him. Beatty's appearance turned an incipient disaster into a victory but it was a victory that relied on luck and chance rather than professionalism. In the Pacific, the Admiralty cast away the chance to destroy Von Spee by attempting too many tasks before the German squadron had been hunted down. At the same time they drove the most loyal of Dominion governments to the brink of resignation because of their arrogant assumptions about the strength of troop escorts. There is some irony in that it was the Japanese who came to their rescue. The orders to Cradock were a grim farce which saw the destruction of a squadron of (admittedly) obsolete ships and the drowning of 1,660 sailors. (If the 1,400 lost in the sinking of the three cruisers are added, the Naval Staff by their incompetence caused 3,000 men to drown in the first three months of warfare.) In this instance the Admiralty not only ignored the opinion of the admiral on the spot that his squadron was inadequate for its task, they also ignored Churchill, who as First Lord should have had an opinion that counted for something. The despatch of the battlecruisers that saw the end of Von Spee owed nothing to the Naval Staff and everything to Fisher and Churchill, whose decision it was. It was fortunate that two battlecruisers were sent, given Sturdee's tactics, and perhaps fortunate that Sturdee even came within hailing distance of Von Spee. The success at the Battle of the Falklands, like that of the Heligoland Bight, owed more than a little to luck. As for Beatty at Dogger Bank, it demonstrated that even an aggressive commander could struggle to make his thoughts clear and struggle even harder to instil some initiative into his subordinate captains. That story in fact had longer to play out.

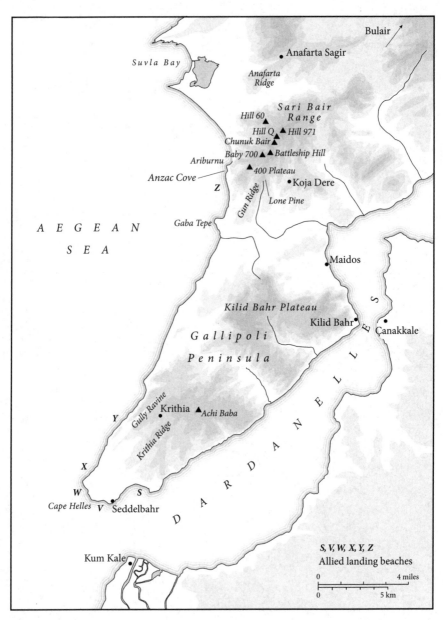

Map 2. Gallipoli.

CHAPTER 4

GALLIPOLI – THE
POLITICIANS' HOUR

IN THE LAST MONTHS of 1914 various members of the War Council expressed themselves unhappy with the level of casualties and lack of progress on what was becoming known as the Western Front. Balfour, an ex-leader of the Conservative Party who had been seconded to sit on the Council by Asquith, thought the aim of winning by 'assaulting one line of trenches after another ... a very hopeless affair'.[1] Asquith agreed. He considered 'the losses involved in trench-jumping operations ... out of all proportion to the ground gained'.[2]

Churchill had actually visited the front and observed the result of a failed trench attack with the ghastly spectacle of soldiers impaled on the barbed-wire entanglements that were becoming more and more common. He had also learned from a friend of 'the absolutely indescribable ravages of modern artillery fire' on troops attempting to advance.[3] He wrote to Asquith that he saw the navy (of which he happened to be the head) as Britain's salvation. Surely, he thought, the power of the navy could be 'brought directly to bear upon the enemy'.[4] If naval predominance could be used to capture an island (Borkum was the usual target put forward) off the German coast, the German fleet would be forced to fight a large naval battle that Britain was certain to win. Then with the Germans expelled from the North Sea the Grand Fleet could enter the Baltic and with the assistance of the Russians attack the north German coast. This would force Germany to divert troops from the west, which might make an advance in that area an easier prospect. In any case this strategy was more appealing than sending the new armies that Britain was raising to 'chew barbed wire in Flanders'.[5]

Meanwhile, Maurice Hankey, formerly Secretary of the Committee of Imperial Defence and now Secretary of the War Council, had also written a memorandum to Asquith. He drew the Prime Minister's attention to the deadlock on the Western Front and suggested a number of mechanical devices (including a type of weapon that would evolve into the tank) which might help to break it.[6] He went on, however, to suggest that other theatres offered more attractive prospects. In particular he conjured up a coalition of Balkan states that 'might weave a web round Turkey and end her career as a European Power'. The demise of Turkey would open up communications with Russia through which could flow munitions and food, allow a more efficient prosecution of the war by Russia and thus ease pressure on the Western Front. Three British army corps combined with Balkan and Russian forces could achieve these ends.[7]

Next in the field was Lloyd George. He too looked to the Balkan states. But he considered that an alliance with them could best be achieved through landing the new British armies (totalling between 1.4 and 1.6 million men) on the coast of Dalmatia (or perhaps Salonika) and attacking the weaker enemy, Austria. A lesser scheme might be to land troops at Alexandretta in Turkish territory to cut off any forces attacking the Suez Canal. This would also relieve Turkish pressure on Russia in the Caucasus.[8]

These memoranda had a cumulative effect on Asquith, who was also becoming increasingly disillusioned about the lack of progress in Flanders. He thought highly of Hankey, whom he considered 'a good opinion', and on receipt of the missives from Churchill and Lloyd George he determined to summon the War Council to review the whole situation.[9]

But there was a problem with all the schemes put forward to Asquith. None offered a practical military operation. Churchill's Borkum/Baltic plans had never found wide acceptance at the Admiralty and in particular had been resisted by Jellicoe, who had no intention of risking the Grand Fleet in waters dominated by mines and submarines. Moreover, no one had asked the hard-pressed Russians whether they had a contingent of highly trained troops to spare for such risky operations. As for Hankey's 'web' strategy, there was no hint of how the internecine hatreds of the Balkan states might be reconciled in order to construct a winning coalition. The same criticism could be applied to Lloyd George's scheme, which had the additional problems of deploying 1 or 2 million men in the railway-less wilderness of the Balkans and the hazards of landing them on the Dalmatian coast in near proximity to the Austrian fleet.

Fisher proved the unwitting catalyst in breaking the impasse posed by these impractical schemes. He abandoned a plan of his own to land in the Netherlands, which he seemed to forget was neutral, and expressed enthusiasm for Hankey's Turkey plan in the most extravagant terms. He proposed moving over 100,000 men from the Western Front to land in Anatolia while enticing Greece to attack the Gallipoli Peninsula with a similar number of troops.[10] Simultaneous with these landings, the British would force the Dardanelles with squadrons of pre-dreadnought battleships, of which it had thirty to forty to spare.[11]

Churchill read this memorandum with interest. He realised that any Greek army operating against Turkey was a pipe dream and that removing 100,000 men from the Western Front was hardly practical politics. But the idea of naval action at the Dardanelles appealed to him. He could use the obsolete British battleships, thus circumventing the argument that his naval plans might endanger the Grand Fleet. Also, because it did not involve troops, its conduct lay within the scope of the Admiralty. So on 3 January he called a meeting of the Admiralty War Group (which consisted of himself, Fisher, Admiral Oliver, the Chief of the Naval Staff, and Admirals Wilson and Jackson – both employed in an advisory capacity) to consider that aspect of the Fisher/Hankey plan. At the conclusion of that meeting, a telegram which almost certainly had the approval of the whole group was sent to Admiral Carden, commanding the British squadron off the Dardanelles:[12]

Do you consider the forcing of the Dardanelles by ships alone a practicable operation.

It is assumed that older battleships fitted with minebumpers would be used preceded by Colliers or other merchant craft as bumpers and sweepers.

Importance of results would justify severe loss.[13]

Carden's reply was rather grudging. He could hardly refuse to carry out an operation of such importance that it justified 'severe loss'. But he deprecated a rush at the Dardanelles. He thought the straits *might* be forced by *extensive* operations by a *large* number of ships.[14] Despite these caveats this was enough for Churchill. He telegraphed back that Carden's opinions were agreed with by 'high authorities' in Britain and asked him to produce a plan.[15] This arrived on 7 January. In essence it was hardly a plan at all, merely the sequence in which the forts at the Dardanelles should be attacked.[16]

Churchill was not bothered by the vagueness at the centre of Carden's plan. Perhaps he did not even notice it. On 13 January he presented it to the War Council and urged it on his colleagues. They received it with sufficient enthusiasm to conclude that the Admiralty should prepare a plan 'to bombard the Gallipoli Peninsula with Constantinople as its objective'.[17]

Churchill was soon to find that he had a problem as well as a plan. Some of those 'high authorities' whom he had invoked in favour of the plan were starting to have second thoughts. Jackson was now emphasising that the loss of ships in such an operation might be very severe.[18] And Fisher was starting to behave erratically. On the one hand he added the newly minted *Queen Elizabeth* (the most powerful battleship in the world) to Carden's fleet, on the other he abruptly resigned his post as First Sea Lord on the bizarre grounds that the Admiralty had not prepared the public about impending raids on London by Zeppelins.[19] Captain Richmond, a member of the Naval War Staff, thought the pressure of the job was becoming too much for Fisher. He considered him old and worn out, a man who merely wanted to enjoy the prestige of his office without risking his reputation by an adventurous policy that might fail.[20] Indeed, on 25 January Fisher wrote a paper to Churchill deprecating all extraneous operations by the fleet and urging the First Lord to allow the steady pressure that it was exerting against Germany via the blockade to wear it down gradually.[21] A few days later he wrote to Asquith that as he could not assent to the Dardanelles operation he would not attend future meetings of the War Council.[22] In reply, Asquith ordered Fisher to attend the meeting scheduled for that day but arranged a preliminary talk between Fisher, Churchill and himself to iron out differences.[23]

Whatever Asquith thought this meeting had achieved, he was soon made aware that very little ironing had taken place. When Churchill introduced the Dardanelles plan, Fisher interjected that he had understood that the matter was not to be discussed that day and that the Prime Minister was well aware of his views on the subject. With that he left the table and walked towards the window. Kitchener followed and slowly coaxed him to return. This was an unusual incident, to say the least. Yet no one at the meeting asked Fisher to expand on what his views might be. This might well be because most members of the Council already knew that Fisher had strong reservations about the naval attack. Churchill, Asquith and Kitchener obviously knew. Crewe, Lloyd George and Balfour testified before the Dardanelles Inquiry that they knew. Haldane and Grey, who met Asquith frequently on other matters, almost certainly knew. Yet this knowledge did nothing to dampen the politicians' enthusiasm for the operation at Gallipoli. Indeed when summing up the plan, Balfour enumerated the views of most of them:

> It would cut the Turkish army in two;
> It would put Constantinople under our control;
> It would give us the advantage of having Russian wheat and Russia could resume exports [to pay for Entente munitions];
> It would also open a passage to the Danube;
> It was difficult to imagine a more helpful operation.

At which point Grey chimed in suggesting that the operation might break the diplomatic deadlock in the Balkans in favour of the Entente.[24]

Against this onslaught of enthusiasm Fisher stood no chance. At this stage of proceedings the enthusiasm of the civilian members of the War Council for the naval attack held the field. They were just not interested in his doubts.

Admiralty opinion was, however, hardening against the plan. Jackson, Richmond and Fisher were now insisting that it would be necessary to land troops on the Gallipoli Peninsula to aid in knocking out the forts and to enable the minefield to be swept at leisure when the peninsula was occupied.[25] No authority was suggesting a major military operation, merely that it would be prudent to have troops on hand to assist if required. Hankey shared these opinions and passed them on to Balfour and Asquith.[26] He also informed Asquith that Churchill's judgement on the naval-only operation was not to be trusted.[27]

Churchill too seemed to be having doubts about the naval-only plan. He too began to push for troops, in fact first-class troops, to be in close proximity to the Dardanelles.[28] Kitchener at first resisted this demand on the reasonable grounds that he had been assured great things could be accomplished without the use of troops. But in the end he too weakened and the 29 Division (the last of the British Regulars) was earmarked for the east.

What no one seemed to be noticing was the potential that these decisions had to change the nature of operations at Gallipoli. There were already 30,000 Australian and New Zealand troops training in Egypt before despatch to the Western Front. In addition there were 10,000 from the rag-tag Royal Naval Division formed by Churchill which was to be despatched with the bombarding squadron. Now 17,000 British Regulars were going. And as soon as that news reached Paris the French added 17,000 troops, lest Britain carve up the Turkish Empire single-handed. This added up to an army of 74,000 men in close proximity to the Dardanelles. What perhaps the politicians were not noticing was that, should the navy fail, the imperatives to use these men would be very great indeed. Troops are rarely accumulated to provide an audience for failure.

* * * * *

The Admiralty was now required to give substance to the naval attack at the Dardanelles. Their deliberations plumbed new depths of tactical incompetence. The Turkish defences at the Dardanelles consisted of three interlocking elements. First there were over 100 heavy guns in forts along the European and Asiatic sides of the straits.[29] Then there were the minefields consisting of 271 mines laid in nine lines to a depth of 14 feet across the straits. Protecting these mines were eighty-seven medium howitzers deployed on both sides of the straits, concealed from view from the sea and with the mobility to shift position as required.[30] The task to be undertaken by the navy was never simply that of destroying the guns in the forts. To get through the straits it was necessary to sweep most of the mines which were protected by the mobile howitzers while at the same time dealing with the fire from the forts.

Yet, to accomplish this complex task, the Admiralty provided Carden not with fast minesweepers from the fleet but with a series of Grimsby trawlers manned by civilian crews. The ships had such modest speed that, with their sweeps out, they could hardly make headway against the 4-knot current which ran down the straits.[31] Other Admiralty instructions ensured that these makeshift sweepers would not be closely protected by the guns of the heavy ships. Oliver and Jackson insisted that the bombardment of the forts be carried out at such a distance as to keep the ships beyond the range of the guns in the forts.[32] At this range it was essential to provide aircraft to signal to the ships the accuracy of their fire and direct adjustments to ensure that their shells actually hit the forts. But the few venerable seaplanes despatched by the Admiralty, when equipped with the heavy radios then in use, lacked sufficiently powerful engines to enable them to gain enough height to avoid even Turkish rifle fire. Yet without radios the planes were almost useless. After observing the fall of shot, they would have to return to their ship and drop the necessary corrections in waterproof pouches.[33] By the time this information was retrieved by the ships the adjustments required would in all probability be out of date, as conditions of wind and weather would have changed.

Then there was the bombarding squadron itself. Carden was provided with twelve battleships, ten pre-dreadnoughts plus the modern battlecruiser *Inflexible* and the *Queen Elizabeth*. In addition the French agreed to add six of their older ships to Carden's force. The problem here was the age of the ships. Most had been constructed in the nineteenth century. The barrels of the guns were all worn (to varying degrees) when the ships arrived at the Dardanelles. Wear on the rifling of a gun barrel was of supreme importance in modern gunnery because it determined accuracy. A worn barrel might cause a shell to wobble as it left the gun, which could affect its range and dictate whether it deviated to the left or right. Hitting a small target such as a gun in a fort at long range under these conditions was a matter of chance. Even a modern ship like the *Queen Elizabeth* could on average only hit an enemy gun 3 times in 100 from 12,000 yards. For the older ships this number was much lower, probably not much more than 1 in 100.[34] To destroy the 100 heavy guns in the forts, then, would have required an enormous supply of ammunition. No one at the Admiralty seemed to notice that this was just not available in the Mediterranean in 1915.

To sum up, the Admiralty plan gave Carden no sure way of sweeping the minefields. Nor could the flat trajectory of naval guns take out the concealed howitzers that protected the minefields. As for destroying the guns in the Dardanelles forts that kept the Allied heavy ships at long range, the task they had been set was impossible. The naval attack was set fair for failure before it began.

The great naval attack on the Dardanelles began on 19 February when seven British and three French battleships opened fire on the forts at the entrance to the straits. They fired for eight hours without hitting a single gun.[35] Bad weather then intervened, delaying further firing until the 25th. This day proved the most successful of the entire operation. Four Turkish guns were destroyed, two by the *Queen Elizabeth* and two by the pre-dreadnought *Irresistible*. Euphoria swept through the fleet. Carden was emboldened to land parties of marines near the entrance forts. They succeeded in blowing up six heavy guns. French troops landed on the Asiatic coast and destroyed three smaller pieces.[36] In the days that followed, landing parties demolished sixteen heavy and thirty-two lighter guns at the entrance forts.[37] After this success the Turks moved troops to the toe of the peninsula in some numbers. Further landing parties were beaten back.

Unfortunately for the Allies, destruction of guns by the ships did not prove as successful as the landing parties. Each day from 26 February to 8 March the battleships entered the straits and attacked the forts. At the end of this period precisely no guns had been hit. All the negative factors mentioned earlier were in play. Spotting by aircraft was woefully inefficient because the craft could on most occasion not carry radios; the weather was often bad; and the old guns of the pre-dreadnoughts just did not have the accuracy to hit small targets from long range.[38]

Nor was the sweeping of the minefield proceeding well. The sweepers had been in action since the first day of the attack. Overall they made seventeen attempts to sweep the mines. In total they swept just 2 out of the 387 mines that the Turks had now laid. The reasons for failure have already been suggested. The current often proved too strong for them to even reach the mines. On two occasions (27 and 28 February) the trawlers were actually blown, by a combination of wind and current, backwards out of the straits. On other occasions the fire from the concealed howitzers protecting the minefield proved too fierce. Sweeping at night proved no more successful as the Turkish defenders had strong searchlights which made the almost stationary trawlers sitting ducks for the guns. By mid-March the minefield was still intact.[39]

Faced with the utter failure of the ships to subdue the forts and the sweepers to deal with the mines and under pressure from Churchill to demonstrate some progress, Carden called a council of war for 13 March. The upshot was a decision to use sixteen battleships inside the straits against the forts while a concerted effort was made to sweep the mines.[40] In the event this operation would not be conducted by Carden. On 16 March, two days before the great attack, he collapsed. Admiral de Robeck, his second in command, was immediately appointed by Churchill to conduct the operation.

The concerted naval attack was carried out on 18 March. The idea was that the battleships would form up in three lines which would engage the forts sequentially. Then the sweepers would advance and, taking advantage of the battering of the forts and the destruction of their guns, attempt to sweep the mines unhampered. The result was a fiasco. At the end of the day three ships (*Bouvet*, *Ocean* and *Irresistible*) had been sunk and three more badly damaged. Just one heavy gun had been put out of action and no mines swept.[41] De Robeck immediately offered to resume the attack, but the situation was dire. One third of his battleship fleet had been put out of action for no result. Some authorities have asserted that renewed action might have succeeded as the Turkish forts were almost out of ammunition. There is no warrant for this. The Turks had sufficient ammunition to fight off another two British attacks, by which time, if 18 March is anything to go by, there would have been no serviceable heavy ships remaining. Moreover, it was not the forts that really mattered but the mines – and they were still intact.

All this led the men on the spot (including de Robeck, who had always had doubts about a naval-only operation) to call for the landing of troops on the peninsula to capture the forts and then remove the minefield.[42] This was not a sudden reversal of strategy. As noted, many authorities in London had been calling for such landings for some weeks. Indeed, when the decision was finally made to send the 29 Division to the east, a commander, General Sir Ian Hamilton, previously in charge of Eastern Command, had been despatched to observe events. He witnessed the disaster of 18 March and rapidly came to the conclusion that troops were required if the strategic aims in the area were to be met.[43] Only Churchill now adhered to a continuation of the naval attack. But he was overruled by the Admiralty War Group.[44] De Robeck and Hamilton were as one on the landing of troops and the War Group insisted that the men on the spot were in the best position to judge. Kitchener agreed. There 'must be no going back', he decreed, 'the effect of a defeat in the Orient would be very serious'.[45]

Having decided on a military landing, what thought was given in London to such an operation? Many questions required exploration. The objectives for the troops would be the forts and howitzers protecting the minefield and, as these were located on both sides of the straits, did this mean a divided landing? Then there was the Turkish army to consider. In total it could muster about 500,000 men and it was equipped with some modern artillery and machine guns. Not all of it could be deployed at Gallipoli because of operations in other parts of the Empire (See Chapter 7). Nevertheless, an operation to facilitate the arrival of a hostile fleet before the Turkish capital would represent a serious threat to the Ottoman Empire and it was a reasonable assumption that as many divisions as possible would be deployed against it. In this situation would 74,000 men be sufficient? No answers to any of these questions were given by the General Staff in London, for the simple reason that Kitchener never placed the prospect of a military landing before them. Nor did the War Council meet to insist that such a process be observed. All were apparently happy to leave the matter to the man on the spot, Sir Ian Hamilton. The fate of the whole venture was now squarely in his hands.

Hamilton began to develop his plan soon after the definitive failure of the naval attack. He did this in spite of cautionary warnings from two of his senior commanders. Major-General Archibald Paris, C-in-C of the Royal Naval Division, pointed out to Hamilton that the Turks had 250,000 men within striking distance of the peninsula and that he regarded the whole affair as 'hazardous in the extreme under present conditions'.[46] General Aylmer Hunter-Weston, in command of 29 Division, went further. He noted that Hamilton's forces were deficient in artillery and that they risked being held up by Turkish entrenchments dug across the peninsula. He concluded that the whole affair was likely to turn into a second Crimea and prove 'a disaster to the Empire'.[47] There was never any possibility that such warnings would be heeded by Hamilton. Whatever his own thoughts, and he was an optimist by nature, he was under instructions from Kitchener to land. Hamilton was well used to obeying Kitchener. He had served as his Chief of Staff in the South African War, but no general, even of stern disposition, would in 1915 have queried an order from such a source.

When Hamilton studied the topography of the peninsula he found that favourable landing beaches were few. Much of the coastline consisted of low cliffs that descended to the very water line. He finally decided to make his main landing with the 29 Division at five beaches near the foot of the peninsula around Cape Helles.[48] Once ashore they would be assisted by the guns of the fleet to advance on the narrows forts. To the north, the Anzac contingent would make a secondary landing at what later became known as Anzac Cove, advance across the peninsula and thus prevent Turkish reinforcements reaching Helles. The French would make a diversionary landing on the Asian shore near Kum Kale and later join the 29th in the advance up the peninsula. The Royal Naval Division would sail close to the Bulair (the narrowest point of the peninsula) in the hope of attracting reserves away from the Anzacs but would then withdraw and act as reinforcements as required.[49] Many questions were left unanswered by this plan. How would the forts and howitzers on the Asiatic shore be dealt with? And if they were not dealt with, how would the mines be swept? Was Paris's point about the large Turkish force that could be directed against the landings taken into account by Hamilton; or Hunter-Weston's that trenches could turn the peninsula into a version of the Western Front, the avoidance of which had been a large rationale for the operation in the first place? Was there lurking at the heart of Hamilton's plan a form of Orientalism, an assumption that troops from the 'sick man of Europe' would flee in the face of the might of the West?

Whatever the case, having made his plan Hamilton set about the preliminaries required to implement it. The ships that were to carry the forces and their stores and equipment to the peninsula had now to be tactically packed for orderly disembarkation. This delay is often given as a reason for the failure of the operation as it gave the Turks time to strengthen their defences. But the re-ordering of the ships was inevitable and, in any case, the Turks were already in the process of sending more men to the area. In addition the weather was just too bad to land troops any earlier than late April.

The landings on the Gallipoli Peninsula took place on 25 April. The feint attacks can be dealt with briefly. French forces managed to destroy some guns at Kum Kale but were soon withdrawn under Turkish pressure and prepared to take up their positions on the right of the British at Helles. At Bulair the demonstration had no effect because the German commander of the Turkish forces at Gallipoli (General Liman von Sanders) was already holding men there in anticipation of a landing. These attacks therefore diverted no Turkish troops from the main events at Helles and Anzac.

At Helles around 7,000 men were landed in the first wave. There were three flank landings on the left and right of the foot of the peninsula at S, X and Y beaches. The main landings were at W and V beaches (see map). At V Beach the British used the expedient of running aground an old collier, the *River Clyde*, packed with troops – which, it was hoped, might give protection against Turkish gun fire. The covering fire from the ships that was supposed to subdue the defenders, however, had utterly failed. The old guns were so inaccurate that one shell fired to assist the landing at S Beach landed near Y. The first to land at V (the Dublin Fusiliers) were met with devastating rifle and machine-gun fire from the old fort of Seddelbahr and some nearby trenches. The same fate awaited those that left from the sally-ports cut into the sides of the old collier. In the end common sense prevailed and it was decided to withhold the 1,000 men who remained in the *River Clyde* until nightfall.[50] At W Beach the initial landings had fared no better. The ships' fire had again proved ineffectual and the Lancashire Fusiliers in their small boats ran into barbed-wire obstacles that protruded well into the sea.

At the apex of the attack all was confusion. On the flanks landings had been much more orderly. At S Beach, inside the straits, opposition was quickly brushed aside, as it was at X on the other side of Helles.[51] Further up the coast the landing at Y was unopposed and 2,500 troops were soon ashore in good shape. There appeared a chance for the troops on the flanks to redeem the position at V and W by mounting converging attacks on the few hundred Turkish defenders who were holding up the main body. But the orders for these flanking forces were to remain in position until the main contingents arrived from V and W. And the fact was that these troops had little idea of the situation at the southern beaches and only rudimentary maps of the peninsula. Striking out across unknown ground defended

76

by an unknown number of Turks was asking too much of junior officers in their first operation. Nor was the command nimble or well informed enough to take advantage of the situation. Hunter-Weston and Hamilton were off shore on their command ships and in any case Hunter-Weston's every instinct was to throw more men to where the attack seemed to failing at V and W. So the flanking forces remained stationary except at Y, where attacks on some contingents had seen a drift back towards the beach that ended in a general evacuation from the peninsula. If salvation was going to come to those at V and W it would not come from the flanks.[52]

Eventually initiative on the part of some officers at W, the reinforcements landed at X and darkness, which allowed debouchment from the *River Clyde* to proceed, told on the Turks. Their strong defence of hillocks at Helles gradually slackened and sheer weight of numbers at last saw a toehold on the southerly peninsula secured by the 26th. The cost had been high – 3,800 men from 29 Division became casualties that day, about 20 per cent of their strength.

At Anzac, Australian and New Zealand forces, under Lieutenant-General William Birdwood, also established a toe-hold. Here there was much confusion about where the troops were to land. Many accounts maintain that they were landed in the wrong place and this ruined their entire operation. This is not the case. The fact was that General Birdwood's instructions for the landing were so vague as to give little guidance to the first waves. In the event, these men were landed almost exactly in the centre of the mile-long stretch of coast that he had designated (see map).[53] What caused confusion on the beaches was the fact that in the darkness (the landings took place before those at Helles) the tows bunched together, causing units to be landed on a very narrow front and much intermixed.[54] While these men were sorting themselves out, under fire from some 200 Turkish riflemen, the second waves landed on a much broader front.[55] Did this mean that the operation was in good shape? It did not. At this point the absurdly ambitious nature of the plan began to manifest itself. The troops had two main objectives: on the left they were required to occupy the high ground of the Sari Bair Range from Hill 971 in order to protect those troops advancing across the peninsula; on the right they were required to capture Gun Ridge to block Turkish reinforcements thought to be in the area. When these movements had been completed, the cross-peninsula march could begin. In fact the force did not have sufficient men to accomplish even one of these objectives. Groups of men, often from disparate units, struggled up the tortuous slopes of Sari Bair. Others proceeded towards Gun Ridge.[56] The country alone would have made these tasks formidable, but from around mid-morning Turkish reinforcements began to arrive on the battle-field in numbers. Mustapha Kemal (later Ataturk) led a contingent that drove the Anzac forces from Battleship Hill and Baby 700, while on the right a force commanded by Sami Bey stopped the men struggling across 400 Plateau towards Gun Ridge.[57] In these circumstances a force to cross the peninsula could not be formed. The Anzac forces which landed later were absorbed as soon as they landed in the fighting on the hills to the right and left. Indeed, so bewildering was the situation that Birdwood and some of his commanders seriously considered evacuating the force at nightfall.[58] The navy refused to countenance such a hazardous venture and cooler heads soon prevailed on land.[59] The Anzacs would remain but the plan to cut off Turkish reinforcements to the south lay in ruins.

The various commanders from Hamilton down were not dismayed by the lack of progress on the first day. After all, they were ashore and it was now a matter of arranging some concerted advances inland. Attention first turned to Helles. Hunter-Weston was anxious to be off. Perhaps he had observed that the Turks had as yet few trench defences on the peninsula and thereby lay the chance to avoid his predicted second Crimea. But his preparations were hasty; the fire support for the troops rudimentary, as few artillery pieces had yet been landed; in addition what guns he had available lacked ammunition; coordination among the units launching the attack broke down; there were no reserves and in any case the participating troops were exhausted by their efforts in establishing themselves ashore. The result, dignified by the name of the First Battle of Krithia, was a fiasco. As at Ypres a few months previously, machine-gun and artillery fire from the most hastily dug positions proved devastating to troops attacking in the open. By the end of the day (28 April) the troops were back at their start positions. The British had suffered 2,000 casualties and the French 1,000.[60]

Early in May the Turks tried their hand. They adopted the expedient of attacking at nightfall. It availed them nothing. The surprise of a night attack saw them penetrate the Allied line in a few places but British and French reserves were soon rushed forward and restored the situation. So confused did the night fighting become that in the end the Turks were not certain whether they were advancing or retreating. Another night attack a few days later met the same fate. The Turkish commander had certainly had enough. One more night attack, he announced, and he would resign.[61]

Hunter-Weston was not deterred by Turkish aggression. Despite the exhaustion of his own troops, he deemed the Turks to be at the end of their tether. It was a grand opportunity to launch another attack. On this occasion some fresh troops in the form of the British 42 Division were made available to him. Further, a composite brigade of Australian and New Zealand troops were sent down from Anzac to bolster his line. And he had more guns – seventy, an increase of fifty over those available in April.

The Second Battle of Krithia began on 6 May. The French infantry started late, thus missing any protection their guns could provide. They were shot down.[62] So were the British, hit by a nest of concealed machine guns, well short of the main Turkish line. Not a yard of ground was gained. The following day the orders listed the same objectives as for the 6th. The results were also the same. No ground gained at heavy cost. A prudent command might have at this stage called off the battle. But prudence was a virtue unknown to Hunter-Weston. He ordered the New Zealanders forward over the bare slopes of the Krithia Ridge. Their commanders were given the most rudimentary orders at the last minute. They were unsure about even the location of the Turkish line. Not surprisingly they failed. At this very moment, Hamilton, who had been following events from his office on the *Queen Elizabeth*, determined that the Turks were ripe for defeat. He ordered 'bayonets fixed' and an attack along the entire line. This ludicrous and ignorant order brought disaster to 2 Australian Brigade, who at the time it was issued were 1,000 yards behind the front. There was no time to explain such fine detail as the objectives or even the direction of the attack. The Australians lost 50 per cent of their infantry strength without really understanding what they were required to do. Thus ended the Second Battle of Krithia.

It would be tedious indeed to describe the third battle. A brigade of Indian troops was sent from Egypt as reinforcements for this unfortunate affair. They suffered appalling casualties from unsubdued Turkish machine guns and artillery in Gully Ravine on the left of the peninsula. In the centre, however, a brigade of 42 Division actually broke through and seemed on the brink of capturing the village of Krithia. Rapid reinforcement might have seen it fall. But Hunter-Weston was nothing if not consistent. He sent his reserves to reinforce failure on the flanks. That they did, by making the failure greater than it already was. Without further men to deploy, the battle fizzled out.[63]

The three battles of Krithia were unalloyed disasters, relieved not even by a single ray of common sense. But something did emerge from them. Hunter-Weston and the French commander, General Henri Gouraud, met to discuss future plans. They hit on the expedient of pooling their heavy guns and attacking only along a length of front that could be covered by them. Objectives would be limited. They had discovered a method that was called 'bite and hold' on the Western Front. Gaining ground was not the objective; killing Turkish soldiers was. Between 21 June and 13 July this method was tried. It worked. The ground captured was insignificant; the losses inflicted on the Turks, impressive.[64] Then Hunter-Weston was invalided home with heatstroke and Gouraud grievously wounded by a shell. No one in the high command seemed to notice what they were accomplishing. Further advances in the south were put on hold. Birdwood had produced what seemed to be a much more imaginative scheme for an attack in the north.

In one way this change to the northern battlefield made sense. The aim of the British in the south was to capture the heights of Achi Baba. Artillery would then be brought forward and the defences of the straits laid bare to the British guns. The flaw was that the forts at the straits could not be seen from Achi Baba because of the intervening (and heavily defended) Khilid Bahr Plateau. The capture of these heights would have represented only a tiny step forwards. Much hard slogging would have remained.

The north was not without its problems, however. The country was much more difficult than at the foot of the peninsula. The Sari Bair Ridge was dissected by numerous gullies and ravines, difficult enough to traverse in good weather without riflemen and machine-gunners trying to impede progress.

Birdwood had answers to these objections. He would attack at night but he would not attack the strong Turkish defences that hemmed in the Anzac perimeter. He would undertake a gigantic left hook around those positions with three columns of troops which would capture the dominating heights of Hill 971, Hill Q and Chunuk Bair. From these positions he would assault down the ridge, taking the Turkish defenders in flank and scattering them before him like chaff. There would then be no impediment to that advance across the peninsula thwarted on the first day.[65] With the peninsula isolated, the Turkish army facing the British at Helles would wither on the vine. The straits would be cleared. The fleet would proceed through to Constantinople. A Turkish surrender would follow.

Hamilton and the staff at GHQ accepted this plan with alacrity. At a stroke it would restore a war of movement, which had been one aim of the Gallipoli venture. But they insisted that such would be the number of troops required to carry it out that a base for supplies must be established. The troops would be landed to the north of the Anzac perimeter at Suvla Bay, an area of flat ground ideal for the accumulation of stores.[66]

The main problem for Hamilton and his plan was: would the many additional troops he required be provided? The War Council to which Hamilton's request was directed was defunct by the time it arrived. In May there had been an upheaval in British politics. The combination of the shortage of shells for the Western Front (see Chapter 5) and the final resignation of the increasingly erratic Fisher over the Gallipoli operation had forced Asquith to restructure the government. The Conservatives were brought into a coalition. One of their demands, which indicated their scepticism about the Gallipoli operation, was Churchill's removal from the Admiralty. Asquith retained for him a seat on the War Council, now renamed the Dardanelles Committee, but with the lowly position of the Chancellor of the Duchy of Lancaster. His influence over operations at the Dardanelles was at an end.

Despite the reservations of the Conservatives about the whole Gallipoli operation, the three divisions of troops requested by Hamilton were despatched without debate. They would arrive at Gallipoli at the end of July.[67] At the next meeting, when Churchill suggested that three might not prove sufficient, the committee decided to send two more.[68] Again there was no debate. Two additional divisions would be sent. Hamilton was to have five additional divisions – more troops than the number with which he had commenced in April. Despite the lack of progress, the new coalition government was determined to persist.

Birdwood's great assault began on the night of 6 August. A feint attack to the south at Lone Pine failed at high cost. Its doleful contribution was to propel Turkish forces towards the Anzac perimeter at a faster rate.[69] Meanwhile Birdwood's three assaulting columns assembled on the beaches and foothills within the perimeter and set off. The low foothills to the north were soon secured but then all columns became lost in the dark in the tortuous twists and turns of the ravines and nullahs. The most northerly column, led by Brigadier John Monash, became so disoriented that it eventually faced 180 degrees away from its true destination on Hill 971.[70] Consequently it played no further role in the operation. The two other columns also lost their way. But on 8 August a few New Zealand troops captured the summit of Chunuk Bair and on the 9th some Gurkhas from the Indian Brigade ascended the summit of Hill Q.[71] They did not remain on the heights for long. The New Zealanders were soon counter-attacked in overwhelming numbers and fell back to the lower slopes. On Hill Q the Gurkhas were hit either by the misdirected fire from a British ship or by their own artillery. In the confusion they too were driven from the heights.

Ever since, some authorities on the battle have claimed that the men on two important summits brought the operation to within an ace of success. This is not the case. There were no available reinforcements for these two groups and without them the Turks always had the numbers to drive them back. Even had they held on longer, this fate always awaited them. And such was the nature of the country that supplying even small forces with food and ammunition was a matter of extreme difficulty. This leads to a larger question. Had the entire ridge fallen to Birdwood's force, how would it have been supplied? The logistical problem was almost certainly insoluble. Even a success in capturing the ridge would have led, sooner rather than later, to a major retreat. As for sending a strong force across the peninsula, it first relied on the capture and holding of the ridge and then on there being enough additional troops to mount such an operation. None of these conditions applied in August 1915. The failure at Anzac was always destined to be comprehensive.

While these movements were taking place, the force to secure a base at Suvla Bay landed. Two divisions of Kitchener's New Army (10 and 11 Divisions) were landed under the command of Lieutenant-General Sir Frederick Stopford, chosen because of his seniority rather than for any innate military virtues. Against the odds, the operation succeeded in capturing enough ground for a base to be established. This was despite

Stopford's lack of control of events on the ground and the supine nature of his lower-order commanders. The troops, terribly mixed because of the confused nature of their landing, inched their way towards the Anafarta Ridge, a height thought to be essential to secure the base.[72] As it happened, Turkish reinforcements who had been rushed to the area forestalled them. Then it was found that the Turks did not have sufficient artillery to destroy the accumulation of stores that formed the base. Nor could they mount a sufficiently concerted counter-attack to drive back the British into the sea. The base remained intact until the end of the campaign.

Yet the overwhelming consensus is that Suvla was a resounding defeat. This strange attitude came about in this way. In his original orders for the attack, Hamilton gave Stopford the task of assisting the Anzac attack after he had established his base. On arrival on the peninsula Stopford protested that he had insufficient troops for this task.[73] The orders were then changed. Stopford was to confine himself to securing the base.[74] Historians, in general, have not noticed this change. They condemn Stopford for not moving with speed against the Turkish forces holding up the Anzac attack. Stopford was not a general ever to act with celerity, neither did he have the junior commanders to provide such impetus. Progress at Suvla was glacial. But it was never part of Stopford's remit to assist at Anzac, and a glance at a map reveals that because of the distances involved, the nature of the country and the perennial difficulty of bringing forward water, food and ammunition, such a task was beyond the capacity of any troops to accomplish, even with a first-class commander at their back. Turkish reserves, in close proximity to the battlefield, were always likely to forestall the attackers in reaching the high ground and once there deny further advances with machine guns and artillery.

The attempt to capture the Sari Bair Ridge was really the last hurrah of the Gallipoli campaign. The two additional divisions were landed and took part in a great deal of confused fighting around Hill 60 at the end of August. They were badly handled and suffered high casualties, but nothing of significance was at stake in these operations. There would be no more large attacks on the peninsula.

Back in London the Dardanelles Committee decided on a change of command. Hamilton was sacked and replaced in October with the dour General Sir Charles Monro from the Western Front.[75] After Monro surveyed the scene, he recommended evacuation, though he considered that this would cost 40 per cent of his force.[76] The politicians baulked. Kitchener was sent out, possibly to remove him from the war-making machinery, possibly to bring a seasoned eye to the war in the east. He confirmed Monro's decision.[77] Then the politicians received a plan from Commodore Roger Keyes, in charge of the lighter naval forces at the Dardanelles. He offered to rush the straits, using destroyers as minesweepers. A few in the Dardanelles Committee, led by Lord Curzon, waxed enthusiastic, insisting that the Keyes plan be given a chance.[78] But high naval authorities would have nothing to do with it. Indeed Keyes's plan was fatally flawed – there were never enough destroyers to sweep the large number of mines still in place. It was quietly abandoned.[79]

Evacuation was then the only policy. In December troops from Anzac and Suvla were lifted from the peninsula under cover of darkness. In January those at Helles left. Casualties, far from being 40 per cent of the entire force, were under 100. Whether the cunning plan to retreat by small groups at night devised by Colonel Brudenell White at Anzac and Lieutenant-General Francis Davies at Helles baffled the Turks or whether they realised that it was good policy to let the invaders go quietly has never been satisfactorily resolved. In any case the Gallipoli strategy was at an end.

The campaign had not been cheap. The British suffered over 70,000 casualties, the Australians and French about 25,000 each, New Zealand over 7,000 and the Indian Brigade 5,500, a total of 135,000 which included at least 46,000 dead. Turkish casualties were certainly higher than this figure but the object of the exercise had hardly been to replicate the attritional warfare of the Western Front.[80]

The civilian-inspired strategy at the Dardanelles had in fact been based on a series of fallacies. The first had been that old, worn-out battleships could somehow affect the war on land by knocking out a major belligerent. Any sober analysis by the Admiralty should have provided their political masters with information that should have stopped the operation before it started. The state of the ships' guns meant that few hits on the forts would be made, which in turn meant that ammunition in a quantity that the navy did not possess would be required, and the amount of wear on the old gun barrels that this amount of firing implied would mean that the ships would get less and less accurate as the operation progressed. The mines were never considered a major factor by the naval planners, yet, as we have seen, they were the key to the entire defensive system at the Dardanelles. In 1915 the Naval War Staff had just not gelled into the kind of organisation that could provide this level (or indeed any level) of expert advice.

The second fallacy was that somehow the Turkish army would not respond to the military landings with the utmost vigour. Yet these landings could have but one aim – to clear the way for the fleet to proceed to Constantinople. To a threat of this nature the Turkish command had every reason to throw their most experienced divisions into the fray. And these divisions were equipped with modern machine guns and at least a quantity of quick-firing artillery. The British military command took no heed of these factors. Perhaps they were counting on the Turks to surrender. But if the Turks did not surrender, their modern weaponry would enable them to replicate at least to some extent the trench warfare of the Western Front. The conditions of warfare in 1915 could transform the army of a second-class power into a first-class defensive force. This fact escaped British military planners entirely. It was therefore not surprising that it escaped the politicians as well.

The third fallacy was that if by some chance the operation succeeded and the fleet arrived at Constantinople, the Turkish government would surrender. There is no evidence to support this view. Trenches were being dug in Constantinople and contingencies were being made to continue the war from Anatolia.[81] In fact the British fleet, in those more civilised times, had strict instructions not to bombard Constantinople. Had the British reached the city and the Turks not surrendered, what would have happened? Could the fleet have been kept supplied or would it have been forced to sail back down the straits? No one asked these questions. In fact the sober Hankey produced a paper entitled 'After Constantinople: The Next Steps'. At this point it might be thought that delusion could proceed no further.

Yet it could. And this brings us to the final fallacy. Some on the British side (and we must include Churchill, Lloyd George and Grey among their number) considered that the appearance of an Allied force at Constantinople would galvanise the Balkan states to join the Entente, unite their armies into a force of over a million men and advance along the Danube, smiting the forces of the weaker of the Central Powers (Austria) and forcing Germany to withdraw such forces from the Western Front as would shorten the war. It is difficult to retain equanimity in the face of such arguments. Suffice it to say that the Balkan armies in question (those of Bulgaria, Romania, Greece and even Montenegro) were hardly equipped for modern, mobile warfare. Romania, for example, had just one shell factory, which produced two heavy shells per day. Moreover, it beggars belief that these states, who hated each other much more than they loved the Entente, would have buried their differences or even allowed their territory to be traversed by the armies of neighbouring states. Then there was the large matter of logistical support for an army of 1 million men in an area with few railways. Even had a leviathan of this kind got underway, how would it have dealt with such obstacles as the Julian Alps? Would their ox-drawn artillery have coped? The whole idea was fantastical and no doubt would never have come to pass.[82]

What was certain after Gallipoli was that civilian-directed strategy was for the moment at a discount. Military planning would in 1916 return to the military. Whether this would prove advantageous to Britain remained to be seen.

CHAPTER 5

1915 – LEARNING AND NOT LEARNING

THE GALLIPOLI EXPERIMENT WAS intended by the politicians to be an alternative strategy to what they increasingly regarded as the killing fields of the Western Front. Yet that front could hardly remain quiescent while the western Allies waited to see if operations in Gallipoli would be successful. After all, in the west the German armies occupied French and Belgian soil. The French alliance demanded that Britain play its part in driving them out. So while Gallipoli proceeded, most British divisions were still sent to the Western Front. By January the BEF had grown from the original four infantry and one cavalry divisions to twelve infantry and six cavalry divisions, organised into two armies – the First commanded by Sir Douglas Haig and the Second commanded by General Horace Smith-Dorrien.[1] Around the time that Gallipoli was evacuated, the BEF had grown further to twenty-eight divisions of infantry and still six divisions of cavalry with the addition of a Third Army commanded by Lieutenant-General Edmund Allenby. The force held a continuous front of 60 miles from Ypres to Lens and a 20-mile front astride the River Somme around Albert. The whole force now amounted to almost 1 million men.[2]

There was no doubt that this army would see action when the atrocious winter weather improved; the question was where and when? At this stage of the war, planning between the Allies was rather rudimentary. Various schemes for an Anglo-French offensive were canvassed but all came to nothing. Eventually it was decided by French and Joffre that they would go their own way. The British would launch a minor attack in March while the French would launch their offensive in Artois in May.

Haig was first off the mark with a plan for the British. He suggested to Sir John French that it might be useful to straighten the British line around the village of Neuve Chapelle.[3] This was a modest but useful proposal. The German line bulged into the British positions, which would allow the British to bring artillery fire to bear from three sides.[4] The approval of the politicians for this small affair was not sought or required – it was after all only a matter of straightening the line. The detail of the planning of this attack will be followed, however, because it had lessons that were to remain valid for the rest of the war.

In framing their plan the British commanders had at their disposal the lessons of the fighting in 1914. Two main factors stood out. The first was that the cavalry as a shock weapon was obsolete. Troops in the open could still be dealt a blow by horsed soldiers – if they possessed the element of surprise – but the appearance of trenches protected by barbed wire meant that such a scenario was less and less likely. The second was that the fire and movement tactics rehearsed by the infantry so often in pre-war manoeuvres and enshrined in *Field Service Regulations* were also obsolete. Groups of infantry attacking in the open, even in superior numbers, could not sufficiently protect each other from defenders lurking in modest trenches and armed with magazine rifles and machine guns and backed by artillery.

These were sobering lessons. The army's main weapon of exploitation (cavalry) was defunct. And a substantial infantry advance even across the stretch of ground between trench lines was a dubious proposition as countless attempts at the Aisne and Ypres had proved.

There was good initial evidence that Haig, the Army Commander, and Rawlinson, IV Corps commander at Neuve Chapelle, paid some attention to these unpalatable lessons. Their task, in the first instance, was to capture the German front line to remove the bulge. This line, though rudimentary by later standards, was an advance on anything seen at Ypres. It consisted of sand-bagged earthworks, 4 feet high and 5 feet in width. Protecting it was a double row of barbed wire, varying from 6 to 15 feet wide. In the village an attempt had been made to fortify some of the houses. Behind the front were a number of strongpoints, some of which contained machine guns.[5]

Haig and Rawlinson realised that to capture this line the wire in front of it would have to be cut and a sufficient proportion of the trench and its inhabitants destroyed to enable enough of their own troops to survive the perilous journey across no man's land to occupy it. The key to the process of destruction, they decided, was the artillery. Haig immediately called for calculations from his artillery experts to establish how many shells would be needed to capture a section of enemy trench.[6] Rawlinson analysed these figures and divided the artillery tasks into two. The lighter guns would cut the wire with shrapnel. The heavier guns would demolish the trench. The length of front to be attacked was determined largely by the number of trench-demolishing guns (6″ howitzers and above) that were available. The time required for the bombardment was calculated from carefully studied practice attacks on sections of trench. Taking these factors into account, Rawlinson arrived at a front of attack of 2,000 yards (800 yards for his own IV Corps and 1,200 yards for the Indian Corps which would attack along-side) and a bombardment time of forty-five minutes – ten minutes to cut the wire and then thirty-five minutes to demolish the German trenches.[7] Then the artillery would drop a curtain of fire to the east of Neuve Chapelle village to hamper the Germans from reinforcing their front positions. This was a remarkable achievement for such inexperienced commanders as Haig and Rawlinson. The artillery calculations were sophisticated and methodical. And the barrage (literally barrier) was an innovation in this type of attack.[8]

There were further innovations. By 7 March (the offensive was to begin on the 10th) the RFC, at Haig's behest, had photographed the German posi-tions to a depth of 700 to 1,500 yards. Between 1,000 and 1,500 maps had been assembled from these photographs to assist the infantry and the artil-lery.[9] Haig was lyrical, speaking of 'the wonderful maps of the enemy's trenches which we now had as a result of the aeroplane reconnaissances . . . enabling us to make our plans very carefully beforehand and with the full knowledge of how the enemy's trenches run, his communication trenches etc.'[10]

Rawlinson also turned his mind to the matter of communication. From his earlier experiences he had observed that staying in touch with troops when they went over the top was fraught with difficulty. So he ordered that all telephone cables to the infantry and the artillery be triplicated to provide some insurance against them being cut by hostile gun fire. He carefully collected the 340 guns to be employed without alerting the enemy to their presence and camouflaged the weapons and the ammunition. Registration of the guns on their targets, which took some days, was carried out as discreetly as possible with spotter planes equipped with radios for the long-distance pieces.[11]

So far all promised fair for this small enterprise. Then Haig's ambitions grew. Just a few days before the battle, he decided that Aubers Ridge, some 1,500 yards in rear of Neuve Chapelle, must also be captured. Rawlinson protested that this was going too far but Haig was determined:

> The idea was not to capture a trench here, or a trench there, but to carry the operation right through; in a sense to surprise the Germans, carry them right off their legs, push forward to the Aubers . . . ridge with as little delay as possible, and exploit the success thus gained by pushing forward mounted troops forthwith.[12]

This statement revealed that while Haig had learned something from the experiences of 1914, he still had some way to go. By introducing distant objectives he was attempting to push the infantry beyond the reach of the supporting artillery. And by foreshadowing the use of horsed soldiers he seemed to be forgetting that the cavalry charges in 1914 against unsubdued defences, especially if they contained machine guns, had proved a recipe for disaster. Haig was certainly aware that there were a number of strongpoints behind the front at Neuve Chapelle and from the aerial photographs that they did indeed contain machine guns. Probably he was relying on the artillery to subdue them, but they offered very small targets for guns firing at long range. Rawlinson was also aware of this problem and in the days that followed did all he could to limit the attack. Haig would have none of it. The more ambitious scheme would stand.[13]

The day of battle dawned fair but cold. Three brigades, two from 8 Division and one from the Meerut Division of the Indian Corps would lead the attack. At 7.30 a.m. the bombardment started. At that moment the first of the 12,000 assault troops climbed the specially placed ladders and moved forward over what was already being called 'no man's land'.

On the right the Garhwal Brigade had some early success. The enemy trenches were flattened by the artillery and the Indian troops proceeded to occupy the ruins of Neuve Chapelle. The Dehra Dun Brigade followed them and advanced to the edge of a large wood, well beyond the main German defences. Then two things happened: machine-gunners from the vicinity of the wood opened fire on them and the 25 Brigade from the 8 Division did not appear on their left. They fell back, though not far and still occupied a small brook just beyond the ruined village.[14]

The 25 Brigade were in fact just in rear of the Indian troops but obscured by smoke and dust. They too had carried their chief objectives and were occupying what was left of the main street of Neuve Chapelle. The real hold-up had occurred in the area of 23 Brigade. There the men had found the wire uncut and the trenches un-bombarded.[15] The howitzer batteries designated for this part of the front had arrived in the line too late to be properly registered.[16] In the event, the Middlesex Battalion from 23 Brigade eventually cut the wire by hand and subdued the German defenders. The whole of the original objective was in the hands of IV Corps.[17]

The plan now was for two brigades from 7 Division (21 and 24) to pass through 8 Division and on to Aubers Ridge. But, despite Rawlinson's best efforts, most communications between his headquarters and subordinate units were now cut. By the time runners conveyed the orders personally it was late in the day. Some battalions did receive the orders and attempted to attack but they were not supported by the artillery, which was not certain of their exact location or by their fellow infantrymen to right and left. Some ground was gained but the strongpoints which were still holding up the Garhwal Brigade took a heavy toll on the units of 7 Division. The first day at Neuve Chapelle was over.

If the affair had ended there the British could have claimed a modest success. After all, the original objectives as set out by Rawlinson had been captured. But the imperative was now to press on to Aubers Ridge. And on this occasion the artillery had insufficient time to register on their new targets. And because of a shortage of ammunition, the bombardment would last just fifteen minutes. In addition the Germans had not been idle. At the fall of Neuve Chapelle they had rushed thirteen companies of troops towards the village, so on the morning of 11 March the British were confronting twice as many enemy troops as they had on the previous day.[18] Their resulting attack was a fiasco. The first wave could hardly leave its trenches because of the severity of enemy fire, the artillery having missed all their targets.[19] A second attack, insisted upon by Rawlinson in the afternoon, got no further but with heavier casualties.[20] Haig's conclusion was that 'the troops had done nothing'.[21] In fact they had died in considerable numbers because of the stubbornness of the command to push on whatever the circumstances.

Day three at Neuve Chapelle was a dismal affair for both sides. In the morning the Germans counter-attacked the well-dug-in British line. Ten thousand Germans went over the top, following a bombardment that had also missed all its targets. The results were disastrous. German dead lay in rows in front of the British trenches.[22]

But the British were not to be outdone. They launched no fewer than three attacks themselves that day. All failed. At one point Haig telegraphed to his corps commanders, 'The 4th and Indian Corps will push through the barrage regardless of loss.'[23] This order was to include some of the hapless cavalry which had been brought forward for the great attack. Luckily for the cavalry, all roads leading to the front were blocked by the infantry. Some foot soldiers did attack. Most were shot down.[24] Others were held back by cooler heads at the divisional and brigade level. Even as darkness fell, Rawlinson contemplated night operations. Only poor communication, the exhaustion of troops and in one case a refusal by a brigadier to obey such orders prevented further useless slaughter.[25]

The cost of Neuve Chapelle was considerable. Total British casualties were 11,652. Only the German policy of recapturing lost ground kept the balance sheet reasonably even – they lost about 10,000 casualties.[26] For the British the lessons were obvious. If defences were accurately registered by the artillery and the objectives strictly limited, some progress was possible. If objectives were extended beyond the range that the guns could cover, troops without automatic weapons could not hope to get forward against those who possessed them. The initial battle was well planned but Haig's desire to win further territory had cost his troops dearly. Nevertheless, this was a first attempt. There was much to be absorbed.

Rawlinson seemed to be learning these lessons. He told Kitchener that it had been a mistake 'to go on hammering at the enemy's defences' through the last three days of the battle. The army should have been content with the capture of the village.[27] And he went on to explain to the King's Private Secretary in greater detail the kind of operation he had in mind:

> What we want to do now is what I call 'bite and hold'. Bite off a piece of the enemy's line, like Neuve Chapelle, and hold it against counter-attack. The bite can be made without much loss, and, if we choose the right place & make every preparation to put it quickly in a state of defence there ought to be no difficulty in holding it . . . and inflicting on him at least twice the loss that we have suffered in making the bite.[28]

No wiser words were written in the course of the war on the tactical problem facing the British.

There would soon be an opportunity to put these new methods to the test. After Neuve Chapelle Joffre had revealed to Sir John French his plan to capture the Vimy Ridge and then advance across the plain of Douai, forcing the German line back some 12 to 15 miles.[29] In the north he required assistance from the BEF to widen the breach in the German line and to prevent reinforcements from being despatched south against his main advance.[30] Sir John French immediately offered ten divisions of infantry and five of cavalry for the new enterprise.[31]

The ensuing Battle of Aubers Ridge (9 to 10 May) was a disaster. The German defences in this area were considerably stronger than those at Neuve Chapelle – three or four trench lines instead of one, and considerably more strongpoints behind those lines.[32] And the British had fewer heavy guns to deal with these stronger defences than they had deployed at Neuve Chapelle.[33] It might be thought that all this would be revealed to Haig and Rawlinson when they carried out a set of detailed artillery calculations for this battle similar to those done before Neuve Chapelle. But for reasons that are not clear, no artillery calculations at all were undertaken. They seemed merely to assume that the guns they had would prove sufficient. Their new plan was therefore based on hope rather than calculation. In the event, though, it had no hope. The rather feeble bombardment (one-fifth of the intensity of Neuve Chapelle) hardly touched the strong German defences. As a result, when the men left their trenches they were shot down in large numbers.[34] Then on the second day of battle it was discovered that there was insufficient ammunition even for the guns they did have. The battle was promptly called off. Not a yard of ground had been gained at a cost of 11,000 men. Rawlinson, who should have noted the error in the plan, instead blamed the men. They had got cold feet, he said.[35] It might have been pointed out that in the case of the 11,000 dead, the cold extended well beyond their feet. Not for the last time the high command failed to identify their own plan as the source of failure.

Their next chance not to learn came soon enough. Joffre, whose large plan had also failed, insisted on trying again and insisted that once more the British play a part. The Battle of Festubert (15–16 May) was the result. Some learning was evident. The British, on one part of the line, tried a night attack without a bombardment. The Germans were caught by surprise and two lines of enemy trenches fell.[36] But once again no detailed artillery planning had been carried out and Haig and Rawlinson's forces ran into German strongpoints that had not been touched by the artillery – or in some cases even identified as targets. Slaughter resulted. The initial gains were retained but at a cost of 16,000 casualties.[37] And no enemy troops had been diverted from Joffre's force, which had suffered another reverse.

The First Army's three efforts to the south of Ypres had cost just short of 40,000 casualties for derisory gains, none of which provided any useful help to their allies. What were the authorities in London making of all this? The answer was, in terms of controlling the military events at the front, virtually nothing. It was clear that the War Council considered that military operations on the Western Front were a matter for negotiation between Sir John French and Joffre. It did not help that their chief military adviser on that body was a cipher. General Sir James Wolfe Murray has not proved a name to conjure with in British military history. Yet at this moment he found himself Chief of the Imperial General Staff (CIGS). He had had a distinguished military career, serving in prominent positions in India and South Africa. But he found himself in his present position only because the previous incumbent (General Sir Charles Douglas) had died suddenly in October 1914 and it then was discovered that all other likely candidates – Archibald Murray, Henry Wilson, William Robertson and French and Haig – had decamped to France. As an artilleryman Wolfe Murray (inevitably called Sheep Murray by Churchill) might be thought to offer some insights as it gradually became clear that artillery was proving to be a major factor in Western Front fighting. But Wolfe Murray remained silent on this issue and indeed on most other issues that were brought before the War Council. Apparently he saw it as his task to provide advice only when asked. But the fact was that no one on the War Council asked his advice. Anyway, present on that body was Kitchener, a soldier acting as a civilian and in addition a hero and a legend and well capable of silencing a much stronger character than Wolfe Murray.

It was not surprising then that when events on the Western Front did not develop as promised the ire of some on the War Council (particularly Lloyd George) was directed at Kitchener rather than Wolfe Murray. And in this they were aided and abetted by none other than Sir John French, still smarting from Kitchener's intervention during the Battle of the Marne and increasingly worried that Kitchener had him in his sights for the sack. So when the 'shells scandal' broke after Aubers Ridge, French leaked to the military correspondent from *The Times*, Charles Repington, that it was mishandling by the Minister of War (Kitchener) which had brought this sorry pass about. *The Times*' story caused a sensation in London and that, coupled with Fisher's sudden resignation from the Admiralty over disagreements with Churchill about Gallipoli, forced Asquith to reconstitute his government by bringing in the Conservatives under Bonar Law. The big winner was Lloyd George, who was given a new post as Minister of Munitions; the big loser Kitchener, who had munitions production removed from the War Office.[38] The politicians found that if they did not pay attention to matters at the front those matters had a way of attracting their attention anyway.

Even before the formation of the coalition government, however, the British army found itself involved in a new crisis, this time not of their own making. The Germans had been closely following developments on the Western Front and concluded that they had not the required firepower to break through the increasingly sophisticated trench defences. What they thought was required was a new weapon altogether and they thought they had hit upon it in the form of poisonous gas.

The German army had been experimenting with various gases since shortly after the outbreak of war. They had used a form of tear gas against the French in October 1914 but conditions were so unfavourable that the French seem not to have noticed. Similar experiments on the Eastern Front in January 1915 failed because the weather was so cold that the gas failed to vaporise. In December 1914, however, Fritz Haber, an army officer but also a research chemist at the Kaiser Wilhelm Institute in Berlin, suggested using chlorine. This gas was poisonous and also heavier than air. It would settle in trenches and force defenders out into the open where they would become easy targets for artillery and machine guns. The idea was put to Falkenhayn, who agreed. The use of such gases had of course been made illegal by the Hague Convention of 1898, but that convention was brushed aside by the Germans, the major factor for them not being illegality but the calculation that such was the primitive state of the British chemical industry that early retaliation was not to be expected. The proposition was then put to the five German army commanders on the Western Front. Four refused to countenance the move but Duke Albrecht of Württemberg, who commanded the German Fourth Army around the Ypres Salient agreed.[39] In some ways the salient was a less than ideal testing ground. On most days the wind blew west to east in this area, and in the very north of the salient there were only eighty-six days of the year when it blew north to south – that is, towards the city of Ypres. Yet Falkenhayn was impatient. He was to launch his major offensive in the east in the spring and he was anxious to attempt the gas experiment before large troop movements took reserves away from the west. All this accounts for the fact that the German troops who were to release the gas were only given the simplest protection (gauze masks taped over the nose) and that only one large-scale test was tried, on 2 April, before the chlorine was used operationally.[40]

The day of battle depended on a favourable wind, the vagaries of which led it to be postponed from 14 April to the 19th, to the 21st and finally from the early morning of the 22nd to the late afternoon. On that day at 5 p.m. some 149,000 litres of chlorine gas from 6,000 cylinders was released on a 7,000-metre front over a period of ten minutes. It struck the French Algerian and Territorial divisions in the northern section of the salient. The cloud advanced at 0.5 metres per second, starting as white in colour and turning yellow-green as the volume increased.[41]

Its effect was immediate. A French colonel reported: 'Everywhere were fugitives ... without weapons, haggard, greatcoats thrown away or wide open, running around like madmen, begging for water in loud cries, spitting blood, some even rolling on the ground making desperate efforts to breathe.'[42]

The front collapsed as the troops streamed back to attempt to escape the gas. Five batteries of guns were immediately lost to the German troops following close behind the cloud. By the end of the day fifty-one guns had been captured, which rendered Allied artillery bombardments ineffective for some days to come. From Poelcapelle in the east to the Yser Canal to the west the front sagged back. The entire northern section of the salient had been scalped. Ypres probably lay open, but, as night fell, the Germans commenced digging in. There were no follow-up troops to take advantage of the great hole ripped in the Allied line. This has puzzled many observers since. Yet there is no puzzle. The gas attack was an experiment. No one on the German side was certain of the outcome. Moreover, the reserves which might have converted the attack into something larger might also have given away that an attack was in preparation. If as a result of this the Allies had shelled the German positions and hit the gas cylinders, the German troops would have been gassed instead of their opponents. When using a new weapon in haste there was room for caution.

To the immediate right of the gas attack stood the Canadian Division. They attempted to re-establish the Allied line but were beaten back by the Germans dug in on low ridges. Other attacks by British reserve units followed the next day and the day after that. All were hastily arranged. None had sufficient artillery support. All failed with heavy loss.[43]

On 24 April a new gas attack was directed against the Canadians. They fell back. Events then followed a familiar pattern. Counter-attacks of a shambolic type went in. They all failed. Casualties mounted.

After these episodes Sir John consulted his army commanders. Smith-Dorrien put before him a cogent case for withdrawing the salient back to the so-called GHQ Line, which would save men, deprive the Germans of the utility of any gas cylinders installed in their own front line and eliminate the need for the costly counter-attack policy.[44] It was never likely that Sir John would listen to Smith-Dorrien – their relationship had not improved since he had 'disobeyed' Sir John's order at Le Cateau and saved the day by so doing. On 30 April, however, Haig also advocated withdrawal to straighten the line. If the French would not attack 'it was the C-in-C's duty to remove his men from what was really a "death trap" '.[45]

In the end Sir John bowed to the wishes of Smith-Dorrien and Haig. But it would not be Smith-Dorrien who would oversee the withdrawal. Late on

27 April, Sir John French effectively sacked the Second Army Commander towards whom he bore a grudge which went back to the Battle of Le Cateau where Smith-Dorrien had (rightly) ignored Sir John's strictures to continue the retreat. Smith-Dorrien therefore handed over the troops in the salient to General Sir Hubert Plumer. The withdrawal to the GHQ Line was gradually undertaken. In this period the Germans launched four more gas attacks, three of them in the area of Hill 60 in the southern section of the salient. The last attack took place around Bellewaarde Lake on 24 May. There the fighting was most intense, with the Germans accompanying the release of the last of their gas with a ferocious artillery bombardment. In yet more futile counter-attacks three brigades of troops, largely from the 27 and 28 Divisions were wiped out. Finally, it was the ammunition situation on both sides which caused the fighting to die down. By 25 May the British were left with virtually only shrapnel shell available. At the same time the Germans were having to turn their attention to the large French offensive in Artois. In any case most of their reserve divisions had now left for the Eastern Front and those in the line were exhausted.

The Second Battle of Ypres had cost the BEF dear – almost 60,000 casualties or a quarter of its entire strength. By contrast, the Germans – who had after all, launched no fewer than six attacks – probably suffered only 35,000 casualties. The disparity in numbers, it needs to be emphasised, came not from the unleashing of poisonous gas which probably accounted for just 3,000 casualties, but from the uncoordinated, poorly thought-out, narrow-front counter-attacks launched by the British to re-establish a salient that had become untenable after the first day. No commander on the Allied side exercised any grip over this dismal affair. Not even the appointment of Plumer stopped the incessant counter-attack policy but he did preside over a movement to smooth out the salient, which by then all were agreed was necessary.

The melancholy fact was that after four battles on the Western Front the BEF had suffered over 100,000 casualties and lost more ground around Ypres than it had gained around Neuve Chapelle. There was also no question that the British had inflicted fewer casualties on the Germans than they had suffered. All this pointed to a period of defence until more artillery, machine guns and troops could be trained and made ready for an offensive in the spring of 1916. For the British there was an additional reason to remain quiescent on the Western Front – they had not yet given up on Gallipoli and were in the process of making a decision about whether to reinforce the troops on the Peninsula.

By early July John French was extremely pessimistic about the prospects of an offensive, All the BEF could do for the moment, he considered, was take over more of the French line, thus freeing their ally's troops for an autumn offensive.[46] Kitchener would not even go that far. Two days later he told the War Council that although the French wished to launch an autumn offensive, he was determined to talk them out of it – the Western Front should remain quiescent for the remainder of the year.[47] An Anglo-French meeting to discuss strategy for the summer was convened in Calais on 6 July, and at a meeting of French and British staff officers at Chantilly the next day Kitchener thought he had made his point. Certainly many on the British side thought that the meetings had decided that there would be 'no great offensive' on the Western Front that year.[48] But Joffre was playing his cards close to his chest. On the French side, though no definite decision for an offensive had been made, planning would continue for just such an operation.

The location which Joffre had in mind for the British part of his offensive was the area around Lens where the British and French lines intersected. After examining it, Haig noted that the area was 'covered with coal pits and houses', quite unsuitable for military operations.[49] Rawlinson agreed.[50] Joffre's main offensive was to be made in Champagne but his Tenth Army would attempt a converging attack to the south of Loos and he required the British to extend this attack to the north by capturing the village of Loos and points north.[51] In an attempt to stave off a large attack, Sir John French deprecated the entire scheme, offering instead an 'artillery plan' whereby all the guns at his disposal would support the French but no infantry would go over the top.[52] Joffre rejected this at once. He wanted 'a large and powerful' attack 'composed of the maximum force you have available'.[53]

Enter Kitchener. The Minister of War had opposed Joffre's plan earlier in the year and since then he had been told by Lloyd George that there would be insufficient ammunition to support it.[54] He was now also aware that the commanders on the spot were against it. Yet he now agreed to it. What seemed uppermost in his mind was the situation of the Russians.

They had reeled back under an enormous German offensive at Gorlice-Tarnow in May. By 4 August Warsaw had been lost. Kitchener thought the Western Powers must attack to relieve the pressure. He told Haig, 'we must attack with all our energy . . . even though by so doing, we suffered very heavy losses indeed'.[55]

Kitchener laid this extraordinary policy before the Dardanelles Committee on 20 August. Churchill vigorously protested. He pointed out that the Germans had strengthened their defences since the last offensive. All that we would achieve, he said, was the loss of 200,000 or 300,000 lives for no advantage. Kitchener admitted that there was a great deal of truth in what Churchill said but he was not moved. 'Unfortunately', he said, 'we had to make war as we must, and not as we should like to.'[56] The Committee capitulated. The great offensive would go ahead.

Yet that did not mean that the Battle of Loos as eventually fought was set in stone. Indeed many plans were discussed before settling on the final design. Initially Rawlinson proposed capturing Loos village and Hill 70 which dominated it in a cautious step-by-step battle lasting several days.[57] This was soon swept aside as not conforming to Joffre's 'large and powerful' attack. Then a combined effort by I Corps (Lieutenant-General Hubert Gough) and IV Corps (Rawlinson) was suggested. Four divisions would be in the line and two in reserve. But there would be a gap between the corps of some 3,000 yards. This reminded the corps commanders of the disastrous enfilade fire at Aubers and Festubert that had been poured into the assault troops from an un-attacked section of the line. The two reserve divisions (1 Division in IV Corps and 7 Division in I Corps) were then incorporated into the attack, which would now be carried out by six divisions. But this arrangement left no reserve at all. This was solved by impressing a new corps then being formed (XI) to act a reserve. This force consisted of 21 and 24 Divisions, which had no experience in the line, and the Guards Division to add experience. But in a peculiar arrangement, this force would not be under the direct orders of Haig, who would conduct the battle, but Sir John French, who would be many miles distant from the front at GHQ.[58]

The British attack had now grown from a two-division affair, favoured by Rawlinson, into a six-division attack with three divisions in reserve. As a consequence the front of attack had increased from 2,000 yards to 7,500 yards. Even that is not the entire picture. Behind their front, the Germans had dug a strong second line running from La Bassée in the north to Lens village in the south. Moreover they had dug an additional 2,000 yards of trench to protect Loos village and between these lines had constructed about 20,000 yards of communication trenches. The British therefore had at least 17,000 yards of trench to bombard and probably a total of well over 20,000 because machine-gun strongpoints could as easily be placed in communication trenches as in the first or second line.[59]

Did the British have the firepower to deal with these defences? The short answer is no. Measuring artillery resources by the successful Neuve Chapelle standard, the artillery available at Loos was only one third as strong.[60] Yet the situation was actually worse than revealed by these figures. At Loos, because of the lack of cover, wire cutting would have to take place at a much greater range than at Neuve Chapelle, with a consequent reduction in accuracy.[61] Moreover, the German second line, which was also wired, was out of range of most of the wire-cutting guns and situated on a reverse slope so that any damage done by heavier guns was difficult to observe.[62]

There was yet another artillery problem. The bombardment was to be fired over four days but to maximise efficiency – which the shortage of ammunition demanded – it would be only fired each day during the twelve hours of daylight. This gave the Germans at least some chance to repair the wire at night, when they would face only sporadic British harassing fire.

The British command were well aware of these problems and in particular the paucity of heavy guns. They had therefore taken the decision to complement the artillery bombardment with that of (for them) a new weapon – poison gas. As Haig explained to his corps commanders, the gas would cause a panic in the German ranks and this would enable the British to overrun the second German line before they recovered.[63] No one apparently thought to inform Haig that many German troops opposite the British at Loos had respirators, a fact that was well known to the lower-order commanders.

Of course in one way poison gas, however lethal against troops, was no substitute for artillery. All German trench lines at Loos had considerable wire defences which no gas, poison or otherwise, could hope to cut.

There was another problem with gas. The French attack, and therefore the British, had to be set days in advance – the attack had to commence the moment the last of the bombardments ceased. That is, at zero hour an obliging wind had to be gently blowing towards the German lines. But no weather forecast could anticipate this with any accuracy. In this sense the British attack was dependent on an element over which the command had no control.

Another aspect of the planning process was reminiscent of that at Neuve Chapelle. Haig kept extending the objectives. Rawlinson's original idea to capture Loos village and Hill 70 only had been discarded. The main objective was now the Haute Deûle Canal, at least 2 miles further east. Then on 6 September Haig urged his corps commanders to push on well beyond that objective to the plain of Douai, which would convert a tactical victory into something larger. To this end the Cavalry Corps was concentrated for the breakthrough.[64] In this way Rawlinson's limited objective 'bite and hold' operation was converted by Haig into something much more grandiose.

But as the planning progressed, there emerged a powerful reason to proceed with caution. Falkenhayn's prediction that the British would struggle to retaliate with poison gas was wrong but not altogether misplaced. British industry did find it difficult to produce a sufficient amount of chlorine quickly. What was required in the plan was an amount of gas that could be discharged along the front of attack for longer than thirty minutes – a length of time that would overwhelm the primitive respirators worn by some German troops. But the extension of the front and the slow response from the factories meant that only twenty-four minutes of gas would be available for release. A partial solution to this problem was thought to be to supplement the gas with smoke. The plan adopted was that gas would be released for twelve minutes, followed by eight minutes of smoke, another twelve minutes of gas and a final eight minutes of smoke. It was hoped that the defenders would not risk removing their masks during this entire period. Yet the flaw in the plan was that the neutralising chemicals in the German respirators would not be exhausted by twenty-four minutes of gas. The troops in the trenches and dug-outs would therefore not succumb to gas poisoning, though the smoke might help conceal the advance of the attacking infantry from them.[65]

On the night of 18 September the difficult process of transporting 5,000 gas cylinders to the front began. It took three men to carry each cylinder, but by the 21st the gas was in place.[66] As Army Commander, Haig was required to make the decision to release the gas. On the day before battle, conditions seemed favourable and the troops were ordered into their attack positions. Then on the morning of the 25th it was obvious that the wind had dropped. The latest data indicated that it might increase later. It was now 3 a.m. Zero hour was imminent. Haig gave the order. The attack would go over the top at 6.30 a.m.[67] Despite this agonising, Haig had in fact extremely limited parameters. The preliminary bombardment (both British and French) had been underway for four days. The French were not using gas and would attack, come what may. They were expecting their left flank to be protected by the British. Haig's options were to leave his ally in the lurch or not. In these circumstances there was virtually no choice.

In the area of I Corps in the north the consequences of this decision ranged from disastrous to indecisive. The 2 Division found that the fluky wind blew the gas back on their own troops, in some areas before they had left their own trenches.[68] Then they discovered that the bombardment had missed the wire and the troops were shot down by machine guns which the artillery had failed to supress. By 9.40 the survivors were back in their own trenches.[69]

Further south, due to an accurate bombardment of a strong German position by two of the corps' heaviest guns (9.2" howitzers), progress was made. The first German line was captured and the troops moved on the second position. But elsewhere men ran into their own gas and the bombardment had not been comprehensive or accurate enough to deal with the many German positions in slag heaps and the numerous miners' cottages. Here too the wire had not been cut. When Gough was informed of this check, he immediately ordered a re-bombardment and a further attack. The result was a disaster. The infantry were only vaguely aware of what was required of them; the bombardment missed its targets and the result has been well described as 'a tragic example of how *not* to conduct an attack on fortified trenches manned by an alert, determined defence'.[70] One battalion lost 85 per cent of its officers and 70 per cent of its men in the first three minutes of this futile endeavour.[71] In short order the brigade of 9 Division which made the attack was reduced to a shambles, back in their own lines, incapable of further effort.

The 7 Division, on the right of the I Corps attack, carried the first German line but as with most divisions that day found the second line strongly held with the wire intact. They halted before the village of Hulluch but were saved from the fate of 9 Division by the sensible decision of their divisional commander, General Capper, to dig in where they were and await the new day.[72]

In IV Corps area the real action took place on the right where 47 and 15 Divisions were attacking. (On the left, wire and gas had held up 1 Division.[73]) The 47 Division was required to establish a defensive flank on the very southern portion of the British front between two large slag heaps. To achieve this feat they had to capture two German defensive lines and advance through a valley vulnerable to flanking fire from Loos village to the north and from Lens to the south. Yet by midday all objectives were in their hands for less than 1,000 casualties.[74] In this sector the artillery had 'completely' cut the wire and the speed of the advance of the Territorial soldiers was so rapid that many German defenders were caught in their dug-outs and the enemy reserves could not arrive in time to assist.[75] The gas cloud had moved at appropriate speed but had caused few casualties (just five, by one estimate) but the smoke had concealed the troops from German machine-gunners in Loos and Lens.[76] Indeed the villages were still blanketed in smoke at 1.30 p.m. when the troops dug themselves in.[77]

To the north of 47 Division, 15 Division had the greatest success of the day. They too had a series of difficult objectives. They had to capture the German front line, an additional line protecting Loos village, fight their way up Hill 70 which dominated the village, force the German second line and push on past it to the high ground 3 miles beyond. All did not go the way of the Scottish soldiers, one of the first Kitchener Divisions to see action. Some were gassed by wind changes; others ran into enfilade machine-gun fire because of the failed attack by 1 Division to their north. Yet, as for 47 Division, the gas and smoke had given a measure of cover to the 15th; the wire had been well cut, and many German defenders had been caught in their dug-outs. Loos village fell at 7 a.m., just thirty minutes after zero and by 8 a.m. columns of troops were streaming up Hill 70.[78] By 9.30 a.m. Hill 70 had fallen, but all attempts to advance beyond that point came to nothing. Communication with the rear had been lost, so no new artillery bombardment could be ordered.[79] Once again the thick wire in front of the German second line was intact. There was nothing to be done but to dig in on the forward slope of the hill and await reinforcements.

Unfortunately for 15 Division, German reinforcements arrived first. Four battalions of the enemy forced the British back.[80] They lost the summit of the hill but the reserve brigade stabilised the situation. The fact remained, however, that – although no one knew it – the British advance at the Battle of Loos had reached its limit.

There is no warrant to think that the 1,500 troops who swept over Hill 70 brought the British to within a reasonable distance of success at Loos. The Germans had mustered around 800 defenders, the trenches were intact and so were the thick belts of wire protecting them. The gas and smoke soon dispersed and the enemy was amply supplied with machine guns with clear fields of fire. And IV Corps had no more reserves.

Plans now had to be made for the continuation of the battle on 26 September. Of all the planning sessions held so far by the command during the war, this was the nadir. The battered, reduced, remnants of I and IV Corps were ordered to capture those positions which had not fallen on the 25th: the German second line from the north of Hulluch to beyond Loos. In addition the 21 and 24 Divisions would push beyond to the Haute Deûle Canal and points east. This plan plumbed the depths of almost criminal irresponsibility. It should have been obvious, even to a relatively inexperienced command, that the Germans would rush forward reserves to hold their second line – after all, this is what they had done in every other battle so far fought by the British on the Western Front. And Loos was to prove no exception. During the night of the 25th they brought up two additional divisions which meant that the second line was now more strongly held than their original line had been on 25 September.[81] This line was now to be attacked by exhausted or green troops without the benefit of an accurate artillery bombardment which would in any case only last one hour due to ammunition shortages. There would also be no gas or smoke, all supplies having been expended.

The result was a predictable disaster. Much debate on this operation has hinged around the placing of the reserve divisions which attacked late in the day after it was obvious that the original attack had failed. Were these men held too far back? Was Haig or Sir John French largely responsible for this? In fact this debate entirely misses the point. The reserves should not have been used at all. By then, having beaten back an attack by the exhausted troops that had made the first attack, the defenders were thoroughly alert, well equipped with machine guns and artillery of their own, untroubled by an inaccurate and brief barrage and well able to fight off troops of any description whenever they attacked. The inexperience of the reserve divisions, advancing in thick masses across the open made the carnage worse but it did not affect the result of the battle. So devastating was the result that the war diaries were hard put to explain what had happened. The diarist of 21 Division commented:

> About 10.45 a.m. some of the troops . . . began to retire, and their retirement was followed by that of most of the other attacking troops . . . The cause of this retirement is not clear and there was no appreciable German advance. Most of the troops were rallied just east of Loos.[82]

There indeed had been 'no appreciable German advance'. Without leaving the safety of their trenches the defenders had inflicted 8,200 casualties in just over an hour. The troops fled to the rear and were 'rallied' by the Guards Division rushed forward to stem the rout.[83] The divisions were withdrawn from the line and had to be reconstituted.

The misuse of the reserves at Loos had wide repercussions. Rawlinson was quick to tell anyone in authority who would listen that the fault in holding them too far back lay with Sir John French.[84] So did Haig.[85] It had an effect. In London no politician had sufficient military knowledge to question the whole basis of the operation on the 26th – to which Haig and Rawlinson had raised no dissenting voice. It was probably the last straw for Sir John, in any case. He had lost a battle too many after raising expectations too high. In December Asquith sacked him.[86] The new commander of the BEF would be Sir Douglas Haig. Wolfe Murray was also replaced – by another Murray (Archibald) who would prove just as incapable of standing up to Kitchener. His tenure would not be long; he was replaced by Sir William Robertson in December 1915.

The casualty figures for 1915 on the Western Front were of themselves a reason to change the command. For no useful gain of ground the BEF had suffered about 80,000 killed and 225,000 wounded. In addition there were 577,000 sick or injured. This represented a battle casualty rate of about 30 per cent and a total casualty rate of 130 per cent of the total strength of the force.[87]

Why had the results been so barren, especially after an excellent beginning on the first day of Neuve Chapelle? The answer was that the conception of battle outlined by Rawlinson of biting off a section of the German line and then holding it against counter-attack had not been grasped – not even fully by Rawlinson. Instead, an earlier conception of battle was attempted where a period of tough pounding followed by sweeping breakthroughs capturing an immense amount of ground forced the enemy out of their fixed defences, causing a rout. In 1915 there were at least three major problems with this scenario. First, it tended to spread available artillery fire too thinly. Secondly, it was predicated on there being a weapon of exploitation that could sweep through the rear enemy defences. In 1915 there was no such instrument. The cavalry, as the experience of 1914 had shown, was a broken reed, unable to withstand rapid infantry and machine-gun fire. Moreover, the appearance of great belts of barbed wire and more sophisticated trench systems in 1915 made mass cavalry charges quite impracticable. Without this weapon of exploitation, if trench defences, magazine rifles, machine guns and artillery had exponentially increased the power of the defence, strategy in terms of large movements of armies across great swathes of ground was a dead letter. The problem was tactical. How were the enemy to be blasted from one position to another until either they lost the will to carry on or lost so many soldiers that they had no means of carrying on? Rawlinson had put a tentative finger on this problem at Neuve Chapelle but showed little fixity of purpose in pursuing it. Haig had also started with a concept of artillery concentration but soon abandoned it in favour of an outdated Napoleonic view of warfare. Sir John French certainly never grasped the issue at all. Neither did Joffre or any of the French command.

Neither, of course, did the political leadership in Britain. The realities of the Western Front, which some such as Churchill had grasped, led them to believe that British strategy was misguided but that the solution lay in attacking somewhere else – that the way to victory lay through various corners of increasingly obscure foreign fields accompanied by increasingly dubious allies. This is not a matter of great surprise or even of criticism. If soldiers at the front had failed to identify the problem facing them, it was asking a great deal of politicians in London to point them in the right direction. War might be too important to be left solely to the generals, but tactical problems are usually an exception. In 1915 excuses can be made about a group of politicians who had never presided over a major war against a first-class European Power. But if 1916 was to reveal a more sophisticated approach to battle, planning it would have to come from the new commander appointed by the government. The political class turned their faces – perhaps with some apprehension, but also with some hope – towards Sir Douglas Haig.

CHAPTER 6

THE YEAR OF THE SOMME

1915 HAD BEEN A barren year for the western Allies. All their offensive operations had failed. Gallipoli was about to wind down. In the west, German armies everywhere stood on French or Belgian soil. In an endeavour to perform more effectively in the future, two conferences were called in France in the last weeks of the year. The first, among the British and French premiers, called for a committee to 'co-ordinate the action of the Allies'.[1] The second conference was between the military representatives of Britain, France, Russia and Italy. They came to three main conclusions. First, it was agreed that large attacks by the four Allies should take place as near simultaneously as possible in 1916 in order to prevent the Germans switching forces from one front to the other as they had so successfully done in 1915. Secondly, these major offensives would be launched by the Italians on the Isonzo, the Russians in the northern section of their front and by the Anglo-French side-by-side in Picardy, the French providing the majority of troops. The third was that all secondary fronts would be provided only with the minimum of resources – Mesopotamia, East Africa and Salonika would be defensive efforts only.[2]

On the British side, the two military figures who had decided this policy were soon no more. The services of Sir John French as C-in-C and Sir Archibald Murray as CIGS had been dispensed with. Murray had already laid out a course to be followed in the new year but the change in personnel did not change his strategy. The new CIGS, Sir William Robertson, and the new commander in France, Sir Douglas Haig, endorsed it. There would be a large Anglo-French offensive in the spring on the Western Front. The War Committee approved this paper on 28 December. They concluded:

(i) From the point of view of the British Empire, France and Flanders are the main theatre of operations.
(ii) Every effort is to be made to prepare for carrying out offensive operations next spring in the main theatre of war in close co-operation with the Allies and in the greatest possible strength.

Other conclusions involved the minimum forces needed to sustain lesser theatres.[3]

Here, then, was a clear political agreement to a joint Anglo-French summer offensive on the Western Front. Yet four months later Sir Douglas Haig, whose armies had been concentrating to the north of the River Somme, was still waiting for a clear directive from his political masters on what action he should prepare for.

In the intervening period interminable discussions in the War Committee had failed to make any decision on this matter at all. Just twenty-four hours after the commitment had been made, Balfour (now First Lord of the Admiralty) noted that, considering defence had proved stronger than attack, it would be prudent to allow the Germans to attack first and thus wear themselves down.[4] Asquith reminded the Committee that they had given no commitment at all but merely agreed to 'make every effort' to mount an operation. The final decision was still open.[5] Lloyd George agreed that they should not attack 'until we were really strong enough'. As Minister of Munitions he could assure the Committee that any superiority could not occur in spring.[6] McKenna, as Chancellor of the Exchequer, worried that a failed offensive might see Britain short of funds with its overseas credit rating in peril. Austen Chamberlain, Secretary of State for India, was concerned that any plans for the west might in any case come to nothing if the Germans struck in the east.[7]

Discussion rambled on. In February the gigantic German attack on the French at Verdun might have provoked a reconsideration of strategy on the

Western Front but the War Committee seemed barely aware that their major ally was under threat. In these weeks the Committee discussed many things: the provision of machine guns to Romania, the supply of artillery to the Russians, food production for the home front, the state of the Grand Fleet – almost every topic, that is, other than the Western Front.

Finally Haig crossed to Britain to seek a decision. He was told that the War Committee were committed to a western offensive. He also gathered that their approval was rather lukewarm. He returned to the front muttering about the pusillanimity of politicians and with no clear direction on whether the projected offensive would go ahead.

Over the next weeks the Committee debated the new offensive. All grasped that success depended to a large extent on the ability of the heavy artillery to destroy enemy trenches and those who inhabited them. To that extent they could hardly have been reassured by the comment from their senior military adviser General Robertson, who told them that while heavy artillery 'frightened' soldiers it did not kill them.[8] Perhaps Robertson considered that once heavy shelling commenced troops would shelter in dug-outs impervious to the ordnance being thrown at them. If so, he had raised an important point about the effectiveness (or non-effectiveness) of bombardments. Perhaps on the other hand the Committee regarded his statement as simply bizarre. In any event they did not seek amplification and Robertson's gnomic remark remained uninterrogated.

Instead the Committee turned to Lloyd George, Minister of Munitions since May 1915, to reassure them that Britain was producing enough shells to ensure that the new offensive would be successful. He was happy to oblige. Since he had become minister, munitions programmes had greatly increased. The list of War Office 'approved suppliers' was scrapped and a series of National Shell Factories was constructed, organised and run by the government. 'Dilution' of skilled workers was also introduced, largely by employing almost 1 million women in munitions production.

These measures were a great success. Lloyd George was able to inform the Committee that in shell production, from January to June 1915, 2.3 million shells had been produced but in the next six months this figure had increased to 5.4 million and in the next six, 14 million. The same growth applied to guns. In 1914 the British had produced 91 guns, only two of which were classified as heavy. In 1915 it produced 3,194 guns but fewer than 100 were heavy. In 1916 4,314 guns were manufactured and now over 1,000 were heavy.[9]

There was a certain irony here. The efficiency that civilian control brought to munitions production allowed campaigns such as that being prepared on the Somme to be fought. The army could now expend the 'unlimited' supply of high explosive that it had asked for. Lloyd George assured his civilian colleagues that his efforts would ensure the success of the campaign. He produced aerial photographs showing that German trenches in other parts of the British front had been obliterated by heavy ordinance. When he was asked whether the same could be done to all German trenches he answered, 'certainly'.[10]

But this was a hollow claim. Neither Lloyd George nor any other member of the War Committee had any idea of the plan for the new attack that was being developed by Haig. As with Festubert and Loos and indeed all offensives against trench systems, it was not high explosives alone that would decide the outcome – it was the manner in which they were used. And, as the War Committee deliberated, this matter was the subject of furious debate between the army commander who would fight the battle (Sir Henry Rawlinson) and the Commander-in-Chief (Sir Douglas Haig).

As it happened (and as we have seen in 1915), these two men had quite different conceptions on how to wage war on the Western Front. Rawlinson had been one of the first to put forward the 'bite and hold' operation. The aim was not to gain ground necessarily but to 'bite' off a section of the enemy line, allow them to wear out their troops by trying to regain it by counter-attack and then move the guns forward and repeat the process. That is what he put forward for the Somme campaign. He would attack on a front of 20,000 yards between Serre and Mametz and aim in the first instance to capture only the German first line. The determinants of his plan were that 20,000 yards was the maximum amount that could be successfully bombarded by the 200 heavy howitzers at his disposal and that the strength of the German trench system and the relative 'greenness' of his troops would allow no more ambitious objective.[11]

There was much sense in this plan. The German front 'line' was now really a trench system consisting of three lines of trenches 200 yards apart. In front of the trenches the Germans had placed two belts of barbed wire, each 30 feet wide. Deep dug-outs about 30 feet below the surface had been constructed along much of this system, each of which could hold twenty-five men. In addition the Germans had incorporated a number of fortified villages, solidly built of stone (Beaumont Hamel, Thiepval, Ovillers) into this system and utilised the cellars in the houses for dug-outs and machine-gun posts. Not content with the strength of the front line, the Germans had constructed a second system some 2,000 to 4,000 yards back and placed a series of strongpoints between the two systems. Certainly this line was not as strong as the front but it had been constructed mainly on a reverse slope, out of direct sight from British artillerymen and incorporating high ground where possible such as that around Pozières. They had even begun the construction of a third system 3,000 yards beyond the second but it was still in a rudimentary state at the start of the battle.[12]

These were formidable obstacles and Rawlinson was thinking in Neuve Chapelle terms when he argued that it was important to ensure that the front system fell before any further penetration of the German trench systems were planned. Haig was unimpressed. He thought that, with the large Franco-British armies available, 'we can do better than this by aiming at getting a large force . . . across the Somme and fighting the enemy in the open'.[13] So Haig aimed to capture both the German first and second systems in one rush. This would assist the French in the main endeavour south of the River Somme and maximise Britain's contribution to the battle.

Rawlinson might have been expected to resist Haig's new plan on the solid ground that the Fourth Army did not possess the artillery resources to carry it out. A comparison with Neuve Chapelle would have revealed that if the bombardment was spread, as Haig was insisting, it would be reduced to half the intensity of that battle against much stronger German defences. But after the rejection of his initial plan Rawlinson did not so argue. Probably he realised that it was a matter of bowing to the inevitable. In the end there could only be one winner in these debates. The views of the Commander-in-Chief must prevail. The objective would not be limited to 'bite and hold'.

It was this factor that made Lloyd George's assurances to the War Committee irrelevant. Had his precious shells been concentrated on the German front line, his promise that it would be demolished would prob-ably have proved correct. But if those same shells were spread over an area three times that size there was no hope that major demolition would take place anywhere. It may be thought that such fine military considerations were beyond the ken of civilian politicians, but one of their number had discerned exactly this problem as far back as December 1915. Winston Churchill had then produced a document for the War Committee entitled 'Variants on the Offensive' in which he explained that it was not the capture of the enemy's front line that was the major problem on the Western Front. The difficulties arose from trying to do anything beyond that. What he suggested was a series of what were in effect 'bite and hold' operations, forcing the enemy to counter-attack to win back the ground and thereby suffering heavy casualties.[14] This paper was also submitted to Major-General Earl Cavan, who happened to be Churchill's divisional commander during his period on the Western Front. Cavan commented that he was 'in entire agreement' with Churchill's paper and 'methodical progression from point to point is the *Book* and it is absolutely true and will lead to victory'.[15] Cavan would eventually rise to the post of CIGS and was one of the most thoughtful soldiers on the Western Front, but there is no evidence that anyone – politician or military – took his endorsement of Churchill's suggested strategy seriously. Perhaps Churchill's Dardanelles experiment proved fatal to his subsequent military ideas. More likely the members of the War Committee had not the cast of mind to grasp his point. In this case a little military knowledge would have been a very good thing.

* * * * *

Back at the front there was one major factor in play that might have given Haig pause to reconsider his 'unlimited' offensive. This was Verdun. On 21 May Joffre informed Haig that the thirty-nine French divisions initially devoted to the Somme offensive would have to be reduced to thirty because of the need for reinforcements for Verdun. By 20 May the number had become twenty-six, by the end of the month twenty and by early June twelve. In other words, the operation would now be a mainly British affair with the French Sixth Army offering only six divisions as flank support.[16]

Astoundingly, this did change Haig's perspective but not in the way that might be thought. Rather than toning down his ambitions, the demise of the French saw them increase. So on 14 June Rawlinson was instructed to issue new orders. The first objective was the German second line, as Haig

114

had already specified. But now he went further. A second objective some thousands of yards beyond the German second system was specified, and yet another some distance beyond that.[17] Moreover a combined force of cavalry and infantry under General Gough had been grouped into a 'Reserve Army'. Its objectives were no less than Bapaume, some 20 miles from the German front line and then Monchy and Douai some 70 miles away.[18]

These orders contained within them the seeds of disaster – not for the cavalry, because it was difficult to imagine that the horsed soldiers would even be able to negotiate the trenches, barbed wire, shell holes, collapsed dug-outs and other obstacles around the German first system, let alone deal with surviving machine-gunners and advance to more distant destinations. The potential for disaster lay with the infantry. It was because, unlike Rawlinson's initial plan, which would have concentrated the fire of the available artillery on the first system, that fire would now have to encompass all three German lines, an enormous area which would substantially dilute Rawlinson's fire plan. And compounding the problem was the fact that Haig would have no more guns capable of reaching the distant defences than were available initially.

Just one example will show what this meant. The great killer of infantry in the attack was the enemy artillery. It was therefore of the utmost importance to attempt to neutralise the German guns before zero hour. Haig was always deficient in the kind of gun suitable for this purpose. In fact, of the 1,500 guns in his possession, just 180 could perform what was called counter-battery duties. But with the extended objectives it was found that many of the lighter wire-cutting guns did not have the range to reach the distant wire protecting the second and third objectives. So a proportion of the precious counter-battery pieces were switched to these objectives. As a result, in the initial attacks on the Somme, the enemy guns would be attacked by fewer guns than at Loos, which had been a substantially smaller operation than the Somme.

Haig had another problem with guns that seemed to pass unnoticed. Rawlinson not only had insufficient guns to destroy enemy batteries – he had far too few heavy guns to destroy German trenches – in all he had just 233 guns of 6" calibre or above for this task. During the preliminary bombardment these guns fired 188,500 shells weighing 34.5 million pounds.[19] This seems a prodigious amount of shells. However, taking into consideration the length of trench that had to be demolished in the complex systems constructed by the Germans at the Somme, it is less than half the intensity delivered at Neuve Chapelle. No comment by either Haig or Rawlinson was made on this matter in the lead-up to the great attack.

Artillery problems did not stop here. Prolonged firing wore out many of the springs on the 18-pounder guns, rendering their accuracy dubious; fuses for some heavier-calibre pieces such as 8″ and 9.2″ howitzers were faulty and often failed to explode; shells for 6″ guns varied so much in length that it was impossible for artillerymen to calculate their range with any certainty.[20]

What was the result of all this? It was lamentable. Even after a seven-day preliminary bombardment which fired 1.7 million shells at the German defences, much of the wire protecting the German trenches remained uncut – either because it was too distant or because the gunners did not possess sufficient accuracy to burst the shrapnel shells at exactly the correct height or distance for optimal efficiency. Moreover there was inadequate heavy artillery to demolish anything like the number of deep dug-outs which protected the German infantry. And the counter-battery guns made almost no impression on the German artillery. The enemy guns remained ready to throw deadly barrages of shells into no man's land. None of this was unknown to the command. Patrol reports gathered during the bombardment revealed that the state of the dug-outs was in general good and that much wire was still intact.[21] The German artillery retaliation was obvious to the Corps Intelligence officers. It was described by many as 'heavy' and by others as 'active' or 'considerable'.[22] Why did the command not act on these reports? We can never know with any certainty, but it seems likely that the timetable for the attack, agreed with the French, produced a fatal inevitability as to when the attack would commence. There were anyway insufficient shells to prolong the bombardment, so the alternatives seemed to be that the attack went in on the designated date or it was called off until the situation was reassessed. In the event there would be no reassessment and the infantry would pay the price.

The soldiers left their trenches at 7.30 a.m. on 1 July. In the north they were shot down in swathes, the VIII Corps alone suffering 13,000 casualties. The X and III Corps to their south also suffered severely for no gains.

Only in the south, aided by the French artillery and where creeping barrages were fired by the artillery to protect the infantry, were gains made. There the first German trench system fell and considerable ground was won towards the second. For these small advances almost 60,000 casualties were suffered, of which almost 20,000 were dead. Contrary to general belief, these casualties were not caused because the troops that day slowly walked in solid ranks to their doom. In fact the instructions for the best methods to traverse no man's land issued by Fourth Army were vague to the point of incomprehensibility. In these circumstances battalion commanders devised a variety of complex and innovative ways of crossing that killing zone. Their expertise went for nothing. So many enemy machine-gunners, batteries and riflemen had been left intact by the feeble bombardment that the attackers were mown down in whatever formation was chosen. Indeed, so lethal was the hail of fire directed by the Germans that around 30 per cent of British casualties were suffered *before they reached their own front line.*[23]

* * * * *

This disaster was viewed with more equanimity by the command than might be thought appropriate. They had presided over the greatest single disaster in British military history. Haig, however, merely remarked that 'on a sixteen-mile front of attack varying fortune must be expected'.[24] Rawlinson noted that while the casualties had been heavy there were 'plenty of fresh divisions behind'.[25] One matter was not discussed by either of them: no mention was made of how far short of expectations the results of the first day had been. Rawlinson quietly dispersed the cavalry during the evening; Bapaume or Douai or Arras were not referred to.

The immediate question was, where to attack next? Joffre, whose armies had made more progress north and south of the Somme, thought he knew. Haig should attempt to take that ground in the north where the German trench systems had not been captured. This was not only a foolish suggestion, it was impossible to execute. The dead and wounded lay in such quantities in this area of the British front that military operations had become impossible until they were cleared. Haig rightly rejected Joffre's proposal. He would continue to try to make ground in the south in order to be in a position to mount a concerted attack on the German second line between Pozières and Longueval.[26]

Haig was being sensible here. His execution of the plan was anything but sensible. During the next two weeks (2 to 13 July) Rawlinson's Fourth Army made a total of forty-six separate attacks.[27] All were hastily organised, on a small scale and on a narrow front. This allowed the Germans to concentrate their artillery and machine guns on one minor operation after another. They therefore maximised their resources and minimised their casualties while the British did the opposite. All told, the British suffered 25,000 casualties in these operations. On occasion multiple attacks were made on the same location with what troops that could be assembled. Eight times the British hammered at Trônes Wood. All were made by just one or two battalions. All failed with heavy casualties except the last.[28] These operations were characterised by poor coordination with the available artillery and haste – whereby assaults were launched without much knowledge of the exact locations of German strongpoints that had held up previous attacks. More deliberation and more attacks on a wide front were called for. They did not eventuate. Whole divisions were consumed, such as the 38 Welsh Division which suffered so many casualties in attempting to capture Mametz Wood that it had to be withdrawn from the line for the remainder of the Somme campaign.[29]

Nevertheless, the command was relatively happy to be in a position to mount a major attack by 14 July. The plan on this occasion mainly came from Rawlinson. It had some extraordinary features. This time Rawlinson was not content with capturing a large section of what had been the second German line. Aerial reconnaissance had revealed to him the existence of a third German line some 3,000 yards beyond the second. Photographs also showed that the line was not completely wired and not strongly held. Rawlinson therefore incorporated the two cavalry divisions in his plan with orders to gallop through after the initial objective fell and take this position.[30] Haig protested and ordered the cavalry withdrawn into reserve.[31] It is worth noting at this point that the two commanders had almost totally reversed the positions they had held regarding the initial attack. In the event Rawlinson took no notice of Haig and the cavalry aspect of the plan remained. There was, however, one large difference from 1 July. Rawlinson's entire artillery resources would concentrate on the German front line. He reasoned that after it had fallen, the cavalry would meet no resistance, apparently not even from the odd machine-gunner or artillery battery that might have survived the bombardment. Another innovation that he insisted upon, rather against Haig's wishes, was that the attack be launched at night, thus concealing the approach and traverse of the infantry across no man's land.[32]

In the event, the operation was a qualified success but not in the way anticipated by Rawlinson. The crushing intensity of the bombardment – by far the most severe fired by the British army in any operation so far – wiped out whole sections of the German line.[33] The five assaulting divisions, with varying amounts of opposition, managed to capture the German front system from just south of Longueval on the right to Contalmaison on the left. Units of the 2 Indian Cavalry Division were ordered forward. They found extreme difficulty in negotiating the war-torn ground with its barbed wire, shell holes and trenches. Nevertheless they managed a charge between High Wood and Delville Wood. Soon they ran into machine-gun and artillery fire and were forced to dismount. Though suffering few casualties themselves, they could make no headway and were withdrawn.[34] Once more the utility of the cavalry on a modern battlefield had proved dubious, to say the least. With that the operation came to an end. The 'bite and hold' aspect of it had proved yet again that artillery was the determinant of success. What was also on display was the usefulness of attacking on a wide front in order to force the enemy to disperse their defensive firepower. But what had also been demonstrated was the futility of aiming at distant objectives without a weapon of exploitation.

The first phase of the Somme campaign was now over. Haig had gained derisory amounts of ground for a casualty bill that was approaching 100,000. This was hardly what the politicians in the War Committee expected. How did they receive the news of what amounted to the greatest disaster in British military history? Although Hankey reported a meeting between Lloyd George and Balfour where they had expressed concern about casualties,[35] discussion of the campaign is almost absent from the official record. On 6 July Lloyd George merely observed that British gunners were shooting very well, despite their inexperience.[36] The fact that the Germans must have also been shooting well to inflict 60,000 casualties on the first day went unremarked. On 11 July Robertson announced that

British casualties were now 80,000, which was accurate enough, but again there was no discussion on whether this was a reasonable price to pay for a gain of 5 or 6 square miles.[37] Moreover, he added that the Germans had only been required to move one division from Verdun to the Somme and that they were now less than 3 miles from the French city.[38] Though the French were obviously in dire straits, this news produced no consternation at all. In general the response of the War Committee to the unprecedented carnage was silence.

The next phase of the Somme campaign lasted from 15 July to 14 September. It is one of the strangest episodes in the history of the British army on the Western Front. After the battle of 14 July the British line ran from the boundary with the French south of Guillemont almost due north to the village of Longueval. Then, in a sharp right-angled turn, it ran east–west until it crossed the Albert–Péronne Road. It then entered what had become the zone of a new Reserve Army under General Gough, the control of the entire front being thought beyond a single army commander. In this zone the line ran north-east to Serre.[39] The line therefore faced three different directions: due east from the junction with the French to Longueval, due north from Longueval to Contalmaison and north-east in the area of the Reserve Army. With this configuration GHQ needed to coordinate operations between the Fourth and Reserve Army to ensure that they did not pull in mutually different directions and that an attack by one corps directly aided that of another.

Nothing of the kind happened. In the period in question the Reserve Army on the left attempted to advance north-east while the Fourth Army was trying to advance north in the central section of the front and east in the rightward section. Had any of these operations succeeded, the only result would have been the rending of the British army into three quite disparate sections, each unsupported by the other. The only thing that held it together was the abject and almost total failure of any operation to advance the line at all. GHQ, as a coordinating body, did not fulfil its function in this period. Haig has been criticised for commanding from a chateau, but from the perspective of coordination he might as well have been on the moon.

What then did happen? In the sector of the Reserve Army the Australian Corps entered the line on 17 July with orders to capture the heights and village of Pozières. This they accomplished on 23 July after a well-thought-out attack, amply supported by accurate artillery fire. Then for the next six weeks they struggled north-east with the vague idea of capturing Thiepval from the rear but actually inching towards the blasted ruins of Mouquet Farm. Their operations were characterised by great ineptitude on the part of the higher command, both British and Australian. The ground over which they fought was featureless, which made pin-point artillery support difficult. In addition they were assailed by German artillery from three quadrants of a circle. Finally, each attack was made on a narrow front with limited support on either side by groups that rarely exceeded battalion strength and which were so difficult to supply that on occasion the number of rifles fell well below the number of soldiers. The attempt to advance on the farm was incessant. Day after day these men forced their way forward a few yards, only to be driven back on a subsequent day. Sometime during this period, Gough decided to capture Thiepval frontally, meaning that all purpose in the Mouquet Farm operations had ceased. But this information was not imparted to the Australian command so their blighted attacks continued. In eight months at Gallipoli the Australians had lost about 25,000 casualties. At Pozières/Mouquet Farm they lost almost as many in six weeks.[40]

This is not to say that the Australians were in any way singled out as sacrificial lambs by the command. Operations on the front of the Fourth Army in this period were at least as badly thought out and as costly. Rawlinson, in attacking Intermediate Trench, High Wood, Delville Wood, Longueval, Ginchy and Guillemont, proceeded in much the same way as the Reserve Army – that is, his attacks were made by small packets of men, on narrow fronts, without decent fire support. There was also no attempt to coordinate these operations by the Fourth Army command, so that an attack on (say) Delville Wood and one on Longueval would take place on different days at different times despite the fact that the objectives were side-by-side. These conditions allowed the German defence to concentrate the maximum amount of artillery and machine-gun fire against very small targets and to keep up these tactics day in and day out as the British struggled to get forward.

Let one of these futile endeavours illustrate many made during this period. On 4/5 August the 13 Durham Light Infantry from 23 Division (see

Map) were ordered to capture Torr Trench, which stood just 200 yards from their own. The attack was unsupported by infantry units to the right and left of the Durhams. The attack was allotted only a derisory amount of artillery fire, most of which in any case missed its targets. This meant that large sections of Torr Trench were not bombarded at all. As a result the leading waves were cut down by machine-gun fire as they left their trench. Follow-up waves received the same treatment. Officers were sent forward in an attempt to rectify the position. At this moment the British artillery shortened its range and inflicted casualties on its own men, something that it had conspicuously failed to do to the Germans. Yet another attack was ordered, but many men refused to go forward and those close at hand were only prevented from copying them by officers with drawn revolvers. The end result was no ground gained, 132 casualties suffered and a fine battalion reduced to near mutiny.[41]

During this period Haig became aware that, as he put it to Rawlinson, 'something is wanting in the methods employed' in directing these attacks.[42] He had already noted that Fourth Army was trying to advance in two different directions and enjoined Rawlinson to hold in the centre while straightening the line on the right. He also observed that many attacks were rushed and poorly thought out and wanted careful and methodical approaches substituted for them.[43] This was very sensible of Haig. The battle, which had patently lacked 'grip' in the last weeks of July, looked as though it was being taken in hand by the Commander-in-Chief. What happened as a result of Haig's memorandum? Precisely nothing. Rawlinson continued to operate as though Haig had not spoken. He therefore kept up attacks on both sections of his front, though they faced different ways. These operations were no better planned than those that had gone before. As for Haig, he made no follow-up inquiries as to whether his army commander was paying attention. No more admonishing memoranda flowed from GHQ. The hapless soldiers could have been no worse off if the command had been totally absent, which indeed mentally it was.

And it must be emphasised these penny-packet attacks were not cheap. From 15 July to 12 September Haig's armies suffered 126,000 casualties.[44] In doing so they gained 6 square miles. This may be compared with the disastrous first day when 60,000 casualties were suffered in gaining 3 square miles. So this middle portion of the Somme Battle was no less a tragedy than the first day. Only the fact that the slaughter was spread out over a longer period has concealed this fact from observers at the time and historians since. Some units in this period were wiped out. In a series of attacks near Delville Wood, 5 Division lost the equivalent of its entire infantry strength (12,000 men). The 1 Division lost 10,000 men; the 3 and 33 over 8,000 each; six others lost between 5,500 and 7,000 each.[45]

Why this phase of the Somme spiralled out of the control of the British command does not admit of an easy answer. Perhaps the size of the army and the scale of operations were beyond those who had begun the war in the relatively lowly positions of corps and divisional commanders. More frighteningly, Haig might have attempted to apply *Field Service Regulations*, the British army's philosophy of war, to the Somme. Haig had written most of this pamphlet but it had been published in 1909 and not surprisingly had hardly envisaged the conditions applying on the Western Front in 1916. Nevertheless, *Field Service Regulations* did contain chilling phrases such as: 'Superior numbers on the battlefield are an undoubted advantage, but skill, better organization, and training, and above all **a firmer determination in all ranks to conquer at any cost, are the chief factors of success**.' Also: '**Half-hearted measures never attain success in war, and lack of determination is the most fruitful source of defeat**.'[46] The sections in bold were in bold in the original and constitute some of the most meaningless words ever written in a military context. What did 'conquer at any cost' actually mean? Did it mean, for example, that an attacking army was required to suffer almost total casualties in order to achieve its purpose? Under these conditions, what would achievement amount to? Was it possible that Haig still actually thought in these terms and that all his army needed was a commander who was not half-hearted – that is, someone awfully like himself – in order to push this ruthless policy through? If this was the case it certainly represented a triumph of thoughtless doctrine over common sense.

Of course there is another side to this. The incessant attacks made upon the Germans by the British represented a shocking episode for the Kaiser's armies as well. From 15 July to 12 September the British artillery fired 7.8 million shells at the Germans.[47] Though these missiles may often have missed particular targets, they often hit other troops, trenches and headquarters. It gradually became clear to the Germans that they were now not fighting just one major industrial power in the shape of the French but two as the British munitions effort began to show results.[48] This had a depressing and wearing effect on the enemy soldiers, as their regimental histories make abundantly clear. Their mood was not improved by the lunatic policy followed by Falkenhayn of ordering every inch of ground lost to be recaptured by counter-attack, often in the most inauspicious of circumstances. Almost all these attacks were beaten off by the British and the balance sheet of slaughter to some extent equalised.

In any case the British struggled forward. By the first week in September it was apparent that they might have straightened their line sufficiently to carry out another major attack. For this new operation Haig would have at his disposal an entirely new weapon of war. For some time the British had been thinking about the problem of transporting soldiers over the killing zone of no man's land. Churchill in his 'Variants on the Offensive' document had projected some form of armoured personnel carrier. But it was viewing caterpillar tractors pulling heavy guns that led Colonel Swinton to develop the idea for the tank – an armoured vehicle which would not provide transport for troops but, if it was armed with cannon or machine guns, could give fire support while the dangerous crossing of no man's land was underway. By September, thanks to the ingenuity of British industry, some tanks had arrived in France and Haig and Rawlinson went to see them in action. The Mark I tank was a cumbersome weapon. Each vehicle weighed 28 tons and was 8 feet high and 32 feet long. It could crush barbed wire and had some ability to operate over rough ground, provided the going was firm. Its maximum speed was, however, just over 2 miles an hour, which made it slower than a marching soldier. It was very vulnerable to artillery fire and its crews were unable to function for more than a few hours because they were breathing in noxious fumes from the engine at very high temperatures. By no stretch of the imagination did these tanks add up to any kind of weapon that could exploit a breakthrough.[49] Some of these limitations were obvious at this first display. Two of the six on show broke down and one of the officer-drivers fainted from engine fumes while at the controls.[50] Nevertheless, both commanders found the new weapon encouraging and Rawlinson agreed to incorporate them 'cautiously' into his battle plan.[51]

Caution was not a word that appealed to Haig. He rejected Rawlinson's initial idea which, as always, was merely to capture the German front position.[52] Very soon a familiar pattern was re-established: Rawlinson presented a cautious 'bite and hold' operation; Haig rejected it. The final plan bore Haig's stamp. It involved the capture of all three German positions faced by the British and a cavalry operation that would burst through these objectives, turn north and roll up the entire German line.[53] These had been the objectives envisioned by Haig for 1 July. So, despite two and a half months of campaigning which left these objectives still distant, Haig had reinstated them for his September plan.

One of the main difficulties with the tank was how to incorporate it into the existing array of weaponry. In particular this applied to the artillery. For example, the creeping barrage which had been used by only a few divisions on the first day of the Somme was now generally used to protect the infantry going forward. The challenge of using the tanks *and* the creeping barrage with the infantry needed careful thought – might not the shells disable the tanks if they were used in the very front of the advance? At the Somme this matter was thrashed out by the corps commanders. Unfortunately for the troops, the solutions arrived at by these men were not optimal. Lieutenant-General William Pulteney of III Corps determined to use his small packet of tanks through the tangled ruins and stumps of High Wood, the very type of ground which would bring the caterpillar vehicles to a halt in short order. General Henry Horne of XV Corps thought a creeping barrage entirely useless. He provided no solution to the problem. Others worried that shells might indeed hit the tanks. Their solution was to leave gaps in the barrage where the tanks would operate. The danger here was that the fifty tanks (all that were available) were positioned to operate opposite the strongest German points in the line – those that contained concreted machine-gun posts and strongpoints. But under the corps commanders' plan, these sections of the line would have no artillery protection at all. The idea was that the tanks would take care of these strongpoints. But, as was obvious from the demonstration, the first tanks were very prone to mechanical breakdown. If they failed to arrive at their allotted places the German machine-gunners would have no barrage of shells to contend with and no tanks. They would therefore be free to fire on any troops advancing towards them.[54] No one on the British side identified this as a problem.

The first tank attack in history began just before dawn on 15 September. In all eleven divisions attacked on a 15,000-yard front. It was one of the few occasions where the offensive involved divisions from the Reserve Army and Fourth Army attacking simultaneously. It made some promising gains but not always due to the tanks. On the left the Canadians swept in behind an accurate and dense bombardment and secured Courcelette and Martinpuich without the assistance of any tanks, all of which broke down.[55] On the right the tanks also failed. Some faced armour-piercing ammunition originally brought forward by the Germans to deal with steel shields employed by British snipers but in the event useful against the tanks.[56] In the centre, however, a substantial advance was made of some 2,500 and 3,000 yards. Here four tanks survived and, followed by the New Zealand and 41 Divisions, captured Flers as the German defenders fled back in terror before the mechanical monsters.[57] In this area the tanks did live up to expectations. But their limitations were also on show. By mid-afternoon all had broken down. At this point only small sections of the German second line had been captured. The infantry, who had suffered severe casualties from the machine-gunners in the lanes where the creeping barrage was not fired, were also at the end of their tether. The successful divisions such as the New Zealanders and the 41 Division had paid a high price for their success and needed rest. There would thus be no great cavalry sweep and Haig's distant objectives still remained distant.

Nevertheless, the battle had been a qualified success. The appearance of the tanks shocked the Germans and in some areas led to larger advances than would have been made without them. Haig has been much criticised for using these vehicles before they were available in great numbers but this is misguided. It was as well to try the tanks in limited numbers in the first instance and not rely on them alone to win the battle. Experience had been gained in their use and their mechanical unreliability confirmed. No fewer than 50 per cent of the vehicles failed to reach the start line and had, large numbers been employed, a shambles might well have been the result. However, the tank had arrived as a weapon of war and Haig immediately ordered 1,000 more from the Ministry of Munitions.

Ten days later the Fourth Army demonstrated what could be achieved without tanks. This time the French would also attack on the right flank, meaning that the operation would take place in daylight as the French did not favour dawn attacks. The British soon decided that the few tanks available would be too vulnerable to artillery fire to be used in the full light of day. Without the tanks, an artillery bombardment could be fired across the entire front of attack. The final plan set no distant objectives. The ten attacking divisions would just attempt to secure the German front line around Gueudecourt. Because the objective was limited, the bombardment was intense, comparable to that fired on 14 July. Advancing behind a creeping barrage, the troops were able to capture the shattered German trenches and occupy the ruins of the villages of Gueudecourt, Lesboeufs and Morval. The divisions taking part had no doubt as to the cause of success:

> Our artillery barrage was excellent, & we advanced with it, practically in it & got to the objective the very second it lifted . . . The Germans . . . were largely in shell-holes, a few in front (who were killed as we went up), the majority were in rear of the trench. The Germans were killed in the shelters & in the trench, & at first, some as they attempted to come forward from the shell-holes – the remainder surrendered.[58]

Thus were the lessons of 'bite and hold' revealed once more. These lessons were again on show on the left of the line on 26 September when Thiepval was also subjected to an intense bombardment and captured by 18 Division. The whole plan had been devised by Major-General Sir Ivor Maxse, who was emerging as one of the most thoughtful generals on the Western Front and had clearly grasped the utility of the limited attack.[59]

The last two weeks of September had therefore seen limited but solid achievements on the Somme. However, it was by now late in the campaigning season. The weather had held up very well in September but October was a month which regularly saw heavy rainfall that could turn the battlefield into a quagmire. This was an important factor because Haig's armies stood on the edge of the Morval Plateau. Any advance would lead to lower ground that was quite swampy at any time of the year, let alone during late autumn. And if the weather turned and the battlefield did become a bog, the two important innovations made by the British – the creeping barrage and the tanks – would be virtually useless. Moreover, the Germans had dug three defensive lines in this are that stretched back to Bapaume. These were all excellent reasons for calling off the offensive, especially as the French had now recovered at Verdun. Would Haig take this sensible course?

The other question was what attitude to a renewed offensive would be taken by the War Council in London. So far they had allowed Haig to plough on for meagre reward. Yet on 1 August they received a paper from Winston Churchill that should have given them pause.[60] Churchill produced a series of figures, obviously provided for him by someone in authority at the War Office, which demonstrated that the British army at the Somme was paying a casualty bill that was higher than the German and out of all proportion to the gains made. His conclusion was devastating:

> In *personnel* the results of the operation have been disastrous, in *terrain* they have been absolutely barren ... From every point of view, there-fore, the British offensive *per se* has been a great failure. With twenty times the shell, and five times the guns, and more than double the losses, the gains have but little exceeded those of Loos. And how was Loos viewed in retrospect?[61]

Everyone of course knew how Loos was viewed in retrospect – so disastrous that its commander had been sacked.

The response by the War Committee to this document was outstanding in its obfuscation. Robertson produced his own series of figures which amounted to nothing short of a tissue of lies. He claimed that the Germans had already lost 1.25 million men as against British losses of 160,000; that is, against all intuitive reasoning, the defence had cost eight times as many men as the attack – and one third of the German army in the west had been wiped out – just by the British on the Somme.[62]

There was no reason for a group of seemingly intelligent men to fall for this nonsense. Yet not one of them called for any inquiry into the discrepancy between Churchill's and Robertson's figures. Indeed, when they received a missive from Haig stating that British losses 'could not be considered unduly heavy', they pronounced themselves well satisfied and instructed Robertson to send Haig a message stating that he could count on full support from home.[63]

Emboldened by this response, Haig immediately wrote to Robertson asking for authority to continue to press the attack with the utmost determination.[64] This brought forth a furious riposte from the new Minister of War, Lloyd George, who had replaced the drowned Kitchener in July. But his target was not Haig or his ambitions in the west; Lloyd George pointed with indignation instead at the collapsing Allied effort in the Balkans.[65] He called for an Allied conference to examine the Romanian situation and to consider how 'our honour might be saved'. (Romania had joined the Allied side in August 1916 and had immediately been crushed by the Germans). An acrimonious debate between Lloyd George and Robertson followed which led to a clear threat of resignation from the CIGS. Lloyd George was not to be deterred. He kept up his attack on Robertson until it was obvious that Romania was past salvation.[66] What seemed beyond Lloyd George's grasp was that so far as Britain was concerned, what happened to Romania, tragic though it may be, was of minor importance. It was what happened in the west that was of concern. Yet while the Minister of War fulminated about Romania, the request from Haig to carry on attacking on the Western Front remained unanswered. It never was answered and Haig, reasonably, took this silence for assent. The Battle of the Somme would continue.

This decision was disastrous. It takes a very large-scale map to see the derisory gains made between the beginning of October and the end of the Somme campaign. Once again Haig's objectives were grandiose. Early in the month he planned an attack by three armies (from south to north, Fourth, Reserve and Third) that would converge between Cambrai and the River Sensée – a distance of some 30 miles for each army.[67] Despite the modest gains made over a period of three months, Haig was still thinking in terms of gigantic cavalry sweeps as if he was planning Napoleonic operations.

Needless to say, these ambitions came to nothing. Rain began to fall before the bombardment could even begin. So bad was the weather that no spotting for the artillery from the air could be carried out. On 7 October when the attack commenced, the troops could hardly leave their sticky holes that once had been trenches, let alone follow a creeping barrage. The Transloy Line, which was the first objective in Haig's grand plan, remained intact.[68] A similar fate befell repeat performances on 12 and 18 October.[69] Finally, Brigadier Lord Gort, who was one of Haig's liaison officers, and Lord Cavan, the commander of XIV Corps, entered strong protests about the conditions in which the troops were being asked to operate.[70] Cavan concluded by saying that 'no one who has not visited the front trenches can really know the state of exhaustion to which the men are reduced', which was one way of saying that the high command were completely out of touch with the situation at the front.[71] Even these warnings produced no effect at GHQ. Operations continued until mid-November – costly in casualties, barren in results, damning in terms of the competence of the command. Eventually, on the front of the Fourth Army they stopped because conditions got too bad for even Haig to ignore.

But this did not mean that all operations ceased on the Somme. Haig was to be present at an Allied conference in November. He wished to attend on a winning note so he arranged with the ever-eager Gough for the Reserve (now renamed the Fifth Army) to attack on the very north of the line to capture Beaumont Hamel. This ruined village, of no tactical significance, was eventually captured in operations which lasted from 13 to 19 November. For reasons that remain obscure this attack by Haig was hailed at the time and by some historians since as some kind of victory. In fact minuscule amounts of ground were gained at great cost. Writing to the Official Historian in 1936, one officer unlucky enough to participate in it said, 'It was the very worst instance I came across of what appeared to be a cruel sacrifice of life and the climatic conditions alone made it clear . . . to the very stupidest brain that no success could possibly result.'[72]

By the end of the battle the British had suffered 432,000 casualties and inflicted about 240,000 on the Germans. Churchill was therefore correct in August in saying that Haig's forces were suffering much more than their adversaries. In return for this prodigious slaughter a small amount of ground of no strategic or tactical importance had been gained.

There is a great irony in the fact that the five-month campaign in which the British fired 35 million shells at the Germans was only possible by the munitions effort that resulted from the politicians' wresting control of shell and gun production from the rather ineffective War Office. In this sense it was the War Committee that was directly responsible for the Somme. They were responsible in other ways as well. As a group, perhaps these civilians lacked the forensic ability or military knowledge of a Churchill who in December wrote much good sense on how the Somme might be fought and in August pointed out that it was actually being fought in a way that maximised British casualties while minimising German. His colleagues, by executing some mental gymnastics, could perhaps argue that Churchill alone was responsible for one of the major setbacks of 1915 and that there-fore they wanted no more lectures on strategy from this quarter. But his casualty figures had so obviously come from an official source that some investigation into them should have been ordered. No action followed. Instead the War Committee concerned itself with matters that it could not affect: waning British prestige in the Balkans, stagnation at Salonika and the fate of Romania. In fact, they give the impression during this period of turning their faces from the Western Front, where the choices were unpal-atable and difficult but were of some moment, in order to focus with some intensity on what was of much lesser moment. The lack of military nous by politicians supposedly running a war was never more keenly felt.

As for Haig, he did not fight the Somme as a battle of attrition to wear down the German army or even as the first phase of a process that would lead to that end. On three occasions at least (1 July, 15 September, 7 October) he attempted to win the war or to go a long way towards it in a single battle. His distant objectives reveal this cast of mind; many entries in his diaries confirm it. Haig never possessed the fixity of purpose or the grit for a campaign of attrition. Attrition was merely what was taking place while he was making grandiose plans. There is something to be said for Haig. He was no technophobe and never hesitated to use to the maximum the weapons that were provided to him, even weapons as innovatory as the tank. He also welcomed developments such as the creeping barrage. But he lacked the ability to discern when these weapons could be used to maximum advantage (in the dry) and never ceased to use them in periods when they were bound to fail (in the wet). He also stood too far back from the battle-field and let the campaign run itself. There were few interventions to alter the direction or shape of the battle. And even when there were, in his instructions to Rawlinson in August, there was no follow-up to ensure that his wishes were being obeyed. Admittedly, the Somme was an extraordi-narily difficult battle to manage. There were no easy solutions or quick fixes available to Haig. But it was his responsibility to ensure that his armies were inflicting more damage on the Germans than the Germans were on him. In this he failed. That his soldiers kept on attacking is a wonder. Surely they deserved a plan as well as a cause.

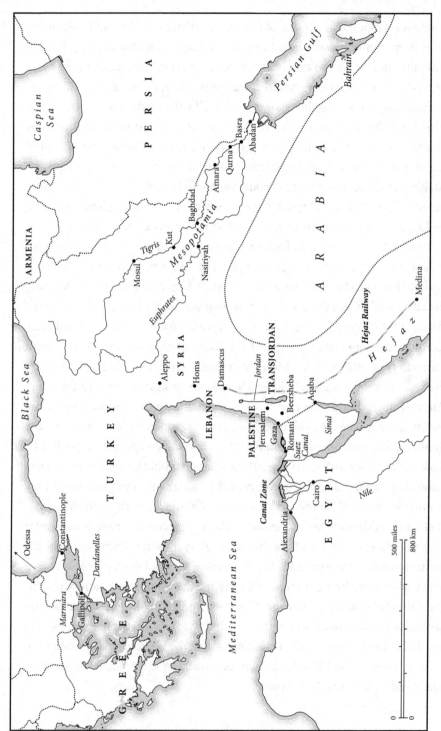

Map 3. The Ottoman Empire.

CHAPTER 7

THE DEFEAT OF THE OTTOMAN EMPIRE 1914–1918

THERE IS SOME IRONY in the fact that the country that mainly prosecuted the war against Turkey had spent the last 100 years attempting to prop up the 'sick man of Europe' against its foes. By the early years of the twentieth century the position had changed. The Young Turk Revolution in 1908 promised much but delivered little in the way of reform. The Balkan wars of 1912 and 1913 saw Turkey lose most of its European possessions. As a result the new regime turned inwards and became more Turco-centric and less tolerant of ethnic and religious differences than the old empire.

One consequence of this was the alienation from Turkey of the tribes in the Arabian Peninsula, a situation which led Britain and France to speculate whether the Ottoman Empire was on the brink of collapse. And if it did collapse, would Britain in particular face a series of hostile states on the flank of its communications with the east through the Suez Canal? Clearly, the British would have an interest in events in the Ottoman provinces and France had a long-declared interest in the fate of what are now the states of Lebanon and Syria. Vultures seemed to be gathering in anticipation that there would be a carcass to consume.

The Young Turk government knew of British and French interest in their fate. In an attempt to shore up their position they staged a coup in Constantinople in 1913, centralising affairs under the triumvirate of Enver Pasha (Minister of War), Djemal Pasha (Minister of the Navy) and Talaat

Pasha (Minister of the Interior). Enver, in particular, was pro-German. He had been Military Attaché in Berlin and was a great admirer of German military efficiency. On the other hand, Djemal leaned towards the French and Talaat towards the Russians. It soon became clear, however, that the Entente Powers were not prepared to accept Turkish conditions, which included the return of the Aegean islands lost to Greece in the Balkan wars and the abolition of the Capitulations – the series of tax concessions forced upon Turkey by the Great Powers. All the Entente was willing to offer was a guarantee of Turkish sovereignty in the event of war, which was a better deal than it looked to the Turks in 1914.

The Central Powers could seemingly offer more. Liman von Sanders was head of the German Military Mission in Turkey, and more assistance in retraining and equipping the army was offered. This suited Enver, who as early as July 1914 had asked the Germans for an alliance, which was signed on 2 August.[1]

However, on the outbreak of war in Europe a month later, Turkey put the German alliance in abeyance and declared its neutrality. The Triumvirate feared that Russia's strength, added to that of Britain and France, might win the ensuing war. The Young Turks bided their time. By October, when in their opinion, Germany was well on the way to winning the war, they decided to trigger the German alliance. The German ships *Goeben* and *Breslau* had arrived in Constantinople after evading the British Mediterranean Squadron. They made useful replacements for the two dreadnoughts being built for Turkey by Britain but withheld for its own use after the declaration of war on Germany. The Germans now promised the Turks that they would abolish the Capitulations and, if Greece intervened, restore the lost islands.

The specific incident which saw Turkey enter the war is shrouded in mystery. On 29 October, Admiral Souchon, with the *Goeben* and *Breslau* (now with Turkish names), bombarded Odessa and attacked Russian shipping in the Black Sea. The Triumvirate had almost certainly agreed in secret to this operation and, after it occurred, dissidents within the government were persuaded to stay as a sign of national unity.[2] On 2 November the Russians declared war on Turkey, followed by Britain and France on the 5th. Indeed the British fleet off the Dardanelles had bombarded its outer forts even before the declaration of war.

Why were Britain and France so eager for war with Turkey? Possibly they saw the break-up of the Ottoman Empire as inevitable and wished to safeguard their interests when it occurred. On the other side, Enver in particular became convinced that the Central Powers would win the war and that Turkey's long-term interests lay with them. This was a fearful miscalculation that took little note of British sea power and Britain's determination to protect its communications with India. But all this lay a long way in the future. Given that Britain and France were having a great deal of difficulty even containing the Germans on the Western Front and that the Russians had received an early thrashing at Tannenburg, exactly what forces did the Entente have to spare to deal with Turkey and how were they to be deployed?

In fact the war against Turkey evolved piecemeal and over disparate areas. In the initial phase (1914–1915), with the exception of Gallipoli, only relatively small forces were involved and many of these did not originate in Britain. By the end of the war, however, 500,000 troops had been committed against Turkey, and Egypt had become the greatest base for British troops outside the homeland. Apart from Gallipoli, which has already been dealt with, there were three main areas of British involvement against the Turks: Mesopotamia, Palestine and the Arabian Peninsula. The considerable conflict between the Turks and Russians, although it often robbed Turkey of reinforcements for the other theatres, lies outside the scope of this book.

The first pressure point came in Mesopotamia because of a decision by Churchill as First Lord of the Admiralty to convert the British fleet from coal to oil.[3] The usual reason given for the British invasion of Mesopotamia was the protection of the oil refineries around Abadan at the head of the Persian Gulf which supplied Britain's Mediterranean Fleet. No doubt this was the immediate aim. But the principal reasons for intervention given at the time were a demonstration to the Turks that the British could strike them in any part of their empire, an encouragement to the Arab populations to rally to Britain, and to safeguard the Persian Gulf, which was seen as an outlier in the defence of India. Oil was a factor but, as it could be obtained freely from the United States, a lesser factor.[4]

The initiative for intervention came from London – which in the light of subsequent events had more than a touch of irony. Some British Indian Army units (a composite force largely consisting of Indian troops but with

British officers and a 'stiffening' of a few British battalions) were being transported across the Arabian Gulf to Europe for service on the Western Front. On the insistence of the Cabinet (but to the annoyance of the Viceroy, Lord Hardinge), a brigade of the 6 (Poona) Division was diverted to the Gulf. It anchored off Bahrain on 23 October awaiting further instructions. On the outbreak of the war with Turkey these instructions soon followed. The 16 Indian Brigade was to proceed to the Shatt al-Arab and then occupy Abadan.[5] That, for the moment, was deemed sufficient by London.

Facing the British were two divisions of the Ottoman army (35 and 38 Divisions). They were not of the highest quality, consisting mainly of Arab and Kurdish troops of dubious loyalty to Turkey, the best troops being grouped much closer to Constantinople.[6] Moreover, most of the troops had been dispersed in frontier posts and were quite unused to fighting as a unit.[7] Each division contained about 5,000 men and had thirty-two pieces of light artillery. Few of these troops were at the head of the Gulf, though, so the British were able to land without difficulty. They then advanced several miles upriver until they were 2 miles north of the oil installations. Abadan was safe.

However, by then the remaining brigades of the 6 (Poona) Division had arrived and its commander, Lieutenant-General Sir Arthur Barratt, had fresh orders. The better to protect Bahrain, he was to occupy Basra. In the event, this was not difficult. Intelligence arrived that the Turks were evacuating Basra. He immediately despatched several battalions of his force and on 21 November 1914 Basra was in British hands.

At this point the factor that plagued British policy in Mesopotamia began to reveal itself. Basra had been captured to protect Abadan; Qurna, 30 miles upriver at the junction of the Tigris and Euphrates, was now deemed essential for the protection of Basra.[8] A British expedition was sent north. Qurna, due more to the incompetence of the local Turkish commanders than the enterprise of the British, capitulated with its garrison of 1,000 men on 9 December.

Another perennial factor that was to hamper the British was also revealed at Qurna. The floods that would turn the whole area of the confluence of the Tigris and Euphrates into a gigantic flood plain were imminent. Yet the British had little water transport. They had a few small gunboats capable of carrying small garrisons and 2 x 18-pounder guns, but that was all. The waters, while ubiquitous, were shallow. The only answer seemed to be to employ hundreds of local canoes called bellums.[9] These could hold around eight men, who were required to row them as well as fight. Thus the novel but anachronistic addition of canoe-borne infantry was made to the British army.

While the British were pondering their next move, the Turks were preparing to recapture Basra. They gathered a motley force at Nasiriyah and began to march (or wade) towards their objective. The result was a fiasco for the Turks. The British had good intelligence about their approach and, reinforced with another division of troops from India, sallied forth to attack them. Three days' fighting in March saw the end of the Turkish thrust. The Turks lost heavily and retreated towards Nasiriyah. However, the lack of transport, which the government in India had done nothing to augment, meant that the British were unable to follow.[10] The Turks would survive to fight another day.

Nevertheless, these easy victories had aroused the interests of the sub-imperialists at Simla. Hardinge noted that his Indian forces had advanced over 100 miles from the entrance of the Persian Gulf with little opposition and were now in control of much of lower Mesopotamia. Might not that whole area be added – not to the British Empire but as a province of a nascent Indian Empire? Could not some of the teeming millions of India be resettled there and at the same time the Arab tribes coaxed away from Turkey to settle along the shores of the Arabian Peninsula?[11] At this point the impetus for military operations in Mesopotamia tended to pass out of the hands of London and into eager hands in India.

But at this time the British were changing their focus to a much more threatening area – that of the Suez Canal zone in Egypt. Egypt was of course still legally part of the Ottoman Empire but actually semi-autonomous under a khedive and in reality (since 1883) controlled by the British. The defence of the Canal Zone therefore fell to the Commander-in-Chief of Egypt, General Sir John Maxwell. At his disposal were about 30,000 troops from the Indian Army and from December 1914 a contingent of Anzacs on their way to Britain but, due to crowded facilities there, training in Egypt.[12] As the British well knew, a Turkish invasion force to attack the canal had long been in preparation. By January 1915 20,000 men and 10,000 camels, some light artillery and a few pontoons had been assembled in the Beersheba area under the nominal command of Djemal Pasha but operationally controlled by the wonderfully named General Friedrich Kress von Kressenstein.[13] The organisation of this force was a far cry from the rabble around Basra. Careful preparations in the form of adequate water and food supplies had been made to cross the desert. Marches were made by night to avoid detection and the heat. As a result of this efficient organisation, the force reached the canal in good shape.

When the Turks arrived at the canal, however, they soon found that organisation was not enough. The defenders were well dug in along its western banks, and the canal was on average 150 feet wide. It was also interspersed with some wider lakes but these were controlled by small British gun boats. The Turks were therefore forced to scramble down the steep banks of the canal and attempt to launch what small boats they possessed. There was never any prospect of success. Most pontoons were holed by rifle and machine-gun fire before they reached the water.[14] By 4 February it was all over.[15] The British awoke to find that the Turks had withdrawn in good order back to Beersheba. The hoped-for rising of the Egyptian population against the British had failed to materialise. By June 1915 Kress's force had been withdrawn from Sinai to reinforce Gallipoli. The canal was safe.

There was no attempt to pursue the Turks. The British forces lacked mobility and supplies of food and water to transverse 100 miles of desert. Indeed water could only be carried by pack animals and as there was a severe shortage of camels stalemate reigned in Sinai.[16]

In Mesopotamia the situation seemed quite promising. With the arrival of the new troops from India in April 1915 a new general had been put in charge, a 'thruster' by the name of General Sir John Nixon. Under him were grouped the 6 (Poona) Division under General Sir Charles Townshend and the 12 Indian Division under Lieutenant-General George Gorringe. (Barratt had been sent home). That Nixon would need all the troops he could get was soon apparent. In April 1915 he received instructions from the Indian government that his main task was now the occupation of the entire province (vilayet) of Basra. This ranged well beyond the territory so far captured and extended to Nasiriyah in the north, a total of 16,500 square miles of territory. More alarming was their next instruction. Even before the vilayet of Basra was conquered, a plan was to be made for the capture of Baghdad. From London's perspective there was not much sense in any of this. The landings at Gallipoli had now occurred and the Suez Canal had still to be defended. The British government was therefore quite satisfied to rank Mesopotamia third in importance and limit its ambitions to the security of the oil refineries. But what London had never grasped were the vaulting ambitions that now drove the Indian government and particularly Viceroy Hardinge. The war against the Ottoman Empire was now being waged from two centres (London and Simla) and with two quite distinct aims.[17]

To carry out Simla's imperial purpose, Nixon reported that he would need more animal transport, a light railway, armoured cars, aircraft and a huge increase in river transport. But he sent these requests to London, which was unaware of the growing ambitions of the colleagues in India. To make matters worse, he sent the requests through the ordinary post. When they eventually arrived no one in London realised that the demands, which they regarded as extraordinary, were designed to fulfil the ambitions of the government in India. Most were turned down.

Meanwhile, despite the priorities of the Indian government, Nixon had to delay all thought of an advance until he had secured the oil pipelines which were threatened by various Arabian tribes. Once General Gorringe had achieved this, Nixon was ready to advance. His first destination was Amara, some distance from Basra. General Townshend, described by one recent authority as 'overwhelmingly ambitious and impossibly immodest', was in immediate command.[18] He was not without talent, however, and soon mastered the amphibious aspects of warfare in Mesopotamia. His canoe-borne troops, accompanied by three shallow-draught gunboats, set off in May. One company commander recorded the scene:

> May 31st. The bellum flotilla started off, each bellum contained eight men with one day's rations and blankets. The 1/Oxford L[ight] I[nfantry] advanced against Norfolk Hill and the 22 Punjabis made for One Tree Hill. At the same time the fleet in the river steamed upstream ... The Oxfords leapt out of their bellum and took Norfolk Hill with the bayonet.[19]

As if to emphasise the strangeness of this war, the attack of the bellum flotilla coincided with the first use of aircraft for reconnaissance purposes by the British in this theatre.[20]

By 3 June Amara had surrendered. Nixon then set off to Nasiriyah, with an ominous coda to his orders that this town would be more secure if Kut, some 120 miles beyond, lying outside the Basra vilayet, was also captured.

Nasiriyah fell as easily as Basra and Amara. There was no doubt that these rapid victories emboldened Nixon to attempt to capture Kut, which he now regarded as a matter of 'strategic necessity'.[21] Reluctantly, the Secretary of State in London (Austen Chamberlain) gave his approval for the next advance. He urged caution but was completely unaware that the Indian government saw Kut as merely a staging post for the ultimate prize of Baghdad.[22]

One matter soon became clear: the commander who was to advance on Kut was against the whole idea. While Gallipoli remained in the balance Townshend thought gains made in Mesopotamia should be consolidated. He knew that his force was chronically short of water transport and that this might endanger his hold on Nasiriyah, let alone anything further upriver. Nevertheless, he had his orders. On 28 August his troops set off – this time not by canoe, because the dry season had arrived, but by foot – in temperatures of 116°F. In these conditions the 6 (Poona) Division began the advance on Kut.

Townshend had good reason to be cautious. After its early failures, the Turkish army was recovering. Two new divisions had arrived and their overall commander, Nureddin Pasha, had dug formidable defences on the left and right banks of the river 7 miles from Kut, thus blocking the British advance.

Townshend took a typically gloomy view of his chances to force these defences. But he developed a clever deception plan which caused the Turks to concentrate their men and guns on one side of the river while Townshend sent his main force against the other. This won the day. After hard fighting, on 28 September the British found that the Turks had decamped. Kut had fallen and Townshend had inflicted heavy casualties on the defenders – some 4,000 men as against just 94 of his own killed. A slow pursuit upriver towards Baghdad ensued; soon the British were within 60 miles of the city. But the advance had failed to trap the retreating Turkish army. Townshend's force lacked sufficient pack animals to make his advance anything but an infantry slog. In that sense the enemy still remained to be beaten.

The question now was could Baghdad be captured? Townshend and the War Office in London thought his lines too extended to take and then hold the city. Consolidation was Townshend's watchword. But soon the prospect of the evacuation of Gallipoli changed the minds of the London decision-makers. By October the Foreign Secretary (Grey) was speaking of a success in Mesopotamia as a suitable antidote to the loss of Gallipoli. Typically, the Cabinet could not come to a definite decision, so they sanctioned a 'raid' on Baghdad, without ever defining exactly what was meant by a 'raid'.[23]

Meanwhile Nixon and Townshend moved cautiously upriver to the approval of the authorities in Simla.[24] The Cabinet, if they even noticed, no doubt felt that these movements fell within their definition of a raid. Hardinge therefore sanctioned the capture of Baghdad if Nixon's forces were strong enough. To encourage him, the Viceroy promised him two additional divisions but notably no time was specified for their arrival. London remained silent. Townshend therefore began the advance on 14 November. Worryingly, he had no more shipping resources to support his advance than had been available in May. Nevertheless, at Ctesiphon (the ancient Assyrian capital) in a clever battle of manoeuvre Townshend defeated a sizeable Turkish force.[25] In the event, this victory meant little. His troops had finally outrun their tenuous supply chain. Townshend had no cookers, no water carts and few pack animals, which meant that the men were always short of rations. He also had few tents, so the sick and wounded were forced to lie in the open, often in wet and freezing conditions. Medical supplies were also running short, which hardly improved matters.[26] So, having arrived at the gates of Baghdad, Townshend promptly ordered a retreat.[27] And the retreat would continue until he could be assured of sufficient supplies; that is, he would return to whence he had come – Kut. He reached the town on 4 December and declared – not without reason – that his force was exhausted. They would stand at Kut and if besieged (which soon followed) await a relief column. In the event the siege would last 147 days until May 1916.

The Turkish attack on Kut commenced soon after Townshend's exhausted force arrived. It was relentless. On Christmas Eve 1915 a major assault was launched. The Turks secured a foothold within a corner of the fort and were only ejected with heavy casualties. Christmas Day was a dismal affair with the officers munching on burnt goose and plum pudding that was described as 'chiefly sand'. Others spent the day in the grim task of cleaning out the human remains from the fort.[28] Rations were progressively cut and on 15 January the first case of scurvy was reported. By February the advantages of mule over horse flesh were being discussed. At the same time bombing by one or two enemy aircraft added to the misery.[29] Meanwhile, there were three poorly thought-out efforts to break through, their failures much publicised by Townshend, which could hardly have raised morale. Townshend also launched a propaganda barrage, blaming the siege on his superiors and protesting that he had been against the whole venture from the start.[30]

The eventual depletion of food supplies and the failure of an attempt to resupply Townshend's force from the river meant that capitulation was the only option. In the end 13,000 men from the 6 (Poona) Division went into captivity. Townshend, through no fault of his own, was treated well and lived in relative luxury on an island in the Marmara. His men were less fortunate. Decades before the German 'death marches' of the inmates of concentration camps, the Turks used a similar policy on British prisoners taken at Kut. About 10,000 men set out from Kut. Marching across the desert in blazing heat with what seems wilful neglect, most of these men died. Indeed the marches seemed so purposeless that this appeared to be their only end. The episode gives the Turks the dubious distinction of both carrying out the first genocide of the twentieth century (in Armenia) and inventing the death march as well.[31]

The government in London quickly responded to the fall of Kut. They took control of the operations from the Indian government, sacked Nixon and replaced him with Lieutenant-General Stanley Maude, one of the few generals who had enhanced his reputation at Gallipoli by his handling of 13 Division.[32] It was determined that he would have a force of four full-strength divisions, so 50,000 men were added to his army. Also the port of Basra, sunk into a mire of inefficiency and ruin, was reorganised. River-transport capacity increased from 450 to 700 tons per day. With this new force, Maude set off for Kut in December. The well-equipped troops advanced in good heart but the real success belonged to the gunboats. Their fire reduced a Turkish retreat to a shambles. In January 1917 the British were back in Kut.[33]

What followed was the inevitable pause because the British, even with improved logistics, had outrun their supplies. But when his resupplied force set out in March, it was not to be denied. The force was far too strong for anything the Turks could spare in this area. On 9 March Baghdad was in British hands.[34]

The remainder of the Mesopotamia campaign was anti-climactic. Maude sent columns beyond Baghdad but the Turks had recovered and offered stiff resistance.[35] In mid-November Maude died of cholera, but his job was virtually over. Allenby's campaign in Palestine was now the main event and in 1918 the Mesopotamia campaign ground to a halt.[36] There was a flurry of activity in November when a British force raced ahead to secure Mosul before the Armistice was concluded, but that was all. Attention had long since shifted elsewhere.

* * * * *

It was the critical situation in Palestine which made Mesopotamia seem irrelevant. After the defeat of the Turkish attack on the canal, the British had cautiously moved into Sinai. Kress had attempted raids against the canal but with many of his troops withdrawn to supply the needs of the Gallipoli campaign these amounted to mere pinpricks.[37] Then, in 1916, with Gallipoli evacuated, Kress made a bolder move. In April he moved towards the canal with 3,500 men. He surprised some advanced posts (the British had sensibly decided to defend the canal from the Sinai Desert). Kress now waited for more German equipment before making his next move. But the British were also being reinforced and a standard-gauge railway line had been pushed across the desert to Romani.[38] In August Kress determined to capture it by a flanking movement around the right. There he ran into one of the British reinforcements – the Anzac Mounted Division. Several attempts to annihilate the horsed soldiers failed. With the Turks tiring, a spirited charge by two brigades of Anzac cavalry proved too much. Some 500 Turks surrendered and with the aid of British infantry (52 Division) the whole Turkish line began to retreat. But darkness was falling; the horses had been without water for a considerable time, so once more Kress escaped.[39]

The question now was: what was British policy in this area to be? By this time Maxwell had been despatched back to Britain and a new commander – General Sir Archibald Murray, former Chief of the General Staff – took his place. Murray was a cautious man and with some reason. He had no desire to fling a force across the wastes of the Sinai Desert only to see it retreat through lack of supplies. In this respect he was the opposite of his fellow generals in Mesopotamia. He would advance across the Sinai but only at the pace that a water pipeline, a railway and an improvised wire-based road could be built across the sandy wastes. The pace of all this was glacial. By December 1916 British forces were still in Sinai near El Arish. They were now accompanied by a formidable cavalry component in the form of the Desert Column and the Anzac Mounted Division. Indeed, these forces played a major role in the action at El Arish which saw Turkish forces expelled from Egypt.

The next prize was Gaza, the position which anchored the Turkish defence of southern Palestine. Murray's plan for the First Battle of Gaza was imaginative. He would attack the city frontally while at the same time outflanking it with his mounted troops. It started promisingly on 24 March 1917. The mounted troops carried out their role to perfection and were well to the north of Gaza. But then an intelligence failure led them to believe that the frontal attack had gone disastrously wrong, which it had not. As a result the mounted troops withdrew and the Turks were left in full possession of Gaza.[40]

In London, the Cabinet were not pleased with this outcome and urged Murray to try again. Murray pleaded lack of reinforcements and guns as a reason to delay. Political pressure won out. The Second Battle of Gaza commenced on 17 April with weapons such as handful of tanks and poison gas – the first time this weapon had been deployed outside Europe. (So ineffective was the gas that it dispersed quickly in the warm desert air and the Turks were unaware that it had even been used.) The plan was, however, unimaginative. Three divisions were to assault Gaza frontally. This they did to no effect whatsoever. British losses amounted to 6,500 men.[41] Turkish losses were only a third as many. That was the end of Murray. He had proved an excellent administrator and a disastrous general. Lloyd George wished to replace him with Jan Smuts, but when the South African turned down the command, General Allenby, then commanding the Third Army on the Western Front, got the job. It was to prove a fortunate circumstance.

As he took up his command, Allenby was to discover that he had an energetic and sometimes troublesome ally at the base of the Sinai Peninsula at Aqaba. This was T.E. Lawrence, unofficial officer with Arabian forces in Hejaz. The Arabian army was nominally commanded by Sharif Hussein of the Hejaz. Hussein had been induced to join the war against Turkey in 1916. There had been an exchange of letters between Hussein and the British High Commissioner in Cairo, Sir Henry McMahon. These letters have a certain desperate opaqueness about them but, on the surface anyway, they promised Hussein certain territories around modern Syria and the Arabian Peninsula in return for support. Hussein, with the encouragement of Lawrence, then a member of the Arab Bureau in Cairo, was happy to oblige. Arabian nationalism had grown in the nineteenth century and disillusionment with Turkish rule had grown with it.

The Arab uprising against the Turks began in the Hejaz on 5 June 1916. The Turks had just a single division in this area and Hussein and his four sons – the most notable of whom was Feisal – were able to capture Mecca within a few days. Feisal, who increasingly took the lead on the Arab side, then besieged Medina but his forces, though large in number, were short on discipline and firepower and failed to take it.

The return of Lawrence to act as a kind of chief of staff to Feisal changed the way operations were conducted. Lawrence developed a double strategy. He would allow just enough material to pass down the Hejaz railway to sustain the Turks but not enough to increase their strength. This would confine most Turkish troops to the Hejaz while Lawrence with Feisal's Arab army advanced along the coast northwards to Aqaba.[42] Lawrence knew that it was necessary to link up with British forces in Palestine as quickly as possible if the Arabs were to have the territory seemingly promised them by McMahon. And Lawrence knew this because he was privy to another division of the Middle East decided by Britain and France in the Sykes–Picot Plan of April 1916. Under this plan France would be pre-eminent in Syria and Lebanon, while the British would be the dominant power in Palestine, Jordan, Mesopotamia and the Persian Gulf. Clearly, if this agreement was put into practice there would be little room for the Arab states already agreed to by the British. The best way, Lawrence considered, to make certain that the Arabs got their due was for them to occupy such key points as Damascus, Aleppo and Homs.

Lawrence accomplished his first purpose. With the aid of the Royal Navy, Arab forces with British supplies advanced along the Red Sea coast and by 6 July 1917 were occupying Aqaba. The next question for Lawrence was how the newly appointed Allenby would deal with the situation.

Allenby's arrival saw an immediate lift in British morale. He stayed in close touch with his troops and moved his headquarters from Cairo into the Sinai. He also ensured that time was taken to prepare the third assault on the Gaza–Beersheba position. This time the plan showed some imagination. Gaza would be attacked frontally but only as a feint attack. The main operation would occur on the right with three infantry divisions, securing the Turkish line while mounted troops would seize Beersheba and its precious water wells by *coup de main*. The Turkish line would then be rolled up from Beersheba to Gaza while the mounted forces cut off any Turks attempting to flee. In all Allenby would have seven infantry divisions, three mounted divisions, 300 guns and six tanks. He would also have air superiority due to new types arriving in the Middle East from Britain.[43] There was another factor: Allenby would also use gas but in much greater quantities than at the Second Battle of Gaza and of a more lethal type. In all he would have over 10,000 chemical shells, some being the choking and blistering agent phosgene. The gases were to be used against crossroads, troop bivouacs and trench strongpoints.[44]

The operation began on 31 October 1917 with a 3-mile cavalry charge against the left of the Turkish line at Beersheba. The capture intact of the wells there ensured a good supply of water for the entire centre-right force. The report on this famous charge is most matter of fact:

> Both the 4th and 12th L[ight] H[orse] Regiments went forward at a gallop and took successive lines of trenches until reaching the Wadi at Beersheba. The left flank of the 12th Regiment came under heavy machine gun fire [but] ... the M.G. Squadron immediately opened fire in this Redoubt and the Brigadier ordered Major Harrison. O.C. Notts. Battery, R.H.A. [Royal Horse Artillery] to open fire on these trenches. It was practically dark [but the Notts Battery] found the range with their second shot, and quickly drove the Turks from the ridge ... The rapidity of the attack seemed to demoralise the Turks and also avoided their artillery fire.[45]

So when the Western Front was distant, the machine guns were few and with a little help from the artillery, the cavalry charge could still prove useful.

The Turkish positions from Beersheba to the coast were subjected to a six-day bombardment by more than sixty medium and heavy guns, supplemented by a naval bombardment from craft in the Mediterranean. In all it was the heaviest bombardment on an enemy position outside the Western Front. What effect gas had as a part of this bombardment is controversial. Some Turks were apparently killed by it, but gas hardly rates a mention in the official accounts.[46] In any case the conventional bombardment dealt severely enough with the Turkish defences. The three centre-right British divisions (53, 74 and 60) made some headway. Then an attack on the coast by three more divisions (62, 54 and 75) begun merely as a feint attack turned the flank of the whole Turkish line and, with the successes on the right, forced a general retreat.[47] Turkish counter-attacks were beaten off but lack of good supplies of water prevented the mounted troops from cutting off the Turks.[48] Nevertheless, the advance continued but at a slower pace. By 16 November the British had gained an average of 50 miles and were within striking distance of Jerusalem.

Jerusalem presented a problem to Allenby. A city regarded as holy by three major religions could hardly be stormed or subjected to bombardment. He planned an encircling movement to the east of the city but the Turkish defence was too strong and it was beaten back.[49] A second attempt to the west met with more success. The Turkish Seventh Army with 16,000 defenders had to be overcome but the series of defeats already inflicted by the British had sapped its morale. So on 8 December, this potentially formidable fighting force withdrew from Jerusalem and Allenby famously entered it bare headed and on foot the following day. Lloyd George's self-serving wish to present the capture of Jerusalem to the British people by Christmas had been fulfilled.

Winter now settled over the area and the British army needed rest and recuperation as well as resupply. Conventional operations were therefore temporarily suspended.[50] Lawrence, meanwhile, was continuing to launch nuisance raids on the Turks. The most spectacular of these – the attack on the Yarmuk railway bridge – failed. Nevertheless, Lawrence's operations did tie down a number of Turkish troops to the east of the River Jordan while Allenby got on with the main business in Palestine.[51] While Lawrence's contribution has been wildly overblown (mainly by himself), there is no doubt that he played a role in the Turkish retreat.

Allenby, in Jerusalem, began to plan his campaign for 1918. The War Cabinet, perhaps impatient with Allenby's progress, sent out General Smuts to report on the situation. In February 1918 Smuts recommended that operations in Mesopotamia be defensive and that two divisions from that theatre be transferred to Allenby to enable him to take the offensive.[52] Several factors delayed it. The first was the failure of the British to capture the important junction of Amman to the east of the Jordan.[53] But at least the failure convinced the Turks to concentrate more forces in the area, taking them from the coastal strip along which Allenby always intended to make his final thrust.[54] The other factor was the situation in France. Ludendorff launched the first of his great offensives on 21 March and Allenby was soon required to free two British divisions (53 and 74) for the Western Front, followed by artillery batteries and more battalions of troops as shipping became available.[55] Apart from small-scale raiding operations of dubious value, this saw an end to major British activity in Palestine for four months.

In fact the next major British battle in Palestine did not take place until 19 September 1918. Allenby, having coaxed most of the Turkish forces to the east of the Jordan, struck along the coast. The force at his disposal was formidable. The British had 35,000 infantry, 9,000 cavalry and 383 guns on a front of only 15 miles. The Turks who faced them had just 10,000 men and 130 guns. Before the battle the Royal Air Force (as the air service was now called) had played a significant role. By repeated bombing, it had cut all railway traffic from the north to Palestine, thus making reinforcement of the Turkish army virtually impossible. The outcome of the battle was never in doubt. Not even the presence of Falkenhayn, 'genius' of Verdun, as the new Commander-in-Chief of the Ottoman armies, could stem the tide. The preliminary bombardment dropped 1,000 shells per minute on the Turkish defenders. The infantry broke through near Megiddo (the ancient Armageddon) and this time the cavalry did manage to encircle the retreating Turks. By 21 September the Turkish Seventh and Eighth Armies had ceased to exist. Allenby, sensing that victory was within his grasp, pressed on. The 3 Australian Light Horse entered Damascus on 1 October, closely followed by Lawrence's Arab forces eager to stake their territorial claims. What followed was a diminuendo. British troops pursued the increasingly disintegrating Turkish army to Aleppo, which was taken on 26 October without a shot. Armistice negotiations commenced on the same day and were concluded on 31 October. The war against Turkey had been won.[56]

How was it that a handful of British divisions had been able – eventually – to overthrow the Ottoman Empire while almost all British resources were deployed on the Western Front? The Ottomans faced a difficult situation. They had in 1915 four major fronts with which to contend: Gallipoli, Egypt, Mesopotamia and the Caucasus. Gallipoli was a defensive victory but the remaining elements of the Turkish army did not have the capacity to undertake successful offensive campaigns. Against the Suez Canal, logistics were a nightmare. It took the British two years and a major industrial effort (the construction of the railway and the water pipeline across the desert) to establish a base from which to push on. In Mesopotamia it was their ability to employ gunboats as much as any military factor which saw them victorious. Moreover in this far-flung Turkish province the troops were not of the best, nor could the loyalty of some be counted on, let alone the loyalty of the local population. The British had little trouble in recruiting many Arabs to their side, a factor which virtually opened a fifth front. When Allenby arrived in Palestine he was able to build on the solid foundation of communications already in place. He could also deploy guns almost at a Western Front standard and he had an efficient mobile arm always able to threaten the Turkish flanks. In the end, though, the Turks were overwhelmed by industrial production and an army that was more efficiently managed. In many ways, the victory against the Ottomans was remarkable. Although it had taken four years and suffered some considerable setbacks, the British had overthrown an empire with the remnants it could spare from its army on the Western Front and because it could mobilise considerable numbers from its Indian Empire to assist.

That the war against the Ottomans became a political war where the clashing ambitions of Britain, France, the Arabs and the government in India became intertwined is beyond doubt, and the ramifications of these competing ambitions beyond the scope of this book. Yet the war came about in a rather old-fashioned way – because factions in the Young Turk government in 1914 decided that the Central Powers would win the war. And that this government had ambitions of its own is revealed by their prompt move on the Suez Canal. Before the conflict began, Britain was prepared to guarantee the Ottoman Empire, no doubt content to have a weak power on the flank of its communicant line to India. Once the war had commenced, any desire to keep the Ottoman Empire intact vanished. The Western Powers were dividing up the empire in various and devious ways. In this carve-up the government of India came a bad last – its imperial ambitions trumped by those of Britain, France and Lawrence's Arabs. After 1917 the Jews also should be placed in the mix due to the Balfour Declaration that they should have a national home, though not at the expense of anyone else who might have been promised the same territory.

CHAPTER 8

RUE MORGUE – 1917

THE BATTLE OF THE Somme formally ended on 17 November 1916. In the weeks that followed, it claimed its two most prominent casualties. In France, Joffre's policy to continue this barren offensive in the spring terrified the French government, which promptly sacked him. His replacement was the little-known General Robert Nivelle. The new man, who had won two minor battles at the very end of the Verdun campaign, put forward a formula for victory – he would stun the Germans with a series of rapid-fire offensives by the French along the Chemin des Dames. The British would play a supporting role by attacking 70 miles further north at Arras. Most importantly, he guaranteed that, should these operations falter, he would close them down. To a government that had endured 750,000 casualties in 1916 for no gains of note this was very appealing.

In Britain the change was political. On 6 December 1916 Lloyd George replaced Asquith as Prime Minister. Lloyd George's ascent to power was to some extent inevitable. He had galvanised munitions production, supported conscription (introduced by a reluctant Asquith in May 1916) and generally favoured a more vigorous prosecution of the war. To an American journalist he had stated that the war must be fought to a finish – 'to a knock-out'.

This seemed a straightforward policy. Yet Lloyd George was a man of many contradictions when it came to running the war. He had a deep-seated antipathy towards the military and especially to the British military leadership that he had inherited. He thought the CIGS (Robertson) a dullard and Haig a butcher who had presided over a battle that had cost more British casualties than any other in its history – and for no tangible result. He told his secretary: 'Haig does not care how many men he loses. He just squanders the lives of these boys. I mean to save some of them in the future . . . I am their trustee.'[1] The circle Lloyd George had to square was how to prosecute the war vigorously while conserving lives, a feat no commander on the Western Front had yet managed.

His first opportunity arrived at an inter-Allied conference in Rome in January 1917. Without revealing his plan to the French or to Robertson, he came forth with the idea that the Italians, lavishly reinforced with British and French artillery, should carry out the main Allied offensive in 1917 against the Austrians. That would certainly conserve young British lives, but the Italians refused even to discuss it.

With the Italians out and Russia struggling to maintain an army in the field, somewhat reluctantly Lloyd George turned towards the French. He knew of Nivelle's plan but was disinclined to countenance further bloodletting on the Western Front. Now he was forced to reconsider. Nivelle was invited to London, where he placed his 'formula' before the War Cabinet. He proved an attractive personality – one who could explain his plan with verve and eloquence. Robertson and Haig, who were also present, were not charmed, noting, rightly, that there seemed little that was new in this so-called formula.[2] But Nivelle's exposition won over the politicians; Haig was instructed to play his supporting role.

Indeed, Nivelle offered Lloyd George a way of squaring his circle. The French would carry out the main offensive under a commander who seemed to be concerned to limit casualties. Perhaps placing Haig under such a commander would limit British casualties as well. This arrangement might ensure that there were no more battles such as the Somme.

In the weeks that followed, Lloyd George's attitude towards the military hardened. Perhaps he was irritated by Haig and Robertson's response to the new plan; perhaps he was annoyed by an interview given to the press by Haig where he seemed to cast aspersions at the efforts of the Ministry of Munitions; perhaps he merely thought back to the blighted hopes and high cost of the Somme. Whatever the reason, he now determined to place Haig under Nivelle's control.

On 17 January the War Cabinet took the extraordinary step of instructing Haig to carry out his share of Nivelle's plan 'at the date laid down in the . . .agreement, or even before that date, with the forces available at the moment . . . On no account must the French have to wait for us.'[3] In other words the offensive was to take place whether Haig considered his forces adequate or not – an assertion of civilian control that was reckless in the extreme. Robertson fought back. At a meeting on 13 February he reminded ministers that in this situation they – not Haig – must bear the responsibility for any ensuing disaster, and he also reminded them that the current state of the French railways might make it unfeasible for Haig to adhere to the original plan because of the impossibility of accumulating supplies.[4]

Lloyd George regarded this merely as a manoeuvre to abrogate Haig's subordination to Nivelle, so on 24 February he called a War Cabinet. On this occasion Robertson was told not to attend. The conclusion reached was that French generals and staffs were cleverer than their British equivalents and that in particular Nivelle was far cleverer than Haig.[5] Therefore the original arrangement must stand.

To reinforce this decision a conference was called at Calais among senior French and British politicians and military leaders. The ostensible reason for the conference was to attend to the state of the French railways; the real reason to subordinate Haig to Nivelle. With Lloyd George's connivance the French produced a paper that gave Nivelle control over Haig, leaving the British general little but administrative matters to deal with. A furious row between the Prime Minister, Haig and Robertson followed. Overnight Hankey drafted a compromise. Haig would 'conform' to Nivelle's plan but have the right of appeal to London in the case of disagreement. He would also retain considerable freedom in conducting his own operations. Lloyd George and the military leaders reluctantly accepted Hankey's draft. Bad blood remained on both sides.[6]

On return to London the Prime Minister found his position had been undermined by none other than Nivelle. The French commander had sent a number of high-handed, indeed peremptory, telegrams to Haig about how to conduct the coming offensive. The Conservatives in the War Cabinet (and particularly Lord Derby, the Minister of War, who had been kept away from Calais) rebelled. They insisted on another Anglo-French conference where Lloyd George was forced to announce that the War Cabinet retained 'full confidence' in Haig, who was 'regarded with admiration in England'.[7] Thus was reached for the moment a low point in relations between the politicians and the military in Britain.

Meanwhile the general in whom Lloyd George had 'full confidence' set about planning the diversionary battle that would be a prelude to Nivelle's offensive. The attack out of Arras was to be carried out by the Third Army (Allenby) with the First Army (Horne) to capture Vimy Ridge as flank protection on the left. The Fifth Army (Gough), on the right of the First, was to mount a subsidiary operation to divert German reserves.

The German defences to be attacked were very strong. In the area of the Third Army, the Germans had constructed a front system of three to four trench lines 75 to 100 yards apart, all protected by belts of wire. A support line of similar strength lay just further back and a reserve line, also strongly wired, was several hundred yards in rear. Finally, 4 miles back lay the Drocourt–Quéant Switch Line which was part of the Hindenburg Line and cunningly placed on a reverse slope, well suited for resolute defence and out of direct artillery observation.

The plan as eventually developed was to attack these defences with four-teen divisions. In the north, the Canadian Corps of four divisions and one British division would seize the heights of Vimy Ridge. Further south, nine divisions of the Third Army would attack on either side of Arras. They would capture the three enemy trench systems in distinct stages, with a pause between. Then they would advance on the quite formidable Drocourt–Quéant Line and ultimately capture Cambrai, some 25 miles distant. The cavalry were given a role. If the infantry plan went well, they would sally forth and seize the high ground around Monchy. Only forty rather unreliable Mark II tanks would be available. All were allotted to the Third Army.[8] If the opportunity arose the Fifth Army to the south of the Third was to capture Bullecourt, which lay in the Hindenburg Line proper.

The artillery resources supporting these armies were formidable, sure evidence that the Ministry of Munitions was delivering the goods. In all 4,500 guns were disposed by the First and Third Armies. Five hundred of these were heavy pieces of 8" calibre and above. They would be lavishly supplied with ammunition. In the first quarter of 1917 the Ministry of Munitions produced no fewer than 5 million shells, all of a much higher quality and reliability than had been attained at the Somme. Against this array the Germans counted just 1,000 guns, of which only 220 could be considered heavy.[9]

There were other artillery refinements since the Somme. The command had at last grasped that the two main killers of infantry (enemy batteries and machine guns) had to be given top priority in any bombardment scheme. So, counter-battery fire was placed at the head of artillery duties at Arras. And for the first time enemy batteries would be deluged with gas shell that was now available in quantity.[10] Next in importance were enemy machine guns. Those in the trench systems were to be dealt with by a heavy creeping barrage. The enemy machine guns placed behind the trench systems, which had caused havoc to the advancing infantry in earlier encounters, were to be the target of a separate barrage fired by concentrated British machine guns.[11] Moreover, the exact length of trench to be destroyed and wire cut was carefully calculated from aerial photographs (along lines developed at Neuve Chapelle in 1915 and then forgotten at the Somme) and the appropriate number of guns assigned to deal with each section of the German defences.[12]

There were also improvements in artillery accuracy. Much more attention was now paid to weather conditions which could affect the flight of a shell. Three 'meteor' telegrams were received by the batteries each day giving wind speeds and air temperatures so that guns could make relevant adjustments during the bombardment.[13]

The British had now developed a 'graze' fuse – a fuse that would detonate on first impact. Such a fuse (No. 106) could now be placed in high-explosive shells and used for wire cutting, a method that allowed much more wire to be cut per shell than with a standard shrapnel round.[14]

The intense bombardment was to begin on 2 April, with much preliminary work against batteries and particularly difficult positions commencing on 20 March. The day of battle was to be 8 April, but bad weather delayed it until the 9th, Easter Monday.

Despite the improvements in artillery planning and accuracy and the better quality of shells in use, some familiar problems remained unaddressed. Monchy, an objective for the first day, was 5 miles distant and protected by huge belts of wire that only the heaviest guns could reach. Then there were objectives such as Cambrai, 25 miles distant, twice the distance gained in the entire five-month campaign on the Somme. And how was Cambrai to be captured? It was to be taken by the cavalry, a weapon that had so far proved incapable of a major advance even against rudimentary defences in 1914. In the matter of distant objectives GHQ were simply incapable of reining themselves in. It is sobering that three years' fighting on the Western Front had not taught them that such objectives were chimerical.

The Battle of Arras was launched in the grey light of early dawn, amidst scuds of snow, at 5.30 a.m., 9 April. Fourteen attacking divisions plus the two leapfrogging units moved forward on a 16-mile front from Vimy Ridge in the north to the River Sensée in the south. Though it was a subsidiary operation, designed to attract reserves away from Nivelle, Arras was a larger front of attack and involved more divisions than the first day of the Somme.

In the north, the four Canadian divisions and one British division assaulted Vimy Ridge, a major obstacle to any advance further south. Let us follow the fortunes of the 3 Canadian Division, directly opposite the town of Vimy. Before the battle the progress of the bombardment had been carefully checked by raids, groups of forward artillery observers and a plethora of aerial photographs. By zero hour confidence was high that excellent results were being obtained. At 5.30 a.m. the two attacking brigades rose from their trenches and advanced close under the creeping barrage. Wire in front of the enemy line had been entirely destroyed. The new 106 fuse had worked well. Enemy artillery retaliation was described as 'fairly heavy' but too late to catch the waves of infantry. The German front system was captured with few casualties. The defences had been obliterated, and what remained of the demoralised garrison (79 German Reserve Division) offered little resistance. The only difficulty came in recognising the objective, so thoroughly had the artillery done its work. A pause of forty minutes followed as the infantry consolidated and prepared for the next advance. Then at 6.45 a.m. the troops moved towards their final objective. By 8 a.m. it became clear that in the 3 Canadian Division's area, the enemy had been driven right off the ridge. Communications to the rear were excellent and some concentrations of enemy troops were quickly dealt with by bombardments from the heavy artillery. Consolidation took place all along the line, with the exception of the left flank, where the 4 Canadian Division had been held up by German troops clinging to the very top of the ridge. But the 3 Canadian Division's day was over. They dug in, the artillery dealing with several attempted enemy counter-attacks.[15]

And so it was all along the line. With the exception of two strongpoints, Vimy Ridge was in Canadian hands by the evening of 9 April. The advance had not been cheap. By 11 April the Canadian Corps had suffered 11,297 casualties.[16] But on this occasion they had inflicted heavy casualties on the Germans – the two defending German divisions lost 6,604 killed, wounded and missing, and 4,000 prisoners. In addition the Canadians captured 54 guns, 104 trench mortars and 124 machine guns.[17] The whole operation was an excellent example of what could be achieved by a 'bite and hold' approach. The corps commander (General Byng) has been accused of missing opportunities to make further advances.[18] This criticism entirely misses the point. Byng was not seeking to advance further. He had secured the left flank. He had captured Vimy Ridge. That was enough.

Further south the main attack was launched by Allenby's Third Army with ten divisions in the line and two more ready to leapfrog. Here let us take the example of the 9 Scottish Division, the experience of which serves as a microcosm of the Battle of Arras as a whole.

The 9 Division had played its part in the Battle of the Somme and had featured prominently in the night attack of 14 July. Its artillery commander, General Tudor, was one of the first to develop the tactic of the creeping barrage as a form of infantry protection. In January 1917 the division came under XVII Corps and took up a position just north of the city of Arras. Here it was entrusted with preparing the ground for battle for the entire corps. So in the next six weeks the division dug communication trenches, built light tramways, headquarters for brigades and battalions, laid cable and constructed platforms for field artillery and trench mortars. Eight days of training were devoted to the battle. Each brigade rehearsed its role: 'Models in clay of the German positions were built on the training ground and all ranks made themselves familiar with every detail connected with the German trench system'. Later such methods became routine but in the winter of 1917 they represented a great advance.

As with other divisions in this area the 9 Division was to capture three German trench systems with a pause between each capture. Then the

4 Division would leapfrog through and capture a fourth system, including the village of Fampoux.

The division was supported by a prodigious amount of artillery: 54 trench mortars, 168 field guns and 47 heavy pieces. In addition twenty machine guns would fire a barrage directly behind the creeping barrage and four tanks would support the division.[19]

Tudor once more demonstrated that he was an artillery innovator. The creeping barrage in the 9 Division area would consist of high-explosive shell instead of shrapnel, which was (rightly) thought to give the infantry more protection. In addition one shell in four fired in this barrage would be smoke shell designed to conceal the infantry as they advanced.[20]

At exactly 5.30 a.m. the men of the three brigades of 9 Division (the South African Brigade was in the centre) climbed out of their trenches and followed the creeping barrage of high explosive and smoke. Apart from the occasional machine gun which had survived the bombardment, the German defences had been reduced to ruins. The 8 Black Watch actually crossed no man's land without casualties, surely a record for the Western Front. In no time the first objective had been captured. By 8.45 a.m. the second objective had been overrun, aided by the presence of a tank 'which caused a panic amongst the enemy'. The third German line might have presented a problem – the wire in front of it remained largely uncut – but the enemy were so demoralised that they surrendered in large numbers, passages were cut through the wire and the position taken. By this time (3 p.m.) the brigades of 4 Division had moved through to capture the fourth German position and Fampoux. The 9 Division's day was over. This single division had captured 51 officers and 2,086 other ranks, 17 guns, 24 machine guns and 3 trench mortars.[21]

Overall, it was the same story. The ten divisions of Third Army advanced an average of 3,000 yards on a 10-mile front – the greatest advance achieved in a single battle since the Western Front had solidified. Careful planning, massive fire support and an infantry that were well versed in their tasks had carried the day. Two cavalry divisions were on hand but had been quartered well back. If they had been forward, 'experienced officers' of the 4 and 9 Divisions believed the cavalry would have had some opportunities in their area.[22] As usual this was wishful thinking. The distant wire, as we have seen, was not uniformly well cut. In addition, a company commander in the 4 Division noted that at this time: 'The enemy fire was very heavy now, especially machine-gun fire at long range from Greenland Hill, beyond the Hyderabad Redoubt ... The German shelling was [also] now becoming very heavy.'[23] Yet this was the very area in which the cavalry would have been required to operate. It is worth noting that the very detailed contemporary account from the 9 Division makes no mention of cavalry opportunities.

There is a German side to this great success. In the main area of attack the Germans had not pulled back to the Hindenburg Line. Their positions were largely on forward slopes and therefore very vulnerable to intense artillery fire. They were also in the process of changing their defensive structures, the idea being that counter-attack divisions would be held back beyond all but the heaviest British artillery fire. This was in place at Arras/ Vimy. There were no fewer than seven counter-attack divisions behind the front of attack.[24] They were too far back, though. The British had overrun all four trench systems before these units could be propelled forward. However, their very presence is yet another caution against the view that larger advances could have been made that day. These fresh divisions would have come into play sooner rather than later. And they had more than enough stopping power to deal with cavalry.

There was no question that the action around Arras would be renewed the next day. The French offensive would commence on the 16th, so if the British were to pin the Germans to their section of the front they would have to be continuously engaged. As with most periods of battle after a major push, the action at Arras was ragged. Guns had to be moved forward, the position of the infantry established with some accuracy and the movements of the enemy accounted for. North of the River Scarpe only the most meagre advances could be made. The line inched forwards but no major objectives were taken as tired troops struggled with increasing enemy resistance. South of the river there was better progress. Under a well-fired creeping barrage, troops captured the Wancourt–Feuchy line and advanced on Monchy. But the village was sited on a hilltop and well dug-in machine-gunners prevented further gains across ground that was open and where the troops had very little fire support. Once more the cavalry were called forward but a snowstorm saved them from useless sacrifice. However, this day saw some solid progress. The enemy's last outpost before the Drocourt–Quéant Switch section of the Hindenburg Line had fallen, a feat that on the Somme would have been regarded as a triumph.[25] But that was the end of the successful phase of the Battle of Arras.

11 April was a day of desperation and disaster. Haig had visited the army commanders on the 10th and 'urged on Allenby the importance of keeping the Enemy on the move during the next 24 hours, before he can bring up reserves to meet our advance'.[26] Allenby needed no urging. Indeed he seemed in a mood of extreme over-excitement. His orders for the 11th stated: 'The A.C. wishes all troops to understand that Third Army is now pursuing a defeated enemy and that risks must be freely taken'.[27]

It seems likely that the troops had no such understanding because it was patently obvious to them that they were not in any sense in 'pursuit' and that the enemy, though dealt some hefty blows, was far from beaten. Therefore it was not some pitiful remnant of a battered enemy that the British 37 Division – with the considerable aid of a number of tanks – forced from the high ground at Monchy, but the advance battalions of a division fresh from reserve (3 Bavarian). It seemed that these tired and increasingly disorganised British groups might be driven from the town by counter-attack. Enter the cavalry. Almost inevitably two divisions of cavalry had been sent forward by Allenby to mop up what he considered to be the remains of the German army. They endeavoured to pass north of the village to begin the rout, when they were forced back by heavy artillery fire. They found shelter in the ruins of Monchy, where, dismounted – that is, acting as infantry – they saved the day. Although the Germans directed all the guns they could muster on the village, the cavalrymen hung on. It was one of the finest feats of the war.

Meanwhile, to the south, in the area of Fifth Army, one of the most miserably conceived operations ever conducted on the Western Front was taking place. The plan, put forward by Gough, the Army Commander, was for a division to occupy the Hindenburg Line just south of Bullecourt to facilitate a cavalry sweep north to join hands with Allenby's cavalry and complete the rout of the German army after Arras. The scheme had many counts against it. The corps commander who was to carry it out (Birdwood) and his Chief of Staff (White) thought it impossible of execution; a single-division attack on a narrow front repeated the worst aspects of the Somme battle where all such endeavours had failed; the Fifth Army did not have artillery forward in sufficient quantities to demolish the defences and cut the wire; the tanks which were to smash down the wire in place of the artillery were few in number (there were twelve), mechanically unreliable and untested against defences as strong as the Hindenburg Line; in order to break through, the cavalry would be required to negotiate shattered and shell-pocked ground, twelve lines of deep trenches and any wire not flattened by the tanks; finally, it should have been obvious to Gough that by 11 April when the operation was carried out there was no British cavalry operating to his north and that the whole affair had therefore lost its purpose.

Extraordinarily, the 4 Australian Division, without the benefit of tanks, which had either broken down or been held up by the impossible ground, managed to find sufficient gaps in the wire to force their way into the Hindenburg Line and secure over 1,000 yards of it. They were then subjected to severe counter-attacks from enemy holding the line on their flanks and from the German reserve line. So intense was the German bombardment that ammunition-carrying parties could not get through to the Australians and, because the exact position of the troops was not known, friendly artillery support spluttered to a halt.[28] By the end of the day the division had lost more than 3,000 casualties, over 1,000 of which were prisoners – the greatest capture of Australian soldiers in the war. The incompetence of Gough, which had been on full display at the Somme, was thus reinforced at Bullecourt.

Back at the main front a second push was being prepared. Here the divisions which had done so well on the first day were all given limited objectives in order to keep pressure on the enemy. Haig's view was that 'now we must try to substitute shells as far as possible for infantry'.[29] This was a sensible policy; it was just impossible in the circumstances to carry it out. The fact was that there was not sufficient artillery forward to provide the kind of barrage that had so assisted the advance on the first day. Then there was the state of the troops. Consider the 9 Division. It had been in the line for four days without sleep or hot food.[30] It was now required to capture the village of Roux and a chemical factory. The South African Brigade reported that it was not in a fit condition to attack, so just two brigades advanced. They were heavily shelled by the enemy before they left their trenches. One brigade was required to negotiate 1,750 yards of open ground in full view of the enemy. They asked for a smoke barrage to cover them but communications with the rear were in disarray and the message arrived too late. The creeping barrage was fired at a speed which outpaced the tired troops. The exhausted South Africans were then sent in. The result was a fiasco – no ground gained for heavy casualties.[31]

And so it proved all along the line – on this day and on the 13th and 14th. The command seemed incapable of realising that it was one thing to make long preparations for the first day of battle – quite another to coordinate subsequent actions when artillery and communications were not robust and the troops were exhausted. The ground gained from the evening of the 9th to the end of fighting on the 14th could only be discerned on the most detailed of maps. The Third and First Armies did not materially improve their positions after the capture of Monchy and they suffered heavy and unnecessary casualties.

On 16 April Nivelle launched his offensive on the Chemin des Dames. It was not totally disastrous. He took some ground and captured 2,000 prisoners. But he did not break through and he did not fulfil his promise to stop operations. By the end of the month Haig was aware that Nivelle had failed, therefore there was no reason to continue operations around Arras which had only been designed to assist the French. Yet Haig persisted. And it should be emphasised that he did not persist because of the incidents of 'collective indiscipline' in the French army because he was quite unaware that any had occurred. (In fact the French army had staged a conditional mutiny; they would hold the line but not attack.) Haig continued the battle because he always acted that way. The enemy were always on the run, they were always short of reserves; wearing down must continue.[32]

So the battle wore on. Operations exhausted the First and Third Armies at a greater rate than they did the Germans. Attacks went in on the 23/24 April and 28/29 April but reached their nadir on 3 May. The 9 Division was back in action by then and found themselves part of a three-army attack from Vimy in the north to Bullecourt in the south. The assault was to take place at 3.45 a.m. – in the dark. Its objectives were familiar: Roux and its chemical works, the same target as on 12 April. This time there would be no South Africans, just the 26 and 27 Brigades. So heavy had been its casualties that it was left behind when the division returned to the front.

When the troops went over the top they found that the enemy front line had been missed by the barrage. Heavy machine-gun fire cut down many of these first waves. Then the troops lost direction in the dark. In particular the 5 Cameron Highlanders swung to their right and were identified as enemy troops by the neighbouring 4 Division. A furious fire-fight ensued, but between two British battalions. Further along, the 9 Scottish Rifles swung so far to the right that they advanced firing from the hip on men from the 26 Brigade who were still in their own front line. Thus four friendly battalions engaged each other while the Germans watched on. During the day various attempts were made to get forward but there was no cohesion and even the brigadiers near the front had little idea of the exact position of their men.[33] Yet one brigadier knew precisely who to blame – his troops. He opined that the troops of the 'old army' would have made progress and that the troops at his disposal displayed:

Want of leadership
Want of initiative
Want of elasticity and scope in training
Want of training.[34]

He failed to explain that the troops were also wanting a decent plan that did not commit them to unknown territory in the dark and that they had insufficient fire support to help them on to their objectives. In addition he omitted to explain how either greater training or the 'old army', which was hardly bulletproof, could possibly have compensated for such a poorly thought-through plan of attack.[35]

Gradually it became clear that divisions to the right and left had failed. Overall, Third Army gained no ground that day. In all the 9 Division lost 88 officers and 1,770 other ranks, not all inflicted by the Germans.[36]

On that same day the martyrdom of Australian forces at Bullecourt resumed. This time the wire in front of the Hindenburg Line had been well cut in front of the Australians but not in front of the neighbouring British division. The Australians once again entered the Hindenburg Line but on a very narrow front. The Germans counter-attacked down the trenches to right and left of them as well as from the front. Five days of intense fighting ensued. On 8 May the 5 Australian Division replaced the 2 Division, with no better results. Gradually German resistance in Bullecourt crumbled and the 62 British Division moved in to occupy it. A small, tactically useless village had been captured, well after the main battle had ceased. It had cost 7,000 men. Gough had once more been at the helm of a fiasco.

The Battle of Arras has been described in some detail to establish the nature of the offensive over which the War Cabinet in London was presiding. Essentially there had been two days of success followed by over a month of failure. The total cost in terms of casualties was not light – some 80,000 men. It so happened that the politicians had an opportunity to discuss these matters with the Commander-in-Chief. On the very day of the disaster at Bullecourt and further north at Arras (3 May), a meeting took place between the British Prime Minister and Haig at the C-in-C's headquarters. Lloyd George was visiting France to 'put some ginger into the French' and took the opportunity to see Haig. It was a scenario for confrontation when an indignant Prime Minister might take Haig to task for his repeated failures since 10 April and order him to cease operations at once. Nothing of the kind happened. Instead Lloyd George expressed the greatest confidence in Haig, stating that the Commander-in-Chief had the 'full power to attack where and when he chose'.[37] What had brought about this extraordinary praise? Perhaps Lloyd George had been mightily impressed with the capture of Vimy Ridge on the first day of battle, a feat that had eluded all other armies on the Western Front up to now. Perhaps he was unaware that the slogging match that followed was bare of results and costly in casualties. Or perhaps he thought of his own position: he had backed Nivelle and Nivelle (though not yet sacked) had clearly failed. Haig had at least had some success and Lloyd George was well aware that Haig still had the strong support of his Conservative colleagues in the War Cabinet. Perhaps he therefore thought that he must cling to Haig to retain some credibility at home. Whatever the reason, on this visit, all was sweetness and light between the two men. We must be careful not to ascribe to this one-night stand the attributes of a marriage. Lloyd George still retained his suspicions of the military. On his return to London he established a War Policy Committee, a body designed to scrutinise Haig's plans for the summer (which the Prime Minister knew to be gestating) in the greatest possible detail.

Certainly Haig had given much thought to his post-Nivelle plan. It would consist of an attack from the Ypres Salient in order to drive the Germans from the Belgian coast and then roll up their entire line from the north. To that end he had already consulted Plumer (whose Second Army occupied the area around Ypres) and Rawlinson from the Fourth Army about developing a plan.[38] He was disappointed on both counts – Plumer and Rawlinson advised careful 'bite and hold' operations of limited scope. Haig required an operation planned on bolder lines so he turned to a man whom he thought could deliver more far-reaching results. He turned to Gough.[39] Why he thought Gough, the architect of the disastrous First Battle of Bullecourt and about to preside over the even more disastrous second attempt, was the man to elevate to command an entire campaign is puzzling. Perhaps Haig thought he had no option, given the responses of Plumer and Rawlinson. Maybe, against any evidence, he thought highly of Gough. In any case, Gough got the job. Plumer would lead off the campaign by capturing the Messines Ridge which dominated the Ypres battlefield, and then the main event would kick off with Gough advancing on the Passchendaele Ridge and points east.

Of course in Britain, it is as well to remember that the sanction for a large offensive did not lie with the Commander-in-Chief. It was the government that would decide. That was why Lloyd George had formed the War Policy Committee. It consisted of himself, two senior Conservatives (Lords Milner and Curzon) and Jan Christian Smuts, the South African statesman. Robertson and Andrew Bonar Law, the Conservative leader, also attended many meetings. It met for the first time on 11 June to consider Haig's plan and to suggest alternatives.[40] No perceptive discussion ensued. Milner argued that it would be worth 500,000 casualties to clear the Belgian coast but then mused that such a bill would greatly wear down the British army.[41] Lloyd George returned to the fantasy of an Italian offensive, to be reminded by Robertson that the Italians were 'miserably afraid of the Germans'.[42] So much for alternative plans; Haig's plan remained. Lloyd George hated it. He predicted that the operation stood 'no decent chance of success and that great losses would result' which would 'jeopardise our chance next year, & cause great depression'. Having thus predicted the outcome of the Third Ypres campaign with some precision he lamely concluded that 'the responsibility for advising in regard to military operations must remain with the military advisers'.[43] In the end he thought the responsibility just too great for the committee he had specifically set up to be responsible. He would spend the rest of his life and much space in his memoirs trying to justify this abdication.

Nevertheless, the War Policy Committee did add a feeble coda to this supine position. They would authorise only the first phase of Haig's operation. Should it become bogged down into something resembling the Somme, they would call it off.[44]

As finally determined by Haig the operation would take the following form. The first attack would seize the high ground on the Messines Ridge, essential because it overlooked the entire Ypres Salient. This would be entrusted to Plumer, who knew the ground and had been preparing for just such an operation for two years. Once Messines was secure, Gough would attack out of the Ypres Salient, with the sequential objectives of the Passchendaele Ridge, Roulers and Thourout and the Belgian coast. But Haig had created a huge problem in appointing a commander who was unfamiliar with the territory around Ypres. It was in one sense entirely reasonable that Gough could familiarise himself with the ground over which he was to operate. In another sense the seven-week gap determined by Haig to be necessary for this process was disastrous. The Messines operation would surely draw the attention of the Germans to that area of their front and any preparations for a full-scale assault from Ypres could not be concealed from an enemy that, even after Messines, would hold ground such as the Gheluvelt Plateau and the Passchendaele Ridge that overlooked the salient. This disadvantage called into question the whole idea of any offensive from such an unpromising area. Nevertheless, Haig convinced himself that the Germans could be deceived about the true nature of his intentions. Messines would be attacked in the first week of June and the Ypres operation would commence around the end of July.

Planning for the Messines operation seemed straightforward. Since 1915 companies of tunnellers had placed twenty-one mines under the ridge, containing 1 million pounds of TNT. After a preliminary bombardment of four days Plumer intended to explode the mines and occupy the devastated ridgetop, an advance of some 1,500 yards. Haig was not satisfied with this modest proposal. As always he wanted more than 'bite and hold'. He told Plumer that he must not only capture the ridge but advance down its opposite slope and capture the German guns clustered around a position called the Oostaverne Line.[45] At a stroke Haig had doubled the distance the infantry would be required to travel and he had added an objective on the reverse slope of a ridge out of direct artillery observation from the British front.[46]

Still, there were some hopeful signs concerning Messines. First, inter-rogation of German prisoners revealed that they had no conception that their entire position had been undermined.[47] Secondly Plumer had available 1,510 field and 756 heavy guns to cut the wire and subdue the German batteries.[48] And he had enormous stockpile of shells (144,000 tons) to fire.[49] Against this array the Germans had just 344 field and 404 medium to heavy pieces.[50] Moreover, new aeroplanes in the form of the Sopwith Scout had arrived to address the debacle of 'Bloody April' when inferior British machines had been shot out of the sky at Arras. The Second Army could deploy 300 aircraft, almost double the German total.[51] Finally, a burst of fine weather allowed Plumer to benefit from thousands of aerial photo-graphs of the German positions.

The bombardment began on 21 May with counter-battery fire and the destruction of German strongpoints in Messines and Wytschaete villages. German artillery retaliation was at first robust but from 1 June enemy fire started to slacken as British superiority began to tell. Stunned prisoners described their defences in many aspects as non-existent.[52]

At 3.10 a.m. on 7 June 1917, the order was given to explode the mines. Their detonation was at that point the largest man-made explosion in history. People in London heard it as a muffled roar. In Lille, 15 miles away, residents thought they were experiencing an earthquake.[53] Following the explosion the infantry from nine divisions advanced behind a barrage 700 yards in depth. The capture of the German front line happened without incident, the mines and the artillery having absolutely devastated the German positions. The soldiers who survived 'fled in all directions' and effective British counter-battery fire ensured that German artillery retali-ation was feeble.[54] The fall of the ridge soon followed. The New Zealanders had some resistance to overcome in Messines while the 16 Division occu-pied the rubble of Wytschaete with hardly a shot fired.[55]

The next phase, the advance to the Oostaverne Line to capture the German guns, did not proceed smoothly. Most German guns had in fact been moved back before the British attack and now these batteries opened a murderous fire on the British troops advancing down the slope towards them. In addition these troops were hit by British guns still firing the protec-tive barrage but firing it blindly over the crest of the ridge. In this period the 25 Division suffered 2,750 casualties, mainly caused by the artillery fire of one side or another. In any case, once the ridge which overlooked it was in British hands the Oostaverne Line was untenable. Later in the week, the Germans pulled back. The second part of the Messines operation, wished on the Second Army by Haig, proved unnecessary. It was also when most of the 25,000 casualties caused to Plumer's men occurred. 'Bite and hold' had yet to win any friends at GHQ.

In the meantime two men who would fundamentally affect the Third Battle of Ypres had arrived in the salient. On 1 June General Gough established his headquarters at Lovie Chateau and on 14 June the German defensive expert General von Lossberg arrived at Roulers. While Gough pondered his new attack, Von Lossberg acted. The German defences facing Ypres were already formidable. There were three trench systems, each about 2,000 yards apart. Behind them ran the Flandern Line which encompassed the high ground of the Passchendaele Ridge and the Gheluvelt Plateau. For Von Lossberg, after the experience of the first day at Arras and Messines, this was not enough. He ordered the construction of two more lines behind the Flandern 1 Line and an additional line along the Gheluvelt Plateau. The British would now have at least five defensive lines to penetrate. He also ordered the construction of many more pillboxes. Because of the low-lying nature of the Ypres terrain there were no deep dug-outs similar to the Somme. Instead the pillboxes took their place. These were low concrete shelters built up several feet above the ground and covered with turf and soil. They could hold machine-gun nests, a garrison of a maximum of forty men or some field artillery. Hundreds of these constructions were placed chequerboard across the entire defensive area between the front line and Passchendaele. Worryingly for the British, the pillboxes were impervious to the creeping barrage fired from the field artillery.

What Von Lossberg anticipated was that any British attack would be fragmented by the resistance encountered in the first two defensive positions. The troops in these areas were expected to fight it out until help arrived. That help would come in the form of counter-attack formations, not held as far back as at Arras and propelled forward the moment a British attack commenced. In total the defensive layout facing Gough was 10,000–12,000 yards in depth, manned by nine divisions in the area of attack and four further back.[56] It needs to be added that, had Haig not insisted on a new commander, with its consequent delays, most of Von Lossberg's new defences would not have been completed.

Gough's plan of attack on these defences was surprisingly modest, an attribute not usually associated with the commander of the Fifth Army. He would aim to advance in three jumps to a distance of 3,000 yards with suitable pauses between jumps. He would then aim for a fourth jump of between 1,000 and 2,000 yards as circumstances admitted. His final objective for the first day was a line Polygon Wood–Broodseinde–Langemarck. Gough's plan was in fact not all that different from the first day at Arras on which it was probably built. The interesting point is this: Haig had insisted on Gough because of his distant horizons and his liking for the attack *au fond*. What he got was more Plumer-like. Even the cavalry was not massed for a breakthrough, perhaps a necessary caution given the boggy state of the ground and the pillboxes.

One aspect of the plan, however, seems to lie in the realms of science fiction. Sir Henry Rawlinson, who had been sidelined for the main operation, had after all been given a command. He was put in charge of a force placed on the Belgian coast which would outflank the Germans as Gough's force swept forwards. In addition one division, equipped with tanks that could allegedly climb sea walls would land from the sea behind the German front. Thankfully for those involved, D-Day 1917 never occurred.[57]

For the battle Gough had nine divisions of infantry in the front line, approximately 100,000 men. And he had two French divisions that would operate on the very north of the battlefield, an indication that French morale had markedly improved since the Nivelle disaster. Training had proceeded along lines established at Arras. Replicas of the battlefield had been created behind the front and the troops rehearsed in their part of the plan. Officers were also shown the Arras battlefield, and the notes made by the Canadian Corps on their success at Vimy Ridge were widely circulated. Aerial photographs of objectives to be captured were distributed in their tens of thousands. Such methods indicated a steady advance in sophistication in training.[58]

Gough would also have 120 tanks of the newer Mark IV model. But on this occasion nothing spectacular was expected of them. Because of the poor state of the ground they would not be put in the front line but used by follow-up troops to help subdue strongpoints missed by the bombardment.[59]

What of the artillery, the effectiveness of which would allow the skills of the infantry to be displayed? Gough had at his disposal 1,422 field guns and 752 heavies, approximately the same as disposed at Messines and over a similar front of attack (14,000 yards).[60] The problem, as ever, lay with the more distant German defences. So deep were they that the heavy artillery would be required not only to cut the distant wire but to provide a creeping barrage for troops advancing beyond the range of the field artillery. Were there sufficient guns to perform these tasks and demolition and counter-battery duties? Perhaps Fifth Army Intelligence thought there were. But they had made one drastic miscalculation. They had identified 185 heavy German guns opposed to Gough's array. In fact there was double that number, a mistake that was to cost the troops dear when they went over the top.[61]

The preliminary bombardment commenced on 16 July. Haig was well satisfied, underlining in his diary General Birch's (his artillery adviser) remarks that by the 28th the British gunners 'have gained the upper hand over the hostile artillery'.[62] This was far from the truth. Fifth Army Intelligence commented two days later that 'the enemy shelled our battle areas and forward communications on all corps fronts, from time to time firing heavy concentrations'.[63] In particular, the batteries behind the Gheluvelt Plateau, which in number were certainly underestimated by the British, were proving difficult to locate in the shattered woods which characterised the area. Nor was the weather for much of the bombardment period conducive to aerial spotting. At the end of the bombardment many batteries in this section of the front remained untouched.

Zero hour was at 3.50 a.m. to take advantage of the first streaks of dawn. Even then the weather did not oblige. Low cloud obscured the rising sun and the troops went over the top in pitch dark.

The story of the first day of battle can be told in two parts – the left and right of the front. On the left around Pilckem Ridge, where the French, the XIV, XVIII and XIX Corps were operating, the immediate German defences had been obliterated. Indeed the French attack was supported by more artillery than any French assault yet mounted.[64] The Pilckem Ridge fell to XIV Corps and the Steenbeek River was crossed by XVII Corps. Tanks provided useful service and all seemed set for an advance on Gravenstafel, just a few thousand yards short of the Passchendaele Ridge.[65]

There was a problem, however, on the right opposite the Gheluvelt Plateau. After some initial successes, troops from II Corps ran into the boggy ground in the twisted remains of the woods. In these circumstances they soon lost the creeping barrage. Then they were heavily shelled by those un-attacked and unidentified batteries just beyond the plateau. They also found that many pillboxes and strongpoints were still intact.[66] Soon II Corps were stalled, well short of any important objectives on the Gheluvelt Plateau.

This had serious consequences for those in advanced positions on the left. Many of the batteries on the plateau could now swing their fire around and enfilade the men of XVIII and XIX Corps. Moreover, the German counter-attack formations near the Passchendaele Ridge had survived the bombardment unscathed, and at around 11 a.m. they moved to the assault.[67] And as it happened, the three most advanced British divisions (15, 55 and 39) were not in good shape. The fighting in the latter part of their advance had been heavy and the men were somewhat scattered. More importantly, the divisional commanders had little idea of the exact location of their troops, which made it impossible for them to direct reinforcements precisely to where they were needed.[68] Finally, communications with the artillery were tenuous and in any case the forward troops were beyond the range where they could be supported by an accurate or dense standing barrage. Not surprisingly the counter-attacks succeeded. The British forces were driven from St Julien, London Ridge and a number of fortified farms.[69] These locations would in coming weeks take much fighting to regain.

The 31 July was, though, by no means a disaster for the British. On the left they had overrun two German defensive positions, advanced 3,000 yards and now held the Pilckem Ridge, thus denying the Germans some good observation points over the salient. The attack across the plateau had gained some 1,000 yards but could progress no further and the tangled wilderness of woods still lay before them. The cost had been 27,000 casualties, hardly cheap but only half those suffered on the first day of the Somme. Also 18 square miles of ground had been gained compared with 3.5 on 1 July 1916. And, unlike that day, they had inflicted almost an equal number of casualties on the defenders.

Yet the achievements of the day had fallen well short of the command's expectations. It was obvious that positions such as the Passchendaele Ridge could not easily be taken. An enormous expenditure of ammunition had carried the troops between 1,000 and 3,000 yards. To achieve something similar the guns would have to be brought forward (no speedy task over the churned-up battlefield) and the troops reorganised for another attack. In time some distant objectives might be captured but not rapidly and not cheaply. The great strategic vision of Sir Douglas Haig was nowhere in sight.

And matters were about to get considerably worse. Most war diaries recorded that rain started to fall around noon on the first day of battle. It hardly stopped for a month. Only on three days in August was no rain recorded. The low-lying battlefield became a quagmire, a swamp and then, in part, a lake. This type of weather always had a disastrous effect on military operations in the First World War and this was particularly so in 1917. In that year British artillery superiority began to assert itself – at Arras, at Messines and in the preliminary bombardment at Ypres. Also, with the significant exception of Arras, newer types of aircraft provided the army with air superiority. In addition newer artillery methods, both in ensuring the accuracy of its own guns and locating with accuracy the position of enemy guns, were starting to be more widely used. Older forms of infantry protection, such as the creeping barrage, had been refined. This kind of barrage now contained more shells, heavier shells and proceeded at a slower pace in order for the infantry to advance immediately behind it. Finally the Mark IV tank was proving more mechanically reliable than its predecessors.

But all these advancements had one thing in common – they were almost always nullified by bad weather. In particular, in wet and cloudy conditions aircraft could often not fly. Even in the air they had great difficulty in observing the fall of shot for the artillery and could send back few corrections to the guns. Similarly, aircraft had difficulty identifying the position of forward troops and could offer little guidance to the command on the requirements for reinforcements or to the artillery on where to place protective barrages. The artillery itself often had to fire blind in these conditions and the spotters who helped locate enemy guns by noting their flash were useless. In short, in conditions of poor weather artillery superiority either in numbers or in accuracy often counted for little. The same applied to the creeping barrage. If troops could scarcely clamber out of their trenches because of the ooze and barely walk upright in the mud of no man's land they could hardly follow a barrage, at whatever pace it proceeded. Of course, tanks needed good going to operate effectively; in the conditions that applied around Ypres in August 1917 they could often not even reach their own front line.

These points had been demonstrated to the command in one failed battle after another. By 1917 the lesson should have been obvious. When the weather deteriorated, major operations should cease. Yet three years of warfare on the Western Front had taught them no such thing. Whatever else they had gleaned about the effectiveness of accurate artillery fire, however much they had welcomed innovations such as tanks, Lewis guns and rifle grenades, this lesson eluded them. Once operations commenced they were expected to continue even though the artillery would be blinded, though the troops would sink into the mud, though tanks would stick in the swamp. By their persistent obtuseness in this area they managed to render nugatory the lavish supply efforts of the Ministry of Munitions and to condemn their soldiers to operations where bravery and training might mean nothing.

So it was in August in the Ypres Salient. Large-scale operations were launched on the 10th, 16th, 19th, 22nd, 26th and the 27th. Minimal distances were achieved. Not all operations were absolute failures. On the left flank the French gained some ground. On the British front Maxse's XVIII Corps captured a few fortified farms utilising some dry roads that allowed the tanks to operate. The line advanced just over 100 yards.[70] Against the Gheluvelt Plateau no ground at all was gained. Gough knew who to blame: it was the troops. Haig recorded him saying after a disastrous attack on 16 August that cost the 16 and 36 Divisions 7,800 casualties 'the men are Irish and apparently did not like the shelling'.[71]

Haig was in no mood to blame the troops. On 25 August he interviewed Gough and Plumer and informed the latter that the front of the Second Army would be extended leftwards to encompass the Gheluvelt Plateau. Gough's Fifth Army would merely provide flank protection to the north. Gough had thus been sidelined, an admission that his appointment had been a disastrous mistake in the first place. Bizarrely, this was not accompanied by an edict forbidding Gough from further attacks. So penny-packet attacks in Gough's section of the front continued, as did Haig's policy of leaving such matters to the discretion of the Army Commander, thus incidentally completely abrogating his own responsibilities as Commander-in-Chief.[72] After Gough's fifth failure Haig finally 'suggested' but did not order that he desist.[73] Gough took the hint. Plumer's moment had arrived.

Plumer submitted his proposed plan to Haig on 29 August. It called for a three-step advance across the Gheluvelt Plateau, with Gough and the French providing flank support on the left. Plumer requested that his first step only be launched after three weeks of fine weather, a condition that was immediately granted by Haig. Presumably Gough's four-week slog through the mud had concentrated Haig's mind on the matter of weather. Plumer also demanded and received unprecedented amounts of artillery and shells. In all, his first attack would dispose 575 heavy and 720 field guns for an attack on a 5,000-yard front. Gough would have 300 heavy and 600 field guns for an attack on a similar front. Plumer also had available 3.5 million shells, which gave him an overall artillery concentration of three times that of 31 July.

He proposed to use his artillery in the following manner. For the strong-points – pillboxes, fortified farms – destructive fire was to begin at the end of August and employ the heaviest pieces. Counter-battery fire would commence at the same time, with the added accuracy provided by sound-ranging and flash-spotting sections to assist in accurately establishing the position of enemy batteries. To protect the infantry a creeping barrage which slowed as the attack progressed would reflect the realities of the churned-up battlefield. In addition four more barrages, each 200 yards in depth, would be placed ahead of the creeping barrage to provide a wall of shells of 1,000 yards' depth – almost the entire zone to be captured. When the objective was reached the whole 1,000-yard barrage would continue for nine hours to allow the infantry to dig in, safe from coordinated counter-attacks.[74] This was industrial warfare with a vengeance.

He would also deploy some fresh troops. Against the Gheluvelt Plateau, two new corps (totalling four divisions) would be employed – X and I Anzac. Operating to the left of the Australians would be V Corps with the experienced 9 and 55 Divisions.

Nevertheless this battle was largely an artillery one. To paraphrase the Australian Official History (not a work given to underplaying the achieve-ments of the infantry), the artillery would conquer the ground and the infantry would occupy it.[75] And so it happened. On 20 September the Battle of the Menin Road advanced the British line and captured such strong points on the Gheluvelt Plateau as Inverness Copse and Glencorse Wood that had resisted the efforts of the Fifth Army for over a month. At the end of the day, territory to an average depth of 1,250 yards had been gained. The victory had not been cheap, costing the British 21,000 casualties. Many of these had been inflicted by the German artillery, which had by no means been mastered, despite being outnumbered four to one by the British. Periods of poor weather had not assisted the British gunners and in the Fifth Army, map errors produced erratic shooting. In addition, as always, not all machine-gun strongpoints had been neutralised by the bombardment and the German infantry were tenacious in defence. In the main, however, Plumer's tactics had worked. German counter-attack divisions, held back beyond the British bombardment, had been unable to penetrate the protective artillery wall in sufficient numbers to dislodge the consolidating British forces. It seemed that at last the products of industrial Britain were prevailing on the battlefield.

The next two encounters seemed to ram that message home. On 26 September at Polygon Wood, employing the same methods as at Menin Road, Plumer advanced a further 1,250 yards across the Gheluvelt Plateau and on 4 October an advance of 1,000 yards was made at Broodseinde. The casualties were again not insignificant – 15,000 at Polygon Wood, 20,000 at Broodseinde. Yet the Germans had no answer to these tactics. If they held counter-attack forces too far back they would be unable to penetrate the protective artillery barrages. If they packed men into the front system of trenches (as they did at Broodseinde) in an attempt to bring the attack to an immediate halt, they merely provided more targets for the bombardment.

But Plumer's methods had their drawbacks. With all the artillery at his disposal he could not locate accurately enough sufficient of the German batteries that lay behind the Gheluvelt Plateau or the Passchendaele Ridge to provide relatively cheap victories. So his three steps had cost the British army 56,000 men and after the Somme and Arras it was doubtful how many more Broodseinde-type offensives could be borne in 1917.

And after 4 October there was an excellent reason to halt the offensive. Rain had again started to fall and it continued until the very eve of the next push on 9 October. The results were predictable. The artillery was again blinded. Indeed it was even difficult to obtain stable platforms for the guns in the mire. More importantly, it was difficult to get sufficient guns forward across the moonscape battlefield to support the attack. Yet Haig and Plumer persisted. They persisted on 9 October at the Battle of Poelcapelle and they persisted again at the Battle of Passchendaele on 12 October. Further desperate actions to capture the Passchendaele Ridge followed on 26 and 30 October and on 4 and 11 November. The end result was that the village of Passchendaele and part – but not all – of the ridge were captured. For this meagre achievement a fearful toll had been exacted on Australian, New Zealand, Canadian and British troops. In the conditions, which more resembled a muddy lake than a battlefield, there was never a chance that much progress would be made. Haig, as always insisted that the Germans were on the brink of collapse. When the War Office had the temerity to query whether this was actually the case, Haig accused the Chief of Intelligence (Lieutenant-General Sir George Macdonogh) of being gulled by tainted Catholic sources because he himself was a Roman Catholic.[76] Any comment is superfluous. There is in fact little evidence that the German army was on the brink of collapse. The Plumer battles had certainly exacted a heavy toll on the enemy and the seemingly inexorable progress of the British must have dampened German morale. But the historian of the German army in this period can find no evidence to support a breakdown. The majority of the troops fought with a stubborn determination that never weakened during the entire campaign.[77]

The more bizarre aspect of this period is the enthusiastic endorsement of Plumer for these profitless enterprises. The master of 'bite and hold' paradoxically seemed to disregard those aspects of his battle plans which had brought him some success. In truth there is no paradox. Plumer's three steps were designed to gain ground across the difficult Gheluvelt Plateau merely as a preliminary to launching a great offensive against the Passchendaele Ridge and points east. It is questionable if Plumer really grasped that the essential of 'bite and hold' was to kill the enemy rather than gain any particular ground. He was, in fact, as one with Haig in his territorial ambitions. His reputation as the one general on the Western Front who had grasped the essentials of warfare there has perhaps been rather inflated.[78]

But the question has to be asked as to why all this occurred. Why did tens of thousands of soldiers flounder forwards in such appalling conditions, which in this last phase were worse than anything encountered at the Somme when Britain's civilian leaders had specifically stated that these were the very circumstances in which they would refuse permission to continue? The answer reveals one of the most lamentable lapses in civilian control of the military in modern British history. The body that had made the emphatic declaration that no more Somme-type offensives would be tolerated, The War Policy Committee never met during August or the first three weeks of September. This dereliction was not offset by the actions of the War Cabinet, which did meet regularly and had almost the same membership as the War Policy Committee. This lapse did not occur through lack of information. Hankey tried to draw members' attention to the fact that Haig was continuing to attack in dreadful conditions of weather, and Robertson made regular reports of what he dignified as the progress of the offensive. The War Cabinet just seemed uninterested. They spent much time on affairs in Italy and the desirability of sending heavy artillery to assist the Italians, much time on air raids on London and eventually even more time on the possibility of a renewed offensive against Turkey.[79] Even when Plumer's successes seemed to brighten the scene, their interest was minimal, Lloyd George remarking that the effect of such limited advances on a war-weary country would not last long.

Finally, on 3 October, the Prime Minister turned a withering eye on the Flanders campaign. He noted that Haig had still not captured the 'Klercken Ridge' (by which he presumably meant the Passchendaele Ridge).[80] On 11 October he predicted that the ridge would not be captured and that he would bring this fact to the attention of the War Cabinet in three weeks' time.[81] In essence, the War Cabinet was making a fearful decision. By its inaction it sanctioned the continuation of the Third Ypres campaign. It failed to stop it in the dreadful conditions of August and it failed again in the even worse conditions that applied in October and November. Indeed it predicted disaster and promised to reassemble to confirm the accuracy of that prediction. On occasion the civilian leadership is offered a safety line by the argument that Haig held such a strong position that it was impossible to sack him. This is a category error. It was not a matter of sacking Haig – merely one of ordering him to desist. And there is little doubt that if such an order had been sent it would have been obeyed. Whatever his faults, disobeying a direct order from the government would not have crossed Haig's mind.

Why then was such an order not issued? Two explanations present themselves. The first is that while the War Cabinet or the War Policy Committee might flirt with operations in Italy and Turkey they shied away from tampering with the Western Front because they knew that it was the only front that mattered; in the end they did not have the internal fortitude to impose their will on the military in such a vital area. Second, Lloyd George and at least some of his companions hankered, like Haig, after the knockout blow. And if Germany was to be knocked out, the Western Front was where it would have to take place. Haig therefore must continue in case he delivered a miracle.

What the War Cabinet's decisions amount to is a dereliction of duty of staggering proportions. These men were in a position to know the perilous state of the Entente. Russia was sliding into rebellion; France, as a major contributor to operations on the Western Front, was – temporarily anyway – out of the picture; the Americans had not yet arrived. Yet the War Cabinet did nothing while Haig set about casting away the best army that the Entente could field. That the Third Ypres campaign had to be attempted need not be doubted. That it was allowed its barren progression and its casualty bill of 275,000 men beggars belief. The absence of those men would prove desperate in the coming months.

* * * * *

The balance sheet for the Third Battle of Ypres is therefore unambiguously negative and it might be thought that as far as the British army was concerned 1917 had seen enough fighting. But this was not to be. Since September Haig had fixed on a new battle, opposite Cambrai, where the rolling, unscarred countryside provided the good going that was absent for much of the Flanders campaign.[82] The bloodletting in that theatre in October and November did not cause him to reassess his design.

There were novel aspects of this operation. The most important concerned the artillery. New developments such as sound ranging and flash spotting allowed the position of German batteries to be known with exactitude. This meant that the artillery could remain silent until zero and then have an excellent chance of destroying or neutralising the German batteries.

There now need be no preliminary bombardment. Surprise could be returned to the battlefield.[83]

The second novel feature concerned tanks. The Mark IV tank still had many problems – it took four men to steer it, visibility was poor, it was desperately slow (about 4 mph) and an interior temperature of 120°F would strictly limit the endurance of its crews. It was certainly no weapon of exploitation. Yet the Mark IV was now being manufactured in numbers; no fewer than 450 would be available for the coming battle. It was a reasonable supposition that the appearance of these mechanical monsters, whatever their shortcomings, might en masse cause the enemy infantry to flee the scene.

There was a further novelty of this operation that did not reflect well on the military high command. Haig had not bothered to inform Lloyd George or anyone in the War Cabinet that the battle was to take place. Indeed the Commander-in-Chief had only informed Robertson a few weeks before the battle that it was to commence on 20 November. And Robertson, knowing with what determination the War Cabinet were looking for offensives outside the Western Front, did not see fit to inform them either. This would have large repercussions later.

Despite its novel aspects, any attack in the Cambrai region would face severe difficulties because its defences were part of the Hindenburg Line. Here the defences consisted of a well-wired outpost zone with chequer-board machine-gun nests often incorporated into fortified villages. Behind this was a battle zone with trenches 10 feet wide, protected by four belts of wire each 12 yards wide. In rear of the battle zone was a support system of similar strength. Further back was a third line, protected on the right by the considerable obstacle of the St Quentin Canal. On the left the uncompleted Canal du Nord would prove a constricting obstacle.[84]

Much ingenuity on the part of the tank experts was shown in dealing with these obstacles. There was no doubt whatever that the weight of a tank (about 30 tons) could crush the wire. Traversing the trenches was another matter. In the end enormous bundles of sticks, held together by chains, were carried by every third tank, the idea being that the carrying tank would drop these bundles (or fascines) into the trenches to provide rudimentary bridges for other tanks and the infantry.[85]

The infantry component of the attack consisted of six divisions in the front line and one in reserve, with two flanking divisions offering protection left and right. Because of the depredations of the Third Battle of Ypres and the need to send two and then four infantry divisions to Italy to prop up that front after the Austro-German breakthrough at Caporetto in late October, no more reserves were available. This was a boon in the sense that it was often the presence of infantry reserves that indicated to the enemy that an attack was imminent but in no other respect.[86]

What has been described so far seems to be the preliminary of a perfect 'bite and hold' scenario designed to deal a heavy blow to the Germans by throwing them out of a section of the Hindenburg system with little loss. But this is only the first part of the plan as conceived by General Julian Byng (the commander of the Third Army, which would carry out the attack) and Haig. In their design there would be a second and a third stage. After the first-stage break-in had created a gap, the cavalry would seize any river or canal crossings and capture Bourlon Ridge, on which there was a wood and a village. Then there would be a further advance to capture Cambrai and trap any Germans caught in a pocket by such rapid action.[87] After that, who knows what havoc might be wrought?[88]

In the event the first phase of the attack by and large went to plan. The 1,000 guns of the Third Army blanketed the German batteries at zero, allowing the tanks and infantry forward. The 378 serviceable tanks that attacked certainly shocked the enemy. Fascines were dropped; the tanks and infantry progressed; the Germans surrendered in numbers. A few men were even on the far side of the St Quentin Canal. By the end of the day two strong sections of the Hindenburg Line were in British hands on a front of 6,000 yards. The cost had been modest by Western Front standards – some 4,000, which as it happened was slightly less than the number of German prisoners. In addition two enemy divisions had more or less ceased to exist.[89] This was 'bite and hold' with a vengeance; if the battle had been called off at this point it would have been hailed as a triumph and as a pointer to a new kind of operation.

But it was not called off. On the 21st it resumed along the lines of what had become a pattern for the second day of battle in trench warfare. Attacks were attempted all along the line but they were uncoordinated, usually made without artillery support and without many tanks, for about half of the mechanical vehicles were out of action due to German gun fire or breakdown. The action was utterly profitless. The German reserve line remained intact and those few men across the canal could only be reinforced in driblets. On the left the tanks and cavalry worked together to capture Fontaine village but every effort to take Bourlon Ridge, in the absence of artillery or concerted tank support, failed.

Now was the time to call off the battle but Haig thought he detected, in the words of the Official Historian, 'on somewhat slender evidence', signs that the Germans were about to pull back.[90] Fresh attempts to gain Bourlon Ridge persisted for the next five days. No progress was made. This kind of operation continued until 27 November, producing a sharp, narrow salient on the right of the British line. If Byng and Haig were oblivious to the danger this represented, the Germans were not. A German counter-attack, using new infantry tactics which no one on the British side seemed to notice, eventually involving fourteen divisions, went in on 30 November. It came as a complete surprise. The Germans gained much ground despite a desperate defence. In the end the British were only able to stabilise the line just in advance of where they had started on the 20th.

The ringing of bells in Britain after the initial gains had indeed been premature. Lloyd George was furious, firstly because he had not been told about the original attack, secondly because of the excessive enthusiasm with which the military had trumpeted the early success, thirdly because all the gains had been undone and fourthly because Robertson and Haig had repeatedly assured him that the Germans had lost all offensive capability. Even Robertson was unnerved. Haig's troops, he noted, 'were pretty well used up in the Ypres salient and therefore he is rather hard put to it to hold his own'.[91]

The Prime Minister had already taken steps to marginalise his military advisers by ramming through with the French a Supreme War Council, a body that would meet at Versailles and provide alternative military advice to the British and French governments.[92] As British representative he placed the oily Henry Wilson, an officer much disliked by Haig and Robertson. He now moved against GHQ. Haig's Chief of Staff (Lieutenant-General Launcelot Kiggell) and his Chief of Intelligence (Brigadier-General John Charteris) were sacked as well as lesser functionaries.[93] There was no doubt the Prime Minister would have liked to go further and remove Haig and

Robertson themselves. He asked Henry Wilson and the rather discredited ex-C-in-C of the BEF, Sir John French, to prepare proposals for an alternative strategy but their papers came to nothing. He raged at the shadowy Viscount Esher about the intrigues of the army against him, knowing full well that Esher would pass this back to Haig.[94] He even sent Smuts and Hankey on a tour of the Western Front to find a successor to the Commander-in-Chief.[95] Unhelpfully they returned without a credible name.

So in the end Haig and Robertson kept their jobs. But here was a pretty pass. The civilian leader of a democratic state had lost all confidence in his military leadership in the middle of a war. That military leadership had cost Britain around 800,000 casualties in 1917 for derisory gains of ground – or at Cambrai no gain of ground at all. Of these men 230,000 were dead and a considerable percentage of the wounded would never return to the battlefield. Britain had probably permanently lost 500,000 fighting men. Clearly, the 'trustee' of the soldiers was failing in his duty. Such a situation could not continue. As 1918 dawned and discussion commenced about the shape of a new campaign, this impasse would require resolution. The question remained as to how Lloyd George was to do it.

CHAPTER 9

THE WAR AT SEA 1916–1918

As far as the British and German battlefleets were concerned, after the Battle of Dogger Bank, quiet reigned in the North Sea. The Grand Fleet performed regular patrols. No German heavy ships were sighted.[1] In April 1916 the seaside resort of Lowestoft was bombarded by the High Seas Fleet, showing perhaps the greater enterprise of its new commander, Admiral Scheer. The Grand Fleet put to sea but the Germans had long gone before it could intervene. Then on the last day of May 1916 a major action took place. To the British this brief encounter is known as the Battle of Jutland.

The battle may be quickly described. On 28 May the Admiralty, which was regularly reading German naval codes, became aware that Scheer was to put to sea in an enterprise designed to trap and sink a section of the Grand Fleet.[2] They therefore ordered Jellicoe to intercept him, with Beatty's battlecruisers scouting ahead in order to lure Scheer onto the main British battlefleet. But, due to a delay in signals decoding, the British commanders were told that Scheer was in fact still in port.[3] As Scheer was also unaware that the British were at sea, any encounter between the fleets was likely to come as a surprise to all. The battle had the potential to be gigantic. All told, the British could dispose 151 warships with a total crew of 75,000 men. The Germans had 99 ships crewed by 45,000 men.[4]

The first ships to encounter each other were the battlecruiser squadrons led by Beatty and Hipper. Just after 3.30 p.m. firing began. Beatty ought to have had the best of it because he had the four powerful dreadnoughts of the 5th Battle Squadron in company with his six battlecruisers, while Hipper's squadron had just five battlecruisers. Instead, two British battlecruisers exploded on being hit by German shells. Shortly afterwards the British realised that the entire High Seas Fleet was at sea so Beatty turned north and headed towards Jellicoe.

Of all this Jellicoe remained largely in the dark. Beatty's messages to him were infrequent and lacking in detail. When he finally became aware that the entire High Seas Fleet was steaming towards him he had but a few minutes to deploy his twenty-four dreadnoughts. This he did with admirable composure, directing his fleet to form a single line putting them between Scheer and his base. The only adverse event in this period came when yet another British battlecruiser (commanded by Rear-Admiral Horace Hood) blew up.

Scheer was in dire peril as the fire of twenty or so dreadnoughts descended on his outnumbered force. He immediately turned away and fired torpedoes at the British fleet. To avoid these, Jellicoe himself turned away and the two forces lost contact in the descending North Sea gloom. As night fell the two fleets were thus steaming on roughly parallel courses with Jellicoe between Scheer and his base. The Admiralty were, however, in a position to enlighten Jellicoe as to the whereabouts of the German fleet. They were still reading German naval messages and picked up at 9.14 p.m. that the German fleet had been ordered home and gave Jellicoe Scheer's course and speed.[5] Jellicoe, however, ignored this message on the grounds that it was probably out of date, and he sailed on. Even the sound of firing at the rear of his battle line, which was in fact the German fleet crashing through his cruiser screen and making for home, did not divert him.[6] In the morning the Germans were gone and Jellicoe was sailing the North Sea alone.

A statistical balance sheet of Jutland comes out on the German side. The British lost fourteen ships, of which three were battlecruisers; the Germans lost eleven, of which only one was a heavy cruiser. In terms of men, the British lost just over 6,000 killed, the Germans 2,500.[7]

Because it was a chance encounter and in duration hardly lasted more than eighteen hours, there was no opportunity or wish on the part of the politicians to take any part in the North Sea Battle. But in a sense they had already played their role in building the Grand Fleet and appointing its commanders – Jellicoe in overall command and Beatty in command of the battlecruisers.

At Jutland the Grand Fleet consisted of thirty-six dreadnought-type heavy ships – twenty-three dreadnought battleships, four super-dreadnoughts (the *Queen Elizabeth* Class) and nine battlecruisers.[8] The Germans had just seventeen dreadnought battleships and four battle-cruisers.[9] The prodigious feat of building the British ships fell to the Balfour government of 1905 but substantially to the Liberal governments of Campbell Bannerman and Asquith between 1906 and 1915. The latter effort is most remarkable in that a party dedicated to 'peace, retrenchment and reform' presided over the greatest naval building programme in British history. The fact is that the threat to British naval supremacy presented by the German decision to build a large navy soon converted the Liberals to naval expansion. Churchill, once a severe critic of armament expenditure under the previous First Lord of the Admiralty, Reginald McKenna, soon became an advocate for dreadnought-building when he became First Lord in 1911. This was not so much a matter of boosting his own department as realising that naval supremacy was for Britain non-negotiable. He remarked that the difference between the British fleet and that of the Kaiser was the one was a necessity, the other a luxury. The statement caused much offence in Germany but accurately summed up the determination of the British to maintain naval supremacy. If Jutland showed anything, it was that this supremacy remained intact. Scheer's 'battle about-turn' when faced with the totality of the Grand Fleet demonstrated that fact very well.

The most important criticism made of the Grand Fleet is that while the politicians might have built the ships, the loss of three British dreadnoughts at Jutland indicated that they had built them very badly. This criticism, for some, extended a lament about the state of British technological know-how to a wholescale condemnation of the incurable decadence of British society. In fact even the lesser criticism of giving the sailors a 'flawed sword' is misplaced. The three battlecruisers that blew up at Jutland did so for the same reason – the flash of a shell hitting deck armour could travel down the gun shaft to the magazine. Unless the doors to the magazine were shut, the flash could ignite the shells and any cordite lying about and the ship would explode. This was a design fault common to German battlecruisers as well as British. However, at Dogger Bank in 1915 the Germans had been alerted to the problem when the *Seydlitz* came within an ace of destruction due to this circumstance. The Germans promptly introduced rigorous control of their magazine doors; the British did not.[10] It was chance, therefore, not British manufacturing deficiencies (or irreversible decadence) that led to the destruction of three ships at Jutland. When this factor is removed from the equation, it is found that British ships stood up quite as well as German to the pounding they received.

What of the performance of the command at Jutland – especially Beatty and Jellicoe, both of whom were appointed by Winston Churchill? Beatty has received much heavy criticism in the battlecruiser phase of the battle. He seemed to forget that he had the powerful 5th Battle Squadron with him. In any case he failed to keep them fully informed of his intentions and entered the fight with Hipper without these ships being able to contribute to the fight.[11] In this phase due to Beatty's negligence the British engaged Hipper's ships seriatim instead of as a combined unit. In doing so they paid a price and failed to inflict what could have been a crippling blow on the Germans. Beatty's signalling in this period plumbed new depths and he was once again incapable of making his intentions clear. In particular he seemed reluctant to use his radio to keep in touch with other ships, sticking to flags that were difficult to see in the murk.[12] Altogether, it was a poor performance. In the second phase of the battle Beatty failed again in signalling. It was desperately important that he keep Jellicoe informed of events yet he failed to do so until the last minute.[13] However, overall his tactics to lure the Germans onto the main body of the Grand Fleet were correct and, had the encounter happened earlier in the day when the light was better, the Germans might have suffered considerable losses.

Jellicoe has also come in for heavy criticism. Three main areas may be identified. His deployment of the fleet has been said to have lost an opportunity to close with the German fleet for a decisive encounter; he is castigated for turning away from Scheer during the German torpedo attack and consequently losing contact with the enemy fleet; and he is criticised for apparently being oblivious to the fact that Scheer was breaking through his cruiser screen at night and heading safely home, thus missing another chance for a decisive battle. None of these criticisms has any merit.

In the deployment phase, if Jellicoe had deployed closer to the German fleet, he would have risked the end of his line lapsing into confusion because of the crowding that would have taken place. He would also have had the worst of the light as Beatty had had in the battlecruiser encounter and, as he expected the German torpedo boat flotillas to be leading Scheer's columns, he worried that part of his line would be subjected to close-range torpedo attacks. We now know that these flotillas were well to the east of the German battle-fleet but it must be remembered that because of Beatty's poor signalling, Jellicoe was forced to deploy without knowing with accuracy the position of a single German ship. As it was, his deployment placed the Grand Fleet squarely between Scheer and his base, while also crossing the German T, which meant that only the forward guns of the leading German ships could be brought to bear on the British while the entire Grand Fleet could attack Scheer with broadsides. Let the Germans have the last word on Jellicoe's deployment:

> Suddenly the German van was faced by the belching guns of an intermi-
> nable line of heavy ships extending from north-west to north-east, while
> salvo followed salvo almost without intermission, an impression which
> gained in power from the almost complete inability of the German ships
> to reply to this fire as not one of the British dreadnoughts could be made
> out through the smoke and fumes.[14]

What of Jellicoe's turn away during the torpedo attack? This was merely prudent. A turn away minimised the risk of his dreadnoughts being torpedoed and in any case the light was so bad at this point that even a turn towards Scheer might not have revealed his location with any accuracy.

As for Jellicoe's stubbornness in ignoring both the Admiralty signal about Scheer's whereabouts and the evidence of fighting in the rear of his line, prudence was again his watchword. The likelihood is that Jellicoe chose to ignore the Admiralty message and evidence of night fighting for the same reason: he was utterly opposed to any kind of night action. The Grand Fleet had not practised such a manoeuvre and, besides, it was too great a risk. He must have realised by this time that Scheer would not stand and fight in a line of battle. If the Germans were heading for home, so much the better. Naval supremacy remained with the British while Jellicoe kept his fleet intact. Why risk a night encounter where responsibility would devolve from Jellicoe to the commanders of individual squadrons or ships? Jellicoe had deliberately centralised control of the Grand Fleet on himself for good reasons. While it kept together as a unit he calculated that it could not be beaten and he had (rightly) not much confidence in the initiative or skill of his subordinate commanders. In all this he was surely correct. At

Jutland Jellicoe ensured that he did not lose the war in an afternoon by ensuring that all major decisions were made by him. In choosing Jellicoe, Churchill had chosen well, though in his subsequent writings on Jutland he was at pains to distance himself from the Grand Fleet commander. As regards Beatty, he did not perform well at Jutland but justified his suitability for high office when he became C-in-C of the Grand Fleet after Jellicoe went to the Admiralty as First Sea Lord. Neither man was Nelson but their ultimate vindication was that they maintained British naval superiority against the considerable German challenge.

* * * * *

While the surface ships of the Grand Fleet and the High Seas Fleet were having these inconclusive encounters, another war was being waged at sea that potentially had far more serious consequences for Britain than Jutland. The idea of a vessel that could operate *under* the sea had a long history – one authority places it back as early as 400 BCE.[15] But as a weapon of war its development had to wait until the industrial revolution. In the 1860s Robert Whitehead, an English engineer, designed a 'locomotive torpedo', essentially a tube with an explosive tip that could be fired from a submerged ship and strike the hull of a surface warship and potentially sink it. All naval powers showed an interest in this development and by the end of the century an underwater metal-hulled ship which could fire this weapon was under design in many countries. By the beginning of the war these countries had all added flotillas of 'submarines' to their order of battle.

The power most concerned with this development was Britain. With by far the largest, and most expensive, fleet of surface warships and the largest fleet of merchant ships, it provided the most targets for these relatively inexpensive undersea boats. And with the rise of the Anglo-German naval antagonism from the building of the 'Tirpitz Fleet', the underwater vessels that most concerned Britain were German U-boats.

The early German models were of about 400 tons displacement with two torpedo tubes in front and rear. They had a range of 1,500 miles and a speed of around 10 knots on the surface and 5 knots submerged. They could cruise at a depth of 98 feet, had a crew of twenty-two and no gun armament. They were just 138 feet long and stood 21 feet out of the water.

Each boat had a periscope that could be raised when the ship was near the surface to allow the captain at least some view of conditions on the surface.[16] Later types were larger (1,000 tons), faster (16 knots on the surface) and carried guns as heavy as 105 mm and sixteen torpedoes.[17]

Later in the war when the Germans seized sections of the Belgian coast and inland ports such as Bruges, they developed two smaller types of U-boat that could operate in coastal waters. The UB variety carried six torpedoes and was merely a smaller version of the oceangoing types. The UC class was equipped with sixteen mines which they could lay in coastal seaways, although they also carried some torpedoes.[18] Though small, these coastal boats were to cause the British much anxiety as the war went on.

All submarines built during this period had considerable drawbacks. The quarters were very small and the crews lived a cramped and claustrophobic existence. Operationally, U-boats had to surface regularly. While underwater they ran on electric batteries; on the surface they used diesel engines. The batteries had a very limited life-span, especially if the submarine was operating at full speed, yet to charge the batteries the diesel engine was needed. This meant that a submarine had to spend long periods on the surface recharging its batteries so that it could spend at least some time submerged. These boats were really submersibles rather than genuine submarines.

There is no evidence that any but one of the naval commanders of the Great Powers foresaw the danger posed by submarines. The exception was Fisher. He well knew that the laws of war, such as they were, prevented the use of the submarine against civilian ships. He concluded, however, that in a war such niceties would disappear. He wrote in 1914:

> The question arises as to what a submarine can do against a merchant ship when she has found her. She cannot capture the merchant ship; she has no spare hands to put a prize crew on board; little or nothing would be gained by disabling her engines or propeller; ... in fact it is impossible for the submarine to deal with commerce in the light and provisions of international law ... What can be the answer to all the foregoing but that (barbarous and inhuman as, we again repeat, it may appear), if the submarine is used at all against commerce, she must sink her captures?[19]

This paper brought forth a storm of criticism from the Admiralty. Churchill was unconvinced. He did not think that submarines would ever be used in such a manner by a civilised power and he thought Fisher's paper marred by such thoughts. Jellicoe and Keyes agreed with Churchill.[20] Richmond commented that 'the submarine has the smallest value of any vessel for the direct attack upon trade.'[21] Fisher, who was of course out of office when his paper was written, was ignored.

When war broke out, Fisher's fears were not immediately realised. In the first four months of the war fifteen ships were sunk by submarines, of which eleven were warships. Just four were merchant steamers and all four were sunk by gun fire from U-boats on the surface after the crews had been given the opportunity to take to lifeboats.[22] And on the positive side for the British, this rather meagre total had cost the Germans five U-boats, two attempting to attack the Grand Fleet at Scapa Flow, two that probably struck mines in the Channel and one that disappeared in the North Sea.[23]

But the U-boat campaign was about to receive a fillip from a great source of frustration to the German government – the British blockade. As the war progressed, the British had extended the list of contraband goods that they were entitled to seize if they were bound for Germany in neutral ships. So far, though, the extensions had never included food. Then, on 25 January 1915 the German government announced that it was taking over control of all foodstuffs, so the British immediately added food to the list of contraband.[24]

German retaliation was swift. On 4 February Admiral von Pohl, the Chief of the German Admiralty Staff, issued a proclamation which said:

[T]he waters round Great Britain and Ireland, including the entire English Channel are hereby declared a military area. From February 18 every merchant ship [of whatever nationality] found in these waters will be destroyed, even if it is not always possible to avoid thereby the dangers which threaten crews and passengers.[25]

In other words any shipping, British or neutral, might be sunk without warning by submarines if they were found in these waters. A counter-blockade of Britain by the U-boats had begun.

The policy had an immediate effect. In February 1915 just nine ships totalling 23,000 tons had been sunk by submarines. In March those figures jumped to forty-two ships, totalling 79,000 tons, almost all of them sunk in the declared war zone.[26] The Admiralty response was supine, still mired in pre-war complacency. In 1914 they had actually dissolved their Submarine Committee.[27] It was the return of Fisher as First Sea Lord that saw this committee re-established and it set to work to find methods to combat the U-boats.[28] These included large nets fitted with buoys which might enmesh a submarine – the disturbance of buoys alerting nearby warships; mine-fields, especially across the Strait of Dover; underwater listening devices called hydrophones; explosive bomb lances; trawler and destroyer patrols at such choke points as the Strait of Dover, St George's Channel and the Irish Sea; the arming as far as possible of trawlers, drifters and yachts and the development of the decoy (or Q ship) whereby an innocent-looking merchant vessel would uncover concealed guns and engage submarines that had surfaced to sink what they took to be a sitting duck.[29]

Apart from the mine barrages, all of these methods had one common thread: they were designed to hunt out a submarine and sink it. Ironically, only the Dover Barrage proved of any utility, not because it was an effective barrier but because the Germans thought it was. At an early period in the campaign they forbad their oceangoing submarines from attempting its passage, thus forcing them to travel across the North Sea and around the coast of Scotland to find that wealth of targets that were traversing what were called the Western Approaches to Britain. This added some 1,450 miles to their journey, and as the Germans had just twenty-nine U-boats, only about one third of which could be at sea at any one time because of the repeated repairs necessary to keep these fragile vessels seaworthy, it severely limited the scope of their campaign.[30] Table 1 shows the sinkings of all ships in the remainder of the first submarine campaign.[31]

Table 1: Ships sunk by German U-boats, April–December 1915

Date	April	May	June	July	Aug	Sept	Oct	Nov	Dec
Ships sunk	39	66	124	103	126	70	47	69	51
Tonnage	62,000	158,000	122,000	121,000	201,000	146,000	85,000	157,000	119,000,000

From the figures it appears that an initial burst of success by the Germans soon fell away to more manageable totals. However, this is deceptive. The neutral states received the changed German policy with some apprehension – none more so than the United States, which was even in 1915 supplying Britain and France with much-needed war materiel. A crisis seemed to have been reached in May when the 35,000-ton *Lusitania* was torpedoed with the loss of 1,198 lives, including 128 Americans, but vociferous US protests left the Germans unconcerned.[32]

Then in August the Germans sank another passenger liner. On the 19th the White Star liner *Arabic* was torpedoed 40 miles from the Head of Kinsale off Ireland; forty-four lives were lost, of which three were American.[33] On this occasion the US government, perhaps seeing no end to the sinking of passenger liners, entered the stiffest protest. Unwilling to risk further strained relations with the great neutral, the Germans largely withdrew their submarines from the Western Approaches, where they were likely to encounter US ships or harm US passengers, and concentrated on the much less American-infested waters of the Mediterranean. As Table 1 reveals, here they found many fewer targets and the tonnage sunk plummeted. Indeed in this period the Allies added more merchant tonnage built or seized from the Central Powers than they lost – about 1.8 million tons added to 1.3 million lost.[34]

There was another side to this equation – the Germans were constructing more U-boats than they were losing. In 1915 the Germans had built sixteen oceangoing U-boats and forty-one smaller coastal craft. At the same time they had lost thirteen U-boats, two of which they possibly torpedoed themselves. Generally however, British counter-measures were not working. The decoy trawler had proved the most effective British counter-weapon with six submarines destroyed but the extensive network of mines and nets had sunk just two.[35] For the Germans, considering the paucity of boats and the protests from the US, this was a fair return – thirteen U-boats lost for 1.3 million tons of shipping sunk or 100,000 tons sunk for every U-boat destroyed. For the Allies, whatever they might tell themselves, it was American pressure rather than any of their counter-measures that had proved the most successful deterrent.

The threat from the US gave the Germans pause but by no means halted their submarine campaign. They continued to build U-boats at an increasing pace. By the end of 1916 they had increased their total of U-boats from 64 to 157.[36] And the sinkings rose. In January thirty-seven ships were sunk, in February fifty-six and in March eighty-one.

As noted, not all of these boats could be at sea at once, but it took very few U-boats to disrupt trade. On 6 April 1916 a British steamer, the *Zent*, was sunk off Fastnet Rock. There were no destroyer patrols in the area because they had been recalled to convoy Canadian troops to Britain. Westbound shipping was immediately halted by the Admiralty. Vessels underway were sent to Portland or Spithead. Then another ship was torpedoed off the north coast of Ireland and shipping to the Clyde was halted. It was not until 11 April that a general resumption of shipping could be ordered. In the meantime great congestion of ships had built up on the western ports and much damage done to the smooth passage of trade.[37]

Nevertheless, due to American pressure, an increasing percentage of the sinkings were in the Mediterranean, a somewhat lesser concern to the British. And the number could have been lowered had not they placed a quite unwarranted confidence in the so-called Otranto Barrage, a series of nets and minefields placed across the bottom the straits that led to the U-boat bases (both German and Austrian at Pola and Cattaro). In fact the barrage more closely resembled a sieve, the submarines passing through its holes to destroy shipping in all parts of the Mediterranean at will.[38]

Once more the British counter-measures continued to destroy very few U-boats. During these three months of 1916 they had scored just one kill, with the U68 lured to its doom by a Q ship off the coast of Ireland. This dismal pattern was to continue for the entire year, with just six more U-boats destroyed, and one of those by its own mine.[39]

However, American pressure continued to be effective. From May to August just twenty-three large British steamers were sunk in waters around the British Isles and forty-three in the Mediterranean.[40] These losses were sustainable given the output of new ships.

But the failure to dent British naval supremacy at Jutland led to a change in German policy. A new U-boat campaign was approved and the main target area was shifted from the Mediterranean back to the Western Approaches, though care was to be taken to avoid US ships or ships that contained US passengers. An added boost to this campaign was given by the design of a new 'coastal' boat, the UB II of the Flanders Flotillas, which could operate well beyond the normal range, even into the Western Approaches and the Bay of Biscay.[41]

The results were immediately apparent. In the last quarter of 1916 almost 500,000 tons of shipping was lost.[42] And in December 75,000 tons were sunk in the Channel alone. This threatened the vital link with France and the Western Front.[43] Clearly, the anti-submarine measures put in place in 1915 were not working and this was all the more surprising given that the British were reading wireless traffic from the submarines and had been from almost the beginning of the war. The German U-boats had excellent radio transmitters that could send and receive signals over several hundred miles – an enormous advantage. But British Naval Intelligence found that direction-finding towers placed around the coast could intercept these messages and they could also decrypt them with the broken German naval codes. By the end of 1916 all German submarine messages from the Heligoland Bight were intercepted and those in the Baltic and the Mediterranean as well.[44]

Why then could the British not locate and sink the U-boats? The main factor was that the 'fixes' obtained from direction finding were only accurate within a radius of 20 miles for submarines in the North Sea and within 50 miles in the Atlantic.[45] And in the time taken to transmit this information to trawler groups or destroyers, the U-boats might well have changed course. This left the hunting patrols to cruise blindly around the Western Approaches, an area of 40,000 to 60,000 square miles. This area was just too large and the patrol vessels too few to obtain any sightings.

One example (from early 1917 but relevant to this period) illustrates this dilemma. Hunting patrols and Q ships had been traversing the major Western Approaches for a week, but given the huge area to be covered, the U-boats could still operate with impunity. During this period four German U-boats (U70, U49, U44 and U62) sank thirteen 'fair sized' ships in this area.[46]

Other anti-submarine devices were proving useless. Towed explosive charges such as the paravane would of course also only work if the ship was in the near vicinity of the U-boat. Nets were quite ineffective, as the U-boat traffic through the Channel and the heavy sinkings in those waters demonstrated. Hydrophones could not distinguish the noise of a U-boat from that of nearby ships.[47] Aircraft, which were to make a substantial impact later, were no more useful than hunting patrols in this period. Their patrol areas were too large and their numbers too small to make an impact.[48] At the end of 1916, therefore, the British were no closer to solving the U-boat problem than they had been at the beginning of the war. What had got them through this period were the paucity of U-boats, pressure from neutral powers and the relative restraint shown by the U-boat commanders. They were about to find that if any or all of these restrictions were lifted, their situation would be dire indeed.

And in late December 1916 the Germans finally decided to lift all restrictions on their U-boats. Their reasoning ran as follows: Britain was clearly the main enemy, yet after Verdun and the Somme the prospects of a successful land offensive against the British looked slim. Germany would therefore stand on the defensive in the west and seek to overwhelm the tottering Russians in the east. However, that left Britain untouched. So, for the first time in their history, the Germans looked to the sea for salvation. A document was compiled by the head of the Admiralstab (Admiral Henning von Holtzendorff) which claimed after a lengthy and dubious statistical argument that if U-boats could sink 600,000 tons of British shipping per month for six months such a campaign might also keep 40 per cent of neutral shipping from sailing. With these accumulative losses of imports, Britain must seek peace.[49] The risk of war against the United States must be accepted and in any case a successful U-boat campaign might prevent American troops from being deployed in Europe before Britain gave up the ghost. The final decision was made on 9 January 1917 that the unrestricted campaign would begin on 1 February.[50]

In one sense Britain's political leaders were ready for the coming campaign. The rise in sinkings in October 1916 had induced them to consult with the C-in-C Grand Fleet. On 2 November Jellicoe attended a meeting of the War Cabinet which was largely taken up with the submarine question. But the War Cabinet soon realised they had wasted their time: Jellicoe had little to offer. He suggested arming merchant ships (which was happening anyway) and generally seemed negative and gloomy. Finally Lloyd George asked him directly 'if he had any plan against these submarines'.[51] In the light of what was to come his answer should be given in full:

Sir J Jellicoe said he had not. They only had armed merchant ships, and these could not act offensively because they did not see the submarines. He suggested having floating intelligence centres to direct the routes of shipping if found needful.[52] He did not approve of convoys, as they offered too big a target.[53]

This was pitiful from Jellicoe, who was hardly aided by the contributions of his Naval Staff. When Bonar Law tried to return to the convoy question he was told by the Chief of the Admiralty War Staff (Admiral Oliver) that if convoy was implemented, every merchant ship would require its own escort. Lloyd George protested that surely a dozen ships could be convoyed by three warships but Jellicoe had the last word:

> [He] said they would never be able to keep movements of ships suffi-
> ciently together to enable a few destroyers to screen them. It was
> different with war ships, which they could keep in a locked up forma-
> tion. Submarines would get round the rear of merchant ships.[54]

And there for the moment the matter of action against submarines stalled.

As losses increased through December. Hankey entered the debate. He thought the situation so serious that the war against U-boats must be 'a first charge on our resources'. He went on to suggest the arming of all merchant ships and that an enormous mine barrage be laid across the North Sea to hem in the submarines.[55] Jellicoe, now promoted to First Sea Lord, was quick to dash the latter idea. He informed Hankey and the Prime Minister that Britain only possessed 1,000 mines, very inferior to German types.[56] What Jellicoe meant was that while German mines exploded when a ship hit them, British mines more often than not did not. In any case Jellicoe thought mines hardly effective against submarines.[57]

A few days after this meeting, the Germans announced unrestricted submarine warfare. In the absence of any ideas from the Admiralty the government had already introduced some measures of their own. In December Lloyd George had appointed Sir Joseph Maclay, a Glaswegian shipowner, Minister of Shipping with wide powers to purchase and construct merchant ships.[58] This measure was opposed by Jellicoe as a trespass on an Admiralty remit but his objections were swept aside by the War Cabinet, and Maclay was soon ordering dozens of merchantmen from the United States and Japan as well as diverting naval construction into civilian shipping.[59]

Meanwhile, sinkings rose to 320,000 tons in January and to 140,000 tons in the first week of February alone.[60] And of the seventy-five ships sent to the bottom in this week no fewer than twenty were neutrals.[61] The losses had an immediate effect and went a long way to meeting the German aim of paralysing trade with the neutrals. Within a few days 360 neutral ships were tied up in British ports, refusing to sail.[62] Ruthless measures were immediately put in place by the government to alleviate this situation. The neutral ships were detained and released 'only when they arranged to return with an approved cargo to a British or Allied port'.[63] The Dutch and Scandinavian countries, which made up a good proportion of the neutral shipping, were treated more harshly. They were only permitted to sail their vessels 'on the arrival at a British port of a similar vessel of the same flag'.[64] In the end the neutrals bowed to this force majeure but, as was pointed out at the time, there was little point in them sailing merely to be sunk.

While the carnage continued at sea and the Admiralty wrung its hands, a second intervention was made by Hankey. In his diary he records that on 11 February he had had 'a brain wave on the subject of anti-submarine warfare' and as a result submitted to Lloyd George a memorandum on convoy.[65] In it he suggested that objections to the convoy system had been exaggerated. The objection that the arrival of convoys would clog the ports could be overcome by a careful system of scheduling. The 'big target' objection was also misplaced – unless a U-boat could anticipate the exact course of a convoy the (say) twenty ships in it might escape detection, while if the same twenty ships straggled into port one by one, a submarine was more likely to find and sink at least one ship and probably more. The problem of keeping formation would be lessened if ships in a convoy were grouped to be of approximately the same speed. In any case, he pointed out, the most valuable of cargo – troops – had been convoyed since the beginning of the war without the loss of a single man. And as far as anti-submarine patrols were concerned, even if 3,000 to 4,000 ships were deployed they could only cover a tiny fraction of the most dangerous areas.[66]

Lloyd George was so impressed by Hankey's memorandum that he called Jellicoe, Lord Edward Carson (First Lord of the Admiralty) and Rear-Admiral Alexander Duff (the head of the Admiralty Anti-submarine Division) to breakfast to study it. According to Hankey the Admiralty authorities 'resisted a good deal' but 'they admitted that they were convoying transports, and agreed to enquire about the results of a big convoy of transports coming in from Australia'.[67]

The upshot of all this seems to have been that the Admiralty continued to resist a good deal. There is no evidence that they ever reported on the fate of the Australian convoy (it arrived intact) or that they took any of Hankey's other points very seriously. Surprisingly, they were not prodded by Lloyd George. The inattentiveness of the Prime Minister probably came about because of the considerable distraction of Western Front command disputes with the French which were happening at this exact time. Perhaps, as he later admitted, he had never regarded the submarine menace as seriously as Hankey.[68]

Whatever the Prime Minister's attitude, continued sinkings kept the submarine war before the War Cabinet. On 16 February they were forced to restrict imports on a wide range of goods in order to reserve space for vital commodities such as munitions and wheat.[69] Then on the 19th Jellicoe was asked to report on the question of convoys. He stated that the Admiralty was 'going into' the issue and that he was assembling some experienced merchant captains on the matter of station keeping.[70] This meeting was held at the Admiralty on 23 February and was entirely negative. The masters assured Jellicoe that they would not be able to maintain station and that 'they would prefer to sail alone rather than in company or under convoy'.[71] Despite the seriousness of the sinkings (over 500,000 tons were sunk in February), Jellicoe waited two weeks before reporting this finding to the War Cabinet. No one challenged it or the delay in reporting it, or the representative nature of the captains Jellicoe had assembled.[72]

Jellicoe was certainly regarding the situation with some complacency. In mid-March he tabled a comparison of losses during the periods 1–13 February and 1–13 March. The table indicated that 205,000 tons had been lost in the February period and 193,000 in March. These were staggering losses and the reported improvement was relatively minor. Yet Jellicoe told the War Cabinet that in his opinion 'the position in regard to losses from submarines was rather more satisfactory than he had expected'.[73] This rather too optimistic view seemed to accord with the mood of the War Cabinet. They had ordered a review of the shipbuilding programme and were relatively satisfied that Britain could hang on. They concluded that the survey 'did not support the theory that Britain would have to make peace by the end of the year, provided we restricted imports and increased food production'.[74]

Then came April. In the first six days alone 110 ships were sunk, the highest total for any six-day period so far. At the end of that time the Germans, by their submarine policy and their crude diplomatic attempt to lure Mexico into attacking the United States, had induced President Woodrow Wilson into declaring war. In effect the Germans had now lost the war – unless the U-boats could sink so many ships that American industrial might and military potential could be prevented from reaching Britain and the battlefields in France and Flanders.

Did the entry of the United States into the war affect the Admiralty's attitude to convoy? One of the obstacles put forward was that the Americans would not make available ports where convoys of twenty or more ships could assemble. Now that objection was gone. And in April it was decided to convoy the trade with Scandinavia across the North Sea.[75] However, regarding Scandinavia, the impetus for convoy came from Beatty and it was adopted partly so that ships would be less vulnerable to attacks from the High Seas Fleet which was on the flank of this trade. There is in fact little evidence that the Admiralty had a changed attitude to convoy in early April. On 10 April Jellicoe met the American representative Admiral William Sims, who had been rushed over from Washington to report on the state of the naval war. In their first talk Jellicoe did not mention convoy but thoroughly alarmed Sims by gloomily remarking that he thought it impossible to go on if losses continued at their present rate. Sims enquired if there was any solution to the submarine problem: 'Absolutely none that we can see now', Jellicoe announced. He described the work of the destroyers and other anti-submarine craft to the American but he showed no confidence that they would be able to control the depredations of the U-boats.[76]

Moreover, when Jellicoe reported the conversation to the War Cabinet the next day, the only proposal for dealing with the crisis that he could put forward was to build a series of 50,000-ton ships specifically to carry such bulky items as wheat. Maclay protested that ships of that size would take too long to build. All that was decided was that the two departments should confer on the subject of giant ships.[77]

As the losses in April accelerated in the latter half of the month, the War Cabinet became alarmed. They discussed the whole matter on 20 April and decided that the possibility that the Salonika operation should be abandoned to save shipping must be considered. They also asked Jellicoe for a weekly review of the facts on shipping and the import of raw materials.[78] A full consideration of the submarine was, however, deferred because the Prime Minister was in Paris at a conference with the French.[79]

Lloyd George's absence may have had one fortuitous result. Travelling with him was Hankey, who took the opportunity to present the Prime Minister with a detailed paper on the strategy of the war which stressed the danger of the shipping situation and the need for convoy to overcome it.[80] Hankey noted that Lloyd George had read the paper and 'at last seemed to have grasped the danger of the submarine question.'[81]

Indeed this seems to have been the case. When the War Cabinet reassembled on 23 April Lloyd George immediately turned to the question of shipping losses and 'referred to the possibility of adopting the convoy system which, he said was favoured by Admiral Beatty and Admiral Sims.'[82] This surely was meant as a direct challenge to Jellicoe to take up the issue. The First Sea Lord merely replied that the question of convoy 'was under consideration', the same remark he had made on 19 February. The shortage of destroyers as escorts was a major problem and even with the help of American vessels he thought 'a much larger number would, however, be necessary before any system of convoy could be introduced'.[83] He was also negative about the Scandinavian convoys, which he described as not 'altogether successful'.[84] In the event discussion just petered out, the members resolving to reconvene in the late afternoon to discuss a paper on the subject from Jellicoe. This paper was entitled 'The Submarine Menace and Food Supply'. It was a most frustrating document. The First Sea Lord began with the premise that the shipping situation was dire. But all he recommended was the provision of more vessels for hunting patrols, mining the German submarines in the Heligoland Bight and the building of those monster ships. These recommendations rapidly led nowhere. There were no more vessels for patrol; the British did not possess an effective mine and the monster ships had already been ruled out by the Minister of Shipping. Once again the meeting (and the issue) was adjourned.[85]

However, it is clear that the War Cabinet was losing patience with Jellicoe. At its next meeting their frustration was manifest:

There was a general feeling that the Cabinet were not sufficiently informed on all the varying aspects of the [submarine] question, e.g. anti-submarine warfare, protection and control of shipping, priority of the various claims on shipping, our own requirements of food and munitions and those of our Allies, shipbuilding, steel etc. Recent enquiries by the War Cabinet have made it clear that there is not at present sufficient co-ordination in these matters. It was decided that –

(a) The Prime Minister should visit the Admiralty with a view to investigating all the means at present in use in regard to anti-submarine warfare.

(b) Milner to investigate the claims on shipping in order to accumulate the largest possible stocks of food.

(c) Curzon to investigate shipping output, including priorities for steel and the prospect of building mammoth 'unsinkable' ships.[86]

It is impossible to view these conclusions as anything but a massive vote of no confidence in the Admiralty. Three of the five permanent members of the War Cabinet were directed to inquire into aspects of work the Admiralty should already have had in hand. Further, a personal visit to the Admiralty by no less a personage than the Prime Minister would ensure that the matter required urgent attention.

In the end all was anti-climax, Jellicoe and his senior staff being bailed out in the nick of time by their more junior colleagues. One version has the key player being Commander R.G. Henderson. For some weeks he had been investigating the matter of the number of ships that arrived in British ports per week. He found that the Admiralty had been gulled by its own propaganda. The tables he examined suggested that thousands of ships arrived each week but on closer examination he found this included multiple voyages by small coastal vessels and fishing boats added to the statistics only to induce neutral opinion to accept that the percentage of sinkings was vanishingly small. In fact just 280 of these were ships over 1,600 tons engaged in overseas trade.[87] This was a number that, with American help, could be found.[88] In this version it was this paper that led to Duff, the head of the Anti-submarine Division at the Admiralty, to change his mind and support convoy. Another version claims that the Admiralty were well aware that overseas trade was conducted by relatively few ships but rejected convoy because grouping ships would disrupt trade.[89] Whatever the case, Duff was still opposed to convoy as late as 19 April. Then he wrote a paper stating that an escort would have to be provided for every two ships convoyed and that convoys passing over the same area 'must prove the easiest preys to the submarine'.[90] Yet just seven days later Duff decided that convoy would be feasible after all, and in a note to Jellicoe dated 26 April he proposed 'the convoy of all vessels – British, Allied and Neutral – bound from North and South Atlantic to United Kingdom'.[91] Jellicoe approved the plan the next day (27th) and Hankey noted in his diary on the 29th that the Admiralty were undertaking convoy on '*their own initiative*'.[92]

The chronology of these events has been taken by many authorities to indicate that the Admiralty had the matter of convoy in hand before Lloyd George's visit on the 30th. In some ways this seems to have been the case. Duff's paper to Jellicoe contained detail about the number of ships which would require convoy, the number of destroyers which should accompany them, the ports where the escorts should be based and the frequency of convoy sailings.[93] It is not reasonable to assume that he assembled these details as a result of the War Cabinet's decision made just the day before that Lloyd George should visit the Admiralty. On the other hand, Churchill's view that this visit represented 'a menace' to the Admiralty also seems incontrovertible.[94] What probably happened was that Duff's paper on convoy was in hand before 26 April but its production and approval by Jellicoe were hastened by the War Cabinet's decision. Moreover, Henderson, whether his paper influenced Duff or not, had been in touch with Hankey over convoy issues for some time and it is impossible to believe that he and other members of the Admiralty Staff were unaware of the War Cabinet's increasing impatience over the matter. So by the time that Lloyd George and Jellicoe met on the 30th, the First Sea Lord was able to present Duff's paper to the Prime Minister as a settled Admiralty policy and this is why Hankey's notes on the meeting and his later diary entries do not record any conflict over convoy.[95]

Yet we may doubt that Jellicoe's conversion to convoy was wholehearted. He was reported by Robertson on the 26th as giving an almost daily pronouncement that the naval situation was hopeless and in a paper written for the War Cabinet on solutions to the submarine problem convoy was only one of a number of measures he mentioned. Much more important in Jellicoe's view were the curtailing of all imports other than food, the elimination of the Salonika expedition to save shipping and placing essential materials and food in troop convoys sailing to Britain.[96] As the Official Historian noted, 'the writer of this ultimatum was far from believing that the great problem of the war had been solved.'[97] It must be concluded that if convoy had been left to Jellicoe and senior members of the Admiralty Staff, it would have been a long time coming. The civilian members of the War Cabinet and especially Hankey made no greater contribution to Britain's war effort than in concentrating the minds of the sailors on convoy and the urgency of its introduction.

Once Duff's paper had been accepted as policy, the navy acted with reasonable despatch in organising the first convoy. It sailed from Gibraltar on 10 May, consisted of sixteen steamers escorted for the entire voyage by two Q ships and in British waters by six destroyers. It was a total success. No ships were lost and station keeping proved well within the competencies of the merchant captains. No submarines were sighted despite the fact that there were a number operating in the waters through which the convoy travelled. This highlighted one aspect of convoy protection that all parties had tended to neglect. One of the secrets of the success of convoy only slowly became apparent but existed from the first. The objection that a convoy would present a large target to a submarine was to be turned on its head. A convoy of (say) twenty ships proved difficult for U-boats to find for this reason, as explained by Henry Newbolt:

> The visibility circle of a dozen or twenty ships in convoy formation was much smaller than the collective circles of the same number of ships sailing independently and the actual chance of any given submarine sighting the group was much less than the chance of her sighting one or more of the ships, if they were brought in along various routes and at various times.[98]

There were other benefits for ships sailing in convoy. Naval Intelligence found that while they could not contact every merchant ship that sailed independently because many of them did not have a wireless, *every* convoy had at least one ship with wireless. It was possible then for Naval Intelligence to divert whole convoys away from known positions of U-boats. Evasive routing saved innumerable ships from attack and further emptied the seas around which U-boats gathered.[99] It is remarkable that no one on the Naval Staff gave the slightest consideration to this measure.

Despite these significant advantages there is no indication that the Admiralty sought to institute general convoy as a matter of urgency. Losses in May had declined from 850,000 tons in April to 550,000 tons but this was still very high. If British losses only are considered, the figures of 550,000 tons and 350,000 tons were well in excess of new construction.[100] Yet a committee appointed by the Admiralty to report on the implementation of convoy in April only submitted its scheme on 6 June.[101] And although by the end of July thirteen homeward convoys consisting of 245 ships had been convoyed across the Atlantic for the loss of one ship, ships outward bound from Britain were still not being convoyed, despite clear evidence that the U-boats had now turned their attention to these ships.[102] In the event, outward-bound ships were not convoyed until mid-August.[103]

This glacial speed was maintained. Convoys from Dakar were commenced in mid-August, from Sierra Leone towards the end of September. In the Mediterranean there were additional obstacles. Jellicoe had by this time become converted to convoys and at an inter-Allied Naval conference in London in September had urged the adoption of universal convoy for all ships.[104] It was then discovered that the French and Italians were by no means converted to this measure and it was not until early October that outward convoys to the Mediterranean could be commenced and not until mid-November that homeward convoys from Port Said were started.[105]

By November ocean convoy had at last become general. Yet losses at a level higher than replacement building continued. In May 550,000 tons were lost, in June 632,000 and in October the figure was still 492,000.[106] What was going wrong? The fact was that U-boats, unable to find convoys, had shifted their area of operation. In the first six months of 1917 just 18 per cent of shipping losses occurred within 10 miles of land. In October that became 38 per cent and by November 63 per cent.[107] The explanation was that ships were being convoyed until they reached a major British port, then many ships would sail independently around the coast of Britain until they reached their final destination. It was these independent sailings that provided the easy pickings for the U-boats. And as usual the Admiralty were slow to respond. In February 1918, such was the slaughter in the Irish Sea, that convoys were extended into west coast ports. But it took until August 1918 before a complete system of east coast convoys was instituted and until October 1918 for a north Cornish coastal convoy to be started – just about in time to coincide with the end of the war.[108]

One final point should be made. In the First World War a convoy did not attract U-boats to it and then destroy them. In all about 180 U-boats were sunk during the course of the war. Of these probably fewer than forty were destroyed by escorting warships.[109] The main causes of loss were mines, followed by ramming and Q ships. In the main the U-boats could not locate the convoys, thus denying their escorts much opportunity to sink them. This needs to be borne in mind when we consider the campaign in the Second World War.

The spectacular success of convoy can be summed up with a few figures. In the unrestricted period, from February 1917 to the end of the war 83,958 ships were convoyed. Of these just 257 or 0.3 per cent were lost to submarines. In contrast, 1,500 ships, 5.5 per cent of independent sailings, were sunk by U-boats. Thus in this period 85 per cent of total losses were from ships sailing alone.[110] Nevertheless, the Germans caused great inconvenience with the submarine campaign and Britain was required to ration food and restrict non-war cargoes to see them through.

The Admiralty under Jellicoe does not emerge well from this picture. They were slow to implement and slow to extend the convoy system; the demise of Jellicoe, fired by Lloyd George in June 1917, comes as no surprise. The caution and indeed pessimism that had served him well at Jutland was a hindrance in a situation that required new thinking. It was the politicians and the civilians – especially Hankey if he can be so called – who saved the day. Without ascribing Lloyd George's visit to the Admiralty the entire credit for the introduction of convoy, there seems little doubt that it was the Admiralty's awareness that their civilian masters in the War Cabinet were unhappy with their response to convoy that concentrated the minds of the more astute members of the staff on this problem. And it was Hankey's ability to focus the ever-wavering attention of the Prime Minister to use the prestige of his office to ram this point home that produced results. Without this civilian pressure, convoy would have been much delayed – had it been introduced at all.

CHAPTER 10

1918 – THE WHIRLWIND

THE DISAPPOINTMENTS OF 1917, Arras, Passchendaele, Cambrai and perhaps disappointment with himself for presiding over these disasters, reduced Lloyd George's relations with the military to a low ebb. Whatever he did to curb their power came to nothing. After establishing the inter-Allied General Staff at Versailles to act as an alternative source of advice to government, he found that the War Cabinet absolutely refused to grant that body executive power. His man Wilson might be sent to Versailles but he could only act as an adviser.

Thus thwarted, the Prime Minister tried another manoeuvre. He suggested that the generals assembled at Versailles be formed into an Executive War Board and given control of all the reserve forces behind the front. This was a clever move to hobble Haig because, once an engagement started, one of the few ways a Commander-in-Chief could influence a battle was to decide where or when to commit his reserves. However, the fact was that in early 1918 there were no central reserves. Haig had been forced to take over a section of the French front to relieve pressure on his ally and that had used up the small number of divisions available for a strong reserve. The Americans were arriving but not in sufficient numbers to have reserves. And the French, under their new commander, General Pétain, were quite unwilling to spare the few reserve divisions they had to multinational control. In the end, therefore, there were no central reserves for the

Executive War Board to manipulate. On the British front Haig would retain control of the few reserves available.

But Lloyd George did score one success. Robertson had complained at length at the potential power that Wilson might have at Versailles. In the end the Prime Minister outmanoeuvred him by offering him the post. Robertson refused. Lloyd George then ordered him to Versailles. Robertson again refused. Haig, sensing which way the wind was blowing, urged the CIGS to go. But Robertson dug in. The only way out was resignation. It was hastily accepted. Wilson was brought back from Versailles as CIGS. Haig also moved quickly. Rawlinson, Haig's man, replaced Wilson at Versailles. Lloyd George's one step forward was followed by half a step back.

Regardless of the underhanded nature of some of Lloyd George's manoeuvres, there was a desperately serious purpose behind them. Casualties of the scale of 1917 were not sustainable. If Haig and Robertson were to conduct offensives in 1918 of the type of the Somme and Passchendaele, there might not be an army of any size and ability left by the end of the year. So Lloyd George's attention turned from command to the control of manpower. The department overseeing this question was the Ministry of National Service. In the autumn of 1917 it had been totally reorganised by a new minister, Auckland Geddes. Under former ministers (one of whom was Neville Chamberlain) the department had merely been a cheer squad for the voluntary system of allocating labour to the armed forces or industry. Under Geddes its remit was widened to encompass manpower planning for the entire economy. One matter became rapidly apparent to the new minister: if the bottom of the manpower barrel had not yet been reached, it was certainly in sight.[1]

Lloyd George had been alerted to this situation by Geddes at the same time he had received from the military a note that they would require 1.3 million men in 1918, of which 600,000 were to be category A1 men (the top level of fitness) for the infantry.[2] The Prime Minister was well aware that Haig's plan for 1918 was to 'continue our offensive in Flanders' – that is, to revive the disastrous Third Ypres campaign.[3] If the army was granted its manpower requirement it would be in a position to conduct exactly that type of campaign. The trustee for British youth in the form of the Prime Minister intervened. Lloyd George determined to seize control of manpower allocation. A small committee of the War Cabinet was set up for this purpose in December 1917. Its findings were bad news for the military. The Committee, with Geddes as an adviser, after surveying the needs of the entire war economy, established a list of priorities for the allocation of manpower in the new year. First priority was given to shipbuilding and manning the new naval craft needed for convoy. Next was placed the need to manufacture more aircraft and tanks. Third in importance came the need to increase food production on the home front to ease the import burden. When these needs had been taken care of, the wishes of the army could be considered. It was found that there were very few men available. Haig would be given only the thinnest gruel. He was to receive not 1.3 million men but 190,000: 150,000 for the infantry and 40,000 for menial tasks on the lines of communication. In return the army was required to consolidate what force it had by reducing infantry divisions from twelve battalions to nine and to reduce the number of what the Committee considered to be obsolete cavalry units.[4]

The import of all this needs to be stressed for it amounted to the reassertion of civilian control over strategy. With the numbers of men made available to him, Haig could hardly embark on offensives of the nature of the Somme or Passchendaele. The options, imposed upon him by the War Cabinet, were either to remain on the defensive or to find new and cheaper ways of conducting his offensives. Haig, Robertson and the military in general railed against this policy but there was nothing that they could do about it. They might have reflected on their wasteful offensives in 1917 but there is no evidence that this crossed their minds. Civilian control of the military was part of the British system and it had now been reasserted. This was arguably the most important decision made by the Lloyd George government in the entire course of the war.

And there was no question that the civilians were correct. Giving the army the 1.3 million men it asked for risked deindustrialising the BEF. That force, if the military authorities had not noticed, now needed tanks, machine guns, aircraft, artillery and machines of all kinds that had not been imagined in 1914. Workers were required to make those products and they, along with the home population, had to be fed. In the nick of time the civilians were obliged to remind the army that modern war was a more complicated business than filling up infantry battalions. A wider view of warfare was now necessary, as Haig and Robertson had now been told in no uncertain terms.[5] And if critics of Lloyd George need to see an example of what havoc untrammelled military control of a war economy can wreak, they need look no further than what was to happen to Imperial Germany at the end of 1918.

How, then, was Haig to handle, with the force he now had available, the impending German offensive, for from mid-December on there was no doubt that there would be a German offensive. Whatever the other failings of Haig's Intelligence service, calculating the build-up of enemy divisions along the Western Front was not among them – they counted 157 in early January, 172 on 1 February, 183 by the end of the month and 200 by mid-March. Also noted was that of these, ninety-two were concentrated against the fifty-seven of the BEF.[6]

Haig's reaction to this situation was ambivalent. On the one hand he said that he 'was only afraid that the Enemy would find our front so very strong that he would hesitate to commit his Army to the attack with the almost certainty of losing very heavily'.[7] And when alerted by the French to the fact that the Germans were practising deep breakthrough tactics, he merely remarked that this reminded him of Nivelle's optimism of the previous year – that is, if the Germans tried such tactics they were doomed to fail.[8] On the other hand, he pointed out to anyone who would listen that he was critically short of manpower and that by June the situation would be desperate, while at the same time contemplating with apparent equanimity the fact that in mid-March 88,000 men from the BEF would be in Britain on leave.[9] Probably his attitude can be explained by his knowledge that while the German build-up opposite the BEF was of enormous proportions, no offensive on the Western Front, certainly none conducted by himself, had yet made a deep or rapid penetration of an enemy line.

The disposition of his armies, however, revealed at least some concern about a possible German breakthrough. In the north, where the front line was just 50 miles from the Channel ports, there was little room in which to conduct a major retreat. Here he chose to be strong. Here the Second and First Armies were given twenty-six divisions for a front of just 56 miles, or one division approximately every 2 miles. In the centre, around Arras, where the distance to the coast was little more than in the north, the Third Army disposed fourteen divisions over 28 miles, also 2 miles per division. In the south, where the line arced away from the coast, Haig chose to be weaker. There the Fifth Army held a front of 42 miles with just twelve infantry and three cavalry divisions, a ratio of 3.2 miles per division, but in an area where a retreat of some distance could be contemplated without compromising vital communication centres or ports. In addition Haig held just eight divisions in reserve, parcelled out at two divisions per army, a thin enough complement.[10]

There was a way in which he could have accumulated more reserves. In the north Rawlinson, who had temporarily taken over command of the Second Army from the absent Plumer, declared the salient around Passchendaele 'a really untenable position against a properly organised attack' and realised that it would have to be evacuated rapidly in such a circumstance. This would have saved three or four divisions, yet no such authority came from GHQ.[11] Another few divisions could have been placed in reserve by evacuating the Flesquières Salient formed after Cambrai. Again no such move was made. So the eight divisions Haig had in hand could have been increased to at least fourteen had the Commander-in-Chief chosen to evacuate dangerous and wasteful salients.[12]

With these exceptions, Haig produced a sensible distribution of divisions across the front. But what he was not to know was the manner of attack the Germans had decided to throw against him. For some time new infantry tactics had been featuring, to some extent at least, in German offensive operations. At Riga on the Eastern Front, at Caporetto in Italy and at Cambrai, some German divisions had given up any kind of linear advance in favour of what came to be known as 'storm troop tactics'.[13] By early 1918 these tactics had been fully developed. Divisions were now divided into two types: attack and trench divisions.[14] In an attack division, a battalion might have a trench mortar company, some flamethrowers, a battery of light artillery and four light machine-gun teams.[15] Such formations were to advance in groups, bypassing any Allied strongpoints or centres of resistance. They were to penetrate as deep as possible into enemy positions and not wait for flanking support to left or right. Reserves were to reinforce success, not attempt to redeem failure as in previous battles.[16] Any mopping up of the bypassed enemy would be left to the trench divisions.[17]

To accompany these new infantry tactics the Germans, under the direction of General Georg Bruchmüller, developed new artillery methods. Unlike the colossal bombardments that accompanied battles in 1916 and

1917, Bruchmüller's approach aimed not at total destruction but at neutral-isation and paralysis. Enemy batteries would be neutralised by a deluge of gas shells to prevent the guns from being manned. Paralysis of enemy command, control and communication centres would be achieved by intense bursts of fire from as many guns as could reach those areas. Finally, in the hours before zero, hurricanes of fire would fall on enemy infantry concentrations.[18] The accuracy of all artillery fire would be assisted by sound-ranging and flash-spotting sections, coming into use in the German army as they were in the British.

In many ways these were startlingly modern developments, certainly on the infantry side, far in advance of anything developed by the Allies. And the idea of artillery as a neutralising rather than a totally destructive weapon was also new. But in other ways Ludendorff's tactics were desperately old-fashioned, to the extent of almost harking back to pre-industrial war. The main problem lay with the new infantry tactics and the disconnect with the weapon of breakthrough – the artillery. If the new tactics worked and the defensive crust of the enemy was broken, the infantry were to continue to advance. But the further they advanced, the more they would outrun the fire-support weapon that facilitated their progress in the first place. True, they would carry machine guns and flamethrowers with them but the like-lihood of getting even light artillery forward across cratered ground scat-tered with trenches and barbed-wire entanglements was remote. Some advantage might be obtained if the attacking infantry could overrun the enemy's guns in the first rush but in truth many of the heavier artillery pieces lay many miles beyond the front. If these could be pulled back and reinforced by artillery in reserve, the fire-control equation would soon swing against the attackers. Increasingly, infantry weakened by inevitable casualties would be opposed by an enemy with an growing number of guns and with fresh troops brought from areas so far in the rear that the attackers could not reach them. In effect, the German tactics must in the last analysis have relied, after the initial breakthrough, upon winning the war by infantry alone.

Ludendorff of course did not see his operations in this light. His main aim was to destroy the most efficient army on the Western Front: the BEF. He would attack the British with three armies – from north to south, Seventeenth, Second and Eighteenth. All armies were to penetrate the

British defensive systems. Then the Seventeenth Army would attempt to cut across the rear of the British northern armies and head towards the Channel coast. The Second and Eighteenth Armies would act as a flank guard to hold off the French to the south and provide reinforcements to the Seventeenth as required.[19] If the BEF could be rounded up against the coast before the Americans arrived, he could turn on the French, whom he now regarded as the lesser enemy. Once they had been dealt with, peace on German terms could be negotiated.

What manner of defences would these new German tactics face? In theory each section of the British front was divided into three zones – the forward zone, the battle zone and the rear zone. While such a configuration might have looked similar to the flexible German defence in depth, adopted from 1917 on, there were significant differences. There was nothing particularly flexible in the British system. The troops holding the front zone were expected to maintain their positions and use their machine guns to compel the enemy to employ strong forces in its capture. If the enemy entered the zone, local counter-attack forces were expected to drive them out.

There were also differences between the defences in the north and those in the south. In VI Corps (Third Army) the forward and battle zones had complete networks of trench lines. Here defence and retreat could be conducted in the same old way, with lines of soldiers moving back from one completed position to the next. In XVIII Corps, further south, many 'posts' or 'forts' were placed in the forward and battle zones with all-round wire and trench defences, and these were expected to break up the enemy attacks and, if surrounded, to hold out and thus absorb the assaulting forces for as long as possible. One problem with this style of defence was that many of these areas were isolated from each other with little hope of any mutual support. If an attack succeeded, each area could be mopped up seriatim.

But the main problem with the British defence system was that it was incomplete. The forward zones were fully developed on the northern section of the British line but that was all. Further south, because of lack of labour, they were far from complete. As for the battle zones, in most areas they consisted merely of two trench lines with few interconnecting trenches or strongpoints. Even less impressive were the rear zones, placed some 4 to 8 miles behind the battle zone. Any troops in this area were to reinforce the battle zone as required but in most areas of the front its functions were never fully developed because, again due to labour shortages, it was little more than a line marked on the ground.[20]

One notable and mournful feature of the entire British system was that no less than two thirds of all troops would be within range of the great majority of German artillery fire, the British having many more troops in the forward zone than was thought necessary by the Germans at this time of the war.[21] The system had other failings. Machine guns, which were to be the main weapon of defence, were not, in general, located in concreted posts; there were no pillboxes; nor were there any strong counter-attack formations. The whole system showed the baleful effect of the blighted 1917 offensives and the general point that the BEF had not stood on the defensive for almost the entire war – it had either retreated (1914) or attacked (1915–1917). It had no experience and its commanders had no interest in defensive warfare, a factor that should be kept in mind in what follows.

A German attack in the area of the Third and Fifth Armies had been long anticipated by British Army Intelligence. In early March Fifth Army Intelligence expected a heavy attack near Cambrai; by 13 March the impending attack was thought to extend from Arras to St Quentin.[22] Of all the higher commanders, Gough had come closest to divining German intentions. He took the presence of Von Hutier, one of the victors of the Riga offensive, opposite his Fifth Army as a warning sign and he suggested concentrating what labour there was on the Fifth Army front.[23] Haig, however, had to spread his labour corps across all his defensive positions and so was in no position to comply with Gough. Then on 17 March the weather turned, with cloud and rain blinding aerial reconnaissance of the German preparations. Still, prisoners alerted the British that a major attack was planned for 21 March and that it would extend across the fronts of Fifth and Third Armies. Gough had it right when he told his wife on the 19th that he expected the bombardment to begin on the 20th with an infantry attack to follow six to eight hours later on the 21st.[24]

How did Haig instruct the British to fight the forthcoming battle? His instructions to the northern armies were simple and direct: fight for each of the three defensive zones. Give as little ground as possible – because there was little ground to give behind the northern British front.

For Gough the instructions were more complicated; indeed they bordered on the inscrutable. On two occasions Haig impressed on Gough that it might prove impossible to reinforce his forward and battle zones because reserves might have trouble getting forward across areas immediately behind those zones which had been devastated by the Germans in their retreat after the Somme battles. He was told to fight for his defensive zones but not to commit large reserves for their recapture should they fall, unless the 'general situation' (which was undefined) required it. This was vague enough but worse was to follow. On one occasion Gough was told that it was 'for consideration' whether he should retreat to the east of the River Somme, some 30 miles in rear, and make his main stand there.[25] Some days later he was told that he was to hold the line of the Somme 'at all costs'. That is, he was not to retreat to the east of the river at all. In fact he was now required by GHQ to establish a defended bridgehead to the west of the Somme at Péronne. Instructions followed about how to construct such a work but, as Gough had no labour, that was all rather irrelevant.[26]

So Gough was to fight for his zones but be prepared to retreat rather than commit reserves to hold on. He was to either give up the line of the Somme or fight to the death for it. And he was to establish a strong bridgehead at Péronne though he had not the means to do so.

In these circumstances it was surely open to Gough to call in the strongest terms for clarification from GHQ because the scenarios they had laid out were obscure, contradictory and in some instances impossible to fulfil. Gough did nothing of the kind. Perhaps he thought that after his performance at Bullecourt and the Third Battle of Ypres he was fortunate to hold any command at all and that GHQ might not take kindly to a statement to the effect that their instructions were nonsensical. In the event all Gough did was mull over these instructions with his corps commanders – with what effect we will see later on.

What neither Haig nor Gough nor anyone on the Allied side was expecting was the ferocity of Operation Michael. At 4.40 a.m. on 21 March, from the rivers Sensée in the north to the Oise in the south, a front of over 40 miles, sixty-seven German divisions supported by 6,608 guns and 3,534 trench mortars opened fire on the twenty British divisions in the front line. On that first day of battle the Germans fired 3.2 million rounds of ammunition, one third of which was gas – mustard and other types – against the British defenders.[27] Communications were cut, batteries could not be manned due to the gas and headquarters were in many cases unable to calculate where to direct what few reserves they had. Bruchmüller's methods had proved successful.

At 9.40 a.m. a creeping barrage began, followed closely by the infantry in storm groups. As it happened, the infantry were also protected by the gas clouds and a heavy fog which lay over most of the battlefield that morning. There seems little doubt that the fog aided the attackers more than the defenders. Certainly, at times, the Germans ran directly into uncut wire or defended machine-gun posts, but most often the Germans overran the British before they realised what was happening. The fog also effectively blinded that main British weapon of defence, the machine gun. Those Germans advancing across open ground, who might have been shot down in large numbers on a clear day, traversed no man's land in many places unseen and unharmed.[28]

There is neither space nor time to detail every action of the thirty or so British divisions involved that day. There are, however, some generalisations that can be made. By 11 a.m. the forward British defensive zone had been overrun. The overwhelming numbers of German storm troops, the effectiveness of their artillery, the isolation of many British defensive redoubts, the new infiltration tactics – all proved decisive. In those few hours it has been estimated that the Third and Fifth British Armies lost forty-seven battalions of infantry or about one fifth of their total strength.[29] Some groups fought until they had expended their ammunition; some 'didn't fight very hard'.[30] Surrenders occurred all over the battlefield to the extent that by the end of the day the British had lost 20,000 men captured. Many of these men were isolated by the fog and stunned by the ferocious bombardment. Many may have formed part of the 90,000 new conscripts supplied to Haig between January and March but barely trained.[31] Others, such as the men of the 16, 36, 58 and 30 Divisions, were shell-like formations, worn down at Passchendaele. Others yet had many inexperienced troops just nineteen or twenty years of age. In any case, most were civilians in uniform of a type who did not fight to the last man or the last round. Few armies in history have ever done so.

This is not the whole story. When the fog began to lift and the gas dissipated, the British artillery and machine-gunners began to exact a fearful toll on many German units. By evening the results had begun to even up. Everywhere, except in the 59 and 6 Divisions of the Third Army and in the 16 Division and III Corps of the Fifth Army, the British clung to their battle zones. In one area, the Flesquières Salient, the Germans gained no ground at all.[32] Moreover, although the Germans had broken the British front on a length of 40 miles, an unprecedented advance in terms of the Western Front, they were rather disappointed with the day's work. They had, for example anticipated overrunning most British artillery positions on the first day. Instead the German Second Army had captured just fifty guns,[33] the Eighteenth Army which had made some of the most rapid gains that day only eighty,[34] the Seventeenth Army hardly any because it remained stuck 4.5 miles short of its objectives.[35]

The overall casualty figures for the day are also instructive. The Germans had lost almost 40,000 men, 11,000 of whom were dead and 29,000 wounded. The British had also lost around the same number overall but only 7,500 were dead and 10,000 wounded. The attack, despite the element of surprise, had once more proved more costly in men killed and wounded than the defence. Where the numbers evened up is in prisoners – the British 20,000, the Germans 300.[36] Nevertheless, many of those German wounded would not fight again. Even on the first victorious day Ludendorff was paying a high price for progress.

During the next few days the critical developments took place in the Fifth Army in the south and in the boundary between the Fifth and Third Armies in the centre. In Gough's area, what reserves he had were moved forward – 39 Division to VII Corps, 20 Division to XVIII Corps and 3 Cavalry Division (Dismounted) to III Corps. No French troops were yet in sight and it would take many days for divisions from the un-attacked Second and First British Armies to arrive. Clearly, Gough's main concern was to retreat to a supposedly more defensible line. In the morning Lieutenant-General Richard Butler (III Corps) had discussed with Gough that such a line might be the St Quentin Canal, some 3 to 5 miles behind the battle zone. Gough accepted that suggestion and by midnight the move back had been made 'without interference'.[37] By midday on the 22nd further moves were in train. Lieutenant-General Maxse's XVIII Corps, on the left of III Corps, was ordered by Gough to fight a rearguard action back to the rear zone and then to the Somme. Maxse soon decided that this was not far enough. 'During the afternoon' of the 22nd he ordered his corps to withdraw straight to the left bank of the Somme – that is, behind it – because the rear zone turned out to consist of a single trench just 18 inches deep.[38] More shocks followed for Maxse. When his corps reached the Somme at Péronne they found it had no defensible positions at all. Nor was the 20 Division, in reserve at Péronne, aware that it had to be held at all costs. So Péronne fell with hardly a shot fired. And the rapid move back of Maxse's corps unhinged the defence to its north. There all Watts, commanding XIX Corps, knew was that Maxse's men had disappeared and that as a consequence his right flank was open. He too beat a hasty retreat back to the Somme.[39] By the end of the 23rd the entire position in which Gough was to make a stand, from Ham on the Somme to the north of Péronne, was in German hands.

This rapid withdrawal of the Fifth Army had grave consequences for the Third Army to its immediate north. Because the corps of Fifth Army (XIX) which linked it to the Third Army had retreated, the VII Corps of Third Army was under the same compulsion or it would completely lose touch with Gough's men. But on its other flank the V Corps of Third Army occupying the Flesquières Salient had not given an inch of ground. A command decision was desperately needed here. The obvious choice was to evacuate the salient, which would allow VII Corps to maintain contact with Gough's troops and their own V Corps and thereby keep the armies together. Such a move would also create a small reserve which could be used to backstop the retreat. But the Third Army Commander (Byng) seemed to regard the Flesquières Salient, the only ground retained during the disastrous Cambrai offensive, as in some way sacred. Haig had himself given approval for the evacuation to take place but for forty-eight hours Byng ignored him.[40]

Finally, on 23 March Byng capitulated to reality and gave the order to withdraw. The Official Historian, not one usually given to flights of rhetoric, describes the state of the men thus:

Tiredness is not strong enough an expression to describe the state of the troops, most of whom were still suffering from gas shelling . . . No words also could convey any picture of confusion of the night of the 23rd/24th March: troops wandering about to find their brigades and battalions, in an area without landmarks, devastated a year before by the enemy; dumps burning and exploding; gaps in the line; the Germans attacking almost behind the V Corps front; the atmosphere charged with uncertainty, and full of the wildest reports and rumours.[41]

One rumour that happened to be true was that Byng's boneheaded decision to delay withdrawal had opened up a gap between the Third and Fifth Armies. From the Flesquières Salient for a distance of some 3,000 yards, there were no troops at all, and that situation applied for the next twenty-four hours. Almost as bad was the situation to the south of this point. There, the retreat of VII Corps had fallen into disarray, because of the confusion about whether to maintain touch with the Fifth Army to its south or the Third Army to its north, with considerable distances now appearing between battalions.[42] In sum, from southward of Flesquières to just north of Péronne the BEF consisted of a straggling disorganised rabble rather than an army. As it happened, this was the very area where Ludendorff was to propel his Seventeenth Army through to Arras and then the coast in order to separate the entire BEF from the French and bottle it up against the Channel.

At this point of greatest danger to the British Ludendorff made one of his fateful interventions. A glance at a map revealed to him a new situation: the great advances by the Eighteenth Army in the south far exceeded anything gained by his two northern armies. He therefore changed his plan. No longer was the main effort to be made to drive the British into the sea – though minor operations in that direction would continue. Now his main objective was to separate the BEF from the French by exploiting the successes in the south. What this meant in practice was that the German offensive began to dissipate. The northern attacks would continue due west but with less weight, while his Eighteenth Army would be reinforced and head south-west to round up the remains of the Fifth Army and to block any French attempt to come to their rescue.[43]

None of this was obvious to the troops in the line. Gradually the eight divisions in Haig's reserve were fed into the battle. Gradually French divisions, though often without artillery, replaced the worn-out British units south of the Somme. Indeed, by 24 March the Fifth Army was placed under French command (General Fayolle) and the boundary between the national armies was established along the River Somme. Meanwhile the retreat continued. On 24 March Bapaume, an important road and rail junction, was lost and soon the British found themselves retreating across the old Somme battlefield. Le Sars, Combles and a host of other wrecked villages, so familiar to the troops of 1916, fell once more into German hands. Nevertheless, with some difficulty a more or less continuous line between the French and the British Fifth and Third Armies was maintained. Ludendorff's attempt to drive a wedge between the Allies had failed.

The next crisis concerned the command rather than the troops. On 24 March Haig and Pétain met. The outcome was mutual misunderstanding. Pétain was uncertain that the British Third Army would hold and thought that in that situation Haig would withdraw north-west away from the French towards the Channel ports. Haig had certainly investigated this possibility but his strategy was to withdraw if necessary *along* the Channel coast while maintaining touch with the French via the Third Army, which he was convinced *would* hold. At the same time Haig became convinced that Pétain was intent on retiring westward on Paris at the cost, if necessary, of losing touch with the British. Pétain actually only intended to follow that course if the British Third Army collapsed. Both men, however, were certain that the actions of the other risked a split between the coalition armies and defeat in detail.[44] A close reading of the various accounts and orders issued by the two men reveals that their true intentions were to keep their respective armies in touch but the heat of battle is not an ideal time for such an exercise.

Ludendorff's best hope of victory, indeed his only hope of victory, was that such misunderstandings would persist and that he would be able to defeat one national army and then the other. But any misunderstandings were soon overcome at an inter-Allied conference. From Britain the Minister of War (Milner) and the CIGS (Wilson) were en route to France, and Georges Clemenceau and General Ferdinand Foch were on their way to meet them. Pershing, the American Commander-in-Chief, joined them – a new factor to be taken into consideration. At a conference in Doullens on 26 March, which was also attended by Haig and Pétain, Foch was charged 'with the coordination of the action of the British and French armies (on the Western Front)'.[45] Under extreme circumstances Lloyd George had at last attained unity of command though hardly in the manner he had envisaged. There was an immediate change. Now not a yard of ground must be voluntarily ceded; the French and British armies would stay linked together.

Foch insisted that a large blocking force be placed in front of the rail centre at Amiens, through which supplies to such a high percentage of British forces flowed and something that Haig had been pointing out for some time.[46] If Ludendorff had ever possessed a chance of victory it had now passed.

It needs to be emphasised yet again that the improvement in the Allied position was not obvious to the soldiers in the front line. All the men knew was that they were still retreating. On 27 March Albert, a town to the north of the Somme that had been behind the British line at the opening of the Somme campaign, had now fallen – the Germans capturing in six days what the Allies had struggled to secure in 140.

Nevertheless, there were some positive signs for the Allies. By 26 March the German infantry seemed to be running out of steam. German prisoners complained that they were being thrown into battle at the end of long marches by which time the limit of their physical endurance had already been reached. They also stated that they were given no particular objectives but merely told to push on as far as possible. Their supply trains were often far in the rear and there was a lack of cover in the devastated area from aerial bombing now that the RFC had appeared over the battlefield in numbers.[47] From the 21st to 25th, on average the Germans had advanced 5 miles per day. From 26th to 30th March that had been reduced to 2.5 miles per day.[48] The German infantry were not only running out of puff but more importantly out of fire support as well. Their breakthrough had been achieved by an unprecedented concentration of artillery. Most of those guns, especially the heavier types, had not been able to keep pace with the infantry advance, a factor made so much more difficult by having to traverse two areas of devastated land.

Conversely, the British had managed to save many of their guns and they were falling back on considerable reserve stocks of artillery well beyond the distance of the German advance. So while the Germans had captured 859 British guns in the first week of their offensive, this still left them with a sufficiency in all categories except 12″ howitzers.[49] And reserve infantry divisions were being employed in increasing numbers. Nine divisions from Army Reserve and GHQ Reserve had entered the line by 26 March.[50] In addition, Plumer had bowed to the obvious and evacuated the Passchendaele Salient around Ypres. This freed up the 62, New Zealand

and 3, 4 and 5 Australian Divisions for operations in the south. Moreover these divisions had maintained their twelve-battalion structure, as had the four Canadian divisions which were around Vimy, had not yet been attacked, and also represented a powerful reinforcement.[51] Finally, French divisions had begun to replace units from the III and XVIII British Corps to the south of the Somme. Parts of twelve French divisions and two cavalry divisions were in the line and five more French divisions and a further cavalry division were approaching. Many of these units had no artillery and were short in various other types of equipment but they maintained an unbroken line and allowed many shattered British formations to fall back in reserve.[52]

And on the German side Ludendorff continued to waver. He was aware that many French units entering the line south of the Somme were weak, so he once more reinforced Eighteenth Army to assist its advance against them. This took his strongest army south-west. At the same time he ordered one corps of the Eighteenth Army to advance due west towards Amiens, perhaps belatedly realising that this was indeed a strategic objective worth seizing. Simultaneously he ordered an attack some 50 miles to the north of these operations by Seventeenth Army on either side of Arras called Operation Mars. Ludendorff's grand plan had now dissolved into a series of scattered affairs that were to advance in three different directions and not be contiguous. Moreover, though most additional infantry reserves were directed to the southern Eighteenth Army, so much of the heavy artillery was moved north for Mars that the army carrying out this attack (Seventeenth) had more heavy weaponry than the Eighteenth, which had the most infantry. Thankfully for the Allies' fixity of purpose was not Ludendorff's greatest attribute.

In the event, the Mars operation was a complete failure. Nine German divisions attacked four British divisions to the north and south of Arras. The artillery preparation had been rushed and most Allied artillery survived the bombardment intact. Weight of infantry numbers forced the British back to the rear zone but their guns fired 750 rounds per 18-pounder and 650 per 4.5″ howitzer that day and took a devastating toll on the enemy infantry. To this was added the fire of their heavy artillery further back and massed machine guns that had also been missed by the German artillery. The slaughter was immense. Two Canadian divisions had been summoned to backstop the British but by the end of the day it was clear that German operations in that area were at an end.[53]

Meanwhile, south of the Somme changes were being made to the British command. On 26 March Henry Wilson informed Gough that he was to be removed from command. Clearly a scapegoat was required and the most precipitate retreat had been on the front of the Fifth Army. Some harsh things have been said about Gough in the course of this narrative but it is somewhat ironic that he was sacked for the only efficient operation he ever conducted. In addition to the gnomic instructions emanating from GHQ, the weight of the attack by the Eighteenth Army would have made it impossible for any commander to hold the line.

His replacement was Henry Rawlinson, and the situation he took over was dire. His new 'army' (quickly renamed Fourth Army) consisted of little more than five weak divisions of XIX Corps with a nominal fighting strength of little more than 9,000 men.[54] In addition he had a rag-bag of units: 'Carey's Force' – an improvised group of stragglers of about 4,000 men – the 1 Cavalry Division, rushed south by Gough before his dismissal and now entering the line south of the Somme, and a brigade from 3 Australian Division moving towards the vicinity of Villers Bretonneux.[55] The final throw of the Germans in the area of the Somme was directed against this town which promised good artillery positions from which to bombard Amiens. Initially the Germans made ground but on 4 April a ferocious counter-attack from battalions from the 3 Australian Division accompanied by men from a Canadian motor machine-gun battery, a British cavalry detachment (17 Lancers) and some remnants of the 18 British Division, which had been fighting since 21 March, drove them back.[56] The front stabilised, Villers Bretonneux remained in Allied hands and there were no more immediate attacks by exhausted German forces in this area. Attention once more moved to the north.

Among the plethora of attack plans developed by the German army in late 1917 was Operation Georg – an advance around Armentières to cut off the British in the Ypres Salient and capture the important rail centre of Hazebrouck. With the ascent of Operation Michael, this was gradually reduced to Klein-Georg and finally Georgette. With Michael fizzling out along the Somme in early April, Ludendorff decided that Georgette would be carried out. It was to be a smaller affair than Michael but still formidable.

The attack was to be delivered by IV Army Corps with 1,686 guns against a British force of nine divisions (one being an understrength Portuguese division) supported by just 511 guns.[57]

The battle was launched on 9 April. Once again, Bruchmüller's artillery methods and the storm troop tactics proved effective in places (although there were far fewer storm divisions in Georgette because of the enormous casualties caused to these leading formations in the earlier offensive). In some areas the Germans gained 23 miles of territory and came within 4 miles of Hazebrouck, one of their main objectives. These were much smaller gains than had been secured in Michael and by the end of the month the German command admitted failure and called the offensive off.

Why did this second German effort fail so precipitately? The first factor was that in the north the British defensive zones were almost complete. In fact many areas between the zones had also been honeycombed with switch lines, defended localities, concreted machine-gun posts and deep dug-outs for some of the infantry.[58]

It will be useful to concentrate on one division (55 West Yorkshire Territorials) to demonstrate what a well-practised division with sufficient time could achieve in such a defended area. This division lay at a particularly important point in the line near Givenchy on the extreme left of the German attack – if the Germans were to make progress towards Hazebrouck and turn the British position, they would need to overrun the 55 Division. Here the commander, General Jeudwine, had divided his troops into two groups: the first group consisted of garrisons whose task it was to fight to the last whether outflanked or surrounded; the second group were for immediate counter-attack to win back all strongpoints taken by the enemy. Two brigades occupied the front defences. The third brigade was to carry out counter-attacks or set up defensive flanks. Each move had been practised to the extent that they would move forward on the issue of a single code word.[59] The division had also constructed many belts of wire throughout its defensive scheme to funnel the German attackers into channels that were well covered by machine-gun fire.

When the German attack went in, some strongpoints succumbed to Bruchmüller's artillery. The church in Givenchy village was captured. But the remaining garrisons, though surrounded, held on and poured a withering machine-gun barrage into the attackers. Then local counter-attacks conducted on the initiative of company, platoon or section commanders resulted in the recapture of the lost ground and a large number of prisoners and machine guns.[60] Meanwhile the belts of wire had completely baffled a group of German assault troops, to the extent that they could not find a way through them to retreat. Eventually 641 troops, two battalion commanders and 100 machine guns and automatic rifles were captured. To cap it all off a marching band that was to have played the Germans into Béthune was also secured, along with their instruments.[61] This story was repeated on the front of 55 Division for the remainder of the battle. They stood fast, Givenchy did not fall, the left of the German attack completely stalled.[62]

The second factor which halted the Germans was the strong British reserves behind the front. For example, to the north of the 55 Division were placed the two divisions of the Portuguese Expeditionary Force, no doubt baffled by the decision of their government to send them to the cold waste-lands of the Western Front. In fact just prior to the German attack, one of these divisions was drawn into reserve and the other was thinly spread across the front to cover its withdrawal. At that moment the Germans attacked. The undermanned and under-gunned Portuguese were routed and a hole torn in the British line. The immediate British reserves (50 and 51 Divisions), alerted to the possibility of a collapse by the Portuguese, were thrown into the gap, but they could only slow the German advance. Then two more divisions from reserve (39 and 61) arrived and slowed it even further. Even so, the Germans were now approaching Hazebrouck. Haig ordered the 5 Division, newly arrived from Italy, and 1 Australian Division to fill the gap.

These two divisions turned the tables. Both were strong units, still consisting of twelve well-rested battalions. They were well dug in a few miles in front of Hazebrouck when the Germans arrived. As the Australians recount, 'many vain' and 'futile attempts' were made to rush these positions in the following days. 'All proved of a most costly nature to the enemy.' The Australians even counter-attacked some German positions, capturing pris-oners and machine guns but no marching bands.[63] The German attempt to capture Hazebrouck was over.

The third reason for the Allied success in April lay more on the German side. As Ludendorff's troops approached Hazebrouck he diverted some of them to capture some hills (including Kemmel Hill) to the north. This movement caused great anxiety on the British side and on 25 April Kemmel fell. But the dispersal of effort slowed the German advance and in the lull Plumer acted. He quickly drew back from the Ypres Salient (thus giving up every inch of ground won in the Passchendaele campaign) and with the reserves so created by shortening the line stopped any further German advance. Also in this period French forces had arrived and in a counter-attack restored Kemmel to Allied hands. These efforts were no doubt worrying, but the German tactics dispersed the efforts of their increasingly weary troops and made no strategic sense.[64]

The fourth reason for the German failure was one of resources. They simply did not have the capacity to launch two major offensives in the west in the space of a few weeks. Bruchmüller found many batteries unprepared when he arrived in the north. He did his best, but there was just not time to adjust. The whole affair was rushed, many aircraft not arriving on time and some troops having to march all the way from the Somme.[65] Tactically, the Germans still showed some of their usual skill in Flanders but even if Ludendorff was slow to recognise it, there was a limit to what skilled infantry tactics could achieve.

There is no doubt that the German offensives in March and April 1918 represented one of the major crises of the war. The Allied armies were pushed back over distances unprecedented in the four years of fighting on the Western Front. Gains of 40 or 50 miles were made by the Germans, distances only to be found in the most outlandish plans made but not executed by Sir Douglas Haig. But the German plans had one quality in common with Haig's. Neither army had a weapon to exploit a breakthrough. The Germans had only a handful of lumbering heavy tanks of very short endurance. They had long given up on the cavalry sweep. And, despite their innovatory infantry and artillery tactics, they had not yet discovered that it was sheer folly to push attacking infantry beyond the protective cover of the artillery. All they managed when they did break through was to shift the zone in which their infantry could be slaughtered 40 or 50 miles to the rear. In other words the German offensives were bound to fail while the Allied armies held together and kept their nerve. This, in spite of a fearful battering, they managed to do.

The only other possible path forward for the Germans therefore lay in a failure of nerve on the part of the Allied political or military leadership.

This too was never on the cards. The misunderstandings between Haig and Pétain might have caused some anxiety but were soon sorted out. On the part of Clemenceau and Lloyd George there were never any misunderstandings. Both were resolved to fight the war out to the end – to a knockout blow, to use Lloyd George's phrase. And the appointment of Foch to the Supreme Command was masterly: he was the French general in whom the British had the most confidence.

So in March 1918 Lloyd George achieved one victory – there would be unity of command. His other wish was that there be no more offensives of the type endured in 1916 and 1917. How that wish would play out in the summer of 1918 remained to be seen.

CHAPTER 11

1918 – VICTORY

LUDENDORFF'S ATTEMPTS TO DESTROY the British army had by the beginning of April 1918 failed. The German command, with a less than impeccable grasp on logic, maintained that while the British were still the main enemy, the best way to strike against them was by attacking the French. So between May and July 1918 it was the French who would bear the brunt of the German assault. In May the Germans struck the French between Noyon and Reims, which included the old Chemin des Dames battlefield. Tactically the results were spectacularly successful. On 27 May on a front of 40 miles Bruchmüller opened the bombardment with 5,263 guns and 1,233 mortars. The results were unprecedented – an advance of 37 miles in four days. But, as in Operation Michael, the results led nowhere. No great strategic objective was captured and the French clung to the important communications junction of Reims. In all, the Germans suffered 105,000 casualties for no important gains.

They soon determined to try again. This time they attacked on either side of Compiègne in an attempt to straighten their line and save divisions. They comprehensively failed, suffering 25,000 casualties for derisory gains.[1] In July they attacked to the east of Reims with almost no gain of ground at all. All they managed was to completely exhaust what attack divisions remained in their army.[2]

That was to be the last major German offensive on the Western Front. The distinct German bulge across the Marne to the east of Soissons had attracted the attention of the French. In secret, French forces had been gathering to the west and south of this position. On 18 July the Tenth Army struck. Accompanied by more than 300 of the new Renault light tanks, the infantry attacked on a front of 28 miles and advanced 3 miles. In the next few days other French armies attacked from the south. The Germans escaped north but this was a victory of the greatest significance.[3] The French had recaptured much ground lost to the Germans earlier in the year – the first army to do so. Still, their armies were tired and after bearing the brunt of the war for three years could not be expected to play a major role in 1918. Whether Allied momentum could be maintained rested largely with the BEF.

What was the state of the British army in July 1918, after its ordeal in the early months of the year? It had lost about 350,000 casualties: 175,000 in Michael, 142,000 in Georgette and the remainder in those divisions unlucky enough to have been rested in the French areas where subsequent German attacks had taken place.[4] In the face of these losses reinforcements were sent from Britain, within the numbers agreed in the Geddes plan. So 110,000 of the 190,000 earmarked for the army were sent immediately; the remainder were sent in June. Two divisions had been returned from Italy and the Middle East (5 and 74) and many of the 88,000 soldiers on leave returned to the front. Furthermore, the army received 40,000 category B men (unfit for first line infantry). In total then the BEF received about 300,000 men from March to June, which made it slightly smaller than it had been on 20 March 1918. However, many of the new conscripts had received little training and others were lads under the age of nineteen. Haig's army in that sense was a much greener group than at any time during the war.

As one of the first divisions to see action when offensive operations returned to the British sector in late April 1918, we may consider the 8 Division. This was one of the last of the Regular divisions of the old BEF. It had served on the Western Front since 1914 and its personnel had seen many changes. The division fought on the disastrous first day of the Somme, where it was almost wiped out, suffering about 9,000 casualties. Then it returned in time to experience some of the worst fighting in the first stage of the Passchendaele campaign. In early 1918 it was considered too weak to remain in the front line. In the March/April emergency it did return to combat, only to be involved in the general rout of the Fifth Army. It was then sent to rest on a 'quiet' section of the French front, where it was almost immediately attacked by the Germans near the Chemin des Dames, suffering 7,800 casualties.[5] Finally it was sent out of the line to be reconstituted once more near Amiens. The division, now consisting of the greenest recruits, was moved up to Villers Bretonneux where the German advance had been driven back earlier in the month. But the Germans had not finished with Villers Bretonneux. On 24 April, perhaps to cover their move on Kemmel in Flanders, they attacked with mustard gas and a number of their huge tanks (AK7) and drove 'the children' who now constituted the 8 Division back and occupied the town.[6] This brought the Germans dangerously close to the junction at Amiens and Rawlinson insisted that it be recaptured immediately. On hand was the 5 Australian Division. On the night of the 25th a brigade of this unit advanced to the north of the town and one to the south, reinforced by men of the British 58 Division. The night attack was one of the most ferocious of the war. Few prisoners were to be taken. 'Only', states the Official Historian, 'as men tired of killing, prisoners came back in droves.'[7] Villers Bretonneux village was then cleared and remained in Allied hands. It was not to be lost again.

After the French offensive of 18 July, it was obvious that the Germans had lost the initiative on the Western Front. The question arose as to how the Allies would regain it. The American armies were arriving in France in numbers, the majority of them convoyed by ships from the Royal Navy taken from other duties.[8] Yet by the time of the March offensive there were just 300,000 US troops in France and many of these were barely trained or battle hardened. Their commander, General John Pershing, was loath to feed them piecemeal into the existing battles. How they would have coped with a Bruchmüller bombardment under foreign commanders did not admit of a positive answer. Lloyd George and Clemenceau might rail at Pershing but his reasons for holding his men together were militarily sound.[9]

With the Americans not yet a force to be reckoned with and the French still recovering, attention turned to the British. Between March and July the question of reinforcing the BEF and revising the manpower allocations decided on before the German offensive had constantly been on the agenda of the War Cabinet. They resolved to take men from the mines, munitions industries and to lower the age at which conscripts could be sent overseas. The numbers discussed were minuscule – a few thousand here and there. Overall they stuck to the Geddes plan; the industries and services that supported the army were to be maintained at their present levels. Haig would have to make do with shrinking infantry numbers. In early 1917 a British division might contain twelve battalions of around 900 men. Now, an average British division might contain 650 men in its nine battalions – a decrease from 10,000–12,000 riflemen to just 6,000.[10]

There were some British commanders at the front who saw the answer to this problem in a more mechanised army. Haig had always wanted more tanks than could be supplied by the Ministry of Munitions. Now Rawlinson pointed out that, 'bearing in mind the limitations of our manpower' – that is, bearing in mind that Britain was running out of men – machines in increasing numbers would from now on have to determine the victory.[11]

The difficulty was that the great retreat forced on the British in March and April had cost them much equipment captured or destroyed. In terms of artillery pieces the British had lost 975 guns, half of which had been heavy weapons of 6" or higher.[12] Thousands of machine guns, Lewis guns and many tanks had also been lost.

The solution lay with the British Ministry of Munitions. It had grown through 1917 and 1918 into the largest manufacturer of munitions in the world. Much to its surprise and horror Germany found itself out-produced by a country where a munitions industry had scarcely existed in 1914. Such was the output of this organisation in 1918 that Churchill (now returned to government as Minister of Munitions) could promise that by 6 April all equipment lost could be made up by supplies in Britain and in munitions parks in France.[13] In fact while on 1 January 1918 the BEF had 5,931 guns, despite the March and April losses, they had 6,709 by the beginning of June.[14]

Weapons production in other areas had also increased. The output of machine and Lewis guns was 80,000 in 1917 and 121,000 in 1918. Light trench mortars which could be carried forward by attacking troops had increased from a yearly supply of 3,000 to 5,000. Rifle grenades, a weapon unknown at the beginning of the war, had reached stockpile numbers of 4,000,000 by June 1918. Aircraft production had been 14,800 in 1917 but was 31,000 in 1918. Tank production only increased from 1,100 to 1,360 in these years but the new models were more sophisticated and much less likely to break down than earlier types.[15]

All this meant that the reduced size of an infantry battalion in 1918 would pack a considerably greater weight of firepower than one in 1916 or 1917. So while in 1916 a battalion might have four Lewis guns and one or two light trench mortars and no rifle grenades, by 1918 each battalion included thirty Lewis guns, eight light trench mortars and sixteen specialist rifle grenadiers. In addition battalions would be accompanied by more reliable tanks and many more close-support aircraft.[16]

Along with these prodigies of production came greater sophistication in using the available weaponry. Flash spotting and sound ranging as means of determining the exact whereabouts of German batteries could be done without firing a long preliminary bombardment. Fire could now be opened at zero and thus return surprise to the battlefield, as had been done at Cambrai. These methods had been more widely adopted and had increased in accuracy by 1918.

More refinements had also been introduced into aerial photography. Cameras had improved and the clearer pictures which they produced were being subjected to sophisticated analysis by staff experienced in identifying small and camouflaged targets.[17] Of course the use of aerial photography relied on the achievement of aerial superiority but that was a factor that British production made more likely in 1918.

One other factor should be mentioned. By 1918 GHQ had assembled a network to distribute information to lower levels of command. Whereas in 1916 the creeping barrage might have been confined to the few units that had developed it, by 1918 all new procedures and discoveries were disseminated to corps and divisions with great rapidity. In addition, pamphlets already issued were now regularly updated to take in the latest findings. In general the British army was becoming a more knowledgeable fighting machine.

What then was the state of their opponents? From 1 January 1918 to the end of July 1918 the Germans suffered between 712,000 and 778,000 casualties.[18] It seems certain that this number was not fully replenished and that the reason was that the Germans were also running out of men. There was no Auckland Geddes in Berlin or a War Cabinet keeping a close eye on the civil/military balance. So when Ludendorff asked for more men he was sent 350,000, whether or not they could be spared from the home front.[19]

One of the first units to realise that all was not well on the German side seems to have been the Australian Corps. South of the Somme opposite Hamel they noted that the Germans were not maintaining their defences to their normal standard; nor did Australian raiding operations, which managed to gain some ground permanently from the enemy, reveal a high state of morale among the German defenders.[20] This state of affairs was brought to the attention of the Army Commander under whom the Australians were serving, General Rawlinson. He was aware that he would soon have a new tank at his disposal – the Mark V. This was a modification of the Mark IV and an improvement. It was slightly faster than its predecessor, could be steered by one man instead of four, and had greater endurance and mechanical reliability.[21]

Rawlinson therefore invited Lieutenant-General John Monash, now commander of the Australian Corps, and Brigadier-General Hugh Courage of the Tank Corps to put forward proposals to straighten the line north of Hamel village and generally test the resolve of the German defence.[22] Monash and Courage's plans were based on the British experience at Cambrai. Both of them would use the new artillery methods to effect surprise and at zero 600 guns would shell unsuspecting German batteries and strong points. Then fifty to sixty new-model tanks would advance, covered by a moving barrage of heavy shells fired some 300 yards in front of them. Behind the tanks would come two brigades of infantry which would advance 2,000 yards to their final objective, where they would be relieved by two fresh brigades to beat off any German counter-attack.[23]

These plans did not meet with the approval of two of the second-rank commanders. Brigadier-General Thomas Blamey, Chief of Staff to Monash, and Major-General Ewen Sinclair-Maclagan (4 Australian Division), who was to command the attack, both entered a strong protest. They had been present at the ill-fated Battle of Bullecourt when tanks had been substituted for the creeping barrage as a means of infantry protection. When the tanks failed to arrive, the soldiers had been shot down in large numbers. Neither man wanted any repetition of that. They suggested to Monash that the infantry and the tanks advance together and that both be protected by a creeping barrage fired immediately in front of them. The heavy guns could then be removed from 'tank protection' and be used to fire on likely centres of resistance well behind the German front.[24]

These proposals were immediately accepted by Monash and then Rawlinson. This planning process shows a much greater degree of sophistication than many that had preceded it. Haig, in his lofty role as Commander-in-Chief, had no role in planning such a small operation. Rawlinson, as Army Commander, played a much smaller role than usual, merely calling for plans and then giving the end result his final approval. Monash was more willing to listen to his subordinates and be guided by their advice than many corps commanders in previous years. And so the end plan was the production of a committee of experts with close knowledge of the local conditions rather than one or two men in remote headquarters.

From their raiding activities, the Australians knew a great deal about their opponents at Hamel. They knew that they faced about 2,500 infantry from low-grade divisions of poor morale. They also knew that the German defences consisted merely of a single line trench, with some shell holes and a few dug-outs, with little barbed-wire protection.[25]

The date for the operation was set for 4 July. Appropriately, Rawlinson and Monash, after a certain resistance from the American command, had incorporated several US battalions into the attack. The artillery plan was almost completely successful. Two hundred guns blanketed the German batteries, 'silencing for some hours after zero the hostile artillery on the main battle front'.[26] Then the infantry and tanks, protected by the creeping barrage, made short work of most of the enemy defenders in their inadequate trenches. One trench, in Pear Wood, had escaped the attention of the artillery and the supporting tanks had lost their way. This was captured in the old way by frontal assault, resulting in considerable casualties to the Australians.

Notwithstanding this setback, the troops were digging in on their objective in just over ninety minutes from the beginning of the barrage. The new method of air dropping supplies to the advancing troops had worked perfectly. The operation had cost 1,000 casualties. On the German side 1,000 men were dead or wounded and 1,000 in captivity – almost the entire force had been wiped out.

Rawlinson was so taken by the operation that he immediately suggested to Haig that another attack south of the Somme be made to advance the line still further. Haig noted that his reserves at the moment were small but that

Rawlinson should go ahead and prepare a plan should troops become available.[27] Rawlinson submitted his plan to GHQ on 17 July. It called for an eleven-division attack astride the Somme and was based on the assumption that the Canadian Corps (then in reserve) would be available to fight alongside the Australians, with one British corps operating to the north of the river.[28]

Haig took this plan to a meeting called by Foch with his national army commanders (Pétain, Pershing and Haig) on 24 July. Pershing was eager but not ready; Pétain also asked for more time. On this basis the Haig/Rawlinson plan held the field.[29] On 26 July another meeting was held to formalise the arrangements. Foch insisted that the French First Army (General Debeney) also take part and, rather against Rawlinson's judgement, they were placed under Haig's command for the battle.[30]

There were no cosmic objectives set for this operation. Its purpose was merely to remove Amiens from long-range German artillery fire, yet it was to be a harbinger of great things. It was the first of many operations conducted by the BEF that would see the Germans routed on the Western Front and the war ended. These British battles were:

> The Battle of Amiens (Fourth Army), 8–15 August
> The Battle of Albert (Third Army) 21–26 August
> The Battle of the Scarpe (First and Third Armies) 26–30 August
> The Battle of the Hindenburg Outpost Line (Fourth Army) 18 September
> The General Western Front Offensive (First, Second, Third, Fourth Armies) 27 September – 5 October
> The Battle of Cambrai (Third, Fourth, First Armies) 8–9 October
> The Battle of the Selle (Fourth, Third, First Armies) 17–25 October
> The Battle of Sambre (Fourth Army) 4 November

This list is by no means comprehensive. The Second Army in Flanders was more active than the list indicates but for some of the time is was merely following the German retreat, as was the Fifth Army. In addition the French, Belgian and American armies were in action – in the Argonne, Champagne, the Aisne, Flanders, St Mihiel and other areas.[31] The main British armies were also by no means quiescent between the battles listed above. They were pursuing retreating German units or hustling them out of positions that needed to be held for future major operations. These minor actions are too numerous to detail, and even the major battles represent a challenge to a general history of this nature. Each action was so large and one followed another with such rapidity that a full description even of the main features of each one cannot be attempted: the canvas is too large; the detail too crushing to fit neatly into the structure of this book.

Moreover there is one question of overriding importance that demands an answer: why did the BEF prove so successful in this period when it was led by the same Commander-in-Chief and – with one exception – the same army commanders who had presided over such barren enterprises as the Somme, Arras and Passchendaele? Had these men, or others, hit upon a formula for success in the latter part of 1918 that helped bring the conflict on the Western Front to a successful conclusion?

The answer is that they had. But a formula, like a recipe, can contain many ingredients. One of the most important of these in the battles of August to November 1918 was the development of a coordinated weapons system. This was not developed out of thin air in 1918. The British had been groping towards such a system for some time. At Cambrai they had used artillery and tanks together but had complicated matters first by including weapons that could not be combined in any meaningful way (such as cavalry) and secondly by negating their artillery and infantry components by setting objectives that were too distant for either of them to deal with comprehensively.

The most startling example of the new weapons system came in the Battle of Amiens. Its main components were artillery, portable infantry weapons of some potency and tanks, all used in the context of an operation with a limited objective. This last factor deserves a brief comment. After viewing the final plan, Haig, as always, became convinced that Rawlinson's objectives were too modest – he suggested an advance on Roye (5 miles distant) and Ham, some 15 miles beyond that.[32] In the past instructions such as these had completely disrupted the artillery plan, spreading its fire too thinly to subdue any objectives. Roye and Ham, however, were beyond all but Rawlinson's heaviest guns. The artillery plan therefore remained intact although Rawlinson was forced at least to note Haig's desire for deeper objectives. The old Haig (he of the smashing breakthrough and the one decisive battle) had not yet disappeared from the scene.

At Amiens the British artillery best demonstrated what role it could play in a weapons system. There would be no preliminary bombardment in this battle. The sound rangers, aerial photographers and flash spotters had identified with great precision the location of 95 per cent of the 530 enemy guns that the Fourth Army faced.[33] And knowing with some certainty the number of guns ranged against the Fourth Army enabled its artillery experts to assign an appropriate number of counter-battery guns to deal with them. To make sure that all guns fired accurately they were taken out of the line before battle and adjusted for wear and any other factors that might affect their range.[34] On this occasion, as at Cambrai, the aim would be not to destroy every German gun, but to neutralise it for the duration of the infantry advance.

All these methods worked on almost all areas of the front. Walking over the battlefield on 9 August Major-General Charles Budworth, the Fourth Army's artillery commander commented:

> Some guns had been hit and some dumps of ammunition blown up, but . . . in the majority of cases, the detachments had evidently either been driven from their guns or had failed to man them. Some guns were captured with camouflage material over them, and muzzle and breech covers still on. Where attempts had been made to keep the guns in action or to limber up, the havoc wrought amongst personnel and horses was generally great, and afforded excellent testimony to the accuracy of the fire and the destructive effect of the shells.[35]

The significance of this hardly needs to be stressed. British infantry and tanks could proceed to the attack generally without the interference of hostile artillery. And some 450 captured guns would play no further part in this war.

The second part of the artillery formula was of course the creeping barrage. This method of infantry protection had been introduced in 1916 but had suffered many teething problems. The initial pace of the barrages was too fast for the infantry, there were too few shells to neutralise enough of the defenders, the barrages were not accurate enough and there were often insufficient guns to cover the entire front of attack. By Amiens these issues had been addressed. Before the battle, careful calculations had been carried out to ensure that there would be one field gun for every 25 yards of front attacked and that each gun would have enough ammunition to fire four rounds per minute for the period of the assault.[36] And so lavish was the provision of munitions that for this battle there were assembled more guns and shells than were required by the formula.[37] In addition, because of the factors already mentioned, the barrage would be fired more accurately than had often been the case in the past.

So when the infantry went forward at 4.20 a.m. on 8 August the counter-batteries ensured that they would not be met with a hail of shells. Indeed in some areas the enemy barrage was described as 'very weak and, as the attack progressed [it] ceased altogether'.[38] Most enemy machine-gunners were neutralised or killed by the creeping barrage. In this it must be said that they were aided by the stringent measures adopted by the Fourth Army to ensure surprise and the heavy fog that blanketed so many battlefields in the early mornings in 1918.[39]

Nevertheless, as always, some strongpoints survived the barrage. But now the attacking infantry had the means of dealing with these centres of resistance without resorting to frontal charges. With Lewis guns, rifle grenades and light trench mortars, groups of men could flank these German forces and deal with them at a distance.[40]

So far we have a weapons system consisting of heavy and field artillery and portable infantry weapons that could be quite lethal at short distance. The other component, especially at Amiens, was the tanks. Tanks were always going to be part of the Amiens plan but Brigadier-General J.F.C. Fuller, who was temporarily in charge of the Tank Corps, suggested that the entire corps – ten battalions of heavy tanks and two battalions of lighter 'whippet' tanks – be used.[41] As the fog lifted at Amiens these machines emerged. The sight of over 400 tanks lumbering out of the murk was too much for some Germans who had survived the earlier artillery onslaught. They either surrendered or fled in large numbers.[42] Within two hours the tanks had carried the advance forward to the second of its three objectives. This was the most significant tank action of the war. Another component had been added to the weapons system.

There was a further aspect to the planning of the Amiens Battle that enabled the advance to be carried further than in previous encounters. Units capturing the first objective paused to allow fresh units to leapfrog through them onto the second and third objective.[43] This drew on the experience of Cambrai, where it had been found that the troops who had secured the first objective had reached exhaustion but were then expected to move forward to more distant points. The result in that battle but not at Amiens was that they fell behind the barrage and stalled.

One important lesson from the Battle of Amiens was to influence all other battles fought by the British in the next four months. As the troops struggled towards Roye and Ham, the battle soon became ragged as units and commanders became uncertain or confused about the exact position of their troops, and artillery support consequently also became problematic or non-existent. The tanks, which had proved of such assistance to the final infantry advance on the 8th, had been reduced to merely a handful by the 11th. Communication between the forward troops and Fourth Army headquarters became difficult and orders for start times for the next day often failed to reach the forward troops. Even units within the same corps could not communicate with any certainty because lateral communication links had been cut. As a result, on the 9th the sixteen attacking brigades employed thirteen different start times, allowing the enemy the chance to recover.

After the blow on the 8th, the Germans rushed reinforcements in troops and artillery to the front.[44] In the next few days confusion on the Allied side got worse at the same time that German resistance stiffened. In the past this would have been a recipe for disaster as a period of ill-coordinated, hastily planned and inadequately supported attacks followed. On this occasion the resolution of a corps commander altered the pattern: when Rawlinson visited the Canadians on the 13th he was startled to find that their corps commander, Lieutenant-General Sir Arthur Currie, regarded further operations 'as a rather desperate enterprise and anticipates heavy casualties'.[45] He strongly deprecated any further advance. Rawlinson took careful note. Currie commanded a national contingent and had the right to appeal to his government should he consider orders from above to be endangering his force. So on the 14th Rawlinson confronted Haig and pressed him to postpone further operations. Haig, who was also clearly learning, abandoned his insistence on distant objectives and immediately agreed. When Haig informed Foch, the generalissimo at first urged and then ordered Haig to attack.[46] In reply, Haig 'spoke to Foch quite straightly and let him understand *that I was responsible to my Government and fellow citizens for the handling of the British forces.* Fs attitude at once changed.'[47]

That would be the last occasion that Foch would ever attempt to issue direct orders to Haig and a battle would not again be pushed beyond what the local commanders thought reasonable. Operations in 1918 therefore proceeded very differently from those of 1916 or 1917. There would be no more Somme or Third Ypres offensives. 'Bite and hold' had at last bitten and held with the British command.

For major set-piece battles, these tactics were the basis of all the British victories in 1918. There were of course many variations. In the Battle of Albert (21–26 August) tanks played a lesser role because there were only 183 available.[48] Moreover, because of the more broken nature of the ground, Byng paused after the first day in order to give time to bring forward his artillery before he recommenced the advance on the 23rd. But, looking at the Third Army operations orders, the timing of the attack (4.55 a.m.), the opening of the bombardment at zero, the thickness and pace of the creeping barrage and the use of light infantry weapons in the advance bear a striking similarity to those used by the Fourth Army.[49] However, on this occasion, when the Third Army approached a major obstacle in the Canal du Nord, there was no imperative instruction to continue from Haig. GHQ immediately ordered a pause to rest the troops and regroup for the next phase.[50]

The Battle of the Scarpe was fought in much the same way, this time with Horne's First Army operating to the north of the Third and Fourth Armies. What is notable about this battle is that the capture of the Drocourt–Quéant Line, a position that had held up many an attack in 1917, rated just one sentence in the War Diary of the unit that captured it: 'The 1st C[anadian] Div [with the 3 Brigade on the right and the 2nd on the left], preceded by a rolling barrage and supported by Tanks, attacked and captured the Drocourt-Queant Line.'[51] Progress, not stalemate, was now becoming normal.

Meanwhile at the other end of the advancing British line another vital link in the German defensive system fell. After the pause on the 15th, the Fourth Army had resumed its advance on 22 August. By the end of the month the line of the River Somme and the town of Péronne were in sight. The key to the German defence in this area was Mont St Quentin, a height just north of the village. On this occasion field artillery were pushed up to the very head of the advancing infantry columns to lend fire support. As one participant relates, in the situation of semi-open warfare the infantry were coming to rely to a great extent on the weapons they carried with them:

> The attack would . . . commence and it would not be long before the Germans in the post would find themselves under a heavy, accurate and destructive high-angle fire from rifle grenades. The length of time they stood this depended on the range, their moral[e] and their casualties, but generally the effect of the rifle-grenade fire was to cause them to bolt. As soon as they did this the Lewis gun sections were given their opportunity and they would open fire on the targets thus forced from cover.[52]

The fall of Drocourt–Quéant and Mont St Quentin unhinged the German defence. The German High Command had no alternative but to order a retreat of forces facing the First, Third and Fourth British armies to their last strong position in the west – the Hindenburg Line.[53]

But around Ypres, facing the Second Army, were those powerful defences, still complete with pillboxes which had proved so difficult, even with the Plumer methods, to overcome in 1917. The British army's methods would now be put to a stern test – they had succeeded against the flimsy defences the Germans had managed to construct at the high tide of their offensives in 1918. Could they succeed against more formidable fortifications?

In this case the answer was yes. In only two days the Second Army, operating with the Belgians, had advanced from just east of the Ypres ramparts to a line in front of Roulers in the north and Menin in the south. This was a greater distance than the British had managed to advance in three and a half months over the same ground at the Third Battle of Ypres in 1917. This time Passchendaele fell to the Belgians on the second day of operations.

Various explanations can be put forward for this extraordinary result. The artillery resources available to the Allies must play a prominent part. The British fired 250,000 rounds in a creeping barrage in the support of just one division (14) and around 1,500,000 shells in total.[54] It would take a formidable infantry to withstand an onslaught of this proportion. For the heavy artillery bombardment we have no precise figures but at this stage of the war the artillery was much more accurate. As a consequence the German artillery response was 'weak, and soon died away'.[55]

The Anglo-Belgian success was probably aided by some additional factors against the German side. Since August the action on the British front had been well to the south of Flanders, and the Germans had certainly moved some of their better divisions to meet the attacks there. In fact, of the divisions left in the line on 28 and 29 September (12 Bavarian, 40, 6 Bavarian, 11 Reserve, 52 Reserve, 39, 13 Reserve, 23) only one was rated by Allied Intelligence as 'First Class'.[56] Indeed, Crown Prince Rupprecht (the commander of the German Fourth Army) reported that his troops 'can no longer stand up to a serious enemy attack' and should pull back to a line that could be stiffened by reinforcements.[57] However, not too much should be made of the low level of the German infantry. Looking at the infantry on the Allied side reveals significant weaknesses here as well; for example, 14 Division instructions to troops include the following:

> The bulk of our Field Artillery barrage . . . will consist of shrapnel, and troops must be warned that shells bursting just over their heads are not directed at them, and are not short, but that the bullets will strike the ground some distance in front of them. The men will be warned, too, that out own machine guns will be firing over their heads; this may be disconcerting to troops not accustomed to it.[58]

It goes without saying that experienced troops who had served for some time on the Western Front would not have required such warnings. The 14 Division contained very few such men; the division had been badly knocked about in the German April offensive and hastily rebuilt with green drafts from Britain. Despite this rebuilding, its brigades were weak: 43 Brigade – one of those leading the attack – had a strength of only 1,720 as against a nominal strength of 3,000. This is detailed in its battle report: 'Although battalions were very weak and the men belonged almost entirely to "B" category [not fit for general service], yet they were filled with keenness and confident of success. They moved across the ground with energy keeping close to the creeping barrage.'[59]

One may imagine that the confidence and keenness shown by these men was somewhat increased by the amount of firepower that was supporting them. It may also be noted that the category B men who captured some significant German defences that day were thought quite unsuitable for action by the army and there were many cries of protest when the government despatched them to the front. In the end, despite the greenness of the troops and the lack of tanks, the combination of fierce, accurate artillery and an array of infantry weapons overcame an enemy that had slowed the progress of seasoned troops in 1917 for a period of months.

Meanwhile the Germans were simultaneously being assailed on many other sections of the Western Front. The French and the Americans were attacking in the Argonne, and the British First, Third and Fourth Armies were making progress towards the Marcoing Line and, more importantly, the Hindenburg Line.[60] The most significant of these operations was the attack on the strongest section of the Hindenburg Line by the Fourth Army. Here the Australian Corps, the IX Corps and to a lesser extent III Corps had made significant progress on 18 September by capturing an outpost line that protected the main line.[61]

The Hindenburg Line defences were daunting – concreted machine-gun posts, dug-outs, huge belts of wire and systems of trenches and communication trenches linking the rear defences with those further forward. In addition, in the southern section of the front lay the St Quentin Canal. This was a formidable obstacle. Its sloping sides had a steep gradient and fell away 50 feet to the water. The bed of the canal was 35 feet wide and a series of dams maintained a level of water or mud to a depth of over 6 feet.[62] Monash, who made the original plan, sought to avoid this obstacle altogether by confining the attack to the section of front where the canal ran through a tunnel.[63] Rawlinson, however, thought this front of attack (6,000 yards) was too narrow and extended it to 9,000 yards by insisting that a division from IX Corps (46) attack across the canal.[64]

The attack plan as developed would make its main effort across the canal tunnel. Here two American divisions (27 and 30) – both double the size of a British division – accompanied by eighty-six tanks would seize the main defensive system. Then two Australian divisions (3 and 5) accompanied by seventy-six tanks would leapfrog through them and take the Beaurevoir Line, the last in the German defensive system. Any exploitation eastwards would be carried out by cavalry, a rather anomalous addition to a modern battlefield plan. In the north III Corps would provide a flank guard for the US/Australian effort. In the south, IX Corps, aided by 3,000 lifebelts, portable rafts, ladders and collapsible boats, would send 46 Division across the canal and then leapfrog the 32 Division through it to capture the high ground to the east of the canal.[65]

There could be no surprise in this battle. So strong were the defences that a bombardment of four days was considered necessary to break down the German positions. All told, the artillery would have over 800,000 shells available to it.[66] In earlier battles against defences of this strength, this weight of artillery would have been insufficient, but in late 1918 it was a different matter. Now it could be assumed with some confidence that most shells would find their targets. Furthermore, in capturing the Hindenburg Outpost Line the British had seized positions with excellent observation over many German artillery sites.[67] Additionally, in August the Australians had captured detailed plans of that section of the defences that lay between Bellicourt and St Quentin. These gave the exact location of pillboxes, dug-outs, battery positions and many other aspects of German defensive arrangements.[68]

Nevertheless, the results of this bombardment were not uniformly successful. In the north, the American 27 Division had attempted to seize some important outlying positions prior to zero hour, but the artillery was not certain exactly where these US soldiers were and so they left many important strongpoints un-bombarded. In addition, the creeping barrage started 1,000 yards ahead of where the Americans actually were; the attempt to advance here soon stalled, with much slaughter.[69] Nor could the follow-up Australian forces redeem the situation. An insistence by Monash that all objectives *had* been taken merely led to more futile attempts to advance and higher casualties.[70] Tanks were knocked out in numbers and stalemate set in. Further south the American 30 Division was aided by the bombardment; Bellenglise did fall and the 5 Australian Division managed to make further gains as they leapfrogged through the Americans.[71] Then enfilade fire from the unsubdued Germans to the north stopped them in their tracks.[72] The whole attack across the tunnel was in danger of stalling.

Stalemate was prevented by the actions of the 46 Division attacking across the St Quentin Canal. Here the artillery concentration was unparalleled. For every 500 yards of front attacked the British infantry were protected by 50,000 shells per hour for the entire eight hours of their attack.[73] No defence could stand punishment on this scale and the infantry was able, with the assistance of their nautical paraphernalia, to cross the canal, scramble their way up the shattered banks and seize a bridge near Riqueval intact.[74] In short order the men of the 32 Division leapfrogged through and seized the high ground and in the process relieved pressure on the Americans and Australians to the north. The Hindenburg defences had been breached by IX Corps to a depth of 6,000 yards. Only the relatively weak trenches and wire of the Beaurevoir Line stood between the Fourth Army and open country.[75]

In a series of scrappy, rather uncoordinated actions over the next few days the Fourth Army eventually captured the Beaurevoir Line. At times the Germans resisted strongly but on those occasions there was a pause by the British as artillery was brought forward and a heavy bombardment fired on the centres of resistance.[76] Then, often accompanied by what tanks could be mustered, the infantry would go forward and another line would fall.[77] In earlier years the German command would have rushed reserves to the front, but with the whole Western Front from the Channel to St Mihiel erupting there were no reserves available. Many local 'divisions' that entered the battle were little more than reinforced battalions.[78] Being too weak to counter-attack, all these formations accomplished was a longer casualty list. The Hindenburg Line at its strongest point was no more.

With the Hindenburg Line now outflanked, the front of attack was widened to include the Third Army and the Canadian Corps of the First Army. Action commenced on 8 October and considerable gains were made. Caution was the watchword. If there was a hold-up or if artillery protection was not present, no attempt was made to advance until the infantry could receive proper protection.[79] Some old habits died hard, however: both the Third and Fourth Armies attempted to push some cavalry through to hasten the German rout. Few got past the infantry front line and those that did were set upon by German machine-gunners who showed no reluctance to wreak havoc on this sort of hapless enterprise.[80]

Nevertheless, it was quite obvious that the German army was starting to disintegrate. As early as 28 September Hindenburg and Ludendorff had agreed that President Wilson should be approached for an armistice. A Peace Note was conveyed to the Americans on 4 October and the troops at the front were told of this on the 6th. Fighting still went on while negotiations were taking place to end the war. A considerable battle was fought on 17 October on the River Selle, but the Germans were now generally in retreat and the most difficult matter for the Allies was keeping in touch with the enemy rearguards in deteriorating conditions of weather, and poor and inadequate roads which were further and further from the nearest railheads. Even so, on 4 November the British First, Third and Fourth Armies together with the French First Army launched an attack on a 40-mile front. There were severe obstacles lying across the path of this operation – the Forest of Mormal was 40 square miles in extent and there was the Sambre and Oise Canal, 75 feet from bank to bank and surrounded by low ground which had been flooded by the retreating Germans. But there were weaknesses as well. None of these obstacles had prepared defences – either in the form of trench systems or strong belts of wire.[81] Once more the artillery was the key. The creeping barrage protected troops crossing the canal while in the forest whole areas or 'blocks' were deluged with shell and any survivors set upon on all sides by the infantry.[82] In its part of the attack the Fourth Army alone fired 20 million pounds of shell and the German army had long passed the state where it could take that amount of pounding.[83]

The last days of the war in the west were a matter of supply rather than fighting. The distance between the advanced troops and the railheads grew ever longer. The use of roads became more and more of a problem as the weather deteriorated. Mobile workshops found it almost impossible to deal with breakdowns and repairs, and horse transport had to be relied upon to keep the armies going. Most, like the Fourth Army, formed a composite force of infantry field artillery, armoured cars and some cavalry and sent it forward just to maintain touch with the enemy. It proved sufficient and, had the German envoys not signed an armistice on 11 November, there is little doubt that the Germans would have continued to be pursued. In the event, they did sign and the guns fell silent on the Western Front.

The politicians back in London were certainly keeping pace with events at the front. They had found CIGS Sir Henry Wilson a reassuring figure who would spell out exactly what the British army was accomplishing. This does not mean that they were following the planning of battles in great detail. Indeed, Wilson was quite surprised when told by Haig that the Battle of Amiens was under way. However, he rushed out to France soon after and interviewed the successful corps commanders in some detail. He told the War Cabinet that he had met Currie, Monash and the five Australian divisional generals, who:

> were all much pleased with the result of their recent operations, more especially with the smallness of the losses incurred. The casualties of each of the five [Australian] Divisional Generals had only amounted to 600 apiece ... The total number of German prisoners taken by the British and French in these operations amounted to about 30,000, together with some 400 to 500 guns. The total losses of the Allies had been about 30,000, of which British losses were about 20,000.[84]

It says something about the ferocity of warfare on the Western Front that 20,000 casualties could be thought 'small'. But Wilson knew his audience. These were men who had sat through accounts of the Somme and Third Ypres, where hecatombs of casualties had won hardly a square inch of territory, so the casualties suffered in a major advance would seem acceptable.

Wilson rammed this point home to the War Cabinet during the 'Hundred Days' from August to November. After the Battle of Albert on 23 August he continued to inform his masters of the difference between earlier campaigns and what was happening on the current battlefront:

> Our losses in the recent offensive had been remarkably slight ... The Chief of the Imperial General Staff then gave a comparison between our losses and captures in the attacks on the Passchendaele Ridge last autumn and those during the last nineteen days on the Arras–Somme front. In the attacks on the Passchendaele Ridge we suffered 265,000 casualties and took 24,000 prisoners and 64 guns. Since the 8th of August we had suffered 58,000 casualties and taken 47,000 prisoners and between 500 and 600 guns.[85]

The War Cabinet were so pleased with this information that they had it published as an official report.

However, as the British armies approached the Hindenburg Line, the fretting of the politicians increased, such was the fearful reputation of the German defensive system. Wilson was alert to the situation. On 1 September he sent a personal note to Haig which said in part: 'Just a word of caution in regard to incurring heavy losses in attacks on Hindenburg Line ... The War Cabinet would become anxious if we received heavy punishment in attacking [it] WITHOUT SUCCESS.'[86] Haig was furious to receive such a note but, considering his efforts in 1916 and 1917, it was no more than sensible of Wilson to alert the Commander-in-Chief that he was being watched. As it happened of course, the operations at the Hindenburg Line were a success and it is noteworthy that with the increasing rate of advance on the Western Front Wilson had to issue no more warnings.

* * * * *

1918 was the most extraordinary year of the war. From March to June the German army made advances that were unprecedented on the Western Front. In total they gained more territory in three months than the Allies had in three years. Then in the 'Hundred Days' the Allies made a series of advances that ended the war in the west. Why was it that after suffering such setbacks the Allies prevailed in such a short span of time? Many explanations for this phenomenon have been put forward over the years. Some of these concern the effect of the Allied blockade of Germany and the alleged crippling effect this had on the German war economy. However, no explanation of this kind so far put forward is satisfactory. The statistical material necessary to examine the state of the German war economy in the detail required is either missing or too intractable to be submitted to analysis. As a result, many of the economic explanations of German demise rely on assertions or in some cases wild speculations.

If we put these economic arguments aside there is a simpler explanation for the German collapse: the German army was in the end outfought by the Allies on the Western Front. The great German advances in the first six months of the year seem spectacular and were made possible by a combination of innovative artillery methods and infantry tactics. But at their heart, these operations had fatal flaws. In all of them the infantry was propelled forward with no particular objective. Ludendorff's was not a guiding hand; he hacked his holes and nothing followed. The battles meandered on, first in one direction, then another, and finally and fatally in many directions at once. All of these attacks eventually petered out for the same set of reasons.

The infantry eventually outran the fire support which had enabled them to break through. The Allies fell back on stockpiles of artillery, which, with the guns they managed to bring back, enabled the fire equation to gradually swing in their favour. Moreover, the German infantry were marching and fighting their way forward. They were soon encountering Allied troops that had been brought up by rail or at least had not been required to fight to reach the front. In this situation, facing fresh men supported by artillery, it is no matter for surprise that the German attacks ground to a halt.

When it came their turn to advance, the British army did not follow the German path. The considerable difference between the two armies was that the British chose not to replicate the elite German storm troops or their tactics. In general the British chose not to divide their army into elite units or push any unit beyond the range that could be protected by the artillery. Tanks could increase the territory gained by some measure but First World War tanks lacked the mobility to gain great swathes of ground. The British advances behind a deluge of artillery shells might have lacked panache and limited advances to modest proportions, but the Germans never discovered any means of stopping them.

The most significant difference, then, in approach to attack between the two armies was the adoption (finally) by Haig of the limited objective. This of course was 'bite and hold' – a method that had been around since 1915 but then discarded because it failed to capture much ground. Haig returned to it (under some pressure) at Amiens and it stuck for the remainder of the war. British operations therefore developed into a series of fairly shallow advances, each followed by a pause while the guns were brought up to enable the next stage to be undertaken. So on the British front (and elsewhere as well) the Germans were pushed back and then pushed back again. In addition, by switching from one area of the front to another, but in no case attempting to advance too far, momentum could be maintained without exhausting the troops. By contrast, when Ludendorff moved his battlefront, by always insisting on objectives that were unlimited, all he achieved was the wearing out of a fresh set of divisions.

The impulse behind these different methods needs to be emphasised. On the British side it was the political leadership that made a series of decisions concerning manpower that were crucial. On the other side, by 1918 Ludendorff *was* the political leadership. Haig, despite his grumbling, made the best of the situation created by Lloyd George. Haig's smaller 1918 battalions would have to be used more economically than heretofore or there would be no more BEF. Happily for Haig, the political leadership also provided the means to allow him to fight more economically. The immense output of the Ministry of Munitions equipped those smaller battalions with an incredible array of portable firepower. The question then became, could Haig use this array of weaponry in an appropriate manner? The answer was in the affirmative. While he had the men, Haig, all his army commanders, and many at the lower levels, were quite willing (or thought it necessary) to use massed battalions in poorly thought-out battle plans that were prodigal in casualties. Happily, however, Haig was never a technophobe. He was always enthusiastic about the tank and technical developments such as the creeping barrage, sound ranging, the use of air power for reconnaissance and photography and many new developments. When, very late in the day, Rawlinson observed that the army was running out of men, the army turned to machines to great effect.

Despite having a weapons system and the technical ability to use it to crushing effect, aspects of the old Haig remained. For Amiens he set objectives that were just as ludicrous as those he had set at various times during the Somme offensive. It took a corps commander of courage (Currie) to put an end to the ragged, indefinitely prolonged battles of yesteryear. And it is staggering to find that as late as 4 November 1918, Haig was massing the cavalry for the breakthrough just as he had done to no effect in 1915, 1916 and 1917. Luckily for the horsed soldiers, they were not needed. Haig therefore can be credited with enabling the British army to develop into a most efficient fighting machine. Whether he ever grasped the principles of the limited offensive which stared him in the face for over two years is much more doubtful.

INTERLUDE 1919–1939

AT THE ARMISTICE BRITAIN and its empire possessed the largest navy in the world, the largest air force and the most efficient army. Everywhere it stood triumphant – on the Western Front its armies had delivered to the Germans the most crushing blows; the High Seas Fleet was about to sail for British ports, not to engage the Grand Fleet but to be interned; in the Middle East the Ottoman Empire was no more and ships of the Royal Navy would finally traverse the Dardanelles to occupy Constantinople. 11 November became known as Armistice Day but really the Central Powers had surrendered on terms dictated by the Allies.

Yet, twenty years later, on the outbreak of the second German war Britain found itself with an army in readiness of just five under-equipped infantry divisions. From leading the world in armoured warfare it now had insufficient tanks to deploy even one armoured division. The navy, which could deploy sixty dreadnoughts in its battlefleet in 1918, though still impressive in size, consisted of a dozen Great War-vintage battleships, many of which were outgunned by its enemies and too slow ever to catch them. In addition, in spite of the deadly nature of the U-boat war, there were few oceangoing warships that could provide escorts for the convoys that would again need to provide Britain with many of the sinews of war.

Only sections of the air force had aspects of modernity. Fighter Command had in the Hurricane and Spitfire modern single-wing fighters of great speed and manoeuvrability, backed up by a system of control that represented the most advanced air defence system in the world. But the main weapon according to the Air Staff was a bomber force ready to strike terror into the Germans and perhaps even deter them from launching bombing raids on Britain. However, on examination the bombers were almost entirely made up of slow, ageing types or light bombers carrying derisory bomb loads of no penetrative power. If Britain had been the dominant power in 1918, it was certainly an ailing giant by 1939. How had it come to this?

Much of the decline of Britain in the inter-war years as *the* Great Power has a certain inevitability about it. The level of expenditure on armaments in the last years of the war was clearly unsustainable and increasingly reliant on loans from the United States. These loans accumulated debt, which with the internal borrowings that largely financed the war, had to be paid back. In addition, the gigantic civilian armies had to be demobilised at some speed to prevent unrest and to return men to the workforce in order to restore the economy to healthy levels of industrial production. There was also no appetite to maintain bloated armed forces. The shock of over 700,000 dead and 1.7 million wounded induced cries of 'never again' and there was hope throughout the 1920s anyway that the League of Nations and various peace initiatives might lead either to the abolition of war or to any hostilities that broke out being nipped in the bud through acts of 'collective security'.

As well as these matters there were extraneous shocks to the British system. As the 1920s and 1930s progressed, it became obvious that British manufacturing was out of kilter with world requirements. The old staples – cotton, steel and others – were either not in demand or subject to competition or tariffs from other countries. The 1920s in Britain certainly did not roar; the workshop of the world was on half time. Then in 1929 the Depression hit, throwing millions into unemployment, crippling exports and making loans impossible to secure without savage cuts in government expenditure.

With this background the armed forces were always going to suffer. The army was to fare worst of all. With the reduced budgets it had in the years following the Armistice, it was required to take on new responsibilities, policing newly acquired areas of chronic instability in Palestine, Iraq and

Persia as well as encountering what amounted to external wars on the Afghan–Indian border or internal wars in Ireland. Yet in the 1920s the forces of modernisation in the army seemed to prevail. Britain had after all invented the tank, and the establishment of a mechanised force in the mid-1920s, with tanks, artillery and aircraft acting in combination, seemed to point the way towards the armoured divisions of the Second World War.

In the event, the forces of conservatism, both military and economic, won out. In 1929 the armoured force was disbanded. An armoured component would be formed – not by expanding the existing force, but slowly by mechanising the considerable number of cavalry units still in existence in Britain in the mid-1930s. Much evil flowed from this decision. The process took years and the attitudes of the senior officers of the cavalry gradually penetrated into the armoured units. Tanks were seen as petrol-fuelled horses and their role adapted to pre-Western Front conditions. In this view tanks en masse could be used to provide the shock once delivered by cavalry charges. The tanks could penetrate deep into enemy lines and operate as an independent force able to paralyse the enemy command without the support of masses of infantry, guns or close air support. This was very far from the German conception of armour, where anti-tank guns and air support would be far forward in support of the panzers. Many a doubtful battle would be fought by British armoured formations before the shortcomings of this approach was realised and to some extent, as Montgomery and others were to find, they never were.

It might be thought that the rise of Nazi Germany from 1933 would provide the required shock to modernise the army, as we shall see it did to the air force, but this was not the case. Despite the best efforts of the Defence Requirements Committee chaired by Maurice Hankey, the government refused to incur the cost of modernisation and the various CIGSs were in any case lukewarm. Indeed, in later years of the decade the incredible decision was made that a future army would play no role in the affairs of Europe. The term 'Expeditionary Force' was banned. The 'Field Force' was now to confine itself to policing the Empire, anti-aircraft duties and to providing a garrison at home. This decision hardly fostered modernisation, for what were the use of masses of tanks and guns on the North-West Frontier of India or against tribal groups in the Middle East?

To reinforce this policy, Basil Liddell Hart, now chief adviser to the new Minister of War, Leslie Hore-Belisha, declared that contrary to most of his previous teachings, the defence was after all stronger than the attack. The French could therefore hold any German thrust without help from the British who, if they became engaged at all, would supply the required naval units and no doubt subsidies to allies, as in the Napoleonic period. Apparently all forgot that in that period, as in others, it usually required a European-based British army to finish off putative European expansionists. In any case the turn away from Europe proved congenial to the government, which, especially under Chamberlain, deemed that the policy of appeasement would mean that there was no enemy to fight, Hitler presumably getting all that he wanted without fighting.

It was the air force, also starved of funds and – except for Iraqi tribesmen – enemies in the 1920s and early 1930s, which responded most rapidly to the rise of Nazism. Until 1933, under the leadership of Air Marshal Hugh Trenchard, the main weapon of the RAF was the bomber force. This made a certain amount of sense. Bombers in this period were faster than fighters and a great deal more robust. From 1933 and especially 1935 when Hitler announced the existence of the Luftwaffe, the 'shadow of the bomber' loomed over British policy. The RAF's answer was to build up their own bomber force to such an extent that the threat of unleashing it against a future enemy (that is Germany) would deter the Germans from bombing what Churchill referred to as the 'fat, tethered cow' of London. The problem here was that the bomber force never reached these dimensions. For the whole of the 1930s it consisted of increasingly obsolescent machines (financial stringency also hit new designs) designated 'heavy' bombers though most were 'medium' at best and the remainder 'light' with little navigational capability and incapable of finding even large targets in the dark. Increasingly too, the speed of such machines fell below those reached by the newer fighter monoplanes (with which the Luftwaffe was amply equipped). The deterrent was looking able to die gallantly but not much more.

Two factors proved vital in rescuing the RAF from oblivion in any future war. The first was the decision to switch production to fighters in late 1937. This choice was made partly for economic reasons. It was thought that the Luftwaffe had expanded beyond the point where air parity with Germany could be regained, but the most rapid way to increase numbers was by building fighters, three of which could be constructed for every bomber. This policy also dovetailed with other developments. By 1937 the Hurricane fighter was about to enter service and the even faster Spitfire was in prospect. In addition, experiments with radio direction finding (radar) had detected aircraft at some 60 miles and a chain of radar stations was being built around the coast of England. It remained a formidable prospect to link radar with fighter stations and convert the result into a modern early-warning system but the genius of Air Marshal Sir Hugh Dowding and others carried this through. The whole policy proved popular with Chamberlain. The switch to fighters would save money, and the system of detection as developed would be confined to Britain and therefore avoid continental entanglements. Fighter Command was in this sense appeasement's deterrent.

The other factor that was to place the RAF at the centre of the next war was a scheme put forward by the Air Staff in November 1938. This was for the development of true heavy four-engine bombers (the Halifax and the Stirling). These, together with another type (the two-engine Manchester which became, when modified, the four-engine Lancaster), carried much heavier bomb loads than any German bomber and would wreak a considerable amount of havoc on Germany from 1942. Both the wartime Fighter and Bomber Commands therefore had their origins in the appeasement years of the 1930s.

In the navy inter-war attention remained focused on the battlefleet. Here the British did particularly badly. Financial stringency ensured that few of these expensive craft would be built, and poor design work by the Admiralty resulted in the six battleships that were constructed between 1919 and 1939 being inferior in almost every way to their Japanese and German equivalents. Eventually the British entered the war with no fewer than ten of their fifteen battleships being of First World War vintage and five of these being so slow as to be almost useless.

Although hardly anyone seemed to notice, this ageing Main Fleet obviated a major British inter-war initiative – the construction of the Singapore naval base. Most of the obsolescent Main Fleet would have to kept in home waters to counter the small but more lethal number of German battleships, a situation that only worsened with the addition of Italy, which also possessed a modest but newer battlefleet. The Singapore base, despite many pauses and hiccups in construction, was completed in time for war. Britain just did not possess a Main Fleet to occupy it.

Two factors also diverted attention from the most deadly aspect of the First World War at sea – the submarine peril. The first of these was the invention of an underwater detection device – ASDIC. What was astonishing about this development was that, while after 1932 all destroyers were fitted with the device, no practice was ever carried out to test its ability to defend merchant convoys against submarines. The test of war would prove that for optimum use this device needed experienced operators but they were given no opportunity to hone their skills in the inter-war period.

The second aspect was the obsession of senior officers in this period with the non-event that was the Battle of Jutland. In staff exercises this battle was fought over and over again, though Britain rapidly did not have the wherewithal ever to refight it. This resulted in a lack of emphasis on the navy's anti-submarine role. This in turn led to a neglect of the kinds of ship that would be needed to escort convoys. For example, no modern escort sloops were constructed before 1936 and even then the Hunt Class in particular was found to have poor sea-keeping capabilities, which made them difficult to handle in the North Atlantic. Other attempts such as the Flower Class corvettes were found to be too slow to catch submarines running on the surface. These deficiencies were not overcome in peace time. Only the exigencies of war focused the Admiralty on the need for reliable escorts.

In one area the navy seemed to have an advantage. On the eve of war it possessed seven aircraft carriers – although admittedly some of these were of obsolete design or converted battle cruisers. But the advantage in numbers was cast away through continual disputes between the Admiralty and the RAF as to which service should supply and man the aircraft the ships carried. In the end there was no resolution to this dispute, which basically meant that the Fleet Air Arm came last in terms of design of new aircraft. As a result the navy went to war with more carriers than any other power but equipped with Swordfish biplanes that proved surprisingly robust but were obsolete compared to American and more importantly Japanese types.

There were few disputes in the inter-war period between the military and their civilian masters. Drastic cuts were imposed on the services from

1919 to 1932 but the military were conscious enough of Britain's financial position to enter no more than mild protestations. As for the looming threat of Nazi Germany and later fascist Italy and Japan, the Chiefs of Staff were at least as paralysed with fear as the government. There is evidence that they welcomed Chamberlain's appeasement policy and spent as much time appealing to the government to reduce the number of enemies facing Britain as on urging rearmament. Their craven attitude to the carve-up of Czechoslovakia and their chronic inability to decide on the function of a future BEF rank at least as high as appeasement in the explaining the general unpreparedness of Britain for war. These attitudes on the part of the British political and military leadership would deeply affect the way Britain made war in 1939 and would indeed persist to haunt the first months of Churchill's premiership. It would take immense skill and determination on his part to change this rather defeatist mindset.

CHAPTER 12

APPEASEMENT AND WAR

IN 1914 GREY HAD charted a carefully calibrated path through the July crisis. He determined from the first that, while offering Britain's good offices to help solve the crisis in south-eastern Europe, it was not in Britain's interests to intervene. Only when it became clear that German war plans involved the invasion of France and Belgium did Grey call for Cabinet and Parliament to back intervention on the grounds that Britain's national interests were now under threat.

In 1939 there was no such clear-cut road to war. Partly this was because in contrast to the six-week crisis in 1914 there had now been a six-year crisis during which the appeasement governments of Stanley Baldwin and Neville Chamberlain had ducked every opportunity to halt Hitler's aggression. From the first days of the Nazi regime in 1933, it had been obvious that Hitler had no intention of abiding by the Treaty of Versailles, the Locarno Agreement or indeed any of the conventional norms of diplomacy. Thus the German withdrawal from the League of Nations in October 1933, the elevation of Hitler to Führer in August 1934, the admission of the existence of the Luftwaffe and the introduction of conscription in Germany in March 1935 all pointed to a future fraught with danger but were met with silence from the Western democracies.

The first overt territorial move from Hitler came in March 1936 when, in direct contravention of Versailles and Locarno, he occupied the

Rhineland. At least some members of the French Cabinet wished to respond militarily to this act. No fewer than thirty French divisions were available, a far greater force than Germany had at the time. But the French were divided. All depended on British support and it soon became clear that there would be no such support. The Foreign Secretary (Anthony Eden) deprecated any intervention and he was backed by a supine paper from the Chiefs of Staff (COS) which stated that any move against Germany could only be carried out by disengaging from all commitments in the Mediterranean.[1] Given Benito Mussolini's menacing attitude and his recent invasion of Abyssinia, this Britain was not prepared to do. When it became clear to the French that no support would be forthcoming from Britain, they too folded. A protest note was sent to Hitler. He ignored it. His scratch force in the Rhineland began digging fortifications. The French divisions that certainly could have removed it remained stationary. What was needed, London and Paris decided, was not more confrontation but more appeasement.

The opportunity to look the other way as Hitler tore up more sections of the Treaty of Versailles came in April 1938 when he incorporated Austria into the Reich. No one in Britain thought of intervention in this instance. Churchill at least wanted to send a note to Hitler that the invasion of any further country would result in British intervention. Chamberlain, now Prime Minister, resisted. Hitler could still be appeased, perhaps by the return of colonies, despite the Führer's total lack of interest in colonial matters.[2]

The crisis for appeasement came over Czechoslovakia in the summer of 1938. Here an almost entirely artificial crisis in the form of the treatment of the German minority in the Sudetenland had been fabricated by Hitler and some compliant Czech Nazis. The solution, worked out by Chamberlain and to a lesser extent the French Prime Minister Edouard Daladier without Czech participation, was to cede the Sudetenland to Germany. Appeasement had now descended to giving away sections of foreign countries to divert any threat from your own. Moral bankruptcy hardly sums it up. And on this occasion it met with stern resistance from within Parliament. Czechoslovakia, it was pointed out, was a functioning democracy with an alliance with France. It had an effective military and the largest armaments works (the Skoda works) in Europe. It was not a 'faraway country'. If it was a cause not worth fighting for, what was? In Parliament, Alfred Duff Cooper,

258

First Lord of the Admiralty, in his resignation speech made the comparison with Belgium in 1914. 'We were fighting then', he said, 'as we should have been fighting last week, in order that one great power should not be allowed . . . to dominate by brutal force the Continent of Europe.'[3] Churchill characterised it as 'a defeat without a war' and went on to prophesy:

> I venture to think that in future the Czechoslovak State cannot be maintained as an independent entity. You will find that in a period of time which may be measured by years, but may be measured only in months, Czechoslovakia will be engulfed in the Nazi regime.[4]

As it happened the period of Czech independence lasted only months. In March 1939, after another manufactured crisis, Hitler sent in the troops. Prague was occupied; the eastern section of the country was hived off – Slovakia became a puppet state. Chamberlain merely remarked that Britain could not be expected to intervene on behalf of a state that had ceased to exist.[5] All was over.

Chamberlain found that the popularity generated in Britain by the avoidance of war at Munich soon disappeared. He needed a new policy, especially when it became clear that Hitler's ambitions were by no means quenched. Nazi attention turned to Poland, the corridor that separated Germany and East Prussia, at the apex of which stood the Free City of Danzig under the increasingly precarious supervision of the League of Nations. A plan was soon thrashed out and announced in Parliament of 31 March:

> In the event of any action which clearly threatened Polish independence, and which the Polish Government accordingly considered it vital to resist with their national forces, His Majesty's Government would feel themselves bound at once to lend the Polish Government all support in their power. They have given the Polish Government an assurance to this effect.[6]

Thus was Polish independence, but not necessarily its territorial integrity, guaranteed by Britain, with France shortly to follow with the same guarantee. Conscription was introduced also introduced in April. All this seemed a massive change in Britain's traditional policy, which did not usually regard events in Eastern Europe as being vital to its national interest.

But as the Poles were to learn to their cost, the guarantee was not really about them – it was about stopping Hitler from dominating Europe.[7] The hope of the appeasers was that the guarantee alone would stop Hitler. The problem was, if it did not, how was the guarantee to be redeemed given that neither the British nor French COS considered military opposition against Germany a possibility? One answer to this problem lay with making an arrangement with the large state bordering Poland to the east – the Soviet Union. The Russians seemed amenable. On 18 April 1939 they suggested that a three-power pact between themselves, Britain and France be made to render assistance to any Eastern European state threatened with aggression.[8] But as the Foreign Secretary Edward Halifax was quick to point out, Poland might object to such a scheme on the grounds that once Russian forces entered their territory it might prove impossible to get them to leave. Halifax also noted that the British COS in any case thought the value of Russian military intervention slight.[9] On these grounds discussions with Russia stalled.

Over the next four months talks with Russia, for a number of reasons, never really succeeded in overcoming these problems. On the British side Chamberlain and Halifax always regarded a Russian alliance with 'misgiving'.[10] This manifested itself in various ways, the most obvious being the British reluctance to send their top people to negotiate with the Russians. So in June a middle-level diplomat, William Strang, was despatched to Moscow to undertake the political discussions.[11] Then, very late in the day, in August a military delegation was sent by slow ship (the *City of Exeter* took twelve days to reach Leningrad from Britain), and in charge was an admiral (Drax) of no great prominence.[12] Neither Halifax nor the Prime Minister (who had flown on three occasions to meet Hitler) ever suggested that they meet the Russians in person. Yet the difficulties to be overcome, which all revolved around the reluctance of the Eastern European states to be guaranteed by the Soviet Union, were so serious that they could only be solved, if they could be solved at all, at the highest level. Not even rumours of an impending détente between Russia and Germany could inject any life into the British/Russian discussions.[13] In the end Stalin concluded that the western Allies were not serious about an alliance and made his pact with the Nazis. Halifax's response to this move, one of the greatest blows ever delivered to British diplomacy, was stupefying: 'The situation is not so enormously changed', he thought, 'both we and they [Poland] have always discounted Russia.'[14] In fact everything had changed. With Russia neutralised Poland lay at Hitler's mercy and he was not slow in ratcheting up the pressure.

At least Halifax thought it prudent to recall Sir Neville Henderson, the British Ambassador to Germany, for consultations. (Henderson was able to pass on to Cabinet the invaluable information that his butler, who was a German, was 'very indignant about the [Nazi–Soviet] Pact').[15] In a more substantial gesture, Britain and Poland signed a five-year military assistance pact. Meanwhile in Danzig, the Germans were continuing to smuggle in arms to the fifth columnists already there. Accordingly, Hitler increased his demands – he now wanted a minimum of Danzig and the Polish Corridor – and there were ominous rumblings about the so-called mistreatment of the German minority within Poland.

In the Cabinet interminable talks ensued in attempting to construct a message to Hitler. Eventually the letter was brought to Hitler by Henderson on 28 August. It suggested talks should commence on all outstanding issues between Germany and Poland and that agreement be the subject of an international guarantee. The note also reminded the Führer that Britain could not acquiesce in any deal which threatened Polish independence. Hitler promised a reply by the 29th.

Yet when the 29th came there had been no reply from the Führer. He had almost certainly decided to invade Poland but was hardy going to disclose that to the British. All Chamberlain could do was make a lame speech to Parliament saying that he was waiting on events.[16]

Next day Henderson wired that Hitler wanted a Polish emissary to appear in Berlin with full powers to negotiate a settlement. This sounded very much the formula for intimidation that had been applied to President Kurt Schuschnigg of Austria and President Emil Hácha of Czechoslovakia. The Cabinet deprecated any such move.[17] Stalemate resumed.

It was soon broken by Hitler. In the early hours of 1 September 1939 German troops attacked Poland on a wide front. The Cabinet met to consider this at 11.30 a.m. To begin with, the discussion was anything but resolute. Argument seemed to hinge on whether Warsaw was being bombed, never mind that Hitler had announced over German radio that the invasion was underway.[18] Despite this the Cabinet concluded that it was desirable not to take any 'irrevocable action' until they had greater assurance that Poland had actually been invaded.[19] Later in the meeting Halifax could inform his colleagues that the invasion of Poland was indeed a fact. This sobered the members. It was now concluded that unless Germany withdrew its troops Britain must fulfil its obligations to Poland. The problem was, however, the French. Astoundingly they were worried that if Britain declared war on Germany before they did it would seem that they (the French) had been dragged into the war by Britain. They asked therefore to be the first to declare war. Chamberlain was having none of this. A declaration must be simultaneous. Cabinet was adjourned so that the French could be consulted.[20]

This process was to lead to the most excruciating delays and hesitations. The French, it turned out, wanted to delay any declaration for forty-eight hours while they completed the evacuation of women and children from Paris. They were also taken with an idea for a conference put forward by Mussolini. Halifax was not keen on Mussolini's initiative, which sounded too much like an attempt to re-run Munich, but he was persuaded by the French Foreign Minister (Georges Bonnet) that any note sent to Hitler not contain a time limit for reply – that is, it not be an ultimatum.[21]

The House, which was unaware of the difficulties with the French, assembled at 6 p.m. expecting a declaration of war. They did not get it. All Chamberlain could say was that if Germany did not withdraw its forces from Poland 'the United Kingdom will without hesitation fulfil its obligations to Poland'. At this point a member shouted out 'Time limit?', to which the Prime Minister lamely replied that if the answer was unfavourable the British Ambassador would ask for his passports.[22] This hardly satisfied members, and Arthur Greenwood (acting leader of the Labour Party as Clement Attlee was ill) and Archibald Sinclair (leader of the Liberals) made strong speeches exhorting that an ultimatum be delivered to Germany with all despatch.[23] The House then set about discussing defence measures and was adjourned until the 2nd.

The Cabinet met at 4.15 p.m. on 2 September; its members had certainly noted the restlessness in Parliament the previous day. Halifax began with a long-winded explanation of where Britain stood, with the alarming conclusion that in the event of German/Polish talks commencing, an extension of a time limit to midnight on the 3/4 September for Hitler could be considered. He was to find that the Cabinet were in no mood for such an act. The Home Secretary, Sir Samuel Hoare, demanded immediate action and he was backed by the three service ministers (Leslie Hore-Belisha, Lord James Stanhope and Kingsley Wood). Oliver Stanley (Board of Trade), Lord Ernle Chatfield (Co-ordination of Defence), Leslie Burgin (Supply) and Sir Thomas Inskip (Dominions) joined in. Chamberlain was forced into a rapid back-flip. The Germans were to be given to midnight on the 2/3 September to withdraw troops. This was at last an ultimatum. Action was to be coordinated with the French. With this understanding the Cabinet adjourned.[24]

Dramatic events followed. It was announced that the Advanced Air Striking Force and the first units of the Field Force were crossing to France and that Churchill had been invited to join a War Cabinet. So when the House met at 6 p.m. they expected Chamberlain to announce the declaration of war. Once more there was no such announcement. Chamberlain merely told them that Henderson had delivered a warning message to Joachim von Ribbentrop (the German Foreign Minister) but that no reply had been received from Hitler, the delay possibly caused by the Italian peace conference proposals.[25] This went down very badly. When Greenwood rose to protest, Leo Amery shouted to him to 'Speak for England'.[26] This Greenwood endeavoured to do, pointing out that Poland had been under attack for thirty-eight hours and that immediate British action was required. He was cheered for his efforts, alarmingly for the Prime Minister, most loudly from the government benches.

The government was now in great danger of being overthrown. Groups of dissidents gathered after the House had been adjourned – one group in Churchill's flat, another, containing many members of the Cabinet, in a room in the Commons. Churchill contacted the French Ambassador and barked at him that the French must act in concert with the British.[27] But the real action was in the meeting of ministers chaired by the previous arch-appeaser, the Chancellor of the Exchequer Sir John Simon. They demanded to know why Chamberlain had departed from the previously agreed Cabinet decision that an ultimatum be delivered to Germany. He explained that the problem lay with the French but that he had told them that it would be impossible to hold the situation in London. There could be no further delay. He suggested that an ultimatum be presented to Germany at 9 a.m. the next morning with a three-hour timetable. If no satisfactory reply had been received, it was war. Chatfield stated that the COS preferred an overnight ultimatum but were most concerned that the timetable be short. Simon, seeking to avoid a repetition of what had just occurred in the House, stated that the time limit must be shortened to 11 a.m. British time to ensure that, when he addressed Parliament, he would be in no doubt as to the position.[28] This was agreed.

On 3 September it only remained for the scenario sketched out by the Cabinet to be played out. At 11.10 a.m. Chamberlain heard from Henderson that no reply had been received to the ultimatum. The BBC in the form of Alvar Liddell was standing by. At 11.15 a.m. Chamberlain broadcast to the nation in his tired, grey voice, announcing that Britain was at war with Germany and that all he had striven for had come crashing down. A more dispiriting performance is hard to imagine. Most who heard the broadcast commented on Chamberlain's 'sad' voice. Evelyn Waugh, however, thought he did 'very well'.[29]

There is no question that the entire responsibility for the outbreak of the Second World War must rest with Hitler. He was determined on war and it was only a matter of time before he got one. Having said that, it is difficult to feel much enthusiasm for Britain's path to war in 1939. If the Rhineland came too early in the rearmament phase for Britain to respond and if there were certain ambiguities with the Anschluss, there should have been no such reservations over Czechoslovakia. Here was a democracy willing to resist unprovoked aggression. Instead of encouraging resistance, Britain and France coerced it into ceding some of its defensible frontier and much of its land in order to appease Hitler. This was an unconscionable act which actually tilted the balance of power against Britain and France. If there was a time to go to war it was in September 1938. The occupation of the remaining Czech lands in March 1939 demonstrated just what Hitler's word was worth. The guarantee to Poland saw the beginning of a diplomatic debacle. Little thought was given to the act and none at all to a mechanism whereby the Soviet Union could be brought into the picture, even though it was an essential player. The half-hearted way that negotiations were conducted with the Russians spoke to Chamberlain and Halifax's dislike of them and their confidence that in the last analysis they could ward off conflict with Germany by some backhanded deal with Hitler.

The drama of the last week of peace revealed above all how the reputation of the appeasers had sunk. There seems little doubt that many of the hesitations and mistimings of that period were brought about by the difficulty of coordinating actions with the equally unimpressive French government. But what stands out is how little Chamberlain and Halifax were trusted to do the right thing. When that lack of trust extended to their Cabinet colleagues (partners until then in appeasement) and the House of Commons, there was the making of a true crisis. Only some fancy footwork by the Prime Minister on 2 September saved his government from extinction – in retrospect probably a bad thing for the initial leadership of the war. Appeasement was only ever a policy of capitulation to force and when it failed, it failed absolutely. So, when the war came, it was to be directed by men not attuned to conflict; indeed everything about them recoiled from it. Yet now they were to preside over large military operations. And they were still not trusted. It was hardly a recipe for success.

* * * * *

On 3 September after his speech to Parliament Chamberlain called together his War Cabinet, which he had formed the day before. His only startling addition had been to bring in Winston Churchill as First Lord of the Admiralty. Lord Hankey was also added, but in the lowly position of Minister without Portfolio. The other members of the War Cabinet were the same men who had presided over the failed appeasement policy in the 1930s – Lord Halifax (Secretary of State for Foreign Affairs), Sir John Simon (Chancellor of the Exchequer), Leslie Hore-Belisha (Minister for War), Sir Samuel Hoare (Lord Privy Seal), Sir Kingsley Wood (Secretary of State for Air) and Lord Chatfield, who had been Admiral Beatty's Flag Captain at Jutland, as Minister for the Co-ordination of Defence.

While Chatfield's post seemed important, until the outbreak of war he had been given few consequential duties to perform. Now he proposed setting up a Military Co-ordination Committee (MCC) with himself as chair. Attendees would include the COS and the three service ministers. The idea was that this would provide a forum for the service ministers to exchange ideas with the Chiefs of Staff. In practice the MCC was a fifth wheel. It had no executive authority and the ultimate decision-maker (the Prime Minister) did not attend. Churchill was in favour of it but quickly became disillusioned as the myriad of subjects it dealt with had to be discussed all over again by the War Cabinet, which to a large extent consisted of the same personnel.[30] If anything the MCC slowed down decision-making because of this duplication. Matters did not improve when Churchill took over from Chatfield as chairman in April 1940. Churchill did his best, persuading the Prime Minister to chair the Committee when possible. That gave the Committee more clout but the experiment was short-lived as the Chamberlain government fell shortly afterwards. The whole affair, however, demonstrated to Churchill that this was not the way to run a war.

The fact was that it was not the war-making machinery that was the main problem for the appeasement government – it was that they hardly wanted to prosecute the war at all. Churchill was of course different and soon made his intentions clear. He was keen for immediate action. Britain had gone to war to fulfil its obligations to Poland and he thought that: 'Every means possible should be employed to relieve the pressure [on Poland]. This could be done by operations against the Siegfried Line, which was at present thinly held. The burden of such operations would fall on the French Army and our Air Force.'[31]

The War Cabinet suddenly realised that they were quite ignorant of what the French intended to do in this situation. CIGS General Sir Edmond Ironside and Air Marshal Sir Cyril Newall, the Chief of the Air Staff (CAS), were immediately despatched to France to meet the French Commander-in-Chief, General Maurice Gamelin. He informed them that he intended to concentrate a force of about eighty divisions and begin a slow, methodical advance towards the main French fortifications along the Maginot Line. He would then 'throw out' a reconnaissance force to test the German frontier defences of the Siegfried Line. This phase would not be rushed. It would consist of another slow, methodical advance supported by a heavy concentration of artillery. By 'X' day – which he could not specify – Gamelin would be ready to commence, not a full-scale attack, but 'leaning against the Siegfried Line' – whatever that meant. These actions – if they can be so described – would provide no help for the Poles, as Gamelin made clear. He thought Polish resistance would soon be overcome and that the Allies must conserve their forces for the 'main struggle' and 'not be led astray by popular outcry'.[32]

What Gamelin's plan did was render inoperative an assurance he had given to the Poles that the Allies would intervene against Germany in the first fourteen days of the war. Whenever 'X' day arrived, it would clearly lie far outside that period. Germany must be beaten but as it turned out this would have little to do with the fate of Poland.

Back in London it might be expected that this plan would have been greeted by the War Cabinet with an outcry of the type that Gamelin feared. Nothing of the kind happened. There was general agreement that nothing could be done. When the French were ready, the RAF would be made available to support them. Only Churchill dissented. He urged that Germany should be bombed immediately to relieve pressure on the Poles. His was a lone voice; the decision for inaction won the day.[33]

Given Gamelin's attitude, it was obvious that there would be little immediate action in France. In September four divisions of the BEF had crossed to France and were digging in along the Franco-Belgian border. Six more Regular British divisions were to follow and then an unspecified number of the Territorial divisions. That in the first six months of the war was the entire contribution of the army in France. The remainder of the front, from the Franco-Belgian border to the Swiss Alps would be handled by the French.

What of intervention from the air as Churchill had suggested? Only in fighters were the British well placed. The squadrons of Fighter Command were being equipped with modern single-engine Hurricanes and Spitfires, equal to anything the Germans had and superior to the latest French types. But fighters were essentially a defensive weapon, and they could only operate with security in 1939 behind the British radar chain that could give warning of an enemy attack. In France there was no radar. A few squadrons were sent there but only to provide cover to the BEF. A small force of light bombers was sent to operate with the French but as the French had no intention of bombing Germany these aircraft remained idle.

In terms of attacks against German industry and communications it was the bomber force that was important. On the outbreak of war Bomber Command could muster 272 aircraft. Of these 30 per cent consisted of the Fairey Battle single-engine light bomber which could carry just 1,000 lbs of bombs.[34] Other types, the Hampden, the Whitley and the Wellington, could carry up to 7,000 lbs in bombs but the Hampdens were old, having first been laid down in 1932, and the Whitleys unstable.[35] All were slow. To some extent this hybrid and obsolescent force was the product of the rapid changes in bomber and fighter design in the 1930s.[36] Certainly the Air Staff realised that it had many drawbacks. The bomb loads could not crack concreted targets, they had no long-range fighter capable of protecting the bombers in incursions into Germany, the crews had received little training in navigation, bomb-aiming or even flying and there was a doubt if the skill existed even to fly in formation, which made a concentrated blow against a target a dubious proposition.

What is striking about the British bomber force is that the War Cabinet considered it to be a fearsome weapon of mass destruction. Their discussions were not a lament that the RAF had a bomber force of great feebleness, vulnerability and inaccuracy, but whether the awesome weapon they possessed ought to be unleashed against the Ruhr and other areas of German industrial production.[37] This presented Chamberlain with a dilemma. He was determined by temperament to delay an actual shooting war for as long as possible. Initially he was bailed out by President Franklin Roosevelt, who just before hostilities commenced issued a plea to all belligerents to refrain from bombing civilian targets.[38] An Anglo-French declaration accepting the restriction was issued the following day and Hitler followed shortly after-wards with a similar statement.[39]

Not everyone on the British side accepted this policy. On 9 September the CAS asked the War Cabinet that the RAF be used more extensively. He reported that in Poland the Luftwaffe had attacked not just munitions factories but power stations and civilian works of all kinds. Chamberlain's response was to 'consider' these reports and meanwhile to get the Ministry of Information to publicise the type of attack the Germans were making. The restrictions on bombing Germany were to remain.[40] Churchill also thought British policy too restrictive and urged that the synthetic oil plants in Germany be attacked. He too was overruled.[41]

One might have thought that the massive attacks carried out on Warsaw on 24 and 25 September would have altered Chamberlain's perspective on bombing. Surely this meant that Roosevelt's appeal had failed and that a new situation now applied. Yet over the next few months the War Cabinet was to discuss bombing and the circumstances in which it might be used without shaking Chamberlain's initial position.

One problem concerning Bomber Command was the subject of repeated discussion: how to decide what action by Germany would be so dire as to warrant the unleashing of the strategic bombers. Clearly Poland did not qualify, but what of an invasion of Belgium? Strangely, although keeping Belgium out of foreign hands had been a cornerstone of British policy since the state had been formed in 1830, Chamberlain doubted that such an action by Germany would justify bombing the Ruhr. Even after the CIGS, General Ironside, assured him that such an action by Hitler could certainly be regarded as 'decisive', Chamberlain cavilled. Would bombing Germany, he enquired, make the difference between the success or failure of an attack upon Belgium? Hore-Belisha, the Minister for War, came to Chamberlain's aid by stating that from his conversations with Gamelin he had adduced that the French were opposed to bombing the Ruhr in any circumstances and that in any case they did not view the invasion of Belgium as necessarily constituting a 'decisive' event. Now was surely the time to indicate to the French that Britain placed a rather higher value on the integrity of Belgium than Gamelin, but Chamberlain sided with the French. The War Cabinet came to the utterly lame conclusion that they should inform the French that they indeed had a plan to bomb the Ruhr but that it would be implemented only if the battle in the west 'looked decisive'.[42] In short, they would decide not to decide and wait on events.

Months of debate on this topic did nothing to move Chamberlain. In December he was still saying that 'an attack on the Ruhr in consequence of Germany's violating Belgian neutrality would be a departure from our previous ideas'.[43] And Halifax was still supporting his leader by asserting that if Britain attacked the Ruhr it would be accused of being the first to 'take the gloves off'.[44] In the light of discussions such as these, it is necessary to affirm that Chamberlain and Halifax were aware of the bombing of Warsaw and the widespread massacres that had taken place in Poland.[45] The 'gloves', for those who had eyes to see, were well and truly off, but it would take more than widespread massacre in the east to divert Chamberlain from his inflexible resolve to do nothing.

The decision not to bomb Germany did not mean that the bomber force would not traverse enemy territory. The bombers would not, however, drop bombs; instead they would drop information leaflets. These generally urged the German people to overthrow Hitler and make peace without annexations.[46]

The leaflets were dropped by the million but as early as 16 September Halifax was beginning to doubt their efficacy. Chamberlain considered the programme 'good and useful'.[47] Not surprisingly the Prime Minister's view prevailed and the leaflet war continued.

A glance at Bomber Command operations between September 1939 and April 1940 confirms that this was so. During the first 250 days of the war not a single bomb fell on German territory, except poorly directed projectiles aimed at ships in port. The records reveal that there were so many leaflet raids that the historians of bomber operations felt compelled to group them into periods to avoid constant repetition. Thus between the nights of 4/5 September and 23/24 December 1939 there were twenty-two leaflet raids; between 4/5 and 19/20 January 1940 there were probably about the same number, and so on.[48] If, in the 1930s, British policymakers lived 'in the shadow of the bomber', the German people, in the first eight months of the war, merely lived in the shadow of the leaflet.[49]

What of the navy? Here the British were better placed. From 1933/4 to 1937/8, the navy received the highest percentage of the defence vote; only in 1938/9 and 1939/40 was the RAF given more money.[50] On the outbreak of war the Home Fleet (the more modestly named equivalent of the Grand Fleet in the Great War) had in British waters: eight battleships, two battle-cruisers, four aircraft carriers, three cruiser squadrons, nine destroyer flotillas and numerous other craft such as submarines, minesweepers and trawlers.[51] In addition, the British had five battleships and six aircraft carriers under construction.[52] Compared with this array, the Germans had four capital ships and two more under construction, five cruisers, twenty-five destroyers and no aircraft carriers. Only in submarines were the Germans ahead for the simple fact that the British navy and Merchant Marine provided many more targets for them than did the small number of German ships for the British.[53]

Certainly the navy was a less troublesome weapon of war for Chamberlain than the bomber force. There would be no Cabinet discussions on using the navy to bombard Germany because there were few targets on the short German coastline and its waters were anyway protected by minefields, submarines and destroyers. Churchill's rather madcap idea that the heavy ships of the Home Fleet could be rendered mine-, torpedo- and bomb-proof and thus dominate the Baltic (Operation Catherine) had no support within the Admiralty or outside it. It forever remained in the planning stage.[54]

His other idea was to drop mines into the River Rhine and thus disrupt the considerable amount of traffic that flowed down it. The problem here was the French – they opposed such action lest the Germans retaliate. Churchill pushed hard but in the opening months of the war they would not budge.

However, there was a way in which the navy could be used offensively without risking the nightmare of the Chamberlain government, an actual shooting war. The navy could blockade the Third Reich – denying Germany essential war materials and food. From the outset, blockade was the one warlike policy adopted by the Prime Minister with something approaching enthusiasm. Chamberlain was not alone in expecting much from the blockade. There was a school of thought – encompassing military experts from both Britain and Germany – that held that it was the blockade that brought Germany to its knees in 1918. We now know that this quite misread the situation. Gerd Hardach and others have demonstrated that if the German people were short of food and other consumables at the end of the Great War, it was the usurpation by the military of the greater part of the resources of the country as well as the transport system that was the root cause.[55]

This is not to say that the blockade had no effect in the Great War or that it was without value in the first eight months of the Second World War. When it was implemented on the first day of the war, it had an immediate effect on some of the 'choke points' in the German economy. One of the most important was the supply of oil. Oil was a constant worry for the Germans for the whole of the Second World War. Germany manufactured 120,000 tons of synthetic oil per month in 1939–1940 and had stockpiles of 2.1 million tons. This, they estimated, represented five months' consumption for most of the economy under wartime conditions and just three months' for the Luftwaffe.[56] The British had reasonably accurate intelligence on German oil supplies, so their attention turned to the one European country that produced oil in quantity – Romania. In one sense both Britain and Germany (and for that matter France) all faced the same problem in pursuing Romanian oil supplies – all were short of hard foreign currency to pay Romania for its oil. In the case of the Allies, what hard currency they had went to the United States, which from November 1939 allowed commodities such as oil to be purchased on a cash and carry basis. The Germans were also chronically short of hard currency and were prevented by the blockade from accessing any part of US production. However, they could offer Romania weapons with which to modernise its military. Messerschmitt fighters were accordingly exchanged for oil. After the conquest of Poland, the geographic proximity of the German army to Romania induced the government to release more oil.[57] By 1940 Germany was receiving 1.56 million tons of oil per annum from Romania.[58]

This was one leak in the blockade that the Allies were powerless to stop. There was another. Under a clause of the Nazi–Soviet pact, premier Joseph Stalin had undertaken to supply Germany with strategic materials of all kinds. In this way shortages of other critical materials such as copper, manganese, chrome and phosphates flowed into Germany from Russia. As Adam Tooze has noted, the Quarter-Master General of the German army considered that this pact allowed the conquests of 1939–1940 to be made.[59] The economic blockade was thus neatly circumvented. Chamberlain's main weapon of war was a broken reed.

What further action could the navy take? The answer in terms of an offensive was very little. When a German raider, the pocket battleship *Graf Spee*, was located in the southern Atlantic it was pursued relentlessly by three lighter British warships and forced to scuttle itself in Uruguayan waters. Most other actions were defensive. The most important was the attack on British ships by U-boats. The first weeks of the war saw the few boats of Admiral Karl Doenitz's fleet score some spectacular victories. On the first day of war they sank the passenger liner *Athenia* and a few weeks later the battleship *Royal Oak* within the defences of the main navy base at Scapa Flow. However, apart from these headline-grabbing successes, the balance of the attack on seaborne trade by the U-boats favoured the British. Certainly the Germans had some early success against British trade: in the first four months of war over 400,000 tons of merchant shipping was sunk by U-boats.[60] On the other side of this equation some nine U-boats were destroyed, around 20 per cent of the entire German fleet.[61] And it is notable that many of these losses occurred before Britain could fully implement its convoy system, not through tardiness on the part of the Admiralty but because it took time to assemble a convoy and its escorts. Coastal convoys began in the first days after the declaration of war, and oceangoing ones a few weeks later. The system worked. Of the 114 ships sunk by U-boats from September to December 1939 just 12 were sunk in convoy.

For the First Lord these figures were unsatisfactory. Churchill took a keen interest in the U-boat war and surrounded himself with charts and statistics showing German losses, convoy sailings and the like. In January 1940 he became dissatisfied with what he was reading. He upbraided his admirals for claiming just nine U-boats sunk (the correct figure), insisting that the true total was at least thirty-five.[62] He set up a 'Committee for Assessing Enemy Submarine Losses' only to find that it agreed with the original Admiralty figures. It also (correctly) concluded that between 4 December 1939 and 30 January 1940 no U-boats at all had been sunk.[63] Churchill then launched a personal attack against Captain Victor Danckwerts, who was a member of this Committee and Director of the Plans Division at the Admiralty. He instructed the First Sea Lord, Admiral Dudley Pound, to 'remodel' the Plans Division and assign to it an officer of 'vigour and positive temperament' – that is, someone who agreed with him.[64] This rather discreditable affair ended with Danckwerts being removed from his position a few weeks later.[65]

On one other matter Churchill was more favourably disposed to his admirals. In November sinkings due to German mines suddenly increased from about 30,000 tons per month to 120,000. The Germans were using a new type of mine that threatened to play havoc with shipping close to the British coast. This was the magnetic mine that exploded when in close proximity to the magnetic field of a nearby ship.[66] A special section of the Admiralty was set up by Churchill to tackle the problem.[67] Soon an intact mine was recovered from the Thames mudflats and yielded its secrets. A counter-measure was discovered in January 1940 – degaussing – which involved coiling a cable around a ship which decreased the force of its magnetic field. By March 600 ships had been fitted with such coils.[68] This process continued throughout the war and though losses from mines continued, they never threatened to disrupt British trade. There is no doubt that Churchill's drive and Admiralty expertise could at times produce rapid results.

* * * * *

Meanwhile Chamberlain was straining every nerve to avoid a shooting war against Germany. He generally held to the view that the Hitler regime would collapse either because of the palpable insanity of the Führer, or through an uprising of the German people, or via a military coup. However, throughout this period he also held to the view that there was one far away theatre in which, at little cost, the war against Germany might be prosecuted. If fields in Flanders or France repelled him, he was attracted by the fiords of Norway.

The attention paid to Norway in late 1939 and early 1940 was due to its role in shipping Swedish iron ore. Germany was not self-sufficient in this material, so vital for its war economy. In 1938 it imported 22 million tons of ore – 5 million tons from France (now hardly a source), 3 million tons from Spain (a country very susceptible to the British blockade) and 9 million tons from Sweden, much of it via Norway. The crucial importance of Swedish ore to the Reich need hardly be emphasised.

The ore was despatched to Germany by two routes. The principal one was through the Gulf of Bothnia from the Swedish port of Luleå. This trade (consisting of about 5 million tons) flowed from spring until late autumn, when the waters of the gulf iced over. During the remaining months (November to April) the Swedes sent the ore by rail to the Norwegian port of Narvik. From there it travelled down the coast, largely within Norwegian territorial waters, and then through the Kattegat to Germany. In 1938 about 4 million tons travelled by this route.[69]

At the beginning of the war, the newly formed Ministry of Economic Warfare (MEW) pointed to various weaknesses in the German economy, including the ore situation. Churchill almost certainly read their report for on 19 September he put the issue before the War Cabinet:

> Our policy must be to stop this trade [in ore] going to Germany, and at the same time provide it with an alternative market. The First Lord

warned the War Cabinet that, if the desired result could not be attained by pressure on the Norwegian Government, he would be compelled to propose the remedy which had been adopted in the last [war], namely, the laying of mines inside Norwegian territorial waters, which had driven the ore-carrying vessels outside the three-mile limit.[70]

He added that this expedient had not been adopted until after the United States had joined the war, showing that he was well aware of the need to satisfy American opinion before such a policy was implemented.

The War Cabinet 'noted' Churchill's plan for Norway but took no action. Indeed Churchill had not called for action, merely foreshadowed a future policy. The question of the iron ore trade was set aside while the War Cabinet discussed issues such as the defence of Waziristan and what to do about Hong Kong in the event of a Japanese attack. Then in November Churchill returned to the subject. Late in the month he had several discussions with the Admiralty Staff, as a result of which he told Admiral Pound, the First Sea Lord, that despite the MEW's enthusiasm for stopping the trade, other authorities had thrown doubt on its importance. He wanted an independent study made of the effect on Germany of stopping the Narvik trade.[71]

Apparently as a result of the favourable conclusions produced by this study, Norway was on the agenda for the War Cabinet of 30 November. Churchill argued that the time was coming when the laying of a few small minefields to disrupt the Narvik trade would have to be considered. Halifax raised 'serious' doubts about the operation. The Norwegians, if asked, would probably refuse permission to lay the minefields and the Germans might retaliate. He also noted the importance of American opinion, which Churchill agreed might be 'critical'. The end result was to ask the COS to prepare a paper on the implications of the mining; and to satisfy Churchill's doubts the MEW was to be asked for a paper on the importance to the German economy of stopping the traffic.[72]

Before the War Cabinet came to any sort of decision about Churchill's statement, the Soviet Union attacked Finland. This caused an outcry in Britain and France and a demand that something be done to help the gallant Finns. General Ironside developed a plan which he considered could resolve the iron ore dilemma and at the same time 'aid' the Finns. As

Ironside told his military assistant: 'We should go to help Finland by landing at Narvik and thence by the railway to Gallivare and Finland. While only one brigade group would enter Finland . . . there would be four or five divisions on the lines of communication including Gallivare.'[73] It should be noted that this plan would involve British forces traversing two neutral states (Norway and Sweden). How that was to be arranged was not specified by Ironside. It also involved deceiving those states. The stated aim was to help the Finns but they would receive just one brigade group. The real purpose of the operation, that of occupying the Gällivare ore fields in Sweden in strength (five divisions), would be concealed. As an example of the cynicism with which great powers 'assist' small ones, this could hardly be bettered.

Norway was now continually on the agenda of the War Cabinet. On 22 December they considered the report requested by Churchill from the MEW. The Ministry concluded that only if *all* Swedish iron ore was denied to Germany would the consequences be 'fatal' to their industry.[74] Another report to Hitler from the German industrialist Fritz Thyssen, obtained by French Intelligence and passed to the British, reached a similar conclusion.[75] This meant that not just the Narvik trade but also ships proceeding from Sweden to Germany down the Gulf of Bothnia should be stopped. The reports therefore implied that Gällivare must be occupied and were accordingly favourable to Ironside's scheme. They also raised the question of exactly how the Norwegians and Swedes were to be induced to cooperate. After much discussion the War Cabinet decided that Halifax should send notes to the Scandinavians asking that British and French troops be allowed to traverse their countries on the way to Finland.[76] The fact that most of the troops would in fact proceed no further than the Swedish ore fields was not to form part of the note.

The Norwegian and Swedish replies to this note arrived in short order. They were generally unfavourable. Technical missions made up of volunteers could cross to Finland but no troops. Ironside's project seemed doomed.[77]

At this moment the report asked for by the War Cabinet from the COS arrived. It did not recommend Churchill's smaller project of laying minefields off Narvik. The COS thought this action might provoke German retaliation against such centres as Oslo and Stavanger which the British

could do nothing to prevent and would spell the end of Scandinavian cooperation in Ironside's scheme, which they did favour.[78] The COS were silent
on the matter of how Norway and Sweden could be induced to cooperate
but their report put the whole issue back on the table.

Churchill read these reports carefully. While he considered it important
to cut off Swedish ore supplies to Germany through the Gulf of Bothnia by
sowing magnetic mines or other unspecified means, he thought minelaying
off Narvik could be implemented immediately. If this provoked a German
attack on Norway or Sweden or both, so be it. 'We have more to gain than
lose' by such actions, he concluded.[79]

His views had hardened at the next meeting of the War Cabinet. He
thought that as the Finns were now in desperate trouble, Norway and
Sweden should be urged to give them all possible assistance. In return the
British and French should offer a guarantee of aid if the Scandinavians were
attacked by Germany or Russia. In the meantime mines should be laid off
Narvik, and the COS asked for plans to enable all Swedish ore to be cut off
from Germany. The War Cabinet agreed, with a significant rider: no mining
off Narvik should take place until the Swedish and Norwegian reactions to
such a policy was gauged.[80]

This proviso frustrated the First Lord. He pointed out to his colleagues
that inaction was allowing ore to flow through Narvik to Germany and that
Norway should be informed that minefields would be laid early in January.[81]
Two days later he wrote a further paper noting that the larger plan of seizing
the ore fields was actually knocking out his smaller scheme when there was
no prospect of Sweden or Norway acquiescing in any kind of Anglo-French
military operation on their soil.[82]

In the first week of the new year the War Cabinet met virtually every day
to consider the Scandinavian problem. No conclusions were reached,
Ironside now doubting whether the British and French had the type of
troops that could traverse the deep snow to Gällivare. It was suggested that
Canadian troops might be tried but there was uncertainty about their skiing
ability. Snowshoes were mentioned as an alternative but then the debate
just fizzled out.[83] By 12 January Churchill was at the end of his tether. He
told his colleagues that discussion of the Norway problem had been
proceeding for six weeks. Every negative argument had been canvassed
against his Narvik scheme but, as for the larger plan, 'he saw no reason at

all why the Scandinavian countries would allow us to send troops to the north'. Britain should lay a minefield off Narvik and be done with it. Chamberlain would have none of it; the mining operation was to be cancelled. He proposed instead to send a mission to Scandinavia.[84] At a later meeting Halifax strongly supported the idea of a mission. He stated that the Scandinavians must be made to understand 'the true problem of the war'. Churchill pleaded to send a destroyer flotilla to Narvik first, and then a mission. By the following week, however, opinion had hardened against a mission. Instead, Halifax was to see the Scandinavian ministers in London.[85]

Needless to say these meetings produced no results. The Norwegians were evasive. They had signed an agreement allowing the Allies to charter their considerable merchant shipping fleet. This, they pointed out, would provide substantial assistance to the Allies. They were not prepared to go further.[86]

Despite this rebuff the War Office were making plans. In mid-January, they outlined a three-pronged operation for landings in Norway and Sweden. In the north (Operation Avonmouth) two divisions would land at Narvik and occupy the Swedish iron ore fields.[87] There would then be a second landing of five battalions (Operation Stratford) in central Norway around Trondheim and Bergen to protect the rear of this force by denying these ports to the Germans.[88] Finally, to forestall a German landing in the south, a third force of two divisions (Operation Plymouth) would be made available to assist the Scandinavian defence of this area. To provide protection for the troops eleven British aircraft squadrons (six bomber, three fighter, two army cooperation) would be needed.[89] The reports all stressed that Scandinavian cooperation was essential.

Towards the end of the month the COS reconsidered the whole matter. They thought the number of troops provided in the War Office plan too modest. Two brigades would land at Narvik but a further five divisions would be required to reinforce the north or south as required. These troops would require 380,000 tons of shipping for transport and be escorted by forty destroyers and twenty-five trawlers. The remainder of the Home Fleet would also be in attendance. Only in the matter of air cover did the Chiefs scale back the British effort. They considered two bomber, three fighter and one army cooperation squadron were all that could be sent. They noted that this force would be inadequate to satisfy the Scandinavians but offered no solution as to how to win them over.[90]

At this point the French intervened, but not in a way congenial to the British. The Daladier government declared themselves under great pressure to help the Finns. As a result the French General Staff had devised a plan of landing a force in northern Finland at Petsamo.[91] The British wanted nothing to do with this scheme, which not only ran a great risk of involving the Allies in war against Russia but also ran counter to their own plan (not divulged to the French) of using aid to Finland as a cover for seizing the Swedish ore fields.[92] In the end the British gained from the renewed French interest in Scandinavia. While extracting from the French a promise to provide mountain troops and a contingent from the Foreign Legion and some Poles who had formed a brigade of infantry in France, they went through the motions of considering the Petsamo scheme. Not surprisingly, their answer to the French was negative but the French promise of troops remained.[93] The available force for intervention in Scandinavia now stood at five and a half British divisions and approximately two divisions from France.

The proposed Franco-British expedition to Scandinavia had now reached substantial proportions, involving seven to eight divisions of troops, hundreds of thousands of tons of shipping, the Home Fleet and a modest six squadrons of aircraft – all of which would have to be withdrawn from British home defence, an extremely unlikely circumstance.

Then an incident occurred which turned attention back to Norwegian territorial waters. On 16 February 1940 the German merchant ship *Altmark* was intercepted by the navy just off the coast of Norway. Churchill ordered the *Altmark* boarded; 300 British sailors who had been captured by the *Graf Spee* and were being transported back to Germany as prisoners onboard the *Altmark* were released. Norwegian warships had just stood by, giving the impression that Norway could not defend its territorial waters. The *Altmark* incident focused attention in Britain on the ease with which Germany could avoid the British blockade by transporting Swedish ore along the Norwegian coast.[94]

Churchill therefore immediately took the opportunity to reintroduce his mining scheme to the War Cabinet. He now had an ally in Ironside, who had given up on Scandinavian cooperation and was hoping that German retaliation to Churchill's minelaying plan might eventually allow his military expedition to intervene in Scandinavia after all.[95] But even the combined weight of the First Lord and the CIGS could not prevail. The War Cabinet deferred discussion of a paper on the subject by Churchill on 18 February and was still considering it on the 22nd.[96] Then on the 23rd Chamberlain intervened:

> The Prime Minister said that, although his instincts were in favour of taking action, he could not take the proposed step [the mining operation] light-heartedly. We had entered the war on moral grounds, and we must be careful not to undermine our position, else we might lose the support of the world. In any case, it would be necessary to make quite certain that the Dominions were with us, and it would be advisable to consult the Leaders of the Opposition.[97]

Chamberlain had clearly developed cold feet. Up to this point in the war he had shown scant consideration for Dominion opinion and nothing but contempt for the Opposition. It sounded like what in fact it was: an attempt to buy time until he could squash the scheme definitively. This he did on the 29th. He had consulted the Dominions and found that they had no strong opinion for or against, the leader of the Liberals was for it but the Labour leaders thought it might lower Britain's moral standing. Therefore Chamberlain was:

> not at all convinced that the measure proposed would be opportune at the present moment . . . He had reached the conclusion that it would be advisable to postpone taking this measure . . . He had reluctantly come to the conclusion that he could not advise the War Cabinet to take action in Norwegian territorial waters for the present. The project could be put on one side and its execution could be reconsidered as the situation developed.[98]

Churchill tried to talk the Prime Minister around, using the *Altmark* incident as a justification for British action, but to no avail.[99] The Narvik scheme was off the table.

The Prime Minister had, however, reckoned without the French. At this point Daladier was so desperate to show that his government could take some action somewhere that he had promised the Finns that French *and British* troops were prepared to force their way through to Finland even if the Norwegians and Swedes resisted.[100] If Narvik was off, Ironside's larger scheme had suddenly reappeared.

In London an outraged War Cabinet met to discuss what was considered to be a deceptive proposal by the French. No one thought to mention that British policy towards Finland also had its deceptive aspects. The Chief of the Air Staff – representing the CIGS, who was in France – pointed out the difficulties involved in an opposed landing: the expeditions' equipment would have to packed to enable it to be used tactically when the troops disembarked. Nevertheless, the British found themselves in an awkward position. A refusal to back the French might result in Finland suing for peace with Russia. Despite their misgivings, the War Office was given the green light to prepare for an opposed landing – that is, for war with Norway or Sweden or both.[101]

When Ironside returned to London he was appalled by this decision. He called the whole thing 'nonsense'.[102] 'To try to get up the Narvik railway [to the Swedish iron ore fields] without any help from the Swedish and Norwegian railway personnel is madness . . . We simply cannot do it. I must reiterate this to the Cabinet'.[103]

That there would be no help from the Scandinavians seemed perfectly clear. They had rejected yet another request for help by the Allies on 2 March.[104] Yet, despite Ironside, the Norwegians and the Swedes, opinion in London seemed to be turning in favour of the French scheme. Even Pound, usually the most cautious of the Chiefs, waxed enthusiastic. On 8 March he told the War Cabinet that Britain should not give up the Gällivare scheme just because Sweden said no. If our troops arrived off Norway and were turned away, this would be less damaging than dropping the scheme altogether. Also the very fact that troops had arrived might induce the Norwegians to allow them to land. Astonishingly, the Minister for Co-ordination of Defence, Chatfield, agreed with this less than logical proposition. Even more surprisingly, so did the Prime Minister[105]

There were some voices of caution. Halifax produced figures which showed that the amount of ore shipped from Narvik in the first two months of 1940 was only one third of that shipped in the same months of 1939.[106] Churchill deprecated the proposed landings at Trondheim and Bergen. He suggested that this might have the appearance of a full-scale invasion and wanted any action confined to Narvik.[107] The British also remained under heavy pressure from the French. Daladier was 'showering the British authorities with telegrams, notes, appeals aide-memoirs and memoranda' to commence operations.[108] To reinforce the message the French Ambassador, Corbin, upbraided the Foreign Office for their reluctance to aid the Finns.[109]

Finally, the War Cabinet was told that a military commander (Brigadier-General Pierse Mackesy) and a naval commander (Admiral Edward Evans) had been appointed for the expedition. The meeting then grappled with the question of what instructions to give to these men, should the Norwegians show resistance. The result was high farce. In their final form the instructions read:

> The attitude of the Norwegians and Swedes to our arrival in their country is uncertain. HMG earnestly desire to bring to pass their moral obligations to bring help to Finland without any serious fighting with Norway or Sweden.
>
> It is possible that our reception may be friendly . . .
>
> Should, however, active hostility be encountered your action must be governed by the following considerations [that is] those which apply to military action in aid of the civil power within the British Empire.
>
> Should they open fire upon your troops a certain number of casualties must be accepted and your counter action should, within limits, rest upon the use of might, discipline, the rifle butt and fist.
>
> You should not open fire except as a last resort and fire must only be opened on the order of a Platoon or higher commander.
>
> Subject to the above you are given discretion to use any degree of force necessary to ensure the safety of your command.
>
> So long as you act with good intent within the above limitations you can count upon the complete support of your commanders.[110]

Surely, no soldiers in modern times have been sent to war with instructions such as these.

In the end events in Finland intervened to end Franco-British enthusiasm to invade the northern neutrals. The day after the War Cabinet had fixed their 'rules of engagement' Finland capitulated. As the Naval Staff noted with appalling frankness: 'Our real objective was, of course, to secure possession of the Gallivare ore fields . . . up till now we have had the assistance of Finland as "cover" for such a move on our part, but we had now lost this justification for intervention in Scandinavia.'[111]

This meant the end of the larger plan. Ironside argued that the Stratford, Avonmouth and Plymouth forces should be kept in being. Chamberlain, however, thought they should be dispersed. In the end there was a compromise. The force to assist the Swedes (Plymouth) was dispersed and within a few days two of its divisions were on their way to France.[112] The Stratford and Avonmouth forces remained concentrated. The fact was that Chamberlain had not quite given up on Norway. He stated that Germany could not be allowed to reap the advantages of Swedish and Norwegian neutrality unchallenged. Suddenly, Churchill's mining scheme was back on the agenda.[113] The Prime Minister considered that forces should be available in case the Germans reacted. For Narvik the British had two brigades and the French the Chasseurs Alpins Brigade and two battalions of the Foreign Legion. For Trondheim, Bergen and Stavanger there were five battalions of the 48 Division. Nevertheless, no one in authority really expected an opposed landing. The troops, Chamberlain considered, would be invited in by the Norwegians to protect them from unspecified German retaliation.[114]

All the British had to do to put their mining plan into action was gain the assent of the French. In one respect this was not difficult. With the collapse of Finland, Daladier had become a sudden convert to the Narvik plan. But the British, for reasons that remain obscure, had decided to link this plan to an earlier Churchillian idea to sow mines in the Rhine (Operation Royal Marine) to disrupt German internal trade. But this was too close to home for Daladier. He demurred, only to be told by an angry Chamberlain, 'No mines, no Narvik.'[115] The French seemed to cave in and a timetable was finally set. The Scandinavians were to be told that the Allies intended to take action on 1 April – which was somehow appropriate. Royal Marine would commence on 4 April and the minefields laid in Norwegian territorial waters the next day.[116] In the event there was a slippage in these dates because the French baulked at Royal Marine at the last minute. Reluctantly, the British agreed to proceed with Narvik alone. The notes were delivered to the Scandinavians on the 5th, Royal Marine was postponed to a later date and the Norwegian minefields would be laid on the night of 8 April. No one thought that these few days' delays meant anything. Hitler had other ideas.

During its eight-month tenure Chamberlain's government did not perform well. On land the British were tied to French policy and it is impossible to see what action was open to them independent of the French. It is also clear that Chamberlain was quite satisfied with being in this situation. The last thing he wanted was a shooting war in France. As for the Poles, to whom promises had been made, they were hardly mentioned. The air was a slightly different matter. The British, for reasons that are not clear, regarded themselves as having a bombing weapon of ferocious power. Certainly the French were not keen they use it lest the Germans retaliate. Once again, it seems certain that Chamberlain saw this as a convenient excuse for inactivity. Roosevelt's concern about bombing civilians can be placed in the same category. After the German bombing of Warsaw it surely did not apply. And if Chamberlain did not consider a German invasion of Belgium reason enough to unleash the bombers, it was doubtful if under his leadership they ever would be unleashed. At sea Chamberlain could hardly prevent action but not much of it was consequential during this period.

At the Admiralty, Churchill had an uneven start to the war. On the plus side, the blockade was brought into action with some efficiency. However, German pressure on Romania for oil supplies soon had an effect and in other areas the blockade proved almost entirely useless, though this was hardly Churchill's fault. The magnetic mine was quickly mastered. Convoys were also speedily introduced and played their role in keeping sinkings down, even if the First Lord was unhappy with the kill rate against U-boats. On the negative side, Churchill's Baltic scheme to dominate that sea with 'unsinkable' battleships and stop that section of the iron ore trade was a fiasco waiting to happen. It took many hours of Admiralty time to ensure that it never took place.

The main action of the appeasement government concerned Norway. Here Chamberlain seems to have initially welcomed the idea because it was so far removed from France but developed cold feet any time a plan looked as if it might reach fruition. It is interesting to note that at one time or another the entire War Cabinet, including Churchill, contemplated war with Russia in order to use aid to the Finns as a cover plan to capture the Swedish ore fields.

It is also notable, however, that action along these lines mainly depended on receiving an invitation to invade by the Scandinavian countries – an invitation that most were certain would never be given. As for Churchill's plan to mine Norwegian territorial waters, it could have been implemented at any time from late December 1939 onwards. Churchill himself listed eight areas of obstruction to the plan: the economic departments who regarded it as insufficient, the Joint Planners who wanted to think bigger, the COS who at times embraced the larger plans, the Dominions and their consciences, the French, the United States, the morality question, and finally the Cabinet.[117]

The fact was, though, that the main centre of obstruction was the Prime Minister, who was merely using some of the eight areas mentioned by Churchill for his own purpose – which was to take as little action as possible. In some senses, Churchill was trying to run the war from the Admiralty but in the end the power of the Prime Minister was such that he could not prevail. With the shooting war about to begin, that fact was to become a great deal more important.

Map 4. Norway.

CHAPTER 13

THE NORWAY CAMPAIGN

WHILE THE BRITISH WERE dithering about Norway, the Germans were not. They had long prepared a plan to invade Denmark and Norway should the British be seen to be moving on their iron ore supplies.[1] In mid-March 1940 the breaking of some British naval codes revealed that the Home Fleet at Scapa was preparing to convoy troops.[2] Norway was a likely destination so Hitler ordered Admiral Raeder to implement Operation Weserübung during the next full moon (7 April).[3] The plan was as follows. About 9,000 troops were to be embarked on warships for Narvik, Trondheim, Bergen and Oslo. Stavanger was to be captured by paratroops. Denmark was also to be occupied to protect communications and to provide forward airfields for the Luftwaffe. The *Scharnhorst* and *Gneisenau* would escort ten destroyers carrying 2,000 troops to Narvik. Other heavy ships would escort contingents to the other destinations. Air Corps X with 1,000 aircraft of all types would also be used.[4]

British Intelligence sources had picked up various reports to the effect that German naval preparations might be aimed at Norway. They disagreed on their interpretations, though, the Foreign Office commenting that 'I wish I could believe this story. German intervention in Scandinavia is just what we want,'[5] while the War Office merely noted that the intelligence involved 'the usual rumours'.[6] Subsequent reports became more specific. On 7 April the Admiralty signalled to the C-in-C Home Fleet (Admiral Forbes):

Recent reports suggest that a German expedition is being prepared. Hitler is reported from Copenhagen to have ordered the unostentatious movement of one division of ten ships by night to land at Narvik with simultaneous occupation of Jutland. Sweden to be left alone. Moderates said to be opposing the plan. Date given for Narvik was 8th April.[7]

This report was quite accurate and might have propelled the Home Fleet to sea had not someone at the Admiralty appended a note which said, 'All these reports are of doubtful value and may well be only a further move in the war of nerves.'[8] Even then, reports that British aircraft had attacked German ships in the Skagerrak and that *Scharnhorst* was at sea might have alerted Forbes but they were not passed on to him for many hours, by which time it was too late to intercept any German convoys.[9]

Some British warships were at sea. Vice-Admiral William Whitworth with the battleship *Renown* and attendant destroyers was escorting the eight destroyers that were to lay the much-delayed Narvik minefield. In very bad weather and poor visibility they made contact with the *Scharnhorst* and *Gneisenau* escorting the troop-laden German destroyers making for Narvik. The German heavy ships turned away but the 15″ guns of the *Renown* crippled the *Gneisenau* with three well-aimed shots before the German ships were lost in the murk.[10]

This was the only chance the British had to disrupt the German invasion plan. By the time Whitworth turned back to Narvik the German destroyers had slipped through and enemy troops were now occupying the town. As for the other landings, Admiral Forbes was too distant to affect them. The German occupation of Norway was now an accomplished fact.

Back in London, Churchill was by no means disappointed at the turn of events. He ignored, or was unaware, of the intelligence failures, noting that 'we could not have prevented the landings without maintaining large patrols continuously off the Norwegian coast'. He told the War Cabinet that 'our hands were now free' and that Britain could apply overwhelming sea power to the situation. Altogether 'we were in a far better position than we had been up to date'.[11] Noticeably he made no mention of enemy air power.

Later that day, Churchill also chaired the Military Co-ordination Committee, where he had taken over from Chatfield as chairman. Attention quickly turned to what action the British could take. It was thought that German possession of shore batteries ruled out naval action in the south but that a force of destroyers should immediately be sent to Narvik to attack any German warships found there. As for military operations, Ironside considered the forces at his disposal (the 13,000 troops that had been concentrated for an attack through to Finland) should be used to retake Narvik, which he also thought doomed to failure if it was rushed. When pressed he promised to attack at 'the earliest possible moment'.[12] The next day the Committee met again. Ironside explained that a base near Narvik would be seized and the troops, which would now also include the French Chasseurs Alpins, would be sorted into formation for the attack on Narvik which might take place around 23 to 25 April.[13] Plans continued to develop rapidly. Churchill explained to the War Cabinet that Harstad, on an island just 15 miles from Narvik, had been chosen as a base. Ironside said that Major-General Pierse Mackesy had already left for Harstad, that four battalions of troops would follow and then the remainder of the forces including the French.[14]

Meanwhile the Admiralty (or Churchill) had decided that the German destroyers at Narvik must be dealt with. They instructed the captain of their own destroyer flotilla, Captain Bernard Warburton-Lee, to attack. Warburton-Lee was outnumbered five destroyers to ten and he could have asked Whitworth (who had not been informed by the Admiralty of their instructions to his subordinate) for reinforcements. Instead he decided to use surprise and attack 'at dawn high water'.[15] This he did, sinking two German destroyers and damaging three more. On the way out of the fiord, however, he encountered the remaining enemy destroyers, losing two of his own craft and his life.[16] The Admiralty ordered Whitworth on the newly arrived battleship *Warspite* to clean up the Germans. On the 13th the *Warspite* and nine destroyers entered the fiord and put an end to the remaining German warships. In all ten enemy destroyers (half of their entire stock) went down in the two actions. The German troops in Narvik were now cut off from resupply.[17]

At the same time that these actions were taking place, the British were learning that they had an ally. The Norwegian government (and the King) had fled before the Germans entered Oslo. They now wished to be installed at Trondheim, the ancient capital of Norway. Halifax drew this to the attention of the War Cabinet, noting that however successful the proposed landing at Narvik was, it would not have the political impact of retaking Trondheim. Churchill responded that an opposed landing at Trondheim would be very difficult and would require careful preparation while the Narvik plan was well advanced. He promised, though, that the Naval Staff would examine the project and report back.[18] While the Admiralty dithered, Churchill came under intense pressure from Halifax and Chamberlain to carry out the Trondheim plan. Although 'apprehensive' about weakening operations at Narvik, Churchill was inclined to shift his position.[19] The next day in writing to the French, Churchill asserted, while 'nothing must interrupt the vigour of this [the Narvik] operation' . . . we must consider the extreme importance and urgency of operations against Trondheim'. He went on to say that the British were proposing to land 4,000 troops near Trondheim to secure a lodgement from where larger forces might be directed on the ancient capital.[20] And he asked the French if they might divert some of their own troops from Narvik for this operation.

Later that day Churchill heard from Whitworth that the *Warspite* operation had thoroughly frightened the Germans in Narvik and that he recommended the town be occupied without delay.[21] Churchill called a meeting of the MCC. The consensus was that both Narvik and Trondheim could be captured. Narvik was now an easier proposition than first thought, so some part of the Narvik force could be diverted to Namsos to the north of Trondheim with instructions to march on the capital. Ironside was to direct the military to study the feasibility of this new plan and the putative commander (Major-General Carton de Wiart) was to be flown to Namsos to scout out the ground.[22]

An operation in the Trondheim area was clearly now in prospect, so Churchill sought to gauge from Forbes, then off Bergen with the Home Fleet, the practicability of taking the city direct. In a telegram that sounded eerily similar to the 'ships alone' signal sent to Carden at the Dardanelles, he asked:

Do you consider that the shore batteries [protecting Trondheim fiord] could either be destroyed or dominated to such an extent as to permit transports to enter? And, if so, how many ships and of what type would you propose to use. Request early reply.[23]

Forbes, unlike Carden, was not buying in. His fleet had been under air attack at Bergen, the *Rodney* had been hit by a bomb, other heavy ships had received near misses and a modern destroyer (the *Gurkha*) had been sunk. In his reply Forbes stressed that, while the shore batteries could be dominated, that was not the main problem. It was the domination by the Germans of the air that was the issue. He concluded that he did not consider the operation feasible 'unless you are prepared to face very heavy losses in troops and transports'.[24] Churchill was not quite prepared to give up. He suggested that the RAF might put the nearby airfield at Stavanger out of action and promised Forbes that a supply of 15″ high-explosive shell be made available for this purpose. 'Pray', he persisted, 'therefore consider this important project further'.[25]

Forbes replied with a series of questions – what size landing force was being contemplated? where were the troops to land? how were the transports to be protected from land-based aircraft flown from Denmark or Germany?[26] These were good questions, hardly met by the Admiralty's promise to use Regular troops in the landing or to provide biplanes flown from carriers to neutralise first-class German-based fighters.[27] But cooler heads were starting to exert an influence in London. First the COS came out against a direct attack on Trondheim and then the Admiralty backed down. Operation Hammer, as the attack on Trondheim was called, was aborted on 20 April. Other options would have to be tried.

Meanwhile the expedition against Narvik was underway with a brigade of Guards setting sail on the 9th. Then it was discovered that thousands of German troops might be in occupation of the port. Narvik might not be a pushover, so the War Office added another brigade (146 Territorials) to the force. Its embarkation was bungled. The cruisers (*York* and *Berwick*) in which it was to sail were ordered into the North Sea on a rumour that German heavy ships might be making for the Atlantic. Unfortunately these cruisers contained most of the 146 Brigade's equipment. Three days passed before alternative shipping could be arranged for the brigade on the passenger liner *Empress of Australia* but without its equipment, which was still on the *York* and *Berwick*.[28]

While the brigade was at sea the Admiralty received a hopeful telegram from Admiral Whitworth suggesting that Narvik might after all be a soft target requiring just the Guards to secure it. Churchill passed this information on to the War Cabinet and suggested that the second brigade could be diverted to Namsos, where de Wiart with an advanced guard was soon to arrive. If the French Chasseurs Alpins were also sent to reinforce him they could land a force to the south of Trondheim as well as at Namsos to the north. In all the Allies would have 23,000 men against the Germans 3,500. Might not the old capital be captured after all?[29]

All this looked from London quite neat. At Narvik a blast from the guns of the *Warspite* would herald a relatively easy opposes landing. Further south there would be an attack on Trondheim from Namsos by 146 Brigade from the north, perhaps accompanied by a converging attack from the south. The Norwegian government could then be installed and other operations contemplated.

On the ground, however, things were far from neat. At Namsos the 146 Brigade was not only without most of its equipment, it was without its commander, Brigadier Charles Phillips. The brigadier, for obscure reasons, had left for Narvik on a different ship to his men. When the destination was changed from Narvik to Namsos the seas were so rough he could not tranship, so he made his way north while his men headed for central Norway. Then, when the *Empress of Australia* approached Namsos it was apparent that the ship was too large to dock at the small pier. A plan was therefore made to transfer the troops to the smaller escorting destroyers but this could only take place in calm waters well to the north of Namsos. Immediately the process of transhipping the men began, the destroyers were attacked by the Luftwaffe. This forced them back to Namsos – with the troops but without the little equipment they had with them.[30]

It is worth pausing at this point to consider where the brigade's equipment was. Much was in the cruisers *York* and *Berwick*, dashing about the North Sea in pursuit of the non-existent German heavy ships; a small amount was with Brigadier Phillips on its way to Narvik; some was on the *Empress of Australia*, which had not been able to transfer all of it to the destroyers before the Luftwaffe attacked; and some had been left to the north of Namsos when the destroyers had to dash back there in the middle of transhipping the men.

By 17 April events took a briefly more hopeful turn. The 146 Brigade had finally disembarked at Namsos. De Wiart and Phillips had arrived, and the commanders set off to Steinkjer to catch up with their men on the road to Trondheim.[31] Soon the French also arrived at Namsos but when de Wiart returned to greet them he found a shambles. The Luftwaffe had destroyed the town and much of the French stores, including their transport. The French were therefore immobile and were without anti-aircraft guns with which to fight off the Germans. De Wiart could not help them; his only transport (a few 3-ton trucks) was too wide for the narrow Steinkjer road. When he returned to his men, de Wiart found another disturbing situation: the Germans had landed troops equipped with artillery south of Steinkjer on the flank of his force and were shelling the advanced contingents and threatening his line of retreat. He immediately signalled to London for support before the 'situation becomes untenable'.[32]

Back in London this signal was received by Lieutenant-General Hugh Massy, whom Ironside had placed in command of all operations in central Norway. He told de Wiart to remain on the defensive until help arrived. Ominously he added that this might take several weeks.[33] But the position of 146 Brigade was already 'untenable'. De Wiart's force was being attacked in flank by German troops equipped with skis, they had no transport, no anti-aircraft guns, no artillery; their base was in ruins and the French were unable to support them.[34] On 27 April Massy accepted that de Wiart's force must be evacuated and then added to the confusion by telling the commander that this movement must be 'gradual but rapid'.[35] De Wiart chose the rapid option. His force was withdrawn between 29 April and 1 May with remarkably little loss.[36]

So ended the sorry affair at Namsos. In a bitter entry in the brigade's war diary, Brigadier Phillips (he of the travails at Narvik) summed up the reasons for failure. He noted that no advance plan had been made, that he had no maps of the area in which he was to operate, no snowshoes, no skis, no anti-aircraft guns, little artillery, gunners who had never fired a shot in anger and in any case had no ammunition to fire. He had troops with no transport, many of whom had never fired a rifle or a mortar. They had received no brigade training, had no air support and no communications, having been forced to use local Norwegian telephone exchanges. He ended by saying:

This was a campaign for which the book does not cater. Big frontages, great distances, a mixture of the NWFP [North-West Frontier Police],

Palestine and Gallipoli with air the dominant feature. Finally I am forced to the sad conclusion that not only the lessons we learnt so dearly at Gallipoli, Salonika and Mesopotamia have been forgotten but we now make even more mistakes of a most elementary nature.[37]

Whether Churchill noted the reference to Gallipoli is not known.

While events at Namsos were being played out, equally disastrous operations were occurring to the south of Trondheim at Åndalsnes. Here a naval reconnaissance force had visited and deemed the place suitable for a base, whereupon the War Office despatched the 148 Brigade to it. In fact only a portion of the brigade arrived. One half of a battalion remained in Scotland awaiting shipping, while another battalion had already been despatched to Narvik to reinforce the Guards.[38] So only 1,200 men under Major-General Harold Morgan disembarked at Åndalsnes. Morgan's orders were prodigious. He was to block any German move from Oslo in the south and operate with any Norwegian force around Lillehammer. He was then to turn north and advance on Trondheim.[39]

Morgan soon found out where his priorities lay. The British Military Attaché in Norway (Lieutenant-Colonel Edward King-Salter) informed him on landing that the Norwegians would collapse if they were not supported, a message reinforced by General Otto Ruge, the Norwegian Commander-in-Chief.[40] Faced with this information, all thought of the Trondheim advance vanished. Morgan turned south towards Lillehammer. But he turned without most of his equipment. The ship carrying it had been sunk in the North Sea; down with it went the entire motor transport of the brigade, four anti-aircraft guns, 25,000 rations and a huge amount of ammunition.[41] Morgan's advance met with a certain inevitability. It soon encountered German forces equipped with artillery, motorised machine guns and supported by dive bombers.[42] The result was a rapid retreat. By 23 April Morgan's force was down to 400 men. Evacuation seemed certain. Seemingly unaware of the situation, the War Office had decided to reinforce him, however. As the remnants of 148 Brigade flooded back to Åndalsnes, a brigade of Regulars (15 Brigade) was just landing.

Here seemed salvation, but all was not well with 15 Brigade. Such was the haste with which it had been despatched that in the first instance it had no artillery, anti-tank equipment or maps; nor would there be any air support.[43] Moreover, there were docking problems – the wharf being too small for even destroyers to tie alongside. Many of these ships had to proceed to Molde (15 miles away) and have the unloaded stores brought back by ferry. This did not make the embarkation of the division any less chaotic. By 26 April the administrative staff were reporting:

> Position here confused ... Office and Signal Office confused in one room with Naval Signal Officers and ratings ... The rest of the house is being used for sleeping and messing. Candle illumination. Many people coming and going without apparent purpose. Many men hanging about doing nothing.[44]

This confusion escalated when the Luftwaffe bombed the base, setting fire to stores and partially destroying the port. Under the strain the Chief Administrative Officer cracked. His revolver was quietly removed and morphine administered. When that wore off, he broke away but was chased down by a naval medical officer, given another shot of morphine and removed to hospital.[45] It was not an auspicious beginning.

In charge of 15 Brigade was Lieutenant-General Bernard Paget, who had spent the first days of his command scouring bookshops in London for maps or tourist guides of Trondheim.[46] He landed on 25 April and set off to find Morgan. The good news was that 263 Squadron flying Gloster Gladiators had arrived at a nearby lake. The good news rapidly vanished. The Luftwaffe attacked the squadron before it could get airborne, destroying many of the aircraft and sinking others as they blasted holes in the lake. Of those few who managed to take off, some ran out of ammunition only to find there was no reserve. Thus ended British air support.[47]

Paget with Morgan then met General Ruge and ascertained that the situation was indeed desperate. The War Office had also arrived at that conclusion and they signalled Paget to prepare for evacuation but not to inform Ruge. To his credit, Paget disobeyed this order and told the Norwegian Commander what was afoot. However, German pressure meant retreat was inevitable, so – covered by Ruge's ski troops – the British began the trek back to Åndalsnes. Paget dashed off a series of signals to the War Office to provide air cover for his evacuation but to no avail. On 28 April Paget's force began evacuation from Norway. By 2 May they were gone, miraculously without a single casualty.[48] The British incursions into central Norway were at an end.

In London the politicians were well behind the flow of events in Norway. Early on, though, Ironside had described the operations around Trondheim as 'no picnic'. However, there was general relief that de Wiart's contingent and then Morgan's had got ashore with few casualties.[49] There was speculation about whether Morgan's force should turn south to aid the Norwegians or set out against Trondheim, without any knowledge that that decision had already been made on the ground.[50] Gradually reality began to dawn. By 21 April Churchill was noting the lack of air cover at Namsos and the despatch of the soon-to-be-destroyed Gladiators.[51] On the same day he read de Wiart's first telegram suggesting evacuation but still thought the situation could be rectified.[52] By the 25th (the anniversary of Anzac Day) he had finally realised that the pincers from Namsos and Åndalsnes were doomed. His solution was curious: to reinstate Operation Hammer, the direct attack on Trondheim, a plan that Admiral Forbes had vetoed some ten days before.[53]

Churchill was having difficulty in translating his wishes into action. If he was to reinstate Hammer he required the concurrence of the COS (Ironside). But only the Prime Minister could direct the COS. Churchill therefore tried the expedient of asking the Prime Minister to chair the Military Co-ordination Committee himself. Chamberlain agreed but the whole move backfired because at the next meeting of the MCC the Prime Minister made it clear that he did not favour Hammer in any form. Neither, as it happened, did the COS. What they both favoured was renewed emphasis on Narvik. Churchill, sensing which way the wind was blowing, immediately changed course – Hammer was off, Narvik was on.[54]

The state of play at Narvik was this: General Mackesy was on his way there to take command of a force of Chasseurs Alpins and the Guards brigade. His instructions from the War Office were decidedly ambiguous. He was told that his primary objective was to expel the Germans from Narvik and that he should take advantage of any naval action against the port. 'Boldness', he was told, 'is required.'[55] But then they added that 'it was not intended to land in the face of opposition'.[56] As there were up to 3,000 Germans thought to be in occupation of Narvik the manner in which he was to fulfil his orders was not obvious.

Churchill, for one, seemed unaware of these orders. On 10 April he had appointed an admiral (the splendidly named Admiral Lord Cork and Orrery) to command all naval forces around Narvik to support the army in what he described as their 'impending attack'.[57] Certainly Cork was unaware of Mackesy's orders for he wrote to the General on the 14th saying:

> Following for General. In view of successful naval operation on 13 April [the *Warspite* attack] enemy appear frightened – suggest we take every advantage of this.
> I should be most willing to land military force now in *Southampton* at Narvik at daylight tomorrow from HMS *Aurora* and destroyers.[58]

Mackesy was having none of this. On arriving at his base at Harstad he found, as so often in Norway, that the small port was unsuitable to unload stores even from the destroyers. As a result he had to employ over 100 Norwegian small ships called 'puffers' to do the job. These craft were slow and the Norwegian crew inexperienced, so the stores were unloaded in no particular order.[59] He had also reconnoitred Narvik and found 'concrete pill boxes and trenches covering the landing places'. He had no doubt that they were manned by at least 3,500 Germans.[60] Mackesy was probably being too cautious here. Had he got in touch with elements of the Norwegian 6 Division who were in the vicinity they could have told him that there were no more than 600 German troops in the town – the remainder were in perimeter defences some miles away. But Mackesy made no attempt to contact the Norwegians.

Churchill was still expecting rapid action. On 16 April he told the MCC that Narvik might be 'settled' by the 20th.[61] Next day, however, he received a telegram from Cork making it clear that Mackesy intended not to act until the snow melted, around the end of the month, and that even then he was counting on the Chasseurs Alpins which in the meantime had been diverted to Namsos. Churchill regarded this information as 'unexpected and disagreeable'.[62] At the War Cabinet he suggested a note be sent to the commanders telling them to get on with it:

> Your proposals involve damaging deadlock at Narvik. We cannot send you Chasseurs Alpins. HMS *Warspite* will be needed elsewhere in two

or three days. Full consideration should therefore be given by you to an assault upon Narvik covered by *Warspite* and the Destroyers . . . Send us your appreciation and act at once if you consider right. Matter most urgent![63]

On 18 April Mackesy and Cork met for the first time at Halstad. The meeting did not go well. Mackesy stated that his force was inferior to the German garrison at Narvik, that he had no troops which could operate in 4 feet of snow and that many Norwegian civilians might die in any naval bombardment of the town. He was willing to reconnoitre the port to ascertain whether the garrison was sufficiently demoralised to surrender but he was not prepared to go further. Cork reluctantly agreed.[64] He then communicated his views direct to the Admiralty:

> General and Senior Army Officers are strongly opposed on military grounds to an assault. Narvik is still under snow and apprehension felt as to possibility of even advancing once ashore. I have urged assault but feel obliged to accept soldiers view which seems unanimous, at least until snow disappears.[65]

Meanwhile Mackesy set out for his reconnaissance but he warned the War Office that whatever the result, no military operation could take place for some weeks owing to the deep snow. He also pointed out that at the moment he had no artillery, no anti-aircraft guns and no mortar ammunition.[66]

This was the last straw for Churchill. After securing Ironside's permission, he wrote to Cork and Mackesy stating that from now on Cork would be placed 'in absolute command' and that there should be no delay in the capture of Narvik.[67] On receiving this news Mackesy immediately offered to resign.[68] Cork thought another conference in order. He told Mackesy of Churchill's idea to warn the inhabitants of Narvik before operations commenced; if the Germans refused to allow them to leave, the odium of causing civilian casualties would fall on them. He also informed the general that, as he (Cork) was now in charge it was his opinion that the attack should be carried out immediately, as London had requested.[69] Mackesy yielded to the extent of allowing a battalion of troops to accompany a naval bombarding force but he did not disclose to Cork that he had instructed the battalion thus: 'should the German forces NOT surrender it is NOT intended to force an opposed landing'.[70] Thus the only circumstance in which a landing would take place was following a German surrender.

Narvik was bombarded in a blinding snowstorm on 24 April. Cork could see no sign of a white flag – indeed he could hardly see anything at all. The deep snow even made damage assessment difficult. Cork had recent experience with deep snow: he had stepped ashore on the 23rd and disappeared into a deep drift; naval ratings were rushed up to dig him out. He admitted to Churchill that there was nothing for it but to wait until some French ski troops (now back on the agenda) arrived and the snow melted.[71]

Relations between Cork and Mackesy had inevitably deteriorated. On 26 April Cork pressed Mackesy to produce at least some kind of a plan for a landing when the snow permitted.[72] Mackesy prevaricated, telling the War Office that Cork's military knowledge was 'exactly NIL' and adding that he hoped the French commander was aware that his troops would be placed under the command of a 'sailor without any military knowledge'. With this missive Mackesy had certainly overstepped the mark and the Vice Chief of the General Staff (Sir John Dill) was brought in to admonish him. He was told to support Cork's plan and to do nothing to undermine confidence in him.[73] The requisite assurances were received from Mackesy, who nevertheless could not refrain from adding details about the 'absurd' bombardment of 24 April 'which had done no damage at all'.[74]

Despite this unapologetic front, Mackesy seems to have been shaken by Dill's strictures. Cork next demanded a timetable and Mackesy finally supplied one. He would reconnoitre the beaches on 7 May, assemble his ships on the night of the 9/10th and attack on the night of 10/11th.[75] If this seemed the end of the affair, it was not. When Mackesy gave the commander of 24 Guards Brigade (Brigadier Thomas Trappes-Lomax) his orders, he received a furious response. Trappes-Lomax pointed out that he had insufficient landing craft, that the landing beaches were too small, that surprise would be impossible because of the long Arctic days and that there was nowhere to dig in on the rocky shoreline.[76]

By this time even Cork was having second thoughts. The French troops (with skis but without their artillery) had arrived, but he passed

Trappes-Lomax's report on to the Admiralty and put to them the real question about Narvik – the port had been thoroughly wrecked by three naval actions and the harbour was blocked with sunken ships. No iron ore or anything else would flow through it for a considerable time. Was not the capture of Narvik merely symbolic?[77]

In London, where the authorities seemed to be considerably behind the action, or lack of action, this was not the view. Churchill had sold the French on the fact that the evacuations from central Norway could be redeemed by the capture of Narvik.[78] Even an advance from Narvik towards the Swedish border and the Gällivare ore fields was back on the agenda.[79]

Then on 30 April Churchill was promoted. He would not only chair the MCC, he would give 'guidance and directions to the Chiefs of Staff Committee'. For that purpose he could summon the Chiefs for personal meetings any time he considered necessary.[80] In all but name this act by Chamberlain virtually made Churchill Prime Minister but of course without the real powers that accrued only to the top job.

It was all too late. Before Churchill could settle into the office, events overtook it. Lieutenant-General Claude Auchinleck had been despatched to Narvik in an attempt to overcome the Cork–Mackesy stand-off. In addition the French had landed and were trekking towards the town. Also closing on the town was the Norwegian 6 Division, a unit from the French Foreign Legion and some Polish battalions under French command.[81] Finally Narvik fell, not to troops commanded by Auchinleck, Cork, Mackesy or Trappes-Lomax but to this late-arriving heterogeneous group. The assault cost the Allies 150 dead, of whom 60 were Norwegians.[82]

The victory, as Cork had predicted, was largely symbolic. The town, port and harbour were destroyed and no iron ore went to Germany from there for some time. It only remained to evacuate the force. Even that was botched. The troops were removed safely but covering the last convoy was the aircraft carrier *Glorious*. For reasons that have never been satisfactorily explained, the commander asked to proceed direct to Scapa Flow escorted by just two destroyers. Equally baffling, he was granted permission. Directly the carrier left the security of the Home Fleet it was set upon by the *Scharnhorst*. The *Glorious* was soon a burning wreck. The two accompanying destroyers were also sunk but not before one had severely damaged the German heavy cruiser with torpedoes. In all 1,500 men were lost.[83] But by then the authorities in London had larger matters to deal with.

* * * * *

At the top level no one on the British side comes out very well from the Norwegian campaign. The decision-making in London was sclerotic at best. The COS found it difficult to make their voices heard in the over-large Chamberlain War Cabinet. When they acquired more opportunity in the MCC, the Committee had no authority to enforce their opinions without agreement from the War Cabinet and in particular the Prime Minister. The cobbled-up committees with Churchill as chair failed to meet these deficiencies. In the end he had to call in the Prime Minister in order to get decisions made. The last inept move – to allow Churchill to direct the Chiefs of Staff (whatever that meant) – only lasted a few days. It is difficult to see that it would have made much of a difference.

The campaign revealed other flaws. Liaison between the Admiralty and the War Office fluctuated from adequate to quite disastrous. Ships continually left port with cargoes required by the army with seemingly no one capable of coordinating these actions. Commanders, equipment, ammunition and most other war stores either failed to turn up or turned up in the wrong place. No one seems to have had adequate maps and the vision of high-ranking army officers touring Charing Cross Road to find them is pure farce.

The navy acting alone generally performed well. Warburton-Lee might have been foolhardy but his and Whitworth's actions at Narvik gave the German navy a taste of what resolute command could do. In other actions the navy managed to cripple most German heavy ships and at the end of the campaign the German fleet had been reduced to a skeleton. Forbes, in standing up to Churchill's hazardous Hammer operation against Trondheim, saved the navy from a probable fiasco. Only the incident with the *Glorious* dented the navy's prestige; overall they were the one service to have a good campaign.

On the ground it was quite different. The troops, many of whom were poorly trained, found themselves in action with inadequate artillery and air support, often with conflicting or fluctuating objectives and pitted against an enemy of the first rank. The fact that in central Norway they hung on so long is the matter for wonder, not the fact that they were forced to evacuate.

At Narvik the troops were better trained but in an impossible environment often once more without proper equipment. They could not fight in deep snow and they nothing that would equip them for an opposed landing. It was little wonder that Narvik was captured by ski troops from the landward side while the British watched on helplessly.

Churchill has received much blame for the fiasco. Certainly he endeavoured to run the campaign from London with only a vague idea of the conditions faced by those on the ground. He prodded for action at times when no action was possible. The farcical arrangements between Cork and Mackesy can be largely laid at his door. Yet there is another side to all this: in the absence of Chamberlain, who was to run the war? The Prime Minister certainly, by his own actions, thought that he was not up to the job. Nor did Ironside reveal any desire to grip the situation. The other service ministers (Stanley and Hoare) were ciphers whose voices are hardly discernible in committee. Given this vacuum it is hardly surprising that Churchill stepped in. And it must be said that a great deal of this fiasco was beyond the power of anyone to rectify. Once the Germans had seized the initiative and landed, they had the inestimable advantage of overwhelming air superiority with front-line aircraft. It certainly took Churchill too long to realise this but he was hardly alone in this myopia. What emerges from the episode is that the politicians may have directed the campaign disastrously but that Churchill had at least made the attempt. In fact he emerged, despite some missteps, as the only member of the government capable of running a war. In what was to follow it is notable that many members of the House of Commons grasped this fact. He might have blundered but he was a 'war man' of the type not thick on the ground in Britain in 1940.

Map 5. Northern France and Belgium, 1940.

CHAPTER 14

1940 – CRISIS YEAR

THE HOUSE OF COMMONS was quick to recognise that Churchill had the qualities to be a war leader. On 8 May Chamberlain called a debate on Norway. Here was Churchill's chance, but there was also some danger for him in the debate. He had been responsible for more than one error in the Norway campaign. How would the House react? Churchill need not have worried. He did his best to defend the government of which he was a part; the House was having none of it. The most scathing speeches about Chamberlain's conduct of the war came from his own side. Leo Amery and Admiral Keyes thundered at the government and deliberately excluded Churchill from their philippics. In reply Chamberlain was feeble, not helped by such nonentities as Henry Page Croft, who rose to support him. At the vote, which Labour forced, Chamberlain's majority fell from 200 to just 80. In those days, when negative sentiment in the House of Commons had an effect on the government, Chamberlain felt he must resign. There was a brief flirtation with Halifax for the top job but his position in the House of Lords and his own doubts that he was up to the task saw him sidelined. In any case Labour in the end favoured Churchill and on 10 May as the panzers rolled across the French border he became Prime Minister.[1]

Within just two days Churchill had chosen a War Cabinet of five permanent members (himself, Attlee, Greenwood, Chamberlain, Halifax) and established himself as Minister of Defence as well as Prime Minister. At the same time the BEF, as had been anticipated, was invited into Belgium. The plan was that the British, under General Gort, would advance its ten divisions to the River Dyle, well inside Belgium, with the Belgian army on its left and the French First Army on its right. There it would stand and, it was hoped, ward off the advancing German hordes. The advance, which started on 10 May, was uneventful – indeed even the Luftwaffe was largely absent. What of course neither the British political nor military leadership realised was that they were advancing into a trap. On their front they would encounter the German Army Group B, made up largely of infantry. Further south the Germans had concentrated most of their armour opposite the hilly Ardennes, the idea being that this force would cut through the French frontier divisions and execute a large encircling movement which would pin all the northern armies, including the British, between them and the sea.

On the British side all seemed to progress smoothly until 15 May. The Germans had been encountered on the 14th but their outposts had been driven back and the Dyle position occupied. Then disturbing news arrived from the French: German columns had pierced their defences at Sedan. By the 16th the gap was reported to be from 5 to 12 miles wide.[2] Equally disturbing news then came from the north: Germany had invaded Holland and the Dutch army was said to be rapidly disintegrating. Later that day General Gaston Billotte, commander of all armies in the northern section of the front, called a conference. Because the armies to the south were falling back, he would have to issue orders to the French First Army to swing back to maintain a solid front. As a consequence the BEF and the Belgians would also have to fall back. He thought the Dutch were beyond redemption. Indeed they had already surrendered.[3]

Events at the front were moving too rapidly for the politicians in London to keep pace. On the 13th Churchill discussed sending air reinforcements to the BEF. But then on the 14th he received an alarming telephone call from the French Prime Minister Paul Reynaud.[4] The gist of the message was that the Germans had broken the French line and only an injection of mass fighters from Britain could restore the situation.[5] Churchill was more sanguine and sent Reynaud a note saying that the problem was being studied.[6] Then on the 15th Reynaud telephoned again. In an 'excited mood' he told Churchill the French line had collapsed, the road to Paris was open and 'the battle was lost'. He even talked of giving up the struggle.[7]

This message was received with the utmost alarm in London. A series of meetings of the COS and the War Cabinet followed, the general consensus being that four squadrons of fighters were all that could be spared.[8] By the next day, however, another two squadrons were readied for despatch at 'short notice' if it was so decided.[9] Then Churchill learned that the BEF might also have to fall back. He announced that this could not possibly be contemplated (actually it was already happening) and that he must fly to France immediately to discuss the situation.[10]

Churchill found the scene in Paris one of utmost despair. At the Quai d'Orsay, where he met Reynaud, he found the archives being burnt and the government dejected to the point of defeatism. A spirited debate, largely between Churchill and the French C-in-C (Gamelin) followed, Churchill insisting that the French were far from beaten, Gamelin suggesting that the situation was far worse than Churchill imagined. On the position of the BEF the French could give the Prime Minister no information. Gradually it became clear to Churchill that the French had little idea of how to respond to the German attack and that if they received no additional help they could collapse.[11] He therefore asked the War Cabinet to approve the sending of six additional squadrons of fighters.[12] The War Cabinet demurred. Six squadrons would be committed to the battle in France but they would fly from British airfields and only operate in shifts – three in the morning and three in the afternoon.[13]

Meanwhile at the front the BEF had retreated from the Dyle to the line of the Escaut Canal, some 30 miles in rear. That this movement was carried out with celerity owed nothing to the C-in-C. During this period Gort showed an alarming tendency to be absent from GHQ, either at his Advanced Headquarters or just visiting the troops. However, the corps commanders (Lieutenant-Generals Alan Brooke, Michael Barker and Roland Adam) managed this retreat quite well. The problem was that as they arrived on the Escaut more alarming news arrived from Billotte. On the afternoon of the 16th he managed to find Gort and told him of a movement of German armour to the south of the BEF at Arras. This threatened to cut the BEF's lines of communication, which stretched back to Rennes in western France. Gort reacted. He sent an improvised force towards Arras and next day sent another.[14] He also alerted the three 'digging' divisions that had been hurried from Britain to dig defences, to deploy around Amiens. As the situation continued to deteriorate, the 50 Division was sent to secure the Vimy Ridge just to the north of Amiens.[15] For the moment that was all that could be spared if the Escaut line was to remain safe.

In the light of these moves GHQ set about reviewing the position of the BEF. The results of their deliberations are contained in a note written during the night of the 18/19 May. It is of the utmost importance:

> If our right rear [south of Arras] becomes filled with Germans we should be cut off from the French except for the remnants of 3 French Corps [around Lille]. To go South West was not possible [because the Germans were already there]. To go west is almost as bad. By going north west we should get flank protection of the Douai–La Bassee Canal Line. A series of water obstacles on th[is] line of retreat gave some hope of conducting the withdrawal in an orderly manner. The [narrow] corridor would end at the sea at Dunkirk from which hopes of evacuation of personnel with French & of operational material [would be possible.][16]

This note contains no mention of conducting a counter-attack to restore the situation. Indeed it concludes that the only available action is escape through Dunkirk and it indicates that Gort had already given up on the French.

This was not what the War Cabinet wanted to hear. On this very day Churchill had spoken in Parliament about the stabilisation of the front in his 'conquer we must' speech.[17] Later Ironside in the War Cabinet advised members that he had told Gort that his proposal 'could not be accepted at all'. The BEF must fight its way through the Arras area and join up with the French south of the Somme.[18] Churchill 'fully agreed' with Ironside's objection. The BEF must move back but in concert with the French.[19] This directive was thrashed out that evening by the Defence Committee, which instructed Ironside to proceed to GHQ with the message that the BEF must retire on Amiens, attacking all enemy forces encountered and take station on the left of the French army.[20]

Ironside arrived at GHQ on the 20th. Gort soon convinced him that the situation was much worse than was realised in London. Almost all the BEF was in contact with the enemy. He therefore had no substantial reserves for an attack south-west – he might at best provide a few battalions. Gort and Ironside then motored to French HQ to see what Billotte could provide.

They found the French commander in a state of nervous collapse. He suggested that any troops he put into the line would not face an attack.[21] Any operation towards Amiens from Arras would have to be undertaken with what troops Gort could spare.[22]

The Arras counter-attack took place on 21 May. All that Gort could spare were two battalions of infantry and fifty-eight tanks, sixteen of them the heavy Matilda type. The French in the end provided some flank protection. The attack had some success; it destroyed a German column of troops and took a heavy toll on some German light tanks. But it was soon stopped by Rommel (who happened to be on the spot) deploying some anti-aircraft guns (the first use of the deadly 88s in this role).[23] In any case Gort had given his small force very limited objectives and it soon withdrew north of Arras. The attack was not made entirely in vain. The Germans overestimated the amount of British troops in the area and came to the conclusion that some of their panzer divisions must be halted to deal with them. The British would find this delay useful in the coming days.

Meanwhile Churchill had a burst of optimism. On the 20th the French had reconstituted their government. Gamelin was sacked and General Maxime Weygand, Foch's staff officer in 1918, was installed. The new commander met with General Sir John Dill (Vice Chief of the General Staff) on the 20th and promised a converging offensive from north and south to cut off the German columns. Dill warned Churchill that nothing was likely to come of this,[24] but the Prime Minister was enthusiastic, telling Reynaud that he had 'entire confidence' in Weygand.[25]

Churchill crossed back to France on 22 May to meet Weygand to establish if he was in fact the man for the hour. At a meeting of the Supreme War Council later that day Weygand convinced the Prime Minister that he was.[26] After the meeting Churchill issued new instructions to Gort:

(1) The Belgian army should withdraw to the line of the Yser and flood the ground behind them.

(2) The BEF and First French Army should attack southwards at the earliest moment – certainly tomorrow.

(3) The RAF should give maximum support.

(4) The French should attack north from Amiens to meet the Anglo-French attack advancing southwards.[27]

It is reasonable to assume that Gort did not receive these orders with equanimity. The Belgians, far from being able to conduct an orderly retreat in the face of a superior enemy, were showing every sign of collapse. As for the BEF, the German armour was already across their lines of communication; the French First Army showed no signs of cooperation and Gort did not have the luxury of diverting large forces to this attack because most of his force was still in contact with the enemy. Lieutenant-General Henry Pownall, Gort's COS, fumed at these 'impossible' Churchillian orders.[28] Considering this situation, Gort took the bravest decision of his career. He completely ignored Churchill's directive. Instead he withdrew forces from the Escaut to shorten his line and sent two of the divisions to the west to aid his improvised forces along the Canal Line. And instead of attacking out from Arras, he ordered the forces there (5 and 50 Divisions) to evacuate the area and head north to plug a gap around Menin that was appearing as the British sidestepped from the Escaut.[29] In effect what he was doing was carrying out the plan laid down on the night of the 18/19th – he was withdrawing on Dunkirk.

What was happening was this. The Regular divisions of the BEF were sidestepping northwards from the Escaut to Menin and Ypres. The Territorial divisions and the improvised forces on the Canal Line were attempting to hold off the panzer divisions that – having passed to the south of the BEF – were now turning north towards the Channel ports of Boulogne and Calais. The area held by the BEF resembled an area shaped like a U which was ever-decreasing in size but remained open.

Luckily for the BEF, Dill was still on the spot in France and Gort had no difficulty in convincing him that there was no alternative to his plan. He also had no trouble in convincing the Minister of War in London (Eden) that this was the only course. Eden immediately told Gort that he could expect a maximum effort from the RAF and the navy.[30] He also contacted Churchill, who had finally realised the seriousness of the situation and had authorised Gort to operate towards the coast.[31] Evacuation was now inevitable.

The only action that Churchill could now take was to shore up the defence of the Channel ports. Late on the 23rd, 20 Guards Brigade was sent to Boulogne and 30 Brigade to Calais. On the 24th the War Office ordered that Calais be evacuated, but Churchill reversed the decision, furious at what he regarded as defeatism in the General Staff.[32] Instead the commander of 30 Brigade was ordered to fight to the last.[33] That the Guards did, only surrendering on the 26th when they had run out of ammunition. Churchill has been criticised for sacrificing these men but in truth they did delay the panzers by at least two days, buying useful time for the BEF as it crowded around Dunkirk.

The evacuation of the BEF from Dunkirk took place between 26 May and 4 June.[34] There was little that the politicians in London could do to influence events. Churchill had made an early intervention when, after receiving Gort's note on the BEF on 19 May, he ordered the Admiralty 'as a precautionary measure' to 'assemble a large number of small vessels in readiness to proceed to ports and inlets on the French coast'.[35] This was done under the command of Vice-Admiral Bertram Ramsay who was given control of what became Operation Dynamo. From then on it was a matter for the local commanders. The navy, ably led by Captain William Tennant at Dunkirk, organised the army into units at the Dunkirk mole and several improvised piers and started shuttling them home, largely in navy ships but also utilising the 'small ships' that Churchill had ordered assembled. Within the fire and confusion at Dunkirk, an orderly process evolved which eventually saw over 560,000 men returned to Britain – 390,000 from the BEF and 170,000 French troops. Churchill ordered that due consideration be given to the French who manned much of the perimeter around Dunkirk and who were keeping the Germans away from the beaches.[36] The commanders on the spot (Gort and, after him, General Harold Alexander) ignored these instructions and gave the BEF priority. Eventually, none of that mattered as the beachhead held for three days longer than expected. The additional time gained allowed the remaining French troops to be lifted.

For much of the ill-fated campaign of the BEF in France Churchill remained out of touch with the fast-moving events at the front. Had Gort obeyed his instructions, the BEF may well have been lost. When Churchill at last realised the true picture he made some decisive interventions regarding the Channel ports. He watched the evacuation at Dunkirk closely, adding up the daily totals of men evacuated, but could do little to influence events. His real worth in these days lay not so much in influencing events abroad but in countering defeatism at home.

The first inkling that all was not as robust at home as it could be came from the military. Shortly after Churchill came to power, the COS had been working on a paper, 'British Strategy in a Certain Eventuality' – the eventuality being the collapse of France. Churchill had strong views about what Britain would do should that eventuality come to pass. At every meeting with the French, and at many meetings of the War Cabinet and Defence Committee at home, he had stated that whatever happened to France, Britain would fight on. Then on 25 May, as the evacuation from Dunkirk was getting underway, the COS produced their paper. It was intensely gloomy. They concluded, perhaps not unreasonably, that the BEF would be largely lost in France. They also asserted that they held grave doubts about whether the RAF could hold on, even behind the British radar chain, if the Germans occupied the French coast. In these circumstances all depended on whether the navy could prevent an invasion; the Chiefs were doubtful if it could. In essence the COS could see no path to victory without full American military and financial involvement.[37]

There is little doubt that Churchill was shocked by this paper, especially the downbeat assessment given to the role of the RAF and the navy. The document came at a difficult moment for him; it was to be circulated to the War Cabinet, with which, as we will see, Churchill was having problems. He therefore immediately declared that circumstances had changed since the document had been drafted and he gave the COS new terms of reference, including this statement: 'In the event of terms being offered to Britain which would place her entirely at the mercy of Germany ... what are the prospects of our continuing the war alone against Germany and probably Italy.'[38] This was clever wording because it gave the Chiefs little option, unless they embraced the prospect of being 'entirely at the mercy of Germany', of fighting on. In giving new terms of reference he also rendered the old paper obsolete.

The tactic worked. The Chiefs produced a new paper, 'British Strategy in the Near Future', in which they concluded that Britain could indeed hold on. Churchill then muddied the whole position of the COS by debating at length in War Cabinet their statistics on the relative strengths of British and German air power. In the end the matter became so bogged down in detail that the substance of the two papers was never discussed by the

War Cabinet. By default, Churchill's policy of fighting the war out became the Chiefs' policy.[39]

At the same time that Churchill was bringing the COS to heel, he was fighting off Chamberlain and Halifax (particularly Halifax) in the War Cabinet. This story has often been told and will not be repeated at length here. Suffice it to say that on 26 May (when Churchill was also dealing with the crisis in France) Halifax introduced the idea of seeking peace negotiations through Mussolini. He thought this a fruitful line of approach because 'it was not in Herr Hitler's interest to insist on outrageous terms'.[40] The idea that Hitler would seek anything other than outrageous terms was indeed a novel prospect but Chamberlain also thought the Mussolini idea worth following, and the very inexperienced Labour members at this point had little to say. Churchill dodged and weaved his way through many tense meetings of the War Cabinet in the next few days. He bolstered his position by inviting the leader of the Liberal Party (and a sure ally) Archie Sinclair to attend the meetings. He then addressed the wider Cabinet and obtained their approval for his policy of no talks and fighting on. Then the Labour members found their voice and expressed strong disagreement with Halifax's proposition. In the end the Prime Minister prevailed. The war would be fought to the end but in these days in May the whole future of liberal democracy hung in the balance.[41]

While all this was happening, the war in France continued. The French armies along the Somme were still intact, as was a considerable British force consisting of an armoured division, the 51 Highland Division and lines of communication troops, in total about 150,000 men. Churchill thought there remained a slim chance of keeping France in the war. He crossed to meet the French leaders on 11 June, not in Paris, which was deemed insecure, but in Briare on the eastern Loire. He was to be disappointed. He reminded the French of 1918 and how they had clung on after the German assault in March. But Pétain, who had now joined the government, pointed out that in 1918 he had sufficient reserves to call upon. Now he had none. Weygand was no more optimistic, 'I am helpless', he lamented. Then he asked that Britain commit all of Fighter Command to the battle immediately. Churchill was not buying. He pointed out to the French that they were now a secondary consideration. Fighter Command must be kept intact for the coming battle for Britain. Some extra squadrons might

313

intervene but they would be based on airfields in Britain. None would be sent to France.

This agreement lasted hardly a day. On the 13th Churchill was summoned back to France, this time to Tours, well west of Briare, in itself an indication that the situation was deteriorating. French resolve was also deteriorating. Reynaud put two questions to Churchill: would he intervene with Roosevelt to secure immediate aid for France? what would Britain's attitude be if the French sought terms? On the first question Churchill promised to contact Roosevelt but made it clear that the French could expect little from that quarter in the immediate future. On the second question he said if the French made terms Britain would fight on and blockade the French, as it would the rest of Nazi-occupied Europe. Churchill then left for London with an offer to commit a few more squadrons to the battle.[42]

The Prime Minister immediately contacted Roosevelt but the President told him that there was no prospect of American intervention. All seemed lost. However, Attlee then came up with an idea for an Anglo-French union, a prospect that had been floated by some of Churchill's inner circle for some time. A truly remarkable declaration was drafted which proposed that there be one Franco-British nation with common citizenship, that the war would be fought out under the direction of a single War Cabinet and that the union would concentrate its whole energy against the enemy, wherever that may be.[43]

This offer was conveyed to the French government, now at Bordeaux, by the British Ambassador, Sir Roland Campbell. Reynaud was enthusiastic but his Cabinet was now largely defeatist and they turned it down. The whole episode has something of farce about it, yet the offer was no doubt sincerely made. How long the union would have lasted is open to question but no country, especially Britain, gives up sovereignty on a whim.[44]

This was effectively the end of the Anglo-French alliance, but there was one more matter to deal with. In the June days, one issue was of increasing concern to the British: the fate of the French fleet, second only in size to the Royal Navy in European waters. What Churchill required from the French was that their fleet should not fall into German hands. To that end he sent the First Lord of the Admiralty (A.V. Alexander) and the First Sea Lord (Dudley Pound) to Bordeaux to obtain such assurances. Admiral François Darlan brushed aside any suggestion that the fleet would sail to

British-controlled waters but told Alexander and Pound that on no account would he surrender the fleet to the Germans. In the next few days, however, Reynaud resigned, Pétain became premier and an armistice was signed with Germany.[45] Regarding the fleet, the terms stated:

> The French war Fleet – with the exception of that part left at the disposal of the French Government for the protection of French interests in its colonial empire – will be assembled in ports to be specified and there demobilised and disarmed under German or Italian control.[46]

This was hardly reassuring. German control might easily morph into German possession. At this Churchill ran out of patience with the French. No one had worked harder to keep them in the struggle and on more than one occasion the Prime Minister had ignored military advice and committed more fighters to the battle. Now he took steps to recognise General Charles de Gaulle's Council of Liberation as representing France. And he put to the War Cabinet that the French fleet must be dealt with – either it could sail to a British port or to a neutral or American port well away from Europe or it should be sunk. On 30 June the War Cabinet made the fateful decision: these options should be put to the French by the commander of the British Mediterranean Fleet and if the first two were rejected the third should be carried out.[47] The admiral in question, Vice-Admiral Sir James Somerville, cavilled at these instructions and insisted that hostilities between the two fleets should be avoided at all costs.[48] He was overruled by the War Cabinet and told to get on with it. On 3 July he put the propositions to Admiral Gensoul at the French Mediterranean base of Mers-el-Kabir. After lengthy negotiations the French refused to sail to a British port or to anywhere else. At 5.54 p.m. Somerville opened fire. Many ships were either sunk or damaged but one of the heavy French ships (*Strasbourg*) escaped to Toulon. Elsewhere the battleship *Richelieu* was put out of action by torpedo bombers and *Jean Bart* at Casablanca was discovered to have no ammunition. In Britain, French ships in harbour were taken over. At Alexandria the French squadron was demobilised without loss of life after a masterly piece of diplomacy by the British commander on the spot, Vice-Admiral Cunningham. Over 1,000 French sailors died at Mers, a matter that would cause lasting bitterness between France and Britain.[49] All told, however, it is difficult to see what else Churchill could have done. Assurances from Pétain's Vichy regime were worthless; a large French naval presence in the Mediterranean dangerous. For Churchill this was a hateful task but the ruthlessness with which it was carried out was at least a sign to those at home and in the US who doubted Britain's resolve, that indeed this war would be fought to a finish.

In July attention in Britain turned to invasion: would the Germans come by sea or air or both? Churchill had already made changes in the high command to meet invasion – if it came. Ironside was moved to command the Home Army and Dill became CIGS, probably a better match than their original roles. Ironside had little to work with; most equipment had been lost on the beaches at Dunkirk. There were just 300 x 25-pounder guns in the country in June and 140 Matilda tanks, the only British tank that had proved its worth in France. On paper Britain had enough men – 1,270,000 by mid-June – but of these 500,000 were still in training and of the trained troops 275,000 were just back from France with little or no equipment. Ironside distributed most troops around the southern and eastern coasts and established a GHQ line from south of London to the Midlands, incorporating waterways and canals. Along it he placed anti-tank obstacles to break up any German armoured thrusts that broke through the coastal crust.

Churchill considered Ironside's approach misguided and soon (20 July) replaced him with Alan Brooke (II Corps commander in France). Brooke had talked Churchill out of a half-baked idea of establishing some kind of 'redoubt' in Brittany which might be held by those British troops which remained in France after Dunkirk. Instead Brooke insisted that the men be evacuated, which they were. Churchill perhaps remembered the good sense exhibited by Brooke on this occasion and perhaps also that here was a soldier quite willing to stand up to him. On the matter of invasion dispositions, however, they were as one. Both favoured a much thinner coastal crust of troops than Ironside. Brooke in particular wanted as many troops as possible to be withdrawn from the beaches for training and to provide more depth to the defence.

Apart from this intervention Churchill left the general aspects of invasion planning to the service chiefs. Brooke got on with the business of training the troops, which he oversaw with some efficiency. Forbes (C-in-C

Home Fleet) had to be persuaded and then ordered by the Admiralty to have his heavy ships far enough south to intervene should invasion come, but eventually he hammered out an appropriate plan. Air Chief Marshal Sir Hugh Dowding, C-in-C Fighter Command, had already, as we will see, a well-honed organisation to deal with the Luftwaffe.

The Prime Minister kept a very close eye on invasion preparations. On occasion his interventions could only be marginally useful. For example he insisted that long-range guns be installed near Dover to counter similar batteries of German guns near Calais. After much effort this was done but there was no evidence that these guns caused the Germans any harm (or that their guns did much damage in Britain).[50] Air power, not artillery, was the key to controlling the Strait of Dover.[51]

Other interventions had more impact. In June the COS decided that they wished to deploy General Bernard Montgomery's 3 Division, then guarding the south coast, to Northern Ireland to counter a likely German invasion of Eire. Churchill considered such a German move to be highly unlikely and in any case he considered the 3 Division to be essential for the defence of southern England. The Chief of the Air Staff (Newall) assured Churchill that the move had been 'carefully weighed up'. Nevertheless, the Prime Minister took the matter to the War Cabinet and in the end the 3 Division remained where it was.[52] Similarly, Churchill prevented the redeployment of 2 Canadian Division to Iceland, which had been occupied by Britain as a counter to the fall of Denmark and Norway. He regarded this division highly and wished it to remain in England for invasion duties – which it did.[53]

In general the Prime Minister insisted that he be kept informed of all aspects of invasion planning. He admonished his Military Secretary, Major-General Hastings Ismay when he considered that vital service telegrams were not getting through to him.[54] He asked the COS to provide him all kinds of information, from the number of tank-carrying barges the enemy might have at Calais, to the number of troops held back in reserve, to the assurance that destroyer forces were well placed to intercept any invasion force.[55]

One example may be quoted. After inspecting the defences in East Anglia, Churchill wrote to the Minister of War (Eden) and the CIGS (Dill):

I was much concerned to find that the 1st Division which has an excep-
tionally high proportion of equipment and include a Brigade of Guards,
should be dispersed along the beaches, instead of being held in reserve
for counter-attack. What is the number of Divisions which are now free
and out of the line, and what is the argument for keeping Divisions with
a high equipment of guns, etc on the beaches?[56]

The 1st Division was shortly thereafter moved back in reserve.

If Churchill made one error of judgement in this period it came from his
desire to take the offensive. He backed the rather hare-brained French
scheme to invade the Vichy-controlled colony of Senegal in West Africa.
De Gaulle thought that the arrival of a French-led expedition might rally
the French colonies and seize the useful port of Dakar. The troops were
largely French but the force had a considerable British naval component
from the Mediterranean – which it had to have because the British had
sunk a considerable proportion of the French fleet.[57] All told, two battleships, an aircraft carrier, three cruisers and ten destroyers accompanied
the expedition and were therefore absent from early September to early
October, thus depriving the Home Fleet of a considerable reinforcement
in invasion season. This fact was noted by the Assistant Chief of the
Naval Staff but Churchill insisted that the ships go. Perhaps luckily, the
expedition failed with some rapidity and the ships were quickly returned
to Gibraltar.[58]

* * * * *

While anti-invasion planning was underway Britain prepared for an
onslaught from the air. Air strategy in the inter-war period had been dominated by the 'shadow of the bomber'. Certainly many in Britain had believed
that an enemy bomber force might be capable of delivering a knockout
blow to the life of the country. The most sophisticated air defence system in
the world was the result. In 1940 the radar chain had two components –
a Chain Home system of towers that could see enemy aircraft forming
up in western Belgium and Northern France and a Chain Home Low system
that could see low-flying aircraft assembling over the Channel. These
'blips' on the screen were sent by underground cable to Fighter Command

headquarters at Bentley Priory, north of London, where the C-in-C of Fighter Command, Hugh Dowding, presided. There this information, along with that from the 30,000 personnel of the Observer Corps (who tracked raids once they had crossed the coast) was 'filtered' into specific raids. The raid intelligence was then passed on to Fighter Group headquarters, where the decision was made about which squadrons from the main or 'sector' airfields might be directed against the raiders. When they received this intelligence the sector commanders scrambled the designated squadrons or those from satellite airfields under their control. The system was so efficient that it might take just five minutes or less from information arriving from the radar chain at Bentley Priory to 'squadron airborne'.

In 1940 Fighter Command was divided into four groups. 13 Group, based on Newcastle, covered the north of England and Scotland. The Midlands was defended by 12 Group based at Nottingham, and 10 Group based west of Bristol covered the West Country. But the most important group was 11 Group, based on Uxbridge. Its airfields were scattered across south-eastern England and included London and many of the south coast ports. Essentially 11 Group fought the impending battle. It was commanded by Air Vice Marshal Sir Keith Park, a tactician of genius; he and Dowding were the key figures in the Battle of Britain.

In terms of numbers the British seemed well outmatched. The Germans had a total of 2,462 serviceable aircraft in July 1940, of which 900 were single-engine fighters and 1,000 were bombers (the remainder were dive bombers or twin-engine fighters). In contrast the British had just 752 serviceable fighters, of which 469 were Hurricanes and 283 Spitfires.[59] Numbers do not tell the entire story. The Germans had little idea of how the British air defence system worked. They knew the large towers around the coast were radar towers because they were developing radar of their own, but they had no idea of how the radar chain was linked to Fighter Command headquarters or how the information it provided was sent to the squadrons. In particular the Germans had no idea about the crucial role played by sector airfields or even that there were sector airfields. In addition the Luftwaffe was led by Hermann Goering, who had no fixity of purpose and was incapable of giving strategic direction to his Luftflotte commanders (Albert Kesselring and Hugo Sperrle). The Luftwaffe therefore tended to bomb at random and to switch targets at a whim.

The Battle of Britain may be divided into three sections: overture, crisis, and diminuendo. The overture began on 10 July 1940 when large numbers of enemy aircraft began bombing targets along the southern coast of England. Typically, there was no concentration of German effort in this phase. From 10 July to 7 August there were forty-five major attacks in this area, but apart from Dover – which was attacked on twelve occasions – there were no repeated raids on other targets. In all the Germans achieved very little in this period. They sank only 24,000 tons of shipping in the Channel, they put no airfields out of commission and they failed to destroy even one of the towers in the vital radar chain.

All this allowed Park to fight the battle as he wanted. On receipt of information from Bentley Priory he scrambled just enough squadrons to interfere seriously with any one raid. The radar chain gave him about thirty to forty minutes' warning of an impending attack, and that proved enough for the sector airfields to get their aircraft aloft and to a sufficient height to intercept (or be 'vectored on') to the incoming enemy. It was an advantage in this period that the German command sought to commit no more than 16 per cent of its total force to the battle on any one day. This allowed Park, with his much smaller force, also to economise. At no time did he commit more than 50 per cent of his available squadrons on one day in this period. This meant that on any given day the British pilots might well be outnumbered (hence 'the few') but in enough strength to break up the German bombers. In a typical raid on 10 July, for example, a force of just eight Spitfires attacked at least eighty German aircraft, destroyed three of them and damaged four others at a cost of just one Spitfire damaged.

The system, it should be noted, was far from perfect. Many personnel at the radar stations were relatively inexperienced and made mistakes both in estimating the number of incoming aircraft and the height at which they were flying. Also the Observer Corps initially had difficulty in accurately identifying the kind of aircraft overhead or was unable to identify them at all because of cloudy conditions – a situation not unknown during an English summer. Nevertheless at the end of the 'overture' period the British had more aircraft available and more pilots to fly them than when the battle commenced.

This desultory battle was ended by Hitler. His new instructions to Goering were to concentrate on the destruction of the RAF – in the air, on the ground and through an attack on aircraft factories. Goering immediately outlined a new plan against Britain. It was to open on 5 August, named Eagle Day – proving if nothing else that the Nazis were good at grandiloquent kitsch. The list of targets, however, showed little sign of a determined plan. Certainly the RAF was given high priority (how could it not be?) but ports, merchant ships, warships and other installations were included in the list. In other words the Germans were about to make the same mistake as previously by spreading their targets too wide, not that either Hitler or Goering seemed to notice. The only specific direction came from the German High Command (Oberkommando der Wehrmacht – OKW), which suggested that the radar chain be attacked in the first wave.[60]

Even regarding the RAF, Goering's plan had many problems. The Germans could hardly destroy the force on the ground in some kind of surprise attack as they had the Polish and French air forces because the warning given by the radar chain would allow most aircraft to be in the air. Nor if airfields were attacked did the Germans know which ones belonged to Fighter Command rather than Bomber Command or Coastal Command. Indeed, in this period the Luftwaffe spent an inordinate time in rendering Eastchurch Airfield inoperable – a field which belonged to Coastal Command and contained no Hurricanes or Spitfires. Even if Fighter Command airfields were hit, the Germans had no idea which were the vital Sector airfields or that the crucial targets there were the huts that allowed them to communicate to Group HQ for radar intelligence. And, should the runways of some airfields be cratered, in many instances the fighters could take off from grass strips. As for aircraft factories, Luftwaffe Intelligence only had the vaguest idea of where they were, evidenced by the facts that during the entire battle just one factory was hit (the Spitfire factory at Southampton), that the bombers that hit it were probably aiming for another target and that the Germans never realised that they had hit a vital target – evidenced by there being no follow-up raids.

This is not to say that German pressure on the RAF did not increase during this period. As an overture to Eagle Day a specially trained unit of the Luftwaffe with excellent navigational skills attacked the radar chain. In a matter of minutes on 12 August four radar towers (Pevensey, Rye, Dunkirk (Kent) and Dover) were bombed before a single British fighter could intervene. Shortly after this, Ventnor on the Isle of Wight was virtually destroyed.

Though three of these stations were only out of action for some hours (Ventnor was out for eleven days), it was a sign of serious intent on the part of the Luftwaffe and if continued spelled great danger for the British air defence system. But these raids were not continued. Goering apparently questioned the value of the attacks and they stopped.

Eagle Day (13 August) turned out to be a fiasco for the Germans. Cloudy conditions caused Goering to call it off, but only the fighters received the recall. The bombers flew on unescorted and a massacre was only averted when the RAF failed to find them in the cloud. At the end of the day the Germans had lost forty-three machines; Fighter Command just fourteen. More directed attacks by the Luftwaffe increased after this, however. The next month saw the most concentrated attack on Fighter Command airfields of the entire battle. In all, sixty-seven airfield attacks were made although twenty-seven of them were against airfields that contained no fighters. Nevertheless, some sector airfields were seriously damaged in this period. Kenley was put out of action on 18 August; Biggin Hill reduced to a shambles between 30 August and 1 September; Hornchurch disabled on 31 August. But no further raids against these followed, and by various means of improvisation the airfields were returned to working order within a few days. Once again the Luftwaffe dispersed its effort attacking such non-RAF targets as Portland, Chichester, east coast convoys, Yarmouth, Ipswich and many other targets.

One change in German tactics proved disastrous to them. In mid-August it was decided by Goering to attack the Midlands using squadrons based in Denmark and Norway. Because of the great distances involved, the bombers would be escorted only by the twin-engine Me 110s. The result was a massacre. The radar chain picked up the attack well out to sea and squadrons from 12 Group were scrambled to deal with it. The raiders lost twenty-seven aircraft for no losses from the RAF. The experiment was never repeated.

By 6 September Fighter Command in 11 Group was certainly feeling the strain. Five of its six sector airfields had been dealt savage blows and the strain on the pilots was intense. Park made all this very clear in a report to Dowding where he noted that the efficiency of his group had been severely degraded and that the situation was grave. Dowding agreed but replied that despite the incessant attacks 11 Group was still functioning and that the temporary expedients to overcome various aspects of the destruction were working well. In short, he thought that Fighter Command could continue to absorb punishment for some considerable time.

As it happened, Fighter Command was about to receive a reprieve. On 7 September 1940 the Luftwaffe turned its attention to London in a massive daylight raid that marked the beginning of the Blitz. It is often suggested that this raid was in reprisal for raids that the RAF had carried out on Berlin in late August in retaliation for bombs dropped (accidentally) on the outskirts of London. This is not correct. Luftwaffe Intelligence was telling Goering that the RAF was at the end of its tether and that the way to finish it off was to select a target that the few remaining fighters were bound to defend; that target was London.

London was to suffer some grievous raids in the next few days but the turn to the capital worked decisively against the Luftwaffe. In the first instance, the additional distance which the Me 109 fighters had to travel gave them just ten minutes over the capital before they had to turn back to refuel, and this allowed the Hurricanes and Spitfires to take a fearful toll on what were, for some of the journey, unescorted bombers. Moreover, the appearance of the Luftwaffe over London allowed those squadrons from 12 Group just north of the capital to engage the enemy in numbers, thus taking some pressure off Park's hard-pressed formations. In addition the extra time taken to reach the capital allowed Park to send his squadrons up in successive waves to engage the waves of bombers both on their way to London and returning. This meant that the fighters had in total a longer period of time to engage the enemy than was possible in the tip-and-run raids of the earlier periods. And while the enemy were engaging London they were not attacking the fighter airfields which could use this period for repair and maintenance work.

This is not to deny that this period also took a heavy toll on 11 Group and especially its pilots. In some cases the availability of pilots in front-line squadrons fell alarmingly. Dowding reacted to this situation by rotating pilots from squadrons in quieter areas into 11 Group and ensuring that those rotated were the best pilots. So while pilots available per serviceable aircraft did fall from July to August, they began to rise thereafter and ended the battle with a higher figure than they began with. And, as Park noted at a crisis meeting held in early September, while his own position was parlous, he thought the position of the Luftwaffe both regarding pilots and aircraft was worse. Park was correct. The main German problem was the drop in serviceable aircraft. From early August until the end of September serviceability in single-engine fighters and in bombers fell by 28 per cent. This was not sustainable, especially as Hitler had already made the decision to invade Russia, where a flourishing Luftwaffe must play a major role.

As a result of all this Goering changed tactics once again. The bomber force would now be used sparingly by day. Instead of bombers he would equip Me 109s with bomb racks to make tip-and-run sweeps over southern England. These sweeps proved difficult for Fighter Command to counter, but the bomb capacity of the aircraft was very low (250 lbs) and they did very little damage. They were in fact a recognition that Germany had lost the Battle of Britain.

Churchill's most decisive intervention in the Battle of Britain came just as it commenced. Sometime in early July Sinclair told Churchill that he was considering removing Dowding from his post as head of Fighter Command when his tenure ran out in four months. Churchill told Sinclair that he was 'much taken aback' by this proposal and continued:

> Personally, I think he is one of the very best men you have got, and I say this after having been in contact with him for about two years. I have greatly admired the whole of his work in the Fighter Command . . . In fact he has my full confidence. I think it is a pity for an officer so gifted and so trusted to be working on such a short tenure . . . and I hope you will consider whether it is not in the public interest that his appointment should be indefinitely prolonged.[61]

Needless to say, after this missive Sinclair's obtuse decision was reversed.

With this confidence in the leadership, Churchill rarely intervened in the way Park and Dowding fought the Battle of Britain but he kept a very close watching brief. It is clear from many sources that he received the daily 'score' of aircraft shot down, remarking as early as 13 July that the balance was very favourable to the RAF.[62] He also pored over the charts and diagrams produced for him by Frederick Lindemann, his scientific adviser, and identified in early August that British production of fighters must be overhauling that of the Germans.[63] In this he was correct. In 1940 Britain produced many more aircraft than Germany. During the Battle of Britain the Germans lost ground in every type of aircraft involved except dive bombers, which were entirely withdrawn from the battle after catastrophic losses in August.[64]

As usual, Churchill was concerned with many of the details of the battle. He was aware of the pilot shortage and sought reassurances that it was being met. He noted that Dowding was adding aircraft to squadrons instead of creating new squadrons in an effort to save on administrative manpower and again sought confirmation that this was the best procedure.[65] He was concerned to develop small rockets to protect airfields and put considerable energy into this weapon, which proved in the end to be a complete flop.[66] And as always he urged commanders to comb out administrative personnel to increase numbers at the sharp end, although there is no evidence that this amounted to anything substantial.[67] More importantly he halted the movement of pilots to Canada and South Africa for training, insisting that the crisis demanded that other facilities in Britain be found for them so that they could be thrown into the battle as soon as possible. This was done and overseas training only resumed when the battle had been won.[68]

One intervention produced immediate results. On 28 August Churchill visited Manston Airfield, which had been cratered so often that it had been abandoned. He was shocked to learn that just 150 staff were available to fill in craters for the whole of Fighter Command. He insisted that four crater-filling companies be established with 250 personnel with motor transport to move them rapidly from station to station as required. He also insisted that stations had supplies of gravel and other filling materials on hand so that there should be no delay.[69] It might be thought extraordinary that it took a prime ministerial intervention to rectify this oversight.

During the height of the Battle of Britain Churchill made nine visits to Fighter Command stations: one to Manston, two to Kenley, two to Dowding's headquarters at Bentley Priory and four to Park's 11 Group headquarters at Uxbridge.[70] During the visits to Dowding's and Park's headquarters Churchill followed the action on the large maps which recorded data received from the radar chain and the reactions by the flight controllers to send squadrons to intercept the raiders. There is a famous description of his 15 September visit to Park in his memoirs which perhaps indicates that he was not aware of a controversial aspect of Dowding's strategy during the battle. At one point when the display in the control room indicated that Park had scrambled all squadrons in 11 Group and some adjacent squadrons in 12 Group also, Churchill asked about additional reserves. Park replied there were none.[71] On the day this was literally true. There were no more fighters in the vicinity that could be called upon. But the fact was that were many more Spitfires and Hurricanes within Britain than those in 11 Group and adjacent squadrons in 12 Group. At no time during the battle did Park have more than 43 per cent of the available front-line fighters in his group. If the squadrons near to London in 12 Group are added, the figure does not climb much above 50 per cent.[72] Some of the remainder were in 10 Group in the west of England but most were in 13 Group covering northern England and Scotland. No doubt Dowding wanted to keep some aircraft beyond the range where escorted German bombers could harm them, but could not some of these aircraft have provided the reserves that were absent on 15 September? It was no doubt possible for Dowding to move some fighters south. Park certainly thought so and wrote to Dowding after the rout of the German attack from Scandinavia asking for additional squadrons.[73] Dowding resisted and in the end his policy appeared justified. Park, with a little help from 12 Group and 10 Group, won the battle and Britain emerged with a Fighter Command that was stronger than it had been when the battle started. However, it is hard to doubt that if Churchill had got wind of this policy, he would have instructed Dowding to move at least some fighters south. Of course it is possible that he realised and approved Dowding's strategy and just wrote for dramatic effect in his memoirs about the lack of reserves, but the absence of any mention of those northern 'reserves' in the documents indicates that, master of detail though he was, this aspect of the battle escaped the Prime Minister.

* * * * *

The last campaign in 1940 with which Churchill had to deal was the Blitz. This began with the day attack on London on 7 September 1940 and continued against London and many other British cities until May 1941, when most of the Luftwaffe was withdrawn from the west and deployed against Russia. There is no need to give a detailed account of the Blitz. The story is too well known and the operations of the Luftwaffe were beyond the control of any British politician.[74] It must be emphasised, however, that the bombing of civilians on the scale suffered by London and other cities was unprecedented. In London, for example, over 13,000 people were killed in 1940–1941 and 18,000 wounded. In just September and October 1940 178,000 homes were destroyed and in the period September 1940 to April 1941 there were never fewer than 20,000 people homeless on any given night.[75] Other cities of lesser size such as Coventry and Liverpool suffered even more in proportion than London. There was thus no precedent to indicate what effect this onslaught would have on Britain's ability to wage war.

Although widely anticipated, the aerial attack on London found the government largely unprepared. Shelters had been built before the war but they were built above ground and shoddily constructed. It was soon found that they were death traps.[76] There was little that Churchill could do other than to order that better shelters be constructed. What he could do was break a bureaucratic deadlock that had arisen about whether people should be allowed to use Underground stations (the Tube) for shelter. He wrote a scathing letter stating that he was in favour of this form of shelter, that tickets should be provided to those who wished to use the Tube and in general that the Home Secretary should get on with it.[77]

Britain also did not have an effective night fighter in this period. But a method was discovered that at least prevented some German aircraft from finding their target. In May a young scientist, R.V. Jones, discovered that the Germans were using radio beams to direct bombers onto their targets. There was widespread scepticism about Jones's findings until Lindemann drew Churchill's attention to the discovery. Jones (aided by an Enigma intercept, though Jones was not to know this) convinced the Prime Minister that the Germans were in fact using beams, and research was begun on a method of countering them. Soon jamming devices were in place that managed to confuse some German raids (though it must be said that most cities were obvious enough targets without directional beams). Without Churchill's interest, however, jamming would have been much delayed.

Churchill's main contribution during the Blitz was no doubt his touring of the blitzed cities to see the damage for himself. From Mass Observation and Home Morale reports we know that these visits had a positive effect on the population. There also seems to have been a determination on the part of those visited to ensure that Churchill was providing the strong leadership they required, that there would be no slackening of resolve to prosecute the war and that Germany would be bombed in retaliation. Churchill provided all of this and Germany would in the years to come reap the fruits of that resolve.

1940 was Churchill's year, yet not perhaps in quite the way that is commonly thought. On military operations he had little influence. Events in France unfolded at such lightning speed that he was often well behind the action at the front and some of his instructions to military commanders might have led to disaster had they been followed. Similarly, in the Battle of Britain he could observe closely but only intervened at the margins. No doubt the confidence he had in Dowding and Park was a major factor here. He hardly felt the need to involve himself in a battle that was being well managed, as his daily perusal of statistics revealed. His attempts to keep France in the war were persistent, heartfelt but unavailing.

He was of course the vital man in this year of crisis. Though hard pressed by Halifax and to a lesser extent Chamberlain to make some form of cobbled-together peace which must have ended disastrously for Britain, he outmanoeuvred them and ensured that his policy of victory at all costs prevailed. He also outmanoeuvred the Chiefs of Staff who showed much less confidence in Britain's chances of survival than the facts warranted. In this area Churchill demonstrated rather more military realism than the experts advising him. Above all he gave single-minded, strong and clear leadership of a type that was in tune with the stern will of the people that this war should be vigorously prosecuted. His speeches, his visits to ruined cities and the fact there could be no doubt about the way the country was being led made him the indispensable man. Churchill, in 1940, ensured that whatever 1941 brought, the war would be fought to an end.

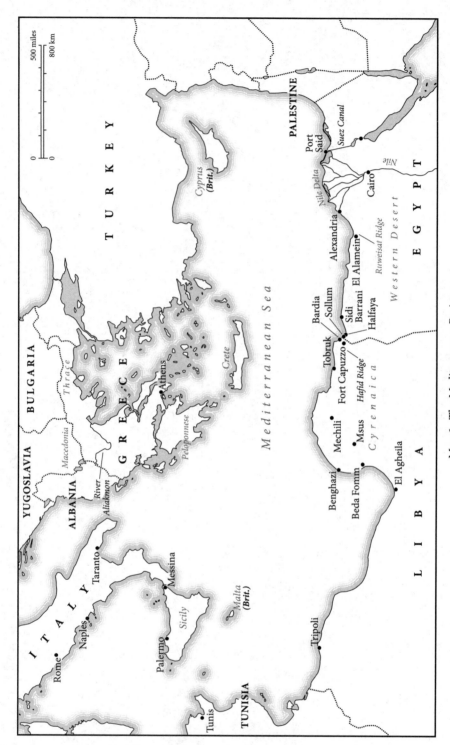

Map 6. The Mediterranean Basin.

CHAPTER 15

THE DESERT – WAVELL'S WAR
1939–1942

AFTER DUNKIRK THE BRITISH were not to engage the main army of their main enemy for four years. Indeed, in the weeks that followed the evacuation it was not at all clear how they were to engage an enemy army of any kind. Mussolini soon provided the answer. On 10 June 1940 he declared war on Britain and France. France soon left the scene, concluding an armistice with Germany on 25 June. Britain now faced Italy alone in the Mediterranean. And this situation saw Britain well outnumbered in most areas. In capital ships, for example, the Italian navy outnumbered British capital ships eight to one. In troops Mussolini had seven times the force in Libya that Britain had in neighbouring Egypt. At least in this area of adjoining colonies, Britain had a chance of engaging an Axis army, even if it was regarded as a second-rate one. Indeed Britain, if it wished to maintain any presence in the Mediterranean at all, was required to engage and defeat the Italians.

Yet in June 1940 Britain had just 30,000 troops in the Nile Delta – hardly sufficient force, it was thought, to take on the Italian Tenth Army of 250,000 men in Libya. Obviously, to conduct offensive operations from Egypt, the British would need to reinforce the Egyptian garrison. The question was – where were the troops to be found, given that the remnants of the BEF and the newly forming armies in Britain would be on anti-invasion duty for some time? The reinforcements would come from the Empire and the

Dominions – from the Indian Army and from Australia, New Zealand and South Africa. Without these forces a substantial Mediterranean campaign would have been unthinkable. If Britain could not strike back, the Empire could.

Reinforcements soon started to arrive. From August to October 1940 (while Britain was still under threat of invasion) just four convoys with a mere 30,000 troops and equipment were sent from Britain to Egypt. In the same period six convoys arrived from India and Australia with an additional 46,000 men from the Indian Army and Anzac forces.[1] At the same time that troops were flowing into Egypt, aircraft of various types were shipped to Takoradi on the Gold Coast and then flown by a circuitous route to the Sudan and then to Cairo.[2] Meanwhile, the fleet in the Eastern Mediterranean was increased from one battleship to three, from three cruisers to six and flotillas of destroyers and submarines were despatched.[3] Admiral Pound thought that the fleet might have to abandon its base at Alexandria but this was vetoed by Churchill, a decision that was thoroughly approved by the local commander, Vice-Admiral Andrew Cunningham.[4]

The attraction of increasing British forces in Egypt was that the Egyptian/ Libyan border was the only area where the British were actually in direct contact with Axis forces. Considering the vast literature about Britain's so-called Mediterranean strategy, this needs to be emphasised. The British fought in the desert, not because they considered the Mediterranean the most appropriate theatre, not because they saw Italy as an easy target and certainly not because they saw the Mediterranean as a route back to mainland Europe. They were fighting there after June 1940 because they could fight the enemy nowhere else.

In command of these troops was General Sir Archibald Wavell. He had taken up his command at Cairo in June 1939 but found himself in charge of British forces in Palestine, the Sudan, Transjordan and Cyprus. He was also to be responsible for all war plans in British Somaliland, Aden, Iraq and the Persian Gulf.[5] These enormous responsibilities were not changed on the outbreak of war with Germany or on Italian belligerency. Wavell was left with an impossible task. He was in charge of the entire British Middle East. He also lacked any guidance from London as to what his priorities should be.[6] However, as the war progressed and Italy became an enemy, he began work on a plan to invade Libya from the Western Desert.[7]

This is how matters remained until Churchill brought his mind to bear on the situation in Egypt in July 1940. Already Churchill was unhappy with what he thought of as the lack of action from Cairo. He considered that matters were being run in a 'dead-alive' manner and he therefore invited Wavell, whom he had never met, to London to explain his situation.[8] This meeting is said to have gone badly because Wavell's inarticulateness reminded Churchill of Haig. Nevertheless, Wavell gave a clear exposition of the Middle Eastern position to the Chiefs of Staff in which he emphasised that if the Italians advanced in force he would have to withdraw but that he doubted, given the state of the Italian army, that any serious threat to Egypt would develop.[9] Wavell then had a pleasant meeting with Churchill at Chequers, after which the Prime Minister informed his colleagues in the War Cabinet that 'he had taken a great liking to General Wavell' and that a convoy of armour should be sent through the Mediterranean rather than around the Cape to reinforce him.[10] This last suggestion led to a long debate between the Prime Minister and the Chiefs of Staff, who in the end over-ruled Churchill – the armour would proceed via South Africa.[11]

Meanwhile Churchill had written a Directive to Wavell making it clear to him that the defence of Egypt was his primary task and that the Western Desert must be fortified so as to withstand a major invasion by Italian forces.[12] There was not long to wait. On 13 September, after heavy shelling of positions that had already been abandoned by the British, the Italian Tenth Army crossed the Egyptian frontier. They then inched forward to Sidi Barrani, where they halted for lack of good roads to carry supplies and water. The commander of the Italian forces, General Rodolfo Graziani, announced that he would not be ready to make a further move until mid-December.[13]

Other Italian forces were ready to move before this date. On 28 October Italy invaded Greece from positions in Albania which they had occupied in 1939. Britain under Chamberlain had guaranteed Greek independence and Churchill was hardly likely to repudiate that policy. However, Churchill was also impatient that Wavell launch an offensive against the Italian invaders of Egypt, so he attempted to pressure Wavell by saying that in the absence of an attack in the Western Desert, aid to Greece would become his first priority. If an attack in the desert was launched, on the other hand, only token forces need be sent to Greece. He concluded:

Trust you will grasp situation firmly, abandoning negative and passive policies and seizing opportunity which has come into your hands. Safety first is the road to ruin in war, even if you had the safety which you have not. Send me your proposals earliest or say you have none to make.[14]

In fact, as Eden – who was on a visit to the Middle East as Minister of War – was soon to find out, Wavell needed no prodding. He had been planning for some time to attack the Italians but in a misguided sense of security had not felt able to impart this secret to Churchill during his visit to Britain. Even now Wavell instructed Eden that he could only pass the information to the Prime Minister verbally, which Eden did on 8 November when he returned to London.[15] This information, the fact that the Greeks had halted the Italian advance, and the destruction of a number of Italian warships in harbour at Taranto, convinced Churchill that the time was ripe for Wavell to implement his plan.[16] What in particular worried him was that Enigma intelligence was indicating that the Germans were building up forces in Bulgaria. One obvious purpose for such a build-up would be to invade Greece from the north-east to help out the struggling Italian armies.[17]

Churchill was keen that Wavell launch his attack before the Germans could strike in Greece. He demanded a timetable from Ismay and insisted the role of the navy in the operation incorporate landings from the sea behind the enemy front.[18] He also pestered Wavell for details of the attack and pointed out to him that the sooner 'Compass' (the code name of the attack) was undertaken the better.[19] Indeed, so often did Churchill write to Wavell that Dill and Eden had to intervene, Dill becoming 'very angry' with the Prime Minister's interference.[20] In Churchill's mind Greece now very much took second place to an attack in the desert. Munitions and some squadrons of Gladiator fighters were despatched to Athens but Hurricanes hitherto earmarked for Greece were diverted to Wavell on Churchill's instructions.[21] Yet, although Wavell was clearly determined to take action in the desert, Churchill was not satisfied with his preparations. He took exception to the Commander-in-Chief describing the operation as 'a raid' and told Dill that he was afraid Wavell was failing 'to rise to the height of circumstances', adding, 'I never worry about action, but only inaction.'[22] There must have been a sense of relief all round when Operation Compass began in the early hours of 9 December 1940.

Churchill's relief might have been short-lived if he had realised that Wavell was attacking with just two divisions – the 7 Armoured and the 4 Indian – about 36,000 men. The infantry division would, however, be rein-forced by heavy tanks (Matildas) from the 7 Royal Tank Regiment, the armour of which could not be penetrated by Italian artillery. Facing them was the Italian Tenth Army with around 250,000 troops of varying quality.[23] British patrols had established an ascendancy over their Italian opponents in the summer, though, and the British commanders (Wavell and Major-General Richard O'Connor, who was in operational control) were aware that their artillery and tanks were far superior to anything that the Italians possessed.[24]

The British also had air superiority with a motley force consisting of 48 fighters (Hurricanes and Gladiators) and 116 bombers (Wellingtons, Blenheims and a squadron of obsolescent Bombays).[25] This superiority was essential to keep British preparations from the Italians and concealing the approach march of the attacking force.

The battle had been carefully planned by O'Connor, 'a wisp of a man, with a bold spirit and a shrewd brain'.[26] The 4 Indian Division would carry out a shallow left hook through the desert and then turn north and attack a number of Italian advanced positions or camps. These consisted of rectan-gular walled structures, surrounded by an anti-tank ditch but with a gap in it, usually on the north-west corner, to allow easy resupply – a fact that was known to the British from their summer patrolling. While these camps were being dealt with the 7 Armoured Division, equipped with lighter cruiser tanks, would operate on the left flank of the Indians to protect them from interventions from rearward Italian formations around Sollum and in the desert at Safaris and Rabia. Further operations would depend on results. A small group of men (Selby Force) would advance along the very edge of the coast as a distraction from the main battle to the south.[27]

The ground across which these operations would be conducted deserves some comment. Although the area was colloquially known as the 'Western Desert' it should not be thought of as a wilderness of sweeping sand dunes as found in the Sahara. The strip of land which hugged the coast from Alexandria to Benghazi was rather an area of rock and gravel with low clumps of salt bush under thin layers of sand. It rose from the coast to a feature of varying width known as the 'escarpment'. This higher ground was passable to wheeled vehicles and tanks although the going could be very tough.[28] The area was cursed with strong winds which whipped up sand storms of some ferocity. Alan Moorehead describes one of these thus:

> At Bagush [near Mersa Matruh] it blocked visibility down to half a dozen yards ... The dust came up through the engine, through the chinks of the car body and round the corners of the closed windows. Soon everything in the car was powdered with grit and sand. It crept up your nose and down your throat, itching unbearably and making it difficult to breathe. It got in your ears, matted your hair, and from behind sand goggles your eyes kept weeping and smarting ... I have known soldiers to wear their gas masks in a [sand storm], and others to give way to fits of vomiting. Sometimes a [sand storm] may blow for days, making you feel that you will never see light and air and feel cool-ness again.[29]

Through this hell tanks had to manoeuvre, trucks haul equipment, artillery be positioned and men prepare to fight and kill.

O'Connor's plan worked about as well as any battle plan can. There were occasional mistakes and mis-directions, but the Italian camps could not face the fire from 72 x 25-pounder artillery pieces and an attack by skilled infantry supported by tanks impervious to Italian guns. This is not to say that the Italians immediately surrendered. Some did, but in general their artillery fought hard and fired with some accuracy against armour which they had no hope of denting. After the camps had fallen the infantry turned north and took Sidi Barrani. It was then that O'Connor decided there was scope for further operations. He had now 20,000 prisoners under rudimen-tary guard for a loss of 700 of his own men.[30] The small port of Bardia now called, as did the larger and more significant harbour at Tobruk.

These operations would not be conducted by the 4 Indian Division. One rather bizarre aspect of Wavell's planning had been his intention to remove this division from the desert after the capture of the Italian camps and transfer it to operations in the Sudan where Italian forces had overrun the British-held fort of Kassala. Its place would be taken by the untested 6 Australian Division, the first battles of which would be against two defended ports.

The 16 Australian Brigade captured Bardia on 7 January 1941. An interesting note in its War Diary records that the 6 Division troops were mocked as they trained in Sydney as being the worst representatives of the layabouts and the unemployed.[31] If that was the case, nine months' training in Palestine had hardened them and they captured the town as though on a training exercise. Nor did the Italians meekly surrender:

> They ONLY threw down their arms after our troops had weathered the storm of their f[iel]d guns and SAA [small arms ammunition] barrage and then at bayonet point. The Italians shot it out with our men right up to their own doorsteps. It was then, at the last moment ... that the enemy's morale collapsed.[32]

Tobruk was the prize, however. Its extensive port would allow supplies to be shipped to the forward troops faster and in much greater quantity than via the coast road. Any advance beyond Tobruk that left it in enemy hands did so at its peril.[33]

The defences constructed by the Italians around the port were extensive, if incomplete in some areas. Around the 30-mile perimeter which defended the port was a double wire fence, 5 feet high. Outside the fence was an anti-tank ditch 20 feet wide and 12 feet deep. It was, however, unfinished in the western and southern sections, where it was very shallow. In front of the incomplete sectors of the ditch the Italians had laid minefields and in front of those a series of booby traps triggered by trip wires. Along the wire was a line of strongpoints, concreted – except on top – but surrounded by their own wire and ditches. Five hundred yards behind them stood a second line. Each strongpoint had one or two machine guns and an anti-tank gun. The whole defence, with the 61 Division and units from other formations, was backed with 140 field guns and 68 heavier pieces, 120 tanks and an infantry counter-attack battalion.[34] The main weakness of the defences was that they lacked depth. A break-in of a few miles would see enemy troops overlooking the port.

For the Australians Tobruk presented a considerable problem: not only were they required to capture it, as the only infantry in the rebadged XIII Corps, but if the British advance was to continue they had to capture it cheaply. The attack was to be made in the southern sector where the anti-tank ditch lay unfinished. The plan was for 16 Brigade to break into the perimeter, roll it up and capture any advanced field guns. The 19 Brigade would then advance through the ground captured and thrust deeply into the heart of the defences. The port area was to be taken by the second day.[35]

The key to the plan lay with the artillery. The 6 Division had available 144 guns of various calibres. They also had an artillery commander of great skill. Brigadier Ned Herring had been an artilleryman in many of the major battles of the First World War, including the successful Battle of Amiens. Although he was not a Regular officer he had retained much of what he had learned. At Tobruk he faced the same problems as any artilleryman on the Western Front: how to minimise the amount of hostile shell fire during the attack; how to neutralise sufficient of the enemy defences while the troops moved to capture them; and finally how to protect the attacking formations as they went forward. Herring's solutions were methodical. He located the enemy batteries by a combination of the flash-spotting techniques used in the First World War, aerial photographs (it was a considerable help that the British had aerial superiority during the entire Compass operations) and using those photographs with survey techniques to give the exact coordinates of enemy batteries on the artillery maps. The same combination of photography/survey techniques was also used to locate the Italian strongpoints. The attacking troops would be protected by a creeping barrage, fired by the 25-pounders, which lifted at 100 yards per minute and lasted until the attackers were well within the enemy defensive zone.[36] An important point was that the attack would be covered by the entire complement of divisional artillery.

The plan was studied and altered and discussed at a series of conferences attended by the commanding officers of the division and the brigades. Zero hour was fixed at 5.40 a.m. on 21 January 1941.[37] To familiarise the men with the ground across which they would attack, scale models were made for them to study.

The first men to move into no man's land were sappers sent forward with sharp sticks, scissors and a revolver. These men were to remove the booby traps and 'delouse' the belts of mines. To distract the enemy while this work was underway there was a naval bombardment of the port, bombing from low-flying aircraft and demonstrations from the 7 Armoured and the 17 Brigade of 6 Division, which were not taking part in the attack.

At exactly 5.40 a.m. the 25-pounders and 6″ howitzers opened on the enemy strongpoints. The troops moved forward behind the creeping barrage which was fired with great accuracy. Enemy artillery replied but 'did not appear to be heavy'.[38] Behind the infantry came the Matilda tanks, which were able to deal with those machine-gun posts still firing after the artillery barrage. The advance was carried out with incredible speed. By 8 a.m. the brigade had penetrated some 2.5 miles into the defensive zone. Through this area moved the 19 Brigade. It reached its start line at 8.40 a.m. and then moved forward behind another accurate creeping barrage. By midday the leading troops were across the Bardia Road and within hailing distance of the port.[39]

Not all was plain sailing however. The 2/8 Battalion had the task of advancing on and capturing Fort Pilastrino, a strongpoint on the left of the attack. In the course of their advance they came under fire from dug-in tanks and mobile tanks. There was also severe hand-to-hand fighting, especially from an area protected by low stone walls called sangers. The attacking troops were assisted by a machine-gun barrage fired by a section of Northumberland Fusiliers attached to the brigade. In the end this barrage, followed closely by rapid fire and movement tactics, overcame all resistance.[40]

The next day was an anti-climax. The Italian admiral in the port surrendered on behalf of the entire garrison. Tobruk was in British hands.

O'Connor had by no means finished with the Italian Tenth Army. Benghazi, the most important Italian base before Tripoli, was now a prospect. O'Connor's plan was to propel the 7 Armoured Division through the desert via Mechili to the coast at Beda Fomm while the 6 Australian Division pursued the retreating Italians along the coast road towards Benghazi. Ideally, the enemy would be trapped by these two movements and forced to surrender.

Across the desert the going proved to be the worst yet. 'Rocks and steep wadis caused much delay, especially to the light tanks', and there were daily sand storms.[41] Meanwhile the Australians, carrying Italian binoculars, pistols, suitcases and occasionally dressed in Italian uniforms replete with gold braid and no doubt sustained by captured 10-lb tins of tomato paste, chianti, spaghetti, mineral water, cheeses of all types and other delicacies, set off around the coast.[42]

In the end the plan worked. After hard fighting at Beda Fomm, on 7 February most of the enemy surrendered. The news was sent back to Wavell in Cairo:

> Have just seen staff officer returned from Benghazi. March by Armoured forces of 150 miles in 30 hours over bad tracks in blinding dust storm was amazing performance. Support Group [of 7 Armoured Division] reached road about 50 miles south of Benghazi and took up position just before head of enemy column arrived. After tank attack and counter attack lasting 15 hours enemy gave up. Our casualties believed to be very light . . . Italian commanders state that they had examined advance of armoured force by southern route but had ruled it out as impossible in time. Italian force was accordingly surprised . . . Australians also made great effort and brigade group arrived in enemy rear just as action closed.[43]

Operation Compass was over. In all a force of just two divisions had advanced 500 miles. Its losses were light – 500 killed, 1,400 wounded and 55 missing. In return it had captured 130,000 prisoners, 400 tanks and 850 field guns. The Italian Tenth Army of ten divisions had been totally destroyed.[44]

In the light of what was to happen later in the desert war, it is useful to pause and reflect on what were the main ingredients of success in Compass. From the very beginning the divisions involved (7 Armoured, 4 Indian and 6 Australian) acted as divisions. That is, the attacks conducted were supported by the full range of divisional artillery, tanks and other forms of firepower. This method gave a concentration of fire which overwhelmed each target (the desert camps, Bardia, Tobruk and the Italian forces at Beda Fomm) in turn. Equally important was the fact that the attack plans were very thoroughly thought out. At Bardia and Tobruk it was the infantry in the form of sapper patrols that led the way, followed later by armour. And the armour was only called on to operate after the defences had been softened up or neutralised or destroyed by carefully calculated artillery barrages. What the armour in these battles did not do was race all about the desert seeking out enemy armour in order to bring about an all-tank battle. The armour generally operated within the range where it could be protected by the artillery. Only when the enemy had been thrashed and was in precipitate retreat was the armour unleashed. It was the artillery not the armour, then, that was the key weapon in all this because it not only protected the armour, it also protected the infantry advances and kept casualties to a minimum. It is also worth noting that one division which employed these sophisticated tactics was not made up of Regular soldiers. As mentioned, 6 Australian Division had been raised on the outbreak of war. Many of its officers (including the artilleryman Herring) were civilians in uniform. What remained to be seen was whether subsequent operations would exhibit the same professionalism as demonstrated by the forces in Operation Compass.

* * * * *

The question of what the desert army would do after Benghazi was decided in London. On 8 January the Defence Committee had been told by Churchill that 'the campaign in Libya must now take second place' – the imperative was to help the Greeks against the Germans.[45] The Prime Minister's reasoning was this: Ultra intelligence since late October had indicated that Germany was building up armoured and air forces in Romania and Bulgaria with the intention of aiding the struggling Italians in dealing with the Greeks.[46] Churchill thought German domination of Greece intolerable and that such an event would convince Turkey and Yugoslavia to remain neutral: 'They would be likely to see whether yet again one of our friends [Greece] was able to be trampled down without our being able to prevent this.'[47] The main game in the war was to fight Germans in Europe rather than Italians in Africa. Moreover, Britain had guaranteed Greek independence; that guarantee must be upheld. In any case, the Italians had been defeated.

The Defence Committee asked the Chiefs of Staff what form British aid to Greece ought to take. The Chiefs agreed with Churchill that Greece should have first call on British forces in the Middle East and suggested that modern fighters were the most urgent need and that as many Matilda tanks as possible should be passed through the Mediterranean to Greece.[48] Wavell was then despatched to Athens to determine what aid the British might give. Here came the first stumbling block. The Greek dictator (General Ioannis Metaxas) decided that, while Britain might provide just enough ground forces to provoke a German attack, it could not provide sufficient to deter or repel it. He therefore asked for equipment only – especially modern aircraft.[49] What is interesting about this rebuff is that it had no immediate effect on British policy. Wavell was still instructed to build up a force of 4 divisions for despatch to Greece.[50]

Shortly after this Metaxas died. The new man was Alexandros Korizis. No one in London knew what line he would take on the matter of British assistance. The Defence Committee continued to debate the issue but could reach no other conclusion but that Britain must assist Greece if such assistance was sought.[51] Eventually it was decided to send out a high-level delegation consisting of Eden (now Foreign Minister) and Dill (CIGS) to report to the Committee on what action should be taken.[52]

Even before this delegation arrived, both the COS and the Defence Committee were quite resolute about assistance to Greece. The COS informed Wavell:

> The Defence Committee consider that if Greece were to yield to Germany without fighting, Turkey also would not fight, and consequently that the only way of making sure that the Turks do fight is to give sufficient support to the Greeks to ensure that they fight. Accordingly, the Defence Committee have decided that it is essential for us to place ourselves forthwith in a position to send the largest possible land and air forces from Africa to the European Continent, in order to assist the Greeks against a probable German attack through Bulgaria.[53]

This was an extraordinary communication. By the time it was sent it was known that Turkey did not intend deviating from its position of neutrality. Notwithstanding that, the Defence Committee considered that if the force committed to Greece was sufficiently large, both Turkey and Greece (whose position on British help was still not clear) would be bound to enter the war. Apart from the cloud-cuckoo-land thinking about the importance and strength of a Balkan bloc that this document revealed, there were two serious matters that were being overlooked. The first was that the British did not have available in the Middle East a force of sufficient size to counter a full-scale German attack on Greece. The second was that what force they did have was woefully deficient in modern aircraft and armour, the very factors that would decide an encounter with a force that was armed with such weapons.

Wavell was quick to point all this out to the COS. He told them that he deplored the fact he was being directed to send three squadrons of modern fighters from the desert to Greece. He emphasised that 'nothing (repeat) nothing we can do from here is likely to be in time to stop German advance if really intended . . . I am desperately anxious lest we play the enemy's game and expose ourselves to defeat in detail.'[54]

Meanwhile Churchill had been having second thoughts. Correspondence with Wavell had revealed the reality of what British forces were available in Egypt. It was not a matter of adding up numbers, as Churchill seemed to think, because many of these men were administrative and support troops. Of the fighting formations only two divisions, an armoured brigade group and two regiments of medium artillery were available for Greece. And this would leave the Western Desert to be held by just one infantry division, an armoured brigade group and an Indian motor brigade.[55] Churchill now knew that the forces for Greece 'would not be very numerous.'[56] He passed this information on to Eden and added:

> Do not consider yourselves obligated to a Greek enterprise if in your hearts you feel it will only be another Norwegian fiasco. If no good plan can be made please say so. But (placing a bet each way) of course you know how valuable success would be.[57]

The fact was that no good plan was made. Detailed military discussions on 22 February indicated that the Greeks would fight if invaded. In that instance Greek forces would be withdrawn from exposed positions in Macedonia and Thrace and form one defensive line along the Aliakmon River with the British contingent.[58] Later, however, this plan was overturned by the Greeks. They now thought that they must continue to fight the Italians along the frontier and that they must also hold the line of the Bulgarian frontier against any incursions from there. They therefore promised a much smaller force to join the British along the Aliakmon.[59] This was disastrous. An attack on a wide front by the Germans would now meet three scattered forces instead of a single concentrated one. The risks in this plan were so great that Dill considered withdrawing the British offer completely but in the end accepted the compromise, as did Eden and Wavell, so recently an advocate of sending nothing to the Greeks.[60] The British were therefore committed to Greece against the better judgement of those on the spot making the plan and an increasingly hesitant Prime Minister in London. Apparently what swayed everyone involved was that to win the war the British ultimately would have to inflict a military defeat on Germany somewhere and that some kind of front might yet be established in the Balkans with Yugoslav and Turkish participation.[61] If this was the case it was a matter of ends trumping means.

In the event, the Greek campaign was a predictable disaster. Despite an anti-Nazi coup in Belgrade, on 6 April the German Twelfth Army invaded Yugoslavia and Greece on a front which stretched from Macedonia in the east to Albania in the west. In all the Germans deployed five army corps, which included crack mountain troops and four armoured divisions.[62] In addition they had available 900 aircraft.[63] This force overwhelmed the Greeks and the 60,000 Anzac and British forces rushed to assist them. The nine squadrons from the RAF proved quite inadequate to supply constant air support. The fighting soon developed into a staged withdrawal which was carried out with some skill. Of the 60,000 troops, just over 50,000 were lifted by the navy from various beaches in the Peloponnese.[64]

From there 35,000 men were shipped to Crete, which was rightly thought to be the next German objective. Here the Germans attacked first with airborne troops and then from the sea. Again, after much hard fighting, the Germans prevailed. About 20,000 men were rescued from this debacle, leaving a total of 25,000 troops or about two divisions and all their equipment lost. If the British required a futile gesture at this point of the war the Greek campaign certainly provided it. It is a wonder that no military voice was raised against it. The Chiefs of Staff and Wavell, after his hesitations in January, uttered not one cautionary word. As for Churchill, one of the reasons he supported the decision was to impress on the Americans that Britain stood by its allies. On frequent occasions the Prime Minister informed the President of the state of affairs in Greece. No reply was received. Finally, when the fiasco was over, Roosevelt told Churchill that British action in Greece was a 'worthy effort' and highly admired.[65] For the moment that was the only comfort he was to receive.

* * * * *

Meanwhile what of the Western Desert? Here there had been a further series of failures. The Intelligence community had been very slow to realise that German forces in number had crossed to Africa. It came as some surprise when British forces in the desert announced on 22 February that they had encountered German troops at El Agheila.[66] At this point, it needs to be emphasised, no British troops had been despatched to Greece. The appearance of German forces in the desert was not sufficient to encourage a rethink of that policy. Indeed Churchill could tell Roosevelt that he was aware that the Germans were in the desert but that he was 'not unduly anxious about the Libyan–Egyptian position'.[67] To a large extent this optimism was based on an appreciation from Wavell which acknowledged the German presence but went on:

> Tripoli to Agheila is 471 miles and to Benghazi 646 miles. There is only one road and water is inadequate over 410 miles of the distance; these factors together with lack of transport, limit the present enemy threat. He can probably maintain up to one Inf. Div. and Armd Bde. along the coast road in about three weeks, and possibly at the same time employ a second Armd. Bde. if he has one available . . . Eventually two German Divisions might be employed in a large-scale attack. This with one or two Inf. Divs. would be the maximum maintainable via Tripoli. Shipping risks, difficulty of communication and the approach of bad weather make it unlikely that such an attack could develop before the end of the summer. Effective interference by sea with convoys and by air with Tripoli might extend this period.[68]

In other words the situation in the desert could be managed for at least the next few months.

Wavell had, however, not counted on General Erwin Rommel. The German commander arrived in Africa on 12 February. He was followed by a reconnaissance battalion, some artillery and then by the 5 Light Division. In addition he had some Italian units and dive bombers and fighters from X Air Corps.[69] Against all advice and orders he decided to attack the British as soon as possible.[70] Rommel divided his force into a number of mobile columns; Some were to head up the coastal road to Benghazi; others to advance through the desert to Msus and Mechili.[71]

The forces he faced were hardly formidable. The infantry unit on the coast was the 9 Australian Division (Lieutenant-General Leslie Morshead), but it was without one brigade (left in Tobruk through lack of transport), without its artillery (accompanying were just two batteries of First World War-vintage guns), without its signalling equipment, with few anti-tank guns and quite inadequate air support.[72] The armoured unit was labelled the 2 Armoured Division but it consisted merely of the 3 Armoured Brigade (its other brigade having been despatched to Greece) and the Support Group of artillery and a battalion of infantry.[73] The entire 'armoured' unit could muster just fifty-six British tanks, the 6 Royal Tank Regiment being equipped with repaired Italian M13 tanks of a type that had proved of doubtful utility to the Italians during Compass.[74] Moreover, many of the cruiser tanks of the 3 Armoured had broken down on the trip from Cairo or were in a worn-out condition. Both units were quite new to the desert, with inexperienced commanders and were out of touch with each other due to a lack of wireless equipment.[75]

In this situation, Rommel's probes soon turned into a rout for the British, whose armoured units drifted to and fro in the desert trying to find fuel dumps or acting on false reports of enemy movements. Soon they were cannibalising their poorer tanks to keep their better ones going. In the end just two tanks remained.[76] The remainder were forced through lack of fuel and ammunition to surrender at Mechili. With no flank support, the Australians had to retreat via the coast road, warding off several attempts to cut them off with the help of some units of British artillery. By 11 April they were back in Tobruk.[77] Wavell's interventions in the battle had undoubtedly made a bad situation worse. He had no confidence in either General Philip Neame, who was in overall command, or in Major-General Michael Gambier-Parry who commanded (if that is the right word) what was left of the 2 Armoured Division, so he rushed O'Connor from Cairo and attempted to insert him into the command structure. O'Connor did his best but the dispersion of command only added to the confusion, as did the orders issued by Wavell himself. Then in the midst of battle O'Connor and Gambier-Parry took a wrong turning in the desert and were captured by the Germans. This took the already shambolic situation to new heights (or depths).[78]

The only bright spot came from Tobruk. Yes, Rommel had besieged it but his attempts to capture the port all ended in failure, although he could deploy many more tanks than could the besieged garrison. Here the actions over Easter 1941 (12–15 April) are instructive. The garrison consisted basically of Australian infantry from the 9 and 7 Divisions and various units of British armour and artillery that had retreated inside the defensive perimeter around the port. The commanders were first General Lavarack from the Australian 7 Division and then, for most of the siege, Lieutenant-General Morshead, commander of the 9 Division. Their tactics were innovative. When Rommel launched his Easter offensive the relatively thin crust of infantry allowed the thirty or forty assault tanks through and concentrated their energies on stopping the following German infantry. Then the isolated tanks were set upon by the artillery grouped ahead of the tanks in batteries of 25-pounders and on either flank by mobile 2-pounder batteries. These soon took a devastating toll on the German tanks and forced a withdrawal. Other attempts by Rommel to crack the increasingly deep and sophisticated defences also failed and the Tobruk garrison kept wrong-footing their besiegers by aggressive patrolling which often penetrated some thousands of yards into enemy territory. They in fact inflicted the first check that the panzers received in this war. The lesson of well-placed artillery and infantry manoeuvring with some imagination, first demonstrated at Bardia and Tobruk itself, was there for all to see. Whether anyone did see it was another question.[79]

Churchill was watching these events closely. When he learned that German forces were advancing in Libya he telegraphed Wavell asking about his dispositions and in particular the position of the 7 Armoured Division.[80] Wavell was in Eritrea when this telegram arrived but Churchill was informed that the 7 Armoured was refitting in Cairo.[81] Next day the Prime Minister was reassured by the Commander-in-Chief that there were few Germans in Libya and that the attacking forces were mainly Italian. He told Churchill that the Support Group of the 7 Armoured Division (its artillery and motorised infantry) had been sent forward but that the armoured component had no tanks other than those that were being repaired. Wavell said he had had to run great risks in Cyrenaica in order to aid Greece and that there was only one weak armoured brigade and a partly trained Australian division there.[82] Churchill's concern mounted. On 2 April he told Wavell that while a 'rebuff' to Rommel would have 'far-reaching prestige effects', withdrawal from Benghazi 'would appear most melancholy'.[83]

At the same time Churchill informed Eden, who was then in Athens. that the idea that British forces could not face the Germans 'would react most evilly throughout the Balkans and Turkey'.[84] Nevertheless, when the reverse in Cyrenaica came, Churchill reacted mildly, telling the Commander-in-Chief, 'I warned the country a week ago that they must not expect continuance of unbroken successes and take the rough with the smooth . . . be quite sure that we shall back you up in adversity better than in good fortune.'[85] Churchill was no doubt aware of the many issues that flooded in on Wavell at this period of his command, which included the campaign against the Italians in East Africa, an incipient Vichy revolt in Syria and the possibility of trouble in Iraq led by the pro-fascist Rashid Ali.[86]

Nevertheless, what Churchill required of Wavell was the conquest of Libya and the relief of the besieged forces in Tobruk. The essential matter was supply. Wavell, as he had informed London, had no spare armour and by the end of the Cyrenaica campaign was woefully short of aircraft as well. In Churchill's view the solution was to run a convoy containing as many tanks and crated Hurricanes as possible directly through the Mediterranean using Force H at Gibraltar and the Eastern Mediterranean Fleet from Alexandria as cover.[87] With some hesitation the Chiefs agreed, perhaps unwilling to thwart Churchill a second time over through-Mediterranean convoys. Churchill then, against the express wishes of the CIGS, added another ship to the convoy (codenamed Tiger) with an additional sixty-seven tanks.[88] The risk proved justified. Just one ship was sunk but 238 tanks and 43 Hurricanes were delivered to Wavell on 12 May, thus saving forty days over the Cape route.[89]

Strangely, the very day these reinforcements arrived, Wavell, with Churchill's concurrence, decided to launch a preliminary attack in the Halfaya–Sollum areas to test the strength of the German defence (Operation Brevity).[90] That defence proved stronger than anticipated. For a derisory amount of ground, which was soon lost, eighteen tanks which could have taken part in the major operation were damaged or destroyed.[91] Why such a futile operation was ever sanctioned is a mystery.

Churchill apparently accepted Wavell's assertion that Brevity had been a 'near success'.[92] What was agitating the Prime Minister were other matters. He railed at the long delays in getting the Tiger convoy tanks off the ships and into the desert.[93] Wavell attempted to explain that there were hold-ups at the wharf due to equipment deficiencies and that there were delays in obtaining essential equipment such as sand filters to make the tanks desert-worthy.[94] This rather bad-tempered dialogue continued until the very eve of battle: Churchill (and, it must be said, the CIGS) reminding Wavell of how much materiel and how many men they had sent him; Wavell noting that his command stretched from Ethiopia to Iraq, which areas tied down many of his troops and equipment.[95]

Iraq was, of course, the other matter. On April Fools' Day a proto-fascist, Rashid Ali had launched a coup against the British-backed government in Baghdad. German intervention threatened and Churchill and the COS pushed Wavell to send a relief column to the now-besieged British airport at Habbaniya near Baghdad.[96] Wavell refused, citing lack of resources and the fact that he was having to prepare yet another army to capture Vichy-controlled Syria. Given these pressures, he suggested negotiating with Rashid Ali instead. Churchill had not become Prime Minister to negotiate with fascists – which he pointed out to Wavell in no uncertain terms. Eventually, and with much reluctance, Wavell assembled a column (Habforce) which set off for Iraq in early May 1941. Meanwhile an enthusiastic C-in-C India (General Claude Auchinleck) had despatched an Indian brigade to Basra.[97] The contrast between Wavell's and Auchinleck's attitudes was noted by the Prime Minister and it boded ill for Wavell's future prospects. In the end Wavell offered to resign and Churchill suggested that he should do so if he was not prepared to carry out the policies decided in London. Eventually the imminence of the desert battle halted these bad-tempered exchanges.[98]

* * * * *

Churchill's exasperation with Wavell's gloomy (or realistic) assessment of the multifaceted pressures of his command is very evident in the correspondence at this time. However, the main game for the Prime Minister was not Iraq or Syria but a victory in the desert. All would be redeemed for Wavell if he succeeded there. His battle plan (called not very imaginatively, Battleaxe) was planned by Lieutenant-General Noel Beresford-Peirse. It was a considerable regression from O'Connor's efforts in Compass. The troops would consist of the 7 Armoured Division and the 4 Indian Division.

Yet in this battle they would not operate as divisions. For example, one of the principle tasks of the 4 Indian Division was to capture the German defensive position at Halfaya Pass. The force that was to attack the pass (11 Brigade) was split in two: one section driving along the coast and another attacking the pass frontally. Nor was that all. On its left, the 4 Armoured Brigade was also to be split into two columns, as the 22 Guards Brigade, which was to operate between the 4 Indian Division and the 7 Armoured Division. In fact, one column of this brigade was to advance on Sollum and the other on Fort Capuzzo. As a result, the attacking forces on the right would be split into five groups. The consequent dispersal of firepower of these forces could not have been more disastrous.[99]

The deployment of 7 Armoured Division was no more coherent. Its task was 'to draw the enemy armoured forces into battle and destroy them'.[100] The area in which this destruction would take place was Hafid Ridge, actually a series of sand dunes to the south of Capuzzo.[101] It would not act as a unit. Its Support Group (its infantry and artillery) would act separately as a flank guard for both the Armoured Division and the Indian forces to its south. The result was that the forces deployed for Battleaxe would consist of no fewer than seven columns.

What this meant for the firepower resources at Beresford-Peirse's disposal was disastrous. In terms of field guns, sixteen were allocated to the direct attack on Halfaya, sixteen were with the armoured brigade deployed against Capuzzo and sixteen were with the Support Group on the flank of 7 Armoured. The fifty-two anti-tank guns were similarly split. As for the medium artillery, eight of its 6″ howitzers were to be used at Halfaya and eight were with the Support Group.[102] Thus a force which could in any case deploy only 112 guns in total ensured that there was nowhere on the battlefield where they could deliver a concentrated barrage. The armour was likewise dispersed. The 4 Indian Division had eighteen Matildas to help with Halfaya; the 4 and 7 Armoured Brigades had around another ninety Matildas and ninety cruisers divided between them.[103]

The shortcomings of the plan went beyond dispersion. Its commander, Beresford-Peirse, placed himself 50 miles in the rear at Sidi Barrani, a position from where he could have little influence over a moving battlefield. The tanks of the Armoured Division would have no direct or immediate artillery support at all. They were expected to take on whatever Rommel threw at them and defeat it. The other point to be made concerns the size of the force. It consisted of only two divisions, yet it was expected to capture strongly defended localities, destroy the enemy armour, advance across Cyrenaica, relieve Tobruk and pursue Rommel across Libya. As Wavell remarked to Churchill, it would be fortunate if the force at his disposal accomplished just one of these tasks.[104]

In the event Battleaxe was a sad failure. The attack on Halfaya came unstuck at once – eleven of the twelve Matildas closely supporting the Indian infantry were put out of action by well dug-in anti-tank guns, some of them the deadly 88-mm first deployed in this role by Rommel in France. Wireless communication between the infantry and the supporting 25-pounders then broke down, leaving the troops with virtually no protecting artillery. Shortly after that four of the six remaining Matildas ran into a minefield. No progress was made.

On the desert flank 7 Armoured Division advanced in three bounds to what it thought was the Hafid Ridge. It then discovered that this feature consisted of three groups of dunes, and as it attempted to advance further it ran into Rommel's tanks, anti-tank guns and infantry concealed behind the second group. The 88s and other German artillery pieces took a heavy toll, while its own artillery was too distant to intervene. In no time the 7 Armoured Brigade had been reduced to just forty-eight cruiser tanks.[105]

In the centre there was a modicum of success. The armour outflanked Halfaya and took Fort Capuzzo. The infantry (22 Guards Brigade) was slow to come up, but eventually the fort was held strongly enough to fight off counter-attacks and prepare all-round defences.

This modest achievement turned out to be the high-water mark of Battleaxe. Rommel responded immediately by sending an armoured group around the Hafid Ridge in an attempt to outflank the 7 Armoured. The British turned south to counter this move and an armoured *pas des deux* resulted which saw the two forces moving in parallel back to the old front line. This manoeuvre, though necessary, left the Indian force around Capuzzo danger-ously isolated and Major-General Frank Messervy (commanding 4 Indian Division) ordered that it too retreat. By 17 June the British were occupying the positions from whence Battleaxe had started.[106] Casualties were relatively light – about 700 killed and wounded. But in tanks the story was quite different. Of approximately 200 that started the battle ninety-one were lost to the enemy by destruction or breakdown. The Germans had just twelve tanks destroyed – those damaged were gathered from the battlefield and repaired.[107]

Churchill tried to portray the battle in a reasonable light, telling Smuts that the enemy losses had been heavy.[108] Then the CIGS somehow discovered that this statement, based on a communiqué from Wavell, was not correct. A furious Dill told the Commander-in-Chief:

> it is very difficult, if not impossible to get away with your communique about Battleaxe of 18th June. Nobody really believes it and it will certainly not deceive the enemy . . . Prime Minister has postponed any statement until next Tuesday. Whatever he says, it will clearly have to be something nearer the truth than the Middle East Communique.[109]

Whether this played any role with Churchill's decision to swap Wavell with the Commander-in-Chief, India (General Auchinleck) on 21 June is not known. Probably the reasons given by Churchill at the time were reasonable enough: that Wavell was tired and irritated beyond measure by the ever-expanding demands of his command which in May had active fronts in Crete, Abyssinia, Iraq and Vichy Syria as well as the Western Desert. Indeed Wavell had a good case for limiting his jurisdictions but no one in London seems to have reached this conclusion. In the end Wavell's post-battle decision to spend three months on the defensive in order to rebuild his forces after Battleaxe was not congenial to the Prime Minister, and he was dismissed.[110]

Wavell's dismissal was to have one knock-on effect later in the year. At some stage (probably late June or July) Churchill read Wavell's detailed account of the action of the 2 Armoured Division's actions during Rommel's first offensive. He reacted strongly. Essentially he considered the orders quite negative (the words 'retreat' or 'withdrawal' were mentioned five times in the two pages of orders) and concluded that Wavell was 'resigned to disaster should the enemy press hard'. Overall he was disturbed by the fact that Wavell had assigned such an important role to an inexperienced unit when the experienced 7 Armoured Division were refitting over an inordinately long period in Cairo.[111] He went on to claim that Wavell had kept him in the dark concerning all these matters and that he intended to circulate a memorandum to this effect to the War Cabinet.

In fact many of Churchill's claims were not true. Wavell's telegrams to Churchill detailed every action he took and elicited no response from the Prime Minister at the time. The CIGS, Dill, felt moved to point this out to Churchill. Dill particularly objected to the 'resigned to disaster' phrase and declared himself 'shocked' by Churchill's attack on Wavell.[112] Dill also told the Minister of War, David Margesson, that he was 'horrified' by Churchill's approach, which he considered 'frightfully unfair'.[113] Margesson agreed with Dill and suggested to Dill that he ask Churchill to circulate his (Dill's) note as well as Wavell's orders to the War Cabinet. At some point Dill proposed this to Churchill; he received a stinging rebuke. Churchill told Dill that he reserved the right to circulate to his Cabinet colleagues such information as he deemed fit. He did, however, agree to circulate Wavell's orders but went on to renew his assertion that Wavell had not informed him of the parlous state of the desert force.[114] Dill back-pedalled but held to his point that Churchill had treated Wavell unfairly.[115] This was the beginning of the end for Dill. He had already clashed with the Prime Minister over a telegram from Churchill to Wavell setting out the tactics that might be employed in Battleaxe, the CIGS suggesting that it was unwise to interfere in operations to this extent.[116] The second clash was one too many for the Prime Minister. As soon as it was convenient he sent Dill to Washington as his representative on the new Combined Chiefs of Staff Committee and replaced him with the more robust and cannier General Alan Brooke.

After the failure of Battleaxe there was a considerable debate about what lessons could be gleaned from the defeat. Astonishingly, given the thrashing that the British had just endured, most discussion focused on the shortcomings of the Germans. The 7 Armoured Division in particular considered Rommel's tactics to be rather 'rigid'. His only aim, they stated, was to draw 'our tanks on to his anti-tank guns and then attack with his tanks when our intentions are clear'.[117] They did not go on to make the obvious point that Rommel's tactics had worked rather well. Instead, they concluded, the German armour was held to be 'slow to adjust to altered circumstances'.[118] The answer to all of this, they considered, was rapid manoeuvre against the enemy armour by mixed columns of tanks, artillery and infantry – that is, the use of 'Jock' Columns of later notoriety.[119] How these deductions were reached is a matter of wonder. There seems nothing at all 'rigid' about tactics that within three days forced the British back to their start line. And in what sense was luring a tank force to its destruction 'rigid'? As for adapting to changed circumstances, the rapid deployment of outflanking armour against the 7 Armoured on Hafid Ridge would suggest the very opposite. Moreover, the solution offered to these supposed deficiencies – small, mixed columns of tanks, artillery and infantry – had considerable drawbacks. Might they not be picked off by an enemy operating in mass or at least in divisional groups?

The 4 Indian Division's conclusions were much more sensible. They deprecated frontal attacks without sufficient artillery to soften up the defences. They also urged rapid consolidation of positions captured and the deployment of anti-tank artillery at the front to ward off attacks by enemy armour. They also drew attention to the poor performance of the British wireless sets and correctly suggested that the Germans were intercepting what wireless messages the British had managed to send and were therefore apprised not only of the attack but of the subsequent manoeuvres during it.[120]

The post-mortems in London took no notice of the sensible suggestions from the 4 Indian Division. Indeed they agreed with the rather bizarre conclusions reached by 7 Armoured Division. In this politicians and the military were united. Churchill considered the 'divisional system' 'ill-adapted' to desert warfare and thought 'a system of self-contained Brigade Groups . . . would be operationally and administratively better'.[121] Brooke, one of Britain's most thoughtful soldiers, held to this view well into 1942, noting for the Prime Minister that he too much preferred brigade groups to armoured divisions.[122]

What no one seems to have realised is that there were lessons to be drawn from the capture of Bardia and Tobruk and the later siege of Tobruk, some of vital importance. The fighting around these towns demonstrated that carefully used concentrated artillery fire and the imaginative use of tanks and infantry could be successful in attack and defence. The single most important lesson (which Rommel had already grasped) was that artillery could outfight tanks and overcome fixed defences when concentrated. Perhaps it was the fact that these lessons were learned around defended ports that obscured this point and perhaps the British commanders thought it did not apply to warfare in the expanses of the desert. But even the 7 Armoured had grasped that it was Rommel's anti-tank guns that had destroyed them on Hafid Ridge – which was in fact located in the expanses of the desert. Perhaps therefore it was a view inherited from France that tanks were the key to success that blinded the desert generals to this lesson. Perhaps the capture of the general (O'Connor) who had presided over the first of these victories was important. On the other hand, almost all the armoured commanders were cavalrymen, wedded to mobility at all costs. Whatever it was, there was now a new commander and it remained to be seen what influences he could bring to bear on the desert war: would he favour columns with small numbers of tanks, guns and infantry or would he prefer the concentrated power of divisions? Would the desert war proceed along the lines of Bardia or Battleaxe?

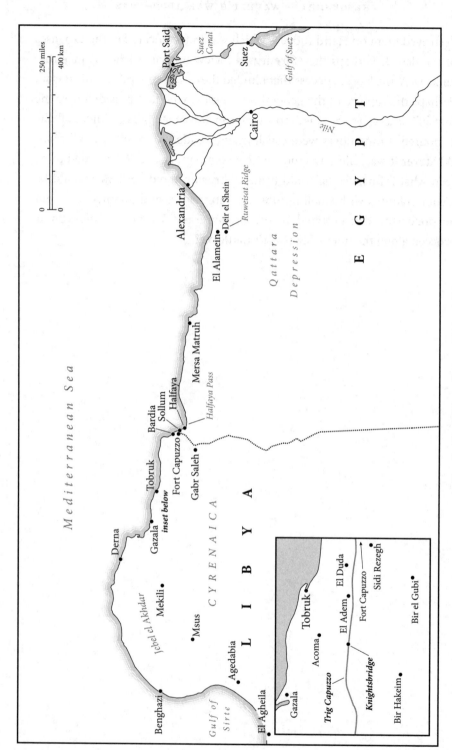

Map 7. The Western Desert, 1940–1943.

CHAPTER 16

THE DESERT –
AUCHINLECK'S WAR 1941–1942

GENERAL AUCHINLECK, THE NEW Commander-in-Chief Middle East, had spent his entire career in the Indian Army. He had come to the attention of Churchill in 1940 when he had assisted in cleaning up the fractured command (which Churchill had created) at Narvik. Then in May and June 1941, as C-in-C India, Auchinleck had proposed energetic responses to the crisis in Iraq. Churchill no doubt compared this response with Wavell's reluctance to get involved in Iraq at all, so when he was casting around for a replacement for Wavell, Auchinleck seemed to have the energy required.

The relationship between the Prime Minister and his General began as it was to continue for over a year, with Churchill insisting that any decision to launch an offensive was Auchinleck's alone and then providing a list of reasons (German preoccupation with Russia, the necessity to relieve Tobruk) why that launch was a matter of urgency.[1]

Auchinleck, however, urged caution. He noted that fighting against the Vichy French in Syria was still continuing and that this campaign must be ended before attention could be focused on the desert. He was also worried that the Germans might seize Cyprus by airborne assault and thus outflank the British position in Palestine. Turning to the desert army, he stressed the need to rebuild the shattered 7 Armoured Division and for adequate training for new troops before they were committed to battle. He then went into some detail about the kind of army he needed to defeat Rommel.

Infantry divisions, he declared, 'however well trained and equipped, are not good for offensive operations in this terrain against enemy armoured forces'. What he required were '2 and preferably 3 armoured divisions with a motor division' to pit against the Afrika Korps.[2] As we will see, this was a highly contentious proposition – infantry divisions were to play a key role in the defeat of Rommel – but at the time neither Churchill nor the Chiefs of Staff questioned it. What they did question was the need for so much armour, for if Auchinleck's demands were to be met, such was the slow rate of tank production in Britain and such was the shortage of shipping, that there would be no offensive in 1941 and a struggle to mount one in the first half of 1942.

A flurry of telegrams followed. The gist of them was always the same – Auchinleck pointing out that he would have no more than one or perhaps one and a third armoured divisions ready by the end of October, Churchill replying that the situation at Tobruk, Malta and the German effort in Russia demanded a more rapid response.[3] In the end Churchill and the COS insisted that Auchinleck return to London to discuss the entire situation and at the end of July he arrived.

Auchinleck's first appearance was at a rather inconclusive meeting with the COS.[4] The main event was at the Defence Committee, where he faced an intense grilling from the Prime Minister. Churchill opened by noting that with the Germans preoccupied in Russia, now was the time to bring on the battle. Auchinleck replied that he had no superiority in tanks and that he needed a superiority of two to one to succeed. The discussion then moved on to when additional tanks could be sent out but Auchinleck pointed out that it was not just a matter of unloading tanks; defects (of which there were many) had to be repaired, the tanks had to be made desert-worthy (sand filters and the like) and then the crews required a period of training. Only then could they be used in battle. He added that the last battle (Battleaxe) had failed because it had been launched prematurely. At this point Attlee entered the debate. He deemed it essential that the battle take place within the next two months, adding that Battleaxe had failed because not 'everything' had been thrown in. Disputes then followed about the strength of the Desert Air Force and whether, given Auchinleck's reluctance to fight, the 1 Armoured Division might be better employed elsewhere. It was to no avail. Auchinleck stuck to his guns – or rather to his lack of them.[5]

Next day Auchinleck met Churchill at Chequers. He had been warned by Ismay not to judge the Prime Minister by ordinary standards; that he was carrying an enormous burden and that in the end he would support his general.[6] At the meeting both men stood their ground but in the end Churchill admitted that there were 'strong practical arguments advanced' to delay the offensive until November and with some reluctance he accepted Auchinleck's position.[7] As the general wrote, he had 'won his case'.[8]

That was not the end of the matter, however. Churchill was largely consumed during the next few weeks with the determination of the Australian government to remove its 9 Division from Tobruk. Despite Churchill's efforts, this occurred in October and it was replaced with the 70 British Division and a Polish brigade. In the meantime his attention had returned to the Western Desert. He had received a message from Auchinleck in late August moving the date for the new offensive back from early November until the middle of the month. He told Auchinleck that he was 'depressed' by this news and hoped the C-in-C was 'aware of the dangers of delay, and the very high price which may have to be paid for it'. He declared 'it . . . inexplicable to the general public [i.e. to him] that we should remain absolutely inert during these months when the enemy is involved in Russia'.[9] The answer covered no new ground. Mid-November was the earliest that the 7 Armoured Division could be fitted with new tanks and had time for training. Moreover, only the first brigade of the 1 Armoured Division would be able to participate in the battle by then. Dumps of fuel and stores had to be sent forward (the gap between the British forward troops and the Afrika Korps was about 90 miles) and training with the new American Stuart tanks had to take place.[10]

The fact was that Auchinleck's arguments were irrefutable. Battleaxe had virtually worn out the 7 Armoured and it had to be rebuilt. Additional armour could not be rushed through the Mediterranean and had to take the six-week journey around the Cape. The unreliability of the British made tanks meant that, as Auchinleck said, much work on them had to take place on arrival. Then there was the matter of making not just armour but all vehicles, especially motor transport, robust enough to survive the sand storms and rough roads of the desert. All this took time. Churchill, of course, had many valid points too. Five months was a long time to wait when Britain's major ally, Russia, was reeling from the Nazi invasion. And, in those days, when politicians held themselves accountable for their actions to Parliament, there was a certain restlessness in the Commons about the delay. In the event, it was not the delay as much as the type of plan being developed in the Middle East that should have concerned the politicians because it was little more than a re-run of Battleaxe.

The planning for the new battle (Operation Crusader) would be carried out by a newcomer to the Western Desert, Lieutenant-General Alan Cunningham, the conqueror of Ethiopia and Somaliland, the brother of the naval commander in the Mediterranean. His plan, which Auchinleck approved, looked very much like Battleaxe on a larger scale. This time there were to be two corps operating – the XIII (Major-General Alfred Godwin-Austen) consisting of two infantry divisions (4 Indian and 2 New Zealand) plus a brigade of Infantry tanks – and the XXX (Major-General Willoughby Norrie) with the 7 Armoured Division (Colonel William Gott), the 1 South African Division (Colonel Brink) and the 22 Guards Brigade. In all there would be 118,000 troops, 629 medium, 129 light and 205 Infantry tanks (963 total), 849 guns (field, medium and anti-tank) and 612 aircraft.[11] Essentially all the mobile tanks would be concentrated in XXX Corps, while XIII Corps was an infantry formation.

This was a formidable force but the plan it was to implement left much to be desired. The XIII Corps aspect was reasonably straightforward. Here the 4 Indian Division (Messervy) was to attack Halfaya Pass and tie down or capture the German/Italian defenders on the frontier. Meanwhile the New Zealanders would carry out a left hook to cut off these defenders from their base, capture Fort Capuzzo and Bardia and prepare to move west towards Tobruk. It was stressed, however, that this corps would do 'the absolute minimum' until the location of the enemy armoured forces became clear.[12]

XXX Corps would advance to a non-descript area south-west of Capuzzo called Gabr Saleh, more a point on a map than a location of any importance. There they would wait until the location of Rommel's panzer divisions was known and then destroy them. After that, destruction the two corps (now called the Eighth Army) would move on Tobruk, the garrison of which place would have driven a wedge out to El Duda to meet them.[13]

This sounded straightforward but it was not. The 7 Armoured Division would for a start not have its entire armour concentrated. One of its brigades

(4) would try to provide a link by protecting the left of XIII Corps, where the New Zealanders were operating, and the right of the bulk of 7 Armoured. Thus its 166 tanks would occupy a weird kind of no man's land between the two corps.[14] Nor would the remainder of the division be unified. On the left, 22 Armoured Brigade (128 tanks) was to divert to prevent the Italian Ariete Armoured Division from intervening. That left at the sharp end just the 7 Armoured Brigade with its 129 tanks. And this unit would not have the immediate support of its divisional artillery. The 7 Support Group, with its anti-tank guns and motorised infantry, would lag somewhat behind the spearhead ready to support whichever brigade needed it most.

This bizarre layout goes to the heart of much that went wrong for the British in the desert in 1941 and 1942. There was clearly never a conception that their armoured divisions should fight as a unified body. The separation of the artillery from the tanks was especially egregious because it was only the artillery (including anti-tank guns) nestled among the tanks that could prevent a Battleaxe-type slaughter. As the British had noted, the Afrika Korps fought as a whole and always had its anti-tank guns and artillery well forward.[15]

This was not the only weakness in the XXX Corps plan. The infantry supporting the armour was the 1 South African Division. It had performed well against the Italians in East Africa but its only experience in the desert was digging defences around Mersa Matruh. It had had so little time to train for the battle that the entire operation was delayed three days to allow for additional training. Indeed the army commander threated to replace it with the more experienced 4 Indian Division; it might have improved prospects slightly if he had.[16]

Another notable feature of the XXX Corps plan was that the corps commander (General Willoughby Norrie) thought aspects of it contemptible. Norrie had first protested about the dispersal of his armour. He was also scathing about the selection of Gabr Saleh as a point which might bring on 'a sort of Armageddon', noting that 'it takes two to make an armoured battle' and that 'Rommel had no reason to fight for this unimportant point'. Finally he argued against the inclusion of the half-trained South Africans in XXX Corps.[17] All his objections were noted by Cunningham but none was accepted. Norrie would therefore be called upon to implement a plan in which he had no confidence.

Thus the newly badged Eighth Army would attack but not as one formation. In total Britain had assembled a formidable force for this battle. They had about 700 tanks, 600 field guns, 68 medium guns and almost 400 anti-tank guns.[18] This was many more than Rommel could deploy. He had just under 400 tanks and many fewer guns.[19] Yet, as the plan stood, the British weapons would be dispersed over two quite distinct areas. On the coast, XIII Corps, doing 'the absolute minimum', had just 122 tanks but more importantly 170 field guns, 48 medium guns and over 100 anti-tank guns. Inland, the widely dispersed XXX Corps would have the remainder but split up into five groups – three armoured brigades, each operating separately, the Support Group and the South African infantry.

An alternative plan might have employed the entire army in a short left hook to capture the coastal frontier defences, Sollum and Bardia. In this manner the firepower of the entire army could have been used unified to blast a way through the German defences. Then the army could have dug in with its anti-tank guns forward, ready for Rommel's riposte. If Rommel suffered a reverse in this encounter the relief of Tobruk (in any case a secondary objective in Cunningham's plan) might have followed. But so fixated were the desert generals on conducting a mobile battle along what they thought were the methods used by the Afrika Korps that no one thought in terms of massed firepower and modest gains. As it stood, the only real hope for the British was that Rommel might have a bad battle. In this, as we will see, they were not to be disappointed.

At 6 a.m. on 18 November 1941 a bombardment opened on the German defences at the frontier, and the Indian and New Zealand troops crept forward. The attack was not a success. Many of the Infantry tanks (Matildas) were put out of action by dug-in German anti-tank guns which the artillery had comprehensively missed. The Indian attack stalled and the New Zealanders could only inch forward towards Fort Capuzzo.[20]

Also, early in the morning the 450 or so tanks of the 7 Armoured Division crossed the wire marking the Egypt/Libya border. By early next day the leading armoured brigade (7) had reached Gabr Saleh. There was no reaction from Rommel, mainly because he was busy with preparations to attack Tobruk. Even when he eventually noticed that there was British armour in this vicinity, he took no action, deeming it merely a reconnaissance in force. In any case, the occupation of a map point by the enemy was

1. Sir Edward Grey speaking to a packed House of Commons, 3 August 1914. His speech swung the House behind the government's decision for war. Churchill, Asquith and Lloyd George are prominent on the front bench.

2. Mr Asquith taking an interest in the war or at least in an aeroplane.

3. General Sir John French, C-in-C of the BEF, with his ADCs in 1915. As with his plans, his reputation hardly survived contact with the enemy.

4. Lloyd George with his Cabinet colleague Lord Reading and Albert Thomas (French munitions minister) visiting the front. Lloyd George and Thomas seem to be doing their best to ignore their military guides.

5. Generals Rawlinson and Haig during the Battle of the Somme. No cloak could disguise their differences on how the battle should be fought.

6. Admiral Sir John Jellicoe. He mastered the German battlefleet at Jutland but was utterly baffled by the enemy U-boat campaign.

7. Soldiers at the Battle of the Menin Road, 1917. This is what victory looked like during the Third Battle of Ypres.

8. 'The guns standing wheel to wheel pounding home the lessons of democracy.' This quotation (probably apocryphal) is ascribed to Lloyd George, but if the quote is apocryphal the guns were not. More than anything else, guns were the determinant of victory on the Western Front.

9. Trenches at Gallipoli, exactly the type of warfare the campaign was designed to avoid.

10. Troops wading into battle in Mesopotamia. These conditions led to the formation of a new arm of the British army – canoe-borne infantry.

11. Churchill with the King and the War Cabinet, 1943: Mr Morrison (Home Office), Lord Woolton (Reconstruction), Sir John Anderson (Exchequer), Mr Attlee (Deputy Prime Minister), King George VI, Winston Churchill (Prime Minister), Mr Eden (Foreign Affairs), Mr Lyttelton (Production) and Mr Bevin (Labour).

12. Keith Park. His tactical genius guided the few to victory in the Battle of Britain.

13. Generals O'Connor and Wavell. Their plans in 1940–1941 destroyed the Italian 10th Army.

14. Changing the guard in Cairo. Sitting: Smuts, Churchill, Auchinleck, Wavell; standing: Tedder, Brooke, Harwood, Casey. Eventually, the new commander in the desert would prove no more congenial to Churchill than the old one.

15. British troops at the invasion of Sicily in July 1943. The order on the beach indicates that this image was taken well after the often shambolic landing.

16. Cassino and its dominating monastery. Polish troops captured its ruins during the great Allied offensive of May 1944.

17. General William Slim. He re-conquered Burma while Churchill and the Chiefs of Staff made other plans.

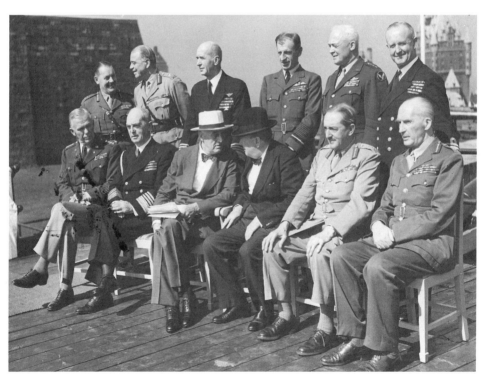

18. The Grand Alliance at Quebec, 1944. Front row: Marshall, Leahy, Roosevelt, Churchill, Brooke, Dill; back row: Hollis, Ismay, King, Portal, Arnold, Cunningham. Brooke's face bears out the exhaustion detailed in his diary.

19. The D-Day commanders. From the left: Bradley, Ramsay, Tedder, Eisenhower, Montgomery, Leigh-Mallory, Bedell Smith. Separating Tedder and Montgomery was not an unusual position for the Supreme Commander during the Normandy campaign.

20. Sherman tanks from the 3 Canadian Division pass through the village of Reviers shortly after the D-Day landings.

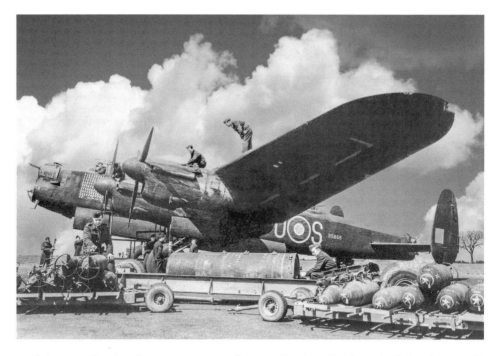

21. A Lancaster bomber, the true instrument of strategic bombing. It is being loaded with a 4,000 lb blockbuster bomb as well as other heavy ordnance.

22. A convoy in mid-Atlantic, finally with air cover.

hardly a matter for concern.[21] No one on the British side had considered what to do in the event of complete indifference by the enemy. Eventually Cunningham ordered an advance towards Tobruk. Here the dispersal of 7 Armoured Division started to exert a doleful effect. On the left 22 Armoured Brigade ran into the Ariete Division and, despite some vigorous action, could not dislodge it. On the right 4 Armoured Brigade was halted by a battlegroup from the Afrika Korps, whose commander, General Ludwig Crüwell, unlike Rommel, had realised that the British were conducting a major operation.[22] The Germans took a heavy toll on the light Stuart tanks and halted any forward movement. This left the 7 Armoured Brigade to advance towards Tobruk alone. It had some initial success, capturing the Sidi Rezegh aerodrome and destroying nineteen planes on the ground.[23] But it was without its Support Group (that is, most of its artillery), which was at Gabr Saleh, still deciding which grouplet of the division it should support. In the event the advance of the 7 Armoured Division was stopped by screens of anti-tank guns to the west and north of Sidi Rezegh and could make no progress. Eventually the Support Group joined them, but too late to affect the battle.

So far the British, though dispersed, had been assisted by Rommel's dithering. Only a few units of the Afrika Korps had been engaged and those piecemeal. On the 20th, however, Rommel grasped that a major offensive was underway and that one of its purposes was to relieve Tobruk. He therefore ordered units of the Afrika Korps to disengage and attack the British around Sidi Rezegh where they threatened to break through to the besieged port.[24]

The next three days proved to be a race between the Afrika Korps and XXX Corps to concentrate their forces — in the first case to remove the British from Sidi Rezegh; in the second to capture the escarpment beyond the airport and push on to Tobruk, where the garrison was to make a sortie to link hands. The race proved more difficult for the British. In the first place they had to rearrange their forces. One of their armoured brigades (22) had to be sent to the right rear to assist the 4 Armoured Brigade, which was still under attack. To take its place a brigade of the South African infantry had to be moved up to keep the Ariete Division away from any force advancing from Sidi Rezegh. Confused fighting occurred on all three days. By the 23rd the 7 Armoured Division was 'in a very crowded position with its HQ jumbled up with [the motor transport] of the South African Brigade and units crammed on the ground in no sort of position or formation.'[25] At this moment a concentrated attack by the 15 Panzer and the Ariete overran the South African brigade and smashed into the remnants of the 7 Armoured Brigade and the Support Group. In all the South Africans suffered 3,400 casualties and the brigade ceased to exist.[26] But the South Africans had their artillery with them and between those guns, the guns of the Support Group and (belatedly) some help from 22 Armoured Brigade a heavy toll was taken on the Germans with perhaps some seventy tanks being destroyed.[27] No one who took part in these battles had an accurate idea of the outcome. As the 7 Armoured narrative said: 'In all the big tank battles, dust and smoke created by movement and gunfire produced a veritable fog in which visibility was often less than one hundred yards.'[28]

No such uncertainties disturbed Rommel. He knew that he had inflicted heavy casualties on the British. He declared them decisive and ordered the Afrika Korps to dash for the Libya/Egypt border to round up the remnants of the Eighth Army.[29] This 'dash to the wire' was quite premature. The 7 Armoured Division was still in being, as was the other brigade of South African troops. Still, in no time at all, elements of 21 Panzer Division were across the border. They were also without orders or direction of any kind. They therefore huddled for the night, surrounded by British troops who were unaware that the enemy was among them. Behind this group lay a long, straggling line of various units of the Afrika Korps and their supply trucks.[30] A few were under Rommel's orders; others were under Crüwell; most were following the tank or truck ahead. The end result was the rather farcical situation where the bulk of the Afrika Korps were closer to Cairo than most of the Eighth Army.

Units of the 7 Armoured Division noticed this movement without having the slightest idea of what was occurring. The 4 Armoured Brigade and the Support Group attacked the enemy columns, causing much damage among the soft-skinned motor transport.[31] Nevertheless, Rommel persisted with his enterprise until the 26th. In truth his forces merely flailed about in the desert to not much effect. Then he learned that New Zealand troops had recaptured Sidi Rezegh and had linked up with the sortie by the 70 Division from Tobruk. Immediately, he assembled all the forces on the frontier and headed west.

What had happened on the British side was that Cunningham had changed his plan. Despairing that the much-reduced 7 Armoured Division would make it through to Tobruk, he ordered the armour to consolidate to the south of Sidi Rezegh and the New Zealanders forward to the escarpment and then, if possible, on to Tobruk.[32] He had unleashed the infantry. They succeeded. Two brigades (4 and 6) of New Zealand troops occupied the ridge and drove back those Germans who had not joined, and were probably unaware of, Rommel's movements. Then, in an amazing feat, the 19 New Zealand Battalion with Bren-gun carriers improvised the first night attack with tanks ever attempted. In the words of their historian: 'There was no time to stop or to go back to mop up, bayonets were used effectively throughout the advance, and grenades were tossed . . . The enemy casualties were considerable – ours were nil.'[33] In no time this battalion with six Matilda tanks had advanced 10,000 yards to El Duda to join with the Essex battalion from 70 Division. One aspect of the plan had, for the moment, succeeded.

This was Cunningham's last act as C-in-C Eighth Army. On 25 November 1941 Auchinleck visited Advanced Headquarters. He found Cunningham 'perturbed' by the situation and uncertain whether he should keep attacking or switch to defence. Auchinleck went back to Cairo but then returned to the desert and relieved Cunningham of command. This presented a difficulty. Churchill urged Auchinleck to take command himself, but he deemed his wider responsibilities to the Middle Eastern theatre precluded that.[34] Nor was he willing to promote either of the corps commanders in the middle of a battle. In the end he decided to promote his Deputy Chief of the General Staff, Lieutenant-General Neil Ritchie, who certainly knew Auchinleck's mind and would be resolute to continue the offensive.[35] There would be now no question of defence. Crusader would continue.

As these changes in the British command were taking place, Rommel and the Afrika Korps were heading west to deal with the New Zealand infantry, who were now at risk of being trapped between the garrison surrounding Tobruk and the rapidly closing Afrika Korps. The British armour was hastily reorganised to protect the New Zealanders, the 4 and 22 Armoured Brigades being consolidated under the 4. These blocking tactics worked – the 100 tanks in this force allowed the New Zealanders to escape. The 4 Armoured Brigade then found itself surrounded by the

Germans, but when the German armour drew back for the night the British tanks found the gap and fled south. The connection with Tobruk had, however, been lost and Sidi Rezegh was back in German hands. The siege of Tobruk resumed.[36]

Meanwhile the Support Group had divided itself into four small columns composed of field guns, anti-tank guns and motor infantry. Operating on information obtained by its armoured cars, the columns proved highly effective in harassing the enemy, whether the Germans were attacking or defending. Many casualties were inflicted on Rommel's forces in this way and these actions may well have helped swing the battle. Their effect was certainly noted by the commanders of the armour, and 'Jock Columns' (they were named after the commander of the Support Group, Brigadier Jock Campbell) were to be a permanent feature of British armoured actions until Alamein.[37] What was not noted was that the columns were only of use in a very fluid situation when the Afrika Korps were also split into groups. When Rommel's force was unified (as it usually was) he could pick off these columns seriatim; this was what occurred in the next year of war in the desert.

By the beginning of December weight of numbers on the British side was beginning to tell. Ritchie could introduce some reserves – 22 Guards Brigade into the battle and a brigade from the 4 Indian Division. He had well over 100 tanks up and running.[38] On his side, Rommel had nothing to add; his position was becoming critical. On 2 December an ill-advised attempt to cut off the New Zealanders along the coast road failed with heavy losses to 15 Panzer Division. By 4 December the Afrika Korps had fewer than fifty tanks.[39] By 7 December Rommel ordered a retreat back to the Gazala position.[40]

As Auchinleck's report makes clear, cutting off an enemy determined on retreat proved impossible:

> The first reports that the enemy were withdrawing came in during the early hours of 8th December. The [4] Armoured Brigade, directed to advance on Knightsbridge, a track crossing about 18 miles due west of El Adem, came up against the main enemy delaying positions . . . It was hoped that their centre line would bring the Brigade round or against the western flank of the enemy. In fact it led them to the centre of the

position which was strongly held by field and anti-tank guns behind which the enemy tanks took cover hull-down when engaged. Repeated efforts by the Armoured Brigade to turn the position on either flank were unsuccessful, and when evening came the enemy were still holding the ridge.[41]

As it happened, Rommel had decided on a much longer retreat – Gazala was only a way station. On the night of 16/17 December he slipped away. By Christmas Day he was south of Benghazi, pressed not very hard by 22 Guards and 4 Armoured. Indeed when the advance guard ventured too close to Rommel they received a bloody nose. On 28 December the 22 Guards were turned on by the retreating Afrika Korps. The Guards lost sixty tanks and had to be taken out of the line.[42] By early January Rommel reached his chosen stopping place El Agheila, the equally exhausted British lagging behind.[43] Operation Crusader was over.

Rommel's retreat was greeted with great enthusiasm in London. Churchill was cautious, however. He noted the severe nature of the fighting and the heavy cost in armoured vehicles that the British had paid.[44] He was right to be circumspect. Over this victory, as Michael Carver has noted, hung the feeling of failure.[45] This partly came about because there was a general perception that, in the larger armoured battles, Rommel had managed to concentrate a force that usually outfought the British. This occurred in the battles between 23 and 27 November near Sidi Rezegh where the British had two brigades of infantry (5 South African and 6 New Zealand) almost wiped out. Overall casualties were approximately even – about 10,000 killed and wounded on either side – just short of 10 per cent of the total numbers engaged.[46] In terms of tanks, the British definitely lost more than the Axis – probably the figures are just over 500 for the British and 300 for the German/Italian armies.[47] There was certainly a feeling on the British side that their tanks were inferior to the German. Generally, though, the British 2-pounder gun had as much penetrative power as the main German Mark III and IV tanks, but some German tanks had improved armour protection and against these the British tank guns were useless (except broadside on), and this may have led to the feeling of inferiority.[48] Most tank casualties were caused not by other tanks but by artillery and anti-tanks guns. Here the Germans had an advantage because of their

88-mm anti-tank gun which had much greater stopping power than the British 2-pounder.

In terms of generalship the battle was practically a draw with egregious errors on both sides. The British never fought united but on this occasion they were almost matched by the Afrika Korps. Initially this was because Rommel refused to believe that a large-scale offensive was taking place. Later his lunatic 'dash for the wire' dispersed his force and laid it open to attack, both advancing and retreating. If he was the consummate desert general, he was hardly at his best during Crusader. The retreat was a different matter. Here he demonstrated great skill but it has to be noted that no retreating army was ever overwhelmed in the desert war.

It also should be borne in mind that no army recovered from adversity as rapidly as the Afrika Korps. On 21 January 1942 Rommel turned and smote the advance units of the Eighth Army (the Guards Brigade and 1 Armoured Division) and drove them back. By 28 January they were fighting on the outskirts of Benghazi; by 4 February they were back at Gazala, just south of Tobruk. How had this volte-face occurred? The fact was that the strength of Rommel's retreating force had been much underestimated by Eighth Army Intelligence, which had also missed the fact that he had been reinforced with a large shipment of tanks. The underestimate was caused by overestimating the casualties suffered by the Germans in Crusader. Eighth Army thereby calculated that Rommel had fewer than 50,000 troops in the Afrika Korps when in fact he had 80,000.[49] On the matter of tanks, Auchinleck had deduced from Enigma decrypts that a convoy of six ships averaging 7,200 tons had reached Tripoli. The decrypt specified that the ships contained a large consignment of fuel for the Afrika Korps and the Luftwaffe and went on to state that it also contained material 'of great importance to the D.A.K [Deutsche Afrika Korps]'.[50] For reasons that are obscure the Middle East authorities concluded that this must mean motor transport and ammunition. Why they did not conclude that tanks might be 'of great importance' to Rommel is incomprehensible. In fact a consignment of between fifty-four and eighty tanks (estimates vary) had arrived. Again Eighth Army Intelligence compounded this error of judgement by crediting Rommel with far fewer tanks than he had. Their estimate was 90; the true number was 173, now boosted to well over 200 by the arrival of the convoy.[51] It was this force that swept aside the much outnumbered British forces on 21 January.

This whole episode is puzzling and made more so by the fact that authorities in Cairo were well aware that Rommel's supply problem must ease in the face of the deteriorating British position at sea. In December 1941, Force K, consisting of four cruisers based on Malta and preying on Rommel's cross-Mediterranean convoys, had sailed into an Italian minefield. Two cruisers were sunk and two badly damaged. In addition, just before the commencement of Crusader, the *Ark Royal*, the only aircraft carrier in the Mediterranean, had been torpedoed and sunk. This was followed by the sinking of the battleship *Barham* and the cruiser *Galatea* a week later, which was in turn followed by an attack inside Alexandria Harbour by an Italian human torpedo squad which put the battleships *Queen Elizabeth* and *Valiant* out of action for six months. In the light of the collapse of British naval power in the Eastern Mediterranean, the insouciance with which Rommel's supply position was regarded in Cairo is astonishing.[52]

The authorities in London, military naval and intelligence sent no warnings to Auchinleck regarding the balance of forces in the desert. The only person who did pass on such a warning was Churchill, who was in Washington to concert action with Roosevelt, now his ally. Churchill, however, was still reading Enigma. On 11 January he alerted Auchinleck of the arrival of the vital convoy, only to be told of 'the great losses in the recent fighting [suffered by Rommel]' and that as a result 'the enemy is hard pressed more than we dared to hope'.[53]

The 'hard-pressed' enemy was by the end of February on the Gazala line where Ritchie quickly improvised a defensive position. The 1 South African Division was hastened forward from reserve and the 50 Division was summoned from the delta.[54] To the south a brigade of the Free French were placed at Bir Hacheim. As a backstop the armour of the XXX Corps (7 and 1 Armoured) were placed behind the front. Mines were then laid in profusion. The South African Division placed no fewer than 150,000 and there were similar densities along the remainder of the front.[55] Towards the end of February, apart from a few raiding columns, Rommel paused. For the moment the situation had stabilised.

Back in London this was not to Churchill's taste. And on this occasion he was not alone. On 24 February 1942 Brooke addressed the Chiefs of Staff on the position of Malta, the island bastion athwart the supply lines from Italy to Africa, vital in disrupting supplies to Rommel. Enigma decrypts might provide the details of enemy convoys but only forces directed from the island could act on this information. Malta had been relentlessly attacked by the Luftwaffe and the Italian air force since early 1941. The only method of resupply was via convoys run into the island by the navy – often at great cost. As time went on, the view of Malta held in London became more complex. It was gradually seen as not only a base for offensive operations against the Axis armies in Egypt but also as a symbol of British defiance. It was therefore thought to be worth preserving in its own right as well as a base. Indeed, after Dunkirk and Singapore and the colossal reverses in the Western Desert there were those in the government who thought they might not survive the capitulation of an island of 300,000 people. With the loss of Force K and Britain's diminished naval presence in the Mediterranean, the easiest way of supplying Malta was from the aerodromes around Benghazi. The problem was that those aerodromes had recently been lost in the great retreat. The way to get them back was to counter-attack in the Western Desert. This is what Brooke suggested to the Chiefs of Staff: that a telegram be sent to the Commanders-in-Chief Middle East 'drawing their attention to the need for offensive action in the Western desert at the earliest possible date' to relieve Malta.[56]

This telegram was followed by one from Churchill stating that the 'most drastic steps' should be taken to maintain Malta and that the last date he would accept for an offensive was early April.[57] Auchinleck, however, had been counting tanks. After Crusader he had concluded that German armoured superiority precluded an early attack. He would not move before he had obtained a superiority of two to one in tanks; a target that would not be reached until June.[58]

The COS and Churchill were greatly disturbed by this appreciation. The Chiefs noted that Malta must be resupplied in May and that therefore the attack would have to precede that date. They reminded Auchinleck that without Malta Rommel could be reinforced at will and suggested in particular that German air reinforcements were flowing into Africa. In their stark view, 'it is now or never'.[59] Churchill was even blunter, telling

Auchinleck that 'the delays you contemplate will seal the fate of Malta'. He continued:

> The reputation of the British army now lies unhappily very low. We do not seem to be able to fight the enemy on even terms or man for man. I was looking to the Eighth Army, on which everything we have has been lavished, to repair the shame of Singapore. Surely it is possible to move forward into close contact with the enemy and engage him continuously till a decision is reached.[60]

From Auchinleck's point of view it was not possible to move forward. He put to the COS that the point was not whether he could save Malta but whether he might jeopardise Britain's entire Middle Eastern position if the battle went against him. July was now mentioned as a start date for the offensive.[61]

This proved too much for Churchill. He wanted to meet the C-in-C to thrash the situation out: 'I should be glad . . . if you would come home for consultation at your earliest convenience – bringing an authority on tank maintenance.'[62] The Chiefs of Staff were of the same mind – Auchinleck must return to London for consultation. But Auchinleck would not return.[63] He wrote to Churchill:

> Am certain I cannot leave Mideast in present circumstances. Situation is entirely different from that obtaining in July, and I am not prepared to delegate authority to anyone while strategical situation is so fluid and liable to rapid change. I can give no more information regarding tank situation than I have already given, nor would my coming home make it more possible to stage an earlier offensive.[64]

This was poor judgement on the part of Auchinleck. Churchill in particular craved personal contact with his generals and was entitled to ask for it. Moreover, Auchinleck's best chance of persuading the Prime Minister of the soundness of his case lay in a face-to-face meeting. Also Brooke, Auchinleck's front-line defence against Churchill, had requested a meeting and was not amused by this refusal.[65] It was naive of Auchinleck to think that his refusal would end the matter; Churchill rang Brooke in a fury and suggested sacking the C-in-C.[66] Brooke headed that off but Churchill told Auchinleck that his attitude had raised the 'deepest anxiety' in London, that he was 'endangering Malta', that his tank numbers showing a German superiority were not believed (Churchill had Enigma decrypts that showed Rommel was inferior to Eighth Army in tanks) and that he would be visited by the Vice Chief of the Imperial General Staff (Major-General Archibald Nye) and a member of the War Cabinet (Stafford Cripps, on his way to Delhi to solve the intractable question of Indian independence) and would be expected to explain himself.[67]

The Nye visit would not be a casual affair. Churchill compiled a quiz of twenty questions that he required Auchinleck to answer to Nye's satisfaction. Nye would then transmit the answers with comments back to the Prime Minister in London. These questions were not the anodyne platitudes that generals often receive from politicians. For example, Question 7 on tank strengths said in part:

What is the detailed evidence to support [your] ... figures of 475 Medium enemy Tanks by 1st March, and 630 by 1st April, even accepting this as the best possible case for the Axis? ... We believe [from Ultra decrypts] that two German and two Italian divisions at their respective 'North African' establishments would total 542 Tanks, that is, 266 German and 276 Italian Tanks.[68]

Or Question 17:

'What progress has been made in the repair of Tanks? Why has Commander-in-Chief not allotted sufficiently high priority to ensure shipping of 3rd Echelon Ordnance Workshop Units which have been standing by in this country awaiting despatch for three months?[69]

Whatever one might think of questions at this level of detail, it cannot be said that the Prime Minister was not well acquainted with the minutiae of the desert war. Nye passed on Auchinleck's answers to these questions. He detailed the basis on which Auchinleck and the Middle East command had arrived at their estimates and why damaged tanks were not coming out of the workshops in greater numbers. Overall Nye sought to reassure Churchill that all was well in Cairo and that Auchinleck was doing his best to hasten towards an offensive.

Stafford Cripps had the same message for the Prime Minister. He told Churchill that Auchinleck had insufficient strength in tanks and aircraft to attack immediately. He concluded:

> That the mid-May date be accepted as the target and that everything possible be done to prepare for that date both here and at home. I am not suggesting that there is any want of effort here, as I am sure there is not, but merely that an effort should be organized for that particular location.[70]

Churchill was not convinced. He sent a blistering reply to Nye:

> I do not wonder everything was so pleasant considering you seem to have accepted everything they said and all we have got to accept is the probable loss of Malta and the army standing idle while the Russians are resisting the German counter-stroke desperately, and while the enemy is reinforcing himself in Libya faster than we are.[71]

Nye was enjoined to stay and go into matters more thoroughly. He did this but his conclusions were the same. On 31 March the Defence Committee 'reluctantly' accepted a mid-May date for the British offensive, thus taking a gamble that Malta would hang on.[72]

The discussion on tank strength continued throughout April, Churchill and Auchinleck batting back and forth numbers mainly derived from the same Enigma source.[73] Gradually it became clear that the mid-May date had slipped. On 6 May Auchinleck declared that he must insist on a three to two ratio in tanks and that he would not be in this position until mid-June.[74] Churchill was now apoplectic. He railed that Malta would be lost, 'a disaster of the first magnitude to the British Empire and probably fatal in the long run to the defence of the Nile Valley'. He insisted that Auchinleck attack in May and that the War Cabinet would take the entire responsibility.[75] Auchinleck held his ground and, despite the COS the Defence Committee and the War Cabinet insisting that Malta must not fall, in the end they agreed that Auchinleck could start his offensive in mid-June.[76]

373

In fact by this time the entire debate had become academic. Enigma was revealing that Rommel was preparing his own offensive. Evidence accumulated during early May, when it became clear that the Afrika Korps would move to the attack sometime after 22 May. On 26 May the code word 'Venezia' was intercepted and this was 'correctly interpreted . . . as being the enemy's pre-arranged signal for the start of his attack'.[77]

In truth, whatever Auchinleck's protestations, Eighth Army was superior to Rommel in all departments. On the eve of the Battle of Gazala it had 100,000 men, 849 tanks and 604 aircraft. Rommel had 90,000 men, 561 tanks and 542 aircraft.[78] Nevertheless it is possible to identify the basis for Auchinleck's reluctance to attack earlier than June. Whatever the state of Malta, he was in charge of an army that had just taken part in a colossal retreat. The Afrika Korps and attendant Italian forces had hustled Ritchie's men from one position to another over a distance of 500 miles. Only exhaustion had brought this rout to a halt in February. In the line at Gazala he had the 1 South African Division, a new British division (50) and a brigade of Free French soldiers. Behind them he had the 1 and 7 Armoured Divisions and some smaller Indian units. In many ways this was not an attractive line-up. The South African commanders had proved reluctant warriors in Crusader and their new commander (Major-General Dan Pienaar) had proved the most reluctant of all. The 50 Division was new to the desert; its previous post had been garrison duty in Cyprus during a quiet period. The armoured divisions were being partly re-equipped with a new tank (the Grant) but they had not proved all that effective in stemming Rommel's advance and their commanders were yet to show their worth against the panzers. All this made Auchinleck cautious. He could not be sure that such a layout would stop the Afrika Korps, let alone launch a major operation against it.

It seems certain that these negative factors were exacerbated by the way in which the Eighth Army was deployed. At Gazala the drift from divisions fighting as complete units had quickened. The front-line infantry were now organised in brigade boxes with all-round defences. This immediately dispersed the artillery resources of a division into smaller packets. Worse still, many of these boxes were not mutually supporting. The South Africans were reasonably closely grouped but 150 Brigade of 50 Division was some 7 miles from its neighbour (69 Brigade), and the Free French at Bir Hacheim were 20 miles further south. Other 'keeps' at Acroma, Knightsbridge and Point 209 were out of range of the front line and out of range of each other. None had a garrison of any strength. The armour was no better placed: the 7 Armoured Division was in the south and the 1 Armoured Division some 25 miles to the north. And each division was not concentrated. So in the south there was a considerable gap between the 7 and 4 Armoured Brigades and in the centre a smaller but still significant gap between the 2 and 22 Armoured Brigades.[79] Some of this confused layout came about because Ritchie and Auchinleck had different ideas about where Rommel would attack – Ritchie considered a right hook in the south most likely and Auchinleck a direct attack on the centre north. Auchinleck had recently told Ritchie that he wanted the armoured divisions to fight as divisions, yet he was either unaware of Ritchie's dispositions or he allowed them to stand.[80] Either way it was a major command failure, for the whole disposition of the Eighth Army positively invited defeat seriatim. Unless the widely dispersed units acted with great speed to support each other, Rommel might eat them up one by one.

The destruction of the divisional structure might well have raised the greatest concerns among the military authorities in London when they ran their eyes over Auchinleck's dispositions for battle. Far from this – his tactics won approval. Brooke noted Auchinleck's changes:

> that the unit of organisation was now the brigade group which would now be self-contained.
> and that the armoured divisions would be similarly broken up into smaller units.

He passed this information on to Churchill, adding that he agreed in principle with the changes.[81] Churchill replied the same day: 'I have long preferred Brigade Groups to Divisions as you know. I cordially approve the change.'[82] Thus all authorities, from army commander to Prime Minister were as one in breaking up the standard unit of the British army and dispersing its considerable firepower all over the desert.

All the evils that had first revealed themselves at Battleaxe and Crusader were therefore to be repeated at Gazala. Rommel attacked concentrated; 90 Light Division, 21 and 15 Panzer Divisions and the Ariete coming in a gigantic right hook (as Ritchie had predicted) around the minefields that protected the British front from the coast to the south of Bir Hacheim. They met the brigades of the 7 Armoured Division (Messervy) dispersed and dealt with them seriatim, also overrunning the Advanced Headquarters of the division, thus decapitating it. Next it was the turn of 22 Armoured Brigade, moving slowly and well away from its sister brigade which was immobile around the Knightsbridge box. In short order it lost thirty tanks, including many of the new Grants.[83] Apart from the Free French at Bir Hacheim who were successfully warding off the Ariete Division, the entire British southern front had collapsed. Nevertheless this success had not proved costless to Rommel. The British armour, though defeated, had managed to take a heavy toll on 15 and 21 Panzer Divisions, which had probably lost about 200 tanks between them. Worse still for the Germans, the scattered units of 7 Armoured had launched various counter-attacks on what turned out to be Rommel's supply columns. These thin-skinned vehicles were easy prey and their destruction meant that the German armoured columns were now jammed between the remaining British armoured units and the minefields, with supplies of petrol and ammunition running short.[84]

Rommel's response was rapid. He had already ordered the Italians facing the minefield to the north of the Trig Capuzzo to create gaps in the minefield through which supplies could be directly sent to his armour. Now he abandoned his plan to head towards the coast and turned his force due west to link up with the Italians and widen any gaps they had created. The idea was that 15 and 21 Panzer Divisions would form a screen between the British box at Knightsbridge and the minefields (this area quickly became known as the Cauldron) while his infantry dealt with the mines.

None of the above was known to Ritchie, the commander of the Eighth Army. He knew, of course, the outline of Rommel's movements and considered that his armour had inflicted heavy casualties on the Germans. More worryingly, he deemed himself quite satisfied with the situation, which he claimed 'was foreseen and . . . planned for.'[85] This was cloud cuckoo land. No one had foreseen or planned for the bulk of the Afrika Korps to be rampaging around behind the British lines after scattering the bulk of two armoured divisions. Nor had Ritchie grasped the intent of Rommel's turn to the west. He conceived this as a desperate enemy attempting to escape through a hostile minefield.[86] In Ritchie's mind, Rommel was trapped. In this circumstance it might be thought that the imperative was to concentrate every available armoured unit and crush the embattled enemy. Nothing of the kind happened. On 29 May the 22 Armoured Brigade alone moved against Rommel, only to be beaten back by the screen of guns which now surrounded the panzers. Other piecemeal attacks followed. None was successful. Still, the fact was that Rommel's position was worse than he had initially thought. Between him and the minefield lay the 150 Brigade entrenched in their box with a group of infantry tanks, some artillery and a battery of the new 6-pounder anti-tank guns. Rommel's initial attacks on this isolated brigade by the panzers, 90 Light Division and (from outside the minefield) the Brescia Italian Division were all repulsed, the defence being described as 'skilful and stubborn'.[87] Eventually weight of numbers told: by 1 June after heavy dive bombing and bitter fighting, the 150 Brigade was overcome; 3,000 troops became prisoners. No unit of the Eighth Army had come to their rescue.

The blame for this fiasco must be spread widely. The Official History's explanation that by the time corps and army headquarters realised the 150 Brigade was in trouble 'it was too late to do anything effective to help' is quite unbelievable.[88] The position, if not the intention, of the Afrika Korps was known. The position of the 150 Brigade was also known. It surely took no genius to realise what might eventuate. Lieutenant-General Herbert Lumsden, commander of 1 Armoured Division, sent encouraging words to the brigade but no tanks. Other units of the XXX Corps wandered down to Bir Hacheim, to no great effect. A column from the Knightsbridge box ventured towards the Cauldron and was stopped by the anti-tank screen. XIII Corps did nothing. Ritchie spent many hours in conference with his corps commanders but little action followed. In truth Ritchie, Norrie, Gott, Lumsden and Messervy proved collectively and individually incapable of reaching rapid decisions or indeed any decisions. The Eighth Army think-tank was disintegrating at the same rate as their armour.

What followed has been described by one authority as 'a long series of committee meetings' between Ritchie and his corps and divisional commanders.[89] Various plans were discussed. Typically, Pienaar refused to have anything to do with any of them. Ritchie eventually decided on a frontal attack on the east face of the Cauldron. Gott refused to participate, apparently on the grounds that it was reminiscent of Western Front operations. Norrie was then given the task but he promptly passed it to Messervy and Colonel Harold Briggs, the commander of 5 Indian Division, now brought forward from reserve.[90]

The consequence was as a 'lamentable fiasco'.[91] The attack was not launched until the night of 5/6 June. This gave Rommel ample time to consolidate his position. It also gave the British ample time to reconnoitre but they failed to do so. As a result their artillery bombardment fell well short of the enemy's defensive positions. When the tanks went forward through the advancing infantry they ran into an undisturbed German artillery and anti-tank screen. When Rommel moved to the attack, the destruction of British forces in the Cauldron was complete. With many of their artillery and anti-tanks guns out of action and sixty tanks destroyed, the Indian infantry scattered, as did the remains of 22 Armoured Brigade.[92]

This failure allowed Rommel to concentrate on the French garrison at Bir Hacheim. The French had put up a spirited defence and it took the transference of 15 Panzer Division to the south after the British disaster in the Cauldron to force an evacuation of the isolated post. This was successfully accomplished on 11 June and, despite German efforts, over 3,000 of the garrison escaped. Yet the whole affair was another damming indictment of the policy of scattering so-called strongpoints all across the desert.

The end was now in sight. Confused and swirling fighting (as well as a dust storm) enveloped the area around Knightsbridge, another isolated box where the Guards Brigade had observed but had hardly taken part in the previous battles. The concentrated efforts of the Afrika Korps now forced a general retreat. The Guards, the remains of the armoured divisions and the Indian infantry streamed back north-west. The only matter for consideration was where the British forces might find a defensible line and whether the two divisions in the northern section of the front (1 South African and the remains of 50 Division) would be able to escape.

Churchill, as usual, had been following developments. Based on Auchinleck's optimistic summaries he had made a statement in Parliament on 2 June to the effect that while there had been hard fighting, the Eighth Army had inflicted serious casualties upon Rommel and that Ritchie and his generals were doing well.[93] But as the battle progressed he grew anxious. On hearing that Ritchie had been forced to retreat he asked Auchinleck:

To what position does Ritchie want to withdraw the Gazala troops? Presume there is no serious question in any case of giving up Tobruk. As long as Tobruk is held no serious enemy advance into Egypt is possible ... [but] do not understand what you mean by withdrawing to 'old frontier'.[94]

Auchinleck's reply revealed orders to Ritchie that were riddled with ambiguity:

Although I do not intend the Eighth Army should be besieged in Tobruk, I have no intention whatever of giving up Tobruk. My orders to General Ritchie . . . are –
    (a) To deny general line Acroma – El Adem – El Gubi to the enemy.
    (b) Not to allow his forces to be invested in Tobruk.
    (c) To attack and harass the enemy whenever occasion offers.[95]

Attempting to untangle this message is not easy and, as a hard-pressed Army Commander, Ritchie was surely entitled to greater clarity. What Auchinleck seems to have meant is that he expected Ritchie to hold a line (north to south) Tobruk–Acroma–El Adem–El Gubi rather than merely falling back on Tobruk and undergoing another siege. Should that line not hold, however, Auchinleck's intentions for Tobruk were not clear: should Ritchie abandon the port (not allow his forces to be invested there)? If this was the case, what of Auchinleck's statement that he had no intention whatever of giving up Tobruk?

Back in London the War Cabinet tried to make sense of it cabling Auchinleck:

We are glad to have your assurance that you have no intention of giving up Tobruk. War Cabinet interpret paragraph (b) of your telegram to mean, if the need arises, General Ritchie would leave as many troops in Tobruk as are necessary to hold the place for certain.[96]

That is, Tobruk would not undergo a siege unless it was necessary that it should.

This interpretation turned out to be correct. Ritchie would only place sufficient troops in Tobruk to hold it temporarily should it become isolated. The bulk of the Eighth Army (including the 1 South African Division and the 50 Division, which had both extricated themselves from Gazala) would hold the Acroma–El Gubi line until they could counter-attack and relieve Tobruk of its temporary embarrassment.[97]

There were (at least) two problems with this policy. The first was that there was no strong defensive line south of Tobruk to hold. Having been forced out of a much stronger position at Gazala and now running desperately short of armour and guns, what made Auchinleck think he could hold what amounted to little more than a line in the sand? Secondly, the defences of Tobruk were not what they had been when held by the Australians the year before. Many of the mines had been shifted to bolster the Gazala defences, the anti-tank ditches had largely collapsed and many of the local strongpoints had fallen into disrepair.

These factors soon came into play. By 17 June the Acroma 'line' had been abandoned as Rommel's forces advanced on Sidi Rezegh.[98] As for Tobruk, the COS anxiously asked the size of the besieged garrison. They were reassured by Auchinleck that there were over 30,000 troops around the port and that Ritchie and Gott had 'great confidence' in Major-General Hendrik Klopper, the South African in charge.[99] By the 20th Rommel had turned on Tobruk. The attack went in from the east with the 15 and 21 Panzers and two Italian divisions, including the Ariete. Massed attacks by Stukas accompanied the advance. Klopper announced his intention to fight to the last but he was out of touch at the western end of the perimeter and had managed to convey no fighting spirit to his troops.[100] His last message summed up his command: 'Situation shambles. Terrible casualties would result. Am doing the worst. Petrol destroyed.'[101]

The next day Klopper and 30,000 troops surrendered. In reality there was little chance of any commander withstanding an attack of the scale mounted by Rommel. A resolute commander might have made some kind of stand to delay the inevitable. Klopper was not that man. In fact he had not even managed to destroy the petrol mentioned in his last message. His worst had been not nearly good enough – 1,400 tons were captured by Rommel, a bonus that would allow him to pursue the Eighth Army into Egypt.[102]

In the middle of the siege Churchill had left for Washington to concert future policy with Roosevelt. He was in the Oval Office when a slip of paper was handed to the President announcing that Tobruk had fallen. Not only that – another message soon arrived from Vice-Admiral Henry Harwood at Alexandria stating that he was moving the entire Eastern Mediterranean Fleet south of the Suez Canal 'to await events'.[103] Churchill records this as 'one of the heaviest blows I can recall during the war'. He pondered, with some reason, whether any British army could fight a modern battle. What he did not know was that neither Auchinleck nor Ritchie had really intended that Tobruk withstand a long siege. What they had not done was make this clear to Churchill. Auchinleck's great failure was not to realise that Tobruk was a political matter as well as a military one and that his political chief needed to be kept in the loop. Churchill now had not only Singapore to explain but Tobruk. And he would have to account for these events to a House of Commons that was becoming restive to the point of laying down a censure motion. The desert generals were showing that not only were they incapable of fighting battles, they were endangering the war leadership as well.

There was little time to weigh these matters. Rommel was now advancing into Egypt. How was he to be stopped? Whatever the method, it would not be carried out by Ritchie. It is difficult to know exactly when Auchinleck lost confidence in his army commander but by 25 June he had had enough – he relieved Ritchie and took command himself.[104] His first plan had been to fight a kind of delaying action at Mersa Matruh and then conduct an orderly retreat to the so-called El Alamein Line. This misfired immediately – Rommel broke through at Matruh.

The retreat was accompanied by the further break-up of the divisional structure of the army. Ritchie had decided and Auchinleck confirmed that every infantry brigade would be split into battlegroups, which were little more than improvised columns of whatever artillery, infantry and other ad hoc formations of armour could be gathered together.[105] The so-called static aspects of the division were sent back either to the Alamein position or in some cases to the delta. Thus in the midst of chaos the Eighth Army 'was told to change its organization and its tactics'.[106] There seems little question that Rommel's advance was hastened by this shambles. South of Matruh he swept aside two of these Jock Columns (Leathercol and Gleecol) and headed east.[107] Even Gott was losing his grip. The New Zealand Division had been brought up and, because of its commander Lieutenant-General Bernard Freyberg's protests, had not been split into columns. It therefore had a reasonable chance of blocking Rommel, at least in the southern section of the front. However, Gott was under the impression that it had been overrun and ordered all other units, including the 1 Armoured, to retreat. The New Zealanders were therefore left quite alone and to some extent surrounded by the Afrika Korps. Amazingly, the New Zealanders staged a breakout.[108] At the cost of over 900 men they lived to fight another day, but it must be said that their relations with XIII Corps and the British armour reached a new low.[109]

The Eighth Army was soon back at Alamein but their retreat had hardly been orderly. The line to which they retreated also barely existed. Some attempt had been made in 1941 to construct some defensive boxes in the area but little work had been carried out. The one advantage of the position was that it was limited in size. To the north there was the sea and 50 miles to the south lay the Qattara Depression, a region of impassable sand. Thus Rommel's favourite manoeuvre of a right hook around the defences would not be available to him; he would have to attack frontally. What confronted him were a series of low ridges and depressions which were to some extent defensible but the troops holding them were very few. In the north, around the railway siding of El Alamein, 1 South African Division held the best constructed box, with some minefield and trench defences. Just to the south the 18 Indian Brigade, which had been rushed forward first from Iraq and then Palestine, held the saucer-shaped Deir el Shein Depression. Further south still was the New Zealand Division with much experience of desert warfare but short of men thanks to the disastrous handling of their retreat by XIII Corps. Behind these forces was the 1 Armoured Division with around 100 tanks.

On the other side, Rommel was also in no great strength. The 15 and 21 Panzer Divisions could muster just fifty-five tanks between them, though he still had some 300 guns, of which twenty-nine were 88s and thirty-nine captured British 25-pounders. The most serious shortage was in infantry. The panzer divisions had fewer than 600 men each, 90 Light Division had just over 1,000 and the Italian Corps 5,500 – a very limited number in the wastelands of the desert.[110]

Rommel's plan for 1 July was to drive through what he thought was a gap south of the Alamein box with 90 Light while the Afrika Korps headed south probing for another gap in the defensive boxes. As it happened Rommel's intelligence was deficient: across the path of the Afrika Korps lay the 18 Indian Brigade at Deir el Shein. These men, the Essex, Sikhs and Gurkhas, put up a stiff resistance. Their artillery aided by nine Matilda tanks took a heavy toll of the panzers. Soon over a dozen had been disabled, quickly followed by six more. As the fighting progressed, the brigade was finally overrun but the panzers could go no further; the armoured thrust had been stopped. In the north the Germans fared no better. As 90 Light skirted the Alamein box, concentrated fire from the South Africans rained down on them. Exactly who organised this devastating riposte is not certain. What is clear is that it caused a panic (the word is used in their War Diary) in 90 Light that was only stopped by vigorous action by upper-level commanders and by Rommel himself.[111]

Convinced he had the Eighth Army at the last gasp, Rommel tried again the next day. This time he attempted to capture the Ruweisat Ridge. He was stopped by the guns of an improvised column and 1 South African Brigade. The column was overrun but the South Africans and later the New Zealanders hung on and indeed managed to give the Ariete Division a bloody nose. In the end Rommel was forced to the conclusion that for the moment the Afrika Korps had run out of steam – he would halt for a fortnight to regroup.[112]

Auchinleck now seized what he thought was his chance. During the remainder of July the Eighth Army moved to the attack. In all they launched seven attacks on the Afrika Korps. All failed except the first, where the 9 Australian Division, in its return to the desert, managed to capture a piece of insignificant ground on a narrow front. The remainder, poorly organised and coordinated, gained no significant ground while wearing down the units involved. In July the New Zealand Division suffered 4,000 casualties, the 5 Indian Division 3,000 and 50 Division 2,500.[113]

These battles, from Gazala to Alamein, demonstrate the Eighth Army leadership at its nadir. There is much discussion in the literature as to whether Auchinleck or Ritchie or Norrie or Gott or the armoured commanders were at fault. The truth is that they all were. Auchinleck continually breathed down Ritchie's neck by frequent visits to his headquarters, only to fly back to

Cairo and allow Ritchie to conduct his ill-starred operations. Ritchie by all accounts hardly made a move before consulting Norrie and Gott at length. Even then Gott was able, without repercussions, to opt out of battles in which he had no confidence. In turn Pienaar would hardly speak to Gott, and Freyberg would rarely swap a word with the armoured commanders, whom he blamed – with some justice – for continually letting his New Zealanders down. In short the leadership of the largest British army in contact with the enemy was a rabble. And they were an incompetent rabble. They had broken up the structure of the army to no good purpose, dispersed its firepower all over the desert and proved incapable of acting with the precision and speed required in armoured warfare. They seemed to grasp, at one point or another, that Rommel generally operated with his armour united, made decisions with celerity and never advanced his tanks without an attendant screen of anti-tank guns and artillery. Yet no British commander at a senior level ever managed to replicate Rommel's tactics or devise anything new to counter them. What is surprising in the scenario was not that morale was low but that it held up at all. That it did hold up is shown by the 18 Indian Brigade and the South Africans on 1 July, by the New Zealanders on numerous occasions and the Australians when they re-entered the battle. This demonstrates conclusively that it is quite possible to fight hard with less than optimum morale. If the leadership was a rabble, the troops of the Eighth Army never were. They never broke and they only surrendered when there was no other choice.[114] What they required was competent leadership that was capable of developing a decent battle plan. After Gazala and Alamein, the political and military leadership in London were determined that leadership changes were in order. Churchill and Brooke prepared to fly to Cairo.

CHAPTER 17

SLOUCHING TOWARDS A STRATEGY – ANGLO-AMERICAN PLANNING 1940–1942

IN THE WAR IN the desert and in Britain's defensive strategy against invasion, Churchill and the Chiefs of Staff could definitively decide British responses among themselves. Certainly they were obliged (sometimes grudgingly) to consult the Dominions about troop movements and reinforcements but these rarely affected strategic decisions. If the Prime Minister and the COS differed – for example, on the desirability of running convoys to the Middle East through the Mediterranean – their views could be thrashed out in the Defence Committee, the COS Committee and in the War Cabinet. Within the Empire, strategy in this period was almost always decided in London.

From the beginning of Churchill's premiership, however, the United States loomed large. Despite many bursts of confident rhetoric from the Prime Minister, he knew that the vast resources of America must be thrown onto the scales if Britain was not just to ward off German invasion but defeat the Hitler regime. His expectations of the Great Republic ran high. On 11 September 1939, while First Lord of the Admiralty, Churchill had received a letter from Franklin Roosevelt, the American President:

My dear Churchill,
    It is because you and I occupied similar positions in the World War that I want you to know how glad I am that you are back again in the

Admiralty . . . What I want you and the Prime Minister to know is that I shall at times welcome it if you will keep me in touch personally with anything you want me to know about.

    Franklin D. Roosevelt[1]

Churchill was so anxious to take up this offer that he telephoned the President to accept.[2]

There is no question that this overture from Roosevelt raised false hopes in London. Roosevelt, although sympathetic to the British cause, was merely seeking information. His original letter and subsequent correspondence when Churchill became Prime Minister implied nothing else. Yet when the first great crisis of the war came on 15 May 1940, with the French premier's gloomy predictions of defeat, it was to Roosevelt that Churchill turned:

I trust you realise Mr. President that the voice and force of the United States may count for nothing if they are withheld too long. You may have a completely subjugated and Nazified Europe established with astonishing swiftness, and the weight may be more than we can bear.[3]

He went on to ask for American destroyers and various other war materiel.

This letter not only sought American resources, it sought an immediate entry into the war. From Churchill's perspective American entry into the war made sense. Of the few democratic states remaining in the world only the United States had the potential power to defeat Hitler. For Roosevelt this was asking too much. In 1940 the country's small armed forces were unready. In his view, public opinion was also unready, and he still had an over-optimistic estimate of British power. Britain was the Great Power of his childhood, with the resources of a vast empire. Surely it would prevail. If it did not, should America throw good resources after bad?

Roosevelt's response to Churchill's entreaties reflected all these factors. He was hesitant on the destroyers, vague on the supply of other war-related stores, and silent on the matter of a Nazified Europe. Churchill's immediate hopes were dashed. Nevertheless, over the next eighteen months they would from time to time soar. A rousing speech by the President indicating full support for the Allies would be made. Churchill would respond enthusiastically, only to discover that there had been no change in US policy. This was typical of Roosevelt. As he said of himself:

> You know I am a juggler, and I never let my right hand know what my left hand does . . . I may have one policy for Europe and one diametrically opposite for North and South America. I may be entirely inconsistent, and furthermore I am perfectly willing to mislead.[4]

Churchill never grasped this aspect of the President, either in the dark days before America entered the war or indeed after that point.[5] What he was to discover was that Britain could not dictate strategy to a neutral state, however much he considered that the interests of that state were inextricably bound to the fate of Britain. This is not to say that Britain was friendless in the United States. Roosevelt hardly wanted Britain to be overrun by the Nazis, and Britain did receive as much aid as the President deemed fell within the limits of what public opinion would bear. The problem for Britain was that the President's deeming did not amount to much. Fifty old destroyers were eventually delivered but not in time for the invasion season; American naval patrols extended into the Atlantic but not far; Iceland was occupied by US forces in June 1941, freeing up a few British troops to return home. Then there was the lend-lease bill which was passed in March 1941 – a guarantee that the resources of the United States would be available to Britain 'without the dollar sign', but very little materiel flowed to Britain in the short term. And in the short term Churchill feared Britain might be dead. Meanwhile, until the summer of 1941 the dollar sign was still operative.

In various secret manoeuvres Roosevelt continued to raise British hopes. In June 1940, in relation to the destroyers deal, the British Ambassador to the US (Lord Lothian) suggested that staff talks between the two countries might be appropriate. The President reacted at once, saying 'he thought that this would be a good thing and it ought to take place at once'.[6] Churchill was not so sure. Roosevelt's letters to him had concentrated on the fate of the British fleet should Britain fall, and Churchill felt that 'staff talks' were just another mechanism to pressure him on this issue.[7] However, Halifax and the COS persuaded him to relent, noting that Britain should take up any offer by the President of military discussions.[8] Typically, Churchill then became enthusiastic, suggesting that he should see the delegation as soon as they arrived and offering a dinner at No. 10.[9] Meanwhile the American Military Attaché in London, Colonel Raymond Lee, had got wind of the delegation from 'cocktail party gossip'. He had no idea of the origins of the mission or what they were to discuss.[10] He quickly moved to dampen down expectations, telling Ismay that the delegates (whoever they were) 'should be treated as ordinary visitors coming to this country to study war conditions'.[11] Ismay cancelled Churchill's dinner party but Churchill immediately un-cancelled it and instructed the Cabinet Secretary (Sir Edward Bridges) to 'get on with it'.[12] These were staff talks. The end result must be to get America more deeply involved.

There was no doubt in general terms, however, that Lee was right in describing the US delegation (Generals Strong and Emmons representing the army and army air force and Admiral Ghormley for the navy) as 'fair but no heavyweights'.[13] When they met the Vice Chiefs of Staff on 20 August (disguised under the cover of the Anglo-American Standardization of Arms Committee) Ghormley immediately remarked that the Americans in no way represented a joint mission. They had merely been appointed observers. It should also be understood that none of these observers had been authorised to make any commitments on behalf of their government.[14] Then, when war production was suggested by the British as a useful matter to discuss, Ghormley and Strong said that they 'were not in a position to enter into detailed technical discussions on the subject of production. Nor did they wish to do so.'[15]

This rather left hanging what their purpose actually was. On close interrogation Lee could not discover it. Ghormley could only tell him that they had come to 'look and learn' and that they had had typically 'no instructions at all' from Roosevelt.[16] Further questioning on the part of Churchill's staff got no further; Lee repeated that the Americans had no instructions. Non-plussed by the vagueness of the American response, the Vice Chiefs quickly arranged a series of visits to fighter, bomber, naval and military sites in the hopes that the visitors would be impressed with British defence preparations, or perhaps just to fill in their time.[17] After the tour the Americans met with the COS, Ghormley thanking them for it but noting that they 'as yet not had the time fully to digest the results of this experience'.[18] This response stifled further discussion and most of the remainder of this meeting was taken up by a survey of the strategic situation given by the Chief of the Air Staff, Newell. After that the meeting just fizzled out. The Americans met with the COS again on 31 August. Newell gave yet another strategic survey but a feeling of lassitude permeated the remainder of a rambling discussion. The only lively point came when Ghormley asked what plans the British had if they failed to withstand a German invasion. He was tersely informed by Newell that there were no such plans as the whole nation assumed that such an attack would be withstood.[19]

Perhaps the whole rag-tag business had not been entirely useless. On their return to the US, Generals Strong and Emmons reported favourably to General George Marshall about British chances of survival, and Strong gave an interview to the press where he noted that Germany was in for a 'nasty surprise' if it invaded.[20] No doubt this raised British stocks in the United States to some extent, but firm commitments remained a long way off.

More substantial staff talks commenced in January 1941 and continued through March. Their origins are also murky. In late October 1940 the US Military Attaché met with Major-General Roger Evans, the commander of the 1 Armoured Division. Evans told him that he had been instructed to 'get ready to be the Military member of the delegation slated to travel at an early date to the United States for joint staff talks and plans'.[21] Nothing was to happen, Evans emphasised, until after the presidential election in November. Indeed, it was not until the end of that month that Lee heard from Ismay that talks would probably take place in the new year.[22] It seems likely that the idea for formal staff talks were initiated by the Americans. The timing (after the November 1940 election and while lend-lease was being negotiated) clearly reflected some sensitivity in the administration about being seen to be tied too closely to Britain. The other impulse was the redirection of American strategic plans. In late October 1940 Admiral Harold (Betty) Stark, the newly appointed head of the US navy, produced a document commonly known as Plan Dog.[23] Stark's paper indicated a change in American strategic priorities. Previous American war plans (known as Rainbow and Orange) had concentrated on responses to a crisis in the Pacific. Now Stark concluded that in any war against the Axis powers the US should pursue a 'Germany first' policy while remaining on the defence against the Japanese.[24] The implication here was that the British and the

Americans recognised that they had a common interest. In this circumstance Stark thought that a common strategy should be thrashed out between the proto-allies. Roosevelt's response was typical. On being shown Stark's plan he dodged giving it his approval but made it clear that staff talks should proceed.[25]

Once again Churchill held high hopes for these conversations, although he could hardly have thought that they were a prelude to immediate US intervention.[26] The British sent just a middle-level delegation (Rear-Admirals Bellairs and Danckwerts from the navy, Brigadier Edwin Morris from the army and Air Commodore John Slessor from the RAF). Stark and Marshall attended the first meeting with the permanent American delegates Generals Embrick, Miles and Gerow from the army and army air force and Admirals Turner and Ghormley from the navy.[27] The American selections were to cause the British some difficulty. Embrick and Turner thought the US had been somehow 'tricked' by the British into entering the First World War and were on the look-out to prevent this re-occurring on their watch. Moreover, the US delegation did not speak with one voice, the Americans having no COS system where differences in the services could be thrashed out before the meetings. The British therefore found the Americans to be suspicious and prickly at times. At other times it was difficult to establish what authority remarks by the navy might have when they were repudiated by the army.[28]

Nevertheless, the meetings started on a reassuring note for the British. By Meeting 2 (21 January 1941) the minutes state that: 'There was general agreement that the European Theatre was the vital theatre where a decision must first be sought, and that the general policy should be to defeat Germany and Italy first, and then, if necessary deal with Japan.'[29]

Many of the subsequent meetings discussed the Pacific theatre, the British wishing the US to base some of the Pacific Fleet at Singapore, the Americans resisting.[30] Another trial balloon floated by the British that North Africa might be a suitable theatre for the deployment of US ground troops, providing that the Vichy French were agreeable, was met by silence from the American delegates.[31] In the end a rather anodyne report was issued. It committed to an exchange of military missions between the two powers, agreed that any future joint force should be commanded by the power with the predominant interest in that theatre, and that if Japan entered the war the US would employ a defensive strategy until Germany had been defeated.[32]

In general the British delegation was satisfied with the talks. Germany had been recognised as the major foe and if Singapore had been scorned by the Americans the mere fact that the talks had occurred was at least a step towards future integration. The political leadership on both sides, though, paid little attention to these meetings. Churchill merely noted that he had read the final report and passed it to his secretariat without further comment. This was more attention than the Americans paid to it; neither Roosevelt nor the Secretary of State (Cordell Hull) read the report. Neither man embraced or repudiated the 'Germany first' strategy or commented on any other aspect of the talks.[33]

However, the establishment of military missions in both countries did take place, although the US was careful to retain the name 'observers' for members of their mission.[34] These missions grew in size to over 100 military personnel and clerks, but their purpose was never clear and they held few meetings. Nor did the meetings come to any important conclusions or indeed to any conclusions at all.[35] All were agreed that liaison was an important aspect in establishing orderly processes and priorities for war production now that lend-lease was to play a major role. But the American mission overlapped with the Averell Harriman and Harry Hopkins missions sent by Roosevelt to discuss the same matters and it was never clear to the British as to which mission had the President's ear or if any of them did.[36]

The next series of talks between the British and the Americans took place off Newfoundland in August 1941. Roosevelt and Churchill held several meetings and their respective military staffs met separately. The impulse for these talks also seems to have come from the Americans. Two matters concerned Roosevelt: the increasing intensity of the Battle of the Atlantic and the danger it represented to the US now that they had taken over from the British in occupying Iceland; and the implications of the German attack on Russia for the war as a whole and for US supply if Russia was to be included in lend-lease. Once again the talks were set up through informal channels. Early in January 1941 Roosevelt had decided to send his confidant Harry Hopkins to Britain for the outstandingly diffuse reason 'to communicate to this Government any matters which may come to your attention'.[37] One matter that immediately came to his attention was that both Churchill and Roosevelt desired a meeting.[38] It was arranged that such a meeting might take place in April aboard a cruiser. In the end events such as the German invasion of Greece and the Western Desert offensive delayed the meeting until August, but it did take place on a cruiser (or cruisers) off Placentia Bay in Newfoundland.

At the time Churchill made much of this series of meetings. Afterwards his private secretary noted that following the joint declaration between Britain and America (the Atlantic Charter) 'America could not honourably stay out'.[39] Looking at the records, it is difficult to see the Atlantic meeting as much of an advance on previous efforts. In their joint talks, Roosevelt and Churchill mainly concentrated on the exact wording of the Atlantic Charter, a very general statement of war aims in which Churchill attempted to exempt the Empire from the clause stating that 'all peoples' had the right to self-government and Roosevelt attempted to break Empire free trade by insisting that nations should have access 'without discrimination and on equal terms to the markets and raw materials of the world'.[40] Both men no doubt entered silent caveats on these clauses.

As for the talks between the staffs, they took the usual form. The British wished to know what US strategy might consist of should the Americans enter the conflict, and General Marshall, Admiral Ernest King, Admiral Ghormley and others refused to commit to anything specific. Tensions arose over what the Americans thought was an excessive dependence on heavy bombers and were reluctant to supply the British with the numbers requested. This proved not to matter a great deal. The British were on the cusp of producing a heavy bomber (the Lancaster) that was far in advance of anything the US had on the drawing board and would therefore not have wanted the Flying Fortress. The Americans also questioned the British decision to invest so heavily in the Middle East. The answer the British gave (they fought there to protect their oil supplies) was rather circular (they needed oil supplies from the Middle East in order to build up large armies there) and raised the suspicions of the Americans that they were maintaining a strong position in the Middle East for imperial reasons. Perhaps the obvious answer – that Britain was fighting the Axis in the Middle East because they did not have the strength to fight them anywhere else – was too embarrassing. The American view that the British were following some kind of peripheral strategy for reasons of imperialism in the Middle East had been born.[41] This would cause the British much grief in the future.

There was never any possibility of a coherent Anglo-American strategy while the US remained even a benevolent neutral. The decision to defeat Germany first was in fact a major step and probably all that could be hoped for. Everything changed in December. On 7 December 1941 the Japanese attacked at Pearl Harbor and on the 11th Hitler declared war on the United States. As Roosevelt said to Churchill, 'we are all in the same boat now'. Churchill was desperate to shape the kind of strategic boat they were in. He immediately suggested a meeting in Washington and set about gathering a British delegation to attend. On 12 December they left on a transatlantic crossing on the battleship *Duke of York.*

On this voyage Churchill penned a number of strategic documents. Much of these were taken up with the Allied position in the Pacific and will be dealt with in due course. The one strategic option which dominated his thoughts on operations on the Atlantic littoral was a landing in French North Africa. This strategy had a long history. As early as December 1940, in a letter to the Canadian Ambassador to Vichy France, Pierre Dupuy, Churchill had suggested that he approach the governor of French North Africa, General Weygand, and sound him out to the possibility of moving to the Allied side. The British, Churchill assured Dupuy, had a 'strong and well-equipped' expeditionary force standing by to assist Weygand. The result could lead to the clearing of the Mediterranean and a saving of shipping.[42]

Nothing came of that particular initiative but Churchill persisted with the idea. In October 1941 he relayed the plan to Auchinleck, thinking that it might fit well with the impending Crusader operation.[43] In that letter he also noted that a successful Crusader might lead to an invasion of Sicily – Operation Whipcord. The Chiefs of Staff immediately declared Whipcord a logistic impossibility, so Churchill switched back to his North African idea, urging them to prepare a force of two divisions and an armoured division to take advantage of the rapidly vanishing possibility of Weygand joining the Allies.[44] From then until the entry of America, the COS worked on a plan, known as Operation Gymnast. By 7 November it was ready. It called for two and a half infantry divisions, one armoured division, twenty-two fighter and eight bomber squadrons to be deployed to assist Weygand repel any German or Spanish incursions.[45]

Some thought had been given to US participation in this plan. Indeed, it had been floated in Washington by the British Joint Staff Mission. Indeed it had been suggested that North Africa was a possible theatre for the first deployment of American troops in the eventuality of war.[46] The US planners thought the French very unlikely to cooperate. Nevertheless, the British planners felt the scheme should be further developed as a contingency and the US observers in London apprised of its progress.[47] Because of the impending crisis in the Far East no further work seems to have been carried out on Gymnast until Churchill revived it on the *Duke of York*. Here he waxed lyrical about it:

> We ought . . . to try hard to win over French North Africa, and now is the moment to use every inducement and form of pressure at our disposal upon the Government of Vichy and the French authorities in North Africa. The German setback in Russia, the British successes in Libya, the moral and military collapse of Italy, above all the declarations of war exchanged between Germany and the United States, must strongly affect the mind of France and the French Empire. Now is the time to offer to Vichy and to French North Africa a blessing or a cursing. A blessing will consist in a promise by the United States and Great Britain to re-establish France as a Great Power with her territories undiminished. It should carry with it an offer of active aid by British and United States expeditionary forces, both from the Atlantic seaboard of Morocco and at convenient landing-points in Algeria and Tunis.[48]

He went on to suggest that Britain land the 55,000 men earmarked for Gymnast and that the US land 150,000 men at Casablanca and elsewhere. This was the campaign, he concluded, that must be fought in 1942 and concluded by the end of the year.[49] Interestingly, he looked no further forward than that. There was no mention about what might happen in 1943.

The Chiefs of Staff agreed with Churchill's analysis. After reading his paper they prepared one of their own entitled 'Anglo-American Strategy'. They noted that 'Germany first' held the field and that 'it does not seem likely that in 1942 any large-scale land offensive against Germany, except on the Russian front will be possible'.[50] They thought that the Allies must be prepared to take advantage of any serious German weakness but that they should only anticipate returning to Europe in 1943 from across the Mediterranean or from Turkey or the Balkans.[51] From London, Brooke, the newly appointed CIGS who had been left at home to mind the shop, agreed. It had been his policy for some time to invade North Africa as a first step to returning to Europe.[52] British strategy for 1942 in what might loosely be called the 'European sphere' had been decided. It only remained to sell it to its American ally.

The Prime Minister wasted no time in raising the prospect of operations in North Africa with the President. At their first meeting at the White House the two men agreed that plans should be made 'for going into North Africa, with or without [an] invitation from Vichy France'.[53] The project was to be studied by the staff, with the President adding that he 'was anxious that American land forces should give their support as quickly as possible . . . [and] he favoured the idea of a plan to move into North Africa in any event'.[54] The next day the British and American COS met in what would later develop into the Combined Chiefs of Staff. North Africa was raised but the cautious Marshall now attached a rider that the expedition would only be undertaken if the French invited the Allies in. He also said American participation was contingent on the marines who would land in North Africa (some 4,500 men) being released from garrison duties in Iceland and that he doubted if the US could meet the British target date of landing in mid-February. A study should be made by the Joint Planning Staff.[55]

The British had anticipated this move and were able to produce a plan the following day.[56] Further discussions followed – between the Joint Planners, the Chiefs of Staff and between Churchill and Roosevelt – but no conclusions were reached. Shipping, or shortage of it, emerged as the key factor. The Americans had insisted on doubling the troop numbers for their part in the operation from 150,000 to 300,000, which made the transport of the force almost impossible. Any attempt to reduce this number ran up against Marshall's statement that this would be the first time that US troops had encountered the German army and 'it was very important to avoid a reverse'.[57] Nevertheless, the Joint Planners whittled back the figures to the original 150,000 and by early January it seemed that the shipping might be found.[58] Yet within a week Gymnast was in doubt. The US, it turned out, had no overall view of their shipping capabilities and a plethora of tasks to fulfil – troops to reinforce the garrison in Iceland, the despatch of three divisions of infantry to Northern Ireland, Atlantic convoy, and many divisions to despatch to the Pacific theatre. The British were certain that the ships could be found for Gymnast but until the Americans sorted out their various responsibilities there was little that they could do and nothing that they could insist on.[59]

The final report of the Washington conference summed up the situation:

> It was found that lack of shipping, particularly American shipping, the need for reinforcing the Far East, and, to a lesser extent, the despatch of troops to Ireland and Iceland, would not enable a large force to be put quickly into North Africa. After much discussion ... it was found that D1 [D Day] for Super-Gymnast could not be before 25th May and the whole operation would take about 6 months to complete ... Planning is to proceed.[60]

The planning was to proceed under a new organisation set up by the conference. This was the Combined Chiefs of Staff (CCS) – the US Joint Chiefs and representatives of the British COS led by Dill, meeting in Washington, thus incidentally indicating that the centre of gravity of the war had shifted across the Atlantic. The CCS was a new organisation but they soon confronted an old problem: shipping. At their first meeting Marshall emphasised that the only way to supply Russia and to reinforce the Middle East and the Far East was to use ships earmarked for Gymnast.[61] Dill was forced to agree. Within a month, on 17 February 1942, he told the CCS that the British shipping position had deteriorated to the extent that they might not be able to reinforce both the Middle and the Far East. Could the US find some excess shipping?[62] In the event, the US could find enough ships to send 40,000 British troops to the Middle East and India, but this was contingent on the cancellation of Gymnast.[63]

The British had laboured for months over this operation as the only viable strategy for 1942 and the only way of deploying US forces in the (vaguely defined) European theatre in that year. It had come to nothing. During all the meetings about Gymnast there was a sense that the Americans were never wholly behind the operation in the first place. The President expressed the most enthusiasm for it but Marshall and King and some of the other American Chiefs only ever saw difficulties. The President had said that planning should go ahead with or without an invitation from the French, but the military had consistently made a French invitation a prerequisite. With the French not forthcoming, and then with the British reverses in the Western Desert in January and February making any link with an invading force unlikely, the American military simply seemed to lose interest. This raised the question of what strategy the Anglo-American planners were to pursue in the western theatre in 1942. This was a question that had already occurred to the American planners. As Gymnast faded from the scene they came forward with an alternative. By the end of the month both Marshall and the President had approved it and Marshall and the trusty Hopkins were bound for London to sell it to the British.[64]

The plan originated in the Operations Division of the US army and was largely the work of the soon-to-be-famous Dwight 'Ike' Eisenhower. It called for a year-long build-up of American forces in Britain (Operation Bolero) in advance of a cross-Channel attack in the spring of 1943 (Round-Up). The landings would be extensive (six divisions) followed by twenty-four additional divisions (total of 1 million men), while the British contributed eighteen divisions. In the interim another US plan (Sledgehammer) was to be considered. This was for an emergency cross-Channel landing in 1942 to be undertaken if the Russians seemed on the verge of collapse or if the Germans were so preoccupied on the Russian front that an opportunity for such a landing presented itself. Two factors limited the scope of this operation and its timing. First, there was a shortage of shipping and landing craft. Second, in 1942 the US would only have a handful of divisions in Britain that could participate in the operation. This meant that mid-September of that year was the earliest date on which Sledgehammer could be executed.[65]

The British had themselves contemplated what action might be carried out in Europe to relieve pressure on the Russians. As early as 28 March 1942, the COS had met with the head of Fighter Command (Air Marshal Sholto Douglas) and the head of the Home Army (General Bernard Paget) to discuss a 'second front'. Brooke doubted the wisdom of any landing, which he thought would have to take place in the Pas de Calais, the limit of fighter cover, where the Germans were just too strong.[66] As he later recorded:

'[This is] a difficult problem – this universal cry to start a western front is going to be hard to compete with, and yet what can we do with some 10 divisions against the German masses?'[67]

A variation of this plan was again put forward the next month by Vice-Admiral Louis Mountbatten (who had joined the COS as head of Combined Operations) and Paget. Brooke thought the plan 'thoroughly bad'. He vetoed it on the grounds that no conceivable landing could be held. The Germans were just too strong.[68]

Later that day Brooke met Marshall and Hopkins, and Marshall laid his plans for 1942 and 1943 before the COS. He emphasised the importance of aiding the Russians and noted that no considerable American forces would be available in Britain under Operation Bolero until 1943. He thought circumstances might arise, though, where the Allies might have to stage 'emergency operations on the Continent to help [the Russians] before then'. For this 'some' US forces would be available but every effort should be made to prepare for a landing in the autumn of 1942.[69] This 'emergency' plan was very similar to the one put forward by Mountbatten and Paget the day before, which Brooke had described as 'thoroughly bad'. In dealing with the Americans he was, however, more diplomatic:

> If events developed badly for the Russians, we had been considering what we could do to relieve the pressure on them. **We were doubtful whether anything could be achieved by land operations,** but we might be able to use land forces as a bait to bring on air battles advantageous to ourselves. The German fighter margin was a small one and we might be able to inflict a very serious drain on it, and so take the pressure off the Russians, at all events in the air.[70]

He was still firm in rejecting the US plan:

> If we were forced to land on the Continent this year to relieve the pressure on the Russians, we might be able to put ashore a force of some 7 divisions and 2 armoured divisions. **This force was, however, not strong enough to maintain a bridgehead against the scale of attack which the Germans could bring against it, and it is unlikely that we could extricate the forces if the Germans made a really determined**

effort to drive us out. The loss of this force would dangerously weaken the defence of the United Kingdom, where we were by no means strong at present. Moreover, we were encroaching on the strength of Home Forces by sending divisions to the East.[71]

This was the first occasion on which Marshall had encountered Brooke. What he made of this intense little man with his jabbing finger to emphasise points and his rapid, clipped speech is not clear. Certainly he had not taken Brooke's measure, for what the CIGS was saying was that in no way would he accept Marshall's 'emergency' operation. Despite this rebuff, Marshall pressed on:

> He could not press for an 'emergency operation' before September as American assistance could not be given before that date on any scale. He again emphasised the great value to American troops of battle experience and said that they were ready to take their part in any operation. He realised that even with good judgment, losses might be sustained and these they were ready to accept.[72]

This was an extraordinary statement. Marshall was suggesting that combat experience be obtained through an operation Brooke had just said would probably end in the loss of the entire force. As Brooke commented later, 'Marshall had a long way to go at that time before realizing what we were faced with'.[73] Nevertheless, Marshall stuck to his plan. At the end of the day 'emergency Sledgehammer' was still on the table.

This left the British in an awkward position. Obviously they wanted American troops in Britain as soon as possible – as a hedge against invasion if Russia collapsed, to free their own troops for the Far East and for large-scale operations in Europe in 1943. They were therefore delighted with the Bolero–Round-Up aspect of Marshall's proposals. What they were not delighted with was Sledgehammer, even if there was a small American component. The trick was, how to accept a build-up for 1943 without using those troops in 1942? The COS mulled this over on 10 April without arriving at a definite answer. The best that they could come up with was to attempt to persuade the Americans of the legitimacy of the British position. Thus they 'agreed that the various staffs concerned should afford every assistance to the United States Staff Officers, who had accompanied General Marshall, on strategical, tactical and technical matters and instructed the secretary to arrange accordingly'.[74] How they were to arrange this without sounding as patronising as the minute secretary was not discussed.

The COS met Marshall again on the morning of 14 April. Marshall completely ignored the rather condescending offer to educate his staff on matters strategic and moved attention to Sledgehammer. He went over much the same ground as previously: the necessity of giving US troops combat experience, relieving pressure on Russia and emphasising that 'operations on the Continent should not be reduced to the status of a "residuary legatee" for whom nothing was left'. In short, subsidiary operations in the Middle East should not interfere with the main game. Again the British put forward objections; Mountbatten stressed the lack of landing craft, Brooke the fact that any operation in 1942 must be small and its value measured against the possibility of the Germans and Japanese linking up in the Indian Ocean area. Once more it was decided to have further staff talks.[75]

In the evening the Defence Committee (chaired by Churchill) met with Marshall and Hopkins. This was the first formal occasion on which the Prime Minister was able to comment on the Marshall memorandum. He began effusively, describing Marshall's proposals as 'momentous'. 'For himself, he had no hesitation in cordially accepting the plan. The conception underlying it accorded with the classic principles of war – namely concentration against the main enemy.'[76] But he then went on to say that despite the principle of concentrating against Germany, 'it was essential' to defend India, the Middle East, Australia and the island bases that connected the latter country to the United States. Regrettably that left no troops available for Marshall's Sledgehammer plan.

Hopkins attempted to come to Marshall's aid by directing a none too subtle warning to the British. He told them that if public opinion in America had its way the US would concentrate on defeating the Japanese. To counter this, the President wanted American troops in action against Germany at an early date – Sledgehammer would fulfil that role. Churchill then attempted to sum up the discussion:

> Full preparations should now start and we could go ahead with the utmost resolution. It would gradually become known that the English

speaking peoples were resolved on a great campaign for the liberation of Europe, and it was for consideration whether a public announcement to this effect should in due course be made. He could assure Mr. Hopkins and General Marshall that nothing would be left undone on the part of the British Government and people which could contribute to the success of the great enterprise on which they were about to embark.[77]

In summing up thus Churchill had not agreed to any operation in particular. His statement was in fact pure flannel. All the reservations about action in 1942 entered by the Prime Minister, Brooke, Air Marshal Sir Charles Portal (Chief of the Air Staff) and others still applied but were not here spelled out. Marshall chose to read this verbiage in his own way. After the meeting he told Henry Stimson (Secretary of War) that 'PM in impressive pronouncement declared a complete agreement and a deep appreciation of the purpose and time of our visit.'[78]

Of course Churchill was not in 'complete agreement' with the American proposals. He had been very careful not to commit to Sledgehammer in 1942. In fact at this time he told another of Roosevelt's special envoys (Averell Harriman) that he thought the operation 'impossible, disastrous'.[79] Brooke agreed with him, noting in early May that a force of the size contemplated for Sledgehammer 'would not hope to maintain a bridgehead on the Continent indefinitely. No effort that we could make this year could be likely to draw off land forces from the Russian front.'[80]

Two days later Brooke emphasised that the conditions that must obtain for this operation to take place in 1942 were 'unlikely to arise', but a plan should be prepared in case they did.[81]

There matters rested until June. Then Molotov, the Russian Foreign Minister, arrived in London with demands that a landing in France of a similar nature to Sledgehammer be carried out immediately. The British maintained their position. Such an operation was unlikely that year. They provided Molotov with an aide-memoire which spelled out their position:

We are making preparations for a landing on the Continent in August or September 1942. As already explained, the limiting factor to the size of the landing force is the availability of special landing craft. Clearly, however, it would not further either the Russian cause or that of the

Allies as a whole if, for the sake of action at any price, we embarked on some operation which ended in disaster ... We can therefore give no promise in the matter, but, provided that it appears sound and sensible, we shall not hesitate to put our plans into effect.[82]

Molotov left for Washington to canvass Roosevelt. Here he was more successful. After a series of meetings Roosevelt wrote to Churchill on 31 May:

> [Molotov] has made very clear his real anxiety as to the next four of five months, and I think this is sincere and not put forward to force our hand. Therefore I am more than ever anxious that Bolero [Roosevelt actually meant Sledgehammer] proceed to definite action in 1942. After talking to our Staff, I believe German Air Forces cannot be defeated or indeed brought to battle to an extent which will bring them off the Russian front until we have made a landing. I have great confidence in the ability of our joint airforces to gain complete control of the channel and enough of the land for appropriate bridgeheads to be covered.[83]

Churchill must have been startled by this missive, especially as his own views and those of the COS had, if anything, hardened against any kind of cross-Channel operation in 1942.[84] But in Washington they were working on Marshall's premise that the British had agreed to both Sledgehammer and Bolero–Round-Up. Much work had been done by the Americans on the planning of these operations and Roosevelt had been kept informed of the preparations. The two Allies were therefore working for some months at cross-purposes, but the first clear indication that this was the case was Roosevelt's letter to Churchill of 31 May.

Churchill's response was to despatch Mountbatten to Washington in an attempt to discover to what extent Roosevelt was absolutely wedded to a cross-Channel attack in 1942. Mountbatten concluded that Roosevelt's views were flexible. While the President thought that a plan should be prepared in case Sledgehammer proved practicable, his greatest concern was that American troops should fight in the European theatre as soon as possible and that as far as Gymnast (the plan to land in North Africa) was concerned, he had definitely not ruled it out.[85] This gave Churchill an opening he thought he could use. He telegraphed the President immediately suggesting they meet in Washington.[86] Churchill's purpose was clear: he would attempt to persuade Roosevelt in regard to Gymnast and dissuade him from Sledgehammer.

The British delegation arrived in Washington on 18 June and a series of meetings ensued through the next week. The two sides found little common ground. At a CCS meeting on 19 June, Brooke stated quite categorically that 'some form of "Gymnast" should be considered' while at a later meeting between Marshall and Dill, both of whom had been present earlier, it was decided that 'Gymnast should not be undertaken under the existing situation'.[87] Then at a CCS meeting on the 20th the Americans came out strongly against Gymnast while Brooke came out strongly against Sledgehammer – with no conclusion being reached by the end of the meeting.[88]

Meanwhile both sides were working on Roosevelt. On 20 June Churchill told him:

No responsible British military authority has so far been able to make a plan for September 1942 [for Sledgehammer] which had any chance of success . . . Have the American Staffs a plan? At what points would they strike? What landing-craft and shipping are available? Who is the officer prepared to command the enterprise? What British forces and assistance are required?[89]

The Prime Minister concluded that in this context the alternative of landing in North Africa should be revived.[90]

At the same time, however, Stimson (Secretary of War), Marshall and Lieutenant-General Dwight Eisenhower (Operations Division) were writing to Roosevelt, stating their categorical objection to Gymnast and urging him to stick with the Sledgehammer–Bolero plan.[91]

In the end the staff talks were side-tracked by the British collapse at Tobruk. Meetings were held to discuss what form American aid to the Eighth Army might take and how rapidly troops or equipment could be despatched. Then Churchill had to fly home to meet a vote of censure regarding the fall of Tobruk. What no one seemed to notice was that no conclusions on strategy had been reached. Was it to be Sledgehammer or Gymnast or Bolero? As events were soon to show, no one was really certain.

These uncertainties morphed into a full-blown crisis in July. When Brooke returned to London he had another study undertaken of operations in 1942. Not surprisingly it came to the same conclusions reached previously – that no cross-Channel attack was a feasible operation and that Gymnast should be carried out in its place.[92] The matter then went to the War Cabinet. That body decided that the Americans must be told in unequivocal terms that Sledgehammer was off. Churchill was instructed to tell the President, the assumption being that Roosevelt would wish to proceed with Gymnast.[93] Churchill duly informed the President and Brooke the British members of the CCS.[94]

The result was explosive. Marshall immediately informed Roosevelt that in his opinion this meant the cancellation not just of Sledgehammer but Round-Up as well and that in that case the US should 'turn immediately to the Pacific with strong forces and drive for a decision against Japan'.[95] This furious reaction, a decision in effect to leave Britain to prosecute the war against Germany alone, was not congenial to Roosevelt. He turned on Marshall, asking 'this afternoon' for Marshall's detailed plan for operations against the Japanese and the effect such an operation would have on Russia and the Middle East during the remainder of 1942.[96] There was of course no such plan – Marshall's bad-tempered bluff had been called by the President. When calm was restored, Marshall was instructed to go with Hopkins and King to London at once with a view to bringing US ground troops into operation against Germany in 1942.[97]

Marshall interpreted these rather vague instructions as a means of resurrecting Sledgehammer, which was clearly not Roosevelt's intention. Nevertheless, Marshall found an ally in Eisenhower, then in London as Commander-in-Chief, European Theatre. Eisenhower regarded Gymnast as a 'strategically unsound' operation that would provide no help to Russia and divert Allied resources from the decisive Western European area.[98] He went on to suggest that there were four possible landing points for Sledgehammer: Pas de Calais, Le Havre, Cherbourg and Brest.[99]

Armed with the Eisenhower memorandum, Marshall, Hopkins and King met the British COS on 20 July. The Americans put forward two operations – to proceed with Sledgehammer, or if that was not possible, to establish a bridgehead on the Cotentin Peninsula (Cherbourg) that could be held until a full-scale invasion could take place in 1943. Brooke was appalled. He thought that the first would merely result in the loss of six divisions and the second impossible to achieve because no bridgehead could be held for long against the forces that the Germans could bring against it.[100]

The meeting was adjourned without result and resumed the next day. Again little progress was made, except Brooke believed that King was deadly serious about transferring operations to the Pacific. A third meeting also got nowhere, the Americans putting up an outline plan for landing at Cherbourg, the British resisting. Appeals by the Americans to put their position to the Prime Minister and that he then put their position to the War Cabinet were rejected.[101] Finally it became clear to the US delegation that the British were just not going to attempt any form of cross-Channel attack in 1942 and that – as any such operation had to be largely British in composition – debate was at an end. The Americans then appealed to Roosevelt for guidance. In short order they were instructed to accept Gymnast.[102] This they did at a meeting on 24 July.[103] They accepted it with a bad grace. Marshall and Eisenhower were furious with the British for vetoing Sledgehammer.[104] King deprecated any operations in Europe in 1942. Hopkins was ever the pragmatist; he had pushed for Sledgehammer but now urged Roosevelt to switch to Gymnast. A united front should be developed behind this operation as the British would have no other.[105] By the end of the month the British staff mission in Washington noted that the operation, renamed Torch, 'is catching on well here'.[106] The final irony was that in command of the operation, as European theatre commander, would be one of the men who opposed it so resolutely, Dwight Eisenhower.

* * * * *

Two points can be made about this debate. The first is that the COS and the Prime Minister found that it was a great deal easier to make strategy on their own. The introduction of an ally, especially one with most of the resources, complicated matters a great deal. Nevertheless, and this deals with the second point, the British maintained a united front. There was never a major difference between Churchill, the COS and the War Cabinet on this issue. No one thought that a cross-Channel attack was possible in 1942 for the good reason that the German forces were too many and the

Allied too few to ensure even a vague prospect of success. The other factors which were repeatedly noted by the British were that the short range of single engine fighters confined the landing area to the Pas de Calais, the very area in which the Germans were at their most formidable, and the lack of specialist landing craft.

What has bedevilled this debate, perhaps at the time, and certainly ever since, is that the operations under consideration have not been seen in terms of practicalities. Rather they have been portrayed as operations that conformed to one or another strategic theory: that of the direct versus the indirect approach or a direct strategy versus a peripheral one. The damage this does is that it quite misrepresents what the British were about. They were not suggesting a landing in North Africa as part of some Liddell Hartian indirect approach. They were suggesting it because they could not see the possibility of engaging US forces against the Germans with advantage anywhere else. They had had two years' experience in fighting the German army – in France and Flanders, in the Western Desert, and in Greece and Crete – and they had not fared well. Even when they had an advantage in manpower and armoured vehicles they had not managed to prevail. When they looked across the Channel they saw a formidable foe with twenty-five divisions of troops and sufficient aircraft to give them strong support. They had never yet managed to fight with advantage against a fraction of such a force.

The Americans, and particularly Marshall, were heavily discounting these factors when they urged Sledgehammer on the British. And they had no well-thought-out plan that might convince the British that the factors that had so far defeated them would not apply to this operation also. Marshall and Eisenhower in particular seemed to think that it was merely a matter of propelling the massive American industrial resources across the Atlantic and then across the Channel – that materiel in that quantity must overcome whatever strategy and tactics the Germans could bring against it. In the long run they were probably correct – brute force does overcome many obstacles – but they were not correct in 1942. The force they had was not brute enough to overcome the Wehrmacht. In seeking to land elsewhere the British were not playing some elaborate peripheral game with a view to their post-war position in the Mediterranean. They were merely landing where they considered they had a decent chance of success. To see the Anglo-American strategic debate in terms of strategic theory is to miss the point. And it is greatly to exaggerate British power and cunning.

The period between June 1940 and the autumn of 1942 saw on the British side a shift in the nature of the debate between the politicians and the military. In the early days of his premiership, when Churchill and the COS disagreed over matters strategic, they thrashed out their differences in committee and usually reached satisfactory compromises. During 1941 and especially after Pearl Harbor the debate became one between the British leadership and the Americans. Churchill and the COS were as one in thinking cross-Channel operations impossible in 1942. The American military thought otherwise and said so on many occasions. Consensus on strategy came about because the President and Hopkins eventually forced the military to accept the British point of view in the interests of Allied unity. Marshall and Eisenhower complied, albeit with a bad grace. If Churchill thought he could persuade the President to adopt this position on other occasions, he was misguided. Roosevelt was persuaded this time because he wanted to be – it was in line with his 'Germany first' policy. On other occasions Churchill would find that the President's thinking had developed its own momentum along with American power.

Map 8. Malaya and Singapore.

CHAPTER 18

SINGAPORE

IN THE PRE-WAR YEARS the cornerstone of British defence policy in the Far East was the so-called 'Singapore Strategy'. A 'main fleet' made up of capital ships and attendant destroyers and cruisers would be despatched east to occupy the Singapore naval base, where it would either act as a deterrent to a hostile power (the Japanese) or engage in a major fleet action should the enemy venture so far south. This fleet would also be well placed to interpose itself between an enemy from the north and Australia and New Zealand.

This strategy was effectively dead the moment Britain declared war on Germany on 3 September 1939. Admittedly the German fleet was much smaller than the British in all classes of warships, but the German heavy ships were much newer than their British equivalents and would confine most of the twelve British capital ships to home waters in order to watch the Germans and prevent them raiding the Atlantic trade routes.[1]

In any case the Singapore Strategy suffered a catastrophic blow with the collapse of France and the Italian declaration of war against Britain in June and July 1940. The Mediterranean, instead of being a friendly route to the Far East, became a hostile lake and the only Allied fleet that sailed it was the British, the considerable Italian fleet now being an enemy and much of the French fleet being at the bottom of the sea, sunk by the British. Moreover, the Germans now had bases on the French Atlantic coast from where they could place submarines and heavy ships to attack cross-Atlantic shipping, vital for Britain's survival.

The Chiefs of Staff soon drew the appropriate conclusions: no fleet could now be sent to Singapore. Malaya and all points east would now have to be defended by the army and the air force. And such forces could not come from a Britain threatened by invasion. Army units might be found in India or Australia. Where an air force was to be found was passed over in silence.[2] The COS's conclusions were sent to the Dominions. They could now be under no illusions – the Singapore Strategy upon which so much time and money had been lavished was no more.

Churchill, however, did not agree with the Chiefs' downbeat assessment. He thought the Japanese very unlikely to declare war but that, if they did, it would not be necessary to send a fleet eastwards immediately. Fortress Singapore could withstand a siege. In the meantime a fleet could be scraped up from the Mediterranean. In the last resort, he concluded, 'our course was clear':

> We could never stand by and see a British Dominion overwhelmed . . . and we should at once come to the assistance of that Dominion with all the forces we could make available. For this purpose we should be prepared if necessary to abandon our position in the Mediterranean and the Middle East. An assurance on these lines might form the basis of a telegram to the Dominions.[3]

Whether the Dominions were reassured by this message is not clear. Certainly, at the time of this meeting in August 1940, Britain's position in the Middle East was precarious. The British had no large army in Egypt and faced a seemingly formidable Italian foe in neighbouring Libya. Yet there was no real indication they were prepared to abandon that position. Indeed, Churchill was doing all he could to build it up while also urging Wavell to take offensive action against the Italians. Moreover, there was not a single staff study into the consequences of liquidating their position in Egypt or what shipping might have been required to move men and equipment east.

The varying statements by the Chiefs and Churchill seemed to foreshadow a major split in strategic goals. But they did not. Churchill maintained his position that the threat to Singapore was not 'unduly alarming'.

The Chiefs, however, were alarmed. They considered that it was not just the naval base that should be defended but the entire Malay Peninsula – one could not be defended without the other.[4] Given that they could see no situation in which the naval base would have any heavy ships, this was a rather strange position.

Despite the Chiefs' pessimism and Churchill's optimism, no one made a move substantially to boost the defences at Singapore or Malaya or to enquire under what circumstances Britain's position in the Middle East might be wound up. Notwithstanding differences in rhetoric, Churchill and his military advisers were essentially of one mind: they would fight the enemy where they could (at home and in the Mediterranean) and they would hope for the best elsewhere. Their collective actions affirm this position. The army and air force at home were given first priority because of the invasion threat, and the army and air force in Egypt were built up to the greatest extent possible given the needs of home defence. The Far East would have to make do with what was left over – if there was anything left over.

This policy was adhered to even as the strategic scene in the Far East darkened. In September 1940 the Japanese army had moved south into Indo-China in considerable force. Naval units and aircraft soon followed. The Japanese were now just 200 miles from Malaya.[5]

This move caused considerable alarm in Singapore. The local commanders demanded an increase in their air forces from 88 to 566 aircraft, a doubling of ground troops, increases in artillery and anti-aircraft guns and some squadrons of tanks, of which they had none.[6] The COS offered sympathy but not much else. A few units were despatched from the Indian Army to Malaya, and Australia was encouraged to send as much of its 8 Division as shipping would allow. As for aircraft, some Brewster Buffalo machines (described by one authority as the worst fighter in the world) might be diverted from Australian supply. In line with earlier thinking, there would be no fleet.[7]

This pattern continued – Churchill assuring the Australian Prime Minister Robert Menzies that tensions in the east had 'eased';[8] the Chiefs worried by Intelligence and Staff reports that indicated that Malaya could be attacked by six Japanese divisions within nine days and that Singapore was deficient in weaponry of all types. Indeed the Chiefs declared that the

Malay Peninsula must be held because of its 'vital' supplies of rubber and tin.[9]

Though the Chiefs made no moves to bolster Malayan defences, in light of this report the Prime Minister was at least jolted out of his complacency about the imminent danger of Japanese moves in the Far East, which he now considered a 'serious menace'.[10] Despite this, Malaya and Singapore slipped even further down Britain's priority list. On 21 June 1941 Hitler invaded Russia. Churchill promised immediate aid, including 'any technical or economic assistance which is in our power'.[11] The first convoy of materiel, including Hurricane fighters, left Scapa Flow for Murmansk on 21 August. For the remainder of the year similar convoys followed. Regardless of Churchill's assurances to Menzies and the encroachments of Japan, the policy of providing materiel to fighting fronts continued. Given the immediate need to keep Russia fighting there was little else that could have been done. Churchill's move was instantly endorsed by the COS.[12]

In any case Churchill thought he saw a solution to the Japanese threat in the United States. He was to meet with Roosevelt in August to discuss the whole war situation. The problem of Japan was sure to arise. He would hammer out a joint message with the President that would be bound to deter the 'prudent' Japanese from carrying out any plans for aggression that they might be hatching.

The main result of the August meeting was, of course, the Atlantic Charter, but discussions about Japan were also prominent. In the early days of the conference the draft of a protest note to be handed to Japan was written by Sir Alexander Cadogan (Foreign Office) and then passed to the Americans for comment. In part it said: 'Any further encroachment by Japan in the South-West Pacific would produce a situation in which the United States Government would be compelled to take counter measures even though these might lead to war between the United States and Japan.'[13]

At a later meeting between Churchill and Roosevelt the President agreed to incorporate this note, word for word, in any warning given to the Japanese.[14] The Prime Minister jubilantly reported this matter to the Cabinet and set out for London well satisfied with this result.[15] He hastily told Menzies about the note, informing him that it was at last clear that if Japan attacked British possessions it would find itself at war with the United

States.[16] He concluded by saying, 'I feel confident that Japan will lie quiet for a while.'[17]

All was not as it seemed. Roosevelt had shown the British-drafted note to Hull. The State Department thought it much too stern. In its final form the American note to Japan read as follows:

> The Government now finds it necessary to say to the Government of Japan that, if the Japanese Government takes any further steps in pursuance of a policy or programme of military domination by force or threat of force of neighbouring countries, the Government of the United States will be compelled to take any and all steps necessary towards safeguarding the legitimate rights and interests of the United States and American nationals and towards ensuring the safety and security of the United States.[18]

This not only watered down the British note, it changed its whole tone. Now a crisis would only arise if unspecified American interests or nationals were threatened. There was not even a hint that the US would take action if third parties were attacked. This was a strange response on the part of the Americans. They had taken actions in July (embargo of scrap metal, the freezing of Japanese assets in the US and finally the oil embargo) that tended to make war in the Pacific more likely. Yet, not for the first time, the Prime Minister had read these actions as a certain prelude to, if not war, then a much more resolute stance towards war by Roosevelt. He had once more been too certain that Roosevelt would see that British and American interests were identical. With his confident assertions to the Dominions rendered worthless he was bereft of a policy for the Far East.

When he returned to London he passed this issue to the COS. After much consideration they announced that they had no additional troops that could be sent east and no front-line aircraft.[19] Essentially they had concluded that Singapore/Malaya was indefensible with the resources at Britain's disposal. Rather in desperation, Churchill reverted to the position of sending some ships. Instead of a 'main fleet', though, he asked Pound if the despatch of just one modern British battleship (say the *Prince of Wales*) night deter the Japanese?[20] Pound thought not but considered that a squadron of four old R Class battleships might do the job. Much debate followed. Eventually a compromise was reached. The *Prince of Wales*, the battlecruiser *Repulse* and an aircraft carrier would be sent.[21] This was hardly a 'main fleet' to Singapore but it was all Churchill could do in the way of a Far Eastern policy.[22]

In Australia the new policy cut very little ice. The Dominion had a new government led by the Labor leader John Curtin. On taking office he immediately asked Sir Earle Page (Australian Liaison Officer in London) to approach the War Cabinet to find exact details about British policy towards Singapore. Page attended the War Cabinet on 12 November and opened with a strong statement – there were two brigades of its 8 Division in Malaya and they lacked any kind of a decent air force to protect them. What was Britain to do about it? Portal reassured Page that the air force at Singapore had sufficient squadrons for defensive purposes, ignoring the fact that the obsolescent craft were useless for any purpose. Page, who was clearly not au fait with the air museum assembled to defend Singapore, seemed reassured.[23] Then Churchill made a remarkable statement:

> He was not one of those who believed that it was in Japan's power to invade Australia. Nevertheless he would renew his assurance that if Australia were gravely threatened, we should cut our losses in the Middle East and move in great strength to Australia's assistance. Such a decision, however, was not to be taken lightly.[24]

Page might have noticed that the previous discussion had been about Singapore and not about the invasion of Australia. He might also have noticed that Churchill's pledge was hedged around with many qualifiers. He might also have questioned how a commitment of such gigantic size to the Middle East (500,000 men, over 1,000 aircraft and hundreds of tanks and other equipment) was to be wound up. He might lastly have questioned where the shipping was to be found to move such a force to the east. What the Chiefs made of Churchill's declaration is not clear. Perhaps they thought that Australia would never be invaded and that therefore Britain's position in the Middle East would be retained. Perhaps they had nothing to offer Page. Perhaps they wished to maintain British solidarity in the presence of a Dominion representative. In any case they said nothing.

The outcome of this meeting revealed that British policy concerning the defence of the Far East was pretty threadbare. Britain would send three ships and hope it was enough. At this last desperate moment Roosevelt threw the British a lifeline. He had remained silent on Japan since the August meeting with Churchill, but in early December in a casual conversation with Halifax, the British Ambassador, he said, 'in the case of any direct attack [by Japan] on ourselves or the Dutch we should obviously all be together'.[25] Churchill urged caution, having been burnt more than once by such declarations from Roosevelt. Nevertheless a note to Roosevelt was despatched with lightning speed agreeing with his position and no dissenting note was received.[26] At the last minute the British did have a Far Eastern policy – they would rely on the United States.

In the event, they would all be in it together. On 7 December the Japanese attacked the US at Pearl Harbor and in the Philippines as well as the Dutch in the East Indies, Thailand and the British in Malaya. The 'mad dog act' that Churchill had assured the Dominions would not happen had come to pass. The greatest surprise was the attack on Pearl Harbor which eliminated the US battleship fleet at a stroke. However, the immediate problem for Churchill was Malaya. All in London knew it was under-resourced. How would the deficiencies be made up?

Churchill moved to send reinforcements immediately. He now had a fighting front to support. The problem was that there was not much war materiel or men at hand. He despatched two brigades of an Indian division and alerted the British 18 Division, then rounding the Cape, that it might be diverted east. In addition anti-aircraft and anti-tank guns were to be sent and light bomber and fighter squadrons from the Middle East.[27] Then tanks and modern fighters (Hurricanes) were added to the list, also to come from the Middle East. Churchill further promised that two divisions of Australian troops (6 and 7 Divisions) would make their way east as well as an armoured brigade.[28] Later four aircraft carriers and four R Class battleships were promised as replacements for the now-sunk *Prince of Wales* and *Repulse*. All of this amounted to a considerable force. There was never a question about 'cutting losses' in the Middle East. Churchill was careful to tell the COS: 'There could course be no question of taking anything away from Crusader [the offensive against Rommel in the Western Desert then in full swing] until the victory was won.'[29]

There was of course another caveat. It would take some time to assemble all the shipping required to send such a force to the east. Much of the men and materiel mentioned would not arrive until February 1942. Meanwhile the forces already in Singapore and Malaya would have to hold the enemy at bay.

In the meantime Churchill discovered that his worldwide search for reinforcements for the Far East found no favour with the Australian government. On 23 December Curtin wrote Churchill a blistering note which he copied to Roosevelt. In part it said:

> The reinforcements earmarked by United Kingdom Government for despatch seem to us to be utterly inadequate, especially in relation to aircraft, particularly fighters.
>
> At this time small reinforcements are of little avail. In truth the amount of resistance to Japan in Malaya will depend directly on the amount of assistance provided by Governments of United Kingdom and United States . . . It is in your power to meet the situation.[30]

The problem was that it was not in Churchill's power to meet the situation. He could certainly be held accountable for the situation pertaining in Malaya but since the Japanese attack he had assembled as many reinforcements as possible for which he could obtain shipping to send east. Indeed the COS looked at the position again on 24, 27 and 31 December and could find nothing more that could arrive expeditiously.[31] In reply, all Churchill could do was to repeat to Curtin what reinforcements had been assembled and that he was coordinating all actions taken (including the reinforcement of Australia) with the President. He told Curtin, 'we do not share the views expressed . . . that there is a danger of early reduction of Singapore fortress.'[32]

The reinforcement question, however, rested on one rather large assumption: that Singapore Island and at least some of Malaya would still be in British hands when the additional troops arrived. Churchill had no doubts:

> We expect . . . Singapore island and fortress will stand an attack for at least six months, although meanwhile the naval base will not be usable for either side. A large Japanese army with its siege train and ample

416

supplies of ammunition and engineering stores will be required for their attack upon Singapore.[33]

Yet in London questions about the longevity of 'Fortress Singapore' were creeping in. On 15 December, Brooke, the new CIGS, doubted whether Malaya would last a month.[34] Later that day the Joint Planners produced an outlook which said that Japan could deploy up to ten divisions in Malaya as well as 240 land-based and 155 carrier-based aircraft.[35] This more or less decided Brooke. As early as 17 December he was saying, 'I do not feel there is much hope of saving Singapore.'[36]

As for Churchill, towards the end of December his early optimism about Singapore, no doubt under the influence of the retreat down the Malay Peninsula, was starting to slip. In Washington he told his wife Clementine:

> Not very good news has also come in from Malaya. Owing to our loss of the command of the sea, the Japanese have an unlimited power of reinforcement, and our people are retreating under orders to defend the Southern tip and the vital Fortress of Singapore. I have given a good many instructions to move men, guns and aircraft in this direction [but] we must expect to suffer heavily in this war with Japan.[37]

Then, when asked at a press conference with Roosevelt on 23 December, 'Isn't Singapore the key to the whole situation out there?' Churchill deflected the question by answering, 'the key to the whole situation is the resolute manner in which the British and American Democracies are going to throw themselves into the conflict'.[38] He was still describing Singapore as a 'fortress', however, and it was not until mid-January that, still in Washington, he began to express real fears about the situation. At that time he signalled to Wavell, who was, as we shall see, about to take up his forlorn command:

> Please let me know your idea of what would happen in the event of your being forced to withdraw into the Island. How many troops would be needed to defend this area? What means are there of stopping landings as in Hong Kong? [the island had fallen after a brief siege on 25th December]. What are the defences and obstructions on the landward side? Are you sure you can dominate with Fortress cannon any attempt

to plant siege batteries? Is everything being prepared, and what has been done about the useless mouths? It has always seemed to me that the vital need is to prolong the defence of the Island to the last possible minute, but of course, I hope it will not come to this.[39]

Despite the doubts evident in this message, Churchill was unprepared for the answer from Wavell:

Until quite recently all plans based on repulsing seaborne attack on island and holding land attack in Johore or further north, and little or nothing was done to construct defences on north side of island to prevent crossing of Johore Strait . . . Fortress cannon of heaviest nature have all round traverse but flat trajectory makes them unsuitable for counterbattery work. Could certainly not guarantee to dominate enemy siege batteries with them. Supply situation unsatisfactory.[40]

As Raymond Callahan states: 'This finally pricked the bubble. There was no "Singapore Fortress".'[41]

Churchill confessed to being 'staggered' by this news. He told the COS that he had thought the island enclosed with all-round defences with searchlights, wire and batteries with the right type of ammunition that would have been able to dominate any siege batteries the enemy brought up. He now realised Singapore had none of these things. He added:

How was it that not one of you pointed this out to me at any time when these matters have been under discussion? More especially should this have been done because in my various minutes extending over the last two years I have repeatedly shown that I relied upon the defence of Singapore Island against a formal siege . . . It is most disquieting to me that such frightful ignorance of the conditions should have prevailed.[42]

Churchill surely has a point here. He had repeatedly referred to Singapore as a fortress in his minutes to the COS and in discussions with them. And the fact is that over this extended period no one did correct him. Mainly the responsibility for this falls to Dill, who, as CIGS, was surely obliged to have detailed knowledge of the cornerstone of British defences in the Far East.

The awful truth seems to be that Dill also regarded the island as some kind of fortress. Even Pound might have made it his business to find out how the naval base was to be defended from a landward attack, but there is no record that he contemplated such an operation. And Portal, on the appointment of an airman (Air Chief Marshal Robert Brooke-Popham) as C-in-C Far East, which at least implied a primacy for that arm of the services, might have busied himself far more than he did on the air requirements of the so-called fortress. In the event none of them did anything and in 1942 Singapore remained what it had always been – a naval base – only in that year it was a naval base without ships.

The question now arose as to the utility of the forces, guns and equipment that Churchill had directed towards Singapore. He instructed Ismay to call a Defence Committee on 21 January to discuss Wavell's 'bad' telegram and to discuss the following questions:

> What is the value of Singapore if its defences were thoroughly demolished?
>
> Is not Burma and the Burma Road [the main Allied supply route to China] now not more important strategically than Singapore?
>
> If Singapore can only be defended for a few weeks is it worth losing all reinforcements and aircraft at presently directed there?[43]

The Committee met at 10 p.m. on 21 January 1942. Churchill led off by saying that the 'object of the meeting was to focus on the position in the Far East':

> It was now apparent that we could not consider Singapore as a fortress. If the battle in Johore went against us it was possible that a prolonged defence of Singapore island could not be made. .... Taking the widest view, Burma was more important than Singapore. It was the terminus of our communications to China which it was essential to keep open. The Americans had laid the greatest stress on keeping the Chinese fighting on our side. Burma was badly in need of reinforcement. If it looked as though Singapore could only hold out for a few weeks it might be that some of the reinforcements which were destined for Malaya ought rather to be sent to Burma. We did not wish to throw good money after

419

bad; on the other hand if there was a reasonable chance of holding the position in Malaya and thus allowing further reinforcements to arrive, then these should be sent as arranged.[44]

A short discussion followed on the relative importance of Burma and Malaya, but in the end no decision was reached. It was merely agreed to see how the situation developed in a few days.[45]

The decision about whether to reinforce Singapore would not be made in London. It would be made in Canberra. Earle Page had attended the Defence Committee meeting on 21 January. What struck him was the importance given to Burma. Malaya (and particularly Singapore), in his mind, was the key to Britain's and Australia's position in the Far East. Burma was a far away country about which he knew nothing. After the meeting he quickly telegraphed Curtin that the British were thinking of cutting and running from Singapore. This was not strictly accurate but Page (who, according to Brooke, had the mentality of a 'greengrocer')[46] had grasped well enough which way the conversation was drifting. Curtin's reply was direct:

> After all the assurances we have been given, the evacuation of Singapore would be regarded here and elsewhere as an inexcusable betrayal. Singapore is a central fortress of the system of Empire and local defence. We understood it was to be made impregnable; and, in any event, it was to be capable of holding out for a prolonged period until the arrival of the main fleet . . . On the faith of the proposed flow of reinforcements we have acted and carried out our part of the bargain. We expect you not to frustrate the whole purpose by evacuation.[47]

It appears that the Australian government had been labouring under the same illusions as Churchill in thinking Singapore a fortress. Worse, they had not yet realised, as he had, that it was not. Moreover, they had not taken on board the clear statement in June 1940 by the COS that there would be no 'main fleet' arriving in Singapore. Here was a stern message which went to the heart of Empire solidarity. Although Churchill was already furious with Curtin about a newspaper article Curtin had written suggesting that Australia should turn towards America and away from Britain for defence purposes, he seems to have buckled. Neither the Defence Committee, nor the COS, nor the War Cabinet again discussed the destination of those troops and equipment nearing Singapore. So the remainder of the 18 Division, the reinforcements for the 8 Australian Division and various aircraft and supplies landed in Singapore when in fact it was too late. Those troops who survived the campaign would spend the remainder of the war as Japanese prisoners. Had a decision been made merely on military grounds, the reinforcements would either have gone elsewhere or not have been sent. The myth of 'Fortress Singapore' cast a long shadow.

In the end what was available to defend Malaya and Singapore? In aircraft there were just 243 machines – mainly obsolete or second-rate types, from Vildebeest torpedo bombers (1928 vintage) to Buffalo fighters to Blenheim and Hudson light bombers (well out of date in Europe). No aircraft then in the east were a match for the Japanese Zero.[48] Even the Hurricanes, many still in their shipping crates, were not in this class. The army had about 90,000 men to defend the peninsula and the island. Two thirds of them were from the Indian Army – good material but under-trained and especially lacking experienced officers. There were also two brigades of the Australian 8 Division which were rather in the same category. No unit in Malaya had supporting tanks (though a few had armoured personnel carriers) and they were all light on anti-tank guns. Artillery was the strongest supporting arm but, like the infantry, it tended to be dispersed with the brigades. More materiel was of course on the way – guns and the untested British 18 Division, another brigade of Australians and two brigades of Indians.

The dispositions of the troops already in situ were hardly optimal. Generally they had been spread in brigade groups throughout the peninsula to guard the many airfields scattered across Malaya. Hardly anyone seemed to notice that much of the air force was held back on Singapore Island to guard the naval base, which left many brigades in Malaya guarding airfields that were bereft of planes. The end result was that the brigades were often too widely separated to support each other and therefore likely to be picked off one at a time if they were attacked in force.[49]

Compounding the problem of obsolete equipment and faulty dispositions was the quality of the command. It almost goes without saying that the leadership of a non-fighting front would consist of the second eleven. In overall command was Air Chief Marshal Brooke-Popham, chosen in 1940 possibly more because of his seniority in the service than for any outstanding performance in command. When told of his selection he noted that he would not 'press for facilities that cannot be given', which was at once an accurate summing up of the place of Singapore in Britain's overall defence stance and a depressingly accurate forecast of the lack of drive that characterised his tenure.[50] In charge of the army was Lieutenant-General Arthur Percival, who was far from the donkey of legend. However, almost his entire career had been spent in staff positions and he lacked the drive and personality that strong leadership requires. He realised quite early that Singapore and Malaya were under-resourced but was hardly the type to cause a fuss about it. Air Vice Marshal Conway Pulford was in charge of the antique air force but seems merely to have accepted that fact without much comment. All told, these were sleepy commanders in what had been a sleepy zone.

A reconnaissance aircraft sighted a large Japanese convoy in the Gulf of Siam on 6 December 1941.[51] On board were the 5, 18 and Imperial Guards Divisions of the Japanese army. These were not, as legend would have it, seasoned jungle fighters – which was in any case irrelevant because by and large it would not be jungle that they were fighting in but rubber planta-tions, coconut groves and mining areas. All divisions, however, were seasoned, fully trained and had seen action in China. Possible destinations for the ships were the northern beaches of Malaya around Kota Bharu or those around Singora in the Kra Peninsula of the neutral but helpless Thailand. Brooke-Popham had a plan (Operation Matador) to advance into Thailand and forestall the Japanese, but he now dithered. He had been warned on numerous occasions by London not to alienate American opinion by prematurely invading a neutral country. As the Americans had by this time been squared there was no reason to hesitate. But he did. Then the reconnaissance patrols lost the Japanese convoys in heavy cloud. Only on the 8th were the convoys relocated. One was by then landing troops at Singora. It was too obviously too late to pre-empt a landing in Thailand, so Matador was cancelled. A column was ordered into Thailand, not to stave off the Japanese but to hold a tactically important feature called the 'Ledge'. In the event, they failed to reach it before it was occupied by Japanese troops from Singora.[52]

From then on, the scattered dispositions of the brigades told against them. The advancing Japanese were always in superior numbers. In addition the Japanese deployed tanks, a weapon which many Indian soldiers had never seen. Not surprisingly, when they did see them they fled. The divisional commander in the north-west (Major-General David Murray-Lyon) suggested an immediate withdrawal in order to consolidate his forces further south. Percival ordered him to stand and fight. This he did, only to see his brigades defeated one at a time. Nor did Percival's order delay the inevitable – as casualties mounted and forces were outflanked, retreat became inevitable anyway, but such was the haste that there would now be no time to 'consolidate' a new defensive line to the south.

Retreat became unavoidable down the east coast as well. Here the Japanese had landed at Kota Bharu in Malaya. The 8 Indian Brigade put up a stern defence but they were soon outnumbered and forced back. In this manner many of the airfields that had been the object of the defence fell into enemy hands. In any case, the air force that these fields were intended for was soon no more. The Japanese fielded some 180 fighters, well in excess of what the British could send against them. To make matters worse, no Allied aircraft lasted long against the ninety Zero fighters deployed by the enemy. By 10 December air superiority had passed to the Japanese with lightning swiftness.

By this time the fleet had also vanished. The *Prince of Wales* was at Singapore on the 6th when the Japanese convoys were sighted, but the *Repulse* was on its way to Darwin for a short visit. (The aircraft carrier which was supposed to have accompanied the heavy ships ran aground while training in the West Indies and did not make the trip.) The *Repulse* was hurriedly summoned back to Singapore but this meant that the two ships could not be made ready for sea until the evening of the 8th – too late to intervene against the landings. However, when convoys were reported at Singora, Admiral Sir Tom Phillips decided that that he must intercept them. He sailed north with his two heavy ships accompanied by four destroyers. He had been promised fighter cover, but it was not forthcoming. When he was sighted by Japanese aircraft he decided to turn back to Singapore but instead was diverted east to investigate a (false) report of an enemy landing at Kuantan. At this point he had been discovered by Japanese bombers. Phillips's decision to maintain radio silence throughout this period ensured he would continue to have no fighter cover. On 10 December the two heavy ships were sunk, though most of the crew (not including Phillips) were rescued. Air superiority and the fig leaf of naval power had disappeared in a day.[53]

News of the sinkings reverberated around the world. Churchill said it was the worst shock he received during the entire war; Harold Nicolson almost fainted on seeing the headlines in Oxford Circus. Yet there was a certain inevitability about the entire affair. Phillips might with advantage have sailed his ships off to Australia after news that the Japanese were solidly ashore; obligations to assist the local situation ensured he would never have taken that course, although there were few opportunities for his ships at Singapore. Closer to Singora, the Japanese had a watching group of two battleships, two heavy cruisers and some destroyers in the eastern Gulf of Siam. Moreover, the further Phillips moved north the closer he brought his ships to the squadrons of Japanese land-based bombers in Indo-China. The overwhelming probability was that he would have been sunk some-where, perhaps by different methods. Two ships were all that could be scraped up for the Far East; they were never going to be enough.

The remainder of the campaign in Malaya also had a certain inevitability. The retreating Indian units were almost invariably encountered by the Japanese one at a time and defeated one at a time. By 20 December on the west coast Butterworth airfield and Penang Island had fallen, while on the east Japanese forces were well south of Kota Bharu. Japanese tactics had uniformity. They would advance straight down a major road, often with tanks in advance. If checked, patrols would be sent through the jungle or rubber plantations and a roadblock established in rear of the Indian forces, which would then have to fight hard to retain control of the road, which was essen-tial because they were so heavily reliant on wheeled transport. In the west the Japanese were also able to utilise captured boats to employ short amphibious hooks which again brought them in rear of the retreating Indians.

Major battles were few but at Slim River massed Japanese tanks crashed right through Indian defences and inflicted a considerable defeat. Possibly as many as 500 British and Indian soldiers were killed and 2,000 taken pris-oner. The 28 and 12 Brigades were reduced to shattered remnants.[54] After this disaster there was no chance of retaining central Malaya. Kuala Lumpur fell on 11 January 1942 and the road to Johore was open.[55]

Meanwhile London had been trying to regain some control by changing the command. Brooke-Popham was sacked and replaced by Lieutenant-General Henry Pownall, a good appointment made far too late.[56] Churchill, then in Washington, was persuaded, rather against his will, to appoint General Wavell to overall command of what was called the ABDA (American, British, Dutch, Australian) area that encompassed Malaya, Singapore, the Dutch East Indies and northern Australia.[57] Churchill hesitated before offering the job to Wavell because by this time he thought the battle in Malaya well on the way to being lost, but Marshall was insistent and Churchill considered that the plan might calm the increasingly fractious Australians (it did not – the Australians, rather surprisingly, were miffed that Brooke-Popham had been sacked).[58]

London had already made one unhelpful addition to the command structure in the Far East. In September Duff Cooper (a failed Minister for Information) had been sent out as a 'Minister of State', to somehow coordinate the civil/military command in Singapore. The pompous and out-of-touch Duff Cooper, as Churchill quickly recognised, contributed nothing, complicated everything and wrote long-winded appreciations for London telling them that everyone involved in command was incompetent, something they could see for themselves by this time. He was soon ordered home.

Apart from informing Churchill that Singapore Island was not a fortress and probably indefensible, Wavell's contribution to command was decidedly ambiguous. He certainly brought more energy than shown by Percival to the campaign but he was obviously not well informed about the local situation. He quickly grasped that the only hope of stopping the Japanese was to defend Johore. After interviewing the commander of the Indian forces (Lieutenant-General Lewis Heath) and Major-General Gordon Bennett, the Australian commander, Wavell, without consulting Percival, wrote out an operational order. Basically it withdrew the tired Indian troops into reserve, shifted 27 Brigade of the Australian 8 Division to the west and placed the newly arrived 45 Indian Brigade and 9 Indian Division under Bennett's command (now named Westforce). The other Australian brigade (22 Brigade) was to remain on the east coast.[59]

These were disastrous arrangements. Wavell was correct in regarding the Indian troops who had retreated from the north for some sixty days a spent force and correct in thinking the Australians the best troops available to defend Johore. It was, though, a bad mistake to split the Australians into two groups out of touch with each other. This was just perpetuating the dispersal of troops that allowed the Japanese to pick off one brigade after another.

This blunder was soon compounded by the dispositions made by Bennett. For some reason he thought that the Japanese would advance on Johore in a single column down the main central road. He therefore placed most of the 27 Brigade astride that road. This left the untested 45 Indian Brigade to cover 25 miles of tortuous river country on Bennett's left flank.

Initially the 27 Brigade did well. On 15 January they ambushed a Japanese advanced guard – riding bicycles, as was typical – and inflicted considerable casualties on them. A later enemy attack with tanks was stopped in its tracks by the brigade's anti-tank guns, with nine tanks destroyed. Later still the battalion involved (2/30) was forced to withdraw under heavy air and artillery attack. The Japanese – who had received a considerable check – were slow to follow up. Morale in the brigade was said to be 'excellent'.[60]

Bennett's faulty dispositions were soon to nullify this success in the centre. Unremarkably, General Tomoyuki Yamashita, Japanese Commander-in-Chief Malaya, had decided to advance into Johore on two axes. The second one hit the inexperienced 45 Brigade. Muar on the coast was attacked and the Imperial Guards conducted an amphibious right hook which landed in the rear of the Indians. On 16 January Bennett was forced to send first one battalion and then two from the unengaged 22 Brigade on the east coast to the west to attempt to shore up his left flank.[61] It was all too late. Muar was lost and the entire Westforce had no option but to retreat. The recently arrived 53 Brigade from 18 Division was summoned forward to counter-attack, but lack of artillery forced it to abandon its efforts.[62] More disasters followed. On the west coast 15 Indian Brigade from 9 Division was cut off and only remnants survived to be evacuated to Singapore by small boats. Then 22 Indian Brigade was ordered by Bennett to withdraw down a railway line, thus forgoing its wheeled transport. The Japanese were too quick for it, cut it off and captured the greater part of it, only a few stragglers making it back to Singapore.[63] In short order the defence of Johore had collapsed. There was nowhere now to go but back to Singapore Island.

The story of its fall can be quickly told. Percival by his dispositions almost pre-ordained defeat. He determined to defend the entire coast of the island, with the Australians in the north-west, the now almost fully arrived 18 Division in the north-east and the Malay brigades in the south. The remnants of the worn-down Indian troops constituted the only reserve. In trying to be strong everywhere, Percival managed to be strong nowhere. Wavell had suggested that the landings would come in the north-west where the Johore Strait was narrowest. Percival thought the Japanese would land in the north-east astride the now-unimportant naval base.

There were myriad other factors which told against the defence. The lack of artillery was one of the most important. Much had been left on the Malay Peninsula during the long retreat. For example, two battalions of the Australian 22 Brigade had virtually no artillery support and on the 27 Brigade front near the causeway there was just one battery.[64] Nor were the guns guarding the naval base of much use. It is a myth that none of the guns could traverse inland. Some certainly could not, but others could and did fire at Japanese troop concentrations in Johore. However, the fortress guns were designed to stop a seaborne attack. They had low trajectory, excellent against warships, of less use against troops in the open. They also fired mainly armour-piercing shells, again excellent against warships but when they hit soft targets they tended to bury themselves and then explode, thus limiting their destructive value.[65]

Along with a paucity of artillery went a lack of northward-facing defences. Percival had had available to him at least sixty days to dig some form of wired defences but he had refused to contemplate this action on the grounds that it might lower morale. The fact that such defences might have given his troops some protection and therefore raised morale apparently did not enter his thinking. Nor did pressure from Wavell to commence work on them have any effect.[66]

Then there was the state of the defenders. Most had retreated for some two months and were dog-tired and to some extent (though too much has been made of this) demoralised. Others had just arrived – some 2,000 reinforcements for the 8 Australian Division and the last brigade of the 18 Division. In the case of the Australians, they were quite untrained and should have been kept at home. In the case of the men from 18 Division,

427

they had just endured a two-month sea journey and were quite unused to the conditions in which they had to fight. They too would have been better off somewhere else.[67]

Finally, there was the state of Singapore itself. Rather than a fortress it was a city of some 500,000 people which had swollen to 1 million due to an influx of refugees from the peninsula. Much of the water supply for the island came across the causeway from Johore. Now it was cut. Water from reservoirs on the island could have supplied some rations to the swollen population, provided that no pipes were destroyed – a tall order given that the city was under constant artillery pounding and air attack.[68]

The Japanese attacked across the straits in the north-west, exactly where Wavell had prophesied, on the night of 8 February. The British searchlights that were supposed to illuminate any landing failed and the few batteries that were meant to put down a protective bombardment were forced to fire blind. On the front of 22 Brigade the forward troops had instructions to fall back if pressed, which allowed the Japanese to establish a foothold. Further north there was a slight chance that the defence might have held, at least for a time. Here the Imperial Guard attacked on the 9th. The 27 Brigade reported that the enemy had obtained a foothold but were then stopped and heavy casualties inflicted on them from mortars and machine guns. On the 10th they were still reporting that the enemy were held up with heavy casualties and 'our casualties slight'.[69] Then, just as the Japanese commander was seeking permission to call off the attack, the brigade withdrew, apparently to conform to the withdrawal of the 22 Brigade to the south.[70] Probably, given events elsewhere, this did not matter much, but it was the only occasion on which the Japanese might have suffered a considerable bloody nose in the invasion.

With a lack of firepower and a lack of strong direction from the top (there is no indication that Percival or Bennett had any real influence on the battle) the troops were pushed back towards Singapore City. Stands were made: by 22 Brigade on Holland Road, near the causeway by 11 Division and by the 1 Malay Brigade on the south of the island. All to no avail. Water was running out, the civilian populations were being subjected to increasing attack from the air and by artillery, law and order was breaking down behind the lines as a few soldiers looted and spread ill-discipline. Churchill had initially hoped that the army would fight to the end and gave

Wavell instructions accordingly.[71] Now, under the impression of disaster, he telegraphed that Wavell should judge when the moment arrived to surrender and that he should instruct Percival accordingly.[72] That moment came on 15 February. Percival and a small delegation met Yamashita at that symbol of Western dominance, the Ford Motor Factory, on the outskirts of Singapore and surrendered. Some 130,000 men went into captivity. It was the largest surrender in British military history.

* * * * *

Who should bear the responsibility for this colossal military disaster? In the post-war years it was conventional to blame the local military commanders – Percival, Bennett and the almost invisible Heath (commander of the Indian Corps). Certainly they were the second eleven – as they had to be, given that Britain's first eleven were commanding anti-invasion units or were fighting in the Western Desert. There is also no doubt that the local commanders performed an impossible task badly. Still, it is difficult to see how any possible combination of commanders could have turned the campaign from a defeat into a victory or even a stalemate. Park could no more have won the air battle than Pulford. Even had (say) a Montgomery demanded more resources from London, it is very doubtful that he would have got them. There were just insufficient resources available. The problem of Singapore was more far reaching than the competency of the command.

What of Churchill? He could certainly argue that he had been out of office from 1931 to 1939 and was therefore not responsible for what was not done in that period to build up Britain's defences in the Far East. But, as we saw, in the period when he was in power (August 1939 on) he had made two assertions about Singapore and had often repeated them. The first was that the Japanese would not launch an attack on the Western Powers in the east and the second was that even if they did Singapore would hold on until help arrived.

The first of these assumptions seemed reasonable in 1939 and 1940. Japan made no moves against prostrate Western Powers such as France and the Netherlands in 1940 or against Britain when invasion loomed. In 1941 the assumption grew more dubious. As Japan started to encroach on Indo-China and therefore creep closer to Malaya and Singapore, the danger obviously rose. But Churchill stuck to the same mantra, repeatedly telling the COS, the Prime Ministers of Australia and anyone else who would listen that Japan would not launch a war. This attitude was, of course, with the benefit of hindsight, almost wilfully blind. Japanese aggression increased rather than lessened in 1941 and as a result tensions grew, particularly with the United States. And yet the Japanese decision for war was, as Churchill noted, a 'mad dog act'. The economic potential of the United States compared to Japan was hardly a contest. The expectation among the Japanese leadership that a sneak attack was an ideal way of bringing the Americans to the negotiating table was totally irrational. So Churchill was wrong in this matter, though his argument was reasonable and his judgement that after Pearl Harbor the war was won was vindicated by events.

Churchill's second assumption, that 'Fortress Singapore' would hold out until help arrived, also proved false and in some of the literature Churchill is excoriated for thinking in terms of a fortress. It is certainly true that he used this description in almost all his correspondence with the COS and with Commonwealth leaders, and he certainly appears to have believed for some time that the island was indeed a fortress. Here some explanation is required from those who advised the Prime Minister militarily. Did it occur to none of them that Churchill was talking in pipe-dreams? Did none of them think to inform him that the island was merely a naval base with defences that could only protect it from attack from the sea? And did it occur to no commander on the spot (Brooke-Popham, Percival or anyone else) to point this out? There is a strong feeling that Dill and Portal and Pound shared Churchill's delusion that Singapore actually was a fortress. But surely the local commanders knew better? Perhaps they thought the proposition would never be tested because the army and the air force would be able to hold the defenders in northern Malaya. When they were rapidly disabused of that notion in early December, though, they did nothing to even attempt to rectify the problem. The illusion of 'Fortress Singapore' was certainly held by many other than the Prime Minister. The Australian government, as we have seen, continued to hold this view even as Singapore fell.

There is another possible illusion that was widely held about war against Japan, and that involved the underestimation of the enemy. Churchill certainly thought Japan not a first-class enemy, especially in the air and on land. The myth that the Japanese would be outclassed in the air by Western pilots was held by many and might have been the basis of Portal's fantasies about the Buffalo versus the Zero. There was also a view that the Japanese army would not prove formidable. Perhaps this came from the inability of that army to conquer the rather ineffectual Chinese, but that was to misread that war. It was the size of the problem not the incompetence of the army that led to Japan's difficulties in China. However, it was a view widely held, and diaries from soldiers who fought there are replete with derogatory remarks about their opponents, 'the little yellow men'.

Nevertheless, to ascribe to these mistaken assumptions the responsibility for the fall of Singapore misses the point. The time had long gone, if it ever existed, when Britain could fight three well-armed enemies spread across the globe. It certainly was not required to do that in the First World War when future enemies, Italy and Japan, were allies. And yet in that war it took all Britain's strength (and much of its money) to prevail against Imperial Germany, even with the help of France and Italy and eventually the United States. In 1941 the situation was starkly different. It is worth repeating that during this period Britain had no first-class ally. Certainly it had the Commonwealth and Empire behind it, and this allowed it to deploy many more infantry divisions (Australian, New Zealand, Canadian, Indian) than it otherwise could have. Behind these Commonwealth units, though, was very little industrial capacity. Britain had to supply these men with almost everything from rifles to artillery to transport. Against this Britain faced Germany and Italy, which amounted to at least one and a half Great Powers. In addition, in the first half of 1941 Britain was under almost constant aerial bombardment and the threat of invasion. its only active front against the Axis powers lay in the Western Desert, and there – after promising beginnings – the arrival of Rommel and the Afrika Korps saw Britain very hard pressed indeed. The relevance of all this to Singapore is that it is difficult to see where arms and men could have been found to bolster its position in the Far East. Even after the German onslaught against Russia in June 1941 the position was no better. Indeed, for a time it looked worse, as the Russian armies were sent reeling back with losses that were unprecedented in modern war. Churchill's decision to supply Russia as best he could meant that Singapore slipped yet another notch down the priority list. At the time, anything that kept Russia fighting seemed no more than prudent. Arguably, materiel could have been taken from the British armies in the Middle East as well as supplies cut back to Russia in favour of Singapore, but this would have amounted to taking risks on fighting fronts to attempt to bolster a front where there was no fighting. Neither Churchill nor the COS were willing to take this risk. The COS might have made noises in that direction but in the end these were rather empty gestures – the little equipment they sent east was usually obsolescent or inappropriate for home defence or for fighting in the desert. The Vildebeest biplane, for example, would have hardly lasted a day against the Luftwaffe.

But the more important point regarding men and equipment for the east is that no amount that could conceivably have been sent would have stopped the rot in Malaya or Singapore. For their invasion the Japanese deployed three first-class divisions (with reserves available), 550 first-line aircraft and a naval contingent which contained two battleships, two fleet carriers and a plethora of cruisers and destroyers. There was never a possibility that the British could have matched this kind of force. In aircraft alone it would have meant either denuding the Middle East or home defence, or a combination of both. In heavy ships it would have meant despatching not two battleships to Singapore but almost the entire Mediterranean Fleet and a portion of the Home Fleet as well. More half-trained infantry divisions would certainly not have done the job in Malaya. Only the Regulars from the BEF, then on invasion duty, might have stopped the Japanese, but only if they had been sent in 1940 to enable training to take place in the new conditions. It was not, therefore, a matter of redistributing existing materiel from one from one front to another. The problem was that Britain just did not have enough stuff to go round. Singapore and Malaya were only safe if they were not attacked by a first-class enemy. Bluff and inherited prestige alone enabled Britain to maintain an eastern empire. When that bluff was called, it was all over.

CHAPTER 19

THE DESERT –
MONTGOMERY'S WAR 1942–1943

WHILE BRITAIN'S POSITION IN the east was crumbling, affairs in the desert were also not to Churchill's taste. It is difficult to place precisely the moment that he lost confidence in Auchinleck. The wildly inaccurate material provided by the Commander-in-Chief for Churchill's speech to the House of Commons and the fact and circumstances of the fall of Tobruk hardly helped. For a few weeks Churchill, at least publicly, believed that Auchinleck could turn around the fortunes of the Eighth Army. Three days after Tobruk surrendered he told Auchinleck that he still retained his 'entire confidence' and went on to detail the considerable help the US was providing – 300 Sherman tanks and 100 self-propelled 105-mm guns for the desert army.[1] By early July 1942, however, it was obvious that Churchill was greatly disturbed by the situation in the Middle East. On the 9th Brooke records him as running down the army in Egypt in a 'shocking way' and criticising Auchinleck for his lack of offensive spirit.[2] Brooke did his best to shield Auchinleck but was clearly uneasy about the Middle East command himself, particularly Auchinleck's decision to hand the command of the Eighth Army to Major-General Thomas Corbett, in whom Brooke had no confidence.[3] He deemed it essential that he go to Cairo and investigate the situation for himself and was able to win Churchill's approval for the visit.[4] What he was not able to do was prevent Churchill coming with him. By the 30th Churchill had become oppressed by Auchinleck's string of failures on the

Alamein line and was disturbed by his (realistic) decision to go onto the defensive.[5] The visit would therefore be a joint effort.

Brooke arrived in Egypt on 3 August with Churchill just a few hours behind him. They did not like what they found. There had clearly been a 'flap' in Cairo and all kinds of plans were afoot to evacuate the delta and move the Eighth Army either down the Nile or to Palestine. Much was made of this by Montgomery when he assumed command, but most of these plans were contingencies in case Rommel broke through. They did, however, create an uncertain mood which both Brooke and Churchill quickly picked up. Brooke first interviewed Corbett, Auchinleck's choice for the command of Eighth Army and the man who had made the evacuation plans. He thought him a 'small man; the more I saw of him the less I thought of him' – 'unsuited for command of the Eighth Army'.[6] That was the end of Corbett, but who to select in his place? Over the next few days various names were bandied about between Brooke, Churchill and Smuts and Wavell – both of whom attended what amounted to a conference on the command. At first it was assumed that Auchinleck would remain as overall commander. That possibility was probably much diminished after Churchill and Brooke spoke to the divisional commanders in the desert. The field then narrowed to four: Alexander, Montgomery, Gott and Brooke himself. Brooke quickly ruled himself out but Churchill was now determined to replace Auchinleck and he favoured a combination of Alexander and Gott.

Brooke supported Montgomery, who was 'bounding in self-confidence' and known to him as his divisional commander in France and southern army commander in England. He thought Gott tired out after two years in the desert and he also favoured a complete sweep of the Middle East command. Churchill, though, stuck to Gott and Brooke eventually agreed. Potentially this was a disastrous decision. In the Gazala battles Gott had seemed overwrought, but more importantly his tactical judgement had never been sound. It was under his command that the decision was made to split up the divisional structure, and his use of 'Jock' Columns and other unconventional units had only increased since then. Moreover, at Gazala he had found frontal attacks so distasteful that he had refused to carry them out. Yet at Alamein there were no flanks and therefore no alternatives to frontal attacks. Whether Gott could have coped with this situation is open to grave doubt.[7] Churchill was attracted to Gott as an extreme exponent of mobility and, as we saw Brooke was not averse to splitting the British army into small, mobile groups. In the end the situation resolved itself tragically. Gott's plane was shot down as he returned to Cairo and he died attempting to rescue other passengers. The most popular man in the Eighth Army was thus removed from the scene. In his place Montgomery was hastened out from England. In the light of the battles that had to be fought this was just as well.

So the combination of Alexander as theatre commander and Montgomery as Eighth Army commander was put in place. The gigantic Middle Eastern command was dismantled, with Henry Maitland Wilson taking over the Ninth Army command covering Palestine, Syria, Iraq and Persia, something that both Wavell and Auchinleck had long advocated. Montgomery arrived in Egypt on 12 August and, though Auchinleck nominally remained in command until the 15th, immediately took over. This implacable, self-assured and often grating little man summed the situation up with astonishing speed. He countermanded all plans to evacuate to the delta and all plans to remove the Eighth Army from Egypt. Most of these orders were unnecessary given the plans were only to be put in place if Rommel broke through, but Montgomery's orders produced clarity, especially in the minds of the troops. The Alamein position would be held. There might be defeat but there would not be retreat.

The 9 Australian Division, which surely had its fair complement of cynics, recorded the event:

Arrival of new army commander and change in policy

    With the arrival of the new Army Commander, Lt-Gen B. L. Montgomery (who at once visited Divisional H.Q. on 14 August) a new policy of three principal points was promulgated:–

(a) there would no 'looking over the shoulder'. If the enemy attacked Eighth Army would stand and fight in its present position;

(b) sub-units and units were to be assembled into their units and formations and fight under their own commanders. The formation of battle groups was to cease;

435

(c) although the men were brown and looked fit, they required toughening and hardening and units required training. Every opportunity was to be taken to harden the men and to raise the standard of training in units.

The effect of the new policy was quickly apparent. General relief and satisfaction was felt when it became known that the enemy was to be met and fought in the prepared position then held. Confidence and morale increased rapidly. From the first day of its arrival in the desert, the breaking up of the division and its formation into battlegroups with inadequate fire resources and lacking the advantage of the normal system of command and control had been strenuously and continuously opposed. For these reasons the new policy was most welcome.[8]

Montgomery then generalised these thoughts in edicts of startling simplicity and clarity. The first concerned the structure of the army:

The policy of fighting the enemy in Brigade groups, Jock columns, and so on, would cease at once. Divisions would fight <u>as</u> Divisions, and they were not to be split up into bits and pieces all over the desert.[9]

He continued:

Dominating ground must be held strongly by infantry formations with a strong anti-tank defence, and with plenty of artillery,

The armour must be kept concentrated. It must be so positioned on important ground that the enemy will be forced to attack it, i.e. he will have to attack our armour on ground of its own choosing.

The concentrated fire of artillery is a battle-winning factor of the first importance. Artillery command must be centralised under the C.R.A. [Commander Royal Artillery] of the Division so that he can use the Div artillery as a 72-gun Bty when necessary.[10]

These orders amounted to a revolution in desert warfare. First, the division was restored as the main fighting unit. This was a reversal of policy adopted for Crusader and taken to extreme lengths after that. If divisions were now to fight as divisions, unity would be restored to the army, especially as one division would now stand alongside another. There would now be a solid front which Rommel would have to confront instead of a series of boxes which he had always managed to mop up at will.

Montgomery had also restored infantry as a major factor in the desert war. Apart from the successes against the Italians in 1940, subsequent commanders had never known what to do with infantry. Montgomery was clear – infantry would advance to hold dominant ground wherever it could be found. They would then be supported by appropriate firepower to enable them to hold it and to inflict damage on any units attempting to expel them.

The concentration of armour was also vital. This feat had only rarely been managed since 1940. But Montgomery did not mean that concentrated armour would then proceed to dash about the desert looking for enemy tanks to destroy. It too would position itself on important ground that the enemy would be required to attack, thus reversing the situation that had applied through most of 1941 and 1942.

Finally, the artillery would also be concentrated. Of all the factors listed by the new Commander-in-Chief this was the most important. The desert army had often had a mass of firepower at its disposal and in the 25-pounder an excellent weapon with good range. From Crusader on, however, the dispersal of infantry and armoured units had resulted in the dispersal of artillery firepower. Now it would be centralised, at the very minimum at divisional level and on other occasions at the corps or army level. Churchill had detected that something was wrong with desert artillery methods when he said 'renown awaits the commander who first restores artillery to its proper place on the battlefield', but he failed to grasp that his advocacy of brigade groups and mobile columns militated against such a policy. Montgomery realised it from the first and put it into effect.

It is interesting at this point to note that Montgomery was eliminating the very aspects of desert warfare that both Churchill and Brooke had championed. Brigade groups had gone; all kinds of columns had gone; decentralised control had gone. Yet not once did either man criticise Montgomery's decisions on these grounds. Did they not realise what was transpiring in Eighth Army? Or, having appointed Montgomery, were they leaving such matters up to him? No doubt if he had lost any of his major encounters with Rommel such criticism might have returned, but nothing mutes a critic like success.

Montgomery did more than revolutionise the tactics of the desert army. He moved army headquarters to the coast, a more salubrious location and one that placed him in direct touch with the Desert Air Force. He also summoned up a division from the delta (44 Division), which enabled him to complete the line from the coast to the Qattara Depression. To add strength to his line Montgomery also brought forward the 8 Armoured Brigade from the newly arrived 10 Armoured Division.

No doubt he had also thought hard about the ingredients of Rommel's successes. Clearly the key for Rommel was the Afrika Korps, so Montgomery set about creating one of his own – 'a British Panzer Corps' he first called it – consisting of two armoured divisions (1 and 10) and a motorised division.[11] This new unit was not to hold the line but to be ready to exploit success achieved by more conventional divisions.

The other immediate problem for Montgomery was that of senior command. That he did not think highly of the group he had inherited was obvious to all. Moreover, Auchinleck and Corbett had been removed by higher authority and Gott was dead. Other casualties were Norrie, sacked as XXX Corps commander, and Dorman-Smith, removed as Deputy Chief of Staff. In their place Montgomery brought out Major-General Oliver Leese from England to command XXX Corps and Major-General Brian Horrocks to command XIII Corps. Major-General Allan (John) Harding was moved from GHQ to command the 7 Armoured Division. One key appointment was that of Chief of Staff, given to Eighth Army's former Intelligence Officer, Brigadier Freddie de Guingand. Montgomery gave his new COS wide ranging powers and an ability to speak for the army commander in all matters. It was a fruitful partnership that was to last until the end of the war. Also brought out from England was Lieutenant-Colonel Sidney Kirkman to command the centralised Eighth Army artillery. If one appointment pointed towards the type of battle Montgomery was to fight, it was this one. The issue of command of the armoured divisions was more fraught. No one in England had actually commanded armour in battle so Montgomery stuck to those with desert experience: Lumsden to command the new corps (soon to be named X Corps), Briggs to command 1 Armoured Division and Major-General Alexander Gatehouse to command 10 Armoured Division. In retrospect he might have made a clean sweep of these uninspiring men, who had been so damaged by repeated defeats by Rommel, and gambled on new faces from home.

Having chosen his commanders, Montgomery set about preparing for what seemed a certain attempt by Rommel to break through before the new army commander could settle. Montgomery acted quickly. The 44 Division was rushed forward and filled an important gap on the Alam Halfa Ridge, the obvious target for one of Rommel's right hooks. To protect that unit the 8, 22 and 23 Armoured Brigades were placed nearby. Further north were the New Zealanders and 5 Indian Division and closer to the coast the 1 South African and 9 Australian Divisions. More important than the physical dispositions was Montgomery's assessment that the Alam Halfa Ridge and points to the east and west of it would be the target of Rommel's main attack. To meet it he placed along the ridge 44 Division with a heavy screen of anti-tank guns and ample field artillery. He also ordered the armour to dig the tanks in on the high ground and also to have anti-tank guns and artillery with them. The whole area therefore became one of concentrated and concealed firepower. In addition he ordered the armour on the ridge to remain in situ and not in any circumstances to dash after Rommel, even if he retreated.[12] Here was a recognition that he must conserve armour for his own attack – when the time came – and acknowledgement that Rommel would have his own anti-tank weapons and artillery accompanying his tanks in order to take his usual toll on an attacking British tank force.

The battle began on 30 August and from the beginning did not go well for Rommel. As his forces were forming up for the right hook they were hit by repeated sorties from the Desert Air Force, now closely integrated into Montgomery's plan. This delayed the panzers but did not stop them. Then, as they approached the ridge, they were met with a hail of shell fire from an enemy that was difficult to see. The dug-in firepower of tanks, anti-tank guns and artillery took a fearful toll on 15 and 21 Panzer Divisions. Nor did the British venture from the ridge, as they would have in past battles – 'the swine isn't attacking', Rommel complained.[13]

This day was fatal for Rommel. The Panzerarmee was running short of petrol, due largely to British sinkings of German supply ships in the Mediterranean. He attempted to break the British grip on the ridge for two more days but, having been under fire for the entire time, including at night when he was constantly bombed by the Desert Air Force, he was obliged to retreat. This presented an opportunity for the Eighth Army to strike him in the flank and perhaps finish off the Afrika Korps. Like many a British attack in the desert, it misfired. The troops used were green and they had not coordinated their movement with their neighbours. Eventually the German and Italian forces counter-attacked but were stopped by concentrated artillery fire. There was in fact no opportunity for the Eighth Army finally to defeat Rommel at this early stage. The chances to retreat were too great, the troops employed too new. What mattered, more than this was that the Eighth Army had won a battle. Certainly Rommel was short of supplies but the positions on the ridge adopted by Montgomery and the overwhelming firepower he could bring to bear could under any circumstances had stopped the Afrika Korps. As for the debate over whether Auchinleck could have won this battle, it is as sterile as it is long. He did not fight the battle; Montgomery did.

Having seen Rommel off, Montgomery set about developing his own plan of attack. It turned earlier British plans for desert warfare on their heads. Previously armour had attempted to clear the way for infantry. In Operation Lightfoot (Montgomery's name for his plan), the infantry would clear a path for the armour. The initial battle was therefore to be mainly an infantry affair. In the north XXX Corps would assemble four infantry divisions (from north to south: 9 Australian, 51 Highland, 2 New Zealand and 1 South African) and propel them forward some 6 to 8 miles to overrun the enemy forward defended posts on a front of 16,000 yards. Then the X Corps, consisting at this point of two armoured divisions (10 and 1) would proceed through the area captured by the infantry, pivot on the Miteiriya Ridge and swing right 'till the Corps (which would now include the New Zealand Division) is positioned on ground of its own choosing astride the enemy supply routes'.[14] Further operations by the armour would depend on the reaction of the enemy to the original thrust.

In the south XIII Corps (50, 44, 7 Armoured Divisions and the Free French Brigade) would keep the 21 Panzer Division away from the main battle area by breaking through two German minefields and launching an armoured car regiment into the German rear.[15]

One aspect of this plan should immediately be emphasised: the role to be played by the armoured divisions was very modest. In the north the

1 and 10 Armoured Divisions were eventually to position themselves in front of the infantry but not by far. Their first position (Pierson) was in some areas just 1 mile beyond the final infantry objective and nowhere more than 3 miles in advance of it. Their final objective (Skinflint) 'astride the enemy supply routes' was less than 5 miles beyond that. This hardly amounted to a dash through the desert or indeed any form of 'exploitation' at all, for the armour was to wait on Skinflint ('ground of its own choosing') for the enemy to attack it.

Two factors might have induced Montgomery to assign this modest role to the armour. The first was his assessment of British armoured commanders. He had no great faith in them and had at first wanted Horrocks, direct from England, to command the armour. He was eventually won around to Lumsden by dint of the latter's experience in the desert but his approval was not based on first-hand experience. The second factor goes to the heart of the desert war. Montgomery had almost certainly come to the conclusion, again with astonishing speed, that Rommel had won many of his encounters with the British by standing on 'ground of his own choosing' and using a combination of artillery, anti-tank guns and dug-in tanks to defeat the British tanks, which usually attacked alone.

In the matter of leading the attack with the infantry, probably the nature of the enemy defences at Alamein left Montgomery with no choice. After Alam Halfa, Rommel increased his defences in the only manner left to him; he sowed more and more mines in deeper and deeper belts. By the eve of battle some 445,000 had been laid, some of which were anti-personnel mines.[16] The minefields were cunningly designed to leave empty spaces between the belts in which the British armour might be trapped. The full extent of the fields was not known to Montgomery. Aerial photographs provided many clues but patrols could only penetrate the most forward fields and to some extent those behind remained a mystery.[17] In any case it would have been foolhardy in the extreme to send armour into this morass. Instead the infantry, armed with some mine-detectors and some prototype flail tanks, could help clear pathways through the fields, but much mine-lifting would be carried out by small patrols prodding the ground with bayonets. Perhaps this is why Montgomery called the operation 'Lightfoot'.

The main weapon which would blast the infantry through these defences was the artillery. As noted, Sidney Kirkman had been brought out from

England as Commander Royal Artillery (CRA) Eighth Army and supervised the XXX Corps plan. The enemy position in addition to the minefields amounted to three defended positions – outpost, battle and reserve – each of which contained riflemen, machine-gunners, mortars and in some cases anti-tank guns. Each position was wired but with only thin belts of concertina wire. The problem of wire cutting was not therefore a major factor in the artillery programme. The programme had three aspects. Twenty minutes before zero the 408 x 25-pounders and 48 medium guns would fire on the enemy gun positions in an intense counter-battery shoot at the rate of two rounds per gun per minute. In two areas (51 Division and New Zealand Division) a creeping barrage would be fired, partly to enable the troops to keep direction, partly because there was not as much information about the exact layout of the defences in these locations. The last aspect was that fire on the defended areas would lift from locality to locality at a rate of three minutes per 100 yards. Also introduced was a technique for firing a concentration of all guns against a single target. This was called a 'stonk' and would be particularly valuable against important strongpoints or concentrations of stationary tanks. The programme, including counter-battery would last for 205 minutes.[18] Ammunition was plentiful but there was a shortage of medium artillery and an entire absence of heavy pieces.

So far so good. This concentration of guns could bring down a devastating fire on the rather rudimentary defences (apart from the minefields) that were possible in the desert (they were mainly slit trenches). What of the artillery plan for X Corps? Here lay an incredible flaw in the battle plan. In his notes on the battle Kirkman said that there was 'no occasion . . . when the action of armour was supported by heavy concentrations of artillery fire'.[19] The reason for this is startling: X Corps had not incorporated such a fire plan into their operations orders. Their artillery might fire at ad hoc targets but there was nothing which foresaw the need to bring down concentrations of fire on groups of enemy batteries. Nor had they prepared to use smoke shells as a form of concealment when moving forward. All this begged the question of what X Corps was to do when they ran into unsubdued enemy anti-tank guns. The answer seems to be that they expected the infantry to move forward and capture these weapons. Yet this begs another question – if the infantry were to overrun the enemy defences to the extent of capturing their guns, what role was left for the armour? The answer is that the armour saw their role at Alamein as they had always seen their role: that of dashing about the desert in pursuit of an enemy that had already been beaten – a glorified cavalry pursuit in the style of Balaklava. Perhaps this was the unfortunate legacy bequeathed to the British from the 1930s in forming most of their armoured units from the cavalry, thus percolating pre-modern attitudes in what was allegedly the most modern aspect of the army.

There is another mystery here. Montgomery had a low opinion of the armoured commanders, especially Corps Commander Lumsden, who had been a cavalryman. That view was certainly shared by Kirkman, if the tenor of his notes on the artillery is any guide. Yet Kirkman, in overall command of the artillery at Alamein, did not make or even supervise the artillery aspect of X Corps' plan – and therefore only noticed after the battle that there was no plan. And Montgomery, in overall control, and indeed something of a control freak, did not once check Kirkman's plan, as Kirkman has testified: 'between that moment [his appointment as CRA] and the Alamein offensive he never again referred to the gunnery plan.'[20] In the event, then, X Corps had no plan to call down artillery concentrations on unsubdued anti-tank guns, no plan to use smoke shells to conceal an advance, no plan at all to integrate artillery in any way with their operations. Here was a gaping hole that would remain in the Alamein plan throughout the battle and at one point almost prove fatal.

Artillery accuracy was ensured by a number of methods. The main one was the use of aerial photographs to establish the position of batteries and strongpoints with some precision. This was aided by flash spotting. A series of towers had been constructed behind the front to enable the spotters to plot the flashes of guns, particularly those firing at night, and pass the coordinates along to the batteries. There was also a sound-ranging section with a series of microphones that picked up the sound of a distant gun firing and enabled its exact position to be plotted.[21] In almost all cases these methods made it possible for the artillery to hit its target.

As the planning for battle moved forward Montgomery became increasingly worried that he was asking too much of the armour. Then both de Guingand and Leese reported to him that Lumsden, Gatehouse and Briggs had no intention of breaking out on the first day of battle. De Guingand reported Lumsden as saying:

Monty's plan – there's one point I don't agree with: that tanks should be used to force their way out of minefields. Tanks must be used as cavalry: they must exploit the situation and not be kept as supporters of infantry. So I don't propose to do that'.[22]

This was disquieting. If armour was to be used as cavalry, the infantry alone would have to inflict a wholesale defeat on the enemy (including enemy armour) before the tanks could be unleashed. At first Montgomery stuck to his plan. He had Lumsden 'whistled in' and told him 'in no uncertain voice' that the armour must break through the moment the infantry had reached their objectives.[23] But he then had second thoughts and modified his plan.

Montgomery's second plan was issued on 6 October. The main difference between this and the first plan was one of emphasis. In his revised plan Montgomery spoke much more about 'hard and prolonged' fighting, that the 'infantry must be prepared to fight and kill, and to continue doing so over a prolonged period'.[24] The operations of XXX Corps were now more precisely defined. After capturing the enemy 'forward positions' the 9 Australian Division would work north and the other three divisions would work south in order to 'crumble' away the remaining enemy defences. As for the armour, its main task remained the destruction of the enemy's armour but 'if this should not be possible initially, the Corps (10 Corps) will be manoeuvred so as to keep the enemy armour from interfering with the "crumbling" operations being carried out by 30 Corps'.[25] In the south, operations of XIII Corps would remain as in the initial plan with the proviso that the 7 Armoured Division was to be kept 'in being', 'it must not be destroyed'. Nor would the armoured cars be launched into the enemy's rear without the express order of the Army Commander.[26] This was a more cautious approach in line with Montgomery's view that the troops were not in all cases 'highly trained'. After their initial advance, the infantry of XXX Corps would methodically move forward, destroying the remaining enemy infantry as they went. Should the armour not be in a position to destroy the enemy armour, and Montgomery clearly thought that they would not be, they would form a shield probably not in advance of their first objective (Pierson) to protect the infantry as they 'crumbled'. The armour in this layout would be defensively deployed in a position to deal with enemy armoured counter-attacks. As a coda, if X Corps armour were not able to progress, 7 Armoured Division would probably be transferred to the north to assist them, assuming that the Germans also moved 21 Panzer Division north. One additional factor that might have led Montgomery to modify his plan was that Ultra intelligence was telling him that the German additions to their minefield defences were particularly formidable and that there now might be a third line behind the existing two.[27]

In the weeks that followed, the infantry was trained over ground resembling that of the battlefield. Models of particular sections of the front were created and officers and men were given explanations of their particular part in the battle. Most importantly battle drills (common procedures to deal with the various contingencies of battle) were to be instilled in order to produce a uniform and rapid response to any problems encountered.[28]

Meanwhile, Montgomery showed himself to the army, speaking with unbounded confidence to groups of officers and men and assuring all that he would knock Rommel for six right out of Egypt. There has been much derisory comment about the 'Monty' show – his strange collection of hats, his egotism, his arrogance and his love of publicity. However, the Eighth Army was not in good shape when he took command and there was a tendency to look over the shoulder to the next line of retreat. Montgomery needed to radiate confidence and convince the troops that they could have confidence in him. This approach worked. He was able to satisfy his troops that *his* plan, with which he would brook no interference, would defeat Rommel. The centralisation that this implied was welcomed because it was now thought that someone was in command who knew his business. That this was to some extent unfair to Wavell and Auchinleck has been the subject of much comment. That it was necessary for the Eighth Army is now being recognised.[29]

What were the comparable strengths of the two armies on the brink of Alamein? In all the British had seven infantry divisions (9 Australian, 51, New Zealand, 1 South African, 4 Indian, 50 and 44) in the line. There were also three armoured divisions (1, 10 and 7). The Axis had two German infantry divisions (164 and 90 Light), four Italian infantry divisions (Trento, Pavia, Brescia and Bologna), the Ramke (German) and Folgore (Italian) Parachute Brigades and four armoured divisions (15 and 21 Panzer and Littorio and Ariete). In terms of numbers, however, the Allies outnumbered the Axis two to one (220,476 to 108,000).[30] In terms of tanks the

Eighth Army had 1,029, including 252 Shermans and 170 Grants, 194 Valentine infantry tanks and several hundred more obsolescent types. Rommel had just 548, including 120 of the newer, thicker armoured types and 420 older German and Italian models.[31] There was also a discrepancy in artillery numbers with the British having 892 pieces and the Axis 552. In anti-tanks guns the numbers were closer – British 1,451, Axis 1,063. In aircraft the Desert Air Force had 520 serviceable and the Luftwaffe 350. It has to be remembered that on other occasions – namely Crusader and Gazala – the British also outnumbered their foes without startling result.

These numbers and the quality of the new Sherman tanks gave Montgomery great heart as he proclaimed his certainties of victory. However, the main factor, as he must have known, was the artillery. The concentrated fire from the 450 guns available to XXX Corps would be his major weapon. No troops in the defences available to them in the desert could possibly withstand this onslaught. And it mattered little if these troops were German or Italian – the nationality of a human body hardly counted when it was being deluged by a rain of shells.

No battle is tidy and the historian has to realise that the structure he or she brings to an operation might be hardly recognisable to those who fought in it, and to make it intelligible much detail has to be compressed and smoothed out. Nevertheless Alamein has a certain tidiness compared to the rather shapeless form of Crusader and the Gazala battles. The will of the Army Commander imposed a shape to Alamein that is absent from those earlier desert battles because they had no single, overarching commanding presence.

We can detect at Alamein two acts and an interlude, and this is how it will be described here. The first act commenced on 23 October before zero hour with the firing of the counter-battery programme which at once blanketed the German gun positions. Many guns were immediately taken out, sometimes including entire batteries of both field and anti-tank guns.[32] Counter-battery was soon followed by the actions of the Desert Air Force, whose Wellington bombers dropped 125 tons of bombs on the Axis forward positions.[33] Then followed, at 10 p.m., four divisions of infantry usually led by the mine-lifting parties. Let us follow the actions of the 9 Australian Division in this attack. The operation mainly ran smoothly. Under cover of the barrage the enemy listening posts and the first strands of wire were deftly dealt with. A triple band of wire was then blown up using Bangalore torpedoes. Overall, the first line containing the forward defended localities was easily captured, held as it was 'entirely by Italians'.[34] Direction was maintained with the help of a Bofors gun which fired tracer at five-minute intervals. The Germans held the second and stronger line, which was also protected by unidentified minefields. This held up the Valentine tanks of 40 Royal Tank Regiment which on the left was supporting the infantry. On the right all went to schedule, though there was heavy fighting for the second line. Gaps were made in the minefields with the assistance of bright moonlight and by just after 2 a.m. on 24 October the final objective had been captured.[35] On the left the brigade was forced to dig in just short of its objective due to the fire of 'hull-down' (that is dug-in) tanks.[36] Nevertheless, almost all objectives had been captured all along the divisional front.

To the south events had not gone this smoothly. However, 51 Division was stopped only a short distance from its final objective; the New Zealand Division captured the vital high ground of the Miteiriya Ridge; while the South Africans had made ground but were some way short of their objective. Unidentified minefields and the fact that crack German infantry (from 164 Division) was holding most of the front and second positions delayed the final advance and it was not until after daybreak (7 a.m.) that the ridge was secured.[37] All these units had suffered heavier losses than the Australians but overall the artillery had done its job in blasting a hole in the enemy defences.[38]

This was the moment for the armour to break out or at least push forward. Where were they? On the New Zealand front the 10 Armoured Division had been held up by unidentified minefields. Some tanks had in fact gone forward but ran into the mines and then were hit by enemy tanks and anti-tank guns. The remainder of the tank brigade (8) crouched with the New Zealand infantry behind the ridge. All attempts by the 9 Armoured Brigade that was attached to the New Zealand Division to move forward also failed. According to a contemporary New Zealand account, 'it was clear that the bridgehead could not be exploited by our armour at this stage and the day was spent re-organising the position to hold what we had gained.'[39] The armoured accounts indicate that their commanders had reached the same conclusion. The 10 Armoured Division, however, blamed the New Zealand infantry for impeding their progress.[40] What had happened? Not all minefields, it seems, had been accurately plotted and some time elapsed before X Corps engineers had located them and cleared gaps.[41] The other factor was the extreme reluctance of the armoured commanders to venture beyond the ridge into what they regarded as a formidable screen of anti-tank guns.

Montgomery noted this situation with alarm. Finally he ordered the armour on the Miteiriya Ridge forward to an objective know as Pierson – in fact a line in the sand just beyond the ridge. This led to a telephone conversation between the commander of 10 Armoured Division (Gatehouse) and the corps commander (Lumsden) which lasted thirty minutes.[42] Surely all options must have been canvassed during this time, but the only decision was to remain on the ridge and await the new day when Gatehouse, who had always been 'sceptical of the plan', expected the infantry to undertake the advance because tanks 'should definitely NOT be used for this type of role'.[43] There was some merit in the X Corps case; charging a line of anti-tank guns had proved disastrous to British armour in the past. But what stands out is the utter inability of these men to arrive at a decision (a half-hour phone call in the middle of a battle?) or devise any other solution to their problem. And here is where the lacunae in the artillery plan played such a doleful role. The answer to a line of anti-tank guns is a coordinated artillery bombardment. We saw how the initial XXX Corps onslaught took out many of these guns. Now was the time for X Corps, the artillery of which was back under its own control,[44] to fire a bombardment on the enemy anti-tank line before the armour went forward. No such bombardment had been planned, and there is no evidence that such an approach was ever discussed during the long phone call. In other words either Gatehouse or Lumsden had no idea of how to integrate their armour with their artillery or they considered that Montgomery's plan foisted on them a task more appropriate for the infantry and refused to carry it out. Lumsden might have had the command of Britain's equivalent to the Afrika Korps but he was no Rommel.

In the north, 1 Armoured Division with 2 Armoured Brigade leading was also mired in confusion. It had been unable to move through the leading Australian battalions 'due to an enemy Anti-tank screen, although a bridgehead had been made through the enemy minefields'.[45] The problem was that although the Australian infantry knew where the British armour was (with them), the commander of the division (Briggs) – due to a navigation error that would persist throughout the battle – thought they were some 1,000 yards further forward on their objective (Pierson).[46] This led to the puzzled remark in the Australian account that 'their [2 Armoured] own locations seemed to us to be obviously incorrect'.[47] Nevertheless, as far as the armoured commanders were concerned, all urgency in the north had gone – they had achieved their goal.

Meanwhile the southerly attack by XIII Corps had stalled. The 7 Armoured Division had cleared a path through the first minefield (January) but failed to clear the next (February) because of German artillery fire and the complete failure of the mine-clearing tanks. As Montgomery had left strict instructions that the 7 Armoured was not to incur unnecessary casualties, the battle was halted.

The Germans managed to mount no major counter-attacks on 24 October, but the 25th was different. Rommel, who had been in Germany on sick leave when the battle opened, had now returned and began to organise counter-attacks. On the front of the 9 Australian Division alone three major attacks came in, the first with twelve tanks, the second with forty and the third with an unknown number. All were beaten off, mainly by the artillery with some additional fire from dug-in tanks and machine guns. No attack penetrated a British position and as far as Montgomery was concerned this was exactly what he wanted the enemy to do – wear out their armour piecemeal.[48]

Montgomery's plan, however, was in more trouble than he knew. He called in Lumsden and 'impressed on him the urgent need to get his armoured divisions out into the open' in order that the 'crumbling' operations could start.[49] Later he again spoke to Lumsden 'in no uncertain voice' and told him that he must '"drive" his Divisional Commanders [forward]'.[50] He thought this telling off 'produced good results' but it did not. Neither Lumsden, Gatehouse nor Briggs had any intention of obeying the army commander. Eventually a report came in from X Corps headquarters that any progress would require 'full artillery support'.[51] This sounded like progress was intended but in fact Lumsden and his artillery commander were in different parts of the battlefield and (it may be speculated) X Corps either did not have the expertise to lay on a full bombardment or thought any advance should not be their task but that of the infantry. So nothing happened. And despite Montgomery's repeated orders to the armour, nothing continued to happen. By the 25th a crisis had been reached. In XXX Corps the infantry and the armour were more or less where they had been on the early morning of the 24th and no crumbling operations had begun. Worse, most infantry formations had suffered casualties and were not in a position to crumble anything. Further south XIII Corps was stuck. Fortunately for Montgomery there was one exception – the 9 Australian Division had entered the battle at full strength and had only suffered modest casualties. The army commander acted decisively. He pulled 1 and 10 Armoured Divisions and the New Zealand Division into reserve and ordered the Australians to begin operations northward to threaten a breakthrough along the coast. The interlude had begun.[52]

With Montgomery removing three divisions from the line for another major attack, the thinning out of the front to enable this to take place and the stalling of XIII Corps in the south, the whole weight of the battle fell upon the Australians. Their first attack was to capture Point 29, a molehill, but one which gave good observation over the surrounding ground. It was captured in a matter of minutes on the night of 25/26 October with infantry mounted on Bren-gun carriers and a 'large number of Germans' captured or killed. Further operations on the 28th and 29th and 30th/31st followed. Not all ground fought for was gained but the German reaction was everything that Montgomery had anticipated. Rommel, now back in command from convalescence in Germany, considered that the British had shifted their axis of advance and were trying to drive along the coast. If that succeeded, some of his troops would be cut off. He therefore reacted with fury. From 26 October to 1 November no fewer than nineteen counterattacks were unleashed against the Australians. Even the 21 Panzer was brought from the south to participate. Most of these attacks were made with whatever tanks were at hand (eighteen, twenty and forty tanks are mentioned by the Australians) and lorried infantry.[53] In other words they were made piecemeal. All failed, but this was crumbling with a vengeance – the best units of the Afrika Korps were being worn out.

The Australians in the end did not operate exclusively alone. By 27 October the 1 Armoured Division finally managed to get an armoured brigade forward on its southern flank and at its second attempt it captured a number of strongpoints which again produced a furious response from Rommel. The counter-attacks of the Afrika Korps were all beaten off.

This military interlude was accompanied by a political one. Churchill had insisted that he be given the plans for Alamein. When they arrived he had been acute enough to note that:

> [while] the tank was originally invented to clear a way for the infantry in the teeth of machine gun fire now it is the infantry who will have to clear a way for the tanks, and it seems to me their task will be a very hard one.[54]

For the (partial) inventor of the tank, this was a matter of some concern. When Alamein appeared to be bogged down he called a COS meeting and told Brooke that he intended to telegram Montgomery and ask in some detail about the army commander's intentions.[55] Brooke headed that off (though he was also concerned about Montgomery's lack of progress), so Churchill wrote instead to Alexander reminding him that the Torch landings in North Africa were about to take place and that whatever he could do 'to shake the life out of Rommel' would be appreciated.[56] The message startled Alexander. Later that day (29 October) he visited Montgomery's headquarters, accompanied by the Minister of State, Richard Casey. Clearly both men were worried about the lack of progress, but Montgomery's and de Guingand's assurances that all was in hand smoothed the waters.[57] Before Churchill had time to react Eighth Army's second great offensive at Alamein had opened.

In planning Act Two of his great offensive Montgomery's first thought was for XXX Corps to drive north-west to capture Sidi Rahman on the coast. He then changed his mind, probably influenced by intelligence from de Guingand which showed a great concentration of German units in this very area. If he struck further south the opposition would largely consist of the weaker Italian divisions and there would be the chance of hitting the panzers in the flank if they came south to rescue the Italians.[58] Montgomery wanted Lieutenant-General Bernard Freyberg ('easily my best fighting Divisional Commander') to take charge.[59] The problem here was that the New Zealand Division had incurred considerable casualties since 23 October. This meant that each infantry company had been reduced to about 500 men (470 other ranks and 27 officers). This does not sound drastic until it is realised that of these, 300 were specialists of one kind or another (signals, anti-tank gunners and so on) and that this left just 200 riflemen per company at the sharp end of the attack.[60] Montgomery solved the problem by 'loaning' the New Zealanders a brigade from the 51 Division and one from the 50 Division, obtained by his process of thinning out the line. He did more. He placed under Freyberg's command the 23 Armoured Brigade and allowed him to retain the 9 Armoured Brigade, thus giving an infantry commander control over a substantial body of armour. Hence Operation Supercharge would be largely, so far as command went, an infantry affair. Montgomery had sidelined the armoured commanders and ensured that whatever armour the infantry had would cooperate with it by placing it under infantry control.

The timing of the attack was determined by Freyberg, who announced that he would not be ready until the early morning of 2 November. In the meantime models were made of the terrain and a barrage plan worked out.[61] The barrage would actually be more intense than that for Lightfoot. Just 300 guns would open at zero but on the restricted frontage of 4,000 yards. This gave intensity three times heavier than the original attack. Knowledge of the enemy defences was sketchy so it was decided to fire a dense creeping barrage across the entire front, starting from the New Zealand front line, the troops having withdrawn to a safe distance. The rate of advance was to be 100 yards per two and a half minutes. The infantry were to keep up with the barrage at all costs, bypassing tanks or other strongpoints. Anti- tank guns were to advance with the infantry. The 9 Armoured Brigade would be close behind and proceed under a further creeping barrage beyond the infantry objectives until the high ground beyond the Rahman Track had been secured.[62] Montgomery made it quite clear that he was prepared to accept heavy losses in the armour so that a position might be reached where the 1 Armoured Division could be unleashed into the enemy's lines of communication. To what extent he actually believed that this would occur is doubtful. The exact timing of the battle was thus:

Zero – 1.05 am
Objective captured – 3.45 am
Creeping barrage for armoured advance – 5.45 am
1 Armoured to exploit – 6.45 am.[63]

On 2 November the bombardment opened on time and the troops moved forward. Close behind followed seventy-five Valentine tanks to subdue any strongpoints missed by the barrage. On the left all went smoothly and the 152 Brigade from the 51 Division had reached its objective at 4.17 a.m., just thirty minutes late. On the right 151 Brigade from the 50 Division was held up by enemy resistance but was on its objective by 5.25 a.m. This delay led the commander of 9 Armoured to ask for the barrage to be postponed for thirty minutes. Then at 6.15 a.m. the armour advance commenced. All did not go well. The 3 Hussars, for example, could only muster one squadron of heavy tanks (Grants and Shermans) at full strength – that is, fourteen. The other squadrons had just thirteen heavies between them, and a motley bunch of relatively obsolete Crusaders. In the move to the start line nine heavies were either hit by shell fire or broke down. So the 3 Hussars went into battle with eighteen heavies and four Crusaders.[64] These numbers were mirrored across the brigade. In all just ninety-four tanks from 9 Armoured went forward.[65] The 3 Hussars had also lost contact with their motorised infantry, which did not enter the fray with them. Additionally in this area something went wrong with the barrage, their report noting 'apart from a few stray shells, no barrage materialised on our particular front'.[66] Nevertheless, like their counterparts in the remainder of the brigade, they charged the German gun line. Some harsh things have been said about the British armour in this account. Let this New Zealand narrative restore the balance:

> The three tank regiments were out of touch with each other and at first light all were hotly engaged by dug-in tanks and anti-tank guns at close range. In most cases squadron leaders' tanks were blown up; wireless contact was lost and tanks fought individually. 3rd Hussars were reduced to three Crusaders and nine Shermans or Grants, but they knocked out fifteen anti-tank guns from 50 mm upwards, and later a further five tanks and two 88mm guns. The tanks of the Royal Wilts were nearly all knocked out, but they accounted for fourteen anti-tank guns. The Warwicks were engaged on three sides. They accounted for all anti-tank guns firing on them, but had only seven runners left at the end of the battle. It was a grim and gallant battle right in the enemy gun line.[67]

In the end the commander of the 3 Hussars was reduced to walking between his remaining seven tanks and giving them orders individually. All units of the 9 Armoured Brigade continued to fight in this way until the much-delayed 1 Armoured Division arrived.[68] In fact it just had time to dig in its tanks and deploy its anti-tank guns before an attack by the remains of 15 and 21 Panzer Divisions came in. A heavy toll was taken on the panzers, eighteen of which were left burning and another seven knocked out.[69] Although the Axis line did not break, Rommel was in a desperate position. His infantry divisions had been crumbled by the initial assault. The British armour had reduced the panzer divisions to shadows. At most, Rommel would have thirty-five tanks running on 3 November. Nor did he have sufficient anti-tanks guns to hold off a further British attack. And now the 2 Armoured Division, with the 7 Armoured Division in rear (having been brought from the south to accompany the move by 21 Panzer) was unleashed. Rommel had no option but to order a retreat. The Battle of Alamein was over.

* * * * *

In reflecting on this battle it is reasonable to say that almost nothing went according to Montgomery's original plan, even as modified on 6 October. The infantry did not secure their original objectives and only the Australian division was in a position to pursue some serious crumbling. As for the armour, it had lived down to Montgomery's expectations. There was never a serious intent to break through, probably a legacy of being outfought in that department by Rommel for two years. No doubt the task of the armour was difficult and, as Lumsden had suggested, it was a more fragile instrument than the army commander thought. However, it was a weapon of exploitation and it was used without dash or even imagination at Alamein. Montgomery's dream of a corps de chasse was just that. He might have been better served if the armour had been allotted to the infantry divisions as in the case of 9 Armoured Brigade.

On the other hand Montgomery played to the strengths that the British had had on more than one occasion in the desert war and thrown away. His concentration of force and especially the artillery was the key to victory. No desert defences could withstand a wholesale bombardment, as the

Australians had demonstrated long ago at Bardia and Tobruk. To say that Auchinleck was 'about' to concentrate his guns is humbug. He had the opportunity and did not take it. By reverting to infantry plus artillery, Montgomery knew he only had to persist. With these instruments, as long as the panzer army stood and fought, he would win. This was the foundation of his often-insufferable confidence but at least it was a confidence well-based. There was in fact a precedent for Alamein and it was the successful British battles of 1918. At Amiens and the Hindenburg Line the artillery had blasted a hole for the infantry with the tanks playing a minor role. Now armour was more important but not yet as important as men and guns. At none of these battles was a break-in converted to a breakthrough, but at all of them enough damage was inflicted upon the enemy to induce a retreat. And in all cases this was a retreat with no end. Alamein was the beginning of the end for 'Hitler's Mediterranean gamble'. With an Anglo-American army about to land in Morocco and Algeria, the only choices for the Führer were to cut his losses or to fight it out.

There is one other matter worthy of note at Alamein. It was not fought according to the principles that the Prime Minister or the Chief of the General Staff had laid down as appropriate for desert warfare. Their ideas of mobile brigade groups, of improvised columns and of extreme mobility were all discarded by Montgomery. In fact Alamein was, more than anything, a battle of attrition. This word, so redolent of the Western Front, was of course never used by the army commander, though his idea of 'crumbling' came close. Churchill was too acute an observer of things military not to have noticed how the battle was being fought. His instincts were often right, as was his view in the middle of the battle that Montgomery's plan had bogged down. Yet he made no criticism of Montgomery and made a great deal of Alamein as a turning point in the war. Montgomery might not have had the dash that Churchill always appreciated in his commanders, but if he could continue to produce victory after three years of defeat, there would be no prime ministerial critique of exactly how that victory had been obtained.

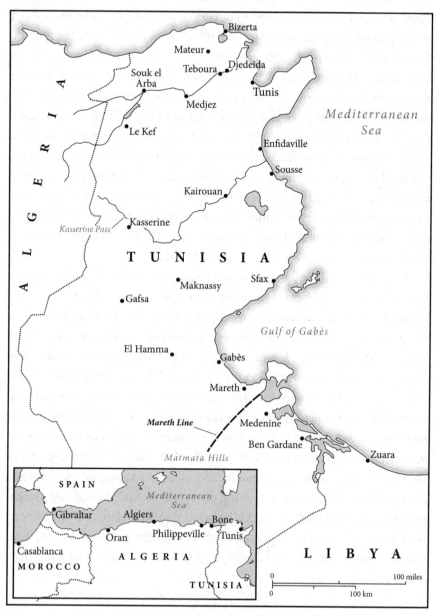

Map 9. North-West Africa and Tunisia.

CHAPTER 20

THE END IN AFRICA

IF THE BRITISH THOUGHT settling on an area of operations with an ally was a difficult task, they were yet to learn that developing an Allied plan for those operations was even more difficult. In July 1942 Dwight Eisenhower was appointed Supreme Commander of the Torch landings. His tasks were embodied in a directive agreed to by the Prime Minister and the President. His force was to accomplish three things:

(1) Establish lodgements in the Oran–Algier[s]–Tunis area and at Casablanca
(2) Rapid exploitation of these lodgement areas in order to control French Morocco, Algeria and Tunisia and to operate against the rear of the Axis forces in Libya
(3) 'Complete annihilation' of Axis forces opposing the British in the Western Desert to ensure safe communications through the Mediterranean and 'to facilitate operations against the Axis on the European continent'.[1]

This seemed clear enough. There would be landings inside the Mediterranean and outside at Casablanca. Then the forces would proceed 'rapidly' to Tunisia and Libya in order to annihilate, in conjunction with the advancing Eighth Army, all Axis forces in Africa. This would free up the Mediterranean and allow the Allies to develop further operations against the Axis in Europe. Notably this last task was left vague, no doubt because the course of the Torch campaign could not be predicted with any certainty.

Eisenhower's plan reflected the priorities he had been given. He envisaged four simultaneous landings – at Casablanca on the Atlantic coast and at Oran, Algiers and Bone inside the Mediterranean – with the ultimate aim of 'the early seizure of Tunisia'.[2] He was fully aware of the need to reach Tunisia with due speed. He told Washington, 'if Axis forces ever beat us to that place their later capabilities for building up strength will far exceed our own and will reduce the campaign to another futile and costly defensive venture'.[3] Indeed on thinking over the problem of reaching Tunisia rapidly he now proposed that all landings take place within the Mediterranean – at Bone, Philippeville, Algiers and Oran, with the latter force proceeding west and taking Casablanca from the rear.[4] Essentially he had pushed the force towards Tunisia.

Before the British COS could consider this plan, Dill arrived from Washington with sobering news. The US Chiefs, he thought, who had only accepted Torch with the greatest reluctance, were now leaning towards reinforcing the Pacific. If Torch was to go ahead they considered it too risky to land the entire force within the Mediterranean because if Spain proved hostile and closed the Mediterranean at Gibraltar the Allied armies might be lost.[5]

Dill was not exaggerating. The US Chiefs had been rethinking their entire strategy. They worried that a naval defeat by the Japanese off Savo Island on 8/9 August had imperilled their landings at Guadalcanal in the Solomons. In this situation shipping could not be transferred from the Pacific for Torch. In addition the reverses suffered by Auchinleck at the hands of Rommel led them to believe that any forces landed in North Africa might well find themselves alone in a hostile continent. This induced them to scale back Eisenhower's plan considerably. There would now be just two landings: one at Casablanca and the other at Oran. Churchill and Roosevelt's grand directive was cast aside. The purpose of the operation would now be to safeguard American supply lines across the Atlantic.[6]

The British were appalled by this turn of events. A study of Eisenhower's plan by the COS had concluded that the force of three divisions to be landed inside the Mediterranean was far too weak to forestall a German reinforcement of Tunisia.[7] Now the Americans proposed ditching those landings and landing a much smaller force some 800 miles from their intended objective. In Washington the British Staff Mission was in despair. A military member (Brigadier Vivian Dykes) recorded in his diary:

> A disastrous day ... the US are asking us to put home a revised draft directive for Torch, giving Casablanca and Oran only as objectives – to be gained as bases from which to conduct a later offensive against Tunisia (800 miles eastward). This is a shattering blow.[8]

So low was the morale of the British staff in Washington that they thought the whole enterprise better abandoned than pushed forward on that basis.[9]

There was never any chance that Churchill would agree to abandon Torch, the operations for which he had fought so hard to get American agreement. Brooke was of the same opinion. He suggested a compromise whereby landings would take place at Oran, Algiers and Casablanca. He thought this prudent in that landings further west at places such as Bone would be difficult to cover from the air, while landing at Casablanca would address US concerns about the Mediterranean being closed. Portal and Pound remained in favour of Eisenhower's original plan but Brooke's voice was decisive.[10] It now fell to Churchill to sell the compromise to Roosevelt.

On 27 August the Prime Minister wrote to the President:

> We are all profoundly disconcerted by the memorandum sent us by the United States Joint Chiefs of Staff ... It seems to me that the whole pith of the operation will be lost if we do not take Algiers as well as Oran on the first day ... not to go east of Oran is making the enemy a present not only of Tunis but of Algiers ... I hope, Mr. President, you will bear in mind the language I have held to Stalin [whom Churchill had visited in Moscow earlier in the month] supported by Harriman with your full approval. If Torch collapses or is cut down as proposed, I should feel my position painfully affected ... I most earnestly beg that the memorandum may be reconsidered.[11]

This was putting it very bluntly indeed. Churchill was saying that Stalin would feel betrayed if the new American proposals for Torch went ahead and that he (Churchill) might consider resignation in this circumstance.

Churchill's threats cut no ice with the American Chiefs of Staff. They met with their British colleagues in Washington on 28 August. Marshall began by saying that even if three landings were desirable (Algiers as well as Casablanca and Oran) there was only shipping available for two and one of the two must be Casablanca to maintain communications outside the Mediterranean and to ensure success by landing in strength against a weak opponent. (The British might have noted that this was the same man who had pushed to the point of desperation a landing against a much more formidable opponent across the Channel.) Cunningham (now First Sea Lord) tried to reassure Marshall that the Germans did not have the strength to close the Mediterranean at Gibraltar and that the key to the whole operation was the early capture of Tunis, but to no avail. King quickly agreed with Marshall, adding that the US navy was heavily committed in the Pacific and that he would shift naval resources to the Atlantic to aid Torch unless he was ordered otherwise. The meeting ended in complete impasse.[12]

In the light of this deadlock, the British COS, Churchill and Eisenhower put forward Brooke's compromise to the President. There would be landings at Casablanca as well as Oran and Algiers, Eisenhower undertaking to attempt to find shipping for Casablanca. In turn the British decided to abandon the easternmost landings at Philippeville and Bone.[13]

The President, probably under the strong influence of Marshall, was not moved. Indeed, in a letter to Churchill (which was clearly written by someone in the military), he introduced a new twist. He now insisted that the first landings (still to be confined to Oran and Casablanca) be made entirely by American troops – the British landing a week or so later.[14] The reasoning behind this position is contained in a letter Marshall wrote to Eisenhower the day before, the contents of which was 'not at any time [to] be communicated to the British'.[15] Why the letter should not be communicated to their ally soon became clear. Marshall worried that a British appearance in the initial landings would provoke the Vichy French into strong resistance with devastating consequences for the untried US troops. Moreover, despite Cunningham's assurances, Roosevelt was insisting that a line of communication be maintained outside the Mediterranean in case (or when) the British were routed in Egypt. Marshall also emphasised that he did not accept the British view that this scenario meant that Tunisia and Algiers would be lost to the Germans.[16]

None of Marshall's reasoning was disclosed to the British by Eisenhower, which was probably just as well because the British regarded Roosevelt's letter as disastrous enough. There was no chance that the British would accept the idea of an all-American landing. The COS drafted what they considered the maximum compromise that they were able to accept: abandonment of landings at Philippeville and Bone, three simultaneous landings at Casablanca, Oran and Algiers, with an American as well as a British component in the latter. On a landing at Algiers they would not compromise.[17]

This was conveyed in a telegram which Churchill sent to Roosevelt on 1 September. On it hung the whole future of Torch. Churchill deprecated the absence of British troops in the first landings and thought that the naval expedition (largely in British ships) would disclose their presence. In any case he noted that in the gloom of dawn 'all cats are grey'. He went on:

> This sudden abandonment of the plan on which we have hitherto been working will certainly cause grievous delay. General Eisenhower says that October thirtieth will be the very earliest date. I myself think that it may well mean the middle of November. Orders were given to suspend loadings yesterday in order that, if necessary, all should be recast . . . It seems to us vital that Algiers should be occupied simultaneously with Casablanca and Oran. Here is the most friendly and hopeful spot where the political reaction would be most decisive throughout North Africa. To give up Algiers for the sake of the doubtfully practicable landing at Casablanca seems to us a very serious decision. If it led to the Germans forestalling us not only in Tunis but in Algeria, the results on balance would be lamentable throughout the Mediterranean . . . I am sure if we both strip ourselves to the bone as you say, we could find sufficient naval cover and combat loadings for simultaneous attempts at Casablanca, Oran and Algiers.[18]

It was vital if Torch was to go ahead that Roosevelt accept most of what Churchill was suggesting. Under the heavy influence of Hopkins, who drafted most of the President's reply, he accepted most of Churchill's compromise proposal.[19] Three landings (Casablanca, Oran and Algiers) would take place although Roosevelt heavily weighted the Casablanca landing – 34,000 troops in the initial landing, followed by 24,000 shortly afterwards, and 25,000 at Oran followed by 20,000 in the immediate follow-up. This left a niggardly 10,000 for Algiers, which was the landing the British considered most important. Further compromises followed. The Americans found 5,000 more troops for Algiers, as did the British; 20,000 men would now land at the easternmost point of the attack.[20]

Torch was to go ahead 'full blast'. But it is important to examine what happened to the operation during what was called 'the great transatlantic essay competition'. In the first plans made by Eisenhower and approved by the British, the vast weight of the operation lay at its eastern end with landings at Bone, Philippeville and Algiers. This had now changed. Now there would be no landings east of Algiers, with just 20,000 men committed to land there. But 25,000 would land at Oran and 58,000 at Casablanca – the weight had definitely shifted westwards. At the sharp end of any advance from Algiers to Tunis would be fewer than 14,000 combat troops, the remainder being support and transport units. These men (well short of a complete infantry division) would be required to advance 500 miles, overcome rocky and hilly terrain, arrive at Tunis as a coherent force and tackle any German troops that had been rushed from Sicily. These were mammoth tasks that had been foreseen in the early days of the planning but rather forgotten in the compromises that followed. Having said that, it was almost inevitable that some component of Torch would be landed outside the Mediterranean. After all, it was not just the Americans who thought this prudent but Brooke as well. The Americans were worried about supply through the Mediterranean and Brooke thought there ought to be a force to watch the Vichy French in Morocco in case they proved hostile. This was perfectly sensible but the slight weight given to the Algiers landing and the cancellations of landings east of that point were not. Tunisia, which was surely the main objective of Torch, would have very few men available to secure it. What had happened to the grand plan outlined in the Roosevelt/Churchill directive in mid-August?

There is no doubt that the British–American discussions had achieved the great virtue of a consensus plan. But if that had been gained, something had been lost. The original aim of the plan was to hustle the Germans out of Tunisia in quick time. But in weighting the attack towards the Atlantic ports – that is, *away* from Tunisia – the consensus plan made that very much more difficult to achieve. Why did the British agree to such a change, which was certainly at odds with Churchill's original conception? There are some obvious reasons. The American Joint Chiefs of Staff were so hostile to the entire concept of landing in North Africa that the British might have seen any compromise which actually resulted in a landing as some kind of victory. Churchill in particular knew that Roosevelt was fighting rather a lonely game on the issue and might well have agreed to the compromise to rescue his partner and the plan from total defeat.

The puzzle, though, is not Churchill in this instance but Brooke. Brooke not only agreed to the compromise but helped bring it about by strongly supporting the Joint Chiefs of Staff in their insistence that there be landings on the Atlantic coast. Brooke must have been aware that this would make the early arrival of the Allies in Tunis less likely. Why then did he push so hard for this option – indeed push it against the opinions of the other service Chiefs? We may find two reasons. The first was merely caution. Brooke knew that this would be the first occasion that the untried Americans encountered German troops, and Brooke well knew from British experience in the Western Desert that these men were able to stymie units with much more experience than the Americans. Therefore he may have reasoned that a slow build-up in French Morocco and Algeria for an extended period *before* the US troops encountered the Germans would be prudent to the extent that in his view this trumped the goal of arriving in Tunis rapidly.

This caution may also have played into Brooke's longer-term strategy. From the discussions with the Americans about Sledgehammer he seems to have arrived at the conclusion that the Allies were not only unready to invade north-west Europe in 1942; they would probably not be ready in 1943. A rapid capture of Tunis (say in January or February 1943) and then a swift conquest of Sicily in the next month or so would leave the summer of 1943 open for such a cross-Channel operation. Proceeding in North Africa at a much steadier pace, on the other hand, would rule out the summer of 1943 for such a risky (in Brooke's view) operation. Perhaps this was the motive behind Brooke's almost unique support for an American strategic idea. We cannot be sure that this was his motivation because he certainly never admitted to it but it does explain why on this one occasion the British Chiefs spoke with divided opinions.

* * * * *

The North African landings took place on the night of 8 November 1942 after a logistic and organisational triumph which saw men delivered from the United States and various parts of Britain to three main landing areas simultaneously. Resistance by the Vichy French was variable. Some naval units in particular fought hard but there was no discernible difference between the opposition offered to American or British troops, which bore out Churchill's dictum about grey cats. Operations at Casablanca and Oran met sporadic but increasing resistance by warships and coastal batteries until, just as Casablanca was about to be stormed by General George Patton's II Corps, the Vichy regime under Admiral Darlan capitulated.

This outcome, so welcome in the fighting zone, caused tension between the theatre commander Eisenhower and Churchill. In Britain, Churchill came under fire for approving the deal reached between Eisenhower and Admiral Darlan for a French capitulation. The refusal of Darlan to sail the French fleet to British or neutral waters in 1940 had not been forgotten. Yet Eisenhower was trying to do the best he could for the troops, and a rapid French capitulation was obviously part of that. Churchill privately approved but had to do some hard talking to the House of Commons in Secret Session to convince his colleagues that this was for the best. In any case Darlan soon departed the scene – and the earth – when he was murdered by a French patriot on Christmas Day.[21]

Meanwhile at Algiers a composite British/American force had landed with only mild opposition. This was the British First Army, rather a grandiloquent name for a force that consisted merely of a British and American brigade group and a scattering of support troops. Two days later they were joined by a second British brigade group, making a total force of no more than 20,000 men.[22]

This was the force that had the job of advancing 500 miles to Tunis and routing any German/Italian force that was sent against them. Lieutenant-General Kenneth Anderson, the commander of First Army, landed in Algiers on 9 November and set about directing his meagre force eastward. Initially he had some success. The 36 Brigade was despatched to Bougie by ship and landed unopposed. Then a small force of commandos and parachutists was sent even further east to Bone, which they also successfully captured. So rapid were these movements that Anderson felt able to order a general advance on 14 November. The task confronting his force was immense. Anderson's small group, which had no more than 12,000 men at the sharp end, was spread out over a front of more than 50 miles. Moreover, there were only two half-decent roads by which a highly mechanised force could advance – one near the coast and the second further south on the other side of a treacherous mountain range from Souk el Arba to Medjez, Djedeida and Tunis.[23] Even then the army would have an open right flank with only some American parachutists and an unknown number of French troops to the south.

Anderson deployed one brigade group and accompanying armour and some parachutists and commandos to each road. In bad going, with an uncertain supply chain, they made good progress. Within two weeks the columns had covered over 450 miles and were approaching Meteur in the north and Djedeida – which was just 15 miles from Tunis – in the south.[24] But the Germans had not been inactive. After the landings Hitler had decided to hold Tunisia as a bridgehead. By 12 November the first group of reinforcements had arrived in Tunis. These were not the second-class troops predicted by Allied Intelligence; they were crack paratroopers and panzer grenadiers. In just a few days 15,000 men and equipment had been flown in while another 2,000, accompanied by some armour, arrived by ship. In addition the number of aircraft in North Africa had increased from 283 aircraft to 445.

The German troops were placed under the command of the energetic General Walter Nehring, who soon sorted them into battlegroups and deployed them against the Anglo-American columns.[25] In early December these forces struck the strung-out Allied columns at Teboura and drove them back. Then they struck further south near the open flank and only a rapid withdrawal saved envelopment.[26]

At this point Eisenhower arrived at the front, for the moment freed from his political responsibilities by the agreement with Darlan. After consulting with Anderson, he decided that the advance must pause while supplies were brought forward and more airstrips made available to ward off increasing German air attacks.[27]

The fighting resumed on 9 December. By this time the French had decided to throw their lot in with the Allies and provided flank assistance to the south to Anderson's forces. Also to the south of the French the US II Corps took its place in the line, giving a more or less coherent Allied front from the sea to the impassable Salt Lake in the south. Then the rains came, which they did regularly in North Africa at this time of the year. By Christmas Eve fog and mud had halted all progress. Anderson called a

465

conference between himself, Eisenhower and Lieutenant-General Charles Allfrey, the newly arrived commander of the British V Corps. Reluctantly the decision was made to halt major operations until the rainy season was over – in effect meaning that an attempt on Tunis would not be made until March 1943.[28] The hope of a rapid conclusion to Torch was gone.

Much opprobrium has been heaped on Anderson and Eisenhower for this decision. Eisenhower, it was said, was too busy being a politician to take a strong grip of the situation on the ground. Anderson was said simply not to be up to the job – a 'good plain cook', 'a man silent in three languages'. It is true that neither Anderson nor Eisenhower were the most inspired ground commanders produced by the Allies in the Second World War. It is also true that the plan for Torch hardly gave them a decent chance of achieving a rapid victory. The American insistence on weighting the attack to the west and enfeebling the force at Algiers proved fatal. It is difficult to see what commanders of any calibre could have done in the circumstances. This was the first opposed landing made by the Allies in Europe and it was made in an area where all supplies, including coal for the railways, had to be brought with them. In addition, troops who had never been in action before had to sort themselves out and advance over great distances in most difficult terrain where air and armoured support were never guaranteed. It is not surprising that, when they encountered crack German troops, their advance was stymied. In fact it is to the credit of the command that they got so far before being halted. Another division of troops might have made the difference, especially if they had been landed closer to Tunis. However, Tunis remained in Axis hands and attention now turned to the other Allied army that was approaching from the east. Could Montgomery and the Eighth Army hasten the end in North Africa?

After Alamein, the Eighth Army continued to push back Rommel's forces as they retreated across Cyrenaica and Libya. By 8 November Montgomery was in Mersa Matruh, by the 13th in Tobruk, by the 20th in Benghazi and by 24th at Agheila. All attempts to cut off Rommel's forces, in particular by the 7 Armoured Division at Bardia and by light armoured forces cutting across the Jebel Bulge, failed. For these failures Montgomery has been castigated ever since. The fact was, however, that Montgomery was determined not to preside over the kind of setbacks that had wrecked Wavell's and then Auchinleck's operations. To this end he kept the Eighth Army concentrated and made sure that it never outran its supply chain. This certainly meant a slow and steady advance but it also meant that he could not be checked by Rommel. Montgomery explained his difficulties to Brooke thus:

> I have advanced over 1000 miles by road since 5 November . . . As far as Tobruk I have one road, one single railway line, and the sea. Beyond Tobruk I have one road and the sea; there is NO railway. I can get a big daily tonnage into Tobruk; but it is 3 days journey by M.T. convoy from Tobruk to Benghazi, or 6 days for the round trip there and back. I am getting 2,000 tons a day into Benghazi but only 500 tons of that is petrol and petrol is 50% of my daily requirements in tons.[29]

There were other factors which also influenced Montgomery to take a cautious approach. The first was his lack of confidence in his armoured commanders, especially Lumsden. He flagged in November that Lumsden ('not fit for high command in the field') was to go. In December he was dismissed and replaced by General Horrocks. In addition, while he thought morale satisfactory, he also felt that this might change rapidly if there was any kind of reverse. Only a continual run of successes would rectify this situation and he was loath to attempt anything that might endanger this state of affairs.[30]

The other thing that needs to said about Montgomery and the desert war is this: despite Rommel's brilliance as a commander, at no time in his victorious romps across the desert did he manage to cut off sizeable portions of the British army. Poorly led though that army sometimes was, it always managed to escape his clutches. This illustrates how difficult it was to get past determined rearguards equipped with machine guns, artillery and a scattering of tanks. Outside the 1940 campaign this was a feat that was not accomplished by any army in the western sphere.

So while Rommel's forces continued to be hard pressed and short of petrol and supplies of all kinds, they were forced back rather than encircled. Attempts by Montgomery to do this at Agheila failed as Freyberg's New Zealanders were thwarted at the last minute by Rommel's withdrawal. The 7 Armoured and the New Zealanders were stymied again by the German withdrawal from Tripoli in January 1943. In the main, however, the Eighth Army observed rather than engaged the retreating enemy. As a situation report in late January 1943 said:

The last four days have seen the steady but slow withdrawal of the enemy's rearguards from Tripoli westwards to Zuara. By 1000 hrs we had passed Giado and reached Zuara–Nalut road. We were within 15 miles of Zuara by last light on 27 January and our patrols were observing the German recce units in the Uotia area. In the same way as on our way up to Benito, the soft sand south of the coast road has hampered our progress considerably; and the enemy has been able to continue his withdrawal towards the confines of Tunisia in good order.[31]

The German retreat into Tunisia did raise the question of how the Allies were to coordinate their plans – was the stalled First Army in Tunisia to deliver the *coup de grâce*, or was the battle-hardened Eighth Army the instrument to end Axis resistance in Africa? The fact is that no one in higher authority seems to have given this any thought. As the two armies approached each other, there was a desperate need to coordinate their actions. But not until very late in the day was the issue addressed. This gave Rommel the chance to strike first at one of his opponents and then the other.

Rommel's first blow was aimed at the First Army. His moment (14 February 1943) was well chosen because at this point the command structure of that army had rather fallen into chaos. Eisenhower was of course in overall command but somewhat removed from battlefield decisions. At the end of January Anderson was given the task of coordinating operations along the entire front, including that held by US forces. In fact, little coordination was achieved. The front was now very long (about 600 miles) and Anderson had no personal aircraft. It took him four days therefore for even short visits to his corps commanders.[32]

It was into this command vacuum that Rommel attacked. Enigma intelligence gave some warning that the Germans were preparing an operation against First Army; it did not indicate the exact time or place.[33] His target was in fact the inexperienced US II Corps, then under the uninspired leadership of General Fredendall. In the van of the attack were the 10 Panzer, 21 Panzer and other units from the Afrika Korps along with some Italian tanks. The Americans, whose first experience of Rommel this was, were slow to react. Then they moved rapidly but backwards. By 19 February the Kasserine Pass had been lost; by the 20th Anderson found himself ordering 'NO Retreat'. Anderson also summoned help. American and British reserves, particularly armour and artillery, were rushed forward; by 22nd Rommel had in fact reached the limit of his advance. Fredendall was sacked and replaced with the more dynamic Patton, who stabilised the front in rapid order. The Americans would take some time to recover from the setback that was Kasserine Pass.[34]

It was now Montgomery's turn. On 6 March Rommel delivered an attack by three panzer divisions at Menedine. But on this occasion the attack, thanks to Enigma, had been anticipated. The armour and following lorried infantry ran into Montgomery's massed anti-tank guns, backed up by artillery. A fearful toll was taken on the panzers, and Rommel's attack immediately ground to a halt with heavy losses. Montgomery hardly lost a tank. As he said later to Brooke, the battle was 'an absolute gift'.[35]

Montgomery now conceived grandiose plans to sweep Rommel out of Africa. He submitted a plan to advance up from the south with his right flank on the coast to deliver 'a 1st class Dunkirk on the beaches of Tunis'.[36] But such operations were premature; facing Montgomery was a considerable obstacle that he would have to overcome before he could enter Tunisia. This was the Mareth Line.

The Mareth Line was an old group of fortifications built in the 1930s by the French against a possible Italian incursion. The position had some strengths. Salt pans and flooded wadis between the coast and the hills made the going difficult for all vehicles. Some strong field works, including concreted boxes, wire and anti-tank ditches, had been incorporated into the front along with some 70,000 mines. The hills were less well defended but the going was tough and the road ran through some easily defended defiles. In short, there was no easy way through and no easy way around.

Montgomery's plan was two pronged. He would attack alongside the coast and at the same time send a force of infantry and tanks around the front in a wide left hook. The problem with the plan was that the attack along the coast was very weak. In fact just one brigade of troops from 50 Division would assault here at the very point where the Mareth defences were strongest. The left hook was stronger – the New Zealand Division, the 8 Armoured Brigade and a force of the Free French (27,000 men and 200 tanks) would advance through the mountains. But as de Guingand said, 'the general plan ... was to try to make a breach in the Mareth Line in the coastal sector'.[37] This aspect of the plan failed dismally. The few attacking troops got bogged down in the wadis and only a few tanks penetrated the flooded areas; no wheeled vehicles could get through. The troops soon lost the barrage, and the defenders – which included the veteran 15 Panzer Division, exacted their price. Because of the narrowness of the front of attack, enfilade fire was poured into the attacking infantry. By the evening of 24 March they were back on their start line.

Meanwhile the New Zealanders, the armour and the French had been making steady progress towards a defile in the hills called Plum Gap. However, the outflanking movement had been discovered by the Luftwaffe and the Germans began to move units away from the coast to stymie it. Montgomery was now in a considerable dilemma with the prospect of the entire operation stalling. To de Guingand at the time he appeared rattled, saying to him, 'What am I to do?'[38] If this was the case, the army commander soon recovered. On the morning of 23 March he announced that the coastal attack would be closed down, 1 Armoured Division sent to the New Zealand force, accompanied by Horrocks who would take command of the entire left hook. Horrocks soon wired Montgomery with three alternatives: a cautious step-by-step attack, splitting the armour to get around the bottleneck, and an all-out 'blitz' attack with maximum artillery and air support.[39] Montgomery quickly decided on the last option and sent de Guingand to consult the air commander, the newly installed Wing-Commander Harry Broadhurst. Out of the discussions came a novel plan. There would be maximum artillery support fired by the New Zealanders and the medium guns that X Corps had available but there would also be massive air support with no fewer than sixteen squadrons of fighter bombers attacking anything that moved in front of the creeping barrage. An additional refinement was that the attack would not take place at night, as was usual for Eighth Army, but in the late afternoon when the blinding sun would be in the faces of the enemy.

The attack started on 26 March. It was entirely successful. The fighter bombers and the barrage proved irresistible, the Axis armour being swept aside as the 1 Armoured charged for the enemy gun line. And these were not ordinary enemy formations – 21 Panzer, 15 Panzer and 164 Infantry Divisions proved quite unable to stem the onslaught. Once again, though, the remains of the Afrika Korps managed to withdraw, first to Gabes and then further north. There was still much work to be done.

In western Tunisia fighting had resumed after the setback at Kasserine. It began under a new command structure. At last the Allies had moved to coordinate the operations of the First and Eighth Armies. They were now combined to form an Eighteenth Army Group, with Eisenhower remaining Supreme Commander but Alexander taking over battlefield operations, his subordinates being Anderson and Montgomery. This sensible move soon paid off with Patton's II Corps attacking as a distraction for Montgomery's operations against the Mareth Line. By early April the armies formed a continuous front and Alexander rightly decided to lay aside Montgomery's earlier plan to sweep Rommel from Tunisia because of the severe fighting at Mareth that the Eighth Army had just undergone. The *coup de grâce* would now be delivered by the First Army. That unit had grown to a considerable size with the US II Corps in the north, the V and IX British Corps in the centre and the XIX French Corps in the south. The new plan was to drive towards Tunis and Bizerta and trap the Germans between the two wings. In these aims the operation failed in the teeth of strong German resistance. However, advances were made everywhere and much German armour was written down. The most intense fighting (often hand to hand, not a regular occurrence for western armies in the Second World War) took place in the centre between V Corps and the Herman Goering Division and the 15 Panzer.[40] Eventually all the enemy's defensive positions were captured, but similar to actions on the remainder of the front, the attacking divisions soon reached exhaustion and Anderson sensibly broke it off on 25 April.[41]

Now came the final act. On 30 April Alexander met with Montgomery and due to the difficulty of the ground facing the Eighth Army, transferred some of its divisions to Anderson. The plan was simple. Three armoured divisions (1, 6 and 7) were concentrated opposite Medjez along with the 4 British Division and 4 Indian Division. Scorpion tanks led the way, clearing mines. Then under a heavy artillery bombardment, which was again extended by fighter bombers shooting up vehicles and guns ahead of the curtain of shells, the infantry and armoured attack went in. For once the German infantry broke and ran, 'throwing away their rifles'. By 7 May British infantry entered Tunis and the Americans Bizerta.[42] By the 12th the unconditional surrender of German and Italian forces in Africa was complete. Estimates suggest that about 240,000 Axis troops surrendered, split more or less evenly between German and Italian troops.[43] Hitler's 'Mediterranean gamble' was now over.

Back in London Churchill followed the progress (or otherwise) of these operations in detail but with a growing sense of frustration. One of his main concerns about the Tunisian campaign had been that it should be over early, so that the operation decided upon at the Casablanca Conference (Husky – the invasion of Sicily) could be advanced. In a letter to Smuts he voiced his frustration that the original British plan was not adopted: 'It was a near thing Anderson's Army Corps did not carry the Tunisian Tip at the first bound. If our original plan had been followed out we should have had the whole place.'[44]

With the advent of coalition warfare Churchill felt much constrained from making his usual detailed interventions in what was largely an American operation. For example, he was much frustrated by Eisenhower's decision in December 1942 to postpone operations for two months, but he did not intervene, merely urging Ike to make haste once his attack recommenced.[45] Ironically, this telegram was sent on the eve of the American setback at Kasserine. Clearly Churchill had a relatively low opinion of the standard of training of US troops at this stage of the war. Nevertheless, the Prime Minister uttered few words of criticism of the Americans. Thus, although he told the King that Kasserine had left him disturbed by events in North Africa, he crossed through a section of his letter which revealed that Enigma had spoken of the 'low fighting quality of the enemy', referring to the US II Corps.[46] Two days later, in a letter to Hopkins all was sweetness and light: 'Tunis battle is good and going to get better and men British and American are fighting like brothers together and side by side.'[47] The fact that North Africa showed Britain and America in action together against what Churchill considered to be the main enemy clearly trumped any negative views he might have about American fighting power.

Perhaps because he felt so constrained about criticising the Americans, he vented his wrath on his favourite battlefield general, Alexander. After the Mareth Battle Churchill became convinced via Enigma that Rommel was finished. He peppered Alexander with telegrams demanding information. He received no replies so on 29 March he wrote to his army group commander: 'I can not understand why you do not report to us what is happening, particularly on the Mareth Front. Boniface [Enigma] shows considerable events are taking place but we hear nothing from you.'[48]

Alexander replied the same day that the fighting in the area was very confused and that he did not want to give Churchill the wrong impression. He ended (rather peevishly) 'please trust me to do my duty in this request'.[49] This provoked a furious response from the Prime Minister. While he said he did not want to 'burden you in the midst of a complicated battle', he was disturbed to receive 'no news from your headquarters for about 30 hours'. He demanded that a dedicated staff officer be appointed to supply him with regular information when Alexander was away visiting the front. Churchill had also heard nothing about US operations and he demanded to know from Alexander if Eisenhower was withholding information from him, 'as in that case I should have to take the matter up with the President'.[50] Alexander rapidly backed away, assuring Churchill that he would receive regular information from the front when Alexander was away and assuring him that he and Eisenhower were on the best of terms and in full communication with each other.[51] From then on Churchill did receive the most detailed military reports from Tunisia, both from Alexander and Montgomery.[52]

Nevertheless there is one overwhelming reason for Churchill's relative restraint in his remarks to his generals during this period – they were winning. No doubt they were winning too slowly for the taste of the Prime Minister, and there is good cause to believe that his bombardment of Alexander about the state of the German army revealed by the Enigma decrypts indicated that he thought his commander ought to be getting on with the job rather more rapidly than he was. But, having witnessed years of setbacks in the Western Desert and having struggled through most of 1942 to get the Americans to adopt his North African strategy, he was hardly going to unleash a litany of complaints about the pedestrian nature of the advances. Despite checks such as Kasserine or the length of time required to win victories such as Mareth, his strategy was working. And having persuaded the Americans that their next action should also be focused in the Mediterranean – that is, the invasion of Sicily – he was not inclined to be critical. That this would not always be his stance will be demonstrated in future chapters.

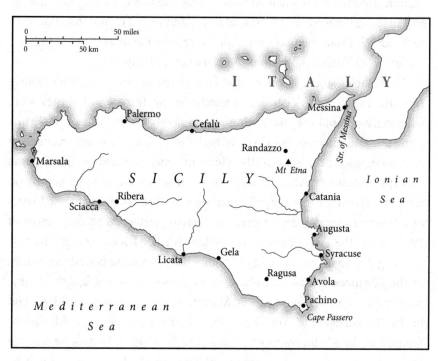

Map 10. Sicily.

CHAPTER 21

INCHING TOWARDS ITALY

EVEN AS TROOPS LANDED in French North Africa, Churchill's fertile mind was pondering further strategic possibilities. On 9 of November 1942 he suggested to the COS that to follow up Torch merely with the capture of Sicily and Sardinia would be 'regrettable'. Surely, he thought, it would be possible to attack Italy 'or better still southern France', bring Turkey into the war and operate with the Russians in the Balkans.[1] After that the invasion of north-western Europe could take place in the late summer. This plethora of operations was anathema to the cautious Brooke, and there is no evidence that the COS ever considered Churchill's paper as a whole. Instead they discussed what operations should follow if the North African campaign was successful. The options were Brimstone (the invasion of Sardinia) or Husky (the invasion of Sicily). The Joint Planners favoured Brimstone but Brooke clearly favoured Husky. Planning for both operations was to proceed, but no mention was made of Churchill's broader schemes.[2] The Prime Minister was not satisfied. Torch, he told the COS, had opened up enormous possibilities. Brimstone or other such operations might be carried out in the first half of 1943 but the main event was a return to Europe via the Pas de Calais or the Biscay ports in August or September. They should re-examine the whole question.[3]

These meetings with Churchill were starting to exhaust Brooke, who did not expect to last another year as CIGS.[4] A few days later Churchill returned to the charge. He pronounced himself to Brooke 'greatly disturbed' by the present outlook. All that was on offer was a small operation in Sardinia. This was far from the great series of attacks he had promised Stalin during his August visit. Brooke (who was certainly showing signs of exasperation) replied that Stalin had not been promised anything of the kind 'in his presence', indicating that perhaps Churchill had made promises behind his back. Brooke and Attlee attempted to refocus the Prime Minister on the Mediterranean but he would not be deflected. 'Only in France', he insisted, could the entire air force based in Britain be brought to bear and in any case he did not think 'invasion would prove so formidable when the time came'. He insisted that the COS carry out his instructions to re-examine the operation.[5]

So fixated on a cross-Channel attack was Churchill that he misinterpreted an American note on shipping to mean that the US had abandoned invasion planning in 1943. He dashed off an indignant note to Roosevelt about this 'most grievous decision' and demanded to know how it had come about.[6] Roosevelt assured him that the US build-up for the attack was not in danger and that the whole matter was a misunderstanding.[7] Churchill was soothed.[8]

The disarray among British decision-makers was threatening to have dire consequences. A meeting with the Americans had been scheduled for early January and there was a real prospect that the British would not present at it a united front – the COS opting for some kind of Mediterranean operation and the Prime Minister going bald-headed for a cross-Channel attack (Round-Up). In an endeavour to sort out these differences the COS met with Churchill on the eve of departure for the Casablanca Conference. Brooke attempted to persuade Churchill that the US build-up in Britain would not provide enough divisions to launch a full-scale attack upon France until at least August and perhaps not even then. This, he thought, would leave a gap of several months between the successful invasion of Sardinia or Sicily and a cross-Channel operation. Germany must be continuously engaged by operations in Sicily, Italy and perhaps the Balkans, thus dispersing German divisions and not staking everything on a Round-Up that might not take place.[9] This would also be the best way of aiding Russia.

For Brooke, there were probably other factors in play. He knew that Montgomery, despite his superiority in tanks, artillery and men, had been required to fight very hard to prevail at Alamein and that following up even a shattered Afrika Korps had proved difficult. He also knew that the Anglo-American forces were making heavy weather of it in Tunisia and that some of the landings had not gone smoothly though they had been virtually unopposed. What troubled him was that an attack on the German army in well-defended positions might be beyond Allied troops in 1943 whereas blows against a weaker enemy (Italy) might well succeed. None of this was he ready to vouchsafe to Churchill, who in his present mood was hardly ready to receive it.

Nevertheless Brooke made some headway. Churchill could certainly see the logic and relative ease with which operations in the Mediterranean could be conducted by armies which were already in the theatre. So while the Prime Minister still asserted that Round-Up was the 'better strategy', he told the CIGS that he would be content with an early Brimstone (invasion of Sardinia) and an invasion of Sicily or southern Italy or both 'with the object of knocking Italy out of the war, preparing for an entry into the Balkans and bringing Turkey into the war on our side'.[10] If this was not quite Brooke's strategy, at least he had moved the Prime Minister some way towards it.

This was the state of play among the British as they prepared to meet the Americans at Casablanca in the second week of January 1943. They soon faced two sobering facts. The first was the meeting between Eisenhower and Anderson on Christmas Eve 1942 at which it was decided that no further operations could take place in Tunisia for two months on account of the rain. This threw out the entire schedule that had been forming in Churchill's mind in which Husky/Brimstone/Italy would be dealt with in the first half of 1943 and perhaps Round-Up in the second.[11] The second was a briefing by Dill in which he informed the British delegation that the Americans, and in particular Marshall, were opposed to *any* future operations in the Mediterranean after Torch. What they wanted was to concentrate more forces in the Pacific and transfer as many divisions as possible to Britain for a cross-Channel attack in August. In fact Marshall had a 'genuine fear of commitments in the Mediterranean, and secondly a suspicion that we [the British] did not understand the Pacific problem'.[12]

Indeed, when the British Chiefs met their American counterparts on 16 January they soon discovered that Dill had not exaggerated the problems. Marshall led off by stating that the US plan to defeat Germany was simple – all available help to Russia and a Round-Up attack across the Channel as soon as possible. What he could not fathom was how the British intended to defeat Germany with a peripheral strategy. Before Brooke could enlighten him, Marshall asked a detailed series of questions about the importance of operations in the Mediterranean and if they formed a part in any plan to win the war. What, he asked Brooke, was 'the main plot'?[13]

The gist of Brooke's reply was that the main plot did not involve a cross-Channel attack in 1943. The Germans had too many divisions in France (forty-four) to defeat the twenty or so divisions that the Allies might bring against them. Mediterranean operations would force the Germans to disperse their forces and, if Italy collapsed, replace Italian divisions in the Balkans with their own. In the meantime the Russian army would have worn down the German army, leaving the possibility of a full-scale Anglo-American invasion of France in 1944. A long discussion followed which ranged widely but not helpfully over many topics, including an invasion of Norway, operations in Burma to assist China and establishing a bridgehead in Brest or Cherbourg. At the end of the day no decisions were reached except that the Joint Planners were to report on the invasion of Sicily.[14]

The arguments sharpened at the following meeting. Brooke accused the Americans of retreating from the 'Germany first' strategy agreed in 1941. He stated bluntly that it was impossible to defeat Germany and Japan simultaneously and that if the Allies attempted it 'we shall lose the war'.[15] Marshall responded furiously. Doing nothing in the Pacific was impossible and, as for Brooke's strategy, 'he was most anxious not to become committed to interminable operations in the Mediterranean. He wished Northern France to be the scene of the main effort against Germany – that had always been his conception.' If there was no cross-Channel attack in 1943 troops could always be redeployed to the Pacific.[16]

The meeting became so heated that it was adjourned. There was no agreed strategy, nothing that could be put to the President and Prime Minister that mapped a way forward.

What happened next is the subject of some debate and mystification. During the adjournment a paper was produced by the British entitled 'Conduct of the War in 1943'. It specified some points that could easily be agreed: the defeat of the U-boats then running amok in the Atlantic, the maximum assistance possible to Russia and an all-out strategic bombing offensive against Germany. Then it went on to specify areas for offensive action:

(1) the occupation of Sicily with the object of opening the Mediterranean for shipping, divert German divisions from the Russian front, put pressure on Italy and entice Turkey into the war.

(2) 'limited' offensive operations across the Channel with the amphibious forces available

(3) the 'assembly' in Britain of the strongest possible forces in 'constant readiness' to re-enter the Continent as soon as German resistance is weakened to the required extent

(4) the allocation of such forces to the Pacific and the Far East to 'maintain pressure on Japan' and to reconquer Burma.[17]

Apparently the document was shown to Marshall by Dill during the break and when the meeting reassembled he immediately agreed that it should be placed before the President and Prime Minister as the stated policy of the Combined Chiefs of Staff.[18] Marshall had conceded much that he had just some hours before argued strenuously against. There now would be a major operation in the Mediterranean, and Marshall's grand 'conception' of a major cross-Channel attack was left without a definite implementation date.

Why did Marshall submit so readily? One matter Dill might have mentioned was that of landing craft, essential to any major seaborne attack. The British had investigated this matter and discovered a worldwide shortage.[19] This meant that at least some craft used in one theatre would have to be transported to another before a further operation could take place. In particular, craft in the Mediterranean that would be used for Husky would have to be shifted to Britain for any major cross-Channel attack. On further enquiry they found that this process would take three months. And although their investigation had taken place in January 1943, at Casablanca it was generally accepted by the CCS that Husky could not take place before Tunisian operations had ended and a period of training undertaken, which made the likely invasion date July. This in turn meant that landing craft in sufficient numbers would not be in place for major operations from Britain until October or even November – too late for a full-scale attack because of the weather. This argument might have persuaded Marshall. In any case there was something in the British document for the Americans. Against their better judgement the British had agreed to launch a Burma offensive, which Marshall deemed vital to open a route to China. Admiral King was also content that the rather large force in the Pacific would remain there to keep 'pressure' on the Japanese, a phrase that obviously did not preclude offensive operations.

This was the substance of the document that was placed before Roosevelt and Churchill, who both quickly agreed to it. The Prime Minister's consent was probably as much a relief to Brooke as that of Marshall. Churchill had certainly arrived at Casablanca with one eye on a cross-Channel attack in 1943, but constant contact with Brooke seems to have convinced him that the CIGS was right. He certainly grasped the point that gambling on a Round-Up operation late in the year might mean that no operation after Tunisia could be carried out at all in 1943. Anyway by 16 January 1943 he had been convinced and was saying to Brooke that he was confident of being able to convince the President of the merits of Husky.[20] This he was easily able to accomplish, largely because Roosevelt still adhered to the 'Germany first' policy and because the rather meagre American planning team that accompanied him to Casablanca could not produce a more attractive operation or indeed one that fell within the realms of possibility. The results are summed up neatly by Brigadier Jacob of the secretariat:

> The Prime Minister and the CIGS being at one on the merits of Sicily, their influence was naturally quite decisive. The task at Casablanca was therefore to sell Sicily to the US Chiefs of Staff. Actually it did not prove very hard [Brooke would have disagreed with this part]. They had no alternative to the Mediterranean as a theatre in which to engage the Germans on a large scale in 1943, and as the President was quite of the Prime Minister's way of thinking, it was not long before everyone accepted Sicily as the thing to do.[21]

In the European theatre, at least for the moment, the British had won the strategic debate despite being the weaker partner. This has often been framed as the cunning British, with hundreds of years of subtle diplomatic skills behind them, outwitting the straightforward but rather simple-minded Americans. Or alternatively the British were playing a long game in the Mediterranean with the aim of dominating the Mediterranean politically to the extent of weaving some former Italian or even French territory into their empire. These arguments are nonsense. What Churchill and Brooke were putting forward was not grounded in some kind of Liddell Hartian military theory of an indirect rather than a direct approach to defeating Germany. What they were doing was merely suggesting an operation that had a decent chance of success. This was no more than realism. Britain's record in fighting the German army had certainly turned a corner in 1943, but only just. Its record in amphibious operations in recent times (apart from evacuations) was hardly glorious, as one of the originators of the Gallipoli adventure was in a good position to know. Yet, whatever operation was in prospect, it involved an opposed landing on a hostile shore defended by Germans. This was no minor matter. The German army was difficult to defeat, as the Americans were soon to find at Kasserine. Some on the American side (such as Walter Bedell Smith, Eisenhower's confidant) recognised this. They had not been out-thought at Casablanca so much as faced with practicalities that they found impossible to overcome. Marshall was no simpleton but his one strategic idea amounted to thinking that production could surmount all problems. (His suggestion that Denmark be invaded as a flanking operation to a cross-Channel attack was greeted with silence by not only the British but by members of his own delegation.)[22] As for British ambitions in a post-war Mediterranean, they were the fevered invention of some anti-British planners in Washington.[23] Britain was already in hock to the United States; its lynch-pin of empire (India) had already been promised Dominion status (effectively independence) after the war; its finances would hardly stretch to holding down yet more territory when the war was won. Not even Churchill thought that way. The strategy decided upon at Casablanca was practical but hardly imperial.

Much had been decided at Casablanca but much had not. Most importantly, the precise date of the Husky operation had been left hanging. This matter immediately sparked an acrimonious debate within Allied ranks. When the British Joint Planners mentioned a possible date for Husky as September, Churchill at once remarked that this would be quite unacceptable, he would like to see the operation 'launched in May'.[24] In the event May would prove impossible as operations in Tunisia continued for a month longer than anyone at Casablanca anticipated. Indeed, after the conference, the CCS issued a directive to General Eisenhower that he would command Husky, Alexander would be his deputy, Air Marshal Arthur Tedder the air C-in-C and Cunningham the naval C-in-C, and they were to aim for a date in June with a more realistic prospect of launching the invasion in July.[25] Eisenhower replied that after thorough investigation a June date could not be met and that in any case lack of time for training and other preparations meant that 'a June assault is unlikely to succeed'.[26] Churchill was appalled. He told Ismay:

> I am most shocked by Eisenhower's [message]. I am telegraphing to the President ... It is absolutely necessary to do this operation in June. We shall become a laughing stock if, during the spring and early summer, no British and American soldiers are firing at any German or Italian soldiers.[27]

He instructed Ismay to have the COS look into the entire matter. And to ensure that the President got the point, Churchill wrote to Hopkins:

> Please see Eisenhower's [message]. I was much upset about this ... I think it is an awful thing that in April, May and June, not a single American and British soldier will be killing a single German or Italian soldier while the Russians are chasing 185 divisions around ... I wish you would put this point to our friend.[28]

Eisenhower tried to appease Churchill by stating that he recognised the necessity of launching Husky at the earliest possible date but that the experience of the Torch landings meant that additional amphibious training was essential if Husky was to succeed. Moreover the CCS agreed with him.[29]

Churchill was not of a mind to care who agreed with Ike. He told the COS:

> In view of the delaying attitude adopted by General Eisenhower certain Americans towards 'Husky', I wish a small Joint Planners Sub-Committee

and the ... Combined Operations department to work out a study of doing it all alone by ourselves in June, and taking nothing from the United States except landing craft, escorts, &c.

There would be great advantages in having it all done by British troops, with the Americans giving us a hand at the landings, with the air force, &c. The Americans could then come in to the ports we had taken and go into action without having to go through the training for assault landings. Anyhow, see how this would work out.[30]

In fact it did not work out. The CCS, perhaps under pressure from Roosevelt, had now instructed Eisenhower to plan for a June attack. This saw the end of an all-British Husky.[31] The incident is instructive, however, in indicating how determined Churchill was to minimise the gap between Allied operations and highlighting the low opinion he had of the abilities of US troops at this time of the war, an attitude that was shared by Brooke.[32]

Eisenhower also now raised an issue in Churchill's mind about the competence of American commanders. In a note to the CCS and the COS in April Eisenhower told them that Husky had a 'scant promise of success' if faced with 'substantial, well-armed and fully organised German ground troops' which he proceeded to define as more than two divisions.[33] A further storm ensued. Churchill immediately commented to the COS:

This statement contrasts oddly with the confidence which General Eisenhower showed about invading the Continent across the Channel, where he would have to meet a great many more than two German divisions. If the presence of two German divisions is held to be decisive against any operation of an offensive or amphibious character open to the million men now in French North Africa, it is difficult to see how the war can be carried on ... I trust the Chiefs of Staff will not accept these pusillanimous and defeatist doctrines from whomever they come. I propose to telegraph, shortly to the President, because the adoption of such an attitude by our Commanders would make us the laughing stock of the world ... I regard this matter as serious in the last degree. We have told the Russians that they cannot have their supplies by the Northern Convoy for the sake of 'Husky', and now 'Husky' is to be abandoned if there are 2 German divisions – (strength unspecified) in the neighbourhood. What Stalin would think of this, when he has 185 German divisions on his front, I cannot imagine.[34]

The COS agreed with Churchill. They told the CCS:

We are resolutely opposed to the view that if the garrison of Husky contains more than two German Divisions of unspecified strength the Operation has little prospect of success. In effect such a view implies that we cannot take on the Germans in a combined operation unless we can attack in overwhelming superiority at all points.[35]

These missives soon concentrated Eisenhower's mind. He assured the COS and Churchill that Husky 'will be prosecuted with all the means at our disposal ... there is no thought here except to carry out our orders to the ultimate limit [of] our ability'.[36] Husky would therefore proceed despite the presence of Germans. It would, however, not go ahead in June. Despite the urgings of the Prime Minister, the delay in bringing operations in Tunisia to an end and the important matter of training raw troops for an opposed landing meant that in the end the earliest possible date was 10 July 1943.[37]

The other matter left unresolved at Casablanca was the nature and date of operations that might follow Husky. These issues had been left desperately vague in the compromise document that was the final report of the CCS to the President and Prime Minister. Regarding post-Husky operations in the Mediterranean the report said nothing at all. In the case of cross-Channel attack, if German morale suffered a severe decline, an operation to secure the Cherbourg Peninsula would be prepared with a target date of 1 August. In the meantime, a staff would be formed to plan for a return to the continent 'to take advantage of a German disintegration'. In the latter case no date could be specified and any attack above the level of a raid hinged on German collapse, of which there was on the horizon no sign.[38]

These were compromises destined not to last. The first rift came in February. Late in the month Marshall informed the senior American general in London (General Andrews) that, 'owing to the urgency of the situation in another theatre', no shipping would be available to lift troops to

Britain during March or April.[39] The 'other theatre' was of course the Pacific. What had happened was that the US planners, and Marshall himself, remained opposed to the Sicily adventure which, in their view, would leave any build-up of troops in Britain bereft of operational employment and therefore 'dormant'. To avoid this possibility he wanted these troops redirected to the Pacific. To the British, however, this broke the agreement to deal with Germany first and threatened entirely to reorient Allied strategy. And as they were uncertain about Marshall's motives they asked Dill to make some enquiries. Dill informed them that the matter revolved around shipping (possibly for General Douglas MacArthur's advance on Rabaul from Guadalcanal) and that he could see no way that the Americans could meet their Casablanca obligations to build up troops in Britain (Bolero).[40] This led to a general discussion of shipping on the British side. After several inter-Allied meetings the COS came to two conclusions: with a reduced Bolero there was no chance that anything more substantial than a large raid could be mounted from Britain in 1943 and that their own shipping shortage made any large-scale operation in Burma, as laid down at Casablanca, impossible.[41]

Most of the Casablanca accords (Bolero, the Burmese operation and some kind of cross-Channel attack) had now collapsed. Whether this was because of bloody-mindedness on Marshall's side followed by retaliation on the British side or whether shipping was as dire as all sides suddenly discovered is hard to untangle. Whatever the reason, the Allied situation was totally unsatisfactory. They now had no major plan for Burma and, more importantly, no major plan for Europe. Most crucially, after Husky all that was in prospect was the possibility of a cross-Channel raid. Between Husky and a return to Europe, which the British COS thought could not take place before spring 1944, lay inaction.

This was of course quite unacceptable to Churchill. He might have been a late convert to Brooke's Mediterranean policy but now, with the downgrading of the cross-Channel attack and the disappearance of anything large in the east, he could see no alternative to Mediterranean operations. The invasion of Italy, he declared, was the operation to consider. If the Germans left the Italians to their fate, there was 'no limit to the amount of Italian territory we may overrun. We might meet the Germans at the Brenner on the Austrian border or in the Riviera. If, on the other hand, an invasion of Italy was beyond our power opportunities might open in the Dodecanese, along the Dalmatian coast or even Turkey.' Regardless, something, he instructed the Chiefs, must be done.[42]

The COS agreed and asked the Joint Planners to consider whether an invasion of Italy was possible after a successful Husky. The planners thought it was because the Germans had a limited number of divisions which they could withdraw from other fronts to prop up their ally or occupy the country in the event of an Italian collapse.[43] The problem here was that no such plan had been agreed with the Americans – indeed they had given every indication at Casablanca that they would oppose such an operation. It was time for some personal diplomacy. Churchill wrote to Roosevelt, proposing a meeting in May.[44]

As usual before inter-Allied conferences, the British COS met to agree a position to put to the Prime Minister. Their opinions were divided, though all saw the Mediterranean as the theatre in which to operate after Husky. Brooke favoured an invasion of mainland Italy as recommended by the Joint Planners, though he thought an attack against Sardinia and the Dodecanese should also be studied. Portal, however, wanted Sardinia attacked after Husky to further free the Mediterranean for shipping, which would in turn facilitate any operations in Burma. It would also provide bomber bases from which north Italy could be attacked. On the other hand, Pound wanted to invade southern Greece to draw German forces away from the Russian front and to allow bases to be established to bomb the Romanian oilfields at Ploesti.[45] In the end the Chiefs decided to instruct the planners to prepare papers on operations in Italy, Sardinia, Greece and the Dodecanese. But, as Brooke had spoken quite bluntly against Sardinia and Greece, and as the Dodecanese was a quite minor matter, the invasion of mainland Italy was clear favourite.

The British party, accompanied by 5,000 German prisoners of war destined for internment in America, left Glasgow on the *Queen Mary* on 6 May. The most important meeting between Churchill and the COS took place on board ship on the 10th. Not surprisingly, Brooke announced that the COS considered that Italy should be invaded after the completion of Husky. In answer to Churchill, he thought Sardinia should be the alternative if the mainland proved impossible. Churchill, who had no doubt spoken to Pound, thought an operation in Greece should be investigated but agreed that the elimination of Italy from the war should be the first charge on the Allies and that this position should be put to the Americans.[46]

The first 'Trident' meeting took place two days later at the White House with the President, Prime Minister and the CCS in attendance. The President invited Churchill to open proceedings, which he did at some length. He stated that:

> The first objective was in the Mediterranean. The great prize there was to get Italy out of the war by whatever means might be the best. He recalled how in 1918, when Germany might have retreated to the Meuse or the Rhine and continued the fight, the defection of Bulgaria brought the whole of the enemy structure crashing to the ground. The collapse of Italy would cause a chill of loneliness over the German people, and might be the beginning of their doom.[47]

He went on to say that invading Italy would take pressure off Russia and that it was impossible to remain inactive between the end of Husky (which he forecast quite accurately to be towards the end of August) and a cross-Channel attack. As for that operation:

> He could not pretend that the problem of landing on the Channel coast had been solved. The difficult beaches, with the great rise and fall of the tide, the strength of the enemy defences, the number of his reserves and the ease of his communications, all made the task one which must not be underrated ... He desired to make it clear that His Majesty's Government earnestly desire to undertake a full-scale invasion of the Continent from the United Kingdom as soon as possible. They certainly did not disdain the idea, if a plan offering reasonable prospects of success could be made.[48]

The President replied as though Churchill had not spoken. He asked 'where do we go from Husky', as if this question had not been the entire point of Churchill's long harangue. He continued:

> He had always shrunk from putting large armies in Italy. This might result in attrition for the United Nations and play into Germany's hand.

He indicated that a thorough investigation should be made of what an occupation of Italy proper, or of the 'heel' or 'toe' of Italy would mean as a drain on Allied resources.[49]

He concluded by saying that any surplus of men should be put into the build-up of forces in Britain for Round-Up and that a date for this operation 'should be decided on definitely as an operation for the Spring of 1944'.[50]

The President had been much more amenable to British strategy at Casablanca than he demonstrated here. Probably Churchill's long disquisition had raised several doubts in Roosevelt's mind. The first was obviously that Britain's one strategic option in 1943 was an invasion of Italy. The other was despite Churchill's rather pompous declaration about the policy of the government being the invasion of France, it was hemmed and hawed about with many qualifications and concluded rather lamely that such an operation was not 'disdained' by the British, which hardly sounded like a ringing endorsement. There was no further discussion that day – Roosevelt and Churchill had spoken for so long that the meeting was adjourned.

The next day the service Chiefs had their say. Brooke suggested that Allied strategy must be looked at as a whole, and that involved 'knocking Italy out of the war'. Marshall countered that on the contrary it 'involved knocking Germany out of the war'. The old arguments were then rehearsed by each side: Brooke stating that the Allies had too few divisions to establish anything but a bridgehead in Europe in 1943 and that the best way to assist Russia was by extending Germany's front and obligations by invading Italy; Marshall replying that Italy would prove a vacuum into which Allied resources would be endlessly sucked, that an Italian campaign would prolong the war and that the American people would not tolerate it. Admiral William Leahy, Roosevelt's naval adviser, weighed in on Marshall's side and Portal on Brooke's. No ground was gained or conceded by either party. The meeting morphed into a discussion on whether the Azores Islands should be seized from Portugal or whether they might be given up voluntarily. There was no agreement on that either.[51] Brooke left, 'thoroughly depressed'. Not even a tour of the new War Department building (the Pentagon) cheered him up.[52]

And so the meetings continued. Papers were written on global strategy which seemed to have sharpened the differences between the two sides.

Brooke tried to maintain calm by saying that he was 'not in entire agreement' with a US paper when in fact he hardly agreed with one word of it.[53] The introduction of Burma into the debate only made matters worse. The British were clearly reluctant to devote resources to what they considered a marginal operation while the Americans thought a major effort was essential there to keep China in the war.[54] The major sticking point was, however, the feasibility of Round-Up. From the British perspective the Allies would not have sufficient strength to carry out a major attack until the spring of 1944, by which time the German army would have been worn down by the Russians and by operations in Italy to the extent needed for a successful invasion. The Americans took this to mean that the British were reluctant to conduct Round-Up at all, would fritter away Allied reserves and when spring 1944 arrived would announce that yet again the time was not yet ripe.[55]

The American position had a weakness, the same weakness in fact that had surrounded the arguments over Gymnast. Then the problem had been that if Gymnast was not carried out there would be no operation involving US troops against Germany in 1942. Now the argument was that if Italy was not invaded there would be no US operations against Germany after Husky in 1943. If this occurred, more American resources would be directed towards the Pacific, making a bigger nonsense of the 'Germany first' policy than was already the case, the US having far more troops in the first half of 1943 engaged against Japan than against Germany.[56] The problem with this was that it might have been congenial to Admiral King and the American planners but it was directly contrary to the policy of the President.

By 19 May – after an entire week of meetings – there was no agreement. Then Marshall, probably prompted by Dill, suggested that the meeting be cleared of all advisers and the six principals meet alone. They assembled in the Federal Reserve Building in Washington at 4.30 p.m. The log jam broke. The Americans had wished to pin the British down to the specifics of a cross-Channel attack. This they did. The British agreed that the operation would be mounted in the spring of 1944 by five divisions, with two airborne and two follow-up divisions, with a further twenty divisions available to reinforce. In turn the Americans agreed that Eisenhower 'should be instructed to mount such operations in exploitation of "Husky" as are best calculated to eliminate Italy from the war and contain the maximum number of German forces'. To ensure that the Mediterranean did not become a bottomless pit, seven divisions (four US and three British) were to be withdrawn from Italy for Round-Up at the appropriate time. To round off affairs the British agreed to mount some kind of attack from Burma towards the end of 1943.[57]

Did these decisions, readily agreed to by the President and Prime Minister, amount to a final meeting of minds? Not really. At the last meeting Marshall indicated that, should Russia collapse or make peace with Germany, he would want the entire suite of policies agreed at Trident reviewed with a view 'to undertak[ing] the defeat of Japan prior to that of Germany'. Brooke agreed that all decisions should be reviewed 'since it was vital to exploit any opportunities which arose. The position in Southern Europe might well be such that we could take advantage of it'.[58]

What the two men were actually saying amounted to this. Marshall was stating that if Britain's Mediterranean policy delayed a proper second front and caused Russia to collapse, the US would turn to a policy to defeat Japan first. Brooke, on the other hand, was stating that Britain's Mediterranean policy would open up opportunities that might see an even greater emphasis put on that theatre in months and years to come. The two sides had compromised but in reality were as far apart as ever.

* * * * *

While the Allies were papering over their strategic differences, planning for Husky was proceeding. The initial operation was sketched out by the Joint Planners at Casablanca. It had many weaknesses. The landings were to take place at no fewer than ten points from just south of Catania on the east coast of Sicily clockwise around to Pachino, Gela and Sciacca in the south, to Palermo and points west in the north. All landings were to be made in small numbers and none were mutually supporting. Each landing was an invitation to defeat in detail.[59] This plan did not long survive the scrutiny of Montgomery. He told Alexander that it had been the result of 'some pretty woolly thinking' on the part of the planners and that he had 'no intention of doing some of the things they suggest'.[60] A few days later he was even more forthright. Alexander was now told that the plan would 'land the Allied Nations in a first class military disaster' and that while he (Montgomery) would be prepared to

participate in the attack he would do so in his own way.[61] However peremptory Montgomery's language, there is no doubt that the plan laid before him
did invite disaster. He soon recast it into a more consolidated punch with
just three landing places grouped around the south-east corner of the island,
near where key airfields needed for immediate fighter support were located.[62]
The Eighth Army (Montgomery indignantly rejected his organisation being
renamed the Eastern Task Force) would land with four divisions on the right
and the US Seventh Army (actually it was II Corps rebadged to match the
British) with three divisions on the left.

One aspect of Husky planning was rather vague. Much thought had been
given to getting ashore and the capture of nearby ports and airfields. But the
plans tended to stop there. What was to be the pattern of advance from these
positions? Would the island be dissected by a drive through to the north
coast and, by which army – the British or the American? Would there be an
attempt to seal the Strait of Messina and force a mass capitulation as had
occurred in Tunisia? None of these questions was answered in the outline
plan, probably because the immediate commanders (Montgomery and
Patton) were still involved in active operations in Tunisia during the planning period. Nor did the overall ground commander (Alexander) seek to
clarify any of these questions. This lack of detail in the plan would have
serious consequences.

What was unusual about the development of the plan was that Churchill
was never at any stage involved. This is worth a pause. For Torch (and all
previous operations) Churchill had been intimately involved in operational
planning, down to such detail as suggesting the number of troops that
should land at each beach. Part of the explanation is that for most of the
planning period Churchill had pneumonia which laid him low and from
which he was slow to recover.[63] Moreover, in Alexander and Montgomery,
Churchill had commanders he could trust to come up with a decent plan.
They had presided over one victory after another since Alamein. Perhaps
the major reason for Churchill's non-intervention in the Husky plan was
that the process was becoming far more complex than in earlier years. Now
enormous air fleets and navies were to be coordinated and troops in the
million organised. While all went well Churchill was willing to step back
and leave the war to the military. As we will see, however, this was not
always to remain his stance.

Sicily was invaded by seven Allied divisions, an airborne division and some air landing units on the night of 9/10 July 1943. Five weeks later (17 August) the island was in Allied hands. Until near the end of the campaign, Churchill made no comments on the progress of the battle, though he was given regular updates by Alexander. This followed a trend set in Tunisia, where almost his only interventions regarded the unsatisfactory speed of the advance. Yet the campaign was not without its controversies and setbacks, which in the past would have provided Churchill with plenty of scope to intervene. There are a number of explanations which can be put forward to explain his rather hands-off approach.

The first is the somewhat Panglossian summaries of the campaign sent to him by Alexander. For example, in detailing the landings Alexander described the Eighth Army efforts thus: 'All initial landings effected according to plan. Little opposition met so far.'[64] In fact the landings were more or less a shambles, saved from defeat in detail by a scattered and in some parts reluctant defence. This is what the commander of 50 Division, which landed near Avola on the south-east coast of Sicily, had to say about the operation:

A study . . . shows beyond any doubt, that so far from the assaulting troops landing as a concentrated wave at a given time and place as planned, they landed in scattered groups at places miles apart and the majority one and a half hours late. To make matters worse Co[mpan]ys and Pl[atoon]s of Btns [Battalions] were landed not as composite groups but almost inextricably intermingled, with in some cases, their com[man]ders landed at an entirely different place. Some assaulting troops were even landed outside the Div area altogether whilst the reserve Btn [was landed in 5 Division area]. . . . It is apparent . . . that skippers of LCTs [landing craft tanks] had not been properly briefed, had not had clear orders and had no knowledge what to do in the event of enemy shellfire, which in any landing operation is inevitable. To make no attempt to land at the proper beach because some shells were falling and to go instead to one that is equally likely to be shelled, but known by the army to be quite unsuitable is to invite failure . . . In our case, the hours spent poring over air photographs to select places for assault were a pure waste of time.[65]

This document has been quoted at length for two reasons: first to ask what Churchill might have made of it had he read it, especially in the light of Alexander's message; and second to make the point that the confusion described reinforces the view of Churchill and especially Brooke that if this scene had been replicated off the shores of northern Europe, with stronger defences and a more resolute defence, the result might well have been a stern rebuff. The Allies obviously had much to learn and it was as well that they did not attempt to learn in 1943 by attacking crack German divisions.

In the case of the British air landings, Churchill asked the air commander, Tedder, to estimate the losses incurred.[66] He was told that the losses were 'very much less than anticipated'.[67] This hardly sums up the disaster that was suffered by air landing force. Their object was to capture a crucial bridge to the north of the British landing area. In fact: 'Sixty-nine gliders landed in the sea and many men drowned. Fifty-nine gliders landed strewn across twenty-five miles of country . . . Twelve gliders landed in the correct zone . . . Two gliders were shot down. Ten had turned back to base before release.'[68] The bridge was not taken. As one American historian has remarked: 'If the courage of those flying to Sicily that night is unquestionable, the same cannot be said for the judgement of their superiors in concocting and approving such a witless plan.'[69]

It is clear that none of this was conveyed accurately to Churchill at the time.[70] Had it been, his reaction can only be imagined. The air operations, which were replicated in the US sector with variations on the theme (of disaster), also indicated that their time for Normandy was not yet.

Churchill did not intervene in the minutiae of several disputes with which the Battle for Sicily was afflicted: the handing over of a crucial road by Alexander to Montgomery, thus stalling a developing US advance and extending Eighth Army's troops too thinly across eastern Sicily; the useless advance by Patton into the western tip of the island when enemy troops had already withdrawn and the over-confidence which led Montgomery to split the Eighth Army into four columns, ensuring in the short run that none had the strength to make progress. They were no doubt even too detailed for his critical eye and would have also involved him in an Anglo-American dispute at a relatively minor level. The one area where Churchill was disturbed enough to make an enquiry was the escape of the bulk of

German and Italian forces on Sicily across the Strait of Messina. He told Cunningham:

> I am naturally distressed to read in the newspapers about the large numbers of Germans said to be escaping across the Messina Straits. I should be obliged if you would let me know the kind of measures you are taking to limit this misfortune. Obviously the difficulties are very great but the prize is also of the greatest importance.[71]

Cunningham replied that the reports were 'equally distressing' to him but that it was impossible to keep his ships close in because of the strength of the coastal artillery and searchlights. He emphasised that the journey across the straits was short, that he would willingly risk cruisers and destroyers for some gain but that he was not prepared to incur casualties without achieving anything. In a swipe at the air force, he noted that during daylight hours he gave the air a free run at the defences but that regular crossings were still occurring.[72]

On other occasions such a reply from an operational commander would have attracted some kind of rebuke or at least a follow-up telegram ordering him to block the straits at all costs. No such message followed here. Yet Churchill was right to have expressed concern. From 1 to 17 August the Germans had evacuated 54,000 troops, 51 tanks, 163 guns and almost 10,000 vehicles to the mainland, and the Italians had withdrawn over 60,000 troops, 41 guns and 230 vehicles.[73] The fact was that the Allies had fair warning that an evacuation had been planned and was underway. As early as 1 August Enigma disclosed that ferrying in the Strait of Messina was being carried out for practice and experimental purposes.[74] From then until the end of the operation decrypts flooded in, indicating exactly what the Germans were up to.[75] Nor were the more immediate formations unaware of what was happening. On 7 August Eighth Army Intelligence revealed that 'enemy landing barges and ferries were active on the north end of the Messina Straits. They are departing loaded from the island.'[76] Montgomery had certainly got the message by then. On the same date he fumed in his diary:

> There has been heavy traffic all day across the Straits of Messina, and the enemy is without doubt trying to get his stuff away. I have tried hard

to find out what the Navy-Air plan is in order to stop him getting away; I have been unable to find out. I fear the truth of the matter is there is NO plan.[77]

Montgomery was right: there was no plan. For this the four senior commanders, Eisenhower, Alexander, Tedder and Cunningham must share responsibility. Admittedly, the task of preventing the evacuation was difficult. On either side of the straits the Axis had placed 123 heavy and 112 light anti-aircraft guns, 150 mobile 3″ or 4″ guns and ten batteries of heavier fixed guns.[78] Yet considering Allied air and naval superiority, the effort at attempting to block the straits seems feeble. In the air, what effort there was fell to the Tactical Air Force with medium bombers well within range of all enemy anti-air ordnance and with insignificant bomb loads. What was missing was any real effort on the part of the 180 US strategic bombers. Although they could fly above the range of the light anti-aircraft guns, they flew just 142 sorties inside the straits and on most of those concentrated on hitting towns and roads. No raid by these aircraft sank any enemy shipping.[79]

As for the naval effort, it hardly existed. Destroyers rarely ventured near the straits and the heavy ships, including heavy cruisers and battleships, were nowhere to be seen.[80] Perhaps as Carlo D'Este speculated, Cunningham, who had been on a destroyer at the Dardanelles, recoiled from risking ships in waters covered by guns and searchlights.[81] Perhaps this is why Churchill, who also had cause to remember the Dardanelles, failed to follow up his enquiry to Cunningham about the evacuation. Whatever the reason, the high command failed in this aspect of the Husky campaign. There seemed to be a distance, both physically and psychologically, between the four of them and this operation. Tedder and Cunningham certainly disapproved of Montgomery's (essential) changes to the plan and their attitude towards Husky thereafter seemed half-hearted at best. Alexander was slow to react to intelligence concerning the evacuation and supine in directing that anything be done about it. Eisenhower was too remote from the action and too tied up with the Italian armistice negotiations to be a factor. Yet it was Eisenhower who allowed military, naval and air headquarters to be so remote from each other. As Montgomery noticed: 'Cunningham is in Malta; Tedder is at Tunis; Alexander is at Syracuse. It beats me how anyone thinks you can run a campaign in that way.'[82]

What no one had planned (including Montgomery) was any operation to land a blocking force on the toe of Italy in order to make evacuation impossible. By the end of July it was probably too late for such a venture, given the state of repair of the landing craft. But, had such an operation been planned for from the start, it might have been possible. The only person who came close to such a suggestion was Churchill when he told Eisenhower and the COS that his wish was that 'we should be able to go from "Husky" directly into Italy'.[83] The Americans were, however, at that time still leery of any adventures into Italy.

In the end Churchill allowed that the Sicilian campaign was successful and was over in the relatively short time of five weeks. That the Allies should have emerged victorious with 450,000 troops against just 70,000 German troops and a somewhat larger number of reluctant Italian troops, whose willingness to fight after Mussolini was overthrown on 26 July was minimal, was hardly surprising. But for Churchill, who had presided over a fair string of defeats, it was still a success to savour. In that sense Sicily was not a bitter victory at all. To the victor went what spoils there were.

* * * * *

The period January to July 1943 saw a marked change in Churchill's strategic outlook. He had started the period convinced that a cross-Channel attack must be undertaken that year, but he had been convinced by Brooke at Casablanca that such an operation was not in prospect and that the invasion of Italy was the best substitute. Again this was a matter of grasping practicalities not the adherence to some theory of peripheral warfare. Brooke's arguments centred on the lack of sufficient divisions in Britain in 1943 to carry through a successful invasion. Brooke also had grave doubts about whether the Allied armies or commanders were ready for a large seaborne landing against German opposition. Operations in Sicily indicated that he was almost certainly correct. This meant that the invasion of Italy became an operational necessity. The geographical proximity of Italy to Sicily and the logistical difficulty of moving armies rapidly to another area may well have forced such a conclusion on the Allied leadership in any case. To this point it seems that the British had had the best of the strategic argument in as much as what they were arguing for was practical and without huge risk. It remained to be seen whether the invasion of Italy would bear them out. But it is worth remembering that the alternative – D-Day 1943 – would have been fraught with danger.

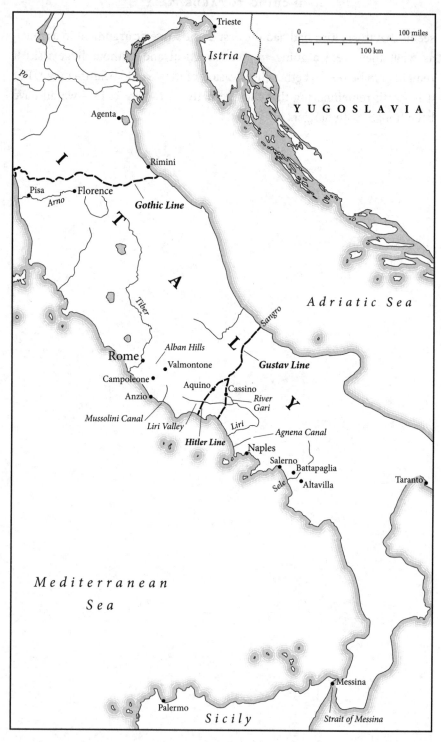

Map 11. Italy.

CHAPTER 22

PIVOT OF POWER –
THE MEDITERRANEAN 1943

THE COMPROMISES AT THE Trident summit in May 1943 hardly sat well with the main players on either side. With Churchill they sat very badly indeed. In particular he disapproved of the vague instructions given to Eisenhower that he 'develop' operations to eliminate Italy from the war. What he desired was to know what specific operations would be developed and to be reassured that they would be substantial. So he proposed to Roosevelt that he and Brooke proceed straight from Trident to Eisenhower's headquarters at Algiers for direct discussions with the Supreme Commander. And lest that appear too blatant for the Americans, he suggested that he be accompanied by General Marshall.[1]

On 29 May the parties met in Algiers and talks began on post-Husky operations. The conference opened on an unusual note, Eisenhower arguing that the seven divisions earmarked to move to Britain for Round-Up (or Overlord, as it was now called) should stay in the Mediterranean and assist in finishing off Italy, Churchill insisting that they must go and that Overlord must have primacy.[2] The old arguments soon asserted themselves, however. Marshall did not want to commit to any operations against Italy until the progress made in Husky was assessed. Churchill, however, soon reverted to his previous position and demanded that some definite decision be made on the invasion of Italy. Eventually Eisenhower produced a compromise where plans would be produced for all eventualities (rapid collapse in Sicily, collapse in Sicily by 15 August, prolonged fighting in Sicily), with operations against Sardinia, in the toe of Italy and in an area around Naples as possibilities.[3]

This hardly satisfied Churchill or, it may be supposed, Brooke.[4] At the next meeting, after a long discussion in which Marshall made it clear that Eisenhower would have no more divisions to prosecute operations against Italy than had been agreed at Trident, Churchill made this impassioned plea:

> The Prime Minister said it would be hard for him to ask the British people to cut their rations again but he would gladly do so rather than throw away a campaign which had possibilities of great success. He could not endure to see a great army stand idle when they might be engaged in eliminating Italy from the war. Parliament and the people would become impatient if the army was not active, and he was willing to take almost desperate steps in order to prevent such a calamity.[5]

He announced that he was prepared to replace the seven divisions to be sent to Britain for Overlord with eight other divisions scraped from around the Mediterranean.[6]

This was certainly putting the issue squarely. Marshall had invoked the American people in arguing for Overlord; Churchill had now invoked the British people (and Parliament) for an Italian campaign. The probability is that no one at these discussions needed convincing that some form of operation against Italy had to follow Husky. The difference lay with Marshall trying to limit the scope of such operations and Churchill and Brooke trying to ensure that they were the largest possible. No one on the British side was arguing against Overlord, only that maximum use should be made of the troops in the Mediterranean in the interval. In the end the discussions ended where they had begun. The decision on what post-Husky operations should be conducted was left to Eisenhower. There was general agreement that he should not so decide until after the progress of Husky was assessed.[7]

Churchill and Brooke then flew off to Turkey in yet another futile attempt to coax that country into the war. War supplies were promised on behalf of the Allies but the Turks were, as usual, not forthcoming. In the meantime Sicily had been invaded by the Allies. After three days Churchill declared the opposition 'less obstinate than expected' and urged a landing as high up the Italian Peninsula as fighter cover would allow. Two or three good divisions, he declared, could seize Naples and he urged the COS to look into the whole matter.[8]

Brooke was only too anxious to agree but wanted a stronger operation. He had heard from the CCS that Eisenhower intended to land three divisions south of Salerno (the maximum distance that could be covered by fighters based in Sicily). He thought this too meagre and wanted the landing boosted to five divisions and the build-up of additional forces speeded up. In the meantime he ordered that British landing craft slated to return to Britain after Husky remain in place.[9] This move immediately raised American hackles – were the British playing their old games and attempting to convert the Mediterranean into the major theatre? In any event the US response was to refuse to commit more troops to the theatre. Eisenhower might invade Italy but he would invade it with what he had. Here was another impasse. And, as was becoming customary, that implied another summit – Churchill and Roosevelt would meet in Quebec in August in what came to be known as the Quadrant summit.

They met in dramatic circumstances. On 25 July Mussolini was overthrown and arrested. The King (Victor Emmanuel III) appointed an interim government under General Pietro Badoglio. What this meant for future relations between Italy and German and Italy and the Allies was unclear. Would the prospective invasion be a walkover? Would the Germans defend the Italian Peninsula and if so where would they choose to stand? What all now agreed on was that the Italian mainland should be invaded. Any thoughts of operations in Sardinia or elsewhere in the Mediterranean were scrapped.

Yet, if all agreed on the invasion of Italy, on the scope and purpose of that operation there was no agreement. Indeed, there was deep division and suspicion. On the British side, Brooke and Portal noted that the invasion of Italy needed to be undertaken by forces strong enough to enable an advance to be made into the northern Italian plain. This would accomplish two things – it would mean that airfields could be occupied from which they could attack German aircraft factories that were too remote to be consistently bombed from bases in Britain, as could the Romanian oilfields at Ploesti. Secondly, such an advance would provoke the Germans to remove divisions from Russia or France or both in order to stem the tide. The Italian operations would therefore assist Overlord by reducing German fighter strength and by reducing the number of German reserves able to be directed against Overlord. Moreover, Brooke added, the forces in Italy must remain in sufficient strength to drive the Germans back and this might mean retaining some of the seven divisions earmarked for Overlord. A decision on that could be made later when the extent of German opposition was assessed.[10]

The American position as stated by Marshall and King was at odds with this. Overlord was the main operation. They agreed that as much of Italy should be seized as possible, but it should be seized by what was at hand in the Mediterranean at the time. No more units should be added to Eisenhower's army and the seven divisions mentioned by Brooke should be despatched to Britain at once. Any delay might fatally weaken Overlord and if there were any additional American divisions available they would be sent to the Pacific, not deployed in Italy.[11] There was no agreement here and not much of a basis for further discussion.

From there the talks deteriorated. The slanging matches are only hinted at in the minutes but Brooke's diary gives the flavour of those 'poisonous days'. On 16 August the secretaries and planners were sent away, as they had been at Trident. Brooke continues:

> I opened by telling them [the Americans] that the root of the matter was that we were not trusting each other. They doubted our real intention to put our full hearts into the cross Channel operation next spring and we had not full confidence that they would not in future insist on our carrying out previous arrangements irrespective of changed strategic conditions. I then had to go over our entire Mediterranean strategy to prove its objects which they have never fully realized, and finally I had to produce countless arguments to prove the close relation that exists between cross Channel and Italian operations. In the end I think our arguments did have some effect on Marshall. Unfortunately Marshall has no strategic outlook of any kind.[12]

At this point in previous conferences Churchill and Roosevelt often stepped in with some kind of compromise. That did not happen at Quadrant. While the conference was in progress, Badoglio approached the Allies seeking terms. This raised difficulties regarding Roosevelt's announced policy of unconditional surrender. The political leaders therefore spent most of their time hammering out just what should be offered. Military operations receded into the background.

In the absence of overall guidance, the Chiefs of Staff realised that they must compromise or they would have nothing to show to their political masters. On Overlord versus the Mediterranean the CCS Final Report to the President and Prime Minister said:

[Overlord] will be the primary United States–British ground and air effort against the Axis in Europe. (Target date the 1st May, 1944.) . . . As between 'Overlord' and operations in the Mediterranean, where there is a shortage of resources, available resources will be distributed and employed with the main object of ensuring the success of 'Overlord'. Operations in the Mediterranean Theater will be carried out with the forces allotted at 'Trident', except in so far as these may be varied by decisions of the Combined Chiefs of Staff.[13]

Here was a statement which, in the fullness of time, everyone could find something with which to disagree.

It was the best Brooke could do, however. But when it was presented to Churchill and Roosevelt he found that the Prime Minister had some reservations. Churchill noted that a date had been set for Overlord but added that unless German air and ground strength had been sufficiently worn down, the operation should be reviewed by the CCS and if these criteria were not met, an operation to invade Norway should be prepared in its stead. This Churchillian ruse (Jupiter) had plagued the British COS for some time. It is clear from their discussions that they had no intention of ever carrying it out, while retaining the idea as a useful threat. In that spirit – but no other – a paragraph was added to their report indicating it would be considered if Overlord was for any reason abandoned. Churchill also asked that the movement from the Mediterranean of the seven divisions earmarked for Overlord be subject to review if the circumstances warranted. Brooke of course agreed with him on that point and suggested that indeed that might prove to be the case. Surprisingly, the Americans remained silent. On another point there was an unexpected silence from the British. For some time the Americans had been re-equipping a French force in North Africa. At Quadrant they suggested that it might be used to invade the south of France simultaneously with Overlord to divert German attention from the main operation. The British agreed, not mentioning that a further operation in the Mediterranean might also have the potential to divert attention from an Italian campaign. It was a silence that Churchill would certainly come to regret.[14]

There was another surprising silence on the British side. At a CCS meeting on 24 August an exposition of Eisenhower's plan to invade Italy was given to the Chiefs by one of the Joint Planners (Major-General John Whitely). He told them that there would be two amphibious assaults. The primary attack would be made south of Salerno by three divisions under the command of the US Fifth Army (General Mark Clark). Another attack of two divisions would be made across the Strait of Messina by the Eighth Army under Montgomery. The Germans were withdrawing from the south and intended, so the planners thought, to hold a line in the north from Pisa to Rimini. The Eighth Army was not therefore expected to meet strong opposition but, all told, the Germans had sixteen divisions in Italy.[15] Other expositions on the detail of the operation followed. The only comment made by the CCS was that they 'took note with interest of the above statements'.[16]

From Brooke's perspective this was an extraordinary silence. He had already suggested that the Salerno operation be boosted to five divisions. Yet the two divisions of the Eighth Army that could have provided the extra weight were to be landed 300 miles to the south, against no expected opposition and would have to crawl a considerable distance up the leg of Italy before they could offer any support to the Salerno landings. Moreover, the primary landings would be commanded not by someone with the experience of Montgomery, but by a general who, whatever his qualities, had never seen a shot fired in anger. It might have been expected that Brooke would have entered the strongest reservation about this plan – that mainland Europe was to be invaded in effect by just three divisions with troops that had no experience with amphibious operations under an inexperienced command, all presided over by Alexander and Eisenhower, in whom Brooke had little confidence and with the only commander in whom

Brooke had confidence (Montgomery) playing a subsidiary role. The whole plan was a recipe for disaster but Brooke's silence can perhaps be explained by a diary entry for the very day that the plan was unveiled.

> The conference is finished and I am feeling the inevitable flatness and depression which swamps me after a spell of continuous work, and of battling against difficulties, differences of opinion, stubbornness, stupidity, pettiness, and pig-headedness. When suddenly the whole struggle stops abruptly, and all the participants of the conference disperse in all directions, a feeling of emptiness, depression, loneliness and dissatisfaction over results attacks one and swamps one! After Casablanca, wandering alone in the garden of the Mamounia Hotel in Marrakash, if it had not been for the birds and the company they provided, I could have almost sobbed with loneliness. Tonight the same feelings overwhelm me, and there are no birds.[17]

Clearly, Brooke was at the end of his tether and probably in no condition to argue the toss over the Italian plan. Possibly he was also counting on Montgomery to play the same role that he had in the Husky plan and adjust any weaknesses. But for Husky Montgomery had had the luxury of time in which the alterations to the plan could be made. Here the plan was presented so late in August that it was almost a fait accompli. Nevertheless, it is strange that Montgomery accepted the Alexander/Eisenhower plan which effectively sidelined the Eighth Army. That he thought little of the plan is obvious from his blunt correspondence with Alexander; that he attempted radically to alter it as he had done to Husky there is not a shred of evidence.

The result was that the three military advisers trusted by Churchill remained silent about the Italy plan; Alexander because he had planned it, Brooke because he was exhausted and Montgomery because he seems to have been sulking in his tent. The Prime Minister would discover soon enough that all was not well with the Mediterranean strategy.

The invasion of Italy began on 3 September 1943 with the non-event of Operation Baytown on the very toe of the peninsula. After an enormous artillery bombardment (29,000 shells were fired) two divisions of the Eighth Army crossed the Strait of Messina to find no enemy in sight. Gradually, they began the slow path northwards, hampered at every turn by German demolitions of roads, viaducts, bridges and anything else that might stall the progress of a highly mechanised army.

Six days later the grandly titled Fifth Army Group landed in the Bay of Salerno, some 300 miles from Montgomery's forces. In fact just three divisions (36 US and 46 and 56 British) landed at widely spaced beaches. The landings were accomplished with relative ease but that was because the German divisions in the area had been held back on the high ground which surrounded the beaches like an amphitheatre. When the Germans moved to the attack, the Allied situation quickly deteriorated. The German battle-groups soon found the gaps between the Allied divisions. They also discovered that a river (the Sele), against all military experience, formed the boundary between the US and British landings, providing an attractively weak corridor down which to launch an attack.[18] By the 12th the situation was dire. As the 46 Division (which was on the left of the British line) narrative comments:

> To the south the 56 Division were driven out of Battapaglia and the Americans were forced to withdraw from Altavilla. On 13 September an even more critical situation arose when the enemy succeeded in driving in the left flank of VI (U.S.) Corps on the Sele river, and was only stopped by the desperate expedient of flinging every available man into a hastily improvised defence. Naval guns were used, and that night 504 Parachute Infantry were dropped to reinforce the line. On our front it came to such a pass that Sapper, mortar and machine gun companies were used as infantry, administrative groups took up defensive positions and reinforcements went straight into action as they landed.[19]

So perilous was the position that Clark ordered contingency plans prepared for an evacuation or at least a movement of US forces to the British sector, where the situation was slightly (but only slightly) better.[20] Still in Washington, the Prime Minister became thoroughly alarmed. He telegraphed to Alexander:

> I hope you are watching above all the battle of Avalanche [the name of the operation] which dominates everything. None of the Commanders engaging has fought a large-scale battle before. The battle of Suvla Bay

was lost because Ian Hamilton was advised by his CGS to remain at a remote central point . . . Had he been on the spot he could have saved the show. At this distance and with time lags I cannot pretend to judge but I feel it my duty to set before you this experience of mine from the past.

Nothing should be denied which will nourish the decisive battle for Naples. Ask for anything you want.[21]

Despite the dubious analogy between Salerno and Suvla Bay, this message revealed that Churchill had at last realised the weakness of the Salerno plan, and it propelled Alexander to the battle front. By the time he got to the beachhead the situation was beginning to stabilise. Naval gun fire, augmented by the arrival of two British battleships and enhanced air activity had beaten the German battlegroups back.[22] The Americans had also stabilised their front and all thought of evacuation had gone by the time Alexander arrived.

Casualties in all divisions, however, had been heavy. Then, as the 46 Division's narrative states:

Towards the end of September further large scale reinforcements came from North Africa to fill the depleted ranks. Some of them were men from 50 and 51 Divisions, both of which were leaving for England. Naturally they were somewhat disgruntled not to be going home with their own divisions, and the short rest before the Volturno crossing was insufficient to recapture the spirit which had distinguished the Salerno landing.[23]

What had happened was that 700 men from these divisions had shown their disgruntlement by staging a sit-down strike on the Salerno beaches and refusing to move into the line. The corps commander (Major-General Richard McCreery) rushed to the spot and addressed the men. As a result 500 responded and moved up while 192 were sent to Africa and court-martialled. The three ringleaders were sentenced to death and the others to imprisonment. All sentences were then commuted on the basis that the offenders return to Italy and earn a reprieve, which they did.[24]

What this incident perhaps laid bare was the fact that the Salerno landing was a poor plan, shoddily implemented. Alexander had urged

Montgomery to bring the Eighth Army into play but it was too distant, its two divisions had supplied for just one day and it was carrying out many administrative functions for the entire Fifth Army Group.[25] Montgomery pushed out light forces as far north as they could be supplied but the armies were too far apart for mutual support. By the time Eighth Army arrived in the vicinity of Salerno, the crisis was over. Defeat had been avoided but only just.

With Montgomery's forces now occupying the right of the Italian Peninsula, the advance northward could begin. It needs to be understood that this movement was fraught from the very start. It was now late in the campaigning season and the German engineers were very skilled at demolishing bridges, ploughing up the few good roads in the area and, as Montgomery knew from the desert, the German rearguards fought with skill and tenacity, making every yard of ground gained contestable. The conventional story is that the soon-encountered mountains held up the Allied forces, but severe difficulties were encountered well before the mountains loomed into view. On the left of the line 46 Division struggled across the River Volturno against considerable opposition. Then:

> The weather broke, turning the tracks into mud. Enemy tanks, now less frequently encountered, were a sufficient threat to compel a slow, methodical progress. The ... farms had to be cleared one by one of odd machine gun posts. The flat fields offered little cover; on the other hand observation was limited to a few hundred yards. Some fifty enemy planes were operating on the front, and air battles were an occasional distraction from the muddy sameness of the countryside ... In the slow advance to the ... Agnena canal there was no major engagement, but a series of probing patrols and platoon and company attacks, which made limited gains. Enemy shelling and mortaring was on a considerable scale.[26]

In other words the Allied advance was slowing to a crawl well before the mountain heights were reached and places such as Cassino were hardly known.

Such a slowing of an offensive was always unwelcome to Churchill. The one aspect of the Italian plan that had caught his attention was the relative slowness of the build-up of Allied divisions – there were to be just twelve

ashore by the end of the year. Alexander was, of course, aware of this disposition and moved to reassure Brooke that everything was being done
to push the advance forward.[27] However Churchill quickly assured his
commander that all was well and he understood that the administrative tail
had to be pulled up before a major advance could be made.[28] The fact was,
however, that Churchill's attention was wandering from operations in Italy
to a small group of islands off the coast of Turkey.

* * * * *

The Dodecanese had been on Churchill's radar since the beginning
of offensive operations in the Western Desert in 1940. These islands
(Rhodes, Kos and Leros were the main three) had been in Italian hands
since the Italo-Turkish war of 1911. Churchill sought to seize them and sent
a number of primitive landing ships (they were Glen passenger liners) to
the Mediterranean in 1941 to land troops. However, the exigencies of the
desert war, the setbacks in Greece and Crete and troubles in Syria, Iraq and
elsewhere meant that such an operation could never be mounted. After
German intervention in Greece in April 1941, small numbers of German
troops joined the Italian garrisons on these islands, making their capture
that much more difficult. All mention of these rather obscure islands then
vanished from British discourse for some two years.

Then, as operations against Sicily made progress, General Sir Henry
Maitland Wilson, Commander-in-Chief Middle East, alerted Brooke that
an Italian collapse might enable Rhodes and the other smaller islands to
be occupied on the cheap.[29] The Chiefs of Staff and Churchill agreed, the
Chiefs signalling that landing craft destined for India under an agreement
reached in Washington should be held in the Mediterranean and Churchill
telling the Chiefs that 'here was a business of great consequence to be thrust
forward by every means'.[30] The means, however, did not seem to be available. Wilson contacted Eisenhower to establish what could be supplied for
a Dodecanese operation from Italy. He received a reply that said nothing
could be supplied. The Vice Chiefs (the COS were by this time in Quebec)
agreed that this was indeed the case, and there the matter rested.[31]

It did not rest for long. Wilson, as it happened, continued with what
preparations he could make with his limited resources. Churchill approved,

telling him to 'improvise and dare'. It was all too late.[32] On 9 September (the day of the Salerno landing) the German commander at Rhodes moved to disarm the much larger Italian garrison. He succeeded and by the 11th the island was under the control of some 8,000 German troops.[33] Britain hung on to some nearby islands (Kos, which had an airstrip, and Leros), but if the Germans established themselves on the Rhodes airfields these would certainly be forfeit.[34]

In fact the Germans soon rushed squadrons to Rhodes and commenced bombing the British airfield and garrison on Kos. Churchill at once asked the COS if anything could be done, adding 'there is only one German Air Force' and 'we might as well fight them here'.[35] The COS agreed and signalled Eisenhower and the CCS in Washington:

(a) Middle East should prepare plan for capture of Rhodes in consultation with AFHQ [African Force Headquarters];

(b) Withdrawal from Kos and Leros cannot be accepted. There is only one German Air Force which is now badly stretched. The more rapidly it is diminished by fighting, the better, and apart from actual battle in Italy, we can fight it as well from Kos as anywhere else. With our superior forces we can afford to disperse better than they can.[36]

Again it was too late. On 3 October the Germans mounted a full-scale invasion of Kos. A flurry of telegrams from Churchill to Tedder and Eisenhower pleading for help and pointing out that Rhodes was in fact key to the whole situation had no effect.[37] Kos surrendered the next day.

The deteriorating British position in the Eastern Mediterranean was considered by the COS with Churchill in attendance a few days later. All agreed that Rhodes was the key to retaking the Dodecanese but to accomplish that feat, it was also agreed, would involve additional assault shipping, landing craft, carrier-borne fighters and more troops. Brooke worried that these resources could only be found in Italy, which might seriously affect the campaign there, but the airmen present (Sholto Douglas and Portal) considered that with the Dodecanese in British possession, 'we could control the Aegean Sea', and Churchill weighed in with the view that it would be 'very wrong' to throw away a chance to restore the Dodecanese. He would contact the President over the matter of retaining landing craft earmarked for Overlord in the Mediterranean if that would make the difference to the capture of Rhodes. Eventually it was decided to ask Eisenhower to call a conference of relevant commanders to consider the whole issue while the COS awaited a report by Cunningham (recently appointed First Sea Lord in place of the dying Pound), who was to return to the Mediterranean the following day.[38]

Overnight, however, the Germans attacked Leros, so Churchill reconvened the COS to consider the problem again. Churchill restated his case, this time arguing that the situation in Italy had eased and that a division could therefore be spared for Rhodes. Brooke disagreed. A division of troops might guard against a 'Rommel' counter-stroke in Italy, but he then went on to claim that if such a force was available it would be better employed in the Balkans than against Rhodes. Cunningham and Portal supported Churchill, stating that they were anxious to see an attack launched against Rhodes. Notably, the meeting reached no conclusions, but in summing up Churchill said:

> A cardinal strategic decision was now at issue. It was intolerable that the enemy, pressed on all fronts, could be allowed to pick up cheap prizes in the Aegean. Rhodes was the key and every effort should be made to capture it provided our position in Italy was not imperilled. The matter required further and urgent study.[39]

Before any further or urgent study could be undertaken, Churchill dashed off telegrams to Eisenhower and Roosevelt. To Eisenhower he said:

> I believe it will be found that the Italian and Balkan Peninsulas are militarily and politically united and that really it is one theatre with which we have to deal. It may indeed not be possible to conduct a successful Italian campaign ignoring what happens in the Aegean ... I have never wished to send an army into the Balkans ... All I am asking for is the capture of Rhodes and the other islands of the Dodecanese. The movement northward of our Middle eastern air forces and their establishment in these islands and possibly on the Turkish shore ... would force a diversion on the enemy far greater than required of you.[40]

And on the same day he wrote to Roosevelt making many of the same points and adding:

> I beg you to consider this [the operation against Rhodes] and not let it be brushed aside and all these possibilities lost to us in the crucial months that lie ahead. Even if landing craft and assault ships on the scale of a division were withheld from the build-up of 'Overlord' for a few weeks without altering the zero date it would be worth while. I feel we may easily throw away an immense but fleeting opportunity. If you think well would you very kindly let General Marshall see this telegram before any decision is taken by the combined Chiefs of Staff.[41]

Roosevelt was already aware that Eisenhower had replied to Churchill that he had no troops or equipment to spare from Italy, so he responded:

> I do not want to force on Eisenhower diversions which limit the prospects for the early successful developments of the Italian operations to a secure line north of Rome.
>
> I am opposed to any diversion which will in Eisenhower's opinion jeopardize the security of his current situation in Italy, the build-up of which is exceedingly slow considering the well known characteristics of his opponent who enjoys a marked superiority in ground troops and Panzer divisions. It is my opinion that no diversion of forces or equipment should prejudice 'Overlord' as planned.
>
> The American Chiefs of Staff agree.
>
> I am transmitting this message to Eisenhower.[42]

This was as bleak and blunt a message that Churchill had ever received from Roosevelt, but it did not constrain the Prime Minister from trying again:

> I earnestly pray that my view may receive some consideration from you at this critical juncture, remembering how fruitful our concerted action has been in the past and how important it is for the future. I am sure that the omission of Rhodes at this stage and ignoring of the whole position in the Eastern Mediterranean would constitute a cardinal error in

strategy ... I am willing to proceed to Eisenhower's headquarters with the British Chiefs of Staff immediately, if you will send General Marshall, or your personal representative, to meet me there and we can submit the results to a searching discussion to you and your Chiefs of Staff. We can be there Sunday afternoon.[43]

Roosevelt replied with what amounted to a slight. He said that he had instructed the conference that the Prime Minister wished to make it clear that he thought they should consider the subject with an open mind.[44] In effect the conference was hardly needed. Eisenhower and Roosevelt (and Marshall and others) had made their decisions. There would be no diversion of men or equipment for the Eastern Mediterranean.[45]

This incident has been dealt with at length, not because of the importance of a campaign in the Dodecanese (of which more later) but because it is indicative of a seismic shift in the Anglo-American alliance. So far in this war the Americans had bowed to British pressure – or common sense – in matters strategic. They had accepted North Africa instead of an attack across the Channel; they had agreed to the invasion of Sicily when yet again at least some of Roosevelt's advisers had felt the call of Northern France; they had seen the logic in the Italian adventure but at the same time inserted Overlord into the equation. Now they were saying 'no' to the British in a most direct, almost brutal, manner. There would be no campaign in the Dodecanese or the Aegean or the Eastern Mediterranean because the Americans did not want such a campaign. The power within the alliance had shifted. And this time it had shifted for all to see. In a sense lend-lease had seen a shift, because the British could no longer prosecute a war without American financial and material help. But in 1942 and most of 1943 it was the British who had by far the larger forces engaging the Axis powers. And these forces fought under British command and were still largely equipped with British war materiel.

That situation began to change in Tunisia with the appointment of Eisenhower as overall commander. Even then most troops had been British and so had the immediate ground commanders (Alexander and Montgomery). At the end of 1943, however, Eisenhower was Supreme Commander and American war materiel in the form of landing craft of all kinds, tanks and even fighter aircraft were now playing a much more important role in operations. Indeed, the equipment Churchill and others were asking for in the Dodecanese was to a large extent American (landing craft, P-38 long-range Lightning fighters and the like).

It seems clear that Churchill was slow to grasp this shift in power. His correspondence with Roosevelt offered the President guidance; when that was initially refused he offered more guidance. In the end it took a telegram that stated directly that Roosevelt not only did not require guidance, he thought the guidance offered by Churchill was dangerous and foolish. Shifts in power can often be accompanied by humiliation, as was indeed the case here. The Churchill/Roosevelt partnership would continue but never on the same basis. The special relationship had lost much that Churchill at least had regarded as special. It indicated something else too. Churchill would now have to win approval for any military schemes he might have not only from the British Chiefs of Staff, he would have to win the approval of the Americans as well. Churchill's and indeed Britain's days of independent power were over.

The whole incident was more painful for the British because the Americans were right. Rhodes, the Dodecanese, the entire area were irrelevant to the successful prosecution of the war. A glance at a map reveals the peripheral nature of these small dots in the Aegean. When Roosevelt said he could not see where the campaign went if these islands were recaptured, surely he had a point. It would hardly entice the Turks into the war. Nor would they be happy if the Dardanelles were to be opened to Russia – a point on which the Joint Planners and the COS agreed.[46] Could Greece be invaded from the Dodecanese? Hardly. It was under solid German occupation – as was Crete, which lay astride any invasion route from Rhodes. In any case, such a plan had been considered by the British in 1943 and rejected (for good reason) in favour of an Italian campaign. What of Bulgaria, the state closest to the Dodecanese, after Greece and Turkey? The answer is that this puny state hardly mattered in the great sweep of the war. Yes, it was a German ally, but its armed forces were weak and in any case the huge mass of the Red Army would deal with Bulgaria sooner or later. There was no urgent reason for the Western Powers even to think of Bulgaria.

As for Churchill's claim that Italy and the Balkans should be thought of as one theatre, it was arrant nonsense. The Italian campaign had been launched without reference to the Balkans and would be won or lost on its own terms. Whether guerrilla or partisan activity in Greece or the Balkans was fostered or ignored by the Allies hardly influenced what happened in Italy. In any case the Dodecanese were a considerable distance from the Balkans and their occupation or non-occupation again hardly mattered to what happened there.

There were thus no great strategic reasons for the British or anyone else to be involved in a campaign in the Eastern Mediterranean. Was this then just a Churchillian obsession? Many have thought so, and books have been produced about this period, one entitled *Churchill's Folly*.[47] Certainly Churchill became obsessed with Rhodes, as his humiliating correspondence with Roosevelt indicates. Brooke's diary is a further source. On 7 October he spoke of 'another day of Rhodes madness' and on the following day:

> He [Churchill] has worked himself into a frenzy of excitement about the Rhodes attack, has magnified its importance so that he can no longer see anything else and has set his heart on capturing this one island even at the expense of endangering his relations with the President and with the Americans.[48]

This seems definitive enough but it was not just Churchill who had set his heart on British action in this theatre. Almost the entire British politico/military leadership was with him.

In September, the Minister Resident in Cairo, Richard Casey, pointed out to Churchill the benefits that would accrue from the capture of Rhodes, noting that General Henry Maitland Wilson was very much in favour of it and concluding that 'your support would be much appreciated here'.[49] Smuts, whose opinion Churchill valued highly, was also all for conducting operations in this area. Among the Chiefs, Portal supported operations in the Dodecanese throughout the period, noting on 30 September 1943 that it would be 'quite wrong' to withdraw from Cos or Leros and on 7 October that he was 'anxious' to get Rhodes.[50] Cunningham was, if anything, even more enthusiastic, saying on 7 October that 'the possession of secure bases in the Aegean would offer our naval forces great opportunities and he would therefore like to see Rhodes in our hands'.[51] Even Brooke, who identified Churchill's 'Rhodes madness' accurately enough in his diary, was not opposed to a Dodecanese operation on strategic grounds but because it might take resources away from Italy. Moreover Brooke was much more enthusiastic about operations in the general area of the Balkans than his diary would suggest. After all, although Brooke opposed diverting a first-class division from Italy to Rhodes, he went on to suggest that such a division might be better employed supporting 'the guerrilla forces now in Albania and Yugoslavia'.[52] Later in the month, in a section of the COS minutes deemed so secret that they had restricted distribution, Brooke stated that his three goals in the Mediterranean were to continue the offensive in Italy, provide small Allied forces to aid Balkan guerrillas and to consider 'what operations could be undertaken in the Aegean with a view of opening the Dardanelles, thus making contact with Russia and enabling us to bring direct pressure to bear on Romania'.[53] So when Brooke, in a post-war note, says that the Americans 'imagined I supported Winston's Balkan ambitions, which was very far from being the case', it should be taken with a grain of salt.[54]

The question remains, then, why did these hard-headed, intelligent men, who had clearly and logically guided British strategy for some years, suddenly go off on an irrelevant and indeed dangerous tangent? There is no easy or obvious answer. Perhaps, after the long arguments with the Americans over North Africa, Sicily and Italy, they yearned to develop a strategy that was purely British which could be run without reference to the Americans – only to find that in the end they needed American aid even for the Dodecanese. Perhaps the Americans had at last got their 'sphere of influence' conspiracy theory right. Having been wrong about Britain desiring to dominate North Africa or having ambitions in the central Mediterranean, they were perhaps correct in thinking that Britain wished to dominate the Eastern Mediterranean. After all, Britain was the dominant power in this area – it occupied Egypt, Palestine and Iraq and had removed the Vichy French from Syria in a hard-fought campaign. It also had a special interest in Greece, as the attempt to forestall the German attack in 1941 demonstrated. Moreover, at Casablanca, Churchill had asked to 'play the hand' with Turkey – that is, attempt to persuade the Turks to enter the war on the Allied side, which they had conspicuously failed to do after two years of protracted and tedious negotiations. The Dodecanese were to be a reward for the Turks for taking the plunge, something that the inhabitants of Rhodes might not have actually welcomed. Perhaps the whole affair hinged on the fact that the expulsion from the Dodecanese was the first British defeat at the hands of the Germans since the First Battle of Alamein in August 1942, a loss often referred to by Churchill.

Perhaps, however, there was a matter which overlay all this, and that is there was a distinct wobble in this period to a commitment that the Americans had extracted from them at Quebec – that there would be a cross-Channel attack on occupied France in the spring of 1944. There are many indications that various members of the COS and Churchill himself were having doubts about the operation. Even before the Quebec meeting Brooke had been examining the plans produced by Lieutenant-General Frederick Morgan who had been appointed Chief of Staff to a yet-to-be appointed Supreme Commander and who regularly reported to the COS on his progress. On 4 August 1943 he noted:

> The estimated rates of build-up gave us a very small margin over the enemy. As regards the estimated rate of advance, he said that the country around Caen [Normandy had been selected by Morgan as the site of the landing] was very broken and was unfavourable to the attack. He felt that the estimated rates of advance were too optimistic. We had not achieved so high a rate of advance in Sicily where circumstances, especially port facilities, were more favourable than we could expect in Overlord.[55]

Although Brooke was not commenting on the feasibility of the operation, this was hardly a ringing endorsement.

It is clear that others among the group of British decision-makers were having their doubts. In early September Smuts told Churchill:

> I suggest our victories in Mediterranean should be followed up in Italy and Balkans instead of our adopting cross channel plan which means switching on to new theatre requiring very large forces and involving grave risks unless more softening has taken place. Preparations for the Channel plan should be slowed down or put into temporary cold storage.[56]

But Churchill, who was still in Washington and very aware of the strength of American feeling about Overlord, was dismissive, replying quite bluntly to Smuts: 'There can be no question whatever of breaking arrangements we have made with the United States for Overlord . . . I hope you realise that British loyalty to Overlord is keystone of arch to Anglo-American co-operation.'[57]

Smuts, though, had not given up. After he met with the King, George VI wrote to Churchill:

> I had a long talk with Smuts yesterday about the Mediterranean theatre of war. He has discussed this with you, & wants us to go on fighting there, & not to switch to a new front like Overlord.
>
> I have thought about this matter a lot since then & am wondering whether we three could not discuss it together, I have always thought that your original idea of last year of attacking the 'underbelly of the Axis' was the right one.[58]

The King received the same reply from Churchill – there could be no possibility of going back on Overlord: 'Both the US Staff and Stalin would violently disagree with us.' He also reminded the King that a cross-Channel operation was the only one in which the strength of the formidable air force accumulated in Britain could be brought to bear on the enemy.[59]

However, Churchill's commitment to Overlord did not, in his mind, preclude the possibility of a purely British operation in the Eastern Mediterranean. Just a few days later he wrote to the COS:

> I should be glad if the Chiefs of Staff would carry out a staff study of the situation in the Mediterranean with particular reference to a growing resistance to Germany, both active and potential, which is developing in varying degrees in all the Balkan countries.
>
> I am fully aware of the engagements into which we have entered with the Americans at Quadrant with particular reference to Overlord and South-East Asia. Nevertheless, we must not shrink from taking a stern view of the policy we ought to adopt as opportunities open themselves to us for exploiting success in any theatre of war.

We cannot lightly disregard the difficulties facing the Germans and their satellites in the Balkan countries and the chance that may lie within our grasp to bring Turkey more actively on our side.

Pray let this enquiry be conducted in a most secret manner and on the assumption that commitments into which we have already entered with the Americans, particularly as regards Overlord, could be modified by agreement to meet the exigencies of a changing situation.

If the Chiefs of Staff advocate a forward policy in the Balkans, I should like to know, in broad terms, what this will involve. It may well be that we need not recant on Overlord except as regards emphasis and the balance of our effort.[60]

No doubt the enquiries had to be highly secret to keep them from the Americans, for if Churchill concluded that 'we need not recant on Overlord' the implication was that 'we might'.

This missive to shift British strategy from north-west Europe to the Mediterranean was not uncongenial to the COS. Brooke noted in his diary:

We received a note from PM to swing round the strategy back to the Mediterranean at the expense of the cross Channel operation. I am in many ways entirely with him, but God knows where that may lead us to as regards clashes with Americans.[61]

Later that day the COS met with the Prime Minister, Smuts and Cadogan from the Foreign Office in attendance. The main agenda item was headed 'Relation of Overlord to the Mediterranean'. Churchill led off by saying that he was worried that neither operations in Italy nor those in north-western Europe would be delivered in enough force to ensure success. The cross-Channel attack well might get ashore but excellent German communications would see them bring overwhelming force against the Allies to 'inflict on us a military disaster greater than that of Dunkirk'. Portal hastened to agree, suggesting that the Americans were convinced that Allied air power could prevent such a concentration, but he assured the meeting it could not. Smuts chipped in that 'it would be quite wrong to jeopardise what was almost a certainty [Mediterranean operations] for the sake of an operation that was not planned to take place for some months and which it already appeared likely to be postponed.' Brooke added to the chorus. War could not be waged according to 'lawyers contracts' (meaning the Quebec agreements); he had insisted at Quebec that the withdrawal of divisions for Overlord be reviewed in the light of military circumstances. Cadogan reiterated that the best action Britain could take was to stir up action in the Balkans. Cunningham and Portal then pushed for opening up the Dardanelles, which implied the capture of the Dodecanese. Churchill summed up (no doubt with his recent correspondence with Roosevelt in mind) by saying:

it was clear that **if we were in a position to decide the future strategy of the war we should agree**

(i)   To reinforce the Italian theatre to the full.

(ii) To enter the Balkans.

(iii) To hold our position in the Aegean Islands.

(iv) To build-up our air forces and intensify our air attacks on Germany.

(v)   To encourage the steady assembly in this country of United States troops, which could not be employed in the Pacific owing to the shortage of shipping, with a view to taking advantage of the softening of the enemy's resistance due to our operations in other theatres, though this might not occur until after the spring of 1944.[62]

Churchill ended by saying that unfortunately they could not make unilateral strategy but a meeting with the Americans must be arranged.

Certainly this meeting represented some kind of declaration of independence, albeit from a group that had already been defeated. Of Churchill's five points, Britain could really only carry out (iv) without reference to the Americans. Point (v), though, was the most startling. It suggested (and there was not a dissenting voice recorded at the meeting) that any invasion of Europe would only take place when Germany was on the verge of collapse and that the troops used would be mainly British accompanied by those US divisions that had not been diverted to the Pacific. This was not Overlord but rather Underling. The meeting ended with a strong resolve that a staff study should be carried out on the relationship between Overlord and the Mediterranean campaign.[63]

Churchill had wanted this study kept secret, presumably to keep it from American eyes. But just a few days later in a letter to Roosevelt he gave away that something of the kind was being undertaken. He opened by saying that 'all our plans for 1944 are open to very grave defects'. He then went on to repeat his fear that Hitler, with the excellent German communications network, could concentrate more divisions against a cross-Channel than the slower Allied build-up would be able to withstand and he ended by throwing doubt on whether Overlord could ever be mounted because he now thought that the conditions for a landing which he had specified at Quebec (attrition of the German army to certain specified levels) 'may very likely not be fulfilled'.[64]

If this did not indicate a significant wobble on operations in Northern France, nothing did. Roosevelt took some time to answer, partly because he had influenza but partly surely because any reply must have reopened the gulf between the two men. When he did respond he noticeably did not deal with Churchill's substantive points but merely deprecated a meeting between the British and the Americans (which Churchill had requested) without the Russians also being present as observers – and of course bolstering the American view of Overlord.

At this point a factor appeared that was to further complicate the already fraught position between Overlord and operations in the Mediterranean. Reports from Alexander and Eisenhower indicated that affairs in Italy represented a danger to the Allied position there. The Allied advance, as we noted, was becoming bogged down in early October. Since then the armies had struggled forward to the mountains without making a great deal of headway. Their progress was now being hampered by rain and poor weather which grounded much of the air force. In addition Enigma had at last thrown light on German intentions. The Germans had changed policy: they would now not execute a slow withdrawal to the Pisa–Rimini line as anticipated by the Allies. They would stand and fight in the excellent defensive country south of Rome. They were also reinforcing their front by bringing divisions down from the north to the extent that they might outnumber the Allied armies by a considerable margin. The removal of landing craft and men for Overlord was hampering the Allied build-up, and Alexander and Eisenhower feared that if this situation continued, there was a chance that a major German counter-attack might succeed.[65] In any case the capture of Rome was now a distant prospect and, if landing craft were not available for a landing behind the German positions, operations must degenerate into a slogging match.[66]

These reports brought forth a flurry of telegrams from Churchill and the COS to the Americans. Churchill told the President that on no account must a stalemate be allowed to occur. The commanders must have what they requested, especially in landing craft, 'no matter what effect is produced on subsequent operations [i.e. on Overlord]'.[67]

The COS were just as direct. They told Dill that they insisted that Eisenhower and Alexander be backed to the full 'even if the Overlord programme is delayed'. They also informed Dill that they were ordering fifty-six British landing craft due to return to Britain to remain in the Mediterranean and they strongly advised that the Americans order their own craft to remain.[68]

In the event, Churchill considered the situation so serious that he summoned the War Cabinet to obtain their approval of the policy laid down by himself and the COS. The Cabinet agreed unanimously, Brooke pointing out the 'folly' of withdrawing forces from the Mediterranean and making the point that a successful Overlord depended on the Italian campaign to wear down the German forces.[69] Cadogan, who attended the Cabinet, claimed that Churchill was so exercised about the position in Italy that if the Americans did not come to the party he was ready to make it a matter of resignation.[70]

After much hesitation the Americans, through the CCS, agreed that substantial numbers of landing craft should remain in the Mediterranean until 15 December. After a protest from Eisenhower that this would not allow him to make a major amphibious landing, they extended the date until 15 January 1944.[71]

For the moment the great Anglo-American debate on strategy went into a holding pattern – after all, it was an American commander demanding the resources and it was hardly the case that anyone on the American side wanted the Italian campaign to end in disaster. Nevertheless, the British flirtation with the Balkan/Aegean strategy in this period had done a great deal of damage to the alliance. Churchill was not unaware that this was the case. On 30 October 1943 Halifax told Churchill that he had held several talks with Roosevelt and Hopkins:

I am struck by the impression I get from these talks which is confirmed by Dill on the staff side, as to the misgivings entertained by your real intentions about Overlord. Both the President and Harry [Hopkins] of course, agreed that the final decision must and could only be made in the light of the actual facts at the time the decision had to be taken but the feeling of doubt in the background of their thought plainly remained. This will not be new to you nor, indeed, was it to me. But I was surprised and a bit disturbed to find the feeling so strong, and I had not much doubt that it colours and discolours their judgement ... [on any?] suggestion made from your side that can appear to have any reaction in Overlord field; e.g. it came out plainly in the President's reference to the exchange you had with him about the Dodecanese.[72]

This perceptive letter on such an important matter surely required a response from Churchill but there is no evidence he ever replied to Halifax. It also surely required a clarification for Roosevelt of Churchill's position, but that did not occur either. Churchill's silence after this warning can only be a matter for speculation. Perhaps he did not wish to be reminded of the painful correspondence over the Dodecanese. Perhaps he did not want to clarify his position on Overlord to the President because his position was so ambivalent. If so, that was unfortunate because in the last analysis Churchill seems to have realised that whatever his own position and that of the British COS, Overlord would be carried out – though not necessarily in May. This is revealed most clearly in an exchange the Prime Minister had with Eden, who was in Moscow during this period, attending a Foreign Ministers' Conference. On arrival Eden told Churchill:

They [the Russians] are completely and blindly set on us invading Northern France and there is absolutely nothing that we could suggest in any other part of the world that would reconcile them to a cancellation of, or even a postponement of Overlord ... Whatever misgivings there may be about Overlord it is impossible to show any weakening on it.[73]

Despite this warning, Churchill sent Eden Alexander's pessimistic letter and got him to read it verbatim to Stalin.[74] This Eden did but reported to Churchill that despite understanding that the setback in Italy had to be dealt with, Stalin still expected Britain to make every effort to carry out Overlord as soon as possible.[75] Churchill replied the next day:

> There is of course no question of abandoning Overlord which will remain our principal operation for 1944. The retention of landing craft in the Mediterranean in order not to lose the battle of Rome may cause a slight delay . . . The delay however would mean the blow when struck would be with somewhat heavier forces.[76]

This is probably an accurate summary of the British position regarding Overlord at the end of 1943. With both the Russians and the Americans being insistent on it being carried out, there was really no other position they could hold. Yet the amount of distrust that this episode sowed and Churchill's failure to reassure Roosevelt as he had Stalin that there could be no question of abandoning Overlord meant that reasonable British requests regarding Italy were treated by the President as a dastardly plan to reinvigorate a wider Mediterranean strategy. And about this the President was not entirely wrong. In committing to Overlord Churchill had by no means given up on other operations in the Mediterranean. In fact, Churchill quite failed to realise that he was beaten and was only too anxious to meet Roosevelt and return to the charge.

It needs to be said, however, that there was no split in the British political and military ranks over strategy in 1943. Brooke might rail against Churchill's obsession with Rhodes but he was quite willing to commit at least some forces to the Balkans and to talk of the opening of the Dardanelles. Portal and Cunningham were gung-ho for the Dodecanese, as was Smuts and Casey. What they all had in common was that they were representatives of a power (Britain) that had borne the brunt of the war in the west but was now declining. If they were not yet prepared to recognise that fact, it is no matter for surprise. No power on the wane ever has been.

CHAPTER 23

ROCK AND A HARD PLACE –
ITALY 1943–1944

CHURCHILL'S PRIORITY FOR THE end of 1943 was to meet Roosevelt and persuade him that greater flexibility was required for the timing of Overlord and of the necessity for more extensive operations in the Mediterranean. Roosevelt dodged the issue. The two Western leaders had agreed to meet Stalin in Tehran in the New Year – surely that meeting was enough. In any case Roosevelt suggested that the British and Americans could not be seen to be 'ganging up' on Stalin.[1] Churchill persisted and Roosevelt eventually agreed to a meeting in Cairo en route to Tehran, but he made sure that his arrival date was so late that just two meetings with the British leader could take place before Tehran. To make certain that he would be as little distracted by Churchill as possible, he invited Chiang Kai-shek to the meeting.

On the way to Cairo Churchill summed up his view of the war:

The allies had denuded the Italian theatre and therefore had failed to take Rome. They had also failed to divert German divisions from Russia, lost opportunities in the Balkans and allowed the Germans to take control of the Aegean. His solutions were to stop all movement of troops and landing craft for Overlord from the Mediterranean, energise the Italian front and capture Rome, capture Rhodes, land forces along the Dalmatian coast to aid the Yugoslav partisans and establish unity of command in the Mediterranean so that it could be seen as one theatre.[2]

Dill saw this memorandum and warned the British COS that the Americans would regard Churchill's strategy as 'a serious drain on the resources for Overlord' and that this would cause tension at Cairo.[3] However, with the exception of operations on the Dalmatian coast, the substance of Churchill's draft remained on the agenda, including the capture of Rhodes.

Essentially Churchill's rather gloomy survey of the war, minus the Dalmatian coast landings, was what he presented to the President at Cairo. There was no dissent from the COS, Brooke thinking the Prime Minister's exposition 'masterly', 'a great help in our deliberations'.[4] The Americans were not impressed. Soon Brooke and Marshall were having 'the father and mother of a row' ostensibly about an operation in the Indian Ocean (Buccaneer) that Brooke was asking to be delayed, but more likely about Marshall's suspicions that Brooke wanted the landing craft earmarked for Buccaneer to facilitate British adventurism in the Eastern Mediterranean.[5]

Cairo really decided nothing. The big decisions would be made at Tehran with Stalin. Tehran as the location of the first meeting of the 'Big Three' was curious. In 1941 Persia was deemed to be in danger of being taken over by pro-German elements, so by agreement the Russians occupied the north of the country and the British the south. Persia thus ceased to exist as an independent power and Tehran, which was conveniently close to Russia (though hardly to the US or Britain) became a location where Stalin was prepared to travel to what was the first 'summit' meeting.

The runes were not favourable to the British. Roosevelt insisted upon being located at the American Embassy, which was well away from the almost adjoining British and Soviet Embassies. Soon, a probably phoney security scare convinced Roosevelt to relocate – not to the British Embassy, which seemed logical, but to the Russian – another sign, no doubt, that he maintained his position of distancing from Churchill.

Having failed to convince the Americans at Cairo of the virtues of operations in the Mediterranean, at Tehran Churchill set about trying to persuade Stalin. Overlord, he proclaimed, would be carried out, but not until the German army had been worn down in Italy and elsewhere. As for the Eastern Mediterranean, Russia should join with Britain to induce (or force) Turkey into the war. Then the Dardanelles could be opened and Russia more easily supplied.[6]

Stalin was pretty clearly not that interested in Churchill's strategy. He replied that:

> It would be a mistake to disperse forces by sending part to Turkey and elsewhere and part to Southern France. The best course would be to make Overlord the basic operation for 1944 and, once Rome had been captured, to send all available forces in Italy to southern France. These forces could then join hands with the Overlord forces when the invasion was launched. France was the weakest spot on the German front. He himself did not expect Turkey to enter the war.[7]

Roosevelt was quick to agree with Stalin – there should be no dispersal of force, especially to the Eastern Mediterranean.[8]

At a third meeting Churchill tried again, emphasising the importance of the Mediterranean, of bringing Turkey into the war and this time including operations along the Dalmatian coast to aid the Yugoslav Partisans. Stalin's reply was emphatic:

> He felt bound to emphasise . . . that the entry of Turkey into the war, the support of Yugoslavia and the capture of Rome were, to the Russian way of thinking relatively unimportant matters. If, as was to be assumed, this conference had been convened to discuss military matters, operation Overlord had overriding importance. The decisions taken must be related primarily to this operation.[9]

Stalin concluded by stating that there were three big decisions to make: the date of Overlord, the date and scope of the landing in the south of France and the matter of the appointment of a Supreme Commander for Overlord. Other matters, such as the capture of Rome, were merely diversions.[10]

That was where matters were left at Tehran. When the British and Americans reassembled in Cairo, the matters raised by Stalin were top of the agenda. It was decided that Overlord would indeed be carried out in May 1944, that the Supreme Commander of that operation would be Eisenhower and that there would be a two-division landing in the south of France. Noticeably, the Eastern Mediterranean was not discussed.[11]

The British had been comprehensively outmanoeuvred at Cairo and Tehran by a Russo-American united front. In the light of this there was never a chance that any British Mediterranean agenda would prevail. But it is notable that the British hardly made the most of their own case. Their main operation in the Mediterranean was in Italy. This was the only front where a force could be deployed that was large enough to wear down or pin a considerable number of German divisions that might otherwise be used against Overlord. Yet instead of concentrating on the benefits of Italian operations, Churchill and the COS lost focus by insisting that operations involving Turkey, Rhodes, the Dardanelles and the Balkans be equally considered. Indeed, the British leadership during this period had tended to ignore the Italian front entirely. But, as Brooke was soon to find, all was not going well in Italy.

* * * * *

After Cairo, Churchill and Brooke planned to visit Italian HQ on the way back to London. In the event Churchill did not go, succumbing to a bout of pneumonia and having to convalesce in Tunis. Brooke therefore called on Alexander alone and was alarmed at what he found. We left the Allied armies in Italy struggling through the mud to the north of Naples. Ahead of them loomed the mountainous hinterland, dominated by the Apennines and intersected by numerous rivers liable to flood in autumn and winter. In these conditions, how were the Allied armies to progress? Or, rather than try to press on, was it a matter of waiting for good campaigning weather in the spring and going on the defensive through the winter? And if a defensive stance was to be adopted, what stratagems might be used to stop the Germans moving divisions away to other fronts?

There is no evidence that these matters were ever faced squarely by the command in Italy. Montgomery certainly thought this was the case. He spoke of there being no grip, 'no policy, no planning ahead; indecision, hesitation, ineffective command'.[12] In his diary he was more specific:

> What we want in Italy is a proper and firm plan for waging the campaign.
> At present it is haphazard and go-as-you-please. I fight my way forward
> as I like; I stop and I pause when I like; I choose my own objectives.

Clark (Fifth Army) does the same; I have very close touch with him and we see that our actions are so coordinated that all is well. But we each do <u>what</u> we like <u>when</u> we like; the total military power in the two Armies is not applied on one big plan. In other words, there is no grip or control by 15 Army Group.[13]

Thus the state of play in December 1943 was that on the left the Fifth Army had struggled up against the main German defences (the Gustav Line) from Cassino to the coast, while on the right the Eighth Army was across the River Sangro but had shut down operations because of extensive rain and flooding. It was at this point that Brooke visited the front. He was not pleased. Montgomery told him 'in no uncertain voice' that neither Alexander nor Clark was 'gripping the show' and that the capture of Rome could not be anticipated before spring 1944.[14] On meeting Alexander he was even more depressed:

My impression of the day is that we are stuck in our offensive here and shall make no real progress till the ground dries, unless we make greater use of our amphibious power . . . The offensive is stagnating badly and something must be done about it as soon as I get back.[15]

Brooke then flew back to Tunis to visit Churchill, who was very ill with pneumonia which had affected his heart. Brooke told him nothing 'about the depressing impression I had gained whilst in Italy . . . I had to keep all these misgivings to myself and look for a cure.'[16] His cure was 'making use of our amphibious power in this theatre by opening up a bridgehead near Rome.'[17]

However tight-lipped Brooke thought he had been, his depressed mood had made an impression on the Prime Minister, who although sick clearly had his wits about him. After Brooke's visit he wrote to the COS:

There is no doubt that the stagnation of the whole campaign on the Italian front is becoming scandalous. The CIGS visit confirmed my worst forebodings. The total neglect to provide the amphibious action on the Adriatic side and the failure to strike any similar blow on the west have been disastrous.

None of the landing craft in the Mediterranean have been put to the slightest use for three months, neither coming home in preparation for Overlord nor for Accolade [Rhodes] nor in the Italian battle.[18]

Given Brooke's already expressed views, the COS were quick to agree with the Prime Minister:

We have discussed the Italian situation with the CIGS [who was now back in London] and are in full agreement with you that the present stagnation cannot be allowed to continue. For every reason it is essential that something should be done to speed things up. The solution, as you say, clearly lies in making use of our amphibious power to strike round the enemy's flank and open up the way for a rapid advance on Rome.[19]

The question, as always, was – were there sufficient landing craft available for such a major operation? The COS were positive about what was needed. They told Churchill that a landing must be a 'standalone' affair as no rapid advance towards the beachhead by the Fifth Army could be expected because of the nature of the country they would have to traverse. In addition the operation would have to be carried out in late January or early February to break the winter deadlock. Two divisions must therefore be landed with a further division as follow-up. They considered landing craft could be found if some from the cancelled Buccaneer (Roosevelt had cancelled it in Cairo) were sent from South-East Asia and others earmarked for Overlord retained in the Mediterranean for some further weeks.[20]

Meetings at Marrakesh between a convalescing Churchill and Eisenhower, Major-General Walter Bedell Smith, Wilson, Alexander and Tedder followed. All were agreed that the operation (Shingle) should be carried out and that the landing craft should be found.[21] The questions now arose as to how many landing craft would be required for Shingle and how long could they be kept in the Mediterranean without endangering Overlord? What ensued was a long and tedious correspondence between Churchill in Marrakesh, the COS in London and the CCS in Washington. By early January 1944 even the Prime Minister was moved to comment, 'are we not making too much of the LST [landing ship tank] business which has become a kind of obsession'.[22] In the end, as was almost inevitable, sufficient landing craft were found – not only to land the initial two divisions but to sustain them and if necessary to land follow-up formations as well.

The amphibious operation behind the German lines took place at Anzio, about 50 miles south of Rome, on the night of 22 January 1944. Two divisions landed – the British 1 Division on the left and the US 3 Division on the right. The force (designated US VI Corps) was commanded by Major-General John Lucas, who was held to have done well in the Salerno operation. The operation achieved complete surprise, mainly because Allied air superiority prevented German reconnaissance aircraft from penetrating the assembly area around Naples and Salerno. After the force landed, its orders were either to establish a beachhead and 'take' or to 'move on' the Alban Hills some 20 miles away.[23] Lucas probably took more notice of Clark when he said, 'Don't stick your neck out like I did at Salerno.'[24] In any case the landing went well, the number of troops ashore shortly climbed to over 10,000 and vehicles and guns came trundling into the bridgehead. There was no sign of any Germans. Kesselring was told soon enough, however, and units from six German divisions began to make their way to the beachhead. Meanwhile Lucas consolidated. He moved his troops gently inland for several hundred yards. Then he stopped. His main concern was to build up supplies, ammunition, vehicles, trucks and tanks either for a further advance or to beat off the counter-attacks that he anticipated from his experience at Salerno. But there were no counter-attacks in the coming days; there were no advances either, except some inching forward beyond the Mussolini Canal and towards some higher ground near Campoleone.

For his supine behaviour Lucas has been excoriated ever since. Indeed, he was excoriated at the time by all comers, including Clark, Alexander, the CCS, the COS and Churchill and Marshall; he was soon replaced by Lucian Truscott. Indeed, Lucas was hardly a thruster of the Patton type. He was a man with little imagination or initiative, but he was no fool. At the landing he had just two divisions, though they would soon be supplemented by follow-up formations which gave him double that number. His objective, the Alban Hills, was 20 miles distant and would expand the area he was required to occupy at least ten fold. In other words, the further he went, the more thinly spaced his troops would be. His four divisions would have had no chance of holding in strength a perimeter which included the Alban

Hills. The further he went, therefore, the more likely he was to be success-fully counter-attacked – perhaps, if the forces had been strong enough, to be driven into the sea. In fact his *initial* task was unambiguously to secure the beachhead, and this is what he did. Certainly a more vigorous commander might have pegged out better claims inland by occupying ground that would have provided a more secure base from which to resist counter-attacks. But with the forces at his disposal that was about the most he could have achieved. .

Yet Churchill expected more. His correspondence with Wilson and Alexander during this period reaches staggering proportions. He insisted on, and received, daily weather forecasts for Anzio and detailed break-downs of exactly which equipment and supplies were landed, and he worried obsessively about the lack of progress.[25] In this he was certainly not alone. His commanders in Italy held the same views. For example, when Churchill asked Wilson to account for the lack of progress from the beach-head, he received the following:

Attributed to:
    (1) Failure of Corps Commander [Lucas] to appreciate the value of surprise he had achieved and to take advantage of it.
    (2) A Salerno complex in that task was to beat off inevitable counter-attacks as a prelude to success.
    (3) Disinclination to risk advance without considerable backing. In this case the arrival of combat team First Armoured Division.
    (4) The conclusion [is] command is only geared to work at slow speed.
    This represents my own personal opinion and had better not be included in reply to Marshall.[26]

Churchill only included a digest of this to Marshall but he wired the entire telegram to Dill, who no doubt informally told Marshall of its contents. It is safe to conclude that the Americans were no more impressed by operations at Anzio than the British.

Churchill continued to obsess about Anzio. He insisted on regular updates about the numbers landed.[27] And, as was usual with him, he demanded to know why the 'tail' of the forces in the beachhead was so large and the numbers of fighting men so small. On being told that 18,000 vehicles had been landed, he caustically remarked that at least 'we must have a great superiority in chauffeurs'.[28] In one sense, however, Anzio was doing its job. It might not threaten the German position in Italy but it was attracting their reserves. Since the landing, elements of five enemy divisions from central Italy, three from northern Italy and a division each from the Adriatic, the south of France and Yugoslavia had been propelled towards the battlefield.[29] If Lucas's forces were not breaking through, they were at least making the Germans redistribute their forces, which after all had been one of the main aims of the Italian campaign all along.

The Germans had soon gathered sufficient troops to attempt a counterattack to drive the Allies into the sea. It commenced on 3 February 1944 and was carried out by three battlegroups containing elements from seven divisions. Alerted by Ultra intelligence, the Allied force beat off these attacks, though some ground was surrendered, especially on the left where the 1 British Division was in a sharp salient.[30] All divisions attributed their success in stopping the Germans to the devastating fire from the Allied artillery and the incessant bombing of German formations from the air.[31] Subsequent German attacks at the end of the month were beaten off in much the same way.[32] These episodes might not have been what Churchill expected of the landing, but in terms of attrition Anzio was achieving one aspect of the Italian campaign: wearing out German divisions.

* * * * *

What Anzio did not do was induce the Germans to retreat from their Gustav positions around Cassino. Alexander had wanted to mount a large-scale attack on the Gustav Line for some time but was bogged down in treacherous mountain country. During January, February and March 1944, fighting in Italy descended to small-scale attacks around the tortuous German positions near Cassino. Operations carried out by the Americans, the French and the New Zealanders all failed, though at various times they came within an ace of success. The problem with these attacks was that they took place on such narrow fronts as to allow the Germans to concentrate their best troops and firepower against them. Interestingly, Churchill hardly commented on these failures. He queried Alexander just once on the penny-packet nature of the operations and made several enquiries about the casualties borne by the New Zealand Corps, knowing the difficulty that country had in finding reinforcements. Perhaps the multinational composition of the force in Italy (apart from US and British troops, there were French, Canadian, New Zealanders and Indian contingents, and the Poles were about to arrive) made it difficult for him to intervene. Perhaps it was his overall (rather misplaced) confidence in Alexander.

Nevertheless Churchill finally recalled Alexander to Britain to discuss his plan for the big battle now scheduled for May. That plan met with his approval. It in fact sprang from the mind of Alexander's new Chief Staff Officer, John Harding. Brooke, who had not the same confidence in Alexander, had appointed Harding to provide some much-needed brains to Alexander's headquarters. Harding immediately identified the need for a full-scale offensive rather than small-scale attacks. On the right, the Adriatic coast was little better than a swamp so he would concentrate all his forces on the centre and the left. He therefore moved the US II Corps and the US-equipped French Corps to the left between the sea and the Liri River, concentrated the British XIII Corps and the British-equipped Polish Corps in the centre from the Liri to north of Cassino, and left the British Fifth Army (which would take no part in the offensive) holding the ground from there to the Adriatic. All this took time and was the main reason for the delay which so vexed Churchill but was an essential part of Harding's plan.[33]

Overall, the operation (Diadem) was larger than Alamein. In terms of troops, twenty-one Allied divisions faced fourteen or fifteen German divisions, each Allied division being of greater strength than its German equivalent. In terms of guns the Allies deployed 1,554, 400 of which were medium or heavy.[34] In contrast, the Germans had around 300 pieces of all kinds.[35] In the air Allied superiority was almost absolute, the Allied air forces disposing 3,960 aircraft, the Germans just 565, 222 of which were located in southern France.[36] The basic plan was to attack from the sea to the north of Cassino with fourteen divisions and then pass reserve divisions through them to carry the attack to the second-line German defences (the Hitler Line) and then exploit north. From Anzio the VI Corps would attack when the southern front had made sufficient progress in order to trap the Germans between the two groups south of Rome.[37]

The bombardment of the German positions opened at 11 p.m. on 11 May. It surpassed Alamein in ferocity, some 500,000 shells being fired in the next six days.[38] However, all did not go well. The British planned a thick smoke component in their bombardment to conceal the troops forming up along the Gari River from enemy positions on the opposite heights. As it happened, most of the battlefield was already covered with a thick mist. In most areas this reduced visibility to a few feet, which soon dislocated the attack and most units lost the cover of a creeping barrage, even though it was fired at the slow rate of advance of 100 yards per six minutes.[39]

The 8 Indian Division may be taken as an example. Its objective for 12 May was the Hitler Line, some 9 miles from its starting position. But the division barely managed to cross the river. Its units became disoriented by the smoke and mist and it was subjected to heavy fire from the fortified ruins of St Angelo village to its north. Tank support was minimal, many being bogged in the marshy approaches to the river and all battling for position to cross the one bridge thrown over it.[40] As the morning went on, the battalions found themselves pinned to the ground by fire from St Angelo.[41] It was quickly arranged that an attack on the village would be put in by the 1/5 Gurkha Rifles, who were by this time across the river. Due to the late arrival of tanks the attack did not eventually go in until 5.40 in the afternoon. It failed and reduced the company that made it to forty men. A second attack had to be postponed until the next day. This time it succeeded, the Germans 'fighting to the last'. Then a warren of fortified dug-outs had to be dealt with, 'only the presence of our tanks and the threat of the Kukri [the fearsome Gurkha knife] coming as it did from behind them, combined to induce the garrison to surrender'.[42] At the end of the day the picture was rather bleak. The Americans and French had got nowhere; neither had the Poles. The XIII Corps was, however, firmly positioned across the river to the south of Cassino.

This cross-river lodgement allowed reserves gradually to be fed into the fighting by XIII Corps. The first was the 78 Division, which, with the 4 British Division, began to gain ground and slowly outflank the Cassino position from the south. Then on 15 May Leese ordered the Canadian Corps to pass through the 8 Indian Division and move on the Hitler Line. All this aided the Poles, whose first attack on Cassino had failed with heavy casualties.[43] In reconnoitring after this failure the Poles discovered that the German positions were situated along ridges in two concentric rings:

> The system of such ring defence can be compared to a Roman amphi-theatre where every single spectator can see the rest of the audience and vice versa. Each single weapon, sited on the circumference of such a ring, could, therefore take part in the battle for any point on the periphery. The capture of a portion of a defensive ring did NOT give the attacking troops any possibilities of holding captured ground, unless this portion was wide enough to eliminate a considerable proportion of sources of enemy enfilade fire.[44]

So, the Poles set out to capture a large enough section of one of these rings to isolate the remaining defenders and then mop them up one at a time. This they managed, with fighting so ferocious that it probably had no parallel in western battles. Even when the German High Command ordered the evacuation of Cassino, German paratroopers and mountain forces clung on almost to the last man, apparently because they thought (incorrectly) that the Poles were not taking prisoners.[45] Finally, on 18 May, the Polish flag was hoisted above the ruins of the monastery and the Poles linked up with 78 Division on Highway 6. The Gustav Line had been broken at its strongest point.[46] It had cost the Poles 3,777 casualties, almost 1,000 of whom were dead or missing. German casualties are not known but the Poles counted 900 German dead around the monastery.[47]

Alexander signalled this success to Churchill but warned him of stiff fighting to come as the Allies approached the German fall-back position, the Hitler Line. This led to one of the very few interventions by Churchill in the battle. He urged Alexander not to pause for too long to bring up his artillery: 'It seems to me very important', he said, 'to keep close on their heels.'[48] He need not have worried. By 23 May the Canadians had the support of 786 guns. And at this stage of the war the guns could perform many different tasks. When enemy fire from the ruined town of Aquino threatened to hold up the attack, it was decided to make that town a 'William Target' – that is to bring every gun the Eighth Army could muster down on the town simultaneously. In this case 668 guns fired 3,509 shells weighing 92 tons on Aquino in a few minutes. All opposition ceased.[49] This 'time on target' firing or firing a 'stonk' became common practice later in the war. With the firepower available to the Allies, the Germans had no chance to hold the Hitler Line (which was quickly renamed the Senger Position by the Germans). By the end of the 23rd it had fallen to 1 Canadian Division.[50] There were no more fixed defences now between the Allies and Rome – and to make matters worse for the enemy, the Anzio bridgehead had sprung to life.

Alexander had held back the attack from the beachhead until the Gustav positions were well and truly broken. On the 23rd the advance from Anzio, led by three US Divisions began. The German army in Italy was now in deep trouble. In the south the Hitler Line had fallen and on the left flank the French and the Americans were making rapid advances. The XIII Corps was also pushing forward, the major hold-up being the difficulty of squeezing two corps, including armour, into the narrowing Liri Valley. Now, with US troops advancing north-west from Anzio, Kesselring's forces risked being trapped between the two Allied armies. Enter Mark Clark. As far as Alexander was concerned Clark was making for a road junction at Valmontone, a clear choke point in the German retreat. But Clark was not. He had turned his VI Corps to the left and was making for Rome, which he triumphally entered on 5 June. Clark had long been obsessed with being proclaimed the conqueror of Rome, a fact he had carefully concealed from Alexander.

Churchill, who – while absorbed with D-Day preparations – was following the Italian battle carefully, noted the point and urged Alexander to move on Valmontone, remarking that 'a cop [that is, trapping the Germans] is much more important than Rome.'[51] By then it was too late – Clark was making for Rome.

Later Clark made no secret of his intentions and told the American Official Historians that he considered Rome 'a gem' that belonged to his Fifth Army.[52] Was the opportunity to crush the German forces in Italy lost? Certainly this outcome could have been a possibility. If US forces had continued to head north towards Valmontone there was a chance of trapping the Germans between two pincers, but trapping a cornered army is a difficult proposition. It hardly ever happened in western battles, and a portion of even the under-resourced Italian army escaped in 1940. Nevertheless, with the Allies in strength in possession of Valmontone there was a chance that at least considerable casualties could have been inflicted on the retreating Germans, even if many would have inevitably slipped through the net. Such a victory, followed rapidly by D-Day, might have had a depressing effect on the German army. In any case, there would have subsequently been fewer Germans to fight. What is extraordinary about this entire incident is that neither Churchill nor Brooke, thanks to the diplomatic Alexander, were aware of Clark's actions at the time. One can only imagine the explosion if they had known.

* * * * *

While Alexander's armies were securing Rome and gathering themselves for an advance northward on the Gothic Line, a disagreement had broken out among the British and Americans over future operations in the Mediterranean. The prospect of a landing in the south of France in support of Overlord had first been raised by the Americans at Quebec in August 1943. It had surfaced again at Tehran, with Stalin an enthusiastic supporter. The British had had little to say about the operation (codenamed Anvil) except to express general agreement that it should be looked at.

The debate sharpened in the early months of 1944. The Americans were concerned that if Alexander's impending operation (Diadem) prised the Germans from the Gustav Line, there would be little to stop them withdrawing to the line of the Alps, holding that line with a skeleton force and sending surplus divisions against Overlord. In this circumstance a landing in the south of France should be made to keep as many German divisions as possible pinned to the Mediterranean.[53]

The British disagreed with this. They thought that the Germans would not withdraw to the Alps, on the grounds that Hitler never withdrew voluntarily from an area he thought he could hold. Instead he would withdraw to the next available defensive position – the Gothic Line between Pisa and Rimini.[54] Alexander would need to retain all his divisions to force these defences and have an excellent chance of destroying the German armies in Italy, which would aid Overlord much more than any diversion in the south of France.

No agreement was reached, each side waiting to see the fate of Alexander's offensive against the Gustav Line and the outcome of D-Day. After the success of those two operations, the debate resumed. But two factors muddied the waters. First Churchill put forward an alternative operation of a large-scale landing (some fourteen divisions) around Bordeaux to trap the German armies in Normandy in a pincer.[55] Then Alexander came forward with a grandiose plan to smash through the Gothic Line and pursue the Germans through the Alps via the Ljubljana Gap and advance on Vienna.[56]

In this atmosphere the British and American staffs met in Britain just after D-Day. Marshall came out very strongly in favour of Anvil. It was now obviously too late to assist D-Day but such an operation could still attract many German divisions away from Normandy. Eisenhower, after a brief flirtation with Churchill's Bordeaux scheme, quickly swung in behind Marshall. Brooke equivocated. He thought the American fears that the Germans would withdraw to the Alps misplaced, given the 'Hitler mentality' to defend everywhere. But he was averse to Alexander's grand plan to advance on Vienna, thinking it a fevered over-reaction to the capture of Rome. Overall he favoured a halt at the Pisa−Rimini Line in Italy and a study made of the southern France and the Bordeaux plans. In the end no agreement was reached.[57]

After the Americans departed, the British set about debating the alternative operations among themselves. Smuts and Portal thoroughly approved Alexander's Ljubljana plan, which he thought must attract German reserves and could cost them the entire region of the Balkans. Brooke disagreed, noting that the country around Istria and further north was well suited for defence. He thought Alexander should concentrate on destroying the Germans at Pisa−Rimini and despatch any forces surplus to that task to the south of France.[58]

Churchill's thoughts are difficult to discern. He found Bordeaux attractive but thought it might not prove practical. He opposed the south of France landing because it would take too long to prepare. As for Alexander's scheme, 'he was not prepared to see General Alexander's armies attempting to storm the Alps', but 'the attractions of the Ljubljana gap were strong.'[59] How he thought Ljubljana was to be reached without traversing the Alps is not clear. Brooke's view of this as a 'lot of disconnected thoughts of no military value' seems an accurate enough summary.[60]

What seems to have concentrated British minds was a series of meeting with Lieutenant-General Sir James Gammell, Alexander's Chief of Staff.

Gammell made three points. The first was that for Alexander's operations to engage the Germans at a tempo which would destroy their armies, landing craft would have to be employed continuously to keep his armies supplied. Second, Alexander would not have excess divisions as Brooke had suggested because of the need to replace divisions that had been in the line for some time with fresh divisions for the decisive battle. Third, if Anvil was to be carried out by early August, as the Americans wished, the seven divisions diverted to it would not be available for the attack on Pisa–Rimini and another stalemate in Italy might be the result.[61]

The fact that Anvil might interfere with Alexander's operations in Italy seems not to have occurred to anyone on the British side until this moment. After contacting Alexander and Wilson, Brooke summoned the COS to consider their options. They were stark. To force a decision, Alexander would need every division he had; the American timetable for Anvil would remove seven of these divisions. The COS concluded: 'Unless, therefore, we were to run the risk of interfering with the attempt to destroy the German forces in Italy, it would not be possible to undertake Anvil.'[62]

Churchill was rapidly summoned by the COS to hear this conclusion. He agreed with them. A note was immediately despatched to Washington:

> We are convinced that the allied forces in the Mediterranean can best assist Overlord by completing the destruction of the German forces with which they are now in contact and by continuing to engage in maximum strength, all German reinforcements deployed to oppose their advance. Any compromising of the enemy armies in Italy at this critical stage of the war, without a compensation of the early destruction of equal forces elsewhere, would in our opinion, be wrong.[63]

In short, for the British, Anvil was off and all forces previously devoted to it would be used by Alexander to destroy the Germans in Italy.

The American Chiefs were not of this mind. They were thinking logistically. Eisenhower had told them that since the destruction of his Mulberry harbour in a storm he required an additional port through which to land men and supplies.[64] Marseilles, although a long way from Normandy, he thought fitted the bill and was an early objective for Anvil. In this mood they were hardly minded to call Anvil off. Their reply was blistering:

The proposal of the British Chiefs of Staff to abandon Anvil and to concentrate on a campaign in Italy is unacceptable ... The fact that the British and United States Chiefs of Staff are apparently in complete disagreement in this matter at this particular moment when time is pressing presents a most deplorable situation. We wish you to know now, immediately, that we do not accept the statements in your paper in general in relation to the campaign in Italy as sound as in keeping with the early termination of the war. The desire is to deploy as many United States divisions in France as quickly as possible. A successful advance by Alexander's force in Italy does not promote this possibility ... The United States Chiefs of Staff do not consider there exists any reason for engaging in further discussion.[65]

The British were incensed by this reply, which Brooke characterised as 'rude'.[66] They were not inclined to take a backward step:

We deeply regret that the United States Chiefs of Staff find the proposal ... unacceptable. We share their anxiety to get an early decision, but it would be unthinkable for want of patient discussion to risk taking a false step ... we are still absolutely convinced that the continuity of the use of maximum force wherever the enemy can be induced to fight must be the foundation of our strategy. In fact, we felt that we should never be forgiven in history if we now invested substantial forces in a project [Anvil] which cannot mature during the next three critical months and even then may only pay a negligible dividend for a further three. In the light of developments since our meeting at Stanwell [10 June] we feel so strongly on this matter that at present we are unable to advise His Majesty's Government in the United Kingdom on military grounds in a sense contrary to what we have set forth.[67]

This amounted to the most serious deadlock reached so far in the Anglo-American alliance. The US found British proposals in Italy unacceptable; the British refused to recommend participation in Anvil (including, presumably, the 300 or so of their ships that were to be devoted to it). In this situation only Churchill and Roosevelt could resolve the deadlock and after meeting with the COS the Prime Minister addressed the President thus:

The deadlock between our Chiefs of Staff raises the most serious issues. Our first wish is to help General Eisenhower in the most speedy and effective manner. But we do not think this necessarily involves the complete ruin of all our great affairs in the Mediterranean, and we take it hard that this should be demanded of us ... I earnestly beg you to examine the matter in detail for yourself. I think the tone of the United States Chiefs of Staff is very arbitrary and certainly I see no prospect of agreement on the present lines. What is to happen then? Please remember how you spoke to me after Tehran about Istria, and how I introduced it at the full conference.[68]

Attached to Churchill's letter was a closely argued note of some length setting out the points in favour of continuing operations in Italy at the expense of Anvil.[69] The reference to Istria was a two-edged sword: yes, Roosevelt had introduced the idea at the Tehran Conference, but now the idea of a landing at the head of the Adriatic only served to remind the Americans of what they regarded as a fatal British tendency to adventurism in the Balkans. Churchill might have been well advised to omit mention of all such operations at this time. In any case Roosevelt was not inclined to overrule Marshall and Eisenhower on such an issue:

> It seems to me that nothing can be worse at this time than a deadlock in the combined staffs as to future course of action. You and I must prevent this and I think we should support the views of the Supreme Commander. He is definitely for Anvil and wants action in the field by August 30th preferably earlier.[70]

Crisis meetings were held – in Washington the CCS were regaled by the British representatives on the virtues of Italy.[71] In London the COS considered their position but refused to budge.[72] Churchill circulated their views to the War Cabinet, who wholeheartedly endorsed them. Finally Churchill drafted the following:

> I really do [not?] know where I am or what orders should be given to the troops. If my departure from the scene would ease matters by tending my resignation to The King, I would gladly make this contribution, but

I fear that the demand of the public to know the reasons would do great injury to the fighting troops . . . There is nothing I will not do to end this deadlock except to become responsible for an absolutely perverse strategy. If you wish I will come at once across the ocean to Bermuda, or Quebec, or if you like, Washington . . . but to agree to the whole great Mediterranean scene, with all its possibilities, being incontinently cast into ruin without any proportionate advantage gained from Overlord, that I cannot stand.[73]

After seeing this draft the COS were in a high state of anxiety. They begged Churchill not to send it, noting that the Americans were determined to proceed with Anvil and would no doubt withdraw troops from Italy for it. They saw no choice but to defer to the President's wishes.[74]

The essence of it was summed up by Brooke in his diary: 'All right, if you insist on being damned fools, sooner than falling out with you, which would be fatal, we shall be damned fools with you, and we shall see that we perform the role of damned fools damned well!'[75]

This was not the end of the Anvil matter, When American armies broke out from Normandy in late July and commenced their drive across central France, Anvil (now called Dragoon by Churchill because he thought he had been dragooned into it) re-entered the picture. On 4 August, according to Brooke, Eisenhower asked for Dragoon to be cancelled and the forces to be employed there switched to Brittany.[76] The same day Eisenhower seems to have told Churchill the same thing. Almost certainly Eisenhower seems to have muddled his message. He probably said that if operations in Brittany went to plan, more US divisions could be landed there than was previously thought possible.[77] Certainly on 5 August he was telling Marshall, 'I will not repeat not under any conditions agree at this moment to a cancellation of Dragoon.'[78]

Churchill, however, had already written to Roosevelt urging him to rethink Dragoon and land the forces in Brittany.[79] The Chiefs of Staff agreed with him and instructed the Joint Staff Mission in Washington to put the case to the US Chiefs.[80] This they did and received a curt reply to the effect that no operation scheduled for 15 August could be re-purposed in the short time available.[81] Meanwhile Churchill had discovered that Roosevelt was incommunicado visiting troops in the Northern Pacific. He immediately tried to convince Hopkins of the benefits of his plan.[82] The reply was direct: the President was out of touch but Hopkins assured Churchill his answer would be negative.[83] Churchill then met with Eisenhower in a final endeavour to influence the Supreme Commander. The meeting was not a success. As the naval aide to Eisenhower recorded in his diary, 'Ike said no, continued saying no all afternoon, and ended by saying no in every form of the English language.'[84] Finally, Roosevelt replied to the effect that Dragoon should be launched as planned at the earliest possible date.[85] That really was the end of the debate. The whole sorry saga seems to have been started by Eisenhower's inability to express himself clearly. But the British, even after Eisenhower had clarified his position, should have realised much earlier than they did that their case was hopeless and that in any case it was too late to redirect a major operation to a different location. That they pushed for the cancellation of Anvil at this point was really just a reflection of how they had felt about the operation since late June.

In fact the British leadership handled the entire debate over Anvil very badly. When the Americans introduced the operation at Quebec and Tehran, no one on the British side realised that this American-led operation might have the potential to affect the British-led offensive in Italy. Perhaps the British were at that time optimistic that their armies in Italy would advance at a rate that would render operations such as Anvil irrelevant. However, Anvil hardly entered their thinking after it became apparent that the fight up the Italian Peninsula was developing into a hard slog.

Moreover, in early June Brooke and Churchill in particular seemed to take their eyes off the Italian ball altogether. In Churchill's case this was not surprising. On many occasions he had developed his own operational ideas; Bordeaux was merely the latest example. At other times Brooke could be relied upon to concentrate Churchill's mind on the main event. This did not happen in the great Anvil debate. Brooke seemed quite attracted to a landing somewhere in the west of France and supported Churchill in having the idea investigated by the Joint Planners. That might have been a diversionary ruse but on other occasions Brooke seemed attracted by a landing in the south of France. Certainly in the joint staff talks with the Americans he did not come out against it and in the COS meetings he mentioned

Toulon as an area where a landing could be effected. Partly, this might have reflected Brooke's lack of confidence in Alexander. He was appalled by his Ljubljana plan, thinking it quite impractical and pointing out to Churchill the difficult country that such an operation would have to traverse. He then described the team of Alexander and Harding as not 'high class ponies' and later bemoaned that fact that 'Harding . . . is not up to his appointment . . . [But] Alex does not realise this fact.'[86] All this may have led Brooke to waver on Italian operations but it does not explain his sudden adherence to them when it belatedly became clear to him that the Americans were going to remove divisions from Italy for Anvil, or the vehemence of his notes to his US counterparts protesting a move that should have been long obvious to him. Brooke was usually a steadying influence on Churchill but his prevarication on this matter let his political master down. If he was as strong for Italian operations as his correspondence with the Americans in late June indicated, he should have made this much clearer to Churchill much earlier than he did.

After all this has been said however, it seems highly unlikely that the British could ever have won over the Americans on Anvil. The operation was a long-standing American idea, it involved largely American troops or American-equipped French troops and they would be landed from American landing craft. Marshall had long held to the position that these craft would remain in the Mediterranean only for Anvil and that if Anvil was cancelled they would be immediately transferred to the Pacific. Given this view, the British were probably always barking up the wrong tree. They could have been clearer, though, on the particular tree up which they were barking.

It is difficult to say which side had the best of this argument. As we will see, when Alexander's reduced forces arrived at the Gothic Line they proved insufficiently strong to break it with celerity. Eventually they did break through but by then the weather had turned and it was eventually decided to close operations down until the spring. If they had had those additional seven divisions removed for Anvil it might have been possible to break through and rout the German armies in Italy in the autumn of 1944. As additional help to operations in north-western Europe this would have proved a boon. Whether it would have shortened the war is too speculative to consider.

The American/French landings in the south of France were conducted efficiently and saw the Germans in rapid retreat up the Rhône Valley. However, by this time the Normandy front had been broken and German troops there were in retreat to the Seine. Any German troops in the south of France would have had to retreat to avoid being cut off. Therefore, as a campaign to force a German retreat the Anvil/Dragoon landings were largely a waste of time. As for the need for a port, as far as landing additional troops is concerned this too was hardly necessary. Just three divisions landed at Marseilles that otherwise would have had to be retained in the United States. The remaining divisions from the US landed across the beaches or small ports in the Normandy area. Perhaps Marseilles was useful as a place from which war supplies could be landed, but no study has any conclusive evidence on this point. It seems that whatever the American justifications for Anvil, they carried out the operation because they wanted to and because they had the means to do so. If Anvil is evidence of anything, it is yet more evidence that power had definitely shifted in the Anglo-American alliance.

CHAPTER 24

THE WEIGHT OF THE WAR – THE STRATEGIC BOMBING OF GERMANY

THE STRATEGIC BOMBING OFFENSIVE against Germany was a protracted campaign that lasted from May 1940 until the end of the war. Only the Battle of the Atlantic lasted longer. The bomber had been much touted as a decisive weapon throughout the 1930s but the attitude of the Chamberlain government and pressure from the French and the Americans not to 'unleash' the bomber force kept it from bombing Germany through the 'phoney war'. That changed with the opening of the German offensive in the west on 10 May 1940 and the appointment of a more resolute government under Churchill on the same day. Other constraints soon disappeared. Roosevelt's plea not to institute the bombing of civilians might have survived the German attack on Warsaw. It did not survive the German attack on Rotterdam. Moreover, the French, under massive attack through the Ardennes, were now calling on Britain to bomb the 'tap-root' of German industry in the Ruhr. The Churchill government was only too happy to oblige. On 12 May Churchill told the War Cabinet that events meant that Britain was not bound by 'our previous scruples'.[1] German industrial targets would be bombed at the first full moon.

On an important matter the new government appeared at one with the old. The Churchill War Cabinet, like that of Chamberlain, considered that in Bomber Command they had a fearsomely destructive weapon to hand. They did not. In May 1940 Bomber Command had just 536 machines, of which no fewer than 300 were light bombers. These fragile planes lacked the range to reach most targets in Germany and in any case were soon shot out of the sky over France as they attempted to support the BEF.[2] That left around 200 Whitleys, Hampdens and Wellingtons. All of these were two-engine bombers with modest bomb loads ranging from 8,000 lbs for the Whitley to 4,000 lbs for the Hampden and just 1,000 lbs for the Wellington.[3] None of them could be classed as 'heavy' bombers, though they were often so described by the Air Staff and politicians. They were also often categorised as 'strategic' bombers but they were only strategic in the sense that they could reach western Germany with a full bomb load and return. Their small number and their puny bomb loads hardly amounted to anything that could enforce a strategic decision on the battlefield.

There were other factors at work that limited the impact that Bomber Command could have in the first months of the war. It was quickly realised that the slow speed of the bombers (200 to 230 mph) would make them unacceptably vulnerable to the German fighters (350 to 400 mph) in daytime. Bombing would therefore be largely confined to the night. Yet these first bombers had no equipment that might aid navigation by night. Most crews had been given little practice at night flying, and when they had it was over the brightly illuminated areas of England and Wales where land-marks were easily identifiable.[4] These lacunae left pilots in a grotesque position when war came. They were now required to fly over a Germany where cities and factories were at least browned out, often covered in cloud or – in the case of the Ruhr – industrial haze, find their target by notori-ously inaccurate dead reckoning navigation (the theoretical working out of the position of an aircraft using forecast winds) and then accurately bomb very small areas in the face of anti-aircraft defence. And all this had to be accomplished alone. Squadrons might take off together but they had been given no practice in night formation flying so they made their way to the target alone and bombed alone. This precluded any kind of concentrated attack on a target and allowed the defences to aim all their fire at one plane at a time.[5]

This meant that Bomber Command would struggle to hit any particular objective at which it aimed its bombs. Was there any sign that the politi-cians and the Air Staff who ultimately controlled its activities realised that this was the case? There was not. Initially, the targets in Germany selected by the leadership for Bomber Command were railway marshalling yards and oil plants in the Ruhr.[6] The first attack on the Ruhr was made by ninety-nine planes (thirty-nine Wellingtons, thirty-six Hampdens and twenty-four Whitleys). The result was that a farmer was killed near Cologne and four people wounded in Münster – not a target for this raid. The eighty-one bombers that reported bombing their targets largely hit open ground.[7] What was later called 'agricultural' bombing had commenced.

While the battle raged in France, Bomber Command kept up this type of attack in an utterly futile attempt to disrupt the economic base of the German military. Targets such as the Ruhr, Hamburg, Bremen and Cologne were frequently visited. Sometimes the listed targets were oil refineries; at other times railways. It mattered little. Most bombs missed the target, and those that did not hardly caused any damage. On one raid a vat of whale oil suffered a near miss which caused the oil to leak out. In what might pass as a comment on bomber operations in this period, almost all of that oil was later pumped back.[8] In all, nearly 2,000 sorties were flown in this period, about 4,000 tons of bombs were dropped and fifty aircraft lost. The loss rate was low but not as low as the amount of damage inflicted upon Germany.[9]

At the end of June 1940 other matters claimed the attention of the politicians and the airmen. Dunkirk, the Battle of Britain and the Blitz shifted thoughts to aerial defence rather than attack. Yet the Blitz in particular also concentrated British minds on how to strike back. On the night of 23/24 August the Luftwaffe accidentally bombed London. Churchill immediately ordered a retaliatory raid against Berlin. Approximately fifty Hampdens and Wellingtons made the journey, which was at the extreme limit of their fuel capacity. Most bombs missed the city entirely. Farms to the south of Berlin were hit and two people wounded.[10] A gesture had been made but hardly an effective one.

Despite these failures, an assessment of Britain's strategic position and the widespread bombing of British cities indicated a response from Bomber Command was needed. Churchill certainly thought this way. In late June he noted that the blockade of Germany, on which such hopes had been pinned, was 'largely ruined' by the occupation of much of Europe and that 'the sole decisive weapon in our hands would be overwhelming air attack upon Germany'.[11] Then on the first anniversary of the war he told his Cabinet colleagues that:

> The Navy can lose us the war, but only the Air Force can win it. Therefore our supreme effort must be to gain overwhelming mastery in the air. The Fighters are our salvation, but the Bombers alone provide the means of victory. We must therefore develop the power to carry an ever-increasing volume of explosives to Germany, so as to pulverise the entire industry and scientific structure on which the war effort and economic life of the enemy depends . . . The Air Force and its actions on the largest scale must therefore . . . claim the first place over the Navy or the Army.[12]

The Chiefs of Staff had already reached a similar conclusion, pointing out the importance of an air offensive and noting that building up a large army might not in itself be sufficient for victory.[13]

The other factor that ensured that the bombing offensive against Germany would continue was, of course, the Blitz. The day after the German switch to the night bombing of London Churchill visited the docks and was told to 'give it 'em back' by a crowd of people.[14] He needed no encouragement. Later in September he broadcast about the 'cruel, wanton, indiscriminate bombings of London' and the 'indiscriminate slaughter and destruction' they caused. And he warned that Nazi Germany would feel the effects of British wrath until their tyranny had been 'burnt out of Europe'.[15] He was particularly incensed by German use of parachute mines. These were very large bombs that drifted down by parachute and because of the vagaries of the wind were by nature indiscriminate in their target. He proposed retaliating by dropping one on Germany for every one dropped on London.[16] Eventually the Chief of the Air Staff dissuaded him by pointing out that the Germans were obtaining quite a poor return for their mines, only one of which could be carried per plane.[17]

The bombing of Coventry on 14 November 1940, where the Germans inflicted more damage in relation to the size of the city than on any other British target, disturbed and alarmed him. He immediately called for retaliation on 'unexpecting' German towns that might provide soft targets for Bomber Command.[18]

The problems in mounting an effective retaliation were two fold. The Germans had been able to inflict such massive damage on Coventry because they bombed with the aid of a radio beam which indicated the exact bombing point. The British had no such aid at this stage in the war. Secondly, the only bombers available were those types with which Britain had begun the war: Whitleys, Hampdens and Wellingtons. True heavy four-engine bombers had been promised in the air plans of 1938 and 1939 but various difficulties had held up their manufacture. By the end of 1940 just forty-one of the new Stirlings and Halifaxes were available.[19]

This meant that operations proceeded as they had since the beginning of the war. Small numbers of the medium bombers were sent to a wide variety of targets in Germany. Priorities changed with bewildering frequency. From July 1940 to March 1941 no fewer than ten directives to Bomber Command were issued by the Air Staff. The priority targets shifted from invasion barges in early July to the German aircraft industry later in the month to power plants at the end of the month. Then in September barges and invasion ports returned as the highest priority targets, soon to be displaced by oil refineries as winter drew on. Then, in a rare burst of consistency, oil remained the priority until March 1941.[20]

Once more, none of these directives changed the fact that Bomber Command found any particular target difficult to hit. During this nine-month period Bomber Command flew 17,000 night sorties and dropped 12,000 tons of bombs.[21] Their loss rate was under 2 per cent but their effective hit rate was hardly much higher.

The inefficiency of Bomber Command in this period was hardly the fault of the pilots and navigators. Without electronic aids, dead reckoning could be rendered useless by a variation in the wind speed or by the sheer difficulty in plotting a course over an unfamiliar and blacked-out country. On the night of 9/10 October 1940, 144 Squadron, flying Hampdens, set out to bomb the Krupp steel works in Essen. The forecast for a clear night was wrong and the whole area of the Ruhr was blanketed in cloud. In the experience of one aircraft, the cold was so intense that ice appeared on the windscreen and wings. Then the ice found its way into the fuel system and the engines began to run rough. When the bombers arrived over the target area the thick cloud and the searchlights made any particular target impossible to identify. After circling the area, the pilot decided to return home and bomb an alternative target on the way. Even that proved difficult and they eventually bombed the Dutch port of Flushing – with what result is not known.[22] Of the twenty planes sent to bomb Krupp just three arrived in the general area of the Ruhr.[23]

Churchill's initial view was that the destruction of German industry should be the primary purpose of the bombing offensive. This opinion was reinforced by assurances by the Air Staff that the bombers were making real inroads into German oil production, and he had repeated this claim in public speeches.[24] However as time went by Churchill, who insisted on daily information on the results achieved by the bombers, became aware that they were not hitting their targets. In July he enquired why repeated attempts to block the Kiel Canal had failed.[25] In September, after examining photographs in *The Times*, he was struck by the inability of the bombers to do much damage to the invasion barges.[26] In December he insisted that the Air Staff investigate reports that raids on Berlin had so far inflicted little damage.[27]

By October 1940 Churchill had foreshadowed a change in bombing policy. He told the War Cabinet:

> Whilst we should adhere to the rule that our objectives should be military targets, at the same time the *civilian population around the target areas must be made to feel the weight of the war*. He regarded this as a somewhat broader interpretation of our present policy, and not as any fundamental change. No public announcement on the subject should be made . . . We should also for the time being take as our primary objectives military targets in built up areas.[28]

The eight permanent members of the War Cabinet and the twelve other politicians and military Chiefs who attended the meeting that day approved the new policy without discussion.

In truth, in terms of targeting, the new policy had little immediate effect. The bombers found even hitting a city a difficult business whatever policy might be promulgated by the War Cabinet. Anyway, winter was setting in and when on the night of 14/15 November eleven bombers were lost over Germany (the highest number of the war so far), Churchill told Archibald Sinclair that the bombing force should not be pushed too far in adverse weather. To ram the point home, he summed up the raid as a 'grievous disaster'.[29] Bombing would be scaled back for the winter.

Nevertheless, Churchill had by no means given up on his policy of making the German population feel the 'weight of the war'. On 12 December the War Cabinet met without the Prime Minister but specifically to discuss his views on widening bombing policy.[30] Portal told them that Churchill had asked him to prepare a plan to retaliate in kind for the Coventry bombing on a German city with 'the object of causing the greatest possible havoc in a built-up area.'[31] He made it clear that while Churchill might not regard this as a change of policy, he did. It was 'the diversion from strictly military objectives to a political objective, namely the effect on German morale'.[32] After a long discussion the War Cabinet agreed with the new policy and Portal produced a list of German cities selected for retaliation.[33]

Mannheim, an industrial city south of Frankfurt, was chosen and 134 aircraft were despatched to burn it down. It was not a success. The most experienced crews were to start fires in the centre of the city at which the others could aim. However, they missed their marks by a considerable distance and the main force scattered their bombs over a wide area. Just 236 buildings were hit, none of them of any military importance. Seven aircraft were lost.[34]

* * * * *

Air Chief Marshal Sir Charles Portal as the new Chief of the Air Staff had ordered the Mannheim raid. The new commander, who would maintain his position until the end of the war, remains perhaps the least well known of Churchill's Chiefs of Staff. Austere (he lunched alone at his club daily throughout the war), articulate, tactful and a man of strong ideas, he handled Churchill with great skill. This was partly made easier by the fact that they both wanted the same end – Germany bombed to oblivion. They would, however, differ from time to time on means. A Defence Committee meeting on 13 January 1941 brought these differences to the fore. Portal put forward his case for attacking oil plants. He told the Committee that at the end of four months Bomber Command could bring to an end production in the seventeen German principal plants, thus drastically curbing the enemy's ability to wage war. Hugh Dalton (Minister of Economic Warfare) and Hankey endorsed the CAS's approach. Then Churchill spoke:

> He said that he was sceptical of these cut and dried calculations which showed infallibly how the war could be won. In the early days of the war

it had been said that if the Royal Air Force were allowed to launch an attack upon the Ruhr, they would, with preciseness and certitude shatter the German industry . . . but there had been only a fractional interruption of work in the industries of the Ruhr.[35]

Portal was not ready to concede. He pointed out that the bombing of the Ruhr had been attempted by day – the attack on the oil plans would be undertaken by night bombers and that in these conditions his forecasts were not unrealistic.

Churchill was not ready to concede either. He said that Portal's approach 'would mortgage the greater part of our air effort for several months ahead on plants, generally speaking removed from the large centres of population'. In other words he wanted to return to bombing cities. The discussion continued, with Attlee, Sinclair, Dill and Geoffrey Lloyd (Petroleum Warfare Department) – who had drawn up the report on which Portal's remarks had been based – all supporting the oil plan. Churchill was overruled. He concluded by saying that he thought there would be no harm in trying the policy though he doubted whether it would be possible to stick to it owing to the certain strengthening of German defences around their oil installations. The meeting therefore adopted Portal's plan.

The policy of attacking oil consequently continued throughout the winter months. By the end of this period Churchill's doubts about the oil plan resurfaced. He insisted that he be given fortnightly reports on progress made.[36] This placed Portal in a difficult position because the fact was that no progress at all was being made. By late February 1941 Churchill had not received the reports but seemed to have forgotten his original request, so the Air Staff decided to 'let sleeping dogs lie' and continue their policy of not giving him the reports.[37]

What saved the Air Staff from Churchill's inevitable discovery that vital information was being kept from him had nothing to do with the bombing war. In January and February 1941 the tonnage of merchant ships sunk bringing vital war supplies and food to Britain rose to 300,000 and then 400,000 tons.[38] In light of these catastrophic figures, on 9 March 1941 Churchill ordered a new directive to be sent to Bomber Command. Centres of U-boat building within Germany were to be attacked as well as Focke-Wulf (the German plane favoured in anti-convoy operations) factories. In addition, a considerable portion of Bomber Command's effort would now be directed against submarine bases such as Lorient, St Nazaire and Brest in western France.[39] Additional targets at Brest were the German battlecruisers *Scharnhorst* and *Gneisenau* which had already sunk twenty-two merchant ships and could outrun any British heavy warships.[40] Surely this would prove more productive than the attempt to bomb the enemy oil plants.

In the event it did not. For the next three and a half months much of Bomber Command's effort switched to the U-boat pens and the warships along the French Atlantic coast. The result was overwhelmingly negative. Almost 2,000 sorties were flown in all, but the bombers lacked the heavy-weight bombs that could have – had the bombing been accurate – penetrated the increasingly thick concreted pens beneath which the U-boats lurked. Nor did the command have much more success against the warships (the heavy cruiser *Prinz Eugen* joined *Scharnhorst* and *Gneisenau* in June 1941 after the destruction of the *Bismarck*). The ships were attacked on at least thirty occasions between March and early July 1941. The *Gneisenau* was crippled for six months on 5 June but by a lone plane from Coastal Command. The one success Bomber Command recorded was hits on the *Prinz Eugen* on the night of 1/2 July which put this ship also out of action for six months.[41] It was a poor return for three months of effort.

By early July 1941 Churchill had had enough. He told Portal that the air situation had now changed. Too much emphasis was now being placed on bombing Brest 'at a time when the devastation of the German cities is urgently needed in order to take the weight off the Russians' by forcing the Germans to return aircraft from the Eastern Front to defend the Reich.[42] Indeed, the arrival of a new ally concentrated Churchill's mind. The Russians were engaging at least 150 German divisions; the British less than a handful. Russia had to be kept in the war and the obvious method that demonstrated British intent was the bombing campaign. So, as early as 7 July Churchill was telling Stalin of the exact number of German towns that were being attacked and the weight of bombs that were being dropped on them. Stalin was also assured that 'this will go on'.[43] Eventually a template was developed into which figures of bombs dropped and towns attacked could be conveniently added.[44] Churchill ensured that Stalin regularly received these statistics for the remainder of the war. Here was an ongoing rationale for strategic bombing.

Meanwhile, during the maritime diversion, frequent raids continued to be made over Germany. The first of the four-engine bombers, the Stirling, took part in some of these operations, but in very small numbers. The results were rather as before; some targets were hit, including Hamburg which was attacked by 188 bombers on the night of 8/9 May 1941. Many serious fires were started and 185 people killed – the highest of any single raid of the war so far. On another occasion Hamburg was bombed when the actual target was Bremen, some 50 miles away.[45] Clearly, navigation to the correct target was still a matter of chance.

Even after the bombers returned in summer to targets within Germany, results hardly improved. A raid on Cologne by ninety-one aircraft on the night of 26/27 August in good visibility failed, with local authorities estimating that only 15 per cent of bombs fell within the city limits.[46] A follow-up raid a few days later fared no better: 103 aircraft including thirteen of the new Stirlings and Halifaxes comprehensively missed the city. In all one person was killed and a few buildings damaged.[47]

German night defences were steadily improving. Anti-aircraft guns were being produced in increasing numbers and gathered around Bomber Command's likely targets. In addition a night defence 'system' under the direction of Colonel Kammhuber was being organised. In brief, this system divided the air space likely to be penetrated by the early bombers into districts or 'boxes'. Each box contained radars, searchlights and night fighters. In its first iteration the night fighter was directed onto the incoming bomber by a ground radar controller. Later (1942) the night fighters were equipped with airborne radar. In the early years all British aircraft had to fight their way through this array with the result that casualties from night fighters steadily rose.

By summer 1941 a report into the effectiveness of British bombing, the Butt Report, was about to be circulated. In early August Lord Cherwell (Churchill's statistical adviser and general scientific éminence grise) had ordered an investigation into the accuracy of Bomber Command. At this stage of the war most aircraft carried cameras which automatically recorded a photograph shortly after bomb release. On 18 August, Butt, a member of the War Cabinet Secretariat, released his survey of over 600 photographs taken by the night bombers.[48] The results were devastating. As Cherwell reported to Churchill, Butt revealed that while two thirds of crews thought they had found their targets just 20 per cent had dropped their bombs within 5 miles of it. In the absence of a full moon only 5 per cent of aircraft achieved the 5-mile radius.[49] Churchill was thoroughly alarmed. He minuted to Portal: 'Action This Day. This is a very serious paper, and seems to require your most urgent attention. I await your proposals for action'.[50]

Portal carefully studied the Butt Report and Cherwell's conclusions and found he agreed with them. He recommended training expert 'fire raising' crews to guide the main bomber stream, rushing the development of the experimental navigation beam called Gee, pushing ahead with some form of airborne radar and in the meantime improving the skills of navigators using existing methods.[51] There was of course one other conclusion to be drawn from Butt that Portal did not include but with which he certainly agreed. That is, if Bomber Command could only drop its bombs onto a wide area, then make such a wide area – such as a city – the target.

Indeed the Chiefs of Staff had flagged such a policy some months before. In a paper entitled 'General Strategy' they had noted:

It is bombing, on a scale undreamt of in the last war that we find a new weapon on which we must principally depend for the destruction of German economic life and morale.

To achieve its object within a reasonable time, the bombing offensive must be on the heaviest possible scale and we set no limits to the size of the force required ... After meeting the needs of our own security, therefore, we give to the heavy bomber first priority in production ... Our policy at present is to concentrate our main effort on the German transportation system [and] as the force increases we intend to pass to a planned attack on civilian morale with the intensity and continuity which are essential if a general breakdown is to be produced.[52]

The stars had now aligned. There was proof that the bombers could hardly hit a target smaller than a city. Churchill had been calling for some time for German cities to be the main bombing targets. The Chiefs of Staff, disillusioned by the total failure of their oil plan, now agreed. They might mention transportation targets – these were mainly railway marshalling yards that in any case lay within the confines of enemy cities – but they also spoke about passing to an attack on German 'morale' – bombing the civilian workers – as soon as possible. In one sense none of this was new. British bombing had been to this point so inaccurate that cities (on a good night) *were* their targets. But now it was official. German civilians would be aimed at. If the enemy had sown the wind during the Blitz they were about to reap the whirlwind.

Portal immediately set about producing a plan. By 22 September it was on the Prime Minister's desk. The paper argued that the weakest part of the German war machine was the morale of the civilian workforce and in particular of the industrial workers. Using the scale of attack on Coventry as a measure, Portal concluded that six attacks in six months would render a town 'beyond hope of recovery'. To wreak such destruction on all German towns was beyond the power of the existing bomber force so he had selected forty-three cities with a total population of 15 million people for sustained attack. Calculations of the tonnage of bombs needed to achieve this result followed. His final calculation stipulated that no fewer than 4,000 heavy bombers would be required to deliver the bomb load.[53] An uneasy covering note was attached:

> I know you do not much like attempts to forecast by arithmetic the prospects of our success in our bomber offensive. Nevertheless I send you the attached paper in the belief that it may interest you if you have the time to go through it.[54]

He then repeated the formula – 4,000 heavy bombers x 6 months equal 'decisive results'. Portal was right to be uneasy. On 27 September 1941 Churchill replied:

> It is very disputable whether bombing by itself will be a decisive factor in the present war. On the contrary, all that we have learnt since the war began shows that its effects, both physical and moral, are greatly exaggerated. There is no doubt that the British people have been stimulated and strengthened by the attack upon them so far. Secondly, it seems very likely that the ground defences and night fighters will overtake the Air attack. Thirdly, in calculating the number of bombers necessary to achieve hypothetical and indefinite tasks, it should be noted that only a quarter of our bombers hit the targets. Consequently an increase in the accuracy of bombing to 100 per cent would in fact, raise our bombing

force to four times its strength. The most we can say is that it will be a heavy and, I trust, a seriously increasing annoyance.[55]

The Chief of the Air Staff was rather taken aback by this rebuke. He protested that all that he was attempting to do was to carry through the Prime Minister's own policy of subjecting Germany 'to a bombing offensive of the greatest intensity' and that if it merely amounted to 'a heavy and growing annoyance' another strategic conception was required.[56]

Churchill disagreed. He told Portal that he hoped the bomber offensive would meet the hopes of the Air Staff but that 'I deprecate . . . placing unbounded confidence in this means of attack, and still more in expressing that confidence in terms of arithmetic.' While he thought it the most 'potent method of impairing the enemy's morale' that Britain had at the moment, he anticipated that if the Americans entered the war the invasion of Europe by armoured forces would be more likely to force a decision. He berated the Air Staff for always placing the effect of bombing too high and pointed out that so far they had always been wrong. He concluded: 'One has to do the best one can, but he is an unwise man who thinks there is any certain method of winning this war, or indeed any other war between equals in strength. The only plan is to persevere.'[57]

This correspondence is important in establishing Churchill's attitude to the bombing campaign. In 1940 he thought it provided the only clear path towards winning the war. By the end of 1941 the close attention he had given to the offensive had left him disillusioned. That did not mean that he was about to give up on Bomber Command. He would continue to insist that it deliver the heaviest possible attack on Germany and he and Portal now agreed in thinking that this attack was best delivered on German cities. This is what he meant by insisting that the German people feel the weight of the war. He had long since ceased to believe that bombers alone would produce victory, though he certainly hoped they could cause chaos. This was a position he maintained until the end of the war.

One point in Portal's original paper – that Britain needed 4,000 heavy bombers to win the war – no doubt infuriated the Prime Minister. Around the time Portal wrote this paper Bomber Command could muster 500 operational medium bombers (if Blenheims were included) and just ninety-nine heavy bombers, of which only eleven were Lancasters. This compared to 535 mediums and five heavies operational one year before.[58] In other words, while the production of medium bombers was keeping pace with the attrition rate, heavy four-engine bombers were appearing at a glacial pace. Churchill had no patience with this. As early as December 1940 he expressed himself deeply concerned about the 'stagnant condition of the bomber force' and asked to receive weekly figures on the expansion programme.[59] Nine months later he was no more satisfied. The Air Staff had promised him 16,500 bombers by 1943 and were now telling him that only 11,000 could be expected. He asked Attlee to look into the matter but, as the minutes of the Defence Committee (Supply) reveal, even the maximum number of bombers that could be expected was no more than 14,000.[60]

On the surface the Prime Minister's impatience seemed to have some merit. The specifications for the Halifax and the Stirling bombers had been issued in 1936. The Stirling (the first true strategic bomber, with a bomb capacity of 14,000 lbs) was plagued with engine and undercarriage problems, and the first prototype did not fly until 1939.[61] The Halifax was also ordered in 1936, but as a twin-engine bomber, the specification being changed to four engines in 1937. The prototype flew in 1939 and, though it did not have the technical problems of the Stirling, was a difficult aircraft to fly and unpopular with crews.[62] The third of the British strategic bombers arose out of a mistake. The Avro aircraft company had designed a two-engine bomber (the Manchester) but the Vulture engines with which it was fitted proved extremely unreliable and as a result just 200 Manchesters were made before it was withdrawn from service in 1941. In the meantime, a brilliant designer at Avro (Roy Chadwick) reconfigured the Manchester with stretched wings to take four Rolls-Royce Merlin engines. This converted it into the Lancaster, the best bomber of the Second World War, which could usually carry 12,000 lbs of bombs but could be modified to carry a maximum of 22,000 lbs of bombs. The delay, however, meant that it did not enter service until 1942.[63]

So, there were technical and design reasons for the slow production of the four-engine bombers. But there were other factors as well. In the first place, the target figures produced by the Ministry of Aircraft Production (especially while it was under the control of Lord Beaverbrook) were always pitched at an unrealistic level, so there was never a chance that they would be met.[64] The main constraint, though, was labour. Aircraft (fighters during the Battle of Britain and bombers after that) usually had a high priority in British war production, but in May 1942, such were the depredations of the U-boats, that the navy became number-one priority for the construction of convoy escorts. Then in the spring of 1944 the construction of various landing craft for D-Day rose to the top. But these were particular episodes; for most of the war the production of heavy bombers received top priority.[65] As a result the percentage of munitions workers employed by the Ministry of Aircraft Production increased from 28.8 per cent in late 1940 to 35.6 per cent in early 1944 – from 1 million to 1.69 million workers.[66] That it rose no higher is an indication of the tight labour constraints under which Britain was operating.

Another drag on production was the introduction of new types of bomber. The replacement of the Whitley and the Hampden, first by the Stirling and the Halifax, and then the replacement of the Stirling by the Lancaster – though necessary if the campaign was to continue with the best aircraft – caused much disruption. Often factories had to be extended to cope with the larger airframes and rejigging and retooling had to be undertaken to meet the new designs.[67] Retooling itself could cause delays. When a decision was made to switch three large factories from making Wellingtons and Stirlings to Lancasters it was found that the machine tools existed only to convert two of the factories. The third continued to make the rather obsolete Wellingtons because the choice was between doing that or closing the factory altogether.[68]

So, while the production of heavy bombers increased quite steeply – from just 41 in 1940 to 4,615 in 1943 – because of heavy losses, the operational strength of the heavies in Bomber Command never increased much beyond 1,000 at any time in this period.[69] This was far from the 4,000 heavy bombers requested by Portal in 1941 or even the seemingly more 'realistic' number demanded by Churchill.

Despite this slow progress, the year 1942 saw the glimpses of a new beginning for Bomber Command. First, its head, Air Chief Marshal Sir Richard Peirse, was sacked. To some extent this was hardly fair; the force he had inherited had done the best it could. But in the end most commanders who preside over failure are replaced sooner or later. So it was with Peirse; his two-year tenure at Bomber Command ended on 7 January 1942. The new commander was a former group commander and had been a delegate to the US urging them to send bombers to the RAF, Air Marshal Sir Arthur Harris. In this latter role Harris had not been a success, his acerbic telegrams a testimony to his lack of diplomatic skills.[70] In any case Harris's forte was operational command, as his retention of his position at Bomber Command until the end of the war indicates. Harris seemed a straightforward if belligerent type but he was more complex than that. His aim was simple: to destroy as many German cities as possible and so win the war. He could be extremely devious in furthering that policy, to the extent of ignoring direct orders given to him by the Air Staff and by Portal. He also proved to be an old-fashioned commander, never visiting his squadrons and ensconced in his headquarters at High Wycombe. He was old-fashioned in another more important way: he had little grasp of technical matters and although he was well aware that his force needed navigational aids and other means to improve its accuracy, it is doubtful if he mastered any of the technology that increasingly became available to Bomber Command – or indeed cared much about it. If his aircraft bombed the city it was aiming for, to a large extent that was good enough for him.

The first matter facing Harris when he took up his command was a new directive from the Air Staff. On this occasion it was one that he was happy to follow. On St Valentine's Day 1942 the Deputy Chief of the Air Staff (Air Vice-Marshal Norman Bottomley) wrote to the head of Bomber Command thus: 'It has been decided that the primary object of your operations should now be focused on the morale of the enemy civil population and in particular, of the industrial workers.'[71] Gone from this directive was any mention of attacking transport or power installations or oil refineries within industrial cities. The targets would be the cities themselves. It had taken two and a half years for Bomber Command to be given a task that it might actually be able to accomplish.

Harris made no immediate attempt to carry out the new policy. There were two good reasons for this. The first was that his fleet of bombers, though increasing, was hardly optimal. When he took over, Bomber Command had about 550 operational medium bombers (Hampdens, Whitleys, Wellingtons, Manchesters) and just sixty-three of the new heavies (twenty-six Halifaxes, twenty-six Stirlings and eleven Lancasters). More of the new types were coming, but this was not yet a formidable force.

Secondly, an aid to navigation was being fitted to some aircraft. This was Gee, a cathode tube which picked up impulses sent from three widely separated stations in Britain. When they intersected on the tube it meant that the aircraft was within 1 to 6 miles of the target. This hardly amounted to deadly accuracy but given the findings of the Butt Report, it was a major improvement. One important limitation was that after approximately 400 miles the curvature of the earth interfered with Gee. It would therefore be useful against the Ruhr and other targets in western Germany, but useless against Berlin and points east.[72]

In any case at almost the same time that Harris took up his command, other forces were questioning whether bombing German cities was an optimal use of the bombers. The navy, concerned about submarine depredations in the Atlantic and the dominance of the Japanese in eastern waters, requested eight and a half long-range reconnaissance squadrons, which could only be provided at the expense of Bomber Command.[73] This was followed by a note from the First Sea Lord (Pound) reiterating the need for the naval use of long-range bombers and reminding the Defence Committee that 'if we lose the war at sea, we lose the war'.[74] This was putting the position very bluntly indeed and there was an added voice for the redeployment of the bomber force from Germany. Across the Atlantic, Roosevelt was under heavy pressure to ease the massive sinkings of US ships along the eastern seaboard of America. He wrote to Churchill in mid-March 1942 to plead for a heavy diversion of bombers to attack the U-boat pens in France.[75] Churchill blamed bad weather for lack of results when in fact Bomber Command had just been redirected from naval targets back to Germany. Roosevelt was not to be fobbed off. He returned to the subject at the end of March with an added threat that perhaps more American bombers should be sent to the Pacific instead of the European theatre.[76] Churchill rather defensively replied that they were doing their best on the U-boat pens and reiterated the need to attack Germany with the increasing accuracy provided by the new navigation aid (Gee).[77]

Meanwhile a long debate on the use of bombers had taken place in the Defence Committee. Pound re-emphasised the need for long-range aircraft to protect shipping in the Bay of Bengal along with six squadrons of reconnaissance aircraft to patrol the Western Approaches. Portal resisted with the claim that these aircraft were needed for Germany and pointed out that

Coastal Command had already received six squadrons from Bomber Command for patrol purpose, but Alexander supported Pound. In the end Churchill concluded, rather lamely, that these questions could not be decided at the present meeting and that the Admiralty and the Air Staff should hold further discussions.[78]

Bombing policy was about to enter a crisis. Clearly Churchill's preferred policy was to continue to bomb Germany. That had always been his preference and in any case the heavy bombers had proved ineffective in their attacks on naval targets. But he could hardly ignore either the Battle of the Atlantic or Roosevelt. At this moment a paper arrived from Lord Cherwell that was meant to clarify bombing policy but in the short term did the opposite. Cherwell had been mulling over the Butt Report and making some calculations on what a more accurate attack on German cities might mean. Based on an analysis of German raids on Britain, Cherwell estimated that, with the heavy bombers coming on stream by 1943, given even 50 per cent accuracy, 22 million Germans living in fifty-eight key cities could be 'de-housed'. The effect on German morale would 'break the will of the people' and end the war.[79] Churchill, as we have seen, was averse to mathematical calculations that demonstrated one way or another that the war could be ended by a single policy, but he also placed a high value on anything Cherwell wrote. So he simply noted on this paper: 'CAS: [Portal] what do you say to this?'[80] Needless to say, Portal was enthusiastic, realising that such a policy would ease the pressure from the navy on Bomber Command. He immediately replied to Churchill that he found the arguments 'clear and convincing' and agreed that what Cherwell suggested was quite possible.[81]

Apparently the Chiefs of Staff, after a note from Churchill, passed Cherwell's paper to the Joint Planners to comment.[82] The result was a paper: 'Effect of Bombing Policy' by the Joint Intelligence Sub-Committee. This paper was of no practical use, being a theoretical piece on what might result if an unspecified number of bombers managed to drop their bombs within a reasonable distance of the target.[83] As might have been expected, the COS had no use for a theoretical report – Churchill would want concrete proposals. More surprisingly the Chiefs ducked the whole issue. Portal wrote to the Prime Minister that they found the question of what might result from the British bombing campaign 'beyond their capacity' and suggested that an independent authority be asked to report.[84] It is quite staggering that instead of Churchill reminding the Chiefs that they were not fulfilling their function, he merely noted 'yes' to the idea of an independent inquiry by Justice John Singleton.[85]

The Singleton Report was not presented to the War Cabinet until 20 May 1942 – five weeks after Churchill's note to Portal. It settled nothing. Singleton had almost no evidence from Germany on which to base a report, and the material from Britain that he did have was of dubious quality. He concluded merely that no great results could be expected within six months and after that matters of accuracy and the number of aircraft deployed might be some of the deciding factors.[86]

In the meantime two events occurred that had the potential to threaten the future of Bomber Command. One was a note by Brooke (CIGS) calling for 2,484 specially designed army cooperation and transport aircraft.[87] Taken with the requirements of the navy, these demands had the potential to end Bomber Command as any kind of major factor in the war, but there was never any chance that Churchill would agree to such a policy. After all, apart from fighting a few German divisions in the Western Desert, the bomber offensive – however ineffectual it might have been – was the only way that Britain could bring the war home to Germany. Moreover, it would hardly be acceptable to Russia and the US to announce that the air campaign against Germany was being shut down. What was Churchill to do?

He was helped out by Harris, who if not a great commander, had a great flair for publicity. By the end of March sufficient aircraft had been fitted with Gee for Harris to initiate a major attack. He chose Lübeck, a Hanseatic town with many wooden buildings in its centre. On 28/29 March 234 aircraft attacked it, damaging or destroying 62 per cent of all buildings and close to 100 per cent in the historic centre. At the end of April four consecutive raids on another Hanseatic town (Rostock) wreaked similar havoc.[88] These targets were rather unimportant in themselves but at least at Rostock significant damage had been inflicted on the Heinkel aircraft works.[89]

Then in mid-May Harris announced to Portal that he had been hatching a plan to attack a single German city on a single night with 1,000 bombers.[90] Portal immediately agreed, as did Churchill.[91] Assembling 1,000 bombers was a considerable feat by Harris. In his main groups he had just 678.[92] But by adding 369 aircraft used for training new crews Harris made the four figures. The scheme was not without risk because if many of the trainers did not survive the operation the impact on the future expansion of the command would be severe. One factor of note was that only 240 aircraft were the new type heavies – the main force would be made up of Wellingtons. It that sense it was one of the last raids without authentic strategic bombers.

There was one major innovation, however. Instead of the bombers flying singly or in small groups to their target, the aircraft would be concentrated into a continuous stream in order to swamp the ever-increasing flak defences and night fighters.[93] The chosen city was Cologne, easily identifiable because of its location on the Rhine and well within the range of those aircraft fitted with Gee. In all 12,840 buildings were hit, of which 3,330 were destroyed. 45,000 people were bombed out and a further 135,000 to 150,000 fled the city. Approximately 480 people were killed. RAF losses were forty-three aircraft, which were light, given the inexperience of many of the crews.[94]

To some extent the thousand plan was a risky stunt but in other ways it pointed to the future. Assembling and deploying such a force without collisions or losses from 'friendly' bombs demonstrated a considerable feat of organisation. Above all it reinforced the views of those such as Churchill and Portal that such a force might pay dividends in the coming months and years. Also it proved a successful propaganda exercise which bolstered the standing of Bomber Command with the public and within its own organisation.

The travails of Bomber Command were not over. Gee, as predicted, had a very short life, the Germans being able to jam it as early as August. From June to December 1942 Harris mounted around sixty raids of a hundred bombers or more, largely against cities in western Germany. Of these Essen was raided seven times, Bremen six, Duisburg five and a host of other cities three times or just once.[95] At least half of these raids were failures which substantially missed the city aimed for or caused minimal damage. Of the remainder just seven inflicted considerable damage on the objectives – the Focke-Wulf factory at Bremen hit on the night of 29/30 June is one such instance. Most raids destroyed a few buildings and killed some civilians but were hardly worth the effort made in mounting them.

Harris was also not helping his own case. One of the recurring problems was accurately locating the target. The Air Staff had put forward a solution: special high-performance squadrons which would find the target for the main bomber force. Harris flatly rejected the idea on the grounds that he wanted no specialised forces within his command, just good average forces. There the idea stalled until eventually Portal ordered Harris to introduce it – as a sop to Harris the new force was to be called the Pathfinder Force instead of the Air Ministry's Target-Finding Force.[96] An acerbic Australian, Group Commander Donald Bennett, was appointed to head the new organisation and took up his command on 5 July 1942.[97] In the immediate term the new force made little difference. Harris ensured that the best crews were not sent to Bennett, and those that were generally lacked experience. A survey of the bombing operations indicates that although more bombers were being sent, better results were only sporadic.

So, once more the utility of Bomber Command's operations was brought into question. Harris sensed the tide might be turning against him and wrote to Churchill suggesting that all aircraft diverted to reconnaissance duties be returned to him in order that he be provided with a force that could win the war alone.[98] He received a curt reply. While sympathising with Harris over the slow build-up of heavy bombers, Churchill reiterated his view that bombing alone could not win the war and that victory would require the largest possible military operations on the mainland of Europe.[99]

Portal entered the debate at the end of September but not in a way that Churchill found helpful. While conceding that military operations in Europe would be required, he proposed building 4,000 to 6,000 bombers – which would leave scope for a relatively small land force to finish the job.[100] Surprisingly, given their earlier negative opinions about the primacy of a bomber force, the Chiefs agreed with Portal. This agreement did not last long. Pound quickly realised that the construction of such an array of bombers would affect the construction of ships and involve the importation of enormous quantities of aviation fuel at the expense of various supplies needed by the navy.[101] He was soon joined by Brooke, who pointed out that the programme would also affect supplies of all kinds to the armies.[102] Portal was now isolated. He wrote another paper in which the size of the enormous bomber force was reduced to realistic proportions, the imperative to invade Europe with significant forces realised, and the needs of the navy acknowledged.

The argument over the place of the air offensive in British strategy lasted almost throughout 1942. Much of it was futile. Churchill, who would make the final decision on the question, was an advocate of all-out bombing when he could not envisage either the navy or the army playing any kind of role in destroying the Axis. In 1942, with two powerful allies at Britain's side, his attitude changed. There were now great prospects of land operations from west and east and south. Bombing in his scheme of things would play an important part in the destruction of the enemy but not the only or the vital part. Harris was worried that his service might be broken up, but that was never Churchill's intention. What infuriated him were papers from Harris and Portal making hugely overrated claims for Bomber Command. Churchill wanted to bomb Germany as intensively and as ruthlessly as possible but not at the expense of other operations.[103] As he said, while the bomber offensive would be maintained, he was not giving way to 'the pleasures of megalomania'.[104] The Germans would feel the full weight of any air offensive he could bring against them but they would feel the weight of land operations as well. If Goebbels was crying out for total war, he would not have long to wait.

The fact was that as 1943 dawned the prospects for Bomber Command were looking up. On 1 January it had 400 four-engine bombers, including 200 of the new Lancasters with their bomb-carrying capacity of at least 12,000 lbs per plane.[105] Then there were two new navigation aids coming on stream. The first of these was Oboe. Two stations in England sent out pulses which were picked up by the aircraft, keeping the aircraft on its set course over the target. When the aircraft retransmitted the signals back to the ground stations, the time taken for the retransmission indicated the aircraft's exact position. By this means course and bomb-release position could be calculated with some exactitude. Indeed if all went well the bomb-aiming error could be reduced to 300 yards.[106] The main shortcomings with Oboe were that, like Gee, the curvature of the earth confined its usefulness to western Germany, and the ground stations could only cope with a handful of aircraft fitted with the device. This second problem was partly overcome by the introduction of a new plane. The Mosquito was an all-wood, very fast fighter bomber. It was ideal as a pathfinder and if equipped with Oboe could lead the main bomber stream to its exact target. The second device was called H2S. It was a type of primitive airborne radar. It gave a rather blurry, flickering picture of the ground below. It worked best when there was some distinctive feature such as a watercourse or a coastline. Outlines of cities could sometimes be seen but it was difficult to work out exactly which part of a city was being viewed. Its great advantage, however, was that it had no range limitations.[107]

Thus Harris now had at his disposal a much more powerful bomber force equipped with navigation aids of some sophistication. However, just as he was to attempt a new campaign, he received a new directive. Such were the sinkings in the Atlantic that the bomber force was once more switched from Germany to naval targets, many of which were on the west coast of France. The main ports listed were Lorient, St Nazaire, Brest and La Pallice. What was unusual about the directive was that it gave War Cabinet approval for 'a policy of area bombing' of these targets. In other words French cities could now be flattened in the same way as those in Germany.[108] Harris reacted with fury at this directive and for once he was justified. The Germans had been constructing U-boat pens of such strength that no bomb possessed by Bomber Command in 1943 could penetrate them. Over 2,000 sorties were carried out against Lorient and hundreds against St Nazaire, with no result. As Harris in his characteristically blunt way noted, 'we did, in fact, uselessly devastate two perfectly good French towns' but destroyed no military targets.[109] In early March the whole venture was recognised as useless. Harris could turn back to Germany.

The one advantage this delay gave Harris was that by March he had even more bombers. At the beginning of the Battle of the Ruhr (his chosen target because it was within the range of Oboe) he had 600 bombers and by the end 800, and 80 per cent of these were four-engine heavy bombers. At last the British could mount a truly strategic attack against Germany. The first target was Essen and the Krupp works, bombed unsuccessfully for more than two years. This time it was different. The Mosquitos equipped with Oboe marked the target exactly, as did the follow-up Pathfinder force. High-explosive bombs were dropped first, blasting the roofs from buildings. Incendiaries in vast numbers followed to start fires in the unprotected factories and houses. Later high explosives with delayed-action fuses were dropped to create more havoc and complicate fire fighting and clearing up. A substantial portion of the Krupp works was hit and before it could be restored an even more devastating raid a few nights later reduced much of it to rubble.[110]

Over the next seven weeks one town after another in the Ruhr received the same type of treatment – Duisburg, Krefeld, Bochum, Düsseldorf,

Dortmund, Cologne, Wuppertal, Barmen, Gelsenkirchen.[111] In all about 34,000 tons of bombs were dropped.[112] The result was devastating: in the first quarter of 1943 steel production fell by 200,000 tons, resulting in an immediate cut in the ammunition programme. As Adam Tooze notes:

> After more than doubling the ammunition programme in 1942, ammu-
> nition production in 1943 increased by only 20 per cent. And it was not
> just ammunition that was hit. In the summer of 1943, the disruption in
> the Ruhr manifested itself across the German war economy in a so-called
> sub-components crisis. All manner of parts, castings and forgings were
> suddenly in short supply. And this affected not only heavy industry
> directly, but the entire armaments complex. Most significantly, the
> shortage of key components brought the rapid increase in Luftwaffe
> production to an abrupt halt. Between July 1943 and March 1944 there
> was no further increase in the monthly output of aircraft. For the arma-
> ments effort as a whole, the period of stagnation lasted throughout the
> second half of 1943. As Speer himself acknowledged, Allied bombing
> had negated all plans for a further increase in production. Bomber
> Command had stopped Speer's armaments miracle in its tracks.[113]

To add to the Germans' misery, in May the 'Dambusters' destroyed two large German dams, flooding a considerable portion of the surrounding countryside. Then in July Bomber Command, using a new invention (thin strips of aluminium foil called 'window') blinded the German night fighter radar defences, allowing the bomber stream to destroy Hamburg, Germany's second-largest city. This resulted in almost as many casualties in one week as the Luftwaffe had inflicted on Britain during the whole of the Blitz and caused 900,000 people to flee.[114]

There were other successes. The raid on the Peenemünde rocket facility in August set back the production of the V-2 rocket by at least two months.[115] Then in October Bomber Command destroyed the centre of Essen, 'de-housing' 123,800 people and putting back the production of Tiger tanks and 88-mm guns by many months.[116]

As Adam Tooze comments, the Ruhr was a 'choke point'; through it Germany was supplied with most of its coal and steel.[117] Many of Germany's most important enterprises depended on it. 'All were united in their dependency on the region for energy and to varying degrees by reliance on it for semifinished goods.'[118]

And yet from August the RAF loosened its grip on the Ruhr in search of other targets within Germany, especially Berlin. The explanation for this shift in priorities is not difficult to discern – none of the three key personnel conducting the bombing war was focused as a first priority on destroying the German war economy. Harris is the simplest to explain. He had a list of German cities that he wished to destroy because he thought that their destruction would end the war. When he deemed a city 'destroyed' (such as Essen) he crossed it off his list and Bomber Command moved on to other targets. This of course ignored evidence from the Blitz, where cities such as Coventry were for a time rendered useless but eventually came back into production. Harris had another argument: the more Bomber Command concentrated on a single area such as the Ruhr the more the Germans could concentrate their air defences there and the higher the cost of each raid might become.[119] This had some force; the Battle of the Ruhr had not been cheap for Bomber Command – from March to July 1943 when it was in full swing, just over 1,000 aircraft had been lost.[120] The fallacy was believing that Harris's new chosen targets would be less expensive to attack. Many of them lay beyond the range of his most reliable navigational aid (Oboe) and would be difficult to bomb with any precision. Other targets such as the German capital, which was the top of Harris's priority list, was surely likely to be as heavily defended as the Ruhr. Nevertheless, Harris's focus on Berlin was typically single-minded. He wrote to Churchill: 'We can wreck Berlin from end to end if the U.S.A.A.F will come in on it. It will cost us between 400–500 aircraft. It will cost Germany the war.'[121]

As for Portal, he was at one with Harris in seeking targets other than the Ruhr. From the Washington/Quebec Conference he cabled the Vice Chief of the Air Staff:

Without wishing to press Harris at all, I should be glad to have estimate of date by which he thinks heavy attacks on Berlin could begin. In present war situation attacks on Berlin on anything like Hamburg scale must have enormous effect on Germany as a whole.[122]

Portal was no doubt hoping that the destruction of Berlin would have a profound effect on German ability to withstand the invasion of Europe. He was certainly not focused on the Ruhr or the German economy. Perhaps he had for too long clung to the idea of the oil offensive and had been rather turned off economic targets by its total failure.

Churchill's lack of attention to the Ruhr possibly combined some of the reasoning of both Portal and Harris. For two years he had been promised that attacking specific targets (marshalling yards, oil, aircraft industry, transport) would bring Germany to its knees. All had proved chimerical. Nor had he ever viewed the air offensive in the all-encompassing war-winning terms that Harris and Portal had held to. He was quite content with Harris's Blue Books showing the devastation of one German city after another. This was the 'weight of the war' that he wished to bring home to Germany and which Harris at last was seeming to achieve. Perhaps he also thought that the mass bombing of Berlin (without accepting the premise that this action would win the war) was payback for the German bombing of London, about which he felt so keenly. He was always of the view that German society would never cope with the bombing with the same fortitude as had the British. Any evidence to that effect was always noted by him with some enthusiasm.[123] For him Harris's policy was enough. There would be no questioning about specific economic targets by the Prime Minister.

So, the Battle of Berlin started in November 1943 and in the main continued until March 1944. It was a failure. It terms of aircraft lost, the total for all targets in this period was just higher than the Battle of the Ruhr (1,117).[124] In terms of damage inflicted it fell far short of that earlier battle. Berlin, like London in 1940–1941 was just too big. In the main, its streets were wide, its buildings solid stone, both of which made the creation of a Hamburg-style firestorm unlikely. Also German night defences had improved. Flak guns were in greater number, but it was the change in German night fighter tactics that was of most importance. In 1943 the Kammhuber defences could be overwhelmed by a single stream of bombers and rendered irrelevant by window. The German night fighters were therefore freed from ground control and equipped with airborne radar. They could now seek out their own targets. They also discovered vulnerability in the bombers. An attack from below with upward-firing cannon was hard to combat and deadly in its effect. In the coming months these tactics were to prove deadlier than those directed by a ground controller.[125]

Turning to the raids on Berlin only, between November 1943 and March 1944 Harris mounted sixteen major attacks on the 'big city'. In all 9,100 sorties were flown and 536 aircraft lost (5.6 per cent of the force). There is no doubt that terrible damage was done. In just two raids (22/23 November 1943 and 28/29 January 1944) 350,000 people were 'de-housed'. On the 16/17 December 1943 the Berlin railway network was hit hard and supplies for the Russian front considerably delayed. In February 1944 many war industries were hit in the heaviest raid of all when 2,642 tons of bombs were dropped. Goebbels's ministry was also hit, as was Gestapo headquarters. Yet many raids, usually because of bad weather, scattered their bombs over a very wide area and did little damage. So Berlin remained as a going concern. Industry still functioned, people went to work, administration continued. Harris's boast had proved hyperbole, as Churchill certainly knew it would. Churchill, however, was satisfied – the capital of Germany had certainly felt the weight of the war.

After Berlin, Bomber Command, against the wishes of Harris and to some extent Churchill, was diverted to assist with the Normandy landings and subsequent operations. This will be discussed later (Chapter 26). The other event that dominated the first half of 1944 was the destruction of the German air force over Germany by the US Army Air Force. The Americans had entered the air war slowly. They were convinced that day bombing was a more fruitful approach and thus limited their first operations to short raids over France where they could be escorted by single-engine fighters. Later, when they ventured over Germany without escorting fighters they suffered horrific casualties. Later still they restored the balance with long-range Lightning and Thunderbolt fighters. Then a US–British aircraft, the Mustang was added. The Mustang (the P-51) had been built in the US for Britain, but the RAF found it underpowered and disappointing. They substituted a Rolls-Royce Merlin engine to it and converted it to the highest-performing long-range fighter of the war. Escorted by these planes (mainly Lightning and Thunderbolts in the first instance), the US air force shot the Luftwaffe out of the sky, reducing its fighter arm to the merest rump by the middle of the year. When the battle for Normandy ended in August 1944 Bomber Command was ready to return to Germany but, thanks to the

Americans, without the strong fighter opposition that had made Berlin and other distant cities such expensive targets.[126]

In September 1944 the strategic bomber forces were released from the control of General Eisenhower and returned to their respective commanders. The fiction that somehow the British and American efforts were under one commander (Portal) was quietly discarded. A new directive to the bombing forces was written, giving the German petroleum industry as top priority, followed by rail and communications, tank and motor transport production facilities.[127] There was, however, an additional clause: 'When weather or tactical considerations are unsuitable for operations against specific primary objectives, attacks should be delivered on important industrial areas, using blind bombing technique as necessary.'[128] The effect of this was of course to give Harris carte blanche; he could adhere to the priorities given to him or he could continue with area bombing. There was little doubt what Harris would do. He could hardly wait to get back to his list of cities. Churchill was also anxious 'for cracking on now to Germany'.[129] Area bombing resumed.

The Allied air forces were virtually unimpeded in their attacks on Germany for the last nine months of the war. In this period the American air forces and Bomber Command dropped three quarters of all the bombs dropped on Germany in the entire war.[130] What Bomber Command could now do is illustrated in the case of Essen. In two raids, on the nights of 23/24 October and 25/26 October, the city was attacked by 1,800 bombers, of which just twelve were lost. About 7,500 tons of bombs were dropped.[131] A new blind bombing device (G-H) allowed for great accuracy even when weather conditions were unfavourable, as they were in the second Essen raid.[132] The result of the attack was devastating. Essen, once the hub of the Ruhr system, ceased to exist as a centre for war production.

And so it went for city after city – Cologne became a ghost town with hardly any inhabitants by 1945; Düsseldorf, Duisburg, Gelsenkirchen, Nuremburg and many more were utterly destroyed as viable cities. Indeed, by 1945 most of the cities on Harris's original list had been obliterated and attacks began on smaller centres such as Bonn, Weimar and Würzburg.[133]

In some ways this was a waste of the power that Bomber Command now wielded. During 1943 and 1944, more experienced crew, better navigational aids and the withering of any real opposition had allowed it to bomb much more accurately than in the early years. It is doubtful whether Harris really grasped this fact or, if he did, whether he particularly cared. Churchill had been burnt too often by the extravagant claims made for the bomber force by both Harris and Portal to take the point on board.

Bomber Command could now achieve great precision in their operations. In September 1944 an entire section of the Dortmund–Ems Canal that supplied the Ruhr was breached, along a 6-mile stretch using 12,000-lb 'tallboy' bombs, although the bombing was carried out in seven-tenths cloud.[134] As for the Ruhr itself, in October 'the Allied air forces flew forty-two major attacks against eighteen bridges and viaducts linking the Ruhr to its hinterland. Ten were completely destroyed; three were damaged and therefore impassable, and only one partly passable.'[135] That was the end of the Ruhr as any kind of industrial hub. Further bombing saw the end of the Reichsbahn as a communications network. As the historian of this aspect of the bombing campaign has highlighted, 'the wheels stopped rolling'.[136] The German war economy ground to a halt.

* * * * *

In the end, then, the bomber did get through and accomplish many things. Before it destroyed the German war economy it distorted it. By the end of the war no fewer than 800,000 Germans were engaged in air defence. The enemy had been forced to deploy 14,000 heavy and 40,000 light anti-aircraft guns, when many of the heavier type were desperately needed as anti-tank weapons on the Eastern Front.[137] Moreover, the entire structure of the Luftwaffe had been distorted to produce fighters. In December 1944, 2,630 fighters were produced but just 262 bombers. In addition, 81 per cent of those fighters were in Germany facing the Allied bombers.[138] This certainly took some pressure off the Russians. Furthermore 30 per cent of the German optical industry and half of electronics output were involved in air defence, thus robbing other sections of the armed forces of these vital products.[139] Bomber Command therefore, although it fell far short of Harris's aim of winning the war single-handedly, played a useful role in destroying the Nazi regime.

Yet it is not so much for the pain inflicted upon the German economy that the bomber offensive is remembered, but for the pain and death inflicted on the German people. Much of this debate is encapsulated in the destruction of

Dresden in February 1945, where a firestorm killed 25,000 people and destroyed utterly the historic centre of the city. Much has been written about this incident, not all of it well informed. For one thing, Dresden was a major manufacturing centre. The Zeiss Ikon works alone, which made precision optical instruments for the military, employed 10,000 workers. In addition there were firms that made parts for V-1 and V-2 rockets, components for torpedoes, aircraft and naval turbines. The city was also a transport hub. Its railways ran to many destinations, but two of them were to the extermination camps of Auschwitz and Belzec.[140] The other point to stress about Dresden was that in February 1945 the war was not yet over and the Germans showed no sign of surrendering. In that sense it was a target like any other.

What of the other aspect of the bombing war – the indiscriminate nature of the destruction and the killing? Churchill had moments of unease about this. In 1943 he exclaimed about the bombing: 'Are we beasts? Are we taking this too far?'[141] He also reacted badly to the Dresden raid, though he helped originate the plan – and had to be sternly reminded of this by Portal, who was certainly not prepared for Bomber Command to be criticised for carrying out the Prime Minister's own policy.[142]

And, as we have seen, it had been Churchill who had driven British policy towards area bombing, and it was Churchill who was content with Harris's policy of destroying German cities because it was really also his own policy. After a brief flirtation with Bomber Command as a war-winning weapon, Churchill settled on this campaign for a number of reasons. The first was that between 1941 and 1944, apart from engaging a handful of German divisions in the Western Desert, bombing was the only way open to Britain to bring the war home to the German people and the Nazi regime. Stop bombing in those years and you practically stopped waging war. The addition of allies in the form of the Soviet Union in June and the United States in December 1941 only made the issue more acute. Britain, as potentially the weakest of the three Allies, had to be shown to be carrying its weight and bombing was the most obvious way of demonstrating it. This fact drove Churchill's policy and redeemed his pledge that Germany would be made to feel the weight of the war.

CHAPTER 25

BATTLE OF THE ATLANTIC

IN CHURCHILL'S FIRST ENCOUNTER with U-boats as First Lord (September 1939–May 1940) there were just not enough enemy submarines at sea to represent any kind of existential threat to Britain. This situation was widely held to have changed with the fall of France and the establishment of U-boat bases in the Biscay ports of Lorient, St Nazaire and others, which saved the U-boats a 500-mile journey around the north of Scotland and placed them directly athwart Britain's transatlantic trade routes. Yet the overall figures tell quite a different story. In the first two years of the war a total of 12,057 ships sailed for Britain from the US, Halifax in Nova Scotia and Freetown in West Africa. Of these just 291 or 2.4 per cent were sunk. A different set of statistics confirms this story. From September 1939 to October 1941, 900 convoys crossed the Atlantic, of which just nineteen lost six or more ships.[1] Why then do the document series during the war and especially the Churchill correspondence continually reiterate the importance of the U-boat war? Why also did Churchill set up first the Battle of the Atlantic Committee and then the Anti-U-Boat Committee, which lasted from 1941 to the end of the war and which he felt the need to chair himself?

The answers to these questions are not so difficult to find. Neither is it hard to understand the level of concern. During the war Britain had to import over half of its food, almost all its oil and a great deal of its war materiel from North America. This was the most abundant source of supply and it provided the fastest route. But by the second half of 1940 the transatlantic route had been reduced to one choke point. By that time all traffic had to come in via Northern Ireland and then head to the west coast ports of Glasgow or Liverpool. The route via the south of Ireland to the British south coast ports was just too close to the U-boat bases in France to remain viable.

Over the next three years shipping losses to U-boats were variable and to some extent unpredictable. So it is not surprising that various U-boat committees held most meetings in times of greatest sinkings, around March 1941 and March and April 1943.[2]

This did not mean that Churchill took his eye off the Atlantic during periods of quiescence. He realised very quickly that what Britain lacked in the Atlantic (and for defence against invasion) was escort craft and particularly destroyers. Here Churchill had not been dealt a strong hand. Only in 1939 was an emphasis in the British building programme placed on convoy escorts, and some of the ships built such as the Hunt Class destroyers were hardly serviceable in the heavy seas of the Atlantic.[3] It was this lack of escorts that led Churchill to push Roosevelt so hard for fifty old American destroyers. His first letter to the US President occurred just five days into his premiership and he kept up a barrage of correspondence on the subject for the remainder of the year.[4] But Churchill was to be disappointed. The destroyer deal was not finally done until September and by the end of the year just nine were in service. Then it was found that many were in such bad condition that they had to be virtually rebuilt to make them seaworthy. They were not therefore ready for invasion season in the autumn of 1940 and accordingly many escort craft which could have been on convoy duty were pinned to the south coast of England in an anti-invasion role.

Despite the shortage of escorts, Churchill insisted that warships be grouped into hunting packs to track down the U-boats. The experience of the First World War should have indicated to the Admiralty that this was a futile endeavour but Pound, among others, needed no prompting and had written such packs into the Admiralty war plans.[5] By August, however, Churchill was not satisfied and demanded a greater concentration of craft in the North-Western Approaches.[6] These endeavours proved futile: in the first two years of the war just one U-boat was despatched by these hunter-killer packs. The lesson of the First World War held good – the best way to destroy U-boats was to attract them to convoys and let the escorts do their job.

Convoy was extended during this period, but 1940 and the winter of 1941 still saw many independently routed ships. It was these ships that provided prime targets for many of the U-boat 'aces' (Prien, Kretschmer, Schepke) and others who were operating in the North-Western Approaches. An Admiralty survey of convoy losses versus ships sailing independently concluded that while just 1.7 per cent of convoyed ships were sunk by U-boats, 5.3 per cent of independent sailings were sunk. For slower independent ships (below 9 knots) the percentage was even higher.

These losses alarmed Churchill. On 26 August 1940 he brought to the attention of the War Cabinet that on just two days 70,000 tons of shipping had been sunk and asked what the Admiralty were doing about it. Pound replied that the enemy were using new tactics (they were not, the first 'wolf pack' tactics whereby convoys were attacked by 'packs' of U-boats was some months away) and assured the Prime Minister that 'suitable countermeasures were underway'.[7] What Pound had in mind here is not at all clear because little changed. In October Churchill noted that the losses – which he followed daily – were continuing but the only solution he put forward was to concentrate more destroyers in the area and await the delivery of the American craft.[8]

Very little was underway. The British had relied on ASDIC to detect submarines underwater but the Germans were well aware of its potential and nullified it during this period by mainly attacking on the surface at night. The other factor was that in the inter-war period the Admiralty had regarded trade protection as consisting of cruisers warding off attacks by enemy warships. They therefore neglected to train destroyer crew in the use of ASDIC, though this sensitive equipment required much skill to be used correctly.[9] Complacency rather than crisis was the prevailing attitude at the Admiralty in the first eighteen months of war.

That attitude changed rapidly in February and March 1941, when no fewer than 132 ships (685,000 tons) were lost in the North Atlantic.[10] Churchill's immediate response was to call a meeting of the Import Executive where various ministers involved in the import and transport of food and war materiel gathered to consider the U-boat problem.[11] As the sinkings intensified, he became dissatisfied with this forum and established a Battle of the Atlantic Committee, over which he would preside. This was a high-powered committee on which sat the service ministers, the Minister of Labour (Bevin) and the Minister of Aircraft Production (Beaverbrook) as well as the Ministers of Transport, Food, Supply, and service representatives from the Admiralty, the army and the RAF.[12]

Churchill issued to this body a Directive. In it he suggested that U-boats should be attacked at sea or in their building yards by bombing. The long-range Focke-Wulf fighters which were also sinking ships must be pursued by fighters or long-range Coastal Command aircraft based in Northern Ireland. Investigations were to be set in train to equip ships with aircraft that could be catapulted to counter the Focke-Wulfs. A trial could be made to sail faster ships (12 knots and above) independent of convoy in order to speed up deliveries and more anti-aircraft guns should be fitted to all ships. The repairing of merchant ships damaged by U-boats was to be expedited, as were methods of streamlining turnaround times in ports.[13]

There was some wisdom and some foolishness in all this. Independently routed craft were the U-boats' prime target; adding to their number would merely add to the toll. Bombing aircraft factories at this time was particularly futile when Bomber Command was struggling even to find cities such as Cologne and when they did find them, struggling to hit them. On the other hand, basing Coastal Command aircraft in Northern Ireland was a step in the right direction, as was speeding up ships' repair and port efficiency.

In any case, with this directive in mind, the first meeting of the Battle of the Atlantic Committee was held on 19 March 1941 with Churchill in the chair. It decided to fit out fifty merchant ships with fighters, construct aerodromes for Coastal Command in Northern Ireland, employ aircraft with longer ranges over the Atlantic, add more anti-aircraft guns to ships and increase efficiency in ports.[14] It cannot be said that the deliberations of the Committee had any marked effect on the situation in the North Atlantic. In April the sinkings fell to 260,000 tons but in May and June the figures were back to over 300,000 tons for each month.[15] One of the problems was that some of the positive measures taken, such as the provision of catapult fighters and the defensive arming of ships, took much longer to fit than first thought – for example, by June just three catapult aircraft were in place.[16] Also turnaround times in ports were slow to improve, relying as they often did on labour having to be transferred from one section of the war economy to another. As for bombing, the Committee was often told – no doubt by Harris, who assiduously attended the meetings – that good results in bombing Focke-Wulf factories were being achieved when in fact not a single factory had been hit.[17] Other measures were found actually to have caused harm. The decision to remove ships of 12 and 13 knots from convoy and sail them independently had merely resulted in more sinkings of this class of ship. At the end of May, Pound had to report to the Committee that this experiment had not proved successful and that such ships were to return to convoy as soon as possible.[18] Churchill resisted this measure and insisted that the experiment be given longer to play out.[19] However, by the end of June he was he was forced to admit that the trial had failed and that all ships of 15 knots and below were to return to convoy.[20]

From July 1941 the sinkings began to drop and for the remainder of the year were kept below 200,000 tons and in November and December were just over 50,000 tons.[21] What had gone right?

A number of factors had contributed to the reduction in sinkings in the latter half of 1941. First was the Battle of the Atlantic Committee decision, reluctantly agreed to by Churchill, to sail the 12- to 15-knot boats in convoy. Second, a number of the U-boat 'aces' were killed or captured in this period. Prien went down in unknown circumstances in late February, as did Kretschmer, rammed by the destroyer HMS *Walker* commanded by Captain Donald Macintyre. This same ship also rammed Schepke's U-boat, thus claiming two aces within a few months.[22] Third was the ability of Bletchley Park to read the U-boat Enigma. They had broken into it in March 1941 and from June were able to read it with a delay which ranged from three days to just a few hours. This enabled the Admiralty to re-route convoys around the increasing 'wolf packs' of submarines to safety.[23] Too much should not be read into this factor, however, because at the same time German Intelligence (B-Dienst) were reading the convoy codes and were re-routing their U-boats to intercept the re-routed convoys.[24] Fourth, during September there were twenty Liberators operating over the mid-Atlantic. These certainly acted as a powerful deterrent to U-boats attacking on the surface. Finally there was the fact that some U-boats had been withdrawn to northern waters to assist with Operation Barbarossa, the German invasion of Russia.

The role of aircraft in anti-submarine operations was not yet fully grasped in London. During October the number of Liberators available for mid-Atlantic patrols had been reduced to ten.[25] Churchill approved, wanting all long-range aircraft operating over the Atlantic redeployed to bomb Germany. Only the intervention of Pound ensured the retention of some aircraft.[26]

Shortly after this the Japanese attacked Pearl Harbor and Hitler declared war on the United States. This had an immediate effect on the Battle of the Atlantic. Doenitz had long anticipated American entry into the war and had developed a plan for it – Operation Drumbeat. In the new scenario five long-range U-boats (Type IX) would head for the eastern American seaboard to prey on coastal traffic. In short order this plan was soon supplemented by additional smaller boats because the U-boat captains found that the Americans had not introduced convoy and that the pickings were good. When in April an improvised 'bucket brigade' of daytime escorts was introduced, the U-boats merely moved south to Caribbean waters and the carnage continued there.[27] By the end of the six-month period – January to June 1942 – 360 ships had been sunk in American waters and fewer than twenty in the broader Atlantic.[28]

There was little that Churchill could do to remedy the situation, which was almost exclusively an American problem. This was doubly frustrating as the sinkings in US waters affected supplies to Britain. On 12 March 1942 Churchill told Hopkins that he was concerned about the number of tankers going down in the Caribbean. He pointed out that continued shortage of fuel would affect Britain's military operations and further reduce its imports.[29] All Roosevelt could offer was to run fewer convoys until the U-boats could be effectively dealt with, which would inevitably mean that British imports would be reduced.[30] It took until July for the Americans to introduce a thorough convoy system.

Churchill also had many other worries at this time, such as the collapse of Britain's Far Eastern Empire, and it is notable that during the period of carnage along the American coast the Battle of the Atlantic Committee met just twice – in February to discuss the import problem and in May when air operations in the protection of shipping were considered.[31] The latter discussion could have proved useful. Pound had already argued to the Defence Committee for a four-fold increase in Coastal Command aircraft for the war at sea.[32] However, the discussion was diverted to the provision of escort carriers for convoy, perhaps because of Churchill's well-known aversion to the diversion of bombers for this purpose or perhaps because there were no very-long-range (VLR) aircraft available at this time. As it happened, the only auxiliary carrier possessed by Britain (*Audacity*) had been sunk in December 1941, and with no others on the horizon the discussion stalled.[33]

In August 1942 the U-boats returned to the North Atlantic. Doenitz informed Hitler that continued action along the US east coast was unprofitable since the Americans had now adopted convoys and also constant air patrols. He therefore started to regroup his boats in the North Atlantic, increasing the numbers there from 124 in September 1942 to 157 by December.[34] The sinkings immediately went up, averaging from August through November just short of 500,000 tons per month and in November Doenitz achieved his goal of sinking over 700,000 tons of Allied shipping.[35] Churchill responded by resuscitating the Battle of the Atlantic Committee as the Anti-U-Boat Committee with much the same membership as previously but with Stafford Cripps as Vice-Chairman.[36]

An early matter considered by the Anti-U-Boat Committee – that of maintaining imports into Britain – weighed heavily on Churchill. So concerned was he that he conveyed his thoughts to the War Cabinet:

> The gravest danger which now confronts us is the U-Boat peril. We must expect attack by increasingly large numbers and spread over wider areas. The highest priority must therefore be accorded to vessels and weapons for use against the U-Boat. No construction of merchant shipbuilding below 1,100,000 tons or slowing down of repair work can be accepted.[37]

If shipping at this level was not maintained, Churchill suggested, imports would fall so low that Britain's war effort would be reduced and food rationing would have to be tightened. Indeed, total imports into the UK had already fallen significantly in 1942.[38] He thought they could fall no further without drastic consequences. In fact the matter was in hand: in Britain more land was being prepared for tilling, livestock numbers were increasing and many other import substitution measures were being implemented.[39] In addition, the Anti-U-Boat Committee had from the first realised the need to make British ports more efficient, and that work was being undertaken. In addition, British production of merchant ships and small convoy escorts did meet Churchill's requirements, never falling in the category of merchant shipping below 1,000,000 tons per quarter for most of the remainder of the war.[40] The real key to the question of imports and shipbuilding in fact lay with the United States. Churchill had alerted Roosevelt to the British problems with shipbuilding and imports, and on 30 November 1942 he received a welcome reply. Roosevelt considered that the relative need of merchant ships versus escort vessels would never be resolved but that 'In this case I believe we should have our cake and eat it too.'[41] He went on to tell Churchill that the US intended to build 18 million tons of merchant shipping in 1943 and that this total would almost certainly be raised to 20 million tons 'after re-examination'. He had also analysed the import figure for Britain in the current year and had concluded that imports could be raised to 27 million tons in 1943. He concluded reassuringly:

> I am well aware of the concern with which your government faces the serious net losses in tonnage to your merchant fleet. It is a net loss which persists, and I think we must face the fact that it may well continue through all of next year. I therefore want to give you the assurance that from our expanding fleet you may depend on the tonnage necessary to meet your import program.
>
> Accordingly, I am instructing our Shipping Administration to allocate through the machinery of the Combined Shipping Adjustment Board enough dry-cargo tonnage out of the surplus shipbuilding to meet your imports, the supply and maintenance of your armed forces and other services essential to maintaining the war effort of the British Commonwealth.[42]

In one sense this message heralded the doom of the U-boat campaign. However many tons of shipping Doenitz sank, he would be overwhelmed by the American shipbuilding effort. Early in the war the German admiral had calculated that he would have to sink 700,000 tons of shipping per month to be successful. The British had more gloomily set the doomsday figure at 600,000 tons.[43] All of this fell away in the face of US shipbuilding. Churchill must have been grateful for Roosevelt's assurances, even if they did place the British shipbuilding effort in some kind of perspective.

While American dockyard workers were determining naval strategy, the Anti-U-Boat Committee continued its work. The question of air cover for convoys arose in its first meeting. Pound was well aware of Churchill's reluctance to divert bombers to Coastal Command. He had unsuccessfully fought a six-month campaign to strengthen patrols over the Bay of Biscay at the expense of Bomber Command.[44] Now he saw a different problem and offered a different solution. He told the Committee that:

> The air had been a great help in meeting the U-boat menace; but there
> was a blind spot in the centre of the North Atlantic where no air cover
> was provided, and it was here that our heaviest losses occurred. Aircraft
> with an overall range of 2,500 miles would be needed to cover this area.[45]

Pound also probably steered the Committee away from using Bomber Command aircraft for this purpose because at the end of this discussion there was a consensus that American Liberator aircraft provided a better solution than modified Halifaxes or Lancasters.[46]

Pound proposed that Britain obtain more Liberators from the US. He also suggested that suitable merchant ships could be converted to primitive aircraft carriers (later known as MAC ships) to carry four or five aircraft to cover the air gap. The appropriate ministries were to report to future meetings on these issues.[47]

The idea of MAC ships was pushed forward but seemingly not with any urgency. The bottleneck seemed to be the provision of arrestor gear for deck landings, but no one appeared to have a solution for this rather trifling matter or took it upon themselves to see what could be done.[48] Thus the first MAC ship (*Empire MacAlpine*) was not ready until April 1943 and others did not come along until the crisis of the U-boat war had passed.[49]

The other solution to the 'air gap' problem – the conversion of American Liberators for VLR work – was strangely bypassed in the next meeting. The matter of VLR aircraft was discussed but in relation to a campaign to attack U-boats at the 'choke point' of the Bay of Biscay. Here it was noted that converted Whitleys, Wellingtons and Hudsons could patrol the 'inner

Biscay zone' but that Catalina flying boats and Liberators were needed for the 'outer Biscay zone'.[50] Of the mid-Atlantic air gap and the need for Liberators to patrol it there was not a mention.

The Committee was soon back on track. On 18 November Pound suggested that the thirty-nine Liberators in Coastal Command should largely be converted to the VLR type and should be concentrated in two squadrons so placed as to cover the mid-Atlantic air gap.[51]

Then the whole debate on the Atlantic air gap just faded out. The Committee considered all manner of anti-U-boat options – from the fitting of low-level bomb sights or the H2S radar in Coastal Command aircraft, to the effectiveness of 30-lb shaped-charge bombs against 100-lb bombs.[52] When they turned to an air gap, it was not the one in the mid-Atlantic but a 'gap' around Cape Town. In November 1942 U-boats had inflicted grievous losses in this area, sinking the troop ships *Oronsay*, *Orcades* and the *Duchess of Atholl*, luckily with very few casualties.[53] What is interesting in this context is the amount of time the Committee devoted to air protection for these convoys in this area while completely ignoring the losses in the central Atlantic.

The question of modifying what Liberators that could be obtained from the US did not return to the Committee until 30 December and then only to inform them that there were delays in the process due to unexpected weaknesses in the undercarriage. Then it transpired that these aircraft were anyway not for anti-submarine duties but for Ferry Command for freight and passenger carriage.[54]

The last meeting chaired by Churchill before he departed to the Casablanca Conference took place on 6 January 1943 and was attended by Roosevelt's representative, Averell Harriman. What is outstanding about this meeting is its irrelevance to the sinkings in the Atlantic, especially as it was known that Churchill would be absent for some time. The sinkings were continuing, though at a lower rate in part because the U-boats had been directed towards the Allied landings in North Africa (Operation Torch). It was time to assess what methods to deal with them were in place, what methods were on the horizon and what was the state of play. No such assessment took place. There were long technical discussions on the type of radar to be fitted to Coastal and Bomber Command aircraft, only for it to be revealed at the end of the meeting that no sets at all were yet available owing to 'non-delivery and technical troubles'. There were the usual ramblings about anti-submarine bombs. When finally it was mentioned that concentrations of U-boats were forming west of the Bay of Biscay and off Newfoundland, the only response was to 'invite' the Admiralty to submit a report on the effect of the bombing of the Biscay ports and to submit proposals on the efficacy of area bombing these bases.[55]

This last item was to lead to one of the most futile endeavours of the war. The navy were concerned about the fate of a recent convoy (ONS 154) from Liverpool to New York. During the night of 28/29 December 1942, ten U-boats fell in with this slow convoy. Over the next twenty-four hours they sank fourteen ships out of forty-six, a total of almost 70,000 tons of shipping. It was one of the 'half-dozen worst North Atlantic convoy disasters of the war'.[56] It led Pound to respond to the Anti-U-Boat Committee's 'invitation' by requesting, not increased air cover for convoys, but the bombing of the U-boat pens in the Biscay ports. Churchill had at first resisted this call, noting that he wanted the bomber effort against Germany increased and that 'in spite of U-boat losses [by which he presumably meant shipping losses to U-boats], this should have first place in our air effort'.[57] He might also have noticed that previous bombing attempts against these targets had proved futile. The matter was then discussed by the War Cabinet who had before them Pound's paper 'asking for the area bombing of the U-Boat bases in the Bay of Biscay and [that] a direction [be given] that these targets should be given priority in the coming months'.[58] There was little discussion, there being 'general agreement that the arguments in the First Lord's Paper demonstrated that area bombing of these ports was likely to have important results in hampering the operation of the enemy's U-boats: and that the operation should therefore be carried out'.[59] The meeting therefore agreed that area bombing of the Biscay ports should take place in the coming months, the only proviso being that the French people in the coastal areas be issued with some kind of general warning.[60] As Churchill told Eden: 'We should warn these ports by leaflets and then do our utmost to make them uninhabitable.'[61]

During the next few months Bomber Command and the USAAF did their best to fulfil Churchill's wishes. In January 1943, 688 heavy bombers pounded St Nazaire, Lorient, Brest and Bordeaux with 1,440 tons of bombs. In February the raids were even heavier with 1,407 heavies dropping

3,452 tons. In this month Lorient alone received over 3,000 tons of bombs.[62] The cities under attack were indeed flattened. In addition mines were laid off the Biscay coast and anti-submarine patrols increased. It was all in vain. The bombing of the bases destroyed not a single U-boat. The mines probably sank one, and the anti-submarine patrols nil. The entire effort was an enormous waste of time and resources. It is indeed staggering that no analysis was carried out in an attempt to match bomb penetration with the thickness of the concrete used in the submarine pens. Had such work been carried out, it would have been that the air forces just did not have bombs with the explosive power to penetrate the pens. Harris of course warned that the effort would prove a fiasco but his single-mindedness on dropping explosive objects only on German targets was so well known (especially by Churchill) that his opinion (which was correct in this case) was no doubt discounted.

While this campaign was being carried through, Churchill and the Chiefs of Staff were in Casablanca. There the conference decided that war against the U-boats was to be 'a first charge' on the resources of the Allies, and they allocated eighty Liberators for the purpose of closing the air gap.[63] There was a general confidence at the conference that the U-boats could be beaten. For example, at a meeting of the Combined Chiefs of Staff on 23 January Roosevelt noted that 'the shipping situation is bound to improve during the coming year as a result of nearly doubling the construction programme and by reason of the more effective anti-submarine measures which are to be taken.'[64] There was no dissenting voice to his statement. Discussion quickly moved on to the invasion of Sicily, operations in the Pacific and the build-up of American troops in Britain for the cross-Channel invasion. No one in the discussion mentioned that this operation might be affected by the activities of the U-boats.[65]

After Casablanca, Churchill embarked on an extensive Middle Eastern tour. He visited the Eighth Army in Tripoli, engaged in extensive (but futile) talks with the Turks in Adana and then visited Cyprus and Cairo. He did not in fact return to Britain until 7 February. During this period, although he was in constant contact with Attlee and the War Cabinet, he never once mentioned the war in the Atlantic. Nor does it seem that he once contacted Cripps, who had chaired the Anti-U-Boat Committee during this time.

On 11 February Churchill made a statement on the war situation to the House of Commons in which he devoted a reasonable amount of time to the U-boat war. He started starkly enough:

> The losses we suffer at sea are very heavy, and they hamper us and delay our operations. They prevent us from coming into action with our full strength, and thus they prolong the war, with its certain waste and loss and all its unknowable hazards.[66]

But then he went on in much more positive fashion, noting that there was no need to exaggerate the danger of the U-boats and that much progress was being made against them. He pointed to the massive US shipbuilding programme, the increasing provision of escorts and air support and the fact that various methods of destroying U-boats had steadily improved in the course of the last year. He ended by assuring the House that he could guarantee that the shipping position would definitely be better by the end of 1943 than it had been at the beginning.[67]

Perhaps Churchill's confidence came from the revelation that Bletchley Park had at last broken into the U-boat Enigma (the 1943 version of the German U-boat code was called Shark) that had kept them at bay since February 1942. The first break came in December and from then on Shark was read with some regularity. But it would be unwise to ascribe the success against the U-boats entirely to Bletchley. For one thing, there were often periods during the bitter convoy battles (February to May 1943) when Shark could not be read. And on some occasions where it was read there were delays of seventy-two hours, during which the position of U-boats could change by some 700 miles or more.[68] Moreover, at the same time that Shark was being read, the German Intelligence service (B-Dienst) were reading the British convoy codes, so that a re-routing of a convoy as a result of Shark might also result in the re-routing of the U-boats by B-Dienst. Only in April 1943 did the Admiralty realise (from decrypted Shark) that their own codes were being read, and changes were not introduced until June.[69] Thus during the 'critical period' the codebreakers were well matched and, although the break in Enigma overall probably favoured the British, other factors that caused the defeat of the U-boats were also in play.

As far as the Anti-U-Boat Committee was concerned, one of these factors – the provision of VLR aircraft – was proving unexpectedly difficult to bring to fruition. The Liberator was generally seen to be the key to closing the air gap, but all Liberators delivered after 1941 had a lesser range than the original model and had to undergo extensive modifications. For reasons that remain obscure, all modifications were carried out at just one location: Prestwick in Scotland. By the end of January 1943 the Committee could report of the thirty-eight slated for modification just three had been completed.[70] The Committee was also informed that there was a two-month gap between aircraft being allocated to the British by the US and their delivery. No solution to this time gap ever seems to have been found.[71] Then it was discovered that the British airfields in Iceland (vital for covering the gap) were not long enough to allow a Liberator fully laden with fuel to take off. Eventually these aircraft seem to have been moved to American Icelandic airfields which had longer runways.[72] Operational issues also impinged on the use of Liberators. In February it was discovered that some patrols were merely making sweeps of the Atlantic in 'areas of probability' instead of closely patrolling convoys where U-boat sightings were more or less a certainty.[73] This was rectified, but little progress was made in speeding up the deliveries to Coastal Command of VLR Liberators. In April Portal could only note that of the eighty aircraft allotted at Casablanca, just forty-five British and eight US Liberators were in operation over the Atlantic.[74]

Meanwhile a return to a second offensive over the Bay of Biscay threatened. The new head of Coastal Command, Air Marshal Slessor, produced a note signed by him, Pound and the US representative on the Anti-U-Boat Committee, Admiral Stark, asking Washington to provide more aircraft for the Bay Patrols. The authors concluded that a decisive blow might be struck there that would cause the entire U-boat campaign to wither.[75] Their letter was addressed to Washington because there was no possibility that Churchill would allow British aircraft to be taken from the mid-Atlantic. As early as 17 March he intervened on this issue: 'The Prime Minister said he agreed that aircraft employed on convoy protection should be given priority over those required for Bay of Biscay offensive patrols which, statistics showed, paid a much smaller dividend.'[76] And at a later meeting he added:

It was clear that the maximum number of aircraft L.R. and V.L.R. must be given to the protection of convoys. As a result of measures taken six months ago the flow of these aircraft were now increasing, and with the longer hours of daylight, opportunities for attacking U-boats in the vicinity of convoys should also be increasing.[77]

But of course Churchill was never one to deprecate offensive action and he went on to say that he also thought that the number of aircraft in the Biscay patrols should be increased but not at the expense of work in the mid-Atlantic or, of course, of the Bomber Command offensive. If additional aircraft were needed, they must be sought from the Americans. The fate of the Anti-U-Boat Committee's note to Washington was rapid. The Americans were not interested in a renewed offensive in the Bay. No additional aircraft for that campaign would in fact be provided until October 1943, by which time the U-boat offensive had been defeated.[78] Churchill's priorities were always clear: Bomber Command always came first, then the mid-Atlantic air gap, then (a poor third) the Bay offensive. The Admiralty's priorities were different: the Bay offensive first, mid-Atlantic gap second and Bomber Command third. But there was never any chance that the Prime Minister would deviate from his policy and, whatever its failings, he at least identified the mid-Atlantic gap as being a more important issue than the Bay offensive.

Of course the mid-Atlantic air gap was not the only issue discussed by the Anti-U-Boat Committee. As they knew, sinkings in the North Atlantic had been going up all year – from 173,000 tons in January 1943 to 289,000 tons in February to a massive 476,000 tons in March. And in March, if losses in other areas were included, the amount of Allied tonnage that went to the bottom was close to 700,000 tons.[79] In the period January–February the Allies had added over 1 million of tons of merchant ships but the margin was getting rather too close for comfort.

One solution was to sail more convoys of a larger size more often. As it was known that most U-boat wolf packs attacked from ahead and could generally only mount one attack before the convoy passed, it was thought that a larger convoy could also get through before the packs could mount second or third attacks.[80] This was done and it is noticeable that while convoys sailing from February 1943 onwards varied in size, the trend was generally upwards.[81] It was also found that with larger convoys economies were possible with escorts. As one escort commander noted, one apparent objection to larger convoys – that they would need correspondingly larger escorts to defend them – was 'met by the elementary mathematical fact that, whereas the area of a convoy is proportional to the square of its dimensions, the length of perimeter to be occupied by the escorts is proportionate only to the length of the radius.'[82]

The next move was to sail more convoys. The transatlantic convoy frequency was reduced from ten days in January–February to eight days in March, six in April and five in May. This rather obvious move had the expected result that more ships got through to Britain more often.

A more drastic solution was reducing the amount of new merchant tonnage built in favour of naval escorts for the convoys. No doubt the British could only take this step because of the enormous size of the US merchant shipbuilding programme, but take it they did. In April 1943 they decided that 93,000 tons of merchant ships would be sacrificed in order to construct twenty more escort vessels by the end of 1944.[83] In the circumstances facing them, this proved a sensible decision.

A further solution, like the Liberators, had been long in gestation but in this instance largely outside the discussions of the Anti-U-Boat Committee. It was realised at a relatively early date by the Western Approaches Command which largely controlled the anti-U-boat war, that by no means all convoys were attacked. What if surplus warships could be formed into hunting groups and come to the aid of convoys that *were* assailed by U-boats? The problem for most of the war was that there were no such surplus warships. The formation of these Support Groups, as they were called, had to wait for the shipbuilding programmes of Britain and the US to come to fruition, and this did not happen until early 1943. Indeed, in early March of that year Pound was complaining that only one Support Group was operating, and that was from the United States.[84] Yet by the end of the month no fewer than five Support Groups had appeared in the Atlantic. Two comprised vessels from the Western Approaches Command that were surplus to convoy escort duties because of the larger size of convoys. Two more comprised destroyers taken from guarding the heavy ships of the Home Fleet. The fifth was an American group which operated out of the Western Approaches during the crisis period in late March.[85]

Most of these groups contained an escort carrier, a small craft which could launch and land up to six aircraft. Four of these had been provided to the Admiralty by the US as early as August 1942 but their use in operations had been scandalously delayed by a plethora of small, largely unneeded modifications. They were then used not in the mid-Atlantic where the need was palpable but in the Torch landings and in Arctic convoys – an indication that the Admiralty had not quite got their priorities in order. Indeed, only a threat by the Americans to withdraw them from British service so that they could be used by the US for their own trade protection purposes saw them appear in the mid-Atlantic.[86]

One important factor on the Allied side was 'the war of gadgets'. We have noted that the Anti-U-Boat Committee had many discussions concerning ship and airborne radar and the optimum size of anti-U-boat depth charges and bombs, and many other matters.[87] These were all important additions to the Battle of the Atlantic and they had a cumulative effect. By spring 1943 many ships had HF/DF (high-frequency direction-finding) equipment. At the beginning of the war such equipment existed only in large land-based towers. These gave a reasonable picture of where U-boats were in the Atlantic and how many. The miniaturisation of the equipment which allowed it to be carried onboard ship obviously meant that much more accurate readings about the proximity of U-boats could be obtained and warships immediately sent to the location to deal with them. The same factors applied to airborne radar. Its miniaturisation in the form of centimetric radar allowed it to be placed on aircraft and greatly added to the accuracy with which aircraft could attack diving or recently submerged U-boats. Other equipment included 'hedgehogs': depth charges that could be thrown from the bows of ships, which gave U-boats less time to crash dive before they were attacked.[88] And by May 1943 some aircraft on escort carriers were equipped with rockets and others with homing torpedoes. The longer the war went on, the further advanced the Allies became in the battle of the gadgets.

The other factor was training. Admiral Max Horton took over Western Approaches Command in 1942 and was in a position to train crews in anti-U-boat warfare. The sailors going into battle from then on certainly had a clearer idea of how U-boats operated and their likely patterns of attack. They also, in the main, had newer and faster ships with which to attack them and – combined with the new detection methods – made life increasingly unbearable or indeed unliveable for the U-boat crews.[89]

The outcome of all these factors in the U-boat war in the North Atlantic in the spring of 1943 can be seen from the statistics. In February even before the arrival of the Support Groups and escort carriers, the rate of U-boat kills had increased. Over the next three months the kill rate was sustained.[90] May, however, was disastrous for the U-boat campaign. In that month forty-four U-boats were destroyed, almost 90 per cent of these (thirty-six) being in the Atlantic. Aircraft could claim eighteen kills, escort ships eleven and a combination of both – five (and two disappeared). In one month Doenitz lost around one third of the U-boat fleet that was at sea and approximately two months' production. The order went out from Lorient for the U-boats to abandon the North Atlantic, although in June nine more were lost in the process of withdrawal. Not that the U-boats abandoned the war. July 1943 saw their second highest losses in a single month of the war when no fewer than thirty-eight went down. But they did not go down in the North Atlantic; only three or four of those losses occurred there – most were lost off the coast of South America and in the Caribbean as they sought easier prey. Even in these climes, however, they were hunted down, nine being lost in those waters, almost all to aircraft.[91]

* * * * *

That in effect was the end of the U-boat campaign as any kind of danger to the successful prosecution of the war. The U-boats continued to sink ships but in 1944 the total dropped to 600,000 tons, which was as much as they had sunk in the four months in 1939 at the beginning of the war. Moreover, U-boats continued to be sunk – 78 from August to December 1943, 234 in 1944 and 136 in the last months of the war in 1945. While Doenitz could hardly alter the outcome (the genuine submarines of the Type XXI and XXII U-boats that could stay submerged for long periods and reach speeds of 17 knots underwater came along too late to have any impact), he could make life uncomfortable and worse for Allied sailors until the last day of the war.

Let us now look at the other side of the equation and examine convoy losses. In the 'danger period', January to May 1943, there were eighty-six convoys that brought war materiel of all kinds and food to Britain.[92] Just under half (thirty-eight) had contact with U-boats. Of these thirty-eight, nine had no losses, leaving just twenty-nine or almost exactly 33 per cent of convoys encountering U-boats and suffering losses. Or to reverse the figures, at the height of the U-boat war, two convoys in three got through with no losses at all.[93]

Despite these figures, which rather modify the conventional view of the Battle of the Atlantic, Churchill was right to pay it close attention. As noted earlier, the Atlantic was the link with the outside world across which food and materiel had to pass if Britain was to prosecute the war. The situation after the fall of France was precarious because, for the first time, the U-boats were perilously close to the main British trade routes. Churchill's moments of greatest concern probably came in 1940 when 1.8 million tons of shipping went down and in 1941 when the total was 2.4 million. In this period the United States had not entered the war and convoy escorts were in extremely short supply due to the woefully inadequate building programme of the appeasement governments in the 1930s. Hence Churchill's desperation to wring fifty obsolete destroyers from the Americans and his frustrations when they proved so slow to supply them.

Yet, as Christopher Bell has said, 'throughout 1941 and 1942, Churchill routinely deprived Coastal Command of aircraft in order to enhance the striking power of Bomber Command.'[94] And, while the aircraft available in these years would not have had the range to close the air gap, they could have at least provided some cover for convoys as they neared the Western Approaches. Likewise, although they were not yet equipped with anti-U-boat measures such as centimetric radar or depth charges with the appropriate settings, their very presence must have prevented at least some U-boat attacks by keeping the boats submerged, a sub-optimal way to engage convoys.

Churchill had information that perhaps explains his decision to direct the bombers over Germany rather than over the Atlantic. He knew that most convoys got through to Britain un-attacked. He also knew that even when convoys were attacked most ships made it to port unscathed. In fact, throughout the war just 3 per cent of ships that sailed in convoy were sunk and only on a few occasions were there multiple sinkings of ships in convoy. Indeed, of the thousands of convoys sailed, in just eleven sinkings ran to double figures.[95] The Prime Minister was therefore concerned with convoy losses but only sporadically so.

After the US entry into the war he continued in this mode. His main concern, that imports be kept up, stemmed only in part from the depredations of the U-boats. The extensive military operations undertaken by Britain in 1942 and 1943 in North Africa and then Sicily and Italy drained imports away from Britain. Yet Churchill never gave any consideration to slowing these ventures down – indeed his continual stance was that they be speeded up.

With America in the war, the battle for tonnage was won. Churchill's only concerns were that the Americans would send to the Pacific ships that he wanted in the Atlantic to carry goods and men to Britain. He need not have worried: Roosevelt, as he repeatedly told Churchill, had the resources to do both.

Certainly the crisis in the Atlantic from November 1942 to May 1943 caught Churchill's attention, and the reconstituted Anti-U-Boat Committee met regularly and discussed many of the issues, including technical ones, that saw the eventual demise of the U-boats. Even in this period there is evidence that Churchill's interest had peaks and troughs, rather like the U-boat sinkings. On 9 January 1943 he relinquished the chair of this Committee to Cripps while he attended Casablanca and other conferences concerned with Mediterranean strategy; he did not resume as chair until late March, when the crisis in the U-boat war had been running for many weeks. During that time he had made no concerted effort to keep abreast of the war in the Atlantic, addressing it on just four occasions in the documents, and when he resumed the chair there were no drastic measures taken, no wholesale reassignment of bomber forces to the Atlantic. Indeed, Churchill did not seem to notice that the Admiralty was dragging its feet over escort carriers or that Coastal Command was not proceeding with the modification of Liberator aircraft in any optimal way. In any case, no prod was given by the Prime Minister to either organisation to get on with it.

In short, it seems that Churchill gave the Battle of the Atlantic the attention it deserved: intense at times of crisis, sporadic at other times. After all, it was not as though this battle was all he had to think about during 1942 and 1943.

CHAPTER 26

NORMANDY

CHURCHILL WAS BY NO means a willing convert to a landing in France in 1944. As he made clear to Roosevelt, he feared the power of the German army and worried about the ability of the Allies to undertake such a perilous operation in the teeth of a German defence system built up over a number of years. Nor he could he, in this instance, look to Brooke for reassurance – it is clear from Brooke's diaries that he held much the same reservations about the operation, which was, after all, the reason he held on to the Mediterranean strategy in the face of American intransigence.

When he was convalescing in Morocco in December 1943, Churchill received the latest Overlord plan. This was produced by the Chief of Staff, Supreme Allied Commander (COSSAC) planners, a small organisation which had been given the task of preparing a preliminary plan for the eventual Supreme Commander of the operation. The planners worked under extreme difficulty: they were forced to estimate both what troops would be available and when the operation might take place. The iteration of the plan which Churchill received in December 1943 suggested a three-division landing on a fairly narrow front in Normandy in the spring of 1944. Churchill did not approve. He thought the attack under-weighted, the front of landing too narrow and the build-up of forces after the landing too slow.

As it happened, Montgomery, who had been appointed overall ground commander for Overlord, called in on Churchill on his way home to Britain to take up his appointment. The Prime Minister showed him the plan, accompanied no doubt, with suitably discouraging words about it. According to the Prime Minister's Military Secretary, Monty and his staff retired to his room and rewrote the plan, increasing the initial punch to five divisions plus two or three airborne divisions.[1]

Next morning he showed the revised plan to Churchill accompanied by these notes:

    (a) The initial landings must be made on the widest possible front.
    (b) Corps must be able to develop their operations from their own beaches, and other Corps must NOT land *through* those beaches.
    (c) British and American landings must be kept separate.
    (d) After the initial landings, the operations must be developed in such a way that a good port is secured quickly for the British and for the American forces. Each should have its own port or group of ports.[2]

More important than these details (although they all made perfect sense) was Montgomery's super-confident manner. Churchill now had a plan in which he could believe, and an army commander who was assuring him that, as long as he was in control, the plan would succeed. From then until D-Day Churchill might express dissatisfaction with aspects of the plan but Montgomery was always on hand to reassure him. Montgomery's arrogance has often been noted but in this case it served a good cause – to convert the Prime Minister to Overlord.

On his return to Britain, Churchill immediately set up an Overlord Committee, over which he presided.[3] There is no need to go through the minutes of these meetings in any detail – they mainly dealt with technical matters such as the various components of the artificial (Mulberry) harbours, rather than problems strategic or tactical.[4] The Mulberries were indeed a potentially important matter, the attempt to capture a port intact at Dieppe in 1942 having failed disastrously. However, operations were now so large, the interlocking parts so complex, that it was almost impossible for those outside the military to have any detailed input. In the smaller encounters of 1941 and 1942 Churchill could intervene at a quite detailed level over such things as the place of artillery on the battlefield. These matters were now beyond him.

His responsibility was to pick leaders in whom he could have confidence. Montgomery in many ways was not Churchill's type of general at all: he could be ponderous rather than dashing, cautious and rather risk averse. But for Churchill in early 1944 he was the general who had won all his battles. That always went a long way to securing political approval.

There was one matter of great importance to Overlord over which Churchill was not prepared to stand aside, and that was the bombing operations which accompanied Montgomery's military plan. On 25 March 1944 Eisenhower met with a collection of air force barons to decide on what specific help Allied air superiority could be to Overlord. He was presented with two plans. The first, delivered by the Deputy Supreme Commander (Tedder), suggested that the air forces concentrate on railway targets and particularly marshalling yards, in order to interdict the Normandy battle-field and prevent the rapid movement of German reserves against the bridgehead. The second, presented by Lieutenant-General Carl Spaatz (C-in-C of the American Eighth Airforce) suggested that oil targets inside Germany should be the focus. He argued that they were few in number, vulnerable to daytime attack now that the German fighters could be dealt with by US long-range fighters, and that all aspects of the German war machine were dependent on regular supplies of oil. Eisenhower decided on Tedder's scheme (which became known as the Transportation Plan) on the grounds that an attack on oil could not yield results rapidly enough to affect the initial landings.[5]

Portal, who agreed with Eisenhower's decision, passed on the results of the meeting to Churchill a few days later, adding:

> There is one point which I should mention to you now. In the execution of this plan very heavy casualties among civilians living near the main railway centres in occupied territory will be unavoidable. Eisenhower realises this and I understand that he is going to propose that warnings should be issued to all civilians living near railway centres advising them to move. I hope you will agree that since the requirements of Overlord are paramount the plan must go ahead after due warning has been given.[6]

Portal was to be disappointed. Churchill asked for an estimate of casualties from his Military Secretary and received the following:

The plan involves attacks on approximately 74 railway centres in France and Belgium. The Ministry of Home Security have estimated that unless evacuation reduced the number of civilian population living near the targets, between 80,000 and 160,000 casualties might be caused by the bombing, of which a quarter would be killed.[7]

Churchill wrote 'Cabinet Monday' on Ismay's note.[8] This was not good enough for Portal, who told Churchill that he required 'immediate' authorisation to bomb targets in France. He had selected three 'least likely to cause heavy civilian casualties'. Reluctantly, Churchill gave permission for just these three sites to be bombed but he warned Portal that any decision to go further must be made by the War Cabinet.[9]

The War Cabinet met on 3 April. Portal put to them the Transportation Plan, along with the likely number of French casualties. Churchill spoke against it, noting that there had been some division in the expert opinion on the plan. Eden was even more forthright. He said that the good repute of the RAF in occupied countries would be lost if the attacks were carried out. He worried that help with sabotage from French railwaymen would cease and that Britain's reputation in France and Belgium would slip vis-à-vis Russia, which might affect detrimentally its place in the post-war world. The end result was that the matter was to be considered by the Defence Committee and in the meantime to restrict raids to areas where the fewest casualties might be caused.[10]

After the meeting Churchill wrote to Eisenhower outlining the War Cabinet's concerns and suggesting the plan would bring 'much hatred upon the Allied Air Forces'.[11] Eisenhower's reply gave little comfort. He told Churchill that the weight of air opinion was in favour of the plan and that indeed it was considered essential to the success of the landings. He thought the casualty estimates 'grossly exaggerated' and that perhaps De Gaulle might be brought in to explain the position to the French people.[12]

The Defence Committee met the following evening. It was well attended. In addition to the COS and the service ministers (P.J. Grigg, Sinclair, A.V. Alexander), Attlee, Oliver Lyttelton (Supply), Eden, Tedder, Air Vice-Marshal Bufton, Bottomley (Deputy Chief of the Air Staff) and Dr Solly Zuckerman (a scientist working for the Air Ministry, whose reports had formed the basis of the Transportation Plan) were present. Generally the discussion fell into two groups: the airmen spoke in favour of the plan and the politicians against. Of the latter Attlee was the most resolute: 'Mr. Attlee said that he was not satisfied that the results likely to be achieved outweighed what we should lose from the antagonism aroused in the French by heavy civilian casualties involved. He did not consider the plan should be adopted.'[13]

Among military ranks Brooke was the exception. He said:

that in view of the terrific amount of destruction which would have to be carried out before the capacity of the French railways would be reduced sufficiently to have a serious effect on enemy military moves, he doubted if the success likely to be achieved by bombing justified the effort which would be entailed.[14]

Attlee's and Brooke's opinions weighed heavily with Churchill, who insisted that the plan be reviewed by the Overlord planners with a view to lessening casualties and taking into account the views expressed.[15]

Meanwhile the bombing of French railway targets went on. But in the absence of agreement from the British, the targets were, to Eisenhower's frustration, much constrained. On 13 April he announced that he had finally got the go-ahead from Portal to implement the entire plan – but he was misinformed.[16] Portal was still being asked by Churchill for figures on French casualties and on the 19th the whole matter came once again before the Defence Committee.[17]

It was soon clear that no one had changed their mind. Portal began on an optimistic note, saying that the casualties for the past week had been less than 50 per cent of those estimated. Tedder supported him and said that early indications showed that the attacks were having a considerable effect. Churchill was not persuaded. He thought the casualties still too high and that the disregarded alternative – the oil plan – offered greater prospects of success. Then A.V. Alexander, Grigg, Lyttelton and Attlee all weighed in against the plan. Churchill summed up by saying that all the Committee was prepared to sanction was another week's bombing, after which the policy would again be reviewed.[18]

The week of bombing had no impact on opinion one way or another. The next meeting of the Defence Committee convened to consider a report from occupied Europe that there was considerable unease in France and Belgium about the bombing policy.[19] Once again Portal led off by stating that the casualties were probably less than had been expected, but the Prime Minister was not impressed. He replied with an impassioned speech:

> He was concerned lest by continuing the attacks over a long period we should build up a volume of dull hatred in France which would affect our relations with that country for many years to come and would lead to the Royal Air Force, which had hitherto been regarded with admiration, being looked upon with odium and accused of killing our friends by blind night bombing attacks. It was one thing to carry out such attacks in the heat of battle but quite another to start them long beforehand and thus wear down the allegiance of our friends and convert those feelings towards us [that] were lukewarm to enemies. His concern would be less if he were convinced of the merits of the plan. He could not, however, believe that the people of this country had yet realised the implications of our present attacks on railway centres and that when they did so, there would be a reaction against our policy which was not in keeping with British morality and resulted in killing large numbers of our friends in France.[20]

Attlee, Eden, Lyttelton and Cherwell were quick to agree with Churchill. The military held out; even Brooke (according to Nye, who attended this meeting in his stead) said events had gone too far to change policy now. It was to no avail. Churchill determined to take the matter to the War Cabinet and if it decided against the Transportation Plan to alert the President to British feeling. In the meantime Tedder should be instructed to consider alternative operations.[21]

The War Cabinet met next day. Churchill reiterated his points, with the additional one that as the RAF were dropping twelve times the bombs that the USAAF were, they would bear most of the odium. Lyttelton now doubted whether the French railways could be knocked out at all. Eden and Attlee considered the risk to French civilian life too great to continue with the policy. It was generally agreed that bombing would be restricted to railway targets where casualties could be kept to 100 to 150. In the meantime Churchill would write to Roosevelt about British concerns and discuss the whole matter with Eisenhower.[22]

Churchill's letter and subsequent talk with Eisenhower produced no result. The Prime Minister rehearsed all the arguments against the Transportation Plan and again suggested that other targets – oil, ammunition dumps, vehicle parks and the like should be bombed instead.[23] Eisenhower replied that military necessity required the railway plan to be implemented. The limit placed on it by the War Cabinet would emasculate it.[24] Brooke by this time (the invasion was only a month away) had shifted. Too much effort had been put into the railway plan to now call it off.[25]

Rather desperately Churchill called another meeting of the Defence Committee. The same arguments were brought forward by the same people. The conclusion was that Churchill should despatch a letter to Roosevelt stressing the political objections to the plan and stating that the number of French casualties killed up to D-Day should not exceed 10,000.[26]

Churchill's letter was sent on 7 May. He told the President that he was 'by no means convinced that this is the best way to use our Air forces in the preliminary period'. He was now assured that 10,000 casualties would probably 'cover the job' but that the War Cabinet had been informed by the Ambassador in Algiers (Duff Cooper) that the whole episode would leave a 'legacy of hate' and therefore he asked Roosevelt to consider the matter 'from the highest political standpoint', stressing that the War Cabinet was 'unanimous in its anxiety'.[27] The reply was dusty. Roosevelt said:

> However regrettable the attendant loss of civilian life is, I am not prepared to impose from this distance any restriction on military action by the responsible military commanders that in their opinion might militate against the success of Overlord or cause additional loss of life to our Allied forces on invasion.[28]

Churchill was extremely unhappy with this result but was not willing to press the matter further. He took out his frustrations on Tedder by sending him weekly notes such as: 'you are piling up an awful load of hatred ... Have you exceeded the 10,000 limit?'[29] Even after operations in Normandy had proceeded for a month he was still asking the Deputy Supreme Commander, 'how many Frenchmen did you kill?'[30] In fact 10,000 French civilians were killed in the campaign, somewhere near the upper limit mentioned by the War Cabinet as acceptable. Who was right – Churchill and the British War Cabinet or Roosevelt and the bomber barons?

Frustratingly, for two main reasons, it is almost impossible to arrive at a definite conclusion. Firstly, the bombing campaign in support of Overlord was never actually confined to railways or marshalling yards. The targets suggested by Churchill and others (ammunition dumps, vehicle parks) were also attacked. So were bridges across the Seine and other rivers, and even oil targets within Germany.[31] Thus a pure 'Transportation Plan' was never carried out, so evaluating the actual plan is also difficult. Secondly, many of the panzer divisions that moved towards Normandy were in fact within the area that the bombers were attempting to interdict. These divisions were attacked and probably delayed to some extent but largely by bombing after D-Day, not by the Transportation Plan.

An attempt was made to evaluate the actual Transportation Plan by one of the economists attached to the staff of 21st Army Group. He came to the conclusion that there were delays in deploying enemy forces against the bridgehead but that the reasons for the delays were complex. Some units were kept in place by the Allied deception plan which convinced at least some commanders that Normandy was a feint and that the real landings were to take place in the Pas de Calais. On the other hand, the move of the 2 Panzer Division from the Albert area certainly seems to have been delayed by the destruction of marshalling yards and blocks in the line at Evreux. Panzer Lehr, however, travelled by road and was not at all hampered by rail bombing. The analyst concluded by suggesting that the Transportation Plan had little effect on the movement of German reserves but that the destruction of bridges perhaps played more of a role.[32]

The whole debate has been obscured by the post-war testimony of the captured German generals. Almost to a man they blamed the Transportation Plan for delaying the movement of German reserves towards Normandy. However, in many cases this seems to have been a cover for their own fractured command structure or for the fact that most of them had been gulled by the Allied deception plan. Overall their testimony must be regarded as suspect.

It seems reasonable to conclude that the British politicians had some basis for their reservations about the Transportation Plan. Churchill, in particular, in wanting the range of targets widened, was pushing a line that was eventually incorporated into the bombing plan. In general British civilians had an additional level of scepticism about bombing due to the large and unfulfilled promises made by the bomber barons over such a long period of time. Certainly they overestimated the casualties (which were frankly horrific) likely to be caused to the French. But then Bomber Command had only in recent times, with the help of such navigation aids as Oboe and innovations such as the Pathfinders, increased their accuracy and could pin-point bomb with much greater certainty. Indeed, perhaps even Harris was not aware that his crews had achieved this greater level of sophistication – neither was Churchill or the civilian members of the War Cabinet. As for the legacy of hate, this too is almost impossible to measure. Villagers 'liberated' by having their dwellings destroyed by the Allied bombers no doubt felt little short-term affection towards them. No doubt this lingered into the post-war years but its overall effect is unknown.

This debate followed the usual British pattern. The military put forward their bombing plan and the civil authorities (Churchill and the civilian members of the Defence Committee and the War Cabinet) rejected it. In Britain that was usually where the debate ended. But by this time the British were not the final arbiters on Allied strategy – the Americans were. And as Roosevelt had backed Eisenhower's Transportation Plan to the hilt, the debate among the British leadership, not for the first time, counted for nothing.

Why did the Americans adopt this line? No doubt lack of direct experience of being bombed played a part, but the fact is that Roosevelt showed little regard for the French throughout the war, neither Lafayette nor the Statue of Liberty modifying his general attitude of contempt for them. Nor was he concerned about the point Churchill was trying to make – that the post-war world needed a strong and friendly France. In the end, it was Roosevelt's interpretation of military necessity, a somewhat slender reed, that carried the day.

* * * * *

While this debate was raging, military preparations for the great attack were gathering pace. Montgomery, since January, had been elaborating his plans. His first full exposition was given to high-ranking officers early in April. There he announced that after consolidating the bridgehead, his first move would be to capture a port. In three months he hoped to be on the line of the Seine. As for detailed operations, the US First Army (Bradley) would land astride the Carentan Estuary, capture Cherbourg, strike south to St Lo with the object of capturing Rennes and then establishing a flank on the Loire. The US Third Army (Patton) would then clear Brittany and cover Bradley's southern flank as the two armies operated towards Paris. Meanwhile, the Second British Army would protect the left flank of the US force while Cherbourg was secured and then 'offer a strong front against enemy movement towards the lodgement area from the east'. Later the Canadian First Army would come in on the left flank of the British with the ultimate task of capturing Le Havre.[33]

Then Churchill arrived and Montgomery took the floor for an additional speech. He explained that the enemy held some vital high ground and communication centres but these must not be allowed to hold up the task of expanding the bridgehead. He explained that the Allies would need to use their armoured and mobile forces to push inland south-east of Caen to capture vital airfields. To add depth to the bridgehead they would need to push mobile forces forward – even a few armoured cars – up to 20 miles inside the German lines to create confusion and make the development of an enemy counter-attack that much more difficult. Churchill, who had possibly not fully recovered from his bout of pneumonia, replied with a poor speech but noted that he was pleased that there was no intention of digging in around the bridgehead, a move which had lost the initiative at Anzio.[34]

Montgomery expanded on this plan to his army commanders, General Omar Bradley and Lieutenant-General Miles Dempsey, later in the month, with copies of his memorandum sent to Eisenhower and Churchill. He again emphasised the need to disrupt enemy counter-attacks by pushing out 'fairly powerful armoured force thrusts on the afternoon of D-Day'. If armoured brigade groups could be got out it would be difficult for the enemy to interfere with the build-up. He was prepared to accept 'almost any risk', even the total loss of the brigade groups to achieve this.[35] Churchill was most impressed. He thought this exactly the spirit in which the operation should be executed and compared it to the stagnation (as he saw it) of the forces at Anzio in a similar circumstance.[36]

A second great run-through of the D-Day plan took place on 15 May. Churchill was again present to hear Montgomery's 'excellent speech'.[37] Montgomery started with a truly frightening catalogue of German forces in France (sixty infantry and ten panzer divisions, four of which were close to the beachheads). He then went on his confident way to assure his audience that he had the matter well in hand. Rommel, he thought, would try to drive the Allied forces back from the beaches with a focus on Bayeux. He went on to repeat his earlier arguments: Rommel must be thwarted by armoured columns rapidly penetrating deep inland; space must be gained into which the follow-up divisions could manoeuvre. While the Americans concentrated on Cherbourg, the British and Canadians would contain the maximum enemy forces on the eastern flank.[38]

It is not difficult to discern what Churchill made of all this. Montgomery had twice said that the role of the British Second Army would be to offer 'a strong front' to the Germans in order to contain 'maximum enemy forces' – that is, to act in a defensive, blocking manner. He had also spent some time on the need to venture inland with armoured columns in order to disrupt Rommel's attempt at mounting a counter-attack. And Churchill had twice commented on how different this was to Anzio, where the battle had bogged down through the lack of rapid action. There seems no doubt what Churchill was expecting. In the days that followed D-Day there would be some kind of armoured advance, the capture of some airfields and a general gain of ground. This was not, as some Montgomery apologists have suggested, an interpretation of a complex plan by an ignorant politician, but a reasonable interpretation of Montgomery's tendency to express tactical aims in very general terms.[39]

Yet Churchill might have pondered Montgomery's expositions in greater depth. In emphasising rapidity of movement inland Montgomery was surely telling the Prime Minister what he thought he wanted to hear. Churchill was always one for fast movement and manoeuvre. Had the Prime Minister cast his mind back to Alamein, the Mareth Line and the invasion of Italy by the Eighth Army, he might have noted that Montgomery had not proceeded thus. All three battles were set-piece affairs, preceded by enormous artillery barrages. Even when the enemy had been smashed, no rapid pursuit or daring manoeuvre followed. How Montgomery's tactics would play out in Normandy remained to be seen.

Montgomery's plan for Normandy was as follows. In the west of the Baie de Seine two American infantry divisions would land – one (4 Division) at the eastern end of the Cotentin Peninsula at Utah Beach, and the other (29 Division) some 20 miles east at Omaha. Two airborne divisions (82 and 101) would be dropped earlier at the base of the Cotentin to support the infantry divisions and to spread confusion among the German defenders. The task of this force (US First Army) was to secure the beachheads, capture the Cotentin Peninsula and to open Cherbourg as a major port through which the Allies could subsequently be supplied. Meanwhile to the east (near the mouth of the River Orne), two British division (3 and 50 Divisions) and one Canadian Division (3 Division) would land at Gold, Juno and Sword beaches. Beforehand the 6 Airborne Division would be dropped to the east of Caen to secure the crossings of the River Orne and to protect the left flank of the landings. The task of the main force was to capture Caen, link up with the Americans and prevent large forces of Germans from interfering with them while they operated on the Cotentin. Two follow-up divisions (1 US and 51 Highland) would land as soon after D-Day as possible to lend drive to the initial assault.

The Normandy operation was the greatest amphibious landing ever attempted. Some 7,000 ships and landing craft, of which 1,200 were warships, crewed by 285,000 naval personnel carried 133,000 troops (75,000 British and Canadian and 58,000 American) to the five landing beaches. Overhead 1,000 heavy bombers delivered 7,000 tons of bombs to the invasion area.[40] The expedition was launched in the teeth of bad weather, with a narrow window of milder conditions prevailing as the Channel crossing was made. Eisenhower made the agonising decision to go and he was vindicated by the result.

* * * * *

Not all went to plan. The American airborne attacks were scattered across the Cotentin and many parachutists struggled or were drowned in the marshy conditions. The wide dispersal of the airborne troops did, however, have the effect of confusing the defenders, especially those near Utah Beach. The British 6 Airborne Division was dropped more accurately and seized some important bridges (Pegasus Bridge is the best known) over the Orne. At the five invasion beaches lodgements were established. At Omaha a desperate struggle ensued as a well-dug-in enemy division occupying the slopes which overlooked the beach caused heavy casualties. Close-support naval fire and the determination of the troops in the end saw a narrow strip of land in US hands.

On the British beaches, Caen, 9 miles inland from Sword Beach, was one of the objectives for the first day. In the event many days would pass before it fell. This is the landing we will examine because it was this so-called failure that was to cause some disquiet among the British and American politico/ military leadership about how Montgomery was running the campaign.

The plan to capture Caen fell to the 3 British Division, landing at Sword. Its three brigades were to land sequentially. The first (8) was to establish the beachhead and secure it. The second (185) was to advance through 8 Brigade and move on Caen. The third (9) was to secure Caen if 185 Brigade was held up or to link up with the Canadians on the right as the situation demanded.[41]

A landing against a fortified coast is one of the most hazardous in modern war. The assaulting troops in the first instance are armed only with light weapons and have no cover. The defenders typically will be protected by either concreted positions, houses along the coast or at least slit trenches. They will also be able to call down fire support from artillery or mortars. To succeed, an assault will have to be supported by sufficient firepower to neutralise or destroy the defenders to an extent which allows the beachhead to be captured without casualties so heavy that they disrupt the attack or render it ineffective.

Defending Sword Beach on D-Day were units (probably about 500 to 600 men) of the German 716 Division, 'a low category formation', 'diluted with foreigners, probably about 20% of all the men in all but specialist units being Poles and other unwilling elements'.[42] Their defences had no depth, just concreted strongpoints and various fortified houses along the seafront. In close support of these troops were 6 x 75-mm guns, 5 x 5-cm anti-tank guns, 2 x 37-mm guns, seven machine guns and five or six mortars. Batteries of field and medium guns some 2 miles back could also be called for support.[43]

The invaders could bring much more firepower to bear than this. Landing in the first waves would be just over 5,000 men. As they approached, the beaches were to be subjected to 'drenching fire' from the eleven destroyers that accompanied 3 Division, plus artillery and rocket fire from weapons on board the landing craft. In addition, the division had a squadron of duplex drive (DD) swimming tanks kept afloat by an elaborate flotation screen, flail tanks to clear minefields and modified tanks (AVREs) to carry engineering stores such as explosives to assist in clearing obstacles. In the event this firepower knocked out between 20 and 30 per cent of all enemy posts and weapons. Moreover, many enemy mortars, machine guns and heavier weapons were found not to be manned, a factor attributed to the fire support given to the infantry by the swimming tanks and perhaps to the low motivation of the foreign troops serving with the Germans.[44]

Hence the assault troops had sufficient firepower available to get on shore with tolerable casualties (the 3 Division had 630 casualties on D-Day) and stay there. Yet the landings were much messier and confused than is painted by this picture. One of the initial assault battalions was the 1 South Lancashire:

Landing Beach Queen Red. 0720 – First wave beached and altogether met by heavy MG fire and mortaring made satisfactory progress. Communications with A and C Coys established by wireless on run-in, and progress report obtained by Bn HQ.

0745 – Second wave (Bn HQ, HQ Coy, B and D Coys) touched down, met by small arms fire, mortar and 88mm. Landing made almost on strong point COD, which was still active. Bn HQ moved towards sand dunes near 88mm gun position, and whilst endeavouring to direct operation the CO, Lt-Col R.P.H. Burbury was killed; Major Stone assuming command of the Bn. B Coy proceeded to deal with strong point COD; their Coy Comnd., Major R.H. Harrison, was killed immediately on landing. Lt. R.C. Bell-Walker assumed command, but was killed during attack on pillbox [COD]. Opposition overcome, apart from isolated snipers. B and D Coys advanced towards Hermanville. Bn HQ followed along main axis, up main road. During the period on the beach, contact was lost with coys due to losses sustained by signallers, or wireless becoming detached, with their operators.[45]

The battalion occupied Hermanville and dug in, though there was street fighting in the small village for the remainder of the day. Overall they had captured the objectives set down for them on D-Day and ejected or dealt with, one way or another, most of the German defenders on their section of beach. They had lost eighteen killed, eighty-nine wounded and nineteen missing, about 20 per cent of their strength, which was tolerable, but three key officers (the battalion commander and two company commanders) had been killed and for much of the day the battalion did not fight united but as separate companies.[46] Such is the shambles of war and the cost of even a successful operation.

Still Hermanville, an essential staging post on the way to Caen, was in British hands by 9.30 a.m. The next stage was for a follow-up battalion (1 Suffolk) to capture two German strongpoints (Morris and Hillman) to allow the advance of 185 Brigade on Caen. Here the plan came unstuck. Morris, which had been subjected to aerial attack and naval gun fire, surrendered easily but Hillman was another proposition. It covered an area of 400 by 600 yards with deep shelters and pillboxes connected by trenches 7 feet deep. It contained two artillery pieces, several machine guns and some anti-aircraft guns that could operate against ground targets. The whole position was protected by two belts of wire and anti-tank and anti-personnel mines.[47] At 11.30 a.m., after an uneventful landing, the 1 Suffolks arrived before Hillman. The fire from a cruiser that was supposed to support their attack was unavailable because the FOB (Forward Observer Bombardment) – the liaison officer between the forward troops and the ship) – had been wounded on the beach and all radio communication with the ship lost. Nevertheless, the wire was soon breached by Bangalore torpedoes. An attack in platoon strength accompanied by a few tanks of the 13/18 Hussars and two batteries of field guns then went in. It was rebuffed by machine-gun fire. A second attack sometime later was 'once again' held up by the enemy machine guns. Then a battalion attack accompanied by eight or nine tanks was planned, but this took time to arrange and in the end Hillman did not fall until 8 p.m. Fifty German prisoners were taken. The Suffolks had six killed and eight wounded for the day.[48]

This hold-up stalled the attempt of 185 Brigade to move on Caen. They attempted to outflank Hillman to the east but this cost them 150 casualties. Other battalions were brought forward but most were without their heavy weapons due to incredible congestion on the landing beaches. The poor weather in which the landing took place had caused the wind to drive in the tide and reduce the width of the beach from over 400 yards to just 200. This meant that many artillery batteries supporting the division were operating in 3 feet of water, which affected their accuracy and rate of fire. As a consequence some units of the 185 Brigade had little fire support. The narrow strip of beach also caused traffic snarls and stores, ammunition and equipment from the LSTs piled up in chaotic heaps. Then reports of enemy tanks, probably from 21 Panzer Division, north of Caen came in as early as 12.15 p.m. By 4 p.m. groups of twenty were reported approaching from the south. Shortly after, the advanced battalion of 185 Brigade (King's Shropshire Light Infantry) were attacked by twenty-four tanks near Biéville. Nine tanks were destroyed by this unit, which happened to have its anti-tank guns forward, but more panzers were noted on the right flank of the division nearer to the sea between Luc and Lion. In this situation the decision was made that 9 Brigade must move to the right to cover the enemy armoured incursion. The 185 Brigade would have to dig in. Caen would be left until another day.[49]

What had happened was this. British Intelligence had been unable to locate precisely where in Normandy the elements of the 21 Panzer Division were. On 21 May it was estimated that they might be dispersed over an area stretching from Bayeux to Lisieux. A few days later Intelligence warned that units from the division might be encountered in 'the forenoon' of D-Day but local intelligence seem to have stuck to the earlier interpretation that they would not meet the panzers until after Caen had been captured. The arrival of the German tanks came therefore as a nasty surprise.[50]

In fact the commander of 21 Panzer (General Edgar Feuchtinger) had had the greatest difficulty in getting his division into action. He knew of the parachute landings shortly after midnight but, because of the fractured German command system, it had taken five hours to obtain authorisation to use his forces against the 6 Airborne. Just as this move commenced, Feuchtinger was warned that the situation to the west was dangerous and that he must despatch his force not against the paratroops to the east of the Orne but towards the enemy advancing to the west of the river. In the end it was 3 p.m. before the division could reorient its tanks and move west.[51] Despite these delays, a group of fifty tanks and a battalion of infantry started probing towards the coast around 6 p.m. Its right flank ran into British anti-tank guns now finally moved from the congested beach to the Perriers Rise and six tanks were quickly destroyed. However, another half-dozen slipped left and reached the coast near Luc. The German defences there were still intact. If reinforced, this wedge of armour between the 3 British Division and the 3 Canadian Division might turn right and attack the lightly armed 6 Airborne. Feuchtinger was quick to realise the possibilities but, just as he was about to swing his tanks eastwards against the paratroopers:

> There came from the Channel the distant drumming of hundreds of aircraft. They flew in like a swarm of bees, skimming low over the gleaming water so that the bright sun setting beyond them would blind the gunners at Le Havre. With two hundred and fifty tugs and two hundred and fifty gliders, escorted by a host of fighters, this was the largest glider-borne force yet to take the air in battle. It carried most of the 6th Air-Landing Brigade, plus ... artillery and reconnaissance regiments including light tanks.[52]

They landed just west of the Orne, almost on top of the panzers. This stopped Feuchtinger's drive to the coast in its tracks. The tanks pulled back, darkness fell and the German opportunity was lost. There would be no more attacks on the British beachheads that day.

There has been far too much hand-wringing at the failure to capture Caen on D-Day. With the 21 Panzer so close to the city there was never really a chance that it could be bundled out by a brigade of infantry. The Suffolks, outside Hillman, for reasons that are not clear, certainly started their operations with 'fiddling attacks' which bore no fruit.[53] Even if Hillman had fallen earlier, the lack of many heavy weapons and artillery support would have made the capture of a Caen, occupied by a panzer division, impossible.

A pattern soon emerged of how the British were to wage war in this campaign. If a strongpoint could not be captured cheaply, the artillery and armour would be called in to obliterate it. This might not be elegant, it might eschew manoeuvre, but it was not out of line with the policy of Montgomery or for that matter Churchill. The British army had plenty of ammunition and plenty of (mainly American) tanks. It did not have, in

1944, plenty of men. Unless divisions were to be broken up as reinforcements for those that remained, this campaign would have to be light on
casualties if Britain was to have any voice when it ended. Chester Wilmot
states that the Suffolks should have taken Hillman 'almost regardless of
casualties'.[54] But the last time the British army had done something like that
was Passchendaele and no one, from the Prime Minister down, wanted the
fields of Normandy to resemble those of Flanders. British soldiers might be
risk averse but with the firepower at their disposal they could afford to be.
If strongpoints could be captured with minimum cost, the last army that
Britain could raise in this war would choose that option.

The success of the early landings did not mean that the Allies were out
of danger. The Germans were rushing reserves to Normandy. The first to
arrive in the Caen sector was the 12 SS Panzer Division, commanded by the
brutal SS commander and war criminal Kurt Meyer and made up mainly of
youths aged between seventeen and twenty, well indoctrinated with Nazi
ideology. For the Germans the ideal scenario would have been to combine
the 12 SS and 21 Panzer Divisions and make a concerted dash to the coast
at the weak point between the 3 Division and the 3 Canadian Division. But
this was not to be. The Canadians, despite much crowding on the beach,
had managed an advance towards the airfields at Carpiquet, west of Caen.
Meyer was obliged to thwart this movement. On 9 June elements of his
division moved to the west of Caen and engaged the Canadians, but this
manoeuvre lacked all coherence. The SS attack, disorganised, piecemeal,
fanatical, ran into Canadian anti-tank guns, forward deployed artillery and
some armour. In a matter of moments nine panzers had succumbed to the
fire of the tanks which were equipped with 17-pounder guns, more than a
match for German Panthers. The infantry were then shot up by well-placed
Canadian machine-gunners and riflemen. The Canadians were pushed
back by weight of numbers, but not far enough to endanger the beachhead.
They had taken a terrible toll on the SS Division.[55] All the SS could do in
retaliation was to murder some 200 Canadian soldiers who had surrendered.[56] It was a timely reminder, if one was needed, about what the Allies
were fighting against.

Montgomery arrived in Normandy on 8 June. There was no doubt that
he had hoped Caen would be in his hands by then but he soon adjusted to

614

the new situation. He told his friend in the War Office, General Frank Simpson:

> The Germans are doing everything they can to hold on to Caen. I have decided not to have a lot of casualties by battering up against the place; so I have ordered Second Army to keep up a good pressure at Caen, and to make its major effort towards Villers Bocage and Evrecy and then S.E. towards Falaise.[57]

His first idea was to envelop Caen from both flanks and at the same time drop an airborne division to the south of the city to encircle all German forces in the area. But Trafford Leigh-Mallory, the overall air commander, thought the air-drop too risky ('gutless bugger', Montgomery called him). Moreover the rather swampy area to the east of the Orne made it difficult to concentrate a sizeable force there, so the Ground Commander had to think again.

At this point events outside Montgomery's control meant that any thought of a British offensive had to be postponed. A major storm in the Channel started on 19 June. It destroyed one of the artificial Mulberry harbours that was offloading troops and supplies of all kinds to the Americans. The British Mulberry at Arromanches was damaged in the same storm. In addition, the rough weather postponed cross-Channel shipping and made unloading over the open beaches virtually impossible. All this delayed the build-up and the prospect of a British offensive.

While the storm raged, Montgomery set about planning his new operation. It was to be a two-corps affair (the VIII Corps had now landed in Normandy) consisting of the VIII and XXX Corps assaulting to the west of Caen. The aim was to force crossings over the River Odon and capture the high ground around Hill 112 to allow an armoured division to 'crack about' south of Caen. Operation Epsom commenced in bad weather on 26 June accompanied by a bombardment from 700 guns. Gains were steady but slow. By the 27th the Odon had been crossed and the 11 Armoured Division had infiltrated some of its units across the river and captured Hill 112. But German resistance was increasing. Two additional panzer divisions had entered the line (1 SS and 2 SS Panzer) and now two more were approaching

(9 SS and 10 SS).[58] In all, the British were now facing eight to ten panzer divisions.[59] In this situation Montgomery ordered his troops onto the defensive. That this was the correct decision was borne out on the 30th, when strong German counter-attacks developed. Hill 112 was lost but not much else. The Germans suffered severe losses from the now dug-in British anti-tank guns and artillery. By 2 July their counter-attack had ceased.

Looked at in terms of 'cracking about' south of Caen, the offensive was a failure, but Montgomery certainly did not view it this way. The British were now engaging a great percentage of the German panzer forces in Normandy. This had allowed the Americans to link up their bridgeheads (10 June), strike across the base of the Cotentin (18 June) and turn and advance on Cherbourg, which fell on 26 June. The American First Army could now turn southwards and prepare for the breakout that Montgomery had always planned. As he told Eisenhower, 'if we can pull the enemy on to Second Army it will make it easier for First Army when it attacks southwards.'[60]

With this policy in mind Montgomery had no intention of letting up. Caen was still in enemy hands and, despite Montgomery's overall satisfaction with his policy, the city blocked Second Army expansion and limited their attacking options to the area west of the city. Montgomery therefore concluded that it was time that the city was captured.

Operation Charnwood (it meant 'burnt wood') began on 7 July. It had the usual Montgomery trademarks, leading off with a bombardment from 656 guns. It had one novel addition: the city would be attacked by the strategic bombers before zero in an attempt to minimise casualties by obliterating the defenders. A total of 467 Lancasters and Halifaxes dropped 2,500 tons of bombs on Caen before zero hour. Then three divisions of I Corps attacked. The six-hour interval between these events gave the German defenders some time to recover. However, by the end of 8 July the area of Caen (or what was left of it) to the north of the river was in British hands. Somehow this operation is usually marked down as a failure on the grounds that not all of Caen had been captured and that the bombing had hampered the troops in getting forward. This is perverse. Most of the town was captured and there is no mention in most war diaries that the rubble caused by the bombing greatly hindered them.[61] In addition the 12 SS Panzer Division was virtually wiped out in the attack, being reduced to just battalion strength. Moreover, the German hold on the southern suburbs of Caen was untenable and they were soon driven out by the Canadians in their part of the Goodwood operation.

There was trouble brewing for Montgomery. At Supreme Headquarters Allied Expeditionary Force (SHAEF) the airmen Tedder, Arthur Coningham and Leigh-Mallory had long had an antipathy to Montgomery, largely it seemed, on personal grounds. Now they declared to Eisenhower that they had grave doubts about the overly cautious strategy he was pursuing.[62] Somehow this was passed on to Churchill. It struck a chord with the Prime Minister. Had not he heard Montgomery declare that armoured forces would in short order be operating south of Caen? Had Montgomery not said that he was willing to pay any price to see mobile columns pegging out claims well inland? Was not Caen an objective for the first day of battle? Armed with this information, Churchill summoned the Defence Committee and announced that Montgomery was being overly cautious. Brooke described what happened next:

> He [Churchill] began to abuse Monty because operations were not going faster, and apparently Eisenhower had said he was over cautious. I flared up and asked him if he could not trust his generals for 5 minutes instead of continuously abusing and belittling them. He said he never did such a thing . . . He was furious with me, but I hope it may have done some good in the future.[63]

What Brooke seemed to overlook was that the person who had most given Churchill room for complaint was Montgomery himself. Churchill, after all, was merely complaining that Montgomery had fulfilled none of the promises made in his pre-D-Day expositions. The Prime Minister had a good memory for these matters and was always on high alert for operations that had stalled, as commanders in the desert and at Anzio could attest.

Brooke soon found that he had not appeased Churchill at all. The Prime Minister was clearly still agitated after this meeting and expressed his anger by asking Ismay a series of detailed questions on the old subject of the excessive length of Montgomery's administrative tail.[64] Montgomery compounded matters by banning all visitors from his tactical headquarters in France, just at the time Churchill was preparing to cross to France to visit him. The Prime Minister's anger rose to fury. He dashed off a letter to Eisenhower stating that he would visit France, but not Montgomery. He intended, however, to take the matter up officially because he, as Defence Minister, 'had a right and a duty to acquaint himself with the facts on the spot'.[65] That is to say, he would visit who he liked when he liked. Luckily for Montgomery this letter was never sent; it would have added to the discontent that was already moving Eisenhower, Tedder and Coningham to call for Montgomery to be sacked.[66] Churchill's letter was sidelined because Brooke had managed to intervene. He had visited Montgomery that day and warned him of the impending storm. He also had Montgomery dictate a note to the Prime Minister specifically inviting him to visit France at the earliest possible moment.[67]

Churchill visited France on 21 July. Montgomery made a great fuss of the visit and went to considerable lengths to explain to the Prime Minister the basis of his strategy – hold the panzers on the left and break through on the right; how he had forced the Germans to concentrate their panzer divisions (eight out of the ten in Normandy) against the Second Army to guard against a British breakout towards Paris; how this had allowed the Americans to clean up the Cotentin, occupy Cherbourg and pivot to break out southwards while the British maintained pressure on their flank.[68] Montgomery's talk, of which we have no record, was no doubt delivered with the general's usual confidence and clarity. The 'acute' Churchill immediately grasped the essentials of the strategy and was mollified. The crisis – which, as so often, had been of Montgomery's own making – was for the moment over.

It was fortunate that Brooke had managed to arrange this tête-à-tête because the general view was that the latest British attack (Operation Goodwood), which took place during Churchill's visit, had failed. The germ for Goodwood had come from the rather anonymous commander of the Second Army, General Dempsey. Epsom and Charnwood, although they had achieved some success, had not been cheap – some 8,000 casualties in the first operation, 3,500 in the second.[69] Dempsey now suggested using the armour in the van of the attack instead of the infantry. This would save lives in the infantry divisions and use to advantage the great preponderance that the British possessed in armour. Dempsey's plan was to group the three British armoured divisions one behind the other (11, Guards, 7) and launch them from east of Caen onto the Bourguébus Ridge and then press on to

Falaise.[70] Montgomery soon modified this ambitious programme. Perhaps harking back to Alamein, he was sceptical that British armour could deliver a penetrating breakthrough. The aim now was to 'write down' the German armour and perhaps to cause alarm by allowing some armoured cars to probe south to Falaise if prospects looked favourable.[71] The only ground Montgomery named as a permanent objective would be the Bourguébus Ridge.

The firepower assembled for Goodwood was greater than for any other single battle fought by the British army in the Second World War. The VIII Corps which would conduct the main operations had 750 tanks and over 600 artillery pieces. Also 1,000 heavy and medium bombers had been coaxed out of a reluctant Harris to pound the area north of the Bourguébus Ridge before zero. In addition, the heavy guns of the navy would bombard all known German battery positions.[72] The battle began on 16 July with 2,500 tons of bombs raining down on the German defences. Then the artillery opened up and the armoured divisions moved forward behind the barrages. Initially all went well. The front defenders were either dead, stunned or completely demoralised by the intensity of shell fire and bombing. Many surrendered to the oncoming tanks. But then, due to appalling traffic congestion in the small bridgehead, the armour fell behind the barrage. Moreover, the German defences were in greater depth than had been estimated and the rearward troops had escaped the worst of the bombardment. Gradually progress slowed. Then on the 20th it halted. Next day the Germans began counter-attacking with troops rushed to the area. Montgomery immediately called off the battle. The armour was to withdraw into reserve. The newly arrived infantry would beat off the counterattacks. Goodwood was over.[73]

Many, at the time and since, regard Goodwood as a failure. Again, Montgomery was not one of them. On 23 July he announced that his troops had achieved a 'break through' south of Caen.[74] This was hardly the case. Even the German armour had not been 'written down' to the extent that he had wanted. Eisenhower was furious with this announcement, especially because the battle had been called off so quickly. Would the British ever break out? Would Monty's forces ever 'crack about' south of Caen? This misread what Montgomery was trying to do: keep the Germans fixed on the eastern flank while the Americans prepared to break out in the west. It also ignores the effect of the battle on the Germans. The 16 Luftwaffe Division had practically ceased to exist; 21 Panzer was down to the strength of a battalion; elements of 125 Panzer Grenadier had surrendered in droves. As Field Marshal Gunther von Kluge (Rommel had been seriously injured in an air strike as the battle began) told Hitler:

> The psychological effect of such a mass of bombs coming down with all the power of elemental nature on the fighting troops, especially the infantry, is a factor which has to be given serious consideration. It is immaterial whether such a bomb carpet catches good troops or bad, they are more or less annihilated. If this occurs frequently, then the power of endurance of the forces is put to the highest test. In fact it becomes dormant and dies.[75]

Von Kluge was acknowledging here that if this type of attack was kept up, the campaign in Normandy was over. And attacks were kept up. Operation Bluecoat (27 July), Operation Totalize (8 August) and Operation Tractable (14 August) followed in short order, as did many smaller operations in between. In the meantime American forces commenced the breakout battle, Operation Cobra, on the western flank. On 24 July they captured St Lo; a week later they were in Avranches and commenced the wide eastern turning movement that Montgomery had always planned. With surpassing folly, Hitler ordered a counter-attack against the Americans at Mortain that had the effect of jamming his forces into an ever-decreasing pocket between the Americans now turning north and Montgomery's Polish and Canadian forces closing the gap at Falaise.

In the end the Falaise pocket was not closed shut. Some German forces escaped in a hasty retreat to the Seine. Some authorities have marked this as yet another failure – largely on the part of Montgomery's armour but also partly because of a lack of coordination between the closing British and US forces. Yet in this war it was rare for an entire army to be sealed off to the extent that there was no escape. This was true at Beda Fomm in the desert and after Diadem in Italy as well as Falaise. In any case it is a strange kind failure that encompassed the destruction of most of the German army in Normandy. In all the Germans lost 300,000 men killed or taken prisoner in the Normandy operations. They also lost most of their tanks, heavy equipment and guns, but most of their higher commanders escaped – something the Allies would rue later in the war.

During this period Churchill made just one intervention. On 27 July he told Montgomery that he had heard that the British had suffered 'a serious set-back' after Operation Bluecoat and he asked for information 'to maintain confidence among wobblers or critics in high places'.[76] Montgomery assured him that there had been 'no serious set back'. He said some small amount of ground had been given up, but that the overall plan was succeeding and that he expected the Americans to secure the breakout shortly.[77] With this Churchill was satisfied.

The Normandy campaign showed just what constraints Churchill was operating under. The dispute over the Transportation Plan indicated that he might summon his political colleagues to overrule the policy of his military advisers, and that this counted for nothing if the Americans took a contrary view. The dynamics in the alliance had changed in 1943 and this episode merely confirmed that. As for military operations, they were now so extensive and had such a large American element that there was little that Churchill could do to influence their course. He might grow impatient with his army commander but Montgomery was after all the one man who determined that Britain would have a large say in how the Normandy campaign was fought. When Churchill grasped the logic of Montgomery's strategy (and if at first he did not Montgomery had no one to blame but himself) he stuck with his general despite the 'wobblers'. Although there were a few ups and downs, this would be his position for the remainder of the war.

Map 12. Burma.

CHAPTER 27

BURMA

THERE WAS GENERAL AGREEMENT among British statesmen and soldiers in late 1941 that war would not come to Burma. An increasingly aggressive Japan might look with envy on the raw materials of the Netherlands East Indies and Malaya but any move in that direction would be stopped either in Johore or 'Fortress Singapore'. The Malay barrier would hold; Singapore would hold. In the event neither held. The islands of Java and Sumatra did not hold either. After the general collapse in the east, the Indian Ocean and the Bay of Bengal lay open to Japanese incursion. Initially, though, the threat to Burma did not originate from the sea. To the north of Malaya, Siam (now Thailand) lay helpless before the Japanese army. An agreement was soon reached between Japan and the Siamese government. The invading troops would be given free passage across Siam into the long, narrow strip of land that was southern Burma. All this happened with remarkable speed. Before Singapore had fallen, Japanese troops were on Burma's doorstep. Tavoy on the coast, defended by a small contingent of the Burma Rifles, fell on 15 January 1942.[1]

There were good reasons that the Japanese incursion might have been expected. In 1941 Burma was the largest exporter of rice in the world. It also had reserves of oil and was the means (via the Burma Road) whereby British and American supplies could be ferried into China. It may be doubted, however, that these concrete rationales played a major role in the

Japanese invasion. More likely the Japanese were shoring up the left flank of their conquests in South-East Asia – Burma just happened to be on that flank.

Some preparations to defend Burma had begun before the outbreak of war in the Far East. In July 1941 the 1 Burma Division had been formed from local troops, and a brigade from the Indian Army had arrived in November.[2] But the air force was in a pitiful state. On the outbreak of war with Japan there was just one squadron of sixteen inadequate Buffalo aircraft in the country and no radar. On the naval side, there was a flotilla of five motor launches.[3]

In the emergency after 7 December 1941 what reinforcements Britain could muster were sent to Malaya and Singapore. But as the situation deteriorated, second thoughts began to emerge. On 19 January 1942, with the Japanese advancing north from Tavoy, the Governor of Burma (Reginald Dorman-Smith) telegraphed to the Secretary of State for Burma (Leo Amery) that reinforcements were desperately needed. He added that Burma must be preserved as a base, with the interesting remark that the loss of Singapore would not be disastrous but that the loss of Burma would be.[4] In London Churchill tended to agree. He told the Chiefs of Staff that the question of the value of Singapore should be put directly to Wavell, whose ABDA Command was disintegrating by the day. He continued:

> The loss of Burma would be very grievous. It would cut us off from the Chinese whose troops have been the most successful of those yet engaged against the Japanese. We may by muddling things and hesitating to take an ugly decision, lose both Singapore and the Burma Road. Obviously the decision depends on how long the defence of Singapore island can be maintained. If it is only for a few weeks, it is certainly not worth losing all our reinforcements and aircraft.[5]

The next day the COS met with the Prime Minister to consider what might be sent to Burma. It was little enough. Three British battalions were to be despatched there immediately and consideration was to be given as to what else might be available from India, the Middle East and Britain.[6] By the end of the week considerable air reinforcements had been found from the Middle East and western India. Of these, eighteen Wellingtons, twenty-one

Hurricanes and twenty-four Lysanders had arrived in India for Burma and a further 128 of these types were on their way.[7] As for troops, the 17 Indian Division, which was about to embark for the Middle East, was halted at Bombay and ordered to Calcutta by rail and then to Burma,[8] and the 7 Armoured Brigade was diverted from Malaya to Burma.[9]

To what kind of environment, political and geographical, were these forces to be sent? Burma is a sizeable country. If a map of the country were superimposed on Western Europe, Tavoy, where one of the first Japanese incursions was made, would be near the Moroccan coast while Rangoon would be near the Pyrenees, Mandalay near Paris, Imphal near London and Kohima in Norfolk. The very north of the country would be in the North Sea somewhere near the coast of Germany.[10] Much of this expanse is jungle but by no means all. Central Burma is flatter and covered with rice paddies. It has little more rain than London and can be extremely hot and dusty in summer. Most other areas such as Arakan are wet, mountainous and receive up to 200 inches of rain per year. The main transport routes were by the three main rivers which flow north to south (Chindwin, Irrawaddy and Sittang). There were few decent roads and none of any note between the north-east of the country and Assam in India. The only port able to take even reasonable-sized ships was Rangoon, the entry point for most Burma–India traffic. Apart from Rangoon there were few towns of note, Moulmein and Mandalay being the largest. The country is dominated by the monsoon, which begins in May and lasts through October. In the beginning of the campaign all armies considered operations during the monsoon impossible.

The political situation was complex. It would have been difficult to find a British colony where the political classes were more hostile to British rule. On the outbreak of the Japanese war the political leaders either fled or were jailed. The population were in general apathetic to the movement of armies but likely to assist in small ways the army which was occupying their territory. It was not only the British who were unpopular. Burma contained many Indians as civil servants, workers in the oilfields and merchants. They tended to look to the British to support them against hostile Burmans and they tended to retreat with the British armies as the surest way to return to India.

The other considerable group in Burma was the Americans, who were to cause endless complications during the war. The Americans were there to supply China with lend-lease material over the Burma Road. This material arrived in vast quantities through Rangoon. The Americans also had three squadrons of aircraft (the American Volunteer Group, AVG) to assist, and some transport planes. There was an understanding with the British that, should Burma be attacked, one squadron of the AVG, flying Kittyhawks, would assist in defence.

The Chinese whom the Americans and the British were helping were Chiang Kai-shek's Nationalists whose capital, Chunking, lay at the far end of the Burma Road. Chiang's army, which had been fighting the Japanese on and off for some years, potentially added to Allied strength but was of dubious utility. Some units of this army stood along the China–Burma border, but only if the mood took Chiang, might he make it available to assist the British. To add a further complication, the Chief of Staff to this army was an American, General J.W. Stilwell (Vinegar Joe), who was also commander of the US armed forces in the China–Burma–India theatre. While his relationship with the British command structure had yet to be determined his Anglophobia was already well developed. The total number of Americans in the theatre was quite small but they were backed by a powerful lobby in Washington. Roosevelt, many in his administration and many in Congress had a sentimental attachment to China that stunned Churchill when he visited the US after Pearl Harbor. The President certainly considered China as one of the Great Powers and Chiang as some kind of emerging founding father to an incipient democracy of 400 million people. The British might be in Burma because they were imperialists; the Americans were there for a much higher purpose – to assist Chiang to defeat the Japanese and to oversee the emergence of China as a great democratic Pacific power. If this was not a recipe for misunderstandings and disappointments, nothing was.

All this lay in the future. The immediate problem was to deal with the Japanese. They had invaded Burma with two divisions of the Fifth Army (33 and 55), well –trained units which had seen service in China. The only force available to meet them south of Moulmein was 16 Brigade of the 17 British Indian Division, trained for the desert, tied to the few roads because of its transport and about to fight its first action. It did not begin well. The Japanese had secured three airports in southern Burma and greatly outnumbered the few Allied aircraft based on Rangoon. The war diaries are full of pleas for 'air action' that could hardly ever be answered.[11] Without aerial reconnaissance the location of enemy forces was practically impossible to determine. In this phase of the battle, therefore, no clear picture of the enemy ever emerged. The Indian forces were bombed, outflanked and brushed aside by a Japanese enemy that was almost invisible to its opponents. Moulmein was under attack before British forces realised what was happening.

There was also little understanding – in high places or low – of the disparity between the skilled, trained Japanese and the 17 Indian Division in these first battles. The Indian Division's own War Diary described the division as 'lacking guts', while the Viceroy (Lord Linlithgow) was telling Churchill that the troops were not fighting with 'sufficient relish'.[12] In fact the troops lacked neither guts nor relish. What they lacked was experience. As in Malaya, the Japanese were always able to outmanoeuvre them. The usual method was a short hook through the jungle and then the establishment of a roadblock in rear of the enemy forces which then had to fight their way through. often facing machine guns and light artillery, to establish a new front. Another short hook and roadblock would then follow.[13] In this manner Moulmein fell and the action moved to the Sittang River and the enormous bridge that crossed it. What happened next is described in 17 Division War Diary:

> This morning [23rd February] owing to heavy pressure and the fact that they [the Japanese] looked to be taking the Bridge with heavy forces, it was decided to blow the Sittang Bridge. At 0830 hrs it was blown. One pier and two spans were collapsed. All day fighting progressed on the East Side of the Sittang and many batches of troops managed to swim the river . . . Groups of men without arms and equipment [came] trickling in from 16, 46 Bdes after swimming river.[14]

What seems to have happened is that those taking the decision to blow the bridge thought most men had already crossed it. In fact the division had been reduced to a shattered wreck before the bridge had been destroyed. Its destruction left many of these men stranded. The following day it was found that just 3,500 officers and men were across the river and only 1,400 of them had rifles.[15] The road to Rangoon was open. This set the scene for one of the most acrimonious exchanges of the war between Britain and one of its Dominions.

On the outbreak of the Japanese war, John Curtin, Prime Minister of Australia, had insisted that the 6 and 7 Australian Divisions return from the Middle East for the defence of Australia. In February they were at sea near Ceylon (now Sri Lanka). Some thought had been given in British official circles as to where these troops might be deployed, neither Singapore nor the Netherlands East Indies having fallen. On 17 February Churchill noted that while it was urgent to reinforce Burma and Ceylon, 'it would be difficult to refuse the Australians' request that their divisions should return home'.[16] The next day Wavell enquired as to the destination of the Australian troops and asked to be kept informed.[17] Then Dill, in Washington, took up the running. The Americans had said that as a US division was being sent to Australia, could not one Australian division be diverted to Burma?[18] The COS considered Dill's request the following day and agreed that the 7 Australian Division was the only considerable force that could arrive at Rangoon in time to shore up its defence. They resolved to enquire if the Prime Minister might telegram Curtin.[19] This Churchill did:

> I suppose you realise that your leading division the head of which is sailing south of Colombo . . . is the only force that can reach Rangoon in time to prevent its loss and severance of communication with China. It can begin to disembark at Rangoon about 26th or 27th. There is nothing else in the world that can fill the gap.[20]

So far this seemed a reasonable request, asked for by the Commander-in-Chief, the COS and the Americans. But Churchill had not had a good week. The *Scharnhorst* and *Gneisenau* had escaped to Germany through the Channel, Singapore had fallen and Curtin, as we have seen, blamed Churchill personally for its fall. Churchill's irritation with all this was soon apparent:

> I am quite sure that if you refuse to allow your troops to stop this gap which they are actually passing, and if in consequence the above evils affecting the whole course of the war follow, a very grave effect will be produced upon the President and the Washington circle on whom you

are so largely dependent . . . We must have an answer immediately . . . I trust therefore that for the sake of all our interests, and above all your own interests, you will give most careful consideration to the case I have set before you.[21]

This has been described by one authority as 'naked blackmail'.[22] It was certainly heavy-handed and hardly designed to elicit a favourable response. To ram home the point to Curtin, Churchill then enlisted Roosevelt, who wrote directly to the Australian Prime Minister stating that he too considered that the 7 Division should be diverted to Rangoon and noting that he was rushing troops to defend Australia.[23] Curtin, who was not well with a gastric ulcer, stuck to his guns, supported by the threatened resignation of Lieutenant-General Sir Vernon Sturdee, the Chief of the Australian General Staff, if the troops did not return to Australia.[24] Curtin therefore replied to Churchill on 22 February, noting his 'rather strongly worded request' and turning it down.[25] This was not the end of the matter, however. While awaiting Curtin's reply, the First Sea Lord (Pound) had sent a signal to the ships carrying the 7 Division diverting them to the north towards Rangoon.[26] Churchill passed this news on to Curtin the same day, expressed surprise at his refusal and asked him to review his decision.[27] Curtin replied in terms as blunt as those used by Churchill:

> Australia's outer defences are now quickly vanishing and our vulnerability is completely exposed. With A.I.F. troops we sought to save Malaya and Singapore, falling back on Netherlands East Indies. All these northern defences are gone or going. Now you contemplate using the A.I.F to save Burma. All this has been done, as in Greece, without adequate air support. We feel a primary obligation to save Australia not only for itself but to preserve it as a base for the development of the war against Japan. In the circumstances it is impossible to reverse a decision which we made with the utmost care.[28]

This bad-tempered exchange came to an end with Churchill accepting responsibility for diverting the convoy and accepting Curtin's decision about the 7 Division, as he had to do. It was revived, though, by the Governor of Burma (Dorman-Smith), who stressed the need for the Australians to land to save Rangoon.[29] Churchill, with all the ill-temper revived, passed Dorman-Smith's note on to Curtin with a comment: 'I have of course informed the Governor of your decision.'[30]

Would the 7 Division have saved Rangoon? Almost certainly not. The city had been bombed by the Japanese on numerous occasions already. The evacuation of civil servants from the capital was well underway. By the time the Australians could have landed (probably the 28th at the earliest) the only forces available for defence were the recently arrived 7 Armoured Brigade and the remains of 17 Division. The Australians had fought in the desert and in Syria but were quite unused to Burmese conditions or to the skill of the Japanese divisions against which they would have been pitted. Given the chaos into which the area had fallen, with the civil administration completely broken down, the railways crammed with deserted trains and general disorganisation,[31] there seems no doubt that the Australians would have soon joined in the evacuation of the area ordered by the new commander, General Alexander, on 6 March. They would have then formed part of the retreat of the entire force and finished up in Assam. Curtin and his advisers were quite correct in identifying a lack of air support as the crucial factor. Without it Rangoon was doomed with or without the Australians.

This seems to have been Alexander's view. The new commander had been rushed out from Britain when it was felt by Wavell that Lieutenant-General Sir Thomas Hutton was not up to the job. Hutton, however, remained as Alexander's Chief of Staff. The decision to evacuate Rangoon was a serious one. It was the only port through which reinforcements could rapidly reach Burma from India. Yet Alexander did not have sufficient troops to hold it and there was a considerable risk that any attempt to do so would result in the whole force being cut off by the Japanese. Indeed Alexander was fortunate to escape from this position himself – only the premature movement of an enemy roadblock allowed him through to the north.[32]

The only course now was to retreat. A line had been selected north of Rangoon on which to make a stand and perhaps a counter-attack but the non-appearance of Chinese forces on the left flank and the sheer inability of Alexander's forces to counter the Japanese rendered this impossible. The next step back was to Mandalay. But that too could not be held. The question then arose: to which area could the British retreat? The choices were unappealing. There were no decent roads that ran from Burma into north-eastern India – all traffic in that area routed across the Bay of Bengal. There were also no dumps of supplies along the road to India, a situation made worse by the lack of transport aircraft for air-drops. On the other hand a retreat into China would make the supply of any such force problematical. There was also a petrol shortage in China and a famine in parts of Yunnan province.[33]

This problem was already being considered by the high command. On 19 March Wavell wrote to Churchill setting out the options. He concluded: 'It seems to me we should keep in touch with Chinese at all costs and I propose instructing Alexander accordingly.'[34] He also informed the CIGS that this was his decision.[35] As a result of these messages, Churchill wrote to Chiang informing him of the proposal that British troops might withdraw to China and stating that while he would be happy to entrust the troops to Chiang, he wanted Chiang's assurance that this move would be welcome.[36] Meanwhile the COS were considering Wavell's proposal. Though inclined to accept the China option they passed the whole question to the Joint Planners.[37] The planners produced a lengthy report rehearsing once more the options and coming to the quite extraordinary solution that the final decision should be left to Chiang.[38]

Meanwhile at the front the hour was rapidly approaching when a decision had to be made. Alexander was inclined to the China option but the promised support from Chiang to shore up the left flank of the retreat had not eventuated, despite a strong recommendation from Stilwell. At a meeting near Mandalay on 25 April the whole issue was thrashed out between Alexander, Stilwell and the commander of the disparate force that was now called Burmacorps, Lieutenant-General William Slim. Slim's intervention was forceful. He thought 'that to send any of our British units in their present state to China would be a grave military and political error'.[39] This carried the day. Alexander agreed and the long retreat over the appalling tracks in north-eastern Burma and Assam began. In the end Burmacorps, with an attached Chinese division (38 Division), arrived in Imphal in Assam just before the monsoon. The Japanese made no attempt in these atrocious conditions to follow up. Fighting and retreating ceased for the time in northern Burma.

The decision to retreat on India was really one of the most critical made in the campaign because the retreating forces were to form the basis of later Indian and British units in Burma. Had they been lost to China the cadre of men who were to fight the Japanese would have consisted entirely of green troops and green commanders. Not for the last time, Slim had saved the day in Burma.

While the great retreat (the longest in British history) was taking place, attention shifted to the Bay of Bengal and Ceylon. With the Malay barrier gone, the Japanese fleet had access to the Indian Ocean. Britain had a considerable fleet there commanded by Admiral Somerville (he of Mers-el-Kabir). But the main units (four slow, old battleships and two aircraft carriers flying Swordfish) were no match for the newer Japanese capital ships and carriers flying Zeros. The worry for the British was that their main naval bases in the area (Trincomalee and Colombo) were open to attack and Ceylon open to invasion. Churchill realised this and ordered Somerville to keep his heavy ships away from any major Japanese incursion. At the same time Ceylon was reinforced with fighters and anti-aircraft guns.[40] This was all to no avail when the enemy fleet attacked Ceylon on 5 April. They destroyed the naval bases and took a heavy toll on the aircraft sent against them. They then sank two heavy cruisers detached from Somerville's main fleet to collect water, and later a small aircraft carrier. After that Somerville was ordered to Kenya, thus conceding the eastern Indian Ocean and the Bay of Bengal to the enemy.[41] The problem that this created for the British was that until sufficient naval strength could be gathered, any attempt to reconquer Burma by amphibious operations across the Bay of Bengal was ruled out.

A focus on the Indian Ocean had, however, led the COS and Churchill to turn their attention to Madagascar. This Vichy-controlled island lay athwart British shipping lanes to the Middle East and to India. It could also provide a base for Japanese submarines to operate against those lanes. Given the supine attitude of Vichy towards Japanese incursions into French Indo-China, might this not be a real possibility? The problem was, as so often, a lack of landing craft, most of which were earmarked for Torch. This meant that operations against the island had to be delayed until the assault shipping could be assembled, which turned out to be 5 May. By this time

Brooke had cooled considerably to the operation (Ironclad), noting in his diary:

> Personally I feel we have little to gain from carrying out the operation. The main object is to deny Diego Suarez to the Japs, and I don't feel they are likely to go there! . . . However Winston decided for it at the present.[42]

Nevertheless, Brooke did not oppose the scheme and Pound was quite in favour so it went ahead. Diego Suarez was easily taken but it proved necessary to occupy other parts of the island as well. All this meant that the troops involved – two brigade groups and an East African brigade destined for India – would not reach Burma until the end of the year, which greatly affected any plans Wavell might be developing for a counter-offensive.

In April, that is even before the great retreat had reached Assam, Wavell had in fact ordered his staff to begin planning for such an operation.[43] He faced a plethora of problems. At his disposal he had one British and six Indian divisions that were under-trained and in some cases (17 Indian Division and 1 Burma Division) divisions only in name. In the air he had four bomber squadrons (three Blenheim, one Wellington) and seven fighter squadrons (six Hurricane, one Mohawk). All fighters were outmatched by the Japanese and he had no forward airfields at all. Close fighter support would therefore rely on capturing airfields in the early days of the offensive, a tall order given the state of the troops.[44] At sea he had a few motor launches and that was all.

There were other difficulties. There were no major roads from Assam into northern Burma or from the base area around Calcutta into Assam; these would have to be constructed before troops in any number could be supported. Then there was the political situation. Churchill had sent Sir Stafford Cripps to India with the bleak task of settling the emerging constitutional crisis. The offer of Dominion status as soon as possible after the war was not sufficient for the Congress leadership, so Cripps left with no deal struck and political unrest continuing.

In the light of all this Wavell decided that he must keep some divisions around India to quell any disturbances. He felt therefore he could do no more than operate some small columns in northern Assam and perhaps gain the line of the River Chindwin and if successful advance further to re-establish a common front with Chinese forces in Yunnan.[45]

This plan did not meet with the approval of the Prime Minister. On 12 June he told Wavell:

> All these minor operations are very nice and useful nibbling. What I am interested in is the capture of Rangoon and Moulmein and, thereafter, striking at Bangkok. For this we should first have to fight our way along the coast amphibiously from Chittagong via Akyab, and at the right time launch overseas expedition of forty or fifty thousand of our best British troops with suitable armour across the northern part of the Bay of Bengal. The object of this would be to carry the war back into southern Burma and Malaya, and strike at the Japanese communications passing northwards into Southern China.[46]

This really was an extraordinary paper. In the Far East at this time there were precisely no landing craft that would allow an amphibious operation along the Arakan coast, let alone a full-scale seaborne attack on Rangoon. Nor did the Prime Minister address how such an operation was to be undertaken in the light of Japanese naval superiority in the Bay of Bengal. Moreover, there were not anything like 40,000 or 50,000 'good British troops' in the area – nor would there ever be. Neither did Churchill address exactly how these operations could be carried out in the face of Japanese air superiority. As for the objectives stated in the paper – Bangkok, southern Burma, Malaya – they were quite ludicrous. There were just not the roads in Burma to support such an advance unless the force was to be supplied from the air. And the fact was that the only considerable body of transport aircraft in the theatre belonged to the Americans, who were busy using them to supply China over the Hump (Himalayas). As Michael Howard has said, this was 'cigar butt strategy' at its worst. As a pattern of operations to be followed after the end of the German war, Churchill's fulminations might have had some merit. As a practical guide for Wavell they had none.

Wavell felt obliged to respond. He announced to Churchill that he had devised a new plan but he insisted that this be conveyed to the COS and the Prime Minister in person by the army commander (the emollient

Alexander), who could not leave India before early July. By this means Wavell bought himself some time.

On 11 July Alexander arrived with Wavell's plan. It consisted of three parts. First, Long Range Penetration Groups (developed by Colonel Orde Wingate as a type of commando) would be airlifted behind enemy lines in northern Burma. Then a division would attack down the Arakan coast, seizing airfields at Akyab that were in range of Rangoon. Finally there would be a two-division assault on Rangoon to cut off Japanese forces in the north of the country. When asked about the timing of the operation, all Alexander would say was that it was dependent on the assault shipping and aircraft being made available.[47]

Alexander, as was to happen so often, seems to have mollified Churchill. The day after the meeting with the COS, Churchill wrote that the planning for what became known as Operation Anakim should proceed immediately, but that its timing depended on events in the desert, in southern Russia and the south-western Pacific. Also, Japanese strength in Burma needed to be whittled down before the operation could be launched. 'We need not commit ourselves' to the enterprise, he concluded. 'Nothing will have been risked or lost, and all the preparations will be helpful in the future.'[48]

Back in Burma Wavell despaired of ever getting the naval and aircraft he needed for the Arakan coast operations. He discussed the issues with Admiral Somerville and Air Marshal Peirse (C-in-C RAF Far East) and concluded that they would not obtain naval or air superiority in time to launch it that year. In a rather desperate move, Wavell decided to launch what parts of Anakim he thought had a hope of succeeding. His initial move was to propel (if that is the right word) the 14 Indian Division down the Arakan coast towards Akyab. This movement began in December 1942 and has been described as 'the worst managed British military effort of the war'.[49] The intention was to hack through the jungles of the Arakan to Akyab and seize airfields in range of Rangoon. Essentially, what happened amounted to a continually reinforced division battering its futile way against a Japanese bunker system well short of Akyab protected by artillery and a mass of interlocking machine guns. The division, which was operating in some of the most difficult mountainous, jungle country in Burma, had been trained for the desert and was made up largely of recent recruits.

It had neither the skill, nor the guns, nor the close air support ever to reduce such a stronghold. This was not Wavell's finest hour and the reason he reinforced the division until it held an unwieldy nine brigades and ordered it to continue attacking, against the advice of the divisional and army commander, is a mystery. Perhaps he felt obliged to do something given the absence of Anakim. He was not, however, obliged to batter away to no effect. In March 1943 the Japanese went on the offensive, driving the British back until in May they were back on their start line. The only positive was that Slim, who was rapidly demonstrating his competence, was ordered in to sort out the mess. By April, Churchill had had enough. Wavell and the Chiefs of the air force (Peirse) and navy (Somerville) were called home for consultations.[50]

Meanwhile Wavell had launched another segment of the Anakim offensive. Major-General Orde Wingate had conducted guerrilla operations against the Italians in Ethiopia. Now he was in Burma selling the idea of Long Range Penetration Groups – mobile columns that could operate behind Japanese lines, be supplied from the air and generally create havoc. In February 1943 the first Chindit operation consisting of eight columns and a total of 3,000 men was launched. It started well. The River Chindwin was crossed and the columns managed to destroy some railway bridges and generally baffle the Japanese. Then Wingate, whose ambitions were growing, crossed the Irrawaddy. This brought his columns into the dry, hot area of central Burma. It also revealed his purpose to the enemy, who increasingly boxed him in between the Irrawaddy and the Chindwin River. In the end the columns, under Japanese pressure, were forced to disperse and make their own way back to India. Of the initial 3,000, just 2,200 made it back and many of them were so badly affected with malaria that they never fought again. Only in the context of Burmese operations could this rather futile exercise be described as a success. Yet it was. There were some positives: Wingate had demonstrated that air supply could work; the Japanese had been somewhat inconvenienced by operations against their rail network. So Wingate's stocks rose (especially with Churchill, who always supported this type of irregular warfare) and Wavell's fell (though the C-in-C had approved the Chindit affair). There would be much explaining to do in London.

So far, operations in Burma had been, for good or ill, British affairs. The Americans were still there, however – Stilwell with Chiang's Chinese just across the border in Yunnan and the air force supplying the Chinese over the Himalayas. The Casablanca Conference in January 1943 marked the point at which the Americans started to take a greater interest in what was happening or not happening in Burma. At that conference the British explained to Roosevelt why the amphibious section of Anakim had to be postponed. The Americans immediately offered landing craft but the lack of aircraft proved insurmountable. There could be no amphibious attack for some time.

The demise of Anakim in any case did not greatly worry the Americans. They were hardly concerned about the British reconquest of one of their colonies. What did concern them was the Chinese. This became clear at the Trident Conference in May 1943. They insisted that the Chinese must be aided – first by vastly increasing the amount of supplies delivered by air and second by 'vigorous and aggressive land and air operations at the end of the 1943 monsoon from Assam into Burma via Ledo and Imphal' as an essential preliminary to reopening the Burma Road.[51]

None of this proved congenial to Churchill, who – as will be seen – was turning towards a quite different suite of operations. He cared little for the Chinese, whom he correctly thought were not prosecuting the war against Japan with any vigour, and he deprecated operations of any kind through the malarial swamps and mountains of Assam.

Here the British were bailed out by the new Commander-in-Chief India. Churchill had lost patience with Wavell and kicked him upstairs to become Viceroy of India. In his place came General Auchinleck, an old India hand and unemployed since his demise in the desert. One of his first duties was to assess the Trident decisions. He quickly deemed that there could be no major operation launched from Assam that year. The communications in the form of roads and forward airfields had yet to be built and the men properly trained in jungle warfare. Nor did he have the resources for any amphibious operations across the Bay of Bengal.[52]

Churchill initially was furious with Auchinleck. How could he explain to the Americans that nothing at all was to be done in Burma during 1943?[53] But as Brooke pointed out, at least Auchinleck had vetoed any large operation from Assam, something that neither the COS nor Churchill wanted. And Churchill had had a brainwave. For the next conference with the Americans (Quadrant, August 1943) he produced Wingate, with his plans

637

for an expanded Chindit operation from Assam. This at least looked like the operation the Americans were seeking without actually committing a large British force to fight in such inhospitable country. The Americans were impressed by Wingate, who for all his faults could present a lucid plan with persuasion and verve. The Americans were at least persuaded enough to agree that Wingate's plan should be further studied while insisting that the emphasis on Burma must be on improving communications to China, which they now thought should consist of an oil pipeline as well as a road.[54] There the Anglo-American debate over Burma ceased for the year.

What is interesting about the Allied debates over action in Burma for 1943 is that, apart from Wavell's truncated and ineffectual Anakim operations, nothing actually took place in the theatre. Plans were produced in number but none was put into effect. There were several reasons for this. The first was that from the British point of view they just did not have the military wherewithal, particularly in assault shipping or warships to back up an amphibious assault or fighter or bomber aircraft to match the Japanese. It also has to be said that the British COS and Churchill had no great interest in major operations designed to reconquer Burma if they risked taking resources away from the invasion of Sicily and Italy and operations in the Mediterranean generally. At all the Allied conferences the emphasis lay with the Mediterranean, and that is what had first call on resources. As far as the Americans were concerned, their only aim in this theatre was to aid China and while the British agreed to one scheme after another with this in mind, they did little to aid the Americans in their pursuits. They were just not interested in China. There was a further reason why nothing happened in Burma in 1943 and that was because the British could not agree among themselves about what kind of operations should be prosecuted there.

The great intra-British debate was started by Wavell. In February 1943, when he must have had more than an inkling that his great Arakan offensive was failing, he wrote to the COS:

So far we have been operating separately from India and the Pacific against the extreme flanks of the Japanese line – the Solomons and New Guinea and Northern Burma. We can only progress very slowly and at considerable cost in these areas. If we could make a sudden combined assault against the centre of the Japanese line we might catch our enemy off his guard and achieve great results.

The objective I have in mind for such a blow is the control of the Sunda Straits between Sumatra and Java. This would threaten Singapore and the whole Japanese position in the Netherlands East Indies. If we could at the same time seize a base in northern Sumatra from which to control the Malacca Straits, we should have gone far towards the defeat of Japan.[55]

Shortly after, the Joint Planners examined the question and found that they agreed with Wavell.[56] Then Leo Amery, Secretary of State for Burma, produced his own paper, 'The South-East Asia Problem (A tentative suggestion)' which also suggested that Burma could best be liberated by landings in northern Sumatra, an operation which could be combined with mobile columns infiltrated into Assam designed to tie down Japanese forces there.[57] In other words: Sumatra plus Wingate.

These ideas appealed to Churchill. He had consistently opposed land operations in Burma and he now insisted that the COS work up plans to put Wavell's ideas and those of the Joint Planners and Amery into effect. In fact both Wavell and the planners immediately back-pedalled on their earlier ideas. Wavell could now see nothing but difficulties in his Sumatra scheme.[58] As for the planners, they produced papers tending to deprecate any large offensives in the Far East, noting that in any case none of them would hasten the end of the Japanese war.[59]

The problem for Churchill was that the COS also deprecated large amphibious operations in South-East Asia. Brooke in particular considered that anything which shifted focus from the Mediterranean was to be discouraged. He also thought (correctly) that the British had not the resources (in shipping or aircraft) to conduct landings in Sumatra and would not have them for some time. This meant that the British did not enter the conference with the Americans with a united front, meaning that they found themselves agreeing to operations to aid China that had no appeal for them. For all these reasons therefore – lack of resources, division in the ranks and the futility with which the American plans for China were regarded – no operations of any note were carried out in Burma in 1943.

Did this mean that 1943 was a wasted year in Burma? From the point of view of the men fighting there it did not. It was obvious to such commanders as Wavell and Slim that the early encounters with the Japanese demonstrated that the British and Indian troops did not have the skill in jungle warfare to match the Japanese. In June 1943 Wavell formed the Infantry Committee to put forward ideas to improve the quality of men entering infantry divisions and to develop training methods that would make them effective jungle fighters.[60] The Infantry Committee recommended that divisions be reorganised. They needed flexible transport, including animal transport, more light equipment such as mortars and towed howitzers, all of which would make them less dependent on roads.[61]

This reorganisation and education of the eastern army continued under Auchinleck, Slim and a number of first-rate divisional commanders who were gradually asserting their authority. One of the latter was Lieutenant-General Frank Messervy who commanded the 7 Indian Division. He noted that the Allied linear defence was continually outmanoeuvred by Japanese infiltration and blocking tactics. He determined that all-round defence was the answer. Positions must be held even if surrounded. The Chindit operations had demonstrated that such positions could be supplied from the air and that the Japanese besiegers could be set upon by units carefully placed on their flanks. He also insisted upon aggressive patrolling, more extensive weapons training, field craft and every other aspect of jungle warfare.[62]

At a higher level, corps commanders and army commanders organised divisional and corps training. For example the 25 Indian Division took part in a divisional exercise in September 1942 (Operation Jove) just a month after it was formed. Exercise Minx followed three months later, then Exercise Fog some months after that. Then corps exercises followed (Operation Barge) and defensive exercises (unfortunately named Trump I and II).[63] This division (and others) would then enter battle with no fewer than six large-scale exercises under its belt, a far cry from 1942.

The situation in the air was also a far cry from earlier days. In 1942 the Japanese ruled the air. By early 1944 the positions had reversed. In January the Japanese had just 220 aircraft of all types while the Allies had 735 (464 RAF and 271 USAAF). In addition the RAF now had Spitfires, which at last provided a superior plane to the Japanese Zero.[64]

Therefore, should the Japanese attack, the army they would encounter would be much more mobile than before, better equipped, not easily distracted by infiltration, ready to be supplied from the air and trained to a decent level of expertise. It is a good question as to who would be most surprised by these developments – the Japanese or the authorities in London.

Auchinleck was soon removed from this equation. Churchill had long taken against India Command and in truth – with famine, floods and civil unrest in the country – they had sufficient problems without concerning themselves with military operations in South-East Asia. He therefore determined to establish a new South-East Asia Command (SEAC) and have a new man in charge of it. That man turned out to be Lord Louis Mountbatten, previously head of Combined Operations and a member of the COS Committee. He had the confidence of the Americans and was thought by the Prime Minister to represent new ideas and not to be averse to amphibious adventures.[65]

* * * * *

The great strategic debate over Burma resumed at the Cairo and Tehran Conferences at the end of 1943. At Cairo the British discovered that Roosevelt had promised Chiang a large-scale amphibious operation in 1944 to retake the Andaman Islands in the Bay of Bengal (Operation Buccaneer).[66] In return Chiang promised to propel his Yunnan army southwards into Burma. This operation did not find favour with Churchill or Brooke. Both worried that it would take landing craft from the Mediterranean and imperil the forthcoming Anzio landing. They were bailed out by Stalin. At Tehran he announced that at the end of the German war Russia would turn its forces against Japan.[67] The war against Japan would now be decided by the forces of America aided by Russia. Roosevelt quickly lost interest in Buccaneer – or indeed any operations in South-East Asia at all.[68]

This did not mean that the debate over Burma was at an end *between* the British. Indeed it got a new life at the Cairo Conference when the COS finally developed a policy of their own for the Far East. Their problem was that this policy was at odds with the Prime Minister's policy, which still involved the invasion of Sumatra. The COS plan also bypassed Burma.

Indeed it bypassed South-East Asia altogether. The COS now wanted a British fleet to operate in the south-west Pacific on the left flank of the Americans. The land component which might reconquer such areas as Borneo would consist of a British army of four divisions and an air component operating from bases in Australia.[69] The COS had agreed 'in principle' to this plan at one of the last meeting of the Cairo Conference.[70] But Churchill had not attended this meeting and at the plenary sessions that he did attend it is by no means certain that the British aspect of operations in the Pacific was clearly laid out.[71] It therefore came as something of a shock to him when the COS unveiled the plan at a Defence Committee meeting in January 1944. He protested that this was the first he had heard of these proposals and he did not agree with them. He noted that Admiral King had told him in Washington in September that British naval help in the Pacific would not be needed and that the only true plan in South-East Asia for 1944 was the invasion of Sumatra (Operation Culverin).[72]

Churchill had instructed the new headquarters (South-East Asia Command) to turn their attention to amphibious operations. Overall, they tended to agree with the Prime Minister. They considered road building to China to be of little benefit compared to the air route. They also favoured Culverin, with advances down the Malay Peninsula and into the South China Sea to follow. This activity would leave few resources for a major campaign in north Burma, so Wingate's LRPGs were brought forward to fill this gap.[73]

Mountbatten determined to be proactive. He established a Mission (Axiom) under his American deputy, General Albert Wedemeyer, to sell his plans to London and Washington. They arrived in London in early February and met with the Prime Minister and the COS on the 14th. Wedemeyer stated that, after study, SEAC had come to the conclusion that a landing in north Sumatra (Churchill's Culverin scheme) was the right operation. It would either pin considerable Japanese resources to the area and away from US operations in the Pacific, or it would facilitate a breakthrough into Malaya which would rob Japan of many natural resources. This was music to Churchill's ears but not to Brooke's. He protested that the wherewithal for Culverin would be difficult to find and that anyway it was not clear that it would do more to shorten the war than the COS's Pacific Strategy. Churchill, however, insisted that the SEAC plan be thoroughly investigated and a committee of the Joint Planners and the Axiom Mission was set up to report on the practicability of Culverin.[74]

The planners, not surprisingly, sided with the COS, stating that Culverin could not be mounted until the spring of 1945 and that the Pacific Strategy might result in the war ending six months earlier.[75] But Churchill, knowing that such arguments were based on assumptions rather than facts, refused to accept them and the debate returned to square one.[76]

The debate continued, interminably, until almost the end of the year, Churchill and his Cabinet colleagues, especially Eden, Attlee and Lyttelton, arguing for Culverin, the COS for the Pacific Strategy. Churchill's position is best summed up in a memorandum to the War Cabinet on 29 February. He stated that the COS position ultimately involved acting 'as a subsidiary force under the Americans'. This in turn raised:

difficult political questions about the future of our Malayan possessions. If the Japanese should withdraw from them or make peace as a result of the main American thrust, the United States Government would after the victory feel greatly strengthened in its view that all possessions in the East Indian Archipelago should be placed under some international body upon which the United States would exercise decisive control. They would feel with conviction: 'We won the victory and liberated these places, and we must have the dominating say in their future and derive full profit from their produce, especially oil.'[77]

In this Churchill was arguing that his strategy had a political aim whereas that of the COS did not, as the Americans would rightly claim that victory in the Pacific was overwhelmingly theirs whether the British participated or not.

The Chiefs did not accept this position. They argued that whatever strategy Britain followed in the Far East the Americans were likely to get the credit for victory and that, as the main action would be the American drive across the Pacific, Britain should ensure that it was part of that action. As for Culverin, Britain was not likely to have the resources to carry it out until six months after Germany had been defeated and perhaps not even then.[78]

Matters came to a peak in early March. Deadlock seemed complete and in an attempt to break it and defuse what he considered a very serious situation, the Secretary of the COS (General Ismay) wrote a confidential note to Churchill:

> There is a clear-cut divergence of opinion between yourself and your Ministerial colleagues on one side, and the Chiefs of Staff on the other, as to the plan that should be followed for the ultimate defeat of Japan. A number of papers have been written on the subject, and there have been a number of discussions. But no agreement has been reached. On the one hand it seems absolutely certain that you and your ministerial colleagues will not agree to the 'Pacific' strategy. On the other hand the Chiefs of Staff, even if their faith in this strategy were shaken by the papers which you have written and the discussions which are to take place, are extremely unlikely to retract the military opinions they have expressed.
>
> Thus we are faced with the practical certainty of a continued cleavage of opinion between the War Cabinet and their military advisors; nor can we exclude the possibility of resignations on the part of the latter. A breach of this kind, undesirable at any time, would be little short of catastrophic at this present juncture [with Overlord just three months away].[79]

He suggested Churchill call a meeting to resolve differences or say directly to the COS that 'political considerations must be over-riding' in this case. He was certain that the COS would accept such a demarche.[80]

That Ismay was not overstating the seriousness of the situation is clear from Brooke's diary. He complained that Churchill was trying to set the War Cabinet against the Chiefs and noted that it 'may well lead to the resignation of the Chiefs of Staff Committee'.[81]

No reply to Ismay's note to Churchill seems to exist. Probably he spoke to him and took up his suggestion of a further meeting with the COS. Three days after his diary explosion, Brooke mentioned that the Prime Minister had called the COS to meet with Attlee, Eden, Lyttelton and Lord Leathers, whom he described as the 'yes men' from the War Cabinet – which is certainly a unique way of describing Attlee.[82] What Churchill did not do was take up Ismay's suggestion of overruling the COS on political grounds. Perhaps he thought that might provoke, rather than dampen, any threats of resignation. Perhaps he remembered the Dardanelles when naval advice was ignored by the War Council and ultimately led to his own demise; no doubt he did not want a major crisis so close to D-Day.

The meeting took place in the evening of 8 March. Churchill led off by stating that the Pacific Strategy had been formulated without his knowledge and that he did not agree with it. He added, however, that much more work was needed on the problem of operations from the Indian Ocean and from the Pacific before a decision could be reached. He was supported by Attlee, Eden, Lyttelton and Leathers. Attlee said that the effect on England and India of the recapture of Malaya and Singapore would be much greater than anything that could be accomplished by Britain in the Pacific. Eden agreed, noting that it was vital to keep up enthusiasm for the war and that shipping was the real issue and Culverin would require much less than the COS's Pacific Strategy. Leathers took up the shipping problem, waspishly stating that the COS did not seem to have any understanding of shipping and that in any case no thorough investigation had been completed. Finally Lyttelton concluded that it was essential that Britain reconquer its lost colonies in South-East Asia. In any case labour might not be available in Australia to build a base for the Pacific Strategy.

For the COS, Brooke did most of the talking. He thought it was possible to get into the action earlier with the Pacific Strategy than with Culverin, which could not be undertaken until the spring of 1945. He thought Australia a better base than India for future operations, largely because 'we should there have to deal with a white population who were accustomed to working at high pressure'. The main action would lie in the Pacific and he thought that if Britain acted promptly enough and built up its forces, a good case could be made for claiming the command in the south-west Pacific. He noted that the COS agreed with the Prime Minister that more work had to be done on the problem before making a decision.[83] It was therefore agreed that there was insufficient data to decide whether the centre of gravity of British operations should be in the Bay of Bengal or in the Pacific. Further work should be undertaken by the COS and the Department of War Transport to resolve the problem.[84]

In the event, not much was resolved. There would be dozens more meetings between the COS and Churchill over Far Eastern strategy in the next seven months. There would be an occasional crisis – Brooke again raised resignation after a paper from the Prime Minister about the merits of Culverin on 20 April 1944.[85] At a COS meeting in August Churchill was still pushing for Culverin and Brooke still suggesting that his Pacific Strategy was much to be preferred.[86] Even at the Octagon Conference with the Americans in September, Churchill was telling Curtin that amphibious operations were under serious consideration.[87] There were various attempts by the planners to square the circle by developing a 'middle strategy' and later a 'modified middle strategy' whereby British forces advanced further to the left in the Pacific than wanted by the COS but not so far left as to be mistaken for Culverin. Such efforts were pretty derisory in strategic terms. They were in fact just desperate efforts to get their masters to come to any kind of agreement.[88]

One outstanding aspect of this debate is that while it was running its course, military operations in Burma were taking place which were quite at odds with Churchill's and the COS views on desirable strategies for Burma. So far the authorities in London had paid little regard to the enemy in making their plans. The Japanese, fully occupied at Guadalcanal and elsewhere, had been relatively quiescent in Burma since the end of 1942. All that changed in early 1944. The Burma Area Army determined to do two things. They would drive the British XV Corps in the Arakan northwards to prevent a seaborne landing around Akyab and they would annihilate the British base at Imphal to prevent it being used as a jumping-off ground for offensive operations across the Chindwin.[89]

Opening moves were made in Arakan in early February 1944 by the Japanese to prevent the transfer of British divisions to Imphal. The attack came as a surprise. It separated the 5 and 7 Indian Divisions and threated 7 Division with encirclement. But Messervy's men, though surrounded, determined to fight it out until help could be summoned. They formed a box defence, manned mainly with administrative staff (the Admin Box). When help arrived from flanking forces, the Japanese were beaten back, the XV Corps securing the first British victory in the Burma campaign.[90]

Further north three divisions of the Fifteenth Japanese Army launched the main attack in the first week of March. The 33 Division attacked Imphal from the south while the 15 Division attacked from the east. Further north still the 31 Division attacked Kohima in an effort to sever the main rail link between India and Assam at Dimapur. The ground across which they attacked was rugged in the extreme – mountainous, malarial jungle with a few winding roads with precipitous drops. Slim and the IV Corps commander (Lieutenant-General Geoffrey Scoones) were wrong-footed by the Japanese plan. Especially at Kohima, Slim thought the country too rugged to conduct operations. The defences were at first rudimentary and the Japanese gained ground towards Dimapur. Slim was not unhappy, however, that the Japanese had launched an offensive. He intended to withdraw to the Imphal plain, reckoning that the Japanese would follow. Then he would use his superiority in numbers to stall the attack and wear them down by attrition. As the enemy weakened, he would drive them back across the Chindwin. Slim's plan worked, though not without some crises.

The immediate use of the reserves around Imphal meant that a division (5 Indian) had to be airlifted from Arakan to shore up the defences. Mountbatten managed this, but only through commandeering American transport aircraft. Other reinforcements took longer to arrive than anticipated due to the rather lethargic response of India HQ. The Japanese obliged Slim, though, by persisting with repeated uncoordinated attacks in some of the worst country imaginable. Their force gradually wasted away, through lack of reserves, disease and persistent futile attacks. On the other hand, Slim gradually gained strength as reinforcements, food and equipment were flown in. By May the tide had turned. The Fifth Army were forced to retreat in the largest reversal for a Japanese land force of the war. Of the 84,000 men who attacked in March, 53,000 had become casualties. The British lost 17,000.[91] By July, despite the arrival of the monsoon, Slim was on the attack. By August he was closing on the Chindwin. The reconquest of Burma had begun.

Back in London the reaction to these events was surprising. It was not that the authorities were unaware of what was happening; Mountbatten kept them fully informed by frequent, detailed battle narratives.[92] Churchill read these closely. For example, on the victory in Arakan at the Admin. Box he noted, 'the new spirit of the forces' involved.[93] He was also told by Mountbatten of the need for American transport aircraft to lift the 5 Indian Division from Arakan to Imphal and he immediately intervened with the President:

Upshot is that Japanese are staging an offensive with the apparent object of capturing Imphal plain. Mountbatten thinks he has a good chance of inflicting a sharp defeat on the enemy greater than that achieved in recent Arakan operations.

Everything depends on flying up from Arakan the operational portion of 5 Division ... To do this Mountbatten needs 30 C47s [Dakotas] or the equivalent in load carrying capacity ... He is going ahead unless contrary instructions are issued. The stakes are pretty high in this battle and victory would have far reaching consequences.[94]

This message demonstrates not only that Churchill was familiar with the course of the battle but that he realised that its result was of some importance.

This close attention to the battle on the part of Churchill persisted throughout its course. In June he noted that the COS were expressing concern about the supply and ammunition situation at Imphal. He assured Mountbatten that he could ask for all the aircraft necessary to maintain the situation and that the Prime Minister's name could be invoked at any time to obtain them.[95]

It is clear therefore that Churchill and the COS followed events in Burma in some detail. What is also clear is that this made little difference to their strategic debates. As far as London was concerned, Slim's victory at Imphal and his preparations to chase a defeated Japanese army back across the Chindwin might have happened on another planet.

Mountbatten did notice. He now saw two strategies for Burma: Operation Capital whereby Slim drove southward on Rangoon or Operation Dracula whereby Rangoon was captured by an assault from the sea.[96] To sort out what to do next, Mountbatten was summoned to London to explain his plans.

Mountbatten arrived on 4 August and discussed his plans with the COS and Churchill. What he unwittingly accomplished was a revival around his plans of the great strategic debate between the Prime Minister and his military advisers. On this occasion Churchill favoured Dracula but combined with Sumatra, while Brooke also favoured Dracula but combined with his Pacific Strategy. Both deprecated operations by Slim. Brooke categorised this as 'eating a porcupine quill by quill' and Churchill as reconquering Burma 'swamp by swamp'.

In the end, British Burmese strategy would not be decided by the British but by the Americans. At the Octagon Conference in September 1944 in Quebec the Americans insisted that Slim's operations continue as the best hope of establishing a link with the Chinese. They also effectively drove a stake through the heart of Dracula by insisting that it be carried out entirely with British resources, knowing of course that the British did not have the resources. The American Chiefs then tried to veto Brooke's Pacific Strategy by making it clear the British fleet was surplus to requirements. The Japanese could be defeated by the US fleet alone. Roosevelt overruled them, however, insisting that a British fleet would be welcome while also conveying to Churchill that this was a good will gesture rather than a strategic necessity.[97]

Slim was of course oblivious to this great strategic debate. He had enough on his hands. He had attempted to incorporate Wingate's second Chindit operation (February–March 1944) into his plans but that operation was soon hijacked by Stilwell to aid his Chinese forces and therefore played no major role in the ejection of the Japanese from Burma. After the death of Wingate in an air crash in May 1944, the whole affair rather fizzled out. Meanwhile it was left to Slim's Fourteenth Army to deal with the main Japanese forces in Burma.[98]

Slim's initial plan was to cross the Chindwin with his two corps (XXXIII and IV) and bring on a decisive battle between that river and the Irrawaddy.[99] The Japanese command, however, decided to withdraw behind the Irrawaddy and fight behind that river line.[100] Slim therefore changed his plan. He now sought to pin the main Japanese army to the Irrawaddy around Mandalay with XXXIII Corps while he sidestepped the IV Corps south along the river and then east to capture the Japanese communications centre of Meiktila. If successful, this movement might trap the Japanese forces around Mandalay between the two British corps and force a decisive battle or (less likely) a Japanese surrender.[101]

The movement of IV Corps was concealed from the Japanese by an elaborate deception plan. The sidestepping divisions of the corps kept radio silence while dummy wireless stations in the north maintained chatter. 'Indiscreet' messages were also broadcast to give the Japanese a quite false impression of Slim's dispositions. In the end all this worked perfectly.[102] Fierce battles by XXXIII Corps in February 1945 forced crossings near Mandalay, inducing the Japanese into continuous counter-attacks. Meanwhile IV Corps crossed the Irrawaddy some hundreds of miles to the south and headed for Meiktila. By 4 March the town had fallen and, despite determined Japanese attacks to retake it, Slim's forces held on.[103]

The Japanese were now caught between the 'hammer' of XXXIII Corps advancing on Mandalay and the 'anvil' of IV Corps at Meiktila.[104] Slim had completely outmanoeuvred the Japanese. As at Imphal they compounded their problems by withdrawing their forces far too late. Their shattered armies, under continual air attack from an air force that could now count over 500 aircraft, fell back towards Rangoon. Slim pursued them, aware of the approaching monsoon – XXXIII Corps down the Irrawaddy Valley, IV Corps along the railway line from Meiktila. As it happened, this period of the campaign ended in farce. Mountbatten determined to capture Rangoon with a much attenuated version of Dracula, employing the few craft he had. He also dropped parachutists on the outskirts of the capital. It was all too late. The Japanese evacuated the city some hours before any Allied troops arrived. Mopping up operations in southern Burma followed. The defeat of 1942 had at least been redeemed in one British colony.[105]

It would be pleasant to report that Slim's progress was followed in great detail in London by Churchill or the COS. But it was not. They continued to receive Mountbatten's reports on the Fourteenth Army and on occasion Churchill would telegraph congratulations on the opening of the land route to China or the capture of Mandalay.[106] Slim's operations remained unwanted in London, even if they were successful. There is barely a mention of them in Churchill's files or in Brooke's diary. Greece, Italy and Western Europe might consume them; Burma hardly rated a mention. Churchill was no doubt pleased with Slim's efforts but they were not the strategy he wanted and they were largely ignored. In the last analysis, Britain's Far Eastern Empire started and remained far down the pecking order in London.

* * * * *

The crisis over British strategy in the Far East is a curious matter. On the main trajectory of British strategy, the COS and the civilian leadership was at one. Britain's principal effort would be in Overlord followed by the Italian campaign. There might be disagreements with the Americans over these issues but there was general unity within the British leadership. For all of them – Churchill, Brooke, Eden, Cunningham – the Far East took third place. Why then fall out over it? Perhaps Henry Kissinger's dictum about academic politics – the infighting is so vicious because the stakes are so small – provides one explanation. In this scenario whether Culverin or Dracula or the Pacific Strategy was adopted was hardly crucial because the Pacific war was being won elsewhere. If this was the case, why push the matter in March 1944 to resignation? Here we seem to be dealing with tired men who had been under strain for some time and that strain was not lessened by the imminence of D-Day, where both Brooke and Churchill held doubts of its success. The Far East was therefore an area where the COS could let off accumulated steam caused by the ever-present prodding of the Prime Minister. Brooke in particular seems to have been irritated beyond endurance by Churchill, especially since the Cairo Conference and Churchill's subsequent declaration that the Pacific Strategy had been developed behind his back. But what after all is notable about the debate is that both sides drew back from the brink. At the 8 April meeting there was an immediate push from both sides to seek further information. That also applied to later stormy meetings. The fact was that resignation by the COS over Far Eastern strategy was unthinkable with D-Day approaching. Ismay's intervention certainly shows that there were serious disagreements, but the actions by the main players indicate that these matters would not in the end cause a rupture.

What of the merits of Culverin or Dracula versus the Pacific Strategy? Certainly Churchill and the members of the War Cabinet were not the amateurs caricatured by Brooke in his diary. The loss of Malaya and Singapore was the worst humiliation of the war. 'Regaining the property', in Churchill's words, made sense. The recapture of these colonies would have raised British prestige around the world and would have been popular at home. Strategy, after all, should have a political aim. Moreover, Culverin and Dracula or some variation of them had not been exclusively a civilian domain. Wavell had suggested Culverin first and later Mountbatten thought it worth an attempt. It was also Mountbatten who first developed Dracula. In this regard Brooke's fulminations about 'puerile arguments' by men who 'did not know their subject' and whose arguments he had no trouble in demolishing can be dismissed as a diarist venting his frustrations.

After all, the COSs Pacific Strategy was not without its problems. There was certainly no identifiable political aim. To act on the left flank of the Americans, as their dash across the Pacific accelerated, would hardly have amounted to much, except to draw attention to Britain's subordinate position. Moreover, Leathers' point about the shipping required to establish a considerable fleet in Pacific waters and an army based on Australia was hardly a minor matter and one to which the COS had given insufficient thought. The huge amount of auxiliary craft for fuel, supplies of all kinds, ammunition and repair required to keep a fleet viable in the Pacific was probably beyond Britain's abilities in 1944. Even the smaller fleet which did eventually operate with the US from the end of 1944 had to have substantial American assistance to keep it in being. Then there was the Australians, who – while they had nothing against a British presence in the Far East – worried about how it might interfere with their by now long-established relations with General MacArthur. If Brooke thought there was any chance in these circumstances of Britain obtaining the command in the south-western Pacific, he was severely deluded. Roosevelt and Curtin would have seen to it that nothing would shift Macarthur if it ever had come to that. What the COS had an eye for was the main event, which did lie with the Americans in the Pacific. As military people they no doubt wanted to be in at the kill. But that alone was an insufficient basis for a strategy. Churchill and the members of the War Cabinet were quite correct in pointing this out, however much it might have irritated the COS.

In truth, neither strategy had much going for it. The problem with Culverin, as the COS were quick to point out, was the lack of assault shipping. Britain alone might have scraped up enough after the end of the war with Germany but it would have taken considerable time to get it to the Far East, and the speed of the American advance across the Pacific might well have made the operation redundant. The only other source for this kind of ship was the Americans. And yet, as early as November 1943, the Americans had announced they 'found themselves unable to provide the additional resources required for "First Culverin".[107] In fact the Americans were never going to divert resources from their Pacific landings to enable the British to regain their lost colonies. It seems fair to say that Roosevelt was not neutral regarding that prospect – he was hostile. The same constraints applied to Dracula; only by this time Britain was running short of men as well as shipping. In the end a minuscule seaborne attack on the perennial objective of Akyab was all Britain could manage. As for the Pacific Strategy, no one really wanted the British in the Pacific. They were not needed by the Americans and in the end only accepted as a gesture of good will. The main problem in all this is that Britain was attempting to fight a three-front war – north-western Europe, Italy, the Far East, with barely enough resources for two of them. No one in the civilian/military leadership during this period fully grasped this. Perhaps the shadows of a great power linger. Shadows, after all, lengthen with the setting sun.

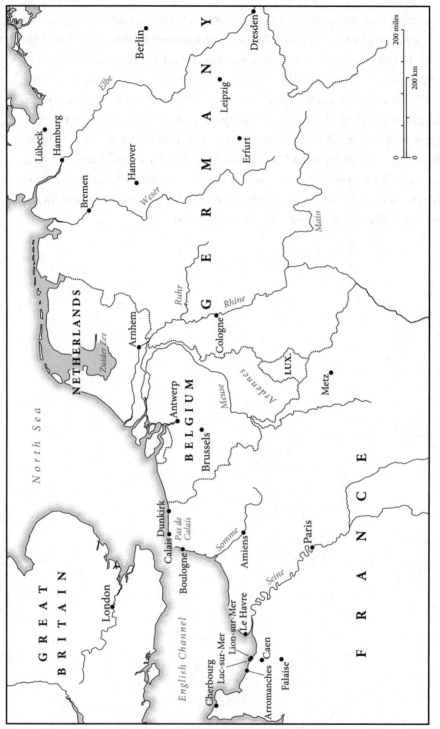

Map 13. France, the Low Countries and Germany.

CHAPTER 28

THE END OF THE WAR IN EUROPE
AUGUST 1944 – MAY 1945

WITH THE CLOSING OF the Falaise pocket on 20 August and the preparations on the same day for penetrating the last major German defensive position in Italy (the Gothic Line), the end of the war seemed imminent. And the war would be won. But for the British political and military leadership, it would not be won as rapidly as they thought possible; it would not be won in the manner which they recommended; and as the months progressed, their armies would play an ever-diminishing role in the victory. In the last nine months of the war only on the peripheries of the conflict could Britain exert much influence and some of that was of dubious utility.

It might be expected that Churchill, generally no bystander in military matters, would be intimately involved in all of the great strategic debates during this period. This was, however, only true of operations in the Mediterranean. On the course that the main campaign in north-western Europe was to take, he hardly participated.

The principal debate in that theatre concerned the shape of the campaign after Falaise. The German armies in the west streamed back from Normandy to the Seine in complete disarray. If the Allies had not managed totally to destroy the German army in the west, they had gone a long way towards it: the German High Command estimated that even before they had retreated to the Seine they had lost 400,000 to 500,000 men, 1,500 tanks, 20,000 motor vehicles and 3,500 pieces of artillery.[1] General Walter Model, who had replaced Von Kluge (who had committed suicide) as C-in-C West found himself with no reserves. The Seventh Army, the defenders of Normandy, now consisted of half a panzer division and two infantry divisions of no more than 3,000 men each. Unless troops arrived, he declared, 'the gateway to Northwest Germany is wide open'.[2]

On the Allied side Montgomery had projected such a scenario. On 18 August 1944, while the fighting at Falaise was raging, he wrote to Brooke:

> Have been thinking ahead about future plans but have not (repeat not) discussed subject with Ike. My views are as follows. After crossing Seine 12 and 21 Army Groups [12 Army Group was a new American formation under General Bradley consisting of the First and Third US Armies] should keep together as a solid mass of some 40 divisions which would be so strong that it need fear nothing.[3]

This mass of troops would be directed towards the Pas de Calais and Antwerp, with the US forces guarding the right flank. One advantage of such a move would be to clear the V-2 sites that were bombarding London.[4]

Montgomery then elaborated this plan for Nye (Vice-CIGS), who happened to be visiting France. He told Nye that the quickest way to win the war was to advance with the force of forty divisions to Antwerp, establish a strong air force in Belgium and then undertake a further advance on the Ruhr. The force must operate as a whole and be under the control of one man.[5] There was no doubt in Montgomery's mind who that one man should be.

But if Montgomery was selling the 'narrow front' advance into Germany, Ike was not buying. Well before D-Day he had elaborated his post-Normandy policy – two army groups (the Twenty-First in the north and Twelfth in the centre) would advance into Germany. Each would have its separate commander and would act under himself as Supreme Commander, which position he would take up on 1 September.[6]

On 23 August Montgomery met Eisenhower. Their accounts of this meeting differ. Montgomery thought he had obtained agreement that he would receive considerable assistance from Bradley in his advance towards the Ruhr which would therefore be made in great strength.[7] Eisenhower, however, in a directive written the following day gave Bradley the task merely of 'supporting' Montgomery's drive on the left while 'advancing eastward from Paris towards Metz'.[8] In other words there would still be two thrusts of more or less equal weight. Montgomery's interpretation of Eisenhower's thoughts might not have been altogether wrong, for on the same day as he drafted his directive to his army group commanders, Eisenhower told Marshall that, due to 'the tremendous importance of the objectives in the northeast we must concentrate on that [i.e. Montgomery's] movement'.[9] Possibly Eisenhower was merely being his usual conciliatory self by trying to please everyone; actually, he managed to please no one. Bradley thought he had given in too much to Montgomery by promising him some flank assistance. Montgomery thought the Supreme Commander had appeased Bradley and dashed any hope of a concerted punch into the Ruhr. In fact what Eisenhower had done, however badly he managed to express it, was stick to his original plan. There would be a broad front advance into Germany along the general lines of 'everybody attacks all the time'. The Rhine would be closed and then encircling attacks made on Germany from north and south.[10]

So far neither Brooke nor Churchill had been involved in the debate. Both had been in Italy attending to the matter of Alexander's forthcoming assault on the Gothic Line. On 28 August Brooke returned to London and noted in his diary that Eisenhower intended to take command and adopt a broad front advance into Germany. He commented sourly, 'this plan is likely to add another six months on to the war'.[11] In the COS Committee he was more conciliatory, merely noting that the Allied left flank (Montgomery) should be sufficiently powerful to fulfil the task allotted to it and that there were no strong reasons for disputing Eisenhower's decision to take command.[12]

Brooke then repaired to Montgomery's HQ and reported that the British commander was 'satisfied' with the situation and that he would have nine American divisions operating on his right flank. They would not be under his orders but he would have the power to coordinate their movements with his own.[13] With this in mind and with Churchill's agreement (he had at last been given the strategic picture by Brooke), a telegram was sent to the British Joint Staff Mission in Washington for the CCS:

1. We are in agreement with the proposed system of command.
2. We are also in general agreement with General Eisenhower's broad strategic conception for the immediate future. In recording this agreement, we desire to lay particular emphasis on a point which, we feel sure, is fully appreciated by General Eisenhower, namely, that the left wing of his Armies must be sufficiently powerful to make certain of accomplishing their first and immediately important mission of destroying the German forces in North East France, observing that the bulk of the enemy strength is in that area. We, therefore, whole-heartedly welcome General Eisenhower's intention that formations of 12th Army group should move on the general axis Paris/Brussels, their principal offensive mission, for the present, being to support 21 Army Group.[14]

It is difficult to know what to make of this message. Did the COS believe that Eisenhower had agreed to some form of the Montgomery 'narrow front' approach? Or were they attempting to impose on the Americans their own interpretation of Ike's ambiguous waffle? Whatever the case, they rapidly found otherwise. They were told by Washington that the 'principal offensive mission' of Bradley's 12 Army Group remained what it always had been: to advance due east of Paris on Metz. Only on its extreme left would it be available to Montgomery and then only if Bradley agreed. The split punch into Germany remained. The British were stuck with a strategy in which none of them believed and which was to deprive Montgomery, at least for the moment, of the forces he believed were required to deal Germany a fatal blow.

To what extent was the scenario favoured by the British a practical operation of war? Could a narrow front, a weighty punch aimed at the Ruhr, have succeeded? The argument is usually framed in logistic terms: could such a force have been maintained given the supply constraints faced by the Allied armies after Normandy? Possibly the forty-division punch first put forward by Montgomery could not have been sustained. But he soon modified that to a force consisting of the First Army Group (twelve divisions) supported by the First American Army (nine divisions). Not even all these units would advance to the Ruhr. The Canadian First Army would advance along the Channel coast, clearing such ports as Le Havre, Calais, Boulogne and Dunkirk. That would leave roughly eighteen divisions for the main attack – nine British and nine American. Could this force have been sustained over an advance of several hundred miles? Some authorities have thought so. Major-General Miles Graham was Senior Administrative Officer in 21 Army Group. He told Chester Wilmot in 1949 that such a drive 'could have carried across the Rhine and isolated the Ruhr, IF GIVEN ABSOLUTE PRIORITY FROM THE END OF AUGUST'.[15] He criticised the estimates of fuel and ammunition used to counter his argument, making the point that no unit ever needs a full complement of both at the same time, because divisions are either moving or fighting.[16] He was insistent that a concentrated attack by the two armies could have been maintained into the Ruhr from the Mulberry harbour at Arromanches and from Cherbourg, without the necessity of opening another major port.[17]

In a more modern study Martin van Creveld, with some modifications, agrees with Graham. He concluded that the eighteen divisions could indeed have been supported into the Ruhr 'though only just'.[18] He too makes the point that those he called the 'pusillanimous accountants' at Eisenhower's headquarters (SHAEF) constantly overestimated the tonnage of supplies needed for an advance, and that indeed Patton and others only got so far as they did by ignoring these calculations.[19] Others have also suggested SHAEF's estimates of supplies were wildly overblown.[20]

Other authorities disagree. Roland Ruppenthal, historian of American logistics in the Second World War, comes to the firm conclusion that without more port capacity, in particular Antwerp, it would have been impossible to develop sufficient logistic capacity to 'attempt a power thrust deep into Germany'.[21]

It is therefore difficult to arrive at a definite conclusion concerning the logistic debate. However, the debate was never really about logistics; it was about politics. One of the authorities above (Graham) noted that for Montgomery's plan to have any chance, absolute priority in supply would have had to be given to the narrow front. This would have meant immobilising Patton's Third Army, which had conducted such a spectacular advance across central France, and diverting its supplies to Hodges' First Army supporting Montgomery.[22] There was no chance that Eisenhower would have contemplated halting an American army to enable a British commander to advance into Germany. There was also no chance that Marshall would have approved of such a policy even if Eisenhower had decided in Montgomery's favour. It was, after all, an election year in the US, they were now the senior partner in the western alliance and the victory was not only theirs, it had to be seen to be theirs. This fed into another factor. Only the British had imperatives to end the war quickly: their manpower constraints, their waning influence within the alliance, the V-2 bombardment of London and general exhaustion as their war approached its sixth year hardly mattered to the Americans. If the war lasted for another six months, so be it.

And yet. There is no evidence that Eisenhower even had Montgomery's rather imaginative plan tested at SHAEF to see if it was practicable. Eisenhower was an excellent conciliator but pretty much a strategic dullard. There is no evidence that he ever grasped how Montgomery planned and won the Normandy campaign. There is no evidence that he grasped the boldness in Montgomery's 'narrow front' approach. Far from having 'a secure grasp of the fundamentals required for success in Europe', apart from the fact that brute force would win through, the Supreme Commander grasped very little.[23] The war would go on. Everybody would attack all the time.

After losing the first post-Normandy strategic debate, Montgomery turned his attention to events at the front. On 26 August his troops were closing on the Seine. He ordered that they should cross it and advance through Northern France and Belgium with all due speed irrespective of the progress of the armies on their flank.[24] The results were spectacularly successful. By 29 August, leading elements of the British Second Army were approaching Amiens, by the night of the 30th/31st they were across the Somme and some 30 miles to the east of that place. By 1 September they were in Arras; two days later they entered Brussels; the next day Antwerp fell. Enemy resistance was described as not being worthy of the name and there were frequent mentions of large pockets of enemy troops sitting, waiting to be rounded up. In all the Second Army had advanced 250 miles in six days. They had lost just 1,400 casualties; the enemy 40,000.[25]

His rapid advance, which covered more ground in a shorter time than any other Allied army in north-western Europe, determined Montgomery to return to the charge of defeating the Germans in 1944. Indeed he had every reason to expect that he might find fertile ground at SHAEF. On 29 August Eisenhower had written a message to his army group commanders that said in part:

The enemy is being defeated in the East, in the South, and in the North; he has experienced internal dissention [the attempted coup against Hitler in July] and signs are not wanting that he is nearing collapse. His forces are scattered throughout Europe and he has given the Allied Nations the opportunity of dealing a decisive blow before he can concentrate in the defense of his vital areas.[26]

In this context Montgomery relaunched his 'narrow front' proposal. He replied to Ike:

I consider we now have reached a stage where one really powerful and full blooded thrust towards Berlin is likely to get us there and thus end the German war.

We have not enough maintenance resources for two full blooded thrusts . . . In my opinion the thrust likely to give the best and quickest results is the northern one via the Ruhr.

Time is vital and the decision regarding the selected thrust must be made at once.[27]

Eisenhower's response was riddled with ambiguity. In one SHAEF directive he stated, 'our best opportunity . . . lies in striking at the Ruhr', which seemed to fit into Montgomery's plan. On other occasions he insisted that a uniform advance would be made on all fronts – northern, central and southern.[28] Montgomery, becoming increasingly annoyed at what he regarded as Eisenhower's failure to express a clear view, insisted on a meeting. That meeting took place in Eisenhower's aircraft on 10 September. Ike had wrenched his knee and was in some pain as Montgomery strode up the stairs to confront him. What happened next is best described by the only witness, Major-General Graham:

The meeting began badly with Monty pulling from his pocket a file of telegrams etc [some were SHAEF directives] and saying to Ike . . . 'Did you send these?'. Ike: 'Yes, of course, why?'. Monty: 'Well they're nothing but balls . . . . sheer balls . . . rubbish etc etc'. G[raham] says that Ike let Monty run on for a while and then lent forward and patted M on the knee and said . . . 'Geez, Monty, you can't speak to me like that, I'm your boss'. Monty pulled up at once and smiled and mumbled an apology. The acrimonious part of the meeting passed.[29]

What was agreed in the less acrimonious part of the meeting was Operation Market Garden, the airborne operation against the Dutch river crossings culminating at Arnhem. Eisenhower had long promised to Montgomery the First Airborne Army, which consisted of the US 82 and 101 Airborne Divisions and the 1 British Airborne Division, bizarrely for operations against the small Channel ports such as Calais which were still holding out against the Canadians as they advanced along the coast. But some time in early September Montgomery had come up with a more startling plan to capture the five river and canal crossings that threatened to impede his advance into Germany.[30] He would thus 'bounce' the Rhine and be well placed for further advances into Germany. Eisenhower, perhaps surprisingly, readily agreed to the Montgomery plan. By doing so he was appearing to cede some priority to the northern thrust, at least temporarily. But in a muddle that was becoming typical of him, the central and southern advances by Bradley and Patton were not halted. Nor was Montgomery to be given any real control over the flanking First American Army. Arnhem (apart from the airborne component) was to be a purely British effort.

What was Montgomery's northern thrust actually supposed to achieve? His plan consisted of a series of steps. First, the Second Army would capture the river crossings culminating at Arnhem. Second it would advance from Arnhem to the Zuider Zee, thus cutting off all German troops in Holland from Germany. Third it would encircle the Ruhr from the north, meeting with the American First Army coming up from the south. In the meantime the Canadian Army would have cleared the approaches to Antwerp and commenced getting the port into working order.[31]

These were rather grandiose objectives to be accomplished by an army of just fourteen divisions. Had Arnhem fallen and the Zuider Zee been reached, the eleven divisions of Second Army would have been strung out over a front of 100 miles. How in this situation a force capable of encircling the Ruhr could have been spared was never specified by Montgomery. Other aspects of the plan were highly dubious. The port of Antwerp was protected by 60 miles of low-lying land, easily flooded and very defensible. Yet Montgomery detailed just three weak Canadian divisions to clear the

Germans from this area. In the end it was to take the Canadians, a considerable force from Second Army, Bomber Command and the navy to clear the path to Antwerp, and it was to take these forces three months to do it. Then there was the American aspect to the plan. The US First Army was not under Montgomery's control and Eisenhower had no intention of directing most of it towards the Ruhr. Under Eisenhower's plan it would head due east on Metz. It would therefore never have appeared as a prong of an encircling force, even had the Second Army reached the Ruhr.

We now know, of course, that the plan fell at the first objective. The bridge at Arnhem was not securely held. Nor could the armoured thrust to a depth of 60 miles astride a single road in a country flat and waterlogged reach the airborne division at Arnhem. Eventually the paratroops were evacuated back across the Rhine with heavy losses. All told, approximately 15,000 Allied soldiers were killed or captured during the operation, 7,500 of them from the 1 Airborne Division.

Why then did the normally cautious Montgomery run this series of risks? Probably he hoped that an initial success in seizing the river crossings and advancing to the Zuider Zee would compel Eisenhower to see a new reality. If the Ruhr beckoned, might not the Supreme Commander detail sufficient American troops to ensure its capture? Might not such events tip the nascent German recovery back into collapse? In this circumstance might not the Germans defending the approaches to Antwerp give up? If any of these events came to pass, the war might be shortened. If they all came to pass, the war might be ended. We now know of course that none of them came to pass. But at that moment in September 1944, for Montgomery, the chance of ending the war seemed worth a try.

Failure at Arnhem did not end Montgomery's determination to press the case for a northern advance. Even while the paratroops were descending, he wrote to Eisenhower pointing out that the Ruhr and Berlin were the ultimate objectives in the west and asked for nine divisions of the US First Army to be assigned to him for these post-Arnhem tasks.[32] There were no takers for this plan. At a meeting with Eisenhower and Brooke, Montgomery was told by both men to get on with clearing Antwerp.[33] But the Field Marshal refused to be deflected. A few days after this meeting he wrote some 'Notes on Command in Western Europe' for Eisenhower's edification. The notes suggested that the command within the Allied forces was far from satisfactory. What was required was a ground force commander who could take charge of the drive into the Ruhr. The short-price favourite for such a post was of course Montgomery himself, but in a show of Allied solidarity he offered to serve under Bradley (no doubt thinking all the time that the plan followed would essentially be his own).[34] This missive irritated Eisenhower beyond measure. He wanted Antwerp cleared and he wanted Montgomery to bend his mind to that task. He also did not want a ground force commander and in particular he did not want a British one. As he had made clear on many occasions, whatever the merits of the northern 'Ruhr' operation, he would continue to advance on a wide front and close up the Rhine. The overall commander of this advance, he felt moved to point out, would be 'myself'.[35] This seemed definitive and Montgomery replied that Eisenhower 'would hear no more of command from me'.[36]

Eisenhower probably took that answer with a grain of salt, but at least Montgomery got on with clearing Antwerp and was for some weeks silent on the matter of command. However, in late November he returned to the charge. The fact was that the broad front approach was making little progress. Patton and the Sixth Army Group (which had landed in the south of France in August) made some ground towards the German border and the Siegfried Line in the south, but in the centre and north the line hardly moved. The Germans had managed to consolidate, the terrain was unpromising for armour and the weather had deteriorated, nullifying Allied air superiority. By November's end, on most sections of the front, the Rhine was still distant. So on 28 and 29 November Montgomery met with Eisenhower and put the familiar arguments for a concentration of strength in the north under a single commander.[37] Eisenhower flatly refused to agree and in fact made a case where progress in the south by Patton might be more acceptable than plugging away in the north to no effect.[38] There the argument might have ended, but Montgomery reported the disagreement to the COS and on this occasion Brooke reacted. He too was well aware that Britain could ill afford the war to be protracted and he believed that Eisenhower's methods would produce exactly that result.

Eisenhower was summoned to London to explain his strategy; to bolster his position Brooke had the Prime Minister chair the meeting. Eisenhower did not perform well. He opened with a long, rambling review of his strategy in which it was difficult to discern which operations were of major importance and which were peripheral. Brooke quite lost patience with him, suggesting that 'there was a dangerous dispersal of forces' in his plans that might lead no particular thrust to succeed. Churchill intervened to state that there was much that Brooke and Eisenhower agreed on; it was all a matter of emphasis. The problem with this is that it was not a matter of emphasis, it was a fundamental disagreement on strategy – Brooke favouring Montgomery's scheme for a strong thrust in the north and Eisenhower, favouring the broad front approach.[39] The meeting ended inconclusively but Brooke was clearly at the end of his tether. He fumed that it was 'Quite impossible to get the PM to even begin to understand the importance of the principles involved . . . He *cannot* understand a large strategic concept . . . Ike also *quite* incapable of understanding real strategy.'[40]

Next day, Brooke found that he had more influence on Churchill than he first thought. The Prime Minister explained to him that he felt obliged to support Eisenhower as he was far outnumbered by the British COS but that he agreed that the situation was serious and should be discussed by the War Cabinet, always Churchill's chosen venue when the going was tough.[41] The War Cabinet duly assembled. Brooke gave them an exposition of Eisenhower's policy which included the fact that the Rhine might not be crossed until May 1945. The Cabinet immediately asked that Brooke prepare a paper to be sent to the Americans asking for a clear exposition of Eisenhower's plan.[42] This all amounted to a massive vote of no confidence in the Supreme Commander.

At this point the entire discussion was stalled by the German attack in the Ardennes. The detail of this encounter need not detain us – it was almost entirely an American affair in which American troops stopped the Germans as soon as clear weather allowed Allied air power and armoured superiority to tell. The whole episode, however, was regarded by the British COS (and of course Montgomery) as proof that Eisenhower's disposition of troops was faulty and that if his broad front strategy continued to be prosecuted the war might go on indefinitely. So, as soon as the front was stabilised, the COS returned to the attack. On 28 December they drafted a note to the Joint Staff Mission in Washington to be passed on to the Americans. In it they made two main points:

(1) There should be a single concentrated thrust across the Rhine from the north.

(2) That operation should be under the operational control of one man.[43]

In other words, they restated what Montgomery had been saying for four months.

Before answering the British, the Americans asked Eisenhower for a short note on his strategy. It arrived on 20 January 1945 and merely restated his previous position: the Rhine would be closed along the entire front and then bridgeheads seized from which various thrusts would be made into Germany. He admitted that the advance on the Ruhr from the north offered the quickest approach to the German heartland but also noted that there were favourable areas further south.[44] A few days later the Joint Chiefs issued a statement thoroughly approving of Eisenhower's plan.[45]

It might be thought that, both sides having restated their case, the argument would have fizzled out. But Brooke in particular would not let up. At a joint meeting with the Americans in Malta at the end of January he once more made the case for a concentrated northern offensive controlled by a single ground commander.[46] Once again the Americans disagreed. Then it became clear that Eisenhower and his Chief of Staff (Bedell Smith, who was at Malta) were putting forward slightly different plans. Clarification was sought but the fact was that these were only differences in minor detail. Eisenhower's broad front plan remained in place.[47] Eventually the discussion became so heated that the room had to be cleared of all but the respective Chiefs. In the end the British could not agree with Eisenhower's plan but were prepared to 'take note' of it, which in plain language meant that they submitted to a fait accompli.[48]

The entire episode of the broad versus narrow front approach to the campaign in north-west Europe is instructive. Initially, the Montgomery–Eisenhower dispute was won by Eisenhower – as it had to be if Ike was to remain Supreme Commander. Brooke's entry, and as a result Churchill's, came very late. In one sense this did not matter in that it is doubtful whether an earlier intervention by the British would have made any difference to US attitudes. On the other hand, it did because by the time the Brooke/ Churchill combination took flight, the Americans were so angered by

Montgomery's interventions that their attitudes had hardened against anyone who attempted to change strategy by raising the old Montgomery issues. This was particularly the case after Montgomery's notorious press conference on 7 January 1945 where he essentially took credit for stopping the German Ardennes offensive. Brooke and Churchill were therefore entering an argument already lost against a group of highly alienated Americans. In the end it was not so much a matter of strategy as it was of Great Power politics. By the close of 1944 the Americans had over twice the number of divisions in the field as Britain. Moreover, the war in the west was being won, albeit considerably more slowly than the British would have liked. In addition Eisenhower's strategy, though unimaginative, was risk free. Even with the setback in the Ardennes there was never a chance that the Allies would not prevail. In warfare waged by an alliance it is not sufficient to have the best strategic argument (which I would argue the British did in this case). There also has to be the strength to impose that strategy on an ally. Given the disparity in strength between Britain and the US in late 1944 and 1945, there was never a chance that this would happen.

There was one final flurry. The approaches to the Rhine took much longer to clear – mainly due to flooded terrain and poor flying weather – than was anticipated and it was not until March that bridgeheads were established across the river.[49] The question then arose about what to do next. Eisenhower had already decided. On 29 March he passed on to the CCS 'for information' a letter he had written to Stalin stating that his immediate aim was to eliminate the Ruhr and then to advance on the axis Erfurt–Leipzig–Dresden.[50] The British were furious with this missive. The COS considered that it relegated Montgomery to a small subsidiary operation in the north which, without attached American forces, he might be too weak to deliver. This would perhaps leave northern German ports and Denmark to be occupied by the Russians. They immediately informed the American Joint Chiefs of their concerns and asked that Eisenhower reconsider.[51] The Prime Minister was also angered. He chided the COS for sending their note to Washington before he had seen it and suggested that no good would come from openly criticising Eisenhower when his armies, which were overwhelmingly American, stood on the brink of success. However, he agreed that Eisenhower was neglecting Montgomery's forces and by implication ruling out any prospect the western Allies had of capturing Berlin.[52]

667

Much has been made of Eisenhower's change of plan and his view that Berlin 'is no longer a particularly important objective'.[53] No doubt he exceeded his pay grade in contacting Stalin direct without consulting either his own government or the British. He was also very naive in thinking that the occupation of Berlin meant nothing to the British who, after all, had been in this war much longer than the Americans. The occupation of the heart of darkness would have nicely rounded off their war. However, the occupation of Berlin, even for Churchill, was only symbolic, a matter of prestige. As he explained to the COS: 'Our zone [of occupation of Germany] is marked out [the zones had been decided at the Yalta Conference in February] and after salutations ... we shall retire to its limits.'[54]

It was therefore not a matter, as some Cold War historians have held, of refusing to retreat from the German capital until the Russians proved more reasonable over Eastern Europe. Churchill knew by then that in all likelihood the Russians would not prove reasonable, whatever the western Allies did or did not occupy, but he was hardly about to confront Stalin with an intransigent stand over Berlin. In the end, Eisenhower's rather bizarre behaviour cost the Allies little. It was just one more indication that Britain was definitely the junior partner in the alliance.

The remainder of the story is soon told. At the beginning of April the breakout of the First Army Group was complete. As the Canadians cleared up the Germans remaining in the Netherlands, Montgomery's spearheads dashed towards the Elbe. By 18 April the army was on Lüneburg Heath and on 24th on the west bank of the Elbe. Later, Bremen was occupied 'not without encountering patches of desperate resistance'.[55] The fact was that the German armies in the west were rapidly disintegrating. The final dash was across the base of Denmark, mainly to stop any Russian designs on that country. This was successfully achieved on 2 May when armoured brigades entered Lübeck. On 4 May a German delegation arrived at Montgomery's headquarters. The Field Marshal stage-managed the surrender much as he had his battles – there was much ceremony and not a little humiliation of the Germans. The war in the west was over.[56]

* * * * *

In this period Churchill and Brooke were only sporadic participants in the strategy of the north-western Europe campaign. Much more of their time was spent on the Italian campaign and the matter of Greece. In some ways this is difficult to explain – these were in 1944 and 1945 very minor fronts. In other ways the explanation is quite simple: the troops on these fronts were overwhelmingly British, as was the command. Britain had a much greater chance of pursuing its own strategy without too much interference from its Allies (the Americans) than it did elsewhere. It is yet another indication of Britain's reduced circumstances that so much effort was expended on what mattered so little to the outcome of the war.

This is not to say that some important issues were not involved in the Mediterranean front in 1944 and 1945. After the fall of Rome, the Allied armies had pursued the Germans northward but all sense of a rout had now disappeared. Alexander had lost his seven divisions to Anvil and the Germans had directed four more divisions to Italy with a further three to follow from Russia. This increase in numbers allowed the Germans to conduct a stubborn retreat and the weakened Allied forces (which, however, had massive air superiority) were required to winkle them out from one defensive position to another. First the Trasimene Line had to be breached, then the Arezzo position and then the Arno Line which covered Pisa and Florence. These were only delaying actions as far as the Germans were concerned. They intended to make their real stand on 'the final blocking line' which ran from Rimini on the Adriatic to just north of Pisa on the Gulf of Genoa. This was the Gothic Line, the outskirts of which the Allies reached in early August 1944.[57]

The defences of the Gothic Line were not trivial. Using conscripted Italian labour, the Germans had erected a position with around 2,500 machine-gun posts, 500 anti-tank and mortar positions, many anti-tank ditches, a number of concreted Panther gun positions utilising the 75-mm guns from Panther tanks and tens of thousands of yards of barbed wire.[58]

The original plan had been to breach the Gothic Line in the central mountainous region. However, the loss of the French mountain troops to Anvil and the difficulty Oliver Leese had working with the Fifth Army and Clark in particular led to a change of plan. Leese's Eighth Army would move to the Adriatic and its three corps (Polish, Canadian and British) would attack there. This would get them away from the Americans but, more particularly, out of the mountains and onto the Adriatic Plain where they would be able to deploy their massive artillery superiority (1,122 guns as against the Germans 351) to better advantage.[59] The Fifth Army would still play a role. After Leese had broken the Gothic Line, Clark would attack in a typical Alexander two-handed punch and capture Bologna. By this time the Eighth Army would be in the Po Valley and the Germans would be well on the way to suffering a rout.

The plan worked well enough. It went in on 26 August 1944 and by the 30th the forward positions of the line had fallen. By 2 September the line had been smashed by the artillery and the Germans were forced to fall back. But by then Kesselring had realised his entire position was in danger. He rushed reinforcements to the Adriatic coast and, in retreating, short-ened his line. Resistance increased and the British, who were chronically short of reinforcements, only advanced with extreme caution.[60] For example, in the 56 Division area (on the left of Eighth Army), advances were mainly conducted at night using artificial moonlight (mass search-lights bounced from clouds to illuminate the battlefield). And to minimise casualties such advances were broken off at daylight and the troops ordered to dig in.[61] Moreover, the enemy were well supplied with artillery. In some areas (in the foothills of the Apennines in particular) supporting fire could not easily be directed against batteries of enemy guns on rear slopes.[62] In other cases features that were found to be heavily held were not directly attacked until flanking advances or an enemy retreat ensured their capture with few casualties.[63] In these conditions there was never a chance that armour might be unleashed to force a major enemy retreat. Ground was gained, but slowly. This was not spectacular but, with divisions unlikely to receive reinforcements in any number, it was a prudent way to approach battle and in the end, with vast artillery and air superiority, sure to win through. The problem for Alexander was that as September drew to a close, winter approached and there was still no sign of German disintegration.[64]

As noted earlier, Churchill and Brooke were visiting Italy in this period and the Prime Minister certainly thought he saw the answer to Alexander's dilemma. At a meeting with Alexander he put forward the idea that in view of the river lines likely to be encountered once the Po Valley was reached, it might be better to think amphibiously and outflank them all by landing in

Istria with a view to advancing on Trieste and points north-east.[65] Wilson and Alexander had in fact already thought of such a plan and, with the Prime Minister's backing, they set about studying it. At the same time Churchill (no doubt thinking ahead about resources such as landing craft) broached the subject with Roosevelt.[66] The President was non-committal – the whole subject could be discussed at the next Anglo-American meeting in Quebec in September (Octagon).[67]

At that meeting Churchill was quick to lay out his wants and his objectives. He told the Americans:

> Our objective should be Vienna. If German resistance collapsed, we should, of course, be able to reach Vienna more quickly and more easily. If not, to assist this movement, he had given considerable thought to an operation for the capture of Istria, which would include the occupation of Trieste and Fiume. He had been relieved to learn that the United States Chiefs of Staff were willing to leave in the Mediterranean certain L.S.T.s now engaged in 'Dragoon', to provide an amphibious lift for the Adriatic operation if this was found desirable and necessary. An added reason for this right-handed movement was the rapid encroachment of the Russians into the Balkans and the consequent dangerous spread of Russian influence in this area.[68]

Brooke elaborated on this point in a subsequent meeting, noting that the Istrian operation would probably not take place until the spring and asking that the US definitely commit to supplying their landing craft for such an operation.[69]

King replied for the Americans: 'He too had in mind the possibility of amphibious operations in Istria . . . Unless a decision to mount an amphibious operation were taken soon the landing craft would be idle.'[70] The result was that Wilson would be enjoined to produce a plan for the CCS by 15 October.

In some ways this was an astonishing result. Roosevelt in particular had resisted any suggestion that the Allies mount operations anywhere near the Balkans. Churchill certainly feared that this might still be the case at Octagon, hence his relief at the US position. What had persuaded the Americans to back an Istrian offensive? Probably it was the fact that they had won all the recent strategic debates. Dragoon had been prosecuted, Eisenhower was now Supreme Commander in Europe and they had no intention of putting more troops into Italy. A small right hook that – if it was successful – would take troops north-east to Vienna rather than into the Balkans seemed suddenly something the Americans could live with. Perhaps too they were persuaded by Churchill's concern about the Russians. In this instance Roosevelt was as aware as Churchill about how intransigent the Russians were proving about the likely composition of a Polish government. In the event the British were not even required to push their case. What they needed now was a plan.

This as it turned out was no easy problem. Alexander's armies (both Eighth and Fifth) were running short of men. They had received no reinforcements except an inexperienced Brazilian Division and just one division from the US. Alexander asked Churchill for three more US divisions, but Brooke doubted if any American reinforcements for Italy would be forthcoming. As a compromise, Churchill undertook to ask Roosevelt for two divisions. The other problem was that troops would have to be withdrawn from this shrinking army for amphibious training and Alexander thought this impossible with the front held so lightly.[71]

A further problem was the weather. After the Gothic Line had been breached, the Allied armies found themselves in the low-lying country south of Ravenna. Had there been any Classical scholars in the forces they could have pointed to the fact that the Romans had moved their capital to Ravenna for a reason. The soil in that area becomes for many months of the year greasy and glutinous, nullifying to certain extent Allied superiority in armour. There were also many small rivers in the area that turned into torrents in the autumn. As the chronicler of 46 Division recorded:

> Heavy rain turned ankle-deep streams into raging torrents in a night, fords became impassable and bridges were swept away, so that supply, particularly of ammunition for the artillery, was a constant source of anxiety . . . The first flush of enthusiasm, engendered by the magnificent news from France and our own successes, began to wane as men found themselves confronted by the prospect of another winter campaign in Italy. There seemed to be no end to the numbers of rivers that had to be crossed [and] desertion became more frequent.[72]

From October there was another problem – Greece. It had become apparent to the British as early as August 1944 that if the Russians continued to advance across Eastern Europe, the Germans would eventually have to withdraw their forces from the Balkans or risk having them cut off. Churchill worried that when the Germans withdrew, a vacuum would exist in Greece which might well be filled by the most active of the Partisan groups – the left-leaning or communist, depending on your perspective, EAM/ELAS.[73] Initially, Churchill had supported the exiled King of Greece, George II, but he had become aware that the King was not likely to be well received in Greece and his new policy was that Britain should establish order in the country while elections were held, which he was also assured that the communists would not win.[74] The Prime Minister therefore instructed Brooke to organise a force of no more than 10,000 men which could be rushed to Athens to secure the central government area in the event of a German retreat.[75] He also sought to square the Americans by signalling to Roosevelt exactly what he intended to do.[76] Roosevelt took his time in replying but agreed that the British should preserve order and that American transport aircraft could be used to supply any force sent.[77]

On 15 October the Germans evacuated Athens. Immediately Operation Manna was put into effect. The 2 Parachute Brigade was despatched from Italy with the 23 Armoured Brigade from the Middle East, along with various Special Forces.[78] Soon, however, it was found that the unrest in Greece and the determination of ELAS/EAM to seize control had been underestimated. It is not the intention here to dip into the murky waters of the Greek civil war. It is noteworthy, though, how determined Churchill was to prevent what he saw as a communist takeover, even at the expense of the Italian campaign. By the end of October the 4 Indian Division and the Greek Mountain Brigade, both of which had fought in the Gothic Line battles, had been despatched to Greece from Italy. In November a brigade from the 46 Division followed, as did the 4 British Division, also from Italy. In early January the remainder of 46 Division went and in mid-February it had been joined by the 5 British Division from the Middle East.[79] In all 80,000 British troops were sent to Greece, supported by many squadrons of aircraft and warships and supply vessels of all kinds.

The point to be made is that all these forces either came from Italy or were potentially available to reinforce Italy at a time when the Allied armies there were desperately short of men. Churchill, of course, knew all this but he was determined that communist or communist-inspired forces would not seize control in Greece. It demonstrates that, between the months of August 1944 and February 1945, anyway, he rated this action a higher priority than keeping Alexander's army at maximum strength. By his actions (including his Christmas dash with Eden to Athens in order to install Archbishop Damaskinos as Regent) he was prepared to incur the odium of a significant part of the Labour Party and the Americans. The debate in the House of Commons on the matter, which Churchill easily won, was the most bitter of any of the votes of confidence held throughout the war.[80] As for the Americans, Churchill was criticised by the newly installed Secretary of State, Edward Stettinius, for intervening in what he described as the internal affairs of Greece. In addition, Admiral King ordered that no ships should support what he regarded as British imperial adventures in Greece. Churchill immediately dashed off a letter to Roosevelt stating that, unless the order to the American ships was withdrawn, he would be forced to mention in the House of Commons that there was a fundamental breach between the United States and Britain.[81] Cooler heads prevailed and the letter was not sent.[82] Instead Churchill made a telephone call to Hopkins.[83] He smoothed things over with Roosevelt and a letter from the President was sent, offering qualified support to Churchill but warning him he could not openly stand with him on Greece because of adverse American public and Press opinion on the subject.[84] Churchill thanked the President for his 'kind' reply and directed him to a speech given by Ernest Bevin to the Labour Party Conference in which Bevin had noted that the Labour members of the War Cabinet agreed with Churchill's stance.[85]

In the end a truce was cobbled up in Athens between the various factions and no communist regime ever came to power in Greece. Churchill never regretted his actions concerning Greece and in some ways he was merely being consistent with the attitude he had held throughout the war. In 1941 he had supported intervention in Greece despite the disasters he foresaw. In 1943 he had pushed Roosevelt extremely hard on intervention in the Dodecanese, which he saw as outposts of Greece and was humiliated by the eventual refusal of the President to support him. Then he had signed the notorious 'spheres of influence' document with Stalin which assigned

Britain a 90 per cent interest in Greece. Whatever the precise meaning of the percentages agreement, Churchill was determined that it would be Britain that intervened in Greece despite (or because of) the installation of communist governments in Bulgaria, Romania and Albania and what he regarded as the dubious nature of the Tito government in Yugoslavia. Overall he risked much for Greece. And on this occasion he won out over the Americans, probably because they had stopped caring much about the Eastern Mediterranean. But his Greek venture also signalled something else – he had finally given up all hope of much coming from the Italian campaign.

In fact, with the deteriorating weather and with Churchill's attention focused on Greece, the Italian campaign inevitably shrank in importance. Wilson, who was soon despatched to Washington to replace Dill (who had died) on the CCS, had already concluded that no amphibious operations outside Italy were now possible with his reduced army. He therefore proposed that Alexander (soon to take over the role of Supreme Commander Mediterranean) confine himself to operations designed to contain or destroy the German forces in Italy.[86] Istria, the Ljubljana Gap and Vienna vanished into the mists. A new directive to Alexander was soon agreed with the Americans and despatched on 2 December: 'The introduction of major forces into the Balkans . . . is not favourably considered at this time. Your first, and immediate objective should be to capture Bologna, then to secure the general line Ravenna–Bologna–Spezia and thereafter continue operations with a view to containing Kesselring's army.'[87] In reality Alexander could do little else. His armies took any opportunity to inch forward but the weather and lack of reserves meant that progress was slow and on narrow fronts.

Churchill, preoccupied with Greece as he was, gave up his wider schemes for Italy with the greatest reluctance. Brooke had been working on him for some time to transfer troops to Montgomery to keep up, at least to some extent, the ever-diminishing British effort in north-western Europe. He told the COS: 'He had with great regret given up hope of a British right-handed thrust into the armpit of the Adriatic. He agreed that it would be right in principle to transfer troops from Italy to the Western front.'[88]

What disappointed him was the two and a half months that it would take to transfer the troops north.[89] The Prime Minister certainly had a point here. He worried that the troops might leave the Italian front without the strength to mount an attack while not arriving in time to influence events on Montgomery's front. On looking at the situation more closely the COS suddenly found that they could relocate the divisions within six weeks, and with that Churchill was satisfied.[90] Thus it was decided at the CCS meeting at Malta to withdraw in total five divisions from Italy. In the first instance three would go, followed at an appropriate time by two more. No American divisions were to go – mainly because Eisenhower was having difficulty in absorbing in northern Europe the reinforcements coming directly from America. In the end just two divisions were sent north, weakening the Italian front to bolster now the only front that mattered.[91]

Alexander, however, still had ambitions to destroy Kesselring's army and in January 1945 planning began for a spring offensive in Italy. He wanted at least three months devoted to training and firm ground on which to conduct an offensive. As it happened, though, Alexander would not be deciding these matters. He was now Supreme Commander and Clark was the new commander of Fifth Army Group. Under Clark were two commanders with firm views – General Lucian Truscott for the largely American Fifth Army and McCreery, who had taken over Eighth Army from Leese in October – and it was these two men who substantially made the plan. The plan boiled down to this: on the Adriatic coast the Eighth Army would lead off with a two-pronged right hook across a series of river lines and (most awkwardly a lake, Lake Comacchio). A few days later the Fifth Army would attack to the west of Bologna with the idea of linking up with the Eighth Army and trapping the Germans south of the considerable obstacle of the River Po.[92] Clark made his mark; he insisted that the operation take place in April rather than May.

Nothing was left to chance in this operation. The Eighth Army alone had over 1,000 guns and 2 million rounds of ammunition available.[93] In addition, the Mediterranean Air Force had 3,750 fighters and bombers as against the Germans, who had fewer than 100.[94] The Eighth Army attack began on 9 April with a devastating display of firepower:

Heavy bombers dropped thousands of 20 lb fragmentation bombs on the . . . defences and on rear areas. This was followed by rocket firing Typhoons, medium bombers and strafing fighters. The final 'softening

676

up' was provided by flame on a scale never before approached in this theatre. Apart from the fire bombs dropped by aircraft, flame throwing tanks and WASP carriers [flamethrower fitted armoured troop carriers] saturated enemy positions with great waves of flame. It was the use of fire, so prisoners stated afterwards that broke them.[95]

Such was the ferocity of the advance on the left of the Eighth Army that the enemy was bustled from one river line to another. Fighting was heavy but the New Zealanders in particular were not to be stopped. Within a few days the series of rivers was breached and Allied troops were closing on the south bank of the Po.[96]

Meanwhile, on the right, the attack across Lake Comacchio had completely surprised the Germans as the Allied used several hundred DD tanks, called in Italy 'Fantails', to ferry troops across the swampy ground.[97] After hard fighting the British finally seized the Argenta Gap (an area of solid ground between lakes and flooded locations) and streamed northward. By this time (16 April) the American Fifth Army to the west of Bologna had commenced their attack, which, led by the newly arrived 10 Mountain Division, made rapid headway. Soon the two forces met up at the well-named village of Finale to the south of the Po. In all 100,000 German troops were rounded up. This was the end in Italy. Allied armoured divisions followed by infantry streamed across the Po. On 23 April they reached Modena, on the 28th Verona, the next day they entered Venice. By 2 May Lake Garda was in American hands and the British were approaching Trieste. By this time negotiations, which had been underway for some time with Karl Wolff, the SS Commander in Italy, could only have one conclusion. On 3 May he surrendered all troops south of the Alps. Perhaps around 400,000 Germans in total were captured or killed by Allied forces. The war in Italy was over.

* * * * *

We noted that Churchill spent most of his time during the last period of the war in Europe concerned with matters in Italy and Greece. Was he correct to do so? The probable answer is yes. He certainly intervened late in the Montgomery/Eisenhower disputes, and part of the reason for that was his focus on the Mediterranean could be all-encompassing. But there is no reason to believe that an earlier intervention would have altered matters. Especially after 1 September, when Eisenhower assumed ground command in north-western Europe, there was little Churchill (or the COS, for that matter) could have done to divert American strategy down their preferred path. All the series of interventions by Montgomery, Churchill and the COS achieved in the end was to irritate the Americans. The broad front strategy remained in place until the end of the war and, with Marshall and Roosevelt backing Eisenhower to the hilt, there was never a chance that this would vary.

In the Mediterranean Churchill had more scope. Not that all his schemes were practicable. In the end, even with American acquiescence, Alexander was unable to launch an amphibious operation, not for the usual reason of a lack of landing craft, but because the British forces were too few. What he could do in the end with his depleted army was, however, considerable enough. First he broke the Gothic Line and in the last campaign utterly destroyed the German armies south of the Alps. Nor can this final victory be put down to sagging German morale. The Germans fought hard in this final campaign. They were destroyed by an imaginative plan carried through with a ferocity of firepower unseen up to that time in Italy. And they were destroyed by an army no larger in number – but of course larger in firepower resources – than their own. Alexander therefore, despite his straitened circumstances, fulfilled his mission to keep as many German troops away from north-western Europe as possible.

As for Greece, Churchill's intervention certainly had military implications in that it took troops away from Italy. But from Churchill's perspective, he secured what he wanted in Greece – the defeat of ELAS/EAM and the risk of some kind of communist takeover. Whatever the future political orientation of Greece, this perhaps ensured that it would not be communist.

In some ways therefore Churchill got what he wanted in the Mediterranean – a successful final campaign in Italy and a non-communist government in Athens. And to the extent that Eisenhower's strategy, whatever its flaws, won the campaign in north-western Europe, Churchill got what he wanted there as well. He was just not able to call the shots and win it in a way that optimised British national interests – an early end to the war and a more prominent role in shaping post-war Europe. But perhaps that was beyond British power anyway.

CONCLUSION

IF THERE IS A general view about politicians and the military in Britain in two world wars it is this: in the First World War politicians presided over untrammelled slaughter on the Western Front as they let the military go their own way. In the Second World War Churchill in particular interfered too much in military matters and was only kept on the straight and narrow by frequent interventions by strong-willed generals such as Alan Brooke. It is possible now to say that both these views are caricatures while containing some elements of truth.

In the First World War the politicians certainly asserted at the outset the primacy of politics in a liberal state. Grey, the Cabinet and then Parliament set out their diplomatic policy without recourse to the military. Despite the best efforts of Henry Wilson to insert himself into the proceedings, it was the politicians who decided what Britain's national interests were and declared war when they considered them to be threatened. Then they cast a sceptical eye at the plans for cooperation with the French developed by Wilson and others over a period of two years and only agreed to them with reluctance and because there seemed nothing better. Even then they held back 25 per cent of the BEF for 'home defence' against the insistent wishes of the military that it all should be sent to France. Furthermore, when Sir John French announced his intention to pull the BEF out of the line because of its efforts in the great retreat, he was instructed by the Cabinet in no uncertain terms that he would remain in the line and carry out his part in Joffre's plan for the Marne.

What neither the politicians nor the military seemed to identify was that the nature of warfare as revealed at Mons, the Aisne, Ypres and elsewhere represented something new. Defensive firepower in the form of machine guns, quick-firing artillery and magazine rifles had transformed the battle-field, making every attempt to push home an attack fraught with difficulty and heavy in casualties.

Churchill was one of the first to realise that quick victories and rapid advances were not likely in these conditions. He saw the result of an abortive attack on the Western Front and determined that there must be a better way of making war than 'chewing barbed wire in Flanders'. The Dardanelles was his answer and he was supported by the entire War Council, despite the fact that naval advice (in the person of Lord Fisher) was opposed to the venture.

The problem here was that the Turks did not lack for modern weaponry. Mines and shore-based artillery could stop a naval attack as convincingly as machine guns and artillery could stop the infantry (or the cavalry) on the Western Front. But the naval setback only caused the politicians to reach higher. Troops were summoned and a back door into Germany through the Balkan states was identified. The war could, in this perspective, be won on the cheap. The difficulty here was that the same defensive firepower, now employed by the underestimated Turkish army, could stop an advance before it reached an important ridge on Gallipoli, let alone before it reached Constantinople or the Balkans. By August 1915 the peninsula was starting to resemble, in the form of trenches, barbed wire, machine guns and artil-lery, the dreaded Western Front. In this case the liability of the British turned out to be strictly limited. Failure had to be squarely faced because alliance politics demanded that it be so.

While the adventurism of Gallipoli was playing out, the fact that the German army stood everywhere on the Western Front on French or Belgian soil dictated that this was where the main body of the BEF must be located. The French would not stand for the diversion of Britain's main effort anywhere else. And so here the British army stood. The problem was that by the end of the year it was standing on much the same ground that it had occupied at the beginning. Neuve Chapelle, Aubers Ridge, Festubert,

Givenchy and Loos had seen no substantial gain of ground, even as the defensive battle around Ypres had seen very little loss. The casualty rate had been horrendous – just over 300,000 men, of whom about 85,000 were dead.

Something had to be done and for the political class this added up to changing the command. There was warrant for this. Sir John French had displayed neither grit nor fixity of purpose nor enterprise. Indeed the best that could be said about him was that he played little part in the planning and execution of the increasingly disastrous Western Front battles. But in focusing on a change of command, the politicians were missing an important point. The candidates for the top job, Generals Plumer and Haig, *had* played a large part in the British effort on the Western Front and they had not covered themselves with glory either. Haig, in fact, was as responsible as anyone for the mishandling of the reserves at Loos, the very matter that precipitated the removal of Sir John French. And Plumer, at Ypres, had played a vigorous but useless hand in attempting to recover ground that – had it been successful – would have seen the British in a worse position than they already were.

What else could the politicians have done? They had hardly grasped that large-scale offensives with distant objectives were passé in the conditions prevailing on the Western Front. Even Haig and Rawlinson had difficulty recognising this point, despite demonstrating a fleeting encounter with reality at Neuve Chapelle. The politicians had to choose someone to command. And Haig had many attributes. He was considered a thinker – anyway to the extent that he had rewritten *Field Service Regulations* in the pre-war period. Surely that must count for something. In addition, he was well-connected with the Palace – hardly an intellectual powerhouse – but perhaps useful in other ways. Also he seemed a steady hand in as much as he had presided over a series of shambolic battles without losing his equanimity. Finally, there seemed no other. Haig it was.

The appointment of Haig would see the nadir of civil/military relations in Britain in either of the world wars. A decision among the Allies led to the expectation of a major offensive in the spring of 1916. The major issue here was exactly how such offensives would be conducted, given that so far no great attack had achieved anything like the objectives set for it. This issue, which boiled down to one of tactics, proved beyond the civilian leadership in Britain to comprehend. The basic choices were a limited 'bite and hold' operation similar to that conducted on the first day of Neuve Chapelle or an unlimited offensive with distant objectives. This mattered because the first concentrated the power of the artillery to destroy trench defences and the second dissipated it. Churchill understood this but he was out of office and his advice post-Gallipoli was at a discount. The members of the War Committee did not grasp it and were unaware that such a debate was proceeding between General Rawlinson, who would conduct the Somme offensive, and Haig as Commander-in-Chief.

In the event the politicians became mere spectators to what would unfold as the worst military disaster in British history: the first day of the Somme. Afterwards they seemed transfixed, like rabbits caught in a spotlight. They neither commented on the enormous casualties nor even enquired as to what had gone wrong. Haig would continue to batter his ineffectual way slowly forward at great cost without any interference from the political leadership in Britain. Churchill attempted to tell his ex-colleagues that whatever damage the British army was inflicting on the Germans (and it was considerable), it was suffering higher losses itself. And when Haig gave his civilian masters an opening by asking permission to continue the campaign, they refused to take it – in the end not even replying to the Commander-in-Chief, which he took (rightly) as warrant to continue. For 450,000 casualties Haig hardly gained the ground mooted for the first day of battle. To preside over this amounted to the greatest dereliction of duty by any civilian authority in a world war. It was not a matter of sacking Haig (they could hardly do that, having just appointed him) but telling him to cease and desist. Why they felt unable to do so remains a mystery. Perhaps Asquith's grip on power or (after the death of his son during the campaign) on events in general was slipping. Perhaps there was an inability to decide what course to take.

In any case Asquith's War Committee seemed out of its depth, and the end of the campaign in the dog days of winter saw the end of the Asquith government. A firmer grip was needed and Lloyd George and a majority of the Conservative Party decided that he was the man to provide it. The war would be fought to a knock-out, he announced.

Unfortunately for the British army, it was the entity that was almost knocked out. Lloyd George's premiership initially continued down the path set out by the Somme. Despite some shards of optimism generated by the occasional success at Vimy Ridge, Messines and perhaps the Plumer phase of the Third Battle of Ypres, the overall trajectory was the same. The campaigns at Arras and later Third Ypres (or Passchendaele) were in no way improvements on the Somme. Indeed, the attempted use of the cavalry at Arras and the continuation of the campaign whatever the weather at the beginning and the end of Passchendaele were rather tactical throwbacks.

This was a bewildering set of circumstances. If the definition of stupidity is repeatedly doing the same thing but expecting different results, then Haig's behaviour falls within that definition. But Haig was not stupid, so how do we account for his actions? It seems that his mind and his military theories worked within very limited parameters. In some aspects his thinking had kept in line with battlefield developments: he welcomed heavy artillery, the creeping barrage and the tank as useful, indeed necessary, innovations. Yet overall he rigidly adhered to Napoleonic concepts of the breakthrough, the unlimited objective and the decisive battle. Territory must be gained for victory. These concepts should have collapsed under the weight of defensive firepower in 1914, with the lessons only rubbed in further in the battles of 1915 and the Somme. But even at the end of this period, at the battles for Passchendaele Ridge and Cambrai, the old Haig lived on – one more push and the Germans would collapse. One more offensive and the breakthrough would be achieved. What he failed to grasp was that territorial gains and breakthroughs were no longer on offer: 'killing Germans' – true attrition, as Rawlinson had pointed out to him – was now the only way to win, but Haig would not listen.

In parallel with this set of circumstances was another just as bewildering. On the civilian front Lloyd George, despite having seen the Somme unfold at close hand, presided over this second round of unrewarding slaughter. The Prime Minister might twist and turn – inveigle the French into taking the major role and then attempt to place Haig under French command. He might try to convince the Italians that they must lead the Entente in offensive action – a futile and indeed ludicrous policy given the state of the Italian army. He might rail against Haig; he might bemoan the lack of progress made. But he would not intervene – not to sack Haig or more reasonably to order him to stop the offensive. There is no reason to doubt that Haig would have obeyed such an order; he was a sound

683

constitutionalist. Such an order never came. What was it about Lloyd George that prevented him from acting? Was it his unfamiliarity with military affairs? Was it a lack of confidence in dealing with the military? Was it his misplaced backing of Nivelle? Whatever it was, it rendered him ineffectual.

There was an unedifying conspiracy of silence surrounding these futile endeavours on the Western Front. Since the opening of the Somme campaign, the British army had incurred over 1.2 million casualties for utterly derisory gains of ground. Yet neither the military nor the political leadership entered into any detailed discussion of the casualty rate and whether the country could sustain that rate without serious unrest. We must remember the context in which the British army was operating. After the Nivelle offensive the French army entered a state of collective indiscipline or conditional mutiny. The Russians were about to leave the war altogether. The Italians were in almost permanent collapse. The American armies were not yet seriously involved. Yet the disaster of the first day of the Somme and the terrible casualties incurred later in that battle and at Arras and at Third Ypres were never the subject of serious military/civilian discussion. No one asked if this level of casualties could be sustained. No one asked if the country might crack. No one commented that the casualty rate was badly out of kilter with Haig's designated objectives. So the military proceeded to cast away the last, best army that the Entente could field and the politicians wrung their hands but refused to intervene. Here indeed was a pretty pass.

There was a certain irony in the fact that it was Haig who precipitated a solution to this problem. His plan was to continue the Passchendaele campaign into 1918 and he required 1.3 million men to do it. This concentrated Lloyd George's mind wonderfully. If he could not control Haig's offensives by direct intervention, he would control them by another – the withholding of manpower. In some ways the Prime Minister had no choice in this matter. His manpower planners were telling him that the level of casualties was unsustainable if Haig's soldiers were to be supplied with the requisite level of weaponry and the country, in the light of U-boat depredations, fed.

Haig would therefore be required to fight smarter. But before any of this could be revealed, the Germans attacked on the Western Front. These battles were handled reasonably well by Haig, his pre-battle dispositions allowing him to give ground in non-vital areas while retaining a firm hold on the approaches to the Channel ports, which was vital. In effect in these battles Ludendorff had become the new Haig. His objectives were unlimited, his regard for the well-being of his armies non-existent. He certainly gained more ground than ever before, but not anywhere that mattered. The British and French armies fell back but retained sufficient cohesion to maintain some kind of front. Both armies also had un-attacked reserves just sufficient to plug any gaps.

Meanwhile the civilians and the military came together at Doullens and determined to fight the battle out and to impose some form of unified command across the entire front. Lloyd George, who had already achieved one objective by manoeuvring the increasingly useless Robertson out of his position of CIGS and manoeuvring in the politically flexible Henry Wilson, now also had Foch as at least nominal commander over Haig. It had taken two years but effective civilian control seemed to have been re-established.

What of the navy? Civilians had little control over the early battles, though Churchill did his best – with varying results – to control events from the Admiralty. The admirals also varied in efficiency: from dismal with Berkeley Milne in the Mediterranean, to adequate regarding Sturdee at the Falklands, to wildly inconsistent of Beatty at Heligoland Bight and Dogger Bank. Luckily in the encounter that might have mattered, Jellicoe at Jutland through rigid control and over-centralisation preserved the Grand Fleet and gave the Germans no choice but to flee back to base. He did not lose the war in that afternoon and thus did his job.

The U-boat war is another matter. Jellicoe's rigidity here regarding convoys ran Britain into perilous waters, though it has to be said that most of the Admiralty were as averse to convoy as a solution as he was. Lloyd George's claim to have imposed convoy on a reluctant Admiralty might have expanded in the telling, but there is no doubt that – prodded by Hankey, who for his part in this affair deserves the gratitude of his country – his threat to intervene concentrated minds and hastened the introduction of the one method that saw off this moment of peril. Overall, the Admiralty did not have a good war but, in some measure thanks to civilian leadership, did not have a disastrous one either.

The battles that followed the great Allied retreat in the spring of 1918 that saw the British army (with considerable help from the French and some from the Americans) victorious on the Western Front did not quite play out as Lloyd George envisaged. The British army, though seemingly under Foch's command, went its own way for all intents and purposes under the control of the dreaded Haig. But what Lloyd George had wrought, probably without realising it, was a revolution in tactics on the part of the British. Without men, as Rawlinson noted, there was no alternative but to turn to machines. This Haig had always been prepared to do and now, thanks to the Ministry of Munitions and to scientific operational research, he had an abundance of weaponry that was more efficient, more accurate and – used in combination – more able to overcome German defensive systems than ever before. Guns could now hit what they aimed at, tanks were more mechanically reliable and the infantry had weapons that in conjunction with accurate barrages could outflank and subdue even well-dug-in trench dwellers. Haig deserves some credit for presiding over this process and not interfering with those experts who were refining this 'weapons system'. The old Haig maintained a shadowy presence in that at Amiens he attempted to extend the objectives to unrealistic distances, but he was certainly more willing than in earlier years to leave the planning of battles to those at lower levels of command who developed the new ways of making war.

It was these lower levels of command that insisted on bringing to a halt battles that had ceased to prosper. Thus in 1918 battles shifted from one army to another as original attacks became bogged down. GHQ, to their credit, facilitated this development and made sure armies kept up with the latest changes in weaponry and their application. Finally, there were messages sent to the front by the civilian masters in London warning of the need to conserve men with an implied threat of what might happen if the warnings were not followed. In the end the Germans were worn down and, though not an inch of German soil was occupied by Allied armies, eventually the enemy could stand the strain no longer. Victory came and even if Ludendorff had played a major role in wearing out his own armies, Haig and Lloyd George could both claim some measure of success, though that process had taken an inordinate amount of time.

In general it can be said that the civilians intervened more in military matters in the First World War than is often thought. This process started in the early days of the war in 1914 and persisted throughout the entire war.

Indeed the First World War provides the only example in the two world wars where the civilians selected an entirely different front (Gallipoli) and attempted a quite different strategy for winning the war than the military would themselves have chosen. The failure of civilian control came in the long, drawn-out slogging matches from the Somme to Cambrai where there were long intervals when, despite the paucity of results, there was no civilian intervention. The politician as spectator went on for far too long in this period. It remained to be seen whether – if ever Britain was involved in another world war – any lessons would be drawn from this barren period.

The road to the Second World War was far less straightforward than that to the first. In 1914 Grey identified British national interest with some clarity and, when it was threatened, determined on war. In 1938 and 1939 the Chamberlain government had a great deal of difficulty in identifying threats to the national interest, except believing that war in almost any circumstances would run counter to it. In adhering to this policy Chamberlain in particular had entirely failed to realise that Hitler might not be amenable to rational argument or that, whatever concessions he was given, war might be his ultimate aim. Nor could Chamberlain identify the right moment to intervene. In Czechoslovakia, Britain (and France) had a democratic country with reasonably strong defences, a considerable armaments industry and the will to defend themselves. Any assessment of the strategic situation might have identified the Czech crisis as the moment to act. But so fearful was Chamberlain of war that he ducked it. Not only was Chamberlain's action in this crisis morally repugnant (giving away vital sections of another people's country), it was strategically illiterate.

Chamberlain realised this almost at once and flung out a guarantee to the much more ambiguous Polish state. This was done in the utmost haste without a thought that the Great Power which bordered Poland to the east (Russia) needed to be taken into account. In fact the accommodation of the Soviet Union was at the one time necessary and probably incapable of fulfilment because of Polish hesitations. In any case Chamberlain made no sustained attempt to 'appease' Russia, rendering his guarantee useless to the Poles and dangerous to Britain. In fact, of course, the guarantee really had little to do with the Poles. Chamberlain knew that further German expansion without intervention by the Western Powers would not be tolerated either by the British people or more immediately by the House of Commons. The guarantee was therefore more about his own survival than that of Poland. In a final unedifying scramble the Chamberlain Cabinet was dragged kicking and screaming into war. Hitler certainly had to be stopped at some time, but the elegance and realism of Grey had sadly departed from British counsels at this time.

The appeasement government might have been shoe-horned into war but by and large they proved incapable of waging it. In another cosmic misjudgement, Chamberlain was averse to overt action because he thought Hitler in imminent danger of overthrow. So Germany was not bombed and the Allied armies did not advance. And when a strategic opportunity – fortunately to be waged off Norway, far from Western Europe – appeared, the government proved incapable of making any decision at all. As was typical, when a decision was eventually made, it was made too late and the Allies were forestalled by the Germans. The ensuing Norwegian campaign was plagued from the outset by lack of preparation, divided counsels and plain incompetence. The beneficiary of all this was Churchill, who made his share of mistakes in this period but was identified by the House of Commons and particularly the Labour Party as the only man with the determination and the military nous to lead his country. In the vital vote on 9 May 1940, Chamberlain retained a majority, but in the days when the House and the Prime Minister would still act with some honour, he resigned and Churchill was raised to the premiership.

Of all the decisions made in the Second World War this was one of the most vital. Churchill first fought off the rather defeatist Chiefs of Staff who, until he pointed out the path ahead, could see no clear way forward for Britain. Then he fought off the efforts of Halifax (with some support from Chamberlain) to cobble together a peace deal via the slippery help of Mussolini. What he could also convey to the people was his utter determination to continue the war and keep hope alive when events turned against Britain at Dunkirk and during the Blitz. These were his contributions. What he could not do was have much effect on military operations. By the time he was established in power the situation on what was briefly the Western Front had deteriorated to such an extent that Dunkirk came to be seen as a kind of victory, though in fact it was signal defeat. During the battle he struggled mightily to keep France in the war but was unable to overcome the deep-seated defeatism within Reynaud's government. He could keep a close eye on the Battle of Britain but by necessity had to leave the course of events in the hands of Dowding and Park. Fortunately these were capable hands and required no intervention from the Prime Minister – though such an action would surely have come if it had been needed.

After Dunkirk another important decision was required from Britain: if the enemy could not be fought in Europe, where could it be fought? The obvious answer was Africa – not for imperial reasons but because there British-occupied Egypt had a common border with Italian-occupied Libya. Churchill and the Chiefs of Staff had little difficulty in deciding that the small British garrison in Egypt would be increased with the prospect of eliminating Italy from Africa and perhaps from the war.

There was no dispute among the politico/military elite on this matter. Differences could have arisen over the issue of whether to assist Greece when the Germans invaded in April 1941 but Wavell, Dill and Eden on the spot thought such assistance a moral as well as a military obligation, as did Churchill, though he was increasingly sceptical about the outcome. The ensuing disaster therefore was a shared responsibility between the politicians and the military, although in the popular literature Churchill continues to be castigated for the affair.

The desert war is a more complicated matter. It is in fact a good example of the influence and limitations of attempts by politicians (really, we are taking about Churchill here) to oversee military events. Wavell's first, spectacularly successful, offensive (Compass) was rather discounted because it was fought against Italian troops. But the concentrated firepower that was its feature would (and eventually did) work against German troops as well. Later battles, first under Wavell and then Auchinleck, failed to use this method and split up divisions into smaller and smaller columns or brigade groups. They also failed to grapple with Rommel's main tactic: the luring of British armour onto screens of anti-tank guns before unleashing his own armour. Churchill in particular realised that there was something wrong with the methods being employed by the desert generals. As early as October 1941 he had written about the need to restore artillery to its rightful place on the battlefield as against the heavy tanks which he surmised had usurped it.[1] He had, though, failed to realise that the main problem with the use of artillery in the desert was that its power had been dispersed by splitting divisions into smaller groups that had an increasing tendency to operate independently. Indeed he seemed thoroughly to approve of this process on the grounds that it gave more mobility to the army, without realising its dire consequences. He also failed to see that Rommel's tactics were not primarily based on the tank but the ability of his anti-tank guns to destroy the British armour sent repeatedly against them. This is one of the few examples of a politician examining military affairs down to the level of tactics, but Churchill then failed to discern why the masses of artillery sent to the desert were not succeeding to do the job he required, and he failed to follow through his initial insight with further enquiries.

Still Churchill was one step ahead of his military advisers on this issue. Even Brooke approved Auchinleck's decision to substitute small units for divisions and produced no paper suggesting a change of tactics was in order in the desert.

Regardless, there was never any chance that the desert war would develop into any slogging match like the Somme. For one thing Britain could not now field an army of the size deployed on the Western Front in 1916. Secondly, Churchill paid much closer attention to military events than had Asquith or Lloyd George. Thus when Wavell failed to deliver the goods he was sacked, and Auchinleck followed him after another string of failures. Nor was there any dispute between Churchill and the COS about these decisions. Dill and Brooke might be endlessly irritated about Churchill's tendency to interfere with every level of military affairs in the desert but they agreed with the necessity to change the command in both these instances. In fact Brooke seemed more shocked than Churchill with the state of the desert army under Auchinleck when they visited Cairo in August 1942.

The choice of the new command raises many interesting issues. It is difficult to see Gott, Churchill's first choice for the Eighth Army, being any improvement on Auchinleck. He was cut from the same cloth, without perhaps Auchinleck's tenacity. Montgomery was no doubt a better general than either of them. Even a cursory glance at Alamein demonstrates that he did indeed restore artillery to the prime position in warfare. But in many ways he was not Churchill's type of general. He was methodical, not given to dashing about the desert and risk averse. What he was doing at Alamein and afterwards was fighting First World War battles better. Attrition was his game, but this was true attrition where the enemy was actually worn down at the faster rate. Churchill had some inklings of what Montgomery was about – as his intervention when Alamein seemed to be descending into stalemate indicated. However, victory was an effective antidote against a possible Churchillian intervention, and so it proved for the remainder of the desert war. Montgomery might not have the dash that Churchill so appreciated but he kept winning, and that ensured that Churchill would continue to back him.

The entry of the Americans into the war gave Britain (politicians and the military) hope that they would win after all and at the same time threw up challenges that would remain for the rest of the war. After Roosevelt's period of indecision (or rather a period of decision which the British did not welcome), the US entry into the war revealed that the American military held decisive views on how it should be fought. It was a relief for the British that fighting Germany first was not one of the issues over which they had to haggle – the Americans had arrived at this conclusion themselves. On the other hand, if a careful count had been kept about whether American resources were deployed towards Europe or the Pacific, the British would have found that delineating a strategy was one thing, implementing it under the pressure of events quite another. More alarmingly, the British found that the Americans were determined to launch an invasion of Europe across the Channel almost immediately. The second great service performed by Churchill, ably and at times vehemently, supported by Brooke, was to fight off this impulse. There might be various views on the likelihood of a cross-Channel success in 1943; there could be none about an invasion in 1942. Such an operation would almost certainly have failed with consequences that are difficult to imagine.

In this period Churchill and the British Chiefs were certainly not following some Mediterranean strategy designed to further imperialistic ends at the war's conclusion. There is absolutely no evidence for this view. What they were doing in selecting North Africa as the next combat zone was fighting the Germans in an area where they thought they had a decent chance of defeating them. Roosevelt's determination that his forces should engage the Germans somewhere in 1942 was a considerable aid to Churchill in this period but it left sections of the Anglophobe American military disgruntled for the remainder of the war.

That disgruntlement only grew with what increasing numbers of the American military regarded as a plot to keep their forces away from Western

Europe. The decisions to invade Sicily and Italy roused grave suspicions among Marshall and his acolytes that the British were playing for post-war supremacy in the Mediterranean. Again, this is difficult to swallow. The British were already dependent on the Americans, via lend-lease. One crucial aspect of Montgomery's victory at Alamein had been an American willingness to send 300 of their Sherman tanks to the Western Desert rather than equip their newly formed armoured divisions with them. In short, what kind of post-war power Britain would be was already strictly dependent on the Americans.

What the end of this period also demonstrated was that American willingness to follow British strategy had its limits. Operations in Sicily and Italy, it could be argued, were central to any Mediterranean campaign. Talk of diverting British and American resources to the Dodecanese was quite something else. Many in the US already regarded the Mediterranean as peripheral warfare – the Dodecanese were in every sense to them the periphery of a periphery. For the first time they refused to cooperate. There would be no campaign in the Dodecanese because the Americans did not want one. The British were slow to observe this turning tide and slower still when the US insisted on its campaign in the south of France rather than keeping all divisions united in Italy. The argument as to which strategy was correct hardly mattered. It was the campaign decided upon by the stronger power that mattered, and that power was no longer Britain. Churchill and the Chiefs went into a huff about this and talked (privately) about following their own path and only invading Western Europe when they were ready. This was just moonshine. They knew full well that they did not have the resources to decide strategy independently. They might rail against the Americans but in the end they would follow the path set down by Marshall and Roosevelt. There would be a landing in the south of France and there would be a landing in north-western Europe in the late spring of 1944. The position was slightly redeemed for the British when, by some fancy foot-work, one of their own generals (Montgomery) was made overall ground commander. If Eisenhower was in charge, events on the ground would be dictated by Monty – a coup, of a kind.

The real battle from 1942 to 1944 in the European theatre then was not between Churchill and his military Chiefs. It was between Churchill and the Chiefs versus the Americans.

This is evident in the planning of the Normandy campaign. Churchill, the COS and the War Cabinet were united in their opposition to the US pre-invasion bombing plan which they all considered might inflict intolerable casualties on the French. Nevertheless the Americans won the argument, only the increased skill of Bomber Command preventing the projected casualties from coming to pass.

With the invasion itself the British in the form of Montgomery wrested back some control. The battle was fought as he wanted, the British bearing the brunt of the panzers on the eastern flank so that the Americans could break through in the west. Churchill wobbled slightly in his support for Montgomery but was reassured by Monty's confidence and his ability to describe his plans with great clarity to the Prime Minister.

The war at sea and the strategic bombing campaigns demonstrate different aspects of Churchill's interventions in military matters. With the war at sea, and in particular the submarine war, the Prime Minister's interest was sporadic. In the crisis periods of 1941 and 1942–1943 he formed Anti-U-Boat Committees and kept a close eye on events and paid great attention to even the most technical aspects of the anti-U-boat war. At other times he had no hesitation in switching Bomber Command from attacking Germany to attempting to destroy the German bases along the Biscay coast. Nevertheless, there was no great crisis of the type dealt with by Lloyd George in 1917. Convoy was instituted early and the overwhelming number of convoys got through to Britain unscathed, even counting March to May 1943. Churchill knew all this and he also knew that the US shipbuilding effort would overwhelm the number of U-boats that Doenitz could put to sea. He paid appropriate attention to this war, but it was not the obsession with him that he later claimed in his memoirs.

On the other hand, the bombing war was continually on his mind. He had decided quite early in the war that Britain would devote a considerable amount of its industrial capacity to building up a strategic bombing force. He was endlessly frustrated by the slow development of this force and its inability to hit anything much when it was unleashed. In Harris he found a commander with the ruthless determination that he required. The Prime Minister demonstrated equal ruthlessness in directing most bombers onto targets in Germany rather than using them as anti-U-boat weapons. He saw the bomber offensive as a way of demonstrating British power to the increasingly strong Americans and Russians. He also (rightly) saw it as the only way from 1941 to 1944 that Britain could bring the war home to the German people. In this regard he was at one with Harris and Portal in attacking one German city after another. But the Prime Minister was rather let down by his bomber barons. In mid-1943 Bomber Command was achieving such accuracy that its attacks on the Ruhr threatened to choke the German economy. Neither Harris nor Portal seemed to grasp this fact. In any case they rapidly switched Bomber Command's effort to Berlin, thus frittering away any chance of causing widespread economic dislocation in Germany. Un-alerted by his commanders, Churchill approved the switch. Probably all three men had seen too many unfulfilled promises of economic disruption during the rather futile and feeble bombing campaigns of 1941 and 1942. Anyway, the attempt was not made and in the end city destruction only came to an end when there were no more cities to destroy. Churchill badly needed guidance in this campaign and, for all the attention he paid to it, he did not get it.

The collapse of Britain's Far Eastern empire (Malaya, Singapore and Burma) played a strange role in civil/military relations. Before Japan's entry into the war there was fairly unanimous agreement between Churchill and the COS that little could be spared for a front where there was no fighting. They were correct in their assessment that in no sense could Britain fight three major powers. Indeed, it was having trouble enough fighting two. At times the Chiefs seemed to agree that more resources should be deployed to the east, but when the chips were down and priorities had to be established, only niggardly reinforcements were sent. Indeed, Britain never had the wherewithal to withstand a major Japanese attack, even had a greater propensity to reinforce the east existed. Along with this, however, Churchill consistently denied that Japan would attack. Whether he actually believed this or whether it was whistling in the wind is unclear. He certainly said it many times and managed to convince the Australian authorities (among others) that he was correct. This was to cause great (though temporary) bitterness between the two countries when Churchill's prophecies turned out to be false. There were certainly assumptions in Britain that were shared by the political and military authorities that Japan was not a major power or that aspects of the Japanese war machine (in particular its air force) were sub-standard. In fact, the entire British position in the Far East was based on bluff, which Brooke (though not Churchill) quickly realised. Churchill's view, that with America in the war, victory was certain, was no doubt correct but it was thin gruel for Australia and New Zealand.

The debates over the war in Burma are some of the strangest in the entire war. Once more Britain did not have the capacity to defend Burma, which was quickly overrun. But from 1942 through 1943 a gigantic effort by Wavell, Slim and others managed to build up the British Indian Army into a force to be reckoned with. Although this represented a major turning point in the war, it received scant attention in Britain among both the military and political leadership. In fact, given this backdrop, the strategic discussions over Burma that were held in London take on rather a surreal air. The major point at issue was not really about Burma at all but where other than Burma the war in the east might be prosecuted, the Chiefs favouring the Pacific, Churchill a flanking movement via Sumatra to win back Singapore and Malaya. While all this was proceeding, Slim with the aid of Mountbatten was actually winning a hard-fought ground war in Burma with the forgotten Fourteenth Army. London hardly noticed, the debates over whether to deploy in the Pacific or Sumatra becoming so heated that the COS, for the only time in the war, threated to resign en masse.

No one, except those on the ground in South-East Asia, comes out very well from this episode. What is worthy of attention, however, is the choice made between prosecuting the war in Europe or in the Far East. Whenever a choice had to be made, Churchill and the Chiefs chose Europe on every occasion. The loss of power in the Far East might have been lamented in London but it was not where their priorities lay. If Britain was to cut any kind of figure in the post-war world, it would cut it in Europe.

Even in Europe, though, the end of the war showed British power in steep decline. Montgomery's strategy for a British-led single thrust into the heart of Germany made sense to Britain in that it held out the promise of an early end to the war. It was overruled by the Americans and, although Churchill might protest to Roosevelt, in the end he was obliged to follow the American broad front strategy and see the war prolonged into 1945. Only on the peripheries, in Italy and in Greece, could Britain play much of a role. In Greece certainly Churchill's intervention snuffed out any chance (if chance there was) of a communist takeover. In Italy a victory was finally achieved by a largely British or British-led force but only at a time when the war was being won elsewhere.

Are there any general lessons to be gleaned from the world wars about civil/military relations in democracies? One is that the primacy of politics is essential. Between 1916 and 1917 the British military trod their own path with (potentially) disastrous consequences. That campaigns such as the Somme, Arras and Passchendaele were allowed to continue without civilian interference is a black mark against the political leadership. Only when Lloyd George seized back control (via manpower allocation) were results achieved at an acceptable (or anyway lower) cost.

This leads to a second point: that a little learning in the case of civilian leadership of the military is a good thing. Churchill, in the Second World War, was able to provide effective leadership because he was sufficiently schooled in military matters to be able to deal with the military with some confidence. This was vital in 1940 when he recognised that whatever the views of the COS, Britain had an excellent chance of continuing the war. This confidence also helped in numerous instances in replacing commanders and in backing his military men against the Americans and thus preventing a potentially disastrous invasion of Europe.

In the end, however, it is difficult for civilians to have that depth of knowledge of military affairs to be able to intervene effectively when affairs on the battlefield go awry. Even Churchill could not penetrate the inwardness of the repeated defeats of the desert army. What he could do was keep replacing generals until he found a winner. And what politicians in general could have done was ask before great armies were deployed, how their generals intended to fight and how they intended to achieve victory.

What the world wars do demonstrate is that democratic politicians are quite capable of waging war with the required level of ruthlessness to combat totalitarian states. And because in Britain's case the politicians acted with the support of their populations they were able to mobilise their states more effectively to fight protracted wars than any dictatorships. When Lloyd George promised the 'knock-out blow' he knew he had been raised to the premiership to deliver it. When Churchill proclaimed 'conquer we must', he knew he would be supported to the last. Democracies at war can be fearsome.

NOTES

1. A Liberal State Declares War

1. G.P. Gooch and Harold Temperley (eds), *British Documents on the Origins of the War 1898–1914, Vol XI* (London: HMSO, 1926), no. 9, p. 12 (this volume collated and edited by J.W. Headlam-Morley). Hereafter *B.D. Vol. XI*.
2. Sir M. de Bunsen to Sir Edward Grey 28/6/1914 (received 6 p.m.), *B.D. Vol. XI*, no. 10, p. 22. The modern spelling of Serbia has been adopted throughout.
3. Grey to de Bunsen 29/6/1914 (despatched 12.50 p.m.), *B.D. Vol. XI*, no. 14, p. 13.
4. Grey to Mensdorff 29/6/1914, ibid, no. 15, p. 13. Note, for reasons of brevity, Austria rather than the correct Austria-Hungary has been used throughout.
5. Grey to de Bunsen 24/7/1914 (despatched 1.30 p.m.), ibid, no. 91, p. 73.
6. De Bunsen to Grey 2/7/1914, ibid, no. 28, p. 20.
7. Grey to Sir H. Rumbold (Berlin) 6/7/1914, ibid, no. 32, pp. 24–5. Rumbold was the acting ambassador while Sir Edward Goschen was on holiday.
8. Ibid.
9. Grey to Sir George Buchanan (British Ambassador to Russia) 8/7/1914, ibid, no 39, pp. 30–1.
10. Benkendorff to Sazanov 9?/7/1914, quoted in T.G. Otte, *The July Crisis: The World's Descent into War, Summer 1914* (Cambridge: Cambridge University Press, 2015), p. 146.
11. For a detailed discussion of these meetings see Otte, *July Crisis*, pp. 72–89.
12. Hoyos memorandum quoted by Luigi Albertini, *The Origins of the War of 1914, Volume II* (London: Oxford University Press, 1952), p. 147. The Germans wanted the Austrian attitude to be immediate to forestall a Russian response in support of Serbia. Did they not know that the state of the Austrian military ruled out an immediate response to anything?
13. De Bunsen to Grey 16/7/1914 (received 3.15 p.m.), *B.D. Vol. XI*, no. 50, pp. 50–1.
14. Ibid.
15. Grey to Sir George Buchanan 20/7/1914, ibid, no. 67, pp. 53–4.
16. Grey to Buchanan 22/7/1914, ibid, no. 79, p. 64.
17. Grey to Rumbold 20/7/1914, ibid, no. 68, p. 54.
18. Grey to Sir Francis Bertie (British Ambassador in Paris) 21/7/1914, ibid, no. 72, pp. 59–60.
19. In his arresting assessment of the July crisis Christopher Clarke suggests that throughout the crisis Grey looked at events through the perspective of the Entente. See Christopher Clarke, *The Sleepwalkers: How Europe Went to War in 1914* (London: Allen Lane, 2012), p. 495. My own view is that this period suggests a different reading of Grey – that of a man striving to keep all the Great Powers out of a Balkan conflict. What he is certainly not doing, even on Clarke's own evidence, is sleepwalking.

20. Grey to de Bunsen 23/7/1914, *B.D. Vol. XI*, no. 86, pp. 70–1.
21. Ibid.
22. Grey to de Bunsen 24/7/1914, ibid, no. 91, pp. 73–4.
23. Ibid.
24. Grey to Rumbold 24/7/1914, ibid, no. 99, p. 78. See also Grey to Bertie on the same date (no. 98), where he suggests the same thing.
25. Communication by the German Ambassador 24/7/1914, ibid, no. 100, p. 79.
26. Ibid.
27. Sean McMeekin, *July 1914: Countdown to War* (London: Icon, 2014), p. 204.
28. Winston S. Churchill, *The World Crisis, Volume 1* (London: Odhams, n.d.), p. 155.
29. Asquith to the King 25/7/1914, CAB 41/35/20, The National Archives, Kew (TNA).
30. Michael Brock and Eleanor Brock (eds), *H.H. Asquith Letters to Venetia Stanley* (Oxford: Oxford University Press, 1982), p. 123. Venetia Stanley received much more detailed accounts of the Cabinet meetings than did the King.
31. Ibid.
32. Grey to Bertie 24/7/1914, *B.D. Vol. XI*, nos 98–9, pp. 77–8 and Grey to Rumbold 24/7/1914, ibid, no. 99, p. 78.
33. Ibid.
34. Buchanan to Grey 24/7/1014, ibid, no. 101, pp. 80–1.
35. Minute by Crowe 24/7/1914 on the above note in ibid, pp. 81–2.
36. Minute by Nicolson 24/7/1914 on the above note in ibid, p. 82.
37. Minute by Grey on the above Minutes in ibid.
38. Grey to Buchanan 25/7/1914, ibid, no. 132, pp. 97–8.
39. Keith Robbins, *Sir Edward Grey: A Biography of Lord Grey of Fallodon* (London: Cassell, 1971), p. 290.
40. Buchanan to Grey 25/7/1914, *B.D. Vol. XI*, no. 125, pp. 93–4.
41. Nicolson to Grey (Itchen Abbas) 26/7/1914, ibid, no. 139, p. 100.
42. See Grey to Bertie 26/7/1914, ibid, no. 140, p. 101, for an example. The notes sent to the other Powers were identical.
43. Otte, *July Crisis*, p. 283. This is one of the few occasions where I take issue with this splendid book.
44. Clarke, *The Sleepwalkers*, p. 464.
45. Minute by G.R. Clarke (Senior Clerk at the Foreign Office) 27/7/1914, *B.D. Vol. XI*, no, 171, p. 121.
46. Communication from the French Embassy 27/7/1914, ibid, no. 174, pp. 122–3.
47. Grey to Goschen 27/7/1914, ibid, no. 176, pp. 124.
48. Communication by the Swiss Minister 27/7/1914, ibid, no. 172, p. 122.
49. Grey to Goschen 27/7/1914, ibid, no. 176, p. 124.
50. Goschen to Grey 27/7/1914, ibid, no. 185, p. 128.
51. Herbert Samuel to his wife 27/7/1914, quoted in Cameron Hazlehurst, *Politicians at War: July 1914 to May 1915* (London: Cape, 1971), p. 77. Samuel was president of the Local Government Board.
52. Asquith to the King 28/7/1914, CAB 41/35/21.
53. Edward David (ed.), *Inside Asquith's Cabinet: From the Diaries of Charles Hobhouse* (London: John Murray, 1977), p. 177. Hobhouse was postmaster-general.
54. Asquith to the King 28/7/1914.
55. De Bunsen to Grey 27/7/1914, *B.D. Vol. XI*, no. 199, pp. 189–90.
56. Goschen to Grey 28/7/1914, ibid, no. 215, pp. 147–8.
57. Grey to Goschen 28/7/1914, ibid, no. 218, p. 149.
58. Minute 28/7/1914, ibid, p. 140. Churchill has a detailed discussion of this meeting in *The World Crisis, Vol. 1*.
59. Otte, *July Crisis*, pp. 331–3.
60. Goschen to Grey 28/7/1914, *B.D. Vol. XI*, no. 249, p. 164.

61. Churchill has a detailed discussion of this meeting in *The World Crisis, Vol. 1,* pp. 38–46.
62. Michael Brock, 'Britain Enters the War', in R.J.W. Evans and Hartmut Pogge von Strandemann, *The Coming of the First World War* (Oxford: Clarendon Press, 1988), p. 146. In footnote 3 on this page Brock helpfully includes a list of periodical articles in which this scenario was discussed.
63. Asquith to the King 30/7/1914, CAB 41/35/22.
64. Burns Diary 29/7/1914, quoted in Otte, *July Crisis,* p. 387.
65. Jack Pease Diary 29/7/1914, in K.M. Wilson (ed.), 'The Cabinet Diary of J.A. Pease 24 July–5 August 1914', *Leeds Philosophical and Literary Society Proceedings,* vol. 19, part 3 (March 1983), p. 6.
66. Asquith to the King 30/7/1914.
67. Hansard 30/7/1914, col. 1574.
68. Otte, *July Crisis,* p. 390.
69. Ibid.
70. Grey to Goschen 29/7/1914, *B.D. Vol. XI,* no. 286, pp. 182–3.
71. Grey to Bertie 29/7/1914, ibid, no. 283, p. 180.
72. On the contentious question of Russian mobilisation I rely on Marc Trachtenberg, 'The Meaning of Mobilisation in 1914', in Steven E. Miller, Sean Lynn-Jones and Steven van Evera (eds), *Military Strategy and the Origins of the First World War* (Princeton: Princeton University Press, 1991), pp. 195–225. Sean McMeekin considers Grey to have been culpable in not knowing about Russian mobilisation and then, when he did know, doing nothing to stop it. See his *July 1914,* pp. 214–16 and 238–9. Grey was aware of Russian actions on 27 July but it seems to me that Grey had precisely no leverage in this matter except to declare British neutrality. That he would not do so was because of his deep and well-founded suspicions of German military plans in Western Europe.
73. Goschen to Grey 30/7/1914, *B.D. Vol. XI,* no. 293, pp. 185–6.
74. Grey to Goschen 30/7/1914, ibid, no. 303, pp. 193–4. The number of this telegram is no doubt a coincidence but also a portent.
75. Ibid.
76. Grey to Bertie 30/7/1914, *B.D. Vol. XI,* no. 319, p. 201.
77. Pease Diary 31/7/1914, p. 7, is the best account of this meeting. Such was the press of events that no communication to the King was made of this Cabinet. Asquith still managed a short note to Venetia Stanley, however.
78. Harcourt Cabinet Note 31/7/1914, quoted in Otte, *July Crisis,* p. 456.
79. Pease Diary 31/7/1914.
80. Ibid.
81. Asquith to Venetia Stanley 31/7/1914, in Brock and Brock (eds), *H.H. Asquith Letters,* p. 136.
82. Margot Asquith Diary 31/7/1914, in Michael Brock and Eleanor Brock (eds), *Margot Asquith's Great War Diary 1914–1916: The View from Downing Street* (Oxford: Oxford University Press, 2014), p. 7.
83. Asquith to Venetia Stanley 30/7/1914, in Brock and Brock (eds), *H.H. Asquith Letters,* p. 135.
84. Ibid.
85. Grey to Buchanan 31/7/1914, *B.D. Vol. XI,* no. 335, p. 213.
86. Grey to Goschen 31/7/1914, ibid, no. 340, pp. 215–16.
87. Ibid.
88. Hansard 31/7/1914, col. 1787. As with Russian partial mobilisation, Grey had no leverage over full mobilisation except to frighten the Russians by declaring Britain neutral, something he would not contemplate lest it spur on the Central Powers. In any case Russian mobilisation did not mean war, a fact well known to the German High Command. For a fuller discussion than can be attempted here see Trachtenberg,

'Meaning of Mobilisation', in Miller et al. (eds), *Military Strategy*; Dominic Lieven, *Towards the Flame: Empire War and the End of Tsarist Russia* (London: Allen Lane, 2015), ch. 7. McMeekin, against the evidence I think, remains a sceptic, see *July 1914*, chs 19 to 21.

89. Grey to Bertie 31/7/1914, *B.D. Vol XI*, no. 348, p. 218. An identical note was sent to the Germans.

90. Note by Eyre Crowe on Grey to Bertie telegram, ibid, p. 222 and memorandum by Sir E. Crow 31/7/1914, ibid, no. 369, p. 228.

91. Note by Nicolson on Grey to Bertie telegram, ibid, p. 222 and Sir A. Nicolson to Sir Edward Grey 31/7/1914, ibid, no. 368, p. 227.

92. Grey note on Nicolson to Grey 31/7/1914, ibid, p. 227. Grey never formally replied to Crowe.

93. Asquith to Venetia Stanley 1/8/1914, in Brock and Brock (eds), *H.H. Asquith Letters*, pp. 139–40. The message is to be found in *B.D. Vol. XI*, no. 384, pp. 235–6.

94. Bertie to Grey 1/8/1914 (received 2.15 a.m.), ibid, no. 382, p. 234.

95. Bertie to Grey 1/8/1914 (received 2.05 a.m.), ibid, no. 380, p. 233.

96. Asquith to Venetia Stanley 1/8/1914, in Brock and Brock (eds), *H.H. Asquith Letters*, p. 140.

97. Asquith in the above letter so described him, as did Harcourt. See Otte, *July Crisis*, p. 456.

98. This list has been pieced together from Asquith to Venetia Stanley 1/8/1914 and an undated entry in the Hobhouse Diary that probably relates to this Cabinet. See David (ed.), *Inside Asquith's Cabinet*, p. 179.

99. This list has been compiled from Samuels's letters to his wife, Hobhouse Diary, Birrell's autobiography and Pease Diary. Note, however, that Pease was not present at this Cabinet, Hobhouse's opinion relies on an undated diary entry written after Britain had declared war. Cameron Hazlehurst includes Runciman in the peace group and McKenna in the waverers. See his *Politicians at War*, pp. 54–6.

100. Asquith to Venetia Stanley 1/8/1914, in Brock and Brock (eds), *H.H. Asquith Letters*, p. 140.

101. Trevor Wilson, *The Political Diaries of C.P. Scott* (London: Collins, 1970), p. 92.

102. The phrase is Bright's at a speech in Birmingham in 1865. See Brock, 'Britain Enters the War', in Evans and Von Strandemann (eds), *Coming of the First World War*, p. 167.

103. In Randolph S. Churchill, *Winston S. Churchill, Volume II, Companion, Part 3, 1911–1914* (London: Heinemann, 1969), pp. 1996–7 there are some Cabinet Notes passed between Lloyd George and Churchill. They are dated 1 August 1914. However, the first note (from Lloyd George to Churchill) states in part 'would you commit yourself in public *now* (Monday) to war . . .' although the Cabinet meeting of 1 August was held on a Friday. Monday would refer to 3 August not the 1st. Further, the next note (again from Lloyd George to Churchill) states in part 'do not press us too hard tonight . . .'. The only Cabinet meeting to take place at night in this period was held on Sunday 2 August, not on the 1st. This second note is dated by the reliable Otte (*July Crisis*, p. 474) to 1 August but the quotation omits the word 'tonight'. Altogether I have decided not to use these Notes.

104. Churchill, *The World Crisis, Vol. 1*, p. 175.

105. Grey to Bertie 1/8/1914, *B.D. Vol. XI*, no. 426, p. 253. Grey had already been reminded about the French coast issue by Arthur Nicolson earlier in the day. See 'Communication by the French Ambassador' in ibid, no. 424.

106. Otte, *July Crisis*, pp. 474–80 has an excellent discussion of this affair.

107. Grey to Goschen 1/8/1914, *B.D. Vol. XI*, no. 448, pp. 260–1.

108. Grey to de Bunsen 1/8/1914, ibid, no. 412, p. 247.

109. Grey to Buchanan 1/8/1914, ibid, no. 422, p. 251.

110. Buchanan to Grey 1/8/1914, ibid, no. 445, p. 259.

111. For the surreal background to German military planning see the superb book by Annika Mombauer, *Helmuth von Moltke and the Origins of the First World War* (Cambridge: Cambridge University Press, 2001), especially ch. 4.
112. Grey to Bertie 2/8/1914, *B.D. Vol. XI*, no. 447, p. 260.
113. Pease Diary 2/8/1914, p. 8.
114. Pease Diary 2/8/1914, pp. 8–9. Pease has the best account of this Cabinet.
115. Note to Pease 2/8/1914, quoted in Hazlehurst, *Politicians at War*, p. 95.
116. Samuel to his wife 2/8/1914, quoted in Otte, *July Crisis*, p. 492.
117. Runciman memorandum 2/8/1914, quoted in Hazlehurst, *Politicians at War*, pp. 92–3. Churchill had already made overtures to the Unionists via his friend F.E. Smith.
118. Pease Diary 2/8/1914, p. 9.
119. Grey to Bertie 2/8/1914, *B.D. Vol XI*, no. 487, pp. 274–5.
120. Margaret MacMillan, *The War that Ended Peace* (London: Profile, 2013), p. 584.
121. Pease Diary 2/8/1914, pp. 9–10.
122. Crewe to the King 2/8/1914, CAB 41/35/23. Crewe took over this duty from Asquith due to the press of events. Emphasis added.
123. Hobhouse Diary August 1914, quoted in David (ed.), *Inside Asquith's Cabinet*, p. 179.
124. Hazlehurst, after much diligence, cannot work him out. See *Politicians at War*, pp. 59–60.
125. There is much talk by Grey and others about 'public opinion' in the Cabinet discussions and in the diplomatic documents. Clarke, in *The Sleepwalkers*, suggests by public opinion Grey meant 'published opinion' i.e. the press (see p. 492). There is no doubt that he kept an eye on what the newspapers were saying. But by 'public opinion' I think Grey meant 'Parliamentary opinion'. After all, in the days before opinion polls, the views of members of Parliament might be a better proxy for public opinion than the press. In any case Grey thought Parliament the final arbiter of his policy, not the press.
126. Villiers to Grey 3/8/1914 (despatched 9.31 a.m., received 10.55 a.m.), *B.D. Vol. XI*, no. 521, p. 288.
127. Some authorities have Grey reading out the telegram to the Cabinet. See Otte, *July Crisis*, p. 494. Otte says the news 'made a profound impression on the Ministers'. But in the official record of the meeting, the Pease Diary and other letters and notes written by members of the Cabinet, not a single one mentions Grey giving them this news. And it will be clear from what Grey said later in the day in Parliament that he was unaware of the telegram at this meeting.
128. Asquith to Venetia Stanley 3/8/1914, in Brock and Brock (eds), *H.H. Asquith Letters*, p. 148.
129. Pease Diary 3/8/1914, p. 10.
130. Ibid. Chronology is difficult here. The Foreign Office had received notification of the German ultimatum to Belgium at 10.55 a.m. but the Cabinet records indicate that this had not yet been transmitted to Grey.
131. Asquith to the King 3/8/1914, CAB 41/35/23.
132. Viscount Grey of Fallodon, *Twenty-Five Years 1892–1916, Vol. II* (London: Hodder & Stoughton, 1925), pp. 12–13.
133. All excerpts from Grey's speech are taken from Hansard 3/8/1914, cols. 1809–29. Grey received the news of the ultimatum at around 4 p.m. It had taken the Foreign Office five hours to get him even a garbled version of this vital document. Sean McMeekin has this point; see *July 1914*, p. 369. He is the only historian who seems to have picked up on this issue.
134. The 'ragged edges' phrase is Asquith's. See Asquith to Venetia Stanley 3/8/1914, in Brock and Brock (eds), *H.H. Asquith Letters*, p. 148.
135. Hazlehurst, *Politicians at War*, p. 46.
136. Hansard 3/8/1914, vol. 65, col. 1833.
137. Grey, *Twenty-Five Years, Vol. II*, p. 17.

138. Grey to Goschen 4/8/1914 (despatched 2 p.m.), *B.D. Vol. XI*, no. 594, p. 314.
139. For Wilson's antics see Charles Callwell, *Field-Marshal Sir Henry Wilson: His Life and Diaries, Vol. 1* (London: Cassell, 1927), pp. 151–6.

2. 1914 – The New Warfare

1. War Council Minutes 5/8/1914, CAB 42/1/2.
2. Callwell, *Henry Wilson, Vol. 1*, p. 158.
3. War Council Minutes 5/8/1914, CAB 42/1/2.
4. Ibid, 6/8/1914, CAB 42/1/3.
5. Brigade War Diary August 1914, WO 95/1352/1, TNA.
6. Timothy Bowman and Mark Connelly, *The Edwardian Army: Recruiting, Training, and Deploying the British Army 1902–1914* (Oxford: Oxford University Press, 2012), p. 9.
7. Ibid, p. 42.
8. Edward Spiers, 'Rearming the Edwardian Artillery', *Journal of the Society for Army Historical Research*, vol. 57, no. 231 (1979), pp. 167–76.
9. This information has largely been drawn from Brigadier-General Sir James E. Edmonds, *Military Operations: France and Belgium, 1914, Vol. 1* (London: Macmillan, 1933), Appendix 2, pp. 485–7.
10. Bowman and Connelly, *Edwardian Army*, p. 102.
11. Edmonds, *1914, Vol. 1*, p. 486.
12. Walter Raleigh, *The War in the Air, Vol. 1* (London: Hamish Hamilton, 1969), pp. 282–98. Reprint of the British Official History, 1922 edition.
13. Richard Holmes, *The Little Field-Marshal: Sir John French* (London: Cape, 1981), p. 206.
14. Elizabeth Greenhalgh, *The French Army and the First World War* (Cambridge: Cambridge University Press, 2014), p. 42.
15. Holmes. *Little Field-Marshal*, pp. 208–9.
16. Edmonds, *1914, Vol. 1*, p. 63.
17. Raleigh, *War in the Air, Vol. 1*, pp. 301–2.
18. Wilson Diary 22/8/1914, in Callwell, *Henry Wilson, Vol. 1*, p. 163.
19. French Diary 22/8/1914, in Holmes, *Little Field-Marshal*, p. 213.
20. E.L. Spears, *Liaison 1914: A Narrative of the Great Retreat* (London: Heinemann, 1930), pp. 148–9.
21. Ibid, p. 149.
22. John Terraine, *Mons: Retreat to Victory* (London: Batsford, 1960), p. 86; Don Farr, *Mons: The Beginning and the End* (Solihull: Helion, 2008), p. 14, map 2.
23. Mark Osborne Humphries and John Maker (eds), *Germany's Western Front: 1914 Part 1, The Battle of the Frontiers and Pursuit to the Marne* (Translations from the German Official History of the Great War) (Waterloo, ON: Wilfrid Laurier University Press, 2013), pp. 120–2.
24. Edmonds, *1914, Vol. 1*, p. 77.
25. Ibid, pp. 77–9.
26. Brigade War Diary 23/8/1914, WO 95/1416/1.
27. Edmonds, *1914, Vol. 1*, p. 93.
28. Holmes, *Little Field-Marshal*, p. 216.
29. Humphries and Maker, *Germany's Western Front 1914*, p. 225.
30. For a good discussion of the limited opportunities the cavalry might have in future warfare see Spencer Jones, *From Boer War to World War: Tactical Reform of the British Army 1902–1914* (Norman: Oklahoma University Press, 2012), pp. 182–5.
31. Bowman and Connelly, *Edwardian Army*, p. 103.
32. This eyewitness account is to be found in Richard Holmes, *Riding the Retreat: Mons to the Marne 1914 Revisited* (London: Pimlico, 1996), p. 140. Holmes gives by far the best account of this episode. It should be compared with the sanitised version in the Official History, Edmonds, *1914, Vol. 1*, pp. 108–9.

33. Holmes, *Riding the Retreat*, p. 140.
34. Marden's Diary, quoted by Jerry Murland, *Battle on the Aisne 1914: The BEF and the Birth of the Western Front* (Barnsley: Pen & Sword, 2012), p. 120.
35. David Lomas, *Mons 1914: Britain's Tactical Triumph* (London: Praeger, 2004), p. 63.
36. Nikolas Gardner, 'Command and Control in the "Great Retreat" of 1914: The Disintegration of the British Cavalry Division', *Journal of Military History*, vol. 63, no. 1 (January 1999), pp. 46–7.
37. Major-General Sir F. Maurice, *Forty Days in 1914* (London: Constable, 1925), p. 106.
38. Brigade War Diary 26/8/1914, WO 905/1416/1.
39. Terraine, *Mons*, pp. 148–55. This remains the most lucid account of the battle.
40. Trevor Wilson, *The Myriad Faces of War* (Oxford: Polity, 1986), pp. 45–6. Chapters 4, 5 and 6 of this splendid work has the best account of the retreat from the point of view of the ordinary soldier.
41. Brigade War Diary 2/9/1914, WO 95/1352/1.
42. Ibid.
43. Brigade War Diary 28/8/1914 to 5/9/1914, WO 95/1/2.
44. This account quoted in Maurice, *Forty Days in 1914*, p. 155.
45. Holmes, *Riding the Retreat*, p. 256; Edmonds, *1914, Vol. 1*, p. 258; Humphries and Maker, *Germany's Western Front 1914*, pp. 411–12.
46. Gary Sheffield, *The Chief: Douglas Haig and the British Army* (London: Aurum, 2011), pp. 261–2, 76–9 puts Landrecies in proper perspective. For Villers-Cotterêts see Edmonds, *1914, Vol. 1*, pp. 260–2.
47. Holmes, *Little Field-Marshal*, p. 229.
48. Asquith to the King 31/8/1914, CAB 41/35/38.
49. Holmes, *Little Field-Marshal*, p. 231.
50. Asquith to the King 1/9/1914, CAB 41/35/39.
51. Holmes, *Little Field-Marshal*, pp. 233–4.
52. Elizabeth Greenhalgh has a brief account in *French Army*, pp. 42–9. For a comprehensive account see Holger Herwig, *The Marne, 1914: The Opening of the World War and the Battle that Changed the World* (New York: Random House, 2009).
53. Brigade, 'Action at Hautevesnes', War Diary September 1914, WO 95/1352/1/1.
54. Brigade War Diary 13/9/1914, WO 95/1416/1/1.
55. Edmonds, *1914, Vol. 1*, p. 399.
56. Australian Military Forces, *Operations of the British Expeditionary Forces in France and Belgium* (Melbourne: Government Printer, 1934), p. 200. Edmonds's narrative lapses into incoherence at this point. The Australian army seems to have had a better sense of this confused fighting, however.
57. Murland, *Battle on the Aisne 1914*, pp. 126–8.
58. Brigade War Diary 14/9/1914, WO 95/1352/1/1.
59. Edmonds, *1914, Vol. 1*, p. 408.
60. Ibid, p. 411.
61. Gary Sheffield and John Bourne (eds), *Douglas Haig: War Diaries and Letters 1914–1918* (London: Weidenfeld and Nicolson, 2005), p. 71.
62. Edmonds, *1914, Vol. 1*, pp. 445–6.
63. I Corps War Diary, 'Report on Operations 1 to 16 October 1914', WO 95/588/1.
64. Bowman and Connelly, *Edwardian Army*, pp. 84–6. Budworth, later commander of Fourth Army artillery at the Somme was one who identified the problem. For its consequences at the Aisne see Murland, *Battle of the Aisne 1914*, pp. 170–2.
65. Robin Prior and Trevor Wilson, *Command on the Western Front: The Military Career of Sir Henry Rawlinson 1914–1918* (Oxford: Blackwell, 1992), p. 12.
66. Brigadier-General Sir James E. Edmonds, *Military Operations: France and Belgium, 1914, Volume 2* (London: Macmillan, 1925), p. 92.
67. Ibid, p. 7.
68. Greenhalgh, *French Army*, p. 51.

69. Edmonds, *1914, Vol. 2*, pp. 121–4.
70. Ian F.W. Beckett, *Ypres: The First Battle, 1914* (Harlow: Pearson, 2004), p. 68. The best book on the subject.
71. A.H. Farrar-Hockley, *Ypres 1914: Death of an Army* (London: Pan, 1970), pp. 98–9.
72. Beckett, *Ypres*, p. 78.
73. I Corps War Diary 22/23 October 1914, WO 95/588/5.
74. Farrar-Hockley, *Ypres*, pp. 96–7.
75. Rawlinson Diary 22/10/1914, Rawlinson Papers, Churchill College, Cambridge.
76. Edmonds, *1914, Vol. 2*, p. 282.
77. Beckett, *Ypres*, p. 95.
78. Statement by Captain Andrew Thorne, Staff Captain 1 Guards Brigade, in I Corps War Diary October 1914, WO 95/588/5.
79. Farrar-Hockley, *Ypres*, p. 96; Beckett, *Ypres*, p. 70.
80. Edmonds, *1914, Vol. 2*, p. 92.
81. 'Brief Accounts of the Operations of the Cavalry Corps 12 October to 2 November 1914', Cavalry Corps War Diary October 1914, WO 95/572/1.
82. Beckett, *Ypres*, ch. 7 is a clear account of this episode.
83. Shelford Bidwell and Dominick Graham, *Fire-Power: British Army Weapons and Theories of War 1904–1945* (London: Allen & Unwin, 1982), p. 49. The chapters on the pre-war army are highly recommended.
84. Raleigh, *War in the Air, Vol 1*, p. 341.
85. Some of the British trenches at Langemarck had some wire put in front of them on the night of 21/22 October. See Edmonds, *1914, Vol. 2*, p. 173, n. 1.

3. The Navy Goes to War 1914–1915

1. These numbers are based on Paul Halpern, *A Naval History of World War 1* (London: UCL Press, 1994), p. 8.
2. Ibid, p. 7.
3. Report of the Standing Committee on North East Coast Defences 29/11/1912, CAB 38/22/41.
4. War Staff Paper on Scapa Flow Defences November 1913, ADM 116/1293, TNA.
5. Naval Staff Monographs, Volume 1, Monograph 4, 'Goeben and Breslau', pp. 178–9. Issued by the Admiralty in 1920, this is one of a series of Naval Staff Studies on various aspects of the naval war.
6. Ibid, pp. 179–80.
7. Note by Rear-Admiral Hood 10/7/1914, ADM 1/8384/184.
8. Admiralty to Milne 30/7/1914, ADM 137/19.
9. Milne to the Admiralty 4/8/1914, ADM 137/879.
10. Arthur Marder, *From the Dreadnought to Scapa Flow, Volume 2* (London: Oxford University Press, 1966), p. 23.
11. Troubridge to Milne 7/8/1914, ADM 137/19.
12. Ibid.
13. The Troubridge court-martial proceedings can be read in E.W.R. Lumby (ed.), *Policy and Operations in the Mediterranean 1912–1914* (London: Navy Records Society, 1970).
14. Halpern, *Naval History of World War 1*, p. 57.
15. A. Temple Patterson, *Tyrwhitt of the Harwich Force: The Life of Admiral of the Fleet Sir Reginal Tyrwhitt* (London: Macdonald, 1973), pp. 50–1.
16. Eric W. Osborne, *The Battle of the Heligoland Bight* (Bloomington: Indiana University Press, 2006), pp. 42–3.
17. Admiralty to Jellicoe 27/8/1914 quoted in Naval Staff Monographs, Volume 3, 1921, Monograph 11, 'The Battle of the Heligoland Bight, August 1914', p. 149.
18. James Goldrick, *Before Jutland: The Naval War in the Northern European Waters 1914–1915* (Annapolis, MD: Naval Institute Press, 2015), p. 114.

19. Beatty Signal 27/8/1914, Naval Staff Monograph 11, 'Heligoland Bight', p. 149.
20. Goldrick, *Before Jutland*, p. 114.
21. Ibid.
22. *Lurcher* Report 29/8/1914, ADM 137/551. *Lurcher* was Keyes's flagship.
23. *Arethusa* Report 30/8/1914, in ibid.
24. Goldrick, *Before Jutland*, p. 125.
25. Temple Patterson, *Tyrwhitt*, p. 63.
26. Churchill to Prince Louis 18/9/1914, ADM 137/47.
27. Admiralty to Admiral Christian (officer in charge of the patrol) 19/9/1914, in ibid.
28. Court of Enquiry into Loss of *Aboukir*, *Cressy* and *Hogue* on September 22, 1914 – Minutes 30/9/1914, in ibid.
29. Naval Staff Monographs, Volume 1, 1920, Monograph 2, 'German Cruiser Squadron in the Pacific', pp. 57–8.
30. Ibid, p. 55.
31. Admiral Patey Report on Operations 23/10/1914, ADM 137/45.
32. Secretary of State for the Colonies to the Governments of Australia and New Zealand 6/8/1914, ADM 137/45.
33. Ibid.
34. Patey's Report 23/10/1914.
35. Patey to the Admiralty 13/10/1914, ADM 137/16.
36. Admiralty to Patey 14/10/1914, in ibid.
37. Note by Admiral Jackson 31/8/1914, ADM 137/7; Minute by Churchill 21/9/1914 in ibid.
38. Lord Liverpool (Governor-General of New Zealand) to the Colonial Secretary 17/9/1914, in ibid.
39. Lord Liverpool to the Colonial Secretary 1/10/1914, ADM 137/16.
40. A.W. Jose, *The Royal Australian Navy 1914–1918*, 6th edn (Sydney: Angus & Robertson, 1938), p. 158 – the Official History.
41. Naval Staff Monograph 2, 'German Cruiser Squadron in the Pacific', p. 114.
42. Admiralty to Cradock 14/9/1914, ADM 116/3486.
43. Admiralty to Cradock 5/10/1914, in ibid.
44. H.T. Bennett, 'Twenty One Years Ago: The Tragedy of Coronel', *Argus* (Melbourne) 2/11/1935. Bennett was navigating officer on the *Canopus* at the time of Coronel.
45. Cradock to the Admiralty (received 12/10/1914), ADM 116/3486.
46. Churchill to Prince Louis [First Sea Lord] 14/10/1914, ADM 137/26.
47. Admiralty to Cradock 14/10/1914, ADM 116/3486.
48. Cradock to the Admiralty 18/10/1914, in ibid.
49. Cradock to the Admiralty 24/10/1914, in ibid.
50. Cradock to the Admiralty 27/10/1914, in ibid.
51. Admiralty to Cradock 28/10/1914, in ibid. There is some doubt about whether Cradock ever received this message. The Admiralty records imply that he did not, the Paymaster on the *Glasgow* is sure that he did.
52. Log of *Glasgow* 1/11/1914, ADM 53/42828.
53. Churchill to Admiral Superintendent, Devonport 9/11/1914, ADM 137/43.
54. Marder, *From Dreadnought to Scapa Flow*, Vol. 2, p. 121.
55. H. Hickling, *Sailor at Sea* (London: Kimber, 1965), p. 66. Hickling was an officer on the *Glasgow*.
56. Diary of an Officer on the *Gneisenau*, ADM 137/1018.
57. *Canopus* Report 15/12/1914, ADM 137/304.
58. *Inflexible* Log 8/12/1914, in ibid.
59. Sturdee's Report 16/12/1914, in ibid.
60. R. Verner, *The Battlecruisers at the Action of the Falkland Islands* (London: John Bale, 1920), p. 10. Verner was on board the *Inflexible*.
61. Admiralty to Jellicoe 23/1/1915, ADM 137/1943.

62. 'Report of Vice-Admiral Sir David Beatty on the Action in the North Sea, January 24, 1915', ADM 1/8413/54.
63. *Lion's* Signals, ADM 137/305.
64. Battle Cruiser Squadron Signals, in ibid.
65. *Lion's* Signals, in ibid.
66. John Brooks, *The Battle of Jutland* (Cambridge: Cambridge University Press, 2016), p. 91.

4. Gallipoli – The Politicians' Hour

1. Blanche E. C. Dugdale, *Arthur James Balfour 1906–1930* (London: Hutchinson, 1936), p. 130.
2. Asquith to Venetia Stanley 30/12/1914, in Brock and Brock (eds), *H.H. Asquith Letters*, p. 345.
3. Valentine Fleming to Churchill November 1914, in Martin Gilbert (ed.), *Winston S. Churchill, Volume 3, Companion, Part 1, Documents July 1914–April 1915* (London: Heinemann, 1972), pp. 272–3. Hereafter *CV3*.
4. Churchill to Asquith 29/12/1914, in ibid, pp. 343–5.
5. Ibid.
6. Lt-Col Hankey Memorandum 28/12/1914, *CV3*, pp. 337–43. All other quotations come from this source.
7. Ibid.
8. Lloyd George to Asquith 31/12/1914, ibid, pp. 350–6.
9. Asquith to Venetia Stanley 1/1/1915, Brock and Brock (eds), *H.H. Asquith Letters*, p. 358.
10. Fisher to Hankey 2/1/1915, Hankey Papers, CAB 63/4.
11. Fisher to Churchill 3/1/1915, *CV3*, pp. 367–8.
12. The secretary of this meeting recalled no signs of dissent about the matter. See Greene Note, August 1916, Greene Papers, GEE/11, National Maritime Museum, Greenwich.
13. Churchill to Carden 3/1/1915, *CV3*, p. 367.
14. Carden to Churchill 5/1/1915, ibid, p. 360. Italics added.
15. Churchill to Carden 6/1/1915, ibid, p. 267.
16. Carden to Churchill 11/1/1915, ibid, pp. 405–6.
17. War Council Minutes 13/1/1915, CAB 42/1/16.
18. Jackson Memorandum 5/1/1915, *CV3*, pp. 376–7.
19. Fisher to Churchill 4/1/1915, ibid, pp. 373–4.
20. Richmond Diary RIC 1/9, National Maritime Museum, Greenwich.
21. For this memorandum see *CV3*, pp. 452–4.
22. Fisher to Asquith 28/1/1915, ibid, p. 461.
23. Churchill to Fisher 28/1/1915, ibid, p. 462.
24. War Council Minutes 28/1/1915, Cab 42/1/26.
25. Jackson, 'Attack on Constantinople' 13/2/1915, *CV3*, pp. 506–12; Richmond, 'Remarks on Present Strategy', RIC 1/9.
26. Hankey to Balfour 13/2/1915, *CV3*, p. 500.
27. Asquith to Venetia Stanley 13/2/1915, Brock and Brock (eds), *H.H. Asquith Letters*, pp. 512–13.
28. War Council Conclusions 13/2/1915, *CV3*, p. 516. Hankey was not present at this meeting so there were no formal minutes. Asquith later conveyed to him the gist of what was said and Hankey thought them important enough to record them.
29. 'Report of the Committee Appointed to Investigate the Attacks Delivered on and the Enemy Defences of the Dardanelles Straits', London, Naval Staff Gunnery Division, 1921, Australian War Memorial, AWM 124, chapter 2, pp. 3–20 (hereafter Mitchell Committee Report).

30. Ibid.
31. Ibid, p. 51.
32. See the papers written by Jackson on 15/1/1915 in *CV3*, pp. 419–21. There are also various papers by Oliver in the same volume on pp. 478–80 and 485–90.
33. For the lamentable performance of aerial spotting during the naval attack see HMS *Ark Royal* (a proto-aircraft carrier) Report in ADM 116/1352.
34. Mitchell Committee Report, p. 78.
35. Mitchell Committee Report, pp. 34–5.
36. Ibid, pp. 38–41.
37. Ibid.
38. Ibid, pp. 44–55.
39. Ibid, pp. 51–9.
40. See Godfrey Papers, Churchill College, Cambridge 69/33/1 and Notes made by Captain Dent in WO 95/4263. Godfrey and Dent seem to have been the main instigators of the plan.
41. There is a vivid description of this operation by a junior officer on the *Prince George*, one of the pre-dreadnought battleships. See the account of Lt. D.H. Hepburn, P322, Imperial War Museum, London. See also de Robeck's Report 24/3/1915, de Robeck Papers 4/4, Churchill College, Cambridge.
42. See de Robeck's paper, 'Appreciation of present position in Dardanelles and proposals for future operations', in Godfrey Papers 69/33/1, Churchill College, Cambridge.
43. Hamilton to Kitchener 19/3/1915, *CV3*, p. 710.
44. See his letter to de Robeck 23/3/1915 ordering him to resume the naval attack. The letter was never sent because of the objections of the Admiralty War Group. See *CV3*, pp. 724–6.
45. War Council Minutes 3/3/1915, CAB 42/2/3.
46. Appreciation by General Paris 19/3/1915, Hamilton Papers, Liddell Hart Centre for Military Archives, King's College, London, 17/7/31. There is no evidence that Hamilton ever replied to Paris.
47. Hunter-Weston to Hamilton 30/3/1915, Hamilton Papers 17/7/30.
48. For the geography of Gallipoli see Peter Chasseaud and Peter Doyle, *Grasping Gallipoli: Terrain, Maps and the Failure at the Dardanelles 1915* (Staplehurst: Spellmount, 2005).
49. Hamilton, 'Force Order No. 1', in C.E. Aspinall-Oglander, *Military Operations: Gallipoli: Maps and Appendices* (London: Heinemann, 1929), Appendix 3, pp. 7–11.
50. See the graphic account of the landing given by Captain G.W. Geddes in the 86 Brigade War Diary April 1915, WO 95/4310.
51. For S Beach see 2 South Wales Borderers War Diary 25/4/1915, WO 95/4311; for X, 87 Brigade War Diary 25/4/1915, in ibid.
52. Aspinall-Oglander, *Military Operations: Gallipoli, Vol. 1*, pp. 202–8. The Official History.
53. Birdwood, 'Operation Order No. 1, 17/4/1915', Aspinall-Oglander, *Military Operations: Gallipoli: Maps and Appendices*, Appendix 14, pp. 37–41.
54. Robert Rhodes James, *Gallipoli* (London: Batsford, 1965), pp. 104–7 rehearses most of the theories about why the Anzac forces landed where they did.
55. Australian Division Report 7/5/1915, AWM 4/1/42/3, Part 2.
56. C.E.W. Bean, *Official History of Australia in the War of 1914–1918, Vol. I: The Story of Anzac – From the Outbreak of War to the End of the First Phase of the Gallipoli Campaign, May 4, 1915*, 3rd edn (Sydney: Angus & Robertson, 1942), chs XII–XVI.
57. Turkish General Staff, *A Brief History of the Canakkale Campaign in the First World War, June 1914–January 1916* (Ankara: Turkish General Staff Printing House, 2004), pp. 69–71.
58. Bean, *Official History Vol. I, The Story of Anzac*, p. 458.
59. Ibid, pp. 460–1.

60. Aspinall-Oglander, *Gallipoli, Vol. 1*, pp. 288–92.
61. Turkish General Staff, *A Brief History*, pp. 132–3.
62. Division, 'Report on Operations from 6th to 7th May, 1915', 29 Division War Diary, WO 95/4305.
63. VIII Corps War Diary, June 1915, WO 95/4274.
64. See VIII Corps 'Report on Operations Eighth Army Corps June to August 1915 in VIII Corps War Diary June and July 1915, WO 95/4274; French Official Account, translation in the Rayfield Papers, Imperial War Museum (hereafter IWM) 69/61/6.
65. Birdwood to Hamilton 8/6//1915, in Anzac Corps War Diary, WO 95/4281.
66. Note by General Braithwaite (Chief of Staff to Hamilton) 22/7/1915, WO 158/576.
67. Dardanelles Committee Minutes 7/6/1915, CAB 42/3/1.
68. Dardanelles Committee Minutes 17/6/1915, CAB 42/3/4.
69. C.E.W. Bean, *Official History of Australia in the War of 1914–1918, Vol. II: The Story of Anzac – From May 4, 1915, to the Evacuation of the Gallipoli Peninsula* (Sydney: Angus & Robertson, 1942).
70. Battalion War Diary 8/8/1915, AWM 4/23/32/10; 15 Battalion War Diary 8/8/1915, AWM 4/23/31/10.
71. For the New Zealanders see New Zealand Brigade War Diary 8/8/1915, WO 95/ 4352; for the Indian Brigade see their War Diary 9/8/1915, WO 95/ 4272. See also Col. Allanson's evidence to the Dardanelles Commission 19/1/1917, CAB 19/33.
72. IX Corps War Diary August 1915, WO 95/4276.
73. Memorandum by Stopford 31/7/1915, WO 158/576.
74. GHQ to Stopford 31/7/1915, in ibid.
75. Dardanelles Committee Minutes 10/11/1915, CAB 42/4/6.
76. Monro to Kitchener 2/11/1915 in Dardanelles Committee Minutes, CAB 42/4/6.
77. Kitchener to Asquith 15/11/1915, CAB 42/5/20.
78. Curzon memorandum 27/11/1915, CAB 42/5/24.
79. For details of the Keyes Plan see Paul G. Halpern (ed.), *The Keyes Papers 1914–1918, Vol. 1* (London: Navy Records Society, 1972), pp. 194–201.
80. Casualty figures in the sources vary. I have used those in Major T.J. Mitchell and G.M. Smith, *Medical Services: Casualties and Medical Services of the Great War* (London: HMSO, 1931), ch. XIII.
81. Answers given to the Mitchell Committee, ADM 116/17/4.
82. For the Romanian Army see C. Kiritescu, *La Roumanie dans la Guerre mondiale 1916–1919* (Paris: Payot, 1936), pp. 54 and 265.

5. 1915 – Learning and Not Learning

1. For these details see Brigadier-General J.E. Edmonds and Captain G.C. Wynne, *Military Operations: France and Belgium, 1915, Vol. 1* (London: Macmillan, 1927), ch. 1.
2. These details can be found in Brigadier-General J.E. Edmonds, *Military Operations: France and Belgium 1915, Vol. 2* (London: Macmillan, 1928), pp. 111–33.
3. Haig Diary 6/2/1915, Sheffield and Bourne (eds), *Douglas Haig*, pp. 98–9. Unless otherwise stated, entries come from this edition. Other Haig Diary entries come from a typed manuscript edition in the National Library of Scotland (hereafter NLS).
4. Haig Diary 25/2/1915, NLS.
5. G.C. Wynne, *If Germany Attacks: The Battle in Depth in the West* (London: Faber, 1940), pp. 20–2; G.C. Wynne, 'The Other Side of the Hill, No, XVII: Neuve Chapelle 10th–12th of March, 1915', *Army Quarterly*, vol. 37 (1938–1939), pp. 30–46.
6. Haig Diary 24/2/1915, NLS.
7. 'Artillery Problem of Neuve Chapelle', IV Corps War Diary Mar–Apr 1915, WO 95/708.
8. Edmonds, *1915, Vol. 1*, p. 78, n. 2.
9. 'Memorandum on the Attack on Neuve Chapelle by First Army', IV Corps War Diary March 1915, WO 95/708.

10. Haig Diary 22/2/1915, NLS.
11. Rawlinson, 'Remarks on VIII Division Scheme', 24 Brigade War Diary, WO 95/707.
12. 'Notes on Conference on 5/3/15' in IV Corps War Diary March 1915, WO 95/708.
13. Rawlinson Diary 6/3/1915.
14. Garhwal Brigade War Diary 10/3/1915, WO 95/3943/4.
15. 'Report on the Operations of the IV Corps from the 10th to the 14th March, 1915', WO 158/374.
16. Division HQ Royal Artillery, 'Remarks on Experiences on 10th–13th March' in 8 Division War Diary Sept 1914–Mar 1915, WO 95/1671.
17. IV Corps Report, WO 158/374.
18. Wynne, *If Germany Attacks*, pp. 34–5.
19. Brigade Narrative, om 24 Brigade War Diary 11/3/1915, WO 95/707.
20. IV Corps Report, WO 158/374.
21. Haig Diary 11/3/1915, NLS.
22. Wynne, *If Germany Attacks*, p. 38.
23. First Army War Diary 12/3/1915, WO 95/154.
24. IV Corps Report, WO 95/374.
25. Brigadier Carter of the 24 Brigade was the hero in this case. See 24 Brigade Narrative, WO 95/707.
26. Edmonds, *1915, Vol. 2*, p. 151; German General Staff, *Der Weltkreig, Vol. 7* (Berlin: Mittler, 1936) p. 59.
27. Rawlinson to Kitchener 21/4/1915, Rawlinson Papers 5201/33/17, National Army Museum (NAM).
28. Rawlinson to Ralph Wigram 25/3/1915, in ibid.
29. Edmonds, *1915, Vol. 2*, p. 3.
30. Ibid, p. 4.
31. Ibid.
32. Ibid, pp. 14–15.
33. See Haig Diary 19/4/1915, NLS and Edmonds, *1915, Vol. 2*, Map 4.
34. For the experiences of the Indian Corps on this day see I Indian Corps War Diary 9/5/1915, WO 95/1089/5.
35. Rawlinson Diary 10/5/1915, Churchill College.
36. See 2 Division War Diary 15/16 May, WO 95/1285/1.
37. David M. Leeson, 'An Ecstasy of Fumbling: A Reassessment of British Offensives on the Wester Front 1915', PhD Thesis, University of Regina, Saskatchewan, 1998, p. 132.
38. This account relies on Wilson, *Myriad Faces*, pp. 201–5.
39. L.F. Haber, *The Poisonous Cloud: Chemical Warfare in the First World War* (Oxford: Oxford University Press, 2002), pp. 25–8.
40. Ibid, pp. 29–30.
41. Ibid, pp. 32–4.
42. Colonel Mordacq quoted in J. McWilliams and R.J. Steel, *Gas! The Battle for Ypres, 1915* (St Catherine's, ON: Vanwell, 1985), p. 48.
43. See V Corps War Diary 23/24 April 1915, WO 95/743/3.
44. A.J. Smithers, *The Man who Disobeyed: Sir Horace Smith-Dorrien and his Enemies* (London: Leo Cooper, 1970), pp. 252–5.
45. Haig Diary 30/4/1915.
46. Nick Lloyd, *Loos 1915* (Stroud: History Press, 2008), p. 36.
47. War Council Minutes 5/7/1915, CAB 42/3/7.
48. Hankey Notes, quoted in Lloyd, *Loos 1915*, p. 29.
49. Haig Diary 20/6/1915, NLS.
50. Rawlinson, 'Proposals for the Attack of Loos Village and Hill 70', IV Corps War Diary Sept 1915, WO 95/711.
51. Lloyd, *Loos 1915*, pp. 33–8.

52. Ibid, p. 38.
53. Joffre to French 12/8/1915, quoted in Haig Diary 14/8/1915, NLS.
54. Dardanelles Committee Minutes 5/7/1915, CAB 42/3/7.
55. Haig Diary 19/8/1915, NLS. Haig underlined the passages quoted.
56. Dardanelles Committee Minutes 20/8/1915, CAB 42/3/16.
57. Rawlinson, 'Proposals for the Attack on Loos Village and Hill 70', IV Corps War Diary Sept 1915, WO 95/711.
58. Holmes, *Little Field-Marshal*, pp. 300–1.
59. Rawlinson to First Army 9/10/1915 on the artillery lessons at Loos, IV Corps War Diary Oct–Dec 1915, WO 95/712.
60. The figures are taken from two documents in the Rawlinson Papers: 'Neuve Chapelle: Gun Ammunition, Total Rounds Expended on 10/3/15' and 'IV Corps 'Ammunition Expended, estimated and allotted for operations from 21st to 30th September 1915'. Rawlinson Papers 1/4, Churchill College. There seem to be no equivalent figures for I Corps but there is no reason to assume that the allocation of ammunition was not similar to that of IV Corps.
61. 'The IV Corps Artillery at the Battle of Loos', Montgomery-Massingberd Papers, Folder 45, Liddell Hart Centre for Military Archives.
62. Wynne, *If Germany Attacks*, p. 64.
63. Edmonds, *1915, Vol. 2*, p. 154.
64. 'First Army Conference on Monday, 6 Sept. 1915', Butler Papers, 69/10/1, IWM.
65. C.H. Foulkes, *Gas! The Story of the Special Brigade* (Edinburgh: Blackwood, 1936), pp. 42–69.
66. Haber, *Poisonous Cloud*, p. 52.
67. Haig Diary 24/9/1915 and 25/9/1915, NLS.
68. I Corps War Diary 25/9/1915, WO 95/592/1.
69. Ibid.
70. Lloyd, *Loos 1915*, p. 129.
71. Edmonds, *1915, Vol. 2*, p. 242, n. 1.
72. Ibid, p. 234.
73. Division War Diary July–Sept 1915, WO 95/1229.
74. Edmonds, *1915, Vol. 2*, p. 191.
75. Division War Diary 25/9/1915, WO 95/2698.
76. Division, 'Report on the Use of Gas' by Lt-Col Hitchcock, 2/10/15, First Army War Diary Sept 1915, WO 95/158.
77. Division War Diary 25/9/1915, WO 95/2698.
78. For these events see 46 Brigade, Operations 25/26th [September 1915], 46 Brigade War Diary July 1915–July 1916, WO 95/1948; 44 Brigade, 'Report on Operations September 21–30th', 15 Division War Diary July–Sept 1915, WO 95/1911.
79. IV Corps, 'Report on Communications During the Fighting at Loos and Hill 70, on 25/9/15', IV Corps War Diary Oct–Dec 1915, WO 95/712.
80. G.C. Wynne, 'The Other Side of the Hill, No. III: The Fight for Hill 70: 25th–26th of September 1915', *Army Quarterly*, vol. 8 (1924), pp. 264–5.
81. Edmonds, *1915, Vol. 2*, pp. 177–8.
82. Division War Diary 26/9/1915, WO 95/2128/1.
83. Edmonds, *1915, Vol. 2*, p. 342.
84. See for example Rawlinson's letter to the King's Private Secretary (Stamfordham) and the Minister for War, Lord Derby on 28/9/1915, Rawlinson Papers 5201/33/18, NAM. Rawlinson also wrote to Kitchener along the same lines.
85. Rawlinson's diary entries for 10/10/1915, 22/10/1915 and 5/11/1915 make it clear that Haig had made his views known to the King, Asquith and others.
86. Holmes, *Little Field-Marshal*, pp. 307–10.
87. These figures are taken from Mitchell and Smith, *Medical Services*, ch. VII, pp. 134–7.

6. The Year of the Somme

1. Brigadier-General Sir James E. Edmonds, *Military Operations: France and Belgium, 1916, Vol. 1* (London: Macmillan, 1932), p. 4.
2. Ibid, pp. 4–5.
3. War Committee Minutes 28/12/1915, CAB 42/6/14.
4. Balfour's Memorandum dated 29/12/1915 is to be found in the War Committee Minutes, CAB 42/7/5.
5. War Committee Minutes, CAB 42/7/5.
6. Ibid.
7. Ibid.
8. War Committee Minutes 10/3/1916, CAB 42/10/9.
9. Ministry of Munitions, *The Official History of the Ministry of Munitions, Volume X, The Supply of Munitions* (London: Naval & Military Press/Imperial War Museum, n.d.), p. 96. This is a reprint of the original.
10. War Committee Minutes 21/6/1916, CAB 42/15/10.
11. 'Plan for Offensive by Fourth Army 3/4/1916' in IV Army Summary of Operations, WO 158/233.
12. The detail on the German defensive systems is taken from Wynne, *If Germany Attacks*, pp. 100–1.
13. Haig Diary 5/4/1916, NLS.
14. Churchill, 'Variants on the Offensive 3/12/1915', CAB 42/7/3.
15. Cavan remarks on the above paper in ibid.
16. Elizabeth Greenhalgh, *Victory through Coalition: Britain and France during the First World War* (Cambridge: Cambridge University Press, 2005), p. 41.
17. Fourth Army Operation Order No. 2, 14/6/1916, Fourth Army Papers, Vol. 7, IWM.
18. Haig to Rawlinson 16/6/1916 in Brigadier-General Sir James E. Edmonds, *Military Operations: France and Belgium 1916, Appendices, Volume 1* (London: Macmillan, 1932), Appendix 13, pp. 86–7.
19. Rawlinson Papers 1/6, Churchill College. The figures come from a document, 'Artillery Shells Fired on 1 July 1916'. Actually the figures give the amount of shell fired by each calibre of gun during the entire preliminary bombardment.
20. On problems with guns and ammunition see Edmonds, *1916, Vol. 1*, pp. 122–3, 356, n. 5 and the unpublished manuscript by Brigadier E.C. Anstey, 'History of the Royal Artillery 1914–1918' in the IWM.
21. For wire-cutting reports see Fourth Army, 'Summary of Operations from June 27 to 30; Wire Reports on the Night of 27/28 June' and 'Patrol Reports on the Night of 28 June', General Ivor Maxse Papers 69/53/6, IWM. For dug-outs see Fourth Army Intelligence Summaries for 29 and 30 June 1916, Fourth Army Daily Intelligence Reports 1 May/30 June 1916, Fourth Army Papers, Vol. 11.
22. Fourth Army Summary of Operations, 1 July 1916, Fourth Army Papers, Vol. 1.
23. For a detailed discussion of these points see Robin Prior and Trevor Wilson, *The Somme* (London/New Haven: Yale University Press, 2005), ch. 11.
24. Haig Diary 1/7/1916, NLS.
25. Rawlinson Diary 1/7/1916.
26. Haig Diary 3/7/1916, NLS. General Sir Sidney Clive Diary 3/7/1916, CAB 45/201/2. Clive was a liaison officer with the French.
27. See Chris McCarthy, *The Somme: Day-by-Day Account* (London: Arms & Amour Press, 1993).
28. See XIII Corps, 'Narrative of Events 1st July–15 August 1916', WO 95/895.
29. Colin Hughes, *Mametz: Lloyd George's Welsh Army at the Battle of the Somme* (Gerrard's Cross: Orion Books, n.d.), p. 67.
30. Fourth Army Operation Order No. 4, 8/7/1916, Fourth Army War Diary July 1916, WO 95/431.

31. Haig Diary 10/7/1916, NLS.
32. 'Note of discussion as to attack of Longueval Plateau and the Commander-in-Chief's decision thereon [11/7/1916]', Fourth Army Papers, Vol 1.
33. Fourth Army, 'Summary of Events, 14th July, 1916', Fourth Army Papers, Vol. 2.
34. Secunderabad Cavalry Brigade, 'Narrative of Events – 14th July' in their War Diary, WO 95/921.
35. Hankey Diary 3/7/1916, CAB 63.
36. War Committee Minutes 6/7/1916, CAB 42/16/5.
37. War Committee Minutes 11/7/1916, CAB 42/16/6.
38. Ibid.
39. The Reserve Army under General Gough took over the areas of the VIII and X Corps, leaving the Fourth Army with the III, XV and XIII Corps.
40. For an excellent account of this whole episode see Meleah Hampton, *Attack on the Somme: 1st Anzac Corps and the Battle of Pozières Ridge, 1916* (Solihull: Helion, 2016).
41. Durham Light Infantry War Diary 4/5 August 1916, WO 95/2182.
42. Haig to Rawlinson 24/8/1916, Fourth Army Papers, Vol. 5.
43. 'Notes of an Interview at Querrieu, at 11.00 a.m., 9th August, 1916, between [Rawlinson, Kiggell, Montgomery and Davidson]', Fourth Army Papers, Vol. 2.
44. The casualty statistics for the Somme are summarised in an untitled document in the Australian War Memorial, AWM 52.
45. Ibid.
46. *Field Service Regulations* (London: HMSO, 1909), Section 99 (1) and (2).
47. 'Fourth Army Ammunition Expenditure'. To the figure given here I have added a quarter, to include shells fired by the Reserve Army.
48. German General Staff, *Der Weltkreig, Vol. 10* (Berlin: Mittler, 1936), p. 374.
49. See GHQ, 'Notes on Tank Organisation and Equipment', in Captain Wilfrid Miles, *Military Operations: France and Belgium 1916, Appendices, Volume 2* (London: Macmillan, 1938), Appendix 15, pp. 39–45; Trevor Pidgeon, *The Tanks at Flers, Vol. 1* (Cobham: Fairmile, 1995), pp. 34–5; David J. Childs, *A Peripheral Weapon? The Production and Employment of British Tanks in the First World War* (Westport, CT: Greenwood, 1999), p. 127.
50. Haig Diary 28/8/1916, NLS; Rawlinson Diary 28/8/1916.
51. Rawlinson Diary 28/8/1916.
52. Haig Diary 29/8/1916, NLS.
53. Haig to Rawlinson 31/8/1916, Fourth Army Papers, Vol. 3.
54. 'Notes of a Conference Held at Fourth Army Headquarters, 5th September 1916', Fourth Army Papers, Vol. 6.
55. See an account by Lt-Col. Coulte (42 Canadian Battalion) quoted by Paul Reed, *Courcelette* (London: Leo Cooper, 1998), p. 56; 5 Canadian Brigade War Diary 15/9/1916, WO 95/3820.
56. 'Operations of 169th Brigade on the Somme Front', AWM 26/6/44/43. See also account in 56 Division War Diary 15/9/1916, WO 95/2949; Note by GOC [General Officer Commanding], 6 Division to XIV Corps, 6 Division War Diary Sept. 1916, WO 95/1582.
57. 'Report of Action at Flers by 122 Infantry Brigade' (41 Division), 122 Brigade War Diary, WO 95/3693; Operations of the New Zealand Division 15/9/1916, Fourth Army Papers, Vol. 2.
58. Norfolk (5 Division) War Diary 25/9/1916, WO 95/1573.
59. See General Maxse, 'The 18 Division in the Battle of the Ancre', 18 Division War Diary Sept. 1916, WO 95/2015.
60. This entire document is to be found in Churchill, *The World Crisis,* Volume 3 (London: Thornton Butterworth, 1927), pp. 187–92.
61. Ibid.
62. War Committee Minutes 18/8/1916, CAB 42/17/11.

63. War Committee Minutes 5/8/1916, CAB 42/17/3; Robertson to Haig 8/8/1916, CAB 42/17/3.
64. War Committee Minutes 18/9/1916, CAB 42/20/3.
65. Robertson to Haig 7/9/1916, quoted in David R. Woodward (ed.), *Military Correspondence of Field-Marshal Sir William Robertson: Chief of the Imperial General Staff, December 1915–1918* (London: Army Records Society, 1989), p. 85.
66. The correspondence can be followed in ibid, pp. 90–6.
67. Haig to Third, Fourth, Reserve Armies 29/9/1916, WO 158/246.
68. For just one example of the conditions see 124 Brigade (41 Division), 'Report of Operations 7/10/1916', 124 Brigade War Diary Oct 1916, WO 95/2640.
69. For examples of these disastrous attacks see 4 Division, 'Narrative' 12/10/1916, in their War Diary, Oct 1916, WO 95/1445 and for the 18th see the same war diary.
70. Major Gort report 3/11/1916, AWM 45, Bundle 31.
71. Cavan to Rawlinson 3/11/1916, AWM 45, Bundle 31.
72. L.W. Kentish to Edmonds 19/11/1916, CAB 45/135.

7. The Defeat of the Ottoman Empire 1914–1918

1. Ullrich Trumpener, *Germany and the Ottoman Empire* (Princeton: Princeton University Press, 1968), pp. 15–16.
2. Ibid, p. 54.
3. Royal Commission on Fuel and Engines, First Report, Vol. 1, January 1913, ADM 116/1208.
4. 'Brief History of British Operations in Mesopotamia from 5th November 1914 to 31 March 1916', WO 32/5195; 'Critical Study of the Campaign in Mesopotamia up to April 1917', WO 106/923, p. 6.
5. 'Brief History of the British Operations in Mesopotamia from 6th November 1914 to 21st March 1916', WO 32/5215.
6. 'Critical Study', p. 10.
7. Bombashi Armin, 'The Turco-British Campaign in Iraq and our Mistakes', CAB 44/32.
8. 'Critical Study', p. 22.
9. Ibid.
10. Ibid.
11. N.S. Nash, *Betrayal of an Army: Mesopotamia 1914–1916* (Barnsley: Pen & Sword, 2016), pp. 24–5.
12. Jeffrey Grey, *The War with the Ottoman Empire* (Melbourne: Oxford University Press, 2015), p. 26.
13. Field Marshal Earl Wavell, *The Palestine Campaign*, 3rd edn (London: Constable, 1931), p. 28.
14. Lt-Gen. Sir George MacMunn and Cyril Falls, *Military Operations: Egypt and Palestine, Volume 1* (London: HMSO, 1928), p. 41.
15. Ibid, p. 43.
16. Wavell considers that a pursuit might have routed the Turks. His opinion must be taken seriously but I differ from it. See his *The Palestinian Campaign*, pp. 32–3. I am convinced by MacMunn and Falls, *Military Operations: Egypt and Palestine, Vol. 1*, pp. 48–9.
17. Ibid, p. 32.
18. Nash, *Betrayal of an Army*, p. 36.
19. Diary of Captain A.J. Shakeshaft, CAB 44/92.
20. Ibid.
21. Viceroy to Nixon July 1915, quoted in 'Critical Study', p. 35.
22. Austen Chamberlain to Nixon July 1915, quoted in 'Critical Study', p. 36.
23. See War Committee Minutes 21/10/1915, CAB 42/4/15.
24. 'Critical Study', p. 52.

25. See Townshend's despatch in WO 32/5195.
26. 'Critical Study', p. 67.
27. Ibid.
28. Shakeshaft Diary 25/12/1915.
29. (Poona) Division War Diary, 'Siege of Kut-el-Amara', WO 95/5112/1.
30. Townshend's communiqués are printed in the above document.
31. See Charles Townshend, *When God Made Hell: The British Invasion of Mesopotamia and the Creation of Iraq 1914–1921* (London: Faber, 2010), pp. 304–23 for these details.
32. Ibid, p. 208.
33. See Edmund Candler, *The Long Road to Baghdad*, 2 vols (London: Routledge, 2016), vol. 1, pp. 76–9. Reprint of 1919 edition.
34. Townshend, *When God Made Hell*, p. 367.
35. 'Critical Study', p. 321.
36. There was a quixotic attempt by the British to rally anti-Turkish forces in the Caucasus. A force under General Dunsterville was despatched to the southern Caucasus but withdrew after accomplishing nothing. See 'Operations of the Mesopotamian Expeditionary Force from 1st April to 30 September 1918', WO 106/916.
37. Wavell, *Palestine Campaign*, pp. 33–4.
38. Ibid, p. 45.
39. Anzac Mounted Division War Diary 4/8/1916, AWM 4/1/60/6.
40. MacMunn and Falls, *Military Operations: Egypt and Palestine, Vol 1*, pp. 305–7.
41. Ibid, p. 348.
42. Ibid, pp. 234–7.
43. See General Allenby, 'The Advance of the Egyptian Expeditionary Force: July 1917 to October 1918', CAB 44/12.
44. Alan H. Smith, *Allenby's Gunners: Artillery in the Sinai and Palestine Campaigns 1916–1918* (Barnsley: Pen & Sword, 2017), pp. 150–1.
45. 'Report on Operations (Attack on Beersheba) by 4th A.L.H. Brigade, 31/10/17', 4 Light Horse Brigade War Diary [October 1917], AWM 4/10/4/10.
46. Smith, *Allenby's Gunners*, pp. 151–2.
47. Allenby, 'Advance of the Egyptian Expeditionary Force'.
48. Ibid.
49. Ibid
50. 'Resume of Operations in Palestine from 12th July to 8th October 1918', WO 106/722.
51. Ibid.
52. Ibid.
53. Allenby, 'Advance of the Egyptian Expeditionary Force'.
54. Ibid.
55. See 'Palestine and Hedjaz' 27/3/1918 and 4/4/1918, WO 106/722.
56. Allenby, 'Advance of the Egyptian Expeditionary Force'.

8. Rue Morgue – 1917

1. A.J.P. Taylor (ed.), *Lloyd George: A Diary by Frances Stevenson* (London: Hutchinson, 1971), p. 139.
2. Haig Diary 16/1/1917, Sheffield and Bourne (eds), *Douglas Haig*, p. 268.
3. War Cabinet Minutes 17/1/1917, CAB 23/1/36.
4. War Cabinet Minutes 13/2/1917, CAB 23/1/64.
5. John Grigg, *Lloyd George: War Leader 1916–1918* (London: Allen Lane, 2002), p. 41. The definitive study.
6. Hankey Diary 26/2/1917.
7. David Woodward, *Lloyd George and the Generals* (East Brunswick, NJ: Associated University Presses, 1983), p. 152.

8. The whole plan is well set out in the First Army War Diary, March 1917, WO 95/168.
9. Cyril Falls, *Military Operations: France and Belgium 1917, Vol. 1* (London: Macmillan, 1940), p. 182 and n. 1.
10. Sandars Marble, *British Artillery on the Western Front in the First World War: 'The Infantry Cannot Do with a Gun Less'* (Farnham: Ashgate, 2013), p. 178.
11. Ibid, p. 179.
12. Lieutenant-Colonel A.F. Brooke, 'The Evolution of Artillery in the Great War', *Journal of the Royal Artillery*, vol. 53 (1926–1927), p. 243.
13. Marble, *British Artillery on the Western Front*, p. 163.
14. Ministry of Munitions, *Official History, Vol. X, Part IV*, p. 48.
15. Canadian Division, 'Narrative of Operations in connection with the Attack and Capture of Vimy Ridge – From April 9th to 14th, 1917', MIKAN 1883111, National Archives of Canada, digitised record.
16. Jonathan Nicholls, *Cheerful Sacrifice: The Battle of Arras, 1917* (London: Leo Cooper, 1990), p. 89.
17. Jeffrey Williams, *Byng of Vimy: General and Governor-General* (London: Leo Cooper, 1983), p. 167.
18. Ibid, p. 161.
19. Division War Diary, 'Narrative of Events from April 9th to April 12th, 1917', WO 95/1738/3.
20. Ibid.
21. Ibid.
22. Falls, *1917, Vol. 1*, p. 237.
23. Diary of Captain Monypenny, quoted in Nicholls, *Cheerful Sacrifice*, p. 126. On the very next page the author of the book is lamenting that 'a golden opportunity for the cavalry' went begging. There is a book to be written called 'Yearning for the Cavalry' on this recurring delusion.
24. Falls, *1917, Vol. 1*, sketch facing p. 241.
25. For these details see ibid, ch. IX.
26. Haig Diary 10/4/1917, Sheffield and Bourne (eds), *Douglas Haig*, p. 278.
27. Quoted in Falls, *1917, Vol. 1*, p. 259.
28. See 4 Australian Division War Diary April 1917, AWM4/48/13, Part 4.
29. Haig Diary 12/4/1917, Sheffield and Bourne (eds), *Douglas Haig*, p. 281.
30. Division War Diary, 'Narrative of Events from April 9th to April 12th'.
31. Ibid.
32. Haig Diary 26/4/1917 to 1/5/1017 gives a selection of these homilies.
33. Division War Diary, 'Narrative of Events of 3rd of May', WO 95/1739/1.
34. Infantry Brigade, 'Account of the Battle of May 3rd, 1917', WO 95/1739/1. The brigade commander was Brigadier-General J. Kennedy.
35. There is an excellent thesis by Trevor Gordon Harvey, 'An Army of Brigadiers: British Brigade Commanders at the Battle of Arras 1917', University of Birmingham, 2015. The thesis gives five case studies of the command of brigades at Arras. The detail is compelling but I wonder, however, given the comments of the 26 Brigade commander, how representative those five are?
36. Division War Diary, 'Narrative of Events of 3rd of May 1917'.
37. Haig Diary 3/5/1917.
38. See Second Army to GHQ 30/1/1917, WO 158/38; Haig Diary 10/2/1917.
39. Haig Diary 30/4/17, Sheffield and Bourne (eds), *Douglas Haig*, p. 288.
40. War Policy Committee Minutes 11/6/1917, CAB 27/6.
41. Ibid, 19/6/1917.
42. Ibid, 23/6/1917.
43. Hankey Diary 30/6/1917, CAB 63.
44. War Policy Committee Minutes 25/6/1917, CAB 27/6.

45. 'Note on the Messines–Wytschaete Attack 5/5/1917', AWM 51. It is worth noting that some information on the planning of Messines has survived in the Australian War Memorial and not in TNA.
46. Second Army Operation Order No. 1, 10/5/1917, AWM 26/6/187/9.
47. Second Army Intelligence Files May 1917, AWM 26/6/187/14.
48. Anstey, 'History of the Royal Artillery 1914–1918', p. 160.
49. Ibid, p. 161.
50. Ibid.
51. Brigadier-General Sir James E. Edmonds, *Military Operations: France and Belgium 1917, Volume 2* (London: HMSO, 1948), p. 42.
52. See the Second Army Intelligence Reports for the first week of June 1917, AWM 26/6/187/14.
53. Grigg, *War Leader*, p. 161.
54. Division, 'Narrative of Events in Connection with Second Army Attack on 7th June', 1917, AWM 26/6/190/1.
55. Colonel H. Stewart, *The New Zealand Division, 1916–1919: A Popular History Based on Historical Records* (Auckland: Whitcombe and Tombs, 1921), p. 194; 'Report on Operations for the Capture of Messines–Wytschaete Ridge by IX Corps', AWM 26/6/189/10.
56. For Von Lossberg see Nick Lloyd, *Passchendaele: A New History* (London: Penguin, 2017), ch. 2. Lloyd has made excellent use of Lossberg's memoirs and other German sources. Essential reading.
57. Colonel W.G.S. Dobbie, 'The Operations of the 1st Division on the Belgian Coast in 1917', *Royal Engineers Journal* (June 1924), pp. 190–3.
58. 'Third Battle of Ypres: Operations of XVIII Corps on 31st July, 1917', Maxse Papers 69/53/8/33, IWM; 'Report on the Operations of the 51st (Highland) Division on 31st July, 1917', in ibid.
59. 'Report on Action of Tanks on 31st July, 1917, Tank Corps War Diary, AWM 45/24/6.
60. Edmonds, *1917, Vol. 2*, pp. 108–9.
61. See the Fifth Army Intelligence Summary 28/7/1917, in AWM 26/6/189/2 and the figures given in the German Official Account of the Third Ypres Campaign held in the Imperial War Museum, London, p. 54. Lloyd, *Passchendaele*, quotes GHQ intelligence to show that the British had accurately estimated the number of German guns (p. 327, n. 7). There is every indication however that Fifth Army was operating on its own Intelligence figures, not those of GHQ.
62. Haig Diary 28/7/1917.
63. See the Fifth Army Intelligence Reports, in AWM 26/6/189/3.
64. Ministère de Guerre, *Les Armées françaises dans la grande guerre, Tome V, Volume 2* (Paris: Imprimerie Nationale, 1933), p. 664.
65. The details of these actions can be found in Robin Prior and Trevor Wilson, *Passchendaele: The Unknown Story* (London/New Haven: Yale University Press, 2016), ch. 9. The footnotes refer to the individual war diaries of the corps involved.
66. See ibid, footnotes to ch. 9.
67. Edmonds, *1917, Vol. 2*, p. 171, n. 2.
68. Brigade, 'Report on Operations: Ypres – 29/7/1917 to 3/8/1917', 15 Division War Diary August 1917, WO 95/1915.
69. See, for example, ibid.
70. 'Preliminary Report on Operations on 19th Aug. 1917', Maxse Papers, 69/53/8; Tank Operation Reports Jul–Sept 1917, WO 158/839.
71. Haig Diary 17/8/1917, Sheffield and Bourne (eds), *Douglas Haig*, p. 317.
72. 'Summary of Operations of Fifth Army for Week Ending 7 and 14 September, 1917', Fifth Army War Diary Jun–Aug 1917, WO 95/520.
73. Haig Diary 11/9/1917.

74. For an example of a corps artillery plan see X Corps Artillery Instructions No. 39, 2/9/1917, in X Corps Artillery War Diary, WO 95/865. Note that cutting belts of wire plays little role in this plan. By September no continuous belts of wire remained across the German front.

75. C.E.W. Bean, *Official History of Australia in the War of 1914–1918, Vol. IV: The Australian Imperial Force in France, 1917* (Sydney: Angus & Robertson, 1938), p. 756.

76. Haig Diary 15/10/1917.

77. Jack Sheldon, *The German Army at Passchendaele* (Barnsley: Pen & Sword, 2007), p. 243.

78. Among those who have inflated it is the present historian.

79. See Woodward, *Lloyd George and the Generals*, ch. 9 for these discussions.

80. War Policy Committee Minutes 3/10/1917, CAB 27/6.

81. Ibid, 11/10/1917.

82. Haig Diary 16/9/1917, Sheffield and Bourne (eds), *Douglas Haig*, pp. 325–6.

83. Captain Wilfrid Miles, *Military Operations: France and Belgium, 1917: The Battle of Cambrai* (London: Imperial War Museum/Battery Press), pp. 10–13. Reprint of 1948 edition.

84. Ibid, pp. 2–4.

85. Bryn Hammond, *Cambrai 1917: The Myth of the First Great Tank Battle* (London: Weidenfeld & Nicolson, 2009), pp. 71–4. The diagrams in this section are excellent. This is the best book on Cambrai.

86. Wilson, *Myriad Faces*, p. 489.

87. Haig Diary 31/11/1917, Sheffield and Bourne (eds), *Douglas Haig*, p. 341.

88. Miles, *Cambrai*, p. 17.

89. Hammond, *Cambrai*, ch. 5. An excellent account of the first day.

90. Miles, *Cambrai*, p. 115.

91. Robertson to Plumer 10/12/1917, quoted in Grigg, *War Leader*, p. 316.

92. Woodward, *Lloyd George and the Generals*, pp. 222–3.

93. Grigg, *War Leader*, p. 317.

94. Woodward, *Lloyd George and the Generals*, pp. 210 and 231.

95. Grigg, *War Leader*, p. 318.

9. The War at Sea 1916–1918

1. See Henry Baynham, *Men from the Dreadnoughts* (London: Hutchinson, 1976), p. 217. See also the non-adventures of Geoffrey Harper in the Grand Fleet in Wilson, *Myriad Faces*, ch. 6, pp. 685–93.

2. V.E. Tarrant, *Jutland: The German Perspective* (London: Brockhampton, 1999), pp. 54–5.

3. The story is complicated. The best detective work on what happened is to be found in Brooks, *Jutland*, pp. 163–6.

4. Marder, *From Dreadnought to Scapa Flow*, Vol. 3, p. 204. Marder has only 60,000 British sailors but he has the numbers wrong. The number of ships comes from Brooks, *Jutland*, p. 161.

5. Brooks, *Jutland*, p. 411.

6. Jellicoe was aware of the rearwards firing. See his proposed appendix to his book, *The Grand Fleet* in the Jellicoe Papers, Add/MSS 49040, British Library.

7. John Campbell, *Jutland: An Analysis of the Fighting* (London: Conway Maritime, 1986), pp. 337–9.

8. For these details see Antony Preston, *Battleships of World War 1* (New York: Galahad, 1972).

9. Lawrence Sondhaus, *The Great War at Sea: A Naval History of the First World War* (Cambridge: Cambridge University Press, 2014), pp. 205–6.

10. For good discussions of the battlecruiser problem see Campbell, *Jutland*, pp. 372–8 and Brooks, *Jutland*, pp. 455–8.

11. A.C. Waller, '5th Battle Squadron at Jutland', *RUSI Journal* (November 1935), pp. 791–9. Waller was the captain of the *Barham*, one of the ships in the Fifth Battle Squadron.

12. Jellicoe pointed this out to the commander of the Fifth Battle Squadron, Admiral Evan-Thomas, after the war. See Jellicoe to Evan-Thomas 2/6/1923, Evan-Thomas Papers, Add/MSS 52504, British Library.

13. Beatty's signalling gaps leap out from the official record. See *Official Despatches to the Battle of Jutland 30th May to 1st June 1916 with Appendices and Charts* (London: HMSO, 1920), pp. 450–3.

14. Georg von Hase, *Keil and Jutland* (London: Skeffington, 1921), p. 295.

15. William Jameson, *The Most Formidable Thing: The Story of the Submarine from Its Earliest Days to the End of World War 1* (London: Rupert Hart-Davis, 1965), p. 17.

16. All technical details have been taken from https://uboat.net. This invaluable resource has technical details of the different kinds of U-boat models built, the career of every U-boat, sinkings, U-boats lost and much more.

17. Ibid.

18. Ibid.

19. Quoted in Lord Fisher, *Records* (London: Hodder & Stoughton, 1919), pp. 183–5.

20. See Ruddock Mackay, *Fisher of Kilverstone* (Oxford: Clarendon Press, 1973), pp. 453–4 and 449.

21. Richmond, 'Memorandum on Submarines 11–13/7/1914', quoted in Marder, *From Dreadnought to Scapa Flow, Vol. 1*, p. 364.

22. See uboat.net and A.J. Tennent, *British Merchant Ships Sunk by U-Boats in World War One* (Penzance: Periscope Publishing, 2006) for these figures.

23. Dwight R. Messimer, *Verschollen: World War 1 U-Boat Losses* (Annapolis, MD: Naval Institute Press, 2002). This is the most up-to-date book on this subject.

24. Sir Julian Corbett, *Naval Operations, Volume 2* (London: Longmans, 1921), pp. 268–9. The Official History.

25. Naval Staff Monographs Volume 13, 1925, 'Home Waters, Part IV', p. 29.

26. uboat.net. The March total includes six very small ships sunk by Austrian U-boats in the Mediterranean.

27. Memorandum by Admiral Tudor in ADM 137/1159.

28. Memorandum by Admiral Tudor 24/11/1914, ADM 137/968.

29. See Naval Staff Monographs Vol. 13, 'Home Waters IV' for discussions of all these stratagems.

30. Halpern, *Naval History of World War 1*, pp. 296–7.

31. Figures from uboat.net.

32. Marder, *Dreadnought to Scapa Flow, Vol. 2*, pp. 344–5.

33. Tennent, *Merchant Ships Sunk*, p, 177; Marder, *Dreadnought to Scapa Flow, Vol. 2*, p. 345.

34. Halpern, *Naval History of World War 1*, p. 303.

35. Figures taken from Messimer, *Verschollen*.

36. All figures taken from uboat.net.

37. Naval Staff Monographs, 1926, Monograph 15, 'Home Waters', pp. 112–15.

38. Marder, *From Dreadnought to Scapa Flow, Vol. 3*, pp. 275–7.

39. Figures taken from Messimer, *Verschhollen*.

40. Tennent, *British Merchant Ships Sunk*, p. 197.

41. Halpern, *Naval History of World War 1*, p. 335.

42. Marder, *Dreadnought to Scapa Flow, Vol. 3*, p. 270.

43. Naval Staff Monographs, 1923, Monograph 18, 'Home Waters', p. 38.

44. Patrick Beesly, *Room 40: British Naval Intelligence 1914–1918* (London: Hamish Hamilton, 1982), pp. 30–1.

45. Ibid, p. 254 n. 1.

46. Figures from ships sunk, uboat.net.
47. Naval Staff History, 'The Defeat of the Enemy Attack on Shipping 1939–1945: A Study of Policy and Operations' (London: Historical Section, Admiralty, 1957), p. 6. This document has a useful introduction to U-boat warfare during the First World War.
48. Ibid.
49. There is a good summary of the statistical argument in Halpern, *Naval History of World War 1*, pp. 337–9.
50. Ibid, p. 338.
51. War Cabinet Minutes 2/11/1916, CAB 42/23/3.
52. I cannot find any further discussion of this rather bizarre idea in the War Cabinet or Admiralty papers.
53. War Cabinet Minutes 2/11/1916, CAB 42/23/3.
54. Ibid.
55. Hankey to Lloyd George 8/12/1916, War Cabinet Minutes, CAB 42/19/2.
56. Hankey Diary 22/1/1917.
57. Halpern, *Naval History of World War 1*, p. 345.
58. War Cabinet Minutes 6/12/1916, CAB 23/1/1.
59. See the War Cabinet Minutes for 15/12/1916, 20/12/1916, 251/1917 and 8/2/1917 for these measures.
60. uboat.net.
61. Ibid.
62. War Cabinet Minutes 2/2/1917, CAB 23/1/52.
63. Halpern, *Naval History of World War 1*, p. 341.
64. Ibid, pp. 341–2.
65. Hankey Diary 11/2/1917.
66. Henry Newbolt, *Naval Operations, Volume 5* (London: IWM/Battery Press), pp. 10–14. Reprint of 1931 edition.
67. Hankey Diary 13/2/1917.
68. Hankey Diary 22/4/1917.
69. War Cabinet Minutes 16/2/1917, CAB 23/2/70.
70. War Cabinet Minutes 19/2/1917, CAB 23/2/73.
71. Reprinted in A Temple Patterson (ed.), *The Jellicoe Papers, Volume 2* (London: Navy Records Society, 1968), pp. 149–51.
72. Grigg, *War Leader*, p. 52.
73. War Cabinet Minutes 14/3/1917, CAB 23/2/28.
74. War Cabinet Minutes 2/4/1917, CAB 23/2/31.
75. See Sondhaus, *The Great War at Sea*, pp. 256–7, where he discusses this issue.
76. Quoted in Marder, *From Dreadnought to Scapa Flow*, Vol. 4, p. 148.
77. War Cabinet Minutes 11/4/1917, CAB 23/2/35.
78. War Cabinet Minutes 20/4/1917, CAB 23/2/41.
79. Maurice Hankey, *The Supreme Command, Volume 2* (London: Allen and Unwin, 1961), p. 649.
80. Ibid.
81. Hankey Diary 22/4/1917.
82. War Cabinet Minutes 23/4/1917, CAB 23/2/42.
83. Ibid.
84. Ibid.
85. War Cabinet Minutes 23/4/1917 (5 p.m. meeting), CAB 23/2/43.
86. War Cabinet Minutes 25/4/1917, CAB 23/2/44.
87. Naval Staff Monograph 18, 'Home Waters', pp. 377–9.
88. Marder, *Dreadnought to Scapa Flow*, Vol. 4, pp. 150–1. I am not able to date Henderson's discovery with any precision. Marder says it was early in April (p. 150), the Naval Monograph quoted above merely says April. No authority gives a more precise date.

89. Nicholas Black, *The British Naval Staff in the First World War* (Woodbridge: Boydell Press, 2009), pp. 174–5.
90. Ibid, p. 180.
91. Duff to Jellicoe 26/4/1917 in Temple Patterson (ed.), *Jellicoe Papers, Vol. 2*, pp. 157–60.
92. Stephen Roskill, *Hankey: Man of Secrets, Volume 2* (London: Collins, 1976). The italics are Roskill's. The very valuable discussion of this whole issue by Roskill on pp. 376–85 should be consulted.
93. Duff to Jellicoe 26/4/1917, Temple Patterson (ed.), *Jellicoe Papers, Vol. 2*, pp 157–60.
94. Winston Churchill, 'The U-Boat War', in Winston Churchill, *Thoughts and Adventures* (London: Odhams, 1947), p. 98. Reprint of 1932 edition.
95. Roskill, *Hankey, Vol 2*, pp. 382–3.
96. Robertson is quoted in Andrew Suttie, *Rewriting the First World War: Lloyd George, Politics and Strategy 1914-1918* (London: Palgrave Macmillan, 2005), p. 132. On Jellicoe's paper see Newbolt, *Naval Operations Vol. 5*, pp. 21–4. Note that the version given by Temple Patterson in the *Jellicoe Papers, Vol. 2*, pp. 160–2 seems to be a compressed version of the same paper.
97. Newbolt, *Naval Operations Vol. 5*, p. 24.
98. Ibid, p. 141.
99. Beesly, *Room 40*, p. 261.
100. Marder, *Dreadnought to Scapa Flow, Vol. 4*, pp. 181–2.
101. Newbolt, *Naval Operations, Vol 5*, pp. 48–9.
102. Marder, *Dreadnought to Scapa Flow, Vol. 4*, pp. 258–9.
103. Ibid.
104. 'Report of a Naval Conference of Powers United against Germany, September 4th and 5th, 1917', in Temple Patterson (ed.), *Jellicoe Papers, Vol. 2*, pp. 203–8.
105. Marder, *Dreadnought to Scapa Flow, Vol. 4*, p. 261.
106. See Marder, *Dreadnought to Scapa Flow Vol. 4*, p. 182 for the May and June figures and p. 277 for the October figure.
107. The figures for October have been taken from an analysis in uboat.net. Other figures come from 'The Defeat of the Enemy Attack on Shipping, 1939–1945', an unpublished account compiled by the Admiralty in 1957. This unpublished record contains a useful summary of events from 1914 to 1918 and some very useful tables. The figures above come from Table 1, 'Comparison Between the Number of Ships Convoyed, Losses in Convoy, and Independent Losses through U-Boat Attack in the Atlantic & Home Waters from the Introduction of Convoy Feb. 1917 to the End of the War Nov. 1918'.
108. See the notes included in ibid, Table 1.
109. See Messimer, *Verschollen* for the manner of destruction of each U-boat.
110. See 'The Defeat of the Enemy Attack on Shipping', Table 2.

10. 1918 – The Whirlwind

1. Much of this section relies on the excellent Keith Grieves, *The Politics of Manpower 1914-1918* (Manchester: Manchester University Press, 1988). See in particular ch. 7, pp. 149–76.
2. Ibid, p. 168; Brigadier-General Sir James E. Edmonds, *Military Operations: France and Belgium, 1918, Volume 1* (London: Macmillan, 1935), p. 52, n. 1.
3. Haig Diary 7/11/1917.
4. Grieves, *Manpower*, pp. 173–5.
5. David Woodward, 'Did Lloyd George Starve the British Army of Men Prior to the German Offensive of 21 March 1918?', *Historical Journal*, vol. 27, no. 1 (March 1984), pp. 241–52 makes this point. I have not here dealt with the rather tangential point surrounding the 'Maurice Debate', of which the central matter is whether Lloyd George misled Parliament about the strength of the BEF in January 1918. The fact is that the

military supplied three sets of quite misleading sets of statistics to the Prime Minister and he chose the set that suited his own purpose. For more on this see Woodward, *Lloyd George and the Generals*, ch. 12, pp. 282–309; Grigg, *War Leader*, ch. 27, pp. 489–512. See also John Gooch, 'The Maurice Debate 1918', *Journal of Contemporary History*, vol. 3 (October 1968), pp. 211–28.

6. These figures are taken from the minutes of the War Cabinet which faithfully noted the GHQ tally at each meeting. The figures for German concentration against the BEF are to be found in the minutes of the meeting of 11/3/1918, CAB 23/5/55.

7. Haig Diary 2/3/1918, Sheffield and Bourne (eds), *Douglas Haig*, p. 385.

8. Haig Diary 21/2/1918, Sheffield and Bourne (eds), *Douglas Haig*, p. 384.

9. Haig Diary 14/3/1918, Sheffield and Bourne (eds), *Douglas Haig*, p. 387; Woodward, 'Did Lloyd George Starve the British Army', p. 251.

10. Edmonds, *1918, Vol. 1*, pp. 114–15. The three cavalry divisions under Gough's Fifth Army have been equated with one infantry division.

11. Memorandum by Rawlinson 10/12/1917, Rawlinson Papers 1/10, Churchill College.

12. It might be thought that by the time Edmonds was compiling the Official History he might have reflected on these matters. He did not. He was too busy fulminating against Lloyd George and his 'starving' of the BEF to focus on the weaknesses of the high command.

13. H. Essame, *The Battle for Europe 1918* (London: Batsford, 1974), p. 37.

14. David Zabecki, *The German 1918 Offensives: A Case Study in the Operational Level of War* (London: Routledge, 2006), p. 70.

15. Wynne, *If Germany Attacks*, p. 295.

16. For an extensive examination of these tactics see Bruce Gudmundsson, *Stormtroop Tactics: Innovation in the German Army: 1914–1918* (New York: Praeger, 1989).

17. Zabecki, *German 1918 Offensives*, p. 69.

18. Ibid, pp. 54–6. For a fuller treatment of Bruchmüller see David Zabecki, *Steel Wind: Colonel Georg Bruchmüller and the Birth of Modern Artillery* (Bridgeport, CT: Praeger, 1994).

19. Zabecki, *German 1918 Offensives* has by far the best discussion of the turns and twists of Ludendorff's thinking. See his Chapter 6 for a detailed discussion of what has been summarised above.

20. Edmonds, *1918, Vol. 1*, pp. 41–2. Robertson thought that most British divisions were 'not good at digging trenches'. See War Cabinet Minutes 24/12/1917, CAB 23/4/79.

21. Zabecki, *German 1918 Offensives*, p. 133. Broodseinde was an exception where the Germans did pack the forward trenches with troops, but this was unusual.

22. Fifth Army War Diary 13/3/1918, WO 95/521/1.

23. Edmonds, *1918, Vol. 1*, p. 97.

24. General Sir Hubert Gough, *The Fifth Army* (London: Hodder and Stoughton, 1931), p. 251.

25. 'Principles of Defence on Fifth Army Front' 4/2/1918, quoted in Gough, *Fifth Army*, pp. 232–3.

26. Lawrence (Chief of Staff to Haig) to Gough 9/2/1918, quoted in ibid, pp. 234–5.

27. Zabecki, *German 1918 Offensives*, pp. 135–40.

28. Martin Middlebrook, *The Kaiser's Battle: 21 March 1918: The First Day of the German Spring Offensive* (London: Allen Lane, 1978), pp. 184–6.

29. Ibid, p. 204.

30. Ibid, p. 213, remark of Fusilier Willy Adams, Lehr Infantry Regiment.

31. Grieves, *Manpower*, p. 217.

32. See maps accompanying Edmonds, *1918, Vol. 1*.

33. Jonathan Boff, *Haig's Enemy: Crown Prince Rupprecht and Germany's War on the Western Front* (Oxford: Oxford University Press, 2018), p. 210.

34. Zabecki, *German 1918 Offensives*, p. 140.

35. Ibid.
36. I have used Middlebrook's best estimates. See *Kaiser's Battle*, p. 322.
37. 'Report of the Operations of the III Corps from March 21st to April 1st 1918', III Corps War Diary March 1918, WO 95/678/3.
38. XVIII Corps narrative in their War Diary March 1918, WO 95/953/3.
39. Edmonds, *1918, Vol. 1*, p. 301.
40. Haig Diary 21/3/1918, Sheffield and Bourne (eds), *Douglas Haig*, p. 389.
41. Edmonds, *1918, Vol. 1*, pp. 380–1.
42. Ibid, p. 367.
43. Zabecki, *German 1918 Offensives*, pp. 143–5.
44. This account follows Greenhalgh, *French Army*, pp. 274–6; Sheffield, *The Chief*, pp. 273–5; Edmonds, *1918, Vol. 1*, pp. 448–9.
45. Edmonds, *1918, Vol. 1*, p. 542. The words 'Western Front' replaced 'the British and French armies in front of Amiens' at Haig's suggestion.
46. Greenhalgh, *French Army*, p. 277.
47. 'General Situation', Third Army War Diary March 1918, WO 95/369/7.
48. Derived from Table 6.10 in Zabecki, *German 1918 Offensives*, p. 161.
49. Ian Brown, *British Logistics on the Western Front* (London: Praeger, 1998), p. 190.
50. Brigadier-General Sir James E. Edmonds, *Military Operations: France and Belgium, 1918, Volume 2* (London: Macmillan, 1937), p. 4.
51. Edmonds, *1918, Vol. 1*, p. 447.
52. Edmonds, *1918, Vol. 2*, p. 4.
53. Third Army War Diary March 1918, WO 95/369/6; Edmonds, *1918, Vol. 2*, pp. 72–3.
54. See Table 'March 30th 1918' in Rawlinson Papers 1/10, Churchill College.
55. Edmonds, *1918, Vol. 2*, p. 25.
56. Edmonds, *1918, Vol. 2*, pp. 126–7; C.E.W. Bean, *Official History of Australia in the War of 1914–1918, Vol. V: The Australian Imperial Force in France During the Main German Offensive, 1918* (Sydney: Angus & Robertson, 1938), ch. XI, pp. 298–354.
57. Zabecki, *German 1918 Offensives*, p. 184.
58. Edmonds, *1918, Vol. 2*, p. 160.
59. 'Narrative of Events on 55th (West Lancashire) Division Front – 9th to 16th April 1918', 55 Division War Diary, WO 95/2905.
60. Ibid.
61. Edmonds, *1918, Vol. 2*, pp. 174–5. The inhabitants of Béthune were at least spared one of the horrors of war.
62. 'Narrative of Events', 55 Division War Diary, WO 95/2905.
63. Australian Division, Intelligence Summary No. 1 15/4/1918, AWM 4/1/42/39, Part B.
64. Boff, *Haig's Enemy*, p. 222.
65. Ibid, p. 221.

11. 1918 – Victory

1. These brief accounts of German actions against the French are taken from Zabecki, *German 1918 Offensives*, chs 8 and 9. There were British and American troops involved in these operations. They have been omitted in my brief accounts to emphasise the contribution of the French and to keep the overall focus on the British army.
2. Ibid.
3. Greenhalgh, *French Army*, pp. 316–18.
4. Great Britain, War Office, *Statistics of the Military Effort of the British Empire During the Great War 1914–1920* (Uckfield: Naval and Military Press, n.d.), pp. 267 and 328. Reprint of the War Office edition. Note that the figures in these two tables differ slightly but not significantly. The German figures are from Zabecki, *German 1918 Offensives*.
5. Sir James Edmonds, *Military Operations: France and Belgium 1918, Volume 3* (London: Macmillan, 1939), p. 159.

6. Rawlinson to Henry Wilson 24/4/1918, Rawlinson Papers 5201/73/44, NAM. Some British tanks were present and so the first tank-on-tank battle in warfare took place here.
7. Bean, *Official History Vol. V, 1918*, p. 604.
8. David Stevenson, *With Our Backs to the Wall: Victory and Defeat in 1918* (London: Allen Lane, 2011), p. 345.
9. Essame, *Battle for Europe 1918*, p. 54.
10. 'Composition of a British Division 1918', Supreme War Council Papers, CAB 25/94.
11. Rawlinson, 'Increase in our Offensive Power by Additions of Machine and Lewis Guns', Rawlinson Papers 5201/33/77, NAM.
12. Ministry of Munitions, *Official History, Vol. X*, Part 1, p. 40.
13. Churchill, *The World Crisis, Vol. 3*, pp. 1264–5.
14. Great Britain War Office, *Military Effort*, p. 487.
15. These figures come from vols X and XII of the *Official History of the Ministry of Munitions*.
16. Captain A.D. Ellis, *The Story of the Fifth Australian Division* (London: Hodder and Stoughton, n.d.), pp. 3–4.
17. Guy Hartcup, *The War of Invention: Scientific Developments 1914–1918* (London: Brassey, 1988), p. 75.
18. This is not the place to enter into a detailed discussion of the fraught subject of casualty statistics. However, a comparison between the figures given by Churchill in *The World Crisis, Vol. 3*, p. 1265 (712,000), the article by James McRandle and James Quirk, 'The Blood test Revisited: A New Look at German Casualty Counts in World War 1', *Journal of Military History* (July 2006), Table 6, p. 683 (778,000) and Jonathan Boff, *Winning and Losing on the Western Front: The British Third Army and the Defeat of Germany in 1918* (Cambridge: Cambridge University Press, 2012), p. 45 (770,000) are remarkably similar. Zabecki, *German 1918 Offensives* gives a lower figure of 566,000 but his source seems to have been the German Official History, which is unreliable on this subject.
19. Jonathan Boff has covered this aspect well. See his *Winning and Losing*, p. 45.
20. See Bean, *Official History Vol. V, 1918*, chs 2 and 3 for a detailed account of these events.
21. R.E. Jones, G.E. Rarey and R.J. Icks, *The Fighting Tanks from 1916 to 1933* (Greenwich, CT: W.E. Publishers, 1969), pp. 5, 16 and 31. Reissue of 1933 edition.
22. Rawlinson Diary 18/6/1918.
23. Tank Corps Hamel Plan 21/6/1918, Monash Papers DRL 3, 2316, Book 18, AWM; Australian Corps, 'Hamel Offensive', 21/8/1918, AWM 26/10/361/2. The two brigades consisted of battalions from four Australian divisions in order to even out casualties.
24. Paper by Blamey 22/6/1918, AWM 26/10/361/2. See also 4 Division Conference in the Monash Papers.
25. Australian Corps, 'Estimate of German strength opposite Hamel' 22/6/1918, AWM 26/10/361/2.
26. Rawlinson, 'Operations by the Australian Corps Against Hamel, Bois de Hamel and Bois de Vaires July 4th 1918', Rawlinson Papers, 5201/33/77, NAM.
27. Haig Diary 5/7/1918, Sheffield and Bourne (eds), *Douglas Haig*, p. 426.
28. Rawlinson to GHQ 17/7/1918, Rawlinson Papers, 5201/33/77, NAM.
29. Haig to Henry Wilson 24/7/1918, Sheffield and Bourne (eds), *Douglas Haig*, p. 434.
30. Haig Diary 26/7/1918, Sheffield and Bourne (eds), *Douglas Haig*, p. 435.
31. It is not the intention of this book to claim that the British army won the war single-handed in 1918. Other national armies played significant roles but this is a book about the British and I leave it to other historians to complete the picture.
32. Haig Diary 5/8/1918.
33. Fourth Army Fortnightly Army Reports for July and August, Fourth Army War Diary July and August 1918, Fourth Army Papers, Vols 43 and 44.
34. Major-General C.E.D. Budworth, 'Fourth Army Artillery in the Battle of Amiens, August 8th, 1918', IWM.

35. Ibid.
36. See for example Australian Corps Amiens Plan 31/7/1918, AWM 26/12/361/4.
37. See Budworth, 'Fourth Army Artillery in the Battle of Amiens'. The formula required 640 field guns and 350,000 shells. The Fourth Army had 1,236 field guns and had stock-piled 700,000 shells.
38. Australian Division, 'Narrative of Operations, 8th August to 13th August 1918', AWM 26/12/528/9.
39. Colonel G.W.L. Nicholson, *The Canadian Expeditionary Force 1914–1919* (Ottawa: Queen's Printer, 1962), pp. 399–401.
40. Sir James Edmonds, *Military Operations: France and Belgium 1918, Volume 4* (London: Imperial War Museum, n.d.; reprint of 1947 edn), pp. 48–50. Nicholson, *Canadian Expeditionary Force*, p. 400. See also 5 Australian Division, 'Report on Operations', AWM 26/12/559/6.
41. Fuller to Fourth Army 23/7/1918, Fourth Army Papers, Vol. 49.
42. Australian Division, 'Narrative of Operations, 8th August, 1918', AWM 26/12/528/9.
43. Rawlinson to GHQ 17/8/1918, Fourth Army Papers, Vol. 50.
44. German General Staff, *Der Weltkrieg, Volume 14* (Berlin: Mittler, 1936), p. 566.
45. Rawlinson Diary 13/8/1918.
46. Rawlinson Diary 14/8/1918.
47. Haig Diary 14/8/1918. Emphasis in the original.
48. Boff, *Winning and Losing*, p. 25.
49. Third Army War Diary 21/8/1918, WO 95/372/1.
50. Boff, *Winning and Losing*, p. 29.
51. Canadian Division Account 2/9/1918, MIKAN 2005715, National Archives of Canada.
52. Colonel J.M.A. Durrant, 'Mont St Quentin; Some Aspects of the Operations of the 2nd Australian Division from the 27th of August to the 2nd of September, 1918', *Army Quarterly*, vol. 31 (1935), pp. 91–2.
53. Boff, *Haig's Enemy*, p. 237.
54. 'Report on Operations 28th Sept. 1918', in 14 Division War Diary September 1918, WO 95/1876/3.
55. Sir James Edmonds, *Military Operations: France and Belgium 1918, Volume 5* (London: Macmillan, 1948), p. 95.
56. See the classifications given to these divisions in United States War Office, *Histories of Two Hundred and Fifty-One Divisions of the German Army Which Participated in the War (1914–1918)* (London: London Stamp Exchange, 1989). Reprint of the 1920 US War Office publication which first compiled this information.
57. These remarks from Rupprecht's published diary have been supplied to me by Jonathan Boff. I am very grateful for his help on this and other matters.
58. Division Instructions No. 216/1 22/9/1918, in 14 Division War Diary September 1918, WO 95/1876/3.
59. Brigade, 'Report on Operations. 28th September 1918', in 14 Division War Diary September 1918, WO 95/1876/3.
60. The Fifth Army was the weakest of the British formations and was following up the Germans forced to retreat by events on other parts of their front.
61. For the Australian operations see, for example, 'Fourth Australian Division Report on Operations 10th–20th September, 1918', AWM 26/12/547/4.
62. Edmonds, *1918, Vol. 5*, p. 102.
63. Monash to Fourth Army 18/9/1918, Fourth Army Papers, Vol. 69.
64. Rawlinson to GHQ 18/9/1918, Fourth Army Papers, Vol. 50.
65. Ibid.
66. Major-General Sir A. Montgomery, *The Story of the Fourth Army in the Battle of the Hundred Days, August 8th to November 11th, 1918* (London: Hodder and Stoughton, 1931), Appendix G.

67. 'Artillery Appreciation of the Various Divisional Sectors of the Siegfried Line' (translation of a German document), Fourth Army Papers, Vol. 53.
68. 'German Defence Scheme: St. Quentin Sector of the Siegfried Line', AWM 26/12/490/6.
69. 'Operations Report of the 27 Division A.E.F., Covering the Period Sept. 23rd to October 21st, 1918', AWM 26/12/487/2.
70. Peter Pedersen, *Monash as Military Commander* (Melbourne: Melbourne University Press, 1985), p. 289.
71. Division AEF, 'Report on Operations of 30th Division against Hindenburg Line September 27th–September 30th, 1918', AWM 26/12/487/3.
72. Montgomery, *Fourth Army*, pp. 162–3.
73. Major R.E. Priestley, *Breaking the Hindenburg Line: The story of the 46 Division* (London: Fisher and Unwin, 1919), p. 143.
74. 'Offensive Operations Undertaken by IX Corps from 18th September 1918 to 11th November 1918', Fourth Army Papers, Vol. 63.
75. Ibid.
76. Edmonds, *1918, Vol. 5*, pp. 159, 164.
77. Tank Corps, 'Summary of Operations', WO 95/94.
78. C.E.W. Bean, *Official History of Australia in the War of 1914–1918, Vol. VI: The Australian Imperial Force in France During the Allied Offensive, 1918* (Sydney: Angus & Robertson, 1942), pp. 1005–6.
79. See Third Army War Diary 8/10/1918, WO 95/374/1 and Edmonds *1918, Vol. 5*, p. 191 for examples of this.
80. Edmonds, *1918, Vol. 5*, p. 196.
81. 'Fourth Army Intelligence Summary 27th Oct–1 Nov 1918', AWM 26/12/475/1.
82. 'Fourth Army Summary of Operations, 4th November 1918', Fourth Army Papers, Vol. 46.
83. Ibid.
84. War Cabinet Minutes 13/8/1918, CAB 23/7/20.
85. War Cabinet Minutes 27/8/1918, CAB 23/7/27.
86. Haig Diary 1/9/1918.

12. Appeasement and War

1. N.H. Gibbs, *Grand Strategy, Volume 1* (London: HMSO, 1976), pp. 247–9.
2. Graham Stewart, *Burying Caesar: Churchill, Chamberlain and the Battle for the Tory Party* (London: Weidenfeld and Nicolson, 1999), p. 290.
3. Quoted in ibid, p. 328.
4. Robert Rhodes James (ed.), *Winston S. Churchill: His Complete Speeches 1897–1963, Volume VI, 1935–1942* (London: Chelsea House, 1974), pp. 6004–13. The entire speech should be read. It is one of Churchill's best.
5. Cabinet Conclusions 15/3/1939, CAB 23/98/1.
6. Cabinet Conclusions 31/3/1939, CAB 23/98/7, Appendix.
7. This is made clear in Chamberlain's Birmingham speech of 17 April. See Nicholas Fleming, *August 1939: The Last Days of Peace* (London: Peter Davies, 1976), p. 12.
8. Cabinet Conclusions 26/4/1939, CAB 23/99/3.
9. Ibid.
10. Cabinet Conclusions 24/5/1939, CAB 23/99/9.
11. Cabinet Conclusions 14/6/1939, CAB 23/99/11.
12. Cabinet Conclusions 2/8/1939, CAB 23/100/8.
13. Cabinet Conclusions 26/7/1939, CAB 23/100/7.
14. This 'private information' was relayed to Halifax's biographer Andrew Roberts. See Andrew Roberts, *The Holy Fox: The Life of Lord Halifax* (London: Phoenix, 1997), p. 167. For Halifax's reputation Roberts would have done well to keep it private.

15. Cabinet Conclusions 26/8/1939, CAB 23/100/11.
16. Hansard 29/8/1939, cols 111–16. Halder (head of OKW) indicates that on 29 August Hitler had a three-day timetable for war, with invasion to take place on 1 September.
17. Cabinet Conclusions 30/8/1939, CAB 23/100/14.
18. Quoted in Terry Charman (ed.), *Outbreak 1939: The World Goes to War* (London: Virgin, 2009), pp. 77–8.
19. Cabinet Conclusions 1/9/1939, CAB 23/100/15.
20. Ibid.
21. Fleming, *August 1939*, pp. 186–7.
22. Hansard 1/9/1939, col. 131.
23. Ibid, cols 133–9.
24. Cabinet Conclusions 2/9/1939 (4.15 p.m.), CAB 23/100/16.
25. Hansard 2/9/1939, col. 280.
26. Amery Diary 2/9/1939, Leo Amery, *The Empire at Bay: The Leo Amery Diaries 1929–1945* (London: Hutchinson, 1987), p. 570. Amery's remark is not recorded in Hansard but there is no doubt about the timing or about what he said.
27. Fleming, *August 1939*, p. 197.
28. Cabinet Conclusions 2/9/1939 (11.30 p.m.), CAB 23/100/17. The minutes give little flavour as to the tension in the meeting. They do say, however, that the Cabinet was called together at very short notice and that some ministers did not arrive until considerable time had passed.
29. There is a good survey of listeners to Chamberlain's broadcast in Charman, *Outbreak 1939*.
30. Churchill to Chamberlain 22/10/1939, Martin Gilbert (ed.), *Churchill War Papers, Volume 1, At the Admiralty* (London: Norton, 1993), pp. 278–9.
31. War Cabinet Conclusions 4/9/39, CAB 65/1/2.
32. War Cabinet Conclusions 5/9/39, CAB 65/1/3.
33. Ibid.
34. Malcolm Smith, *British Air Strategy Between the Wars* (Oxford: Oxford University Press, 1984), pp. 253–7. Smith's extensive account of the development of the Fairy Battle is well worth reading.
35. Ibid, pp. 257–8.
36. The British air staff realised that their bomber force hardly amounted to a strategic weapon. In 1936 they began a programme of designing four-engine bombers which would result in the Halifax, the Stirling and the Lancaster bombers. None would be ready in numbers until 1943. The Germans, however, never reached this conclusion.
37. Richard Overy, *The Bombing War* (London: Allen Lane, 2013), p. 246.
38. J.R.M. Butler, *Grand Strategy Volume 2* (London: HMSO, 1954), Appendix 1, 'Bombing Policy', p. 567.
39. Ibid.
40. War Cabinet Confidential Annex 9/9/39, CAB 65/3/2.
41. Ibid.
42. War Cabinet Confidential Annex 14/9/39, CAB 65/4/13.
43. Ibid 14/12/39, CAB 65/3/26.
44. Ibid.
45. See War Cabinet Conclusions 16/11/39, CAB 65/2/19 for a discussion of German atrocities in Poland.
46. So said Chamberlain in the War Cabinet 3/9/39, CAB 65/1/1.
47. War Cabinet Conclusions 16/9/39, CAB 65/1/17.
48. M. Middlebrook and C. Everitt, *The Bomber Command War Diaries: An Operational Reference Book 1939–1945* (Leicester: Midland Publishing, 1996), pp. 22–4, 28.
49. The quotation is the title of Uri Bialer's important book *The Shadow of the Bomber: The Fear of Air Attack and British Politics* (London: Royal Historical Society, 1980).

50. George Peden, *Arms, Economics and British Strategy: From Dreadnoughts to Hydrogen Bombs* (Cambridge: Cambridge University Press, 2007), Table 3.9, p. 152.

51. Stephen Roskill, *The War at Sea, Volume 1* (London: HMSO, 1954), Appendix, pp. 583–4. There were many other warships in the nearby Mediterranean Fleet.

52. Ibid, Appendix D, p. 577.

53. Ibid, Table 3.6, p. 141.

54. See, for example, Admiral Pound, 'Notes on C[atherine]' 20/9/1939, in ADM 205/4 which throws a large douche of water on Churchill's scheme. There would be many more such notes.

55. See Gerd Hardach, *The First World War 1914–1918* (London: Peter Smith, 1983) for this analysis.

56. W.N. Medlicott, *The Economic Blockade, Volume 1* (London: HMSO, 1952), p, 51.

57. Talbot C. Imlay, *Facing the Second World War: Strategy, Politics and Economics in Britain and France 1938–1940* (Oxford: Oxford University Press, 2010), pp. 113–14; Adam Tooze, *The Wages of Destruction: The Making and the Breaking of the Nazi Economy* (London: Allen Lane, 2006), p. 309.

58. Medlicott, *Economic Blockade Vol. 1*, p. 254. A bizarre Buchanesque plan was hatched by a committee under Hankey to sabotage the Romanian oilfields and to block the Danube to prevent any remaining supplies from reaching Germany via this route. The one snag was that Romania would have to cooperate in destroying its own oilfields. To the consternation of the British, they refused to have anything to do with the scheme. See Medlicott, *Economic Blockade, Vol. 1*, pp. 254–9.

59. Tooze, *Wages of Destruction*, p. 321.

60. Roskill, *War at Sea, Vol. 1*, Appendix R, p. 615.

61. Axel Niestle, *German U-Boat Losses during World War II* (London: Frontline Books, 2014), p. 188.

62. Churchill to Admiral Godfrey (Director of Naval Intelligence) and others 22/1/1940, Chartwell 19/6.

63. Churchill to Pound and others 10/2/1940, Chartwell 19/6.

64. Churchill to Pound and others 16/2/1940, Chartwell 19/6.

65. 'Royal Navy Officers 1939–1945', www.unithistories.com, accessed 9/11/2020. Churchill's hostility to Danckwerts did not last, however. He appointed him as a member to the important Anglo-American staff negotiations committee later in 1940, where Danckwerts performed creditably.

66. Churchill to Pound and Phillips 19/11/1939, ADM 205/2.

67. Churchill to Pound and others 22/11/1939, Chartwell 19/3.

68. Churchill, 'Degaussing of Merchant Ships', Memorandum for the War Cabinet 15/3/1940, Chartwell 19/8.

69. Medlicott, *The Economic Blockade, Vol. 1*, p. 32.

70. War Cabinet Conclusions 19/9/39, CAB 65/1/20.

71. Churchill to Pound 27/11/39, Chartwell 19/3.

72. War Cabinet Conclusions 30/11/39, CAB 65/2/33.

73. R. Macleod and D. Kelly (eds), *The Ironside Diaries 1937–1940* (London: Constable, 1962), p.185. His military assistant was Roy Macleod, one of the editors of the Ironside diaries.

74. Quoted in 'A Review of the Campaign in Norway', AIR 41/20.

75. Butler, *Grand Strategy Vol. 2*, p. 100.

76. War Cabinet Confidential Annex 22/12/39, CAB 65/4/29. The confidential annexes to War Cabinet meetings consisted of those sections of the meetings where the minutes were circulated to a restricted list of members. In TNA they have been given separate catalogue numbers but it should be emphasised that they are part of the same meetings as the more widely circulated War Cabinet Conclusions.

77. Geirr Haarr, *The German Invasion of Norway (April 1940)* (Annapolis, MD: Naval Institute Press, 2009), p. 29.

78. COS Report, Scandinavia 2/1/40, CAB 80/7.
79. Churchill, 'Norway Iron Ore Traffic, Notes for the War Cabinet' 16/12/39, CAB 66/4.
80. War Cabinet Conclusions 22/12/1939, CAB 65/4/29.
81. Churchill, 'Memorandum for the War Cabinet 29/12/1939, Gilbert (ed.), *Churchill War Papers, Vol. 1*, pp. 584–5.
82. Churchill, 'Swedish Iron Ore', War Cabinet Paper 31/12/1939, CAB 66/4.
83. War Cabinet Confidential Annex 2/1/1940, CAB 65/11.
84. War Cabinet Conclusions Confidential Annex 12/1/40, CAB 65/11/10.
85. Ibid, 17/1/40, CAB 65/11/1.
86. Haarr, *The German Invasion of Norway*, p. 31.
87. See the details of the plan in WO 106/1858, dated 16/1/40.
88. WO 106/204B.
89. 'A Review of the Campaign in Norway', AIR 41/20.
90. COS, 'Intervention in Scandinavia: Plans and Implications', CAB 80/7.
91. War Cabinet Confidential Annex 7/2/40, CAB 65/11/25.
92. Macleod and Kelly (eds), *The Ironside Diaries 1937–1940*, entry for 31/1/40, p. 234.
93. War Cabinet Confidential Annex 3/2/40, CAB 65/11/24.
94. Roskill, *War at Sea, Vol. 1*, pp. 152–3.
95. Ironside Diary 19/2/40.
96. War Cabinet Confidential Annex 18/2/40 and 22/2/40, CAB 65/11/32 and 65/11/ 36.
97. War Cabinet Conclusions 23/2/40, CAB 65/5/50.
98. Ibid, 29/2/40, CAB 65/5/55.
99. Ibid.
100. François Kersaudy, *Norway 1940* (London: Arrow, 1990), p. 31.
101. War Cabinet Confidential Annex 1/3/40, CAB 65/12/1.
102. Ironside Diary 2/3/40.
103. Ibid, 4/3/40.
104. Quoted in 'A Review of the Campaign in Norway', AIR 41/21.
105. War Cabinet Confidential Annex 8/3/40, CAB 65/12/8.
106. War Cabinet Conclusions 9/3/40, CAB 65/6/9.
107. War Cabinet Confidential Annex 12/3/40, CAB 65/12/11.
108. Kersaudy, *Norway 1940*, p. 32.
109. David Dilks (ed.), *The Diaries of Sir Alexander Cadogan 1938–1945* (London: Faber, 2010), p. 97.
110. WO 168/83.
111. War Cabinet Confidential Annex 14/3/40, CAB 65/12/12.
112. Ironside Diary 14/3/40.
113. War Cabinet Conclusions 27/3/40, CAB 65/6/21.
114. 'Norwegian Operation – Planning and Operations 5th February 1940–8th June 1940', WO 106/1979.
115. Chamberlain Note 31/3/40, ADM 116/4240.
116. War Cabinet Confidential Annex 29/3/40, CAB 65/12/14.
117. Churchill to Halifax 15/1/1940, Gilbert (ed.), *Churchill War Papers, Vol. 1*, pp. 642–3.

13. The Norway Campaign

1. Vice-Admiral Kurt Assmann, 'The German Campaign in Norway', German Naval History Series BR 840(1), Naval Staff, Admiralty, Tactical and Staff Duties Division, 1948, p. 1. This is one of a number of studies commissioned by the Admiralty from captured German officers using original documents.
2. Ibid, pp. 6–7.
3. Ibid, pp. 7–8.
4. Haarr, *The German Invasion of Norway*, p. 14.

5. F.H. Hinsley, *British Intelligence in the Second World War, Volume 1* (London: HMSO, 1979), p. 116.
6. Ibid, pp. 117–18.
7. Admiralty to Forbes 7/4/1940, in Gilbert (ed.), *Churchill War Papers, Vol. 1*, p. 977.
8. Ibid.
9. Home Fleet War Diary 7/4/1940, ADM 199/361.
10. Home Fleet, C-in Cs Report, ADM 199/393.
11. War Cabinet Conclusions 9/4/1940, CAB 65/6/30.
12. Military Co-ordination Committee (MCC) Minutes 9/4/1940, in Gilbert (ed.), *Churchill War Papers, Vol. 1*, pp. 996–9.
13. MCC Minutes 10/4/1940, in ibid, pp. 1004–5.
14. War Cabinet Confidential Annex 11/4/1940, CAB 65/12/20.
15. Home Fleet, C-in-Cs Report, ADM 199/393.
16. David Brown (ed.), *Naval Operations of the Campaign in Norway April–June 1940* (Portland, OR: Cass, 2000) p. 29.
17. Ibid, pp. 36–8.
18. War Cabinet Confidential Annex 12/4/1940, CAB 65/12/22.
19. War Cabinet Confidential Annex 13/4/1940, CAB 65/23.
20. Churchill to Reynaud and Daladier 13/4/1940, in Gilbert (ed.), *Churchill War Papers, Vol. 1*, pp. 1051–2.
21. Whitworth to Admiral Forbes 13/4/1940, in ibid, p. 1054.
22. MCC Minutes 13/4/1940, in ibid, pp. 1054–6.
23. Home Fleet, C-in-Cs Report, ADM 199/393.
24. Ibid.
25. Ibid.
26. Ibid.
27. Ibid.
28. Brigade War Diary April 1940, WO 168/25.
29. War Cabinet Confidential Annex, CAB 65/12/26.
30. This account is drawn largely from 146 Brigade War Diary, April 1940, WO 168/25.
31. 'Operations at Namsos', file in CAB 44/73.
32. De Wiart to War Office 21/4/1940, WO 168/93.
33. Massy to De Wiart 24/4/1940, WO 168/6.
34. Norway – 'Historical Notes', WO 106/1894.
35. Headquarters North-Western Expeditionary Force War Diary 27/4/1940, WO 168/2.
36. Brown (ed.), *Naval Operations in Norway*, pp. 95–7.
37. Brigade War Diary May 1940, WO 168/25.
38. Joseph Kynoch, *Norway 1940: The Forgotten Fiasco* (Shrewsbury: Airlife, 2002), p. 18. Kynoch was a member of 148 Brigade.
39. War Office to Morgan 16/4/1940, WO 168/93; CIGS to Morgan 19/4/1940 in ibid.
40. Kersaudy, *Norway 1940*, pp. 115–16.
41. Note in 148 Brigade War Diary April 1940, WO 168/93.
42. 'Notes on the Norwegian Campaign', CAB 146/3. These notes were prepared for the Official Historian in 1951.
43. Brigade, Administrative War Diary 20–22/4/1940, WO 168/94.
44. Brigade Administrative War Diary 26/4/1940, WO 168/94.
45. Ibid.
46. Sickle Force War Diary 23/4/1940, WO 168/94.
47. 'Review of the Campaign in Norway', AIR 41/20, pp. 59–60.
48. Sickle Force Narrative of Events, WO 168/93.
49. MCC Minutes 18/4/1940, in Gilbert (ed.), *Churchill War Papers, Vol. 1*, p. 1088.
50. MCC Minutes 19/4/1940, in ibid, pp. 1094–5.
51. War Council Confidential Annex 21/4/1940, CAB 65/12/30.

52. Churchill to Chamberlain 22/4/1940, Gilbert (ed.), *Churchill War Papers*, Vol. 1, pp. 1116–17.
53. Churchill to Pound 24/4/1940 and 25/4/1940, in ibid, pp. 1130–1.
54. MCC Minutes 26/4/1940 in ibid, pp. 1139–41.
55. War Office to Mackesy 11/4/1940, Narvik Telegrams, WO 106/1870.
56. Ibid.
57. Churchill to Pound and others 11/4/1940, Chartwell 19/6.
58. Cork to Mackesy 14/4/1940, WO 168/83.
59. Kersaudy, *Norway 1940*, pp. 124–5.
60. Mackesy to War Office 16/4/1940, Narvik Telegrams, WO 106/1870.
61. Churchill, Note to MCC 16/4/1940, in Gilbert (ed.), *Churchill War Papers*, Vol. 1, pp. 1076–7.
62. Churchill Note to MCC 17/4/1940, in ibid, p. 1080.
63. Churchill to Cork and Mackesy 17/4/1940, Chartwell 19/2.
64. Cork–Mackesy Conference 18/4/1940, WO 168/83.
65. Cork to Admiralty 18/4/1940, WO 168/83.
66. Mackesy to the War Office 19/4/1940, Narvik Telegrams, WO 106/1870.
67. Admiralty to Cork and Mackesy 20/4/1940, in Gilbert (ed.), *Churchill War Papers*, Vol. 1, p. 1197.
68. Mackesy to the War Office 21/4/1940, in ibid, pp. 1108–9.
69. Cork–Mackesy Conference 22/4/1940, WO 168/83.
70. Guards Brigade, Operation Order No. 1 22/4/1940, WO 168/24.
71. Cork to Churchill 24/4/1940, WO 168/93.
72. Cork to Mackesy 26/4/1949, ibid.
73. Dill to Mackesy 29/4/1940, ibid.
74. Mackesy to Dill 29/4/1940, ibid.
75. Mackesy to Cork 3/5/1940, WO 168/93.
76. Trappes-Lomax Report 6/5/1940, War Office Telegrams, WO 106/1917.
77. Cork to the Admiralty 7/5/1940, ibid.
78. Supreme War Council Minutes 22/4/1940, CAB 99/3.
79. MCC Minutes 26/4/1940, in Gilbert (ed.), *Churchill War Papers*, Vol. 1, pp. 1139–42.
80. Churchill Memorandum, in ibid, p. 1169.
81. Geirr Haarr, *The Battle for Norway: April–June 1940* (Annapolis, MD: Naval Institute Press, 2010), pp. 281–96.
82. Ibid, pp. 289–90.
83. Ibid, pp. 329–47. See also Roskill, *War at Sea*, Vol. 1, pp. 194–6.

14. 1940 – Crisis Year

1. For a fuller exposition of these events see Robin Prior, *When Britain Saved the West: The Story of 1940* (London/New Haven: Yale University Press, 2015), ch. 2.
2. GHQ War Diary 15/5/1940, WO 167/5.
3. GHQ War Diary 16/5/1940, WO 167/40; Advanced Brassard War Diary 16/5/1940, WO 167/82. Advanced Brassard was the strange name Gort gave to his advanced headquarters.
4. COS Minutes 13/5/1940, CAB 79/4/29.
5. COS Minutes 14/5/1940, CAB 79/4/31.
6. Churchill to Reynaud 14/5/1940, Prem 3/188/1, University of Adelaide Library.
7. Churchill, Conversation with Reynaud 15/5/1940, Prem 3/188/1.
8. War Cabinet Minutes Confidential Annex 15/5/1940, CAB 65/13/9.
9. War Cabinet Minutes Confidential Annex 16/5/1940, CAB 65/13/10.
10. Cadogan Diary 16/5/1940, p. 256.
11. Supreme War Council Minutes 16/5/1940, Cab 99/3.

12. Churchill to the War Cabinet 16/5/1940, in Martin Gilbert (ed.), *The Churchill War Papers, Volume 2, May 1940–December 1940* (London: Norton, 1995), pp. 61–2.
13. War Cabinet Minutes 16/5/1940, CAB 65/7/19.
14. GHQ War Diary 17/5/1940, WO 167/5.
15. Division War Diary 19/5/1940, WO 167/300.
16. GHQ War Diary Night of 18/19 May 1940, WO 167/5. The directions available to the BEF have been spelled out.
17. Churchill Broadcast 19/5/1940, in Gilbert (ed.), *Churchill War Papers, Vol. 2*, pp. 83–90.
18. War Cabinet Confidential Annex 19/5/1940, CAB 65/13/12.
19. Ibid.
20. Defence Committee Minutes 19/5/1940, CAB 69/1.
21. GHQ War Diary 20/5/1940, WO 167/5.
22. Command Post [Advanced GHQ] War Diary, WO 167/29.
23. See Summary of Events May–June 1940, CAB 106/284; Rommel Diary 21/5/1940 in B.H. Liddell Hart (ed.), *The Rommel Papers* (London: Collins, 1953), pp. 32–3.
24. Dill to Churchill 20/5/1940, in Anglo-French Liaison Folder, CAB 21/1289.
25. Churchill to Reynaud 21/5/1940, in Gilbert (ed.), *Churchill War Papers, Vol. 2*, p. 102.
26. Supreme War Council Minutes 22/5/1940, CAB 99/3.
27. Churchill to Gort 22/5/1940, Chartwell 20/14.
28. Brian Bond (ed.), *Chief of Staff: The Diaries of Lieutenant-General Sir Henry Pownall, Volume 1* (London: Leo Cooper, 1972), 22/5/1940, p. 325.
29. Battle Post War Diary 24/5/1940, WO 167/27.
30. Eden to Gort 26/5/1940, in 'Telegrams: Secretary of State–BEF', WO 106/1689.
31. Eden to Gort 26/5/1940 in ibid.
32. Churchill to Eden and Ironside 25/5/1940, in Gilbert (ed.), *Churchill War Papers, Vol. 2*, p. 141.
33. Churchill to Ironside 25/5/1940, in ibid, pp. 149–50.
34. For a full account of Dunkirk see Prior, *When Britain Saved the West*, ch. 5.
35. War Cabinet Minutes 20/5/1940, CAB 65/7/26.
36. Churchill flew to Paris on 31/5/1940 and told Reynaud that the two forces would be evacuated 'arm in arm'. See Supreme War Council Minutes 31/5/1940, CAB 99/3.
37. COS Papers, 'British Strategy in a Certain Eventuality 25/5/1940', CAB 80/11.
38. War Cabinet Confidential Annex 26/5/1940, CAB 65/13/20.
39. COS, 'British Strategy in the Near Future', CAB 80/11; War Cabinet Confidential Annex 26/5/1940, CAB 65/13/20.
40. War Cabinet Confidential Annex 26/5/1940, CAB 65/13/21.
41. See John Lukacs, *Five Days in London* (London: Yale University Press, 2001); Christopher Hill, *Cabinet Decisions on Foreign Policy: The British Experience* (Cambridge: Cambridge University Press, 2002); and Prior, *When Britain Saved the West*, ch. 3.
42. Supreme War Council Minutes 13/6/1940, CAB 99/3.
43. See Avi Shlaim, 'Prelude to Downfall: The British Offer of Union to France, June 1940', *Journal of Contemporary History*, vol. 9, no. 3 (1974), pp. 27–63; War Cabinet Minutes 16/6 1940, CAB 65/7/63.
44. See Eleanor M. Gates, *The End of the Affair: The Collapse of the Anglo-French Alliance, 1939–1940* (Berkeley: University of California Press, 1981), pp. 277–9.
45. 'Record of Conversation Held at Bordeaux on 18th June, 1940, Between First Lord, First Sea Lord and Admiral Darlan, First Sea Lord's Records 1939–1945, ADM 205/4.
46. Gates, *The End of the Affair*, p. 247.
47. War Cabinet Confidential Annex 30/6/1940, CAB 65/13/56.
48. A.J. Marder, 'Oran,3 July 1940' in his *From the Dardanelles to Oran* (London: Oxford University Press, 1974), p. 228.
49. See Marder, *From the Dardanelles to Oran*, for these details.
50. Churchill to A.V. Alexander 8/8/1040, Chartwell 20/13.

51. Roskill, *War at Sea, Vol. 1*, p. 246.
52. War Cabinet Confidential Annex 2/7/1940, CAB 65/14/2.
53. Churchill to Eden 7/7/1940, Chartwell 20/13.
54. Churchill to Ismay 9/8/1940, Chartwell 20/13.
55. Churchill to Ismay 30/6/1940, Chartwell 20/13.
56. Churchill to Eden and Dill 9/8/1940, Chartwell 20/13.
57. For a short account of Dakar see Roskill, *War at Sea, Vol. 1*, pp. 308–20.
58. Note by Assistant Chief Naval Staff (ACNS) 29/8/1940, ADM 223/484.
59. See Prior, *When Britain Saved the West*, tables on p. 192.
60. Kurt Maier et al., *Germany and the Second World War, Volume 2* (Oxford: Clarendon Press, 1991), p. 380.
61. Churchill to Sinclair 10/7/1940, Chartwell 20/2.
62. John Colville Diary 13/7/1940, quoted in Gilbert (ed.), *Churchill War Papers, Vol. 2*, p. 513.
63. Ibid, p. 644.
64. Luftwaffe Strength and Serviceability Tables, compiled from the records of VI Abteilung Quarter-Master General's Department of the German Air Ministry and translated by the Air Historical Branch, AIR 20/7706.
65. Defence Committee (Operations) Minutes 13/8/1940, CAB 69/1.
66. Churchill to Sinclair 17/8/1940, Prem 3/347.
67. Churchill to Sinclair 25/8/1940, in Gilbert (ed.), *Churchill War Papers, Vol. 2*, p. 721.
68. Churchill, 'Training of RAF Pilots', Cabinet Paper, 26/8/1940, CAB 66/11.
69. Churchill to Sinclair, Newell and Ismay 29/8/1940, Chartwell 20/13.
70. These visits are recorded in Martin Gilbert, *Winston S. Churchill: Finest Hour: 1939–1941* (London: Heinemann, 1983). They are: Kenley, 12 July, p. 661; Dowding, 3 August, p. 711; Dowding, 15 August, p. 735; Park, 16 August, p. 736; Kenley, 17 August, p. 739; Park, 31 August, pp. 735–6; Park, 1 September, pp. 767–8; Park, 15 September, pp. 783–5. There is also a visit to Manston on 28 August.
71. Gilbert, *Finest Hour*, pp. 293–6.
72. T.C.B. James makes this point in his *The Battle of Britain* (London: Cass, 2002), p. 322.
73. Park to Dowding ?/9/1940, AIR 16/330.
74. I recommend the superb Juliet Gardiner, *The Blitz: The British under Attack* (London: Harper, 2011) for the full story.
75. Richard Titmus, *Problems of Social Policy* (London: HMSO, 1950), pp. 270–2.
76. Mass Observation, 'Shelter in London', 3/10/1940, File 436. Mass Observation Archive Online.
77. Churchill to Bridges, Sir John Anderson (Home Secretary, and Sir John Reith (Minister of Works) 21/9/1940, in Gilbert (ed.), *Churchill War Papers, Vol. 2*, pp. 850–1. Reith called this memo 'silly', which says a lot about Reith.

15. The Desert – Wavell's War 1939–1942

1. 'Middle East Convoys', CAB 120/402.
2. Ismay to Newall (CAS) 4/8/1940, CAB 120/300.
3. Major-General I.S.O. Playfair, *Mediterranean and Middle East, Volume 1, The Early Successes against Italy* (Uckfield: Naval and Military Press, 2016), p. 91. Reprint of 1954 edition; the Official History. Also Roskill, *War at Sea, Vol. 1*, p. 295.
4. Churchill to A.V. Alexander and Pound 15/7/1940, Chartwell 20/13.
5. 'Army Council Instructions to the General Officer Commanding-in-Chief in the Middle East' 24/7/1939, quoted in Playfair, *Mediterranean, Vol. 1*, pp. 457–9.
6. Wavell to Ironside 18/8/1939, WO 201/2119.
7. Wavell to Ironside 12/11/1939, WO 201/2119.
8. Churchill to Eden 17/7/1940, Chartwell 20/13.
9. COS Minutes 8/8/1940, CAB 79/6/5.

10. Gilbert, *Finest Hour*, pp. 718–19; War Cabinet Minutes 13/8/1940, CAB 65/14/21.
11. War Cabinet Confidential Annex 26/8/1940, CAB 65/14/25.
12. 'General Direction for the Commander-in-Chief Middle East' 15/8/1940, Chartwell 20/13. Churchill has been much criticised for writing this kind of directive but, as was noted, Wavell had earlier complained about lack of direction from London. He had now been given the direction he lacked.
13. Playfair, *Mediterranean, Vol. 1*, pp. 257–8.
14. Churchill to Wavell 3/11/1940, Chartwell 20/14.
15. Gilbert, *Finest Hour*, p. 479.
16. Churchill to Wavell 13/11/1940, Chartwell 20/13.
17. Hinsley, *British Intelligence, Vol. 1*, pp. 348–9.
18. Churchill to Ismay 18/11/1940, Prem 3/288/1.
19. Churchill to Wavell 22/11/1940, ibid.
20. Eden Diary 4/12/1940, quoted in Gilbert (ed.), *Churchill War Papers, Vol. 2*, p. 1179.
21. Churchill to Ismay 25/1/1940, Prem 3/214.
22. Churchill to Dill 7/12/1940, Prem 3/288/1.
23. Gerhard Schreiber et al., *Germany and the Second World War, Volume III, The Mediterranean, South-East Europe and North Africa 1939–1941* (Oxford: Clarendon Press, 1995), p. 646.
24. For descriptions of some British patrols in July 1940 see WO 201/340.
25. Barrie Pitt, *The Crucible of War: The Western Desert 1941* (London: Book Club Associates, 1960), p. 88.
26. Chester Wilmot, *Desert Siege* (Sydney: Penguin, 2003), p. 2. A reprint of the 1944 edition, which was called *Tobruk 1941*.
27. Playfair, *Mediterranean, Vol. 1*, pp. 238–9.
28. Ibid, p. 115.
29. Alan Moorehead, *African Trilogy* (London: Four Square, 1959), p. 13.
30. Pitt, *Western Desert 1941*, p. 116.
31. Brigade War Diary Jan–Feb 1941, AWM 52/8/2/16.
32. Ibid, 14/1/1941. For an excellent account of the Battle of Bardia see Craig Stockings, *The Battle of Bardia* (Canberra: Army History Unit, 2011).
33. The war diaries, both Australian and British, spell it 'Tobruch'.
34. This detail is taken from the lucid account in Wilmot, *Desert Siege*, pp. 5–8.
35. See 16 Brigade War Diary Jan–Feb 1941, AWM 52/8/16/6; and 19 Brigade War Diary Jan 1941, AWM 52/8/3/8/7.
36. See Wilmot, *Desert Siege*, pp. 13–15 and 6 Division Operation Order No. 7 (Artillery Plan) in 19 Brigade War Diary Jan 1941, AWM 52/8/3/8/7.
37. See, for example, 'Notes of Conference 18/1/1941', 19 Brigade War Diary.
38. Brigade War Diary 21/1/1941, AWM 52/8/2/16.
39. Brigade War Diary 21/1/1941, AWM 52/8/2/19/3.
40. 'The Battle of Tobruch: B Coys Part by Captain Coombes' 28/1/1941, 19 Brigade War Diary, AWM 52/8/2/19/3. The account also notes an incident where an Italian soldier had surrendered but then threw a hand grenade and shot one of the Australian troops. 'Suitable action was then taken', the account says.
41. Playfair, *Mediterranean, Vol. 1*, p. 357.
42. Brigade War Diary Jan–Feb 1941, AWM 52/8/2/16/6; Moorehead, *African Trilogy*, p. 55.
43. Compass Operations, WO 201/349.
44. Playfair, *Mediterranean, Vol. 1*, p. 362.
45. Defence Committee (Operations) Minutes 8/1/1941, CAB 69/2.
46. Hinsley, *British Intelligence, Vol. 1*, p. 259.
47. Defence Committee (Operations) Minutes 8/1/1941, CAB 69/2.
48. Ibid 9/1/1941, CAB 69/2.
49. COS Committee Minutes 16/1/1941, CAB 79/8/61.
50. Defence Committee (Operations) Minutes 20/1/1941, CAB 69/2.

51. Ibid 10/2/1941, CAB 69/2.
52. Churchill, 'Note for Anthony Eden' 12/2/1941, Chartwell 20/36.
53. COS to the Commander-in-Chief Middle East 11/2/1941, FO 954/11.
54. CAS to Wavell 9/1/1941, Wavell to CIGS 10/1/1941, CAB 120/404.
55. Playfair, *Mediterranean, Vol. 1*, pp. 374–5.
56. Churchill to Cadogan 19/2/1941, Chartwell 20/36.
57. Churchill to Eden 20/2/1941, Chartwell 20/49/2.
58. 'Decision to Send British Troops to Greece', Note by CIGS 21/4/1941, FO 954/11A.
59. Ibid. The meeting which modified the original plan took place on 2/3 March.
60. Ibid.
61. Ibid.
62. Schreiber, *Germany and the Second World War, Vol. III*, p. 489.
63. Ibid, p. 493.
64. Butler, *Grand Strategy, Volume 2*, pp. 456–7.
65. Roosevelt to Churchill 10/5/1941 in Warren Kimball (ed.), *Churchill and Roosevelt: The Complete Correspondence, Volume 1, Alliance Emerging* (Princeton: Princeton University Press, 1984), p. 184.
66. Hinsley, *British Intelligence, Vol. 1*, p. 388. The intelligence failure is admitted by Hinsley.
67. Churchill to Roosevelt 16/4/1941 in Kimball (ed.), *Churchill and Roosevelt Correspondence, Vol. 1*, p. 171.
68. Wavell to the War Office 2/3/1941, Prem 3/288/5.
69. Schreiber, *Germany and the Second World War, Vol. III*, p. 673.
70. Ibid, p. 674.
71. Pitt, *Western Desert*, pp. 254–6.
72. Australian Division, 'Operations in Cyrenaica and Tobruk', WO 201/353.
73. 'Report of the Action of the 2 Armoured Division during the Withdrawal from Cyrenaica March–April 1941', CAB 66/17/32.
74. Ibid.
75. Australian Division, 'Operations in Cyrenaica'.
76. Playfair, *Mediterranean, Vol. 2*, pp. 23–4.
77. Australian Division, 'Operations in Cyrenaica'.
78. Douglas Porch, *Hitler's Mediterranean Gamble* (London: Weidenfeld and Nicolson, 2004), pp. 222–3. This excellent book gives a whole new perspective to the debate on the Mediterranean strategy.
79. This brief account of Tobruk is taken from Wilmot, *Desert Siege*; Robert Lyman, *The Longest Siege: Tobruk, the Battle that Saved North Africa* (London: Pan, 2009); William F. Buckingham, *Tobruk: The Great Siege 1941–1942* (Stroud: History Press, 2009); and 9 Australian Division, 'Operations in Cyrenaica and Tobruk'.
80. Churchill to Wavell 26/3/1941, Prem 3/309/2.
81. Middle East Command to Churchill 26/3/1941, ibid.
82. Wavell to War Office 4/4/1941, ibid.
83. Churchill to Wavell 2/4/1941, Chartwell 20/39.
84. Churchill to Eden 3/4/1941, Defence Committee (Operations), CAB 69/2.
85. Churchill to Wavell 4/4/1941, Chartwell 20/37/4.
86. These issues which greatly plagued Wavell and caused tension between the COS, the Prime Minister and Wavell cannot be dealt with within the scope of this book.
87. Churchill to Ismay 20/4/1941, CAB 69/8.
88. Defence Committee (Operations) 21/4/1941 Confidential Annex, CAB 69/8.
89. Playfair, *Mediterranean, Vol. 2*, p. 119.
90. Wavell to Churchill 13/5/1941, Prem 3/309/4.
91. Playfair, *Mediterranean, Vol. 1*, p. 162.
92. This was Wavell's contention in a telegram to Dill 17/5/1941, Prem 3/309/4.
93. Churchill to Wavell 21/5/1941, ibid.

94. Wavell to Churchill 21/5/1941, ibid.
95. The arguments can be found in Prem 3/309/5.
96. Churchill to Ismay for COS Committee 6/5/1941, Chartwell 20/36.
97. Defence Committee (Operations) 9/4/1941, CAB 69/2.
98. For these peripheral but important matters that cannot be dealt with here, see Robert Lyman, *First Victory: Britain's Forgotten Struggle in the Middle East, 1941* (London: Constable, 2006). Lyman deals with Iraq, Syria and Iran in this excellent survey. See also John Connell, *Wavell: Scholar and Soldier* (London: Collins, 1964), ch. XIII is good on this matter.
99. 'Notes on Action of 7 Armd Div 14–17 June, 1941', in 'Lessons – Battleaxe June–Nov 41', WO 201/357.
100. Playfair, *Mediterranean, Vol. 2*, p. 165.
101. 'Notes on Action of 7 Armd Div'.
102. 'Order of Battle and Organization of the Force' in 'Lessons – Battleaxe June–Nov 41', WO 201/357.
103. Wavell to Churchill 29/5/1941, Prem 3/309/5.
104. Wavell to Churchill 28/5/1941, Prem 3/309/5.
105. 'Notes on Action of 7 Armd Div'.
106. Ibid.
107. Playfair, *Mediterranean, Vol. 2*, p. 171.
108. Churchill to Smuts 18/6/1941, Prem 3/287/2.
109. Dill to Wavell 19/6/1941, Prem 3/309/5.
110. Churchill to Wavell 21/6/1941, Chartwell 20/40.
111. Churchill Note 11/7/1941, printed in CAB 66/17/32.
112. Dill to Churchill 14/7/1941, WO 216/14.
113. Dill to Margesson 14/7/1941, ibid.
114. Churchill to Dill 16/7/1941, ibid.
115. Dill to Churchill 17/7/1941, ibid.
116. Churchill to Wavell 28/5/1941, Chartwell 20/39; Dill to Churchill 29/5/1941, Prem 3/309/4.
117. Armoured Division, 'Lessons – Battleaxe June–Nov 41', WO 201/357.
118. Ibid.
119. Ibid. 'Jock' columns were named after Jock Campbell, the immensely brave but tactically illiterate leader of the 7 Armoured Support Group.
120. Indian Division, 'Operations 15–17 June, 1941', WO 201/357.
121. Churchill to Margesson and Dill 2/7/1941, in Martin Gilbert (ed.), *The Churchill War Papers, Volume 3, The Ever-Widening War 1941* (London: Heinemann, 2000), pp. 892–3.
122. Note by Alanbrooke to Churchill 12/2/1942, Prem 3/291/7.

16. The Desert – Auchinleck's War 1941–1942

1. Churchill to Auchinleck 1/7/1941, CAB 120/628.
2. Auchinleck to Churchill 4/7/1941, ibid.
3. The telegrams between Churchill and Auchinleck are in CAB 120/628. Most of them can also be found in John Connell, *Auchinleck: A Critical Biography* (London: Cassell, 1959). In truth there is not much that is critical of Auchinleck in this book.
4. See COS Minutes 31/7/1941, CAB 79/13/26.
5. Defence Committee (Operations) Minutes 1/8/1941, CAB 69/2.
6. Gilbert, *Finest Hour*, p. 1151.
7. Churchill to Smuts 3/8/1941, quoted in Gilbert, *Finest Hour*, p. 1152.
8. Auchinleck note, quoted in Connell, *Auchinleck*, p. 268.
9. Churchill to Auchinleck 31/8/1941, Prem 3/.291/3.

10. Auchinleck to Churchill 19/9/1941, in Connell, *Auchinleck*, pp. 299–301.
11. 'Report on Operations: Eighth Army: Sept.–Nov. 1941', WO 201/358.
12. Ibid.
13. Ibid.
14. Armoured Division in Operation Crusader, WO 201/361.
15. See 'Lessons – Battleaxe June–Nov 41', in WO 201/357.
16. South African Division Operations November–December 1941, WO 201/515.
17. '30 Corps Report December 1941', WO 201/518.
18. 'Guns in Crusader', Prem 3/291/7.
19. Schreiber, *Germany and the Second World War, Vol. III*, p. 726.
20. 'Report on Eighth Army Operations Sept–Nov 1941'.
21. Pitt, *Western Desert 1941*, pp. 344, 345 and 358. Pitt is scathing about the selection of Gabr Saleh as a point which might bring on a decisive clash of armour. For Rommel's lack of concern see Liddell Hart (ed.), *The Rommel Papers*.
22. Schreiber, *Germany and the Second World War, Vol. III*, p. 730.
23. Armoured Division in Operation Crusader, WO 201/361.
24. Schreiber, *Germany and the Second World War, Vol. III*, p. 731.
25. Rifle Brigade at Sidi Rezegh, WO 201/356. The 2 Rifle Brigade was an infantry component of the Support Group.
26. Playfair, *Mediterranean, Vol. 2*, p. 50.
27. Ibid. See also in 7 Armoured Division in Operation Crusader, WO 201/361.
28. Armoured Division in Operation Crusader, WO 201/361.
29. Schreiber, *Germany and the Second World War, Vol. III*, pp. 739–40.
30. Ibid, p. 741.
31. Armoured Division in Operation Crusader, WO 201/361.
32. 'Report on Operations: Eighth Army: Sept.–Nov. 1941', WO 201/358.
33. D.W. Sinclair, *19th Battalion and Armoured Regiment* (Wellington: Historical Publication Branch, 1954), p. 210.
34. Churchill to Auchinleck 27/11/1941, Chartwell 20/45.
35. Auchinleck to Churchill 25/11/1941, Connell, *Auchinleck*, pp. 372–3.
36. Armoured Division in Operation Crusader, WO 201/361.
37. Ibid. Note that this narrative was written by General Gott, the commander of 7 Armoured.
38. Ibid.
39. Schreiber, *Germany and the Second World War, Vol. III*, p. 744.
40. Ibid, p. 747. Bletchley had temporarily lost the German Army Enigma key and were thus not able to warn Auchinleck of Rommel's decision. See F.H. Hinsley, *British Intelligence in the Second World War, Volume 2* (London: HMSO, 1981), p. 311.
41. Auchinleck, 'Report on Operations of the Eighth Army 26 November–10 December 1941', WO 201/359.
42. Schreiber, *Germany and the Second World War, Vol. III*, p. 750.
43. Pitt, *Western Desert 1941*, pp. 460–1.
44. Churchill, Speech to the House of Commons 11/12/1941, in Gilbert (ed.), *Churchill War Papers, Vol. 3*, pp. 1601–5. By the time he made the speech, of course, Churchill had many other matters on his mind.
45. Michael Carver, *Dilemmas of the Desert War 1940–1942* (London: Batsford, 1986), p. 51.
46. Ibid.
47. Playfair, *Mediterranean, Vol. 3*, p. 100. Reprint of 1960 edition. The figures are difficult to calculate, as damaged tanks were often returned to the battlefield by repair crews.
48. Carver, *Dilemmas of the Desert War*, pp. 51–2.
49. Hinsley, *British Intelligence, Vol. 2*, p. 334.
50. Ibid, p. 335.
51. Ibid, p. 336.

52. There is a very useful summary of all this in the Hinsley volume quoted above. See pp. 324–6. I have drawn heavily on it.
53. Churchill to Auchinleck 11/1/1942, Chartwell 20/88; Auchinleck to Churchill 13/1/1942, in Connell, *Auchinleck*, p. 424.
54. South African Division at Gazala Jan–June 1942, WO 201/391.
55. Ibid.
56. COS Minutes 24/2/1942, CAB 79/18/29.
57. Churchill to Auchinleck 27/2/1942, CAB 120/628.
58. Auchinleck to Churchill 27/2/1942, in Connell, *Auchinleck*, p. 457.
59. COS to Auchinleck 27/2/1942, CAB 120/628.
60. Churchill to Auchinleck 1/3/1942, ibid.
61. Auchinleck to COS 4/3/1942 and 5/3/1942, ibid.
62. Churchill to Auchinleck 8/3/1942, ibid.
63. CIGS to Auchinleck 6/3/1942, in Connell, *Auchinleck*, p. 463.
64. Auchinleck to Churchill 9/3/1942, CAB 120/628.
65. Field Marshal Lord Alanbrooke, *War Diaries 1939–1945*, ed. Alex Danchev and Daniel Todman (London: Phoenix, 2002), 13/3/1942, p. 239. I have relied heavily on this splendid edition of the diaries. All references to Alan Brooke's diary are to this paperback edition (hereafter *Brooke Diary*).
66. Ibid.
67. Churchill to Auchinleck 15/3/1942, CAB 120/628.
68. 'Questionnaire and Replies by the Vice Chief of the Imperial General Staff', CAB 120/628. Churchill had this document printed and distributed to the War Cabinet.
69. Ibid.
70. Cripps to Churchill 20/3/1942, CAB 120/628.
71. Churchill to Nye 22/3/1942, ibid.
72. Defence Committee (Operations) Minutes 31/3/1942, CAB 69/2.
73. See Auchinleck to Churchill 13/4/1942; Churchill to Auchinleck 26/4/1942; and other exchanges in CAB 120/628.
74. Auchinleck to Churchill 6/5/1942, CAB 120/628.
75. Churchill to Auchinleck 8/5/1942, ibid.
76. Churchill to Auchinleck 10/5/1942, ibid.
77. Hinsley, *British Intelligence, Vol. 2*, pp. 364–6.
78. Niall Barr, *Pendulum of War: The Three Battles of El Alamein* (London: Pimlico, 2005), p. 13.
79. See Playfair, *Mediterranean, Vol. 3*, Map 25.
80. Auchinleck to Ritchie 20/5/1942, quoted in Barrie Pitt, *The Crucible of War: Year of Alamein 1942* (London: Cape, 1982), p. 37.
81. Brooke to Churchill 12/2/1942, Prem 3/291/7.
82. Churchill Note 12/2/1942, ibid.
83. Pitt, *Year of Alamein 1942*, p. 45. It is interesting to note that there exists no account by the Eighth Army for the fighting around Gazala. Even the war diaries are incomplete and often very confusing as to dates, times and orders.
84. Playfair, *Mediterranean, Vol. 3*, pp. 224–5.
85. Auchinleck to Brooke 28/5/1942, Prem 3/310/4. Auchinleck is quoting Ritchie.
86. Auchinleck to Brooke 29/5/1942, ibid. Once again Auchinleck is quoting Ritchie.
87. Playfair, *Mediterranean, Vol. 3*, p. 228.
88. Ibid, p. 229.
89. Pitt, *Year of Alamein 1942*, p. 62.
90. The above account is derived from ibid, p. 63. Carver, in *Dilemmas of the Desert War* (p. 94), confirms that Gott declined to participate but does not say why. The Official History is silent on the matter.
91. Pitt, *Year of Alamein 1942*, p. 63.

92. Playfair, *Mediterranean, Vol. 3*, pp. 232–4.
93. Hansard 2/6/1942, cols 528–34.
94. Churchill to Auchinleck 14/6/1942, Chartwell 20/76.
95. Auchinleck to Churchill 15/6/1942, Prem 3/310/4.
96. Churchill to Auchinleck 16/6/1942, ibid.
97. Auchinleck to Churchill 16/6/1942, ibid.
98. Auchinleck to Brooke 17/6/1942, ibid.
99. COS to Auchinleck 18/6/1942; Auchinleck to COS 19/6/1942, ibid.
100. Pitt, *Year of Alamein 1942*, pp. 98–103.
101. Ibid, p. 109.
102. Playfair, *Mediterranean, Vol. 3*, p. 274.
103. Winston S. Churchill, *The Hinge of Fate* (London: Cassell, 1951), p. 343.
104. Playfair, *Mediterranean, Vol. 3*, p. 285.
105. Ibid, pp. 286–7.
106. Ibid, p. 287.
107. Pitt, *Year of Alamein 1942*, pp. 120–1.
108. Major-General H. Kippenberger, *Infantry Brigadier* (London: Oxford University Press, 1949), p. 135.
109. Lieutenant-Colonel J.L. Scoullar, *The Battle for Egypt* (Wellington: War History Branch, 1955), p. 132.
110. Pitt, *Year of Alamein 1942*, p. 131.
111. Barr, *Pendulum of War*, pp. 69–82. Barr really is the last word on the July 1942 actions.
112. Playfair, *Mediterranean, Vol. 3*, pp. 342–5.
113. For a superb account of these desperately inconclusive battles see Barr, *Pendulum of War*, chs 5–10.
114. In his ground-breaking book, *Fighting the People's War* (Cambridge: Cambridge University Press, 2019) chs 4 and 6, Jonathan Fennell demonstrates beyond the shadow of a doubt that morale in the Eighth Army was very low at the end of July 1942. My point is not to contest that conclusion but to state that, however they felt about their many reverses, the troops fought on.

17. Slouching Towards a Strategy – Anglo-American Planning 1940–1942

1. Roosevelt to Churchill 11/9/1939, in Kimball (ed.), *Churchill and Roosevelt Correspondence, Vol. 1*, p. 24.
2. Ibid, p. 25.
3. Ibid, p. 37.
4. Roosevelt 15/5/1942 quoted in Warren F. Kimball, *The Juggler: Franklin Roosevelt as Wartime Statesman* (Princeton: Princeton University Press, 1994), p. 7.
5. For a more extensive treatment of this subject see Prior, *When Britain Saved the West*, ch. 13.
6. Lothian to Churchill 11/6/1940, Prem 3/457.
7. Churchill to Eden 24/6/1940, ibid.
8. Halifax to Churchill 27/8/1940 and Dill to Churchill 28/6/1940, ibid.
9. Churchill to COS 10/8/1940, ibid.
10. James Leutze (ed.), *The London Observer: The Journal of Raymond E. Lee 1940–1941* (London: Hutchinson, 1971) (hereafter *Lee Journal*), pp. 29 and 32.
11. Ismay to Churchill 12/8/1940, Prem 3/457.
12. Bridges to Churchill and Churchill's reply 19/8/1940, ibid.
13. *Lee Journal* 8/8/1940, p. 33.
14. COS Minutes 20/8/1940, CAB 79/6/23.
15. Anglo-American Standardization of Arms Committee Minutes 20/8/1940, CAB 99/16. Note the American spelling adopted by the British secretary of the meeting.

16. *Lee Journal*, p. 36.
17. See the minutes for 20/8/1940 for the itinerary, CAB 79/8/1940.
18. Minutes 29/8/1940, CAB 99/16.
19. COS Minutes 31/8/1940, CAB 79/6/39.
20. *Lee Journal* 23/9/1940, p. 68.
21. Ibid, 28/10/1940, p. 111.
22. Ibid, 30/11/1940, p. 147.
23. For the origins of Plan Dog see Mitchell B. Simpson III, *Admiral Harold R. Stark: Architect of Victory 1939–1945* (Columbia: University of South Carolina Press, 1989), ch. 4.
24. For the evolution of this plan see Mark Stoler, *Allies and Adversaries: The Joint Chiefs of Staff, the Grand Alliance and U.S. Strategy in World War II* (Chapel Hill: University of North Carolina Press, n.d.), pp. 29–35.
25. Ibid, pp. 34–5. Stoler should be consulted on the anti-British attitudes of many of the American military (Eisenhower included).
26. Churchill to Roosevelt 28/1/1941, Chartwell 20/49.
27. The confidant of Lee (Roger Evans) who had first told Lee about the talks did not make the final cut, largely due to the intervention of Lee himself, who thought Evans too inflexible. See *Lee Journal* 10/12/1940, p. 167.
28. See the Report of the United Kingdom Delegation of the British-United States Staff Conversations, April 1941, CAB 99/5.
29. British-United States Staff Conversations (hereafter ABC-1) Minutes 31/1/1941, CAB 99/5.
30. See ABC-1 Minutes 10/2/1941 for an agreement to disagree on this point.
31. ABC-1 Minutes 6/2/1941.
32. ABC-1 Report 27/3/1941, CAB 99/5.
33. Stoler, *Allies and Adversaries*, p. 41.
34. Anglo-American Liaison, CAB 99/9.
35. Between May and November 1941, seven 'American Liaison' meetings (as they were called) took place. Those with time to kill can consult them in CAB 99/9. There is no indication that Marshall ever saw the minutes of these meetings.
36. *Lee Journal* should be consulted on Roosevelt's chaotic approach to administration. See entries for June and July 1941 in particular.
37. Roosevelt Note, January 1941 in Robert E. Sherwood (ed.), *The White House Papers of Harry L. Hopkins, Volume 1, September 1939–January 1942* (London: Eyre & Spottiswoode, 1948), p. 233.
38. Hopkins to Roosevelt 10/1/1941, in ibid, p. 239.
39. Colville Diary 30/8/1940 in John Colville, *The Fringes of Power: Downing Street Diaries 1939–1955* (London: Weidenfeld & Nicolson, 1985), p. 434.
40. See Churchill to Attlee 11/8/1941 giving the text of the charter, Prem 3/485/1.
41. See the minutes of the various meetings, CAB 99/18.
42. Churchill to Pierre Dupuy 23/12/1940, in Gilbert (ed.), *Churchill War Papers, Vol. 2*, pp. 1280–1.
43. Churchill to Auchinleck 16/10/1941, Chartwell 20/20.
44. Churchill to Ismay 28/10/1941, Chartwell 20/44.
45. COS Minutes 11/11/1941, CAB 79/15/29.
46. COS Minutes 13/11/1941, CAB 79/15/36. Note by the Joint Planners.
47. Ibid.
48. Churchill, 'Memorandum on the Conduct of the War: Part 1 – The Atlantic Front' 16/12/1941, CAB 69/4.
49. Ibid.
50. COS, 'Anglo-American Strategy' 22/12/1941, CAB 99/17.
51. Ibid.

52. *Brooke Diary* 20/12/1941, p. 213.
53. Churchill to the War Cabinet and COS 23/12/1941, Chartwell 20/50.
54. Ibid.
55. Minutes of Anglo-American COS Meeting 24/12/1941, CAB 99/17.
56. See Alex Danchev, *Establishing the Anglo-American Alliance: From the Second World War Diaries of Brigadier Vivian Dykes* (London: Brassey, 1990) (hereafter *Dykes Diary*), pp. 77-8. Dykes was a member of the British Joint Planning Staff. His diaries are essential reading on the Washington Conference.
57. Combined Chiefs of Staff and Advisors meeting 27/12/1941, CAB 99/17.
58. *Dykes Diary* 4/1/1942, p. 84.
59. See Dykes despairing diary entry of 14/1/1942 and the British COS meeting on the same day, CAB 99/17.
60. Washington War Conference Report January 1942, CAB 99/17.
61. Minutes of the CCS 23/3/1942, CAB 88/1.
62. Minutes of the CCs 17/2/1942, ibid.
63. Minutes of the CCS 7/3/1942, ibid.
64. Larry Bland and Sharon Stevens (eds), *The Papers of George Catlett Marshall, Volume 3, 'The Right Man for the Job', December 7, 1941-May 31, 1943* (Baltimore: Johns Hopkins University Press, 1991), p. 157.
65. See Eisenhower to Marshall 25/3/1942 in Alfred Chandler (ed.), *The Papers of Dwight David Eisenhower: The War Years, Vol. 1* (Baltimore: Johns Hopkins University Press, 1970), pp. 205-7, and Maurice Matloff and Edwin M. Snell, *Strategic Planning for Coalition Warfare 1941-1942* (Washington: Government Printing Office, 1953), pp. 183-7.
66. *Brooke Diary* 28/3/1942, p. 242.
67. Ibid 29/3/1942, p. 243.
68. COS Minutes 8/4/1942 Confidential Annex, CAB 79/56/21. It is worth repeating that the numbering system used by TNA can be misleading. This meeting is a continuation of the same meeting indexed under CAB 79/20/9. The 'Confidential Annexes' had a smaller distribution list than the main meetings.
69. COS Minutes 8/4/1942, CAB 79/56/21.
70. Ibid. Emphasis added.
71. Ibid. Emphasis added.
72. Ibid.
73. *Brooke Diary*, notes on 9/4/1942, p. 246. His other comment that Marshall did not impress him 'by the ability of his brain' probably arose from Marshall's response to him at the 9 April meeting.
74. COS Minutes 10/4/1942, CAB 79/56/24.
75. COS Minutes 14/4/1942, CAB 79/56/25.
76. Defence Committee (Operations) Minutes 14/4/1942, CAB 69/4.
77. All reference to this meeting come from ibid.
78. Marshall to Stimson 15/4/1942, in Bland and Stevens (eds), *Marshall Papers, Vol. 3*, p. 162.
79. Harriman's recollection is quoted in Martin Gilbert (ed.), *The Churchill Documents, Volume 17, 1942* (Hillsdale, MI: Hillsdale College, 2014), p. 545. Here a note of clarification is necessary. The first three volumes of the Churchill War Papers were originally published by Heinemann in London. Publication was then taken over (after a long interval) by Hillsdale College in the US. Hillsdale republished all the Churchill documents originally published in Britain but with their own numbering sequence, hence the 1942 volume being Volume 17 instead of, by the previous British system, being Volume 4. They also renamed the series from Churchill War Papers to Churchill Documents. The Hillsdale numbering system will be used from here on.
80. COS Minutes 5/5/1942, CAB 79/56/36.
81. COS Minutes 7/5/1942, CAB 79/56/38.

82. War Cabinet Papers, Aide Memoire 10/6/1942, CAB 66/25.

83. Roosevelt to Churchill 31/5/1942, Kimball, *Churchill and Roosevelt Correspondence*, *Vol. 1*, p. 503.

84. See COS Minutes 5/5/1942, CAB 79/56/36; and Churchill to Ismay 9/6/1942, Chartwell 20/67.

85. Mountbatten Report to Roosevelt and Churchill, quoted in Sherwood (ed.), *White House Papers of Harry Hopkins, Vol. 1*, pp. 587–8.

86. Churchill to Roosevelt 13 6/1942, Chartwell 20/76.

87. CCS Meeting 12.30 p.m. 19 June and informal meeting at 2 p.m. 19 June, CAB 99/20.

88. CCS Meeting 20/6/1942, CAB 99/20.

89. Churchill to Roosevelt 20/6/1942, Kimball (ed.), *Churchill and Roosevelt Correspondence*, *Vol. 1*, p. 515.

90. Ibid.

91. See the editors' notes in Bland and Stevens (eds), *Marshall Papers, Vol. 3*, p. 243.

92. COS Minutes 8/7/1942, CAB 79/56/69; Note to the Prime Minister 7/7/1942, War Cabinet Minutes 8/7/1942, CAB 65/31/2.

93. War Cabinet Minutes 8/7/1942, CAB 65/31/2.

94. Churchill to Roosevelt 8/7/1942, Kimball (ed.), *Churchill and Roosevelt Correspondence*, *Vol. 1*, p. 520–1; *Dykes Diary* 10/7/1942, p. 166.

95. Marshall to Roosevelt 10/7/1942, Bland and Stevens (eds), *Marshall Papers, Vol. 3*, p. 271.

96. Roosevelt to Marshall 10/7/1942, in ibid, p. 272.

97. Roosevelt to Marshall 15/7/1942, in ibid, p. 277.

98. 'Conclusions as to Practicability of Sledgehammer' 17/7/1942, in Chandler (ed.), *Eisenhower Papers: The War Years, Vol. 1*, pp. 388–90.

99. Ibid, p. 389.

100. *Brooke Diary* 20/7/1942, p. 282. Note that these discussions were held 'off the record' so there are no official minutes of them. It seems, however, that they proceeded much as Brooke has described.

101. The debate can be followed in *Brooke's Diary* from 20 to 23 July.

102. Ibid 23/7/1942, p. 284.

103. CCS Minutes 24/7/1942, CAB 99/21.

104. *Dykes Diary* 22/7/1942, p. 178.

105. Hopkins to Roosevelt 24/7/1942, in Sherwood (ed.), *White House Papers of Harry Hopkins, Vol. 2*, p. 611.

106. *Dykes Diary* 31/7/1942, p. 184.

18. Singapore

1. Corelli Barnett, *Engage the Enemy More Closely: The Royal Navy in the Second World War* (London: Hodder & Stoughton, 1991), pp. 60–1.

2. COS, 'Immediate Measures Required in the Far East', 25/6/1940, CAB 66/9/2.

3. War Cabinet Confidential Annex 8/8/1940, CAB 65/14.

4. Churchill statement, COS Minutes 19/9/1940, CAB 79/6/67; Pound Statement in the same meeting.

5. Butler, *Grand Strategy, Vol. 2*, pp. 339–40.

6. C-in-Cs Singapore, 'Tactical Appreciation of Defence Situation in Malaya', CAB 80/22.

7. 'Reinforcements – Malaya', Note by the CIGS, CAB 80/22.

8. Defence Committee (operations) Minutes 9/4/1941, CAB 69/2.

9. Joint Intelligence Committee, 'Future Strategy of Japan'. See COS Minutes 3/5/1941, CAB 79/11/19; Joint Planners, 'Situation in the Mediterranean and the Middle East'. See COS Minutes 10/5/1941, CAB 79/11/33.

10. Churchill to COS 16/7/1941, Chartwell 20/36.

11. Churchill Broadcast 22/6/1941, in Gilbert (ed.), *Churchill War Papers, Vol. 3*, p. 837.
12. COS Draft Note to the Prime Minister 27/8/1941, CAB 79/14/1.
13. J.M.A. Gwyer, *Grand Strategy, Volume 3, Part 1* (London: HMSO, 1964), p. 134.
14. 'Record of Conversations Between the Prime Minister and the President' 11/8/1941, Prem 3/485/5.
15. Churchill to Attlee 12/8/1941, Chartwell 20/48.
16. Churchill to Menzies 15/8/1941, Chartwell 20/49.
17. Ibid.
18. Gwyer, *Grand Strategy, Vol. 3, Part 1*, p. 137.
19. COS Minutes 19/9/1941, CAB 79/14/23.
20. Churchill to Pound and A.V. Alexander 25/8/1941, Chartwell 20/36.
21. Defence Committee (Operations) Minutes 17/10/1941, CAB 69/2.
22. Raymond Callahan, *The Worst Disaster: The Fall of Singapore* (Newark: University of Delaware Press, 1977), p. 157.
23. War Cabinet Minutes Confidential Annex 12/11/1941, CAB 65/24/4.
24. Ibid.
25. Halifax to the Foreign Office 1/12/1941, Prem 3/156/5.
26. See the cables in ibid.
27. COS Minutes 8/12/1941, CAB 79/16/12.
28. Churchill to Curtin 15/12/1941, Chartwell 20/47; COS Minutes 26/12/1941, 'Reinforcements for the Far East – Summary of Recommendations', CAB 79/16/35.
29. COS Minutes 13/12/1941, CAB 79/16/21.
30. Graham Freudenberg, *Churchill and Australia* (Sydney: Macmillan, 2008), p. 335. It is notable that this document is not to be found in the published Churchill War Papers.
31. See Defence Committee (Operations) Minutes for those dates in CAB 69/2.
32. Churchill to Curtin 27/12/1941, Chartwell 20/47. The document quoted by Freudenberg in his *Churchill and Australia* is dated 25 December. They are, however, the same document.
33. Churchill, 'Memorandum on the Conduct of the War: Part II – The Pacific Front' 17/12/1941, Defence Committee (Operations) Minutes, CAB 69/4.
34. *Brooke Diary* 15/12/1941, p. 211.
35. COS Minutes 15/12/1941, CAB 79/16/22.
36. *Brooke Diary* 17/12/1941, p. 212.
37. Churchill to Clementine Churchill 21/12/1941, in Gilbert (ed.), *Churchill War Papers, Vol. 3*, p. 1663.
38. Churchill, Press Conference 23/12/1941, in ibid, pp. 1669–70.
39. Churchill to Wavell 14/1/1942, Chartwell 20/88.
40. Wavell to Churchill 16/2/1941, in Callahan, *Worst Disaster*, p. 235.
41. Ibid.
42. Churchill to Ismay for COS 19/1/1942, Chartwell 20/67.
43. Churchill to Ismay 21/1/1942, Chartwell 20/67.
44. Defence Committee (Operations) Minutes 21/1/1942, CAB 69/4.
45. Ibid.
46. *Brooke Diary* 19/12/1941, p. 212.
47. Curtin to Churchill 23/1/1942, quoted in Freudenberg, *Churchill and Australia*, p. 365. Curtin, who had not been well and was recuperating in Perth, did not in fact write the telegram. It was sent out under his name by the Cabinet.
48. Major-General S. Woodburn Kirby, *The War against Japan, Volume 1: The Loss of Singapore* (Uckfield: Naval and Military Press, 2016), pp. 162–3. Reprint of the 1957 edition.
49. Ibid, Appendix 10, pp. 512–13.
50. Brooke-Popham to the COS, 'The Defence of Singapore' 26/10/1940, CAB 80/21.
51. Kirby, *Loss of Singapore*, p. 180.

52. For Matador see Brian P. Farrell, *The Defence and Fall of Singapore 1940–1942* (Stroud: Tempus, 2006), ch. 4.

53. Roskill, *War at Sea, Vol. 1*, pp. 564–7.

54. Alan Warren, *Singapore 1942* (Singapore: Talisman, 2002), pp. 143–5.

55. Ibid, pp. 148–50.

56. Churchill to Curtin 15/12/1941, Chartwell 20/47.

57. Churchill to Wavell 28/12/1941, Chartwell 20/47.

58. Churchill to W.M. Hughes 29/12/1941, ibid.

59. Callahan, *Worst Disaster*, p. 254.

60. Brigade War Diary 15/1/1942, AWM 52/8/2/27.

61. Division War Diary 16/1/1942, AWM 52/1/5/17.

62. Division War Diary 21/1/1942, AWM 52/1/5/17; 'Actions of the 53rd Brigade Jan 20/22', in Appendix to 8 Division War Diary.

63. Kirby, *Loss of Singapore*, pp. 338–9.

64. Ibid, pp. 375 and 382.

65. See K. Hack and K. Blackburn, *Did Singapore Have to Fall?: Churchill and the Impregnable Fortress* (London: Routledge, 2004), ch. 5 for a gun-by-gun analysis of the fortress guns. It is a great piece of detective work.

66. Kirby, *Loss of Singapore*, p. 360.

67. Hack and Blackburn, *Did Singapore Have to Fall?*, Appendix A, pp. 190–1.

68. Kirby, *Loss of Singapore*, pp. 411–13.

69. Brigade War Diary 9 and 10/2/1942, AWM 52/8/2/27.

70. Ibid.

71. Churchill to Wavell 10/2/1942, Chartwell 20/70.

72. Churchill to Wavell 14/2/1942, ibid.

19. The Desert – Montgomery's War 1942–1943

1. Churchill to Auchinleck 24/6/1942, CAB 120/629.

2. *Brooke Diary* 9/7/1942, p. 278.

3. Brooke, notes on diary entry 15/7/1942, p. 280.

4. Ibid.

5. Ibid 30/7/1942, p. 287.

6. Ibid 3/8/1942, pp. 289–90.

7. See Bidwell and Graham, *Firepower*, pp. 244–5 for an admirable summing up of Gott's strengths and weaknesses.

8. Australian Division at El Alamein, WO 201/2495.

9. Montgomery Notes 13/8/1942, Montgomery Papers BLM 27/1, Australian Defence Academy Library.

10. Ibid.

11. 'Address to Officers – Eighth Army 13/8/1942', Montgomery Papers BLM 1/92.

12. Armoured Division at Alam Halfa, WO 201/653.

13. Nigel Hamilton, *Monty: Life of Montgomery of Alamein, Volume 1, The Making of a General 1887–1942* (London: Hamish Hamilton, 1981), p. 680.

14. Lightfoot – General Plan of the Eighth Army, Montgomery Papers BLM 28/3.

15. Ibid.

16. I.S.O. Playfair, The *Mediterranean and Middle East Volume 4* (Uckfield: Naval and Military Press, 2016), p. 29. Reprint of 1966 edition.

17. Ibid.

18. Brigadier Sidney Kirkman, 'RA Notes on the Offensive by Eighth Army from 23 Oct–4 Nov on the El Alamein Position', WO 201/555. For more on the origin of 'stonk' see Barr, *Pendulum of War*, pp. 292–3.

19. Ibid.

20. Kirkman interview in Nigel Hamilton, *Monty: Life of Montgomery of Alamein, Volume 2, Master of the Battlefield 1942–44* (London: Hamish Hamilton, 1983), pp. 749–50.
21. Kirkman, 'RA Notes on Alamein'.
22. Sir Francis de Guingand, *Operation Victory* (London: Hodder & Stoughton, 1953), p. 200.
23. Hamilton, *Monty, Vol. 1*, pp. 752–3.
24. 'Lightfoot' – Memorandum No. 2 by Army Commander, 6 October 1942, Montgomery Papers BLM 28/5.
25. Ibid.
26. Ibid.
27. Hinsley, *British Intelligence, Vol. 2*, p. 431.
28. Eighth Army Training Memorandum No. 1, quoted in Hamilton, *Monty, Vol. 1*, pp. 721–3.
29. Fennell, *Fighting the People's War*, ch. 7. This should be read as an extensive discussion of the impact Montgomery had on the Eighth Army.
30. Pitt, *Year of Alamein 1942*, p. 285; Barr, *Pendulum of War*, p. 276.
31. These statistics and those that follow are taken from Barr, *Pendulum of War*, p. 276.
32. Counter-Battery at El Alamein, WO 201/2821.
33. Pitt, *Year of Alamein 1942*, p. 297.
34. Australian Infantry Brigade, 'Resume of Ops EL ALAMEIN 23 Oct–5 Nov 42', AWM 52/8/2/20/56.
35. Australian Brigade, Operation Lightfoot, WO 201/652.
36. Brigade, 'Resume'.
37. New Zealand Division in Egypt and Libya, 'Lightfoot and Supercharge', WO 201/654. This account was apparently written by Freyberg.
38. Playfair, *Mediterranean, Vol. 4*, p. 38.
39. New Zealand Division, 'Lightfoot and Supercharge', WO 201/654.
40. Armoured Division, 'Lightfoot and Supercharge', WO 201/653.
41. Ibid.
42. Armoured, 'Lightfoot and Supercharge'. The conversation took place between 3.50 a.m. and 4.20 a.m.
43. X Corps and New Zealand Division at El Alamein, WO 201/437. 'Not' is in capitals in the original.
44. Armoured, 'Lightfoot and Supercharge'. Their artillery, lent to XXX Corps for the opening bombardment, was back under X Corps control by at least 8 a.m.
45. Brigade, 'Resume'. All abbreviations have been expanded.
46. Barr, *Pendulum of War*, p. 329. Barr has an extended discussion of this egregious error.
47. Brigade 'Resume'.
48. Ibid.
49. Montgomery Notes 24/10/1942, Montgomery Papers BLM 28/1.
50. Ibid.
51. X Corps War Diary 24/10/1942 quoted in Hamilton, *Monty, Vol. 1*, p. 784.
52. Hamilton, *Monty, Vol. 1*, pp. 804–5.
53. Australian Division at El Alamein.
54. Churchill to Alexander 23/9/1942, Chartwell 20/80.
55. Churchill to Brooke 28/10/1942, Chartwell 20/67.
56. Churchill to Alexander 29/10/1942, Chartwell 20/81.
57. Hamilton, *Monty, Vol. 1*, pp. 824–5.
58. This whole issue is discussed at length in Hamilton, *Monty, Vol. 1*, pp. 827–9.
59. Montgomery Diary 28/10/1942, Montgomery Papers BLM 28/1.
60. Barr, *Pendulum of War*, p. 364 has an excellent description of this problem.
61. New Zealand Division, 'Lightfoot and Supercharge', WO 201/654.
62. Ibid.

63. Ibid.
64. The Kings Own Hussars, 'Note on the Action Fought on 2nd November 1942', WO 201/424.
65. Playfair, *Mediterranean, Vol. 4*, p. 66.
66. Hussars, 'Note on 2nd November'.
67. New Zealand Division, 'Lightfoot and Supercharge'.
68. Hussars, 'Note on 2nd November'.
69. New Zealand Division, 'Lightfoot and Supercharge'.

20. The End in Africa

1. See COS Minutes 14/8/1942, Appendix A, CAB 79/57/1.
2. Eisenhower to Marshall 9/8/1942, in Chandler (ed.), *Eisenhower Papers: The War Years, Vol 1*, p. 453.
3. Eisenhower to General Handy (US Operations Division) 13/8/1942, in ibid, pp. 461–2.
4. Ibid.
5. COS Minutes 21/8/1942, CAB 79/57/7.
6. Marshall to Eisenhower 24/8/1942, Bland and Stevens (eds), *Marshall Papers, Vol. 3*, pp. 316–18. See also Michael Howard, *Grand Strategy, Volume IV* (London: HMSO, 1972), p. 124.
7. COS Minutes 23/8/1942, CAB 79/57/9.
8. *Dykes Diary* 25/8/1942, p. 193.
9. Howard, *Grand Strategy, Vol. IV*, p. 125.
10. COS Minutes 26/8/1942, CAB 79/57/13.
11. Churchill to Roosevelt 27/8/1942, Kimball (ed.), *Churchill and Roosevelt Correspondence, Vol. 1*, p. 578.
12. CCS Meeting 28/8/1942, CAB 88/1.
13. COS Minutes 29/8/1942, CAB 79/57/16.
14. Roosevelt to Churchill 30/8/1942, Kimball (ed.), *Churchill and Roosevelt Correspondence, Vol. 1*, pp. 583–4. Kimball is crucial on this because he includes the sections that Roosevelt added to a previous draft.
15. Marshall to Eisenhower 29/8/1942, Bland and Stevens (eds), *Marshall Papers, Vol. 3*, pp. 325–6.
16. Ibid.
17. COS Minutes 31/8/1942, CAB 79/57/18.
18. Churchill to Roosevelt 1/9/1942, Kimball (eds), *Churchill and Roosevelt Correspondence, Vol. 1*, pp. 585–6.
19. See ibid, p. 581 for this vital detail.
20. All this can be found in ibid, pp. 587–92.
21. Keith Sainsbury, *The North African Landings 1942* (London: Davis-Poynter, 1976), pp. 145–8.
22. Rick Atkinson, *An Army at Dawn: The War in North Africa 1942–1943* (London: Little, Brown, 2003), p. 176.
23. See Playfair, *Mediterranean, Vol. 4*, Map 20.
24. General Anderson's Despatch, *London Gazette*, 6/11/1946, pp. 5449–54.
25. Ibid, p. 5463.
26. Ibid.
27. Eisenhower to Churchill 5/12/1942, in Chandler (ed.), *Eisenhower Papers, The War Years, Vol. 2*, pp. 801–4.
28. Anderson Despatch, p. 5455.
29. Montgomery to Brooke 13/12/1942, Montgomery Papers BLM 49/6.
30. Montgomery Diary notes 23 October–7 November 1942, Montgomery Papers BLM 28/1. Jonathan Fennell's work seems to bear out the fact that Montgomery assessment of his army was correct. See *Fighting the People's War*, ch. 7.

31. Eighth Army, 'Advance to Mareth' 27/1/1943, WO 201/592.
32. Anderson Despatch, p. 5456.
33. Hinsley, *British Intelligence, Vol. 2*, pp. 586–7.
34. Playfair, *Mediterranean, Vol. 4*, pp 296–301.
35. Montgomery to Brooke 6/3/1943, in Nigel Hamilton, *Monty, Vol. 2*, pp. 169–70.
36. Montgomery to Brooke 16/2/1943, Alanbrooke Papers, 14/62, Liddell Hart Centre for Military Archives.
37. De Guingand to General Steele [War Office] 28/3/1943, WO 201/627.
38. Interview with de Guingand 22/4/1978, quoted in Hamilton, *Monty, Vol. 2*, p. 193.
39. Ibid, p. 197.
40. Apparently fifty men of the Hermann Goering surrendered and then took up arms again. They were all shot. See Alexander to Churchill 30/4/1943, Chartwell 20/111.
41. Precis of Operations by First Army, WO 201/821; Anderson Despatch, p. 5460.
42. Operations of the First Army and II US Corps in Tunisia, WO 201/822.
43. Playfair, *Mediterranean, Vol. 4*, p. 460.
44. Churchill to Smuts, Chartwell 20/105.
45. Churchill to Eisenhower 13/2/1943, Chartwell 20/106.
46. Churchill to the King 22/2/1943, Chartwell 4/190.
47. Churchill to Hopkins 24/2/1943, Chartwell 20/107.
48. Churchill to Alexander 29/3/1943, Chartwell 20/108.
49. Alexander to Churchill 29/3/1943, ibid.
50. Churchill to Alexander 31/3/1943, Chartwell 20/109.
51. Alexander to Churchill 1/4/1943, Chartwell 20/109.
52. See Alexander's telegram of 2 April giving the state of play in First and Eighth Armies and Montgomery's letter of 6 April giving a detailed account to the Akarit Battle in Chartwell 20/109. There are many other examples.

21. Inching Towards Italy

1. Churchill to Ismay 9/11/1942, Chartwell 20/67.
2. See COS Minutes for 9, 10, 12, 13 and 14/11/1942, CAB 79/28/26–31.
3. COS Minutes 30/11/1942, CAB 79/58/41. This was an ordinary meeting of the COS which Churchill attended. Around this time the Defence Committee (Operations) met less frequently, the Prime Minister instead attending the COS meetings regularly.
4. *Brooke Diary* 30/11/1943, p. 345.
5. COS Minutes 3/12/1942, CAB 79/58/42.
6. Churchill to Roosevelt 24/11/1943, Chartwell 20/54.
7. Roosevelt to Churchill 26/11/1943, ibid.
8. Churchill to Roosevelt 26/11/1943, ibid.
9. COS Minutes 16/12/1943, CAB 79/58/48.
10. Ibid.
11. Churchill to Ismay 27/12/1942, Chartwell 20/67.
12. See the valuable entry in the Jacob Diaries 13/1/1943 in Martin Gilbert and Larry P. Arnn (eds), *The Churchill Documents, Volume 18* (Hillsdale, MI: Hillsdale College, 2015), pp. 102–8; and COS and War Cabinet Meeting 13/1/1943, CAB 99/24.
13. CCS Minutes 16/1/1943, CAB 88/2. Note that the discussions here have been limited mainly to those concerning European strategy. Matters such as submarine policy and operations in the Far East will be dealt with in subsequent chapters.
14. Ibid.
15. Andrew Roberts, *Masters and Commanders: How Four Titans Won the War in the West* (London: Harper, 2010), p. 329.
16. CCS Minutes 18/1/1943, CAB 88/2.
17. The document is to be found in CAB 99/24.

18. The origins of this document are somewhat obscure. Brooke attributes it to Dill, with some input from Portal, but this is in a note written years after his diary – which makes no mention of Dill. See *Brooke Diary* Note 18/1/1943, pp. 362–3. Michael Howard attributes it to Slessor (the British air representative on the CCS but his source is Slessor's memoirs. See Howard, *Grand Strategy, Vol. IV*, p. 251. Roberts, *Masters and Commanders*, p. 335 accepts that it was Dill.
19. Joint Planning Staff, 'Report on Landing Craft' 1/1/1943, in COS Minutes, CAB 79/59/1.
20. COS Minutes 16/1/1943, CAB 99/24.
21. Jacob Diary 18/1/1943, in Gilbert and Arnn (eds), *Churchill Documents, Vol. 18*, p. 149.
22. CCS Minutes 21/1/1943, CAB 88/2.
23. For an excellent study in paranoia see Stoler, *Allies and Adversaries*, ch. 6, 'Britain as Adversary', which delves into the fantasy world of some of the planners in Washington.
24. War Cabinet/COS Meeting 21/1/1943, CAB 99/24.
25. CCS to Eisenhower 23/1/1943, CCS Papers, CAB 88/8.
26. Eisenhower to CCS, in Gilbert and Arnn (eds), *Churchill Documents, Vol. 18*, pp. 407–9.
27. Churchill to Ismay 13/2/1943, in ibid, p. 427.
28. Churchill to Hopkins 13/2/1943, Chartwell 20/106.
29. Eisenhower to Churchill 17/2/1943, in ibid.
30. Churchill to Ismay 19/2/1943, in Gilbert and Arnn (eds), *Churchill Documents, Vol. 18*, p. 477.
31. COS Minutes 22/2/1943, CAB 79/59/26.
32. *Brooke Diary* 18/2/1943, p. 383. It might be noted that this incident took place in the shadow of the American reversal at Kasserine Pass.
33. Eisenhower to CCS and COS 7/4/1943, in Gilbert and Arnn (eds), *Churchill Documents, Vol. 18*, pp. 933–4. This message is headed Bigot-Husky. 'Bigot' indicated that the recipient was privy to the end purpose of the operation. It was used throughout the war. It was a most unfortunate designation.
34. Churchill to COS 8/4/1943, in ibid, pp. 937–8.
35. COS Minutes 8/4/1943, Annex II, CAB 79/60/19.
36. Eisenhower to CCS and COS 12/4/1943, in Chandler (ed.), *Eisenhower Papers, The War Years, Vol. 2*, p. 942.
37. See Churchill to Ismay 4/3/1943; Churchill to Dill 4/3/1943, both in Gilbert and Arnn (eds), *Churchill Documents, Vol. 18*, pp. 561 and 562 respectively.
38. CCS, 'Report to the President and the Prime Minister' 23/1/1943, CAB 99/24.
39. COS Minutes 24/2/1943, CAB 79/59/28.
40. COS Minutes 26/2/1943, CAB 79/59/30.
41. See COS Minutes 11/3/1943, CAB 79/59/41; COS Minutes 10/4/1943, CAB 79/60/20.
42. Churchill to Ismay 2/4/1943, in Gilbert and Arnn (eds), *Churchill Documents, Vol. 18*, pp. 884–6.
43. COS Minutes 13/4/1943, CAB 79/60/24.
44. Churchill to Roosevelt 29/4/1943, Chartwell 20/111.
45. COS Minutes 4/5/1943, CAB 79/60/43.
46. War Cabinet/COS Meeting, CAB 99/22. Note that the minutes of these international conferences are not numbered in the order in which they took place by TNA. Note also that much of this meeting was taken up with discussions about operations in the Far East. These will be dealt with in due course.
47. Trident Meeting 12/5/1943, CAB 99/22. The collapse of Bulgaria had precisely no effect on Germany in 1918. The Kaiser's regime was brought down by major attacks on the Western Front (see Chapter 10). Churchill's was a widely held view at the time, however.
48. Ibid.
49. Ibid.
50. Ibid.
51. CCS Minutes 13/5/1943, CAB 88/2.

52. *Brooke Diary* 13/5/1943, p. 403.
53. CCS Minutes 14/5/1943, CAB 88/2.
54. Ibid.
55. All these arguments can be found in CCS Minutes 15/5/1943, CAB 88/2.
56. *Brooke Diary* 10/5/1943, p. 401. This entry shows that Brooke had been counting US divisions and their destinations.
57. CCS Minutes 19/5/1943 (4.30 p.m.), CAB 88/2.
58. CCS Minutes 24/5/1943, CAB 88/2.
59. There is a useful map giving the outline of the original plan facing p. 17 in Brigadier C.J.C. Moloney, *The Mediterranean and Middle East, Volume V* (London: Naval & Military Press, 2004). The volume is part of the British Official History and was first published in 1973. It is so badly structured that it might have been written by aliens.
60. Montgomery to Alexander 3/4/1943 in Stephen Brooks (ed.), *Montgomery and the Eighth Army: A Selection from the Diaries, Correspondence and Other Papers of Field-Marshal the Viscount Montgomery of Alamein, August 1942 to December 1943* (London: Army Records Society, 1991), p. 191.
61. Montgomery to Alexander 23/4/1943, Montgomery Papers BLM 36/2.
62. Montgomery to Alexander 2/5/1943, Montgomery Papers BLM 64/5.
63. Andrew Roberts, *Churchill* (London: Penguin, 2018), pp. 770–2.
64. Alexander to Churchill 10/7/1943, Chartwell 20/115.
65. General Kirkman, '50 Div Landing in Sicily', in XIII Corps in Sicily, WO 204/10953.
66. Churchill to Tedder 11/7/1943, Chartwell 20/115.
67. Tedder to Churchill 12/7/1943, ibid.
68. Moloney, *Mediterranean, Volume V*, p. 80.
69. Rick Atkinson, *The Day of Battle: The War in Sicily and Italy, 1943–1944* (New York: Henry Holt, 2007), p. 91.
70. It is clear from the Defence files that Churchill received few accounts of the fighting in Sicily and those that he did receive had a very positive gloss. See CAB 120/594 for details.
71. Churchill to Cunningham 15/8/1943, Chartwell 20/117.
72. Cunningham to Churchill 15/8/1943, Chartwell 20/117.
73. Carlo D'Este, *Bitter Victory: The Battle for Sicily 1943* (London: Collins, 1988), pp. 514–15. This is the most thorough account of the Axis evacuation. I have relied heavily on it.
74. F.H. Hinsley, *British Intelligence in the Second World War, Volume 3, Part 1* (London: HMSO, 1984), p. 96.
75. See ibid, pp. 96–9 for the mass of decrypts indicating evacuation and its progress.
76. Eighth Army, 'Husky Operations', Narrative, 7 August, WO 204/1410.
77. Montgomery Diary 7/8/1943, Montgomery Papers BLM 39/1.
78. D'Este, *Bitter Victory*, p. 502. See also D'Este's detailed map of the straits defences on p. 448.
79. Ibid, p. 535.
80. Stephen Roskill, *The War at Sea, Volume 3, Part 1* (Uckfield: Naval and Military Press, 2004), p. 148. Reprint of 1960 edition. But see also D'Este, *Bitter Victory*, pp. 539–45 for an extensive and excellent discussion.
81. D'Este, *Bitter Victory*, pp. 543–4.
82. Montgomery Diary 7/8/1943, Montgomery Papers BLM 39/1.
83. COS Minutes 31/5/1943, CAB 79/61/15.

22. Pivot of Power – The Mediterranean 1943

1. CCS White House Meeting 25/5/1943, CAB 99/22.
2. COS Minutes 29/5/1943, CAB 99/22.
3. Ibid.

4. Brooke's diary for this period gives no indication of the discussions at Algiers. Brooke seems obviously tired.
5. COS Meeting 31/5/1943, CAB 99/22.
6. 'Background Notes by the Prime Minister and Minister of Defence' 30/5/1943, CAB 99/22.
7. COS Meeting 3/6/1943, CAB 99/22.
8. Churchill to Ismay 13/7/1943, Chartwell 20/104.
9. COS Minutes 20/7/1943, CAB 79/62/33.
10. Brooke's main exposition can be found in CCS Minutes 15/8/1943, CAB 99/23.
11. CCS Minutes 15/8/1943, ibid.
12. *Brooke Diary* 16/8/1943, p. 443.
13. 'Final Report to the President and Prime Minister', 27/8/1943, CAB 99/23. The Americans clearly had their way with spelling.
14. CCS Minutes 23/8/1943, CAB 88/3.
15. CCS Minutes 24/8/1943, CAB 99/23.
16. Ibid.
17. *Brooke Diary* 24/8/1943, pp. 447–8.
18. Moloney, *Mediterranean, Vol. V,* pp. 276–80.
19. Division Operations September 1943–May 1944, WO 204/8248.
20. Atkinson, *Day of Battle,* p. 226.
21. Churchill to Alexander 14/9/1943, Chartwell 20/118.
22. Moloney, *Mediterranean, Vol. V,* p. 318.
23. Division Narrative.
24. Shelford Bidwell and Dominick Graham, *Tug of War: The Battle for Italy, 1943–1945* (London: Hodder and Stoughton, 1986), pp. 92–4. This 'mutiny' is not in the official account. The two historians who recorded it served in the Italian campaign.
25. Moloney, *Mediterranean, Vol. V,* pp. 247–51.
26. Division Operations.
27. Alexander to Brooke 24/9/1943, CAB 120/601.
28. Churchill to Alexander 25/9/1943, CAB 120/601.
29. 'Notes for a Statement on Events in the Mediterranean Since 1 August', CAB 120/601. These notes were compiled by the Ministry of Defence Secretariat in November 1943.
30. Ibid.
31. Ibid; COS Minutes 13/8/1943, CAB 79/63/17.
32. 'Notes on Events in the Mediterranean'.
33. Moloney, *Mediterranean, Vol. V,* p. 538.
34. 'Notes on Events in the Mediterranean'.
35. Churchill to Ismay for COS 29/9/1943, Chartwell 20/104.
36. COS to Eisenhower (repeated Middle East Command and Washington) 1/10/1943, quoted in 'Notes on Events in the Mediterranean'.
37. See Churchill telegrams sent 3/10/1943, in 'Notes on Events in the Mediterranean'.
38. COS Minutes 6/10/1943, CAB 79/65/12.
39. COS Minutes 7/10/1943, CAB 79/65/13.
40. Churchill to Eisenhower 7/10/1943, Chartwell 20/120.
41. Churchill to Roosevelt 7/10/1943, ibid.
42. Roosevelt to Churchill 8/10/1943, ibid.
43. Churchill to Roosevelt 8/10/1943, ibid.
44. Roosevelt to Churchill 9/10/1943, ibid.
45. Eisenhower to Churchill 9/10/1943 and Cunningham to Churchill 9/10/1943, ibid.
46. See COS Minutes 20/9/1943 which contains the JPS Report on the Dardanelles and the COS amendments to it, CAB 79/64/23.
47. See Anthony Rogers, *Churchill's Folly: Leros and the Aegean: The Last Great British Defeat of World War II* (Athens: Iolkos, 2007).
48. *Brooke Diary* 7 and 8/10/1943, pp. 458 and 459.

NOTES TO PAGES 515-527

49. Casey to Churchill 23/9/1943, Chartwell 20/118.
50. See COS Minutes 30/9/1943, CAB 79/65/5, and on 7/10/1943, CAB 79/65/12.
51. COS Minutes 7/10/1943, CAB 79/65/12.
52. Ibid.
53. COS Minutes 20/10/1943, CAB 79/88/27. This is a continuation of the meeting on 20/10/1943 numbered CAB 79/66/10 headed 'Secretary's Standard File' to indicate its limited distribution.
54. *Brooke Diary*, note on entry 8/10/1943, p. 459.
55. COS Minutes 4/8/1943, CAB 79/63/10.
56. Smuts to Churchill 9/9/1943, Chartwell 20/118.
57. Churchill to Smuts 11/9/1943, ibid.
58. King George VI to Churchill 14/10/1943, Chartwell 20/92.
59. Churchill to King George VI 14/10/1943, ibid.
60. Churchill to Hollis for COS 19/10/1943, Chartwell 20/104.
61. *Brooke Diary* 19/10/1943, p. 461.
62. COS Minutes 79/66/11. Clearly this is not an ordinary COS meeting but it is filed with their minutes in TNA. All previous references are to this meeting. Emphasis added.
63. Ibid.
64. Churchill to Roosevelt 23/10/1943, Chartwell 20/122.
65. Alexander to COS 25/10/1943, CAB 120/601; Eisenhower to CCS and COS 25/10/1943, CAB 120/601. For Enigma see Hinsley, *British Intelligence, Vol. 3, Part 1*, pp. 173-4.
66. Eisenhower to CCS and COS 25/10/1943, CAB 120/601.
67. Churchill to Roosevelt 26/10/1943, Chartwell 20/122.
68. COS to Dill 26/10/1943. The telegram is to be found in the War Cabinet Minutes for that day in CAB 65/40/5.
69. See War Cabinet Minutes 26/10/1943, CAB 65/40/5.
70. *Cadogan Diary* 26/10/1943, pp. 570-1.
71. Eisenhower to CCS 31/10/1943, in Chandler (ed.), *Eisenhower Papers, The War Years, Vol. 3*, pp. 1545-6; John Ehrman, *Grand Strategy, Volume V* (London: HMSO, 1956), p. 74.
72. Halifax to Churchill 30/10/1943, Chartwell 20/122.
73. Eden to Churchill 22/10/1943, Chartwell 20/121.
74. Churchill to Eden 25/10/1943, CAB 120/601.
75. Eden to Churchill 28/10/1943, Chartwell 20/122.
76. Churchill to Eden 29/10/1943, ibid.

23. Rock and a Hard Place – Italy 1943-1944

1. Roosevelt to Churchill 11/11/1943, in Warren Kimball (ed.), *Churchill and Roosevelt: The Complete Correspondence, Vol. 2 Alliance Forged* (Princeton: Princeton University Press, 1984), p. 597. See this volume for the extensive interchange of letters between Churchill and Roosevelt about this meeting. Kimball's notes on the letters are well worth reading.
2. Churchill, Draft Memorandum for the COS 20/11/1943, Chartwell 23/11.
3. COS Committee Minutes 22/11/1943, CAB 99/25.
4. Ibid; *Brooke Diary* 24/11/1943, p. 480.
5. *Brooke Diary* 26/11/1943, p. 481; Minutes of CCS (Cairo) 26/11/1943, CAB 99/25.
6. Tehran Conference, Eureka, First Meeting 28/11/1943, CAB 99/25.
7. Ibid.
8. Ibid.
9. Minutes of Eureka Meeting 29/11/1943, CAB 99/25.
10. Ibid.
11. CCS Minutes 7/12/1943, CAB 99/25.; Ehrman, *Grand Strategy, Vol. V*, pp. 200-1.

12. Montgomery to Mountbatten 24/12/1943, Brooks, *Montgomery and the Eighth Army*, p. 348.
13. Montgomery Diary 27/10/1943, Montgomery Papers BLM 46/1.
14. *Brooke Diary* 14/12/1943, p. 499.
15. Ibid 15/12/1943, p. 500.
16. Ibid 18/12/1943, p. 502.
17. *Brooke Diary* notes 20/12/1943, p. 503.
18. Churchill to Ismay for COS 19/12/1943, Chartwell 20/130.
19. COS to Churchill 23/12/1943, CAB 120/127.
20. COS to Churchill 24/12/1943, CAB 120/127.
21. Churchill to COS 25/12/1943, Chartwell 20/130.
22. Churchill to COS 6/1/1944, Chartwell 20/179.
23. Bidwell and Graham, *Tug of War*, p. 139.
24. Ibid, p. 141.
25. The correspondence can be found in CAB 120/602.
26. Wilson to Churchill 7/2/1944, CAB 120/602.
27. See for example Churchill to Brooke 4/3/1943, Chartwell 20/152.
28. Churchill to Wilson 10/2/1943, Chartwell 20/156.
29. Bidwell and Graham, *Tug of War*, pp. 149–50.
30. Hinsley, *British Intelligence, Vol. 3, Part 1*, p. 191.
31. See 1 Division at Anzio, WO 204/8239.
32. Alexander to Brooke 16/2/1944, CAB 120/602.
33. There is a good summary of Harding's plan in Bidwell and Graham, *Tug of War*, ch. 15.
34. 'Cassino', various papers on the battle in the Kirkman Papers, Liddell Hart Centre for Military Archives. See Appendix C for gun statistics.
35. Ibid. See maps for German artillery numbers.
36. C.J.C. Moloney, *The Mediterranean and Middle East, Volume VI, Part I* (Uckfield: Naval and Military Press, 2009), p. 68. Reprint of the 1973 edition.
37. See the lecture by Brigadier Siggers and General Kirkman in the Kirkman Papers. Siggers was in charge of the British artillery during Diadem, Kirkman was commander of XIII Corps.
38. Moloney, *Mediterranean, Volume VI, Part I*, p. 99.
39. Kirkman and Siggers lecture, 'Cassino', Kirkman Papers.
40. See 'One More River: The Story of the 8th Indian Division', Kirkman Papers 32.
41. FFR (Frontier Force Regiment), 'Story of the Gustav Line Battle', WO 204/8305.
42. 'Narrative of the Attack on S. Angelo Village by 1/5 Gurkha Rifles on 12/13/May 1944', WO 204/8305.
43. Janusz Piekalkiewicz, *Cassino: Anatomy of the battle* (London: Orbis, 1980), pp. 172–3.
44. 'Operations of 2 Polish Corps Against the High Ground Monte Cassino May 1944', WO 204/8221.
45. Ibid, section on the second attack.
46. Ibid.
47. Ibid.
48. Churchill to Alexander 17/5/1944, Chartwell 20/164.
49. Moloney, *Mediterranean, Volume VI, Part I*, p. 193.
50. Canadian Division Report, WO 204/8202.
51. Churchill to Alexander 28/5/1944, Chartwell 20/165.
52. Bidwell and Graham, *Tug of War*, p. 336.
53. COS Minutes 22/3/1944, CAB 79/72/5.
54. Ibid.
55. Churchill to Ismay for COS 5/6/1943, Chartwell 20/152.
56. COS Minutes Annex 7/6/1943, CAB 79/75/14.

57. These minutes of the CCS represent a difficulty. The British took no detailed minutes so it is not possible to follow the direction of debate from their records. See, for example, CCS Minutes 10/6/1944, CAB 88/4. The Americans also said they took no detailed minutes but for some meetings they did. These are filed out of order in CCS Minutes, CAB 88/4. The minutes for 11 and 13 June are filed after the minutes of 16 June.

58. This meeting is headed 'War Cabinet: Chiefs of Staff Committee' 21/6/1944, CAB 79/76/13.

59. Ibid.

60. *Brooke Diary* 21/6/1944, p. 561.

61. War Cabinet, Chiefs of Staffs Committee 22/6/1944, CAB 79/76/14. Note that no members of the War Cabinet were present at this meeting, which consisted of the COS and military advisers only.

62. COS Minutes 26/6/1944, CAB 79/76/19.

63. COS for Joint Staff Mission Washington for the US JCS 26/6/1944, Martin Gilbert and Larry Arnn (eds), *Churchill Documents, Volume 20* (Hillsdale, MI: Hillsdale College, 2018), pp. 609–11.

64. JCS to COS 24/6/1944, in ibid, p. 593.

65. JCS to COS 27/6/1944, in ibid, pp. 619–20.

66. *Brooke Diary* 27/6/1944, p. 563.

67. British Chiefs of Staff Memorandum 28/6/1944, in Gilbert and Arnn (eds), *Churchill Documents, Vol. 20*, pp. 635–7.

68. Churchill to Roosevelt 28/6/1944, Chartwell 20/167.

69. 'Operations in the European Theatre: Note by the Prime Minister and Minister of Defence', ibid.

70. Roosevelt to Churchill 28/6/1944, in Gilbert and Arnn (eds), *Churchill Documents, Vol. 20*, p. 643.

71. CCS Minutes 29/6/1944, CAB 88/4

72. COS Minutes 30/6/1944, CAB 79/76/24.

73. Churchill to Roosevelt 30/6/1944, in Gilbert and Arnn (eds), *Churchill Documents, Vol. 20*, pp. 661–2.

74. Annex to COS Minutes 30/6/1944, CAB 79/77/1.

75. *Brooke Diary* 30/6/1944, p. 565.

76. *Brooke Diary* 4/8/1944, p. 577.

77. Eisenhower to Marshall 5/8/1944, in Chandler (ed.), *Eisenhower Papers: The War Years, Vol. 4*, p. 2055.

78. Ibid.

79. Churchill to Roosevelt 4/8/1944, Chartwell 20/169.

80. British COS to Joint Staff Mission 5/8/1944, in Gilbert and Arnn (eds), *Churchill Documents, Vol. 20*, p. 982.

81. Joint Staff Mission to British COS 5/8/1944, in ibid, pp. 986–7.

82. Churchill to Hopkins 6/8/1944, Chartwell 20/169.

83. Hopkins to Churchill 7/8/1944 in ibid.

84. Harry Butcher, *My Three Years with Eisenhower* (New York: Simon and Schuster, 1946), p. 635.

85. Roosevelt to Churchill 8/8/1944, Chartwell 20/169.

86. *Brooke Diary* 11/4/1944, p. 529 and 21/10/1944, p. 613.

24. The Weight of the War – The Strategic Bombing of Germany

1. War Cabinet Confidential Annex 12/5/1940, CAB 65/13

2. Max Hastings, *Bomber Command* (London: Michael Joseph, 1979), p. 56.

3. Ibid, pp. 355–8.

4. Sir Charles Webster and Noble Frankland, *The Strategic Air Offensive against Germany 1939-1945, Vol. 1* (Uckfield: Naval and Military Press, 2006), pp. 110–12. This is a reprint of the 1961 edition of the Official History.
5. Ibid, p. 209.
6. Webster and Frankland, *Strategic Air Offensive, Vol. 4, Annexes and Appendices*, Director of Plans (Slessor) to C-in-C Bomber Command (Portal) 13/4/1940, pp. 109–10.
7. Middlebrook and Everitt, *The Bomber Command War Diaries*, p. 43. This is a reprint of the 1985 edition.
8. Operations 27/28 May, quoted in ibid, p. 47.
9. Ibid, p. 55. The figures are approximate because the war diaries as produced often include sorties flown over France in the totals. A sortie is one flight by one aircraft in one day.
10. Ibid, pp. 76–7.
11. Churchill to Lindemann 29/6/1940, Chartwell 20/13.
12. Churchill memorandum, 'The Munitions Situation', 3/9/1940, CAB 66/11.
13. COS Minutes 31/8/1940, CAB 79/6/39.
14. General Ismay, Recollection, Chartwell 4/198, in Gilbert (ed.), *Churchill War Papers, Vol. 2*, p. 789.
15. Churchill Broadcast 11/9/1940, in James (ed.), *Complete Speeches, Volume VI*, pp. 6275–7.
16. Churchill to Ismay 19/9/1940, CAB 120/300.
17. Defence Committee (Operations) Minutes 24/9/1940, CAB 69/1.
18. Churchill to Portal 17/11/1940, Chartwell 20/13.
19. M.M. Postan, *British War Production* (London: HMSO, 1952), p. 125 and Appendix 4, 'Deliveries of New Aircraft in the United Kingdom by Main Groups 1938-1944', p. 484.
20. These directives can be read in Webster and Frankland, *Strategic Air Offensive, Vol. 4*, pp. 123–33.
21. Middlebrook and Everitt, *Bomber Command War Diaries*, pp. 91, 122, 130.
22. This story is taken from the excellent book by Patrick Bishop, *Bomber Boys* (London: Harper, 2008), pp. 69–70.
23. Middlebrook and Everitt, *Bomber Command War Diaries*, p. 90.
24. See speech 19/5/1940 in Gilbert (ed.), *Churchill War Papers, Vol. 2*, p. 87.
25. Churchill to Ismay 15/7/1940, CAB 120/300.
26. Churchill to the Secretary of State for Air (Sinclair) 23/9/1940, CAB 120/300.
27. Churchill to Sinclair 31/12/1940, CAB 120/300.
28. War Cabinet Conclusions 30/10/1940, CAB 65/9/42. Emphasis added.
29. Churchill to Sinclair 15/11/1940, CAB 120/300.
30. I have not been able to establish why Churchill was absent from this vital meeting.
31. War Cabinet Confidential Annex 12/12/1940, CAB 65/16. Portal's paper of 7/12/1940 is to be found in CAB 120/300.
32. Ibid.
33. Ibid.
34. Ibid, p. 111.
35. Defence Committee (Operations) 31/1/1941, CAB 69/2.
36. Churchill to Ismay 31/1/1941, CAB 120/300.
37. Portal to Brigadier Jacob 18/2/1941, CAB 120/300.
38. Roskill, *War at Sea, Vol. 1*, Appendix R, p. 618.
39. Webster and Frankland, *Strategic Air Offensive, Vol. 4*, Appendix 8, Air Staff to Peirse 9/3/1941, pp. 133–4.
40. Middlebrook and Everitt, *Bomber Command War Diaries*, p. 131.
41. The sorties against naval targets in western France have been calculated from Middlebrook and Everitt, *Bomber Command War Diaries*, pp. 131–73.
42. Churchill to Portal 7/7/1941, Chartwell 20/36.

43. Churchill to Stalin 7/7/1941 quoted in David Reynolds and Vladimir Pichatrov, *The Kremlin Letters: Stalin's Wartime Correspondence with Churchill and Roosevelt* (London: Yale University Press, 2019), p. 27. Underlining in the original.
44. For the Template see CAB 120/300.
45. Middlebrook and Everitt, *Bomber Command War Diaries*, p. 168.
46. Ibid, p. 196.
47. Ibid, p. 198.
48. Webster and Frankland, *Strategic Air Offensive Vol. 1*, pp. 178–80.
49. Cherwell to the Prime Minister 2/9/1941, CAB 120/300.
50. Churchill Minute 3/9/1941, ibid.
51. Portal to Churchill 11/9/1941, ibid.
52. Chiefs of Staff, 'General Strategy' 31/7/1941, Chief of Staff Minutes, CAB 79/13/18.
53. Portal, 'Development and Employment of the Heavy Bomber Force', 22/9/1941, CAB 120/300.
54. Portal to Churchill 25/9/1941, ibid.
55. Churchill to Portal 27/9/1941, ibid.
56. Portal to Churchill 2/10/1941, ibid.
57. Churchill to Portal 7/10/1941, ibid.
58. These figures come from tables 'Weekly State of the Metropolitan Air Force' for January 1942 and January 1941 in Prem 3/29/3.
59. Churchill to Sinclair, CAS and the Ministry of Aircraft Production 30/12/1940, CAB 120/272.
60. See Churchill to Attlee 7/9/1941, Chartwell 20/36. For a typical discussion in the DC(S) see the minutes 23/10/1941, Prem 3/13/4.
61. Overy, *The Bombing War*, p. 270.
62. Ibid.
63. See the excellent Wikipedia entries for these two aircraft.
64. Postan, *British War Production*, pp. 173–4.
65. Ibid, pp. 226–7.
66. P. Inman, *Labour in the Munitions Industries* (London: HMSO, 1957), p. 5.
67. Postan, *British War Production*, pp. 337–9.
68. Ibid, p. 208. There were many other causes of delays. The Air Staff often made modifications to the original design while the machines were being made, which caused inefficiencies. Factories had been dispersed during the Blitz, which caused inefficiencies. New staff had to be trained and some managers could hardly cope with severe demands made on men with little experience.
69. Central Statistical Office, *Statistical Digest of the War* (London: HMSO, 1951), Table 130, p. 152. The monthly operational strength of Bomber Command can be found in Prem 3/29/3–4.
70. Overy, *Bombing War*, pp. 279–80.
71. Bottomley to Baldwin [acting C-in-C Bomber Command] 14/2/1942, CAB 120/300.
72. Webster and Frankland, *Strategic Air Offensive, Vol. 4*, Annex 1, pp. 4–6.
73. Memo by the First Lord of the Admiralty, A.V. Alexander 14/2/1942, to the Defence Committee (Operations), CAB 69/4.
74. Memo by Pound 6/3/1942, ibid.
75. Roosevelt to Churchill 20/3/1942, CAB 120/300.
76. Roosevelt to Churchill 25/3/1942 and Arnold to Portal 26/3/1942, CAB 120/300.
77. Churchill to Roosevelt 29/3/1942, ibid.
78. Defence Committee (Operations) 18/3/1942, CAB 69/4.
79. Cherwell to Churchill 31/3/1942, CAB 120/300.
80. Churchill note to Portal 31/3/1942, ibid.
81. Portal to Churchill 31/3/1942, ibid.
82. I cannot find a copy of this note anywhere. It is clear from Portal's later reply that Churchill did write such a note.

83. Joint Intelligence Sub-Committee, 'Effect of Bombing Policy' 5/4/1942, CAB 79/20/14.
84. Portal to Churchill 10/4/1942, CAB 120/300. For the cursory discussion of the report see COS Minutes 10/4/1942, CAB 79/20/14.
85. Churchill note on Portal's paper 11/4/1942, CAB 120/300.
86. Justice Singleton, 'The Bombing of Germany', 20/5/1942, CAB 69/4.
87. Churchill to Ismay 7/4/1942, Chartwell 20/67.
88. Middlebrook and Everitt, Bomber Command War Diaries, pp. 251–2, 259 and 260–1.
89. Ibid, p. 260.
90. Portal to Harris 19/5/1942 quoted in Ralph Barker, The Thousand Plan (London: Pan, 1967), pp. 59–60.
91. Ibid, p. 60.
92. Middlebrook and Everitt, Bomber Command War Diaries, pp. 271–2. The authors note that figures for the raid vary according to the source.
93. Ibid, p. 269.
94. Ibid, p. 272.
95. Ibid, chs 11 and 12. Bomber Command also made many more smaller raids. The large ones have been included to indicate where the major effort was made.
96. Overy, Bombing War, p. 191.
97. Air-Vice Marshal D.C.T. Bennett, Pathfinder (London: Panther, 1960), p. 118.
98. Harris to Churchill 28/6/1942, CAB 120/301, Webster and Frankland, Strategic Air Offensive, Vol. 1, p. 342.
99. Churchill Memorandum 21/7/1942, Chartwell 23/10.
100. Webster and Frankland, Strategic Air Offensive, Vol. 1, pp. 366–7.
101. Ibid, p. 371.
102. Brooke Paper 26/12/1942, Prem 3/11/7.
103. See the minutes of the Defence Committee (Operations) 16/11/1942, CAB 69/4, for a good summary of the arguments put by Churchill, Portal and Brooke.
104. Churchill to Ismay 18/11/1942, Chartwell 20/67. Did Harris ever see this note?
105. See chart in Prem 3/27/3.
106. Middlebrook and Everitt, Bomber Command War Diaries, p. 334.
107. Webster and Frankland, Strategic Air Offensive, Vol. 4, pp. 13–14.
108. Air Staff to Harris 14/1/1943, quoted in ibid, pp. 152–3.
109. Sir Arthur Harris, Bomber Offensive (London: Collins, 1947), p. 137.
110. Middlebrook and Everitt, Bomber Command War Diaries, pp. 365–6 and 368.
111. See ibid, chapter on the Battle of the Ruhr.
112. Tooze, Wages of Destruction, p. 597.
113. Ibid, p. 598. Tooze notes the almost wilful insistence of post-war Allied commentators to underestimate the effect of the bombing on the German economy. Both the US and the British Bombing Surveys do this. As analysis both are virtually worthless. They have now been faithfully followed by the German official historians. See Horst Boog, Gerhard Krebs and Detlef Vogel, Germany and the Second World War, Volume VII (Oxford: Clarendon, 2015), pp. 20–2.
114. For an excellent account of this episode, see Martin Middlebrook, The Battle of Hamburg: Allied Bomber Forces against a German City 1943 (London: Allen Lane, 1980).
115. Middlebrook and Everitt, Bomber Command War Diaries, pp. 422–5.
116. Tooze, Wages of Destruction, p. 602.
117. Ibid.
118. Alfred C. Mierzejewski, The Collapse of the German War Economy 1944–1945: Allied Air Power and the German National Railway (Chapel Hill: University of North Carolina Press, 1988), p. 33.
119. Harris, Bomber Offensive, p. 165.
120. Middlebrook and Everitt, Bomber Command War Diaries, p. 409.
121. Harris to Churchill 3/11/1943, CAB 120/301.

122. Portal to VCAS 15/8/1943, quoted in Webster and Frankland, *Strategic Air Offensive, Vol. 2*, p. 312, n. 2.
123. See his note in Prem 3/193/6A on a memo from Desmond Morton to this effect.
124. Middlebrook and Everitt, *Bomber Command War Diaries*, p. 488.
125. Antony Verrier, *The Bomber Offensive* (London: Batsford, 1968), p. 179.
126. Overy, *Bombing War* is excellent on the American air offensive which lays outside the purview of this book.
127. Bottomley and Spaatz to Harris and Eaker 25/9/1944, Webster and Frankland, *Strategic Air Offensive, Vol. 4*, pp. 172–3.
128. Ibid, p. 173.
129. Churchill to Harris 1/10/1944, Prem 3/12.
130. Overy, *Bombing War*, p. 378.
131. Middlebrook and Everitt, *Bomber Command War Diaries*, pp. 606–7.
132. Webster and Frankland, *Strategic Air Offensive, Vol. 4*, pp. 15–17.
133. For the details see Middlebrook and Everitt, *Bomber Command War Diaries*, chs 20 and 21.
134. See ibid, p. 588.
135. Mierzejewski, *Collapse of the German War Economy*, p. 171.
136. See ibid, chapter 8.
137. Roger Beaumont, 'The Bomber Offensive as a Second Front', *Journal of Contemporary History*, vol. 22 (1987), pp. 3–19, p. 15.
138. Overy, *Bombing War*, pp. 406–7.
139. Beaumont, 'Bomber Offensive', p. 15.
140. This section is taken from Frederick Taylor, *Dresden: Tuesday 13 February 1945* (London: Bloomsbury, 2004), ch. 13.
141. Quoted in Christopher C. Harmon, *'Are We Beasts?' Churchill and the Moral Question of World War II 'Area Bombing'*, Newport Papers, no. 1 (Newport, RI: Center for Naval Warfare Studies, 1991), p. 3.
142. See Prem 3/12 for the exchange of letters between Churchill, Ismay and Portal.

25. Battle of the Atlantic

1. These figures come from Clay Blair, *Hitler's U-Boat War: The Hunters, 1939–1945* (London: Weidenfeld and Nicolson, 1997), pp. 424–5.
2. See the Committee Minutes in CAB 86/1 and CAB 86/2.
3. Stephen Roskill, *Naval Policy Between the Wars, Volume II, The Period of Reluctant Disarmament, 1930–1939* (Barnsley: Seaforth, 2016), p. 451. Reprint of the 1976 edition.
4. Churchill to Roosevelt 15/5/1940, in Kimball (ed.), *Churchill and Roosevelt Correspondence, Vol. 1*, p. 37.
5. Roskill, *War at Sea, Vol. 1*, pp. 46 and 134.
6. Churchill to Pound and A.V. Alexander 4/8/1940, Chartwell 20/13.
7. War Cabinet Conclusions 26/8/1940, CAB 65/8.
8. Churchill to Roland Cross (Minister of Shipping) 23/10/1940, Chartwell 20/13.
9. Roskill, *Naval Policy Between the Wars, Vol. II*, p. 226.
10. Roskill, *War at Sea, Vol. 1*, p. 618.
11. Churchill to Pound A.V. Alexander and Ismay 25/2/1941, Chartwell 20/36; Import Executive: Minutes 26/2/1941, in Gilbert (ed.), *Churchill War Papers, Vol. 3*, pp. 266–8.
12. Battle of the Atlantic Committee Minutes 19/3/1941, CAB 86/1.
13. 'The Battle of the Atlantic: Directive by the Minister of Defence' 6/3/1941, Chartwell 23/9.
14. Battle of Atlantic Committee Minutes 19/3/1941, CAB 86/1.
15. Roskill, *War at Sea, Vol. 1*, p. 618.

16. Battle of the Atlantic Committee Minutes 8/5/1941, CAB 86/1.
17. Battle of the Atlantic Committee Minutes 26/3/1941, ibid.
18. Battle of the Atlantic Committee Minutes 22/5/1941, ibid.
19. Battle of the Atlantic Committee Minutes 5/6/1941, ibid.
20. Hansard Secret Session 25/6/1941, in Gilbert (ed.), *Churchill War Papers, Vol. 3*, p. 855.
21. Roskill, *War at Sea, Vol. 1*, p. 618.
22. Niestle, *German U-Boat Losses*, pp. 39 and 41. See also Donald Macintyre's book, *The Battle of the Atlantic* (London: Pan, 1961), pp. 77–9. Macintyre modestly does not identify himself as the captain of the ship that ended the careers of Schepke and Prien.
23. Hinsley, *British Intelligence, Vol. 2*, p. 163.
24. Michael Gannon, *Black May* (London: Aurum, 1998), pp. 52–4.
25. 'The Defeat of the Enemy Attack on Shipping', p. 74.
26. Battle of the Atlantic Committee Minutes 22/10/1941, CAB 86/1.
27. Ibid.
28. 'The Defeat of the Enemy Attack on Shipping', p. 84.
29. Churchill to Hopkins 12/3/1942, Chartwell 20/71.
30. Roosevelt to Churchill 16/3/1942, in Kimball (ed.), *Churchill and Roosevelt Correspondence, Vol. 1*, pp. 407–8.
31. Battle of the Atlantic Committee Minutes 11/2/1942 and 20/5/1942, CAB 86/1.
32. Pound, 'Air Requirements for the Successful Prosecution of the War at Sea' 5/3/1942, Defence Committee Papers, CAB 69/4.
33. Brian Lavery, *Churchill's Navy* (London: Bloomsbury, 2006), p. 187; Battle of the Atlantic Committee Minutes 20/5/1942, CAB 86/1.
34. Blair, *Hitler's U-Boat War: The Hunters*, p. 24.
35. Stephen Roskill, *The War at Sea, Volume 2* (Uckfield: Naval and Military Press, 2004), p. 485. A reprint of the British Official History. Hinsley, *British Intelligence, Vol. 2*, p. 233.
36. Churchill to Cripps 19/11/1942, Chartwell 20/54.
37. Churchill, 'Manpower', paper for the War Cabinet 28/11/1942, Chartwell 23/10.
38. Erin M.K. Weir, 'German Submarine Blockade, Overseas Imports, and British Miliary Production in World War II', Appendix 1, Britain's Wartime Imports by Category 1941–1944, *Journal of Military and Strategic Studies*, vol. 6, no. 1 (2003).
39. See ibid for these measures.
40. Central Statistical Office, *Statistical Digest of the War*, Table 113, Merchant Ships Built in the United Kingdom, p. 135.
41. Roosevelt to Churchill 30/11/1942, in Kimball (ed.), *Churchill and Roosevelt Correspondence, Vol. 2*, p. 44.
42. Ibid, pp. 44–5.
43. Gannon, *Black May*, p. xix.
44. Christopher Bell, 'Air Power and the Battle of the Atlantic: Very Long Range Aircraft and the Delay in Closing the Atlantic "Air Gap"', *Journal of Military History*, vol. 79 (July 2015), p. 712–15 is the last word on this subject.
45. Anti-U-Boat Committee 4/11/1942, CAB 86/2. See also Bell, 'Air Gap', p, 715.
46. Ibid.
47. Ibid.
48. See the desultory discussion of the Anti-U-Boat Committee 18/11/1942, CAB 86/2.
49. Lavery, *Churchill's Navy*, p. 186.
50. Anti-U-Boat Committee Minutes 13/11/1942, CAB 86/2.
51. Ibid. See also Bell, 'Air Gap', p. 716.
52. See Anti-U-Boat Committee Minutes for 25/11, 2/12, 9/12 and 16/12/1942, CAB 86/2.
53. Roskill, *War at Sea, Vol. 2*, pp. 269–70.
54. Anti-U-Boat Committee Minutes 30/12/1942, CAB 86/2.
55. Anti-U-Boat Committee Minutes 6/1/1943, CAB 86/2

56. Clay Blair, *Hitler's U-Boat War: The Hunted, 1942–1945* (London: Weidenfeld and Nicolson, 1999), pp. 132–3; Arnold Hague, *The Allied Convoy System 1939–1943* (Annapolis, MD: National Institution Press, 2000), p. 158.
57. Churchill to the War Cabinet 24/10/1942, Chartwell 23/10.
58. War Cabinet Confidential Annex 11/1/1943, CAB 65/37/1.
59. Ibid.
60. Ibid.
61. Churchill to Eden 9/1/1943, in Gilbert and Arnn (eds), *Churchill Documents, Vol. 18*, p. 79.
62. These figures are taken from Blair, *Hitler's U-Boat War: The Hunted*, Appendix 13, 'Allied Heavy-Bomber Raids on U-Boat Facilities', pp. 804–5.
63. Bell, 'Air Gap', p. 717.
64. CCS Minutes 23/1/1943, CAB 99/24.
65. Ibid.
66. Hansard 11/2/1943, col. 1469.
67. Ibid.
68. This account relies on Hinsley, *British Intelligence, Vol. 2*, pp. 550–61. Hinsley is assiduous in detailing the difficulties for convoys even when Shark was being read.
69. Hinsley, *British Intelligence, Vol. 2*, pp. 554–5.
70. Anti-U-Boat Committee Minutes 27/1/1943, CAB 86/2.
71. Ibid. The Ministry of Aircraft Production were to look into this matter but no report by them ever seems to have been received.
72. Anti-U-Boat Committee Minutes 27/1/1943, CAB 86/2.
73. Anti-U-Boat Committee Minutes 17/2/1943, ibid.
74. Anti-U-Boat Committee Minutes 7/4/1943, ibid.
75. Quoted in Gannon, *Black May*, pp. 254–5.
76. Anti-U-Boat Committee Minutes 17/3/1943, CAB 86/2.
77. Anti-U-Boat Committee Minutes 31/3/1943, ibid.
78. Gannon, *Black May*, pp. 254–7.
79. Roskill, *War at Sea, Vol. 2*, p. 485.
80. Anti-U-Boat Committee Minutes 10/2/1943, CAB 86/2.
81. Anti-U-Boat Committee Minutes 3/3/1943, ibid.
82. Macintyre, *Battle of the Atlantic*, p. 155.
83. Anti-U-Boat Committee Minutes 7/4/1943, CAB 86/2.
84. Anti-U-Boat Committee Minutes 10/3/1943, CAB 86/2.
85. Roskill, *War at Sea, Vol. 2*, pp. 366–7.
86. Bell, 'Air Gap', pp. 706–8. See also Lavery, *Churchill's Navy*, p. 187.
87. The minutes for this committee are littered with references to the new methods of detecting and destroying U-boats. It might be said that never did so many civilians spend so much time in discussing matter, the technical detail of which, they knew nothing.
88. See Evan Mawdsley, *The War for the Seas: A Maritime History of World War II* (London/ New Haven: Yale University Press, 2020), ch. 15 for the gadget war.
89. Ibid, pp. 312–14.
90. The figures have been obtained from uboat.net, where the losses are conveniently grouped by month.
91. Again the figures come from uboat.net and have been cross-checked with Niestle, *German U-Boat Losses*.
92. The convoy codes for these groups are HX, SC, ON, ONS, UC and CU.
93. These figures come from a table in Hinsley, *British Intelligence, Vol. 2*, Appendix 8, p. 680.
94. Bell, 'Air Gap', p. 697.
95. See convoy statistics in Hague, *British Convoy System*.

26. Normandy

1. Leslie Hollis, *War at the Top* (London: Michael Joseph, 1959), pp. 268–9.
2. Montgomery, 'First Impression of Operation Overlord Made at the Request of the Prime Minister', Montgomery Papers BLM 72. After the war Montgomery liked to give the impression that he alone had saved Overlord from a thoroughly bad plan. It is certain, however, that Eisenhower and Beddell Smith were thinking on similar lines. The detail added is pure Montgomery, though.
3. Churchill to Ismay and Bridges 13/1/1944, Chartwell 20/152.
4. Lord Ismay, *Memoirs* (London: Viking, 1960), pp. 345–6.
5. 'Final Minutes of a Meeting Held on Saturday March 25th to Discuss the Bombing Policy in the Period Before Overlord', quoted in W.W. Rostow, *Pre-Invasion Bombing Strategy: General Eisenhower's Decision of March 25, 1944* (Aldershot: Gower, 1981), pp. 88–98.
6. Portal to Churchill 29/3/1944, CAB 120/302.
7. Ismay to Churchill, ibid.
8. Note by Churchill 1/4/1944, in ibid.
9. Portal to Churchill 1/4/1944 and PM's note, in ibid.
10. War Cabinet Minutes 3/4/1944, Confidential Annex, CAB 65/46/1.
11. Churchill to Eisenhower 3/4/1944, CAB 120/303.
12. Eisenhower to Churchill 4/4/1944, ibid.
13. Defence Committee (Operations) Minutes 5/4/1944, CAB 69/6.
14. Ibid.
15. Ibid.
16. Eisenhower, 'Memorandum for Diary 12/4/1944', in Chandler (ed.), *Eisenhower Papers: The War Years, Vol. 3*, pp. 1642–3.
17. Churchill to Portal 12/4/1944, Chartwell 20/152.
18. Defence Committee (Operations) Minutes 19/4/1944, CAB 69/6.
19. 'Reactions to Allied Bombing Offensive on W. Seaboard of Europe', CAB 69/6. These reports were derived from radio monitoring and were delivered to the Defence Committee regularly.
20. Defence Committee (Operations) Minutes 26/4/1944, CAB 69/6.
21. Ibid.
22. War Cabinet Minutes 27/4/1944, CAB 65/42/15.
23. Churchill to Eisenhower 29/4/1944, Chartwell 20/137.
24. War Cabinet Minutes 2/5/1944, CAB 65/46/7.
25. Ibid.
26. Defence Committee (Operations) Minutes 3/5/1944, CAB 69/6.
27. Churchill to Roosevelt 7/5/1944, Chartwell 20/164.
28. Roosevelt to Churchill 11/5/1944, ibid.
29. Churchill to Tedder 29/5/1944, Chartwell 20/152.
30. Churchill to Tedder 10/7/1944, Chartwell 20/153.
31. Rostow, *Pre-Invasion Bombing*, ch. 8, 'How Oil and Bridges Got In'.
32. 'German Rail Movement in France in the First Ten Days after D-Day: An Interim Report by Charles P. Kindleberger, June 16–19, 1944', quoted in ibid, Appendix F.
33. Montgomery Presentation 7/4/1944, Montgomery Papers BLM 74/4.
34. Ibid.
35. Field Marshal Montgomery of Alamein, *Memoirs* (London: Collins, 1958), pp. 211–12.
36. Ibid, p. 212.
37. *Brooke Diary* 15/5/1944, pp. 546–7.
38. Montgomery Address 15/5/1944, in Hamilton, *Monty, Vol. 2*, pp. 587–8.
39. See ibid, pp. 570–1 for this reading of Churchill.
40. I am indebted to Peter Caddick-Adams, *Sand and Steel: A New History of D-Day* (London: Arrow, 2019), ch. 19 for these figures.

41. I Corps, Operation Order No. 1, 5/5/1944, WO 171/258.
42. Army Operational Research Group Report No. 292, 'Comparison of British and American Areas in Normandy in Terms of Fire Support and its Effects', Papers of General Sir E. Barker, IWM.
43. Ibid.
44. Ibid.
45. Narrators' Notebook D, D+1, CAB 106/1137. These notebooks were compiled for the Official Historians and consist of entries taken from the various war diaries of the units involved.
46. Ibid.
47. Narratives 3 British Division, D, D+1, 'The Capture of Hillman By 1 Suffolk on 6 Jun 44', CAB 106/999.
48. Ibid.
49. Ibid.
50. This interpretation has been pieced together from F.H. Hinsley, *British Intelligence in the Second World War, Volume 3, Part 2* (London: HMSO, 1988), pp. 839–42.
51. See German Seventh Army Telephone Log, IWM 973/2, for these movements.
52. Chester Wilmot, *The Struggle for Europe* (London: Collins, 1971), p. 286.
53. Wilmot interview with Brigadier K.P. Smith (185 Brigade), Chester Wilmot Papers, 15/15/34, Liddell Hart Centre for Military Archives.
54. Wilmot, *Struggle for Europe*, p. 284. The word 'almost' could use some interrogation.
55. Canadian Division War Diary June 1944, WO 179/2768.
56. The Canadian action in the days following the landing is well covered by Marc Milner, *Stopping the Panzers* (Lawrence: University of Kansas Press, 2014).
57. Montgomery to Simpson 8/6/1944, Montgomery Papers BLM 94/1.
58. Montgomery to War Office 29/6/1944, Montgomery Papers BLM 110/16.
59. Montgomery to Churchill 1/7/1944, Montgomery Papers BLM 110/17.
60. Montgomery to Eisenhower 25/6/1944, Montgomery Papers BLM 110/13.
61. John Buckley, *Monty's Men: The British Army and the Liberation of Europe* (London/ New Haven: Yale University Press, 2013), pp. 89–90. See also War Diary 176 Brigade 8/7/1944, WO 171/ 698.
62. Lord Tedder, *With Prejudice* (New York: Little Brown, 1966), p. 557; Leigh-Mallory Diary 15/16 July, AIR 37/784.
63. *Brooke Diary* 6/7/1944, p. 566.
64. Churchill to Ismay 13/7/1944, Chartwell 20/153.
65. Churchill to Eisenhower 19/7/1944 [NOT SENT], Chartwell 20/138.
66. Hamilton, *Monty, Volume 2*, p. 738.
67. *Brooke Diary* 19/7/1944, p. 571.
68. See Operational Directive, M512, 21/7/1944, Montgomery Papers BLM 107/14, which contains the gist of what Montgomery told Churchill. The idea that Churchill had Montgomery's letter of resignation in his pocket during this meeting is ludicrous. Churchill was not about to sack his most successful general.
69. See Major L.F. Ellis, *Victory in the West, Volume 1* (London: HMSO, 1962), p. 318 for Charnwood. The figures for Epsom are my own estimates based on the war diaries of most of the units involved.
70. Dempsey Diary 12/7/1944, WO 285/9.
71. Dawnay (one of Montgomery's liaison officers) informed the War Office of Montgomery's limited intentions on 14 July. See Montgomery Papers BLM 109/3.
72. Ellis, *Victory in the West, Vol. 1*, pp. 336–9.
73. See various reports on Goodwood in CAB 106/1024.
74. Montgomery, press release 23/7/1944, Montgomery Papers BLM 123.
75. Kluge to Hitler 21/7/1944, Wilmot Papers 15/15/42. See also Wilmot, *Struggle for Europe*, p. 364.

76. Churchill to Montgomery 27/7/1944, Chartwell 20/169.
77. Montgomery to Churchill 27/7/1944, ibid.

27. Burma

1. Major-General S. Woodburn Kirby, *The War against Japan, Volume 2* (Uckfield: Naval and Military Press, 2004), p. 28. Reprint of the Official History first published in 1958.
2. Ibid, pp. 12–13. The British Indian Army was generally led by British officers and had two or three British battalions in each division. The remainder were Indian volunteer troops and NCOs.
3. Ibid, pp. 10–11.
4. Dorman-Smith to Amery 19/1/1942, CAB 120/492.
5. Churchill to COS 20/1/1942, ibid.
6. COS Minutes Confidential Annex 21/1/1942, CAB 79/56/4.
7. 'Reinforcements for Burma' 28/1/1942, CAB 120/492.
8. Indian Division War Diary December 1941, WO 172/475.
9. Kirby, *War against Japan, Vol. 2*, p. 39.
10. See ibid, p. 2, map, where this superimposition has been done.
11. See 17 Indian Division War Diary 18/1/1942, WO 172/475.
12. See ibid; Linlithgow to Churchill 17/2/1942, Chartwell 20/70. This is the only war diary that I have read that describes its own troops in such language.
13. Robert Lyman, *Slim, Master of War: Burma and the Birth of Modern Warfare* (London: Constable, 2019), p. 11. The best book on Slim.
14. Indian Division War Diary 23/2/1942, WO 172/475.
15. Kirby, *War against Japan, Vol. 2*, pp. 72–3. For a detailed narrative of the decision to blow the bridge, see Louis Allen, *Burma: The Longest War* (London: Dent, 1984), ch. 1, 'The Bridge'.
16. Defence Committee (Operations) Minutes 17/2/1942, Cab 69/4.
17. Wavell to Churchill 18/2/1942, Chartwell 20/70.
18. Telegram from Dill 19/2/1942, COS Minutes, CAB 79/18/23.
19. COS Minutes 20/2/1942, CAB 79/18/24.
20. Churchill to Curtin 20/2/1942, Chartwell 20/70.
21. Ibid.
22. Freudenberg, *Churchill and Australia*, p. 381.
23. Ibid, p. 383.
24. Ibid, p. 385.
25. Ibid.
26. COS Minutes 22/2/1942, CAB 79/18/26.
27. Churchill to Curtin 22/2/1942, Chartwell 20/70.
28. Kirby, *War against Japan, Vol. 2*, pp. 57–8.
29. Dorman-Smith to Churchill 24/2/1942, Chartwell 20/88.
30. Churchill to Curtin 25/2/1942, Chartwell 20/70.
31. See 1 Burma Division War Diary March 1942, WO 172/447.
32. Lyman, *Slim*, p. 16.
33. Joint Planning Staff, 'Upper Burma', COS Minutes 30/3/1942, CAB 79/19/29.
34. Wavell to Churchill 19/3/1942, Chartwell 20/72.
35. Wavell to CIGS 21/3/1942, CAB 120/942.
36. Churchill to Chiang 22/3/1942, ibid.
37. Ismay to Churchill 24/3/1942, ibid.
38. Joint Planning Staff, 'Upper Burma', COS Minutes 30/3/1942, CAB 79/19/29.
39. Lyman, *Slim*, p. 47.
40. Churchill to Wavell 19/4/1942, Chartwell 20/88.

41. Craig L. Symonds, *World War II at Sea: A Global History* (Oxford: Oxford University Press, 2018), pp. 235–9.
42. *Brooke Diary* 24/4/1942, p. 252.
43. Howard, *Grand Strategy, Vol. IV*, p. 83.
44. Kirby, *War against Japan, Vol. 2*, pp. 250–2.
45. Ibid, p. 235.
46. Churchill to Wavell 12/6/1942, Chartwell 20/76.
47. COS Minutes 11/7/1942, CAB 79/56/72.
48. Churchill to COS 12/7/1942, Chartwell 20/67. Michael Howard says in *Grand Strategy, Vol. IV*, p. 86, that Churchill only came around to this position after a 'long and acrimonious' debate with the COS. In fact he agreed with the COS on the day after Alexander's meeting with them.
49. Ibid, p. 59.
50. Kirby, *War against Japan, Vol. 2*, ch. XV. But see also Raymond Callahan, *Burma 1942–1945* (London: Davis-Poynter, 1978), pp. 59–64 for a more concise and coherent view. Callahan provides the best analysis of the strategy of the Burma campaign.
51. CCS Minutes 14/5/1943, CAB 99/22.
52. See Defence Committee (Operations) 28/7/1943, CAB 69/5.
53. Churchill to COS 26/7/1943, Chartwell 20/104.
54. 'Report to the President and Prime Minister of the Final Agreed Summary of Conclusions Reached by the Combined Chiefs of Staff' 24/8/1943, CAB 99/23.
55. Kirby, *War against Japan, Vol. 2*, p. 363.
56. Howard, *Grand Strategy, Vol. IV*, pp. 400–1.
57. Amery's paper is attached to the COS Minutes 1/5/1943, CAB 79/60/41.
58. COS Minutes Confidential Annex 22/4/1943, CAB 79/60/34.
59. Two papers from the Joint Planners to this effect are attached to the COS Minutes for 29/4/1943, CAB 79/60/38.
60. Kirby, *War against Japan, Vol. 2*, pp. 386–7.
61. Ibid, Appendix 6, pp. 461–2.
62. Indian Division Operational Notes, Messervy Papers 5, Liddell Hart Centre for Military Archives.
63. 'The Arakan Campaign of the Twenty-Fifth Indian Division, March 1944–March 1945', Messervy Papers 7.
64. Major-General S. Woodburn Kirby, *The War against Japan, Volume 3: The Decisive Battles* (Uckfield: Naval and Military Press, 2004), pp. 386–7. Reprint of the 1961 edition.
65. Churchill to Attlee 9/8/1943, Chartwell 20/129.
66. COS Minutes 23/11/1943, CAB 99/25.
67. Tehran Conference Eureka Meeting 28/11/1943, ibid.
68. Roosevelt to Churchill 5/12/1943, in Kimball (ed.), *Churchill and Roosevelt Correspondence, Vol. 2*, pp. 616–17.
69. Ehrman, *Grand Strategy, Vol. V*, pp. 421–5.
70. CCS Minutes 5/12/1943, CAB 99/25.
71. See these minutes in CAB 99/25.
72. Defence Committee (Operations) 19/1/1944, CAB 69/6.
73. SEAC Memorandum January 1944, CAB 120/700.
74. COS Minutes 14/2/1944, CAB 79/70/16.
75. Ehrman, *Grand Strategy, Vol. V*, p. 437.
76. Churchill to COS 16/2/1944, Chartwell 20/188.
77. Churchill to the War Cabinet 29/2/1944, Chartwell 20/188.
78. Ehrman, *Grand Strategy, Vol. V*, pp. 445–9.
79. Ismay to Churchill 4/3/1944, in ibid, pp. 448–9. There is no copy of this note in the Cabinet Papers or in the Chartwell Papers.
80. Ibid.

81. *Brooke Diary* 3/3/1944, p. 528.
82. *Brooke Diary* 6/3/1944, pp. 528–9.
83. COS Minutes Confidential Annex 8/3/1944, CAB 79/89/7. Note that this file is headed CCS (Combined Chiefs of Staff) meeting. It is not a CCS meeting but a staff conference with the COS and members of the War Cabinet.
84. COS Minutes 8/3/1944, CAB 79/71/19. Note that this is a different number Cabinet Paper from that of the Confidential annex noted above. They refer, however, to the same meeting. Only the level of confidentiality has changed.
85. Churchill to COS 20/3/1944, Chartwell 20/188; *Brooke Diary* 21/3/1944, p. 533.
86. COS Minutes CAB 79/79.
87. Churchill to Curtin 13/9/1944, Chartwell 20/171.
88. Christopher Thorne, *Allies of a Kind: The United States, Britain and the War against Japan* (London: Hamish Hamilton, 1978), pp. 411–13.
89. 'The Japanese Account of the Operations in Burma December 1941–August 1945', Messervy Papers 12. The history was compiled by the Twelfth British Army from captured documents. Whether any kind of invasion of India would have taken place had these operations been successful is not clear.
90. For a detailed description of this action see James Holland, *Burma 44: The Battle that Turned Britain's War in the East* (London: Penguin, 2016).
91. This short account of these battles has been compiled from Lyman, *Slim*; Kirby, *War against Japan, Vol. 3* and Slim's own account, *Defeat into Victory* (London: Cassell, 1956). I recommend Lyman's account as the most lucid.
92. See, for example, Mountbatten to COS and Prime Minister 12/4/1944, CAB 120/700, which is a detailed account of the last weeks' fighting at Imphal.
93. Churchill to Mountbatten 2/3/1944, CAB 120/700.
94. Churchill to Roosevelt 17/3/1944, Warren Kimball (ed.), *Churchill and Roosevelt: Complete Correspondence, Volume 3, Alliance Declining* (Princeton: Princeton University Press, 1984), p. 50.
95. Churchill to Mountbatten 22/6/1944, CAB 120/700. See also Philip Ziegler, *Mountbatten: A Biography* (New York: Knopf, 1985), ch. 21.
96. Ibid, p. 281. The Dracula plan was originally called Vanguard. It was quickly changed, however, and I have used Dracula throughout for simplicity. Similarly Capital was originally called Champion.
97. Octagon, 'Report to the President and Prime Minister' 15/9/1944; Minutes of First Meeting 13/9/1944, both in CAB 99/29.
98. Ehrman, *Grand Strategy, Vol. V*, pp. 415–16.
99. Slim, 'Campaign of the Fourteenth Army 1944–1945', Messervy Papers 15.
100. 'Japanese Account of Operations in Burma 1941–1945', Messervy Papers 12.
101. Slim, 'Campaign of Fourteenth Army 1944–1945'.
102. 'Operations of 4th Corps October 1944–May 1945', Messervy Papers 8.
103. Ibid.
104. Slim, 'Campaign of the Fourteenth Army 1944–1945'.
105. Ibid.
106. Churchill to Mountbatten 23/1/1945, Chartwell 20/211; Churchill to Mountbatten 21/3/1945, Chartwell 20/213.
107. Sextant – 2nd Meeting, 23/11/1943, Cab 99/25.

28. The End of the War in Europe August 1944–May 1945

1. Boog, Krebs and Vogel, *Germany and the Second World War, Vol. VII*, p. 616.
2. Joachim Ludewig, *Ruckzug: The German Retreat from France 1944* (Lexington: University of Kentucky Press, 2012), p. 195.
3. Montgomery to Brooke 18/8/1944, Montgomery Papers BLM 1/115.

4. Ibid.
5. Ellis, *Victory in the West, Vol. 1*, p. 460.
6. Ibid, pp. 460–1.
7. Montgomery to Brooke 23/8/1944, Montgomery Papers BLM 1/115.
8. Eisenhower to Montgomery 24/8/1944, in Chandler (ed.), *Eisenhower Papers: The War Years, Vol. 4*, pp. 2090–1.
9. Eisenhower to Marshall 24/8/1944, in ibid, pp. 2092–4.
10. Eisenhower to Bradley and Montgomery 29/8/1944, in ibid, pp. 2100–1.
11. *Brooke Diary* 28/8/1944, p. 585.
12. COS Minutes 28/8/1944, CAB 79/80/4.
13. COS Minutes 30/8/1944, CAB 79/80/7.
14. COS Minutes 31/8/1944, Appendix to Annex 1, CAB 79/80/11.
15. Chester Wilmot, 'Interview with Major-General Sir Miles Graham', formerly M.G. 22 First Army Group, London 19/1/1949, Wilmot Papers 15/15/48.
16. Ibid.
17. Ibid.
18. Martin van Creveld, *Supplying War: Logistics from Wallenstein to Patton* (Cambridge: Cambridge University Press, 1977), ch. 7. The 'only just' quotation is on p. 227.
19. Ibid.
20. See Brigadier C. Ravenshill, 'The Influence of Logistics on Operations in North-West Europe, 1944–1945', copy in the Wilmot Papers 15/15/48. Originally published in the *RUSI Journal*, November 1946.
21. For a concise statement of this case see Roland G. Ruppenthal, Logistics and the Broad Front Strategy' in K.R. Greenfield (ed.), *Command Decisions*, ch. 18, pp. 419–27. The quotation is on p. 424. For a longer exposition see Roland G. Ruppenthal, *Logistic Support of the Armies, Volume 2* (Washington: US Printing Service, 1953).
22. Some authorities have held that this would have meant diverting US supplies to the British, but this would not have been necessary. The most logical move was to divert them to Hodges, who was after all closer to Patton than the Twenty-First Army Group. This point is covered by Van Creveld, *Supplying War*, p. 229.
23. Niall Barr, *Eisenhower's Armies: The American-British Alliance during World War II* (New York: Pegasus, 2017), pp. 402–3. I have to differ from the excellent Barr on this point.
24. Field Marshall Montgomery, *Normandy to the Baltic* (London: Arrow Books, 1961), p. 123.
25. 'An Account of The Operations of Second Army in Europe 1944–1945', Vol. 1, WO 205/972B.
26. Eisenhower to Commanders 29/9/1944, in Chandler (ed.), *Eisenhower Papers: The War Years, Vol. 4*, pp. 2100–1.
27. Montgomery to Eisenhower 4/9/1944, Chester Wilmot Papers 15/15/48.
28. SHAEF Directive 4/9/1944, Wilmot Papers 15/15/48.
29. Wilmot interview with Graham 12/1/1949, ibid.
30. For a lucid exposition of the Arnhem plan see Martin Middlebrook, *Arnhem 1944: The Airborne Battle* (London: Viking, 1994), ch. 1.
31. Montgomery Directive 14/9/1944, in Major L.F. Ellis, *Victory in the West: Volume 2: The Defeat of Germany* (London: HMSO, 1968), pp. 26–7.
32. Montgomery to Eisenhower 18/9/1944, Montgomery Papers BLM 108/35.
33. Ellis, *Victory in the West, Vol. 2*, p. 83.
34. Montgomery, 'Notes on Command in Western Europe' 10/10/1944, Montgomery Papers BLM 76/9.
35. Eisenhower to Montgomery 13/10/1944, in Chandler (ed.), *Eisenhower Papers: The War Years, Vol. 4*, pp. 2221–4.
36. Montgomery to Eisenhower 16/10/1944, Montgomery Papers BLM 108/65.
37. John Ehrman, *Grand Strategy, Volume VI* (London: HMSO, 1956), p. 35.

38. Eisenhower to Montgomery 1/12/1944, in Chandler (ed.), *Eisenhower Papers: The War Years, Vol. 4*, pp. 2323–5.

39. COS Minutes 12/12/1944 (6.30 pm), CAB 79/84/9.

40. *Brooke Diary* 12/12/1944, p. 634.

41. Ibid, 13/12/1944, p. 635.

42. Ibid; Ehrman, *Grand Strategy, Vol. VI*, pp. 36–7; War Cabinet Minutes 13/12/1944, CAB 65/44/37; *Brooke Diary* 13/12/1944, p. 635. The sources are puzzling here. The War Cabinet minutes record a meeting concerning Eisenhower's strategy and that Brooke was 'fearful' about it. But the official record has no conclusion and it is difficult to recon-struct the flow of discussion. Brooke records the fact that the May date for crossing the Rhine made a profound effect on the Cabinet and that they invited him to submit a paper on the subject. I can see no reason to doubt him.

43. Ehrman, *Grand Strategy, Vol. VI*, pp. 69–71.

44. Eisenhower to CCS 20/1/1945, in Chandler (ed.), *Eisenhower Papers: The War Years, Vol. IV*, pp. 2444–9.

45. Ehrman, *Grand Strategy, Vol. VI*, p. 88.

46. CCS Minutes 30/1/1945, CAB 99/31.

47. CCS Minutes 31/1/1945, CAB 99/31.

48. *Brooke Diary* 1/2/1945, p. 653.

49. The difficulties experienced by Twenty-First Army Group in this period are well described in 'Operation Veritable: Clearing the Area Between the R Maas and the R Rhine', WO 205/1133.

50. Eisenhower to Military Mission Moscow and CCS 28/3/1944, in Chandler (ed.), *Eisenhower Papers: The War Years, Vol. 4*, p. 2551.

51. Ehrman, *Grand Strategy, Vol. VI*, pp. 134–5.

52. Churchill to Ismay for COS 31/3/1945, Chartwell 20/209.

53. Eisenhower to Marshall 30/3/1945, in Chandler (ed.), *Eisenhower Papers: The War Years, Vol. 4*, pp. 2560–2.

54. Churchill to Ismay for COS 3/4/1945, Chartwell 20/209.

55. 'Notes on the Operations of 21 Army Group 6 June 1944–5 May 1945', WO 205/972A.

56. Ibid.

57. W.G.F. Jackson, *The Battle for Italy* (London: Harper, 1967), pp. 258–60. It was renamed the Green Line by the Germans but I have used the conventional Gothic Line.

58. Douglas Orgill, *The Gothic Line* (London: Pan, 1967), pp. 45–6.

59. General Sir William Jackson, *The Mediterranean and Middle East: Victory in the Mediterranean, Volume VI, Part II* (Uckfield: Naval and Military Press, 2004), p. 229. Reprint of the Official History.

60. Wilson to COS 2/9/1944, in Gilbert and Arnn (eds), *Churchill Documents, Vol. 20*, pp. 1251–5.

61. 'Notes on the Gothic Line Fighting', in Reports on Ops from Within Divisions, WO 204/8265.

62. 'Account of Operations: 13 Corps Artillery: Italy August 1944–May 1945', WO 204/7235.

63. 'Records of Operations 'Ind[ian] Div. May 1944 to March 1945', WO 204/8305.

64. Wilson to Churchill 13/9/1944, in Gilbert and Arnn (eds.) *Churchill Documents, Vol. 20*, pp. 1368–9.

65. COS Minutes 21/8/1944, Prem 3/258/3.

66. Churchill to Roosevelt 28/8/1944, in Kimball (ed.), *Churchill and Roosevelt Correspondence, Vol. 3*, pp. 299–300.

67. Roosevelt to Churchill 30/8/1944, in ibid, pp. 301–2.

68. Octagon, 1st Plenary Meeting 12/9/1944, CAB 99/29.

69. CCS Minutes 12/9/1944, CAB 99/29.

70. Ibid.

71. COS Minutes 8/10/1944, in Gilbert and Arnn (eds), *Churchill Documents, Vol. 20*, pp. 1587–90.

72. 'Formation Accounts and Narratives: Italian Campaign: 46 Brit[ish] Inf[antry] Div[ision] – 10 August–12 December 1944', WO 204/7232.
73. ELAS was the military wing of EAM, which was the National Liberation Front.
74. Jackson, *Mediterranean, Volume VI, Part II*, pp. 207–8.
75. Churchill to Brooke 6/8/1944, Chartwell 20/153.
76. Churchill to Roosevelt 17/8/1944, Kimball (eds), *Churchill and Roosevelt Correspondence, Vol. 3*, pp. 278–9.
77. Roosevelt to Churchill 26/8/1944, in ibid, p. 297.
78. General Sir William Jackson, *The Mediterranean and Middle East: Victory in the Mediterranean, Volume VI, Part III* (Uckfield: Naval and Military Press, 2004), p. 22. A reprint of the Official History.
79. For these movements see Jackson, *Mediterranean, Volume VI, Part III*, pp. 22, 84, 85–6, 163 and 170.
80. The gist of the debate can be gathered from the Hansard excerpts given in Gilbert and Arnn (eds), *Churchill Documents, Vol. 20*, pp. 2133–50.
81. Churchill to Roosevelt 10/12/1944, in ibid, p. 2179.
82. There is a discrepancy in the version of this letter in the Kimball edition of the Churchill–Roosevelt correspondence (see *Churchill and Roosevelt Correspondence, Vol. 3*, pp. 453–5 and the version given in the Gilbert and Arnn documents on p. 2179. The House of Commons threat is absent from the Kimball version and Kimball also claims that the letter was sent to Hopkins but not the President, whereas Gilbert and Arnn state that it was not sent to anyone. I have sighted the letter quoted by Gilbert and Arnn in Prem 3/212/5 and it is as they say. I cannot explain Kimball's version but I am satisfied that Gilbert and Arnn are quoting accurately.
83. Note of a phone call between Churchill and Harry Hopkins 10/12/1944, Gilbert and Arnn (eds), *Churchill Documents, Vol. 20*, pp. 2177–8.
84. Roosevelt to Churchill 13/12/1944, Kimball (ed.), *Churchill and Roosevelt Correspondence, Vol. 3*, pp. 455–7.
85. For this incident see Andrew Adonis, *Ernest Bevin: Labour's Churchill* (London: Biteback, 2020), pp. 213–14.
86. COS Minutes 22/11/1944, CAB 79/83/8.
87. Ehrman, *Grand Strategy, Vol. VI*, p. 56.
88. COS Minutes 23/1/1945 6.30 p.m., CAB 79/28/27.
89. Ibid.
90. *Brooke Diary* 30/1/1945, p. 651.
91. Ehrman, *Grand Strategy, Vol. VI*, pp. 94–5.
92. Bidwell and Graham, *Tug of War*, pp. 390–1.
93. Jackson, *Battle for Italy*, p. 302.
94. Jackson, *Mediterranean, Volume VI, Part III*, p. 299.
95. Infantry Brigade [78 Division], 'Account of Operations 9th April to 24th April 1945', 78 Division Operations April 1945, WO 204/8284.
96. New Zealand Division, 'Operations Aug. 44–May 45', WO 204/7238.
97. See, for example, 40 Royal Marine Commando Operations, in 'Reports on Operations from Within Divisions May 1944–May 1945, WO 204/8265.

Conclusion

1. Note by Churchill 7/10/1941, in Gilbert (ed.), *Churchill War Papers, Vol. 3*, p. 1311.

BIBLIOGRAPHY

Primary Sources

Australian War Memorial, Canberra

AWM 4 Unit War Diaries (First World War)
AWM 45 British War Diaries and Other Records
AWM 52 Unit War Diaries (Second World War)
AWM 124 Mitchell Committee Report
DRL 3 General Sir John Monash Papers

British Library, London

Admiral Evan-Thomas Papers
Admiral Sir John Jellicoe Papers

Churchill College, Cambridge

Admiral De Robeck Papers
Admiral Godfrey Papers
General Sir Henry Rawlinson Papers

Imperial War Museum, London (IWM)

Fourth Army Papers
Captured German Documents Papers
General Sir E. Barker Papers
General R. Budworth Papers
General R. Butler Papers
Lt. D.H. Hepburn Papers
General Ivor Maxse Papers
Rayfield Papers
German Official Account of the Third Ypres Campaign (translation)

Liddell Hart Centre for Military Archives, King's College, London

Lord Alanbrooke Papers
General Sir Ian Hamilton Papers
General Sidney Kirkman Papers
General Frank Messervy Papers
General Sir Archibald Montgomery-Massingberd Papers
Chester Wilmot Papers

The National Archives (UK), Kew (TNA)

Admiralty Papers

ADM 1 Admiralty and Secretariat Papers
ADM 53 Ships' Logs
ADM 116 Specific Cases of the Naval War
ADM 137 War History (1914–1918) Papers
ADM 199 War History Cases and Papers
ADM 205 First Sea Lord Papers
ADM 223 Naval Intelligence Division – Intelligence Reports

Air Ministry Papers

AIR 16 Fighter Command Papers
AIR 37 Second Tactical Air Force Files
AIR 41 Air Historical Branch Narratives and Papers

Cabinet Office Papers

CAB 21 Registered War Cabinet Files
CAB 23 War Cabinet Minutes (First World War)
CAB 25 Supreme War Council (First World War) Papers and Minutes
CAB 27 War Policy Committee Papers and Minutes
CAB 38 Committee of Imperial Defence Minutes and Memoranda
CAB 41 Prime Minister's Letters to the King
CAB 42 Photocopies of War Council, Dardanelles Committee, War Committee Papers and Minutes 1914–1916
CAB 44 Historical Section – Official War Histories and Narratives
CAB 45 Historical Section Correspondence
CAB 63 Hankey Papers
CAB 65 War Cabinet Conclusions
CAB 66 War Cabinet Memoranda
CAB 69 Defence Committee (Operations) Minutes and Papers
CAB 79 Chief of Staff Committee Minutes
CAB 80 Chief of Staff Committee Memoranda
CAB 86 Battle of the Atlantic and Anti-U-Boat Committee Minutes
CAB 88 Combined Chiefs of Staff Committee Minutes
CAB 99 Commonwealth and International Conferences Minutes and Memoranda
CAB 106 Historical Section- Operational Reports
CAB 120 Minister of Defence Files

War Office Papers

WO 32 Registered Files
WO 95 Unit War Diaries (First World War)
WO 106 Director of Military Operations Files
WO 158 Military Headquarters (First World War) Correspondence and Files
WO 167 Unit War Diaries BEF France
WO 168 Unit War Diaries Norway
WO 171 Unit War Diaries North-Western Europe
WO 172 Unit War Diaries South-East Asia
WO 179 Unit War Diaries Dominion Forces
WO 201 Headquarters Middle East Files
WO 203 Headquarters South-East Asia Files

WO 204 Headquarters Mediterranean Files
WO 205 21st Army Group Files
WO 256 Photocopy Field Marshal Sir Douglas Haig Diary
WO 285 General Sir Miles Dempsey Papers

National Archives of Canada

Unit War Diaries Online

National Maritime Museum, Greenwich

Greene Papers
Admiral Sir Herbert Richmond Papers

University of Adelaide Library, Adelaide

Chartwell Papers Online
Hansard Online
Mass Observation Archive Online
Prem 3 Prime Minister's Office Operational Files

Unpublished and Internet Sources

Anstey, Brigadier E.C., 'History of the Royal Artillery 1914–1918', Imperial War Museum.
Assmann, Vice-Admiral Kurt, 'The German Campaign in Norway', German Naval History Series BR 840(1), Naval Staff, Admiralty, Tactical and Staff Duties Division, 1948.
Brown, David, 'Naval Operations in the Campaign in Norway', London, Naval Staff, 1951.
Harvey, Trevor Gordon, 'An Army of Brigadiers: British Brigade Commanders at the Battle of Arras 1917', University of Birmingham, 2015.
Leeson, David M., 'An Ecstasy of Fumbling: A Reassessment of British Offensives on the Wester Front 1915', PhD thesis, University of Regina, Saskatchewan, 1998.
Naval Staff History, 'The Defeat of the Enemy Attack on Shipping 1939–1945: A Study of Policy and Operations', London, Historical Section, Admiralty, 1957.
Naval Staff Monographs, Volume 1, Monograph 2, 'German Cruiser Squadron in the Pacific', London, Admiralty, 1920.
Naval Staff Monographs, Monograph 4, 'Goeben and Breslau', London, Admiralty, 1920.
Naval Staff Monographs, Volume 3, Monograph 11, 'The Battle of the Heligoland Bight, August 28th 1914', London, Admiralty, 1921.
Naval Staff Monographs, Volume 13, 'Home Waters, Part IV', London, Admiralty, 1925.
Naval Staff Monographs, Monograph 15, 'Home Waters', London, Admiralty, 1926.
Naval Staff Monographs, Monograph 18, 'Home Waters', London, Admiralty, 1923.
uboat.net.
unithistories.com, Officers 1939–1945.
Weir, Eric M.K., 'German Submarine Blockade, Overseas Imports, and British Military Production in World War II', Appendix 1, Britain's Wartime Imports by Category 1941–1944.

Books and Articles

Adonis, Andrew, *Ernest Bevin: Labour's Churchill* (London: Biteback, 2020).
Alanbrooke, Field Marshal Lord, *War Diaries 1939–1945*, ed. Alex Danchev and Daniel Todman (London: Phoenix, 2002).
Albertini, Luigi, *The Origins of the War of 1914*, 3 vols (London: Oxford University Press, 1952).
Allen, Louis, *Burma: The Longest War* (London: Dent, 1984).

Allport, Alan, *Browned Off and Bloody Minded: The British Soldier Goes to War* (New Haven/ London: Yale University Press, 2015).

Amery, Leo, *The Empire at Bay: The Leo Amery Diaries 1929–1945* (London: Hutchinson, 1987).

Aspinall-Oglander, Brigadier-General C.E., *Military Operations: Gallipoli*, 2 vols and Appendices (London: Heinemann, 1929–1932).

Asquith, H.H., *The Genesis of the War* (London: Cassell, 1923).

Astill, Edwin (ed.), *The Great War Diaries of Brigadier Alexander Johnston 1914–1917* (Barnsley: Pen & Sword, 2007).

Atkinson, Rick, *An Army at Dawn: The War in North Africa 1942–1943* (London: Little, Brown, 2003).

—— *The Day of Battle: The War in Sicily and Italy, 1943–1944* (New York: Henry Holt, 2007).

Austin, Douglas, *Churchill and Malta's War 1939–1943* (Stroud: Amberley, 2015).

Australian Military Forces, *Operations of the British Expeditionary Forces in France and Belgium* (Melbourne: Australian General Staff, 1934).

Ball, Simon, *The Bitter Sea* (London: Harper, 2010).

Barker, Ralph, *The Thousand Plan* (London: Pan, 1967).

Barr, Niall, *Eisenhower's Armies: The American-British Alliance During World War II* (New York: Pegasus, 2017).

—— *Pendulum of War: The Three Battles of El Alamein* (London: Pimlico, 2005).

Barnett, Corelli, *Engage the Enemy More Closely: The Royal Navy in the Second World War* (London: Hodder & Stoughton, 1991).

Baynham, Henry, *Men from the Dreadnoughts* (London: Hutchinson, 1976).

Bean, C.E.W., *Official History of Australia in the War of 1914–1918, Vol. I: The Story of Anzac – From the Outbreak of War to the End of the First Phase of the Gallipoli Campaign, May 4, 1915*, 3rd edn (Sydney: Angus & Robertson, 1942).

—— *Official History of Australia in the War of 1914–1918, Vol. II: The Story of Anzac – From May 4, 1915, to the Evacuation of the Gallipoli Peninsula* (Sydney: Angus & Robertson, 1942).

—— *Official History of Australia in the War of 1914–1918, Vol. IV: The Australian Imperial Force in France, 1917* (Sydney: Angus & Robertson, 1938).

—— *Official History of Australia in the War of 1914–1918, Vol. V: The Australian Imperial Force in France During the Main German Offensive, 1918* (Sydney: Angus & Robertson, 1938).

—— *Official History of Australia in the War of 1914–1918, Vol. VI: The Australian Imperial Force in France During the Allied Offensive, 1918* (Sydney: Angus & Robertson, 1942),

Beaumont, Roger, 'The Bomber Offensive as a Second Front', *Journal of Contemporary History*, vol. 22 (1987), pp. 3–19.

Beckett, Ian F.W., *Ypres: The First Battle, 1914* (Harlow: Pearson, 2004).

Beesly, Patrick, *Room 40: British Naval Intelligence 1914–1918* (London: Hamish Hamilton, 1982).

Bell, Christopher, 'Air Power and the Battle of the Atlantic: Very Long Range Aircraft and the Delay in Closing the Atlantic "Air Gap"', *Journal of Military History*, vol. 79 (July 2015), pp. 691–719.

—— *Churchill and the Dardanelles* (Oxford: Oxford University Press, 2017).

Bennett, Air Vice Marshal D.C.T., *Pathfinder* (London: Panther, 1960).

Best, Geoffrey, *Churchill and War* (London: Hambledon, 2005).

Bidwell, Shelford and Dominick Graham, *Fire-Power: British Army Weapons and Theories of War 1904–1945* (London: Allen & Unwin, 1982).

—— *Tug of War: The Battle for Italy, 1943–1945* (London: Hodder and Stoughton, 1986).

Bialer, Uri, *The Shadow of the Bomber: The Fear of Air Attack and British Politics* (London: Royal Historical Society, 1980).

Bishop, Patrick, *Bomber Boys* (London: Harper, 2008).

Black, Nicholas, *The British Naval Staff in the First World War* (Woodbridge: Boydell Press, 2009).

Blair, Clay, *Hitler's U-Boat War: The Hunters, 1939–1945* (London: Weidenfeld and Nicolson, 1997).

—— *Hitler's U-Boat War: The Hunted, 1942–1945* (London: Weidenfeld and Nicolson, 1999).

Bland, Larry and Sharon Stevens (eds), *The Papers of George Catlett Marshall, Volume 3, 'The Right Man for the Job', December 7, 1941–May 31, 1943* (Baltimore: Johns Hopkins University Press, 1991).

Boff, Jonathan, *Haig's Enemy: Crown Prince Rupprecht and Germany's War on the Western Front* (Oxford: Oxford University Press, 2018).

—— *Winning and Losing on the Western Front: The British Third Army and the Defeat of Germany in 1918* (Cambridge: Cambridge University Press, 2012).

Bond, Brian (ed.), *Chief of Staff: The Diaries of Lieutenant-General Sir Henry Pownall, Volume 1* (London: Leo Cooper, 1972).

Boog, Horst, Gerhard Krebs and Detlef Vogel, *Germany and the Second World War, Volume VII* (Oxford: Clarendon, 2006).

Bowman, Timothy and Mark Connelly, *The Edwardian Army: Recruiting, Training, and Deploying the British Army 1902–1914* (Oxford: Oxford University Press, 2012).

Brock, Michael and Eleanor Brock (eds), *H.H. Asquith Letters to Venetia Stanley* (Oxford: Oxford University Press, 1982).

—— (eds), *Margot Asquith's Great War Diary 1914–1916: The View from Downing Street* (Oxford: Oxford University Press, 2014).

Brooke, Lieutenant-Colonel A.F., 'The Evolution of Artillery in the Great War', *Journal of the Royal Artillery*, vol. 53 (1926–1927), p. 243.

Brooks, John, *The Battle of Jutland* (Cambridge: Cambridge University Press, 2016).

Brooks, Stephen (ed.), *Montgomery and the Eighth Army: A Selection from the Diaries, Correspondence and Other Papers of Field-Marshal the Viscount Montgomery of Alamein, August 1942 to December 1943* (London: Army Records Society, 1991).

Brown, David (ed.), *Naval Operations of the Campaign in Norway April–June 1940* (Portland, OR: Cass, 2000).

Brown, Ian, *British Logistics on the Western Front* (London: Praeger, 1998).

Buckingham, William. F., *Tobruk: The Great Siege 1941–1942* (Stroud: History Press, 2009).

Buckley, John, *Monty's Men: The British Army and the Liberation of Europe* (London/New Haven: Yale University Press, 2013).

Butcher, Harry, *My Three Years with Eisenhower* (New York: Simon and Schuster, 1946).

Butler, J.R.M., *Grand Strategy, Volume 2* (London: HMSO, 1954).

—— and J.M.A. Gwyer, *Grand Strategy, Volume 3, Part II* (London: HMSO, 1964).

Caddick-Adams, Peter, *Sand and Steel: A New History of D-Day* (London: Arrow, 2019).

Callahan, Raymond, *Burma 1942–1945* (London: Davis-Poynter, 1978).

—— *The Worst Disaster: The Fall of Singapore* (Newark: University of Delaware Press, 1977).

Callwell, Charles, *Field-Marshal Sir Henry Wilson: His Life and Diaries*, 2 vols (London: Cassell, 1927).

Campbell, John, *Jutland: An Analysis of the Fighting* (London: Conway Maritime, 1986).

Candler, Edmund, *The Long Road to Baghdad*, 2 vols (London: Routledge, 2016). Reprint of 1919 edition.

Carver, Michael, *Dilemmas of the Desert War 1940–1942* (London: Batsford, 1986).

Cassar, George H., *Kitchener: Portrait of an Imperialist* (London: Kimber, 1977).

Central Statistical Office, *Statistical Digest of the War* (London: HMSO, 1951).

Chandler, Alfred (ed.), *The Papers of Dwight David Eisenhower: The War Years*, 5 vols (Baltimore: Johns Hopkins University Press, 1970).

Charman, Terry (ed.), *Outbreak 1939: The World Goes to War* (London: Virgin, 2009).

Chasseaud, Peter and Peter Doyle, *Grasping Gallipoli: Terrain, Maps and the Failure at the Dardanelles 1915* (Staplehurst: Spellmount, 2005).

Childs, David J., *A Peripheral Weapon? The Production and Employment of British Tanks in the First World War* (Westport, CT: Greenwood, 1999).

Churchill, Randolph S., *Winston S. Churchill, Volume II, Companion, Part 3, 1911–1914* (London: Heinemann, 1969).

Churchill, Winston S., *The World Crisis*, 4 vols (London: Odhams, n.d.).

—— *Thoughts and Adventures* (London: Odhams, 1947).

—— *The Second World War*, 6 vols (London: Cassell, 1949–53).

Clarke, Christopher, *The Sleepwalkers: How Europe Went to War in 1914* (London: Allen Lane, 2012).

Colville, John, *The Fringes of Power: Downing Street Diaries 1939–55* (London: Weidenfeld and Nicolson, 1985).

Connell, John, *Auchinleck: A Critical Biography* (London: Cassell, 1959).

—— *Wavell: Scholar and Soldier* (London: Collins, 1964).

Corbett, Sir Julian, *Naval Operations*, 3 vols (London: Longmans, 1921–1923).

Costello, John and Terry Hughes, *Jutland 1916* (London: Weidenfeld and Nicolson, 1976).

Craster, J.M. (ed.), *'Fifteen Rounds a Minute': The Grenadiers at War August to December 1914: Edited from the Diaries and Letters of Major 'Ma' Jeffreys and Others* (London: Macmillan, 1976).

van Creveld, Martin, *Supplying War: Logistics from Wallenstein to Patton* (Cambridge: Cambridge University Press, 1977).

Danchev, Alex, *Establishing the Anglo-American Alliance: From the Second World War Diaries of Brigadier Vivian Dykes* (London: Brassey, 1990).

David, Edward (ed.), *Inside Asquith's Cabinet: From the Political Diaries of Charles Hobhouse* (London: John Murray, 1977).

D'Este, Carlo, *Bitter Victory: The Battle for Sicily 1943* (London: Collins, 1988).

Dilks, David (ed.), *The Diaries of Sir Alexander Cadogan 1938–1945* (London: Faber, 2010).

Dixon, John, *Magnificent But Not War: The Battle for Ypres 1915* (Barnsley: Pen & Sword, 2009).

Dobbie, Colonel W.G.S., 'The Operations of the 1st Division on the Belgian Coast in 1917', *Royal Engineers Journal* (June 1924), pp. 190–3.

Dobbs, Michael, *Six Months in 1945: From World War to Cold War* (London: Arrow, 2013).

Dugdale, Blanche, E.C., *Arthur James Balfour 1906–1930.* (London: Hutchinson, 1936).

Durrant, Colonel J.M.A., 'Mont St Quentin; Some Aspects of the Operations of the 2nd Australian Division from the 27th of August to the 2nd of September, 1918', *Army Quarterly*, vol. 31 (1935), pp. 91–5.

Edmonds, Brigadier-General Sir James E., *Military Operations: France and Belgium, 1914, Volume 1* (London: Macmillan, 1933).

—— *Military Operations: France and Belgium, 1914, Volume 2* (London: Macmillan, 1925).

—— *Military Operations: France and Belgium, 1915, Volume 1* (London: Macmillan, 1927).

—— *Military Operations: France and Belgium, 1915, Volume 2* (London: Macmillan, 1928).

—— *Military Operations: France and Belgium, 1916, Volume 1* (London: Macmillan, 1932).

—— *Military Operations: France and Belgium, 1917, Volume 2* (London: HMSO, 1948).

—— *Military Operations: France and Belgium, 1918, Volume 1* (London: Macmillan, 1935).

—— *Military Operations: France and Belgium, 1918, Volume 2* (London: Macmillan, 1937).

—— *Military Operations: France and Belgium, 1918, Volume 3* (London: Macmillan, 1939).

—— *Military Operations: France and Belgium, 1918, Volume 4* (London: Macmillan, 1939).

—— *Military Operations: France and Belgium, 1918, Volume 5* (London: Macmillan, 1948).

Ehrman, John, *Grand Strategy, Volume V* (London: HMSO, 1956).

—— *Grand Strategy, Volume VI* (London: HMSO, 1956).

Ellis, Captain A.D., *The Story of the Fifth Australian Division* (London: Hodder and Stoughton, n.d.).

Ellis, Major L.F., *Victory in the West, Volume 1* (London: HMSO, 1962).

—— *Victory in the West, Volume 2, The Defeat of Germany* (London: HMSO, 1968).

Essame, H., *The Battle for Europe 1918* (London: Batsford, 1974).

Evans, R.J.W. and Hartmut Pogge von Strandemann (eds), *The Coming of the First World War* (Oxford: Clarendon, 1988).

Falls, Cyril, *Military Operations: France and Belgium, 1917, Volume 1* (London: Imperial War Museum/Battery Press, 1991). Reprint of the 1940 edition.

Farr, Don, *Mons 1914–1918: The Beginning and the End* (Solihull: Helion, 2008).

Farrar-Hockley, A.H., *Ypres 1914: Death of an Army* (London: Pan, 1970).

Farrell, Brian P., *The Defence and Fall of Singapore 1940–1942* (Stroud: Tempus, 2006).

Fennell, Jonathan, *Fighting the People's War* (Cambridge: Cambridge University Press, 2019).

Fisher, Lord, *Records* (London: Hodder & Stoughton, 1919).

Fleming, Nicholas, *August 1939: The Last Days of Peace* (London: Peter Davies, 1976).

French, David, *British Strategy and War Aims 1914–1916* (London; Allen & Unwin, 1986).

—— *Raising Churchill's Army: The British Army and the War against Germany 1919–1945* (Oxford: Oxford University Press, 2000).

—— *The Strategy of the Lloyd George Coalition 1916–1918* (Oxford: Clarendon Press, 1995).

Freudenberg, Graham, *Churchill and Australia* (Sydney: Macmillan, 2008).

Foulkes, C.H., *Gas! The Story of the Special Brigade* (Edinburgh: Blackwood, 1936).

Gannon, Michael, *Black May* (London: Aurum, 1998).

Gardiner, Juliet, *The Blitz: The British Under Attack* (London: Harper, 2011).

Gardner, Nikolas, 'Command and Control in the "Great Retreat" of 1914: The Disintegration of the British Cavalry Division', *Journal of Military History*, vol. 63, no. 1 (January 1999), pp. 46–7.

Gates, Eleanor M., *The End of the Affair: The Collapse of the Anglo-French Alliance, 1939–1940* (Berkeley: University of California Press, 1981).

German General Staff, *Der Weltkreig, Volume 7* (Berlin: Mittler, 1936).

—— *Der Weltkreig, Volume 10* (Berlin: Mittler, 1936).

—— *Der Weltkreig, Volume 14* (Berlin: Mittler, 1936).

Gibbs, N.H., *Grand Strategy, Volume 1, Rearmament Policy* (London, HMSO, 1976).

Gibson, Langhorne and Vice-Admiral J.E.T. Harper, *The Riddle of Jutland: An Authentic History* (London: Cassell, 1934).

Gilbert, Martin, *Winston S. Churchill: Finest Hour: 1939–1941* (London: Heinemann, 1983).

—— *Winston S. Churchill, Volume 3, 1914–1916* (London: Heinemann, 1971).

—— (ed.), *Winston S. Churchill, Volume 3, Companion Documents, July 1914–April 1915* (London: Heinemann, 1972).

—— (ed.), *Winston S. Churchill, Volume. 3, Companion Documents May 1915–December 1916*, 2 vols (London: Heinemann, 1972).

—— (ed.), *The Churchill Documents, Volume 17, 1942* (Hillsdale, MI: Hillsdale College, 2014).

—— (ed.), *The Churchill War Papers, Volume 1, At the Admiralty September 1939—May 1940* (London: Norton, 1993).

—— (ed.), *The Churchill War Papers, Volume 2, May 1940–December 1940* (London: Norton, 1995).

—— (ed.), *The Churchill War Papers, Volume 3, The Ever-Widening War 1941* (London: Heinemann, 2000).

Gilbert, Martin and Larry Arnn (eds), *The Churchill Documents, Volume 18* (Hillsdale, MI: Hillsdale College, 2015).

—— (eds), *The Churchill Documents, Volume 19* (Hillsdale, MI: Hillsdale College, 2017).

—— (eds), *The Churchill Documents, Volume 20* (Hillsdale, MI: Hillsdale College, 2018).

Goldrick, James, *Before Jutland: The Naval War in the Northern Waters 1914–1915* (Annapolis, MD: Naval Institute Press, 2015).

Gooch, G.P. and Harold Temperley (eds), *British Documents on the Origin of the War, Volume XI* (London: HMSO, 1926).

Gooch, John, 'The Maurice Debate 1918', *Journal of Contemporary History*, vol. 3 (October 1968), pp. 211–28.

Gordon, Andrew, *The Rules of the Game: Jutland and British Naval Command* (London: John Murray, 1996).

Gorodetsky, Gabriel (ed.), *The Maisky Diaries: Red Ambassador to the Court of St James's 1932-1943* (London/New Haven: Yale University Press, 2015).

Gough, General Sir Hubert, *The Fifth Army* (London: Hodder and Stoughton, 1931).

Great Britain, Army, *Field Service Regulations* (London: HMSO, 1909).

Great Britain, War Office, *Statistics of the Military Effort of the British Empire During the Great War 1914-1920* (Uckfield: Naval and Military Press, n.d.).

Greenfield, K.R. (ed.), *Command Decisions* (Washington: Office of the Chief of Military History, 1960).

Greenhalgh, Elizabeth, *The French Army and the First World War* (Cambridge: Cambridge University Press, 2014).

—— *Victory through Coalition: Britain and France During the First World War* (Cambridge: Cambridge University Press, 2005).

Grieves, Keith, *The Politics of Manpower 1914-1918* (Manchester: Manchester University Press, 1988).

Grey, Jeffrey, *The War with the Ottoman Empire* (Melbourne: Oxford University Press, 2015).

Grey of Fallodon, Viscount, *Twenty-Five Years*, 2 vols (London: Hodder and Stoughton, 1925).

Grigg, John, *Lloyd George: From Peace to War 1912-1916* (London: Methuen, 1985).

—— *Lloyd George: War Leader 1916-1918* (London: Allen Lane, 2002).

—— *The Young Lloyd George* (London: Eyre Methuen, 1973).

Gudmundsson, Bruce, *Stormtroop Tactics: Innovation in the German Army: 1914-1918* (New York: Praeger, 1989).

Gwyer, J.M.A., *Grand Strategy, Volume 3, Part I* (London: HMSO, 1964).

Haarr, Geirr, *The German Invasion of Norway (April 1940)* (Annapolis, MD: Naval Institute Press, 2009).

Haber, L.F., *The Poisonous Cloud: Chemical Warfare in the First World War* (Oxford: Oxford University Press, 2002).

Hack, K. and K. Blackburn, *Did Singapore Have to Fall?: Churchill and the Impregnable Fortress* (London: Routledge, 2004).

Hague, Arnold, *The Allied Convoy System 1939-1945* (Annapolis, MD: Naval Institute Press, 2000).

Halpern, Paul, *A Naval History of World War 1* (London: UCL Press, 1994).

—— (ed.), *The Keyes Papers 1914-1918, Volume 1* (London: Navy Records Society, 1972).

Hamilton, Nigel, *Monty: Life of Montgomery of Alamein, Volume 1, The Making of a General 1887-1942* (London: Hamish Hamilton, 1981).

—— *Monty: Life of Montgomery of Alamein, Volume 2, Master of the Battlefield 1942-44* (London: Hamish Hamilton, 1983).

Hamilton, Richard and Holger Herwig, *Decisions for War 1914-1917* (Cambridge: Cambridge University Press, 2004).

Hammond, Bryn, *Cambrai 1917: The Myth of the First Great Tank Battle* (London: Weidenfeld and Nicolson, 2009).

Hampton, Meleah, *Attack on the Somme: 1st Anzac Corps and the Battle of Pozières Ridge, 1916* (Solihull: Helion, 2016).

Hankey, Maurice, *The Supreme Command, Volume 2* (London: Allen and Unwin, 1961).

Hardach, Gerd, *The First World War 1914-1918* (London: Peter Smith, 1983).

Harmon, Christopher C., *'Are We Beasts?' Churchill and the Moral Question of World War II 'Area Bombing'*, Newport Papers, no. 1 (Newport, RI: Center for Naval Warfare Studies, 1991).

Harper, Captain J.E.T., *The Record of the Battle of Jutland* (London: HMSO, 1927).

Harr, Geirr, *The Battle for Norway: April-June 1940* (Annapolis, MD: Naval Institute Press, 2010).

Harris, Sir Arthur, *Bomber Offensive* (London: Collins, 1947).

Hartcup, Guy, *The War of Invention: Scientific Developments 1914-1918* (London: Brassey, 1988).

von Hase, Georg, *Keil and Jutland* (London: Skeffington, 1921).

Hastings, Max, *Bomber Command* (London: Michael Joseph, 1979).

—— *Finest Years: Churchill as Warlord 1940–45* (London: Harper, 2009).

Hayward, Victor, *HMS Tiger at Bay* (London: Kimber, 1977).

Hazlehurst, Cameron, *Politicians at War July 1914 to May 1915: A Prologue to the Triumph of Lloyd George* (London: Cape, 1971).

Herwig, Holger, *The Marne 1914: The Opening of the World War and the Battle that Changed the World* (New York: Random House, 2009).

Hewitson, Mark, *Germany and the Causes of the First World War* (Oxford: Berg, 2004).

Hickling, H., *Sailor at Sea* (London: Kimber, 1965).

Hill, Christopher, *Cabinet Decisions on Foreign Policy: The British Experience* (Cambridge: Cambridge University Press, 2002).

Hinsley, F.H. (ed.), *British Foreign Policy under Sir Edward Grey* (Cambridge: Cambridge University Press, 1977).

—— (ed.), *British Intelligence in the Second World War, Volume 1* (London: HMSO, 1979).

—— (ed.), *British Intelligence in the Second World War, Volume 2* (London: HMSO, 1981).

—— (ed.), *British Intelligence in the Second World War, Volume 3, Part 1* (London: HMSO, 1984).

—— (ed.), *British Intelligence in the Second World War, Volume 3, Part 2* (London: HMSO, 1988).

Holland, James, *Burma 44: The Battle that Turned Britain's War in the East* (London: Penguin, 2016).

Hollis, Leslie, *War at the Top* (London: Michael Joseph, 1959).

Holmes, Richard, *Army Battlefield Guide: Belgium and Northern France* (London: HMSO, 1995).

—— *Riding the Retreat: Mons to the Marne 1914 Revisited* (London: Pimlico, 1995).

—— *The Little Field-Marshal: Sir John French* (London: Cape, 1981).

Howard, Christopher H.D. (ed.), *The Diary of Edward Goschen 1900–1914* (London: Royal Historical Society, 1980).

Howard, Michael, *Grand Strategy, Volume IV* (London: HMSO, 1972).

Hughes, Colin, *Mametz: Lloyd George's Welsh Army at the Battle of the Somme* (Gerrard's Cross: Orion Books, 1976).

Humphries, Mark Osborne and John Maker (eds), *Germany's Western Front: Translations from the German Official History of the Great War: 1914, Part 1* (Waterloo, ON: Wilfrid Laurier University Press, 2013).

Imlay, Talbot C., *Facing the Second World War: Strategy, Politics and Economics in Britain and France 1938–1940* (Oxford: Oxford University Press, 2010).

Inman, P., *Labour in the Munitions Industries* (London: HMSO, 1957).

Ismay, Lord, *Memoirs* (London: Viking, 1960).

Jackson, W.G.F., *The Battle for Italy* (London: Harper, 1967).

James, Robert Rhodes, *Gallipoli* (London: Batsford, 1965).

—— (ed.), *Winston S. Churchill: His Complete Speeches 1897–1963, Volume VI, 1935–1942* (London: Chelsea House, 1974).

James, T.C.B., *The Battle of Britain* (London: Cass, 2002).

Jameson, William, *The Most Formidable Thing: The Story of the Submarine from Its Earliest Days to the End of World War 1* (London: Rupert Hart-Davis, 1965).

Jellicoe, Admiral Viscount, *The Grand Fleet: Its Creation, Development and Work* (London: Cassell, 1919).

Jones, R.E., G.E. Rarey and R.J. Icks, *The Fighting Tanks from 1916 to 1933* (Greenwich, CT: W.E. Publishers, 1969). Reissue of 1933 edition.

Jones, Spencer, *From Boer War to World War: Tactical Reform of the British Army 1902–1914* (Norman: University of Oklahoma Press, 2012).

Jose, A.W., *The Royal Australian Navy 1914–1918*, 6th edn (Sydney: Angus & Robertson, 1938).

Kennedy, Paul (ed.), *The War Plans of the Great Powers 1880–1914* (London: Allen & Unwin, 1985).

Kersaudy, François, *Norway 1940* (London: Arrow, 1990).

Kimball, Warren *The Juggler: Franklin Roosevelt as Wartime Statesman* (Princeton: Princeton University Press, 1994).

—— (ed.), *Churchill and Roosevelt: The Complete Correspondence, Volume 1, Alliance Emerging* (Princeton: Princeton University Press, 1984).

—— (ed.), *Churchill and Roosevelt: The Complete Correspondence, Volume 2, Alliance Forged* (Princeton: Princeton University Press, 1984).

—— (ed.), *Churchill and Roosevelt: Complete Correspondence, Volume 3, Alliance Declining* (Princeton: Princeton University Press, 1984).

Kippenberger, Major-General H., *Infantry Brigadier* (London: Oxford University Press, 1949).

Kirby, S. Woodburn, *The War against Japan*, 5 vols (Uckfield: Naval and Military Press, 2016). Reprint of 1957–1969 editions.

Kiritescu, C., *La Roumanie dans la Guerre mondiale 1916–1919* (Paris: Payot, 1936).

Kynoch, Joseph, *Norway 1940: The Forgotten Fiasco* (Shrewsbury: Airlife, 2002).

Lavery, Brian, *Churchill's Navy* (London: Bloomsbury, 2006).

Lee, John, *The Gas Attacks: Ypres 1915* (Barnsley: Pen & Sword, 2009).

Leutze, James (ed.), *The London Observer: The Journal of Raymond E. Lee 1940–1941* (London: Hutchinson, 1971).

Liddell Hart, B.H. (ed.), *The Rommel Papers* (London: Collins, 1953).

Lieven, Dominic, *Towards the Flame: Empire, War and the End of Tsarist Russia* (London: Allen Lane, 2015).

Lloyd, Nick, *Loos 1915* (Stroud: History Press, 2008).

—— *Passchendaele: A New History* (London: Penguin, 2017).

Lomas, David, *Mons 1914: Britain's Tactical Triumph* (London: Praeger, 2004).

Ludewig, Joachim, *Ruckzug: The German Retreat from France 1944* (Lexington: University of Kentucky Press, 2012).

Lukacs, John, *Five Days in London* (London: Yale University Press, 2001).

Lumby, E.W.R. (ed.), *Policy and Operations in the Mediterranean 1912–1914* (London: Navy Records Society, 1970).

Lyman, Robert, *First Victory: Britain's Forgotten Struggle in the Middle East, 1941* (London: Constable, 2006).

—— *Slim, Master of War: Burma and the Birth of Modern Warfare* (London: Constable, 2019).

—— *The Longest Siege: Tobruk, the Battle that Saved North Africa* (London: Pan, 2009).

McCarthy Chris, *The Somme: Day-by-Day Account* (London: Arms & Armour Press, 1993).

Macintyre, Donald, *The Battle of the Atlantic* (London: Pan, 1961).

Macleod, Roderick (ed.), *The Ironside Diaries 1937–1940* (London: Constable, 1962).

Mackay, Ruddock, *Fisher of Kilverstone* (Oxford: Clarendon Press, 1973).

McMeekin, Sean, *July 1914: Countdown to War* (London: Icon, 2014).

MacMillan, Margaret, *The War that Ended Peace* (London: Profile, 2013).

MacMunn, Lieutenant-General Sir George and Cyril Falls, *Military Operations: Egypt and Palestine, Volume 1* (London: HMSO, 1928).

McRandle, James and James Quirk, 'The Blood Test Revisited: A New Look at German Casualty Counts in World War 1', *Journal of Military History* (July 2006).

McWilliams, J. and R.J. Steel, *Gas! The Battle for Ypres 1915* (St Catherine's, ON: Vanwell, 1985).

Maier, Kurt et al., *Germany and the Second World War, Volume 2* (Oxford: Clarendon Press, 1991).

Marble, Sandars, *British Artillery on the Western Front in the First World War: 'The Infantry Cannot Do with a Gun Less'* (Farnham: Ashgate, 2013).

Marder, A.J., *From the Dardanelles to Oran* (London: Oxford University Press, 1974).

—— *From the Dreadnought to Scapa Flow: The Royal Navy in the Fisher Era 1904–1919*, 5 vols (London: Oxford University Press, 1961–1972).

Matloff, Maurice and Edwin M. Snell, *Strategic Planning for Coalition Warfare 1941–1942* (Washington: Government Printing Office, 1953).

Maurice, Major-General Sir F., *Forty Days in 1914* (London: Constable, 1925).

—— *Haldane: 1856–1915* (London: Faber and Faber, 1937).

Mawdsley, Evan, *The War for the Seas: A Maritime History of World War II* (London/New Haven: Yale University Press, 2020).

Medlicott, W.N, *The Economic Blockade, Volume 1* (London: HMSO, 1952).

Messimer, Dwight R., *Verschollen: World War 1 U-Boat Losses* (Annapolis, MD: Naval Institute Press, 2002).

Middlebrook, Martin, *Arnhem 1944: The Airborne Battle* (London: Viking, 1994).

—— *The Battle of Hamburg: Allied Bomber Forces Against a German City 1943* (London: Allen Lane, 1980).

—— *The Kaiser's Battle: 21 March 1918: The First Day of the German Spring Offensive* (London: Allen Lane, 1978).

—— *Your Country Needs You: From Six to Sixty-Five Divisions* (Barnsley: Pen & Sword, 2000).

Middlebrook, M. and C. Everitt, *The Bomber Command War Diaries: An Operational Reference Book 1939–1945* (Leicester: Midland Publishing, 1996).

Mierzejewski, Alfred C., *The Collapse of the German War Economy 1944–1945: Allied Air Power and the German National Railway* (Chapel Hill: University of North Carolina Press, 1988).

Miles, Captain Wilfrid, *Military Operations: France and Belgium, 1917, Volume 3* (London: Imperial War Museum/Battery Press, 1992). Reprint of the 1948 edition.

Miller, Stephen, Sean Lynn-Jones and Steven van Evera (eds), *Military Strategy and the Origins of the First World War* (Princeton: Princeton University Press, 1991).

Millett, Allan R. and Williamson Murray, *Military Effectiveness, Volume 1, The First World War* (Boston, MA: Allen & Unwin, 1988).

Milner, Marc, *Stopping the Panzers* (Lawrence: University of Kansas Press, 2014).

Ministère de Guerre, *Les Armées françaises dans la grande guerre, Tome V, Volume 2* (Paris: Imprimerie Nationale, 1933).

Ministry of Munitions, *The Official History of the Ministry of Munitions, Volume X, The Supply of Munitions* (Uckfield: Naval and Military Press/Imperial War Museum, n.d.).

—— *The Official History of the Ministry of Munitions, Volume XII, The Supply of Munitions* (Uckfield: Naval and Military Press/Imperial War Museum, n.d.).

Mitchell, Major T.J. and G.M. Smith, *Medical Services: Casualties and Medical Statistics of the Great War* (London: HMSO, 1931).

Moloney, Brigadier C.J.C., *The Mediterranean and Middle East, Volume V* (London: Naval & Military Press, 2004). Reprint of the 1973 edition.

—— *The Mediterranean and Middle East, Volume VI, Part I* (Uckfield: Naval and Military Press, 2004). Reprint of the 1973 edition.

Mombauer, Annika, *Helmuth von Moltke and the Origins of the First World War* (Cambridge: Cambridge University Press, 2001).

Montgomery, Major-General Sir A., *The Story of the Fourth Army in the Battle of the Hundred Days, August 8th to November 11th, 1918* (London: Hodder and Stoughton, 1931).

Montgomery of Alamein, Field Marshal, *Memoirs* (London: Collins, 1958).

—— *Normandy to the Baltic* (London: Arrow Books, 1961).

Moore, William, *Gas Attack: Chemical Warfare 1915–18 and Afterwards* (London: Leo Cooper, 1987).

Moorehead, Alan, *African Trilogy* (London: Four Square, 1959).

Murland, Jerry, *Battle on the Aisne 1914: The BEF and the Birth of the Western Front* (Barnsley: Pen & Sword, 2012).

Nash, N.S., *Betrayal of an Army: Mesopotamia 1914–1916* (Barnsley: Pen & Sword, 2016).

Newbolt, Henry, *Naval Operations, Volume 5* (London: Imperial War Museum/Battery Press). Reprint of 1931 edition.

Nicholls, Jonathan, *Cheerful Sacrifice: The Battle of Arras, 1917* (London: Leo Cooper, 1990).

Nicholson, Colonel G.W.L., *The Canadian Expeditionary Force 1914–1919* (Ottawa: Queen's Printer, 1962).

Niestle, Axel, *German U-Boat Losses During World War II* (London: Frontline Books, 2014).

Official Despatches to the Battle of Jutland 30th May to 1st June 1916 with Appendices and Charts (London: HMSO, 1920).

Orgill, Douglas, *The Gothic Line* (London: Pan, 1967).

Osborne, Eric W., *The Battle of the Heligoland Bight* (Bloomington: Indiana University Press, 2006).

Otte, T.G., *The July Crisis: The World's Descent into War, Summer 1914* (Cambridge: Cambridge University Press, 2015).

Overy, Richard, *The Bombing War* (London: Allen Lane, 2013).

Palazzo, Albert, *Seeking Victory on the Western Front: The British Army and Chemical Warfare in World War 1* (Lincoln: University of Nebraska Press, 2000).

Palmer, Alan, *The Salient: Ypres, 1914–1918* (London: Constable, 2007).

Peden, George, *Arms, Economics and British Strategy: From Dreadnoughts to Hydrogen Bombs* (Cambridge: Cambridge University Press, 2007).

Pedersen, Peter, *Monash as Military Commander* (Melbourne: Melbourne University Press, 1985).

Pidgeon, Trevor, *The Tanks at Flers, Volume 1* (Cobham: Fairmile, 1995).

Piekalkiewicz, Janusz, *Cassino: Anatomy of the Battle* (London: Orbis, 1980).

Pitt, Barrie, *The Crucible of War: The Western Desert 1941* (London: Book Club Associates, 1960).

—— *The Crucible of War: Year of Alamein 1942* (London: Cape, 1982).

Playfair, Major-General I.S.O., *Mediterranean and Middle East*, 4 vols (Uckfield: Naval and Military Press, 2016). Reprint of 1954–1966 editions.

Porch, Douglas, *Hitler's Mediterranean Gamble* (London: Weidenfeld and Nicolson, 2004).

Postan, M.M., *British War Production* (London: HMSO, 1952).

Preston, Antony, *Battleships of World War 1* (New York: Galahad, 1972).

Priestley, Major R.E., *Breaking the Hindenburg Line: The Story of the 46 Division* (London: Fisher and Unwin, 1919).

Prior, Robin, *Gallipoli: The End of the Myth* (London/New Haven: Yale University Press, 2009).

—— *When Britain Saved the West: The Story of 1940* (London/New Haven: Yale University Press, 2015).

Prior, Robin and Trevor Wilson, *Command on the Western Front: The Military Career of Sir Henry Rawlinson 1914–1918* (Oxford: Blackwell, 1992).

—— *Passchendaele: The Untold Story* (London/New Haven: Yale University Press, 2002).

—— *The Somme* (London/New Haven: Yale University Press, 2005).

Raleigh, Sir Walter, *The War in the Air, Volume 1* (London: Hamish Hamilton, 1969). Reprint of the 1922 edition.

Reed, Paul, *Courcelette* (London: Leo Cooper, 1998).

Reynolds, David, *The Creation of the Anglo-American Alliance 1937–1941: A Study in Competitive Co-operation* (Durham: University of North Carolina Press, 1981).

Reynolds, David and Vladimir Pichatrov, *The Kremlin Letters: Stalin's Wartime Correspondence with Churchill and Roosevelt* (London: Yale University Press, 2019).

Robbins, Keith, *Sir Edward Grey: A Biography of Lord Grey of Fallodon* (London: Cassell, 1971).

Roberts, Andrew, *Churchill* (London: Penguin, 2018).

—— *The Holy Fox: The Life of Lord Halifax* (London: Phoenix, 1997).

—— *Masters and Commanders: How Four Titans Won the War in the West* (London: Harper, 2010).

Rogers, Anthony, *Churchill's Folly: Leros and the Aegean: The Last Great British Defeat of World War II* (Athens: Iolkos, 2007).

Rohl, John, *The Kaiser and his Court: Wilhelm II and the Government of Germany* (Cambridge: Cambridge University Press, 1987).

Roskill, Stephen, *Admiral of the Fleet Earl Beatty: The Last Naval Hero: An Intimate Biography* (London: Collins, 1980).

—— *Hankey: Man of Secrets, Volume 2* (London: Collins, 1976).

—— *Naval Policy Between the Wars, Volume II: The Period of Reluctant Disarmament, 1930–1939* (Barnsley: Seaforth, 2016).

—— *The War at Sea, Volume 1* (London: HMSO, 1954).

—— *The War at Sea, Volume 2* (Uckfield: Naval and Military Press, 2004).

—— *War at Sea, Volume 3, Part 1* (Uckfield: Naval and Military Press, 2004). Reprint of 1960 edition.

Rostow, W.W., *Pre-Invasion Bombing Strategy: General Eisenhower's Decision of March 25, 1944* (Aldershot: Gower, 1981).

Ruppenthal, Roland G., *Logistic Support of the Armies, Volume 2* (Washington: US Printing Service, 1953).

Schneer, Jonathan, *Ministers at War: Winston Churchill and his War Cabinet* (London: One World, 2015).

Sainsbury, Keith, *The North African Landings 1942* (London: Davis-Poynter, 1976).

Schreiber, Gerhard, et al., *Germany and the Second World War, Volume III, The Mediterranean, South-East Europe and North Africa 1939–1941* (Oxford: Clarendon Press, 1995).

Schurman, D.M., *The Education of a Navy: The Development of British Naval Strategic Thought, 1867–1914* (London: Cassell, 1965).

Scoullar, Lieutenant-Colonel J.L., *The Battle for Egypt* (Wellington: War History Branch, 1955).

Sheffield, Gary, *The Chief: Douglas Haig and the British Army* (London: Aurum, 2011).

Sheffield, Gary and John Bourne (eds), *Douglas Haig: War Diaries and Letters 1914–1918* (London: Weidenfeld and Nicolson, 2005).

Sheldon, Jack, *The German Army at Passchendaele* (Barnsley: Pen and Sword, 2007).

Sherwood, Robert E. (ed.), *The White House Papers of Harry L. Hopkins*, 2 vols (London: Eyre & Spottiswoode, 1948).

Shlaim, Avi, 'Prelude to Downfall: The British Offer of Union to France, June 1940', *Journal of Contemporary History*, vol. 9, no. 3 (1974), pp. 27–63.

Sinclair, D.W., *19th Battalion and Armoured Regiment* (Wellington: Historical Publication Branch, 1954).

Slim, Field Marshal Sir William, *Defeat into Victory* (London: Cassell, 1956).

Smith, Alan H., *Allenby's Gunners: Artillery in the Sinai and Palestine Campaigns 1916–1918* (Barnsley: Pen & Sword, 2017).

Smith, Malcolm, *British Air Strategy between the Wars* (Oxford: Oxford University Press, 1984).

Smithers, A.J., *The Man who Disobeyed: Sir Horace Smith-Dorrien and His Enemies* (London: Leo Cooper, 1970).

Simpson, Mitchell B. III, *Admiral Harold R. Stark: Architect of Victory 1939–1945* (Columbia: University of South Carolina Press, 1989).

Sondhaus, Lawrence, *The Great War at Sea* (Cambridge: Cambridge University Press, 2014).

Spears, E.L., *Liaison 1914: A Narrative of the Great Retreat* (London: Heinemann, 1930).

Spiers, Edward M., *Haldane: An Army Reformer* (Edinburgh: Edinburgh University Press, 1980).

—— 'Rearming the Edwardian Artillery', *Journal of the Society for Army Historical Research*, vol. 57, no. 231 (1979), pp. 197–76.

Steiner, Zara, *Britain and the Origins of the First World War* (London: Macmillan, 1977).

Stevenson, David, *With Our Backs to the Wall: Victory and Defeat in 1918* (London: Allen Lane, 2011).

Stewart, Graham, *Burying Caesar: Churchill, Chamberlain and the Battle for the Tory Party* (London: Weidenfeld and Nicolson, 1999).

Stewart, Colonel H., *The New Zealand Division 1916–1919: A Popular History Based on Historical Records* (Auckland: Whitcombe and Tombs, 1921).

Stockings, Craig, *The Battle of Bardia* (Canberra: Army History Unit, 2011).

Stoler, Mark, *Allies and Adversaries: The Joint Chiefs of Staff, the Grand Alliance and U.S. Strategy in World War II* (Chapel Hill: University of North Carolina Press, n.d.).

Suttie, Andrew, *Rewriting the First World War: Lloyd George, Politics and Strategy 1914–1918* (London: Palgrave Macmillan, 2005).

Symonds, Craig L., *World War II at Sea: A Global History* (Oxford: Oxford University Press, 2018).

Tarrant, V.E., *Jutland: The German Perspective* (London: Brockhampton, 1999).

Taylor, A.J.P. (ed.), *Lloyd George: A Diary by Frances Stevenson* (London: Hutchinson, 1971).

Taylor, Frederick, *Dresden: Tuesday 13 February 1945* (London: Bloomsbury, 2004).

Tedder, Lord, *With Prejudice* (New York: Little, Brown, 1966).

Temple Patterson, A., *The Jellicoe Papers*, 2 vols (London: Navy Records Society, 1966–1968).

—— *Tyrwhitt of the Harwich Force: The Life of Admiral of the Fleet Sir Reginald Tyrwhitt* (London: Macdonald, 1973).

Tennent, A.J., *British Merchant Ships Sunk by U-Boats in World War One* (Penzance: Periscope Publishing, 2006).

Terraine, John (ed.), *General Jack's Diary* (London: Eyre & Spottiswoode, 1964).

—— *Mons: Retreat to Victory* (London: Batsford, 1960).

Thorne, Christopher, *Allies of a Kind: The United States, Britain and the War against Japan* (London: Hamish Hamilton, 1978).

Titmus, Richard, *Problems of Social Policy* (London: HMSO, 1950).

Tooze, Adam, *The Wages of Destruction: The Making and the Breaking of the Nazi Economy* (London: Allen Lane, 2006).

Townshend, Charles, *When God Made Hell: The British Invasion of Mesopotamia and the Creation of Iraq 1914–1921* (London: Faber, 2010).

Trevelyan, G.M., *Grey of Fallodon* (London: Longmans, 1937).

Trumpener, Ulrich, *Germany and the Ottoman Empire* (Princeton: Princeton University Press, 1968).

Turkish General Staff, *A Brief History of the Canakkale Campaign in the First World War, June 1914–January 1916* (Ankara: Turkish General Staff Printing House, 2004).

Tuttle, Dwight William, *Harry L. Hopkins and Anglo-American-Soviet Relations, 1941–1945* (New York: Garland, 1983).

United States War Office, *Histories of Two Hundred and Fifty-One Divisions of the German Army which Participated in the War (1914–1918)* (London: London Stamp Exchange, 1989). Reprint of the 1920 US War Office publication which first compiled this information.

Verner, R., *The Battlecruisers at the Action of the Falkland Islands* (London: John Bale, 1920).

Verrier, Anthony, *The Bomber Offensive* (London: Pan, 1974).

Waller, A.C., '5th Battle Squadron at Jutland', *RUSI Journal* (November 1935), pp. 791–9.

Warren, Alan, *Singapore 1942* (Singapore: Talisman, 2002).

Wavell, Field Marshal Lord, *The Palestine Campaign*, 3rd edn (London: Constable, 1931).

Webster, Sir Charles and Noble Frankland, *The Strategic Air Offensive against Germany 1939–1945*, 4 vols (London: Naval and Military Press, 2006). Reprint of the 1961 Official History.

Williams, Jeffrey, *Byng of Vimy: General and Governor-General* (London: Leo Cooper, 1983).

Wilmot, Chester, *Desert Siege* (Sydney: Penguin, 2003).

—— *The Struggle for Europe* (London: Collins, 1971). Reprint of the 1952 edition.

Wilson, K.M. (ed.), *Decisions for War, 1914* (London: UCL Press, 1995).

—— (ed.), The Cabinet Diary of J.A. Pease 24 July–5 August 1914, *Leeds Philosophical and Literary Society Proceedings,* vol. 19, part III (March 1983), p. 6.

Wilson, Trevor, *The Myriad Faces of War* (Oxford: Polity, 1986).

—— *The Political Diaries of C.P. Scott 1911–1928* (London: Collins, 1970).

Woodward, David, 'Did Lloyd George Starve the British Army of Men Prior to the German Offensive of 21 March 1918?', *Historical Journal,* vol. 27, no. 1 (March 1984), pp. 241–52.

—— *Lloyd George and the Generals* (East Brunswick, NJ: Associated University Presses, 1983).

—— (ed.), *Military Correspondence of Field-Marshal Sir William Robertson: Chief of the Imperial General Staff, December 1915–1918* (London: Military Records Society, n.d.).

Wynne, G.C., *If Germany Attacks: The Battle in Depth in the West* (London: Faber, 1940).

—— 'The Other Side of the Hill, No. XVII: Neuve Chapelle 10th–12th of March, 1915', *Army Quarterly,* vol. 37 (1938–1939), pp. 30–46.

—— 'The Other Side of the Hill, No. III: The Fight for Hill 70: 25th–26th September 1915', *Army Quarterly,* vol. 8 (1924), pp. 261–73.

Zabecki, David, *Steel Wind: Colonel Georg Bruchmüller and the Birth of Modern Artillery* (Bridgeport, CT: Praeger, 1994).

—— *The German 1918 Offensives: A Case Study in the Operational Level of War* (London: Routledge, 2006).

Ziegler, Philip, *Mountbatten: A Biography* (New York: Knopf, 1985).

INDEX

attacked, 581; reduction in sinkings, 581; role of Enigma, 581, 589; U-boat campaign against the US, 582; 1942 U-boat campaign, 583; its successes, 583; Anti-U-boat Committee, 583–4; impact of US shipbuilding, 584–5; mid-Atlantic gap, 585; MAC ships, 585; VLR aircraft, 585–6, 590–1, 595; bombing of Biscay ports, 587–8; U-boats and Casablanca conference, 588; Churchill's confidence in shipping situation, 589; British convoy codes broken, 589; Biscay air offensive, 590; increased sinkings, 591; convoy sizes, 592; role of support groups, 592; the gadget war, 593; Horton and the Western Approaches, 593–4; success of anti-U-boat campaign, 594; the role of convoy, 595; Churchill and the Battle of the Atlantic, 596; *see also* convoy
Atlantic Charter, 392
Attlee, Clement: in Churchill's War Cabinet, 305; recommends Anglo-French union, 314–16; and Operation Battleaxe, 358; and Mediterranean strategy, 476; supports oil bombing plan, 554; opposes Transportation plan, 601–2
Aubers Ridge, 90–1; battle of, 93, 95
Auchinleck, Lieutenant-General Claude: at Narvik, 300; and Iraqi expedition, 349; becomes C-in-C Middle East, 352, 357; urges caution in new offensive, 357–8; meets COS and Churchill, 358; wins reprieve from Churchill, 358; delays new offensive, 359; approves Crusader plan, 360; replaces Alan Cunningham, 365; promotes Richie, 365; overestimates Rommel's defeat, 368; delays new offensive, 370; criticised by Churchill, 370; summoned home by Churchill, 371; refusal by Auchinleck, 371; Nye and Cripps visit, 372; Churchill losing confidence in, 373; at Gazala, 373–5; disperses British divisions, 375; approved by Churchill, 375; evacuates Tobruk, 379–80; replaces Richie, 381; operations against Rommel, 383–4; C-in-C India, 637; deprecates offensive operations, 637; and reorganisation of Indian army, 640; sidelined by Churchill, 641

Balfour, Arthur James: member of the War Council, 65; aware of Fisher's doubts concerning Dardanelles, 69; enthusiasm for Dardanelles, 69; considers defence stronger than attack, 110; concerned about casualties at the Somme, 119; Balfour declaration, 150
Balkans, in British affairs, 1–2; Second Balkan War, 2
Bapaume, 115, 117, 127, 218
Battle of Britain, 318–26
Battleaxe: plan, 349–50; battle, 351–2
Beatty, Admiral Sir David: commands battlecruiser squadron, 54, 183; at Heligoland Bight Battle, 54; at Dogger Bank Battle, 60–1; at Jutland, 183–4, 186–8; advocates convoy, 199
Beersheba, cavalry charge at, 147
Belgium, British obligations to, 11
Benghazi: captured, 340; evacuated, 347
Benkendorff, Count: assures Grey Russia not hostile to Germany, 3; Grey urges to begin talks with Austria, 4
Bennett, Major-General Gordon: commands Australian troops Malaya, 425; faulty dispositions, 426; in defence of Singapore, 428
Berchtold, Count, pushes for war against Serbia, 3
Berseford-Pierse, Lieutenant-General Noel: plans Operation Battleaxe, 349; little influence on battle, 350; disperses firepower, 350
Bethmann Hollweg: favours supporting Austria, 4; attitude to Belgian neutrality, 13
Birdwood, General Sir William: commands Anzac force, 77; considers evacuation, 78; August plan, 80; the attack, 81–2; Bullecourt plan, 160
'bite and hold' infantry tactic: Rawlinson and, 93, 102, 112; Churchill and, 114; Haig and, 125; and 25 September attack at the Somme, 127; at Vimy Ridge, 157; Plumer and, 166, 176; at Cambrai, 180; in 1918, 239; summary of, 682
Blitz, 326–7; casualties in London, 327; shelters, 327; jamming radio beams, 327; morale, 327–8
Bolero, build-up of US forces in Britain, 397–9, 402–3